KT-230-763

The AUTOBIOGRAPHY of HENRY VIII

The AUTOBIOGRAPHY of HENRY VIII

With Notes by His Fool, Will Somers

A NOVEL

MARGARET GEORGE

MACMILLAN
LONDON

"The Triads" on page 735 are translations from the Irish by Thomas Kinsella: *Thirty Three Triads,* published by Dolmen Press, Dublin, 1955; Atheneum, New York, 1961. Reprinted by permission.

The translation from the Irish of "Cathleen" is reprinted by permission of Tom McIntyre.

"The Hag of Beare" from *The Book of Irish Verse,* 1974, by John Montague, is reprinted by permission of A D Peters & Company on behalf of the author.

Copyright © 1986 by Margaret George

All rights reserved. No reproduction, copy or transmission of this publication may be made without written permission. No paragraph of this publication may be reproduced, copied or transmitted save with written permission or in accordance with the provisions of the Copyright Act 1956 (as amended). Any person who does any unauthorised act in relation to this publication may be liable to criminal prosecution and civil claims for damages.

First published in the United States of America 1986 by St. Martin's Press, New York.

First published in the U.K. 1986 by
MACMILLAN LONDON LIMITED
4 Little Essex Street London WC2R 3LF
and Basingstoke

Associated companies in Auckland, Delhi, Dublin, Gaborone, Hamburg, Harare, Hong Kong, Johannesburg, Kuala Lumpur, Lagos, Manzini, Melbourne, Mexico City, Nairobi, New York, Singapore and Tokyo

ISBN: 0-333-43869-8

Printed and bound in Hong Kong

For
Alison
and
Paul

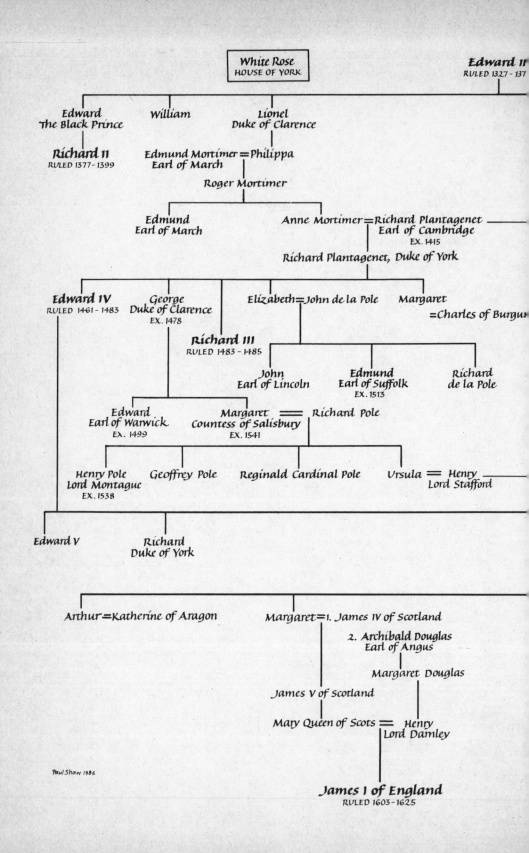

White Rose
HOUSE OF YORK

Edward I
RULED 1327 – 137

Edward
The Black Prince

William

Lionel
Duke of Clarence

Richard II
RULED 1377 – 1399

Edmund Mortimer = Philippa
Earl of March

Roger Mortimer

Edmund
Earl of March

Anne Mortimer = Richard Plantagenet
Earl of Cambridge
EX. 1415

Richard Plantagenet, Duke of York

Edward IV
RULED 1461 – 1483

George
Duke of Clarence
EX. 1478

Elizabeth = John de la Pole

Margaret
= Charles of Burgun

Richard III
RULED 1483 – 1485

John
Earl of Lincoln

Edmund
Earl of Suffolk
EX. 1513

Richard
de la Pole

Edward
Earl of Warwick
EX. 1499

Margaret ══ Richard Pole
Countess of Salisbury
EX. 1541

Henry Pole
Lord Montague
EX. 1538

Geoffrey Pole

Reginald Cardinal Pole

Ursula ══ Henry
Lord Stafford

Edward V

Richard
Duke of York

Arthur = Katherine of Aragon

Margaret = 1. James IV of Scotland

2. Archibald Douglas
Earl of Angus

Margaret Douglas

James V of Scotland

Mary Queen of Scots ══ Henry
Lord Darnley

James I of England
RULED 1603 – 1625

Paul Shaw 1986

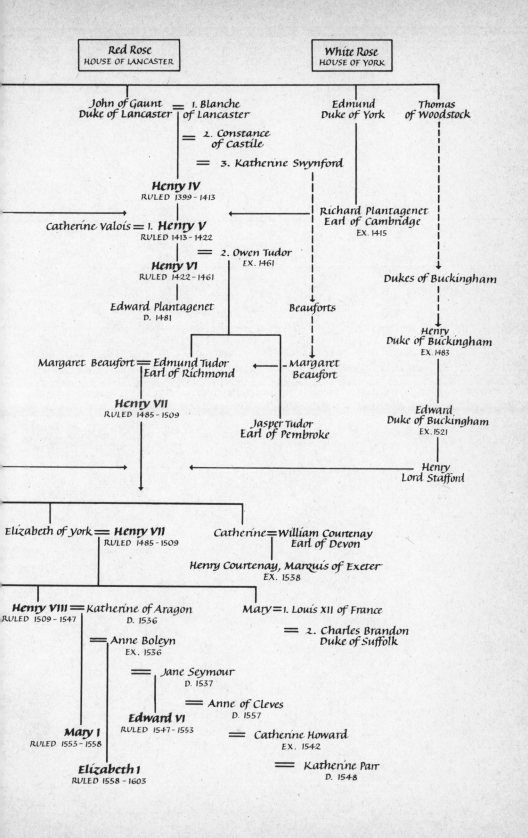

Red Rose
HOUSE OF LANCASTER

White Rose
HOUSE OF YORK

John of Gaunt
Duke of Lancaster = 1. Blanche
of Lancaster

Edmund
Duke of York

Thomas
of Woodstock

= 2. Constance
of Castile

= 3. Katherine Swynford

Henry IV
RULED 1399 – 1413

Richard Plantagenet
Earl of Cambridge
EX. 1415

Catherine Valois = 1. **Henry V**
RULED 1413 – 1422

= 2. Owen Tudor
EX. 1461

Henry VI
RULED 1422 – 1461

Dukes of Buckingham

Edward Plantagenet
D. 1481

Beauforts

Henry
Duke of Buckingham
EX. 1483

Margaret Beaufort = Edmund Tudor
Earl of Richmond

Margaret
Beaufort

Henry VII
RULED 1485 – 1509

Jasper Tudor
Earl of Pembroke

Edward
Duke of Buckingham
EX. 1521

Henry
Lord Stafford

Elizabeth of York = **Henry VII**
RULED 1485 – 1509

Catherine = William Courtenay
Earl of Devon

Henry Courtenay, Marquis of Exeter
EX. 1538

Henry VIII = Katherine of Aragon
RULED 1509 – 1547   D. 1536

Mary = 1. Louis XII of France

= 2. Charles Brandon
Duke of Suffolk

= Anne Boleyn
EX. 1536

= Jane Seymour
D. 1537

= Anne of Cleves
D. 1557

Edward VI
RULED 1547 – 1553

= Catherine Howard
EX. 1542

Mary I
RULED 1553 – 1558

Elizabeth I
RULED 1558 – 1603

= Katherine Parr
D. 1548

The AUTOBIOGRAPHY of HENRY VIII

Prologue

𝒮 William Somers to Catherine Carey Knollys:

Kent, England. April 10, 1557.

My dear Catherine:

I am dying. Or, rather, about to die—there is a slight (though unconsoling) difference. It is this: the dying can no longer write letters, whereas those about to die can and sometimes do. As this letter proves. Dear Catherine, spare me your protestations to the contrary. You have not seen me in many years (how many since you went into exile to Basle?); you would not recognize me now. I am not sure I recognize myself, whenever I am so ill-advised as to actually look at myself in a mirror— proving that vanity lives at least as long as we do. It is the first faculty to come and the last to go. And I, I who have made my livelihood at court mocking others' vanity—I look in the mirror, like all the rest. And see a strange old man who looks decidedly unsavoury.

But I was already twenty-five when old King Harry (who was young then, himself) took me into his household. And he has been dead ten years now, and that is what I am writing about. Let us come directly to business. You know I have never been sentimental. (I think Harry liked that best in me, being so incorrigibly sentimental himself.) I have a small legacy for you. It is from your father. I knew him rather well, even better than you yourself did. He was a magnificent man, and sorely missed today, even by his enemies, so I should think.

I live quietly in the country, in Kent. It is far enough from London to afford one some protection from false accusations, but not so far that one cannot hear the false accusations against others. There have been more burnings at Smithfield; and as you have most likely heard yourself, Cranmer and Ridley and Latimer were roasted. How Mary must have

I

hated Cranmer, all those years! Think of the times when she had to stand near him in some religious ceremony or other . . . such as Edward's christening, where they actually had her bearing gifts! Dear Cranmer—Henry's compliant churchman. If ever there were anyone who seemed an unlikely candidate for martyrdom, it was he. I always assumed the man had no conscience at all. I see I was wrong. Did you hear that first he recanted his Protestantism, in a typically Cranmerian fashion, and then—oh, marvellous!—recanted his *recantation?* It would have been humourous were it not so deadly.

But then, you and those of your . . . persuasion . . . sensed that early, and had the prudence to clear out of England. I will ask you a question, knowing full well you will not answer it, not on paper if you hope ever to return here. *Just how Protestant are you?* You know the old King never saw himself as a Protestant at all, but merely as a Catholic who fell out with the Pope and refused to recognize him. A neat trick, but then Harry had some odd turns of mind. Then his son Edward, that pious little prig, was Protestant. But not the wild sort, the Anabaptist variety. *Are you that sort?* If you are, there will be no place for you in England. Not even Elizabeth will welcome you, should she ever become Queen. You should know that, and not pin your hopes on things that are unlikely to be. Some day you can return home. But not if you are Anabaptist or the like.

England will never again be Catholic. Queen Mary has seen to that, with her persecutions for the True Faith and her Spanish obsession. Harry never punished anyone for anything save disloyalty to the King. As long as you signed the Oath of Succession you could believe what you liked, provided you were gentlemanly about it and did not run about in a sweating fervour, one way or the other. Thomas More wasn't beheaded for being a Catholic (although the Catholics would like people to think that and have nearly succeeded), but for refusing to take the Oath. The rest of his household took it. But More *did* long for martyrdom and went to . . . heroic? . . . lengths to achieve it. He literally forced the King to kill him. And got that so-called heavenly crown he lusted after as old Harry had lusted after Anne Boleyn. Harry found the object of his lust not as palatable as he had imagined; let us hope More was not similarly disillusioned once he attained his desire.

I forget. I must not make such jests with you. You believe in that Place too. Believers are all alike. They seek—what was More's book title?—*Utopia.* It means No Place, you know.

As I said, I live quietly here in my sister's household in Kent, along with my niece and her husband. They have a small cottage, and Edward is . . . I hesitate to write it . . . a gravedigger and tombstone carver. He makes a good living at it. (Just such puns used to be *my* living.) But he tends his garden as others do (we had wonderful roses last year), plays with his children, enjoys his meals. There is nothing the least death-like about him; perhaps only that sort can stomach such a profession. Although I think being a jester is equally bound up with death. Or providing a scent to cover it, anyway.

I came here before Edward had his coronation. The boy-King and his pious advisers had no need of a jester, and I would have stood about like a loose sail luffing in the wind. Neither is Queen Mary's court the sort of place where one makes jokes.

Do you remember, Catherine, that summer when you and I and all your Boleyn family and the King gathered at Hever? You and your brother Henry were brought to see your Boleyn grandparents. Hever is delightful in the summer. It was always so green, so cool. And the gardens had truly the best musk-roses in England. (Do you perchance remember the name of your grandparents' gardener? I am not far from Hever now, and perhaps could consult with him . . . assuming he is still living.) And it was an easy day's ride from London. Do you remember how the King used to stand on that hill, the first one from which you could glimpse Hever, and blow his hunting horn? You used to wait for that sound, and then go running to meet him. He always brought you something, too. You were the first Boleyn grandchild.

Remember your uncle George that summer? He was trying so hard to be the gentil parfit knight. He practised riding about in his armour, ran lists against trees, and fell in love with that sloppy girl at The White Hart. She gave her favours to every man who frequented the tavern, except George, I think. She knew that to do so would stop the flow of sonnets he wrote exalting her purity and beauty, and she enjoyed laughing at them.

Your mother Mary and her husband were also there, of course. I always thought your mother more than her sister Anne's equal in beauty. But of a different sort. She was sun and honey; the other was the dark of the moon. We were all there that summer before everything changed so horribly. The tide has indeed gone out, leaving that little time as a brave clump of ground projecting above the muddy, flat rest of it.

I am rambling. No, worse, I grow romantic and sentimental, something I abhor in others and will not tolerate in myself. Now, to return to the important thing: the legacy. Tell me how I may get it safely into your hands across the Channel. It is, unfortunately, a rather awkward size: too large to be successfully concealed on a person, too small to be its own protection against destruction. In fact, it can all too easily be destroyed by any number of things—sea, fire, air, or even neglect.

I pray you make haste with your reply. I am distinctly less curious to discover at first hand the shape and disposition of my Maker than are you and others of your sect, but I fear I may be honoured with a celestial interview in the near future. The Deity is notoriously capricious in his affections.

Ever your
Will Somers

❡ Catherine Carey Knollys to William Somers:

June 11, 1557. Basle.

My dearest Will:

I beg your forgiveness in taking so long to place this answer in your hands. Messengers who will openly carry things from England to us here in exile are few in these times; the Queen makes sure of that. However, I trust this carrier and equally trust your discretion in destroying this letter once you have read it.

I am distressed to hear of your ill health. But you, as King Henry's favorite jester, were ever prone to exaggeration in your talk, and I pray God this is but a further example of your art. Francis and I have prayed for you nightly. Not in the idolatrous Mass, which is worse than worthless, it is a travesty (O, if the Queen should see this!), but in our private devotions. We do not do badly here in Basle. We have enough clothes to keep us warm, enough food to keep us fit but not fat; more would be an affront to God, many of whose poor creatures are in bodily need. But we are rich in the only thing worth having—the freedom to follow our consciences. You no longer have that in England. The Papalists would take it all away. We pray daily for that tyranny to be lifted from your shoulders, and a Moses to arise to lead you from spiritual bondage.

But about the legacy. I am curious. My father died in 1528, when I was but six. Why should you wait near thirty years to hand it on? It could not have been scurrilous or treasonous. And that is another thing that puzzles me. You spoke of his "enemies." He had no enemies. William Carey was a good friend to the King, and a gentle man. I know this not only from my mother, but from others. He was well regarded at court, and his death from the plague saddened many. I am grateful that you remember now to do it, but if I had had it earlier . . . No, I do not blame you. But I would have known my father better, and sooner. It is good to meet one's father before one becomes an adult oneself.

Yes, I remember Hever in the summer. And my uncle George, and you, and the King. As a child I thought him handsome and angelic. Certainly he was beautifully made (the Devil did it) and had a certain presence about him, of majesty I should say. Not all kings have it; certainly Edward never did, and as for the present Queen . . .

I regret to say I cannot remember the name of the gardener. Something with a *J?* But I do remember that garden, the one beyond the moat. There were banks of flowers, and he (of the forgotten name) had arranged it so that there was always something in bloom, from mid-March to mid-November. And great quantities, too, so that the little manor of Hever could always be filled with masses of cut flowers. Strange that you should mention musk-roses; my favourites were the hollyhocks, with their big heavy bells.

Your news about Cranmer saddened me. So he was one of us after all. I, too, had thought him merely a creature of whoever was in power. I am sure he has attained his crown and is (in the poor misguided Thomas More's phrase) "merry in heaven." More may be there as well, but in spite of his mistaken allegiance, not because of it. If he *had* trimmed his sails to the wind and survived until now, I doubt not that he would have been among the judges that condemned Cranmer. More was a vicious enemy of so-called dissenters; he is not honoured by us. His death diminished the ranks of our persecutors by one. Naturally there are many remaining, but time is our friend and we shall prevail.

This is hard for you to comprehend as you are of the Old Order, and cautiousness has always been your watchword. But as Gamaliel, the Pharisee lawyer, said in regard to the persecution of the first Christians: "For if this council or this work be of men, it will come to nought: But if it be of God, ye cannot overthrow it; lest haply ye be found even to fight against God." It is written in the fifth chapter of Acts. If you have no translation of the Scriptures available to you (as I believe the Queen has had them destroyed), I can arrange to have one brought to you. A trusted friend has business in London, and sees that we can receive things. My messenger here will give you his name, and we can exchange our things. Although I believe that, whatever the legacy prove to be, it cannot be so valuable as the Scriptures.

Ever your servant in Christ,

Catherine Carey Knollys

ℐ Will Somers to Catherine Knollys:

Sweet Catherine:

Your prayers must have had some salubrious effect, as I have made a partial recovery. God has evidently rescheduled our meeting for a more mutually convenient time. As you know, I shun the offices of all doctors as well as priests. Neither has meddled with me in over forty years. To this I attribute my survival. I have never been bled, never had ground-pearl ointments (of which Harry was so inordinately fond), nor have I cared what vestments the current high priest wore. I do not mean to offend you, Catherine. But I am not a believer in anything save the swift passing of things. Religion, too, has its fashions. Yesterday it was five Masses a day— yes, Harry did that!—and pilgrimages to Our Lady of Walsingham; next Bibles and sermons; now, Masses again, with burnings added; next, who knows? By all means pray to that Geneva God you have created in your own image. He is mighty for now. Perhaps there is something that is constant above and beyond mere fashions in worship. I do not know. My job has been always, and merely, to turn people's faces away from change, loss, dissolution; to distract them while the scenery was being changed backstage.

Catherine: *do not* send me any Scriptures, or translations. I do not wish to receive them, nor to be associated with them in any way. Are you unaware of what danger that would place me in? And for nothing. I have read them already (indeed, I had to, in order to banter with King Harry in public, and in private, to fill in whenever Cranmer or his last Queen was unavailable for his favourite pastime: a robust theological discussion). I have remained unconverted and singularly uninterested in *being* converted. As it is extraordinarily difficult to smuggle in these scriptures, give someone else the rewards of your efforts.

I will, however, speak with your man about the transportation of the legacy. I must cease the mystery and tell it plain. The thing is a journal. It was written by your father. It is extremely valuable, and many people would like to destroy it. They know of its existence but so far have confined their efforts to asking the Duke of Norfolk about it, the remnants of the Seymour family, and even Bessie Blount's widower, Lord Clinton. Sooner or later they will sniff their way to me here in Kent.

There, I have told it all, except the last thing. The journal was written not by William Carey, your supposed father, but by your true father: the King.

6

ℐ Catherine Knollys to Will Somers:

September 30, 1557. Basle.

Will:

The King was not—is not!—my father. How dare you lie so, and insult my mother, my father, myself? So you would rake up all those lies from so long ago? And I thought you my friend! I do not wish to see the journal. Keep it to yourself, along with all your other misguided abominations of thought! No wonder the King liked you so. You were of one mind: low-minded and full of lies. You will not muddy my life with your base lies and insinuations. Christ said to forgive, but He also told us to shake the dust off our feet from towns filled with liars, blasphemers, and the like. Just so do I shake you from mine.

ℐ Will Somers to Catherine Knollys:

November 14, 1557. Kent.

Catherine, my dear:

Restrain yourself from tearing this letter to pieces in lieu of reading it. I do not blame you for your outburst. It was magnificent. A paradigm of outraged sensibility, morality, and all the rest. (Worthy of the old King himself! Ah, what memories it brought back!) But now admit it: the King was your father. This have you known always. You speak of dishonouring your father. Will you dishonour the King by your refusal to admit what *is?* That was perhaps his cardinal virtue (yes, my lady, he had virtues) and genius: always to recognize the thing as it *was,* not as it was generally assumed to be. Did you not inherit that from him? Or are you like your half-sister Queen Mary (I, too, regret your relationship with her), blind and singularly unable to recognize even things looming right before her weak eyes? Your other half-sister, Elizabeth, is different; and I supposed you were also. I supposed it was the Boleyn blood, added to the Tudor, that made for a uniquely hard, clear vision of things, not muddied by any Spanish nonsense. But I see I was wrong. You are as prejudiced and stupid and full of religious choler as the Spanish Queen. King Harry is dead indeed, then. His long-sought children have seen to that.

7

𝒮 Catherine Knollys to Will Somers:

January 5, 1558. Basle.

Will:

Your insults must be answered. You speak of my dishonouring the King my father. If he *were* my father, did he not dishonour *me* by never acknowledging me as his own? (He acknowledged Henry Fitzroy, made him Duke of Richmond—the offspring of that whore Bessie Blount!) Why, then, should I acknowledge or honour *him?* First he seduced my mother before her marriage, and now you say he subsequently cuckolded her husband. He does not deserve honour, but disdain. He was an evil man and brought horror wherever he went. The only good he did, he did merely as a by-product of evil: his lust for my aunt, Anne Boleyn, caused him to break from the Pope. (Thus the Lord used even a sinner for His purposes. But that is to the Lord's credit, not the King's.) I spit on the late King, and his memory! And as for my *cousin*, Princess Elizabeth (the daughter of my mother's sister, *naught else*), I pray that she may . . . no, it is too dangerous to put on paper, regardless of the trustworthiness of the messenger or the receiver.

Go thy ways, Will. I want no further correspondence from you.

𝒮 Will Somers to Catherine Knollys:

March 15, 1558. Kent.

Catherine:

Bear with me yet a little. In your wonderfully muddled letter I sensed one essential question; the rest was mere noise. You asked: If he were my father, did he not dishonour *me* by never acknowledging me as his own?

You know the answer: He was taken out of his true mind by that witch (now I must insult you again) Anne Boleyn. She tried to poison the Duke of Richmond; would you have had her try her hand on you as well? Yes, your aunt was a witch. Your mother quite otherwise. Her charms were honest, and her thoughts and manner honest as well. She suffered for it, while your aunt-witch thrived. Honesty seldom goes unpunished, and as you know, your mother did not have an easy berth in life. *He* would have acknowledged you, and perhaps your brother as well (though he was less certain of his parentage), if the Witch had not

8

prevented him. She was jealous, very jealous of your sweet mother, although, God knows, she gave the King ample cause for jealousy: the admiration of all the world was not enough for the Witch, she must have the services of all the male courtiers as well. Well, as she herself said, the King, having run out of earthly honours for her, provided her with the crown of martyrdom. Ha! All who are killed are not martyrs. She sought to ally herself with Thomas à Becket and even Thomas More, but it was not to be. She has failed in her transparent bid for posthumous honour and glory.

And now take this journal, and make peace with yourself. If you cannot, then save it for your . . . relation, the Princess Elizabeth, against the time when . . . I, too, must say no more than this. It is dangerous, and even my wattly old neck does not find the feel of a rope particularly appealing. I cannot give it into her hands now, although as you have made clear, she is the obvious choice. Spies surround her, and she is watched constantly. Mary wants to send her back to the Tower, and make sure she never emerges again.

How I came about the journal is this: I was, as you know (or perhaps you do not; why should we always assume our private histories are of general importance, and known to all?) first seen by Harry, the King, when my master, a wool merchant in Calais, happened to court. I was not a jester then, just a young man with an hour to pass in the galleries. I amused myself as I customarily did when without the more interesting offices of sack or wine: I talked. The King heard; the rest, as the common people say, is history. (*Whose* history?) He took me into his service, gave me cap and bells, bound me to him in more ways than I was at the time aware. We grew old together; but here I must set down what the young Harry was. The eye of the sun, that blinded us all . . . yes, even me, cynical Will. We were brothers; and when he lay dying in that stuffy chamber in Whitehall, I was the only one who had known him young.

But I digress. I was speaking of the journal. When I first came to Harry in 1525 (just before the Witch enthralled him), he was keeping a sort of daily log, all full of rough notations. Later—after the disgrace of Catherine Howard, his fifth so-called Queen—when he was so ill, he began a personal journal to beguile the time and take his mind from the daily pain in his leg and the growing factions about him. Oh, yes, daughter—he felt himself to be losing control. He knew the parties forming about him, waiting for him to die. So he lashed out, in the open; and secretly, he wrote it all down.

Toward the end, he could only make the roughest notes, which he (eternal optimist) planned to expand later. (Why, only one month before

9

he died, he ordered fruit trees for his garden that would not bear fruit, at the earliest, until ten years hence. An irony: I hear they bloomed last year, and Mary had them cut down. If *she* must be barren, then the royal garden must perforce imitate the royal person.) He never did; he never will. I enclose them here, along with the rest, with my own notes and explanations. I hesitated to deface the journal, but when I read it, it was as though Harry were talking once again, and I was ever wont to interrupt him. Old habits persist, as you can see. As well as I knew him, though, the journal showed me an unknown Henry—proving, I suppose, that we are all strangers, even to ourselves.

But I began by saying how I came to possess the journal. The answer is simple: I stole it. *They* would have destroyed it. They have destroyed everything else remotely connected to the King, or to the Old Times: first the Reformers and now the Papists. The Reformers smashed the glass in every church, and the Papists, so I hear, have gone one step further in bestiality, so that even I hesitate to write it. The Queen's agents have taken Harry's body—her own father!—from its grave, burnt it, and thrown it into the Thames! Oh, monstrous!

This journal, then, is his last earthly remains. Will you be so unnatural a daughter as the Queen, and burn it, as well? If you are not his daughter (as you maintain), then be to him a better daughter than his true-born.

How humourless this is. Humour is, indeed, the most civilised thing we have. It smooths all raw edges and makes the rest endurable. Harry knew that. Perhaps I should employ a jester of my own, having evidently outrun my own calling.

The blessings of your enigmatic God upon you,

Will

Enclosed herein is the journal.
I feel constrained to note: Bessie Blount was not a whore.

The Journal of Henry VIII

1

Yesterday some fool asked me what my first memory was, expecting me to lapse happily into sentimental childhood reminiscences, as dotty old men are supposed to enjoy doing. He was most surprised when I ordered him out of the room.

But his damage was done; and I could not order the thought out of my mind as easily. What was my earliest memory? Whatever it was, it was not pleasant. I was sure of that.

Was it when I was six? No, I remember when my sister Mary was born, and that was when I was five. Four, then? That was when my other sister, Elizabeth, died, and I remembered that, horribly enough. Three? Perhaps. Yes. It was when I was three that I first heard cheers—and the words "only a second son."

The day was fair—a hot, still, summer's day. I was going with Father to Westminster Hall to be given honours and titles. He had rehearsed the ritual with me until I knew it perfectly: how to bow, when to prostrate myself on the floor, how to back out of the room before him. I had to do this because he was King, and I would be in his presence.

"You never turn your back to a king," he explained.

"Even though you are just my father?"

"Even so," he answered solemnly. "I am still your King. And I am making you a Knight of the Bath today, and you must be dressed in hermit's clothes. And then you will re-enter the Hall in ceremonial robes and be made Duke of York." He laughed a little dry laugh—like the scudding of leaves across a cobbled courtyard. "That will silence them, show them the Tudors have incorporated York! The only true Duke of York will be my son. Let them all see it!" Suddenly he lowered his voice and spoke softly. "You will do this before all the peers in the realm. You must not make a mistake, nor must you be afraid."

I looked into his cold grey eyes, the color of a November sky. "I am not afraid," I said, and knew that I spoke the truth.

Throngs of people came to watch us when we rode to Westminster through Cheapside. I had my own pony, a white one, and rode just behind Father on his great caparisoned bay. Even mounted, I was scarcely any taller than the wall of people on either side. I could see individual faces clearly, could see their expressions. They were happy, and repeatedly called blessings on us as we passed.

I enjoyed the ceremony. Children are not supposed to enjoy ceremonies, but I did. (A taste I have never lost. Did that begin here, as well?) I liked having all eyes in Westminster Hall on me as I walked the length of it, alone, to Father. The hermit's robes were rough and scratched me, but I dared not betray any discomfort. Father was sitting on a dais in a dark carved seat of royal estate. He looked remote and unhuman, a King indeed. I approached him, trembling slightly, and he rose and took a long sword and made me a knight, a member of the Order of the Bath. In raising the sword, he brushed lightly against my neck, and I was surprised at how cold the steel was, even on a high summer's day.

Then I backed slowly out of the hall and went into the anteroom where Thomas Boleyn, one of Father's esquires of the Body, was waiting to help me change into my rich red ceremonial robes made especially for today's occasion. That done, I re-entered the hall and did it all again; was made Duke of York.

I was to be honoured afterwards, and all the nobles and high-ranking prelates were to come and pay homage to me, recognizing me as the highest peer in England—after the King and my older brother Arthur. I know now, but did not understand then, what this meant. The title "Duke of York" was the favourite of pretenders, and so Father meant to exact oaths of loyalty from his nobles precluding their later recognizing any pretenders—for, after all, there cannot be two Dukes of York. (Just as there cannot be two heads of John the Baptist, although some Papalists persist in worshipping both!)

But I did not understand this. I was but three years old. It was the first time I had been singled out for anything of my own, and I was hungry for the attention. I imagined all the adults would cluster about me and talk to me.

It was quite otherwise. Their "recognition" consisted of a momentary glimpse in my direction, a slight inclination of the head. I was quite lost in the forest of legs (for so they appeared to me; I scarcely reached any man's waist) which soon arranged themselves into clusters of three, four, five men. I looked about for the Queen my mother, but did not see her. Yet she had promised to come. . . .

A bleating fanfare announced that the dishes were being placed upon the long table running along the west wall of the hall. It had a great length of white linen upon it, and all the serving dishes were gold. They shone in the dull light, setting off the colour of the food within. Wine servers began to move about, carrying huge golden pitchers. When they came to me, I demanded some, and that made everyone about me laugh. The server demurred, but I insisted. He gave me a small chased silver cup and filled it with claret, and I drank it straight down. The people laughed, and this caught Father's attention. He glared at me as though I had committed a grave sin.

Soon I felt dizzy, and my heavy velvet robes made me sweat in the close air of the packed hall. The buzz of voices above me was unpleasant, and still the Queen had not come, nor any attention been paid me. I longed to return to Eltham and leave this dull celebration. If this were a festivity, I wanted no more of them and would not envy Arthur his right to attend them.

I saw Father standing somewhat apart, talking to one of his Privy Councillors—Archbishop Morton, I believe. Emboldened by the wine (for I was usually somewhat reluctant to approach Father), I decided to ask him to allow me to leave and return to Eltham straightway. I was able to approach him unobtrusively as I passed the clots of gossiping nobles and courtiers. My very lack of size meant that no one saw me as I moved closer to the King and stood back, half-hidden in folds of the wall-hanging, waiting for him to cease talking. One does not interrupt the King, even though one is the King's son.

Some words drifted to me. *The Queen . . . ill . . .*

Was my mother, then, prevented by illness from coming? I moved closer, straining to hear.

"But she must bury this sorrow," Morton was saying. "Yet each pretender opens the wound anew—"

"That is why today was necessary. To put a stop to all these false Dukes of York. If they could see how it hurts Her Grace. Each one . . . she knows they are liars, pretenders, yet I fancied she looked overlong at Lambert Simnel's face. She wishes it, you see; she wishes Richard her brother to be alive." The King's voice was low and unhappy. "That is why she could not come to see Henry be invested with his title. She could not bear it. She loved her brother."

"Yet she loves her son as well." It was a question disguised as a statement.

The King shrugged. "As a mother is bound to love her son."

"No more than that?" Morton was eager now.

"If she loves him, it is for what he recalls to her—her father Edward. Henry resembles him, surely you must have seen that." Father took another sip of wine from his huge goblet, so that his face was hidden.

"He's a right noble-looking Prince," Morton nodded, so that his chin almost touched his furred collar.

"I give you his looks. Edward had looks as well. Do you remember that woman who cried out in the marketplace: 'By my troth, for thy lovely countenance thou shalt have even twenty pounds'? Pretty Edward. 'The Sun in Splendour' he called himself."

"Whereas we all know it should have been 'The King in Mistress Shore's Bed,' " Morton cackled. "Or was it Eleanor Butler's?"

"What matter? He was always in someone's bed. Remember that derisive ballad about 'lolling in a lewd love-bed'? Elizabeth Woodville was clever to exploit his lust. I do not wish to belittle the Queen's mother, but she was a tiresome old bitch. I feared she would never die. Yet we have been free of her for two years now. Praised be God!"

"Yet Henry—is he not—" Morton was clearly more interested in the living than the dead.

The King looked about him to make sure no one was listening. I pressed further into the curtain-fold, wishing myself invisible. "Only a second son. Pray God he will never be needed. Should he ever become King"—he paused, then lowered his voice to a whisper as he spoke the unspeakable words—"the House of Tudor would not endure. Just as the House of York did not survive Edward. He was handsome and a great soldier—I grant him that—but at bottom stupid and insensitive. And Henry is the same. England could survive one Edward, but never two."

"It will never come to that," said Morton smoothly. "We have Arthur, who will be a great king. The marks of greatness are already upon him. So learned. So stately. So wise—far beyond his eight years."

"Arthur the Second," murmured Father, his eyes dreamy. "Aye, it will be a great day. And Henry, perhaps, will be Archbishop of Canterbury someday. Yes, the Church is a good place for him. Although he may find the vows of celibacy a bit chafing. Do you, Morton?" He smiled coldly, a complicity acknowledged. Morton had many bastards.

"Your Grace—" Morton turned his face away in mock modesty, and almost saw me.

My heart was pounding. I pressed myself back into the curtains. They must not ever know I was nearby, and had heard. I wanted to cry—indeed, I felt tears fighting their way into my eyes—but I was too insensitive for that. The King had said so.

Instead, after I had stopped trembling and banished any hint of tears, I left my hiding-place and moved out among the gathered nobles, boldly talking to anyone I encountered. It was much remarked upon later.

I must not be hypocritical. Being a prince was good sometimes. Not in a material sense, as people suppose. Noblemen's sons lived in greater luxury than we did; we were the butt-end of the King's "economies," living and sleeping in Spartan quarters, like good soldiers. It is true we lived in palaces, and that word conjures up images of luxury and beauty—for which I must take some credit, as I have worked hard to make it true, in my own reign—but in my childhood it was otherwise. The palaces were relics of an earlier era—romantic, perhaps, steeped in history (here Edward's sons were murdered; here Richard II surrendered his crown), but decidedly uncomfortable: dark and cold.

Nor was it particularly adventuresome. Father did not travel very much, and when he did he left us behind. The first ten years of my life were spent almost entirely within the confines of Eltham Palace. Glimpses of anything beyond were, for all practical purposes, forbidden. Ostensibly this was for our protection. But it had the effect of cloistering us. No monk lived as austere, as circumscribed, as dull a life as I did for those ten years.

And that was fitting, as Father had determined that I must be a priest when I grew up. Arthur would be King. I, the second son, must be a churchman, expending my energies in God's service, not in usurping my brother's position. So, from the age of four, I received churchly training from a series of sad-eyed priests.

But even so, it was good to be a prince. It was good for elusive reasons I find almost impossible to set down. For the history of the thing, if you will. To be a prince was to be—special. To know when you read the story of Edward the Confessor or Richard the Lionheart that you had a mystic blood-bond with them. That was all. But enough. Enough for me as I memorized reams of Latin prayers. I had the blood of kings! True, it was hidden beneath the shabby clothes, and would never be passed on, but it was there nevertheless —a fire to warm myself against.

II

I should never have begun in such a manner. These jumbled thoughts cannot stand as a passable collection of impressions, let alone a memoir. I must put things in some reasonable order. Wolsey taught me that: always in order. Have I forgotten so soon?

I began it (I mean this journal) in a vain attempt to soothe myself several weeks ago while suffering yet another attack from my cursed leg. Perhaps I was so distracted by the pain that I was incapable of organizing my thoughts. Yet the pain has passed. Now if I am to do this thing, I must do it properly. I have talked about "Father" and "the King" and "Arthur" without once telling you the King's name. Nor which ruling family. Nor the time. Inexcusable!

The King was Henry VII, of the House of Tudor. But I must not say "House of Tudor" so grandly, because until Father became King it was not a royal house at all. The Tudors were a Welsh family, and (let us be honest) Welsh adventurers at that, relying rather heavily on romantic adventures of both bed and battle to advance themselves.

I am well aware that Father's genealogists traced the Tudors to the dawn of British history, had us descended directly from Cadwaller. Yet the first step to our present greatness was taken by Owen Tudor, who was clerk of the wardrobe to Queen Catherine, the widow of Henry V. (Henry V was England's mightiest military king, having conquered a large portion of France. This was some seventy years before I was born. Every common Englishman knows this now, but will he always?) Henry and the French king's daughter married for political reasons and had a son: Henry VI, proclaimed King of England *and* France at the age of nine months. But Henry V's sudden death left his twenty-one-year-old French widow alone in England.

Owen's duties were such that he was in constant company with her. He was comely; she was lonely; they wed, secretly. Yes, Catherine (daughter to one king, wife to another, mother of yet a third) polluted—so some say—her royal blood with that of a Welsh rogue. They had two sons, Edmund and Jasper, half-brothers to Henry VI.

But Catherine died in her mid-thirties, and Owen's sufferance was up. Henry VI's Protector's Council ordered "one Owen Tudor the which dwelled with the said Queen Catherine" to appear before them, because "he had been so presumptuous as by marriage with the Queen to intermix his blood with the royal race of Kings." Owen first refused to come, but later came and was imprisoned in Newgate twice, twice escaping. He was elusive and supremely clever. After his second escape he made his way back to Wales.

Once Henry VI came to maturity and discarded his Protector, he treated Owen's two sons kindly. He created Edmund Earl of Richmond, and Jasper Earl of Pembroke. And Henry VI—poor, mad, sweet thing—even found a proper Lancastrian bride for his half-brother Edmund: Margaret Beaufort.

To recount these histories is like unravelling a thread: one means only to tell one little part, but then another comes in, and another, for they are all part of the same garment—Tudor, Lancaster, York, Plantagenet.

So I must do what I dreaded: go back to Edward III, innocent source of all the late troubles. I say innocent because what king does not wish an abundance of sons? Yet Edward's troubles, and those of the next generations, stemmed from his very prolificness.

Edward, who was born almost two hundred years before me, had six sons. A blessing? One would have thought so. But in truth they were a curse that echoes to this day. The eldest, Edward, was called the Black Prince. (Why I do not know, although I believe it was from the liveries his retainers customarily wore. He was a great warrior.) He died before his father, and thus his son, Edward's grandson, came to the throne as Richard II.

Now Edward's other sons were William, who died young; Lionel, Duke of Clarence, from whence ultimately sprang the House of York; John of Gaunt, Duke of Lancaster, progenitor of the House of that name; Edmund, Duke of York (later the heirs of Clarence and Edmund married, uniting those claims), and finally Thomas of Woodstock, ancestor of the Duke of Buckingham.

It happened thus: Henry, son of John of Gaunt, deposed his cousin Richard II and was crowned Henry IV. His son was Henry V, who married the Queen Catherine Valois, who afterwards married Owen Tudor.

Does this confuse you? I assure you that in my youth these tangled ancestral webs were known as today one might know the words of a popular ballad or the sequence of the Five Sorrowful Mysteries of Christ. They loomed over our lives, forcing us to take roles on either side; roles that led directly to fortune . . . or to death.

But Henry V's son, crowned in Paris as Henry VI, King of both England and France, could not hold his inheritance. As he grew older, he proved to be inept and half mad.

When the anointed king is weak, there are others who imagine themselves strong. Thus was born the Yorkist cause.

There is a legend that the wars began when Richard Plantagenet (later Duke of York) met with his companions and rivals Somerset, Warwick, and Suffolk in the Temple Gardens. Richard plucked a white rose from one bush, symbolizing descent from Lionel, third son of Edward III, and bade his sympathizers join him; Warwick, of the powerful northern Neville family, also took a white rose. Somerset and Suffolk picked the red, lining themselves up with the claims of John of Gaunt, Duke of Lancaster, fourth son. Then they prophesied that this would expand to encompass the whole realm.

It is a pretty story; whether it be true or not I do not know. Yet it *is* true that within a few years hundreds of people died fighting for either the White Rose or the Red.

Henry VI was deposed, ultimately, by that brave son of the Yorkists, later Edward IV. He fought thirteen pitched battles and lost none: a military genius.

The strands of all three families were, as I said, interwoven. It is difficult for me to tell of the cruelties visited by one upon the other, as the blood of all now flows in my veins.

Yes, Edward IV was a great fighter. I can take pride in that, as he was my grandfather. Yet my great-grandfather was fighting against him, aided by my great-uncle, Jasper Tudor. They were crushed, and Owen was captured after the Battle of Mortimer's Cross in 1461. He was executed—by Edward's orders—in the marketplace of Hereford. Until the axeman appeared to do his office, Owen could not believe he would actually die. The headsman ripped off the collar of Owen's doublet, and then he knew. He looked about and said, "That head shall lie in the stock that was wont to lie on Queen Catherine's lap." Afterwards a madwoman came and took his head and set a hundred candles burning about it.

I tell this so that when I recount that Owen's eldest son, Edmund, married Margaret Beaufort, thirteen-year-old heiress to the claims of the House of Lancaster, you will not imagine they lived quietly. The battles raged all about them. Edmund escaped from all these cares by dying at the age of twenty-six, leaving his wife great with child. That child was my father, born when his mother was but fourteen. It was January 28, 1457.

WILL SOMERS:

Seeing this date chilled me. It was also on January 28 that Henry VIII died. In 1547—the reversal of the numbers—it is like a parenthesis. The father born, the son dying. . . . Yet I do not believe in such things. I leave them for Welshmen and the like.

She named him Henry, a royal Lancastrian name. Yet at that time he was by no means an important heir, merely a remote figure in the overall confusing fabric. This in spite of being the grandson of a queen (on his father's side) and the great-great-great-grandson of a king (on his mother's). But as the battles went on, those with higher claims to the throne were killed (Henry VI's only son, Edward, and Richard, Duke of York), and each battle advanced Henry Tudor closer to the throne. In the Battle of Tewkesbury in 1471, every male Lancaster was destroyed, save Henry Tudor. And he fled to Brittany with his uncle Jasper.

Henry VI was done to death in the Tower that same year. The Yorkists did it. It was a mercy: Henry VI was, perhaps, a saint, but he was not meant to be King. His poem,

> *Kingdoms are but cares*
> *State is devoid of stay*
> *Riches are ready snares*
> *And hasten to decay,*

proves that. A Yorkist sword released him from the cares of his kingdom, and I cannot but say they did him a good office.

But my father's tale is also long to tell: there is nothing simple in these histories. Father went into exile, crossing the Channel to Brittany, where the good Duke Francis welcomed him—for a fee. Edward IV pursued him, tried to have him abducted and murdered. Father outsmarted him—*Edward was stupid*—and outlived him, watching and waiting in Brittany as Edward's cruel brother, Richard, usurped the throne and did away with Edward's sons Edward V and Richard, Duke of York. They say he had them smothered as they slept, and buried them somewhere in the Tower.

Many men smarted under Richard's rule and fell away, joining Father in Brittany until he had a court in exile. And in England there was such discontent that rebellious subjects invited Father to come and claim the throne.

He tried first in 1484; but fortune was against him, and Richard caught and executed his principal supporter, the Duke of Buckingham. The next year things were again ready, and Father dared not wait longer, lest what support he had erode. He set sail and landed in Wales with an army of only two thousand men, against a known ten thousand for Richard III.

What compelled him to do this? I know the story well, yet I also know Father: cautious to the point of inaction, suspicious, slow to decisions. Still, at the age of twenty-eight he risked everything—his life as well—on what looked to be a hopeless venture. Two thousand men against ten thousand.

He was greeted wildly in Wales, and men flocked to join him, swelling his ranks to five thousand, still only half the number of Richard's forces. Still he pressed on through the August-yellow fields, until at last they met a few miles from Leicester, at a field called Bosworth.

There was fierce fighting, and in the end some of Richard's men held back. Without them the battle was lost. Richard was slain, hacked in a dozen places by his own lost supporters as he sought to attack Father himself.

They say the crown flew off Richard's head in the heat of battle and landed in a gorse bush and that Father took it from there and placed it upon his own head amidst cries of "King Henry! King Henry!" I doubt the truth of this, but it is just the sort of story that is repeated and eventually believed. People like simple stories and will twist even the profound into something plain and reassuring. They like to believe that one becomes king by a Sign, and not by anything as inconclusive or confusing as a mêlée. Hence, the crown in the bush.

In fact, it was not simple at all. Despite the battle and the crown in the divinely placed bush, there remained many recalcitrant people who simply would not accept Henry Tudor as King. True it was that he had royal blood, and had made the late Yorkist King's daughter his wife, but diehard Yorkists were not so easily placated. They wanted a genuine Yorkist on the throne, or no one. Thus the treasons began.

There were no Yorkists left, but the traitors would resurrect the smothered sons of Edward IV (my mother's brothers). They did not dare to "discover" the eldest, Edward; even they were not that bold. Richard, the younger, was their choice. Each coterie of traitors found a ready supply of yellow-haired boys willing to impersonate him.

The first was Lambert Simnel. The Irish crowned him as Richard IV. Father was amused and tolerant. After crushing the uprising in the Battle of Stoke in 1487, he appointed the erstwhile King a cook in the royal kitchens. Working before the hot ovens rapidly deflated his royal demeanour.

The next, Perkin Warbeck, was less amusing. The Scots hailed him and provided him with a highborn wife. Father executed him.

And yet the uprisings went on. There was a bottomless well of traitors and malcontents. No matter what Father did, there were always dissatisfied groups somewhere, plotting for his overthrow.

In the end it made him bitter. I can see that now, and understand it. *They* had taken his youth ("Ever since I was five years old I have been either a prisoner or a fugitive," he once said), and even after he had supposedly won his right to peace, they would not let him be. They meant to drive him from the throne, or into his grave.

Father married his archenemy's daughter. He hated Edward IV, yet he had made a solemn vow in Rennes Cathedral that should his invasion of England be successful, he would wed Elizabeth, Edward's daughter.

Why? Simply because she was the heiress to the Yorkist claims, as he was of the Lancastrian. He had never even seen her and knew nothing about her person. She could have been crook-backed or squint-eyed or pockmarked. Yet marrying her would end the wars. That was all he cared about.

As I said, he despised Edward IV. And why not? Edward had tried to have him assassinated. Edward had killed his grandfather Owen. Yet he would marry his daughter. . . . He understood the times. You murdered people, and it was like cultivating a garden: you nipped tender shoots, or the whole trunk, of whatever plant you perceived might be a threat later in the growing season.

I put a stop to all that. No one is put to death surreptitiously in England now. There are no more pillow-murders or poisonings or midnight stabbings. I count as one of the great achievements of my reign that this barbarism has passed forever.

But I was speaking of Father's marriage. Elizabeth, Edward's daughter, was brought out of sanctuary (where she and her mother had hidden from the ravages of Richard III) and given to him as part of the spoils of war.

Thus Elizabeth of York married Henry Tudor. Royal artists created an especial emblem for them: the so-called Tudor rose, combining the red of Lancaster with the white of York. Less than a year later they had their sought-for heir: Arthur. They named him thus to avoid all "claimed" names (Henry was Lancastrian, Edward and Richard Yorkist), and to hark back to the legendary King Arthur. That would offend no one while promising fine things.

Then followed other children. After Arthur, Margaret (named for the King's mother). Then me. (It was safe to give the third child a partisan name like Henry.) After me, Elizabeth. Then Mary. Then Edmund. Then . . . I cannot recall her name, if indeed she had one. She lived but two days.

Father was twenty-nine when he married. By the time he was forty there remained to him four living children—two princes and two princesses—and the survival of his new dynasty seemed assured.

I am told my father was handsome and popular when he first came to the throne. People saw him as an adventurer, and the English always like rogues and heroes. They cheered him. But over the years the cheering faded as he did not respond to it. He was not what they had expected after all. He was not bluff like Edward nor rough and plain as a soldier-king should be. In fact, he was hardly English at all in his thinking, as he had spent most of his life outside the country, or in Wales, which was just as bad. He was suspicious of people, and they sensed it and finally withdrew their affections.

Here I am describing Father as an historian would, trying to note how he looked and how he ruled. Of course, as a child I saw and understood none of this. Father was a tall, thin man whom I saw but rarely, and never alone. Sometimes he would come to where we—the four children—lived, and pay one of his unannounced visits. We hated those visits. He would walk about like a general inspecting his troops, calling on us for Latin or sums. Usually his mother, Margaret Beaufort, was with him, and she was a tiny woman who always wore black and had a sharp face. By the time I was eight years old, I had reached her height and could look her directly in the eye, although I disliked her eyes. They were bright and black. *She* always asked the sharpest questions and was most dissatisfied with the answers, because she fancied herself a scholar and had even left her husband for a time to go and live in a convent so that she could read all day.

It was she who selected our tutors and guided our education. Of course, the best tutors went to Arthur and the second-rank ones served the rest of us. Occasionally I shared some tutors with Arthur. Bernard André taught us both history, and Giles D'Ewes taught us French. And John Skelton, the poet laureate, began by teaching Arthur but later became my own tutor.

Skelton was a profligate priest, and we liked each other immediately. He wrote coarse satires and had a mistress; I thought him marvellous. Until then I had assumed that to be scholarly, one must be like my grandmother Beaufort. The black, the convent, the books were all linked in my mind. Skelton broke those links. Later, in my own reign, scholarship was freed completely from the convents and monasteries. (And not simply because I closed the monasteries!)

We studied Latin, of course; French, Italian, mathematics, history, poetry. I received an extra heavy dose of Scriptures, theology, and churchmen, as I was earmarked for the Church. Well, no learning is ever wasted. I made extensive use of the knowledge later, though in a way that would have horrified my pious grandmother and her chosen tutors.

How we lived: forever moving. Father had—or, rather, the Crown had—eight palaces, and with every change in season, the royal household would move. But we, the King's children, seldom lived in the same palace as the King and Queen. They preferred us to live in the country, or as near to open fields and clean air as possible. Eltham Palace was an ideal site. It was small and set in green fields, but only three miles from Greenwich and the Thames. It had been built for Edward IV, my pretty grandfather, and was all of stone, with a quiet moat and well-kept gardens. It was too small to house a full court, but was perfect for royal children and our reduced household of cooks and nurses and guards.

And we were guarded. In our pretty little walled garden we might as well have been in farthest Scotland rather than ten miles from the center of London. No one was allowed to come and see us without Father's permission; he remembered the fate of the Yorkist princes too well. We did not, and found all the restrictions irksome.

I was sure I could defend myself against any assassin. I practised with sword and bow and soon became aware of how strong and dexterous I was for my age. I almost longed for an evil agent to make an attempt on me, so that I could prove myself to Father and win his admiration. But no obedient murderer appeared to grant my childish wish.

We were to take exercise outdoors. As I said, I early discovered my facility in physical things. I rode easily and well, from the beginning. I am not boasting; if I am to record everything, I must be as honest about my talents as I am about my weaknesses. It is this: I was gifted in things of the body. I had more than strength, I had innate skill as well. Everything came easily to me, on the field or in the saddle. By the time I was seventeen I was one of the ablest men in England—with the longbow, the sword, the lance; in the tourney, in wrestling, and even in that peculiar new sport, tennis.

I realize such a statement is suspect. They let him win, you will say. One always lets the Prince, or the King, win. For just this reason I competed incognito as much as possible. Of course, my enemies twisted that as well, claiming that my doing so was just a childish love of disguises. But no. I, too, wished to test myself and got no satisfaction from any contest I might suspect was controlled. God's blood! Doesn't a prince have honour? Would a prince take pleasure from being "let" win? Why do they assume a prince's honour is less, or his self-knowledge less, than their own? An athletic contest is above all a test—a short, clean test. They would deny me even that, and darken my achievements on the field of my youth.

But I am digressing. I was speaking of our tame little exercises within the palace grounds, not the later tournaments and contests in which I competed. Arthur hated any exercise and would try to avoid it. Margaret and I were most alike physically, and she was my chief companion in climbing trees and swimming in the moat. She was three years older than I, and utterly fearless—I should say even reckless. She never thought before she hurled herself over a fence, or forced her pony to jump, or tasted a strange wild berry. People have accused me of being fearless, reckless, but I am not and never was. I learned that about myself early from watching Margaret. (And her later behaviour as Queen of Scotland was the same as her childhood behaviour in the confines of Eltham. Quite uncontrolled, and finally disastrous.)

If Margaret and I were alike bodily, Mary and I were alike in spirit. We were, quite simply, made of the same stuff and always understood one another instinctively.

No one was like Arthur, and he was like none of us . . . high and solitary and solemn.

III

We joined the court at Christmas and Easter and Whitsun. I used to count the months in between. Christmas was my favourite, and the long months until then (six or seven, depending on how early Whitsun came) seemed interminable.

It was Margaret and I, of course, who most longed to go to court. Margaret because she would get new clothes, be petted, and receive presents and sweetmeats. And I? For those things, yes. But most of all, I would see the Queen my mother. And perhaps, perhaps . . . I never completed the thought, and cannot, even now.

The winter I was seven, the King decided to hold Christmas at Sheen Manor. I had never been there, or, if I had, could not remember it. It was one of the older palaces upstream on the Thames.

Winter had come early that year, and by early December the ground had been frozen for two weeks and was already covered with a light layer of snow.

On the day of our journey from Eltham to Sheen, we moved so slowly that it took us all day to travel the sixteen miles. Those of us on horseback could not gallop, but had to ride in pace with the twelve ponderous wagons carrying our goods. Not until late afternoon did we reach the great forest of Richmond. This was a royal hunting preserve, and there were stag and deer and boar here. But the loud noise of our rumbling carts scared away any game, and I saw nothing as I passed through.

And then we were beyond the forest, looking down on the Thames— a smaller, shallower Thames than the one at Greenwich—bathed yellow in the flat rays of the low sun, with the red brick towers of Sheen Manor rising along the water.

Still, it took a long time to reach the manor. The great carts had to be restrained on the descent and lumbered even more slowly. I looked over at Margaret.

"Shall we run?" she asked, as I had known she would.

"Yes," I said, spurring my horse without looking back, and together we galloped madly toward the manor. Margaret was shrieking and laughing so loudly she drowned out the cries behind us.

We reached the manor gates a mile ahead of anyone else. We had been so intent on our fast ride that we had not noticed that the cries came from the manor as well as from our own party. Now, standing before the gates, we heard the frenzied shouts of a large crowd, then a sudden silence. And no one came to open the gates for us.

Margaret made a face, dismounted, and tethered her horse. "We must find our own way in, then," she said, making for a small service entrance. Disgruntled, I also left my horse and followed her. She put her shoulder to the old door and shoved, but it held fast. Then she eyed the panels and began trying to scale the door. Suddenly it opened and threw her to the ground.

An angry-looking youth stood there glaring. "And who are you?" he said. He was enormous, or so it seemed to me.

"I am Princess Margaret," she replied stiffly, picking herself up from where she lay sprawled in the mud, her skirt up over her buttocks.

He looked disbelieving.

"And I am Prince Henry," I said, hoping to convince him that we were together and truly who we claimed to be. He stepped out of the gate and saw the rest of our party approaching. He looked rather surprised to be able to confirm our claim.

"All right, then," he said. "I will take you to the King."

Margaret scampered after him, but I stood where I was. "And who are *you?*" I asked.

He turned. I expected him to be angry, but his expression was amused. "I am Charles Brandon," he replied, as if I should know him. "At your service, my Prince." He grinned and bowed; that great boy-man, then twice my age, declared himself mine. To my innocent self, it was not just a court-worn phrase, but a personal pledge of service, a bond between us. I extended my hand, and he grasped it.

It was a handshake that was to last us all our lives.

He shouldered his way through the crowd, which was thick. They were all straining to see something, something hidden from us. Then it came into view: four mastiffs being hoisted aloft on ropes. They were being hanged! They danced and jerked on the ropes, whined and then choked, writhing as they frantically clawed at the rope with their helpless paws. Soon they were dangling limply, their tongues protruding. They turned slowly, and no one made a move to cut them down.

Then I saw why. The King appeared. He stepped before the dogs and raised his hands for silence. He was wearing a grey robe trimmed with old fur, and his voice was high and thin.

"Thus you can see: traitorous dogs must not rise against a King." With each word, his breath made a visible puff in the cold, still air.

He stood back and regarded the dogs and then turned to leave. Just then someone stepped forward and whispered to him. "Ah!" he said. "My children are approaching. We must greet them." He made a gesture, and the crowd turned obediently toward the main gate.

Margaret and Brandon and I stood where we were. As the crowd thinned, we saw what was lying on the ground beneath the dogs: the body of a lion. It was maimed and bloody.

"What is it?" cried Margaret. "Why is the lion dead? Why are the dogs hanged?" She seemed merely curious, not sickened. I myself felt a great revulsion.

"The King set the dogs upon the lion. He meant it as a demonstration of how the King of Beasts can destroy all enemies. Well, the dogs had the best of it. They killed the lion instead. So the King had to punish the dogs as traitors. It was the only way to salvage his lesson." Brandon chose his words carefully, but the tone of his voice told me he did not like the King. Immediately I liked Brandon better.

"But the King—" I began cautiously.

"Is very concerned about his throne," replied Brandon, incautiously. "He has just gotten word of another uprising. The Cornish this time." He looked around to be sure we were not overheard. "This is the third time. . . ." His voice trailed off. Or perhaps he sensed a coming welter of questions from Margaret.

But her head was turned toward the crowd and the noise that met Arthur's arrival into the manor grounds. The gates swung open, and Arthur rode in, clutching his saddle. He winced when he saw the eager faces and large numbers of people. A great shout arose on cue. The King stepped forward and embraced Arthur, almost dragging him from his horse. For a moment they clung together, then the King turned to the people.

"Now my holidays will begin indeed!" he proclaimed. "Now that my son is here! My *heir*," he said pointedly.

He never noticed that Margaret and I were there; and a few minutes later we were able to slip easily in with our own party and endure nothing worse than a tongue-clucking from our nurse, Anne Luke.

As we passed through the courtyard, I saw the body of the lion being dragged away.

We were shown to our quarters, and our household servants began unpacking and assembling the furniture we had carted with us. Soon silver ewers of heated water were brought for us to wash ourselves with. The festivities were to begin that evening with a banquet in the Great Hall.

Then Nurse Luke informed me that Mary and I were not to go.

I could understand why Mary must remain in the nursery—she was but two! But I was seven and surely should be allowed to go. All year I had assumed that when this season's Christmas revels began I would be part of them. Had I not reached the age of reason with my birthday that past summer?

The disappointment was so crushing that I began to howl and throw my clothes upon the floor. It was the first time I had ever shown an open display of temper, and everyone stopped and stared at me. Well, good! Now they would see I was someone to take notice of!

Anne Luke came rushing over to me. "Lord Henry! Stop this! This display"—she had to duck as I flung a shoe at no one in particular—"is most unlike you!" She tried to restrain my arms, but I flailed out at her. "It is unworthy of a Prince!"

That had the wanted effect. I stopped and stood, quite out of breath but still angry. "I want to go to the banquet," I said coldly. "I am quite old enough, and I think it unkind of the King to exclude me this year."

"A Prince old enough to attend formal banquets does not throw his clothes on the floor and scream like a monkey." Satisfied that I was under control, she lumbered up from her knees.

Now I knew what I had to do. "Nurse Luke, please," I said sweetly, "I want so badly to go. I have waited for it all year. Last year he promised"—this was pure invention, but it might serve—"and now he makes me wait in the nursery again."

"Perhaps His Majesty has heard about what you and Margaret did this afternoon," she said darkly. "Running ahead of the party."

"But Margaret is going to the banquet," I pointed out, logically.

She sighed. "Ah, Henry. You are a one." She looked at me and smiled, and I knew I should have my way. "I will speak to the Lord Chamberlain and ask if His Majesty would reconsider."

Happily I began picking up the strewn clothes, already planning what I should wear. So that was the way it was done: first a show of temper, then smiles and favour. It was an easy lesson to learn, and I had never been slow at my lessons.

At seven that evening, Arthur and Margaret and I were escorted into the Great Hall for the banquet. In the passageway outside I saw a band of musicians practicing. They hit many sour notes and looked apologetic as we passed by.

As part of our education, all Father's children were tutored in music. We were expected to be able to play one instrument. This was a source of much struggle to Arthur and Margaret. I, on the other hand, had taken as readily to the lute as to horses, and loved my hours of instruction. I wanted to learn the virginals, the flute, the organ—but my tutor told me I was to wait and learn one instrument at a time. So I waited, impatiently.

I had expected the King's musicians to be well trained, and now disappointment flooded me. They were little better than I.

❦ WILL:

This is misleading, as Henry was extraordinarily talented. Most likely at seven he performed better than slipshod adult musicians.

❦ HENRY VIII:

As we came into the Hall there was a fair blaze of yellow light. I saw what appeared to be a thousand candles on the long tables that ran along the sides of the hall, with the royal dais and table in between. There were white cloths for the full length of the tables and golden plate and goblets, all winking in the unsteady candlelight.

As soon as we entered, a man appeared at our sides and bent over and spoke to Arthur. Arthur nodded and the man—all richly dressed in burgundy velvet—steered him toward the royal dais where he would take his place with the King and Queen.

Almost at the same time, another man appeared and addressed himself to Margaret and me. This one was somewhat younger and had a round face. "Your Graces are to be seated near the King at the first table. So that you may see the jester and all the mimes clearly." He turned and led us through the gathering number of people; it looked to me like a forest of velvet cloaks. He escorted us to our place, bowed, and left.

"Who is he?" I asked Margaret. She had been at court functions several times before, and I hoped that she would know.

"The Earl of Surrey, Thomas Howard. He *used* to be Duke of Norfolk." When I looked blank, she said, "You know! He is head of the Howard family. *They* supported Richard III. That's why he's an earl now, and not a duke. He has to show his loyalty by seating the King's children!" She laughed spitefully. "If he seats us often enough, perhaps one day he'll be a duke again. That is what he hopes."

"The Howard family—" I began a question, but she characteristically cut it off.

"A huge, powerful one. They are everywhere."

Indeed they were. Later I was to remember that until that banquet I had never heard the name. The Howard family. As King, I married two of them, executed three, and married my son to one. But they were all unborn that night, and I but a seven-year-old second son awaiting the day I must take clerical vows. Had I known what was to be, perhaps I should have killed Thomas Howard that night and forestalled it all. Or he, me. But instead he turned his back on me and disappeared into the crowd to pursue his business, and I propped myself up on one leg the better to reach the table, and the thing went forward as water running downhill toward its destination.

A sudden fanfare of cornetts and sackbuts (slightly out of time) broke into the babble of the assembly. Instantly the people fell silent. The musicians then struck a slow processional march, and the King, the Queen, and the King's mother filed slowly in, followed by Archbishop Warham, Lord Chancellor; Bishop Fox, Lord Privy Seal; and Bishop Ruthal, Secretary. At the very rear of the procession was Thomas Wolsey, the priest who served as the King's almoner. He must have had little to do, as the King was stingy and gave no alms.

She was here! My heart soared, and I could not leave looking at her—the Queen my mother. From earliest childhood I had been taught to revere the Virgin Mother, Queen of Heaven. There were figures of her in the nursery, and every night I directed my prayers to her. But there was one image I loved above all others: an ivory one in the chapel. She was slender and beautiful and infinitely merciful, and had a sad, faraway smile.

Whenever I saw my mother, she looked so like the ivory figure that my heavenly mother and earthly mother merged in my mind, and I worshipped her.

Now, as I stared at her slowly coming into the hall, it was as though I were glimpsing Mary herself. I strained forward and felt myself becoming dizzy with excitement.

She walked beside the King, but her eyes were straight ahead. She did not look at him or touch him or speak, but walked on, ethereal and remote. Her robe was of blue, and her gold hair was almost hidden beneath her jewelled cap. She reached the dais. Arthur was beside her, and she reached out and touched his face and smiled, and they exchanged words.

I could not remember her ever having touched me thus, and the number of times she had spoken privately to me were fewer than my years in age. She had borne me easily and just as easily forgotten me. But perhaps this time, when we were alone for the gift exchanges . . . perhaps she might speak to me as she had just spoken to Arthur.

The King was speaking. His voice was thin and flat. He welcomed the court to Sheen. He welcomed his beloved son and heir, Arthur—here he made Arthur stand so that all could see him—to the revels. He made no mention of Margaret and me.

Servers brought us watered wine, and the courses began: venison, crayfish, prawns, oysters, mutton, brawn, conger-eel, carp, lamprey, swan, crane, quail, dove, partridge, goose, duck, rabbit, fruit custard, lamb, manchet, and so on, until I lost count. After the lampreys I could take no more and began declining the dishes.

"You are not supposed to take more than a bite of each dish," lectured Margaret. "It is not like eating in the nursery! You filled your belly with prawns, and now there's no room for anything else!"

"I did not know," I mumbled. I was feeling drowsy from the wine (watered as it was), the late hour, and my full stomach. The flickering candles before me and all up and down the table were affecting me oddly. I had to struggle to stay awake and upright. I hardly saw the grand dessert brought in, a sugared replica of Sheen Manor, and I certainly did not want any of it. My only concern was to keep from slipping sideways, lying down under the table, and falling fast asleep.

Then the tables were cleared and jesters and mimes came in for what seemed an interminable time. I could not focus on them and just prayed for it to be over before I disgraced myself by collapsing and proving Father right —that I had been too young to attend the banquet.

WILL:

A candid opinion of how jesters are perceived by their audiences. It was always a mistake to have us follow a banquet; full stomachs make people unreceptive to anything pertaining to the mind. After eating, a man does not want to laugh, he wants to sleep. I have always believed that in place of the old Roman vomitorium (where they could relieve their distended bellies) there should be a dormitorium, where people could sleep and digest. Perhaps royal architects could incorporate this design in their plans. It should, of course, be directly off the Great Hall.

HENRY VIII:

At last it ended. The jesters exited, tumbling and throwing paper roses and paste beads out over the spectators. The King rose and prodded Arthur to do likewise. No one in the Hall was permitted to stir until the Royal Family had left the dais, and I wondered what Margaret and I were to do as I saw the King, the Queen, and Arthur making their way out. Suddenly the King turned and, with a solemn nod, indicated that Margaret and I were to join them. He had known all along, then, that we were present.

They took no notice of us as we trailed along behind them. The King was busy talking to Warham, and the Queen walked alone, seemingly lost in her own thoughts. Behind her, like a raven, came Margaret Beaufort, all in black, straining to overhear the King's private conversation. Beside me my sister

Margaret walked, complaining about her tight shoes and the late hour and the roast swan, which was upsetting her digestion.

The King's apartments were on the opposite side of the Manor from the Great Hall, a matter for great grumbling in the kitchens. But when we finally reached them I felt a sense of disappointment. They were old and shabby, not even as spacious or well furnished as the nursery at Eltham. The ceiling was stained with soot from poor-burning tallow candles, the floor stones pitted and uneven. And it was cold, in spite of the fire. Drafts came from everywhere, making the torches and candle flames sway and flicker. All at once I was wide awake, and chilled.

But the King appeared distracted and oblivious to the discomfort of his surroundings. He gathered Ruthal and Fox to his side and conferred with them for some moments before breaking away and saying in a strained voice, "Now we must make merry! It is Christmastide." He smiled at the Queen, but it was more like a nervous tic.

She stood up, a slender column of white. "My children!" she said, holding out her hands. "Without children, there are no holidays." She turned to Arthur, standing just beside her. "My firstborn," she said fondly, ruffling his hair. Then she looked out into the room. "And Margaret." Margaret strode up to her, grinning. "And Henry." Slowly I made my way up to her. "Ah, Henry! You have grown so. And I have heard such things from André about your progress in your studies." The tone was warm but the words impersonal. They could have been directed at any one of us. For an instant I hated her.

"Thank you, my Lady," I said. And waited for something else. But there was nothing more.

The King sank into an old, slack leather chair. He called for wine and drank two cups before uttering a word. This was a dismal gathering. I began to wish I had stayed in the nursery after all.

Suddenly he heaved himself out of his chair. "It is Yuletide," he reiterated, as if he had forgotten saying it earlier. "And I am thankful to have my family here with me. We will exchange gifts now—or rather, we shall present our gifts to our children." He motioned, and a gentleman usher brought forth a tray of wrapped gifts. "To Arthur." As the name was called, we were expected to come up and receive our gifts. Arthur took the bulky bundle, clutched it in his arms, and returned to his place.

"No, no!" The King's voice was harsh. "Open it!"

Obediently, Arthur began tearing off the wrapping. There was something folded and soft underneath. It was white. It was—I could see it already!—a velvet cloak. With ermine trim. It fell across Arthur's knees. He shook it out and had to stand to do so.

The King was waiting expectantly. "Thank you, Father," Arthur said. "Thank you, Mother."

"Well?" said the King, beaming. "Try it!"

Arthur slipped it on, and there was a hideous pause. The cloak was far too big for him and hung grotesquely. It made him look dwarfish.

The King saw it and waved his hand. "It is for your wedding," he said testily. "Of course, it's a bit large."

"Of course," murmured the few chamber attendants present.

Arthur took it off and folded it.

Margaret received a pearl headdress. "For your wedding also," said the Queen. "It will not be long," she added gently. "In two or three years' time—"

"Yes." Margaret made a rough curtsey and tramped back to her seat. She plunked down, grasping the dainty headdress in her grimy hands and almost twisting it out of shape.

"And for Henry—" I stood as they called my name and walked toward the Queen, who was extending her hand. "Also for *your* marriage." She handed me a slim package, then nodded at me to unwrap it. I did so, and found an exquisitely illustrated Book of Hours. I looked up at her in surprise.

"Your marriage with the Church," she explained. "Now that you have progressed so far with your lessons, perhaps you can make use of this."

I was disappointed for inexplicable reasons. Yet what had I expected? "Thank you, my Lady," I said, and returned to my seat.

The evening continued in such strained merriment. The King spent much time conferring with his mother, and the Queen never left her ornately carved chair to speak with any of us, but fidgeted with her hands and the fastenings of her dress and listened to Margaret Beaufort's urgent whispers beside her.

Occasionally I caught some of her words. *Cornish. Army. Tower. Defeat.*

And still no one had mentioned the lion or the dogs. That was the most puzzling part. I did not understand, but then I understood so little.

I did not understand, for instance, why the King, who was known to be stingy, had had such a sumptuous banquet. I did not understand why, in spite of his words about making merry, he was so obviously glum. I did not understand what the Cornish had to do with all of it.

I was trying to sort out all these things in my mind while dutifully staring at the Book of Hours to please my mother, when a messenger burst into the room. He looked around wildly and then blurted out for us all to hear: "Your Grace—the Cornish number some fifteen thousand! They are to Winchester already! And Warbeck is crowned!"

The King sat, his face a mask. For an instant there was no sound but his heavy breathing. Then his lips moved, and he said one word: "Again!"

"The traitors!" spat the King's mother. "Punish them!"

The King turned an impassive face to her. "All, Madam?" he asked blandly.

I saw her expression change. I did not know then that her husband's brother, Sir William Stanley, had just gone over to the Pretender.

She met him, steel against steel. "All," she said.

Then the messenger went up to them, and there was a huddle of consultation and much alarm. I watched the Queen's face: she had gone pale, but betrayed no further emotion. Suddenly she rose and came toward Arthur, Margaret, and me.

"It is late," she said. "You must to bed. I will send for Mistress Luke." Clearly she wanted us gone, just when I most wanted to stay.

Nurse Luke came promptly, to my great disappointment, and ushered us out. She was full of cheerful questions about the banquet and our gifts. As we walked back to our quarters, I could feel the cold, worse even than in the King's chamber. It seeped into the open passageway like water through a sieve.

The torches on the wall threw long shadows before us. They were burning low; it must be extremely late. As they dwindled down to their sockets, they gave off a great deal of smoke.

In fact the passageway seemed blurred from the smoke, and ahead it was even thicker. As we turned into another passageway, suddenly the cold was gone. That was how I perceived it—not that it was abnormally warm, but that the cold was no longer there. I started to throw off my cloak. I can remember to this day just how it felt as I grasped the worn velvet and pulled open the fastening, and felt the heavy weight go off me. And almost at the same time I first heard the cry—"Fire!"—so that even today, if I grasp my cloak in just that way, I hear again that fearful sound. . . .

And then we could see it—could see the flames in the Great Hall. They were inside, eating as greedily as we had done just hours ago, devouring everything. Already some, impatient for the next course, were licking up toward the roof. As yet there was no alarm raised, no people were pouring out into the courtyard. It was as if the flames were holding their own private revels.

Nurse Luke screamed and turned and fled back toward the King's chamber, with us rushing behind her. Along the way we passed two sleeping guards; she shook them and shrieked about the fire. We reached the King's chamber and Nurse Luke, incoherent with fear by this time, just stood and stammered. The King was still talking to the messenger and looked annoyed at the interruption. Nurse Luke flung open the heavy door and a cloud of black smoke poured in. "Your Grace, Your Grace—" she babbled, pointing.

The King ran to the window and stared outside. The flames had met and embraced above the roof. As we watched, horrified, the roof began to buckle and slowly cave in, like melting candy. Just then the wind shifted and a great wave of heat hit our faces.

Then the King moved. "Outside!" he called, and his voice was no longer thin, but commanding. "Outside!" We all went into the corridor, thick now with smoke and alight with airborne sparks, and then down a private staircase which led outside the Manor walls. The guards followed. The King turned on them. "Raise the alarm! Get everyone out! And not into the courtyard! To the river!" He turned back to us. "Yes, to the river!" he said, pushing us toward the path to the landing-stage.

Now the Manor itself was a torch. It had been dry and was nearly all of wood. Flames leapt from the roof, and as we hurried to the river, we heard a great groaning: the sound of the roof of the Hall collapsing inward. I turned to see it and saw a great arc of sparks fly upward, followed by a roll of smoke. Then I was knocked down by Arthur running behind me.

"Don't stop and stare!" he screamed. "Get up!" I scrambled to my feet and kept my eyes on the river ahead, which reflected the strange red light behind us. The unfrozen portions danced with the flames, indeed, seemed to be aflame themselves.

The King stopped by the riverbank. "We'll be safe here," he said. Silently we all drew together and watched Sheen Manor burn.

"*Sic transit gloria mundi,*" said Margaret Beaufort, crossing herself. She turned her snapping black eyes on me; I noticed, idly, as one does at such moments, how they reflected the flames in miniature. "A sermon for you someday, Henry. A lesson in how fleeting are the things of this earth." Her language grew more florid by the moment. Clearly it was a sermon she herself wished to deliver on the spot. "It was God's doing, to punish us for our vanity."

"It was the Cornishmen's doing," said Father. *"Or their friends."* He took a stone and threw it angrily out into the river. It thudded on the ice, skidded for a few feet, then dropped silently into the cold water. Ripples spread out, each one red-rimmed.

"Now we must go to the Tower. So it will look as if we *had* to take refuge. They planned it well."

Suddenly I understood it all. I understood the little, puzzling things: that Father had had the banquet in order to show the court and powerful nobles what a wealthy and mighty King he was, how secure, how established. He had brought his children to Sheen and obliged Arthur to sit by his side, had pointed Margaret and me out after the revels to show the solidarity of his family, to present his phalanx of heirs.

He had hanged the dogs because there was treason all about, and he wished to warn potential traitors that they could expect no mercy from him. Appearances were important, more important even than reality. People credited only what their eyes beheld; no matter if it were calculatedly false or staged.

And I understood the big thing: the enemy had its own resources and could pull everything down around you in an instant, leaving you to curse and throw rocks into the river. *All enemies must be destroyed. One must ever be on guard.*

And the most frightening thing of all: Father's throne was not secure. That fact hammered itself into my soul with cold nails. Tomorrow, or next week, or next year, he might be King no longer. . . .

"O Henry, why?" wept Arthur, still clutching the white, ermine-furred gift robes against himself. Then he answered his own question. "I suppose it was a careless cook." He pushed his hand across his nose, sniffling. "When I am King, I will make the kitchens safer."

Then I began to cry, too, and not for the burning Manor, but for Arthur, poor, foolish Arthur. . . .

"Aye," I said. "Make the kitchens safer. That would be a good thing."

Sheen Manor burned to the ground. We went to the Tower for safety, and Father's forces defeated the Cornish, finally, but not before they had reached London itself. A great battle was fought across the Thames on Blackheath, and from the high window of the Tower we could see the men milling, see the puffs of smoke from guns. We could see, too, small sprawled figures that no longer moved, until, as the day went on, they outnumbered the moving ones.

The pretender Warbeck was taken and locked securely in the fortress portion of the Tower, and we came out almost as he went in. A simple matter of which side of the walls one was on determined everything. Father was King again and could walk freely where he chose, while Warbeck was confined within the sunless walls.

Father made grand plans to have Sheen Manor rebuilt in the modern style, with great numbers of glass windows. To emphasize his recent victory, he changed its name to Richmond Palace. (He had been Earl of Richmond before becoming King.) He spent uncharacteristic sums on the new palace, and as a result it was surprisingly magnificent.

He also began making plans for Arthur's long-standing betrothal to Princess Katherine of Aragon finally to lead to a wedding. He was determined to see Arthur settled in the marriage bed as soon as possible.

IV

Arthur had been betrothed practically from the font at which he had first been christened Arthur, "in honour of the British race." And what better way to show the honour of the British race than to cross it with another royal house? Father, as always, aimed high. (I have lately come to realize that he would have made an excellent gambler. What a pity—and loss for his purse!—that he did not play, on principle.) Spain was an obvious choice, as Father preferred not to importune our ancient enemy, France, for a bride. If Spain would allow its princess to marry into the House of Tudor, this would constitute recognition that we were, indeed, legitimate rulers. It would be another bit of showmanship for Father, like the treasonous dogs. It would say to the world: Look, look, I am a true King. For the old, established royal houses would never sign marriage contracts with a Perkin Warbeck or his like. And once there were sons from that marriage, all unspoken reservations about the worthiness of the Tudor blood would be stilled. Arthur and Katherine's children would be welcomed in every court in Europe.

I think there persisted a feeling at the time that England was not a country in the civilized sense of the word. We were perceived as backward, remote, and barbarous—the latter because of our horrible dynastic wars, which had been going on since living memory. We were not truly wild, like the Scots or the Irish, but we were not yet an integral part of the rest of Europe.

Everything took so long to reach us. When I was ten, that is, around the year 1500, glass windows in common dwellings were almost unheard of. No bluff, common Englishman would use a fork (or had even seen one), would wear anything but wool, would eat anything but the traditional "three B's": beer, bread, and beef. There were no rugs on the stone floors, nothing but dirty rushes where people spit and threw scraps. Even the King dined on a collapsible trestle table, and only women in childbirth could expect to have a pillow. This while Italian princes lived in open, sunlit villas, worked on inlaid marble tables, and sampled a variety of fine dishes.

The Renaissance, the New Learning—those were but foreign terms to us, and anything foreign was suspect. Our great lords still tried to keep their own private armies of retainers, long after the princes of Europe had begun concentrating all military power in their own hands. Music, even at court, consisted of a small band of poor musicians playing outdated tunes on outdated instruments. Parliament was summoned only in order to raise money for the King, and then, often as not, the people refused to pay up. European ambassadors regarded a posting here as going into exile, where they would have to endure privations and exist among a baffling, unruly people. They prayed to endure until they could be rewarded by being sent to a "real" court.

Of course, the common people would come out and gape whenever the English King would go from one palace to another. To them we were grand. They knew no better; but foreigners did. They used to mock the King and all our shabby, awkward, unfashionable grandeurs.

At ten, of course, I did not know all this, but I sensed it. I saw how reluctant the Spanish were actually to send their daughter here, in spite of the signed treaties promising to do so. I saw that the French King or the Holy Roman Emperor never met Father, never came to his court or invited him to theirs. I saw that the ambassadors who were here seemed to be old and badly dressed, and that some countries sent no ambassadors at all.

It would be different in Arthur's reign, I hoped. I wanted him to be that old Arthur come again—to be a mighty King, so filled with honour and strength and a sort of shining that it would change everything. As I was trying desperately to shape myself for a churchman, I saw his reign as bringing a new Golden Age to the Church as well. Under Arthur, the monasteries would blossom forth in learning, the priests rededicate themselves to the Saviour . . . and so on. Yes, I tried hard to hew myself into a cleric. I have always felt that whatever the station to which one is called, one must embrace it wholeheartedly. Although the religious life had been chosen for me, I believed that it was meant to be. Was not Samuel the Prophet promised to God before he was born? God had chosen me: God must have special work for me to do. And it was true, although not in the way I had first thought. Have I not done God's work as King? Defended the *true* faith and saved the English Church from the errors of Popery? And could I have done it, would I have been *equipped* to do it, had I not spent my childhood in holy studies? Nothing is wasted, nothing is pointless. God directs all. *All*, I say.

WILL:

Have you ever heard such nonsense? Harry was always so tiresome when he got wound up on one of his religious huffs-and-puffs. This is a perfect example. Worse, he really believed himself.

I should have hated Arthur, but I did not. Even envy was forbidden me: if Arthur was to be King, it was God's will, and I must not wrestle with God. Jacob had, but that was long ago, and he had been duly punished. When I studied Genesis I knew that.

Arthur was hailed as a paradigm of princehood: handsome, brilliant, promising. His graces were admired, his looks, his studies. The sicknesses, the painful shyness, the lack of any physical prowess (this in the son of a King who had won his crown in battle!) were ignored. A King-to-be is always a prodigy, a phenomenon, a reincarnation of Alexander the Great.

So, as the years passed and I grew taller and stronger than Arthur, and caught up with him in his studies (he used to ask me secretly to do his Latin translations for him), it was politely ignored, and I was ignored as well.

Only Arthur himself did not flinch from me. He was fond of me and, in a strange way, envious. He thought me free.

"You are so lucky, Henry," he said quietly one day after the King had been to see us—praising Arthur and nodding perfunctorily at the rest of us. "They don't see you. They don't care what you do."

And for that he calls me lucky, I thought sourly.

"You can do what you like," he continued. "You can be whatever you like, do whatever your fancy tells you."

"No," I finally said. "It's *you* who can do that. Because whatever you do, they say it's right. Whatever I do, they say it's wrong."

"But don't you see? That's the freedom—to be wrong! How I wish—" Suddenly embarrassed, he stopped and changed the subject, that early spring day when he was fifteen and I was ten. "I want you to help me, Henry," he blurted out.

"How?" I was taken aback by the sudden, candid request.

"You're so good—such a skilled horseman," he finally said. "You know I've never . . . liked horses. And now I'll have to ride with Father to meet Katherine, my betrothed."

"You'll be twenty before that happens," I scoffed. Like everyone else, I knew that the betrothal to Katherine had been stalemated once again.

"No. She's to arrive this autumn. And we're to be married right after. I know the Spanish prize horsemanship. Katherine's own mother rode into battle when she was with child! I—well, I—"

"You don't want to fall off in front of Katherine," I finished. "But, Arthur, you've ridden for years, had innumerable teachers. What can I do that they could not?" You hate horses and have no feel for them, I thought to myself, and no teacher can make up for that.

"I don't know," he said miserably. "But if only—"

"I'll try to help you," I said. "But if you aren't a good horseman, why don't you avoid horses in front of Katherine? Do something else. Sing. Dance."

"I can't sing, and I'm a clumsy dancer," he said, his face set. *"You* can sing, and *you* can dance, but I can't."

"Recite verse, then."

"I hate verse."

What can you do, then? I wondered. "Then you must let others make fools of themselves dancing and singing and reciting, and look on with amusement."

"And there's something else! The—the wedding night!" His voice sounded higher than usual.

"Oh. *That,"* I said nonchalantly, trying to appear wise.

He smiled wanly. "At least I can't ask your help in that," he attempted to joke—a joke that was to haunt me, literally, for years.

So it was to happen at last. Arthur was to be married straightway, and the Spanish Princess was already en route to England. The voyage would take two months at least. But she was coming! And there would be a royal wedding and festivities, after years of nothing. Father would be forced to spend money as all the eyes of Europe would be focused on the English Court, watching and judging. There must be great banquets and elaborate allegorical arches and statues and pageants in the streets to celebrate the marriage, and the public conduits would have to run with red and white wine all day. (Already my confessor had pointed out that I had an inordinate fascination for the glitter and pomp of this world, as he put it.) Most important to me, I would have new clothes.

I hated Father's miserliness. I hated being in moth-eaten cloaks and wearing shirts whose worn sleeves ended halfway to my wrists. I was now just as tall as Arthur, yet I was put into the clothes of someone many sizes smaller. When I bent, the breeches cut into my backside; when I reached, the shoulders strained.

"You're your grandfather all over," Nurse Luke kept saying. She could not see how I winced at that. "He was outsized, and you will be, too. He was six feet and four inches."

"Handsome, too." I could not resist that.

"Yes," she said tartly. "Perhaps too much so, for his own good."

"One can never be too handsome for one's own good," I teased.

"No? *He* was. Anyway, handsomeness is wasted on a priest. If you're too handsome, you make people nervous. No one will confess to you."

"But the things *I'll* have to confess!" I laughed.

"Henry!" she snorted. "You should not plan your badness in advance."

"You are right, Mistress Luke. I shall just sin spontaneously."

I enjoyed seeing the look on her face as she bustled away. In truth, I hardly knew what sort of sin I was likely to commit, although evidently some of the court serving girls did: I had caught them looking at me with peculiar expressions.

Katherine did not land at Dover, as had been expected. A storm blew her ship off course, and the Spanish were forced to land at Plymouth instead—a long, wet, and muddy ride from London.

Protocol demanded, nevertheless, that Father go to meet her officially and welcome her to England. Arthur could not accompany him, that was plain. He had lately been ill with a racking cough. He must stay indoors, near fires, to conserve whatever strength he had to face the coming ordeal of his wedding. So it was that I was told to go with Father to bring Katherine to her new home.

It was late autumn, foggy and cold. The leaves were already off the trees, and the countryside was brown and bleak, wreathed in ground mists. The ride promised to be long and clammy. Yet I did not care; I was excited to be out beyond the confines of the palace walls. I was wide-eyed and gaping at everything we passed: the cheering crowds, the muddy-pathed villages, the great yellow open fields, the dark forests.

It took days to reach the place where the Spanish had landed. It was a dismal little huddle of tents; rain dripped off the proud corners of the middle tent, the royal one. The royal standard hung drenched and pathetic on the flagstaff.

It was almost evening, the bone-chilling end of the day when the cold wraps around you and the chill seeps in underneath your cloak. I was glad to be within minutes of sheltering inside a warm, dry tent. I dismounted and sloshed along behind Father, who strode up to the door of the tent.

And was promptly turned away. The King—turned away! He laughed, unbelieving. It seemed that the Spanish custom was that the bride must not be seen before her wedding day by any man outside her family.

Father stopped, stock-still. Then, in deceptively quiet tones, he said, "I am King in this land, and in England there is no such law. Spanish law has no force here."

He pushed his way toward the tent-flap, shoving aside the protesting guard. "Do the Spanish think me a fool?" he muttered. "To marry my heir to someone I've never even seen—who might be pockmarked or deformed? I will see her for myself!"

The remaining guard made a halfhearted attempt to keep him out, but he pushed past him and plunged into the tent. I followed.

We found ourselves in a harem. It was clearly a woman's tent, with women's clothes and toilet articles scattered about, and several ill-at-ease serving maids. We felt very large and mud-splattered and clumsy, standing there surrounded by scarves and cushions and perfumes.

Now there was a commotion in the veiled inner part of the tent: the Princess was told that we had blundered into her private quarters. Doubtless she would come out and chastise us. I could already picture her: thin and fussy and tight-lipped—a perfect bride for Arthur.

I heard her voice before I saw her, and it was a low voice, and sweet, not scolding and shrewish. Then she emerged in her dressing gown, her hair still unarranged and free of any headdress; it fell, in thick, golden-brown waves, over her shoulders.

She was beautiful—like a maiden in the *Morte d'Arthur,* like the fair Elaine, the lovely Enid. Or Andromeda, chained to a rock, awaiting rescue by Perseus in the myth I had been dutifully translating. All the heroines of literature came to life for me as I stared at Katherine.

What can I say? I loved her, then and there. Doubtless you will say I was only a boy, a ten-year-old boy, and that I had not even spoken to her, and that it was therefore impossible for me to love her. But I did. I did! I loved her with a sudden burst of devotion that took me quite by surprise. I stood gaping at her, gripped by yet another unknown emotion: intense jealousy of Arthur, who would have her for himself.

And now the betrothal ceremony must be arranged. I was to represent Arthur and be his proxy in the ceremony promising them to one another, and I thought I could not bear it.

But I did. Early the next day we stood side by side and recited dull vows in Latin before a priest in her tent. Although Katherine was already fifteen, she was no taller than I. I could turn my eye just a little and meet hers on the same level.

I found her continually looking at me, and it made me uncomfortable. But then I caught her expression and realized what she was seeing. Misled by my early height and thick chest, she looked at the second son and saw what no one else, thus far, had seen: a man. She saw me as a man, and she was the first to do it. And I loved her for that too.

But she was Arthur's. She would be his wife, and he would be King. I accepted it without question—or so I thought. Can secret wishes, so secret they are not admitted even to the self, come true? Even as I ask the question, I do not want to know the answer.

꽃

The wedding was to take place on November fourteenth, and Arthur was expected to produce an heir within a year. The King never said so, but I overheard the jests and jokes among the servants (they always spoke freely in front of me, as if I were already a priest). They all wanted a baby by Christmas of the following year; indeed, they thought it their due.

For someone charged with such prodigious responsibilities, Arthur was oddly unenthusiastic. As his wedding day approached, he became more and more listless. He shrank; he dwindled; clearly he did not want to be married. One day he came to my chambers, ostensibly to ask my help in trying on his new clothes, but in reality to cry and confess he didn't want it—any of it.

"I don't want to go through a marriage ceremony before thousands of people," he said in a tremulous voice, standing before a half-length mirror and looking pensively at his reflection, swathed in his white velvet cape. Three years later, he had finally grown into it.

"Well, you must, that's all," I said, grabbing his plumed hat off his head and plopping it on my own, making faces at myself in the mirror. "Think about afterwards." I knew something about that business—in a confused sort of way.

"That's the part I *don't* want to think about," he said quietly.

"Then don't. Perhaps it's better that way." I turned and observed how I looked in the hat. I didn't like the curled brim.

"You don't know . . ." He paused, then muttered, ". . . anything."

Suddenly I was angry. "I know that you are afraid. About *what* it doesn't matter. And if other people can see you are afraid, then it will be bad for you. It mustn't show, Arthur. You mustn't let it show."

"Aren't you ever afraid? No, I don't believe you are. . . ."

I had to turn away then, lest I answer him: *Yes. I am often afraid.* Still, I had learned early to mask fear, to stamp it down. I could not help what it did inside me. But I was pleased that Arthur thought I was never afraid. It meant that others could not see what I really felt.

With studied casualness, I tossed the hat across to Arthur, aiming at his head. It landed square on him, ringing his head perfectly. I heard myself laugh, and heard him join in.

He believed me happy. That was enough for me: a minor triumph in the midst of his general victory. It tasted sweet as honey, almost as good as full-bodied wine. Which I was supposed to be too young to drink . . . just as I was supposed to be too young to love Princess Katherine.

November fourteenth was clear and warm—it fell within St. Martin's Summer, the last burst of sun before the drab winter. The warmth would bring the crowds to their height, I thought, surprised at how experienced that made me sound. In truth, I had not appeared before London crowds since I was made Duke of York seven years earlier.

I must escort Katherine from her lodgings at Westminster Palace east into London to St. Paul's, where she would wed Arthur. She must not see him until they met in the Cathedral; to do so was considered unlucky. Thus it came about that I would ride beside her through London and hear the shouts meant for Arthur.

I had a new white velvet suit for the occasion. Both Katherine and I were to ride white horses, and she would be attired in white and cloth-of-silver, as befitted a virgin bride. Together we would make a white spot in the streets, easily seen a hundred yards away even by someone with poor eyesight.

As she was led out on a fine white mare and we met in the Palace courtyard, I reached out to her, caught her hand. She was even more beautiful than I had remembered, and on her pale cheeks glowed two bright spots. Excitement, or fear? I grasped her hand and she tightened the grip. Her hand was cold. So it was fear.

Then the Palace gates swung open. Beyond stretched a seeming sea of people, some of them having waited since daybreak. They broke into cheers as we rode out, throwing late-blooming flowers upon us. I saw Katherine shrink back, but I was exhilarated, felt a strange stirring in my loins. I loved the stares, the people, the cheers, and wanted the ride to last forever. I was thankful that the way to St. Paul's was long.

There were more than a hundred thousand London citizens, according to Father's ever-diligent census-takers. I believe they were all out that day, watching us. Truly, I had never imagined people in such numbers. And all cheering . . .

The road to St. Paul's followed the unpaved Strand running beside the Thames. To our right were the large houses of the nobility and high-ranking prelates, with long, narrow gardens running down to the river where the watergates and boat-landings were. I could see clear across the river to the Archbishop of Canterbury's palace at Lambeth, its weathering bricks looking pink in the midday sun. It stood alone, yet not far away I could make out scattered dwellings and shops. This area was called Southwark, and I knew (from Skelton) that taverns and hostelries and pleasure gardens and houses of prostitution thrived here in the very shadow of the Archbishop's palace and the dwellings of other bishops. In fact the Bishop of Winchester's house was so close to one of the larger bawdy houses that the women there were nicknamed "Winchester geese." Evidently the south side of the river was undecided as to whether its true nature was holy or profane.

At length we approached Ludgate and were abruptly in the thick of the city. It was but a short way up Ludgate Hill to St. Paul's. A raised wooden walkway had been constructed before the Cathedral's entrance and covered with a white carpet which we must walk over all the way down the great aisle to the altar where I was to hand Katherine over to Arthur.

It was dim inside, and after the bright sun I could barely see. The Cathedral seemed to be a great cavern with a gleam of gold and flickering lights somewhere far in the distance. That must be the altar. I reached out to take Katherine's hand and found it cold as death. I looked into her eyes and saw only fear there. Beneath her veiled white headdress her face was blanched.

I longed to be able to speak to her and ease her fear, but her rudimentary English and my equally rudimentary Spanish could not meet. I put both my hands over hers and smiled. Just as she smiled in return, a silver blare of trumpets announced the beginning of the procession. We must walk to the altar, and I must yield her to Arthur. He waited, also attired in white, a pale moth in the vastness of the great nave.

The wedding banquet following the ceremony was splendid. Enormous tables ran down the entire length of the Hall at Westminster, heavy with gold plate and extravagant dishes—three-tiered castles, pheasants, gilded swans, replicas of lakes—all created by the King's clever pastry artists. The Spanish ambassador looked it all over critically. I saw him pacing up and down, pretending he was deciding upon a dish, but in reality inventorying the whole for his report to Ferdinand. He caught my eye once and smiled. He did not have to fear my opinion of him, as I was negligible, a nonentity—so he thought. The French ambassador and the Imperial one also took mental notes. I saw Father observing them from the royal dais. He was pleased that this expenditure would serve him so well in diplomatic reports.

At the conclusion of the wedding feast, servers took away the dishes and removed the tables, clearing the hall for dancing.

Although I had not been formally trained in it, I loved dancing and had managed to teach myself a great deal in the privacy of my chamber. Now I could try my skill with real musicians and real partners, and I prayed not to appear foolish.

My prayers were answered; my self-taught steps served me well, and although I learned moment by moment with the help of my partners, I found I knew much already. I danced a pavane, a basse dance, and even a Burgundian, a difficult step. Soon I had to remove my jacket, I was so hot. I tossed it into a corner, and was surprised to hear cheers.

"Young Lord Henry!" someone called. "Dance on!"

And so I did, until sweat was pouring off me and I panted for breath. Exhausted, I made my way to a corner where I slumped against the wall. I could feel sweat trickling down my face and back, soaking into my shirt.

"D'you want yer fortune?" a voice suddenly whispered into my ear. I turned and saw a well-dressed woman standing beside me. But she had an odd expression in her eye, and she leaned over in a conspiratorial manner. "I ain't supposed to be here. If they find me, I'm gone. But I come to all the royal weddings. I was at the King's, now"—she jerked her head to indicate Father—"as well as at poor Richard's; and Edward's . . . aye, not that one, since he married her secretly—if he married her at all, that witch!"

She was talking about my other grandmother, Elizabeth Woodville. Still I sat stiffly and did not say anything.

"So you are not curious?" she said, as if I had wronged her. Slowly she picked herself up and prepared to go elsewhere. As she stood up, one of the King's guard recognized her.

"That woman!" he choked, hurriedly coming over. "She's a Welsh fortune-teller! A sorceress!" He apprehended her, hustled her toward the door, and shoved her out. He shook his head apologetically in my direction. "They cluster around like flies! I cannot keep them all out!"

That night Arthur took Katherine into his bed. Alone in mine, I thought about what that Welsh woman had said about my grandmother being a witch, to keep myself from thinking what Arthur was—or was not—doing. Strange to think that in years to come that very question was to be debated by scores of learned men.

V

The next morning Arthur called for courtiers to attend him in his bed-chamber. He demanded cups of wine and was full of boasts about how marriage was thirsty work, and so on. He kept repeating this all day. It was the first thing he said to me as he emerged from his room and saw me. He even attempted a manful chuckle.

Arthur and Katherine were at court all during the Christmas holidays, and I found I could not bear to be with them. I sulked and tried to avoid the festivities. This was so unlike me that the Queen eventually sought me out in my secret, solitary spot: an empty room high in the eaves of the palace. I had thought no one knew I went there, but clearly she had noticed.

It was cold there; no fires were ever lit. But I could hear faint music and laughter from the Great Hall below. It was another masque, another dance. I shut my ears against it and looked out the small cobwebbed window, seeing the late-December sun slanting over the Palace grounds, and far beyond. Everything was brown and golden and still. I could see the ships on the Thames, anchored and waiting. Waiting . . .

I wished I could be a sailor and live on one of those ships; spend my life on the water, sailing all over the world. Being a prince—the sort of prince I must be—was dull by comparison. I would . . . I would start going down to the docks and learning about ships. I would go secretly! That way, Father could say nothing against it. I would disguise myself . . . and then, when I had become an expert sailor, I would sail away, forget my life here, disappear, become a vagabond prince—have high adventures! They would never know what had become of me; only *I* would know my true identity. There would be monsters, and sea battles, and—

"Henry?" A soft voice interrupted me.

I turned, guiltily, and saw the Queen.

"Henry, what are you doing here all alone?"

"I am planning my future."

"Your Father has already done that."

Yes. He thought to make a priest of me. Well, they would have to fit the chasubles and albs and cinctures to someone else. I would be sailing the high seas!

"You must not worry about your place," she said, thinking to soothe me, "nor hide yourself from the festivities."

"The festivities bore me," I said grandly. "And the costumes for the masque were moth-eaten!" Somehow this one thing had greatly embarrassed me. I knew that the Spanish ambassador had seen, and laughed at us.

She nodded. "Yes, I know. They are so old—"

"Why doesn't he get new ones, then?" I burst out. "Why?"

She ignored the question and all that lay behind it. "There will be dancing soon. Please come. You are such a talented dancer."

"A talented dancer!" I said grumpily. "I must forget dancing—unless Arthur will permit the clergy to dance in their vestments. Do you think His Holiness might give us such a dispensation?" It was hopeless; it must be the sea for me, that was clear.

Suddenly the Queen bent toward me and touched my face lightly. "Dear Henry," she said. "I disliked it, too. So much."

So she knew, she understood. She had been the eldest, but only a daughter. Unable to be Queen in her own right. Unable. And waiting. Always waiting—to be assigned her secondary role.

I nodded. And obediently followed her down to the Great Hall.

The Hall was hot and crowded, with everyone dressed in satins, stiff jewelled brocades, and splendidly coloured velvets. I was only too aware of my plain clothes. I had been allowed only three new outfits for the wedding and Christmas festivities, and I had long since appeared in them.

Arthur and Katherine sat at one end of the Hall. Arthur was gotten up like a jewelled idol, and he looked frail and doll-like in the overpowering chair. He kept glancing nervously at Katherine. He and his new wife were to leave London as soon as the holidays were over, and go to a cold, horrid castle on the Welsh border to play King and Queen in training. This was entirely Father's idea; he believed in toughening Arthur, tempering him.

Arthur clearly did not want to be tempered. Yet he was willing, because it was his duty. Arthur always obeyed his duty. He seemed to feel that was what distinguished a king, or even was the essence of kingship.

The minstrels took their assigned places in the stone gallery. There were fifteen of them—double the usual number. Their leader announced that they were honoured by the presence of a Venetian lutenist and a shawm player from Flanders. There was a murmur of appreciation. Then he added that a French musician, well versed in French court dances, would play, as well as another artist who had trained at the Spanish court.

Initially they played only English dances, and almost all the lords and ladies and company danced, as these measures were familiar to them. They knew the pavane, the bransle, and the almain.

Arthur would not dance. He just sat, still and solemn, in his great chair, deliberately ignoring Katherine's restlessness and tapping feet. She was longing to dance—it was evident in every line of her body.

Suddenly I was determined to satisfy that longing in her and in myself as well. We were both prisoners of our station: she, wed to a husband who refused to dance; I, a future priest. It was decreed that we must spend the remainder of our lifetimes without dancing. Perhaps so, but there was still a little time. . . .

I made my way over to her and, bowing low before the dais, indicated that I wished her to join me in a Burgundian. She nodded hesitantly; I held out my hand and together we went to the middle of the floor.

I felt drunk. I had done what I longed to do, and in front of everyone! The exhilaration of it . . . it was a taste I was never to lose, was to seek from then on.

I looked at Katherine. She smiled joyfully at having been rescued. And there was something else in her look . . . she found me pleasing, found my person attractive. I felt her acceptance of me, her liking, and it was like the summer sun to me.

She was a stunning dancer and knew many intricate steps unfamiliar to us in England. I had to struggle to keep up with her. Her timing, her balance, her sense of the music were astounding. Gradually the others fell back and watched us as we progressed through a galliard, a dance du Roy, a quatre bransle, and a Spanish dance of the Alhambra that she showed me. When the musicians stopped, Katherine was breathless and her face flushed. The onlookers were silent for an awkward moment, then they began to cheer us.

Alone on the dais, Arthur glowered like a pale, angry child.

VI

Four months later Arthur was dead—of consumption in that drafty Welsh castle—and Katherine was a widow.

And I was, suddenly, the heir—the only thing standing between the young Tudor dynasty and oblivion.

I was alone in my chamber when the news came. One of the pages brought me a brief note from the King, asking me to come to him right away.

"Immediately?" I asked, puzzled. The King never sent for me, and certainly not in the middle of the day, when I was supposed to be doing my studies.

"Yes, Your Grace," he replied, and his voice was different from before. So markedly different that even a ten-year-old boy would take note of it. I looked over at him and found him staring at me.

All along the passageway it was the same. People gaped at me. I suddenly knew that something terrible was about to happen. Was I to be sent away to some remote monastery, ostensibly to study?

I reached the King's Privy Chamber and pulled open the heavy wooden door. Inside it was dark and dismal, as always. Father never lit enough firewood, out of his perverted sense of frugality, unless he expected a high-ranking visitor. He normally kept his quarters so cold that the servants used to store perishable foods behind the screens. Butter kept especially well there, or so I was told.

I saw a shadowy figure standing in the gloom, his back to me. The King. He turned and saw me.

"Henry!" He came toward me, his hands extended. The fingers were slightly blue with the chill, I noticed. His face was drawn as if invisible weights were pulling at the skin.

"Arthur is dead. Your brother is dead." His thin lips spat out the words as if I were responsible.

"When?" was all I could think to say.

"Three days ago. The messenger has just come from Ludlow. It was—

a chill. Consumption. I don't know." He shook his head and made helpless gestures with his hands.

"You sent him there." I heard my own voice; it was a stranger's. "You sent him to Wales, to that horrible castle."

He looked stricken and old: a collapsing leather bag. "To learn to be King—" he protested feebly.

"To die. Of course he would. He was never strong. He couldn't survive that place. And he did not want to go."

Arthur is dead . . . Arthur is dead . . . the words kept beating against my mind, like rain against a window.

"Yes. I sent him to Wales." The King's grey eyes seemed to ice over. "In so doing, it seems that I have made you King."

Until he said it, I had not realized the full implication. Arthur was dead: I would be King.

"This is God's doing," I said automatically, without thinking. It was what priests always said whenever something catastrophic took place.

Father's eyes seemed to bulge, and he took a step toward me, his hand raised as if to strike me. "How dare you imply that God meant you to be King?" he whispered.

"I only meant—" I began, but his blow cut me off.

"Arthur is dead and you live!" he screamed. "I hate God! I hate Him! I curse Him!"

I almost expected to see the Devil materialize in the cold chamber and drag the King off. The priests had told me that was what happened to those who reviled or cursed God. But nothing happened. I was to remember that too, later. . . .

Suddenly the Queen—I had not even seen her in the shadows of the chamber—rushed over to us. "Stop!" she commanded. "How dare you argue and insult each other over Arthur's grave?" Her face was wet and her hair hanging limp, but her voice was hard and strong.

"*He* has insulted *me!* And God," I added as a pious afterthought.

I thought she would upbraid the King, but instead she turned on me. They all turn on me, I thought angrily, and suddenly I was weary of it. . . .

"You will be King, Henry. Do you feel safe and smug, now that you're the heir? But there's nothing to keep you out of the grave as well. Being heir doesn't protect you. It singles you out." She moved closer to me and glared into my eyes. Her own were almost the colour of twilight, some other part of me noticed and recorded. "Now death will want *you* as well. He is hungry for heirs. That is his favourite food. You are now in his fattening pen. Is that your triumph?" With only a few words she was able to strike such fear into me that the history of my kingship would resound with my attempts to still it.

Then she turned to the King, to whom she had always deferred and before whom she had kept silent. "You are mad with grief," she said, drily. "You don't mean what you are saying. You do not mean to insult Henry, your only son. You do not mean that at all."

He nodded, dully.

I had entered the King's chamber a second son and future priest; I left it as heir apparent and future King. To say that everything changed thereafter is to say what any fool could know. By that they would assume I meant the externals: the clothes I wore and my living quarters and my education. Yet the greatest change was immediate, and in fact had already occurred.

As I left the chamber, one of the yeomen of the guard pulled back the door and bowed. He was a very tall man, and I barely reached his shoulder. As he straightened, I found his eyes riveted on me in a most disturbing fashion. It was only for an instant, but in that instant I perceived curiosity—and fear. He was afraid of me, this great, strong man, afraid of what I might prove to be. For he did not know me, and I was his future King.

No one at court knew me. I was to meet that selfsame look again and again. It said: Who is he? Shall we fear him? At length I developed the habit of never looking directly into anyone's eyes lest I again meet that look of wariness coupled with apprehension. It was not a good or restful thing to know that merely by existing I threatened the ordered pattern of others' lives.

They knew Father well and had duly observed Arthur for some fifteen years, grown used to him. But Henry was the unknown, the hidden-away one. . . .

The man smiled, falsely. "Your Grace," he said.

The smile was worse than the look in his eyes, although they went hand in hand. I made some stiff little motion with my hand and turned away.

No one would ever be candid or open with me again. That was the great change in my life.

There were other changes as well, of course. I must now live at court with the King; I must exchange my priest-tutor for a retired ambassador. There were good changes: I was now allowed to practise dancing and even had a French dance-master to demonstrate the fashions in that court, where everything was elegant and perfect (to hear him tell it). I had my own band of minstrels and a new music teacher who taught me theory and composition, and even imported an Italian organ for me to use. Being constantly at court, I began to meet other boys of my own age, noblemen's sons, and so I had friends for the first time in my life.

The bad things: I was not to engage in any "dangerous" activities, such as hunting or even jousting, as my person now had to be guarded against the remotest mishap. As a result, I had to stay indoors and watch my friends at play, or join them outside merely to stand about watching, which was worse.

I had to live in a room that connected to the King's, so that I could go nowhere, and no one come to me, without passing through his chamber first. In that way he isolated me as effectively as one of those maidens in the *Morte d'Arthur,* imprisoned in a turret by her father. The only difference was that as long as my father lived, no one could rescue me or even approach me.

And how long would my father live? He was only forty-five, and seemed healthy. He might live another twenty years, all the while keeping me prisoner in that little room off his own. How could I endure it?

For several months after Arthur's death he was withdrawn and took little interest in anything around him. He used to call for his lutenist to come and play for him. The lutenist was not very good, and his music-making grated on me. I once went in and offered to play for my father instead. He agreed listlessly, and I played several tunes that I had written myself. I could see that he was not really listening, and so I finally got up and returned to my room. He continued staring out the window and gave no sign that he was even aware that I had left.

Stupidly, I was disappointed. I had not yet learned.

But I was learning other things at Father's behest. Every day the old ambassador would come to tutor me. He was Stephen Farr and had served Richard III, Edward IV, and Father on embassies to the Low Countries, to France, to Spain, and to the Pope and Emperor for over twenty years. He had a round face and a high red colouring that belied his years, although he must have been near seventy. Once I mentioned this and he said, "That's my secret, you know. Being fat. People trust fat men. It's the lean ones that seem possible dissemblers. Tell me, Your Grace: whom would you readier suspect of treason or plots—a fat person with a smooth face, or a lean one with a face like a withered apple? Could Friar Tuck have been evil? Or, conversely, could the Sheriff of Nottingham have been plump? Of course not. Employ only fat ambassadors, I beg you."

I laughed. (Some could accuse me of having chosen Wolsey on that basis, had they been privy to our conversation that day.)

"It's no joke, Your Grace, I assure you. People put much stock in appearances. And first feelings and impressions are never erased. The world is full of people who have a peculiar gift for sizing things up immediately. Jealous people call it 'rash judgment.' It is not that at all. I have heard"—he stood up and came toward me, a playful look on his face—"that Your Grace is an expert archer. That you draw the longbow with great accuracy. Tell me—on your best days, do you not hit the mark from the very beginning?"

I nodded. And on bad days, it was just the reverse.

"It is the same with people. The best judges never miss the mark. And from the very first."

"What has this to do with me?" I was anxious to get on with the lesson and impress him with the many facts I had memorized for his benefit since last time.

"Everything. First, you must develop this uncanny skill in yourself, just as you developed your skill at riding or music. There is no greater gift a King can have. And, second, you must play to that gift in others."

"How?" How could I change a stranger's impression of me? I, who could not even change my own father's?

He had turned and walked over to the window. He seemed old and tired. His cloak stirred the reeds. He stopped at the window and heaved a sigh. As well he might. The November rains had come and were pelting against the small panes of glass. His back seemed rounded; I had not realized how old he was.

Suddenly he swung round and was reborn. He walked differently, almost jauntily, and his head was high. Watching him, I forgot November and thought of sun and summer.

"You see?" He stopped in front of me. "It is all in the bearing, the demeanour. Actors know that. With a change of robe and a slight stoop, they go from young to old, beggar to king. It is simple: for a King, do like a King."

He sat down beside me, glancing toward the door. "And now I fear the King will come in and see that we are somewhat behind." He seemed embarrassed at what he had just said, as if he wished me to forget it as quickly as possible.

"Have you learned the things I told you?" he asked.

"Yes," I replied. I glanced over at the fireplace. I wished I could add another log to the fire, as my fingers were chilled. But there were no more there. Father allowed only six logs per day until after New Year's, no matter how foul the weather. I blew on my fingers. "First, France. There are sixteen million Frenchmen. They are the most powerful country in Europe. As late as my father's exile, Brittany was an independent duchy. But when King Charles VIII married Anne of Brittany in 1491, it became part of France. The French are our enemies. Our great King Henry V conquered nearly all of France—"

"Not all, Your Grace," admonished Farr.

"Nearly half, then," I conceded. "And his son was crowned King of France in Paris! And I shall recapture those lands!"

He smiled indulgently. "And how many Englishmen live in the realm?"

"Three million. Three and a *half* million!"

"And sixteen million in France, Your Grace."

"What matter the numbers? An Englishman is worth twenty Frenchmen! They are terrified of us. Why, French mothers frighten their children with threats of *les Anglais!*"

"And English mothers frighten their children with cries of bogy-men."

"We still have Calais," I persisted.

"For how long? It is an unnatural outpost."

"It is part of *England.* No, I mean to pursue my heritage! To recapture France."

"Have you been reading those Froissart things again, Your Grace?"

"No!" I said. But it was not true, and he knew it. I loved those chronicles of knights and their ladies and warfare, and read them late at night, often when I should have been sleeping. "Well—perhaps a little."

"A little is too much. Don't fill your head with such things. They are silly and what is worse, dangerous and outmoded. Any English King who attempts to recapture France now would risk his life, his treasury—and being ridiculed. A King can perhaps survive the first two. But the third, never. Now, then, have you memorized the general map of Europe?"

"Yes. The French have swallowed up Brittany and gorged themselves on Burgundy. And Maximilian, Emperor—"

"Of what?"

"The Holy Roman Empire."

"Which is neither holy nor Roman nor an empire," he said happily.

"No. It is merely a conglomerate of German duchies yoked with the Low Countries."

"But Maximilian has some twenty million nominal subjects."

"United on nothing," I parroted.

"Exactly." He was pleased. "And Spain?"

"Ferdinand and Isabella have driven the Moors out, and Spain is Christian once more. They have eight million subjects."

"Very good, Prince Henry. I believe you have been studying—in between Froissart." He reached out and cuffed me playfully. "Next we will discuss Ferdinand's schemes, and the history of the Papacy. Pope Julius is very much a part of all this, you know. He seems to be personally trying to demonstrate Christ's statement: 'I came not to bring peace, but a sword.' Read further in the notes I gave you and read all the dispatches in the red bag. They cover the correspondence during my years in France." He stood up stiffly. He was pretending we had come to the end of our lesson, but I could tell it was because he was so uncomfortable in that room. The fire was nearly out, and our breath was visible.

"I forgot," he said. "Tomorrow is St. Martin's Day, and so there will be no regular lesson."

That was disappointing. It seemed that whenever we began anything, it was interrupted by the constant procession of saints' days. There were more than a hundred of them in the year. Why couldn't the saints be honoured by going to Mass? Why did they require that everyone stop work as well?

"And Your Grace—please tell the Queen how happy I am with her news, and that I am praying for a safe confinement and a fair new Prince."

He bowed once and hurried out, back toward normal warmth and people. It was no matter; I could not have asked him, even had he stayed. I would never ask my tutor why he knew something I did not. The King had not told me of this, nor had the Queen. Why?

I walked over to the window. The rain had changed to sleet and was pelting against the walls and window. The window was poorly fitted, and small particles of sleet were working their way inside with no hindrance.

The window overlooked not the palace garden, but the ditches and outhouses. I hated all those ugly, straggling things attached to the palace, but especially the open, stinking ditches. When I was King I would have them all covered over. When I was King . . .

The driving sleet had already covered the structures, making them white and smooth. But not pretty. They were no more pretty than a skeleton, which could be equally white and smooth.

A violent shiver drove me from the window to the dying fire.

VII

It was true, what Stephen Farr had said. The Queen my mother was with child. She was confined in February, 1503, on Candlemas Day, and delivered not of an heir, but of a stillborn daughter. She died nine days later, on her thirty-seventh birthday.

Even today I must hurry over those facts, state them simply, lest I stumble and—rage? cry? I do not know. Both, perhaps.

There were many days of official mourning, days while the sculptors worked hurriedly to carve the customary funeral effigy that would sit atop her mourning-car. It must be an exact likeness, so that it would appear that she was still alive, clad in her robes and fur, as the cortege wound through the streets of London from the Tower, where she had died, to Westminster, where she would be buried. The people must see their good Queen again, must carry this last picture of her in their minds. Last impressions, too, were important. I wanted to tell Farr that.

But *I* would not see her again. Never, never, never . . . And when I saw the wooden image I hated it, because it seemed so alive, and yet it was not. They had done their job well, the carvers. Especially as they had had to work from a death-mask and not from life. But then, she was but thirty-seven, and had not thought to sit for her funeral effigy. No, not that.

I heard the King weeping, late at night. But he never came in to my chamber, never tried to share his sorrow with me. Nor did he acknowledge mine, save for a curt announcement that we were all to attend the funeral.

The day of the funeral was cold and foggy. The sun never shone, but turned the mist blue, as if to drown us in eternal twilight. Torches blazed in the London streets even in midday as the funeral procession wound its way from the Tower to Westminster, to the beat of muffled drums. First came the three hundred yeomen of the guard, then the hearse, a built-up carriage some twenty feet high, all in black, pulled by eight black horses, with the (to me) hideous effigy of the Queen all smiling and in royal robes atop it. Then followed thirty-seven young women, one for each year of her life. They wore white, white which seemed like part of the mist, and carried white candles. Then came the King, and Margaret, and Mary, and I.

The ordeal did not end with the procession. Once inside Westminster Abbey, I still had a Requiem Mass and a eulogy to endure. The hearse was driven to the end of the nave where it awaited the next, the awful, part: the burial.

I believe Warham celebrated the Mass; I do not recall. But a young man rose up to deliver the eulogy. Someone I had never seen before.

"I have composed an elegy for the Queen," he said, "which with your gracious permission I should like to read." The man's voice was strangely compelling, yet gentle.

The King nodded curtly. The man began. He had written it as though the Queen herself were taking leave of us all. That had hurt the most; she had said nothing, no farewell to me. Now this man was attempting to repair the omission—as if he had known. But how could he have known?

> Adieu! Mine own dear spouse, my worthy lord!
> The faithful love, that did us both continue
> In marriage and peaceable concord,
> Into your hands here I do resign,
> To be bestowed on your children and mine;
> Erst were ye father, now must ye supply
> The mother's part also, for lo! here I lie.
>
> Adieu, Lord Henry, loving son, adieu—
> Our Lord increase your honour and estate. . . .

His voice, his very presence, brought an extraordinary peace to me. It was not the words in themselves; it was, instead, a great, reaching compassion. Perhaps the first I had ever known.

"Who is he?" I leaned over to Margaret, who always knew names and titles.

"Thomas More," she whispered. "The lawyer."

That night as I prepared for bed, I was more tired than I had ever been. It had been dark for hours; by the time we had left the Abbey the slight daylight was long fled.

At my bedside was a posset. I smiled. Nurse Luke would have seen to it, would have remembered me, even though she no longer had charge of me. I picked up the goblet. The contents were still warm. They tasted of honey and wine, and something else. . . .

I slept. But it was not a normal sleep. I dreamed I was standing at the end of the garden at Eltham. And the Queen came toward me, looking as she had the last time I had seen her—laughing and healthy. She held out her hands to me.

"Ah, Henry!" she said. "I am so happy you will be King!" She leaned forward and kissed me. I could smell her rose-water perfume. "Such a lovely King! Just like my father! And you will have a daughter, and call her Elizabeth, just as he did."

I stood up, and as happens miraculously in dreams, I was suddenly much taller than she, and older, although she remained unchanged. "Stay with me," I said.

But she was fading, or retreating, I could not tell which. My voice changed to desperation. "Please!"

But she had already melted into something else: a strange woman with a pale, oval face. I feared her. The woman whispered, "For a King, do like a King!" and laughed hysterically. Then she, too, faded.

I woke up, my heart pounding. For an instant I thought there must be someone else in the chamber. I drew aside the bed-curtains.

Nothing but six squares of moonlight, exactly reproducing the panes of my window. But it had seemed so real. . . .

I lay back down. Had my mother really come to me? No. She was dead. Dead. They had put her into her tomb that afternoon. Later, Father would erect a monument on the spot. He had said so.

With no one to overhear or stop me, I cried—for the last time as a child.

VIII

How fitting it was, then, that the next change in my life had to do with my coming manhood.

We had left Greenwich and removed to Father's new show-piece, Richmond, where he intended to spend the next few weeks awaiting better weather and attending to affairs of the realm. Each time I came there, I noticed something different. Now I saw that he had put down polished wooden floors on top of the stone. It was a great improvement. And the new panelled wooden walls were far superior to the old-fashioned bare masonry. It would be good to wait for spring here.

But the ice was still on the bare branches of the trees when Father summoned me into his "work closet," as he called it. It was a small panelled room off the retiring room, with its own fireplace which was, as usual, so meagrely lit it was scarcely functional. I always took a surcoat when I received a message that the King wanted me.

He scarcely looked up when he heard me come in. He was bent over an array of papers on the flat, scarred table that served as his desk. I was expected to stand mutely until he decided to acknowledge my presence.

Eventually he did so by muttering, "Another appeal about these cursed vagrants!" He shook his head, then suddenly turned to me. "And what do you say about it? More to the point, what do you *know* about it?"

"About what, Sire?"

"About the poor laws!"

"Which?" There were so many of them.

He raised his hand and pointed to his ear.

"The one against quacks and fortune-tellers? On their second offence they have one ear cut off. On the third offence they lose the other ear." I remembered the Welshwoman at Arthur's wedding feast. I wondered if she still retained her ears.

"But what if the . . . soothsayer wears the cloth and claims his revelations are divinely inspired? What then?"

"It would depend entirely on what his revelations were." I had meant it in sarcasm, but the King nodded in approval.

"You surprise me," he said tartly. "I would have thought——"

He was interrupted by an official from one of the neighboring townships. When Father was at court, he held a sort of business open-house on Tuesdays, and this was Tuesday.

The man entered, dragging something. It was a large, torn net. He held it up in distress. Evidently the King was supposed to gasp when he saw it. Instead he just grunted.

"Well?"

"Your Grace, look at the state of this crow-net!"

"It is unfit for capturing anything smaller than a buzzard. Are you much troubled with buzzards in Oatlands?"

"We need new crow-nets, Your Grace. When we sow this year——"

"Then buy them," he said curtly.

"We cannot! The law says each town must provide adequate crow-nets to trap rooks, crows, and choughs. But we cannot, because of the taxes levied this year—and we cannot afford to pay the taker of crows his accustomed price, and——"

"God's blood!" The King leapt up and looked around accusingly. "Who let this beggar in?"

The man cowered in the midst of his crow-net.

"Yes, beggar!" the King roared. I was surprised at how loud he could speak when he chose. "Where is your licence? Your begging licence? You are required to have one, since you are begging outside your normal township limits. Do you expect *me* to pay for your cursed crow-nets? The taxes are levied on all my subjects! God's blood, you've had a respite for years——"

The man gathered up his spread nets like a woman bringing in laundry before a storm. "Yes, Your Grace——"

The King flung a coin of some sort at him. "Put this in your alms-box!"

When he was gone, the King asked calmly, "And what is the law regarding alms?"

"If one should give alms into any place besides the lawful alms-box, he shall be fined ten times the amount of the alms he gave."

He beamed at me, as his mother used to when I successfully conjugated an irregular Latin verb. "You know the law, then. And will you apply it? No nonsense about the poor, and a Golden Age where we shall all be one and dance on the village green together, festooned in crow-nets?" He looked away. "It is natural, when one is young. . . . I too had ideas, when I was—how old are you?"

"Eleven, Sire."

"Eleven." He had a faraway look. "When I was eleven, I was a prisoner of the Yorkists. Two years later things changed, and poor, daft Henry VI——

my uncle, remember—was on the throne again. My other uncle, Jasper Tudor, Henry's half-brother, took me to him in London. And when the mad King saw me, he said, so that everyone nearby could hear: 'Surely this is he to whom both we and our adversaries must yield and give over dominion.' Henry was a saint, but he was feeble-minded. A prophecy? Should *he* have been punished, then?"

"Clearly it depends as much on the status of the prophet as on his revelation. I amend my earlier statement."

He coughed—not a polite cough, but a true cough. Why *did* he refuse to heat his rooms adequately?

"I pray you excuse me," he said, making for the alcove off his work closet. Another innovation at Richmond Palace: he had had a privy closet built to house a magnificent structure where he could relieve himself. It was a great, throne-like chair, all padded in velvet. Beside it was a huge pewter pot, a royal version of the jordans kept in all bedchambers, that must be emptied every morning. (In the French term, a *vase de nuit*.) He turned to this and proceeded to void into the jordan for what seemed an interminable time, all the while conversing in regal tones.

✥ WILL:

When Henry became King, he tried to outdo his father in everything, and particularly in this area. He had a truly celestial "privy stool" (as he named it) constructed for his own use. It was so decorated, so studded with gems and padded with goose-down, that using it must have been a dazzling experience. How Harry restricted himself to retiring to it only once a day (unless he had some digestive upset, of course) is just one of the many puzzles about him. *I* would have arranged to spend half my day upon it.

In spite of this—now that I think of it—Harry was abnormally fastidious about this subject. He never allowed me to make any references to those functions (a crippling injunction for a jester), nor even to use the good old words "piss" or "fart," or—as he used to say—"the word that rhymes with hit."

✥ HENRY VIII:

"I did not summon you here to talk about crow-nets or mad Henry VI, but about marriage," the King said. I could hardly hear him above the furious sound of his body function.

He turned and I stepped back, making sure my eyes were turned respectfully away. "Marriage!" he repeated, rearranging his robes. "It is much on my mind these days."

He smiled that thin-lipped, smug smile he affected when he thought himself clever. "Margaret will do for me what armies cannot."

He had just arranged the marriage of my sister Margaret to King James IV of Scotland. She would wed the middle-aged but lusty Stuart, and go to live in that barbarous, cold country, whether or not she fancied it (or him). A union of sorts between England and Scotland would result.

He went to his desk and picked up a letter. "I have received . . . an interesting proposal. From Ferdinand and Isabella. That you marry Katherine, their daughter."

I try now to remember my first honest thought. And it was horror, a shrinking. Then, quickly—pleasure. "Arthur's widow?"

"Is there any other Katherine, daughter of Ferdinand and Isabella? The same."

"But she is—she was—"

"The Pope can give a dispensation. *That* is no obstacle. Would it please you? Would it please you, boy?"

"Yes," I breathed. I did not dare to think how much.

"It pleases me as well. To keep the alliance with Spain. To keep the dowry." He shot a look at me. "A woman warms your bed, but money eases your mind. And can buy the woman for the bed to boot."

He disgusted me. And dishonoured my mother, whom he had certainly never bought. "Perhaps," was all I could trust myself to say.

"I will arrange the betrothal, then. And now you had best leave me to the plaintive cries of other crow-net men." He turned back to his work table in exasperation, and indicated to his guard that he was ready to receive the next plaintiff.

I was glad to be gone. I was hungry and knew Father never ate until late afternoon. Once I was back in my own chamber, I asked for some bread and cheese and ale to be brought. While I waited, I walked about restlessly, thinking about Father's proposal. I picked up my lute, but could bring no good music from it. I looked out the window, onto the snowy palace orchard. The trees were writhing black lines against the flat white snow.

A soft sound turned me round to see a server with a tray laden with food. I took it and sat at my small work table and ate. The cheese was exceptionally good, golden and mellow, and not hard as the cheese had been recently. The ale was dark and cold. I finished it all. No matter how much I ate, I never seemed to grow wider, only taller. I was hungry all the time, and at night sometimes my bones seemed to hurt. Linacre, one of the King's physicians, said it was caused by my rapid growth. He said the bones were aching from being stretched. In the past year I had grown almost five inches. I was now taller than the King; I lacked only a little of the six-foot mark.

My favourite time of day approached: the late afternoon, when the boys and young men at court gathered in the enclosed exercise area (yet another innovation) or in the Great Hall for martial exercises. Since it was not dangerous, the King grudgingly allowed me to participate.

From November until March the boys at court were confined indoors. Their only release came during these exercises, which were rowdy, loud, and undisciplined. I was the youngest; most of the others were between fourteen and nineteen. Because of my size and natural ability I was by no means at a disadvantage by age, but because of who I was. At first they had been wary of me, inhibited, but, as always among young people, that wore off as we came to know one another. I was their future King; but I think that was overlooked as we (I can think of no better word) played. I certainly never felt anything except the usual striving the youngest feels to prove himself to his older companions.

✎ WILL:

Perhaps *you* did not, Harry, but I can assure you the others did. Reading this part of the journal saddened me. I never realized how naïve Harry had been, or how desperately a king can seek to convince himself that others are unaware of his position. Or how early the self-deception must, perforce, begin. Certainly the others were well aware that they wrestled and had mock swordplay with the next King. God's blood, they spent the next twenty years using those childhood winter afternoons as the basis for their advancement!

✎ HENRY VIII:

There were a dozen or so of us. The oldest was Charles Brandon, the youth I had first met at Sheen. He was nineteen, but our age difference did not loom so large now. Unlike the others, he had not come to court with his father. His father was dead—killed in the same battle on Bosworth Field where Father had won his crown, singled out by Richard himself because he had held the Tudor dragon standard. Because he could not reward the dead man, the new King honoured his son instead, and brought him to live at court. Thus we were bound to one another by family ties as well as personal affinity.

Nicholas Carew was sixteen. He was very handsome and took a great interest in fashion, saying it was very important to be *au courant* in the French *mode*. He was betrothed to the sister of Francis Bryan, his best friend and companion, an equally avid follower of French fashions. They were always discussing their wardrobes and what sort of feathers might eventually replace fur on caps. Their hearts were more in the banquet hall than on the playing field, and perhaps that is why Francis Bryan was later to lose an eye in a joust.

He simply ran right into a lance. Afterwards he commissioned a jewelled eye patch to be made.

Edward Neville, also sixteen, was a member of one of the most powerful families of the north country and had a more robust appetite for the outdoors than Bryan or Carew. There was an extraordinary physical resemblance between Neville and myself, so that from a middling distance it was difficult to tell us apart. This gave rise, in later years, to an absurd rumour that he was my illegitimate son. Quite an interesting thought, considering that he was about five years older than I.

Henry Guildford, William Compton—they were fifteen, and cared for nothing but reading battle stories and dreaming of invading France. And Thomas Wyatt, son of one of the King's councillors, was even younger than I, and was there only to watch. He was from Kent and, like me, had spent his earliest years in the country. Even at that age he liked to write poetry, although he never showed any of it to me.

WILL:

For which you should have been thankful. One of Wyatt's later pastoral pursuits in Kent was being his neighbour Anne Boleyn's lover . . . perhaps the first? A signal honour, that. Later he wrote a number of indiscreet poems about her, which he wisely refrained from showing to Harry.

HENRY VIII:

When I descended the steps into the Hall that afternoon, most of my friends were already there and trying on their padded doublets. So they intended to use the swords this afternoon, and perhaps do a bit of hand-to-hand combat as well.

Bryan and Carew came in behind me, carrying a large black object, which they set down on the floor with a loud clang. "Look!" they called. "It's the new Italian armour!"

Quickly everyone rushed over to see it. Everyone except Brandon. He just stood, his large arms crossed. "Where did you get this?" he asked.

"We stole it," said Carew.

"No," amended Bryan. "We *borrowed* it. From a knight who came to petition the King. He left it in the guard room when he went in for his audience."

"Return it," said Brandon.

"We will," they chorused. "But we only wanted you to see it. Look, the decorations—"

"I said return it!" bellowed Brandon.

6 7

Carew raised his eyes in appeal to me, as I had feared he would. Yet it was bound to happen, sooner or later. . . .

"Yes. Return it," I muttered. I hated being put in this position.

"Only if you promise to establish an armoury of your own when you become King. There should be one in England, after all."

"Oh, go!" I said, embarrassed. They picked up the half-suit of armour and reluctantly took it back up the stairs.

Afterward, as we watched Compton and Bryan facing each other in hand-to-hand combat across the rush-padded mat, I leaned over to Brandon. "Thank you," I said, "for telling them. I dared not."

He shrugged. "Yet it was to you they turned. Best get used to that, Your Grace."

A thud. Compton had been thrown, and Bryan was bending over him. Neville and another boy took their places. The air was rank now from the sweat and exertion, which mingled with the odours of last night's dinner in the Hall.

Night was falling already. Someone had just come in to light the torches. Soon this must end, and I would have to go back to my solitary room.

I looked at the others around me. They were well-favoured and healthy and—young men. Some were betrothed, one was already married, and most had had women. They talked about it sometimes, casually, which meant it was not even new to them. Like the first time one takes the Sacrament, one anticipates it and thinks much about it afterwards. But as it becomes part of one's life, one says easily: "I have received my Maker." Just so did Bryan and Compton and Carew talk of women.

⚘ WILL:

How like Harry to find a religious simile for the sexual act! The Sacrament, indeed!

⚘ HENRY VIII:

So I would think about Katherine alone. I was to be betrothed. I would not tell anyone yet. And I wondered: when was I to be married?

We were betrothed, formally, three months later, with the provision that the marriage would take place on my fourteenth birthday.

The ceremony of betrothal took place at the Bishop of Salisbury's residence in Fleet Street. It was June then, an exceptionally cool and rainy June. It had been good for the flowers, the gardeners claimed, and certainly the plants continued to bloom an extraordinarily long time.

Father and I and the lawyers were to meet Katherine and her Spanish lawyers directly at the Bishop's. So we rode through London, but took separate routes, lest it appear that we were too familiar already.

In truth, I had not seen Katherine since she and Arthur had left court to go to Ludlow. She had been ill herself of the same fever that had killed Arthur, and had not even attended the funeral or been able to return to London for some time. When she did come, she had been settled in a riverside house on the great open Strand between the city and Westminster. It was called Durham House. There she lived, surrounded by her Spanish household, speaking Spanish, wearing only Spanish clothes, eating Spanish food. For a time everyone had waited to see if she might be carrying Arthur's child, but that soon proved to be merely wishful thinking on the King's part. Arthur was dead indeed.

And now I was to have his leavings. That rainy June day a little over a year since his death, I went to claim the first of them.

We took the royal barge to the water steps of Blackfriars monastery. Horses awaited us there, and we rode up a muddy lane that led away from the river and up to Fleet Street, itself a muddy little path connecting the Strand to the streets of London. We saw few people, as we were outside the main part of London the entire time. It was not a pretty journey, and on the way it began to drizzle, just to complete our discomfort.

At the Bishop's house on that dismal little street, we were ushered into a small room where Katherine and her party awaited us. It stank of wet wool and too many bodies packed into a tight space. It seemed that the number of lawyers required as experts and witnesses had emptied the nearby Inns of Court. And they were all chattering away at once, like a great company of monkeys.

Katherine was somewhere in the midst of them, but it took a moment to see her. When the noise of learned talking and the scratching of pens on parchment was done, they led her out and bade us stand together.

She is so small, was my first thought. She had not grown, whereas I had.

She is so beautiful, was my second.

Katherine was now seventeen, and at her peak of beauty. She was seen by so few people in those days that there remains no legend, no popular memory of that beauty. She spent her young years almost cloistered, and by the time she emerged, some of it had already gone. But then . . . O, *then!*

We stood side by side, stiff and awkward. The King's lawyer thrust a paper into the Bishop's hand on one side, and that of the Spanish lawyer on the other. Then we repeated vows without once looking at each other, long vows in Latin. And signed our names on several pieces of paper.

That being done, we were immediately forced apart by our respective lawyers. We were not to speak to one another, apparently, until we found ourselves in bed together in two years' time. We left the Bishop's residence by separate doors, just as we had come in.

Father said nothing to me until we were safely on the big, clumsy royal barge, crossing the Thames on our way back to Greenwich. The water was a flat, ugly grey-brown, reflecting the overcast sky. Here and there a piece of garbage floated by. People along the banks seemed to consider the river their own private sewer, in spite of an ordinance against "casting any corrupt thing appoisoning the water in and about London." I saw a dead dog turn slowly over and sink from sight in the water. When I was King, I would see that something was done about the misuse of the river.

"You understand," Father suddenly said in a low voice, so that the boatmen could not overhear, "that you must not see or communicate with the Princess in any way. Leave her to her Spaniards in her Spanish house."

"But surely I should send her tokens, write—"

"You fool!" He set his mouth in anger. "Do you see yourself as a suitor? *Tokens!*" He spat out the word. "You will do nothing. Nothing. Leave her be."

"But—*why?*"

"Because this betrothal is on paper only. I doubt that a wedding will ever take place."

"Then why the ceremony? Why the arrangements?"

"It means nothing. What one ceremony does, another can undo. Surely you know *that!* It is nearly the first rule of kingship. The ceremony was merely to buy us some time with the Spaniards, to make a show of our good intentions."

"Which are neither good nor honest nor kind." Another dead animal swept past, churning in the foam. It stank. Everything seemed corrupted to me: the river, Father, myself. Everything except the Princess.

"The Spanish are deceiving us about the dowry. There has been much lying and misrepresentation in the matter. I do not think it will be satisfactorily settled. Therefore I feel that a marriage between you and the Princess will not be feasible."

"Does the Princess . . . participate . . . in these deceptions?"

"She knows nothing. She does as she is told. As you must."

I gripped the carved railing so hard I hurt my hands.

I did not want to do as I was told.

IX

In the end, I had no recourse but to do precisely that. I could get no message to Katherine unless someone would agree to carry it, and no royal servant would go against the King's express wishes. I must say, that loyalty impressed me. Father was well served.

My fourteenth birthday approached, but no preparations were made for my wedding. Instead, I was to have a meagre celebration in honour of my newly attained manhood. (In diplomatic and official parlance, one was considered a man at fourteen, able to sign papers and take a wife and own property in one's own right.)

But I would not be a "man" until the exact date of my birthday, June twenty-eighth. On June twenty-seventh I was still a child, and could be treated as a child.

That evening Father summoned me and peremptorily ordered me to dress myself and prepare to ride into London. He refused to divulge where we were going and why we must go at night.

It was still twilight when we set out, for June twilights linger, and it would not be full dark until almost ten. We rode across the Bridge and found it busier than at noon. There were two-storey houses on both sides, and as dusk fell the people converted the main thoroughfare in between into their own private playground. They sat on benches, and the children played games and fished off the Bridge. They all seemed to know one another. That was the oddest thing to me. Here there were so many of them, such a great gathering of families, yet all so familiar.

It was not that way at court. There were many families at court, to be sure, and often the husband would be in the King's household as an attendant in the Privy Chamber, for example, and his wife serve the Queen as lady-of-the-Bedchamber and his children be pages and maids of honour. They were entitled to lodgings at court, which they usually accepted, and so the Palace might house some two hundred families. But it was not a close group, and there never was such camaraderie as I saw that June night among the bridge-dwellers.

We wound through the streets in the very heart of London. Houses here were closely packed, and each must have sheltered twenty inhabitants, judging from the number pouring out into the street. They were celebrating the end of their working day, and for a few hours would revel in the fading violet light.

As we turned west and went past St. Paul's and then left the city by the Ludgate, I suddenly knew where we were bound. We crossed the little bridge over the stinking, sluggish Fleet River and were soon there, at the Bishop of Salisbury's house.

It was almost full dark now. Father dismounted and bade me do the same. Once we were standing side by side before the Bishop's door, he gripped my arm and said harshly, "Now you will tell the Bishop you are here to make a solemn protestation against your betrothal to Princess Katherine. You will sign papers saying it troubles your conscience. Do you understand?"

"Yes," I said dully. So Father meant to have it both ways: an open betrothal, a secret disclaimer. The dowry business had not been settled. I had heard it from Brandon. People talked freely before him, and he in turn told me what I needed to know.

Father gave me a shove and indicated that I was to knock for entrance. The Bishop opened promptly; it had clearly been arranged in advance.

"The Prince is sore troubled in his conscience about the betrothal to his brother's widow," said Father. "He is here to assuage that conscience."

The Bishop murmured sympathetically and led us in. The papers were already spread out on his work table, neatly lettered, with a large space on the bottom for my signature.

"He is anguished," said Father. He played his part well.

"Ah," said the Bishop. "And what troubles you, my son?"

Father had not rehearsed this with me. I had no idea of what to say, except the truth. "The thought of the Princess in my brother's bed torments me! I cannot bear it!"

Yes, that was true. The thought of her and Arthur together was repugnant to me. I wanted her entirely to myself, for myself. Yet she had lain with *him*. . . .

"Because it would be incestuous," supplied the Bishop. "To uncover thy brother's nakedness, as the Scriptures say."

"No . . ." I wanted to tell him it was not so much because Arthur was my brother as that he was—had been—*a man*. I would have felt the same no matter who it had been.

"He has a lively interest in Scriptures," said Father quickly. "After all, he studied them in preparation for the priesthood. It would be strange, would it not, if he were not strict in his interpretation—"

"Yes. It is an abomination to lie with a brother's wife." The Bishop smiled —an odd reaction to an alleged abomination. "We will put your conscience to rest, my Prince." He drew himself up proudly and rattled off some words for me to repeat.

". . . detest . . . abominable . . . union with our dearly beloved brother's relict . . ."

Then he proffered a pen and made a gesture toward the waiting papers. I signed them, quickly. The pen was a poor one; it blotched the ink and dug into the parchment.

"And by that my conscience is cleared?" I asked. It was a travesty, and I had perjured myself.

"Indeed," the Bishop said.

"So easy," I said. "So easy. One would expect that it should be more difficult. For a matter so weighty."

"The weightiest matters are often dispatched by a simple act," he offered.

"Come," said Father, afraid I might say something else displeasing. "It is over."

✒ WILL:

Although Henry purports to be disdainful of the machinations and underhandedness here, some other part of him must have taken it seriously. I suspect that the first "scruple" in his conscience was planted that night, transforming a perfectly natural sexual jealousy of his predecessor into something profound and scriptural. Henry was a ritualist, and a superstitious one at that. Once he had signed the papers, he must eventually come to believe them. Nothing sent him scurrying like the hint that he had displeased the Almighty. Indeed, he saw God's doing in everything, and strove to keep hand-in-glove with Him. He saw theirs as a special partnership in which, if he did *his* part, God would certainly do His. Do you remember that remark (not *remember*, of course, as you were not yet born)—it was much repeated—of Harry's: "God and my conscience are perfectly agreed." Harry could be comfortable with nothing less.

✒ HENRY VIII:

Shortly afterwards, another wrangle with the dowry forced Katherine to abandon her separate household at Durham House and come to court to live off Father's charity, such as it was. Neither her father Ferdinand, the King of Spain, nor her father-in-law, the King of England, wanted the expense of maintaining her household, and she could live cheaply at court once all her attendants were dismissed. In short, she was to live alone, penniless, friendless, and at Father's sufferance. She was not to "come out" and mingle with the rest of the court, but keep herself apart and separate. Father warned me that on no account was I to attempt to see her, meet with her, or send letters to her. This in spite of the fact that as far as she knew, I was still her betrothed. (The secret of my journey into London on the eve of my fourteenth birthday had been well kept.)

But word reached me of her pitiful state, regardless. She had no money at all, save what Father doled out to her, and he was hardly noted for generosity. If he kept his rightful son and heir in worn clothes and a cold, bare room, what would he do for a girl who could do nothing for him save remind him of the son he had lost, and plans spoiled?

She had had no new clothes since coming from Spain, and those had been mended and turned many times. The fish on her plate was rotten and often made her ill. And she had found a strange confessor, a Fra Diego, upon whom she relied more and more. It was even said that he was her lover, and assigned her penance by day for the unspeakable things they did at night, and that she would do anything he said, so completely was she in his power.

I never believed the more fulsome of these rumours, but the fact that they were being circulated at all meant something. I feared for Katherine, knowing that however difficult my own lot was, hers must be a hundred times more so. I, at least, was in my own country, speaking my own language, with my own friends and my own father (loathsome as he might sometimes be, yet he was mine). I was her only friend here, her only protector. I must see her, must help her.

Now that she was at court, living in another wing only one floor removed from the royal apartments, it was far simpler to get a message to her. I had friends now, and those friends had friends. . . . I did not have to rely on the King's servants.

Where should we meet? I gave much thought to this. It could not be in the open. The ideal place would have been somewhere far from the Palace, some forest or open field, but that required too much cooperation from grooms and horses and even the weather. No, it must be a secret place, where no one would see, but where, if they *did* see us, neither of us could be compromised or suspected.

In the mid-afternoon the Chapel Royal would be deserted. No Mass could be said past noon, and it would yet be too early for Vespers. No priest heard confession at that hour, unless by special appointment. But Katherine was known to be religious. . . .

I sent her a message, asking her to come to the Chapel Royal where I would be waiting in the confession alcove, to help her examine her conscience, at three in the afternoon. I signed it, "T. Wolsey, King's Almoner."

At a little before three I came to the chapel. It was small, as royal chapels are, but richly appointed. There was an image of Saint Margaret there, with a crown of jewels and a cape of pure gold. The chalice and paten and ciborium on the altar were also of fine-wrought gold.

The smell of incense never left the enclosed little chapel. With the doors closed, there was no outside light, no light at all save the candles lit before the images. They winked and fluttered, throwing strange shadows on the carved wooden faces above them.

There was still a little time. I hurriedly knelt and lit a candle to Our Lady, praying that she would have me in her keeping. Then I slipped into the confessional alcove and sat on the stool, pulling a hood up around my head.

I did not have to wait long. Almost as the courtyard clock had finished striking, someone entered the chapel. A crack of light shone in, then the door closed quietly. A rustle of material betrayed the whereabouts of the person, who came closer and then entered the alcove on the penitent's side. I kept my head bowed, so as to hide my face. I heard her sink to her knees on the prie-dieu nearby. Then a hesitation, as she breathed lightly and then began, "Bless me, Father, for I have sinned. I have last confessed—"

"Stop, Kate! I will not hear your confession!" I said, alarmed. I pulled back the hood from my head, revealing my face.

She looked horrified. I could make out a pale face and the great, open O of her mouth. "Henry!" she whispered. "It is a sacrilege—"

"I meant no disrespect for the Sacrament. But oh, Katherine, I *had* to see you!" I reached my hand out and grasped hers. "Three years! Three years they haven't let me see you, or speak to you, or—"

"I . . . know." Her voice was soft and her accent heavy. Possibly she had understood very few of my words.

"And you are my betrothed! I am—I am *responsible* for you." Where I had gotten that notion I cannot say—certainly not from Father. It must have been from the knightly tales I still doted on. "It distresses me that you are alone, and have so little."

She flared. "And who told you that?" Spanish pride—my first glimpse of it.

"It is well known. Everybody says—"

"I have no need for pity!"

"Of course not. But for love, my dearest Katherine—" My other hand sought hers. "I love you!"

She looked discomfited, as well she might. "We must go back," was all she finally said.

"No one will find us here. Not for another hour," I insisted. "Oh, stay a little! Talk with me. Tell me—tell me what you do, how you spend your hours."

She leaned forward. Our faces were only a few inches away in the close, warm darkness. "I—I pray. And read. And do needlework. And write the King my father. And"—this so low I had to strain to hear it—"I think of you, my Lord."

I was so excited I could hardly refrain from embracing her. "Is that true? And I think of you, my Lady." If only I had had my lute and been some other place, I could have sung to her, sung of my love. I had already composed several ballads to that effect, and practised them well. "I will wed you, Kate," I promised, with absolutely no authority to do so. "I swear it! As soon as possible."

"You promised to wed me on your fourteenth birthday. That was a year ago," she said slowly.

"I—" I could not tell her of the hideous "denial" I had made—been *forced* to make. "I know," I said. "But I mean to, and soon. The King—"

"The King does not mean you to wed me. That is clear. I am twenty years old, and *no child*—as others may be."

That seemed unnecessarily cruel to say to her only champion and protector. "I cannot help my age, my Lady. I was not free to choose the day of my birth. But I am not so young as you and others may think." With those cryptic words (I had no idea then, and have none today, precisely what I meant by them), I squeezed her hand once more. "You shall see!" Then I whispered, "We had best leave. Priests will about be soon."

She rose hastily and gathered her skirts. A light lemon scent came to me, floating over the stale incense. Then she was gone.

A moment later I stepped out of the confessional alcove, well pleased with my successful intrigue. I knew now that I loved Katherine and that I must marry her. I was also well satisfied that the scurrilous rumors about Fra Diego were lies. She had been too distressed by the thought of *my* desecrating the confessional by my innocent rendezvous. She was clearly a deeply religious, pious woman.

⌘ WILL:

And better would it have been for Harry had she not been so "religious" and "pious." If only she *had* cavorted with that disgusting friar (who, incidentally, was later deported for gross immorality in London—imagine that!—in *London!*), it would have been worth an earldom to him during Harry's divorce campaign. But no, Katherine was pure. How Harry ever got *any* children on her is one of the mysteries of matrimony. Perhaps the Catholics are right in declaring marriage a sacrament. Sacraments bestow "grace to do that which is necessary," do they not?

It is interesting to note that even at this tender age, Harry used the Church for his own purposes. I have no doubt that, had she consented, he would have cheerfully copulated with her in the shadow of the altar itself.

X

❧ Henry viii:

I now had a Mission: to rescue the Princess from her tower of imprisonment, as a proper knight should do. And being in love (as evidenced by the rush of excitement I felt whenever I pictured her) made it all the more imperative.

Father was preparing to go on one of his summer "progresses," which promised me freedom for the few weeks he was away. Once I had longed to accompany him and been hurt when he excluded me; now I just wished him gone.

Considering that Father disliked going out among the people, detested being stared at, and was uncomfortable when he did not have complete control of everything around him, he made a surprising number of progresses. He viewed them as necessary, and then, the expense spared by living on another's bounty for a month each year appealed to him.

Ostensibly these progresses were to allow the monarch to escape from palace routine and business and go about, simply, in the country. In fact the purpose was to let the King see his land and subjects, and—more important—to let them see *him*. It was necessary to remind the people who their King was, and to show him at his finest. Wherever a royal progress went, people from miles around would line the roadside, waiting for a glimpse of their King. They would hold their children up to see. Sometimes a man with scrofula would stumble up and beg the King to touch him, as the common people believed this could cure the disease.

A royal progress did not wander about aimlessly, enjoying the delights of the countryside, eating wholesomely rough country food by the unspoiled riverbanks. That was the pose. But in fact the route was carefully laid out during the winter months in order that all the wealthy landowners and nobles in the vicinity could prepare to entertain and house the monarch and his retinue. For the King did not travel alone; he took most of the court with him, which precluded simple rustic meals in the meadows. It required prodigious amounts of food, so that any man singled out to host a royal progress two years in a row stood in danger of going into debt.

There was another, darker, reason for Father's progresses: to ascertain the loyalty of the great nobles and to see for himself whether they were complying with his law against liveried retainers. One could never be sure. Edward IV had ordered the dissolution of these private armies maintained by the lords. They were a threat to him for obvious reasons. Once on progress he had stayed with the Earl of Oxford, one of the most partisan of Lancastrians. The Earl had his army of retainers lined up in uniform to greet the King with a great show of loyalty. Edward said nothing until he departed. "I thank you for your good cheer," he told the Earl, "but I may not endure to have my laws broken in my sight." He fined the Earl ten thousand pounds—a far greater sum then than today, when the value of money has eroded so alarmingly.

On August first, the customary Lammas Mass was held in the Chapel Royal, in which a loaf of bread made from the first harvested grain of the season was brought up to the altar. That afternoon the King departed for his progress. He would not return until near Michaelmas at the end of September, when the year had begun to turn and slip toward winter. There was always goose on Michaelmas, a hearty autumnal dish.

I sat in an upper window, watching the royal party gather in the courtyard below. It was hot and sultry, and autumn and Michaelmas seemed a long way off. I felt dizzy with freedom. Everyone was going on the progress. I could see Fox and Ruthal and Thomas Howard and Thomas Lovell, as well as Father's two finance ministers, Empson and Dudley. The King must think of finances, if not in the country sunlight, then late at night.

Only Archbishop Warham had stayed behind, and my grandmother Beaufort. The nobles and court dignitaries not accompanying the King would return to their own estates, as no business would be transacted at court during the King's absence. Business followed him, and court was wherever he happened to be.

But there would be little business, because the whole world, it seemed, was lying idle during those golden weeks of August.

They were golden to me. I spent them in almost continual sport, participating in forbidden jousts and foot combats at the barrier with my companions, risking my person time and again. Why? I cannot tell, even now. Yet I sought danger as a man on the desert seeks water. Perhaps because it had been denied me for so long. Perhaps because I wished to test myself, to see at what point my bravery would break, to be replaced by fear. Or perhaps it is simpler than that. "Youth will needs have dalliance," I myself wrote, and this was one form of dalliance, a knightly, death-defying one. . . .

When I remember those contests, I cannot help but believe that Providence spared me, held me back from a severe punishment. It was that summer of 1506 cost Bryan his eye; and one of my comrades died from a blow in the head while jousting. The curious thing is that immediately after his accident, he seemed well enough. But that night he suddenly died. One of Linacre's assistants (for Linacre had gone with the King) told me it is often so in head injuries. The bleeding takes place inside the skull, where it cannot be felt or stopped.

We were shaken, frightened—and young, so that in just a few days' time we were back riding toward one another on horseback. Thus quickly and naturally do we kill one another in memory as well as in deed.

At night we would sup together, and then play our lutes and talk of our future conquests in France, where we would be brothers-in-arms. It was a good time for us, a little pause between what had come before and what must come after.

Late at night, alone in my chamber, I found myself loth to sleep. Now that I was no longer confined, I relished my solitude after a day of boisterous companionship.

At Greenwich I had two windows in my chamber. One faced east, the other, south. The eastern one had a window seat, and there I found myself often, near midnight. It was always darkest in the eastern part of the sky. By mid-August the slow, lingering twilights had gone, and night came earlier. The stars were exceptionally clear now. I tried to pick them out, as I had been studying astronomy. I knew a great number of the constellations already. The heavens and the stars intrigued me. I was impressed that eclipses and other phenomena could be predicted by mathematicians. I wanted to learn how it was done. Already they knew that the third full moon from now would be partly shadowed. How?

I wanted to learn all things; to experience all things; to stretch and stretch until I reached the end of myself, and found . . . I knew not what.

The small casement window was open where I sat. A hot gush of wind came in, and there was a distant rumble. Far away I could see bright flashes. There would be a storm. The candles and torches in my chamber were dancing.

The wind was from the west. Without thinking, I felt myself at one with that wind, that hot, questing wind. I took my lute, and immediately the tune and the words came, as if they had always been there:

> O Western wind
> When wilt thou blow
> The small rain down can rain?
> Christ, that my love were in my arms
> And I in my bed again.

Summer ended, and the King returned. Within a few hours of his arrival, he summoned me to his chamber. Someone had told him about the tournaments. If I had not expected it, I should have. There are no secrets at court.

I fortified myself for the interview by drinking three cups of claret in rapid succession. (One of the changes I had instigated in Father's absence was an abundant supply of unwatered wine in my chamber.)

Father was in his favourite place: his work closet. (It was popularly referred to as his "counting house" since he did most of his finances there.) He was wrestling with a great mass of chewed papers when I arrived, his head bent over a veritable ball of them. I noticed, for the first time, how grey his hair was. He was without his customary hat, and the torchlight turned the top of his head to silver. Perhaps that was why he never appeared in public without a head-covering of some sort.

"Curse this monkey!" He gestured toward the little creature, now impertinently crouching near the Royal Seal. "He has destroyed my diary!" His voice was anguished. "It is gone!"

Evidently the monkey had decided to turn the King's private papers into a nest, first by shredding the paper and then by trampling it.

"Perhaps you should put him in the royal menagerie, Sire," I said. *Six months ago.* I had always hated the creature, who refused to be trained like a dog for his natural functions, yet could not imitate humans in the matter either.

"Yes," he said curtly. "But it is too late. He has already destroyed that which was most dear to me."

Just then the creature shrieked and began climbing on the wall-hanging. Clearly he belonged elsewhere: if not actually at the bottom of the Thames (my choice for him), then certainly in the royal menagerie at the Tower, where all the other strange (and unwelcome) beasts presented to the King by various misguided well-wishers ended up. There were lions (the symbolism was overworked), large turtles (for perseverance), wild boars (some noble emblem or other), camels (for wisdom, I believe), and even an elephant (for memory?).

"I am sorry, Father."

"You have other things to be sorry for." He abruptly put down the tattered ball of papers. "Your conduct while I was away, for one. Did you think it would remain hidden from me?"

"No, Sire."

"Why, then? Why did you do it?"

"I don't know. I had to."

He snorted. "You are a fool. One of your companions died. And I have been told that—" Suddenly he stopped, racked by a ferocious cough. I had never heard one so deep. When he regained his breath, he went on, "—that you met with Princess Katherine secretly, against my express wishes. No, I will not pause for you to deny it! You are a wilful, perverse boy! You will never make a King, never, never, never—" He was close to tears. Then he put his head down and wept.

I left him in his distress, overcome with my own. Was he correct in what he had said? *You will never make a King, never, never, never.* . . . The words stung and ate at me. He had seen many kings, and he knew.

XI

During the autumn, the King's cough worsened. It was no longer sporadic but became a permanent part of him, waking and sleeping. In November the blood first appeared in the sputum: a signpost pointing to death.

How did he feel, seeing it? Of all the things God does to us, showing us our certain death is the cruellest. I pray that I may be spared such unambiguity when my time comes.

The King carried on. And lived through that winter and the next.

And so I was not to be a fifteen-year-old King. Nor a sixteen-year-old King. For which I thanked God nightly.

I was not ready to be King; I was far too young. Should I become King now, I must inevitably have a Protector, someone who would rule for me in the interim. And how to dispatch that Protector once I came of age? Protectors often usurped the throne. One had to go back no further than Richard III for an example.

I would have to deal with men many years older than myself within my own realm; men publicly my supporters but in truth out only for themselves. And there were the ever-present pretenders and factions. I had several Yorkist cousins; one in particular, the Duke of Suffolk, Edmund de la Pole, son of Edward IV's sister, styled himself "the White Rose" and waited, grinning, in France, to move against me. And abroad, I must face rulers almost triple my age: Ferdinand, King of Spain; Maximilian, Holy Roman Emperor; Louis XII, King of France; Pope Julius. I would be a youth among a pack of veteran intriguers and dissemblers.

Father had assiduously avoided any entanglements on the Continent, but that could not endure much longer, particularly since the French and Margaret of Burgundy (Edward IV's sister, known as "aunt to all the pretenders") persisted in tickling Yorkist fancies and harbouring pretenders and claimants to the English throne. Father had had to fight three pitched battles to win and defend his crown, and I, most likely, would have to do the same. How would I fare on the battlefield? I might make a good showing on the rigorously prescribed area of the tournament field, but a true battle was something else. Richard III had been brave, and a good fighter, it was said . . . but he was hacked in a dozen places, and his naked body slung over an old horse after the battle. His head bobbed and struck a stone bridge in crossing and was crushed, but no matter, he was dead. . . .

There would be fighting, and a test, sometime, of whether I was worthy to be King. And I shrank from it. Yes, I must tell it: I did not want the test and prayed for it to fall elsewhere, at some other time, on some other man. I was afraid. As it came closer, I no longer wished to be King, so acute was my fear of failure. When I was a little younger, I had blithely assumed that since God had chosen me for the kingship, He would protect me in all my doings. Now I knew it was not so simple. Had He protected Saul? Henry VI? He had set up many kings only to have them fall, to illustrate something of His own unsearchable purpose. He used us as we use cattle or bean-plants. And no man knew what his own end or purpose was. A fallen king, a foolish king, made a good example of something, was part of the mysterious cycle.

※ ※

The year I was seventeen, there were but two overriding concerns at court: when would the King die, and *how* would he die? Would he expire peacefully in his sleep, or would he remain an invalid for months, perhaps years, becoming cruel and distracted on account of the constant pain? Would he lie abed carrying on his affairs of state, or would he become incapable, leaving the realm in effect without a King for an unknown stretch of time?

And what of Prince Henry? Who would rule for him? The King had appointed no Protector, although surely the Prince could not rule by himself. Such were their fears.

Outwardly, things went on the same as ever. Father continued to meet with ambassadors and discuss treaties, to haggle over the precise meaning of this phrase or that as if the outcome would concern him in five years' time. He would stop every few minutes to cough blood, as naturally as other men cleared their throats. He kept a quantity of clean linens by his side for this purpose. In the morning a stack of fresh white folded cloths was brought to his bedside; when he retired, a pile of bloody, wadded ones was taken away.

Father convened the Privy Council to meet by his bedside, and I was present at a number of these meetings. They were dull and concerned exclusively with money: the getting of it, the lending of it, the protecting of it. Empson and Dudley, his finance ministers, were unscrupulous extortionists. Evidently a King's main concern (to be attended to every waking moment) was the chasing of money. It seemed sordid. Was Alexander the Great concerned with such things? Did Caesar have to fuss about Calpurnia's dowry?

For Katherine's dowry still had not been settled to Father's satisfaction. He continued to berate Ferdinand's ambassador and threaten to send Katherine back, to marry me to a French princess, and so on. He quite enjoyed it, I think, as other men enjoy bear-baiting. And it kept his mind from the bloody linens.

But the minds of everyone else at court were focused on them. It was a matter of great concern how many he had used today, and how much blood was on them. Was it thick or thin? Red or pink? Or black? The laundryman and washwomen were paid handsomely for this information.

At the Christmas festivities Father continued his slow, agonizing Dance of Death, while by convention all onlookers pretended not to see. It was treason to "imagine" the King's death but at the same time not humanly possible to avoid it.

He continued playing political chess, using his two remaining unmarried children as his principal pawns and collateral. In a macabre (or perhaps only self-deceptive) gesture, he included himself in the marriage negotiations along with me and Mary. Just before New Year's he put the finishing touches on his grand Triple Alliance, a confusing welter of marriages designed to weld the Habsburgs and the Tudors into a splendid family edifice. He himself was to become the bridegroom of Lady Margaret of Savoy, Regent of the Netherlands; I was to marry a daughter of Duke Albert of Bavaria; and thirteen-year-old Mary was to marry nine-year-old Charles, grandson of both King Ferdinand and Maximilian, and in all probability a future Holy Roman Emperor. (Although the Holy Roman Emperor must be elected, the electors seem singularly blind to the merits of any candidates outside the Habsburg family. It is no more an "election" than that of the Papacy, but is for sale.)

WILL:

To the highest bidder, as Henry and Wolsey discovered firsthand when they tried to buy the election of the Holy Roman Emperor in 1517 for Henry, and then the Papal election of 1522 for Wolsey. Those offices do not come cheap, and Henry and his pompous, puffed-up ass of a chancellor were simply not willing to pay the full market value. Henry sometimes showed a streak of perverse frugality—perhaps as a sentimental gesture to the memory of his father?

HENRY VIII:

Happy with this accomplishment, the King retired to his death-chamber. He went into it shortly after New Year's Day, 1509, and never left it again. He chose Richmond as the place where he wished to die.

Yet the outward pose must be maintained. The King was not dying, he was merely indisposed; not weak, merely tired; not failing, merely resting. Every day he sent for me, and I spent several hours at his side, but he stubbornly refused to confide anything of real importance to me. He must play his part, as I mine.

When I came into his chamber, I must not remark upon his one luxurious concession to dying: the logs piled high in the fireplace and the abnormal warmth of the room. Nor must I sniff or allude in any way to the heavy perfumes and incense employed to mask the odour of illness and death. The rose scent was cloying, almost nauseating, but eventually I became used to it—after a fashion. I was to be always alert and cheerful, to appear as blind and insensitive as Father had once pronounced me to be.

In spite of the splendid large windows, with their hundreds of clear, small panes set like jewels in a frame, the hangings were ordered closed, shutting out the abundant light. From where he lay, Father could have looked out upon fields and sky, but he chose not to do so. Instead he lay on his back on a long couch, surrounded by pillows and the ever-present small linens. He would talk idly, or say nothing at all, just stare sadly at the crucifix above the small altar at the opposite side of the room. He was very devout, like all the Lancastrians—although not insanely so, like his half-uncle Henry VI.

"Yesterday I noticed that you used a fork for eating," he suddenly said. His voice was so low I had to strain to hear it.

"Yes," I replied. All the younger men and women at court used forks now.

"French thing," he said dreamily. "The French can be clever. To use a miniature trident at the table—yes—clever. I once had a safe conduct from the King of France. Did you know that?"

"No, Sire." Why do the old always ramble so? Naturally I made a vow at the time never to do so myself.

"King Richard bribed the Duke of Brittany when I was in exile. Or rather the Duke's treasurer, Peter Landois. In exchange for my life, he promised Landois the income not only from my earldom of Richmond, but from all my followers as well. Ha!" He gave a short laugh, followed by a paroxysm of coughing. It ended with a hideous gurgling sound and a soaked linen. He shook and shivered.

"Let me put another cover here," I said hurriedly, pulling up something folded at his feet. Not until it was spread out did I recognize it: the lion skin from that gruesome exhibition so long ago. The tail hung off the side of the couch, its bush of hair looking strangely like an ornamental tassle.

"Better. That's better," he whispered. "The King of France—he said I would be safe there. And so I was. So I was. First I had to escape from Landois, but that was easy. I simply disguised myself as a servant to my own servant.

I changed my costume in the woods. Then we rode as fast as possible for the border of France. Brittany was not part of France then, you know," he added.

"I know." I looked at him, trying to see the young Welsh adventurer somewhere within him. But there was only an old man shivering under the covers in an overheated room.

"Sometimes the French are our friends, sometimes our enemies. They harboured me, but when I became King they also harboured the Duke of Suffolk, Edmund de la Pole."

"The White Rose," I said bitterly. "Darling of the Yorkists."

"Not only did they harbour him, they recognized him as rightful King of England, and honoured him as such! Oh, he had a merry time in the French court. I have finally been able to force the lying French to extradite him. Now he's in the Tower. As long as he lives, you are not safe."

"Even though we have him in captivity?"

"You will have to execute him," he said matter-of-factly. "His life is a luxury you cannot afford."

I was stunned. I could not imagine myself executing someone simply for existing, or for having the wrong (or right?) blood in his veins. "I cannot!" I said in horror. "He has done nothing!"

"He exists. That is enough."

"No!"

"He fled abroad and allowed himself to be honoured as rightful King of England by a foreign court. His intentions are treasonous."

"Intentions are not deeds."

"Henry! In the name of God, this is vital for you to understand: *he is your enemy.* There can be only one King in a land, and if your enemies perceive you to be hesitant or soft-hearted, you will go the way of poor mad Henry VI. They are ruthless; you must be, too. You are all that stands between peace and anarchy. Your life is the one thing keeping another round of chaos at bay. Preserve that life. It is your duty as God's chosen instrument!"

"By taking an innocent life?"

"He is not innocent! He is guilty; a foul, loathsome traitor!" He was becoming so excited that he sat up and beat his fists against the lion skin, feebly. "It does not matter what you know or do not know about finances; you can rely on my finance ministers, Empson and Dudley. Or about the workings of the Privy Council; Bishop Fox, the Lord Privy Seal, can tell you anything you wish to know, and guide you. But in the matter of protecting your throne, you can rely on no one besides yourself." He fell back, exhausted by the exertion. "To be a King is to be an unnatural man. You must be hard where others are soft, and soft where others are hard. And—"

I waited, but nothing followed. In the dim light I could perceive his quiet breathing. He was asleep.

I hurriedly left the chamber. Stepping out into the bright indoor light in the adjoining room, free from the clouds of incense and perfume, was dizzying. A number of servants were waiting in what was in effect an anteroom for the death-chamber. A priest stood ever ready in case of sudden need. Today it was Thomas Wolsey, the King's almoner (whose name I had appropriated to lure Katherine into the confessional). He was reading quietly on a small bench near the window. He nodded at me gravely as I passed through.

I returned to my own chamber, still shaken by Father's order. To execute my cousin de la Pole . . . I went to my work table and took out my writing materials. I found a scrap of paper upon which I had earlier been composing a letter in Latin. I dipped the pen in ink and wrote, for the first time, *Henry Rex*. My hand shook and made a blot. I tried again, then again. By the third time the hesitation was gone, and there were no blots. *Henry Rex.*

The winter passed; an early spring was promised. By late March the skies were blue, and there were bright yellow wildflowers by the banks of the Thames. But in the death-chamber there was no spring; the pulled curtains resolutely kept it away. When the apple trees in the orchard beneath his windows burst into bloom, Father could not see or smell them.

As he became weaker, more attendants clustered about, and we had less opportunity for private talk. Father had left until too late all the things he should have told me. Now we were both bound in the web of court ritual, which extended even into the death-chamber and effectively prevented any confidences between us. Yet at the same time I was expected to be continually present, from the early hour when Wolsey first celebrated Mass, to the evening when the grooms of the bedchamber went through the elaborate sequence of steps in readying the King's bed for the night (such as rolling on the mattress to search for knives, and sprinkling holy water on the coverlet), to the final, surreptitious removal of the day's pile of blood-soaked linens. Then Wolsey came in to say evening prayers, and my day was done.

One night I was not able to leave him before midnight, as he was in pain and could not sleep until his physician administered a poppy-syrup which soothed him. Rather than returning to my own chambers, I felt a great need for cold, fresh air. I descended the small staircase to the door leading outside and found myself in the palace orchard. The trees were in full bloom, and a bloated moon—not quite full—illuminated them. They looked like rows of ghostly maidens, sweet and young. Below me the Thames flowed swiftly with the new spring-water, sparkling in the moonlight as it rushed past.

It was the first time since dawn that I had been alone, and I felt a shuddering relief. Day after day in that death-chamber . . .

I walked slowly through the ghostly orchard. The shadows were peculiarly sharp, and the moonlight almost blue. I cast a long shadow, one that moved silently between the crooked, still ones of the trees.

"—dead soon. He can't last."

I stopped at the unexpected sound of voices. They seemed unnaturally clear and hard in the open night air.

"How old is he, anyway?"

"Not so old. Fifty-two, I believe."

The voices were closer. They were two boatmen who had just tied up their boat at the landing and were walking toward the palace.

"He has not been a bad King."

"Not if you remember Richard."

"Not many care to." They laughed.

"What of the new King?"

There was a pause. "He's a youngling. It is said he cares for nothing but sport."

"And women?"

"No, not women. Not yet! He is but seventeen."

"Time enough if one is disposed that way."

"Aye, but he's not."

They were almost level with me now. If they turned they would see me. But they did not and continued trudging toward the servants' entrance of the palace.

"How much longer, think you?"

The other man made a noise indicating lack of knowledge or interest.

My heart was pounding. In that instant I resolved never to allow myself to overhear talk about myself again. They had said nothing of importance, and yet it had distressed me. The way they spoke so offhandedly about Father's life and my character . . . as though they knew us, had proprietary rights over us.

⌘ WILL:

It was a resolve Henry seemed singularly unable to keep—not to listen in on conversations. (Happily for me, as this penchant of his is what led to our meeting.)

⌘ HENRY VIII:

For them, Father's passing was of little consequence, as they assumed that it did not presage another bloodbath or upheaval.

But to me? I did not want him to die and leave me . . . leave me alone. I loved him. I hated him. I had not known until that moment just how much I relied on his presence, on his being the prow of the boat upon which I rode, protected from the spray and all other discomforts inherent in the voyage. Once he was gone, it would all break upon me.

The men were past. I stood up and continued to walk. I can remember the odd, damp smell of early spring, a sort of musty-earth odour. And the utter stillness of the blossoming branches. In the hard cold light, they looked carved, as though they were made of marble and nothing could shatter them.

I reached up and shook one of the branches, expecting a shower of petals to fall on me. But it did not happen; the flowers had only just opened and were still firmly attached. It was not yet their time to fall. And when it was, they would shower profusely, let go of their branch with an ease I envied.

I was seventeen, and about to be shaken, and fall elsewhere, but I feared I would not do it with ease, or gracefully.

I was no longer afraid. That had passed, replaced by resignation. What must be, must be. In my churchly training I had been told that the great Saint Augustine had asked God to make him pure, "but not yet." God honoured his request, making him holy late in life. My unspoken wish was similar—to be King, but not yet. God had denied my petition. I was to be King before I was ready. I waited for it like a condemned man awaiting the executioner's strike.

But when the blow that severed me from my past came, it came softly and from behind.

I returned to Father's Privy Chamber early the next morning, and the next, and the next. In truth it was no longer a privy chamber; it was swarming with all those whose business it was to attend a dying monarch. Linacre and two other physicians must be constantly by the King's side; two priests must be on the other side, one to hear his last confession and the other to administer extreme unction, while a third intoned Mass at the altar at the far end of the chamber. Lawyers hovered about to consult the King about the usual general pardon for all non-felonious prisoners in the realm, and nurses and servers came in a steady stream like columns of ants marching to and fro, carrying food and medicines and linens. Even his Florentine sculptor, Torrigiano, came to consult about the tomb monument that Father had commissioned for his vault in Westminster Abbey, where his private burial chapel had been under construction for several years. Father was thorough to the end.

There was much left unsaid between us, and doubtless he had meant, in his usual orderly fashion, to leave it to the last. Having never died before, he did not realize that there would be no time, no privacy. As it was, Mary and I (Margaret had married the Scots King James IV six years before and was now in the far north) stood about awkwardly, out of place. The King spent a great deal of time looking at Mary, and I think he was seeing her mother in her. Mary was thirteen then, and a slender, fair girl.

On the fourth day he worsened and could scarcely draw his breath. He lay back on the great mounds of pillows, which were heaped to form an eerie facsimile of a throne, and looked whiter than the bleached linens surrounding him. Clouds of rose-petal smoke rose from a censer nearby, but he no longer coughed in response. It was all I could do to keep from gagging, so pungent was the odour.

He indicated that he wished to say something to me, and I bent near him. "I forgot," he whispered. His breath was foul. "Promise to fight the Infidel." A pause. "No friends. You must have no friends."

When I made no reply, he went on, slowly. "You know about de la Pole. You know the danger. But friends can also be the door through which treason enters. Have no friends. A King has no friends."

I felt great pity for him. His strange vagabond life had precluded any opportunity to have normal boyhood friends, to make those bonds that last for life. I was deeply grateful that I had been given friends such as Carew, Neville, and Henry Courtenay, and I felt privileged, as they were precious to me. I remember the thought, which came to me vividly and insistently. (How honest I am to record it, in light of their subsequent treason. How much more wise I would have myself appear!)

"I would not be a hermit," was all I answered.

"Then you would not be King," he replied softly. "And I see now that you are singularly unsuited to be anything else. You were right—it is God's doing. And you must—" He was interrupted by a fit of coughing so violent that blood flew out of his mouth and splattered on the floor. "A priest—" he whispered, when it had stopped. "Wolsey."

I rushed away from his bedside, seeking Wolsey. In the dim chamber, made more so by the clouds of smoke, I could not see him. Was he at the altar? I ran to it, but did not find him. He must be in the anteroom beyond. I ran at the heavy doors, bursting them open, and stood panting on the other side. Wolsey was sitting on a bench, calmly reading a Psalter. Even at that confused moment, I was struck by his almost unnatural composure.

"My fa—"—I corrected myself—"the King calls you."

Wolsey rose, and together we entered the Privy Chamber.

"Go to him!" I almost pushed Wolsey toward Father's bed. But he did not move toward him. Instead he dropped to his knees by my side.

"Your Highness," he said.

I looked about me. No one was facing Father; they were all turned toward me. Wolsey had seen it, whereas I had been blind.

"The King is dead," said Linacre, coming toward me slowly. I saw Father lying still on the cushions, his mouth gaping open.

"Long live the King!" someone shouted from the back of the chamber, obscenely loud. Then someone else ripped asunder the closed velvet window hangings and wrenched open the casement windows. A flood of sunlight and wind rushed in, dispersing the clouds of sickroom incense.

"Long live the King!" Others took up the cry, until the chamber resounded with it as Father lay unhearing, forgotten.

My sister Mary came to me. I reached out to put my arm around her, to share our strange grief at being orphans. Instead she, too, fell to her knees in homage.

"Your Highness," she said, taking my hand and kissing it.

"Mary! You must not—"

"You are my King, to whom I owe all obedience," she said, turning her shining young face up to mine.

Shaking, I pulled my hand away. I pushed past Wolsey and confusedly sought a little-known door from the anteroom, which led directly to the orchard where I had stood only a few nights ago. I sought it as though it had some magic, some comfort for me.

I pushed open the heavy, studded door and came outside, dazzled by the intense April green. The trees were in full bloom, the soft petals loose now, scattering in the wind and showering over me. At once everything seemed clear, sharp, remote, as if I were seeing through a prism. From far away I heard the herald at the palace gates proclaiming me "Henry VIII by the grace of God King of England and France and Lord of Ireland." His voice floated along in the flower-scented air, a disembodied ghost.

In a few minutes the peculiar otherworldliness passed away, and I was merely standing in a palace orchard I had known since childhood. There was nothing remotely supernatural about the orchard itself, but there was no denying the magic present that afternoon: there is always an element of magic in the making of a King.

XII

Istood there a long time, savouring the illusion of solitude, until voices broke into my thoughts—the voices of a great crowd of ground workers and servants who were converging on the orchard, trapping me.

I turned in surprised dismay and was greeted with a rising shout. "Long live the King!" a large, red-faced gardener yelled. He raised his hands. "Long live King Harry!"

I winced inwardly at the familiarity. Did they see me, then, only as Little Harry? There was no majesty, no dread in that. Just a plaything . . .

"Pretty Hal!" an old woman called. Again I shuddered, remembering another woman's call for Edward's pretty face.

I wanted them to be gone, to stop mocking me. I came toward them, wanting only to get past them and back into the palace. How had they found me so quickly?

Then, as I came closer to them, they began cheering wildly. And rather than fearing them, something changed inside me, and I reached out for them. Another voice than mine (although it came from my own mouth) was saying, "I thank you. I have only one wish: while I am King, may you always be as happy as you are today." The words sprang from within me, unbidden.

"Wine!" I called, to no one in particular, knowing, somehow, that the order would be obeyed. "Wine for all!"

This set them cheering and distracted them so that I could make my way back into the palace. I closed the door behind me, thankfully. I could still hear their shouts outside.

Yet another knot of people—pages and servers and turnspits this time— was waiting on the other side of the door. They instantly fell to their knees and pledged loyalty to me, saluting me as their blessed King. Awkwardly I thanked them and continued on my way back to Father's apartments. All along the passages it was the same: lines of people falling on their knees. How had they heard so swiftly? (I did not know then that within palace walls, news travels faster than the speed of the winged god—some say even before it happens. All I could think was: Will I never be alone again?)

At length (it seemed forever) I reached the guardroom, the outermost of the royal apartments. I wrenched open the heavy door, expecting to find blessed solitude beyond it. And I was not disappointed: the vast room, hung with faded tapestries and outmoded armour, appeared empty. This was where men customarily awaited an audience with the King. The thought crossed my mind that Father had made it as dismal and comfortless as possible to discourage most petitioners before their turns came. Even in late April, the room was chilly.

At the far end was the door leading to the Presence Chamber, the throne room. As I strode toward it, I saw a movement: a priest detached himself from the shadows and made toward the door. It was Wolsey.

"Your Grace," he said. "I stand ready to help you. As the late King's almoner, I am well acquainted—"

Already the self-seekers were at me. "I myself am well acquainted with the late King," I cut him off.

"You misunderstand me, Your Grace. I meant with the . . . distressing business that is attendant upon a royal death. The obsequies, the funeral, the interment—"

"Father has already arranged for that." I pulled at the door, but somehow he prevented me.

"Of course, with the final details," he persisted. He was extremely persistent, this Wolsey. "The magnificent tomb he has commissioned from Torrigiano, the dazzling chapel in the Abbey, already near completed. But the personal details, such unhappy things as the embalming, the lying-in-state, the funeral effigy—"

"Minor things," I said, trying once more to detach myself.

"Distasteful things," he said pointedly. "Things dealing with ugliness, when your mind should be engaged elsewhere. You have much to attend to, have you not? Where is the son who could joyfully oversee his father's funeral? And you must be joyful, Your Grace: you must rejoice, even as the Kingdom does. No gloominess, lest you remind them of—" He broke off tactfully. A rehearsed break. Yet he had touched me on vital matters.

"Then see to it!" I cried in frustration.

He bowed serenely in compliance as I wrenched open the door and at last found myself in the Presence Chamber, alone.

I walked across that large area, strangely plain in spite of the dais with the carved throne-chair upon it. It was situated so that the petitioner must cross the entire length of the room before seeing the King's face. It was effective, no doubt, yet the overwhelming feeling of the room was of greyness, bleakness, which no amount of royal presence could overcome.

And from there I passed into Father's private apartments, where he actually lived. But he was dead, I reminded myself. . . .

The great Privy Chamber, so lately turned into a dying chamber, was already changed. The incense burners were gone, the curtains opened. And the bed was empty.

"Where have you taken him?" I cried.

"The cry of Mary Magdalen," said a voice behind me. I whirled around and saw Wolsey. Again, Wolsey. He must have followed me. " 'They have taken away my Lord, and I know not where they have laid him.' "

"Do you seek to impress me with your knowledge of Scripture?" I said blandly. "All priests know such; I as well. I asked where you have taken him."

Wolsey looked apologetic. "There were things to be attended to immediately. I regret I *did* anticipate my commission. They have taken him to do the death-mask, then to disembowel and embalm him."

"I see." It was sickening. I looked around, feeling a great need of wine. Then I felt a cup pushed into my hand, like a wish fulfilled. Wolsey again. I drank deeply, hoping to dispel the strange sense of inertia and otherworldliness that seemed to have gripped me.

Wolsey vanished, but was replaced by a young red-haired page. It was magic. I almost laughed. It was all magic. I took another draught of wine. Ambrosia. I was immortal now, like a god. No, not immortal, I corrected myself. Kings die. Yet they are gods while they live. . . .

I looked about me. This chamber was Father's no longer, but mine. I walked, a little unsteadily, to the door leading to the King's closet. This was where Father had spent much time, where he had summoned me often. (The term *privy chamber* was a misnomer. It was not private at all, but was the place where everyone personally attendant on the King converged: all the gentlemen and grooms of the chamber, the ushers, pages, servers, barbers, and so on. Beyond that, however, only select persons were allowed entrance. Thus the "closet" was truly the first privy chamber in a series of private rooms.) I flung open the door and stood looking at the bare, pitifully furnished room, recalling all the times I had been humiliated there. The hated monkey still chattered and jumped, even now at liberty to roam.

"Take this creature away," I said to the page. (I regret to record this as my second royal command.) I reached out and grabbed it by the scruff of the neck, thrust it into the boy's arms, and said, "Dispose of it. I care not where!"

The boy took the animal in his arms and carried it away. How easy that was! I stood amazed. Something I had had to endure for years, suddenly gone, swept aside with a word and a gesture. I laughed, delighted. Then I looked about the room, planning other changes. Was it cold? There would be fires. Was the desk old and lacking drawers? There would be a new Italian one, inlaid with rare woods. Was the room old-fashioned? Carpenters would repanel, sculptors redecorate, painters gild.

From there I made my way into the Retiring Room—the first exclusively private royal room, and one to which even I had been denied access—the room where the King took his nightly rest. Father had not slept there in many months, but his great bed (eleven feet on both sides) still squatted in the middle of the room, like a Norman tower. I walked around it, slowly. The hangings were moth-eaten and shabby. I raised my hand and patted one fold, and a great puff of dirt flew out, choking me. Then—I know not what possessed me—I began striking the hangings frantically, beating them, raising clouds of dust. And I felt near tears . . . for what, I know not.

My tears and the dust drove me from the bed, and just then my eyes fell on Father's private meditation alcove. I sank down on his prie-dieu, trying to focus my eyes on the crucifix before me, although my eyes kept turning to the painting of the Virgin on one side, so like my mother. I prayed to be a good King, to be worthy. What else? I fear it was a cry for help, a scream of terror from my soul. Yet I trusted that God would hear. . . .

I reeled away and fell across the bed. The strain, the day, and Wolsey's wine had undone me. I slept, deeply.

And awakened sometime in the dread, empty time of night. I could tell, not from the crier nor by the striking of the chamber clock, but by a feeling deep within me. We *know* that time, know it in ourselves. . . .

I lay on the bed, not covered, still wearing my daytime clothes. It was cold; *I* was cold. I shook. Yet I felt different from before, until I remembered: *I am King.* And almost in the same instant, a half-forgotten saying from the Orient, repeated by Skelton, came to me: *Youth, abundant wealth, high birth, and inexperience: each of these is a source of ruin. What, then, the fate of him in whom all four are joined?*

I was afraid. Then my very youth rescued me, put me back to sleep.

"Your Grace." I heard the voice, felt someone shaking me awake. I opened one eye and saw Brandon. "You must arise."

I sat up, wondering why I was dressed and on this strange bed. Then I knew.

Brandon was standing before me, beaming. "They are waiting."

I was still half asleep, and my face showed it.

"The people. They are waiting!" He gestured toward the window.

I swung myself off the bed and approached the window slowly. Outside I saw people, nothing but people. No trees, no grass, no roads—only people.

"They want a glimpse of you!" he said. "Some of them have been waiting all night."

I started to draw open the window, but he said, "No. They await your appearance, when you ride to the Tower."

Evidently the sound of voices, however faint, signalled permission for others to enter; a slender page burst into the room.

"Your Highness," he said, dropping to one knee. "I wish to—"

He was interrupted by a virtual stream of other servants bringing food upon trays, as well as clothes. One of them bowed low and then began unbuttoning my outer garment. I pushed him away.

"But, Your Grace," he protested, "I am Clerk of the Wardrobe. And it is my duty to attire the King." He gestured proudly toward his assistant. "We have already warmed these before the fire, in accordance with the protocol of the late—"

"Enough!" I cried. "Just get about it." And I was forced to endure the ceremonial dressing, where two men laced and buttoned and pulled and pushed. (Did my great-grandfather Tudor truly have such duties?)

At last it was done and I was able to push them from the chamber. Brandon and I were alone, briefly.

"What must be done?" I asked him. "Father kept it secret."

"You must ride to the Tower," he replied. "A ceremonial taking command, as it were. In the old days, one King was crowned directly an old one died. Now, in our more peaceful, civilized days"—there was a faint smile on his mouth—"there is an interim. The old King must be properly interred, have respects paid. Yet the people still demand an immediate glimpse of their new King. They are impatient and cannot wait the full month until your father is buried. Hence the ride to the Tower." He grinned. "It is a good omen. There has not been a ceremonial ride to the Tower in many reigns. Yours is the first peaceful, uncontested crowning in almost a hundred years."

Sleep still clung to me. "What date is it?" I asked.

The door opened. "St. George's Day," said a voice I already recognized —Wolsey's. "The feast day of England's patron saint. A good omen."

Omens. I was sick of them already. I glared at Wolsey. "As any spring day would be," I replied. "And as for my ride into London—"

"All is prepared, Your Grace. The horses saddled, those who are to accompany you dressed and waiting."

Suddenly I hated him, hated his smug knowledge. "And who are those?" I asked. "I gave you—gave no one!—instructions—"

"Those who love you," he said blandly. "Your dearest companions and your sister. They will ride with you to the Tower, rest with you there. No Council members, no aged ones today. It is a day for youth." He smiled depreciatingly, as if to exclude himself.

"You as well," I said to Brandon. "You must ride with me."

The day was fair, warm, already ripening toward summer. It charged my blood. I came out into the Palace courtyard to see many people waiting: my friends, my supporters and well-wishers. As I appeared, a great shout went up, a deafening roar. They cried themselves hoarse, their lusty voices rising in the spring air.

And suddenly all was swept away: all hesitation, all awkwardness, all fear . . . borne to oblivion on the warm wind. I was King, and glad of it. All would be well; I sensed it, like a promise. . . .

I mounted my great bay, a horse I had ridden in the lists and knew well, and turned him toward the Palace gates. As they swung open, I was stunned to see the unimaginably vast gathering of common people, surrounding the Palace grounds, stretching away on either side of the road to London as far as the eye could see, six, seven deep. Sighting me, they sent up a great cry. And I felt their presence as a kind, friendly thing, nothing to fear. They shouted for me, blessed me, cheered me. Without thinking, I swept off my head-covering and held my arms up, and they cheered all the louder. And I was warmed all over: the sun on my head, their approval around me.

All along the way it was the same: cheering people, standing many layers thick along the riverbanks, as the strengthening sun sparkled the water. We shared that moment, they and I, making a mystic bond between us, exulting in that ultimate luxury: the beginning of things.

We did not reach the Tower until nightfall, so slow was our progress. The city walls of London glowed pink in the setting sun. As we crossed the Bridge, I saw yet more people leaning from the upper stories of their high houses, trying to glimpse me. They had had no time to prepare for this unannounced royal procession, yet they had strung the narrow passageway thick with garlands of fruit-blossoms that swayed in the brisk evening wind, showering us with petals of apple, cherry, pear. . . .

Torches were already lit in the April twilight, great golden flares which turned the fluttering petals to gold as they fell.

Now it all becomes a blur, like the aura from those torches. At the Tower, more trumpets. I am there again, I am seventeen. . . .

I am escorted inside the fortress by the royal guard, costumed in the April green and white Tudor colours. I go to the White Tower, dismount, throw off my cloak, call for wine. Then am overwhelmed by tiredness. The magic is gone; my legs ache, my eyes burn. . . .

The others follow me inside: Brandon, Neville, Carew, Compton. Someone brings wine in great goblets. Neville plucks two from the tray and hands me one in the familiar, careless gesture he commonly uses, turns to clap his hand on my shoulder, suddenly stops, the familiar gesture frozen, the old companions now King and subject. His blue eyes, so like mine, register dismay.

"Your Highness," he says quietly, his hand (again, so like mine) falling limply to his side.

He waits for me to rescue him, to ease this strange moment of transition. I cannot. Then, miraculously, I can.

"I thank you," I answer naturally, and it is as if I have always been King. What takes others years to learn comes to me in that instant. I cannot explain it other than to say that at that moment I *became* King, and there was no turning back. That was my true coronation: the other but a sealing, a confirmation of what had already taken place.

I knew in that instant, also, my goal: to be a *perfect* King, to surpass Henry V and King Arthur in greatness and knightliness.

Afterwards I returned to Richmond until Father's funeral in early May. I was told I must, in fact, hide myself, for a reason both flattering and disturbing: the people had cheered so for me, had been so overjoyed at my accession, that any further public appearance on my part would have been detrimental to the late King's memory and his funeral. I was much amazed.

WILL:

Was Henry really as ingenuous as he paints himself? He records how the people welcomed him, yet purports to be surprised that it would contrast badly with his father's memory. But one must remember his youth. He *was* but seventeen, and unsure of himself, despite the cheers. We who have known him only in his later years must take this into account. I, for one, believe him.

Yet I must confess his self-doubts and hesitancy were well hidden, if indeed they existed. (A triumph of the royal will?) I saw him in London that day; I was upon the Bridge in that great, nameless crowd.

He rode a gigantic horse, gorgeously caparisoned, and he appeared to us as a great golden god—broad-shouldered, handsome, and utterly at ease. He *looked* like a King and rode out among the people with all the eagerness of a boy (which he was, of course), unselfconscious and full of natural grace. The people loved him instantly, and he reciprocated: one of those rare affinities. They loved his beauty, his apparel, his lavishness and colour. Young Harry, who was raised in chill, darkness, and drabness, was to seek light, warmth, and blazing colours all the rest of his life. The people sensed it. And cheered it.

❧ HENRY VIII:

There were many details to be attended to in the dreary interim, details spanning the burying of the old King and the crowning of the new. Everything must be planned simultaneously: there must be both a funeral procession and a Coronation procession, a funeral feast and a Coronation feast, funeral music and Coronation music. This meant, perforce, that the cakes must bake side by side in the royal ovens and the musicians must practise both musics at a single session. While the court wore black in official mourning, fittings were being taken for Coronation cloaks.

What were my duties? I, like all the rest, must be measured for my Coronation robes. Unlike all the rest, I had other, pressing matters to attend to. If I were to be a true King, I must take control of the power Father had just relinquished. I must meet with the Privy Council, learn its ways. And I had much to learn. I, who had always been relegated to a shadowed corner seat during meetings, must now preside over them. Father had left me an intact Council. In a sense, this eased my task; in another, it made it still harder, for they were all Father's men, disappointed that none had been named my Protector and disinclined to yield any power to me.

Of the nine councilmen, all were accomplished. Seven were honest, two were not: Empson and Dudley, Father's erstwhile finance ministers. In spite of the Council's attempts to shield its own, lesser Crown servants managed to reach my ears with information regarding their unscrupulous methods of money-collecting and "law enforcement," and how they were despised throughout the realm by noblemen and poor alike. It was they who had so tarnished my father's reputation amongst the people in the closing years of his reign.

I ordered them arrested, and exempted from the general pardon. I cancelled the bonds they held for the payment of their extorted loans. They were traitors, for their victims were "by the undue means of certain of the Council of our said late father, thereunto driven contrary to law, reason and good conscience, to the manifest charge and peril of the soul of our said late father," as my proclamation said.

They had imperilled my father's immortal soul: for that they deserved to die. They were executed, as befitted their evil.

❧ WILL:

So the tender-hearted youth, who so shrank from "political" executions, could be roused by "moral" crimes? He would not execute for a title, but for a soul. . . .

Of the seven remaining councillors, three were churchmen: Archbishop Warham, the Chancellor; Bishop Fox, Lord Privy Seal; Bishop Ruthal, Secretary. For the laymen, there were Thomas Howard, Earl of Surrey, Lord Treasurer; George Talbot, Earl of Shrewsbury, Lord High Steward; Charles Somerset, Lord Herbert of Raglan, Lord Chamberlain; Sir Thomas Lovell, Chancellor of the Exchequer and Constable of the Tower.

They met at half-noon every day, regardless of the amount of business at hand. The meetings were exceptionally boring: the first one I attended directed itself to an hour-long debate as to whether the expense for the late King's coffin should be deducted from the Crown's privy purse or from general household expenses.

Yet money was important, I realized that. What I did not realize was the extent of the fortune I had inherited, because the Councilmen tried to obscure this information and did everything to keep it from "the youngling," lest he squander it. In the end it was Wolsey who secured the exact figures and presented them to me, totted up in his neat writing.

As I read them, I tried to keep my expression blank. It was a Herculean task—for the figures were so large they were, simply, unbelievable.

"Are these correct?" I questioned Wolsey, evenly.

"Indeed," he replied. "I got them from three separate sources, each one entirely trustworthy. And I have checked them myself four times."

"I see." I put down the small, dangerous paper. It said I was rich, richer than any King of England had ever been—richer, most likely, than any king in the world. (Except the Infidel Sultan, about whose finances even Wolsey was ignorant.) I was numb. "Thank you," I said, finally.

I hardly noticed Wolsey as he turned and exited.

Rich; I was rich. Correction: the *Crown* was rich. Whatever the King desired, he could have. An army? Done, and outfitted with the latest weapons. New palaces? As many as I liked. And people . . . I could buy them, use them to adorn my court, just as I would select jewels.

So whenever I think back upon those first, halcyon days of my reign, I see but a single colour: gold. Shining gold, dull gold, burnished gold, glittering gold. Cloth-of-gold and golden rings and golden trumpets.

I struck Father's treasure chests like Moses striking the rock in the wilderness, and a dazzling river of gold poured forth. The Crown was staggeringly wealthy, as Wolsey had indicated. Wealthy enough that I could invite any subject with a contested debt, an unredressed grievance, or merely a complaint against the Crown to come forward.

We were overwhelmed by the response; hundreds of people came, and I had to appoint extra lawyers just to attend to their claims, most stemming from the cruel extractions made by Empson and Dudley.

The majority of the claims were decided in favor of the plaintiffs, and the Crown paid. So some of the gold flowed directly back into the hands of common men who stood in sore need of it.

It also flowed into the hands of another group too long without means: musicians and scholars and sculptors and artists. (I did not understand why those who elected to follow the calling of the Muse must traditionally embrace poverty as well, whereas a wool merchant can eat and live well. In my court, it would be altogether different.) And so they came—from Italy, from Spain (where the New Learning was sorely repressed), from the Low Countries, from the German duchies. Erasmus. John Colet. Richard Pace. Juan Luis Vives. I wished my court to be an exciting center of learning, to be an academy dedicated to the mind, in the Greek fashion. (I had myself begun studying Greek so that I might read those works in the original.)

✒ WILL:

He certainly succeeded. Henry VII's hard-gotten wealth financed the "learning academy" of Henry VIII, and soon hordes of hungry, high-minded artists from the Continent swarmed eagerly to England and wrote their friends to join them. (Impecunious scholars knew a bargain when they saw it; years of privation had deepened their appreciation of money.) Young Harry's court was an intellectual's dream. Here is an example of how one scholar (Mountjoy) lured another (Erasmus) to England:

> *If you could see how everyone here rejoices in having so great a prince, how his life is all their desire, you would not contain yourself for sheer joy. Extortion is put down, liberality scatters riches with a bountiful hand, yet our King does not set his heart on gold or jewels, but on virtue, glory and immortality. The other day he told me, "I wish I were more learned." "But learning is not what we expect of a King," I answered, "merely that he should encourage scholars." "Most certainly," he rejoined, "as without them we should scarcely live at all." Now what more splendid remark could a prince make?*

And Erasmus came. There he found others of like mind, namely Linacre, John Leland, and Richard Whitford, besides Pace and Colet.

And the young Thomas More, who was even then writing his *Utopia* and struggling to keep himself free from the beguiling royal web spun by Henry. It was composed in equal parts of gold and charm—a deadly combination, which sooner or later trapped everyone he chose to cast it upon. Not that Harry was lacking in intellect or talent. He was gifted; therein lay the danger, the confusion in his own mind and in those of others. He was truly eager for knowledge, in a boyish fashion, all his life. He knew ships and was a good seaman, and was more knowledgeable about French coastal waters than the authorities, for example. As a common soldier from Harry's disastrous French war notes in his diary: "He was learned in all sciences, and had the gift of many tongues. He was a perfect theologian, a good philosopher and a strong man at arms, a jeweler, a perfect builder as well of fortresses as of pleasant palaces, and from one to another there was no necessary kind of knowledge, from a King's degree to a carter's, but he had an honest sight of it."

His passion for theology may have exceeded his actual grasp of it, but nevertheless it was sufficient to impress the Pope himself and many learned bishops. Above all, there is no denying his extraordinary talent as a musician. He composed works of all kinds, from masses to motets and popular tunes and instrumentals. They are still regularly performed today; his motets *O Lord, the Maker of All Things* and *Quam pulchra es* are used even in Queen Mary's Masses.

Just two days ago I heard a pretty young girl in the Cobham market singing "Greensleeves." I asked her where the tune had come from. "I know not," she replied. "Only that 'tis a customary tune." Harry composed it, and common people still sing it. Had he not been King, he could have lived by his music; I am sure of it.

Since that was not to be, he gathered the best musicians and voices in the realm, kept them at court, and organized them into "The King's Musick." They were attendant on him, and under the direction of Robert Fayrefax. They made superb music, and there was nothing remotely resembling them in any other country, any other court. The French (allegedly the leaders in such things) had a dreadful facsimile group, which sang out of time and out of tune, with a "music master" who could not even read music, in addition to being chronically drunk—usually during performances.

HENRY VIII:

There were other, minor things, such as the refurbishing—and refurnishing—of the royal apartments to suit my taste. (I had begun by banishing that stinking monkey, which was the greatest improvement possible.) I ordered carpets from the Turks, glass vessels from Venice, marble and wood-inlaid tables from Italy, and enamel ware from France. (This in spite of the fact that the Infidels were permanently at enmity with all Christian states, that Venice was beleaguered, and France hostile to us. It is curious that merchants never go to war, and resent it only for disrupting the trade routes.) Father's crude furniture and rush floor coverings were to be replaced as soon as the camels and ships could send their successors.

The Audience Chamber, in particular, needed work. *For a King, do like a King,* Farr had said. I now knew this to be impossible without the proper trappings. An Audience Chamber should dazzle the onlooker, and it does no good to be resplendently attired if the canopy above one's head is threadbare or moth-eaten.

WILL:

If his calculated desire was to stun, he succeeded. I remember well the first time I saw him in full panoply, standing beneath the canopy of state. It was as if he were not an earthly man at all, but some other creature entirely. Which a King must be.

We forget, you and I, that being King is an occupation, just as cabinet-joining or road-paving or law-reading. I know the official belief: that Kings are somehow different, springing from a divinely ordained race. Yet Harry's great-grandfather was a Clerk of the Wardrobe. Where was the blood royal in him? At what stage did it miraculously appear? No, Catherine (as you are radical in religion, perhaps this extends into other areas as well?), it appeared in his descendants only when they were called to *be* King. "For a King, do like a King." It is simple, yet not so simple. The truth is that very few men can convincingly "do like a King," try as they will. Harry could; he was a genius in it; a master at capturing and holding men's imaginations and loyalties. He sensed from the beginning the power of physical impressions, and spared no effort to play up his greatest asset: his dazzling appearance. Do you remember that witty Venetian ambassador, Giustinian? He was at Harry's court for four years and wrote a book entitled, appropriately enough, *Four Years at the Court of Henry VIII.* Here is his recording of one of Henry's "audiences":

"His fingers were one mass of jewelled rings and around his neck he wore a gold collar from which hung a diamond as big as a walnut. He received the Venetian ambassadors under a canopy of cloth of gold, wearing a doublet of white and crimson satin, and a purple velvet mantle lined with white satin."

To be a King is to be un-ordinary, extraordinary: *because we will have it so*, we demand it, as we demand our carpenters make smooth-sliding drawers. Much of Harry's behaviour is incomprehensible if judged as the actions of an ordinary man; as King, it appears in a different light. If a man is consciously trying to be an *ideal* King, an outside King, then all the more so.

And there can be no wavering, no half-measures. One must be King every instant, while retiring to the privy stool as well as in state audiences. There is no respite: the mask of royalty must gradually supplant the ordinary man, as sugar syrup replaces the natural flavors in candied fruit and flowers. They retain their original outward appearance, but inside are altogether changed in substance.

Harry bore this burden easily, and wore his regality with a splendid conviction. What this cost him as a man becomes apparent as one reads on in his journal.

✑ HENRY VIII:

At times I felt like the Roman centurion in the Gospel who said to Our Lord: *I am a man under authority, having soldiers under me: and I say to this man, Go, and he goeth; and to another, Come, and he cometh; and to my servant, Do this, and he doeth it.* It was a heady feeling, to be able to command like the centurion, to have men obey me.

Yet I quickly found there was another side to it. Yes, I could command men and women. But unlike the Scriptural centurion, I discovered that ritual surrounded every act of mine, imprisoning me and slowing my movements until they resembled those of a man in a dream. Should I be hungry and require even something so simple as bread and ale, it touched upon the pride and prerogatives of some ten people, each jealous of the other. The messenger must not carry the tray, that was the duty of the Lord Steward's server, who in turn must not enter the Privy Chamber but hand the tray to a groom, who in turn must give it to . . . You see the problem. Rather than ordering someone to "go here" or "come," I often went without things rather than submit to the ponderous ritual attached.

Why, then, did I submit at all? Because I quickly grasped the true purpose of this system: to buffer me from the endless demands of self-seekers and petitioners. The long chain of command stretching between myself and my servers wove a tight web about me, and if I could not break out, neither could outsiders break in.

For whenever I left the royal apartments, I was attacked by swarms of people asking things of me. An appointment for their cousin. A good decision, please, from the court lawyer studying their case. To be sure, they did not physically press in upon me; they were more subtle and wore silks and made sure to keep the required several inches away, and instead of shouting, they whispered their requests. But is it any wonder that I needed time alone to hawk and hunt and ride? At times I felt like an anvil, where all men came to hammer at their desires, and my head rang.

In connection with this, there was yet another meeting I must investigate and attend, at least occasionally: the Lord Steward's so-called Board of Green Cloth. The Lord Steward's staff was responsible for all the creature comforts at court. He oversaw some twenty-five departments, such as the bakehouse and buttery, the saucery and laundry, each with its own staff. These department divisions were time-honoured and thus totally illogical: for example, "poultry" was responsible for procuring lamb, although the "acatary" was in charge of meat, including mutton. The Lord Steward controlled (if that is the proper word, for they seemed quite *un*controlled) a staff of two hundred and twenty. (In peacetime he controlled more expenditure than any other single individual in the realm.) Nevertheless, he attempted to check accounts and inventory supplies every week with his treasurer and controller, while sitting around a table covered with green baize cloth, hence its informal name: Board of Green Cloth.

I attended three of these meetings. One addressed itself to this problem: Was the best wheat to be procured in Kent or in Dorset? (An interesting question, no doubt, but one that hardly required the Royal Presence.) The second worked out an elaborate scheme for collecting used candle-butts and reusing them. And the third discussed the best use for goose-feathers. It seems there was an abundance of said feathers following a palace feast. After that, I went no more, but sent Wolsey in my stead.

But for deeper matters: I lacked yet one thing which I longed for. A wife. Yes, I would have a Queen. And who but Katherine, to whom I had pledged myself so long ago? I disregarded the nebulous marriage treaties that Father had been fashioning: his death rendered them null and void. (Particularly since he pledged himself as a bridegroom in some of the negotiations.) I would have Katherine, or no one.

But I must hurry, so it seemed. Upon hearing of Father's Habsburg marriage plans, the Spanish had finally despaired of the marriage between us, and most of Katherine's possessions had already been transferred out of England by the Spanish ambassador, with her own departure not far behind. She, who had vowed that she would die in England rather than return to Spain unmarried, was about to break her vow.

If she stood ready to break her vow, I did not. She was pledged to me, and I was bound to her. I summoned her to come to the Privy Chamber next day.

She arrived exactly on time. I felt a flicker of disappointment as I saw her, small and poorly dressed, coming toward me across the great floor. She looked much older, and less pretty, than I had remembered. But I had not seen her in full light for almost six years, while I had gone from boy to man. Still, this was my betrothed. . . .

"Katherine," I said, coming to her and holding out my hands. I towered over her. She was . . . squat. No, petite, I corrected myself. "My wife."

She looked confused. "No. You are to marry a Habsburg. De Puebla has begun transferring my dowry to Bruges."

"To hell with the dowry!" I said. "I have been left a fortune, the like of which no English King has ever been bequeathed. I do not need your dowry; I do not want it. It stinks of negotiations, subterfuge, lies, bargains. I want you, Katherine, not your dowry."

She merely stared at me. I had a sudden dread: perhaps she still knew little English? I started toward her, and she drew away.

"Please, Katherine," I said. "I wish you to be my wife."

She stood still. "Very well," she said, and seemed forty years old, cold and dignified. Then she ran toward me, held out her hands. "Henry!" she cried, looking up at me. Tears shone in her eyes. "I wanted—but I thought"—she blinked away the tears—"I thought it was never meant to be."

"No, Katherine. Indeed it *is* meant to be." With all the blind assurance of youth, I said that. "Against all wishes, we will wed! And soon—so that we may be crowned together."

"When?"

"As soon as my father's funeral is past. We will be married privately, and go away into the country for a few days, and be alone—"

"A runaway match!"

I laughed. "Your English is very good. Yes, a runaway match! We will confound them all, all those who advise against it for the sake of treaties, alliances, dowries, dispensations. We are young, and love one another. Nothing else matters."

"No," she agreed. "Nothing else matters."

I bent down and kissed her. Her mouth was firm and sweet. "I am King now," I said. "We have nothing more to fear."

XIII

Katherine and I were married in mid-June, just two weeks before the Coronation. It was a private affair; at a simple Mass in the Chapel of the Observant Friars at Greenwich (where I had been baptized), we were married by Archbishop Warham. Only the family attended.

WILL:

A curious fact: Henry never had a dazzling public wedding like the one his brother Arthur had, although the man normally revelled in public ceremonies. When or where his marriage to Anne Boleyn, Jane Seymour, or Catherine Howard took place remains a mystery to most people.

HENRY VIII:

It was the third time I had stood beside Katherine to recite marriage vows in one form or another. The first time I was ten, the second time twelve, and now I was seventeen.

I try hard to remember that day, as what we later became blots it out. I was proud, and insisted that Katherine wear my wedding gift to her: a necklace of gigantic pearls, each one as big as a marble. I did not know then that pearls are the symbols of tears, and that the common people say that for each pearl the bride wears, her husband will give her cause for weeping. Nor would I have believed it, then. As we stepped out onto the church porch, silvery drops began to fall: a sun-shower. Another omen, pointing the same way . . . you will shed a tear for each raindrop that falls on your wedding day. But to us it felt like the sprinkling of holy water, a special benediction and blessing. Laughing, we clasped hands and ran across the courtyard to Greenwich Palace, where we would have our private wedding feast.

Poor Katherine had no family in England, but no matter, so I thought;

I was to be her family now. My grandmother Beaufort was there, although she was ailing, and my eleven-year-old cousin Henry Courtenay, Earl of Devon. There was my quasi-uncle, Arthur Plantagenet, the natural son of Edward IV and one of his mistresses. He was some nine years older than I. Other members of my family were noticeable by their absence: my cousin Edmund de la Pole, Duke of Suffolk, still imprisoned in the Tower, and his brother Richard, fled abroad to France. It was a small feast.

But it was a merry one. There was almost visible relief on Grandmother Beaufort's face. Her grandson was safely King and had taken a wife, and the future of the family was no longer in jeopardy. She could die now, and she did, just three weeks later.

While I sat beside Katherine, I could not stop staring at her, in disbelief that she was to be mine. Nor could she keep from looking at me—at the ten-year-old boy who had been her friend, now a boy no longer, but a King.

Yet looking at her (all the while the minstrels were playing and the seemingly endless procession of dishes was presented) only made me more anxious and preoccupied. I wished the feast to be over; I wished it to go on forever.

Shall I confess it? I was a virgin. Unlike my companions of the tiltyard and the exercise field, I had never had a woman. How could I, guarded and sequestered as I was, and constantly watched by the King? Oh, there had been the customary invitations from the serving girls. But I had no desire for them—perhaps because they offered themselves so freely. Or perhaps because I was embarrassed to reveal my virginal state, which I assumed would be obvious, and then they would laugh at me in the kitchens and the laundry. In the beginning it was simply that I was too young, and was frightened; then, later, ironically, I was too old.

And now I must take Katherine to bed. The young King, proclaimed a second Hector, another Lancelot, and so on, was as inexperienced as his older, sickly brother had been before him. And with the same woman. I remembered how, with the blithe ignorance of a ten-year-old, I had disdained his timidity and lack of self-assurance.

We were alone in the Retiring Room. The entire humiliating court ritual of "putting the couple to bed" had been duly observed. Our friends and attendants had come especially to undress us ceremoniously (behind separate screens), and mine had crowded around me, telling obscene jokes and making suggestions. I kept drinking wine. Brandon winked and put his hand over the cup and said, "No more of that, Your Grace. You know the proverb: 'Look not thou upon the wine when it is red in the cup; at the last it biteth like a serpent, and stingeth like an adder.' " I hastily put down the wine cup, and they laughed loudly.

Behind the other screen, Katherine's Spanish attendant and dear friend, Maria de Salinas, made her ready. Then we were led out from behind our respective screens (like lambs to the slaughter, I could not help thinking, and our white garments only enhanced the image) and taken to the great bed, with its new velvet hangings. We climbed the wooden steps on each side and got into it, embarrassed and awkward. Maria and Brandon then pulled the covers up over us and the entire company stood back and observed us with satisfaction.

Carew nodded and then shouted, "We have seen it!" and flourished his sword. He was drunk.

At last they were gone, and I turned and faced Katherine. We looked absurdly like two dolls propped up on pillows and attired in ceremonial embroidered nightclothes. There were peculiar scratchy things under the covers. I slid my hand under and pulled one out: a twig of some sort.

"It is betony, from Spain," said Katherine. "To make the sheets smell sweet." She slowly reached up and began to unpin her hair, which fell down heavily and spilled over her shoulders like thick honey.

Something in the action triggered my own response, and I reached out and touched the hair. It was cool and smooth, like new-made satin. And her shoulders under it were warm and smooth as well, and she seemed all the sweetness I had ever known, magically gathered into one being.

I leaned toward her and kissed her; her lips were warm and plump. Her body pressed hungrily against me; I could feel her breasts through the thin nightdress. She had extraordinarily large breasts for such a small, slight girl, I thought, from somewhere outside myself. There was still a part of me detachedly noting such things, but the main part of me was now unhinged, incoherent with excitement. Shyness was forgotten as my desire leaped full-grown into life. I pulled at the straps of her nightdress, impatiently. One of them broke. She grasped it, frowning. "My Lord—" she began.

"I'll give you others!" I said harshly. "Take it off, then!"

"First you must put out the candle."

"No. I want to see you! See your beauty," I added awkwardly.

"No candles," she said. "No lights. Please . . . Henry." She said my name with great hesitation.

I swatted at the candle, and it went out. Then I threw off my own clothing and began tugging at hers. It was so rushed and impatient—but is there any desire, anywhere, as towering as a seventeen-year-old boy's?

She pushed my hands away and carefully took off the nightdress herself, dropping it daintily on the floor. Then, unexpectedly, she turned in the bed and pressed herself against me. "Ah, Henry—" she murmured, sliding her arms up and around me, over my back. She kept kissing me, sighing and making little sounds. Had I died and gone straightway to a pagan paradise?

It was all so very easy, after all. In fact, it seemed to be prescribed: there was nothing else one *could* do effectively to ease that desire.

Katherine seemed to be a virgin. But then, it is hard for one virgin to be sure of another. Thus, years later, when the controversy raged about this very question, I kept a diplomatic silence, lest I betray myself.

XIV

%% WILL:

All of England went on a general holiday for approximately half a year—from old Henry's death in April until the autumn winds blew. There was a great rejoicing among the people, from the lowest (with whom I consorted in those days) to (I assume) the highest. The mood pervaded everything at the time but is very difficult to describe now: a feeling of jubilation and expansiveness. They were ready to embrace Young Harry (as they called him), permit him anything, then forgive him for it. They almost longed for him to sin, so that they could show him their great acceptance.

But he did not sin. He behaved well, as if he were following a private code entitled "The Honour of a Prince." Not only was he young and handsome and rich, but he attended five Masses a day, had honoured his youthful promise to make the Spanish princess his wife, and had turned the gloomy court of his father into a glittering pavilion of wisdom, wit, and talent. The people waited anxiously to see what sort of Coronation he would give them. He did not disappoint them.

%% HENRY VIII:

I chose Midsummer's Day for our Coronation. Midsummer's Day, 1509. Even today I cannot write those words without stirring the scent of green summer from the dry leaves of an old man's memory. High summer almost forty years ago, still preserved like pressed flowers in a few withered minds. . . .

But that day there were thousands upon thousands who saw the young Henry and Katherine winding their way through the London streets to their Coronation in Westminster Abbey. They shrieked and held out their hands to us. I can still see those faces, healthy (perhaps slightly flushed with the wine I had ordered for the populace?) and filled with joy. They wanted me and I wanted them, and on both sides we believed we would live forever in this moment.

When we reached the Abbey, I dismounted while Katherine was helped from her litter by her ladies-in-waiting. She was wearing the costume of a virgin bride, all in white, with her golden-brown hair hanging loose. I held out my hand and took hers. Before us stretched a great white carpet over which we must walk before entering the Abbey. A thousand people lined the walkway.

Suddenly it was all very familiar. Once before, I had led Katherine over just such a walkway and into a great church. For a moment I had a chill, as if a raven had flown across the sun. Then it was gone, so that I could turn to her and whisper, "Do you remember another time when you walked beside me on a state occasion?"

She looked up at me (then, she had looked straight across). "Yes, my Lord. When you were but ten. But already then I sensed that you were—must be—"

She broke off as we reached the doors of the Abbey, where Archbishop Warham waited for us. Just then a great cry went up behind us, and I turned to see the people falling on the white carpet, attacking it with knives and shears. They would cut out pieces to be saved, to remember the day King Henry VIII was crowned, to be passed on to children and children's children. (Where are those pieces now, I wonder?) It was a custom, I was told. Still, the sight of those flashing knives . . .

Within the Abbey, Katherine and I walked slowly down the great nave, with platforms and seats on either side which had been put up to enable the great lords and noble families present to witness the ceremony. Upon reaching the high altar, we separated, and I went to the ancient, scarred wooden throne-chair which had been used for Coronations for centuries. I remember thinking how crudely carved it was, how rough the wood. Then I took my place in it, and it fitted as though it had been constructed just for me.

The Archbishop faced the people and asked them in a clear, ringing voice whether they would have me for King. They shouted "aye" three times in succession, the last so loud it echoed off the great vault. I wondered (it is strange, the thoughts that come to one during such moments) whether it reached my sleeping family in their private chapel behind the high altar—Father, Mother, my deceased siblings Elizabeth and Edmund and the last baby, all interred there.

But this was a day for the living. Warham anointed me, and the oil was warm and pleasingly scented. Then, after my vows, he placed the heavy, jewel-encrusted crown on my head, and I prayed that I might be worthy of it, might preserve and defend it. When he said Mass, I vowed to do only good for England, upon peril of my immortal soul. I would serve her as a good and perfect knight.

Some theorists say a Coronation is but a ceremony, yet it changed me, subtly and forever: I never forgot those vows.

But shortly afterwards, as I looked back on the two months since my accession, I was surprised at how many changes had crept into my being. In April I had been a frightened seventeen-year-old; now (having had my eighteenth birthday, I considered myself much older) I was a crowned King. And nothing untoward had happened, none of the disasters I had feared: no one had challenged my right to the crown (although I had not taken Father's advice about executing de la Pole; he was still healthy in the Tower). I had taken command of the Privy Council and the Board of Green Cloth. I had married. When Katherine told me, a month after the Coronation, that she was with child, I laughed outright. It was all so easy, this business of being King. What had I feared?

And through all those days there ran yet another shade of gold: the gold of my Katherine's hair. Her hair as we spun in dances; her hair flying as we rode across cleared fields and sun-spotted forests; her hair falling over the pillows, her shoulders, my arms, in bed. I was happier than I had ever believed it possible for mortal man to be, so blissfully content I felt it sinful—as indeed it was.

XV

T hen it ended—abruptly, as dreams do. It ended the day Wolsey (who had created a *de facto* position for himself as messenger between me and the Privy Council) came to tell me that "the French emissary had arrived."

What French emissary? I wondered. Perhaps some catastrophe had overtaken King Louis XII? I must confess I half-hoped the old spider was dead.

In the past few years the French had suddenly embarked upon an aggressive policy. In the almost one hundred years since the glorious days of our own Henry V's virtual conquest of France, they had recovered like a moribund man throwing off the plague. First they gained some little strength and rallied their own forces; then they pushed us back—out of Normandy, out of Aquitaine—until we clung only to Calais and a small neighbouring area. Then they began gobbling up surrounding territory: Burgundy, Brittany. Then, again, their appetite grew ever more ravenous, like that of a recovering plague-man. Not satisfied with recovering their own lost dominions, they wished to seize others: Italy in particular. No matter that they were sworn to "universal peace" by the Treaty of Cambrai, which they had signed along with the Emperor, the Spanish, and the Pope; they invaded northern Italy nonetheless, and began threatening Venice as well.

England was also formally bound to peace with France by a treaty concluded between Father and Louis. Yet upon Father's death it became void, and I was not sure I wished to renew it. The Pope had been issuing distressed cries for help as he saw the French encroaching upon Italy; and I had not forgotten that Louis had honoured Edmund de la Pole at court, and even now was harbouring the younger de la Pole brother, Richard. So Louis's death would solve many problems, or at least halt the voracious appetite of the French state for a little while.

I dressed (or rather, put on my "audience clothes"—this involved the ministrations of a good half-dozen men) and made my way to the Audience

Chamber. Wolsey had hurriedly summoned the Privy Council to attend, so that they were awaiting me as I took my place on the Chair of Presence.

The French emissary was ushered in—a perfumed, dandified creature. He made a long-winded greeting, which I cut off, as his reeking person offended me. He stank worse than the rose incense in Father's death-chamber. I demanded to know his business, and at length he disclosed it. He came bearing a letter from Louis in reply to the one I had purportedly written begging my brother the Most Christian King of France to live in peace with me. He handed me the letter. It stank as well—from proximity to its carrier?

As I unrolled the letter and read it rapidly, I could feel my face growing red, as it does in moments of stress, to my embarrassment.

"What?" I said slowly. "The King of France, who dares not look me in the face—let alone make war on me!—says *I* sue for peace?"

The phrase "dares not look me in the face" was, I admit, a trifle overblown, but I was stunned. Someone had written a cringing, demeaning letter in my name, forged my signature, and used the Royal Seal!

"Which of you has done this?" I asked, glaring at the line of councillors on either side of the dais.

Was it Warham, my Lord Chancellor? He looked up at me mournfully, like a sad old dog.

Ruthal, the Secretary? I stared into his blackberry-like eyes, which gave nothing back.

Fox, Lord Privy Seal? He smiled smugly, protected by his churchly vestments—or so he thought.

What of the others—Howard, Talbot, Somerset, Lovell? They smiled back, blandly. None of them had the wherewithal to have done it. It must have been one of the churchmen.

I turned and made to leave the room, shaking with anger, not trusting myself to speak further.

"Your Grace!" called Fox in a clear, imperious voice. "The emissary awaits your reply."

I whirled. "Then give him one!" My voice rang in the large chamber, all freshly bedecked in Flemish tapestry and gilt. "You who are so adept at composing royal utterances—you may continue." I left the room. Behind me I heard the buzz of voices—angry, bewildered.

Had I distressed them, embarrassed them? No matter. I had wanted to kill Fox, to choke his leathery neck, then fling him out into the courtyard and let the dogs fall on him. Yet I had restricted myself to the use of words alone. At least the foppish Frenchman could not report to Louis that the English King had bodily attacked one of his own ministers.

I leaned against the other side of the door and caught my breath. It was all clear now. Father meant to rule from the grave through his three faithful councillors. That was why he had appointed no Protector: this was surer and more secretive, both of which would appeal strongly to him. So now he could lie serenely in his magnificent tomb-monument—"dwelling more richly dead than alive," as one court wit had put it—happy in the knowledge that his untrusted, wayward son would never actually rule.

He is insensitive and stupid. . . . Did he think me so stupid I would not object to others' forging my signature or using the Royal Seal? This was treason. Did he suppose me insensitive even to treason?

Within the privacy of my Retiring Room, I poured out a large cup of wine. (I was free for the moment of the unwelcome ministrations of servers.) Anger and humiliation vied for control within me, both to be eventually replaced by a cold hardness. At length, it was not Fox I wished to punish. He had merely followed orders, remaining obedient to the King to whom he had long ago pledged loyalty. God send *me* such a servant!

I walked over to Father's bed. I had stripped his drab hangings from it, replaced his straw mattress with one of down, had soft-woven woollen blankets put on. I had spent his money, destroyed his furniture, broken his marriage negotiations, negated his dowry correspondence, put logs in his barren fire-places. I had done all this, yet I had not effaced his presence from my life. He was still King in his realm and council.

I flung myself out full length on the bed. What a fool I had been! (Was Father right, then? My mind shrank from that possibility.) So I thought being King was easy? So had it been planned to be, to lull me. . . .

I needed my own men. Or even one man. Someone not a stale remnant from Father's reign, but entirely mine. Who? I lay staring distractedly at the carved underside of the wooden canopy, seeing cherubs and lover's knots and hunting parties, but nothing came to my mind.

"Your Grace?" The door had opened quietly. I sat up, angry. I had not given permission. . . .

It was Wolsey. He bore a scroll of some sort.

"Not now," I muttered, waving him away. I had no wish to read figures. "And I gave express orders I was not to be disturbed!" So I was not obeyed even in my own private quarters.

He bowed. "I know. Yet I was able to persuade your groom . . ."

Wolsey. Yes. Wolsey was my man. *I was able to persuade your groom.* Subtle, golden-tongued Wolsey. Why had I not thought of him? Because I was a little afraid of him, afraid of that awesome efficiency, that inexhaustible energy, coupled with that tireless, amoral mind. Yet I needed him; I must admit that. I was in desperate need of him.

These thoughts flashed through my mind so swiftly that there was no pause before I grunted, "What do you want?"

"To bring you a transcript of what happened after your departure." He smiled. " 'Twas quite humorous. I wish there was some way you could have beheld that Frenchman's discomfiture. Fox said—"

But I was hardly listening, as I observed him critically. How clever to bring me the transcript. And his flattery was subtle. He did not praise my looks, my prowess, did not compare me to Hercules or the like. Rather, he went to the heart of the matter; he knew where I was weakest and sought to shore it up. Yes, Wolsey . . .

Wolsey soon took his place on the Privy Council, by my express command. I told Fox and Ruthal and Warham blandly that perhaps they would welcome another cleric to their ranks, to make an even balance with the laymen on the Council. They seemed pleased. The fools.

In spite of my preoccupation with these matters, I did not wish to neglect Katherine. I arranged entertainments for her, so that she might pass her days serenely. In particular, I went out of my way to obtain good musicians for a season at court.

After a lengthy exchange of letters, I had finally acquired a musical *coup*: Friar Denis Memmo, the organist from St. Mark's in Venice. It required a great deal of gold (everything did, I was learning) as well as a discreet defrocking and reinstatement as a royal priest in my employ. But it was done, and he had come to England, bringing with him from Venice a magnificent organ. I was anxious to examine it, as I was interested in the art and science of organ construction and how this affected its tone. Now the splendid organ was installed in Greenwich Palace, and Memmo was to perform for the entire court.

Wolsey (now in charge of such minute details as well as weightier ones) had assembled all the chairs from all the privy chambers in the palace, so that everyone could be comfortably seated. He had ordered a table of light refreshments to be laid along one wall, and placed fresh candles all about—large, fine ones which would certainly last the entire recital and not make foul smoke to damage Memmo's instrument.

Katherine and I entered the room first and sat in the large royal chairs in front. It was November now, and Katherine's gowns had had to be let out. Her movements were altered, and that made me proud. My heir lay beneath those green silken folds, growing toward his birth.

Memmo's performance was dazzling. He played for almost three hours, and there was no stirring in the court audience. They were enthralled.

Afterwards, although it was not far from midnight, we gathered round the long tables, laid out with prawn jellies and custard and fritters with manchet. The dishes were still moist and fresh: Wolsey's choices. Everyone was talking at once, and Memmo was surrounded by admirers. That pleased me. The well-prepared repast pleased me as well. I must commend Wolsey.

Just then Wolsey appeared from a small side door, as if I had called him up. He stood inconspicuously in the corner, observing his arrangements. Another man saw him and went over to him, and they conferred for a lengthy space.

Curious as to who it was, I made my way to them. Wolsey was listening raptly to the other man, but sensed my approach and broke off.

"Your Grace," he said, bowing.

"Did you hear Memmo's performance, Thomas?" I asked. "He was superb! I hope you did not merely arrange the chairs and supervise the food— which was beautifully done, by the way—without remaining to hear the music."

"I heard," replied Wolsey.

"Thomas hears *everything,*" said his companion. I looked at him: a plain-featured man, yet with an open countenance. Well dressed, but in such good taste that one remembered nothing in particular about it.

"As does *this* Thomas," said Wolsey. "Your Grace, may I present Thomas More? A London lawyer I consult occasionally in regard to setting up this new court that the Privy Council wants held in the Palace." He paused. "You remember. To avoid the harassment and delays in local courts of common law."

"Ah, yes." I had assigned an old room for the purpose, one with a fading celestial scene on its ceiling. They had nicknamed it the Court of Star Chamber.

More smiled. "I fear the artist who painted the ceiling there had never seen the actual sky. The stars are all wrong. He has Castor in Leo. And Rigel is missing entirely in Orion. Still, it makes a pretty picture."

"Do you know astronomy?" Obviously he did.

"My knowledge is poor, Your Grace—"

"Nonsense!" I grew more and more excited. "You must come with me up to the palace roof. Tonight!"

Yes, tonight. Katherine was tired and wished to retire straightway; she had told me so.

"Your Grace, it is late—"

"Just in time for Vega to appear! This is the last week before winter that it will rise at all. And I cannot find it. I tried last night, but it was useless. I have a new astrolabe—"

"His Grace is an enthusiastic star-watcher," said Wolsey. "He sent to Padua and Rome for new star maps and tables, but they are slow in arriving."

"Perhaps I will send you in person to bring them back, Wolsey! Did you know"—I suddenly felt a great desire to confide in More, to joke with him —"Wolsey once carried a message from my father to the Emperor Maximilian in Flanders and back in only four days? 'Tis true. When my father saw him, he chided him for delaying in his leaving, and Wolsey was able to say, 'Your Grace, I have yet gone and returned.'"

"Yes, I heard that," said More quietly. "Wolsey can do the seemingly impossible."

"But come to my roof tonight!" I insisted. I glanced over at the crowd, still milling about the table. "In an hour's time, when all these people are gone to bed."

Now I waited impatiently for More upon the flat roof directly over the royal apartments, which I had fitted up for my observatory. I had an astrolabe, a torquetum, and a solar quadrant mounted there, and a table for my charts and books. This roof afforded an exceptionally unobstructed view of the sky, as the Palace was on high ground far above all the surrounding trees, and the diffuse, distracting lights of London were five miles upstream.

I breathed deeply. It was cold and clear, a pristine autumn night. An ideal time for star-viewing; perhaps the best in the year.

Shortly before one, More appeared. He looked around, surprised at the extent to which my roof had been transformed into a facility for the study of astronomy.

"Thank you for coming, Thomas," I said. I gestured proudly at my equipment. "It does not rival Bologna or Padua, I know, but in time—"

"Your Grace has done marvellously well in assembling this." He strode over to my table with the charts and astrolabe and quickly examined them. "Excellent," he pronounced.

"I have been trying to measure Auriga," I said.

"You must sight Capella first. Then five degrees off that—"

The time passed quickly as More showed me things in the sky I had not seen before, revealed mathematical formulae for deducing the exact time from the height of a star. We talked excitedly and never noticed how light it was growing in the eastern part of the sky. He spent a great length of time figuring precisely where Aldebaran should be, then adjusting the torquetum accordingly to find it. When indeed it was there, we both laughed and cried out in joy.

"A superlative set of brass servants," More pronounced.

"You handle them well," I said. "What sort do you have yourself?"

He smiled and raised his finger slowly to his eyes.

"You shall have one of these! I shall order one to be made straightway, and by spring—"

"No, Your Grace."

That brought me up sharp. "Why not?"

"I prefer to take no gifts."

"But this would help—"

"I prefer not." His voice was quiet, and something in the tone reminded me . . . called forth a painful remembrance. . . . "My good Lord Henry—"

Adieu, Lord Henry . . . yes, that was it. "You recited the elegy to my mother," I said slowly, interrupting him.

"Yes, Your Grace." The voice was the same. Why had I not recognized it earlier? Yet it was a span of nearly seven years since I had heard it. . . .

"And wrote it as well."

"Yes, Your Grace."

"It was—moving." I waited for him to reply, but he merely nodded solemnly. The growing light showed his features now, but I could read nothing on them. "It meant a great deal to me." Again he inclined his head. "Thomas —come to court! Serve me! I have need of men such as you. I wish my court to be filled with Thomas Mores."

"Then the presence of one more or less can hardly matter."

I had said it wrong in my excitement. "I did not mean—I meant that your presence would be precious to me."

"I cannot, Your Grace."

"Why not?" I burst out. All the others had come, even from the Continent, and More was an Englishman whose family had been near the court since Father's time. "Why not?" It was an anguished cry.

"I prefer not, Your Grace. Forgive me." His face was sad, and he said the words slowly.

"I would give you—"

"Do not tell me what you would give me," he said. "Then I should have to say, 'Get thee behind me, Satan.' No fit words to address to one's King!" He smiled, then saw my bewildered expression. "Surely you are familiar with the story of the Temptation of Christ?"

"Yes, but—"

"Read it in Greek," he said. "It is so much clearer in Greek than in Latin." Bowing, he left me standing on the roof alone in the grey light of early dawn. Only later did I remember that I had not given him leave to go.

The next day at noon a beautiful volume of the New Testament in Greek was delivered to me, with a note from More, saying, "I have been both comforted and discomfited by these Scriptures, yet I trust they be true."

Impatiently I thumbed through them until I found the correct passage in Saint Mark. I struggled for two hours to translate it precisely, as my knowledge of Greek was barely up to the task. It read: "Again, the devil taketh him up to an exceeding high mountain, and sheweth him all the kingdoms of the world, and the glory of them; And saith unto him, All these things will I give thee, if thou wilt fall down and worship me. Then said Jesus unto him, Get thee hence, Satan."

As I translated word by word, I became incensed. So More saw me as the Devil, requiring that all worship me? All I had done was ask him to come to court as a lawyer and my sometime companion. What was evil about that? A gift of an astrolabe—a simple thing, something to help him in his pursuit and love of astronomy. Hardly the equivalent of a soul. And, by implication (from the passage he had selected), he saw himself as Christ. I the Devil, he Christ?

Shaking, I put the Greek text aside. More had profoundly disturbed me, as evidently he had intended. But less for myself than for him: I feared he must be unbalanced, demented.

XVI

I resolved to forget More. What matter if he chose not to come to court, but preferred to meet with his scholar-friends in his own house in Chelsea? The only men whose deliberate refusal to come to court would matter were the great nobles like the Duke of Buckingham or the Earl of Northumberland or the Earl of Surrey. But they came, all of them, and pledged their loyalty. (I was "domesticating" them, in Wolsey's word. He always had the appropriate word.)

But even had I wished to (which I assuredly did not!), I could not dwell on More for long, as things of much greater importance were taking place. The French continued their belligerent actions, straining the forbearance of both Maximilian and Ferdinand, who were still honourably bound by the treaty of Cambrai. The Pope had denounced Louis and appealed to me, to Maximilian, and to Ferdinand in turn. He had excommunicated Louis and laid all France under an Interdict: there could be no Masses, no baptisms, no marriages, no burials. A dreadful thing, yet the so-called Most Christian King did not seem unduly concerned, clearly revealing himself as apostate. For who could live without the Sacraments?

Must I declare war on France? Did I truly have any choice? I would be bound by honour to do so. But the army . . .

Unlike other countries, England had no standing army, and each time a war was fought a new one must be raised. An ancient ordinance commanded each able-bodied man to have war weapons at the ready and be prepared to fall into ranks upon the call—in short, a national militia. In fact, very few households kept the required weapons at hand, and of those weapons that were so kept, many were obsolete or in poor repair.

I therefore issued a proclamation (one of my first to touch upon the population at large) ordering everyone to comply with the law and stock the appropriate weapons. There was much grumbling at the expense involved.

WILL:

One curious fact about England, often remarked upon by foreigners: whereas the Kings of other realms sought to limit weapons and keep them out of the hands of common citizens, the English *insisted* that they keep them. Partly it was frugality: standing armies are alarmingly expensive. But mainly it was trust. Harry had no army and only a handful of armed personal guards against a fully armed citizenry. Yet his decrees were obeyed without question and he never feared to go about unarmed among the people, even at the height of his unpopularity.

HENRY VIII:

We talked peace, but readied ourselves for war. This, I soon learned, was customary. Yet the holy season of Christmas interrupted these sordid things, as all the world paused to observe the Saviour's birth.

WILL:

I am sure he would not have put it thus at the time. His title of "Supreme Head of the Church in England" quite went to his head in later years, and caused him to try to emulate Papal pronouncements in retrospect. At the time (he was a mere eighteen, remember!) he undoubtedly said, "It is Christmas and time for the festivities."

HENRY VIII:

I determined that the celebrations in my court would be splendid, for Christmas festivities were important for several reasons. They knitted the court together as a family and dispelled factions, if only for an interval. Those who saw them as mere pomp and display missed their true purpose—for we must have rest and respite from work. And all the world was at rest. The roads were well nigh impassable, and even the Thames froze as far upstream as London, making normal commerce impossible. The fields lay open and frozen, and the common people waited and played. Should not we do likewise?

The weather obliged, and there was a warm spell in December, facilitating the cutting of the Yule log, the seasoning of firewood, the travel of families from far away to court for the festivities. The revels-master was able to assemble his spectacular pageant-machine (all papier-mâché and paint and illusion, to be borne upon a great cart) outdoors.

Then, in mid-December, as if on royal command, the weather changed, turned wintry. Snow blew from the north, driving us indoors, making us glad of the fires and torches.

True, it was not by royal command, yet everything seemed arranged as I would have it, from small things like the weather to more important things, such as finding a servant like Wolsey ready at hand, and finally to my wife, Katherine, who was pleasing to me in every way and now pleasingly great with child. I remember leaning against the window in my work closet (through which I could feel the north wind; the sash was poorly fitted) and thanking God for all my blessings.

Warham celebrated High Mass in the Chapel Royal on Christmas Day, and the entire court attended: the Royal Family and the attendants on the upper level, the rest of the household on the lower level.

Then the secular festivities began. There were masques and miming, and three fools scampered about. A great banquet with some eighty dishes (one of them being baked lampreys, my favourite). Still later, a dance in the Great Hall.

Disguised, as custom decreed, I danced with many ladies to the lively string-melodies of the rebec and the thump of the wooden xylophone. Only one woman made bold to guess my identity: Lady Boleyn, wife of Thomas Boleyn, one of my Esquires of the Body. She was a vain, tiresome woman, much given to flirtation and, as she thought, charm. She began by announcing straightway that she danced with the King; she recognized him by his strength, his manliness, his renowned dancing skill. (A clever move. Should I *not* be King—as her chances were only so-so that I was—then the hearer would be flattered, as she imagined; and if she were, by accident, correct, then the King himself would marvel at her astuteness.) I did not enlighten her, but let her go on about her stepchildren, who were all deserving of accolades and (now it came) positions at court. Mary, George, and Anne. (Cursed names, all! Would that I had never heard them!) I extricated myself as soon as possible.

WILL:

I am sure he did not mean to include Mary in this wish; and certainly he would not undo the children that resulted from his inability to extricate himself truly from the Boleyns. If only the daughters had been as unappealing as the mother! Incidentally, this should lay to rest the old rumour that he dallied with Lady Boleyn as well. Where this got started I cannot imagine; ill-wishers are determined to give the King as large and indiscriminate a lust as Jupiter himself.

HENRY VIII:

It was time for the musical interlude. To everyone's surprise, I myself took my lute and went to the middle of the floor.

"I have composed a song for the season," I announced. It was not strictly true; I had composed it merely for myself, when trying to settle in my own mind exactly what I wished from life. Everyone stared back at me, yet I struck the chord and was not in the least afraid. I sang, boldly:

> Pastime with good company
> I love and shall until I die
> Grudge who will, but none deny,
> So God be pleased this life will I
> For my pastance,
> Hunt, sing, and dance,
> My heart is set,
> All goodly sport
> To my comfort
> Who shall me let?
>
> Youth will needs have dalliance,
> Of good or ill some pastance;
> Company me thinketh best
> All thought and fancies to digest,
> For idleness
> Is chief mistress
> Of vices all;
> Then who can say
> But pass the day
> Is best of all?
>
> Company with honesty
> Is virtue—and vice to flee;
> Company is good or ill
> But every man hath his free will.
> The best I sue,
> The worst eschew;
> My mind shall be
> Virtue to use;
> Vice to refuse
> I shall use me.

It was my own statement, yet as I finished, wild applause greeted me. Evidently it touched the secret feelings of others as well—as any artist must. I was deeply moved.

Unfortunately I suspect you were the only one who was, although your captive audience listened attentively. You must have been so brave and pretty and unexpected, standing out there all alone. It was likely that which touched them, not your banal song.

Incidentally, Catherine, I feel I must apologize for Henry's nasty comments about your entire family. You know he did not always feel that way, and certainly his animosity never carried over to his children.

HENRY VIII:

On New Year's Day, 1510, everyone—from the Duke of Buckingham, the foremost noble in the land, to the lowliest kitchen scullion—assembled in the Great Hall for the formal presentation of gifts. Heretofore this had not been customary, but I meant it to become the highlight of court Christmas festivities. Thanks to Wolsey and his tireless work, the King had a personal gift for everyone: an embroidered handkerchief for the vain assistant to the Clerk of the Wardrobe; a small bottle of Spanish *oporto* for the cook, who loved it; a blessed rosary for the newest priest appointed to the Chapel Royal. For others closer to me, I had selected the gifts myself. To Wolsey, a lush wool carpet from the Turks, procured at great expense and effort (as I already knew how discriminating he was); to Katherine, a jewelled book of Scriptures (as I also knew how devout she was, yet it seemed, still, peripheral to me); to Warham and Fox and Ruthal, sumptuously adorned mass-missals. And then a little personal trick: to More, an astrolabe. He came forward to receive it, ceremoniously, then returned to his place. Etiquette forbade his opening it there. I triumphed at my imaginary picture of his unwrapping it at Chelsea.

Now it was turnabout, and everyone must present gifts to me. More came quickly and handed me a slim package: his *Utopia*.

"Just completed, Your Grace," he said, bending low. "I trust you will find it"—he doubtless longed to say "instructional," but dared not—"amusing." God knows what those words cost him, as he belittled his great work in accordance with court niceties.

From Wolsey, a painting, commissioned from the great Leonardo; from Memmo, a young lutenist from the local Venetian colony to play for us; from Ruthal—but I forget. It was so long ago.

People continued to come forward, bringing gifts until I was standing knee-deep in them. Just when it should have been finished, the doors opened and two Frenchmen appeared (one could identify them as such by the excesses in their costume, so much slashing that their topcoats were virtually nonexistent), carrying something the size of a large trunk by handles on either side.

Every eye in the Great Hall turned toward them as they descended the steps, slowly, carrying their burden solicitously. Their abnormally high heels clicked on the stones.

They came toward me slowly, making their way to within five feet of me. Then they laid their coffin-like weight down and pulled back the covering. It was a pie, the immense size of which no one present had ever seen.

"His Most Christian Majesty Louis, King of France, presents you with this meat pie as a New Year's gift. It is made from a gigantic boar which His Majesty himself took." They bowed.

I stood overlooking the vast pie, as large across as a desk. The pastry was intricate and teased into various shapes, baked a pleasing golden brown.

"A sword," I said, and one was placed in my hands. I slashed open the top of that pretty thing and was greeted with a foul odour: all was rotten within. The boar-meat was decomposing, the filling a green slime.

I backed away. " 'Tis foul," I said.

"As French manners," finished Wolsey, his voice loud in the hush.

We turned toward the grinning Frenchmen. "Give your master our thanks," I said. "But my taste does not run to rancid meat. I have a livelier appetite for *fresh* French things. Such as my title and inheritance. Convey this putrefying mass back to Louis, with our compliments."

They looked sickened, as well they might.

"Yes, it belongs on French soil," I said. "See that it returns to its true source."

I hated Louis. Such a calculated insult must have reply! Yet I would not, must not, upset Katherine. I must laugh at it, belittle the insult. For the time being.

XVII

That night was the appointed time for the "impromptu" invasion of the Queen's quarters by myself and my attendants. (Perhaps you are not aware of this today, but the Queen had her own set of chambers, quite apart from mine. This was, I am told, traditional only in England and had, through the centuries, facilitated adultery on both sides. I record the custom here simply because I foresee its passing into disuse soon. If only Anne Boleyn had not been apart from me . . . or Catherine Howard. . . .)

Twelve of us had costumes of Kendall green, all velvet, with silver visors. We were to invade Katherine's room, to burst in suddenly with a great fanfare of trumpets, to pretend to be Robin Hood and his men abducting the fair maidens. Then, after a mock struggle, we would dance by torchlight. It was arranged, of course, that eleven of Katherine's attendants should be present to make the numbers even.

It went according to plan. We waited outside the Queen's door, then, of one accord, flung open the door. The women shrieked. Katherine dropped a jewel-box, a carved ivory thing, and it broke on the floor. Her hands flew up to her mouth. She had been preparing for bed and was wearing a wine-colored dressing gown over her bedclothes. Her amber hair, combed out, gleamed in the torchlight. I thought her extraordinarily beautiful, in spite of her thickened figure.

"Ah!" I said. "The Queen yields herself to me." I held out my hands (with rings that surely Katherine recognized) and nodded toward the musicians. "Play a pavane, if you please." I took Katherine's hand, and we began to dance.

"I know it is you, my Lord," she whispered, as we came close in one measure.

"Do you?" I was enjoying the game. "Are you sure?"

"Yes," she said, as she passed me, her velvet cloak brushing mine. "I would know your hands, your touch, among ten thousand."

I smiled noncommittally. I had always been fascinated by legends of kings and princes who wandered about disguised—the Roman Emperors and Henry V, before he came to the throne. It could be dangerous (if only for what one overheard), yet I longed to do it.

Suddenly Katherine went pale and reeled against me. She clutched her belly. The music went on, insistently, but she stood rooted. Then she cried out and crumpled to the floor.

We all stood where we were. Only Wolsey (ever-present Wolsey, who had stepped in to oversee that the midnight repast was adequately prepared) knew what to do.

"A physician," he said quietly to a nearby page. He issued orders in a calm voice. "Take Her Grace to the lying-in chamber. It is not prepared? Then to her own bed." The erstwhile Merrie Men picked Katherine up and conveyed her to her own chamber. Attendants, physicians, servitors—they all converged on the Queen's chamber, bringing clean cloths and medicines and instruments, while Katherine cried out in the ancient pain of childbirth.

At dawn all was done: the child was born, a hideous, half-formed thing, three and a half months before its time. Dead. They carried it away in the early blue light and buried it—I know not where. It had no soul, and needed no churchly offices.

Alone in the blue-tinged light, I made my way to Katherine. She lay, white and sweat-stained, upon a couch, while her attendants changed the blood-soaked linen upon her bed. She grasped a crucifix and looked near dead, her mouth half open. I had a dreadful thought: how ugly women look in childbirth. This was not my Katherine, but a woman of fifty, a hard-faced stranger.

I knelt by her side, but she was deep asleep and did not stir. At length I rose and left the room. Although I had not slept, I did not feel tired, but quite the opposite: possessed by an abnormal alertness. I walked stiffly out into Katherine's audience chamber, where the torches from the dancing still burned. I put them out, then continued my restless walk toward my own apartments. It was an ugly dawn. Sleet was whipping against the windows. The passageways were cold.

Earlier I had welcomed this cold. I had wanted a cold Christmas, and so I had it. Anything I wanted, I had only to command, or so it had seemed.

Yet the thing that I had most wanted, that above all I cared to keep, was lost.

XVIII

⌘ WILL:

Yes, he had seemingly lost the magical power to command fate, which had been granted him, teasingly, for such a brief moment. He would spend the next twenty years trying to recapture it—years in which everything happened, and yet nothing happened. They were painful to him without touching him or changing him in essential ways. They left him confused and in that state somewhere between anger and hurt: they left him at the mercy of the Witch.

⌘ HENRY VIII:

Neither could I command happiness to return, and my sadness lingered for weeks afterward, well into the new year. Katherine and I brooded together over our loss, drawing ourselves tightly into a partnership of grief. We ordered extra Masses to be said and increased our personal pieties. I could talk to no one else about my feelings in the matter; it touched me too near my royal person. But Katherine, Katherine, royal herself, *she* understood. . . .

When at length her time of healing was past, I found that our very closeness and sympathy of mind made me approach her differently when we returned to the marriage bed. Why is it, I wondered then (and wonder still), that friendship seems to stifle lust, to smother it under a pillow of intimacy? For lust is not intimate; it thrives on strangeness and mystery, and needs it to survive. Katherine, my mysterious princess from Spain, now my friend in sorrow . . . nevertheless I knew her, as a man should know his wife, so it says in Scripture.

It was Wolsey whom I asked to say extra Masses for Katherine's and my private intentions. Wolsey had already proved himself my man in the Privy Council. It had been politic to appoint him, as he had immediately begun acting on his own initiative to counter some of the Fox-Warham-Ruthal schemes.

Wolsey was subtle; I appreciated that, as when he showed no curiosity upon my request for the extra Masses. Wolsey was discreet, and he was honest. I had acquired a valuable servant. Now I must learn to use him to the best advantage—for both of us.

He sent a steady stream of summaries and memoranda about the shifting politics abroad. He seemed to compile a new report every hour. I was so engrossed in reading a stack of them (as well as a summary of the palace inventories) that I did not hear Katherine enter my workroom one morning late in May. Of course her step was very light. She was standing behind me before I even felt her presence.

"What does my love study so intently?" she asked softly.

"All our property," I answered. "Were you aware, for example, that you—or rather *we*—possess"—I stabbed a finger at the paper and read the word it rested upon—"a dozen painted tiles from Spain?"

"No. But I should love to see them installed. I miss the tiles of home— so bright and clean. Not like the dark wood here."

"Where were they used?" I was curious.

"On the floors. In the walls. Every place where you have paintings and hangings, or wood. Reds and oranges and yellows, they were."

"I shall have them put in the floor of your Privy Chamber at Greenwich, then. With the date entered upon a new tile, to mark the end of the first year of our marriage—and of our reign." I had just been thinking of the date, and how soon it would be a year since the Coronation. "You have made me very happy, my Katherine."

Why, then, did I feel sad even as I said it? I wanted us to stay newly wed forever, never grow into just a husband and wife, yet the end of the first year of marriage was the end of being a bride; everyone knew that.

"Have I? But I, too, have something to give you." She took my face in both her tiny hands and said, "I am with child. Our prayers are answered."

I must have looked as I felt, for she kissed me then, long and sweetly— more like a bride, still, than a true wife.

Midsummer's Day, and my nineteenth birthday, and the end of my first year of marriage came all in June. I could look back on the past twelve months and wonder how I had done as well as I had, considering that I had known nothing of either ruling or marriage when I started. By the grace of God, and my own determination, I had succeeded in making the transition from Prince to King, and now the thing seemed to be running by itself. I would soon venture into the one area as yet untouched: the business of foreign wars and dealing directly with the rulers of Europe. War was the calling of kings, and the *sine qua non* of great kings.

During the extended summer—warm weather lasted even into November—I studied the situation on the Continent like a man watching the steps of a complicated dance and awaiting the proper beat in which to enter it.

It seemed that King Louis XII of France was besieging Pope Julius in Bologna, laying violent hands upon Christ's vicar, and calling a schismatic Council at Pisa to repudiate Julius's authority. Ferdinand of Spain and the Holy Roman Emperor Maximilian solemnly ordered him to desist, or face just punishment. They called their alliance the Holy League, and who could dispute its solemnity? Or that England, as a Christian realm, would be compelled by conscience to join it?

There was no obstacle of desire: *I* desired war, and my subjects would demand it of me. There was no obstacle of opportunity: as soon as the invitation to join was issued, then we would step in. There was no obstacle of means: the war could be easily financed out of the Royal Treasury, without having to bother with Parliament.

"But, Your Grace," Wolsey had said, seeming to know my plans even before I uttered them, "it might be best to call a Parliament, and save your own treasury. The people will grant you anything, in your newness. Later it will not be so easy."

"It would be stingy to do that," I objected. "It smacks of my father, and that I would never do."

"Your father was wise in financial matters. He would never have spent his own money when he could spend someone else's instead. A splendid maxim."

"An old man's maxim! Not a true knight's!" Somehow, to approach Parliament, cap in hand, asking for an allowance, for permission, like a child—no, never! "I hope never to call a Parliament as long as I live," I suddenly thought out loud. "Yes, to be so rich I never have to raise money through them—I want that!"

"Then you will have to find other means, Your Grace," said Wolsey. "For, as I pray God sends you long to reign over us, your treasury can scarcely last for sixty years! No, you must tap another source. Then good riddance to Parliament, I say."

※ ❧ ❧

My son Henry was born on New Year's Day, 1511. He was robust and hearty, his first wails not the piteous mewling a newborn usually makes, but loud and demanding. He entered the world like Hercules.

"Heavy, Your Grace," Dr. Linacre warned as he handed him into my waiting arms. "Very heavy. He must be made all of muscle."

Yes, the bundle was weighty, solid. I could feel the squirming power of the child.

"Praise be to God!" I cried, holding him aloft. "Now the future is assured!" I held my successor in my hands.

Striding in to see Katherine, who was already bathed and resting on fresh sheets, I could scarcely keep from shouting with joy. "Sweetheart," I cried, "you have given England all she wished of you!" There she was, her face radiant, her amber-colored hair falling all about her shoulders—a Madonna, a Madonna whom I adored. I fell to my knees beside her and kissed her hand. "Thank you," I said. "For the great gift you have bestowed on me, and on our country."

"On myself, too," she said.

Then I wanted to raise her up, to pull her from the bed, to dance around the room with her.

"He must be named Henry," she declared. "He is big and strong, like you."

I had not planned to name him Henry, but Edward, after my mother's little King-brother.

"Henry," she repeated stubbornly. "It must be Henry."

"If it means so much to you, then, so it shall be." So long as it was not Alfonso or Felipe or some such foreign-sounding name from Spain. "As soon as you are able, we will invite the realm to celebrate with us. There will be tournaments, feasts, wine from public fountains . . . and commoners can come, too. Into the palace ground," I said on sudden impulse. "He is their Prince, too!"

The Queen's physicians and attendants looked bewildered, and even Katherine shook her head.

"This is not Spain, my love! Here in England the King must go out amongst his people, and let them come to him," I insisted.

"You enjoy playing with them," she said, half-serious, half-smiling. Even then I wondered in which sense she meant "playing." But I did not pursue it.

"In six weeks' time," I promised her. "After the christening."

In six weeks' time Prince Henry had grown amazingly, and was unable to fit into the christening gown Katherine had diligently embroidered. It was meant for an average-sized child, not for this chubby giant. Hastily, extra panels were added to both sides and sleeves.

The baptism, performed by Archbishop Warham, was glittering and splendid. Katherine, giving her Spanish love of lavish celebration free rein, insisted on the excessive number of candles, the double-length cloth-of-gold cape I would wear, and the coloured bonfires afterwards. The infant Prince Henry, wearing his two-yards-long white gown, became a member of the Body of Christ before a hundred witnesses. He cried when the water was poured over his head—a good sign, as it meant the Devil was being chased out of him. A murmur of approval passed around the nave of the church. *That* for Old Scratch.

I watched the child with such deep excitement that it felt like calmness. My beautiful, beautiful son—no puny Arthur, but destined to be the tallest, strongest King that England had ever had. They said that Edward III was a giant, and my grandfather's height of six feet four was verified by men who yet lived. But Henry IX would be a Sun-God, a Helios for England.

Trumpets sounded their silver notes, and the procession made its long, slow way down the nave and out of the church, like a jewelled and languid snake. Outside, in the courtyard, it coiled round itself and waited—waited to pass into the Great Hall of Westminster Palace, where the christening feast was spread.

Did I imply earlier that Westminster was an outmoded palace? So it is, but its Great Hall is a treasure I must be careful not to let Time loot from me. Its dimensions are enormous, so that mounted knights can joust inside, should they so desire. Most arresting of all, the roof is a single span: the ceiling soars overhead in a graceful dance of supporting hammerbeams, scorning any supporting pillars. It was put up in 1395, just in time for the wedding feast of Richard II and Isabella of France. It was the king of its kind; none has surpassed it in size even to this day. Now this marvel welcomed us, with places set for a hundred. Upon the fair white linen the rows of golden platters looked like bright coins in a field of snow.

The dais would include not only the Queen and myself, but my blood relatives. Even those not at court had come to attend the christening of their royal cousin.

There are *those*—and I know who they are—who have claimed that I "killed off" anyone with any touch of royal blood, because I was so fearful of rival claimants to the throne. I can expose this nonsense for what it is by the very list of those I invited to sit at the royal table with me on this occasion. There was Henry Courtenay, my first cousin, the son of Catherine Plantagenet, my aunt on my mother's side. There was Margaret Plantagenet Pole, a cousin of my mother's, and her sons Reginald, Henry, and Geoffrey, my second cousins. There were my St. Leger second cousins, and the Stafford cousins and Henry Bourchier, Earl of Essex, more distant yet. I was happy and wanted to share my joy with all my family, like any normal man.

The prelates had a table of their own, the one farthest to the right. The Archbishop of Canterbury sat at its head, with the other ranking bishops, like Ruthal of Durham and Fox of Winchester, next to him. The rest of the length of table comprised almost the entire membership of Convocation, the "Parliament" of the Church. Wolsey was not at the table. His rank was too low, for at this time he was only an almoner and a lowly canon of Windsor.

The long middle table held the peers of the realm and their ladies. There was only one duke in England left now (except the imprisoned Duke of Suffolk): the Duke of Buckingham, Edward Stafford. There had been other dukes, of course, but they had lost their titles, or their lives, or both, fighting for or against Richard III. Thomas Howard, Duke of Norfolk, had fought my father at the battle of Bosworth Field, and lost. He was then demoted to an earl. His partisans put out a tale that after the battle he went to my father and said, "Richard was King, and as such I fought for him. If Parliament would make a post King I would fight for it, too, as would be my duty." This is absurd, for Parliament does not make kings. And besides that, it is insulting to compare a king to a deaf-and-dumb post, and Howard was more clever than that. Now I was keeping him in the kennel of earldom, until such time as he earned back his title by some noble deed.

Even the number of earls and, below that, marquises, were slim. The wars had thinned their ranks as well. At my Coronation a number of Knights of the Bath had been created, and these knights were now seated at the peer-table. But I considered knighthood to be properly earned only by valour and prowess on the battlefield, and until such time, there would be no new knights.

The third table, on the left side, held those dear to Katherine or myself, for any number of reasons of the heart. There was the Lady Willoughby, who was actually Maria de Salinas, Katherine's faithful girlhood friend from Spain, now married to an old soldier; Lord Mountjoy, Katherine's household chamberlain, and Edward Baynton, her Lord Steward. Also at that table were my friends of the tournament Charles Brandon, Edward Neville, and Nicholas Carew, as well as Thomas More and Wolsey. A curious mixture, and yet they got on well enough, or so it seemed from where I sat.

Katherine was on my right hand and my sister Mary on my left. Whichever way I turned I saw a lovely face, each so different. Katherine's plump and honey-toned, with laughing hazel eyes; Mary's, long and slender, with ivory skin and eyes the color of a cold April sky.

"Ah, sweetheart!" I grasped Katherine's hand and felt excitement there. The six weeks had passed, the ceremony was over. . . . "Thank you. Thank you for this wonderful gift you have given me. A son."

She returned the pressure of my hand. "Not I," she laughed. She had a pretty little laugh in those days—like Spanish bells, I often thought, but never told her so; now I wonder why I never did. "It was God who gave him to both of us."

"No. You. *You.*" I slid my fingers under her belt, out of sight under the linen table-covering, knowing how ticklish she was, wanting to hear her sweet little laugh again. "*You* gave him to me."

She laughed, and I withdrew my fingers. "As you say," she agreed.

I turned to Mary. "I hope you meant it when you promised, as godmother, to 'renounce the Devil and all his works, and the vain pomp and glory of this world.' Did you?" Now I would tease her as well, my favourite sibling. Mary was fourteen, and already past childhood. She saw herself as a princess from old chronicles, to be wooed and won by a Sir Galahad. In truth, she was fair enough. But how can a princess promise to reject "the vain pomp and glory of this world"? It is what princesses are born to.

"They do not necessarily go together," she answered. "I meant the part about the pomp and glory."

I was startled. "I would have thought that was the part you'd stumble over!"

"No. It's the Devil who attracts me, I fear. There is something desirous in me of . . . not evil, exactly, but . . . some of the temptations of the Evil One." She was blushing; oh, yes! It was the Devil's call to her blood that she meant. A yearning our chaste mother had never known—the opposite pole from the Blessed Virgin and her marriage bed with the saintly Joseph. . . .

"We must marry you soon," I said, nodding.

"No! *I* must choose him, it cannot be just anyone, or I shall be the worse—"

"I shall choose wisely," I promised her.

"But I—" Her voice was rising in distress.

"Now, now." I patted her hand as I rose to welcome the company and call upon the Archbishop to bless the feast.

We dined, as the phrase goes, royally. I shall not bore you with a recitation of the courses. Afterward there was to be dancing; and following that, I had invited the common people to come into the Great Hall and see the masquing. Katherine had disliked the thought of allowing the people into the palace grounds, and had tried to dissuade me.

"It is not their place to enter into the private grounds of kings," she protested.

"Nonsense," I had said. "That is a Spanish notion." I had not forgotten that quaint attempt, long ago, to keep Father from seeing Katherine. "Your father and mother may have driven the Moors out of Spain, but Spain remains in the grip of the East, in her veilings between this and that: common people here, virgins there, and so on."

"There must be veilings," she insisted. "And boundaries."

"Aye. But familiarity does not break down boundaries. So long as the essential boundary is not crossed, all others can come down."

Katherine and I would lead the dancing and then seek other partners, until the entire company had joined in the dance. I was proud to lead her out, proud for her to be beheld as my wife and the mother of my child . . . Jesu, how strange it is to write those words! For we became enemies . . . but then, how I loved her!

We danced; broke apart, found other partners. I took my sister Mary. She was a superlative dancer. But as soon as I took her hand, she tried to continue our conversation: the one about her husband.

"To marry without love would kill me," she said.

"You will learn to love him, whoever he is. For he will be royal, and the sacrament of marriage gives grace to love."

Now the music was rising. I hoped to end this conversation.

"You are no priest, however much you strive to sound like one," she scoffed. "Your words are not convincing. Could God have given you grace to love Katherine if she were old and barren?"

A thumping drumbeat failed to drown out her words.

"If it had been His will that I do so," I answered.

She laughed, a short, derisive cough. The music changed, and so did our partners. She chose Charles Brandon; I chose Maria de Salinas.

How gracefully the Spanish danced! Maria was tall and slender, unlike my tiny Katherine, but supple as a blade of the renowned Toledo steel.

"With your English name, one would never suspect the señorita beneath. Until one danced with her," I said.

"We love dancing," she admitted. Her accent had almost disappeared, unlike Katherine's; it lingered only in a certain cadence to her sentences.

"Are you happy here?" I suddenly said. "Are you at home here? Do you ever wish you had gone back, like the others?"

"No. Only I get a longing sometimes, as everyone does, for what I left behind, and remember only in a flawed way. The brokenness of my memories . . . I would like to repair them, someday."

An impossible sea-journey. An impossible wish. "In the meantime you are the Lady Willoughby, and an ornament to your husband," I said pompously. I sensed even then how pompous I sounded.

A change in tempo: time to break, again. This time I chose a young maiden, blond and soft. She did *not* dance well.

"Are you new to court?" I asked. There were many come for the festivities, cousins and relatives of those already in residence.

"Yes, Your Grace. I have come at the invitation of my uncle, Lord Mountjoy." She nodded toward the man Katherine was now dancing with. He was the chamberlain of her household.

"Ah, yes. A Yorkshire man," I said.

"Lincolnshire, Your Grace." She stumbled against me. Her body felt tender.

"You do not dance in Lincolnshire?"

My teasing fell flat. She tried to pull away, thinking I scolded her. I pulled her back. "I will teach you," I said. "Here at court we all dance. You will need to learn, if you stay, Mistress—what is your name?"

"Bessie Blount," she mumbled. Still she tried to pull away, and then stumbled over her feet again. In embarrassment, she stopped dancing entirely. I held her and danced the steps for her, the way a child does its doll. She was as limp and unmoving as any doll. "I shall not stay," she whispered.

"Nonsense," I said. "Do not spend your beauty in Yorkshire. We need you here."

"Lincolnshire, Your Grace."

The beat changed; the drum thumped. She quickly slid away, and not to another partner, but to shadows.

When all the company (excepting only the old and infirm) were at last part of the dance, we went on to other steps and other rhythms. The French ambassador was easily persuaded to demonstrate "la Volta," which he had learned in Louis XII's court only last summer. Everyone danced there, except Louis himself, who was too aged and fragile to bend his knees.

Whilst the company was engrossed in the dances, I slipped away to oversee the preparations for the masquing to follow. As I moved along the high walkway connecting the Great Hall with the antechamber, I could see the huge crowd gathered outside, waiting to be let in, as they had been promised. Beyond them, on the hills surrounding the city, the bonfires blazed yellow, red, pink, ordering the skies themselves to rejoice with us.

"Your Grace."

I turned quickly to see Don Luis Caroz, the Spanish ambassador.

"A word with you, *por favor.*"

"Indeed." I smiled, giving permission for him to proceed.

"I have not had the opportunity to wish you, in person, my congratulations. It is a great day for Spain, as well."

"The daughters of Spain are fair," I said, "and bring Ferdinand fine grandsons." Katherine's older sister Juana had a ten-year-old son, Charles, who was said to be clever, and was likely to become Holy Roman Emperor someday. That is, if he had not inherited his mother's madness: Juana was known far and wide as *"Juana la loca."*

"Sí, sí." Now he could proceed to his true business in seeking me out. "Your Grace, have you settled, finally, on the number of archers you will commit to King Ferdinand in Guienne and also in North Africa against the Moors? He is anxious to know, as he wishes his dear son-in-law to share in all his glorious conquests."

"Ummm. Yes. I believe I had promised"—a glance out the window, at the dancing bonfires, the happy crowd—"fifteen hundred archers. With long-bow, of course." There was no limit; I could do anything now, and I would. Something sang within me, something that had never been there before. "But I think three thousand would be more helpful. With"—go on, do it, you want to—"new cannon as well. We can test them in the field."

"Oh! Your Grace!"

Had I not promised Father on his deathbed to fight the Infidel? Could I do less, now that God had so clearly shown his favour to me? "It is my privilege to fight the enemies of Christ," I assured him.

Outside the crowd moved, like scales of a snake. Snake. I must see to the masque. I nodded to Caroz and indicated that the exchange was over. Still he stood staring at me, his eyes wide and almost fixed. "Your Grace . . ." he said, "your cloak . . . it is magnificent. It blinds me!"

It was a full-circled cape of cloth-of-gold, weighing almost ten pounds. I pictured with amusement the little Spaniard decked with it. Common men think only of the glow of gold, never of its weight. "It is yours," I said, unfastening it, and draping it over his shoulders. He almost buckled, with both the weight and astonishment. O, his face!

Before he could utter a word, I was past him and opening the door to the antechamber, which served as a rehearsal room in which the players were already costumed and speaking.

"Continue, continue!" I ordered them. I could hardly wait to see this idea of mine enacted: the story of the baby Hercules strangling the serpents sent by jealous Juno to destroy him in his crib. I had needed a large child to play the part of the mighty infant; Sir John Seymour's six-year-old son Edward was now wearing an infant's robe and practising throttling the "snakes"—long tubes of multicoloured velvet that had young ferrets inside, so they would move and writhe on their own.

"I hate the infant!" "Juno" proclaimed, pointing toward the crib. "Jupiter has sinned, and this child is the product of this sin. He must die!"

Of course the infant prevailed over the serpents, and the happy conclusion was announced by "Britannia": "Thus perish all the enemies of the King's babe, who seek to harm him. Jealousy, envy, spite cannot stand against the will of the gods, and their protection gives our prince supernatural strength." The company then gathered round the crib, raised their arms, and began an elaborate set-dance. I, as Jupiter, would appear in their midst, bringing the masque to a happy conclusion.

Then we would all come forward, leaving the stage, and present ourselves to Katherine. For it was she I was honouring; she, as the goddess who had brought forth an heir. And if they said it was unseemly for a king to "present himself" to anyone, no matter who . . . well, I would do as I pleased.

The order had been given, and the commoners admitted to the Hall. I could hear them now, the noise resounding, building to a roar.

"Let us begin!" I cried, and the wheeled stage was pushed out into the Hall.

The masque was superlative! Everyone gasped at the costumes, and particularly at the serpents. In the gleam of the leaping torchlight they appeared real: evil, jewel-like creatures, fitting instruments of a jealous goddess. When it was done, and we stood before that vast company, I felt myself overcome. Words I had not known were within me came rushing out.

"Tomorrow I will ride against any knight in the realm," I cried. "Here at Westminster, in the tiltyard, I challenge you. Come and meet your King!" A shore of pebbles before me, each pebble a person. A pretty beach. "All of you here . . . I invite you, as no King has ever invited his subjects: come, help yourself to the gold of my person."

I spread my arms wide, offering myself: *needing* to offer myself. They surged forward, all the people. I was enveloped in their warm bodies, breath, strength—for in numbers they were far stronger than any beast. They stripped, first, the gold letters of my costume—the *H*'s and *K*'s I had attached to my surcoat. Each was made of pure gold bullion. Then the surcoat itself. Then, handling me, they pulled at my very garments. The handling was fearsome, yet oddly arousing and exciting. Like being caressed by a hundred hands—or being crawled upon by a swarm of insects.

They plucked me clean, in unceremonious, unruly parody of the ritual observed every evening in my bedchamber by my gentlemen servers. I was left with only my hose and linen undershirt, both almost transparent. I was naked for all to see. My body was displayed before the kingdom. For an instant I stood there, King and sacrifice. Then they attacked the others, Neville and Carew and Thomas Knyvett, stripping them likewise.

Suddenly it turned ugly. The people were a beast, a beast with fangs, and they turned on the rest of the players, stripping them, and denuded Henry Courtenay, my pretty little cousin. That was enough. I gave orders. The armed yeomen of the guards pushed them back, out of the Hall and back into the common night. It was over for them.

Katherine was rigid with anger by the time I reached her side. "You have turned this celebration into a mockery," she said. "You have dishonoured our son. I am ashamed to have you for a husband."

I laughed. I knew that in spite of her proper words she desired and cherished me. My boldness appealed to something deep and hidden in her Spanish nature. "Then I shall dress myself," I said. "And keep my body veiled forever after."

In the privacy of the wardrobe room, I drew on fresh garments. They had actually stripped me to my very underhose! I chuckled as I pictured them the next morning, wondering what they would do with one patch of the King's vest, or of his sleeve.

⸎ WILL:

It was hard to say which excited the imagination of my fellow villagers more: the idea of enriching oneself by the gold, or of seeing a King and his Privy Chamberers stripped in public.

"He let them *touch* him!" my mother said incredulously. "And he didn't mind—nay, he *invited* it!"

"It was only his wife who made him put them away," put in my father. This discussion took place at the supper table, while they were ladling out a pungent rabbit stew—pungent because the rabbit was past usual consumption time. My father stuck a large piece in his mouth. "Harry would have had himself naked," he said, his words slurred because of his chewing.

My mother tore off a piece of bread from a stale loaf and soaked it in the rabbit juice. "We could have had a gold letter," she said wistfully. "Then our lives would have changed."

"Only for a year," replied Father. "And then what? Back to foul rabbit stew?" He made a face as he chewed up a semi-rancid piece.

Neither of them questioned the fact that the King lived in such wealth that the loss of the gold letters meant nothing to him. On the contrary, they were proud of having such a wealthy King. They did not connect their poor eating with the elaborate court masques designed by the revels-master.

As well they should not, in spite of the current idea held by some that dividing up the Royal Treasury would enable everyone to dine on dainties for the rest of their lives. A mathematician friend of mine has calculated that if the Queen's wealth were distributed equally throughout the kingdom, each person would receive exactly enough to purchase five loaves of bread, shoe one horse, and purchase one blanket. Hardly a luxurious life.

But I digress. I speak now as a man, whereas I was then but a child, and as awed by the story of the King's gold letters as anyone else. I lay in bed that night, imagining myself to be the young Prince. What would my life be like? I would lie beneath soft coverlets (I thought this as I scratched myself against the irritating rough wool), never have to do schoolwork, and have horses and hawks—in short, all the things an ignorant ten-year-old imagines when constructing the perfect life of another child.

Over the next week I thought of the young Prince Henry constantly. When I awakened I immediately thought, "Now *his* nurse is taking him up and dressing him in fine linen." When I went out to play I thought, "They are readying rooms of toys for *him.*"

In truth, I was not far wrong. Upon birth, the infant Prince had been assigned his own household staff. He had his clerk of the signet, his serjeant of arms, and three chaplains, as well as a carver, a cellarman, and a baker—for his entertaining. He even had a special room set aside at Westminster for his future Council Chamber.

I was playing near my house in the muddy main street when my fantasy world was shattered.

"The Prince is dead," Rob said, wiping his nose in the raw weather. Rob was an outsized boy who lived three houses away from me. I remember that the tip of his nose was bright red and his cheeks blotched.

"What?" I said, forgetting to kick the leather-covered ball.

"I said he's dead. The new Prince." Rob quickly took advantage of my pause to capture the ball for himself.

"What?" I broke up the game by trailing after him, demanding, "What?" over and over.

"I said he's *dead.* What's the matter? Are you deaf?" Rob planted his stocky legs in the mud and glared at me. I noticed that his hands had chilblains. There was red oozing between the cracks of his fingerjoints as well.

"Why?"

"Why?" He dismissed my question with the contempt it deserved. " 'Cause God wanted it that way. Stupid!" He pitched the ball at my stomach and knocked the breath out of me.

It was a fine answer—the very one that haunted the King himself, I was to learn years later.

The King gave his son a funeral that stinted nothing. The hearse alone was bedecked with a thousand pounds of candles. Prince Henry, aged fifty-two days, was laid to rest in Westminster Abbey—where the shouts from the nearby celebratory tournaments had rung against the stones only nine days earlier.

Curiously, Henry records the death in an almost Roman, stoic fashion, as if he confused the mood of the masque with the real event. It was most uncharacteristic of him, who was usually so vocal in his outrage.

XIX

⚜ Henry VIII:

But the next morning I had no thoughts for the people or what they would do with the pieces of my clothes, nor did I care. The next morning I had to make funeral arrangements; for Prince Henry had died in his crib even while the play was being enacted. My Hercules had not been able to overcome the serpents (sent by whom?—for we do not believe in Juno) that sought to take his breath.

If he had lived, he would be thirty-five today.

It was here the split began between Katherine and myself. Her grieving took the form of submission, of prostrating herself before the will of God, of devoting herself to His demands, in the form of prayer life and observances. She joined the Third Order of St. Francis, a branch of that discipline for those still in "the world." But it enjoined the wearing of a coarse habit beneath one's regular clothes, as well as rigorous fasting and long hours of prayer. Although its adherents remained physically in "the world," in spirit they began to dwell elsewhere.

I, on the other hand, turned outward. I looked into that inward-turning funnel of spiritual exercises that Katherine had flung herself into, and it frightened and repelled me. It was actions I understood—clean, precise, compelling actions—and it was here I must lose myself . . . or find myself and, in so doing, restore myself to God's favour. I had not been perfect enough in my deeds; I had not gone to war in person against Christ's (and England's) enemies.

Wolsey aided me, here when I most needed him. Despite his office as a priest, it was actions that he, too, understood best: the world of men, not of the spirit. And what was the world of men that was spread out before us, like a box of sweetmeats with its top flipped open?

The Holy League—the Pope's alliance against the French—waited to welcome England into it. His Holiness had drawn up a document recognizing me as rightful King of France, once I had vanquished Paris. Maximilian, the Holy Roman Emperor, stood ready to serve in the field beside me.

I would take my place on the Continental stage, to pursue England's lost dream of conquering France in its entirety. Perhaps that was what God truly required of me; perhaps it was here that I had failed Him. As King, there were certain tasks I must undertake, as surely as a knight at Arthur's Round Table was given them, and to shirk them meant shame and cowardice. England had come close to conquering France, had once held huge chunks of French territory. Henry VI had even been crowned King of France in Paris. But that was nearly a hundred years ago, in 1431. Since then the French had rallied, had pushed us back little by little, while we Englishmen fought ourselves on our own land, until nothing remained of our holdings in France but little Calais and a pitifully small area surrounding it—some nine miles deep and twelve miles wide.

Perhaps, when I conquered France, God would turn His face toward me. I became more and more convinced of it.

My advisors and Council, by and large, were not convinced. Of my desire to redeem myself with God they were unaware; but they were against war with France. Father had spoiled them with his lack of involvement in foreign entanglements, and like any privileged state, they had got used to it. After all, it was Father's leftover councillors who had renewed the peace treaty with France, behind my back. These churchmen—Ruthal, Fox, and Warham—a pacifist trio, continued to thwart me and preach endlessly of the uselessness, the expense, the evil of war. The nobles on the Council—Howard, Earl of Surrey, and de Vere, Earl of Oxford and Lord High Admiral, whose *raison d'être* was making war—were in favour of it. But the Church was not, and even the intellectuals (so carefully imported and cultivated to give a humanist polish to my court!) were not. Erasmus, Vives, Colet—they blathered and wrote such nonsense as "anyone who went to war because of ambition or hatred, he fought under the banner of the Devil."

Disgruntled, at one point I asked Wolsey to ascertain the exact cost of provisioning and equipping a force of thirty thousand men, so I would have true figures with which to argue. I made no muster rolls or correspondence available to Wolsey. By now I knew he was so industrious and resourceful he did not need any direction from me other than a vaguely worded request.

However, as days passed without my seeing him, and as need arose to consult with him about a rumour that the fierce Pope Julius lay deathly ill, I made inquiries as to his whereabouts. At that time he lived in a small suite of rooms in the palace, adjoining the Chapel Royal, with only one manservant and one secretary. I did the unusual thing of going to his quarters myself. But Jonathan, his manservant, told me that his master was "moved to an inn in Kent, thereby to keep counsel with himself for a time." I glanced into the plain, sparsely furnished room. All the table surfaces were bare; he had taken all his papers with him.

"And where is that?"

"At Master Lark's, Your Grace. He has an inn called the . . ." The fellow twisted his face in remembering. ". . . Lark's Morning. Near Chilham."

Lark. Lark. Where had I heard that name? The Lark's Morning. Good name for an inn. I would find it. By God, it would make a fine morning's ride, and I was ready for one. Should I ask Katherine? A gallop together, in the damp March air—but no, this was her prayer-time. Nonetheless, I could ask. Perhaps she would . . . ? No. She would not.

Thus we use our supposed "knowledge" of others to speak on their behalf, and condemn them for the words we ourselves put in their silent mouths.

Having asked Katherine in my mind, and been refused, I was free to go alone.

I enjoyed the ride, galloping over the bare, frost-hardened fields and dull brown earth. March is an ugly month, uglier even than November, its lifeless counterpart. I was glad to reach the Lark's Morning (easy to find, on the main road to Dover), warm myself inside at the fire, and put some heated ale in my belly.

The innkeeper's daughter (she was too young and pretty to be his wife) seemed unusually flustered when she recognized me. I was accustomed, now, to the stir I caused by my presence (odd how easy it is to become used to being taken for a god), but she seemed more frightened than awed. This puzzled me. I made sure I spoke to her gently, to ease her fears.

"I seek Thomas Wolsey, one of my almoners. Tell me, is he hereabout?"

She smiled; or rather, her mouth twitched.

"Father Wolsey," I said. "A priest."

"Aye. He's—he took quarters in the adjoining farmstead."

Farmstead? What possessed him? "My thanks."

The ramshackle building lay some fifty yards behind the inn, hidden by a hedgerow. That was fortunate, as it was such an eyesore it would have kept customers away from the inn.

Outside, two little boys were playing. As always, when I saw male children, pain and (yes, admit it) anger rushed through me. I turned away, making my eyes leave them.

I pushed open the loose, flapping door. Instantly I recognized the characteristic heavy odour of metal. A black-robed figure was moving about inside, stirring up the concentrated smell that was the very essence of war.

"Wolsey!"

He almost jumped—the only time I have ever seen him truly taken by surprise.

"Your Grace!" So abruptly did he turn, the folds of his gown swirled like foam.

"What are you doing here?" My voice was sharper than I had intended. Letting the door swing all the way inward, I saw piles and piles of shields, helmets, lances, mail shirts, swords, and handguns on the dirt floor.

"Testing equipment, Your Grace. I have here a sample of each type available to us, along with its cost and delivery time"—he grabbed a sheaf of papers and began thumbing through them—"speed of manufacture, and accessibility. Before we can place orders, first-hand knowledge of the quality is required. For example, the foundry at Nuremberg . . . its shields seem decidedly flimsy to me, Your Grace." He plucked an oval-shaped one from the pile. "Press here. You see? It indents too easily. However, one must take into account the speed of delivery, as opposed to Milan, from which shipments could take a year to reach us." The facts came spurting out; his voice vibrated with excitement.

"How have you . . . obtained all this?" I had given him his assignment on Tuesday; it was just now only Friday.

"Your Grace! I consider it my privilege to carry out any task with thoroughness and speed."

Thoroughness and speed scarcely described his actions here. Monomania came closer.

"Yes. I see. Well, do you have the figures?"

"Of course."

Of course. I cocked one eyebrow.

"The basic cost in arms, including cannon, would be twenty-five thousand pounds. Then there is the cost of rigging and preparing Your Grace's seven warships. And, you had mentioned commissioning a 'great' ship as well?"

"Aye. The largest vessel since ancient Rome." I had designed her in my mind—a thousand-ton warrior. "I left my plans with the master shipwright at Portsmouth—"

"I have them here." He pointed to a leather portfolio resting on his rickety table. I felt not gratified, but peeved.

"It would take two years to build," he said. "Now, as to the provisioning—the carts, the tents, the food, the horses—oh, that's the headache. Impossible to say. Take ten thousand pounds, and double that. But, oh! I have found something extraordinary! I know how Your Grace loves artillery, particularly cannon . . . am I correct?"

"Yes." My response was guarded.

"*Regardez!*" He pulled out a sheet with sketches of giant cannon—bombards, the type used to break down city walls. "There is a foundry in the Netherlands ready to cast a set of twelve in bronze—beautiful creatures, each named after a different Apostle! Here is Saint John the Evangelist!" He thrust the sketch into my hand.

"And the cost?" I kept my voice calm, although inside I was now ignited with war-desire. Its implements and adornings aroused me like a woman.

"One thousand three hundred forty-four pounds, ten shillings per gun, with an added twelve pounds per gun carriage."

"That is a total of . . ."

"Sixteen thousand two hundred seventy-eight pounds."

Outrageous. More than all the other regular cannon combined. But I must have them, no question of it. I lusted after them.

"How long a delivery time?"

"They are ready to cast them," he said triumphantly. "They can be delivered to Calais by June."

"Well done, Wolsey, well done. But the *total* cost, all these considerations together?"

"Sixty-one thousand two hundred seventy-eight pounds."

More than ten times the total government expenditure of last year! I was stunned.

Reading my face, he said apologetically, "We shall have to ask Parliament."

"No! I shall not! I shall not go a-begging from my own subjects, like a boy! I shall pay for it all from the Treasury!"

He allowed an actual emotion to cross his usually inscrutable face. It was exasperation. "Your Grace, Parliament would readily grant you funds for the war. Why not use the people's money rather than your own?"

"Then it will not be *my* war. I wish to be both its patron and its hero!" There, I had said it, my deepest desire—and surprised even myself.

He spread his hands as if to say, *There you have it. Well, then, there's no remedy.* "As you wish." How beautifully he gave in.

"Forgive me if I tread on painful ground," he said. "But Dean Colet preached a pacifist sermon again, last Sunday at Greenwich."

"I have . . . convinced him." I almost said "silenced."

"A relief for us all." He smiled.

"Pope Julius lies ill. What think you? Is he like to die? And if so, what does this do to our war?"

"My sources say he is not seriously ill, merely diplomatically ill. He will recover. He means to push France out of Italy. Louis's latest victories there—they come too close to home. No, the Holy League will stand."

"England, Spain, the Holy Roman Empire, Venice, the Pope—*everyone* against France!" I said ecstatically.

"And England the only oak," he said. "The only oak in a sea of reeds."

I was startled that Wolsey should speak so derogatorily about my allies. This man who collected and tested all equipment must surely have a reason. "Pray explain yourself."

He made a show of demurring. Then he spoke. "Ferdinand, the Spanish King—how reliable is he? He lured England into that sham of an expedition against the Infidels, which came to nothing."

True. My archers had sat and rotted in Guienne, while Ferdinand decided to attack Navarre instead.

"It is Queen Katherine who inclines you toward her father. But is a son-in-law's duty compatible with a King's?" The words hung on the air between us. "And Maximilian, the Emperor—he is known as a liar. He prides himself on his lies. Why, when Louis accused him of deceiving him twice, he cackled, 'He lies. I deceived him three times!' As for Venice, she has no army. Now, what a rabble—with you as the only true knight!"

"But when an honest knight pursues the course of truth, what matter if his allies are false? God will direct him!" I believed that; truth to tell, I believe it still.

"It is our duty to use our resources wisely against Satan," he agreed. "But this alliance . . . how can you conquer, without unfeigned assistance? A false ally is worse than an enemy."

But I still believed in my allies. Nor did I realize that Wolsey inclined so toward the French. The French were civilised, masters of style, as was Wolsey, the butcher's son. We are surprises to our parents.

I changed the subject. "There is danger from the Scots. They obey no laws of honour or chivalry. They are like to attack whilst we are occupied in France."

"They *are* French allies. The 'auld alliance,' they call it. Although two more unlikely partners I am hard put to imagine!" The brawling Scots with the mincing French. Laughable. "Leave an able soldier behind to contain them."

"Howard," I said. "Thomas Howard, Earl of Surrey. He is from the North, he knows it well."

Just then, two dancing shadows came into the building.

"Father! Father!" they called.

How sweet. The little lads had an affectionate relationship with the visiting priest.

"Mother does not feel well," they whined.

"I am busy." Wolsey's voice was hard.

"She was sick last week, and you not here with us!"

Wolsey was their father. This priest had sons!

"I understand," I said. "I know now what you do at the Lark's Morning! I shall speak with you later." I was shaking with rage, betrayal. "In London."

"No, Your Grace! I dare not leave you!" His face registered alarm. "It is true, I have sinned with the fair daughter of Lark! I loved her—but look you, I shall not keep her! If I have your love, I need no other! Pray, give me that love, and I'll not look elsewhere! Never, never!"

"Abandon her, Wolsey," I said. "Or never look again for any favour at my hands."

I pushed the Wolsey family aside, the warm, clambering boys.

"I abandon her!" he cried. "I will nevermore see her face! Grant me only your love, that is all I desire, all I need—" He almost clutched at my garments.

"See that you do." The pretty Joan Lark was standing in the inn's doorway, sorrow and fear written on her features. Now I understood her agitation at seeing me. All was clear. I hated her, hated Wolsey, hated their sturdy sons.

"They are bastards!" I called, pointing at them. "Worse than bastards, they are the offspring of a priest who has betrayed his vows. The most vile of all things!"

A priest who had betrayed his vows: cursed before God and man. Wolsey himself was a frail reed. "I leave you to God!" I cried. "He alone knows what to do with you!"

All the way back to London, over the same (but how different!) dull, dead fields, I had but one refrain in my head: Wolsey had loved. Wolsey had a passion. Wolsey had sons. That miserable priest! God had given a sinning priest healthy sons and shoved them under my nose! Why was He so cruel? Why would He torment me so?

XX

France. I stood in France, my great army around me. We were besieging Tournai, a fair jewel of a walled city not far from Calais.

Yes, I stood there, and by my own will. Certainly there had been delays, obstacles that would have turned back anyone less determined. But I had overcome them: overcome the problems of raising, equipping, and transporting forty thousand men, the largest English army ever to land in Europe; overcome the reluctance of those who preached "caution" and warned me, "Do not hazard yourself, England cannot lose its King, especially as there is no . . ."

No heir. I had overcome my fears in leaving Katherine, once again pregnant (praise to God!), to act as Queen-Regent in my absence, even though the Scots were gathering at our back.

I had also overcome my innate reluctance to execute the traitor Edmund de la Pole; it was not safe to leave him behind in England, where conspirators stood ready to free him and to proclaim him King. So he perished on the scaffold before we set sail.

WILL:

I notice Henry does not linger on this fact, but records it briskly, as a matter of small note. At the time the people referred to it as "spring cleaning at the Tower."

HENRY VIII:

I had even overcome the timidity and lack of firm plans from my "committed allies." Ferdinand had yet to meet me, and Maximilian had only just shown up, without troops, offering to serve as a soldier under my command whilst we besieged Tournai.

The Holy Roman Emperor was an odd little man, with reddish gold hair and a chin sticking out like a shelf. He appeared so affable that one never questioned his thoughts or his motives. Yet this man controlled the Netherlands, Germany, Austria, and bits and pieces scattered about Italy and France! Now he trotted about in my wake as I inspected cannon and their positions, helped load and fire the bombards (our sulphur from Italy was certainly superior, thanks to the Pope, and gave a nice explosion), and at night he dined with me in my collapsible timber house (which boasted all the amenities of my Privy Chamber at home, including my great bed.) He also relieved himself in my private stool-closet, discreetly attached to the house. After dinner, candles flickering on our massive formal dining table, we spread out maps and discussed strategy.

"Tournai will look pretty, razed to the ground like Thérouanne," chuckled Maximilian. I had besieged Thérouanne for twenty-three days, and when at last it had surrendered, I ordered everyone out and destroyed it.

"I will never raze it," I said. "I plan to incorporate it into the Pale of Calais, make it English. Why"—I thought of this on the spot—"we'll send representatives to Parliament!"

"Your Grace!" laughed Wolsey. "That would mean you would have to garrison them. They'd never go to Parliament otherwise—they're French!"

"Well, *parliament* is a French word," said Brandon, attempting to be jolly. "It means 'let's talk.' And that's all Parliament does—talk, talk, talk!"

"Aye, aye!" The rest of the company laughed, just to be a part of the merriment.

"Thomas More speaks of a silent Parliament," Wolsey said. "He plans to lead one."

"More speaks of many things, most of them preposterous," chimed in Edward Neville. *Sir* Edward Neville: I had knighted him just four hours past for his bravery on the field.

There had been much bravery on this campaign. I was astonished at how very brave an ordinary man can be when confronted with the enemy. The first night we marched, it was pouring rain, and we were bogged down in a sea of mud. I rode round the camp at three in the morning, in my armour, to hearten and encourage my men. "Well, comrades, now that we have suffered in the beginning, fortune promises us better things, God willing."

Suddenly there was a knock at my door. A Scots herald stood outside, come to declare war on England! He concluded, "My King summons Your Grace to be at home in your realm, on the defence." He was wearing his clan badge and hat, and seemed oblivious to the fact that his King, James IV, was acting in a base manner in choosing this time to attack.

"You have come a far way to deliver your cowardly summons," I said at length. "It ill becomes a Scot to summon a King of England. Tell him that never shall a Scot cause us to return! We see your master for what he is. For we never esteemed him to be of any truth, and now we have found it so. Therefore, tell your master I have left the Earl of Surrey in my realm at home to withstand him and all his power." Another thought came to me, directly from God. "This say to your master, that I am the very owner of Scotland. He, being my vassal, rebels against me. With God's help, I shall repulse him from his realm. And so tell him."

The Scotsman began to glower. I turned to my Garter-King-at-Arms. "Take him to your tent, and make him good cheer." The chivalric amenities must be observed.

As soon as he was out, Wolsey asked, "Can Howard hold them? We feared this!"

"God will hold them," I said. Strange that I should be the one to trust in God, whilst Wolsey trusted in details. He had provisioned this French campaign: he had seen to the barrels of tallow to keep the bowstrings supple; the balances and weights to weigh the proportions of saltpetre, sulphur, and charcoal to fire the cannon; vinegar for cooling the guns in action; leather buckets for carrying gunpowder; and so on. But God was not a factor.

True, other churchmen fought. Fox and Ruthal both had battle-armour and commanded one hundred men apiece, and Pope Julius led his troops in person. But they surely carried Christ postilion with them. Wolsey rode alone, in front of his two hundred men.

"God will prosper all our doings," said Sir John Seymour, one of my comrades-in-arms. Steady, reliable, level-headed. A true Englishman.

Tournai fell after only eight days' siege. Each of the Twelve Apostles (for I *had* ordered them, and they had proved magnificent) got to fire only once a day at the city walls, before the white flag waved and a ceremonial surrender was arranged. Tournai gave itself up to us, and we entered it in triumph, with a great procession. The people shouted and called me "Alexander." My men, riding behind me, were heaped with flowers and ribbons.

That day I kept my armour on far past sundown, revelling in its rigid casing and Spartan embrace. Every time I wished to bend, its stiffness reminded me that I was a warrior and a conqueror. I had it on yet when the letter came from Katherine. I remember, because I had to remove the gauntlet, the iron glove, in order to break the wax seals and unfold the parchment. And it was dark then; I had to order more candles to be lit so that I could read clearly.

That day I was indestructible, inviolate. I knew the news could only be good. Therefore it was without surprise or even jubilation that I read that Thomas Howard had met James IV at Flodden Field on September ninth and, by gunfire and arrow-storm, destroyed the Highlanders and their leaders. James

IV and his bastard son Alexander had both perished within a yard of the English standard. The bishops of the Isles and Caithness, the abbots of Inchaffney and Kilwinning (had *they* thought of Christ?), the earls of Montrose, Crawford, Argyle, and Lennox, together with most of the Scots nobility, had been massacred.

Twelve thousand Scots had fallen on that wet and cruel ground of Flodden. They were decimated. Scotland was destroyed for a generation.

"Your Grace," wrote Katherine, "shall see how I keep my promises; sending, in exchange for your banners, a King's coat." I opened the pouch attached; inside was a royal coat, cloth-of-gold, soaked and stiff with a King's blood. It had rents and slashes from battle-axes and swords. Holding it up before me, I felt fear, not joy. I dropped it on the ground.

"Scotland, and its King, have perished," I said, to inform the waiting men-at-arms around me, companions, my fealty-sworn soldiers: Brandon, Neville, Carew, Bryan, Seymour, Boleyn, Courtenay.

They let out a great cheer. "A glorious day!" yelled Brandon.

"Our King is mighty, he destroys his enemies!" cried young Courtenay.

I stepped to the door of my "house" and looked out across the flat plains of France, feeling the wind in my face. Whenever I want to recall that moment, that high moment of military triumph, I have only to close my eyes and open a window and let the wind blow steady and a little cold across my cheeks and lips. I do it sometimes, in moments of uncertainty. Then I become young again, and mighty.

WILL:

Katherine thought she was pleasing him by sending him the bloody Scots King's coat in exchange for the captured Duc de Longueville. As if they were an equal exchange!

Katherine was very devoted to Henry; Katherine was very competent and loyal; Katherine was very stupid in crucial ways.

HENRY VIII:

We landed at Dover, almost four months to the day since we had set sail for France. Then, there had been all the excitement of seeing France—I, who had never seen any of England, save the parts around London—and fighting there, against great odds. France had proved fair; and I had proved a warrior. Now part of fair France was my booty.

All along the Dover-London road, my subjects were waiting. They wished to see us, touch us, call their greetings. We had done well; we had touched a nerve in Englishmen, and aroused a longing in them. And next year we would further satisfy that longing, for we would invade France yet again, this time well coordinated with Ferdinand and Maximilian. This season's campaign had been but the beginning.

WILL:

It was here that I once again saw Henry VIII. I was one of the throng along the selfsame Dover-London road, and I was eager to glimpse him, the Boy-King. I stood for hours, so it seemed, waiting for a hint of movement on the road stretching away on either side. *The King is coming. No, the King will be an hour yet.* It was interminable, yet I dared not leave. At length—it was almost noon, and we had been waiting, standing, since dawn—he came into view, sitting proudly on a great white horse. He was dressed all in gold, and he himself was gold: his hair, his eyes, his glowing skin. He looked fresh, and as full of grace as any knight new-blessed at Jerusalem. My—whatever it is within the breast that expands into life at such moments—pride, for want of a better word, was touched, and I felt ecstatic beholding him, both as if I were King myself, and at the same time awed that we had such a King.

HENRY VIII:

Katherine was awaiting me at the Palace of Richmond. When I reached London, so eager was I to see her I did not bother to change my travel-stained clothes, in which I had lived since boarding my warship at Calais. Instead, I changed horses, so that I might gallop to her on the fastest steed in the royal stables. I had been faithful to her all the time I had been away, even during that time in Lille, between the besieging of Thérouanne and Tournai, when we celebrated our first victory and there were many Belgian ladies eager to "comfort" a warrior-king. . . .

I had never been unfaithful to Katherine. I did not believe it was right. I had pledged myself to her, and I would keep that pledge. My father had never been unfaithful to my mother. I could not have borne it if he had insulted her so.

The towers of Richmond Palace, rising pale and beseeching against the blanched autumn skies. Inside, inside, was my wife. Mother-to-be, victor at Flodden Field . . . oh, truly I was blessed.

Down the walkways (people on all sides pushing, claiming me) I flew toward the royal apartments. And there she was, at the entrance, like any schoolchild, not a royal daughter of Spain. Her hair glinted gold in the murky light. Then it was embrace, embrace; and I felt her warmth in my arms.

"O Henry," she whispered, close by my ear.

"The keys to Tournai." I had carried them on my person. Now I presented them to her, kneeling.

She took them, clasped them. "I knew you would win a city. So many times, as a child, I saw my mother or father return with such keys, keys wrested from the Moors—"

So. She compared the memories. Ferdinand and Isabella driving the Moors from Spain, pushing them back, city by city. Could her husband measure up?

We were traversing the royal apartments. We would go to hers, as the King's were dark and silent and not yet in order. "The Moors are back in Africa, where they belong," I said.

"Yes." Her face was shining. "And the Scots are back in the mountains, where *they* belong."

In her withdrawing room, we stood still a long moment and kissed. Her lips, how sweet!

"You put Moorish honey on your lips," I murmured.

"I do nothing Moorish!" she said, pulling away.

"Surely the Moors had good things to give Spain—"

"No. Nothing." Now her lips, so soft, were set in a hard little line. "There is nothing good from the soft beds of the East."

"Yet you spent your girlhood in the 'soft Moorish East,'" I teased. "Watching the fountains play in the Caliph's Palace in Granada. Come, teach me." I reached out for her belly.

Which was flat. Entirely flat, and hard as her mouth had been when dismissing the Moors.

"He died," she said softly. "Our son. He was born the night after I received word that the Scots were massing. In between midnight and dawn. Warham christened him," she added. "His soul was saved."

"But not his body," I said rotely. "You say—'he'?"

"A son," she said. "A little son, not formed enough to survive. But enough to be baptized! His soul has gone to Paradise."

"Now you do sound like a Moor."

My son. Dead.

"It was the Scots," I said. "They killed him. Had it not been for them, and their dastardly attack, you would not have delivered before your time." I broke away from her. "They stand punished. Their King is dead."

A present King for a future King. Had they truly been punished?

I came back to her and enfolded her in my arms. "We will make another King."

I led her into her sleep-chamber. But it was not duty that called me, but desire, as Katherine was at her ripest and most beautiful: a queen who defended her realm, a mother who mourned a son, a daughter of the East who could give exotic pleasures, no matter how her Catholic conscience denounced them.

XXI

I n recognition of their services on the battlefield, I restored Thomas Howard to his lost dukedom of Norfolk; and I made Charles Brandon the new Duke of Suffolk.

WILL:

A title recently vacated by Edmund de la Pole, as it were.

HENRY VIII:

Wolsey, too, must be recognized. God had opened many Church positions in the last few months, as though anticipating our needs. I gathered them up, making a bouquet of them, and presented them to Wolsey: Bishop of Lincoln, Bishop of Tournai, and Archbishop of York. In one brief ceremony he cata-pulted himself (like one of the cannonballs from the war machines he had helped supply) from simple priest to powerful prelate. "For a man only lately a mere priest, you aim high." I smiled. "I like that."

"What else could I aspire to?" He attempted a look of innocence.

"What else, indeed? And for what do you intend this palace you are planning?"

Wolsey had just acquired the lease of a tract of land far upstream on the Thames from the Knights Hospitalers. He had consulted masons and builders and had twice already braved icy riding paths to inspect the grounds.

"Hampton? 'Tis not a palace, 'tis but a manor house. An archbishop, after all, must have quarters befitting his office."

"There's York Place for that."

"It's old and damp."

"So are my palaces. So, my friend and minister, you aim at something grand. How would you like a . . . cardinal's hat?"

"Yes." No disclaimers, no hesitation. *"Cardinal* Wolsey. *That's* higher than Canterbury. A cardinal would be a worthy representative and minister for you. As King, you deserve no less a man to serve you."

His flattery was so ready. "Oh, yes. I owe it to myself to make *you* Cardinal. Let's see, now. There is a new Pope. What is he like? How best should we approach him for this little favour?" I paused. "We'll flatter Leo. He'll send the cardinal's hat, never fear. By this time next year . . . I'll be King of France, and you'll be Cardinal Wolsey!"

And I would be a father, pray God. The Queen was pregnant again, and surely this fourth time we would have what we—and England—so deeply desired. And urgently needed.

The plans were drawn up. My world was ordered, like a chessboard freshly laid out with new ivory pieces. How the board—the squares and duchies of Europe—gleamed before me! On my side were Ferdinand, Maximilian, the new Pope, Leo. We were to launch our attack on France on many fronts simultaneously, coordinating them by means of the fastest messengers in Christendom (albeit mounted on Arab horses). Katherine and I spent hours imagining the battles Ferdinand and I would fight as comrades-in-arms; she longed to cross the sea with me and fight alongside us. Only the coming child prevented her.

"With the Scots vanquished, I could come," she said wistfully. "Only I would not endanger the child for anything in this world." She patted her stomach tenderly.

"Nor I, my love."

"I am so deeply happy that you and my father will meet at last." True, I had never seen Ferdinand, except through Katherine's devoted eyes. "And that you have chosen—or rather, allowed me to choose—a name from *my* family: Philip Charles."

The men in her family seemed blessed with vigour and longevity; perhaps I had become superstitious about the doomed Henrys, Richards, and Edwards in mine. In any case, it seemed a small enough concession at the time. Anything to keep Katherine happy so that the child might grow in peace.

"Aye, yes."

Her devotion to both Ferdinand and Jesus often interfered with her devotion to her husband's earthly needs. More and more I had found those needs taking on a life of their own, pulsating within me and demanding a hearing. They cared little for Katherine's scruples, or for mine, either. I was twenty-three years old and a man, that was all they knew. Katherine's maids of honour, her ladies-in-waiting, particularly the Duke of Buckingham's married sister, seemed to rouse that imp within me. Satin pulled taut over breasts roused it in me.

The sound of a lute in Katherine's outer chamber called it forth like a cobra rising to a snake charmer's flute. Out there would be the ladies, the maids, playing tunes, passing time, all arrayed in satin and velvet. Like a sleepwalker, I was drawn away. Like a sleepwalker, I was an onlooker only; all that ever happened was in my own head.

The foul letter lay there like a dead fish, stinking with corruption, slime, and rottenness. Ferdinand had played me false, had betrayed me all along. At the very hour when I was entering Tournai in conquest, he was signing a secret peace treaty with the French. His toady and minion, Maximilian, had followed suit.

This whole long winter, whilst plans were being meticulously formulated, munitions ordered, supplies replenished (the precise image of these things danced across my brain!), and my flagship taking shape, board by board, beam by beam, at great cost and rush, so as to be ready for launching in June . . .

And I had even called a Parliament, humbled myself to approach them for money . . .

Ferdinand had already betrayed and abandoned me, leaving me either to call off the war and look the fool to the entire world, or else fight the French alone.

The Judas!

Blood rushed into my head as all these images (the Parliament, the flagship, Ferdinand signing the secret treaty; his partisan daughter, Katherine, singing his praises) clashed at once. I felt I would explode, only no words could utter my rage. Spittle came into my mouth and all but choked me.

Grabbing the letter, I rushed to Katherine's quarters, as maddened as any hashish-chewing infidel. She was, as usual, "at prayer." I pushed aside her wheedling little pet priest, Fra Diego (a Spaniard!); in fact I grabbed him by his pectoral cross and spun him by it, and flung open her chapel door.

Her back was to me, all golden in velvet. I strode over to her and yanked her up off her knees.

"Well, Madam, what say you to this?" I shoved the offensive letter right up against her nose. "You knew it all along! You betrayed me along with him! You're *his* creature, you sneaking little . . . *foreigner!*"

She snatched the letter and her eyes skimmed it. "I knew nothing of it," she said calmly.

"Liar! Liar!" How dare she lie? Did she think me that stupid, that much of a dupe? Perhaps I had been, but no more. God, how I hated her. She had never been anything but a Spanish spy in my bed.

"I know what you are, now! What you have been all along! An agent for Spain, put here to make me clay in Ferdinand's hands, a vessel—a *vassal,* ha ha—for him to piss in! And that's all he's done—from the episode in 1512 with the archers, to the non-appearance last summer, and now this. Tell me— what are his latest instructions to you? What are you to do now, my sweet spy? For I know he's sent you instructions. I know there's a letter here, someplace—" I rushed from the tiny chapel to her work room, with her desk and locked boxes. "Yes, it's here." I tested the little rounded wood box nearest to hand; naturally it was locked. I smashed it open. There was nothing inside but inks and seals.

"But of course, you'd never put it *there*. It's hidden. No, not even that. You're too clever. You memorized it, then destroyed it. It's all in *here*." I put both my hands on the sides of her skull. "If I smash that, too, will the letter pop out?" I squeezed, hard.

"You are behaving like a madman," she said, in a strong, unflinching voice. Courage—she had that Spanish courage. "A madman, not a King."

"What are your *instructions?*" I insisted in a parody of a whisper, close to her ear. "I *will* have them." I turned her to face me. "Were they to wheedle more money from me, for one of your father's causes? Were they to send me to a war alone, to weaken England so that others can claim us? Yes, turn us into meat for anyone's taking . . . he'd like that, wouldn't he?"

"There are no instructions, and I have never acted with loyalty toward anyone but you. If Ferdinand has betrayed you, then he has betrayed me also. From henceforth I renounce him." Her voice was filled with sorrow. Very convincing. "It grieves me that my father should care so little for me that he would do this to my husband."

Father! She was grieved for *him,* not for me.

"Well, you've lost him! Do you understand me? Swear by this cross"— I stepped into the next room and plucked it from the anxious priest's neck— "that you renounce him. With no reservations, no conditions. Else I will divorce you!"

She looked at me in disbelief.

"Yes, divorce you! You are either my wife, and loyal to me, or his daughter. His actions prove you cannot be both, and keep your honour. Swear!"

She clutched the cross. "I swear that I am, and ever will be, a loyal and true wife to my sovereign lord and King."

"That's only half! Renounce *him!*"

She clutched the cross so tightly her knuckles looked like clay marbles. "I—renounce—my natural father, Ferdinand." She seemed to shrink with each word.

"There. That's done. And if you've sworn falsely"—I took the cross from her limp and sweating palm—"you've damned yourself."

"You know . . . there's no divorce." Her voice was small.

"Oh, yes, there is."

"Annulments, yes. But divorce was forbidden by Our Lord."

"As an ideal, yes. Like 'be ye perfect.' Just bring me a son, and there'll be no divorce." Then I thought of something else. "I think it best that you sever all reminders of your former connections to your other life. There'll be no 'Philip Charles' in the Tudor family. I'll find a good English name."

Turning, I left her standing in her work room, tears streaming down her face. But instead of a helpless, frightened woman, all I saw was a tool of the evil Ferdinand, a viper I had nourished in my breast, had crowned and set up in my own household.

I remained in that state for the better part of the evening. Vesper-time, when I was wont to join Katherine at her prayers, came and went. I knew she would be waiting for me. But I could not bring myself to join her. I expected her to send a message to me. But she did not. Good. Just the sight of her handwriting would have inflamed me, as I would have pictured it framing her secret, treasonous letters.

But as the hours passed and I prepared for bed, I began to feel foolish. *Not* at my accusations, for Katherine had been a partisan of Ferdinand's all along—indeed, at one time she had even been empowered to act as his envoy at my court!—but at my wild, naked emotion that had completely controlled *me,* rather than the other way round. I had screamed, I had almost frothed, I had physically harmed the priest. Was I a boy or a man? Shame flooded me.

I mounted the steps up into my great bed. Still no message from Katherine, no appeals to me to return and forgive her. That was a mistake on her part. But I thought it calmly; my anger was cold now.

I settled myself into the mattress. Rest was sweet. I was exhausted from my emotions.

Divorce. Where had I come by that word? There was no such thing for Christians; Katherine was correct. Christ had been quite specific about that, when they—which "they"?—had questioned him concerning divorce. "They" must have been the Pharisees. It was always the Pharisees, wasn't it? But then there *was* an exception, a sort of condition that permitted divorce. It was something Saint Paul had mentioned. I made up my mind to ask Wolsey when I met with him the next morning. He *was* a priest, even if he was no theologian.

After Mass, I went directly to Wolsey's apartments in the Palace, where I found the Archbishop already at work at his desk. The Archbishop, I noted, had not attended Mass himself.

"Read this." I dropped the offensive Spanish letter on his heaped desk. It rolled down a pile of ledgers like a log, coming to rest right at his hands.

His plump fingers smoothed out the parchment, and he read it in less time than it has taken me to write this.

"Abomination!" he whispered. "He is bound for the very lowest circle of Hell, with his fellow traitors: Judas, Brutus, Cassius. Satan will embrace him."

"Yes, yes." His eventual whereabouts did not concern me so much as knowing who embraced him *now:* all the world, so it seemed. "I will be revenged. And sooner than in the Hereafter. What think you to trumping him?"

"What, fighting him? And France as well?"

"I said trumping, not fighting." A plan was taking shape in my mind, a most phantasmagorical plan. "I will outdo Ferdinand in duplicity."

"Impossible."

"I can excel in anything I set my hand to," I insisted. "Even duplicity. Listen"—the thoughts gave instant birth to the words—"Ferdinand has made a secret pact with France? I shall make a public ceremony of brotherhood with France!"

"Your ancient enemy, that you hated up until yesterday?"

"Now I hate Ferdinand more; so *his* enemy has become, on the instant, my friend."

"Your Grace, this is so sudden, it will never be believed."

"What is a *fait accompli* can be believed. What is sealed by marriage can be believed. Tell me—what are the conditions permitting divorce?"

"Whose divorce?"

"Any man's divorce."

"There is no such thing as 'any man's divorce.' There are only particular exceptions to the binding nature of marriage."

"Marriage to a traitor?"

"I assume . . . that the only way one can commit treason against his spouse is by way of adultery. Unless the spouse is a ruling monarch; then other forms of treason would also be marriage-treason. But since thereby the guilty one would be executed for the treason, the remaining spouse would be widowed, not 'divorced.' Death—deserved death—would end the marriage as surely as natural death."

"In short, it would be quicker to execute for treason and become widowed in half a day than to approach Rome for a divorce and wait half a year?" I spoke in theory only, of course.

Wolsey rose from his desk and came toward me. He had begun to put on weight as a result of the official banquets and entertainments he now frequented. "Surely you aren't thinking of—yourself? You cannot divorce the Queen because of her father's deceit. Although, God knows, I think you deserve a French princess on your arm and in your court."

His burst of candour shocked me as much as my proposed turnabout shocked him.

"Why, Wolsey. You don't like the Queen?"

He was all explanations. "No, Your Grace, I *do* like and admire her, I only meant . . . that a graceful French girl would be such an ornament to the court, such a jewel on your arm. Someone who dances and masques, someone who—"

"Yes. I understand." Katherine had become so much more serious in the past year or so. Still, Wolsey had no way of knowing that hidden Moorish side. . . . "France, and its curious combination of elegance and decadence . . . I'd like to sample that in a woman." I had never sampled any woman but Katherine. "But I am married and do not qualify for a divorce. You are correct: Ferdinand's treason does not transfer onto his daughter. Her only 'treason' is in failing to follow the Biblical command to 'leave your mother and your father.' Her heart's in Spain still. But her body's here, and has been technically faithful."

"Besides, she carries a child."

"Yes." But even that seemed tainted.

"However, there are other means of coming close to France." He steered me back onto that subject. He seemed eager; his eyes shone.

"Indeed there are. And other marriages. My sister Mary—to the King of France!"

His face registered the jolt that passed through his whole body. *"Your Grace!"* He licked his lips. "A thought of genius!"

"It came to me, just on the instant. God sent it." I truly believed that.

"We will break Mary's betrothal to Charles of Burgundy," he said.

That would delight her. She had hated the idea of marrying the Habsburg boy, Katherine's nephew, who was four years younger than she. But later she had gotten into the spirit of it and carried his portrait about and attempted to sigh over it. She would be pleased to abandon the effort and go be Queen of France.

❧ ☙

"Queen of France? By marrying that decaying roué with the false teeth? No, no, *no!"* She kicked His Highness's gift: a statue of Venus, with Cupid hovering over one shoulder. *"No!"* The statue toppled over, smashing the marble Cupid's nose.

"My dear sister," I explained, "he *is* a King."

"He is repulsive!"

"Queen of France! Think on it, my dear, think on it well. You will be celebrated in song and verse, will be First Lady of Europe. You will be able to do as you please, wear exquisite clothes, be heaped with jewels."

"And at night?" Her eyes narrowed. "At night I will pay the price."

"What is a quarter-hour of drudgery in exchange for twelve hours of power and luxury?" I helped myself to a cherry from her silver bowl of them, affecting a casual demeanor. By God, if this light touch did not suffice, then I should be forced to use force against my dearest sister.

"When did you become so hard?" she asked quietly. "This is not my brother speaking, not the Henry I have known, but some other man."

She touched on a delicate point. Of late I had felt that hard part growing, taking shape and rising within me like a rock rising from a lake, displacing all the sweet and placid water around it. It had first gathered itself when the word *divorce* had sprung unbidden to my lips, when I had turned against Katherine, if only for a short while. I had not known I harboured such an alien presence within me; but by now it no longer seemed alien, rather an integral part of myself. It was necessary for a King to be hard—at times.

"Yes, the soft-hearted child you knew has gone. In his place is a King," I said. "A child looks only at what he wants, at what he wishes were true. A King looks at what *is,* and how to drive the best bargain."

"And the best bargain for *you* is that your sister be Queen of France."

" 'Tis the best bargain for you, as well. You'll see. Besides"—I blurted this out—"he can't live long. A little investment on your part now would lead to great reward later. You're young. You have decades to enjoy the jewels and titles without the odious presence of Louis himself."

She looked disgusted, not pleased. "To hear you speak thus is a greater loss to me than my virginity to Louis. You are no longer Henry."

"Oh, he's still there." Keep it light, do not venture into this with her. Settle the French marriage.

"Yes, to be brought out whenever charm is required. For the young Henry, my brother Henry, is a winsome man. What has done it to you? Is it Wolsey? A calculating, ambitious priest—"

Everyone wanted to blame Wolsey for everything. He was a handy scapegoat. The "charming" Henry served yet to mask the "new" Henry and his doings.

I sighed, then spoke honestly. "Wolsey does nothing on his own. He has no power I do not grant him. He is entirely my creature."

"Then where did this foreign Henry come from? This Henry who gambles and masques and hunts with worldly courtiers, writes bawdy lyrics, and avoids the Queen's chambers and the scholars he once frequented?"

"My little nun," I scoffed. "I am a man, and I enjoy what other men enjoy." Still, I had yet to find myself in any woman's bed but the Queen's. A popular term for adulterer was "bed-swerver." Well, I had not swerved in that way. "And as for my 'worldly courtiers,' I've noticed that you enjoy dancing with the Duke of Suffolk."

"All women do," she said.

"Aye. He's a ladies' man; he knows what pleases them. He's been married, more or less, to three already, and still maintains his bachelorhood. A neat trick." I envied him.

Mary shrugged. "Shall I become worldly as well? Follow your example?"

"You may as well, and sooner rather than later. While you still have your looks and can drive a reasonable bargain—unlike our other sister."

Poor Margaret, late the Scots Queen, now a coarsening woman with decreasing market value, and frantic for a man. As soon as she had given birth to James IV's posthumous son, she had taken swaggering Archibald Douglas, the Earl of Angus, as her lover.

Mary drew herself up, slender and golden. A most valuable piece on the chessboard. "I shall marry King Louis," she said, each word enunciated as though she were carefully choosing it from a tray of others. "I will take a large number of ladies with me, to form my court. And when Louis dies, I will retain the jewels he has given me." She paused. "From you, I require one thing."

"Name it." Naturally I would grant her anything, any wedding present she might wish. I would even name my new flagship after her, rather than myself.

"When Louis dies, I shall be free to marry whom I will. You may marry me this once. Hereafter I will marry myself."

No. She was too valuable to me, and to England. "No."

"Then I shall not wed Louis. I shall enter a convent instead."

"You would do that, rather than submit entirely?" She was a Tudor—stubborn and ruthless. "I would never let you do that to yourself. Very well, then, I grant you your wish." By the time she was widowed, she'd be more sensible. We all became more sensible in time. Then I had a sudden suspicion. "There isn't someone now that you fancy?"

She smiled a faraway smile. "There are many that I fancy," she said. "As any young girl might."

After we had parted, I could not help reflecting on what she had said. It was true, the company I sought had changed. Instead of Erasmus and Dean John Colet, I wanted Edward Guildford and Edward Poyntz, bluff courtiers. Instead of Katherine, I had Wolsey for my political confidant. I did not want to be alone to pray, or reflect, or compose music. I wanted noise and gaiety and distractions; I wanted power rather than chivalry.

Yet not all of me did. The first Henry, the one who wanted to be a "true knight"—he existed alongside the second one, keeping uneasy watch over him.

XXII

ary and King Louis were to be married by proxy in England, so that she would arrive in France already its Queen. The elegant Louis d'Orleans, Duc de Longueville, taken prisoner in France during the war campaign, was to stand in for Louis and recite his vows for him. Although technically a hostage, de Longueville in fact behaved as a French diplomat, and it was to him that King Louis sent his wedding gift for Mary: a pendant necklace made of a gigantic, pear-shaped pearl so singular that it had a name of its own—the Mirror of Naples. I made a promise to myself to have it appraised by honest English jewellers before Mary left for France.

The ceremony was to take place at Greenwich, with Archbishop Warham presiding, in the presence of the peers of the realm. I had transformed the gathering-room of the royal apartments with cloth-of-gold and silk, so that it glittered like a cave of gold, a treasure-hoard of legend.

Below, at the palace landing, even the piers were swathed in gold tissue, and I could see the lavishly appointed barges of the wedding guests tied up, bobbing gaily on the water.

"Come, Katherine," I said, turning to my wife. "It is time." I offered my arm. Katherine took it, wordlessly and stiffly; that was the way things were between us now.

In my outer chamber, Wolsey was waiting, resplendent in gleaming brocade vestments. As part of the ceremony he was to be recognized by Louis as furthering the cause of France. Katherine nodded stiffly to him. That was how things stood between them, as well.

Mary made a lovely bride. One would never suspect, hearing her lilting voice pronouncing the hastily learned French vows to de Longueville, pledging her love and fidelity, that she had ever desired anything else. The rings were exchanged, the bridal kiss conferred, the papers signed. And now the marriage must be "consummated" by proxy.

This had been my inspiration. A proxy marriage might be repudiated, like a precontract or betrothal. But a proxy consummation—that was another matter.

"An absurd idea," Katherine had sniffed. "Verbal agreements, properly witnessed, or signed documents, are all that honourable men require."

"Like my father and your father? We made verbal agreements and went through a public betrothal. Was it honoured? Why did you have to sell your dower-plate for food, then? You still continue to believe in honour, my duck?"

"I believe in *your* honour," she said.

Wolsey, on the other hand, had appreciated the genius of it.

"The very uniqueness, the novelty of it, will seal it in the eyes of the world," he said. "It will be, in its own way, even more of a consummation than the ordinary kind."

"Quite."

I had had a great state bed set up in the middle of the Assembly Chamber. It was canopied, but no bed-curtains were hung to obscure the view, and no coverlets of fur or wool were arranged there to veil the required actions.

The entire company gathered about the bed, while Mary retired to change into a nightdress. Katherine and her attendants waited until Mary emerged, clad in her magnificent dishabille, then escorted her with stately steps up to the bed, laying her out on her back upon the satin bedcloth, smoothing her hair.

Then the Duc de Longueville approached the foot of the bed, wearing red hose and boots, which he ceremoniously removed, placing them neatly side by side. Assisted by Wolsey and Brandon, he mounted the side of the bed, lay down beside Mary, and touched her bare foot with his naked leg. He remained in that position whilst the onlookers gazed intently and Archbishop Warham peered over them and solemnly pronounced, "The marriage has been consummated!" The witnesses then broke into cheers and showered Mary and de Longueville with flowers.

De Longueville sat up and began making jokes. " 'Twas over in less time than a fifteen-year-old, and here I am of an age with His Highness! Were this all one felt, a man would scarcely hurry home from the fields for it!"

Mary, blushing (as befitted a modest bride), rose from the nuptial bed to change into yet a third costume, her ballgown, for the banquet and ball were to follow. The guests flocked to the Banquet Hall while Wolsey, Katherine, de Longueville, and I lingered, waiting for Mary.

"Well done," I said. "You assisted in the making of a Queen. This will be the Banquet of Two Queens—that of England and France," I said, hoping to cajole Katherine. I had pointedly excluded the Spanish ambassador from all these ceremonies, to her anger.

"If only your other sister were here, there would be three Queens," she answered, irrelevantly. She was determined to be aloof; so be it. I turned to de Longueville.

"You are a free man now. King Louis has paid your ransom." A fat one it was, too, and I had put it right into my private account. "Although I must say you passed your 'captivity' in French style."

He smiled, and answered my implied question. "Yes. Mistress Popincourt is going with me. I shall install her in my apartments in the Louvre." De Longueville had, naturally, acquired a mistress during his brief stay with us. I resolved that it was high time I acquired one, too.

Mary joined us, dazzling in a gown of royal blue silk.

Wolsey bowed low. "You shine like the angels painted by the Italian masters," he murmured. "All blue and gold you are."

"My Queen." De Longueville made obeisance.

Mary looked startled. The transformation from Tudor Princess to French Queen had been so swift, and so absolute.

Katherine moved over to kiss her cheek. "Now we are sister Queens," she said.

Together the five of us entered the Banquet Hall, where all the company awaited us: glowing spots of colour against the creamy stone of the Hall; the candlelight reflecting and magnifying from the gold plate that was displayed everywhere.

Mary was feted again and again, and I led out the first dance with her, Brother King and Sister Queen. I knew we were a stunning sight, our youth and strength and colour making us seem more than mortal. Indeed, I felt myself, that night, to be something beyond an ordinary being, certainly beyond my ordinary self, with all his confines and sensitivities.

Katherine danced only the sedate basse-dances and the pavane, that introductory measure in which all the company paraded their wardrobes. She was now in her eighth month, and all was well. I made sure her thronelike chair was fitted with extra velvet pillows, and that she had a footstool for her swollen feet.

That left me free to dance with whomsoever I pleased, and there were many pleasing women. Katherine's attendants, particularly her maids of honour, were young and unmarried. Yes, it was time I found a mistress. I had been too laggard in availing myself of a sovereign's prerogative. Sovereign's? I looked over at Brandon, smiling at his partner, looking like Bacchus. It was a *man's* prerogative. One did not need to justify it on the grounds of rank.

There was winsome little Kate, from Kent, a niece of Edward Baynton's. She was light as gauze, bright as a butterfly, and as insubstantial. There was Margery, a raven-haired Howard girl, some relation to the Duke of Norfolk, with a big bosom and pudgy fingers. There was Jocelyn, a distant cousin of mine, through my Bourchier relations in Essex. But she was a thin, intense sort, and it was not good to meddle with one's relatives, besides.

There was a Persephone, standing near Lord Mountjoy.

My heart felt a hush as I beheld her. I swear my first thought was of Persephone, of all the ways I had imagined her when I first heard the legend—a sweet nymph with red-gold hair and pink cheeks and a white, simple gown. Gathering flowers, playing on the riverbank so happily . . . all the while unknowingly inciting lust in the lurking god of the Underworld.

We danced. She danced like an accomplished child, all gaiety and abandon. Abandon . . . yes, I longed for that, for abandon in a bedmate. I knew she would be that way, giving and taking with offhanded energy. I lusted for her so acutely that every muscle in my body quivered. Now, now, it must be now, I could not wait even an hour . . . yet I must wait, must endure the dances yet to come, and the other partners, and the speeches, and the leave-taking, and the slow extinguishing of all this company of candles. . . .

"Mistress, you dance well," I murmured. "Perhaps you would care to dance again with me, in private?" How absurd! I knew not the prescribed approach, what phrases to use. Brandon knew all that; he was a practised voluptuary. I was as ignorant as a child.

She looked at me quizzically. "Whenever you may summon me."

"That may be tonight." Was that clear enough? Was that what Brandon would have said?

"I must leave with my uncle," she said hesitantly. Then, suddenly, I knew: she was as unpractised at the art and rules of this thing as I. Did she not realize that I commanded her uncle?

"Who is your uncle?"

"Lord Mountjoy, William Blount."

Katherine's chamberlain! And a friend of Erasmus's and the rest of the humanist scholars! I could not have chosen more unsuitably. But she was so lovely. How could I do other than pursue her?

"Oh, Mountjoy." I flicked my hand in a grand dismissal. "And what is your name?" But even before she said it, I had said it to myself.

"Bessie Blount, Your Grace."

"You have learned to dance," I said softly. "And to like the court, too. I am glad you did not hide your beauty away in Lincolnshire after all."

"I, too, Your Grace. Although until now . . . I was not sure I was right to stay."

Just so simply was it settled. And we both were aware of what had been asked and what had been granted, and the enormous promise that hovered over us.

Oh, would this ball never end?

I was not prepared even as to where to go. A seasoned libertine would have had rooms always at the ready, prepared for impromptu dalliance. I had no such thing. The royal apartments were anything but private. To gain entrance to my bedchamber would require the alerting of at least twenty attendants en route. This had never presented a problem with my lawful wife. Now, suddenly, it was a source of acute embarrassment.

We found ourselves a place in a small chamber behind the musicians' gallery, where the instruments were stored and where consorts often rehearsed. There was a daybed there, and stools, and candles and torches. I lighted a candle and, from that, a torch. We were surrounded by viols, trumpets, drums, and tambourines, all reflecting back the dancing light from their rounded and polished surfaces.

"Bessie," I said, "I am—" I wanted to be kind, warm, reassuring. But lust overwhelmed me, and once I touched her I could not control myself. I covered her face with kisses, plunged my hands into her thick hair, tore out its bindings so that it fell free over her shoulders and even covered her face, all but her parted lips, which I devoured. In a fever-fit of excitement, I undressed her, perplexed by the fastenings of her clothes (for I had never undressed Katherine; her maids of honour did that), trying not to harm them. She had to show me, else I would have ripped them.

When we lay side by side on the musicians' daybed, she turned toward the torch so that the amber-coloured light bathed her body and sweet face. "Bessie—Bessie—" I wanted to master my need, at least draw it out a little, but it mastered me, and I pulled her under me in the ancient act of submission, crushed her beneath me, plunged into her body—O God, she was a virgin!— and in a frenzy, sweat exploding from my whole body, I drove myself into her again and again (hearing dimly her cries in my ear) until I burst open inside her.

I spiralled down into a great darkness, turning, turning, landing softly.

She was crying, fighting for breath, clawing at my shoulders.

"Jesu, Bessie . . ." I released her, pulled her up, embraced her. She gasped for air, crying all the while. "I am sorry, forgive me, forgive me—" The mad beast had gone, leaving a conscience-stricken man to repair the damage. I comforted her, hating myself. Eventually she stopped crying and became calm. I began my apologies again. She put up a shaking finger against my lips.

"It is done," she said slowly. "And I am glad of it."

Now I truly comprehended how ignorant I was of women. "I behaved as a beast, and injured your . . . your honour." I had not even thought of the virginity beforehand.

"If it was this difficult with someone whose body I craved, think how much more difficult it would have been with someone to whom I was indifferent."

"But you would not have found yourself . . . thus . . . with someone you . . . didn't want."

She shook her head. "What do you think marriage is, for a woman?"

Mary. Mary and Louis. God, how could the Mirror of Naples compensate for that?

"But now . . . when you come to your marriage-bed . . . I've robbed you."

"I'll pretend."

"But you can't *pretend*—if it is not so!"

"I have heard . . . that it is easy to pretend, and men are content with that."

I was covered with sweat, the daybed was made rank with her deflowering, I was thoroughly shamed—and yet (O, most shameful of all!) with her words, and the thought of her later in another man's bed, my lust began to flame once more.

Just then she reached over and touched my cheek. "We must go. But oh—let us spend another few moments. . . ." She did not wish to flee? She did not despise me? Truly, I knew nothing of women—or of my own nature, either.

It was dawn when we finally left the musicians' chamber, creeping down the stone stairs and stealing across the silent Banquet Hall, where the flowers still lay scattered on the floor.

XXIII

From that night on I was a changed man: I was a lover, hurrying by light and by dark to Bessie's naked body, seeing how many ways there were of coupling. I had only to imagine something and within hours we would be trying it. The more I created in my mind, the more my ideas doubled and tripled; so lust gives rise to a nation of lust.

I lost no time in setting up a suite of rooms for my purpose. They were to be quite separate from the royal apartments, away from all my watchful attendants. (Bessie's father, Sir John Blount, served as an Esquire of the Body, one who undressed and dressed me. A sense of decency meant that I could not allow him to see the kiss-marks, catch the woman-odour of his own daughter upon the body of the man he served.) My *amour*-rooms were located near Wolsey's suite and consisted of a small dining chamber, a dressing room, and a bedchamber. My locksmith fitted the outer door with a lock to which there were only two keys, one for myself and one for Bessie.

Bessie's hours were such that she must attend Katherine from the midday meal, served with its formal three courses in Katherine's private dining chamber, until Vesper-time at five o'clock, keeping her company, amusing her with music and reading. These days there was much needlework to be done, embroidering new clothes for the baby, whose birth was imminent. Katherine had declined to use any of the clothing from Prince Henry; she had packed it away in sorrow.

Daily I attended Vespers with Katherine, sitting and kneeling beside her, looking with pride at the child she carried. I was able to pray for her, to squeeze her hand lovingly, to feel affection for her . . . and at the same time to imagine Bessie preparing for our assignation, warming the wine, twisting her hair up into that intricate knot I so loved to untie, rubbing perfume into the bends of her elbows and knees . . . oh, I was damned, I was evil, and yet I craved it. Never did it feel better to me than when I crossed directly from Katherine's chapel to Bessie's rooms, words of prayer from my mouth changing to words of carnality.

There was no transition, no polite greeting. Only indecent haste, as we rushed to gratify ourselves upon ourselves, Bessie as much as I. Together we had changed, in the course of only two or three meetings, from awkward, self-conscious youths to shameless voluptuaries.

Should I recount our pleasures here? Should I torture myself by remembering feats I can never hope to match again? We hid sweetmeats in our privates, to be extracted (so our rule was) only by the tongue, never by the fingers. . . . We watched our reflections, watched a hundred Henrys and Bessies copulating, in the window that reflected the mirror that reflected the window that reflected the mirror. . . . We wore masks, and I was a savage and she Diana. . . . I entered her and we turned the sandglass over and counted how many times we could come to the culmination, both together and separately. . . . And there was the time when I decked her naked body with all Katherine's jewels, and that, strangely, felt the most adulterous of all. . . .

After all this, we would take a light refreshment, served by a dim-sighted servant, and then part, almost wordlessly, only to repeat our actions the next day, or as soon thereafter as possible.

That evening I would go over dispatches, confer with Wolsey, and gamble with my companions and attendants of the royal apartments, including Bessie's father. I felt both whole and diminished, as if I were leading only half a life, and at the same time another, added half as well. I both loathed and loved my sin, both cherished and reviled it. My gambling losses mounted. I could not give proper attention to the game, or curb my tendency to escalate the stakes. None of the ordinary things seemed to matter.

Mary had embarked for France with a full court of her own, gloriously dowered and attended. Even children were appointed as pages and maids of honour. The two Seymour lads, aged nine and six, and Thomas Boleyn's two daughters, aged ten and seven, were on board one of the fourteen "great ships" of Mary's flotilla.

It was late one evening in Wolsey's quarters where I first read the name. That name. I had been checking the list in a cursory fashion.

Nan de Boleine.

"Who's this?" I mumbled. I was exhausted from Bessie that afternoon, and needed sleep.

"The Boleyn girl," Wolsey said.

"Why the devil do they affect this spelling? I'd not recognized the name."

"It's 'Boleyn' that's the affected spelling," said Wolsey. "The family name is originally 'Bullen.' But 'Boleyn' or 'Boleine' looks more prestigious."

"Like Wolsey for 'Wulcy'?" I grunted. "All this name-changing is frivolous. I like it not. So both of Boleyn's daughters have gone? And both of

Seymour's sons? There'll not be any young ones left to grow up and attend at *our* court."

"The parents were anxious for their children to acquire French manners."

By God, that rankled! For how long would the world look to France for its standard of elegance and style? I was determined that my court would usurp it. "The court of King Louis is as lively as a grasshopper in November," I snorted. "They'll learn little there."

"They'll learn from the shadow court, the one headed by Francis Valois, Duc d'Angoulême. Unless Mary gives Louis an heir, Francis will be the next King of France. Already he holds court and practises. The little Boleyns and Seymours will learn from him, not from Louis."

"Francis's wife, Louis's daughter Claude, is as holy as Katherine, so they say." My tongue was becoming unguarded with fatigue. "It can hardly be stylish there."

"Madame Claude is ignored. Francis's mistress sets the tone."

Openly? His mistress presided openly? "What sort of fellow is this Francis, of the house of Valois?"

"Much like yourself, Your Majesty." Of late Wolsey had introduced this title for me, saying that "Your Grace" was shared alike with Dukes and Archbishops and bishops, and that a monarch needed his own title. I liked it. "Athletic, well educated, a man of culture." He paused. "It is also said he enjoys a blemished reputation as an insatiable lecher."

"Already? How old is he?"

"Twenty, Your Majesty."

"Are his . . . attentions always welcome?"

"Not universally, Your Majesty. He is most persistent, so it is said, and will not desist once he has his sights set on a prey. When the mayor of the city of Marseille presented him with the keys to that city, he took a fancy to the mayor's daughter—who, being an honest woman, repelled by Francis's looks and manner, refused. He attempted to force her. So great was her repulsion that she held her face over fumes of sulphuric acid to ruin her complexion. Only her disfigurement dissuaded Francis!"

"A tragic deliverance," I said. "For now she'll be scarred forever." I prayed that Mary would conceive a son and spare France from such a ruler.

I glanced at Wolsey's paper-heaped table near the fireplace. "And how proceeds your pleasure-palace?" That table was reserved for documents relating to Hampton Court.

"Very well. The sewers and water-pipes are just being laid. My water will be brought from the springs of Coombe Hill, then pass under the Thames at Kingston, and emerge on my site. A distance of three and a half miles. I'd like you to come next spring, to watch the building. We can cross the river at

Richmond, change horses at Teddington, and then it's just a gallop through the forest."

"There's no point in crossing the Thames twice. The road from Kingston to Richmond is safe, is it not?"

His face took on a peculiar look. "I do not go through Kingston."

"Why? It is certainly the most direct land route."

He rose and made a pretense of stirring the logs in the fireplace. "I cannot say. I know only that Kingston bodes ill for me. I feel it."

"The place? The name? What aspect of Kingston?"

He shook his head. He had the beginnings of jowls, I noted. He was not young, actually. He had begun his climb to power early, but had had many false starts. "I know not. Just 'Kingston.' Do you not have anything like that in your life?"

"A premonition? No. No thing or place seems to promise ill or good. The future is veiled from me."

"You are fortunate, Your Majesty." It was the first time I had ever beheld an expression of true melancholy on his face.

Katherine's time drew near, and all was in readiness. She and her ladies had completed the preparations for the infant, and Richmond Palace had been selected as her lying-in place. I had procured the finest physicians I could find, even paying an Arab to act as consultant—for certain areas of North Africa were known as great centers of medicine, and Al-Ashkar had studied there. They possessed, so it was said, manuscripts of Galen and other Greek physicians, and had access to knowledge lost to us. The knowledge I needed was not something esoteric, but the most basic of all: how to have a living son.

In mid-September, on the eve of Holyrood Day, her pains began, and she was escorted to her lying-in chamber, already stocked with every pharmaceutical aid and surgical instrument known to medicine. Down she lay upon the wallflower-impregnated linens (for wallflower juice was known to ease childbirth pain), and, clutching the hand of Dr. Linacre with her right, and the hand of Dr. de la Sa, her Spanish physician, with her left, she bore each pain with fortitude, her lips moving constantly in prayer. When they offered her a pain-soother, she refused it, keeping her eyes fixed on the crucifix on the opposite wall.

All this while I waited in the outer chamber, Brandon keeping vigil with me. I was as silent as Katherine and prayed just as intently. My prayers began in proper, stiff sentences. *O Lord, Mighty God, grant, I beseech you, a son for my realm.* But as hours wore on, and Linacre appeared, shaking his head, they became frantic, silent cries. *Help her, help me, give us a child, I beg you, please,*

I will do anything, perform any feat, I will go on a crusade, I will dedicate this child to you, like Samuel, here am I, Lord, send me . . .

"It is over." Linacre flung the door wide. I leapt to my feet.

"A son," he said. "Living." He beckoned for me to follow him.

Katherine lay back, like a corpse upon a pallet. She did not stir. Was she—had she—?

De la Sa was massaging her abdomen, which was still distended and puffy. Great spurts of blackish blood shot out from between her legs each time he pushed, where it was caught in a silver basin. The blood was lumpy with clots. Katherine moaned and stirred.

"The child," Linacre indicated, turning my eyes from the grotesque horror on the bed that was my pain-wracked and damaged wife. Maria de Salinas Willoughby was bathing the babe, washing blood and mucus off him.

He was so tiny. Tiny as a kitten. Too small to live, I knew it on the instant.

"We thought it best that he be baptized immediately," said Linacre. "So we sent for a priest."

I nodded, aware of what he was admitting. Baptize him quickly, before he dies. No ceremony. Any priest will do.

A young priest appeared from the outer chamber, having been hurried from the Chapel Royal, where he served with minor duties. He was still adjusting his vestments and carried a container of holy water.

"Proceed," I ordered him. Maria had the babe dried and wrapped in a blanket by now.

"His . . . robe," protested Katherine weakly.

"She means the christening robe she fashioned for him," explained Maria.

"We haven't time." I said the words, feeling nothing. Numb as a hand held against cold metal.

"The robe . . ."

"It is right here, Your Grace, I'll see to it," Maria reassured Katherine tenderly. She pulled the dainty thing over his head, not even straightening it, just so she could comply.

"Godparents?" asked the priest.

"You, Maria, and you, Brandon." What difference? Anyone would do. There would be no duties as the child grew.

"Name?"

"William," I said. A good English name.

"I baptize thee, William, in the name of the Father, and of the Son, and of the Holy Ghost." A trickle of water on his soft forehead.

Quick, now: wrap him warmly, hold him near the brazier, give him heated milk. A miracle if he lives. Lord Jesu, I ask you for a miracle.

Prince William died seven hours later. By the time Katherine's milk came in, the babe had been buried for two days, wearing his little christening robe as a shroud.

✒ WILL:

That winter the news came to us: our King had lost another son. Now, for the first time, people began to worry, and to pray. Their King had been married five years now, and remained childless.

✒ HENRY VIII:

I went to Katherine, and we comforted one another, and I attempted to put all those fearsome doubts behind me. I resolved never to quarrel with her or upset her again. I was deeply sorry that I had said the cruel things I had, and above all, that I had uttered the evil word "divorce" like a curse.

Katherine conceived again. It was a merry Christmas for us in England, and, I hoped, for Queen Mary and King Louis in France.

XXIV

For the past few months I had concerned myself with intensely personal griefs and hopes. But all that ended on New Year's Day, when my attention was called back to matters of statesmanship. For on that ominous first day of 1515, King Louis died. All my carefully constructed plans were overthrown in the final exhalation of a single man's breath. Francis was King Francis I of France now, and my sister no longer Queen but Dowager Queen, as politically useless in the new regime as a pig-farmer in the land of the Turk.

In accordance with French custom, she was taken immediately to the Palais de Cluny, near Paris. There she was to remain, guarded by the nuns and veiled all in white for royal mourning, until her monthly course appeared and assured Francis that there was no heir within her womb to challenge him. She was to be known as *La Reine Blanche,* the White Queen, to distinguish her from Queen Claude, the reigning Queen.

"They are holding her prisoner," I grumbled to Wolsey. "I want her— *and* her dowry jewels, *and* her wedding jewels from Louis—out of France now. I distrust their motives."

"They will not release her until they are sure she is not with child. Francis dares not."

"I like it not! And why have we had no direct word from her? All our communications are passed through the French ambassador."

"I agree . . . there should be an English presence."

I paced the floor, treading softly on the new Turkish carpet that Wolsey had presented me for Christmas. He had insisted that I spread it on the chamber floor, even though it was of silk. It gave me a sense of luxury and power to walk on silk. "You must go. As my representative. Use the pretext of recognizing Francis as King. But spirit Mary, and the jewels, out."

"My presence would alert Francis to something of import. Send the Duke of Suffolk, rather. He is known as a friend of the Dowager Queen's, a boon companion of Your Majesty's, and, begging your pardon . . . he is not the stuff of which intriguers are made." A polite reminder that Charles Brandon was not a man of wit or learning or even much intelligence.

"An excellent subterfuge," I admitted. "Yet he's brave, and loyal. One can count on him to carry out a task."

"As long as he does not have to *think,* Your Majesty, but just be stalwart."

As Brandon made his way to Dover, preparing to take ship and cross the wintry Channel, a messenger arrived carrying a letter smuggled out of the convent. Mary was being assaulted and harassed by Francis, who visited her daily on the pretext of consoling her, but propositioned her, grabbed her, and attempted to woo her. He ordered the nuns to leave them alone and lock the doors, then he tried to seduce her, and failing that, to force her to lie with him.

I shook with rage at the picture of this libertine putting his hands on my sister—his *stepmother*! The very heavens themselves condemned this ancient abomination. The First Gentleman of France, as he called himself, was a perverted beast. Let Mary be found with child, so that France would be delivered from his evil reign! And let Brandon act as her champion to free her from the prison that Francis had put her in.

"Pray God, Katherine," I said, when I recounted Mary's plight to her. "I know he hears your prayers."

"Not always," she said. "But I will pray nonetheless."

God answered her prayers, but in a disastrous way. For Brandon rescued Mary by marrying her himself, with Francis's connivance.

"Traitor!" I screamed, when I read his letter. "Traitor!"

For the tenth time I reread the words:

> My Lord, so it is that when I came to Paris I heard many things which put me in great fear, and so did the Queen both; and the Queen would never let me be in rest till I had granted her to be married. And so to be plain with you, I have married her heartily and have lain with her, insomuch that I fear me lest she be with child.

Now I knew them all by heart. No need to keep this foul document. I flung it into the fire, where it quickly writhed, blackened, and withered.

"He's robbed me of a sister!"

"I think it was rather . . . noble of him to do what he did," said Katherine timidly, for she had learned not to contradict me in my rages.

"In Spain such things may pass for noble. In England they are regarded as foolhardy and dangerous."

"He rescued a princess in distress, whose honour was being threatened."

"He robbed me of a valuable property to be used in marriage negotiations! Now I have no one to use as bait for treaties, no one, as we are childless, and—"

"Can you not rejoice for them, and their happiness? Henry, once you would have. Oh, remember the boy who wrote,

> 'But love is a thing given by God,
> In that therefore can be none odd,
> But perfect in deed and between two;
> Wherefore then should we it eschew?' "

"That boy is dead." When had he died? In my learning to be King?

"He rescued *me*. When *I* was a princess in a strange land."

Oh, she was going to begin on that again. I could tell by the faraway look in her eyes. What a bore. "Well, you are Queen now, and it's a long time past." Impatiently I looked round for escape. "I'll tell Wolsey to devise some punishment for them. Set a fine. Yes, that's it." Quickly I left her alone.

Wolsey did just that. He proposed that Brandon be required to compensate for the loss of Mary's perpetual dowager's pension from France by paying it himself: some twenty-four thousand pounds. If he would agree to this, then they could return to England and I would receive them.

⤷ WILL:

What this did, in effect, was to remove Brandon from any chance of competing for power at court. The heavy fine assured that the Duke of Suffolk could not afford to live at court any longer; he and Mary had to dwell at Westhorpe Manor, in Suffolk, where the living was cheaper. Out of Henry's sight, out of Henry's mind. Or so Wolsey hoped.

⤷ HENRY VIII:

In the meantime I sported myself with Bessie. Brandon's sentence—"I have married her heartily and have lain with her, insomuch that I fear me lest she be with child"—haunted me, mocked me. He, who knew so much about women—how to woo them, win them, bed them—had secrets I did not possess. Whatever his male beauty was, it was sufficient to win a royal princess. Did I have such as that? What *was* it? I did not know, that was the maddening thing of it. It was closed to me, a power I was not sure of. And yet, did we not have the same body, the same parts? Were we not both men, and were there not only a few (far fewer than voluptuaries would admit) common things we could do with our common parts? I drove myself to explore every aspect of the flesh with Bessie, as if to capture that final, elusive thing, sensuality itself. And yet, in the end, my body gave me no further knowledge.

Afterwards, I would return to my outer chamber, where all my attendants and friends gathered. It was known that the King's outer chamber was a place to pass time, to dice and sing and gossip and compare fashions. Then I would join in, become one of them, or fancy myself so. I would order more logs for the fire and more torches, and stronger wine, and the chamber would grow warm and ruddy, as we gambled with cards, playing Primero. In the reddish glow of the firelight and the pleasant aftermath of the misuse of my private parts, I would feel myself a man among men.

Surfeited, I would retire, requesting Bessie's father as my esquire to remove my outer garments. The touch of his hands, his ministering hands, was a perverse victory for me. I savored it, in all its nasty ramifications.

My sleeps were dreamless.

※ ※

In mid-spring, Katherine gave birth to another half-formed, dead son. Al-Ashkar estimated its womb-age to be five and a half months; Linacre, six and a half. What difference? It had missed life by a long margin.

As soon as the physicians permitted, I resumed marital relations with her. That was all it was, now. A duty, a political necessity, like signing state papers in my work room. The fluids still flowed, as impersonally and promptly as the ink with which I signed the documents, *Henricus Rex*. My personhood, my essence. Onto parchment, into my Queen.

Passion—almost equally impersonal—I delivered into Bessie.

※ ※

Mary was arriving back in England, and there was to be a ceremony at Dover to greet her. I made certain I was not there; for to be there was to confer approval on her actions, and that I would never do. Brandon, the (created by me!) Duke of Suffolk, was her protector now. Let him see to her needs.

All communication between us passed through Wolsey. Brandon could not approach me without Wolsey's leave; neither could Mary. Mary I wished to see, therefore I made arrangements for us to meet in London on the royal barge. Together we would be rowed up and down upon the Thames, where we could speak one last time before I relinquished her to Brandon forever.

The woman who approached the landing-ramp was taller, more beautiful, than I remembered. She wore a cloak of deepest blue velvet, gathered about the neck and shoulders, that floated outward like the Virgin's. But she was no virgin. Her very step was changed.

The oarsmen saluted her. "Your Majesty."

I welcomed her, but said pointedly, "Queen no longer, my men. She is Duchess."

"I remain a Princess, regardless of my husband's title," she said, a smile masking her determination.

"Shall we go below?" I took her hand, leading her belowdecks, where the royal stateroom, with all appointments for our comforts, awaited—not the least of which was that we would be insulated from the ears above.

We settled ourselves on the•silken cushions: strangers.

"So you have followed your heart," I finally said, for want of anything else to say. "As you threatened to do."

"I love him!" she cried. "I love him, I love him, I have loved him since I was a child!"

The oars outside the windows made slurping noises as they dipped in and out of the water.

"Can you not see him for what he is? A womanizer, someone who knows all the tricks, all the things to win an unsophisticated heart."

"Is that so?" Her face took on a transcendent, triumphal look. "And what did he win by marrying me? Banishment from court, and from your favour."

"He won England's fairest jewel."

"And your best playing card. Who is the calculating one, Brother?"

I stood accused. Yes, I was worse than Brandon. He had seen Mary and loved her, risking my wrath and banishment from court. I had seen only the loss of a playing card. When had this happened to me? I hated myself, hated that thing I had become: ugly, base, experimenting with my own body as if it were a thing apart from myself.

But a realist. A king who was not a realist cheated his people. That was the truth of it.

A bright arc of foam, spray: the Thames was rising past us. I saw York Place on our port side. Wolsey's residence had gaily fluttering banners planted by the water-stairs, inviting dignitaries to stop and tie up.

"Are you with child?" I asked abruptly.

"Yes." Her voice changed. "It must have happened the first time. When he came to me in that little room in Cluny, where I was a prisoner."

Spare me the recounting, I do not wish to hear it; no, it isn't the *hearing* of it, it is the *imagining* of it, and I cannot stop that. . . . *Jesu, deliver me, torture me not.* . . . I cannot bear the torture of trying to imagine what it is beyond my scope to imagine, and what I long for above all else. The door that cannot open for me.

"I wish you joy." I took her hands. "I wish one of us Tudors joy. Just one, so I can feel that one escaped. We are not a happy family, by and large."

Mother. Arthur. Margaret. And now, added to them, myself, Henry VIII of England, childless.

"Life as a whole is not happy. Only moments. This is my moment. It will pass."

So I could no longer begrudge it to her.

"Yours will come," she said.

She was kind, and loved me, but she did not understand. "Aye." I nodded.

"And will pass, as mine."

"Forget the passing!" I cried, exasperated. "If you think on the passing, you kill the living thing! Stop it, I command you!"

She laughed. "As King?"

"As King."

"You cannot command what cannot be controlled," she replied. "Know you not that?"

Now we were level with Blackfriars, the great, sprawling monastery of the Dominicans. Soon London Bridge, with its nineteen supports, would loom, and we would have to shoot the rapidly swirling white water.

"No. I try always to command, and to control. It is my duty."

"Poor Henry." She laughed, and then it came: the tremendous shaking of the barge, as the water took it over, possessed it, curled it down between the legs of the bridge. In spite of the tightly fitted door, rivulets seeped in around the frame, trickling down the carpeted stairs.

Then, all at once, it was calm. Eerily so. We were on the part of the river below the Bridge, where the Thames suddenly becomes a cheerful public river. Wherries and rowboats plied the water, taverns and docks and shipyards lined the north bank. Rising in back, grimly, was the white rectangular thrust of the Tower.

Greenwich Palace spread itself out on the south bank, with gulls circling overhead. It was a sea-palace, one that seemed to be linked to foreign places and tides rather than to London.

We were almost there. I could see the landing pier, and the waterman at the ready to greet us and tie up the barge.

"Mary, this Francis," I suddenly said, "what is he like?"

"A devil," she said. "With a smiling face and a long snout. 'Le Roi Grand Nez,' they call him."

"How tall is he? Is he as tall as I?"

"Yes. About your height."

Unlikely. I was unusually tall.

"And does he . . . what are his legs like?" I meant what is his *body* like, is it strong and muscular, weak and weedy, fat and soft? Is it as good as mine?

"I did not avail myself of it," she said.

"But surely you could tell—"

"Jewelled raiment and well-tailored clothes disguise bodily defects," she said. "That is what they are designed to do."

They were throwing out the landing ropes. There was not time for an answer, an honest answer.

"Was he a man?" I cried.

She looked puzzled.

The barge bumped against the padded piles. We were there.

"All men are men," she answered. "More or less."

XXV

With the departure of the Duke and Duchess of Suffolk came the arrival of Wolsey's cardinal's hat. The hat, conferred by Leo X, along with a blessed golden rose for me for my fidelity and orthodoxy, arrived at Dover, encased in a regal box. Wolsey arranged that it be conveyed to London with all proper reverence, there to be welcomed by the Abbot of Westminster Abbey. Afterward it was placed upon the high altar of St. Paul's, and then, in a drama designed to dazzle the eye, it was placed upon Wolsey's head, creating a scarlet presence against the ancient grey stones. The chanting of the choristers framed the moment in divine approbation.

"You see what a serpent you have nurtured in your bosom," muttered Katherine, standing stiffly beside me. "He glistens and gleams like the very creature in the Garden of Eden."

A splendid metaphor. Wolsey's satin indeed gleamed by the fluttering candlelight. But he was too plump to pass for a serpent. I said as much, while the chanting covered my low voice.

"A demon, then," said Katherine. "Although Satan himself is sleek, some of his lesser demons must be gluttonous, just as their counterparts on earth."

"Ah, Katherine." She hated Wolsey with such an unreasoning hate, held him responsible for all the changes in me, when in fact he merely facilitated them; they originated within myself.

"How long will you wait before appointing him Lord Chancellor? Will it be a Christmas gift?"

Damn her for her insight! In truth, I had planned a December ceremony, separating the cardinalship from the chancellorship by a decent interval of two months. Archbishop Warham was old and ready to retire. But more to the point, I no longer listened to him on political affairs or considered any of his opinions, so he was useless in his office.

"It is no gift. He has earned it."

Katherine did not reply, merely gave me a withering look of disdain. I did not care to argue. I was keeping my promise to myself, never to fight or hurt or upset her again. Her new pregnancy must be undisturbed, even if it meant coddling and cossetting the bitter and illogically resentful vessel it rested within.

My new Lord Chancellor and I had much to discuss, in February of 1516. The Christmas festivities were over and done with. Archbishop Warham had gracefully surrendered his office and retired to Canterbury to concentrate on his spiritual duties, and Wolsey had assumed the mantle of the highest political office in the realm, along with the highest ecclesiastical rank, as England's only Cardinal.

Did he ever regret the lost Joan Lark and his sons? Or had the sacrifice been well worth it? It had taken only three years to go from the Lark's Morning Inn to this, once the decision had been made. Tactfully, he never referred to it. He was a man of the present. The Welsh longing for unnamable things was not a part of his makeup. I envied him that.

"King Francis has proved himself," he said bluntly, that raw February morning as we settled ourselves before his gigantic Italian work desk.

I knew what he meant. He meant that Queen Claude was pregnant. Francis had proved himself alarmingly, then, both as a warrior and as a getter of children. Within only a few months of his accession, he had taken the field, leading his troops into battle at Marignano in Italy, winning a stunning victory against the Papal forces. Francis meant for northern Italy to become French, and he was well on his way to achieving it.

"Perhaps it will die." I cursed it, then.

"Nothing Francis does seems to die, or not thrive. Truly, he seems to have extraordinary luck on his side." Wolsey was annoyed by this. One could counter stratagems, not luck.

"And all anyone talks of is his wretched court! His styles, his *ballet de cour*, his plans to build *châteaux*."

"A novelty, Your Majesty." Wolsey sniffed daintily at the silver pomander he had affected carrying. "He is the newest king in Europe. 'Twill pass."

"Ah, but he is *not* the newest King!" I produced the telling letter that had arrived only that morning, and handed it to Wolsey.

His eyes attacked it. "Ferdinand is dead." He crossed himself, by rote. "Charles of Burgundy is King of Spain."

"Yes. A sixteen-year-old Habsburg is now the newest—and youngest—King in Europe."

"And that makes you the old fox among them." Wolsey smiled. "We're well rid of Ferdinand. He was useless to us; useless to everyone, in fact. A new king in Spain, a boy-king . . . what possibilities this offers!"

"For manipulation?"

"How well we understand one another."

"That is why you are where you are." And let him understand that it was I who had put him there, not he himself. Without me, he could do nothing, was nothing. "Not all boy-kings can be manipulated. Age is not necessarily a measure of innocence."

"I understand this one is unworldly, peculiar."

"The truth is that he is unknown. As I myself was when first I came to the throne."

"We will make it our business to know his nature, gather information. I have several connections in the Burgundian court, reliable witnesses . . . if paid enough."

In retrospect I cannot help but laugh at Wolsey's primitive methods of spying; at the time they passed for sophisticated. The genius of Cromwell had not yet applied itself to this art.

He continued, "And then there's the Queen. She can make contact with her nephew, and from his replies we can get a sense of—"

"No!" I cried. "Katherine must not be told of her father's death!"

"But it is a fact; it will be known everywhere by tomorrow."

"By tomorrow I will have her immured in her lying-in chamber, sealed off from all contact with court, as custom decrees. She is too near her birthing date. I will not, will *not* have her distressed at this time! Ferdinand will not cost me this child—as he cost me my wife's loyalty and affection! Let him rot, and spare my child!"

Wolsey rose, his robes shimmering. Crimson satin is a passing beautiful fabric. "Your Majesty, this is the Queen's . . . ?" The question was delicate.

"Sixth pregnancy," I cried, my voice rising. "But so near the end now, and she has been well content, and healthy. Pray for me, Wolsey! Do not question me, as a political creature, but pray for me, as a Cardinal!" Or have you quite forgotten how, I wondered. Did Wolsey ever pray? *Had* he ever prayed? Or had he never had a priestly vocation at all, only a burning ambition that drove him to use whatever means were at hand?

"Pray for me, for my child!" I swept all his work papers off the polished surface of his inlaid desk. "That is your business, your only business!"

Katherine was brought to bed on February eighteenth, 1516, and after a short labour, she was delivered of a fair daughter.

I held both of them, flooded with happiness. "We'll name her Mary," I said. After my sister, I thought. May she be as lovely and loved as my sister Mary Tudor Brandon.

"After the Virgin," whispered Katherine.

Outside the chamber doors, all the court awaited the news. I threw open both tall doors, stood, legs apart, in the doorway.

"We have a fair Princess!" I cried. "And if it is a girl this time—why, by the grace of God, boys will follow!"

Our cries of joy reverberated up to the gilded ceiling.

Then the Venetian ambassador, Giustinian, shuffled forward, a sad expression on his face.

"I am sorry, Your Grace, that after all your previous losses, this should be a girl." He looked downcast. "Perhaps God does not intend you to have a male heir," he whispered close to my ear.

The fool! "Am I not a man like others?" I cried.

He seemed not to have heard me. "Am I not a man like others?" I screamed, right in front of the courtiers. I seemed unable to stop myself.

WILL:

Aye, that was the question that haunted Henry: Am I not a man like others? Years later, George Boleyn virtually condemned himself to death at his trial by reading a statement to the effect that he and his sister Anne had laughed at Henry's lack of vigour and manhood. "He hath neither potency nor manhood in him," I believe the words were. Of course that was twenty years after Henry's outburst at Giustinian, but I believe he was always unsure of himself in this regard.

And why not? His first bride ultimately preferred her beads and confessor. His second mocked his potency and cuckolded him with his courtiers. His third soothed him, but soon died. His fourth was so distasteful to him he could not perform—but nonetheless it was humiliating to have to obtain a public annulment on the basis of nonconsummation. The fifth cuckolded him in grand style and held him up to public ridicule. The sixth—he was too ill to use her services for anything beyond nursing, and even she was reported to have said, in response to his proposal, "Sire, it were better to be your mistress than your wife!"

Behold the much-married monarch: he rises up early in the morning. But what of lying down late at night? *Was* he a "man like others," or no?

Certainly in his youth he was lusty. Bessie Blount and Mary Boleyn (begging your pardon, my dear Catherine) could attest to that.

But alas, we cannot ask these damsels, and there are in fact no living witnesses to Harry's potency . . . or lack of it.

The entire subject was one that caused much perturbation, that much we can ascertain. A curious fact: he had more wives than mistresses.

I mention this only because the King is so popularly assumed to have been a satyr. The idea of having six wives titillates the average man. He thinks only of the bed-sport of marriage, never of its inevitable dismal consequences: boredom, bickering, disillusionment, legal entanglements. That is why most kings take mistresses: certainly it is easier and less taxing. But Harry's conscience would not permit him to practise the customary *droit de signeur,* except under exceptional circumstances.

XXVI

HENRY VIII:

Katherine and I were happy together in this child. She brought us to share, once again, all that we had once held in common: our love of music, of scholarship, of quiet camaraderie. The little Princess Mary was precocious and took early delight in the world about her. It was a gladsome thing to find the proper tutor for her, select musical instruments suitable for her, rejoice in her first steps and happy laughter. For she was a bright and winsome child, who never cried. As parents, Katherine and I were at peace with one another.

During the next year she became pregnant again, but had an early miscarriage, even though we took no progress about the home shires that summer, as a precaution.

Wolsey and I had more than enough to occupy us politically, with the struttings and aggressive posturings of Francis upon the Continental stage, and the gentle transfer of power in Spain to young Charles, who remained an enigma—an enigma carefully guarded and schooled by his grandfather, Maximilian. Across the Mediterranean, an arrogant and brilliant new Sultan of Turkey, Suleiman, had begun his reign by conquering all the surrounding territory with terrifying ease. The Papal lands, lying midway between both Francis's and Suleiman's ambitious paths, were presided over by an increasingly jittery and threatened Pope Leo.

It was Wolsey who (I must admit it, must credit his statesmanship here, for it was as a statesman that he found his greatness) proposed that England sponsor a Treaty of Universal Peace, in which all Christians would unite as brothers to fight the Infidel and bar Europe to Turkish military designs.

This treaty, of course, would be signed in London, under my auspices, with Wolsey himself acting as Papal legate.

The proposal was eagerly accepted by Pope Leo, and, using the bait of Tournai, we enticed the French into coming to England to sign the treaty. Not only would we unite in peace, but we would plan and execute a mighty Crusade against the Turk.

The world stood still while the legates, ambassadors, lords, and prelates of all Christendom—England, France, the Empire, the Papacy, Spain, Denmark, Scotland, Portugal, Hungary, the Italian states, the Swiss Confederation, and the Hanseatic towns—gathered in London and signed the treaty. Before the High Altar of St. Paul's, a Pontifical Mass was celebrated by Wolsey, and a general peace within Christendom was proclaimed. Cardinal Wolsey, Lord Chancellor of England, Papal legate, was recognized as "the Architect of Universal Peace." His face shone with triumphant glory.

There were a few private matters to be worked out between England and France. One concerned Tournai. My plans to retain it as a part of England had not fared well. It had proved a dreadful expense, and the attempts to convert its inhabitants from their French perverseness had met with utter failure. I agreed to sell Tournai back to France for six hundred thousand crowns—less than it had taken me to capture and garrison it, but I never begrudge money spent on an idea that seems promising at the time.

The other concerned Francis and myself. Evidently the French King had as burning a curiosity to behold me as I had to behold him. It was a curiosity that we agreed to satisfy. We would meet, with our full courts in attendance, at a place called the Valley of Gold, near Calais, the following summer.

As the last of the diplomats took leave and the ships plied their way across the Channel in the strengthening autumn gales, I was faced with a personal dilemma of a most delicate nature.

Bessie was pregnant.

She had waited until after the treaties were concluded to tell me. I had not seen her throughout the festivities; I had decorously kept Katherine by my side, as good taste, protocol, and respect demanded. There had been no lying with Katherine, however, as she had just begun another pregnancy.

I had looked forward to enjoying Bessie and her incomparable favours again; had found myself thinking on them during the long and tedious banquet that Wolsey gave at York Place, described by flattering chroniclers as "surpassing anything given by either Cleopatra or Caligula," when in truth the spirit of those two lusty goats was to be found within my head, not at Wolsey's table.

How Bessie and I used one another, in fantasy, while the Venetian ambassador droned on in my ear about Adriatic trade routes!

And now, as I was in the very act of reaching for her, my pre-formed desire in the ascendant—

"Your Majesty, I am with child." How calmly those four shattering words came from her lips.

I dropped her arm.

"Yes," she said. "It will be in June."

Seven months. She waited expectantly (in both senses of the word), waited to hear my happy words. *How wonderful. I will make you Duchess of X. What joy. Ask for anything, it shall be yours. You must have your own estates, honours, be recognized as* Maitresse en Titre, *my love, my desire, my pretty one.*

"You must leave court," I said.

"Yes." And?

"I will—I will find you a place to go. Nearby, so I can watch over you until the child is born. Perhaps a priory in Essex."

Her face changed. "But—"

"You must leave the Queen's service immediately. It would be a scandal for you to continue as her maid of honour. It would dishonour all three of us."

"And my father?" she cried. "Surely he should leave your service as well? Does it not dishonour *him* to continue to minister to a—a man who has seduced his daughter?"

"So now you turn sanctimonious? This was not your tune in the beginning. Oh, no, then you dismissed my qualms as overscrupulous, old-fashioned."

"I have honour, too! It is not only you and the Queen who are entitled to it! I have honour, and my father has honour, and now to be treated so lightly—"

How tedious this was, how unpleasant. Why did all pleasure have this rancid aftertaste?

"Come now, Bessie. It was sport, we agreed it was, we've enjoyed one another, but now it is time to observe the proprieties, lest we cause a scandal, and thereby harm ourselves. And the child."

"I loved you! I loved you, and now you treat me as a burden, a problem to be solved."

There it was, the dreaded word: *love.* I did not want to be loved; that was the burden. Unwanted love was the greatest burden of all.

"It is not you that is the burden . . ." I began, but it was too difficult and complicated to explain, and in the end I could not say the only words she truly wished to hear, anyway.

"And after the child comes, what then?"

"Wolsey will find you a husband. Never fear, you will be well married."

"Wolsey!"

"So you see, you will not have been 'dishonoured.' You will be as marriageable as if you had remained chaste the entire time at court."

"You let Wolsey attend to even this . . . personal thing?"

"It is not personal, Bessie."

That was the tragedy of it for her, and the embarrassment of it for me.

There could be no resistance on her part. I would give orders, and in the morning she would be gone.

That night, as I lay alone in bed, I wondered, in horror and fear of what lay within me, why I felt nothing for her. For three years we had joined our bodies, laughed, sung, and exchanged affectionate words. Yet her actions had been real, and mine, evidently, had not.

Toward midnight I fell into a restless sleep. I dreamed that I was passing through a field of poppies in which each flower, if one looked deep within its red center, had a woman's face. The faces were different, yet all the flowers were alike. If I gathered them to make a bouquet, they soon drooped in the silver vases into which I put them, and always withered up during the night. Their scent was beguiling but not addicting. This puzzled me because Arabs used poppy seeds for medicine, which was said to be strongly addicting.

The morning sun dispelled the shreds of this strange dream, but the coming day felt stale already.

XXVII

Katherine wished for our child to be born at Greenwich. Mary had been born there, and Katherine wanted the same chamber, the same attendants, the same everything. A good Christian is not supposed to be superstitious, but I overlooked Katherine's "failing," if it can be called that, because I shared it. I would propitiate anything, because I knew not from which quarter the hostility came.

"I was born here," I told little Mary, as we passed a late April morning walking about the palace gardens. She and I were in front of Katherine, who needed the pathway entirely to herself, so bulky was she. And not just because of the infant. She herself had become very bulky.

Mary looked up at me. She loved hearing my voice; I could tell. "Yes, I was born here, and *you* were born here. Your mother and I were married here! It is a special place."

Overhead the skies were piercingly blue, and I could smell the coming spring in the air: a peculiar sort of blending of sweetness and death. We walked near the water-wall, where the Thames caressed the stones.

Mary pointed up at the gulls. "Birds!"

How well she spoke! How alert she was!

"Yes, sea birds," I said. "You find them wherever there is great water." I looked out at the boats bobbing all about, and especially at the royal wharf where my long-awaited flagship was tied up. "The water is England's greatness," I said. "It surrounds us on all sides and protects us from enemies, but at the same time it allows us to master it and make it our servant. With ships to ride it, as people ride horses, we shall go far."

Mary pointed at *Henri, Grace à Dieu.* "Go see."

"No." Katherine shook her head.

"Let the child indulge herself," I said.

"You mean, let yourself." Yet she was amenable.

I showed our daughter about the great ship, nicknamed *Great Harry.*

Every odour of her planks, every creak of the ropes made something within me sing. I longed to be away, gone, upon open seas. . . .

Mary began fingering the captain's knot-cords. "Those are to measure how fast a ship is moving," I said, opening her fat little fists and making her drop the rope. "But we mustn't mess them."

She began to whine, then to cry. Katherine, waiting upon the docks, looked up. Through a mother's ears, she had heard Mary's faraway cries.

She took the child in hand as we alighted off the gangplank, and forced her to walk obediently along the water-wall separating the palace grounds from the marshy area surrounding it and from the river itself—for Greenwich was a sea-palace, but protected from the ravages of water.

Katherine went to her lying-in chamber in early May, and Mary and I accompanied her with great excitement. I had never imagined how the presence of a child altered all events. What had been a state matter, a public ceremony in the past, now became a part of our family history.

As Katherine took her leave, and the great doors were closed behind her, Mary insisted on giving them a final pat with her hands. Then she put out her hand to me.

"Go pray," she said.

Had Katherine whispered that right before she went in? Or did it arise from Mary's own heart?

"Very well. We shall pray in the best possible place."

I took her to the Church of the Observant Friars, the little chapel of that order where Katherine and I had been married, right next to Greenwich Palace.

I had never been there unceremoniously, and there is a vast difference. This time I came as a private man, with no retinue. The darkness was the first thing I noticed. Without a ceremony of high importance, the interior of the chapel was not lit, and even at midday it was swathed in gloom, except for the glowing windows.

Mary stopped her babbling and stood stock-still in the middle aisle. The magical light had caught her and rendered her silent and awed, as it was meant to.

I took her hand and found not resistance, but ease and cooperation. We knelt side by side facing the reserved Host and the altar. I expected Mary to wiggle, complain, wish to run away. Instead she was rigid with delight and obedience. We prayed together for Katherine's safe deliverance and the gift of an heir. Then Mary slipped away, and I continued my private prayers, begging for a son. The fragmented red and blue light, created from coloured glass but reassembled to form a transcendent whole, seemed to pulsate within the chapel. I had not seen this sort of light even on my wedding day; the artificial brightness of torches and candles had obscured it.

I expected to find Mary fast asleep under a prie-dieu, or playing alone quietly. Instead I found her on her knees, on the worn stones before St. Anne's statue, staring straight ahead with a wide-eyed, fixed stare.

Katherine stayed in her lying-in chamber for the full length of days. This was to be a full-term pregnancy, then. That in itself was a good sign. Of her eight pregnancies, only three others had reached full term. And these past months had been happy ones for her. There had been no health problems, no dropsy, no racing heart, no swollen hands and feet. There had been no discord between us. Ferdinand's death had rendered her mine entirely, and in her heart of hearts, she was glad of it. Or so I believed.

Her labour began exactly on the day predicted. It was a fair, sunny June day, much like the one (so they said) when I was born. All proceeded as it should, and the regular reports issued by the physicians were encouraging. *The Queen is bearing her pains well. . . . The Queen is entering her hard time. . . . The Queen feels that delivery is near. . . .*

Then silence. No physician came to the doors of the chamber. No cries, either of mother or infant. Only an elapse of time, as the long summer day drew to its close. The sun set; twilight began, with its blue-grey haze settling over the river and the palace grounds.

Then, a piercing cry that penetrated all the doors. Katherine's cry.

Still, no announcement, no opening of the outer doors to the chamber. I must enter, even though it was forbidden. I took the door handle in my hand, only to find it being opened from the other side. I shot into the room.

Linacre awaited me. His face told me nothing. It was as bland as old snow in February.

I was relieved. It meant Katherine lived; for if she did not, he would hardly have looked so blank.

"Your Majesty." He gestured. "The Queen wishes you to be with her."

I followed him down the connecting suite of rooms (all muffled with hangings, to keep toxic airs out, and therefore black and stuffy) to the last, darkest one of all: the birth chamber.

Katherine lay in the great bed, her attendants sponging her and combing out her sweat-soaked hair. Physicians were still scurrying about, clicking instruments and gathering bowls and blood-drenched linens. It was as busy as a banquet in there.

"Henry." Katherine gestured to me. I came and took her hand. It was so limp, damp, and hot it felt like a wadded washcloth.

"What has happened?" I had to know. Whatever it was, I had to know. Katherine lived; at least I could be sure of that.

"Dead." There was no need for more than that. The one word said everything.

"A son?"

She shook her head. "A daughter."

Then that was not quite so bad, not an unequivocal sign.

"I am grieved." But relieved. The heavens were yet ambiguous. A clear sign was what I dreaded above all. "May I see her?"

Katherine tried to stop me, but I did not heed her feebly gesturing hands as I turned to the little bundle lying at the foot of the bed, its face covered, denoting death.

Gently I pulled the blanket aside, just to see her face once, to make her mine, before consigning her to the earth forever.

It was no human face that I uncovered, but that of a monster. It had but a single eye; no nose, just a gaping great hole; and mushroomlike, puffy lips, over a mouth with teeth.

"Jesu!" I recoiled.

Katherine reached out for me, clutching. So that was why she had screamed upon first beholding it.

"What have you brought forth?" I am ashamed that those were my words to her, as if the monster were her handiwork.

She closed her eyes. "It is not I. I knew not what I harboured."

"I know. Forgive me." When I remembered all the times we had looked fondly at the swelling of her belly . . . while inside, this horror had been taking shape. "I spoke in sorrow, and stupidly." I looked at the lump. "Thank God it is out of you, and born dead." It must be buried somewhere away from consecrated ground. Deep in the earth, where it could decay and never rise.

I motioned to William Butts, Linacre's young assistant physician. "Call for a priest." I wanted only a priest to handle the thing. Butts nodded, then started to pick up the bundle.

"Stop!" I cried. "Do not touch it!" Let it lie there on the bedcovers, which afterward must be burnt. And instead of a churching ceremony, Katherine and I must be ritually cleansed and blessed.

The priest came and, after muttering a few words, gingerly picked up the dead deformity and put it in a sack. He would know what to do with it. I did not presume to tell him; nor did I want to know where it would lie.

I insisted that a second priest come in to bless and purify Katherine and myself immediately. He did so, whilst the bed was being stripped of its contaminated coverings, and I had to hold Katherine in my arms. But I dared not issue forth from the chamber until it was done. I was trembling with fear—revulsion—premonition.

I carried the limp Katherine all the way through the long wing of the palace to her own apartments, where fresh bleached linens would be laid upon her own bed, where windows were open and healthy summer air could enter. Out of that fetid chamber of contagion and death, and into the daylight of normalcy. She did not protest, merely let me carry her, like a sleepy child past its bedtime.

As I was leaving her quarters, one of the novices from the Priory of St. Lawrence was waiting for me in the guard room. His gentle eyes above his black-hooded robe searched mine.

"The Prior sent me to tell you . . . Mistress Blount is brought to bed. Her delivery is imminent." He waited, not knowing how I would receive the news.

"Then I must come." Like a man in a dream, I heard myself speaking. It had all taken on the features of a dream now. I was being tested, and I no longer knew what God required of me. But I knew that I must see all that was ordained for me to see. I must be at Bessie's side, even if something worse awaited me there. The human requirement was that I bear it with Bessie.

"Lead me," I said.

The young novice—his name was Richard, he told me—and I crossed the Thames directly from Greenwich to the Tower. There I got us fresh horses from the royal stables, and from thence we would ride through the night to the Priory, which lay some thirty miles outside London.

First we had to make our way through the city, sleeping now in the bluish midsummer darkness. Did anyone now follow those ancient midsummer rituals used for foretelling the future? Make a cake, scatter certain flowers about the bed, then walk backwards in silence. . . . The houses seemed quiet. The people therein—my charges—rested secure. O God, if only I could provide them with the one security they needed above all—an undisputed heir to the Throne.

We passed out through the Bishopsgate of the city walls, and directly into the countryside. It was still in that darkest time of night, even at midsummer. I could not see what lay before me. Only Richard, motioning me on, guided me. He knew this road well. It was well worn between the Priory of St. Lawrence and the house of Wolsey, its protector and patron.

Dawn came up early in the eastern skies to our right as we rode. I had tried, all the way and in silence, to banish the picture in my mind of the malevolent child my true wife had borne me. The darkness could not lend itself to this. I could bear to think about it in daylight, no other time. The curse was buried now, safely.

Up came the sun. The countryside about us was fresh. The sun licked all the growing furrows of the fields, encouraging them as children. The intense greenness seemed a promise of explosion into fertility and, beyond that, ripeness. A green goddess presided over these fields.

"Here." Novice Richard reined in his horse and pointed straight into the rising sun.

For a moment I saw nothing. Then the honey-coloured stones took shape before my eyes, growing into a large building.

We galloped along the pathway, blinded by the rising red-gold sun.

At the great gatehouse, a fat monk blinked once as he beheld, then recognized me.

"Your Majesty." He gathered his robes and scurried down to the entrance, where he did obeisance. "The Lady is in the Prior's residence."

The Lady: a euphemistic way of denoting Bessie.

Silently, Richard pointed toward a small house. It stood apart from the rest of the monastery, not attached in any way.

"I thank you," I said. I liked Richard. He seemed to have sensitivity and human love—as distinct from the divine sort, which often does not understand. I dug into my purse to reward him for his twelve hours' journey. He stopped me.

"Pray—make a gift to Our Lady in my name," he said, his eyes boring into mine.

Our Lady. The Lady. The very word was alive with devotion and emotion.

"If you prefer," I said.

I made my way into the Prior's lodging, where Bessie was. Wolsey had made all these arrangements. It was he who had selected this particular priory over any other. I presumed that he had had his reasons. For what characteristics would one select a priory? Worldliness, charity, comfort, anonymity?

The Prior embodied all four. Once again my mind applauded Wolsey, whilst my soul condemned him as a blot on the priesthood.

The Prior, alerted to our arrival, was all attentiveness and discretion.

He was young. That surprised me. His name was Father Bernard (after Saint Bernard of Clairvaux?). He bowed and said, "When Mistress Blount came to us—sent by Cardinal Wolsey, who has a charitable nature and a kind heart—we decided to lodge her as a noble guest in our own quarters. For who, indeed, can judge another? The innkeeper in Bethlehem showed us the way: that all visitors are Divine Guests."

His flattery choked me, and my heart was broken besides.

"Where is she?" was all I could ask.

"In the apartments above," he said, gesturing. "Above my own," he added.

I mounted the stone steps in the ancient quarters. There were carpets on the stairs, and I noticed that only the finest beeswax candles were mounted in the sconces. Unlit, and new: that meant they discarded the half-burnt ends, never using them. But once on the landing above, I forgot all these things, as a novice came forward at once, anxiously.

"Your Majesty!" He fell to his knees.

"Up, up." I gestured. "The Lady?" I might as well use the euphemism, as all the rest did.

"Into her labour. But not at the end yet, Sire, as it is the first."

Yes, the first always took longer.

The novice removed himself; a hovering priest took charge.

"The midwives and infirmarians are with her," he said. His very words made me sure that they disapproved. "They think it will be soon."

Very well. I turned my back, indicating that he should depart from me. I looked out over the grounds of St. Lawrence's, delighting in the order, the simplicity, the production. That was what I longed for in my realm.

I thought of going to the church, which I could see blocked out before me, a great grey building. But I was afraid of missing the end of Bessie's time, and also . . . I was too confused, I cannot write it clearly. But I felt that even cleansed as I was, it was presumptuous to visit the altar of the Lord. . . .

"Your Majesty!" A young novice came to the chamber doors. "Mistress Blount has a fair son!"

A son.

"She calls for you." He smiled. No condemnation there. (Was he too young? Too close to the source of temptation?)

"I come."

I followed the young man through the doors of the waiting room, through the Prior's receiving room, and into the inner guest chamber. I noted, even in my distracted state, that it was lavishly appointed.

A midwife, accompanied by a nurse, came toward me, like a priest elevating a Host.

"Your son," they said, almost in unison. They presented a bundle to me. I peered into it.

It was *his* face. Prince Henry's. Exactly the same.

Jesu! I wanted to cross myself. The dead child brought back to life again, in another child, one who could never inherit the throne—whilst the child of the Queen was born a thing accursed.

"Henry," I murmured, in recognition.

"Henry!" they cried, all the onlookers.

The wrapped bundle felt as heavy and vigorous as the other one. God had returned him to me. But not by Katherine.

Now I shook. I could not think on it. I knew not what it meant.

The midwife indicated that I should follow her. "In this chamber, Your Majesty, she awaits." How delicately she phrased it.

I passed through an adjoining room to find Bessie all bathed, perfumed, coiffed, and awaiting my attendance. Curiously, I did not find her beautiful, but false. Women after childbirth should not resemble perfumed courtesans.

"Bessie," I said, coming to her side. The morning light was streaming in through windows on the right side of the room. Motes danced in the sunlight. The casements were cranked wide open, and the mixed, heady smell of the infirmarians' herb garden below was rolling into the chamber. I fancied that the odour made me drowsy. For I was suddenly and overwhelmingly sleepy.

"We have a son," she said.

"Yes. We have a son. I have seen him." My head was swirling, muddled. "He is . . . perfect." Such a stupid word. Such a word that said everything.

"He looks like you." She smiled, touched my hand. All that filthy passion, made beautiful in an infant. God's grace? I knew not. My head spun.

"We will name him Henry," I said.

"And for his surname?" she gently nudged.

"Fitzroy. A traditional way of saying 'son of a King.'" She smiled. "For this has happened before." She stopped smiling.

The infant had been bathed, swathed, and put in his cradle. I stood looking over him for a long while. His resemblance to my lost Prince Henry was unsettling.

My wife had had a monster. My mistress had had a healthy son.

Clearly, God was giving me a message. One too blatant for even me to ignore.

I spent the remainder of the long summer's day at the Priory. Bessie fell asleep, sleeping the sleep of the young and healthy, undisturbed by conscience, worn out by natural physicality.

The Priory was a neat little community. It nestled in the slightly rolling foothills of Essex, which looked like green knolls. Everything seemed ordered and elevated into more than the everyday. I walked through the stables, the kitchen garden of herbs, the greater vegetable garden. Everything was kept in the most transcendent order, as though the Lord might appear at any moment and call for a stewardship account. In polishing the hinges of the gate between the herb garden and the kitchen, an unknown brother was welcoming God Himself, for who knew when He might come?

Yet, at the same time, the Prior's quarters were meant to exude luxury.

The Prior would claim it was to honour the Priory. Yet would it honour Christ? Would Christ have a bed of down, in case visitors stopped by? Yet He would surely welcome visitors. And we are commanded to make ready for them. Did He require of us a bed of down, or a bed of straw?

Henry Fitzroy was christened in the chapel of the Priory—a dainty thing with stone carvings resembling lace—with Bessie and me in attendance. Wolsey was godfather, and Bessie's sister Katherine and a nun from the nearby convent of Chelmsford acted as godmothers. His christening robe was a Blount one, fashioned and embroidered by a woman on the ancestral Lincolnshire lands. They would make a family legend of Henry Fitzroy. Good for them, as I could offer him little. It was good they could offer him much.

I stood next to Bessie and held her close.

"We have a son," I said, "that will bind us forever."

"Not as I wish, with our hearts. Oh, Henry, I—"

I stopped her. As I could not give her my heart, I did not wish to receive hers. It was not a thing I could keep in trust.

"Bessie, you have had my best."

I touched her hair—her marvellous, rich hair.

I had spoken truth. She had had my best, and it was a sad, unstraight thing, my best. Yet we had a son.

XXVIII

Wolsey and I sat in a private room at York Place. Although it was July, and the sounds of summer on the Thames could be heard through his open windows (and the smells be smelled), Wolsey made no concession to the season. His crimson satin was garnet-coloured in places where the sweat had soaked through, but only his use of a Spanish fan gave any indication that he felt warm. It was a huge one, used in Spanish dancing, which Katherine had once given him, to pretend that she liked him.

"Francis has lost," he said. "The money was not enough." He indicated the letter containing this news.

"Good." Every gold piece out of Francis's treasury gladdened me. "He was a fool to spend it so." Maximilian had died, leaving the office of Holy Roman Emperor open. Francis had tried to buy the votes of the German electors, but had been outbid by Charles. Now Charles was Holy Roman Emperor as well as King of Spain. It was no surprise to anyone except Francis.

"The Habsburg boy has one foot planted in Spain and the other in Germany," murmured Wolsey.

"That positions him to piss all over France." I laughed at my schoolboy humour.

Wolsey smiled indulgently. "Yes."

"What is this business about the mad monk?" I suddenly asked, catching Wolsey off guard. I enjoyed doing that, for reasons I do not care to explore.

"The German? Luther?"

"Yes, that's the one. I would like to read his 'Ninety-five Theses,' the ones he nailed up on the Wittenberg church doors. Obtain a copy for me. You know I enjoy theology." More than Wolsey himself, I daresay.

"Yes, Your Majesty. He has caused quite a stir in Germany. The Church there was—well, quite corrupt. And Pope Leo—really, it was stupid of him to try to raise money for that new basilica of his by selling indulgences. I know, it seemed easy at the time, but it was too visible. Especially since the whole project of a new St. Peter's was questionable. Many sincere people don't see a need for it at all. It was all Pope Julius's idea to begin with. And then Julius died and left Leo stuck with the mess!"

"Inconsiderate. The only way out is for Leo to die. But the Church *does* need reforming. . . ." Against my will, I let myself think back on the Priory of St. Lawrence, with its fat, worldly, and mannered monks. Not a Luther among them. No tortured souls there. "And that Priory of St. Lawrence which you sponsor is a case in point."

He fanned himself rapidly, and the perfumed wood scented the air. "Was it not satisfactory? Was it unclean? Were the accommodations not comfortable?" he asked in alarm.

"Indeed they were. But they smacked more of Herod's palace than of the inn of Bethlehem."

"I plan to close it soon," he said hastily. "And use the income to found the college I had planned, at Oxford."

"Oh, yes. 'Cardinal's College.' So the rich monks will give way to poor scholars. Good. And as for . . . Mistress Blount? Have you . . . ?" I let the question dangle.

"Married a fortnight ago. It had to be with a ward of mine, from Lincolnshire. I took my time, Your Majesty, and looked about, but I had to settle. The property was good." He shrugged apologetically.

"Who was it?"

"Gilbert Tailboys." He paused. "Son of the mad Lord Kyme."

"Lord Kyme was declared a lunatic two years ago! I remember the legal hearings!"

"Yes. Therefore the property went to his son Gilbert, even though Lord Kyme is still alive."

"Is it—the madness—what kind?"

"I don't believe it is hereditary."

But perhaps it was. In youth, Lord Kyme had seemed normal. Holy Blood, what had I sentenced Bessie to? Marriage to a man who might go insane at any moment?

"She was not easy to marry, Your Majesty. It had to be with someone whose background had some question about it."

Just as hers did. Because of me.

"Where are they now?"

"In Lincolnshire. Living in Skelyngthorpe Castle there, on the borders of the great forest of Kyme."

Stuck away in the northern wilds, with only an incipient madman for a companion.

Bessie, forgive me.

No, she could never forgive me. *I* would not, had someone wronged me so.

"Where is my son?"

Again, the uncomfortable admission of things gone awry. "With his mother."

"But—" I had given orders that he be maintained by Wolsey as his ward.

"She begged for him, Your Majesty. So I allowed her to keep him until he is weaned. Then he shall come to me. I made her sign papers to that effect," he assured me.

"It will be impossible to retrieve him."

"Difficult, but not impossible. The advantage is that, far away from court as he'll be, no one need know of his existence—unless you decide to make it known."

"Yes." That was true. Why flaunt him in Katherine's face? His existence served no purpose other than to torment us both, whereas he might bring Bessie some little joy.

Now I wished to speak no more of this painful subject. It was closed forever.

"The meeting with Francis," I said.

Wolsey understood all my meanings. "You will scarce believe this, but yesterday a letter arrived, requesting *me* to make the arrangements for the French meeting site as well." He handed me the letter.

What a strange fellow this Francis was!

"Then do so." The whole business had begun to get out of hand. From a simple meeting between the two of us, it had ballooned into an affair whereby the entire English court would meet the entire French court. Such a thing had never been done before, in either ancient or present-day practice. My courtiers were either wildly enthusiastic about it or disdainful of the idea as a whole. No one was indifferent. Wolsey was one of the enthusiastic ones.

"I suppose since Leonardo da Vinci died, and Francis could not have his services as he'd hoped in designing the tents—" Wolsey attempted a look of modesty.

"He took the next best thing," I assured him.

For once Wolsey did not seem to suspect sarcasm. "I intend to do my best for him."

Suddenly I remembered something that gave me great pleasure: Francis had reputedly bought a substandard painting of Leonardo's just to placate him and entice him to France. Ha! Now he was out his money, out of Leonardo's services, and stuck with the dark painting of the half-smiling woman that everyone agreed was ugly.

"And I am showing my good intentions on my face," I said, fingering my new beard. Francis had proposed that neither of us shave until the meeting, as a token of good faith. I was not sure I liked myself with a beard. Certainly it changed my face.

WILL:

As it turned out, Katherine hated the beard and begged him to cut it, "for her sake." Still trying not to cross her, still half hoping for an heir, Henry succumbed and shaved the beard. This provoked a diplomatic crisis, as Francis was thereby offended, and Henry's ambassadors had to explain the circumstances. Francis's "dear mother" Louise hastened to assure them that "men's love is shown not in their beards but in their hearts," and the incident was smoothed over.

Then, belatedly, Henry started growing the beard again just prior to his departure. Thereby it was not long enough to offend Katherine, but could serve as a token of goodwill toward Francis. Such are the weighty considerations that diplomats must deal with.

HENRY VIII:

June, 1520. I stood on the castle deck of *Great Harry* in the fairest winds God ever sent mortal man. We skimmed across the Channel—nay, we *flew*. The great sails, painted to look like cloth-of-gold (*trompe-l'oeil*, the French say—oh, they have a word for everything!), billowed out and did their duty. We were bound for Calais, to undertake the great meeting between the French and English courts. It had all come about, despite the deep reservations of everyone on both sides.

Including—perhaps most of all?—Katherine, who mounted the steps up to the forecastle to stand, now, by my side. Part of me noted how slowly, how painfully she moved. Her arthritis had made stair-climbing difficult for her in the past two years. The other part of me welcomed her presence as a companion.

"Look, see! There is Calais!" I had sighted it only once before, but took an authority's pleasure in pointing it out to her.

Before us was France and the cupped, fine landing beaches of her northern coast. Behind us, equally visible, were the high white cliffs of England.

"It looks so harmless," she said.

"It *is* harmless. For the land you see is England, the Pale of Calais."

Why did even my wife, the Queen, forget that I was King of part of France?

The plans had been settled to the last detail. I, and all my company, were to land in the Pale of Calais, and thereafter, Francis and I would meet—and all our courts with us—just at the border of the two jurisdictions. Afterwards, each would entertain the other on his own land, and on his own territory. Special cities—temporary, splendid, as those can be only when permanency is not a factor—had been erected on each holding. There were papier-mâché palaces and silken-hung banqueting halls and conduits to dispense red and white wine to the onlookers.

Now we began to make for the harbour, the great, enclosed Calais harbour. I could see the very men standing upon the piers, gesturing frantically.

WILL:

All this time I was growing up. By the time Katherine's last pregnancy ended and Bessie's bastard was born, I was almost a man, ready to make my way in the world, as generations of eighteen-year-olds had done before me. My father had apprenticed me to a merchant in the Calais Wool Staple—a lucrative place, halfway between England, supplier of raw wool, and Flanders, maker of fine woollen textiles. Not that I was burningly interested in it. But the wool trade—buying and selling—suited me better than Father's messy world of dyeing and tanning, and so I fancied myself content.

I lived in Calais, a strange city, compounded of French, English, and Flemings all bent on but one thing: trade. National pride meant little beside a ducat. When the French-English *entente cordiale* was announced, the talk in the taverns was not about the prospects for peace, but about the prospects for profit. Everyone saw great profit in the coming meeting.

The King and his court must, perforce, land and lodge in Calais. That in itself was worth something, all the merchants agreed gleefully. True, they were going on to the fairy-tale palaces to be built from ground up in timber and papier-mâché; but simply building the palaces would require materials and food from the surrounding area.

Their predictions proved true. Construction on the "temporary" palace and banqueting hall began several months in advance, and employed at least two thousand workers—masons, carpenters, glaziers, painters—using local tools and eating local food.

At that time I worked six days for my master, weighing his incoming wool and tabulating his profits; but on Sundays I was free, and so I walked to the area where the "temporary" palace was abuilding. Not that it was a great walk: Guines was only five miles from Calais. (The deepest part of the Pale of Calais penetrated only twelve miles into France.)

The site was easy to find; they had moved great quantities of earth, and there were swarms of workmen about. I found one of them taking his ease under a shade tree, having a picnic lunch. I approached him.

"If there are quarters for only three people—the King, the Queen, and the Cardinal—in this thing you are building," I said, "where is the rest of the court to lodge?"

"That was a problem," he said, eager to talk. "In the end it was decided to have a city of tents. There are to be four hundred of them out in this field." He gestured toward Calais. " 'Twill be a pretty sight. With all the pennants."

"And where will you be? Will you see it?"

"I won't be allowed," he pronounced, proudly. "It isn't fitting that I be there."

"When you finish here—?"

"Then I get to work with the shovel. Moving that hill over there. Y'see, the French King and the English one must meet exactly halfway between Guines and Ardres, and at the halfway point there's a hill in the way. So we're to move it."

"What if the Kings moved instead?" I could not resist asking. I was young, remember.

"The Kings move?" He looked bewildered.

I felt a rough hand on my shoulder, and turned to see the angry face of the building master. He gave me a shove. "Stop talking to my workmen!" He suddenly moved and grabbed the other man by the shoulder. "What was he asking you? Dimensions, designs, secrets?"

"He wanted to know about the hill," the man said slowly.

"Cursed Frenchman!" The master builder looked around wildly for something to throw at me, and found a large dirt clod. He heaved it in my direction. "Go tell Francis he has no hope of bettering us! Go tell your master *that!*"

I would learn no more, and I had seen enough. So I left and continued walking in the direction of Ardres, the first town outside the Pale of Calais. From a hill nearby I watched an identical swarm of workmen building similar structures for the French King. I opened my square of cloth and took out my bread and cheese and last year's softening apple, and ate. I started to laugh at them, but somehow could not. As a child I had promised myself always to answer my own questions and to hold nothing back from myself. Are they not fools? Are they not simpletons? The French King will come, and the English King will come, and then they will go. In ten years they will not even remember the glass in the palace windows. But why should that disturb me?

Because it is wasteful, I answered myself. Because no man should be happy to serve another with no hope of recognition. Because all is temporary, and this reminder of the passing nature of things saddens me.

A blacksmith in my village, reputedly stupid, had once speculated as to why Father's mare had lost her new shoe so unexpectedly. (I had been sent to complain, as Father suspected shoddy work.) "Well now," the smith said slowly, "there's always the reason. And then there's the *real* reason."

I found many reasons for my peevishness and sense of outrage about the royal enclaves being built, but the real one was this: I wanted to be there, and there I could not be.

It would be simplistic to say that my detachment from such things began that day, but certainly I began to distance myself from that world. Everyone wants to feel special in some small way, and mine was to see myself as an aloof observer perched on a wall, watching the parade of human folly—royal and common—passing beneath me. Eventually I convinced myself that I had freely elected that stance.

The day came, in June. The King was arriving, and we must welcome him, every last resident of Calais.

I was there, upon the docks, as my master had directed me. I had dutifully helped him tidy the shop and festoon it properly with Tudor green and white, and flags, and mottoes for the royal visit. For three days street-sweepers had been busy gathering up the trash and offal from the main thoroughfares (it was hoped the King would not take it into his head to go down any others). The populace was anxious to see its King again and to see its Queen for the first time. Deep in everyone's mind was the (futile) hope that if the French and English Kings met in friendship, the peculiar status of Calais would be resolved and the contradictions of our everyday life disappear.

Henry's ship came into harbour—a huge bulwark with golden sails. We all gaped at it. A number of sailors and shoremen tied it up. Then the King himself appeared on the decks.

It was my third sighting of him. I had seen him twice before, once returning from his French wars, and before that, riding to the Tower.

He is not the same, was my first thought. The figure on deck, heavy in majesty, was not that of the boyish soldier-King I had seen on horseback seven years earlier. He was stolid in a way the other never could have been—*fixed,* as in a carved figure.

But he is thirty now, I told myself. *Thirty and almost fifteen years a king.* Time changes men. . . .

He stepped down and strode across the gangplank to the docks. He was wearing clothes that tore one's heart in envy—beautiful, costly things of gold and velvet and satin. He was robust and handsome as mortal men seldom are. I stood in awe of him, at a moment in time when I beheld human perfection—perfection that must, perforce, decay. He raised his arms, and everyone fell silent. He spoke to us, telling us of the forthcoming meeting of monarchs. It was the first time I had ever heard him speak. He had a superb voice, smooth and yet able to carry quite a distance. *What a man,* I thought.

Then Queen Katherine appeared on the decks. She was wearing so many jewels the sun glinted off them and kept her face hidden. She raised her hand and made a gesture to the onlookers. Then she turned and slowly descended the ramp to join her husband.

She was squat and old, and there was a stifled gasp from the crowd. They had expected a beautiful young Queen, someone like Henry's own sister Mary, and instead there was this . . . Spanish warship. Indeed, she did resemble a man-o'-war, with her stiff brocaded skirts and strange, boxlike headdress (standard in the Spain of her youth, some thirty years earlier) and slow, deliberate movements. One almost expected a gust of wind to puff out her skirts and blow her along.

Standing beside her husband, she did not turn toward him or acknowledge him in any way. Instead, she raised her hand in stately fashion (to which we were expected to respond by cheering) and turned her head into the sun.

Which was a mistake. The sunlight on her aged face, in combination with the ugly headdress, reduced the onlookers to silence. *She is so old,* we all thought. (Later it was reported that Francis had observed, "The King of England is young and handsome, but his wife is old and deformed"—a remark for which Henry never forgave his "dear royal brother.") But one can understand Francis's bewilderment, as we were all struck by the contrast. On the one side, Henry, handsome and bursting with physical power; on the other, a woman riddled with gout and troubles.

HENRY VIII:

Katherine and I walked through the streets to a joyous welcome. It was dusk when we set out, and the individual faces in the crowd could be seen by natural light, but by the time we ended the procession, torches had been lit.

We retired to a town house owned by a wealthy wool merchant, on loan for our royal use. We began to settle ourselves for sleep. But then Wolsey appeared. I left Katherine (doubtless she welcomed the privacy to make her personal devotions) and went downstairs to confer with the Cardinal.

He was wearing lesser ceremonial clothes—designed to impress the on-looker, but still permitting some ease of movement and comfort to the wearer. He looked fatter than usual, I thought disdainfully. At the time I was still slim-bodied and hard-muscled, and could not imagine why any man would ever let himself go to fat.

He was ebullient. Two Kings were about to step out upon the stage erected by him, to say lines conceived by him, and sign treaties written by him. Now he was most anxious for us to journey to the first stage of his elaborate set.

I am thus: when someone wishes to impress me, I am determined to remain untouched, whereas when someone clearly does not, I often find myself drawn to him.

WILL:

And you were always singularly unable to tell the difference, mistaking Anne Boleyn's feigned indifference for true. How well she perceived your true nature, and worked it to her advantage.

HENRY VIII:

"All is in readiness. The protocols, to the last raising of an eyebrow, are here." He indicated a leather pouch overflowing with papers.

"I believe I know it all by heart," I said. Just for show, I did not touch the papers or the bag. "Tomorrow I ride out, just to the border of Calais, where the hill has been moved. My court will be behind me. Francis will approach; we will meet exactly halfway, embrace, and then the precisely divided honours and festivities will begin, shifting between Guines and Ardres."

He looked crestfallen.

"Ah, my dear Cardinal," I comforted him. "There will undoubtedly be problems and delays. Nothing will proceed as perfectly as on parchment. Then I rely on *you.*" When had the balance tipped, and he become reliant on my reassurance? When had he ceased to be solicitous of me and the reverse come about? "Tomorrow, early, we sally forth," I said. "Our English party remains divided," I admitted. "Half would not be here."

"They mistrust France to their marrow." He gestured, signifying helpless-ness. "But the ones who said that if they knew they possessed one drop of French blood, they'd cut their veins and let it out . . ." He shook his head.

"A dramatic statement," I said. Could he not appreciate that? "We will be ready, my Queen and I," I told him—or rather, dismissed him. "As the sun rises."

He took his leave, reluctantly. He wished to speak of something else, it was clear. But I did not wish to speak to him. So he must go. I heard his footsteps outside as he sought his silver-bedecked mule—symbol of humility. That made me smile.

But the smile faded as I crossed the empty main room, with its fire still flickering in the corner fireplace. I had no desire to go upstairs and join Katherine, although I was very tired. I wished to be alone.

I sat down on a small chair and stared at the dying flames. They threw eerie shadows, not the least of which was my own, throughout the room. In a strange moment I was envious of the wool merchant who owned this house. I imagined him to have a happy life: a trade he enjoyed, a wife, seven children. Better than being a King with a barren wife and a growing feeling of despair. Yes, despair . . . but of what? There was nothing certain I should despair of. Before such thoughts troubled me further, I got up and left the room, climbing the long staircase up to the waiting bed-chamber.

ᴄ⧉ WILL:

There was no need for him to envy the wool merchant, whom I knew well. He was continually in debt, and his wife was unfaithful. (Only three of the seven children were his!) Yet we always envy others, comparing our shadows to their sunlit sides.

ᴄ⧉ HENRY VIII:

I did not sleep that night. Rather, I reread the plan of my meeting with Francis, and rehearsed it in my mind. Toward daylight I felt drowsy and perhaps slept that strange half-sleep we do at dawn in an unfamiliar place: a sleep that leaves one curiously enervated and worse than no sleep at all. Thus I went forth for the day, with an altered sense of being.

We were to ride forth, all the company of England, and meet the French in the grandly named Camp du Drap D'or. Even in Roman times the vale was known as Vallis Aurea. Clearly it had long awaited a great event, been named for it far in advance. Now we would fulfil it.

As the early morning sun broke over the tightly packed roofs of Calais, it found our numbers overflowing the streets, and we were a high-spirited five thousand. All were wearing furs, gold, jewels: for we came not as warriors but on display. I gave the signal, and we moved out, the hooves of five thousand horses making a great noise upon the cobbled streets.

By noon we rounded a small rise that had obscured our view of Guines. Spread out before us was a city of tents—a city larger than any in England save London, Bristol, or York. They even approximated city streets, with dwellers grouped according to association. Five streets cut through the tent-city, terminating in a great circle where a fountain had been set up.

I heard gasps from the men around me. No one had expected such a thing. Even Katherine smiled. Then I heard it, from someone upwind: " 'Tis the Cardinal's doing."

Rising beside the tent-city was a small, perfect palace. Its rows of windows threw back the sun like a great line of mirrors.

"See where we lodge," I said to Katherine, sitting her horse in expert Spanish style.

She turned to me, the sun behind her, so all I saw was a black outline. She nodded. Then I saw teeth as she spoke. "Wolsey's city," was all she said.

Angry, I reined my horse away from her.

The royal quarters in the so-called make-believe palace were sumptuous. Arabian carpets covered the floor, and intricately carved oaken furniture provided every comfort. A large banqueting house had been erected nearby, with a kitchen and all things necessary for proper ceremony.

We entered our quarters and prepared for our meeting with Francis. There was much dressing to be done; the meeting of two monarchs for the first time decreed that we outdo one another in sartorial splendour.

Although France was the fountainhead of all fashion, my tailors and I had decided not to ape the latest French style (which Francis was sure to surpass in gaudiness, if nothing else) but to draw upon our own English design. I was to wear a fur-trimmed golden cloak over a scarlet doublet, with my white horse festooned in the same cloth-of-gold.

"It is simple, Your Grace," said my head tailor. "But simplicity is the most striking thing on earth."

WILL:

So it proved to be, if you will study the large painting commissioned of the historic meeting. Henry, in gold and scarlet, stands—no, fairly leaps—from the background of a hundred men, riveting the viewer's eye.

HENRY VIII:

We were mounted and ready to set out as soon as the trumpet blared. We were to wait for the French signal, which our own herald would repeat. Then the two great armies of courtiers were to move forward to the sound of drums in carefully measured beats. At all costs a charge—or any suggestion of it— was to be shunned.

Now it came—a tinny bleat from two miles away, to be picked up and repeated by our own trumpeter. We moved forward, the creaking of thousands of saddles filling the air.

It seemed we rode a long way without seeing anything. There was no sign of the French. The flat plain stretched out interminably, green and empty all around. Katherine rode beside me, straight and high in her imported Spanish saddle. She did not look to the left or right, but only straight ahead. My attempts to catch her eye were futile. She was lost in her own thoughts and fears, leaving me to mine.

The sun glinted off something in the distance—a French shield? Yes! Now there was another, then another, until the field sparkled with them. They descended into the vale like a loose-linked necklace, each one momentarily catching the sun.

The men made formations, made a perfect alignment. Then they fell back, leaving a large gap in their center. A glittering figure appeared far back in that central gap—like Moses striding through the Red Sea.

Francis came closer, his great stallion picking its steps carefully while he seemed unconcerned with what his horse did. Once it stopped to accept some sweetmeat from a child, and its rider leaned forward and patted its neck. This while another King waited! I felt anger—and insult—rising within me.

Casually the rider brought his horse back onto the prescribed route (one wondered if he would have dismounted for a picnic?) and faced me again, while riding forward slowly. I did likewise. No one else moved.

Francis and I inched toward one another, with thousands of eyes upon us. I watched him intently as he approached. Now we were within ten feet of one another, and I could see every detail of his costume—a thing overburdened with lace and jewels, altogether too gaudy. We faced each other stiffly. Then he suddenly dismounted, with a surprisingly fluid motion. One moment he was seated on his horse, the next striding toward me, arms outstretched. Then I myself dismounted, strode forward, and embraced him with all the heartinesss that strangers reserve for one another. I could feel the surprising strength in him as he grasped me. Then we drew back and looked full into one another's faces for the first time.

He is not handsome, was my first thought. I noted many flaws in his countenance, flaws I admit I welcomed. His nose was large and long, and made him resemble a ferreting animal of some sort. But he was large—perhaps my own height.

"Brother!" he said, kissing my cheek.

"Frère!" I said, kissing his.

We drew back and held one another at arm's length, and Francis smiled. "I am happy to welcome you!" he said, in oddly accented English.

"Let us all embrace!" he cried, wildly. "Let there be a great ceremony of love!"

Soon all the courtiers were dismounted and mingling, although hardly engaging in a ceremony of love. But they were speaking, which in itself was astounding.

"You will dine with me tonight!" said Francis, in a low voice. His French was much more pleasing than his English. He turned and gestured toward the crowd with pride. "If only our ancestors could have beheld this—and our friendship!" He squeezed my hand with his cold, jewelled fingers.

On the great royal dais in the temporary banquet hall in Ardres that evening, I looked condescendingly at Francis, seated beside me. He was a boy, an overeager child. There was that about his person which was un-royal. It was a pity Louis had not given Mary a son. For true royalty is there from the first moment a child draws breath, and Francis did not possess it, that mysterious substance.

Still, he wore the Crown of France.

Over and over I found myself observing him, noticing his hose and his cap and his facial expressions.

The King of France.

His Most Christian Majesty.

Was it *he* who had fought at Marignano, won Milan, and left twenty thousand Swiss mercenaries dead?

Beside him on the dais sat Queen Claude, her belly puffed up with the eight-months child beneath. She had already borne Francis two sons.

At my right hand sat Katherine, gamely biting her lip and bearing her painful joints.

"Ah! The surprise!" exclaimed Francis, as the servers brought in platters heaped high with yellowish-green pyramidal shapes. The head steward walked stiffly, bearing a golden tray with the artfully arranged fruits toward us. He knelt and presented it.

"La Reine Claude!" announced Francis, plucking the top fruit off the apex of the pyramid, and depositing it ceremoniously upon my plate. "A royal fruit, developed by our own gardeners at the Palace of Blois, which will honour my beloved Queen forever," he proclaimed. A dainty, pearl-handled knife and fork were set out for me to use in eating it, and a pitcher of frothed cream to dribble over it.

The fruit was succulent—sweet, juicy, with just a hint of sourness to give it tang.

"As my Queen," said Francis, when I told him this—in French. Francis's English being poor, we conversed entirely in French. "You must develop a fruit or flower for *your* fair Queen," he said.

All falsehood, as his later ungallant remarks on Katherine made clear!

All about us were our courtiers, purposely scrambled and sitting together at the long trestle tables. Afterwards they would dance together, too, the men and ladies. Up and down the tables, conversation seemed lively.

"I understand you are a formidable dancer," Francis said. "It must be an English talent. For your fair ladies that have remained at my court in the wake of the widowed Queen's hurried departure . . . ah, they dance as if it were their profession!"

Some few unimportant people had remained in France after Mary had eloped with Brandon. But what of them? They were negligible.

"What dance measures do you prefer?" he pressed me. "I will instruct my musicians."

"I dance anything. It is of no matter which begins."

"A monarch without modesty!" he exclaimed. "How refreshing!"

As the tables were cleared away, the musicians began to assemble in the far end of the hall. There were not as many of them as in an English ensemble, but I trusted they would make decent music.

Katherine and I would lead out the first measure, an Alhambra-rhythm, as danced in Spain. She could still do a turn and execute a measure to those melodies, recalling her girlhood.

The company applauded dutifully. Then Francis and his Queen did a slow, dignified dance.

Now both Claude and Katherine could be retired, while Francis and I danced with others, having honoured our spouses.

Francis brought a woman over to me. I had seen her in the French company and at once began speaking French to her, when Francis corrected me.

"She is one of yours, *mon frère*." He touched her bare shoulders lightly. "An Englishwoman. Mary Boleyn."

The lady bowed. She was wearing a May-green gown, as I recall, that wrapt round her shoulders and breasts. Her hair was that honey colour which always aroused me, whether in fabric or hair or just the sun streaming into a room. It was my weakness. How did Francis know?

I took her as my partner. "An Englishwoman, harboured in the very French court?" I murmured. She followed my every movement, as no Englishwoman ever had. It was both maddening and seductive. "How many of you were there?"

"Not many," she replied. "My sister Anne, for one."

I looked about to indicate curiosity. In France, I already felt, everything was indirect, including questions.

"She is too young to be here. She does not yet put up her hair. A wild creature, so our father says."

"Perhaps France will tame her."

"That is his hope. In truth, France does not tame, but refines, boldness."

The message was clear. I took it. "When we return to England, we would take comfort from your presence," I said.

One sentence. So much simpler than the untutored business with Bessie. "As you wish," she replied, looking at me. She did not touch me.

That inflamed me more. She was a clever courtesan.

For courtesan she was. I could recognize one by now. This one had been polished by Francis to a high sheen. Had he enjoyed her? What had he taught her?

I had resolved not to involve myself with women, after the business with Bessie. But a practised courtesan? Surely that was different.

And the truth was that celibacy was irksome. The marital duty was a thing apart from all else, and did not even break one's celibacy. I dutifully did what I should with Katherine. But it did not quiet my blood. This Mary might just do so.

It was well past midnight in the English tent-city surrounding the palace at Guines. Some of the tents in the great assemblage gave off an eerie glow, like resting fireflies: the effect of candlelight shining through cloth-of-gold on a dark night. Even as I watched, some lights were extinguished and faded out into the night.

I dismounted on sudden impulse and waved away my attendant, who was waiting to accompany me to my apartments. I wished to walk alone in the night air.

Is there anything as soft and debilitating as a June midnight in France? The very air seemed voluptuous, but in a sweet sense, like an overripe virgin. Or a fruit left a bit too long on a tree, giving forth a characteristic odour to attract wasps. I inhaled deeply; I had to admit we did not have such nights in England.

Torches illuminated the immediate area of the palace. I moved to the periphery, in darkness on the edge of a ridge between the royal area and that of the courtiers. A warm breeze lifted my hat and blew it from my head. I started to go after it but it tumbled away, into further darkness, the decorative white feathers on its rim making it resemble a playful will-o'-the-wisp as it bobbed along. The apparition was a blackness rimmed by white, and it called something to mind, something unpleasant—but what? Something dark in the center and white beyond, retreating and teasing. . . . I plumbed my mind for images and could find nothing that should so disturb me.

The breeze rose and turned into a wind, tugging at my cape like an impatient lover. I thought of Francis and our meeting this day. The Frenchman had been what I had expected in physical appearance, yet not in manner. He seemed to mock everything, and take pleasure in startling others by his unortho-dox behaviour. He did not convey the dignity of a king, despite his titles and military victories.

Military victories . . . war. I had fought here, against France. *Our ancient enemy*. The French breezes were soft, and the apples juicy, particularly the ones from this region. It would be sweet to own this land. . . .

❦ ❦

I slept as if drugged, and perhaps I was: by the night air, or the apparition? The next morning I slept well past the time when the sun threw squares of light onto the deep red and blue silk carpet by my bedside. Suddenly a clatter of rings accompanied the wrenching open of my velvet bed-curtains, and the face of King Francis stared in at me, a sardonic smile on his lips.

"I am come to be your valet," he said. "I wish to wait upon you." He bowed low.

Where were my regular attendants? How had Francis gained access to my chamber? How dare he intrude upon me to see me at my most vulnerable? If I had not done so already, I would have hated Francis from that moment.

I climbed from the high royal bed and faced this intruder. He stood smiling, fully attired, hands on his hips. He knew I would desire to use the jordan, yet he stayed planted in his chosen place. I was equally determined not to use it in his presence.

"Why are you here? My guards—" I began, aloofly.

"Were pleased to admit the King of France," he finished.

I looked about. Where were my clothes? My Clerk of the Wardrobe had evidently been dismissed along with the rest of my personal attendants. I strode over to the wardrobe room where many garments were hanging, with still more in trunks.

"Since you wish to be my valet," I said to Francis, "select my attire." Let the fool carry out his preposterous mission, then!

Francis stepped up to the long, peg-studded pole. From each peg hung a garment. He made studied poses beside each one. At length he selected a wine-coloured doublet and matching surcoat.

"To enhance your enviable colouring," he said, grinning, as if it were a clever observation.

I dressed in his selections as hurriedly as possible. I have observed that nothing gives one man advantage over another like conversing with him naked, or not in a fit state to receive others. All the while Francis stood staring at me, a smirk on his weasel-like face. He chattered away about everything, omitting the most obvious: the reason for this unprecedented visit.

While awaiting my barber, who daily trimmed and washed my short beard, I asked him, "Why have you come?"

"To know you better, *mon frère*. To know your person."

What a liar he was! I was about to tell him so, when Penny the barber appeared at the door with his customary bowls of scented hot water, towels, combs, scissors, and razors. I settled into a chair and submitted myself to his ministrations.

A great white towel was draped about my shoulders, and then Penny brandished his silver scissors and began snipping my beard. Francis stood where he was, observing. Would he *never* leave? I felt my anger rising.

"Do you still use that type of scissor?" Francis asked, with mock incredulousness. "In France we have a new sort. I am sure you would prefer them, once you had the opportunity to compare."

I truly hated the man. Yet I am not clever with instant retorts, as Wolsey and my jester Will are.

⚜ WILL:

To be lumped with Wolsey! A compliment, or an insult?

⚜ HENRY VIII:

"This does well enough," was all I said. "My beard and it are well acquainted."

"Yet too long an acquaintance can turn to . . . indifference, is that not correct? As in marriage?"

Penny's shears whirled near my throat. I dared not move an inch. "Your own?" I replied.

"I have been married scarce five years," he shrugged. "And already three children—"

"The third is not yet born," I snapped.

"But will be soon," said Francis dreamily. "I hope it will be a girl. I would like a daughter, what with two sons already—"

"You must strive, then, to be as devoted to your daughter as to your mother. Filial love is a sublime thing, blessed by God." All the world knew Francis and his mother had an unnatural relationship, or at least an abnormal one for mother and son. It was said he never made a move without her advice, and closeted himself with her until noon every day for "consultations." She in turn called him, *"Mon roi, mon seigneur, mon César, et mon fils."*

For an instant his smug face altered. Then he smiled. "Indeed," he said. "I shall name her after my beloved mother. I can think of no greater honour."

Evidently, I thought. Pity you cannot marry *mere* yourself. He was truly disgusting.

WILL:

And would Henry not have been closeted with his own mother, had she lived? How closely linked are jealousy and disgust? Why have no learned men studied this? I myself find the question more absorbing than the dreary debates raging today about the true nature of the Eucharist.

HENRY VIII:

Penny being through, I raised myself out of the leather chair and removed the towel. "I have business to attend to," I said pointedly.

Still, Francis continued to stand before me, smiling absurdly. Must I make a banner and wave it before his hooded eyes? "I thank you for your assistance," I said. "But now duties call us in separate directions."

He bowed. "Indeed. Yet we shall meet later—in the afternoon, for the first joust."

Protocol dictated that I accompany him through my private apartments. Reluctantly I joined him and together we left my bedchamber, traversed the inner chamber, and opened the door into the large Privy Chamber. At least a dozen attendants looked expectantly toward us.

"Bon jour," said Francis, lifting his plumed bonnet.

The chamber was some twenty feet wide. Before we had crossed ten, Francis abruptly paused. He put one finger against his cheek and raised his left eyebrow. Then he plucked off his head-covering and tossed it into one corner.

"Wrestle with me, brother!" he cried.

He caught me off guard. Before I could even alter my stance, he came at me, hitting me unfairly, throwing me on my back.

A row of surprised courtiers stared down at my shame. I knew now why Francis had selected a tightly fitting costume for me—it hampered my movements quite effectively.

He stood back, a false look of consternation on his face. *"O! O! Sacre bleu!"* He uttered a string of similar French inanities.

But he did not offer me his hand or help me to my feet. Instead, he stood well back, trying to appear surprised.

I rose to my feet. "In France, do you not customarily give an opponent the chance to prepare for a contest?"

"One must always be prepared for the unexpected, *cher frère."* He rolled his eyes toward the painted ceiling and shrugged. "Life seldom warns us when she is ready to strike a blow. I merely imitate life."

I stripped off the confining surcoat. Let us fight, then, away from public eyes, and defy the protocol banning such contests between monarchs!

"Imitate an athlete, then—if you can!—and let us wrestle properly," I challenged him.

I approached him. Even now my muscles quiver as I relive the moment and remember how I longed to take him.

"I never repeat an act," he said loftily, backing away. "Particularly successful ones."

"You prefer to repeat mistakes?" I advanced toward him.

He looked down at the floor. "How dusty the floor is." His brow furrowed.

"It is French dirt," I said. "It seems to lie everywhere."

"What a pity you fail to appreciate my realm. How fortunate you need never set foot here again. Fate is kind."

"How fortunate that we are 'brothers' and you may bask in your false titles in perfect safety."

He raised that eyebrow again. "Perhaps Edmund de la Pole's younger brother, Richard, might make much the same statement to you." He smiled. "Fortunately such statements are harmless and amusing to us both." He bowed again. *"À bientôt, mon frère!"*

De la Pole! How dare he mention the name of that traitor, who even now was somewhere in France, waiting to be "recognized" as the legitimate King of England? And Francis was shielding him, keeping him in reserve!

I threw the wine-velvet surcoat and doublet (still flecked with floor-dirt from Francis's perfidy!) in a far corner.

"Give them to a French beggar outside the Pale," I ordered my page. As he started away, I added, "Be sure to bestow them on the most ill and deformed person present."

He smiled in admiration. "As the Master Himself would have done." His walk had an added jauntiness as he left the chamber.

An interesting thought: What *would* Christ have done with Francis? It seemed to me that Our Saviour's world had been clearly defined: partisans on one side and enemies on the other. Yet what of someone who spoke fair, yet hated Him in his heart? Was there an example of that in Scripture? There must have been. I vowed to find it. In the meantime, I prayed for fortitude in dealing with a man I now knew to be the nearest approximation on earth to His Satanic Majesty himself.

WILL:

Henry was ever wont to exaggerate, and see things in battleground terms. Francis was not the Antichrist, merely a dissolute Frenchman who saw life as a cosmic joke. He would no doubt be flattered to realize the signal honour Henry paid him in elevating him to such high ranks in the demoniac hierarchy.

XXIX

Whilst we met and took one another's measure on the soft green fields of France, Francis and I, Bishop John Fisher of Rochester fulminated against the gathering, castigating us both.

Although he had attended the meeting as part of Katherine's retinue, he delivered a fiery sermon on the vanity of the entire idea, and while he had some valid points (namely, that all pleasure eventually turns to exhaustion and boredom; that man relies on the borrowed trappings of other animals for his clothes and adornments; that nothing lives up to our expectations) they applied equally to all of life as well, to the very fact of being born a human creature. His last point, that rain and hail and "strange skyward happenings" had wrecked the pretty pretend-palaces, summarized the whole meeting: the *entente cordiale* was insubstantial and immediately destroyed by the first breath of real politics.

That did not stop me from being annoyed with Bishop Fisher, that nattering busybody. He had always been irritating and interfering. My grandmother Beaufort and he had been "thick as thieves," as the saying goes. On her deathbed she had ordered me to "obey Bishop Fisher in all things." Ha! My days of obedience had ended, although she could have no inkling of that. I paid little heed to the cantankerous old theologian, and certainly never sought his advice. But this public preaching on my foreign policy . . . it had to stop. I gave orders.

Everywhere the clergy were publicly debating, denouncing, and pronouncing. The German monk, Martin Luther, had even gone into print with three theological tracts: *On the Liberty of a Christian Man; Address to the Nobility of the German Nation; On the Babylonian Captivity of the Church of God.* The last one was a direct attack on the Church in general and the Pope in particular, claiming that the prophecies in Revelation, Chapter 17, had come true at last. ("And there came one of the seven angels which had the seven vials, and talked with me, saying unto me, Come hither; I will show unto thee the judgment of the great whore that sitteth upon many waters. . . . And upon her forehead was a name written, MYSTERY, BABYLON THE GREAT, THE MOTHER OF HARLOTS AND ABOMINATIONS OF THE EARTH. And I saw the woman drunken with the blood of the saints, and with the blood of the martyrs of Jesus. . . . And the angel said unto me . . . I will tell thee of the mystery of the woman. . . . The seven heads are seven mountains, on which the woman sitteth. . . . And the woman which thou sawest is that great city, which reigneth over the kings of the earth.") It was obviously the city of Rome, on its seven hills, and the Pope, to whom all kings owed allegiance.

Pope Leo had excommunicated him, unless he recanted his opinions within sixty days. Luther's answer was to burn the Papal bull in front of a cheering crowd.

Cheering: for the people of Germany, the Netherlands, and Flanders had embraced Luther's protests. It was as if they had long ago turned from the Church, had existed for a generation awaiting a leader to speak for them. He did not convert them; he discovered them.

Charles, the new Holy Roman Emperor, immediately issued a decree suppressing Lutheranism in the Netherlands. The Humanists (whom he mistakenly believed had sowed the seeds for Lutheranism with their intellectual gibes at the Church) were expelled from the faculties of universities. Luther was called to a hearing before his superiors. He stated his beliefs, then said, "On this I take my stand. I can do no other. God help me. Amen."

The battle lines were drawn, and I found myself facing Luther as an adversary.

Why did I take the Pope's side? There are those who say that I meant merely to curry favour with the Pope, later to throw off my cloak to reveal my true colours—which is to say, no colour at all. To those critics, I have no religious convictions at all; I use religion to further my own ends. An equally insulting interpretation is that I am so inconsistent that I go first to one side and then to the other on the whim of a mood.

The truth (to disappoint my critics and evil-wishers) is neither of these. I found Luther's beliefs to be heretical and dangerous. Taken as a whole, they led to anarchy. They also rebelled against Christ Himself, Who plainly set up the Church.

I believed the Church should be purified, not dismantled. And that is what I have done with the Church in England. It is simple! Why do people make the simple so complicated?

As for my support of the Papacy: my eyes had not yet been opened by my own Great Matter. When I wrote in 1521, I wrote in sincerity and to the extent of my spiritual knowledge at the time. That is all God asks of any man. That he later grows spiritually should not be held against him.

One of Luther's heresies was in claiming that there were not seven Sacraments; that the Church (for mysterious, self-serving reasons of its own) had invented five of them. These five were Matrimony, Holy Orders, Penance, Extreme Unction, and Confirmation. Only Baptism and Communion remained. Under Luther's interpretation, marriage was a legal contract; Holy Orders was unnecessary, for priests had no special powers; confession was something one did directly to God, not to a priest; Extreme Unction was a silly superstition; and Confirmation was a redundant version of Baptism. Christ had not performed any of them, therefore He could not have felt they aided in salvation.

I believed—no, I *knew*—that Luther was absolutely wrong. Each of these Sacraments conferred grace; I had felt it come upon me when receiving them. I also felt called to refute him, on paper, lest he lead more souls to their damnation.

I would find all Christ's teachings on the matter, and those of every one of the doctors and fathers of the Church, from the very beginning up until today.

It proved to be a formidable task. For upwards of four hours a day I laboured on the work. It required a staggering knowledge of theology, I was soon to discover. I had prided myself on my knowledge of the Churchmen and early Fathers, but culling the exact text for a minute philosophical point was an Herculean labour. I began to feel I lived among the dead, concerned only with the obscure opinions of those long since gone to dust, whilst ignoring the living and their distressingly selfish concerns about wages and room allotments. What was real? I began not to know, and as I shuttled back and forth between two disparate worlds, I became disoriented.

In many ways I felt comfortable and soothed in the world of the mind, albeit the minds of dead men, for their thoughts, purified and preserved, were eternal. It would have been so easy to lose oneself here forever; a temptation, a siren call. . . .

These were my labours by day. By night they were of another nature entirely.

As I have said, I brought Sir Thomas Boleyn's daughter Mary back from France, where she had evidently served under Francis—in a minor capacity, for he had a regular mistress already, Jeanne le Coq, a lawyer's wife. In Richmond Palace I established a French suite of rooms (where Father had kept his wardrobe!). "I would explore France further," I said, "and experience those aspects of living in which France is said to excel." Mary must have the accoutrements necessary to duplicate her feats with Francis. She would duplicate, I would surpass. Yes, I carried my rivalry with him even this far. . . .

The walls of the rooms were hung with tapestries depicting not Biblical scenes, but classical ones. French furniture was copied by my cabinetmakers, and the mirrors and sconces favoured by French fashion were installed. Stepping over the threshold into the *Pays de Gaul* suite was like crossing the Channel.

Mary awaited me on Tuesday and Thursday evenings, our assigned time. That in itself was French. The assignation. For the French prided themselves on their logic and rationality, and confined their lovemaking to prearranged trysts. One would think that would diminish the pleasure, but by divorcing pleasure from passion, it both heightened it and lightened it.

All their positions had been catalogued and named, like their ballet steps. How pastel, how artistic they sounded; how far removed from anything to do with sweat, groaning, or fear.

In France, so it seemed, the ancient, natural way of copulation had been entirely abandoned. Everything was from the rear or from the side. The moment of culmination they turned to poetry: *la petite mort,* the little death. Not, as in English, the moment of truth, the great anguish.

Mary led me trippingly through these exercises. "The position for a King who has had a tiring day of Council meetings," she whispered as she demonstrated one method.

"Was it Francis's favourite?" Sharing this woman with him, engaging in exactly the same acts in exactly the same body, was quiveringly arousing. "Did he do this—and this—and *this*—after his meetings?"

Expertly Mary swam under me, bringing herself to *la petite mort* several times in succession, as if to avoid answering. That was another French fashion—no *amoureuse* worthy of the name was satisfied with only one *petite mort*. No, there must be a series, the more of them the better.

"What of Francis?" I kept whispering.

"It was never—he was never—" she murmured obligingly. "He was smaller than you."

Such exercises and flattery were only the beginning of her artful repertoire. There were many other things that decency does not permit me to record, even here.

But in carrying pleasure to its furthest bounds, I exhausted pleasure. It grew to a surfeit. (As Bishop Fisher had predicted in his famous sermon: "First, the joys and pleasures of this life, be they never so great, yet they have a weariness and disgust adjoined to them. There is no meat or drink so delicate, so pleasant, so delectable, but if a man or woman be long accustomed therewith, he shall have at length a weariness of them. . . .")

All this while I was labouring in the theological thickets to complete my *Assertio Septem Sacramentorum*. I found a curious similarity between my two endeavours, in that preciousness ultimately kills all vitality in its subject. Theological hair-splitting and over-refined lovemaking techniques are cousins, bleeding their respective victims dry.

XXX

At length the book was finished. It was two hundred and fifty pages, all in Latin. I was pleased with it. Only then did I show it to anyone else, so that I was in effect presenting them with a *fait accompli*. (See how very French I had become; I thought in French phrases even beyond the bounds of pleasure.) It was to Thomas More and Wolsey and John Longland, Bishop of Lincoln, my confessor, and Edward Lee, canon of Lincoln, that I gave copies. And Wolsey and Longland and Lee returned them with nary a criticism or correction, and with letters attached that praised it.

Only More's did not come back. He held it three weeks past the time the others kept it. I knew then that he was actually reading it, and finding fault with it.

More had lately been lured from his private life as a London lawyer. In Court of Star Chamber he had defended a Papal ship seized as forfeit under maritime law. His defence was so brilliant that Wolsey, who had represented the Crown in the matter, immediately set about to harness More's talents for himself. He induced More to begin serving as Master of Requests—which meant that he must receive petitions presented to me, both at court and on progresses. From there I had named him to the Privy Council and had made it clear that he was to be part of the English party at the Field of Cloth of Gold. Little by little he had been sucked into court life.

More requested to speak with me upon returning the manuscript. I could have received him in the audience chamber, seated upon my throne. But I preferred to speak with him man to man, not King to subject. He should come to my "counting room" and I would have warm, friendly firelight there, not the torches of ceremony.

He was older now. But of course it should be so. A number of years had passed since I had, boyishly, given him the astrolabe to prove a point. He had been a grown man when my mother died. Now we were both men, and things were ordered differently. I did not have to send presents to prove that I was King and master.

He bore the manuscript in a box.

"I hope there are no changes," I said, "as the presentation copies for His Holiness are already being prepared—by monks, of course. They have expertise at these things, at calligraphy."

"Not so much, anymore," he murmured. He handed me the box. "I find only one fault in it. You stress the Pope's authority too strongly. Perhaps it should be more slenderly stated."

Was that all? Relief came in waves.

"Luther attacked it so viciously, I felt bound to shore it up again."

"You overstate the gravity of the office," he said. "Pope Leo will buckle under the weight of it when he reads it. He is not meet to carry it. Nor, I think, is any other man on earth, the way you have presented it."

"But what did you think of the thing as a whole?" The question burst out.

"I thought"—he paused—"it was an admirable work of scholarship. You have clearly shown much diligence in pursuing the references—"

"The thinking! I mean the thinking, the analysis, the deductions! What of *them?*"

More drew back, as if from a physical assault. "They were certainly . . . persuasive. And thorough."

But of course they *should* be persuasive, convincing.

Suddenly I did not care to pursue it further. He had said "admirable," "diligence," "persuasive," and "thorough." Grudging compliments. Not the highest accolades. What he meant was *competent, not stirring.*

He had seen no genius there.

Well, what of it? Was he competent (that word again) to judge?

"I thank you for your time in reading it," I said. "I will take your suggestions into account."

In my head, not in the manuscript, which was even now being copied out on the finest vellum by the obedient monks.

"We were glad of your company in France this summer past," I said. "And of your willingness to undertake the diplomatic mission to Calais, regarding the return of Tournai."

He smiled. Or did he? His face seemed to have no provision for smiling. All its lines were sombre and downward.

"You find yourself in our midst at last," I said.

"Yes. A surprise to myself," he said.

"You will learn to feel at home here," I said. "For it is truly where you belong. The most brilliant minds in the realm should serve their sovereign, as thinking is a higher tribute than rubies. And one that a loyal subject should gladly present his King."

More bowed silently.

I had not meant it to be presented thus. I had meant us to sit before the fire, exchange confidences, gain confidences, foster camaraderie. But he was not warm, despite his amiable manner. Amiability can function as an effective disguise for absolute coldness. I felt his coldness, stronger than I felt the heat of the fire.

"My mind is yours to command," he said.

That was not what I meant, not what I intended at all. It was he who had interpreted it so, twisted my well-meaning into something sullen and sinister.

Oh, let him go! Why did I care so very much what he thought and felt? He was just a man, like all the rest.

WILL:

The book—a great presentation copy bound in gold, with inner leaves of parchment—was dispatched to Leo X. Reportedly the Pope immediately read five pages and said he "would not have thought such a book should have come from the King's grace, who hath been occupied necessarily in other feats, seeing that other men which hath occupied themselves in study all their lives cannot bring forth the like."

The Pope, grateful for the unabashed support of a king, conferred on Henry a long-coveted title: *Defensor Fidei*—Defender of the Faith. Now Henry would no longer feel naked beside his theologically bedecked fellow monarchs.

The little book was an astounding success. Many translations were printed, in Rome, Frankfurt, Cologne, Paris, and Würzburg, among other places, and they sold as quickly as they came from the printing presses. A total of twenty editions was produced before the Continental appetite for it was sated. It was at that point that Luther entered the fray, hurling insults at its royal author. Henry, disdainful of replying, directed More to defend the work.

HENRY VIII:

My theological darts had struck home. I knew that by the vehemence with which the stung Luther responded. The "spiritual" monk unleashed a volley of low-born insults against me in his pamphlet *Martin Luther's Answer in German to King Henry of England's Book*. He called me "by God's ungrace King of England" and said that since this King "knowingly and consciously fabricates lies against the majesty of my King in heaven, this damnable rottenness and worm, I will have the right, on behalf of my King, to bespatter his English Majesty with muck and shit and to trample underfoot that crown of his."

"Well," I said to More, summoned before me, "you can see the level of this Luther's mind. In the privies." More turned the pages of the pamphlet listlessly. Even his expressionless eyes registered surprise (and disdain) when he read the "muck and shit" sentence.

"I want you to respond to him," I said. "In the same manner." He was poised to protest, so I cut him off. "It is beneath the dignity of a King to write in this vein, any more than the Pope could do it. But a subject can write under pseudonymns. As you wrote your *Utopia.*"

"Why me, Your Majesty?" He looked pained. "If all you require is an exchange of excrement, there are others better qualified. I do not use such terms myself, nor think in them. It will be a labour for me to perform what comes so easily to others. I beg you, let me serve you in some other capacity."

"No. For I need someone who can answer Luther at all levels, not merely the scatological. Employ a sailor to help you with the abusive terms; the meat of the argument needs your mind."

He fidgeted a little. I had noticed earlier that he had a tendency to pick at the skin around his thumbs. It was something that could be hidden under legal gowns, something that could be done while keeping an unperturbed face. His thumbs were often raw and bleeding.

"There must be a hidden side of you," I said. "A side that would love to daub the walls of a jakes. Give it rein."

"I am trying not to let my earthly side *reign,* my Lord, but to *rein* it in."

"Give it its head this one last time, then."

With a smile I sealed the command.

More responded satisfactorily. His *Answer to Luther,* by "William Rosse," claimed that Luther should be "overwhelmed with filth." He called him "filthier than a pig and more foolish than an ass," "a toadying buffoon who was once a friar, later a pimp," with "nothing in his mouth but privies, filth, and dung," fit only "to lick with his anterior the very posterior of a pissing she-mule." He called on his readers to throw back into Luther's "shitty mouth, truly the shit-pool of all shit, all the muck and shit which your damnable rottenness has vomited up, and to empty out all the sewers and privies" over his head. Luther, as might be expected, exploded with rage.

"I am pleased," I told More. "I shall bestow a suitable reward on you." The truth was that he had shown scant originality; he had just used "shit" and "privies" to the point of boredom. "The pissing she-mule was an arresting image," I said. The only one.

"Give a stipend to William Rosse to have his stables muck-raked in perpetuity," More said. "Do not connect my name or estates with it in any way."

"Now you have got it out of your system," I said. "That imp, that worldly, physical side of you."

"I may thank you for that," he said sadly.

"Scurrilous, Your Majesty," said Wolsey, glancing at the *Answer to Luther* on my working desk.

"Indeed. I am somewhat embarrassed to have such a fellow as my defender—whoever he may be."

Wolsey sniffed his pomander.

"The stench of literary shit is not blocked by cinnamon and cloves," I said. "Pity."

"Yes, there is almost as much of that about as the common sort, now that every man has a pen and, it seems, access to a printing press." He sniffed again. "I am thankful that you presented your work to Pope Leo rather than to the—Dutchman. And that good Pope Leo did not live to see the pamphlet wars and shit-fights."

I bit my lip to suppress a smile. "You do not care for Pope Adrian?"

The truth was that Wolsey had entertained serious hopes of being elected Pope after Leo's sudden demise. He had attempted to buy the Emperor's votes in the Curia. But instead they had elected Adrian, Bishop of Tortosa, Charles's boyhood tutor. From all reports the man was holy, scholarly, and slow as a "tortosa."

"I do not know him."

He had not told me of his bribery in the Conclave. Spying had become an adjunct to our dealings with one another. Did *he* know that I had commissioned More to write *Answer to Luther?* I hoped not.

Now to the matter at hand: the Parliament I had been forced to call to raise money for a possible war.

Yes, Francis had broken the Treaty of Universal Peace by invading Navarre, wresting it from the Emperor. Now the Emperor prepared for war and called on all those who had signed the Universal Treaty of Peace in 1518 to punish the aggressor, France, as the treaty stipulated.

"What taxes do you plan to ask?"

"Four shillings to the pound, Your Majesty."

"That is a twenty-percent tax! They will never agree!"

"The honour of the realm demands it."

Was he that cut off from what was possible and reasonable? "It is unreasonable. Never ask for something that can be so easily refused. It sets a bad precedent."

He shook his head. His jowls moved along with it. "They will not refuse," he intoned, in a voice suitable for the Masses he never said anymore.

Was it then that I began to entertain doubts about the sanctity, the wisdom, of the office of the Pope? If Wolsey could be seriously considered as a candidate—O, it was good that I had written my book when my faith was as yet untroubled.

The business with Parliament went badly. Wolsey presented the case for the tax, and the noble calling of war against King Francis, the treaty-breaker. He spoke eloquently, as ever. He could have persuaded the birds to come down off the topmost branches of a tree. Any argument offered, he could have countered.

But More, the Speaker of the House, offered the one thing Wolsey could not refute: silence. He claimed that it was an ancient privilege of Commons to maintain "a marvelous obstinate silence" whenever strangers were present. This should suit Wolsey, "forasmuch as my Lord Cardinal lately laid to our charge the lightness of our tongues."

It was a stunning device. Wolsey had no recourse but to leave the Parliament chamber in defeat. In the next session one of his own household members, also in the House of Commons, spoke in a low voice about the ill logic of spending money to fight on the Continent when it could better be spent subduing the Scots at our backs, "and thereby make our King Lord of Scotland as well."

In the end I was allowed a tax of one shilling on the pound.

"Who was the fellow who proposed incorporating Scotland into our Crown?" I asked Wolsey, after the fact, when his pride had stopped smarting.

"Thomas Cromwell," he replied. "A youngling from my household. He speaks when he should keep silent." Thus Wolsey apologized for him.

"I would think you would never hereafter commend silence as a virtue!" The wounds were still open and salt was at hand. "His suggestion had . . . merit." More was a different matter. Did he seek to prove his integrity by this contrariness?

"Cromwell is a man who thinks only in terms of the attainable, not the permissible or the conventional. King of Scotland . . . I'll wager he sees the crown on your head even now."

"As I could be persuaded to, myself." I felt the corners of my mouth go up in the facsimile of a smile. It was a trick I had learned lately to mask impatience or boredom.

In the end we had to go to war, and Parliament had to finance it. Unfortunately for us, Parliament would finance it only so far, and that was not far enough. The war turned out to be a three years' affair, and Parliament would sanction only a year's participation. The result was that we paid our money, suffered losses—but were excluded from the final victory and its glories. For Francis fell in the Battle of Pavia, and was taken prisoner by Charles, in the end. The French army was destroyed. Fighting alongside his patron and master, Richard de la Pole, Edmund's younger brother, the self-styled "White Rose of York" and Francis-styled "King of England," was killed on the battlefield.

"Now we are free of all pretenders!" I cried, when the news was brought me. I rejoiced. But it was a secondhand victory.

In the opening volley of the war, we made great impact. I had recalled Brandon from his estates in Suffolk, where he languished, and put him in charge of the invading army. He and his men came within forty miles of taking Paris itself. But then the money, and the season, ran out. Snow fell and enveloped them, followed by ice. They could not winter over; it would be impossible to sustain an army of twenty-five thousand in the field in winter conditions. (To think that war must obey the trumpet-sound of the seasons!) I beseeched Parliament for the funds to enable them to take up in spring where they had left off. Parliament refused.

So the opportunity to conquer France was thrown away on the smug vote of a few self-satisfied Yorkshire sheep-herders and Kentish beer-brewers!

All English citizens had been ordered to return before the outbreak of the war. That included the few still in Francis's court, such as the Seymour lads and Anne, Mary Boleyn's sister. It was not meet that any loyal citizen remain in the hands of the enemy, where he might be imprisoned or held for ransom. Even the Bordeaux wine procurers hurried home, bringing their provisioning ships along with them.

⌘ WILL:

And thus Anne Boleyn—"Black Nan," as she was known already—came to England. The Witch returned home. . . .

⌘ HENRY VIII:

Going to Parliament had been demeaning in itself (but necessary, as I did not want to exhaust the Royal Treasury completely), but being refused by them was doubly so. Having to call my citizens home, admitting that I was unable to protect them abroad, was tantamount to impotence.

Although I did not suffer from that grave disorder, other aspects of my life concerned with that delicate element were all at odds. I continued to see sweet Mary Boleyn every Tuesday and Thursday (we made the hours sacrosanct!), but Mary had changed.

She grew by turns fretful, then languid, then tearful. In short, it was no longer pleasurable to sport with her. I told her so, like a buyer complaining of shoddy goods.

"Moods and tears are for one's wife, not one's mistress," I grumbled one night, after she had spoiled our tryst. My loins were aching for release, and all I had been offered was a quarrel—about nothing.

"Ah! I am practising," she said bitterly. "It is a skill I must master, and soon."

Now I had it. "You are to marry?"

"Yes," she said glumly.

"Who is he?" The prescribed question.

"William Carey. One of your gentlemen servers."

Carey. I tried to place him. I could fit no face with the name. That in itself was bad. It meant he was unmemorable.

"My father chose him! Paid him, rather! He wants me wed, especially since he sees—or *thinks* he sees—signs that I may be with child."

"Oh." I felt suddenly sad. I would miss Mary; and I hated the idea that I might have a child, a child that was mine and yet was not mine. . . .

"So he paid this fellow to make me respectable. My father wishes to advance at court; it would not do to have a bastard grandchild. Nor be seen as panderer to the King." She laughed spitefully.

"When is it to be? The wedding?"

"Next week. On Sunday."

This was Thursday. So this was our last time. . . .

"Perhaps it will not be as . . . odious to be married as you fear," I reassured her.

"William Carey is a sweet man," she said.

"Then you are fortunate."

"Sweet—and acquiescing."

Suddenly I understood. My first reaction was disgust. Then, close on its heels, relief.

"Then *I* am fortunate," I said.

🕮 WILL:

And, Catherine, you were born within the year, were you not? What say you now?

🕮 HENRY VIII:

After the dreadful, cursed child that Katherine had borne, there had been no others. No pregnancies. It was as if her womb, on bringing forth this monster, had cursed itself.

Katherine had been thirty-three at the time of the vile birth. She was forty now. Although I had continued to fulfil my marital duty to her, she never conceived again.

How fleeting a time is woman's fertility. Katherine's was now over. I had first beheld her when she was just opening that window. Now I held her hand as she closed it. It had not been so very long a time.

XXXI

I was thirty when I presented *Assertio Septem Sacramentorum* to Leo X and he named me Defender of the Faith. It was a stirring moment for me, and I was happy whenever I thought of it.

But it was a happiness set like a jewel against dark velvet. There was little else in my life that showed favour from God, and bit by bit I began to wonder if the Pope were truly privy to God's mind. Rather than being a consolation to me, the Pope's approval served only to throw the integrity of the Papacy itself into question.

For there was little doubt that God had turned His back on me. I had no heir, and the doctors had confirmed what I had long feared: Katherine could bear no more children. My money was spent, yet France remained just beyond my grasp. The Scots had been trounced in 1513, yet they gathered again—Holy Blood, was there no end to them and their troubles? My private vision of England's greatness was clouded. Everywhere I looked, any plan or desire I had cherished had been soundly defeated. It was clear that God did not intend me—and by extension, my realm—to prosper until I had expunged some unknown offence against Him.

But what was it? I could think of nothing so heinous as to merit such banishment from His favour. There had been adultery, which I had confessed. Yet (if I do not seem disrespectful) God seemed to look kindly on adulterers in the Old Testament. Abraham and Jacob and David had "handmaidens" with whom they lay, even bringing forth children. I have always found it puzzling that God was outraged at David's "taking" of Bathsheba, yet evidently condoned Abishag's "comforting" of him in his old age. My own special unhappiness stemmed from the knowledge that I had somehow estranged myself from my Maker. I began to search for the inadvertent action for which I was being held accountable.

I must also face the problems inherent in my situation, should it prove impossible to remove them. I had a daughter, Mary, now nine years old. She was a delight! She excelled at her studies, being quite proficient in Latin as well as Spanish (which Katherine spoke with her) and French. Best of all, she loved music and showed great promise. She was a gentle and loving child.

✒ WILL:

Who grew up to be the bitter, vindictive woman we all now suffer under. When did she change from what she was?

✒ HENRY VIII:

Love her as I did, I was forced to examine the matter in cold terms. She was a woman, and when she married, she would become subject to her husband. When Mary married, England itself would be her dowry.

No! I would not permit it! England to be annexed to either the Holy Roman Empire or France? The very thought choked me! And if she married a lesser prince, someone from a German duchy or an Italian state? What would he know of ruling a great realm? He might try, nonetheless, and thereby bring irreparable harm to England.

Should Mary not live (the very thought was painful, but I must face the possibility), who was next in line for the throne?

My thirteen-year-old nephew, James V of Scotland, little Jamie? I trusted not a Scot.

My other sister, Mary, now had a son and two daughters. Yet their father had been a commoner, and this would inevitably cause questionings and bring forth other contenders and pretenders.

These contenders would be, perforce, distantly related to royalty. But distance, I had found to my surprise and sorrow in the Buckingham affair, was no bar to royal ambition. Let a man's great-great-great-grandfather wear a crown, and he has little trouble picturing himself in it.

Such had been the feelings of Edward Stafford, Duke of Buckingham, descended from the sixth and last son of Edward III. We shared a common great-grandfather, as well: John Beaufort, son of Edward III's fourth son, John of Gaunt. This enabled him to boast that he had more Plantagenet blood in his veins than I.

There was much more besides. He consulted with a monk fortune-teller, who prophesied that he "should have all." Buckingham said, "If aught but good come to the King, I should be next in blood to the Crown." Most chilling of all, he said that God was punishing me (for what?) "by not suffering the King's issue to prosper, as appears by the death of his sons."

After he was arrested, tried, and found guilty of treason, he revealed the full extent of his perfidy. He begged an audience with me, in which he planned to conceal a dagger on his person. He would kneel before me in supplication, then suddenly rise and stab me to death, "using him as his father wished to Richard III." The traitor never had an opportunity to put his fell plan into effect.

⁓ WILL:

Buckingham was rather stupid, as were so many of the long-established nobility. He evidently felt that his titles and lineage conferred some sort of immunity on him, which was curious in light of the fact that three Kings—Henry VI, Edward V, and Richard III—had been murdered within living memory.

⁓ HENRY VIII:

I had other cousins, more distant and numerous the further back one traced the lineage. There were potential claimants aplenty, that I knew.

I could not leave the throne to Mary alone. A woman had never reigned in England but once—Matilda, in 1135. Her cousin Stephen (who stood in exactly the same relation to Matilda as James V to Mary) wrested the Crown from her after a bloody civil war. I could not permit that.

If only I had a son! If only—

But I *did* have a son. Bessie's son throve. I *had* a living son. How could I have overlooked him?

Because he was illegitimate. I had recognized him as mine; but he was not born in wedlock, which barred him from the succession.

I paced my chamber. I remember the sun was streaming in, making patterns on the floor which I disrupted as I passed through the hot golden shafts again and again. Did this truly prevent his becoming King, I wondered. Was there no precedent?

Margaret Beaufort had been the descendant of John of Gaunt's bastard. There was talk that Owen Tudor had never properly married Queen Catherine. I disliked these examples, however, as they undermined my own claim to the throne. There had been William the Conqueror, of course, known as the Bastard. There was also doubt that Edward III was the son of Edward II. Most assumed he was the child of Queen Isabella's lover, Mortimer. Richard III claimed that his brother Edward IV had been the son of a lover, sired while the good Duke of York was away fighting in France.

These were unsatisfactory examples, not apropos to my case. No, this would not do.

My son was my son! All knew him to be such. I could not confer legitimacy upon him. But I could confer titles upon him, make him noble, educate and prepare him for the throne and name him heir in my will. He was but six years old, and there was time to let the people know him and learn to love him, so that when the time came . . .

I stopped stock-still. The answer had been before me all the time. Not a perfect answer, but an answer. I would make him Duke of Richmond, a semi-royal title. I would bring the boy to court. He must be hidden away in the country no longer.

Katherine would be unhappy. But she must recognize that only in this way could Mary be protected against self-seekers lusting after her throne. Our daughter deserved a better fate.

✑ WILL:

One which she did not receive, alas. What Henry most feared has come to pass. The Spanish King Philip II saw Mary only as an opportunity to make England an appendage of Spain. He married her, pretending love; when she refused to put the entire English treasury and navy at his disposal, he left her and returned to Spain. She weeps and pines daily for him. She is the most unhappy of women.

XXXII

🖛 HENRY VIII:

There would be a formal investiture ceremony. Along with my son, I would elevate others: my cousin Henry Courtenay would become Marquis of Exeter; my nephew Henry Brandon, Charles and Mary's nine-year-old son, would become Earl of Lincoln. I would make Henry, Lord Clifford, Earl of Cumberland; Sir Robert Radcliffe would become Viscount Fitzwalter, and Sir Thomas Boleyn, Viscount Rochford. (There are those who snicker at this last appointment, assuming it was made on Mary Boleyn's merit. This is blatantly untrue—Sir Thomas had served me faithfully on many delicate diplomatic missions.)

🖛 WILL:

However skilled a diplomat he may have been, he could hardly have been the man of choice to send to the Vatican to plead your annulment case before Clement! Henry showed remarkable blind spots at times, and Thomas Boleyn was an outstanding example. The man was quite clearly a sycophant, willing to sell his children for the highest title.

🖛 HENRY VIII:

It was held in June, 1525, at Wolsey's magnificent palace, Hampton Court. Yes, it was finished at last, sitting on its banks of the river twenty miles upstream—a good six hours' row—from London. Here the Thames had shrunk to a friendly, smaller stream, with only a slight rising and falling due to the tide. All around was green: green meadows, trees, flowering shrubs. The air seemed clear and purified . . . like Eden itself?

One could glimpse the palace walls as one approached by boat. They were of rich red brick, glowing in the early morning sun. The palace proper was set well back from the boat landing-stage. Not until one disembarked and climbed the steep path up from the riverbank was one rewarded by the sight of the intricate, symmetrical structure, surrounded by its wide, sparkling moat. The moat was ornamental; Hampton Court could have withstood no siege. It was a pleasure-palace, built for beauty and comfort and the delight of all the senses, and it made all older palaces, no matter how opulently appointed, seem dismal by comparison.

WILL:

The French, of course, had already begun building those airy, luxurious palaces now known as chateaux. Not for them the cramped, damp fortresses of days past, where one could have comfort and beauty only at the expense of safety. Katherine was right in her suspicions— Wolsey was more French than English.

HENRY VIII:

I had never been particularly interested in buildings, which is curious in light of the fact that I designed ships. But as I walked up the broad, inviting—and yes, vulnerable—approach to Hampton Court, I felt something leap within me. I wanted—no, needed—a new palace, one I could design myself . . . to be on land what *Great Harry* was on the sea. Immediately a name for it came into existence: Nonsuch.

Even as I began imagining what form my Nonsuch might take, I was diverted by the sights and sounds around me. Wolsey's retainers filed out, their scarlet-and-gold costumes achingly bright in the clear, early-morning light. They formed a human hedge—a well-trimmed one—for us to pass through, for they were all almost exactly the same height. (I knew that Wolsey chose his showpiece servitors for height, and his advisers for wit, regardless of their looks. An admirable division of qualities.) Trumpeters followed, their silver instruments catching the sun. They blew a fanfare. I sat my horse and waited.

I had not long to wait. Wolsey was a master at timing, and I heard the crunch of gravel beneath his mule's feet long before he reached the outer portal, a great gatehouse.

He emerged, his red satin catching the sun even more brilliantly, if possible, than the silver trumpets. He always contrived to have a grand entrance, by one means or another. Yet it was no use. He was fat and old. The yards of red satin merely emphasized the fact, like wrapping a plump turnip in gleaming ribbon.

WILL:

When Henry himself was fat and old, he turned the matter to his own advantage, employing layer upon layer of gold-embroidered velvet, gleaming with jewels, making his shoulders three feet across, a great yoke of strength, while baring his still-thin calves in clinging hose. Aye, Henry knew how to display himself, turning even his physical disadvantages into a stunning triumph of vision.

HENRY VIII:

He dismounted, sliding off his beast like an ungainly sack of meal, and walked—waddled—slowly toward me.

"Your Majesty," he said, bending as low as his girth would permit, "Hampton Court is yours." He straightened and smiled, and I smiled back. All was proceeding according to form. I motioned to my men. But before I could do anything further, Wolsey held up his hands—great white things, like a fish's underbelly.

"No, Your Majesty. What I said, I said truly. Hampton Court is yours." He fumbled in his bosom, and all the while the morning sun glinted off the folds of his satin. At length he stopped and pulled out a scroll.

"It is yours, Your Majesty." He came up to me and put it into my outstretched hand, making a great arc out of the motion.

It was a deed to Hampton Court. Affixed to it was an affidavit, signed and witnessed by two lawyers, that he was offering it as a gift to his sovereign.

I looked about me. All this—a gift? The strengthening sun hit the new red bricks, and already a heat was growing on them. They flamed against the clear June sky. Inside the compound were more apartments, two stories high, circling two inner courtyards. Wolsey's triumph-piece. How could he give it away?

I was embarrassed. To refuse was an insult, to accept was to cause Wolsey great pain.

I lifted my head and tried to look at the throbbingly blue sky overhead, tried to think. But I got no further in my head-lifting than the row of elaborately decorated chimneys I glimpsed, tantalizingly, just beyond the outer courtyard. *I wanted this place!*

"Thank you, Wolsey," I heard myself saying. "We accept your gift, with great thanks."

His face did not change, nor betray any emotion: in that instant, my admiration of him leapt tenfold. A consummate master of dissimulation!

WILL:

A very bad example for Henry, and worse yet that he admired it. At that time, when Henry was presented with Hampton Court, his face was a looking-glass; all men could read by its reflection what passed in his mind. Within a few years he became the man who said, "Three may keep counsel, if two be away. And if I thought my cap knew my thinking, I would cast it into the fire." By the end of his life, he could pass a pleasant evening with his wife, knowing he had just signed a warrant for her arrest the next day. Wolsey gave him his first instructions in the art of subterfuge, deceit, and acting—and as always, Henry soon surpassed his teacher.

HENRY VIII:

I tucked the deed into my belt. "Let us proceed," I said, as if nothing unusual had happened, as if my heart were not pounding and my mind racing with excitement at the thought of owning Hampton Court.

"Of course." Again he bowed. Then he remounted his mule and led us into the inner courtyard.

I was eager to see what lay just beyond the great gatehouse. I was not disappointed: the square expanse of perfect green grass in the first courtyard was surrounded on all sides by beautifully executed double-storey apartments, all in the same red brick, all with wide windows. From the upper storey one could probably see the surrounding meadows, and the Thames itself. And as the sun slanted down in the late afternoon . . .

I became aware that I had stopped, so I urged my horse forward. Wolsey had already mounted the specially assembled platform at the far end of the courtyard where the investiture would take place. The spectators would stand on the grass before it. *And probably tear it up,* was my first fierce thought. I could not bear to have anything mar the perfection of my new possession.

We mounted the platform, Katherine and I. Painful as it was for her, Katherine's presence was necessary to confer approval upon the proceedings. Without her, dissidents could always make a case that the Queen had not concurred, and rally round her as an excuse to foment a war. Katherine knew; Katherine understood; as a mother, Katherine appreciated the threat to her own child that I was trying to avert.

WILL:

Katherine loved you, you blind fool—the only one of your wives who did! She would have walked naked should you have commanded it!

The platform was tastefully laid with Wolsey's Turkish carpets to hide the raw lumber beneath. There was a chair-of-state for me to sit in while I bestowed honours. Wolsey had thought of everything. But then, was that not why I had elevated *him?*

All were assembled. It was near noon, and the sun was straight overhead. Gone was the sweet warmth of early morning. This sun was hot and beat down upon us. I looked longingly at the few feet of cool green grass in a shaded corner of the courtyard. Where was my son?

Again the trumpets sounded, and from yet another courtyard he approached, coming through the arch and then mounting the platform alone.

He was dressed in velvet, and his six-year-old face was so serious. So white. He kept his eyes fixed on me the entire time, and as he came closer I could see the beads of perspiration all across his forehead. The heavy velvet . . . yes, he was hot. And afraid. As I had sweated in the dampness of Westminster so many years ago, as I approached my own father. I could feel it all again, could feel the sword across my shoulders, could feel the fright as I looked into my father's blank eyes. . . .

But I was not like my father! Surely he could not be afraid of me! And such a beautiful boy, too. My heart broke as I beheld him—everything I had longed for in a son, and with the Tudor red hair!

I made him Earl of Nottingham and of Somerset and Duke of Richmond, while Katherine fidgeted beside me, and our own daughter, Mary, stared at him with frank curiosity. He then took his place on the platform beside the only other dukes in the realm—Howard and Brandon. Fitzroy now outranked them both, as Duke of Richmond was a semi-royal title. My sister Mary, Brandon's wife, reached out her hand to the boy and laid it on his little shoulder. She was still beautiful, and had that contented look one wears when one is cherished and in turn cherishes the cherisher. So she was happy with Brandon. Good.

In the front row of court personages I glimpsed Bessie Blount Tailboys, witnessing her son's—*our* son's—triumph. She was still pretty, and her masses of blonde curls accentuated her healthy complexion. I looked at her and smiled. She returned the smile. There was nothing between us, nothing. How had we gotten this son? A miracle!

Now the others must come. Henry Brandon, my nine-year-old nephew, to be made Earl of Lincoln. He was big and boisterous and clumsy, like his father. I glanced once again at my son, standing so still and apart from the others, his face so grave . . . no, Henry Brandon was different, cousins though they might be.

Then came Henry Courtenay, my first cousin. I elevated him from Earl of Devon to Marquis of Exeter. True, there had been suspicion of his family's loyalty, at one time. But he had been guileless and eager for friendship. I remember his clear blue eyes; they looked straight into mine as I pronounced the words that changed his status. They were the color of a faded blue gown, and utterly without malice. I was to remember them years later, they were to haunt my sleep, when he was found to be a traitor. In my dreams they were always looking at me, and at the same time the sun beating down on my head, making rivulets of sweat trickle down my face. His face was clear and one would have thought him at Ultima Thule, so cool was he.

I wanted this over now. I was hot, uncomfortable, and hungry. I must confess I also looked forward to the sumptuous banquet I knew Wolsey would have prepared. His banquets were legendary, and each time he tried to surpass his last effort. Most important, it would be cool inside. The sun was a torch overhead.

There were only a few more. Henry, Lord Clifford, became Earl of Cumberland. Sir Thomas Manners, Lord Roos, became Earl of Rutland. The lowest-ranking ones were last: Robert Radcliffe, to become Viscount Fitzwalter, and Sir Thomas Boleyn, to become Viscount Rochford. As Sir Thomas came forward, I was conscious only of a deep relief that the ceremony was ending. As he approached, I glanced briefly toward his family assembled on the platform.

And then I saw her. I saw Anne.

She was standing a little apart from her mother and her sister Mary. She wore a gown of yellow satin and her black hair fell down over her bodice—thick and lustrous and (I somehow knew) with a perfume of its own. Her face was long, with a pale cast, and her body slender.

She was not beautiful. All the official ambassadorial dispatches, all the puzzled letters later written describing her, agree on that. She had nothing of the beauty I had come to expect of court women, none of the light, plump prettiness that honeyed one's hours. She was wild and dark and strange, and my first awareness of her was that she was staring at me. As I looked back at her, sternly, she did not drop her eyes, as all good subjects are taught to do. Instead she continued staring, and there was odd malice in her eyes. I felt unreasoning fear, and then something else. . . .

I was forced to attend to the ceremonious words and procedure transforming her father Thomas into a viscount, and then it was over, and we could retire to Wolsey's Great Hall for the celebratory banquet.

Katherine said nothing and kept her eyes averted. It had been humiliating for her, I realized—but one must face facts. I reached out and touched her shoulder. She shrank away as if she had been touched by a leper. Mary danced around us, anxious to get to the festivities. She did not care about the Duke of Richmond one way or the other.

Wolsey preceded us, leading everyone to his Great Hall. He himself flung open the door, then stood back for the expected gasps of admiration.

He was not disappointed. The tables, to accommodate some three hundred people, were set in finest linen and gold plate. A special table set apart had been prepared for the King, the Queen, and those honoured by their elevation this day. Tactfully, he had set my son on one side, while placing Katherine and Mary on the other.

I looked forward to having my son beside me so that I might talk to him and know him better. Bessie was relegated to a place at an "ordinary" table. It was a delicate situation. She *was* the mother of the principal guest of honour this day, yet she was not my wife—indeed, she was someone else's. Wolsey had followed the proper protocol.

Henry Fitzroy was clever, although a bit shy. He answered my questions but seemed to have little to say for himself, unlike my nephew Brandon, who talked loudly (with nothing to say) and helped himself to things before they could be passed in proper fashion.

The hall was abuzz with voices. Even in the blessed cool darkness, all this noise was distressing. I looked about me. I did not have to disengage myself from conversation with Katherine, as she did not deign to speak with me, but instead picked daintily at her plate, her eyes downcast. The ceremony had hurt and bewildered her. I knew that, yet what else could I have done?

The hall was shuttered against the noonday heat, and therefore had that strange, seasonless, climateless feeling we experience only rarely . . . sometimes upon waking, when we suddenly think, "What day is this? Where am I? How old am I?" It was June, yet it was cool; it was midday, yet it was dark; I was married, yet the son at my side was not my wife's; and I was in love with Thomas Boleyn's daughter.

Yes. I *knew,* even then, that I loved her, that I must have her. How strange, considering that I had never spoken one word to her. How strange, considering (although I did not consider it then!) that I am a cautious man, seldom making any decision without much deliberation. It is hard for me to take a final action. Yet I knew beyond doubt that I loved Anne Boleyn, that I must possess her, that I would die else.

How I had scoffed at love and lovers! I knew nothing of it. I knew the respect and courtesy I brought to Katherine; the fond laughter and passing lust with Bessie; the awe in which I held my mother. But about this madness I knew nothing.

I had to see her. Where was she? Somewhere in this hall! At which table? The tables must be cleared.

I stood up, and said as much. Wolsey demurred: the dainties had not yet been served. Then there would be gaming and—

"Not at midday," I said. "It is unseemly." I stared out at the crowd; where *was* she? "I wish to dance." Yes, dance. I would meet her there!

"Your Majesty . . . my minstrels have been dismissed, there are no musicians—"

Wolsey had been taken unawares. I laughed. I laughed so loudly that everyone around me turned to stare. "Then let us mingle without music!" I said. What difference? I must find her, and I did not need music to do so.

"But I—"

"Clear the tables, Wolsey. More food will only make us stuporous when we once again face the heat." I hoped that sounded reasonably logical.

"Yes, yes, of course." He scurried away to do my bidding.

Now the hall was cleared and the guests began to mill about and talk— not the least about the King's strange behaviour, first in elevating his bastard son, and then in cutting short the celebratory banquet.

There was no sign of her. No sign of a bright yellow dress among all those revellers, and I searched for yellow; I could see a yellow purse or sash or neckband from a hundred feet away. Yellow danced before my eyes like a mocking field of butterflies. But no one with long black hair in a yellow gown.

I was angry; I was bored; I wanted to be gone. I also felt stifled in the Great Hall. It was too low-ceilinged, and thereby oppressive. The windows did not admit enough light. This was not a confessional, it was a place for gaiety!

I must have light and air! What possessed Wolsey to build such a box? Was it to remind him of his priestly past? I shoved my way over to the side doors and pushed them open. Heat, like a living thing, poured in. It was hot as the Holy Land outside. Even the air was heavy, worse than that inside the Great Hall.

Then I saw them in the garden. I saw a yellow dress, and a slim young girl inside it; I saw her holding hands with a tall, gawky youth, and I saw her—*her!*—lean forward to kiss him. They were standing before the flower garden, and all about them were yellow flowers. Yellow dress, yellow flowers, hot yellow sun, even yellow dandelions at my feet. I slammed the door.

Wolsey came toward me, clutching a yellowed letter. "I thought you might like to read—"

I dashed it from his hands. "No!"

He was stricken. "But it is the history of the land of Hampton Court, when it was still called the Hospitallers' Preceptory, and owned by the Knights of St. John of Jerusalem—"

Poor Wolsey! He had made a grand offering, and I had trampled on it. I retrieved the letter. "Later, perhaps." I swung open the door again; once again the sultry air of a foreign land swam in. The flower garden, some fifty feet away, shimmered in the light and heat. The yellow-clad figure was still there, and the tall boy was no longer letting her kiss him; he was embracing her. They stood very still; only the air danced around them.

"Who is that?" I said, as if I had seen them for the first time.

"Anne Boleyn, Your Majesty," he said. "And Henry Percy. Young Percy is heir to the Earl of Northumberland. A fine lad; he's in my service. His father sent him to learn under me. He and Boleyn's—pardon me, Sire, Viscount Rochford's—daughter are betrothed. Or rather, the betrothal will be announced once Percy's father comes south. You know how difficult it is for those on the border to travel—"

"I forbid it!" I heard myself saying.

Wolsey stared.

"I said I forbid the marriage! It cannot take place!"

"But, Your Majesty, they have already—"

"I do not care!" Ah, but years later how I was to wish I had allowed him to complete that particular sentence! "I said I will not permit this marriage! It is . . . unsuitable."

"But, Your Majesty . . . what shall I tell Percy?"

They were still in the garden, hugging. Now he was toying with her hair. A grin spread over his silly face. Or was it a grin? The rising heat made it difficult to see.

"You, who have no trouble telling kings and emperors and popes what to do?" I began to laugh again, too loudly. "You cannot speak to a—a"—I thought hard for the image the hateful Percy boy evoked in me—"a silly, long-legged bird—a stork?"

I slammed the door and shut out the vision and the heat. Wolsey was discomfited.

"A boy? You fear to face a boy?" I taunted him. "And yet you would have been Pope?"

"Yes, Your Majesty. I'll tell him."

Now I was surrounded by the press of people. Uncomfortable inside, tormented outside. Clearly, I must leave. The banqueting hall was a vise, pressing down upon me. Without thinking, I said, "I'll have it all pulled down, and put up a new Great Hall." Wolsey looked even more unhappy. Obviously something had gone wrong in his plans to impress me.

Agitated and not myself at all, I pulled out the deed to Hampton Court. "I thank you for your gift," I said. "But you may stay here as long as you live. It is still yours."

He looked like a stricken calf spared just as he approaches the slaughterhouse. (Why could I think only of animal images that day?) He had made his gesture and it had been duly registered, yet he did not have to pay the price.

"Thank you, Your Majesty." He bowed low.

"Break the betrothal," I said, pushing past him.

As I rode toward the river, where the royal barge waited, I became uncomfortably aware of the yellow marigolds bordering the courtyard. And once I was on board, bankside yellow buttercups mocked me all the way back to London, as they lay bright and open under the new summer sun.

A month passed. I heard nothing of the matter from Wolsey, did not see the new Viscount Rochford or his daughter. It was high summer, my usual time for sport and athletic practise, yet I found myself unable to lose myself in either. Instead I was sunk in self-evaluation and gloom.

I thought: I am now thirty-five years old. At my age my father had fought for, and won, a crown. He had ended the wars. He had produced a son and a daughter. He had put down rebellions, trounced pretenders. What have I done? Nothing that posterity would note. When latter-day historians wrote my history, they would say nothing beyond "he succeeded his father, Henry VII. . . ."

I was a man imprisoned, feeling helpless, borne along against my will. True, I could command banquets and even armies, and order men to transfer from this post to that—it yet remained a fact that I was a prisoner in the truest sense. In my marriage, in my childlessness, in what I could and could not do. Would Father have been ashamed of me? What would *he* have done under my circumstances? Incredibly, I longed to talk with him, consult him.

Alternating with these dreary moods were acute longings to see Mistress Boleyn. Over and over I pictured her as she stood on the platform (I did not care to think of her in the garden with Percy), until the actual picture in my mind began to fade like a garment left too long to dry in the sun. I had thought of her so much I could no longer see her in my mind.

Clearly, I must see her again. To what end? That I did not ask myself. For yet another fading picture? No. That I knew. If I saw her again, it would not be for a brief glimpse, but for—what?

I sent for Wolsey. His discreet diplomatic summaries had arrived at my work room in a never-ending stream, but there was no mention of the personal commission I had given him. Had he failed to execute it?

Wolsey arrived promptly on the hour. He was, as usual, perfectly groomed and garbed and perfumed. By the time he reached me in my inner room, he was alone and free of his ever-present attendants, of which he had as many as I.

"Your Majesty," he said, bending low, as always. He straightened and awaited my questions on Francis, Charles, the Pope.

"Henry Percy—" I began, then found myself suddenly embarrassed. I did not want Wolsey to know how important this was to me. "The unfortunate affair between the Earl of Northumberland's son and Viscount Rochford's daughter—I trust it has been terminated. I told you to attend to it."

He moved toward me—surprisingly swift for someone so bulky—and made motions for me to come closer.

"Yes. It is over," he said confidentially. "Although it was quite a stormy end. I called young Percy to me and told him how unseemly it was for him to have entangled himself with a foolish girl like Mistress Boleyn—"

By this time he was at my side, breathing heavily. Did I wince when he referred to Anne as a "foolish girl"? I noted his eye upon me.

"—without permission from his father. In fact, I said"—here he drew himself up to full height, and puffed up like a pig's bladder—" 'I myself know that your father will be mightily displeased, as he has arranged another and much more suitable betrothal for you.' Then the lad turned pale and looked as awkward as a child. . . . Your Majesty, are you unwell?" Wolsey solicitously rushed to me as I took a seat in the nearest chair, albeit shakily.

"No," I said curtly. "Pray continue."

"Ah, then. I had to shame him ere he consented. To threaten him, even. He claimed he and the Lady Boleyn had—what were his words?—'in this matter gone so far before so many worthy witnesses I know not how to withdraw myself nor to relieve my conscience.' So I said—"

Had he possessed her? Is that what he meant? I gripped the carved chair-arms until one sharp piece seemed to cut into my fingers.

"—'Surely you know the King and I can deal with a matter as inconsequential as this. We who have dealt with the Emperor, and drawn up the treaty of—' "

"Yes, Wolsey. Then what happened?"

He looked frustrated to be denied yet another chance to recite his diplomatic triumphs. But I could command, where poor Percy was forced to listen. For a moment I sympathized with the lad.

"He wept. He said he loved her. A tiresome business, Your Majesty. He stuck to his contention that he loved the girl and would marry her, regardless. I was forced to send for his father. Aha!" he chuckled, rubbing his cheek. "That did it! His father came down from Northumberland, and castigated him in my presence. I cannot remember all his words, but in essence he threatened to disinherit him if he continued in this misalliance. He called him a 'proud, presumptuous, disdainful, profligate waster' who had 'misused' himself . . . and so on."

"Then where is he?"

"His father took him from my service," Wolsey said, shrugging. He walked across the room without leave and made for pears heaped in a silver bowl. Munching one, he turned and gave me a smug smile. Pear juice dripped from the right side of his mouth.

"Mistress Boleyn," he said, in blurred syllables as he slurped the overripe pear, "was quite angry, so I understand. She made several unseemly displays of temper after Percy's removal. So I ordered her from court." He daintily put the denuded pear stem on a silver platter. "I sent her back home. To Hever."

Anne, gone! Anne, not at court!

"I see," I said.

"She wished evil on me," said Wolsey. "She cursed me and said if it ever lay in her power, she would revenge herself on me." He laughed. "A child like that! If ever it lay in her power—" He stopped, concerned. "Your Majesty! Do you not think it humorous that a child like that should say—?"

"Yes, yes!" I barked. "Very humorous!" What was this woman? For she was no child, that I knew. I heaved myself up from the chair. "Very humorous," I repeated, for want of anything better to say. Suddenly it became important that Wolsey not *know*, not suspect. . . . "You did well. I thank you. Now for the dispatches from the Venetian merchants—"

After he was gone, I paced my floors. Anne was at Hever. Hever was in the hunt country, a day's ride from London. I would go there. Tomorrow? No, I needed more time to be ready. The next day, then.

Out of deference, Wolsey had neglected to tell me one other thing that I learned much later: Anne had cursed me as well as the Cardinal. She hated us equally.

XXXIII

Usually when I went hunting I took several attendants. This day, I decided to take but one, William Compton, and a groom for each of us, and to dispense with the usual retinue. So anxious was I that everything be right that I gave instructions to the stables a full day in advance as to which horses and equipment I desired.

I was awake long before dawn. I lay in bed watching the sky lighten, and thanked God the day would be clear. As I lay there, I was conscious of but one thought: Today I see her. Today I speak with her. Today I bring her to court.

I did not frame my words or rehearse them. I had always had the gift of knowing what to say upon the occasion, and like as not rehearsed words would have been inappropriate. I could picture Anne's face as I told her she was being recalled to court. How happy she would be! And then, once she was there, she would become my mistress. Thinking of that black hair spread round her head on a pillow, knowing that I could bury my face in it . . . Mother of God, would the hour of arising never come? I dared not get up, for fear of disturbing Henry Norris, the attendant who slept on a pallet at the foot of my bed. I was a prisoner in my own bed.

At last there was a stirring. The grooms of the chamber arrived to lay the fire, as they always did at six o'clock. Then came the Esquires of the Robe with my clothes for the day, duly warmed. Norris stirred on his pallet and stumbled sleepily to the door. The day had begun.

By eight I had breakfasted and was in the saddle, attended by Compton and two grooms. Even so, it would be mid-afternoon before we reached Hever. And en route I must stop and pretend to hunt, which would slow us even more.

It was July, but the day promised to be relatively cool and clear. The sky showed not a single cloud, and faint breezes rippled the long grass and made the leaves in the great oaks tremble.

How green it was! The abundant rainfall of the past two weeks had freshened and quickened every growing thing, giving us a second spring. All round me was green—underfoot in the thick grass, overhead in the great trees, turning the very sunlight green as it fought its way through layers of leaves. I was submerged in a sea of green murkiness, alternating with cool, clear openness whenever I emerged from the forest.

At length I stood on the hill above Hever Castle and looked down upon it. It was called a castle, but it was not, being but a fortified manor house, and a small one at that. A ten-foot-wide moat surrounded it, fed by a running stream which sparkled in the sunlight. I could see no one about the grounds. Were they away, then? I prayed that would not be so. But as I approached the manor house I felt more and more dispirited. It looked deserted. I had come all this way for nothing. Yet a prior announcement of my intended visit would have evoked entertainment, a banquet, and every formality I wished to avoid.

The drawbridge was down. We rode across it into the empty, cobble-stoned courtyard.

I scanned the windows on all three sides of the courtyard. There was no sign of movement behind any of them.

A large grey-and-amber mottled cat appeared from an open side door and sauntered across the courtyard. We stood awkwardly, our horses stamping and moving restlessly back and forth, their hooves making loud noises on the stones. Still no one appeared.

"Compton," I finally said, "see if Viscount Rochford is at home." I knew, however, that had he been there, he would long since have appeared in the courtyard, making effusive gestures of welcome. William dismounted and knocked upon the scarred center door. The knocker made a mournful sound, and no one opened the door. He made a gesture of helplessness to me and had started to return to his horse when at length the door creaked open. An old woman looked out. Compton spun around.

"His Majesty the King has come to see Viscount Rochford," he said, grandly.

The woman looked confused. "But—he did not know—"

I urged my horse forward. "Of course not," I said. " 'Twas but an impulse. I was hunting nearby and took a fancy to see the Viscount. Is your master in?"

"No. He—he—went to Groombridge to inspect his tenant cottages there. He said he would return by late afternoon."

I shot a look at the sun. It was halfway down in the sky. "We will await him," I said.

The woman appeared even more upset. "But, Your Grace, there is nothing—"

I dismounted and made for the door she guarded. "I require nothing," I said. "Nothing save a place to rest and perhaps have a sip of ale before returning to London."

She stepped aside and ushered us into the stone-cooled darkness of the house. "The Great Hall is here—" She led us into a large room, hardly a Great Hall. "I will bring refreshment," she said, scurrying off.

The room was sparsely furnished, with an exquisite Flanders tapestry covering the inner wall. The long oaken dining table was expertly carved, and by the great fireplace stood one of the new sort of drawer-cabinets.

My men stood about awkwardly. There was no place for them to sit, and the stone floor was bare. It being July, the fireplace was not in use, denying them the usual time-killing activity of standing before it.

In a moment the old woman returned with a tray containing a golden pitcher and four goblets. She put it down on the table and filled the goblets, handing one to each of us. Then she looked about guiltily: should she leave or stay? It seemed a breach of etiquette to leave the King unattended, but a worse one for a kitchen servant to undertake to receive and entertain him. The dilemma was ended by the sound of hoofbeats in the courtyard: Boleyn was back. In a moment he burst into the house and, having recognized the royal trappings on my horse tethered outside, proceeded to rush to my side.

"Ah, Your Majesty! If only I had known!" he began, ready to string a row of compliments.

"If you had known, then you would be a sorcerer, and such I would not have at court. The truth is that I myself did not know I was coming. How then could *you* possibly have known?"

He beamed, but looked about uneasily, checking to see whether anything was in gross disarray. "I am honoured that you would see fit to come here without notice. It means you regard this as your home, as I hope you always will."

Home? One is not nervous in one's own home; one does not sweat or pace about, or peer out windows. No, Hever Castle was no home to me, nor ever would be.

I smiled. "Thank you. I was hunting, and—" I gestured apologetically toward my hunting clothes.

He twitched a bit and went to inspect the ale. "The ale is superb," I said, sparing him the trouble of asking.

"Would you care for something more? To strengthen you for your return trip? Not that I wish you to return; I would be honoured if you would stay the night, it would be—" He was fairly comical in his frantic desire to accommodate and flatter me.

"No, Thomas," I assured him. "I must needs be in London early in the morning."

His son George strode in, clad all in velvet, and stood stock-still, staring at me.

He was a comely lad of twenty or so, all bedecked in courtier fashion.

I had heard he wrote music and played the lute with talent. I said as much, and requested that he play one of his compositions for me, a request which seemed to embarrass him. He complied, however, disappearing from the chamber and returning a few moments later with a mother-of-pearl-inlaid lute. He sang one melody, a plaintive minor tune to do with lost love. It was quite good. I told him so, and meant it. He showed me his instrument, which he said had been made in Italy, and I duly inspected it.

Lady Boleyn then appeared, and other members of the household. They bustled about and laid a fire, as it would soon be growing dark, and nights in old stone manor houses are damp and cold even in July. But where was Anne? Somehow I could not bring myself to ask.

The sun set, but the light lingered on, as it does in high summer. Boleyn talked to me incessantly, trotting after me like a trained puppy. I did not hear him, and gave noncommittal responses. Still no Anne, and soon we must be gone, or suffer through a long, drawn-out supper laid in our honour.

I passed the small leaded windows along one side of the hall overlooking the tidy Boleyn garden and grounds. The stream which fed their moat trickled through the garden, lined by weeping willows. The wind had risen, as it often does in early evening, whipping about the branches. They were so green they almost glowed, and so thin and whiplike they seemed to writhe like living things.

It was then I saw her, standing by a far willow: a thin figure with long hair that tossed and waved like the branches surrounding her. Anne.

She was wearing green, light green, and her gown billowed in the wind, causing her to sway like the stalk of a flower. She reached out to touch a branch with her hand, and it was the most graceful movement I had ever seen.

I became aware that I had stopped and was staring. Thomas cleared his throat beside me.

"My daughter Anne," he said. "She is back here with us at home, as the Cardinal sent her from court. It was most unfair—"

"I am sure." I turned and pushed past him. "I will speak to your daughter myself." Earlier I had seen the door that opened onto the garden. Now I would avail myself of it.

"Pray do not accompany me," I said to the trailing Thomas. "I will go alone."

Before he could protest, I was out in the garden, slamming the door behind me. It clanged and made that peculiar noise which tight-fitting doors do when suddenly closed. In another part of my mind I thought that the Viscount must enjoy a draught-free hall in winter.

But that was in a small part of my mind, and went almost unnoticed. The larger part was straining toward the slim figure in the far end of the garden. Resolutely, I made my way toward her.

She must have heard me approaching, yet she did not turn. She kept her back to me until I was a scant two yards away. The wind had risen and was lifting her skirts in great swirls. She wore no covering, no shawl. Was she not cold? Still she stood, motionless, save for the tossing of that extraordinary hair.

"Mistress Boleyn," I said loudly, and she turned.

What had I expected? I knew she was not like her sister Mary, yet I was ill prepared for this dark wraith.

She looked at me with wide eyes, great black eyes, child's eyes. "Your Majesty," she gasped, then swooped to the ground like the brushing of a butterfly's wing. All I could see for a moment was the top of that black head, a gleaming part in the middle. As she rose, the wind caught her hair and for an instant her face disappeared, like a pale spring moon covered by fast-moving clouds.

Then she faced me. She was tall, and her magnificent black hair enveloped her like a mantle.

I knew not what to say, yet I must say something. "Will you not join us inside?" The first sentence that ever I spoke to her.

Her eyes met mine boldly. "I prefer the garden just at sunset. The wind comes up, and the clouds become streaked—"

"An artist," I said quickly, not realizing how sharp it sounded. "Yet even artists must have fellowship."

"Yes. I am told that there are certain quarters of London where they . . . congregate and enjoy their own sort of fellowship. I should love to join them!" Her voice was fierce.

I remembered my own longing to run away and sail the seas. We were alike . . . our souls were alike. . . .

"They do lascivious and bold things there, Lady." I was testing her. What would she answer?

"That affrights me not. I could join them or not, as I chose."

She looked at me, her eyes burning into mine. A pale face, rimmed by black hair . . . I shivered, felt an eerie prickling on my neck and arms. . . .

"Would you be a Gypsy, then, and live with the outcasts? For these 'artists' are accounted as the damned."

"No. The damned are here, at Hever, in a great limbo decreed by the Cardinal. He sent me here, for daring to love a man already betrothed!"

"It is your home."

She looked back at the warm, golden stones of Hever. "It was never home to me."

"Then return to court," I said. "Return, and serve the Queen. As maid of honour." I promoted her on a breath. "And your brother George," I added on sudden impulse, "can become a groom of my bedchamber. You should come together."

She smiled, and it lighted her face as the sun shining through a leaf. "Truly?"

"Truly," I said solemnly.

She laughed, and was no longer a fey creature with swirling witch's-hair, but the woman I had been waiting all my life to love. It was terrifyingly simple.

"Will you come?" I asked, shaken.

"Aye," she said.

I held out my hand and she took it, and together we walked back to her father's hall.

It was strange to reenter the hall and find everyone still standing unchanged, whereas I had been utterly transformed. I dropped Mistress Boleyn's hand as her father came toward us anxiously.

"I wish Mistress Anne to return to court," I announced, before he could open his loose-lipped mouth. "And George as well."

"But the Cardinal—" he began, his brow furrowing.

"The Cardinal be damned!" I shouted, causing everyone to turn in our direction. I lowered my voice. "*I* am King, not the Cardinal. If I say Mistress Anne and Master George shall come to court, the Cardinal has nothing to do with the matter. And if I say the Cardinal should depart for his Archbishopric in York, then to York he shall go, and straightway." I was shaking with anger. Did the Cardinal rule, then?

But I knew what he had meant. He feared and *revered* the Cardinal above his King. How many other people in the realm felt likewise?

It was already dark as we mounted for our long ride back to London. We would not reach Westminster until well past midnight. As soon as they were out of eyesight of the Viscount, my companions, having assured him that they were not in the least hungry, dug into the linen-wrapped food parcels the royal cooks had prepared in the morning for them. They ate ravenously as we rode along.

I should have been hungry, but I was not. The moon, in its last quarter, did not rise until we approached the outskirts of London. Even then I was neither hungry nor tired, but strangely filled with energy and purpose. The rising moon illuminated the sleeping city, and from a distance I thought there could be no fairer city, no more fortunate ruler, no more blessed land.

Anne was coming to court!

And once there, she would become my mistress—no, my lover, for "mistress" was too circumscribed, too curtailed. My lover, my confidante, my soul-mate. Yes, my soul-mate. My soul, alone too long, needed this fellow wanderer. Together we would make a whole. And, wandering stars no more, joined, blaze through the sky. . . .

How can I explain it? There was something in her which drew me, as if lying on her breast I would know everything in life I desired to, and the unopened door would open for me. . . .

At base it is inexplicable. Something deep within Anne called to something deep within me. And the calling was powerful; nay, undeniable.

XXXIV

In a fortnight I must go and make my progress about the home shires. And then, when I returned, Anne would be waiting for me, having by that time settled herself at court. Knowing this made each day of the progress (normally so satisfying for me) something that only served to bring me one day closer to my goal, my desire. . . .

But when I returned, and made my customary call on Katherine, I was disappointed to find no hint of Anne's presence among her attendants.

"I had assigned a new maid of honour to your entourage," I said when we were at last alone. "Mistress Anne Boleyn."

Katherine wheeled around and faced me. "Yes. After the other—"

"She is nothing like her sister," I informed her quickly—too quickly.

Katherine, clad all in black, raised her eyes to heaven. "God be thanked for that."

"Mistress Anne is chaste, and very concerned with matters of learning."

"You seem well acquainted with the lady. Is she to be your next mistress?" Katherine cried. Her whole body shook in the noonday light. Part of me wished to take her in my arms and comfort her; another part was repelled by her.

"I do not wish to cause you discomfort," I said. "I merely enquired as to whether she had come to—"

"I will not permit it!" she shrieked, and came at me—slowly, in light of her dignified bulk and the distance. "First that Blount creature, then the Boleyn girl—all at court, all paraded before me—"

"Of course not!" I pushed her back with one hand, summoning all the outrage I could find within myself. "Wife, you forget yourself. I have no mistresses, nor have had for some three years past. I have no wish for mistresses —and if I had, it would not be Boleyn's scrawny younger daughter, fresh from the French court!"

Katherine drew herself up. "Of course not," she agreed.

She is true royalty, I found myself thinking of Katherine in admiration. "Mistress Anne is nothing to excite any man's imagination," I sneered.

Yet she excited mine. Even as I exited from the Queen's inner chambers, I looked for Anne. A flock of young, pretty attendants clustered about, but she was not among them. Wearing an artificial smile, I made my way to the outer doors, wondering all the while where Anne was.

It seemed that Anne was hiding herself from me, if indeed she had come to court at all, as Katherine had cleverly avoided answering. Whenever I called on Katherine, Anne was not there. Whenever Katherine came in state for any special ceremony, Anne was not there. I was near despair, but I could not enquire of Katherine a second time.

The next few weeks were torturous for me. I was so obsessed by Anne, I could hardly give myself to the necessary duties of kingship, such as the day I was to entertain a group of merchants from the Wool Staple of Calais.

I was in no humour to receive the merchants of Calais. Perhaps it was my own failing, but I was in no way sociable. I wished I could take the religious licence and become a hermit for a time. I would not care if I had to give up my fine robes and rooming. To be a hermit, to be utterly alone and responsible only before God, seemed a luxury—more of a luxury than palaces and robes and royal duties.

But such surcease was not permitted me. I was King. Therefore I must be always at everyone's disposal. A common man might become a hermit, but I, never.

And a hermit never burned as I did. I burned to see Anne. And burned with a desire to change things, change myself, change my entire life.

The merchants of Calais paid audience in my Receiving Chamber. They were full of talk of wool quotas, and money exchange, and they bored me exceedingly. As the noise level rose to intolerable levels, I begged leave to retire to my inner chambers for a few moments.

As I waited there, I became aware of voices just outside my inner chamber. A public gallery adjoined the receiving rooms, and I had given leave for the wool merchants' attendants to have access to them.

"Nay, but His Majesty must protect our interests in Calais," one voice said, a high, disagreeable one.

"His Majesty knows nothing of trade, nor of finances," said another. This one was smooth and seemingly knowledgeable. "The Cardinal takes care of all that. Why not apply for a position with him?"

"The Cardinal is not King," said yet a third voice, deep and sarcastic, "although he would like to think himself so. Many things in life bring surprises, and I believe the great Cardinal may come upon one soon."

"The Cardinal is never surprised," said the second voice.

"The Cardinal is intelligent," allowed the third voice, "yet intelligence is not . . . how shall I say it? There is an intelligence beyond ordinary intelligence. By that I mean an ability to see which way things will go, to look at things as they are and predict in what direction they will flow. The Cardinal is sadly lacking in that ability. He sees the immediate, but nothing beyond that."

I must confess that by this time my ears were straining to hear this extraordinary conversation. Keep in mind that for upwards of fifteen years no one had dared to speak truth to my face; therefore I was reduced to hearing it behind my back.

"He does well enough by that."

"For now," said the third voice. "But I predict it cannot last."

"Whyfor not?" began the second voice.

"You know nothing!" cut in the first, querulous voice. "Stuck away in Calais! This is your first time at court, is it not?"

"Aye," said the deep third.

"You cannot know anything beyond stinking wool and an occasional royal visit. These people are different. They behave differently, they think differently—"

"What people, Rob?" The deep third voice again.

"Court people, you fool!"

"Then you're the fool. They are as you." A pause. "Yes, and the King, too. He may look as Apollo come to earth, he may have riches exceeding yours—still he's but a man. With many cares, cares that exceed yours. Withal, he still must use the jordan upon arising."

They all laughed at this.

Did they imagine me using the jordan, then? That thought was offensive. I pressed closer, to hear better.

"We all must use jordans," the first, unpleasant voice said. "Else we be dead. So what does that prove?"

"Nothing. You are correct, Nicholas"—so, first-voice's name was Nicholas—"the jordans are necessary for all. Doubtless even Our Lord had to relieve Himself whilst on earth. That did not detract from His message."

The third voice again. Who was this man? I determined to meet him. Saying that Our Saviour . . . ! Yet He was fully man, is that not what the Church Councils had decided? Then He must have—I slammed my mind on such thought. And charged out into the audience room once more.

The emissaries had ceased their chatter and were expectantly awaiting my re-entrance.

I settled myself into the grand audience chair and nodded for them to continue. They did, as if they had not been interrupted for a passage of time.

"Your Grace, the scales in use in Calais—" A man began.

"I trust your plan to replace the old method of weighing per sheep with the more modern one of pure wool volume," another said.

"And who invented that?" I said. "The French?"

One of the men stepped forward to make apologies. "Aye," he said. "But the French have perfected a new way of weighing wool—"

Always the French! Was I never to be free of them?

"I favour whatever method brings the most money to England," I said. "I leave it to you gentlemen to determine the most efficacious."

They presented several other petitions, and I gave them all due consideration. Then, mercifully, the audience was done. They hurried to the gallery door to admit their servitors, as these important merchants could never carry their own books or cloaks. A large group streamed in.

Which was the deep-voiced speaker? How could I single him out from the swarming rest of them? Not once had he spoken the name of his master; cautious fellow, that. I admired him all the more.

The entire company were gathering up their goods and issuing instructions to their attendants. I began to walk among them. This occasioned stoppage of conversation and much obeisance, which was quite the opposite of my intention. As soon as I came within a length of a man, he turned, smiled, and stood like a frightened rabbit. God's blood! And kings are expected to know their subjects' minds?

I heard no voices, as they fell silent whenever I was near. But as the company prepared to depart (it was time for yet another royal audience for me), near the door I heard a phrase—and a tone—that was reminiscent of the mysterious one I had overheard. I approached the merchant and his assistant, who were engaged in putting on their cloaks and gathering their parcels.

"I beg your pardon," I said. They both stared at me, startled. I turned directly to the assistant. "Were you in the walk-gallery just now?"

"Yes," he said, without hesitation.

"Did you speak to your fellow assistants about the Cardinal? Did you mention that perhaps even the King uses a jordan?"

The man was small and saturnine, and there was no flinching on his part. "Aye." He looked me boldly in the face.

"Think you not that I am an eavesdropper," I said haughtily, "but the voices were clear—" I stopped. Why was I apologizing to this lad? "Your voice was beguiling. Your words made sense. And you had special humour. I am in need of a jester. I invite you to come to court in that capacity."

He remained impassive. Finally he spoke. "My Lord, I am not trained in formal joke-making. Nor would most of my observations be tolerable to court listeners."

"No. They prefer bawdy references over astute comments. But there is room at court for both. I will get a low fellow—"

He grinned. "I can be bawdy far more readily than astute."

"Then you will come?" I asked. "There is great need of such as you."

"Since Queen Katherine has become so pious?"

He was correct, yet out of bounds. "Watch your tongue!" I heard myself saying.

"If I must watch my tongue, what point in being a jester?"

All this time the man's master was staring, as if in disbelief of the exchange.

"In private you may say what you like," I agreed. "But before others, there are certain topics not to be mentioned."

&ℰℛ WILL:

That is how I came into King Henry's employ. It was all happenstance, as the greatest events in our lives are. I can assure you I had no portent that the King himself was hearing my words as I passed the time with some rather dull companions during that audience, nor could I remember my words.

But I do remember seeing the King that day. He seemed burdened, distracted, not at all the young creature I had seen many years ago on his way to Dover, nor even the godlike one I had glimpsed from afar in Calais. This was an older man, one with many cares and envies. I agreed to enter his service for reasons which eluded me at the time. Certainly I had no desire to wear a costume and entertain thick-headed court people. But the King drew me. And needed me, so I sensed. (Vanity?)

He would not permit me to return to Calais with my master, insisting that all my possessions could be sent. In truth, they were not many. I was to become part of court from that moment on.

I quickly perceived that a man could never be free at court. Like a compost heap, this mass of festering humanity was always hot, full of bad humours, and in the midst of colourful decay.

At the top of it all was the King himself, trying to oversee this seething mass. His "household" was also his government, which must be always near at hand. I was surprised at his memory and almost supernatural recall of details. He did not forget me, even amongst the throng, or amid his ever-pressing duties.

⁊ HENRY VIII:

Will never learned that expediency, which is why he eventually became my private jester. He and the court were simply not suitable partners, as consequent events proved. Yet his wit and observations were invaluable to me; I liked to keep him about me.

XXXV

olsey was to have a great banquet and feast for upwards of one hundred guests, to celebrate something or other; I cannot remember what. He surreptitiously circulated the guest list to my chamber. I added several names to it, including Mistress Anne's, then smuggled it back to him, as I was supposed to be ignorant of the proceedings.

Would she be there? Would Wolsey issue the correct invitation? If he did, would she accept? I had at last ascertained that she had come to court. But perhaps she might be too retiring . . . or wonder why she was included amongst the hated Cardinal's celebrations. God's blood! Was there no place on earth where I might see her without being dependent on others to bring it about?

Etiquette demanded that I don a disguise for the occasion (as I was ostensibly not among the guests), and I decided upon that of a shepherd. But I could not arrive unaccompanied, I must have fellow shepherds. Thus I chose them: dear Brandon, my cousin Courtenay, William Compton, Edward Neville, and Anne's father, Thomas.

It was late October, but still mild. A slight row upstream on the Thames would be enjoyable, especially as a fatted moon would soon be rising. My companions and I would row to York Place and wait until the fête was well under way to make our entrance.

The oars dipping in the moon-coated water made reassuring sounds. Water had a soothing effect upon me. *She* would be there; I knew she would. Pray God she would!

We reached York Place in a short time, as it lay near the heart of London. Now that Hampton Court was officially mine, Wolsey was reluctant to entertain me in it, although he continued to live there.

The landing was strung with late-blooming flowers, and there were discreet lights along the walkway. All around me there was a great commotion; my companions were unruly, slapping and hitting one another boisterously, so that they must surely attract attention. I spoke to them sharply, and they subsided, then followed me quietly along the pathway.

Outside the palace we paused. Every window glowed yellow from the torches and candles within. Just as I was gesturing to my men, a deafening roar and tumult drowned our voices. The sound was followed by several loud splashes in the Thames. Small cannon.

"They welcome us," I said. "How kind, as we are all foreigners." I looked around at the faces of my companions, ill-lit by the light from the palace windows. "You all speak French, do you not?" They nodded, not quite in unison. "That is fortunate, as we are lost French shepherds. Come, my friends." I led the way to the Cardinal's great studded door and banged on it. It was promptly opened by a servant who stared at us and pretended to be quite dumbfounded by our costumes and presence.

"Where is your master?" I demanded in my best French. Someone else scuttled up to translate. The servant bowed and gestured that we should follow him.

The Great Hall was brightly lit, more brightly than it had seemed from the outside. Before us stretched long tables, all in readiness for the banquet. An early-season fire crackled in the enormous fireplace, and all about was the buzz of voices—a buzz which silenced itself as we appeared in the doorway.

A server came to our sides and inquired after our business. I played my part and answered in French. He then gestured helplessly toward his master, Wolsey, resplendent in scarlet satin and seated under the canopy of estate. At the sight of us he heaved himself out of his great carved chair and waddled forward—although his robes concealed the waddling and made him seem to float serenely toward us.

"Strangers!" he cried. "How did you come here?"

I answered in French, to which he held up his hands as if in ignorance.

"They are Frenchmen! French shepherds!" he said pointedly. "Yet even though we feel animosity toward their King, we must bid them welcome." He gestured toward one of the long tables.

Long ere he had done so, I had scanned them all. Was *she* there? I could not see her.

I took my place and ate a full banquet, which later was described as "splendid and glittering." I suppose it was, with all its silver and gold plate and sumptuous courses. I knew not, I was so impatient to see if *she* were present. What did I care for food or plates or dainties? I had had fifteen years of them!

After the banquet there would be games of chance—mumchance and shovel-board and Noddy. We must perforce go around all the tables, playing against the guests, at Wolsey's expense. He had bowls and bowls of ducats about. At every gaming table I searched for Mistress Anne, but she was not to be found.

At length, Wolsey had a trumpet blown. "I am ready to retire to my chair of estate," he announced, gathering his glimmering satin folds about him. "But now I perceive that there is one greater than I present in the company, one who rightly may claim the chair. I beg you, if you know him, to identify him, so that I may do him honour."

What a silly game this was! I was weary of such. I was weary of much, truth be told.

"Sir," said Henry Courtenay—ever the eager courtier—"we confess that among us there is such a noble personage; and if you can pick him out, he will be pleased to reveal himself and accept your place."

Now the clever eyes of Wolsey flicked back and forth. He could immediately eliminate the shorter men in their shepherd's costumes. That still left me, Edward Neville, and Charles Brandon. Brandon was broader and thicker than I, so Wolsey could make a distinction there. Neville was bareheaded (although masked), holding his headdress in hand. His thick red-gold hair glinted in the torchlight and drew Wolsey's eye.

The portly Cardinal approached Neville. "It seems to me the gentleman with the black cloak should be even he," he said, offering his chair to Neville.

Neville hesitated, unsure of what further action to take. I rescued him by laughing and pulling off my visor. The entire company joined suit.

The Cardinal turned, discomfited. "Your Majesty," he said quietly. "I see I was deceived in you."

Years later he was to claim that moment as an omen.

But all things are seen in retrospect as omens. I could say Katherine's initial delay in her sailing to England, my having had the dream of a white-faced woman . . . all were omens. Should we think in such fashion, all of life would become one giant omen, and we should fear to stir.

Regardless, the fête must proceed. After the initial embarrassment, Wolsey was able to cover his awkwardness and signal for the festivities to continue.

There was to be masked dancing, and the musicians assembled in the gallery. Twelve of us were to lead partners in an intricate round. We were free to choose unknown ladies.

Where was Mistress Anne? I searched the company and still did not see her. Wolsey had solicitously ordered a number of torches damped. The resulting dim light merely shadowed all faces and turned each person into a trimmed headdress and a gleam of satin. They all stood two and three deep near the walls, and it was impossible to see a single face behind the first row.

Mistress Carew was in front, smiling. She danced well; I supposed she would do as well as any other. I made my way toward her and was on the point of asking her to join me when all at once I saw Anne. At first she was but a row of pearls gleaming like a supernatural halo. Then within that circlet I saw her face.

She was standing well back from the others, as if to forestall being chosen as anyone's partner. There was no torch near her to show her. Nothing betrayed her presence save the luminous pearls encircling her head.

I pushed my way over to her, to everyone's surprise, not the least her own. She stared at me as I approached.

"Your Majesty." She lowered her head. I took her hand and together we went to the middle of the dance-floor.

In the brighter light, I could see that the startling crown of pearls was attached to a small velvet cap. I complimented her on it, and she replied that it was the fashion in France. Her voice was low—unlike the fashionable high voices of our court ladies. Her gown was also different; it had long, full sleeves which almost completely obscured her hands. She had designed it herself. Then I thought it charming. Now I know why she needed to do so—to hide her witch's mark! But as I took her hand to dance, I did not discern the small sixth finger, so skilfully did she conceal it beneath the others. . . .

She danced well—better, in fact, than any of our Englishwomen. When I praised her for it, she shrugged, and once again gave the credit to France.

"I learned there. Everyone dances well in France. There I was accounted of little accomplishment in the art."

"France," I laughed. "Where all is false, where artificiality is elevated to an art form. Because they are hollow at the core, they must celebrate the exterior."

"You are too harsh with France," she said. "Too quick to dismiss its very real pleasures—among them, the ability to appreciate the pretend."

"A polite word for 'the false.'"

She laughed. "That is the difference between an Englishman and a Frenchman!"

"The French King is a case in point," I muttered. What had she thought of Francis?

"Exactly! And he is delightful!"

Francis? Delightful?

"At least your sister thought so," I said censoriously.

She drew back. "Yes, I believe she did," she paused. "And she was certainly in a position to compare."

"As you could be," I said. "Although you must begin on *our* shores." There, I had said it. Her presence, her nearness, inflamed me. I *must* have her! "Unless . . . you know already of Francis's . . . ?" I must know now, it was important that I know now. I did not want that, I could not bear it. . . .

"No. I know nothing, save what Mary said."

She talked? She told? I was thankful, then, that I had not consorted with her after the first year or so of her marriage. A woman who repeated details? Foul, foul!

"I am entirely unschooled in such matters, Your Grace," she said. "I need a teacher."

No regret for the lost Percy, to whom she had pledged herself? Even at that moment I was struck by her disloyalty. But as it benefited me, I did not dwell on it. Rather, I made up excuses for it. *There,* I told myself. *It proves she never really loved him.*

"I could teach you," I said boldly.

"When?" Her answer was equally bold.

"Tomorrow. Meet me"—oh, where to meet?—"in the minstrels' gallery above the Great Hall." When did Katherine dismiss her? "At four in the afternoon." A favourite dalliance-time.

Just then the minstrels ended the measure. Anne quickly disengaged her hand from mine, nodded, and was gone. "I thank Your Grace," she said lightly, before sliding away. For one unpleasant instant the movement reminded me of a quick, dark snake I had once seen near the wall in Eltham's garden. . . .

Tomorrow it would begin. Tomorrow.

All about me the courtiers waited, silver visors in place. We would dance —yea, dance all night. Let Wolsey bring fresh torches!

The minstrels' gallery, overlooking the Great Hall, was shadowy and entirely private. Light exploded into the Hall from the row of windows along its length, but it left the minstrels' gallery untouched. Not that Anne should have anything to fear from the boldest daylight. She was young, and entirely flawless.

I had not yet decided what to do with her. I would make her my mistress, yes, of course, I knew that. But after the coupling . . . curiously, I thought of the coupling more for her sake than for mine. *I* did not need the coupling to bind me to her; that had happened the moment I saw her at Hampton Court; the strange bonding had taken place on the instant. The coupling was for *her.* Women were so literal. Until there was a physical thing, she would not consider herself bound to me.

I waited. The apartments (vacant since Mary Boleyn's gradual decline in my life) stood at the ready. I had ordered them scrubbed, aired, and freshened, and the bed made up with finest Brussels-laced sheets. I would conduct Anne to them within a half hour . . . and within an hour, we would begin our life together. Whatever that meant, whatever that led to. . . .

I waited. I watched the great squares of light from the windows change their shape on the floor of the Great Hall as the sun sank lower. Finally they were long, thin slivers; then they faded and dimness reigned in the Hall.

Anne was not coming. She had broken our tryst.

Perhaps Katherine had detained her. Perhaps Katherine had suddenly needed her presence at some ceremony or other. Perhaps Katherine had even become fond of her and wanted her only to talk, to keep her company.

Anne was so winsome, that was likely.

I was ready to descend, by the little stone steps, when a page approached, hesitantly. "A message," he said, thrusting it into my hand. He bowed and then hurried away.

I unfolded the paper.

"Your Grace," it read. "I could not keep our appointment. I feared for my integrity. *Nan de Boleine.*"

She feared for her integrity? She feared me? She teased me, rather! She had already admitted she would give herself to the artists in their dens! But not to a King! No! She would give herself to Johnny-paint-a-board, but not to King Henry!

And to have agreed to the time and place, and left me waiting! Sending a page in her stead! As if she would disdain to do her own unpleasant business. And the unpleasant business was—me. The King!

I removed Anne from court within a fortnight, sending her back to Hever. It was easily done: the mere writing out of an order, signed, sanded, sealed. As King, I had power to move people about as I would, transfer them from one post to another. But I seemingly had no power over my wife, my daughter, my fantasized mistress. Women! They rule us, subtly if you will, but rule us nonetheless.

XXXVI

At first, as the autumn shrank into winter, I missed her. Whatever had called me to her to begin with continued to call me. As yet I knew not what it was. . . .

But it was not to be. Whatever that thing was, perhaps I was never to taste it. And to what purpose, anyway? I was married, and Katherine was my wife.

There were many diplomatic matters to attend to, foremost among them arranging a proper marriage for Princess Mary. A "proper marriage," of course, meant one that was diplomatically astute. .

O God, I had become like my father!

In early 1527, the "proper marriage" for Mary was with a French prince. Certainly we did not want to ally ourselves with the Emperor; he was too strong, after having so soundly defeated Francis. Even now his unruly troops were holding Rome—and the Pope—terrorized as they looted and rampaged in "celebration." If we allowed him his head, he might become a latter-day Julius Caesar. Julius Caesar belonged in histories, not staring one directly in the face. (And engulfing one. England had been Roman once—and once was enough.)

Gabriel de Grammont, Bishop of Tarbes, came to England to negotiate such a match. Grammont was a great, swelling toad of a man. He began by reading a long proposal to Wolsey and myself, seated as we were outdoors before the fountain in the inner courtyard at Hampton Court. The early-spring sun was making a feeble attempt to warm us, and was doing well, as the encircling courtyards cut off the prevailing winds. I noticed that the grass was green all around the fountain.

"—however, we need to be satisfied as to the Princess Mary's legitimacy," he concluded.

Wolsey a-hemmed and demurred. "I pray you, explain your scruples." He made a face at me, as if to say, "Ah! These legalists!"

"It is this." The toad drew himself up to his full height, swelling out his chest. "Pope Julius issued a dispensation for the marriage of Prince Henry and his brother's widow, the Princess Katherine, who had been legally wed to Prince Arthur. Now we have the case of a brother marrying his brother's widow—expressly forbidden in Scripture! Leviticus, Chapter eighteen, verse sixteen: 'Thou shalt not uncover the nakedness of thy brother's wife; it is thy brother's nakedness.' Leviticus, Chapter twenty, verse twenty-one: 'And if a man shall take his brother's wife, it is an unclean thing: he hath uncovered his brother's nakedness; they shall be childless.' "

He exhaled through his fat lips. "The question is, did the Pope have the right to issue a dispensation? There is only one other instance of such a dispensation being granted, in all Church history. It raises doubts. Is the Princess Mary legitimate? Or is the marriage of her parents—honest and pious—no marriage at all? My master would have these questions resolved, ere he unites himself to such a house."

The dispensation . . . yes, long ago, in that pretend "protestation" I was forced to make . . . the dispensation had been the basis of it. But what exactly were the objections to it? I could not remember.

"Only one other instance of such a marriage taking place?" I asked, with surprise. I had always assumed it was not uncommon.

"Indeed," croaked the toad.

"But the Pope *did* issue the proper dispensation," Wolsey put in smoothly. "So that is a closed issue."

"No, no! There are certain situations, Biblical strictures, which cannot be dispensed with," insisted de Grammont.

"Ah, but Christ said, 'Whatsoever thou shalt bind on earth shall be bound in heaven; and whatsoever thou shalt loose on earth shall be loosed in heaven.' Christ gave Peter—the first Pope—all that power! The Old Testament is not binding for Christians."

"You err! It is—"

It amused me to listen to a Cardinal and a Bishop locking theological horns. Amused, yes . . . but like a black hand seizing me by the throat, the words choked me: *And if a man shall take his brother's wife, it is an unclean thing: he hath uncovered his brother's nakedness; they shall be childless.* And suddenly it was not amusing, suddenly I knew what God had been trying to tell me all these years.

I had complained that I could not read the handwriting of His message, when all the while it was there in Leviticus, written by Moses, waiting for me to see.

I felt ill. Even in the clear, open air I felt closed in, unable to get my breath. I stood up abruptly, pushing back from the table. The plump prelates stared.

"Continue, continue," I muttered. "Finish the debate. I myself want some air—I shall stroll by the riverbank—nay, do not accompany me!"

"Your Majesty," called Wolsey, "there are the new gardens being laid out. Two thousand acres of them. Perhaps you would care to see the work there?"

"Nay, nay." I waved my hand. I was possessed, and could not fasten my attention on anything so mundane as garden plans.

Katherine . . . the marriage . . . it was an incestuous abomination in God's sight. That was why child after child had perished. Eight children, and none had lived but a frail girl.

I passed over the bridge and took the footpath running beside the river.

Living in sin . . . an abomination to God . . .

I know not how long I walked, obsessed with these thoughts. But I found myself in the Thames-side village of Sunbury, with no recollection of how I had gotten there. The cottages were dozing in the late-afternoon sun, under the protection (so they supposed) of their King. *Their King who had sinned a great sin and was being punished.*

I turned round. But at least now I *knew* what the matter was; I could correct it and set things right.

Only on the return walk, with the setting sun on my back, did the rest of the matter come to me.

My marriage to Katherine was no marriage. I was not married to her, and never had been. It was impossible to be married to her; it was divinely forbidden.

I was, therefore, a bachelor.

We sent the good Bishop of Tarbes back to France, enjoining him to consult further with theologians there. But it was a sham, for I knew that there was nothing he could find out which would enable me to return to the state of ignorance and naïveté in which he had found me. I was troubled, yet I would share my thoughts with no one, not even Wolsey. And certainly not Katherine! I must avoid Katherine, especially her bed. I could not defile myself that way again.

৶৾ ৻৾

Now I began to be tormented by thoughts of Anne. I longed to see her, with a fervour that approached madness. The year's absence from her had abated nothing of this yearning.

At night I could not sleep. My mind was filled with her. I wanted to possess her; I *must* possess her, conquer her. And knowing that I had no wife, that I was a bachelor, changed all my fantasies, made me feel very young.

But this possession! This madness! I must somehow master this strange torture in my mind and heart.

WILL:

Henry was, indeed, behaving like a madman. He alternated between elation and absentmindedness. He spent much time making out lists and consulting with theologians. He chuckled and said "Aha!" to thin air. He did not listen to anything I said, but liked to have me about him. He doggedly hid from Katherine.

Usually he burnt up his lists, but this one he carelessly left on his desk.

Virtues	Faults
Dances expertly	Merchant background
Dresses exquisitely	A harlot's sister
Is reputed learned on the lute	Uneducated in either scholastics or the New Learning
Magnificent hair	Sharp tongue
Regal bearing	(Perhaps) yet loves another man

Then I knew: he was consumed with the love-malady, that makes normal men look preposterous, and Kings like asses. But at least it was always temporary.

HENRY VIII:

I must see her! I must have her! She possessed me. Her witch's spells were more efficacious than my practical antidotes.

I would write her a letter, declaring myself. I composed the words during the pre-dawn hours one sleepless night. Upon arising and copying them, I found they did not convey exactly what I wished. (Why are unwritten words so different from written ones?) I must start again. But what tone did I wish to strike, what to say? My own confusion rendered my efforts useless.

Then, one night, I, who had so carefully monitored my letters, rehearsing them in my head, then writing them down, then editing them, and finally discarding them—I retired to my inner chamber after a banquet at which I had partaken of too much wine. In short, I was slightly drunk. I went directly to my writing table and wrote this without thinking:

My mistress and friend,

I and my heart put ourselves in your hands, assuring you that for myself the pang of absence is already too great; and being uncertain either of failure or of finding a place in your heart and affection, which point has certainly kept me for some time from naming you my mistress.

But if it pleases you to do the duty of a true, loyal mistress and friend, and to give yourself body and heart to me, who have been, and will be, your very loyal servant (if your rigour does not forbid me), I promise you that not only the name will be due to you, but also to take you as my sole mistress, casting off all others than yourself out of mind and affection, and to serve you only.

If it does not please you to reply in writing, let me know of some place where I can have it by word of mouth, the which place I will seek out with all my heart. No more for fear of wearying you.

Written by the hand of him who would willingly remain your

H.R.

I had written exactly my feelings, and had great relief upon doing so, after all my agonizing and subterfuge. With a strange impetuousness I sealed it up and, without even reading it over, called a sleepy boy-messenger and sent it off at once. Then I fell upon my bed in exhausted sleep.

In vain I waited for a reply—at first eagerly, bashfully. Then impatiently. Then, after a fortnight, when it became clear she did not deign to even reply, in rage.

So she thought she could ignore a royal letter? As she had ignored our meeting?

The bitch! *I* was King; I could order her to do whatever I wished! Did she not comprehend that? The time for gentleness was past. I would show her just how powerless she truly was.

I sent a curt order, demanding her presence at court for an immediate audience with the King.

Now I stood ready to meet her in my chambers.

XXXVII

It was late April, and unseasonably warm. I had all the casements wide open (even though the bees were swarming) to admit the faint, late-afternoon breeze. Unfortunately, my apartments faced west and so the windows let in not only air but hot, slanting bars of sunlight as well. It was stifling. Was that why I sweated so?

Before her arrival I had appraised myself critically in the wavering beaten-metal mirror in my inner chamber. I was now almost thirty-six—the age when most men began to run to fat, or, worse yet, died. Yet I was the same shape and size I had been twelve years earlier—my tailor had verified it. Waist, thirty-five inches, chest, forty-two. Not a change in near a generation! I had drawn myself up proudly and approached the mirror, sidling up to it like a pickpocket approaching a bulging purse. I meant to wink at it, holding myself in trim. But as my face came clearer in the wavering reflection and gradually straightened, I saw that although my body had remained unchanged, my face had not, particularly the eyes. They stared back at me, and they were hard, with lines radiating out.

I was not young.

To write that is elementary; to feel it for the first time is devastating. *I was not young.*

But I had *always* been young! I had been Arthur's younger brother; I had been the youngest king in Christendom; I had been Katherine's young husband.

The old-young eyes stared back at me. The lighting from behind accentuated the lines in my face.

Arthur is dead, they said. *Francis and Charles are both younger than you. And you are not Katherine's husband, but wish to be that of a girl twenty years younger than she.*

You are old. Nay, not *old*—but no longer young.

Not young? But I had based my entire life on being young!

The hard eyes gazed at me. *The age is in the eyes,* Will had always said.

I can tell any man's age by his eyes. These were not the eyes of a young man.

When did it go? I cried to myself—the ancient lament. No, I am not ready—no, I have so much left to do—I cannot have aged!

Perhaps it was some trick in the lighting! I turned myself another way. That was worse. I rushed to draw the shutters. Any fool knew that light coming from behind was unflattering. (Why, then, did I not consider that in studying my body?)

It did no good. True, the lines were softened. But the look in the eyes—cynical, wary—remained. No twenty-year-old had such eyes.

In such a state was I to meet Mistress Anne.

And what was I to say to Anne? All the things I wished to say, I could not. Why had I summoned her?

For a quarter of an hour I paced. Up and down, up and down. The chamber grew hotter and hotter. A curious thing, as the sun was sinking. Inanely, a common saying played through my mind, *When the days begin to lengthen, then the heat begins to strengthen.*

I poured myself out a cup of watered wine and bolted it. There was no connection between the inordinate heat in the chamber and that saying. What was happening to my mind? Distracted, disjointed. I could not think. Best to concentrate on little things. The gleam of gold on the rounded surface of the flower bowl. And the flowers within: early-blooming apple blossoms, which would wither overnight.

"Your Majesty, Mistress Boleyn is here." The apple blossoms were exiled from my mind. Mistress Boleyn was here.

It took several minutes for her to traverse all the chambers separating us.

She appeared in the doorway of my inner chamber, blocked by a guard. I saw her there, a small yellow figure—yes, yellow again—looking childlike. I motioned to the guard to let her pass.

She was smaller than I had remembered. And more beautiful. As I approached, she smiled—that strange, beguiling smile. Brushing past the guard, she came up to me and curtseyed. Then she rose.

"You sent for me?" Her voice was genuinely puzzled—or managed to sound so.

"Yes." I turned and motioned for her to follow me out of earshot of the chamber guard. He stood, irritatingly staring at us, his legs unnaturally far apart. Evidently he thought it conveyed some standard of soldiery to stand in such a strained pose.

I seemed determined to concentrate on such irrelevant details, to analyze and comment on them—in my own head, at least. Why, now that Mistress Anne was here in my presence at last, after months of imagining her, was I perversely concerned with how a nameless guard placed his feet?

I turned to her. She stared up at me. A mere girl, was my fleeting thought. Face unlined, eyes blank and . . . empty? Then, a goddess. Beautiful beyond all thought. Eyes not empty, but hiding nameless pleasures and depths.

"Sire?" She dipped her head again, displaying the smooth part in the raven's-wing black hair. Upon arising, she still affected that uninformed, puzzled look.

Enough of this! was the first thought coursing through my brain. Careful, was the second. Consequently, my statement was a muddled merger of the two.

"We are pleased that you should have returned to court. We need your presence."

"Is that the royal 'we' or a simple plural?"

She was bold beyond all stomaching! I stared for a second. Then I answered honestly. Why not? "The royal. *I* need your presence. Does that suit you better?"

She chose to disregard the direct question, as the one who loves less is always privileged to do. "What could *you* need me for, Your Grace?"

The girl—nay, she was no girl, I sensed now, but something else, something I knew not—regarded me not as a King, but as a man. Someone to answer back to, rebuke, as long ago others had done. It felt familiar—and hurtful.

"I want you to be my wife," I heard myself saying to this stranger. Yet I had meant to say it all along.

Then came the laughter—high-pitched, ugly. And the turned back: yellow velvet covering the narrow shoulders and waist.

The posturing guard stared balefully at us and clicked his spear manfully upon the floor, as if to remind us that he still existed and was protecting us from harm. The fool!

"Get out!" I yelled. He scurried away.

I turned to Anne and saw that she had now turned to face me, an odd smirk still on her face.

"Your wife?" she said. "You have a wife already. Queen Katherine."

"She is not my wife! Not lawfully! We sinned. . . ." I found myself pouring out the entire process of my growing guilt, laying myself and my thoughts bare to this peculiar girl who seemed at once both the most sympathetic and derisive of persons.

". . . and so," I finished, "the Pope erred in granting us a dispensation to marry. Therefore we are not married, have never been married in the eyes of God. And the present Pope will acknowledge that."

She seemed not to have heard. Or, rather, not to believe. Her long face stared back at me, as if I were reciting some obscure law from the time of Henry I, of no relevance or concern to her.

Finally her lips moved, and she spoke. "When?" A simple, devastating word.

"Immediately," I said. "Within the year, at most. The case is clear. I have simply hesitated because of—because of not knowing your mind."

"My mind?"

"Yes, mistress! Your mind! You have one, I know!" I heard myself exploding and yet was powerless to stop. "Do not play the simpleton with me!" Suddenly I was so angry I was shaking—at her coyness, her elusiveness, her pretended naïveté, her calculating behaviour. I was the *King!* "All these months"—now it tumbled out, all the things I had vowed not to say, had scarce dared admit even to myself—"I have loved you, have wanted to lie with you. Instead you toyed with me, tortured me, made stupid answers to my requests." My voice had risen dangerously (could the attendants in the next chamber hear it?), and she was looking at me in that infuriatingly concerned way. "Well, now I ask you, for the first and last time: Will you be my wife? Will you be Queen?"

There. The thing was said. It seemed to have come of its own accord.

"Your Grace," she answered slowly, "your wife I cannot be, because you have a Queen already. And your mistress I will not be."

"I have no wife!" I yelled. "I tell you, I have no wife!"

She made no reply.

"Clearly, you do not believe me! So you think I lie." I stepped closer to her. I noticed that she not only did not shrink from me, but leaned toward me, as if she wanted my touch. I grabbed her arm, crushing the raised velvet sleeves in order to feel the long, slim arm underneath. "In any case, that is no answer to my question. When the Pope declares me a bachelor—as I am, and as he will—will you or will you not *marry* me?"

She looked up at me. "Yes. I will marry you. When the Pope allows you to be free."

I was aware that I was still holding her forearm in a painful grip. I dropped it, and saw that my fingers had left damp pressure marks on the velvet. Ruined. I must send her another gown.

"Within the year," I said confidently.

"Truly?" she asked. Her voice was doubtful, yet warmer than I had ever heard it.

"Truly," I assured her. She smiled. There seemed nothing left to say. Therefore I gave her leave to depart—two strangers disengaging.

After she had departed, I found myself shaking. Marry her? But I hated her! Quickly I stamped on that thought.

Within a few hours I was basking in the peculiar warmth that comes only rarely in a lifetime—having attained one's heart's desire. The woman I loved was to be mine.

How should I approach the Pope? That he would give me an annulment

I had no doubt. He had given others in less certain circumstances. My wayward sister Margaret had even obtained one from her second husband, the Earl of Angus, on the grounds that three years after the Battle of Flodden her first husband might conceivably still have been living.

I knew all the complexities of my case, having spent many sleepless hours considering them. The Biblical texts were clear, and had they not been, the death of my sons was clear enough evidence. God had not meant me to overlook my transgression.

The night was fully as hot as the day had been. I paced my chamber restlessly. Puffs of orchard-warmed air came into the room. Anne. Anne. Where was Anne? To whom was she talking this very instant?

What difference, I told myself sternly. Soon she would be my wife. Next year at this time we would be alone in this chamber together.

The Pope. He was key to it all. He must grant the annulment straightway. Wolsey. Wolsey would arrange it. I must send for Wolsey.

In the meantime there was this cursed hot, perfumed night to endure.

Wolsey was discomfited; nay, horrified—on him, horror diplomatically registered as mere discomfort.

"Your Grace, the Queen—"

"The Princess Dowager," I corrected him. "Arthur's widow. Her correct title is Princess Dowager."

"Princess Katherine"—he quickly found an inoffensive and correct title —"is the child of a dead King. More important, she is the aunt of a living Emperor. A *devout* Emperor who will doubtless take offence at the implication that his aunt is living in sin."

Exactly what I wanted! Wolsey was always practical. No cant about morality, no obfuscating issues. I could trust Wolsey.

"Facts are often unpleasant. He has faced Luther well enough."

"Two unpleasant facts at one time . . ." He gestured delicately toward a bowl of fruit. I nodded. He selected a last-year's apple—soft, but all that was available this time of year. ". . . are too much for most men to stomach." He bit into the apple, then looked dismayed as he discovered its soft texture. He quickly put it in a bowl.

"Those who would be Emperor must learn to. As you have. As anyone who would be Pope must." At that he lightened. He still had hopes of the Papacy. Ah, if Wolsey had been Pope, then this whole conversation would have been unnecessary. But wishing is futile. An illegitimate Medici cousin of Leo X had succeeded the hapless Adrian as Pope Clement VII in 1523.

"But Popes are men."

"And must die." I smiled.

"And have concerns. Earthly ones," he said sternly.

"Now you sound Lutheran," I mocked. "The Pope, a man? The Pope, swayed by earthly issues?"

Wolsey was in no mood for banter this morning. Oddly, I was; I was in a buoyant, teasing mood. All would be mine. That tends to make a man cheerful.

"Your Grace, this is no matter for humour. To repudiate your wife will be no easy matter. If Your Grace will pardon me, it would have been easier had you done this before Charles become Emperor. . . . Nay, but then her father . . . nay, by then he was dead. In 1518—"

"It is now!" I roared. What was wrong with Wolsey? Had it been the Garden of Eden, things would have been different as well, and what of it? "Now! The year 1527! And I have been living in sin for near twenty years! I want to end it, and instead you blather nonsense."

He looked more alarmed than I had ever seen him. Then he did something I felt was clearly deranged: he sank to his knees.

"Your Grace, I beg you—" Tears began to stream down his cheeks. Stage tears; Wolsey could weep on command. "—do not proceed in this. Thereby lies much tribulation—"

How dare he presume to dissuade me? I looked down at the bulky figure swaying ludicrously on its knees, artificial tears watering my chamber floor.

"Up!"

His tears stopped instantly as he saw that his audience was not touched. Slowly he lumbered to his feet.

"You are Cardinal, and Papal legate," I said. "Well versed in canon law and ecclesiastical procedure. What approach should we use?" I chose to ignore the staged outburst as a mutual embarrassment.

So did he. "Your Grace, I feel that perhaps a small ecclesiastical court here in England should . . . examine . . . the case in question, then give a quiet report to the Holy Father of our foregone findings. That way it can all be a house matter, so to speak; no need to trouble the Vatican with it."

Even weeping on his knees, he had been thinking. Was his devious mind never disengaged?

"Excellent," I said.

"I myself will preside over the court. We need, for appearance sake, one other. What of Warham? He *is* the Archbishop of Canterbury."

"Excellent," I repeated. This was my first—and most momentous—stride down the path I had chosen to take. The first is always the hardest. After that it becomes so much easier.

Wolsey arranged a "secret" hearing of my troubled matrimonial case. He and Warham were to examine the facts and declare that my marriage was indeed invalid. This information was then to be sent to Pope Clement, who would issue a routine annulment. So simple, so easy. Why, then, did everything fail to transpire as we had planned it?

The court met in late May, 1527, at Westminster. Wolsey as *legatus a latere,* Papal representative, and Archbishop Warham as assessor, were chief tribunalers, with Richard Wolman as my counsel. I had high hopes, which came to nothing. Their so-called "findings" were that the circumstances of my marriage were indeed questionable, and must be referred to weightier minds, preferably in Rome. The Pope must examine the entire matter and reach an independent conclusion. In other words, the issue must now be made public.

WILL:

Unknown to Henry, it already was. Rumours of "the King's Great Matter" (as the annulment was euphemistically called) were rife among the commoners. Every ferryman and tart seemed to know the King wished to be free of his wife. Everyone but the person most affected in the matter—Queen Katherine herself.

HENRY VIII:

When my jester, Will, rather shamefacedly brought me a London broadface sheet depicting my marriage bed and trials, I was horrified. Then I realized that if the common people knew, Katherine herself must have heard! I would have to discuss this with her—all the more embarrassing because I had not seen Katherine for a fortnight. She increasingly devoted herself to her charities and her private worship, which I of course did not wish to disturb. Also, I must confess, I had been so preoccupied with thinking of Anne I could scarce collect myself.

To tell Katherine that she had never been my wife would be a hurtful thing and, to one of her pious nature, a shock. I fortified myself with a large cup of wine before I walked to her apartments.

The corridor was unnaturally empty. Usually, swarms of serving-men were loitering about, showing off their latest velvet surcoats. Today it was deserted. Were they all off hunting? I felt the back of my neck; sweat was already gathering. I wished I were hunting with them; I wished I were any place but here. The guard admitted me to the Queen's outer chambers.

There I paced the floor. I wanted to see her. I did not want to see her. At last I was gestured for. I meekly followed Katherine's gentlewoman-usher.

In the back of my mind I reminded myself that this person was serving a Queen who was not truly Queen. I had made her think she was, as I myself had believed her to be.

I faced Katherine. She had been at her devotions and was clearly irritated at being disturbed. After the Mass, she customarily spent an hour on her knees on a stone floor, conferring with her Maker.

"Yes, my Lord?" she asked, coming toward me. She gathered her great skirts in her hands. She still wore the fashion of Spain as it had been when she had left. I thought for a fleeting moment of Anne and her modern gowns, then I shoved the image away.

"So now I must seek an appointment with my Katherine?" I laughed. Yet why was I attempting to be jocular?

"You know the hours of my devotions—" she began.

"They are constant, Madam," I replied.

She stared back at me in anger. I stared at her in wonder. How had we changed so? Two strangers who dreaded to confront one another. She shifted a bit on her feet, looked uneasy. I remembered that she had taken to wearing the coarse habit of a member of the Third Order of St. Francis underneath her everyday clothing. Perhaps it was itching.

"Katherine," I said, "I have come to discuss with you a question of great importance." I thought I should begin thus.

She moved toward me slowly. I noticed that she still wore satins by day. "Indeed?"

"Yes." Then I stopped. How could I broach this subject? She stood in front of me like an army. "The Bishop of Tarbes was, as you know, here recently to consult about the possible betrothal of the Princess Mary to a French prince. He mentioned certain impediments—possible—"

All this time she had been staring at me, her wide eyes already somewhat wider.

"Impediments?"

"Our marriage. As you were married to my brother initially, it seems that many learned figures feel that you and I were never legally married, and therefore there is a question of Mary's legitimacy—"

Before I could say more, she began shouting and rotating her arms like a windmill. "How dare anyone question the dispensation of the Holy Father? Both your father and mine accepted it in good faith. They both—"

Her father and mine? How long ago that seemed! Once they had been of such great consequence in our world; now they were forgotten by all but Katherine.

"—gave their consent to it! Nay, blessed it! And they were holy men!"

Holy men? Certainly not Ferdinand; and as for my father . . . who knew him, truly? They had both been bound by outward obeisance to the Pope, for political show. Was that all?

"Perhaps they were." Give her that comfort. "But even well-intentioned men make errors. And the fact is that God Himself has long ago passed judgment on our marriage. Painful as it is—"

"God?" She drew herself up at that word.

"Yes. All our children have died. We are without issue. Never before has an English King so needed an heir; never before have all his sons died; never before has a King married his brother's wife."

"We have Princess Mary. She lives."

"A daughter. A daughter cannot hold this throne. If she marries—and marries royally, as she must—that means England will thereby come under foreign sway. If she chooses not to marry, then the House of Tudor will end with her, and there will be civil war. The Lancasters and Yorks have many cousins. Which outcome do you prefer, good lady?"

"God's will is that it be so. Whatever He has done, it is His will. We must submit."

Could the woman not understand? "Nay! It is *we* who have violated His law, and His will! It is *we* who have transgressed! And it is *we* who are being punished!"

She began to finger her rosary. Nothing I had said came to rest. In any case, I was a coward. I should have come straight to the point.

"Katherine," I said, stepping toward her. "I have consulted with learned churchmen about our marriage. They have concluded, upon a search of the Scriptures, that it is questionable. We have, perhaps, been living in sin these past eighteen years. Until the matter is cleared, we should separate and live chastely: I as a bachelor, and you as Princess Dowager. You may select any royal residence as your own, and I will—"

She stared at me, and her eyes were like two riveting forces.

"Not your wife?" was all she said, in a quiet voice.

"I do not know," I replied. "The churchmen must decide. In the meantime, my conscience decrees that—"

She burst into tears—loud, wailing tears. I hurried to assure her. Only a formality . . . I still loved her . . . I wanted her to remain my wife. . . .

The tears continued. I no longer knew what I thought, or wanted. I fled from her chambers, seeking a calm refuge of my own.

The tears. Why must there always be tears? And why did I flee?

The next few months were telling for me. I was not married, yet I was not a bachelor. My erstwhile wife was disconsolate; my intended wife was impatient and angry. Wolsey had failed me. His brilliant scheme for the "secret tribunal" in England was a failure. It was worse than a failure; it had alerted all of England—nay, all of Europe—to my situation, whilst solving nothing on my behalf.

In the meantime, how was I to live? With Katherine? As a celibate? Anne was adamant that she would never go to my bed except as my wife.

Therefore I became a celibate. I can understand, now, those who claim that the state heightens one's self-awareness and self-control. During those six years—six years!—that I was celibate, I became a different man. More resolute, more able to command myself. It gives one a strange feeling of control over oneself—and, by extension, over others. I was a true King, at last.

XXXVIII

Daily, Anne and I took walks in the gardens, especially in the bower, of which she was particularly fond. She liked strolling in the vine-sided tunnel, all dark and covered with green leaves, with the sun coming through to make a green murkiness.

Every time she was by my side I could barely restrain the impulse to take her in my arms, to touch her onyx-sleek hair. Yet I did restrain myself, as I knew I must.

In the interest of decorum, Anne insisted that we outwardly maintain our previous states: I as husband to Katherine, she as unmarried, eligible maiden. This was a happier arrangement for her than for me. As a "disguise," she was compelled to surround herself with suitors and courtiers, whereas I must take my place beside the staid but seething Katherine.

In the meantime, in her own quarters, Katherine was hard at work writing secret letters to her nephew, the Emperor Charles, beseeching his help—letters which I had intercepted, with instructions for full copies to be made for my own records. Her means of protecting the marriage was foolhardy: appealing to a foreign power to aid her! She pretended to be fully English, but her actions belied it. She assumed that the Emperor could intervene in English affairs, and that I would cower before his dictates.

For my own part, I was also hard on the track of false hares. I was pursuing the Pope for confirmation that my marriage was indeed invalid. Numerous agents were also sent to Rome to procure a special dispensation allowing the case to be tried in England rather than Rome. They all failed. Pope Clement had no intention of delegating his authority. He insisted that the case could be decided only in Rome.

All the while, months passed as I waited, seeing Anne before me like a flame, surrounded by handsome young courtiers . . . and one in particular, Thomas Wyatt, her cousin.

I liked young Wyatt, otherwise. He was a poet, and a good one. He was, in addition, talented in diplomacy and music. But he was a married man, and as such had no business suing for anyone's favors, particularly his cousin's. They had grown up together in Kent, so Anne assured me. But I liked not the way they acted together and looked upon one another. It was not seemly.

I well remember (well remember? I cannot banish it from my mind!) a fair day in May (a year after Wolsey's foolish "tribunal," and I as far from my heart's desire as ever) when many of the court had gathered for the May bowls. A number of wooden pins were set up on a clipped green, and all men were to compete in tossing a heavy ball to bounce along and knock over the carefully arranged pieces. Katherine was sitting like a chesspiece on a carved chair, to watch us all, and even Brandon and Wolsey had been lured out for the festivities. Brandon had never paid the full fine for his "transgression" and therefore usually avoided Wolsey. Today, however, all was friendly and pleasant. I was especially happy that my sister Mary had come.

It was a lively game of bowls. Brandon still had his strength, though not his old aim. His ball usually went out of bounds with great power. He laughed a great deal about this. He did not care whether he won or not.

Wyatt was a good player, skilfully hurling the ball toward the largest group of pins. Every time he made an accurate hit, he laughed lightly, as if to show how little it meant to him. In the final round he knocked down more pins than anyone before him.

The object of the game was not only to knock down a certain number of standing targets, but to drive through them in such a fashion that one's ball went a fair way down the green. Wyatt's went a great way. The final balls were left to lie where they fell.

As his ball flew toward the targets, I heard a delighted laugh. I turned round. Anne had joined us. She jumped and clapped her hands together when Wyatt bowed, and looked transported. He, in turn, sauntered over to her and kissed her outstretched hand in a semi-mocking fashion. She giggled.

I gripped the wooden ball I held in my hand as tightly as possible, then let fly at the targets. My ball smashed right through the center, scattering the pins like ducks. It then rolled on and on down the green, catching up to Wyatt's.

"Ah! It is mine!" I said, pointing toward the faraway balls with my little finger, upon which was the token ring Anne had given me. Wyatt could not fail to recognize it.

He strolled forward with a smirk. Suddenly I hated the way he walked. "By your leave, Your Grace," he said, "I must measure to ascertain the distance." Then he began twirling something on a long chain, so that at first I could not determine what it was. Then I saw it for what it was: a locket of

Anne's. I had seen it often round her neck. He stretched out the chain mockingly and walked slowly to the balls.

I glared at Anne. She looked back at me, and all I could discern on her countenance was embarrassment. Not shame, not apology.

"I see I am deceived." I turned and began walking back toward the palace. I should not have shown my hurt so nakedly, but I was stunned.

Wyatt continued his walk, his back to me, unaware of my anger. The rest of the gathered ladies and courtiers merely stared, or so I am told. But Katherine heaved herself from her chair and followed me across the newly clipped grass.

"My Lord," she said.

I turned, surprised to find I had a follower. She stood there in the fresh May sunshine, heavily clad in her preferred costume and old-style headdress— a wooden one that encased her head and was overlaid with decorative material. It was so heavy it had made her sweat from the exertion of running only a dozen yards.

"Yes?"

"Stop it! Stop it now!" She was shaking. I said nothing. I could see the beads of sweat on her forehead. "I cannot bear to see you so shamed before all. And for . . ." Her voice trailed off, but with a jerk of her head she indicated Anne, who had not even turned to see me go. "In front of all men. And I must watch."

Suddenly I lashed out at her, as if she were the cause of it, merely for making the wounds deeper. "Then cease to watch, Madam! Cease following me about!"

She looked stricken and stood mournfully rooted as I stalked away, seeking refuge in my privy chamber.

It was cool there, at least. And empty. All attendants had been dismissed, let out into the warm May sun. At last I could pour my own wine without having to request it of some bumbling fool. Must never hurt a server's feelings. No, never. So one must wait a good half hour for a service one could perform for oneself in a half-minute.

The wine was good. I poured another cup, then leaned down to pull off my boots. I flung each one forcefully against the farthest wall. One hit a tapestry and raised a great deal of dust. Of what use were the chamber scourers, then? Filth. Negligence. All was disgusting.

"Your Majesty, Margaret of Savoy would be displeased to see her gift treated so."

I whirled round to face Wolsey's bulk. He had evidently taken the first opportunity to retreat into the shade. From the way he eyed my wine flagon,

I knew he was waiting to be invited to help himself. Instead I grunted. "She cannot see," was all I said.

"Still—" He sidled up to the wine. Suddenly he disgusted me, too.

"Take what you like. Drink it all."

He needed no further invitation. Soon the flagon was empty. He belched —discreetly, he thought. In fact it was not. Then he turned and looked at me with the same mournful expression Katherine had worn.

"Your Grace," he began dolourously, "it grieves me to see you so unhappy."

"Then mend it! End my unhappiness!" I had not meant to scream, but I did. "It lies within your power!"

He knitted his brow in such fashion as to suggest that he was thinking deeply. It impressed those on councils, but I was used to it and knew it was merely a time-serving device.

"You are Cardinal! You are Papal legate! You represent the Pope in England! *Do* something!"

Still he stood with furrowed brow.

"Or, by God, I shall end it myself! With whatever means I must use! I care not what they are!" As I said it, I knew I meant it.

Later that evening, I waited within my chambers. Would Anne send word to me? Would she make amends, assure me that Wyatt meant nothing to her?

No. She did not.

XXXIX

But things changed from that day forward. Wolsey was at last able to badger His Holiness into granting permission for a trial to be held in England, provided another Papal legate sat alongside him. That legate was to be Cardinal Campeggio, who must travel all the way from Rome. This would take months, especially since he was old and troubled with gout, but at last I had within my grasp that which I desired above all else. My case was so clear that judgment was pre-assured, and I would be released from the bonds that grew daily more irksome.

Katherine had become ever more hovering and solicitous, acting more like a mother than a wife. Anne had continued her wayward ways, always assuring me that they were necessary dissimulations.

"If the Cardinal knew we were betrothed, he would not work so diligently on your behalf," she said. "He intends you to take a French princess, Renée, I believe." Her light voice skipped over the name. "He has long hated the Spanish alliance." For some odd reason, I remember her running her slender fingers over the traced carvings of a chair as she spoke. Her touch was so graceful I watched it as I would a swan gliding on a pool. Beautiful, elegant. Like everything she did.

"So we are to deceive the Cardinal? 'Tis not easily done," I warned her.

She smiled. "More easily than you think."

Her eyes had a peculiar look, and I suddenly felt uneasy. Then the look slid away and she was once again the beautiful girl I loved.

"All will be well," I assured her. "In only a few weeks' time it will be over. At last. And we shall be married." I went over to her and took her hand.

She returned my touch and looked up at me. "I cannot wait, I sometimes think, to become your wife."

Was that the happiest moment of my life? The time when I was at the crest, and all else a falling off?

By this time the entire realm knew of my marital dilemma, and awaited the arrival of the Papal legate as eagerly as I. It was early spring, 1529. It had taken nearly two years and countless emissaries and missions to obtain Papal permission to hold this trial in England.

When Campeggio, the Papal legate, arrived in London, he was pleased to tell me that Clement himself had advised Katherine to follow the politically expedient policy of entering a convent, as had the devout Jeanne de Valois, freeing King Louis to remarry for the sake of the succession. His Holiness was bound to release anyone from his or her earthly marriage in order to make a heavenly one.

I was overjoyed. This solution would please all. Katherine was already on the border of the religious life, having taken the vows of the Third Order of St. Francis, and had a great proclivity for it, spending as much time in prayer and devotion as any nun. Clement would be spared a time-consuming and embarrassing trial. I would be spared the possible disapproval of my subjects, who loved Princess Katherine and were already muttering against Anne as a commoner.

In a few days Campeggio, accompanied by Wolsey, dragged himself off to see Katherine, and happily presented his proposal. Katherine refused, saying that she had no "vocation" for the convent life, but that she would agree if I also took monastic vows along with her and went to live as a monk.

The woman baited me! She was determined to mock and thwart me at every turn. It was then I began to hate her. Hate her for her smug Spanish feeling of superiority over me. She was a Spanish princess, I but the scion of an upstart Welsh adventurer. That was how she saw me. And she believed she could serenely command forces that I could not: the Emperor her nephew, the Pope his prisoner. Let little Henry do what he will in his little kingdom, she seemed to be saying with amusement. In the end I will snap my fingers and bring him to heel.

Very well, then. I should meet her in the arena—the arena of the Papal court.

It was the first time such a court had ever been held in England. A reigning King and Queen were to appear on their own soil before the agents of a foreign power, to answer certain charges.

It was to meet at Blackfriars, the Dominican convent, and Wolsey and Campeggio were seated in full array, just below my throne. Ten feet below theirs was Katherine's. Katherine had vowed not to appear at all, as she held any ruling outside Rome to be invalid, even though the Holy Father himself had given permission for it! She was a foolish and obstinate woman!

Yet upon the opening day, she answered the summons from the crier, "Katherine, Queen of England, come into the court."

Ah, I thought. Now she sees the justice and gravity of the case. Now at last she understands.

She came slowly into the room and proceeded to her chair. Then, instead of seating herself, she abruptly turned to her right, bypassed the astonished Cardinals, and mounted the steps toward my throne. When she was within five feet of me, she suddenly knelt.

I felt sweat break out all over my face. Was the woman mad?

"Sire," she began, looking up at me and trying to lock our eyes in an embrace, "I beg you, for all the love that has been between us, let me have justice and right; have some pity and compassion upon me, for I am a poor woman, and a stranger, born out of this realm. I flee to you as to the head of justice within this realm—"

She was truly mad! Everyone was staring, half at me, half at her. Such a thing had never before been seen in court. I myself stared back at her. She still had her eyes raised toward me. I looked at her, hardly recognizing the young girl I had once loved. In her place was an enemy, determined to bend me to her will and make a fool of me.

She continued, "I take God and all the world to witness that I have ever been a true, humble, and obedient wife to you, always conforming to your will and pleasure. I loved all those whom you loved, only for your sake, even though they were my enemies. These past twenty years I have been your true wife, and by me you have had many children, although it has pleased God to call them from this world. . . ." She paused, as this was a painful moment for us both. I ached as well as she. Then she looked up at me once more, and turned the most telling part of her well-rehearsed testimony upon me.

"And when you first had me, I take God to be my judge, I was a true virgin, without touch of man. And whether this is true or not, I put it to your conscience."

She then paused again, and looked at me, her eyes burning into mine. How dare she do this to me? Expose my own inexperience, before all these witnesses? She, as a non-virgin, must have been aware of my state. Now she sought to humiliate me!

I sat silent—a charitable response—until she dropped her eyes and went on with the rest of her speech. It was stupid and irrelevant. At its end she drew herself up and, looking at me once more—only this time in hatred—turned her back and walked out of court. Another piece of unheard-of behaviour.

"Madam!" the usher called. "You are called again!" Three times he repeated it.

"It does not matter," she answered. "This is not an unbiased court for me. I will not tarry." She disappeared from the doorway.

Everyone stared at her, at her short figure receding from view in the shadows of the corridor.

Such a thing was unbelievable in any normal court of law. To appear and then disappear. To refuse to take one's appointed place, but then appeal the case before the other defendant.

And furthermore, to make a fool of me! That was her principal motive. How had she expected me to answer her?

She was pronounced contumacious, and the trial proceeded. It was extremely boring. Many old men gave testimony to their prowess at fifteen (to bolster the claim that Arthur was fully capable), and there was much searching for a witness who could produce irrefutable evidence that Arthur and Katherine had consummated the marriage; but of course no such witness was forthcoming, as none had been lodged beneath the bed. Day after day the trial crept along while Katherine's seat remained empty.

Katherine's defence—Warham, the Archbishop of Canterbury, who had vacillated on the whole issue; Bishop Fisher (him again!); Bishop Standish of St. Asaph's; Bishop Tunstall of London; Bishop Ridley of Bath and Wells; and George Athequa, Katherine's Spanish confessor—presented a muddled case. They made no sense at all. Mine, on the other hand, presented a strong case. But it was no matter; at the end of all, just when the verdict was due, Campeggio rose and announced that as this was a Roman court, and all courts in Rome were suspended, due to the heat, until October, therefore this one was also suspended.

As his quavering voice read this pronouncement, there was a silence, then a stirring, in the room. Clearly the case was closed, without judgment, and given back to Rome.

Then Brandon rose and banged his great hand on the table. "It has never been merry in England since Cardinals came amongst us!" he yelled. The entire gathering broke into discord. I was livid with fury.

XL

WILL:

The poor, indecisive Pope had sent many instructions to England along with Campeggio, but the most important one was: do nothing. Delay the trial as long as possible. Then advoke the case to Rome. Campeggio had merely followed advice, in this case all the more compelling because just the month before, Francis had been soundly defeated in his last desperate attempt to retake northern Italy. The Emperor had decimated his forces at Landriano, and now that all the dust had settled, the Pope and the Emperor had come to terms in the Treaty of Barcelona. The Emperor's troops released Rome, and set the Pope free. The Curia and its Cardinals came flocking back to Rome, and soon the advocation of Katherine's case (always Katherine's, never Henry's) to Rome had been decided in the Signatura and a few days later by the full Consistory. Campeggio had had no choice.

But Wolsey was stunned. This undercut all his power. The Pope, his spiritual master, had betrayed him. His other master, the King, *felt* betrayed. Between them both, he would be ground as fine as grain in a mill.

HENRY VIII:

So they thought they had won. They—Katherine, the Emperor, Pope Clement—thought they could chuckle and dismiss the problem of King Henry VIII and his conscience—never a weighty one for *them*. They were wrong. All wrong. But what to do?

I was finished with the Pope. He had failed me—nay, betrayed me. Never would I consult his court at Rome.

I was finished with Wolsey as well. Wolsey had failed me. Wolsey must have known of all this long ago—after all, he had seen the commissions!

Wolsey—he who was master of all facts, from the herbal remedy used to treat the Papal piles, to who was the Cardinal with the most family connections in the Curia—had proved worthless in this, my greatest concern. He had been nothing but a glorified administrator and procurer after all, not a man of vision or ideas or even insight. He had been meet enough to serve me only in my own green days.

I had outgrown him. I could do better myself.

And I *would* do better myself. I would rid myself of Wolsey and then proceed . . . to wherever the road would take me.

Campeggio was to leave England, and sought permission to take leave of me. At that time I was staying at Grafton, a manor house in the country, and only with great difficulty could I provide lodging for Campeggio. Wolsey accompanied him and was dismayed to find no room for himself. I did not wish to speak with him at this time, but I was compelled. Many of my Council and advisors were eager for me to dismiss him and even have him tried for treason. Their legal excuse was that he had committed "praemunire"—broken an ancient law against asserting Papal jurisdiction in England without prior royal consent. The real reason was that they hated him.

In meeting me, Wolsey was deferential and shaken—a different Wolsey than I had ever seen. He lapped about my hand as a puppy, scampering about, wagging his tail to please. It sickened me and made me sad. I had no wish to witness this degradation.

"Your Majesty . . . His Holiness . . . I did not know . . . I can undo it all. . . ." No, such phrases I did not wish to hear from Wolsey. Not from proud Wolsey.

I gave him permission to retire. Strange it is to think that I never saw him again. When Anne and I returned from our hunt the following day, both he and Campeggio had departed. I knew in what direction Wolsey was bound, so I sent Henry Norris on horseback to overtake him and present him with a ring as token of our continuing friendship.

Evidently the scene was embarrassing. Proud Wolsey leapt off his mule and flung himself upon his knees in the mud, grasping the ring (and Norris's hand) and kissing it wildly, all the while wallowing knee-deep in the mire. I grieved at the vision.

Yet I could not reinstate Wolsey. He had failed me in my Great Matter, and only my clemency saved him from the enemies clamouring for his head. He was of no political use to me now. It was my wish, and command, that he retire to his Archdiocese of York and perform his spiritual duties there, for the rest of his life, quietly and without molestation.

❧ ❧

This Wolsey proved singularly unable to do. He could not bear to be disconnected from power. The wild moors of Yorkshire did not soothe his spirit or speak to him. He was a creature of civilization and artificiality; he longed for the comforts of court: for satins and silver, for golden goblets and intrigues and spies. He judged himself to be still of worth to those in high places—if not to me, then perhaps to the Emperor or the Pope, who might pay him well for what he knew.

We apprehended his letters selling himself, in precisely those terms. His Italian physician, Agnosisti, had served as message-carrier. A clumsy device, but Wolsey was desperate.

My heart was heavy. There was no choice. Wolsey had delivered himself into the hands of his enemies at court and in Parliament, who had long been crying for his elimination; to them, mere banishment was not enough. He had clearly committed treason. And the penalty for treason is death.

For many months thereafter I staved them off. But finally I had to sign my name to the great parchment ordering his arrest for high treason. There was no other way.

By this time Wolsey was already in the far North, within a day's walk of York and his diocese there. And York was where the Percys held dominion.

Thus it was that God arranged it so that Henry Percy (Anne's storklike suitor), as the chief lord in that district, was the only one empowered to arrest Wolsey.

I was not there, of course. But witnesses told me of the heartsick scene: the company coming upon Wolsey in his receiving quarters, his confusion upon seeing them—he is threadbare and almost barefoot. There is no fire in the fireplace, and no wood. Yet he rouses himself as in the old manner, bids them welcome as if they were at Hampton Court. They are strangers to him. Then he sees Percy at the rear of the party, and his tired face lights up. A friend. A familiar face. His worn mind does not remember that he made an enemy of this lad, some five years ago.

He comes forward to embrace Percy, as a friend from his entourage of long ago. He apologises profusely to the company for the quality of their surroundings, as he was wont to do in his great palaces. He then gestures to Percy in a spirit of expansiveness. Percy nervously follows him all the while he is chattering. "I plan to do all the Confirmations in York diocese next May," he says, to the air. "And perform all weddings. There are many in the summer. And to enjoy my simple life, in the country."

"My Lord," says Percy, in such a low voice that Wolsey scarce hears him, and continues talking. "My Lord," repeats Percy, tapping him on the shoulder. "I arrest you for high treason." The voice is a croak.

Wolsey whirls. They stare at each other—the chastised boy, the fallen Cardinal. Revenge should taste sweet, but it does not. Too late, it is rancid.

They take Wolsey away. Master Kingston from the Tower meets them to help keep Wolsey under safeguard en route to London.

"Ah, Mr. Kingston," he says. "So you are come at last." The remark is puzzling to the hearers.

Wolsey never reaches London. Before he leaves his little house at Cahill, he complains of pains in his bowels. (Self-induced? They did not appear before his arrest.) By the end of the first day's journey he is extremely ill, and his party has to beg leave of the monks at Leicester Abbey for a place to rest.

Once within, he makes a great show, predicting his own death. "At the eighth hour of the eighth day," he says piously, after announcing, "I have come to lay my bones among you." This greatly impresses the good brothers. (But how could he know the exact hour, unless he had taken a potion, whose speed of action he knew?)

He is laid upon a simple pallet in a stone cell. He then calls for his gentleman usher, George Cavendish, and a monk. Then he utters his last words: "Had I but served my God with half the zeal I served my King, He would not in mine age have left me naked to mine enemies." He then (as the saying goes) turned his face to the wall and died.

When I heard it I was happy. Wolsey had cheated the wolves at court. There would be—nay, could be!—no trial for treason. Had he taken poison? The more noble and brave he!

And at the end, he had called on God and died in a stone cell in Leicester Abbey rather than the Prior's house at St. Lawrence's. Had he repented in time? Where had his soul flown?

❧ ❧

I was alone. Wolsey was gone. My father gone. Katherine gone—as my advisor. I stood alone. And there was much to do.

Before me stood a road leading to Rome. I knew it well. I could travel it, but it would be time-consuming, expensive, and humiliating. And the verdict was uncertain, for all that.

A smaller, sister road branched off. It led away from Rome, from Wolsey, from everything I had ever known. I could not see where it led, but it could be no less time-consuming and uncertain. Yet it beckoned me. There I would go, regardless of who tried to hinder me. It would not end at Rome, but . . . where? At myself?

XLI

I was in dire need of advice. I had no policy, no plan. I refused to go to Rome and appear before a court. Yet without the Pope's decision I was helpless.

Anne's glee at Wolsey's downfall (she and her friends celebrated his death by staging a masque, "Cardinal Wolsey Descending to Hell," in her private quarters) was premature. In fact his death solved nothing, except for himself.

Anne, determined to supplant Katherine in all ways, including her early function as my advisor, sought to point me toward a possible solution for the Great Matter. She mentioned that her household chaplain, Thomas Cranmer—who was also a scholar and theologian at Cambridge—had proposed putting the prickly question before the great universities of Europe and polling the theologians there as to the niceties of the case. When I had a resounding majority on my side, His Holiness was bound to listen.

Who was this clever man? Whoever he was, he had this sow by the right ear. I wished to meet him, and though he demurred, I insisted he come to court.

Cranmer was not meant for court; that was evident the moment I saw him. He wore the tattered coat of a university theologian, and his hair was all askew. Yet he seemed a gentle sort, as unaffrighted by pomp as by poverty. I liked him immediately.

He seemed to understand the convoluted matter weighing upon my soul. Together we decided upon the universities whose opinions must be sought: Oxford and Cambridge in England; Orleans, Bourges, Paris, and Toulouse in France; Ferrara, Bologna, and Pavia in Italy; and the German and Spanish universities.

I gave him leave to procure the best men for the task, charging all expenses to the Privy Purse—the King's personal exchequer. He smiled hesitantly and backed out.

In the meantime there was Christmas to endure. Anne was lodged in apartments to the right of mine, while Katherine was on my left. Protocol demanded that Katherine and I preside over the court Christmas festivities, even though all the kingdom knew us to be estranged.

Katherine herself pretended there was nothing amiss. Waiting was what she did best. She had waited in Spain while negotiations concerning her marriage to Prince Arthur dragged on for almost ten years. She had waited in England for seven more while the arrangements for ours were worked out. Therefore, the time that had passed since the opening of our Great Matter was nothing to her.

She always enjoyed presiding at the holiday festivities. She planned each detail, down to which kitchen wench should receive which pomander. They appreciated it, knowing that Good Queen Katherine had thought of them.

Good Queen Katherine. That was a sore phrase with me. Every time she appeared—more and more of late—the people cheered her and pointedly called blessings on *Queen* Katherine. The more they did it, the more she appeared. She had taken to waving from balconies and crossing the palace courtyard (public property, and always thronged with people) several times a day. As she traversed the area, she would smile and wave gaily, and toss out tokens and coins, just to hear the people cheer her and revile me. I forbade it. She was most displeased.

But that Christmas—all twelve days of it—we were felicitous and amiable with one another, both ignoring the great rift between us.

Anne was hidden away, as she had no role in the ceremonies, and the time was long past when she could appear as a simple maid of honour. She stayed in her apartments, pacing and brooding. When I joined her of an evening, I found her in a foul mood. One particular evening—it was Twelfth Night—I came to see her, only to find her irate.

All the candles had been snuffed except one, flickering in a lantern. Anne was in her night-robe—a ruby velvet one—and her black hair was down and streaming over her shoulders. In the eerie light she looked half-supernatural, half-mad.

As I stepped in, she rushed toward me—a black and red wraith. A devil. "Are you finished?" she fairly shrieked. Her black eyes reflected odd jumpings of the firelight.

"Aye," I said.

"While I sat here, alone! I could hear the music—" She turned away abruptly.

"Music you have heard many times before. And will hear again." My head hurt, and I was weary. I had looked for comforting, not a harangue.

"When?" She whirled on me. "How many years will I endure Christmas shut up here like a prisoner? You leave me alone—"

My head ached. The bright firelight, once so enticing, now seemed hostile. I drew myself up. "Forgive me, Mistress," I said. "I did not mean to intrude upon you. I also care not to be berated. Good night." Before she could protest further, I turned and shut the door behind me.

Without thinking, I sought Katherine's company. Soothing, kind Katherine.

She was having her hair brushed by a maid of honour when I entered. It was long and, at its ends, still a honey colour. But the rest was the colour of Thames mud.

She smiled to see me, then held out her hand and led me to a padded chair. She sat as near as possible. She leaned forward, and her eyes shone.

"I am so happy that you have come to see me!" she said. I smiled.

A fire was burning steadily. Just as I approached it, I could hear the strange sucking noise of the winter storm outside. The casements rattled. How miraculous to be inside, to be warm.

The fire was a hot one. I could feel it from ten feet away, and held out my hands to be warmed. Katherine came up beside me and held out her hands also—although they could hardly have been cold.

She smiled brightly. In the half-light of the fire I could see the young girl that once was. Then she, too, began to berate me.

You never come to see me . . . you do not eat with me . . . you leave me to sit neglected and forsaken, as lonely as in purgatory. . . .

She reached out and grasped my arm, her fingers digging so painfully into my flesh that all I could think was how to disengage them.

She went on and on, about all my shortcomings and injuries to her person, until I thought her tongue must run dry. Still it did not. Then I became angry.

"It is your own fault if you are neglected and uncomfortable!" I yelled, then lowered my voice. "You are mistress of your own household and can go where you like and live as you like!"

"But not without my husband," she said in mock subservience.

"You have no husband!" I burst out. "Your husband is dead, and has been, almost thirty years! I am *not* your husband. Learned doctors of the Church have assured me of that!"

Katherine drew herself up. "Doctors! They are stupid creatures. You yourself know the truth."

Yes, I did. God had pointed out the truth.

"The Pope will decide," she said smugly. "He will know God's will."

God's will. What did Clement know of God's will? Theologians knew better than he. "The learned theologians in every university will study the case and decide it. And if the Pope does not, thereafter, rule in my favour, I shall declare the Pope a heretic and cease to obey him."

The fire snapped. Had I really meant to say that? Katherine stared. Nonetheless, I *had* said it. I took my leave and went back to Anne.

I told her of what had just happened, of the frightening words I had just said, and what they meant. But she focused only on Katherine, not on my challenge to the Papacy.

Standing in her velvet nightgown at the door to her inner chambers, she laughed. "You should know better than to argue with Katherine," she said, once she got her breath. "Never once have you won an argument with her."

I bridled at that, but she silenced me. She started to say more, but then her face fell and she looked close to tears. "Someday you will be so convinced by Katherine's arguments you will return to her," she said mournfully.

I started to protest, but again she cut me off. Her eyes brimmed with tears; her long, foxlike face was all aquiver.

"I have given up everything for you," she said. "And now I know eventually you will go back to Katherine. You must. And in the meantime"—she kept the door adroitly half-closed, so I could not force my way inside and take her in my arms—"I have given up any chance I may have had for an honourable marriage, now that I am known as the King's Great Whore! My youth has been wasted! There is nothing left for me, except . . . I cannot say what will become of me!" Sobbing, she slammed the door.

I stood, bewildered. And envied the monks, who were free of the snares of women. Had I become Archbishop of Canterbury—

But I had not. We must embrace what we are.

If I ceased to obey the Pope, who would fill his place in my life? It was the very office itself I was questioning, rather than Clement himself. When had the emphasis shifted?

I had said it to Katherine, and suddenly I meant it: I would not obey the Pope, no matter *what* he pronounced. I did not believe in his spiritual authority any longer.

When had that happened? I did not know . . . only that I was sure, in my deepest self, that the Pope was *not* the Vicar of Christ; that the entire office of the Papacy was a man-made thing and carried no more weight than one of those papier-mâché pageant-cars we use at Christmas. Pleasing the Pope had been one of my ways of trying so hard to be the "perfect" King.

What a fool I had been! To tremble before the Papacy and seek its approval! A triple-turned fool—but no more, no more!

You must not suppose that all this time England had been without a Chancellor. England might do without a Pope, but not without a Lord Chancellor. But since touching on his memory is still painful to me, I have delayed recounting the selection of Wolsey's successor in the office.

Immediately after Wolsey's fall, many men clamoured to be Chancellor. It amused me how many saw themselves as fit for the office, when in fact they were not.

The Duke of Norfolk. He had all the prestige of his rank and ancient family name, but he was oddly unimaginative and much too conservative to suit my needs these days.

The Duke of Suffolk. Brandon, my dear friend and brother-in-law. He was a clever and indefatigable soldier, but not a statesman. He would not do.

There were the churchmen: sly Gardiner, aged Warham, fulminating Fisher, smooth-tongued Tunstall. But I wanted no more churchmen. I was moving away from relying on prelates to do my work. I wanted a scholar, a statesman, a layman.

Who else but Thomas More?

Yes, More. I determined to see him straightway. I would visit him at his manor home in Chelsea, to which I had never been invited. Very well, then. I would invite myself.

Chelsea was a small village three miles from London. It took a good hour's row to get there. More chose to live there to escape the hurly-burly of London, as he called it.

The royal barge swung round a bend in the river. Ahead were nothing but open fields and woodlands. We had left London behind. The overhead sun made me sweat and turned the river to a reflection of light.

We approached More's docking. It was meant for small boats, and our large barge could not dock there. I would moor it out in the river. This we did. But even as we dropped anchor, there was much excitement on the shore. The royal barge was something to catch all men's eyes. Every ploughman within a mile had left his plough and come to gape at the barge. As a consequence, the entire bank was lined with men—hardly an inconspicuous entrance for me.

A small rowboat was employed to take me to the pier. I hoped to catch Sir Thomas at home, and at ease. It was most important to find him at ease. I alighted from the small boat and began walking down the pier. The small boat cast off behind me.

The pier seemed very long. Ahead of me lay More's home. It was set far back from the river. A long, sloping green lawn led to the very riverbank. The colour of the grass was so deep it seemed fairly to glow. Was that because it was so well shaded in late afternoon by the giant oaks all around?

I stood at last on the close-cropped carpet. A small flock of goats nearby looked up at me, their slitted yellow eyes appraising me. They soon lost interest and returned to their grass-nibbling.

There was no one in sight. The house sat, drowsy and seemingly empty in the late afternoon sun. Off to one side, I saw a row of beehives and could just catch the slow murmur of bees inside.

I sighed. I had come all this way for nothing. Still, I felt a triumph that I had finally seen More's private place.

Behind me the planks rattled as the boatmen and my few attendants followed me down the pier. They were talking; some were even singing. They would not be so happy when I informed them we must turn around and return to London. Perhaps we should all sit on the lawn for half an hour and watch the swans and small boats gliding past on the Thames. It was a beguiling sight.

Suddenly someone strolled out from the house. It was a serving-maid. She saw us and turned and fled into the house. In a moment several others appeared, and additional faces showed in the windows. I could hear noise from within.

A large wooden door stood square-center in the back of the house; it flew open, and a short, fat woman came scurrying down toward us. She held up her skirts so that she could move faster. Behind her came several others, moving at slower pace.

"Your Grace, Your Grace," she panted as she came closer. I saw then that it was Lady Alice, More's wife. "We are—we are—"

"We are honoured," said a familiar and beloved voice. More's. He brushed Alice aside and smiled easily at me. "Never have we had the pleas—"

"Never have I had the invitation," I heard myself saying, and was mortified. Why, with More, did I always feel as I had in those dark days when Arthur was favourite? Always seeking for approval, always feeling slighted.

More had a curious expression on his face.

"So I decided to make my own," I finished lamely.

"You are most heartily welcome," he replied, in that oddly soothing, rich voice. Yet I knew I was not.

I threw my hand out and gestured wildly toward the house. "Beautiful, Thomas," I said. "So peaceful."

He cocked one eyebrow. Clearly, he thought me a fool. He was not alone. I concurred. I wished myself a hundred miles away.

"High summer is the most peaceful time." You are not a fool, his voice seemed to be saying. You are human, and loved. Ah, that was the danger in More! He always made you feel human, and loved despite it. "Stand still, and listen."

The slight breeze stirred the leaves; the bees buzzed; the river water made small sounds far away. But more than sound, I drank in movement and light. The multicoloured hollyhocks around the house bending slightly; the movement of the bees in and out the golden, woven-straw hives; the dappling of light playing through the trees. And scent: the air here seemed lighter, bearing delicate smells from faraway meadows and nearby gardens. Flowers, cut grass, fertile ground—all blended into some elixir that cleared my head.

"Aye," I said, after what seemed a great while. "Aye."

Dame Alice was gesturing and seemed bothered. "Your Grace . . . if you would care to share a simple meal. You and your—your party—" She looked uncertainly at my retinue. "You see, we are not prepared—"

More silenced her with a look.

"We did not come to dine," I said. "In summer, who thinks of food?"

"Bring out ale, Alice," instructed More. "I am sure the boatmen are thirsty after the long row up from London. Against the tide, too."

They looked grateful, and then he turned to me. His grey-green eyes seemed fairly to burn into mine.

"While she prepares, shall we walk?" His caressing voice issued a command. I obeyed.

He led me off in the direction of the rose garden, which in turn bordered on an orchard. The sun was behind us. Our bodies made long shadows. I remembered trying to avoid stepping on my shadow as a child. It was bad luck. Inadvertently, I kept treading on it this time, try as I would to avoid it.

More pointed out several varieties of roses which he had taken pains in growing, then said simply, "You came about other matters."

"Yes," I said. "I wish you to be Lord Chancellor. In Wolsey's place." If he was simple and straightforward, why should I not be?

I expected either fluster or incredulity. Instead he laughed, a great, ringing laugh. When he stopped, he said, "I? In Wolsey's place? But I am no churchman."

"I do not want a churchman! You are a Christian—more so than most churchmen!"

"Are you entirely positive that you want a Christian, Your Grace?"

Did he mock me? "Yes!"

Instead of replying, he continued walking down the rows of neatly trimmed rosebushes, his hands clasped behind his back. At the end of the row of red roses, he suddenly turned. "I cannot," he said quietly. "Forgive me."

The roses round him made a bloody, flowery frame.

"Wherefore not?" I demanded.

"Your Grace's Great Matter—"

I waved that aside. "The Lord Chancellor is not—"

He cut me off. "The previous Lord Chancellor was deeply involved in this question."

"Because he was a Cardinal and empowered to preside at the legatine trial. Now it has gone beyond that, to—"

"To become a political matter, which would involve your Chancellor more than ever, be he churchman or layman. I cannot—"

"Thomas," I suddenly said, "what is *your* opinion of this entire question?"

He turned and inspected a half-blown rose overmuch. I waited. At length he could delay his answer no longer. "I believe . . ." His usually sure voice was low. "I believe that Queen Katherine is your true wife. And if she be not, I believe only the Pope has the power to pronounce that."

I felt anger rising cold in my neck, working up toward my head, where it would affect and twist my thinking. I fought it.

"So that is why you refuse the Chancellorship." I was surprised—and pleased—at how dispassionate my voice sounded. The coldness was receding, dropping down like water flowing from a pipe. I had overcome it.

"Partly." He smiled. "I cannot be Your Grace's servant unless I embrace all things wholeheartedly."

We had left the rose garden now and approached the orchard. A worn brick wall enclosed it. More opened the wooden door and ushered me inside.

Row after row of pruned and tended trees stretched before me, each about five yards apart from the next. Their branches spread neatly and evenly out, like round tents.

"Plums," said More, gesturing to the farthest row on the left. "Cherries." The next. "Apples." The row immediately before us. "Pears." The last one before the wall on the other side.

More began walking down the space between the apples and cherries. At this stage all the fruit looked much alike. More kept maddeningly silent as I followed him.

"God has pronounced a sentence on it! He has cursed me!" Against my will, I heard my voice rising, coming to an anguished cry. More stopped and turned. Still I continued. "I have sinned! And that sin must be expiated! England will die else! *Die!*"

A quizzical expression on his face, More came toward me. I no longer saw him, nor the golden summer afternoon. All I saw was blackness and despair. Without realizing it, I sank down at the foot of a cherry tree. Yes, England would die. She could not withstand any more wars within herself.

A hand on my shoulder. More was bending down. "Your Grace?"

"My conscience tells me that is true," I finally said. "If all the world disputes it, I still know it to be true."

I got up, humiliated at my outburst. I shot a look at More. He was staring with an expression I had never seen before. One of surprise, awe, yet more than that.

"Then I will be your Chancellor," he said, quietly. "Provided you give my conscience equal deference."

The evening meal was jolly. It was a "picnic," as Lady Alice called it, because it was simple. But long tables were set up on the lawn, covered with white linen, which flapped in the twilight breezes. Simple wooden plates were set down, and earthenware flagons. Great mounds of wild strawberries were brought out, with jugs of fresh cream. Pitchers of May wine, flavoured with woodruff, were passed round.

More's children sang and played the lute. The servants joined us and began dancing with my boatmen. Margaret More, Thomas's eldest and favourite child, held hands with Will Roper, her suitor. More laughed. I laughed. As the shadows lengthened across the abnormally green lawn, I felt I had never been so happy. All would be right.

XLII

O nce I was back in London, the mood dissipated. There was much to be done, and I must set about doing it, for it would never come about on its own. And set about it I did, as I shall now recount.

The verdict of the universities came in, and it was (mostly) in my favour (thanks to golden-coined persuasion). But the Pope was unmoved. (Not that I cared any longer what he thought.) The scheme had been naïve to begin with. Cranmer was not the man, after all, to help me in my Great Matter.

More, Cranmer, Wolsey—all were useless to me in the area of my greatest need. The thought of Wolsey saddened me. Even at this late date, I was still doing business with his estate. The eminent Cardinal had left his books in disarray. But it was time to close them. Wolsey had been dead more than a year.

I had been impressed to discover that there was one former servant who retained all access to, and knowledge of, Wolsey's finances. When others had fled, this Cromwell had stayed on, acting in his late master's name, loyally seeking to clear it. I was further intrigued to learn that he was the same man who had made the point in the Parliament of 1522 that Scotland was near to hand and Europe far away.

I sent for him.

In the beginning I sensed only a keen little man. He had a flattened head —rather like a box all around—and narrowed little eyes. The sort of person one soon forgets, except for the eyes.

He knew all of Wolsey's financial matters, down to every farthing in the household. It was in this capacity that I supposedly consulted him. But one does not merely go over figures. One begins to talk. Therein was I won. Master Cromwell had many interesting tales. In the beginning they were about others; in the end, about himself.

This Cromwell, the son of a Putney blacksmith, had spent hidden years abroad, first as a soldier of fortune in the Italian wars, then as a merchant on the Antwerp market, in the process learning enough common law to qualify for the bar. I received the impression of that rarest of creatures, a totally amoral man, yet ascetic in his wants and needs. Thus he would be singularly resistant to all normal temptations—the satins, the women, the dainty dishes—that had ensnared his master, the Cardinal. Was this the man I sought to help resolve my Great Matter? I hinted of the delicate "problem." He nodded.

A few days later he sent word that he had some "suggestions" for my Great Matter. Thus one euphemism danced with another.

I called Cromwell to meet with me in person and discuss the details of his plan. This he was only too eager to do.

He appeared in my work room promptly after morning Mass, his dark, straight hair wet and combed, his cap in hand. I had not yet had breakfast, and had hardly expected him so soon. A tray of smoked eel, ale, and cheese sat upon my table, awaiting me. I eyed it hungrily. Nevertheless I turned to Cromwell and bade him welcome.

"Your written suggestions were most intriguing," I began, picking them up from my work desk and waving them in my hand. "I have given much thought to them." If I expected an answer, there was none; he stood poised and listening. "I would like a fuller explanation of your plan," I continued. "It is cumbersome to commit all things to paper."

He smiled, knowing what I meant. Then he looked round the room questioningly.

"There is no one here, Cromwell," I said. "You may speak freely." To prove my point—and because I was in a buoyant mood (of late my moods had varied alarmingly, so that I was often elated after breakfast and sunk in gloom by mid-afternoon, quite unlike myself)—I strode over to an arras and thumped it. Nothing but dust flew out.

I sat on a small stool; Cromwell then allowed himself to sit as well, and edged his stool close to mine.

"It is this, Your Grace. I have made an extensive study of the question. And my humble opinion is that it is a much greater issue than the marriage itself. The marriage was merely God's way of opening other ideas to you, of leading you to ponder heretofore unthinkable things."

"What things?" I asked. He was employing flattery, like so many before him. It bored me. The smell of the ale and eel wafted toward me. Let him get on with it!

"That some of Your Grace's subjects are but half your subjects." He paused and lifted his eyebrow significantly. This was supposed to intrigue me, but it was merely silly. I frowned, and he continued hastily. "The clergy. They take a vow of obedience to the Pope. How, then, can they be your loyal subjects? 'No man can serve two masters,' as Our Lord—"

"Yes, yes," I cut him off. "But this has been done always. The heavenly kingdom and the earthly are separate."

"Are they, Your Grace? If, upon pain of death, a subject chooses to obey a foreign ruler over his King—what is heavenly about that? Is it not treason?" A pause. "Does not Your Grace have responsibility for all his subjects? Did not God deliver them into your hands for safekeeping? In days of old there were no Popes, but only Christian princes, who were charged with keeping the True Faith—"

He went on with his extraordinary theory: that the head of each realm was empowered by God to protect his subjects both bodily and spiritually; that he was the highest authority in the land in both spheres; and that the clergy owed allegiance to him, not to the Bishop of Rome, who was a mere usurper. To restore his power to myself was merely to reinstate the ancient, correct, and divinely ordained order of things.

"It is as God wills," finished Cromwell. "He is displeased with the present state. It is a perversion of the truth. That is why prophets like Wycliffe and Hus and Luther have arisen. That is why Rome has been laid low and the Pope reduced to a shivering prisoner by the Emperor. These are all signs. Signs that you must act to restore the rightful order of things. Else the punishments will increase. Remember in Israel, when Ahab—"

"Yes, yes." I could bear the hunger no longer; I reached for the cup of ale. "An interesting theory," I finally said. "Words. Wolsey was also full of words. What of deeds?"

I was curious to know if he had worked this out as well. I was not disappointed. Cromwell leaned forward eagerly, his lizardlike eyes reflecting the morning light.

"The people groan beneath the weight of the monstrous burden," he said.

I must cure him of this extravagant speech he affected. Could no one save Anne speak plain English to me?

"But they are powerless to extricate themselves. Only one person can break their bonds. The King."

I grunted. "How?"

"They will follow you, like the children of Israel following Moses."

This last simile was too much. Why should I not permit myself to indulge in the eel? This would-be orator deserved no deference on my part. I leaned over and selected a tasty-looking piece. "Pray speak plainly," I finally said.

He grinned—something no one had done in my presence for years. Throwing aside the grovelling and hyperbole like a heavy cloak, his voice leapt. "The clergy are helpless to release themselves. The people cannot, save through a general rebellion such as has occurred in Germany, and which above all we do not want. No. The rebellion, the break, must be led from above. And this most of all: *it must seem no rebellion at all*. People—even discarded people— like to feel that the order is eternal. Even while destroying it, we must maintain its outer structure."

His eyes were dancing. He looked demented, delirious. I reached for more eel, as if something in my mouth would subdue the uneasy feeling in my head.

"The Church must be left intact," he continued. "It must retain all the outward semblances of the past. No whitewashed walls, no smashed statues. All will be as always, with one exception: the King, not the Pope, will be Supreme Head of the Church in England. The rebellion will be directed and imposed from above, rather than from below. And the people will follow like sheep, as they always do." He leaned back and folded his hands over his belly, triumphant.

"A pretty picture. And how is this to be achieved?"

"Parliament. Parliament will empower you. Then you may do as you please. Grant yourself an annulment—"

"Parliament is composed of men. All men do not favour my separation from Katherine. In fact," I conceded glumly, "most do not. There is great public sympathy for the Princess Dowager."

"But to a man they resent the privileges of the clergy. Let that be the wedge to separate you from Rome. They can easily be led into attacking the clergy. Once that is achieved, you will have the power to do as you will. Provided you keep them blindfolded until the end."

I merely stared at him, less astonished by his suggestions than by the gleeful way in which he recounted them. He took my silence for compliance, and continued.

"In the meantime you can reduce the Church to subservience. Attack them for some trumped-up transgression; make them pay a penalty and, in so doing, acknowledge you as head of the Church. Thereby they will have set a precedent, will have put themselves in an awkward position. . . . And once all this is accomplished, you can begin to dissolve the monasteries!" he concluded with a flourish.

A look of dismay must have flitted across my face, as Cromwell hastily went on, "Foreign bodies, Your Grace! They send their revenues outside England, draining her as a leech drains blood from a sick man! And lax! The immorality! Rich whores become abbesses, and monks have offspring in all the nearby villages. Their lasciviousness has become a byword! Even in John of Gaunt's time, Chaucer was writing of their immorality. It does this realm no good, as they drain our resources, and it does Christ no good, to have such as His representatives!"

I thought of the luxurious Priory of St. Lawrence, sheltering the King's mistress and bastard. . . . But I also thought of the peaceful, honey-stoned monasteries dotting the land, and of the monks who spent their time tilling the fields, studying manuscripts, raising sheep, spinning wool, providing shelter for travellers, pilgrims, vagabonds. Without them—

"No," I said. "No. They do good."

"They are hotbeds of corruption," hissed Cromwell. "For every good and pious monk, there are ten who spend their days in drunken revelry. It is no accident the best wines come from the monasteries! You imagine they spend their nights in their bare cells, praying, fasting, and flagellating themselves! Only the Lord Chancellor does that. No, the monks . . . I tell you, they loll in a sweaty bed with a village wench while Christ on the crucifix looks down upon them!"

His fervour mounted. What did he mean about the Lord Chancellor? I reached for my ale-cup, but had no desire to offer him a similar cup. He seemed to be edging closer to me. I disliked people to come too near. I moved my stool back.

He sighed and seemed to relax. "I can see you do not believe me. You think only of the kind monks and nuns you have heard tales of. Only allow me to have these 'houses of religion' investigated. That is all I ask. Then judge the findings for yourself." His voice had turned ugly, wheedling.

"Later." I wanted to hear no more of it for now. It pained me. "Parliament," I said, returning to a more comfortable topic. "How do you propose it be used to this purpose?"

He had thought it all out. Parliament would attack the clergy and make laws rendering the Church impotent, thinking all the while that they were merely curtailing the hated clerical privileges and the separate canon law, which allowed churchmen to be tried in their own courts and thus to escape common law.

In the meantime, the clergy was to surrender its power into my hands. The outcome would be that the entire Church would be subservient to the King. The lower clergy would surrender its legal privileges, while the higher would acknowledge the King as its final arbiter. It would be done piece by piece, and only in the end would all be fitted together. Then I could secure power in my own realm. And end Papal jurisdiction in England. And be absolute ruler. And be free of Katherine. And rich.

As Cromwell said jovially on his way out, as if remarking on the weather, "The Church in England has an income two and a half times that of the Crown's. Pity it should go to Rome." He bowed and was gone.

I stared after him. Become head of the Church? Dismantle the ancient structure?

The sun poured in the southern windows, at midday strength now. What Cromwell was proposing was revolution. To change everything in England and in the process free myself.

The chamber was bright. I remembered how I had eagerly chosen furnishings for these rooms, more than twenty years ago. I had been happy to exchange Father's scarred, old-fashioned furniture for the new, polished Italian fashions, to yank down his moth-eaten tapestries and order new.

But to pull down the ancient order of things? To recreate a kingdom? The chaos. The dust. The hurtful transition, the time when all lay bare and ugly, divested of the old and not yet comforted with the new. But if the old were rotten? If God had decreed that it be torn away, as in ancient Rome? The corruptness, the decay, the structure that could no longer support itself?

There was a prie-dieu in one corner of my chamber, a dark corner. Above it in a niche was an ivory statue of the Virgin, with a votive candle flickering beneath it, incongruous in midday. I went toward it, as I knew not where else to go.

The Virgin looked at me, and for one quickly passing instant I saw my mother in her face. Then it returned to smooth ivory again. I prayed, asking guidance. But I felt nothing, heard nothing inside. I could not proceed without guidance; this was too momentous a decision.

I left my kneeler and walked to my Privy Chamber. I would lie down and think awhile, perchance sleep.

There was no one inside, for which I was thankful. My attendants assumed I would not rest in midday; doubtless they expected me momentarily in the outer chamber for dinner. I closed the door softly, and as I did so, something fell with a soft noise. It was Wolsey's medallion, one he had had executed in Italy, showing a Roman scene. It—being of baked clay—crumbled on impact. Gently I gathered up the pieces. Was this the sign I sought? Or was it merely a loose nail in the wall that had caused the falling?

My sleep that night was broken and restless. In the midst of my dreams came wheeling figures of monks and nuns. Some looked at me accusingly. Others just peaceably went about their bee-keeping and wool-weaving and cultivation, sometimes upside down. Then came visions of the Pope, who was sometimes Wolsey and sometimes Father. When Father wore the Papal tiara, he looked at me accusingly. "How has it all been spent? And what have you done with my realm? Given it an heir? Made new and just laws? Nay, that I doubt—" Even as he spoke, mercifully he faded away from my inner vision.

I awoke—had I ever really been asleep?—in the pale sky before dawn. I reflected on the dreams. Father . . . Wolsey . . . the Pope. All my life I had been a dutiful son to one or the other, entrusting my most cherished longings and ambitions to them. Trying to please them and never succeeding. Always I fell short of the mark, some way or other. Then I would try again, only to be subtly told . . . *just this or that is not quite right.*

Now it would end. Now I would begin, at long last, to be my own man. Down with that persecuting trio of nay-sayers. I arose determined to do battle with the only surviving member of the three.

XLIII

I called Convocation to convene immediately. This was important to my plan, as I wanted to take the churchmen by surprise, with no warning of what awaited them. When all the high-ranking churchmen (Convocation was a body representing the Church as a whole) were assembled, they were stunned to hear themselves charged with the treason of praemunire, or bringing Papal bulls into England without prior royal permission. Only the payment of a fine of a hundred thousand pounds could win them a pardon . . . the fine and an innocent document bewailing and acknowledging their evil transgression, signed by them all, and addressed to the King, incidentally titled Supreme Head of the Church in England. Such a simple thing, was it not? So much simpler than the endless plots and ploys of Wolsey's, devised to wring Clement's arm. All those envoys, all those courts, meant nothing compared to that piece of parchment with those seven devastating words.

Convocation balked; it pleaded; it tried to excuse itself. But in the end it capitulated, paid the money, and signed the document. The highest ecclesiastical body in the land had just proclaimed its King to be its head.

I waited for Pope Clement's reaction with curiosity. Surely this would galvanize the stubborn yet weak-willed creature, and let him know I meant to proceed along the course of freeing myself and my country entirely from Rome. It would be so simple for him to sign a parchment freeing me from Katherine, thereby preserving England and its sweet income for the Church—almost as simple as Convocation signing its document.

But no. The recalcitrant goat refused. He issued warnings telling me to cease my actions upon pain of excommunication. He forbade anyone to speak in favour of the annulment until the case had been "decided"—in Rome, presumably. Did the fool not understand that there would be no decision from Rome that would bind me? And if he truly wished things to be impartial, as he made believe, he would have put a ban of silence on *any* discussion of the case, not just on those in favour of the annulment.

"If the Pope issues ten thousand excommunications, I wouldn't care a straw for them!" I bellowed when told of his latest threat.

Cromwell and Anne were present then. Anne looked gleeful; of late she had been questioning my steadfastness to the cause. She believed that I would waver. (They all thought I would. The old Henry would have, but not the new.)

She clapped her hands. "Ah, good!"

Cromwell merely smirked. "Now there'll be jolly stirring in Rome," he said.

"Let the Pope do what he wishes on his side—and then he shall see what I shall do on mine!"

What I intended doing on my side was to continue to disconnect the Church in England from its fountainhead in Rome, using Parliament as the instrument of destruction. I convened Parliament and set them on to the Church.

The Parliamentarians were willing—nay, hot as dogs on a wounded stag's trail. The Church had been injured, and they meant to bring her down.

The first line of attack was to threaten to abolish the traditional Church payments of Annates to Rome. It was the most vulnerable part of the Papal hide. The Pope did nothing. Parliament went ahead and abolished Annates. The first spear had been driven home.

Second came an act forbidding appeals to Rome, because the King was the highest authority and supreme in his own land.

Third came a measure prohibiting Convocation to meet or legislate without royal assent, and allowing the King to appoint a royal commission to reform the canon law.

Pope Clement did nothing but bleat and fulminate.

Fourth came an act that, in effect, empowered the King to appoint all bishops. Close on its heels was another, vitally important to Clement: no longer would England pay tithes (known as "Peter's pence") to Rome.

At bottom we are moved by only two things: love and greed. Both will make us risk our lives, when nothing else will. Surely this kick in Clement's venerable money-bag would bring him to his senses.

But no. He was either a fool or a genuinely good man. Since I knew full well he was not the latter, he must, perforce, have been the former.

A final act concerned heresy charges. Rather than being decided by the Church, they must now be reported and judged by laymen. This measure was immensely popular among the people and caused the Church much discomfiture.

Thus, by the time Parliament had done its work, there was little power left in the Church in England. I was its Supreme Head; its governing body could not meet or even appoint bishops without my consent; all money to

Rome had been cut off. The Pope had lost the island subjects originally won by Saint Augustine in the sixth century.

You must not think that all this happened quickly, or that nothing else transpired while Parliament sat. In fact I was still involved in what the French so charmingly call a *ménage à trois*. I was still, officially, Katherine's husband. We still kept state as King and Queen, still appeared at all festivities and receptions together. At the other end of the palace, Anne was lodged, still serving, officially, as Katherine's maid of honour. It was an intolerable and yet ludicrous situation. The final irony was that this *ménage a trois* was different from all others in one essential respect: I was not sleeping with *either* of the women.

And I was beset on all sides. Many at court who had originally supported me began to waver. People continued to cheer for "Good Queen Katherine" whenever she went outside, and to decry Anne.

Anne and I often attended the Chapel of the Observant Franciscans beside Greenwich Palace. Usually there was a thought-provoking sermon from the pulpit, as well as the ever awe-inspiring Mass. When we came to Mass one blustery February day, however, I was attacked even from there.

It was cold and damp inside the chapel; the braziers failed to keep the chill from sinking in. I saw Anne shiver a bit from time to time. She was so thin that even the furs she constantly wore did little to alleviate her constant shivers and shakes. She had been ill several times since Christmas.

The friar began to speak. But instead of offering an interesting theological premise, he began to shout.

"Do you remember the story of King Ahab?" he screamed. "King Ahab was King of Israel. But he abandoned God and turned to false gods. Yes, a King of Israel worshipped Baal! Evil as he was, there was one by his side still more evil: his wife, Jezebel. She urged him on to even greater abominations.

"Elijah the Prophet tried to warn him. But Ahab was a creature of Jezebel, not the Lord! At length he coveted a vineyard near his palace. It was owned by a man named Naboth. He proposed to buy it from Naboth, but Naboth refused.

"King Ahab was not used to being refused. He was crossed in nothing. So he went home and sulked. Jezebel asked what was troubling him, and when he told her, that wicked woman smiled and said, 'Come, eat and take heart; I will make you a gift of the vineyard of Naboth.'"

Here the friar paused and looked around fiercely, like an owl perched and searching for rodents.

"And what did she do? She arranged a ceremony in which Naboth was given the seat of honour—then paid two liars to come in and charge him publicly with cursing God and the King. The crowd, believing this, dragged him outside the city and stoned him to death. Thus did Jezebel make a 'present' of the vineyard to her husband."

The congregation was silent now, hanging on every word.

"But Elijah went to the King and said, 'This is the word of the Lord: where dogs licked the blood of Naboth, there dogs shall lick your blood. And Jezebel shall be eaten by dogs by the rampart of Jezreel.' "

By now one could hear the wind whistling outside, through the thick stone walls, so silent had it grown in the chapel.

"Now there is in this land a similar thing. A King who has turned his back on God and God's true vicar, and has gone whoring after false gods!

"A King so greedy for money and worldly things that he will rob not only Naboth, but God Himself! A King who is besotted with his own Jezebel, a woman who is bringing about his ruin, and that of the Church.

"I say unto you, as Elijah said unto Ahab: *The dogs shall lick your blood!*"

Anne was pale. The congregation broke out into murmurs. The friar stared balefully at me. He expected me to stamp out, guiltily. I intended to disappoint him, and continued to sit calmly in the royal box.

Later, in her apartments, Anne broke down and sobbed. She flung herself against me and begged me to hold her, in a manner I had never seen before.

"Now, now, sweetheart," I said. "If you are to be Queen, you must learn composure. You must not let every little thing any fool says upset you so. He was but a self-appointed prophet. Next week I shall have someone answer him from the same pulpit; you'll see. Cheer up, sweetheart. Look. I have brought you—"

"There's more—more—I did not want to tell you—it would worry you —but I must—"

She was babbling. Clearly the Scriptural references had upset her. Gently I took her hand and led her over to the fireplace, where we seated ourselves. Then I poured out a cup of wine for each of us and handed it to her. She took it with trembling hands.

"Now, what possible stock can you put in what he said? He was a fanatic, wishing to frighten us. Like that absurd 'Holy Maid of Kent' with all her 'prophecies' who has been wandering round the countryside, proclaiming our doom."

"They hate me," she said. "They hate me, they hate me—oh, it was dreadful!"

"Not so dreadful. I have heard worse."

"No. Not the sermon. The . . . incident. They tried to kill me."

"Who?"

"A mob of women. Last week. I was alone for supper in one of the small royal river-houses near the Tower. Then one of the house-servers came and told me there was a mob of seven or eight thousand women coming, armed with sticks and stones. They meant to set upon me as I left and kill me!

"I looked out the window and saw them approaching. It was true! I rushed to my boatmen and got across the Thames just as they arrived. They set up a great howling and threw stones after me, screaming and cursing me!" She shuddered. "Everyone curses me. With so many curses, how can I hope to escape them all?"

"Why did you not tell me this?"

"Because . . . I did not wish to add to your worries. And because, in a peculiar way, until I told you, I could believe that it did not truly happen. Now it is real."

"A mob of demented women, nothing more. The kingdom is full of them. Remember that one out of every ten men is probably half-mad, and there are more than three million men in England. That makes for many madmen. It means nothing," I assured us both. "It means nothing."

XLIV

B ut of course it did. What she said was true. The people did not like her. This was partly because they were still so loyal to Katherine, and partly because they disliked for a King to marry his subject. My grandfather Edward IV had done so, and there was great resentment over it, even though he had not had to put aside another wife to do so. Yet such was my love and determination that that did not deter me.

Meanwhile, the *ménage à trois* was growing ever more unbearable. On hunting trips and progresses I must be with Katherine, leaving Anne behind. Yet at York Place—Wolsey's vacated London palace—Anne and I lived without Katherine, as there were no Queen's quarters there, it being a former ecclesiastical dwelling. There Anne and I could pretend she was my wife and Queen; she could preside over banquets and entertainments by my side. But by next day, it would be over. There was always some ambassadorial reception for which I must repair to Westminster and the stolid Katherine.

The aggravating situation reached its peak during the summer of 1531. It was now four years since Wolsey had called his "secret" tribunal to hear my case, and two since the ill-fated legatine court with Campeggio and Wolsey. I had just reached my fortieth birthday and was feeling more than usually melancholy about it. I had begotten my first child at eighteen; yet here I was, forty and without a legitimate heir.

The summer months were to be spent at Windsor. Katherine seemed determined to dog my footsteps. If I went to the garden to walk alone, she followed, a bulky black figure in the bright sunshine. If I walked the gallery during a sudden thundershower, when rain fell like javelins on the hollyhocks and roses beneath the windows, I could be sure that she would appear from a door and walk behind me, like a detached shadow.

Not only did she attempt to attach herself to me like the sticky substance glaziers use to hold glass onto leaded panes, she also tried to keep Anne away from me by forcing her to play cards hour after hour. As long as Anne had to sit and play ruff-and-honours with Katherine, she could not walk with me by the river or in the garden. All the time Katherine maintained an outward sweetness; all the time she was writing treasonous letters to the Pope and Emperor. Only once did she reveal her true feelings toward Anne. During one of their interminable card games, Anne happened to hold a king.

Katherine said, "You have good hap to stop at a king, Lady Anne. But you are not like the others. You will have all, or none."

This could not go on. I could bear no more. The very sight of Katherine made me shake with suppressed anger. I knew I had to leave, and the only way to do so was simply—to do so.

I told Anne to make herself ready, and that we would leave early in the morning for a hunting expedition and progress.

That night I felt an immense sense of freedom and exhilaration. One by one I was cutting the ties that bound me to a dead past and made me helpless and angry—Wolsey, the Pope, Katherine. Eagerly, I packed for the progress.

WILL:

Henry has been accused of cowardice for his habit of never seeing his so-called victim after he had made up his mind to rid himself of that person. He sneaked out of Windsor Castle at dawn without ever telling Katherine good-bye; he avoided seeing Wolsey at the end; he stalked away from the May Day joust when Anne dropped a handkerchief to someone Henry thought had been her lover, and never saw her again; he refused to see Catherine Howard or Cromwell after he learned of their "crimes."

But knowing the man as I did, I think it was rather prudence that made him act as he did. Both Katherine and Wolsey repeatedly said that if they could have had just an hour in his presence they could have persuaded him to change his mind. Well, he knew that and chose to absent himself, lest he falter. At bottom, he was rather sentimental and easily moved. Yet he knew what he must do, painful as it might be, and did not want to be dissuaded.

HENRY VIII:

It was July, and even the dawn was warm. I had been dressed for what seemed like hours, and as I stood in the courtyard ready for the horses to be brought out, I waited for the sky to lighten—and for Anne to appear. Eventually she did, wearing a grey hunting gown and cap. Coming through the pale dawn, she was almost invisible. She gave me a smile, and then a yawn. Unlike me, she had slept well.

The small party—just myself, Anne, her brother George and cousin

Francis Bryan, and five grooms—left the cobbled courtyard as the sky began to lighten in the east. The sound of the horses' hooves seemed unnaturally loud to my ears. I suppose that deep inside I was afraid of Katherine hearing.

After the castle was far in the background, I breathed easier. By this time the sun was coming up and shone with all the promise of a high summer day. Anne rode beside me, as I had been aching for her to do on my summer progresses for the past four years. The others rode discreetly behind.

As we passed under the green boughs, heavy now with their full growth of leaves, I looked over at her, marvelling at how well grey became her. There was not one colour that did not suit her—an unusual thing in a woman.

As our horses came close together on one narrow path, I leaned over toward her.

"We are not going back," I said.

She looked puzzled, then ill at ease. I could tell she was thinking of her possessions, clothes, jewellery, books, all still in her apartments at Windsor.

"We can send for your things later. Certainly I have left more behind than you!" Then my voice changed. "Yes, I have left more behind than you have. I have left Katherine behind. Forever."

She stared at me in disbelief. Recklessly, I went on. "I shall never see her again! I hate her! She has done everything within her power to bring about my ruin. And yet she still poses as my solicitous wife. Nay, I shall never see her again!"

Anne smiled. "And where are we bound tonight, my love?"

"Deerfield. To the royal hunting lodge there."

Deerfield was a rather tumble-down, ramshackle building that had been a great favourite of my grandfather Edward's. I liked it because it was so different from the formal palaces. There were only ten rooms, all of them roughly planked, with low-beamed ceilings. The floors slanted, as the old supporting beams underneath had begun to sag. Downstairs a large room with a stone fireplace functioned as a dining hall, as a warming area, and as a place simply to gather and talk.

It gave me the illusion whenever I was there that I was just an ordinary man, a man who went hunting, walked through the woods, ate a simple supper of venison, and sat before the fire with a cup of wine and his beloved beside him. Tonight I was that man, and more.

Anne was beautiful, with the fire playing upon her face. I sat beside her and merely watched her in amazement that such a creature could exist. I thought of the snug bedroom upstairs and the wide, if hard, bed within it. Could not she give herself to me now? I had cast Katherine aside.

We were alone. I reached out for her and kissed her—at first sweetly, then more urgently. Soon I was so aroused I could hardly restrain myself. I fumbled at the strings of her bodice and was surprised when she passively let me undo them and caress her breasts, then kiss them. The fire made strange shadows on her face and body, but that only enhanced the experience. At length I stumbled to my feet and pulled her up. Without a word, we ascended the pitted old wooden steps. By the time I reached my chamber door I was in such a fury to get inside that I would have kicked in the door, had it been necessary. But it was not. The door opened easily; I had not yet locked it. As I took Anne's hand to bring her inside, I felt a resistance. She stood planted firmly outside the threshold.

"No—I must not," she said.

I felt near explosion. "God's blood! Come inside!"

"No. And if I do, I am lost." She gently pulled me back out toward her, looking at me imploringly all the while. "I want you so," she said. "But I cannot. Our child must be lawfully born. Else all this is for nothing, and I am indeed what the people call me—the King's Great Whore."

Before I could say anything further, she slipped away from my grasp and ran down the corridor to her own quarters.

I spent another sleepless night.

The days, nonetheless, were pleasant ones. Hunting from sunup to sun-down, with a fine huntsman's supper each night, lute-playing and games by the fire, and camaraderie.

Then came the expected letter from Katherine. It was another of her sickening "all is sweet" ploys. She was sorry she had not been awakened in time to say good-bye to me. She would be happy to know that I was well.

Never better since I was out of her sight! Hateful bitch! I sat down and immediately dashed off a reply—telling her that she cared little for my peace of mind or my health, since she was bent on destroying both. And, in fact, both were greatly improved when I was away from her. I dispatched it without even rereading it. I had had quite enough of her childish games.

The next week passed peacefully, then came another missive. In this one she took me to task, saying that I owed her a face-to-face good-bye.

Why? So she could berate me? I waited until I had left Deerfield and come closer to London, then called a Council meeting. This was no longer a private matter, as far as I was concerned, but a state one. I wanted everyone to know what I was doing, and why. Together the Council and I drafted a formal letter to the Princess Dowager stating that her disobedience had so displeased me that I did not wish to see her again.

When my progress was completed a month later, the Council sent her another letter, telling her that I was returning to Windsor and wished her to move to Wolsey's old house, The More, before then. While she was there she was then to select a permanent place of residence and thereafter to retire there.

It was done. It was done. I could hardly believe it of myself. Why, then, did I feel such a mixture of euphoria and despair?

The news of my separation from Katherine spread quickly and was not always well received. Unfortunately, it coincided with the beginning of the Parliamentary measures taken to reform the Church. All the old was being dismantled, the people seemed to feel, and there was no secure haven anywhere.

On May fifteenth, 1532, Convocation acknowledged me as Supreme Head of the Church in England. On May sixteenth, More resigned as Chancellor.

He came to me, carrying his Seals of Office, the very ones that Wolsey had been so loth to surrender.

I was, as I remember, reading in my inmost private chamber. I bade More enter—something I rarely allowed anyone to do. Not because of pride, but because it was the only sanctuary I knew, and to have others tramping about it would have spoiled it. But More was different.

"Thomas," I said, coming forward to greet him. "How fortuitous that you should come to see me now!" It was true; I had been feeling sad of late, and Thomas More always had a soothing effect on me. Then I noticed that he had a dolourous look upon his face. And that he had something in his hands. Not a present—from Thomas?

"Your Grace," he began, "it pains me—"

Then I knew. I knew before he had even begun to unroll the wrappings of what he carried. He meant to leave me.

"No, Thomas!" I cut him off, as if by so doing I could make it untrue. "You must not! I need you!"

"Your Grace needs no one who cannot, in good conscience, support your policies. I fear that at last the exigencies of the situation have weighed so upon me that I cannot continue, in good faith, to serve you."

Thomas could not leave me. "Why?" I pleaded.

"Convocation's decision to submit to the charge of praemunire and to acknowledge you as 'Supreme Head of the Church in England' leaves me no choice." His calm grey eyes looked into mine.

"It has nothing to do with the Chancellor!"

"It has everything to do with the Chancellor, Your Grace. I am your chief minister. If I cannot support your measures in my heart, of what good am I?"

"Inestimable good. The people respect you. The peers respect you. Those abroad respect you. There is not a man in England more esteemed."

"In other words, you want me as a figurehead who will give an aura of sanctity to your doings. Your Grace, I love you well, but even for you I cannot sacrifice my conscience. It is the only gem I have. As you know," he laughed, "I have accepted no bribes. I left the Court of Requests as poor as I entered it, and shall leave the Chancellorship a bit poorer, I daresay, as I spend prodigious sums in boatmen's fares from here to Chelsea."

I had no answer. Everything he said was true. I did want him to give a stamp of approval on my course. With More at my side, I could be forgiven anything. I was deeply ashamed.

"Thomas, I want you to stay," I said, simply.

"Your Grace, I cannot," he replied, equally simply.

With that it ended. He handed me the Great Seal and his golden collar, smiled wistfully at me, and took his leave.

Thomas, gone! The clearest head, the most sensible voice, the deepest mind of all those I knew. Did everyone desert me? Must I fight alone? And for *what* was I fighting? There were times when even I did not know. Only that I must go on.

XLV

There was Katherine yet to be disposed of, settled in some way. She had disobeyed my orders to select a permanent place of "honourable estate and retirement," and stubbornly stayed on at The More, in the environs of London.

Very well, then. I would decide for her, and there she would betake herself. I selected Ampthill in Bedfordshire, a manor about forty miles north of London.

I sent a deputation of thirty councillors to give her the following orders: Remove yourself to Ampthill within a fortnight; reduce your household servers by two-thirds; cease to style yourself Queen; acknowledge me as Supreme Head of the Church in England.

As I expected, she refused the last two orders. She said she would gladly release anyone from her service who would not recognize her as Queen, and that her conscience would never permit her to acknowledge her "husband" as Supreme Head of the Church.

Oh! That woman, that stubborn, hateful woman! To cling to something that did not exist—how revoltingly pathetic!

And Mary . . . she proved to be entirely her mother's daughter and none of mine, in her behaviour toward me. She was contemptuous and rude, continually speaking of her mother and the wrongs I had done her, and of the Church and the wrongs I had done *her*. In truth, I knew not what to do with my daughter, as I loved her, but knew her now to be totally against me. In sorrow I sent the sixteen-year-old girl to the manor of Beaulieu in Essex, with a household of her own.

I must put a stop to the incipient questioners and sceptics in the realm. What would silence them better than having Warham, the Archbishop of Canterbury, celebrate my wedding to Anne? As highest prelate in the land, he stood as quasi-Pope to the people. In addition, he had "married" me to Katherine. For him now to officiate at my wedding to Anne would say plainer than anything else that the first marriage was indeed void. I would insist that he do so.

But, astoundingly, he refused. More than that, he denounced me and my "concupiscent desires" and took a grave moralistic stand on the issue of separating from the Pope. I stamped out of his presence.

Alone in my chambers, I paced. Things seemed as hopeless as ever. More had left me. The highest ecclesiastical authority in the land did not see fit to marry me to Anne. The Pope continued to fulminate against me. Only Anne and Parliament stood on my side.

But just when it seemed everything must stay as it was forever, everything changed, as suddenly as a summer squall.

God intervened, and Warham died. True, he was an old man, in his eighties, but I had despaired of ever being rid of him. He had been there since my earliest boyhood, and seemed to be less a man than the office itself, God-given and eternal.

It was August of 1532 when Warham died. I could now find a new Archbishop—one more pliant to my wishes. And whom should I select for the honour? I knew the answer already: Thomas Cranmer.

Cranmer was amazed when I informed him of my decision. He was but a simple priest, he protested. Surely a bishop—

I reminded him that Thomas à Becket had been less; had been only a deacon.

"But, Your Grace," he stammered, "he was truly a holy man, whereas I—I—"

"You also are a holy man. Of that I have no doubt, Thomas. Look! Both your first names are Thomas! Is that not an omen?"

He still stood with a hangdog look. Never had a nominee for Archbishop of Canterbury received the news of his elevation with less enthusiasm.

"I will expedite the bulls from the Pope—I mean, the Bishop of Rome —installing you with all due haste. By this time next year, you will be well acquainted with your duties as Primate of all England!"

Once again he turned his woebegone eyes upon me. I was elated with the decision, and he was downcast!

"Yes, Your Grace," he finally said. "Thank you, Your Grace."

Now I knew in what direction my path lay, and it lay clear. With Cranmer as my Archbishop, duly approved by the hectored (and soon to be discarded) Pope, my Church in England would indeed be legitimate. Free from the Pope, yet sanctioned by him, Cranmer, legitimate Archbishop, would marry me to Anne, and also pronounce on my so-called marriage to Katherine.

Anne was jubilant. At long last, after more than five years of waiting, the end seemed in sight. The bulls should not be long in coming. In the meantime, I had another treat for her: Francis and I were going to meet in Calais, and she must accompany me, just as if she were already my Queen. Francis had shown himself of late to be sympathetic to me and my cause—I suspect because it was against the Emperor's—and was eager to meet and discuss many things.

This would be the first time I had crossed the Channel or beheld Francis since 1520—twelve long years. Since then we had both lost our erstwhile Queens and acquired new ones. We had lost much else, I supposed, and cared not to speculate on it.

Anne was to be my wife and Queen, and it was only fitting that she begin to wear the royal jewels, which were still in Katherine's possession.

I sent a messenger instructing her to surrender them, and Katherine gave me the reply I should have expected. She demanded a written message in my own hand to that effect, since "nothing less would convince her that her husband had so far taken leave of his sense of what was fitting as to demand them of her." She would not give up her jewels "for such a wicked purpose as that of ornamenting a person who is the scandal of Christendom, and is bringing vituperation and infamy upon the King."

Why did she persist in this harassment? Her actions merely annoyed and irritated (but never succeeded in threatening) me. She was petty and pathetic.

There were those who speculated that Anne and I would marry in France. But no. Any marriage must take place on English soil and be conducted by an English priest, thereby making it incontestable.

When I first glimpsed Francis, I thought how he had aged. Then I realized he doubtless thought the same about me. We both stood and stared at one another. This time there was no Field of Cloth of Gold, just a simple royal manor house beyond the Pale of Calais.

Francis was heavier now, and even more gaudily costumed. His youthful gaiety had hardened into a restless sort of cynicism. His stay in the Spanish prison after his defeat by Charles had done little beyond making him more determined to spend himself in hunting and pastimes. Already thirty-eight, he had not yet become a statesman and seemed oblivious to such concerns. I felt a full fifty years older than he. The last five years had seen to that. I had entered them a youth, still under Wolsey's tutelage, and emerged entirely my own creature, much to my own amazement. In a way, I still stood blinking on the rim of the new world I surveyed, not yet used to it.

Things had not gone as I wished. There was much ado over my bringing Anne with me—my Queen, and yet not my Queen. Francis's new wife, being the Emperor's sister (he had had to marry her to gain his freedom), naturally refused to receive her. Francis's own sister, Marguérite, also refused. This hurt Anne, since she had served Marguérite when she was a child in France.

Francis had finally offered, lamely, the Duchess of Vendôme, a lady with —how shall I say it?—a rather tarnished reputation. This insulted Anne more than all the other rebuffs. In the end, Anne met with no one, but remained alone in Calais, bedecked with Katherine's jewels, while I met privately with Francis outside Calais.

We had much to discuss. Mainly it concerned the Pope and Charles: terrors and scourges of us both. Francis suggested that a Papal council concerning my marriage be held in France. He promised to tell His Holiness that I would abide by any decision this council came to. I myself was sceptical of this, but I could not guarantee, even to myself, how I would feel should the Pope grant me my declaration of nullity at this late date.

We retired to Calais, where I found Anne quiet and dispirited. Being almost in France, where she had passed her early girlhood, and yet unable to pass into the land itself, had told on her. Her sister had gone to the French King's bed and been warmly received. Anne herself had refused both Francis and me, and her reward was to be labelled the "goggle-eyed whore" and to be met in France by a whore—presumably her social equal?

When I entered the royal apartments in Calais, I found a strange sight. Anne was asleep in a padded chair. Her head was tilted back and her mouth open, a position suggesting great ardour—except that she was obviously unconscious. On her neck were Katherine's jewels. Coming closer, I saw that she was wearing them all: the earrings, the bracelets, the necklaces. It was as if she had decided to put all on in an attempt to flout the ostracism—to say, in effect, I shall wear the jewels regardless. Even if I must wear them alone.

I stood looking at her. Poor Anne. Asleep, she looked so young, like the girl I had first fallen in love with. She had given up her youth for me; had endured public calumny; had grown into a woman, waiting for me to make a move. Now this humiliating venture into France—meant for her triumph— had ended, once again, as her disgrace. How stubborn, how childlike, to put on the erstwhile Queen's jewels and then fall asleep.

I approached her, supremely beautiful there in the half-light of the large candle standing on the nearby table. The dancing candlelight flickered off the cut surfaces of the gems round her neck.

"Anne." I touched her. She did not stir.

"Anne." This time I shook her, gently. She slowly opened her eyes and looked at me. She seemed confused.

"Oh," she finally said, then looked down at her finery. She had evidently meant to wear it in privacy and take it off long before I appeared. Now she was embarrassed.

"You are practising for being Queen," I heard myself saying. "There is no harm in that."

She shook her head, and tried to reenter the world. "I—I fell asleep. . . ." she mumbled.

"So I see." I laughed. She did not. Instead, she forced herself up out of her chair and began to walk rhythmically up and down the room, twisting a bit of lace in her hands all the while. For a long time she did not speak. She seemed as a madwoman. Finally I interrupted her nervous to-and-fro motions, as one will stop a sleepwalker.

"Anne, what is it?" I asked, as gently as I knew how. Yet she continued to stare at me with blank eyes—open, but uncomprehending.

"Anne," I persisted, "you must tell me what eats away at you so."

She looked at me mournfully, as if she knew but were loth to tell. I had seen the same look in Mary's eyes when she was but seven or eight and had done something wrong.

"It—it is—only that I am sad." She touched her jewels. "I love to touch them. They are royal. And when I am alone, I can believe in all you promised—that I will be your wife, that I will someday be honoured in France, and that the French King himself, not his whore, will receive me.

She came toward me, took my face in her hands. "Ah, Henry. The King of England is my only friend."

"And you will be Queen of England," I assured her. "And then you shall have many friends. So many you will not know which truly are your friends."

She laughed, a half-stifled laugh. "All those in power say such. But I should imagine I will always know *my* friends."

"You think, then, that to be in power is to leave perception behind?"

She spun round. "Indeed it is. For no man will tell you the truth. All seek their own advancement, all come to drink as a horse from the trough. And slobber beforehand."

I winced. "Anne. Be a little kind."

"Never! As *they* were not kind to *me!*"

"*I* was."

"At times." She resumed her walking. "Yet, like all men, you will have both. Trinkets and love-tokens for me, and ceremonial appearances with Katherine. Two wives. I wonder that you do not turn Turk and acquire two others. The Islamic law permits four, so I believe."

I felt anger rising in me. "By Our Lady, Anne! You do push me too far!"

She stood still, at last. In the firelight she looked like a statue; the folds of her gown fell in carved lines. Then she spoke again. "Too far? You who have had women for over twenty years? All sorts—from the pious Katherine to my honeycombed sister, Mary? And I a virgin?" She then moved, came closer. "You sent away the boy I loved, before I was even twenty. And what have you offered me in return? Nothing. Nothing but waiting—and vituperation."

"I offer you myself—and the throne."

"In what order?" Her harsh laughter rang out. I hated her laugh. Then she turned again, and I saw her face by firelight and forgot all else.

"I cannot make you Queen before we are married," I said. "Cranmer will marry us. But until he is empowered by the Pope, his words and ceremony mean nothing. Worse, they will taint our cause. It is only a little time more. We must be patient."

"Patient!" she shrieked, walking quickly across the room. She began feverishly opening coffers and chests, flinging out garments. "All these have I had fashioned since I first came to court! And now they are already judged passé! How much longer? *How much longer?*"

"But a few months, sweetheart." I hoped to soothe her.

"A few months! A few years! A few decades!" She looked ugly, her mouth twisted abnormally.

"This is unseemly," I said. "A Queen must not behave so."

She stopped and pulled herself up. "Yes. A Queen must be patient and long-suffering. Like Katherine. Wait ten years for a betrothal. Wait another seven for a marriage. And then wait another six while the King plays himself out with his paramour . . . the latest in a long list."

"Anne—this is unfair. You know that the others—"

"Were as nothing to you? Why, then, did you bother with them?"

"I cannot—"

"Answer that? Nay, you *will* not!"

She tossed that long heavy hair and smirked at me. Anger mastered me, made me its slave.

"I will answer what I please!" I reached forward and grasped her shoulders. They were thin things; I could feel the bone right through the flesh. I expected her to wince; she did not.

"I have jeopardized my kingdom for you! Alienated myself from the ruling order of things in this world, made an enemy of the Pope, the Emperor, and my beloved daughter—what else can I do to prove to you that you are supreme in my life?" She still kept that aloof, smug expression on her face, until it finally drove me into a fury. "And yet you will not give me the simplest gift—the gift any milkmaid gives her lover. And all the while you wear the royal jewels!"

I reached over and with one adroit movement ripped the jewels from her neck. I did not bother with a clasp, and the string broke; I heard some stones glancing off the floor. Anne's hands flew to her neck; a thin red welt was already appearing where I had snapped the cord. She was outraged. Her eyes followed the bouncing, freed jewels onto the carpet. Already she was marking the place where they might have fallen.

"Such wanton destruction betokens immaturity," she said, gathering up the pearls and rubies hastily. Soon she stood to her full height, her hands brimming with precious stones. I took each of her hands and pried them open, spilling the gems and pearls.

"Such haste betokens greed," I said.

She looked back at me. She was as beautiful as ever, but somehow I now both hated and wanted her.

"You shall hold me in your hands no longer," I heard myself saying, and suddenly it was true. I reached out for her and kissed her. She resisted for an instant, but then suddenly flung her arms around me hungrily.

Never had she inflamed me so. I knew that tonight—this bleak October night in France—was the night I had longed for for six years—nay, all my life.

My kisses fell on her face, hair, neck, breasts. I felt her tremble against me. I carried her over to the pillows and the fine furs heaped up against the wall near the fireplace. At once she was entirely mine.

I was not thinking at all; my mind had died and in its place was a great well of feeling. I knew I loved her; I knew I had waited for her for over half a decade; I knew she was here tonight, and yielding to me. Beyond that I had no thoughts.

She was passive, yet not passive—a yielding sort of presence. She too knew what was coming, and yet could not resist it. She embraced it as she embraced me.

The coming together on the cushions before the fire was like a flame, a shaking of the soul. Even as it happened, in some far-off corner of myself I heard an inner voice saying, *You will never be the same. It is all gone.* Yet at that moment it felt as though all had just arrived. I burst upward into light, freedom, euphoria.

Afterwards . . . there is always an afterwards. Yet this one was surprisingly gentle. I came back to earth to feel Anne next to me, Anne looking into my eyes. Her eyes seemed different from those of only a few minutes past. She stroked my face. Her naked body was half covered with the furs lying near the fireplace. Only her face was as before, with her long hair framing each side of her face and providing a modest cover for her breasts.

"Anne—I did—"

"Shhh." Gently she laid her fingertips to my lips to silence me, then leaned over to kiss me. "Say naught."

What a gift, to be allowed to say naught! To keep one's feelings to oneself.

Together we lay for a long time, wordlessly, until it began to grow chill and the fire was almost down. I roused myself to get another log. She reached out a butterfly-like hand and stopped me.

"No," she said. "Let it die. It is late."

Wordlessly I dressed and left. I could not speak, nor were there any words I wished to say, even to myself.

XLVI

The next few days in France were taken up with petty business. I attended to it all, yet I was hardly there. I could not let myself forget the three hours in Anne's apartment, yet I circled around them in my mind as something too terrifying and sacred to touch upon. Anne herself I saw not at all. Even on our voyage back to Calais she kept to her chambers below decks and sent me no message.

I did not see Anne for several days after our arrival back in England. She repaired to her quarters in the palace and seemed nunlike in her avoidance of company. I assumed she was ashamed and sensitive about her behaviour during our time in France, so I sought her out to reassure her that she had nothing to fear.

She looked more beautiful than ever when she opened the door and stared at me. I had almost forgotten her face, so jumbled up was it with my fantasies. In some demented way I wished I might never see her again. Yet at the same time I longed for her.

She stared at me, as at a stranger. "Yes?" she asked, politely.

"I wish to speak with you alone."

It was early morning. She knew I meant truly to speak and nothing else.

I walked into her apartments. Here at Richmond they were rather sparsely furnished. She kept her best pieces at York Place, her favourite residence.

"I scarce know how to begin," I began.

"Begin at the beginning," she suggested, leaning against the mantle in a relaxed manner. *She* was not nervous; *she* did not dread the encounter, after all.

"Yes. At the beginning," I heard myself saying. "It is difficult. . . ."

"Between those whose hearts are in tune, nothing should be difficult," she finished for me, easily.

I cleared my throat. Nothing could have been less true. But Anne was young.

"I wish you to understand," I began, "that our time together . . . in France . . ."

Now she turned, her green skirts swirling for a moment like sea water, then lying still. "Nay. I understand nothing. Save that I have made a fool of myself."

I rushed over to her (fool that *I* was) and grasped her shoulders. "My dear Anne, I am even now setting plans for a great celebration and Mass—elevating you to one of the highest peerages in the land. You will be the Marquess of Pembroke. Not Marchioness—Marquess!"

She looked shocked. The colour drained from her face, making it even whiter than before.

"You will be a peer in your own right," I continued. "The title will be yours, and in your family forever. There is only one other woman of that rank in England, and she only by right of her husband's title—the Marchioness of Exeter. But you will share yours with no one, and it is a semi-royal title. My uncle Jasper Tudor was Earl of Pembroke."

If I expected her to look awed or indebted, I was mistaken. Instead she looked sad. "Does this mean I am to settle for this? Never to be Queen?"

"No! This ceremony shall serve merely to hoodwink the Pope. For he shall think as you do. And, thinking so, grant the bulls for Cranmer—yes, *your* Cranmer!—to be made Archbishop of Canterbury. That once achieved, we shall be free! Cranmer duly consecrated according to Rome to satisfy the conservatives; Cranmer pronouncing my marriage to Katherine null; Cranmer marrying us. This is subterfuge, my love, nothing else!"

She stopped and mused a bit. Behind that pretty face (albeit strained of late) was a hard, smooth-clicking mind—the equal of Wolsey's. I could almost see her thinking: *I have given myself to him. Even now I could be with child. If it should never come about that I be Queen, in spite of his promises, what then?*

"And my descendants?" she asked coolly.

"It is written in the patent that all heirs *male* of your body will inherit this title. It expressly does *not* say, 'all heirs male legitimate.' "

"Why *male* only? If I can have the title in my own right, why not my daughter?"

"Anne—the entire question of a daughter inheriting on equal terms with a son is what has brought me to my present situation! Can you not see—?"

She cut me off with a smile and a quick question: "And when is the ceremony to be?"

"In only a few weeks' time. At Windsor. Order yourself gowns, my love. Charge it all to the Privy Purse."

She softened, came over to me and kissed me. In only a few seconds' time we had traversed the entire length of the royal apartments to my inner bed-chamber.

I arranged for Anne's "elevation," as it was called, to follow a regular Sunday Mass at St. George's Chapel at Windsor. It was a spectacular building, light and sparkling in the new style, and I thought it would form the proper setting for the unprecedented thing I was about to do.

Truth to tell, it was only the first of many unprecedented things I meant to do, and I was anxious to see how this harbinger would be received. Would the people "murmur" or not? Would they bow to the inevitable and mask their disapproval behind dissembling masks? Or would they openly criticize?

I raised her up, then presented her with her own patent to read. She read it out in a surprisingly loud, clear voice, as if daring the Dukes of Norfolk and Suffolk, the French and Imperial ambassadors, the churchmen, or anyone else present, to find fault with it. She was always that way: reckless, defiant, entirely self-contained. It was that which I loved in her; it was that which I came to hate in her.

She finished the reading. I then stepped down and fastened the ermine-trimmed, crimson mantle of her rank round her shoulders. I placed the coronet on her shining hair and gave her the patent. She thanked me graciously—and so distantly that one might truly have thought us strangers—and then the trumpets sounded once again and she turned and left the chapel.

I looked round, trying to ascertain the reaction of the assemblage. They were uncomfortable: the lack of movement, the absence of spontaneous stirring, betrayed them *en masse*. Curse them! I thought, then caught myself up short. What had I expected? I myself hated the first full day I had to wear new shoes. They never felt quite right. But a week later one felt as if one were born with them. Just so, the people would feel about Anne!

Later in the afternoon I sought Anne out in her apartments at York Place.

She was now simply dressed, in a light gown, and wearing no jewels. The coronet rested on a small table, and the crimson velvet mantle was draped across a chair, as if she were loth to put them away.

I glanced around approvingly. The apartment had been furnished in exquisite taste. She would do the same in my other palaces—banish the dour Spanish influence. I thought with great relish of her having Katherine's confessional and private penance-chapel dismantled and replacing them with a sunny window-seat where one might play the lute.

She rose to greet me, and her face was full of joy. We embraced as lovers, so different from our decorous behaviour only a few hours earlier.

"You look no different as a Marquess," I said.

"Ah, but I *feel* different!" she retorted, twisting away from my grip and almost skipping over to the coronet, which she placed on her head, somewhat askew. She giggled. I came over to her and removed it.

"A crown will become you better." I ran my hands up through her heavy, shining hair, all the way up her neck and to her head. "But the usual Crown of St. Edward will not do for you. Your head and neck cannot bear the weight. I must have a special, lighter crown made for you."

She looked up at me. "Is my neck not strong enough?"

"The crown is extremely heavy. No, you shall have your own. Only those with a bull-neck can bear the present one."

"Like yourself and Katherine?" she laughed. Truly, that afternoon she seemed more like a schoolgirl than anything else. She seemed even younger than the Princess Mary.

"Yes. Not slender willows and daffodils like you."

She threw back her head and laughed. "Then make me one, my love," she said, first holding my hands and leaning back, so that her fine hair tossed and shone, then pulling me after her into her private chamber.

She was laughing; I was laughing; I had never been happier, nor loved her more. I believe we made Elizabeth on that drowsy, yet heightened afternoon.

❦ ❧

New Year's Day, 1533. My feet ached from standing in full state all day, both receiving and distributing the royal gifts in the new Great Hall of Hampton Court. Outside, the sky was a peculiar flat white, while inside all was red and gold and blue—fire and velvet and wine. I gave many spectacular presents—selected by Cromwell, as I no longer had the interest or the time to involve myself—and received many useless and flattering gifts in return.

Returning to my apartments, I was glad to be done with it. I called for Anne, who came within a moment, or so it seemed.

"Happy New Year, my love." I gave her her present—yet another jewel. I expected her to be bored by now with jewels. But she received this one, a sapphire from Jerusalem, with hushed delight.

"I did not have it made into any ring or brooch," I explained. "The stone itself was brought to England by a Crusader who fought alongside Richard the Lionheart. It had lain in the same chest for more than three hundred years, in its wrappings from the Holy Land. Somehow those wrappings seemed something I should not disturb." Would she understand?

She touched the stiff old cloth gently. "Nothing could become it better than this." She folded it back along its creases. "It belongs here." She placed it carefully in its velvet pouch.

Her eyes shone with a peculiar light I had never seen before. "And now I have a gift for you this New Year's Day. Your jewel from the Holy Land serves to bless it—and I shall treasure it forever."

She stood in front of me, but her hands were empty.

"What is it?" I asked.

"It is . . . I am with child."

Her voice was low, and the four words, which meant more to me than all the jewels brought back from all the Crusades, hung on the air. I could not speak, for ecstasy. Yes, ecstasy.

"Anne."

"In the late summer."

Still I could not speak, beyond saying her name.

It was all to be: it was all to come true.

That night I lay in bed, alternating between giddy exultation and dreary practicality, like a man with the smallpox, first sweating, then shivering. The exultation: Anne was with child, with *my* child, the heir I had been longing for. . . .

The practicality: between now and the child's birth, I must be married to Anne, in a marriage that could withstand any legal thunderbolts thrown against it. And it would be pleasing—not necessary, but pleasing—if Anne could have a proper Coronation. Ceremonies had weight in and of themselves, and a regal Coronation might go far in helping the people to replace Katherine in their mind's eye with another Queen. Dislodging Katherine from that inner vision was my greatest challenge.

So . . . first I must address the legal. Without a legal marriage to Anne, nothing else could follow. I must hurry the bulls from Rome, confirming Cranmer as Archbishop. To achieve that, I must reassure and placate Rome—by seeming to lose interest in Anne and by wooing the Papal nuncio, Del Brugio. Clement must be made to feel that allowing Cranmer to become Archbishop of Canterbury was a trifling humouring of a King, a small price to pay for guaranteeing to keep him within the Papal fold.

It was necessary that Anne cooperate in the plan. She must pretend to be cast aside and ready to leave court. I was sure she would be delighted to participate in such a masque.

She was insulted.

"Hide in my apartments? Weep where my ladies can see me? Never!"

"Anne, this is a necessary subterfuge."

"Another 'hoodwinking of the Pope,' as you said in the autumn?"

"Aye."

"It is no such thing!" she burst out. "Whenever you have something you wish to do, you will dress it up in a Papal costume. Do you think I am that much a fool I cannot see for myself what you feel?"

"Anne . . ." Patiently I explained the tangled legal straits we were in, concluding, "And thus the child can be born in legal wedlock."

"The child! The child! Is that all I am to hear from now on? What of Anne? What of poor, wretched Anne?"

She tore herself away and ran for the inner chamber to be ostentatiously sick. I found myself clenching and unclenching my fists. I could fight and manipulate the Pope, Parliament, even the common people. But with Anne as an ally, not as yet another opponent.

Anne emerged from her inner chamber, shaky but under control.

"I think we must be married as soon as possible," she said quietly, coming near. The concentrated essence of rose she had splashed on her throat served to mask the vomit odour. "We must not wait for Cranmer. He can regularize everything afterwards . . . after the fact. That is what archbishops and Popes do. Rearrange things after the fact. Anyone can serve to marry us."

"But a splendid, public ceremony—is that not what you desire, what all ladies of rank long for?"

"Ordinary ladies of rank. But I—I, who have the King's love—require nothing beyond that. Only to be truly your wife, in God's eyes."

Yes. A ceremony conducted by any priest, and duly witnessed, would be as good as a cathedral ceremony. And maybe partake of more magic—be truly *ours*. I felt my blood rising. Just so had my grandfather Edward been secretly married on May Eve to his beloved Elizabeth. . . .

Secret ceremonies—what a luxury for a king! Anne opened door after door of experience and forbidden things to me. . . .

XLVII

I
t was late January, the time when cold creeps into the very walls of all
dwellings, and Bridewell Palace was no exception. The sun did not even
rise until well after eight o'clock, and at five in the morning it was still
dark night. A raft of candles fluttered in the draught of a lonely, unfur-
nished room in the upper regions of the palace. The window was yet a darkened
pane against which sleet drove itself. Chaplain Edward Lee stood there, looking
bewildered, sleepy, and uncomfortable. The other witnesses were there, looking
much the same.

I was dressed in an embroidered moss-green doublet and new fox-furred
cape. The rest were in the things nearest to hand when they had received the
summons to come to this attic room. No one had been notified ahead of time,
for fear of the secret getting out and someone trying to stop the ceremony.

Suddenly Anne appeared. Although undoubtedly as sleepy as the rest, she
appeared radiant and was wearing a light blue gown with a furred mantle over
it. I reached out my hand and took hers, bringing her gently to my side.

"You may proceed with the Nuptial Mass," I told Chaplain Lee.

"But, Your Grace, I have no permission nor instructions from His Holiness—"

"They have been received," I lied. "You may rest assured His Holiness
approves."

Looking discomfited, he began the ancient ceremony. I clasped Anne's
hand. My head was spinning—Anne, my wife at last! No trumpets, no costumes, no eminent churchmen to conduct it. No feast or tournaments afterward.
Instead, a great grey secret, with the winter wind singing outside, and the sleet
flying, and Anne in no wedding gown. The candles kept flickering in the wind
that found its way through the tiny gaps in the mortar. It was deathly cold;
by the time we exchanged rings, my hands were numb.

Then, afterward, no fanfare. The onlookers filed silently from the room,
like shades, and vanished in the early morning grey.

Anne and I were left alone. We faced one another.

"Well, wife," I finally said. I meant to be light, jocular, but all of that faded as I looked at her: her youth, beauty, life—all mine. "Oh, Anne." I clasped her. I was alive at last. It had been a long wait, but all was right, all destined, in that one clasp of flesh against flesh as I held my true wife to my side.

The next few days passed as in a phantasm. I was on earth, yet I was not. By day I signed papers and dressed as a King and behaved as a King. By night I was Anne's husband, her secret husband.

January ended, February began. Still the Pope delayed. Nothing was forthcoming from Rome. To press further now might betray me. So I must wait—the thing I did least well.

Mid-February. The icicles hung long on eaves, the snow rose over boot-tops. Yet the sunset was coming later now, and I could see by the way the shadows fell that spring was not so far away. Ash Wednesday was almost upon us. And once Lent began . . .

I gave a small dinner the Sunday before Lent. I would serve venison and wine and all those things forbidden for the next forty days. I invited only those I truly wished to see: Brandon, Carew, Neville. . . . I lie. The truth is, Brandon, Carew, and Neville were indeed the only ones amongst my guests I truly wished to see, but there were others there: Cromwell, Anne's father and brother, his wife Jane. . . . The Boleyns I must include for Anne's sake; Cromwell so he could give his intelligencers a rest. Anne was seated with her own family, as befitted an unmarried maid, and she kept her eyes properly downcast. It filled me with a voluptuous pleasure to play this part; it inflamed my desire more than if we were alone.

The candlelight barely reached her, and most of her face was in shadow. In fact, most of the room was in shadow. In a great cupboard along one wall was all the silver plate given me by the Venetian Doge, beautifully worked in the Byzantine manner. How it caught the candlelight; how well they knew their craft. . . .

"Is it not a fine dowry?" I said softly to the old dowager Duchess of Norfolk, who was seated next to me. "This silver plate—is not Anne a finely dowered woman?"

She stared back at me like a disgusted hawk.

"How could you have said such a thing?" Anne upbraided me the next day, when my careless remark was already well circulated. Like all wine-remarks, it did not wear well in daylight.

"It was the wine," I said, tired of making excuses, giving explanations. "Thanks be to the Virgin, there will be little wine for the next forty days!"

"By the time this Lent ends, you will walk by my side, publicly, as my wife and Queen." Suddenly it became a pledge. "On Easter Eve you shall go to Mass with me, in all the titles and royal jewels I can give you!"

"On Easter Eve?"

"Aye. So count you these forty days of Lent, pray for a safe delivery and long to reign. For it shall come to pass—I promise that."

Three days later, Ash Wednesday. A creeping cold day. Ashes on my forehead. *Remember, Man, you are dust, and unto dust you shall return.* Dust. I said it with my mouth, tried to pray as if it were true, but I was not dust, that Lent of 1533. I was air, I was feathers, I was blessed—I was King of England and Anne was my wife.

The twenty-second of February. Anne came from chapel early in the morning and chanced across a party of courtiers in the courtyard. Amongst them she spied Thomas Wyatt.

"Tom!" she cried out, rushing toward him and holding out her hands. Her voice was loud and rang out in the cold winter air. "Ah, Tom! Of late I have had such a great longing to eat apples. Apples, Tom! And none to be found! Do you know what that means?" She looked around wildly. "The King says it means I am with child! But I tell him, 'No! No, it cannot be!' " She then began to laugh, and turned her back and rushed away, leaving the courtiers embarrassed and speechless. But they were not speechless for long, as the story was soon circulated about court and reached my ears.

"Anne! What meant you by this?" Now it was my turn to berate her.

"Naught," she said listlessly. She was seated by a window, idly plucking her lute. Everything, even the stabs of murky sunlight coming in the window, seemed enervated with a peculiar late-winter ennui. "I cannot think what came over me."

Her halfhearted excuse was as good as an apology. I did not have the energy to pursue it.

"Doubtless." I looked out over the patchwork fields, drab with dead grass and stale snow. How long? How long must I wait for word from Rome? The roads were clear now, going south.

"Curses to Clement!" I spat.

Anne continued playing her lute.

"Curses to Katherine!" I added, for good measure. "I have sent yet another deputation to her, ordering her to surrender all claims to being my wife. Yet she persists. Like a poll-parrot she repeats, 'I was legally wed to Prince Henry. The Pope's dispensation was good. Henry's wife I was, Henry's wife I am, and Henry's wife I will remain until I die.'"

"Until she dies?" Anne laid down her lute. "Then put her cage someplace where she can sing that song unheard—until that day."

Aye. I looked out across the bleak fields. Put her someplace where it was like this all year round. Let her sing her silly song to the fens!

Buckden was a "comfortable" (by Edward III's standards) red brick palace belonging to the Bishops of Lincoln, and was situated right on the borders of the fen-country, those great grey swamps that make up the eastern coast of England, the ancient land of East Anglia—historic, mysterious, and unhealthy.

I issued the orders immediately. The Princess Dowager would remove herself straightway to Buckden.

There she could rot in the fens!

Within five days a messenger from Ampthill reported that Katherine protested against being moved to Buckden, refused to be addressed as anything other than Queen, and had ordered entire new liveries for her servants with golden *K*'s entwined with *H*'s. As I began to roar with anger, I was handed a letter from the woman herself. It was addressed with the familiar bold black scrawl, as if a staff called me to attention.

I ripped open the missive. It captured her tone perfectly, as if she were standing right beside me. Of course it said nothing, just the usual upbraiding, followed by the usual assurances of eternal love and devotion and fidelity. Ugh! When would she begin to hate me? I looked forward to that day.

Why did she *not* hate me? She had every reason to. Any normal woman would have. But not Katherine of Aragon, daughter of Ferdinand and Isabella, Katherine of Spain, Katherine the proud. It was beneath her. That was what made it so difficult to contend with her on human terms.

I sank down on a cushion and picked up my small harp. Music. I needed music.

I had less than a half hour to myself when Henry Norris, my closest chamber attendant, came in. "Your Grace," he said worriedly, "there is a messenger here from His Holiness."

I leapt up. The long-awaited Papal bulls for Cranmer!

Norris read my face. "No! It is not good news. He has been directed by Clement to deliver into your hands an order to take Katherine back and separate from Anne—on pain of excommunication."

"Excommunication!"

"Aye." Cromwell stood behind Norris in the doorway. I motioned him in. I did not concern myself with how both Cromwell and Norris knew the contents of the "private" Papal letter.

"Does the Papal messenger know that I know he is here?"

"Of course not!" Cromwell was indignant. "That is the point. With your cooperation, we can make sure he never hands you the directive himself. Then neither he nor you need concern yourselves with its whereabouts thereafter. Clement will be relieved—to have spoken clearly without being heard by anyone."

"Very neat."

Cromwell permitted himself a slight smile.

I sent for Anne. I needed her to be my mirror.

Anne came straightway. She was as sweet as honey, yes, as soothing and easy as the melted honey-and-camphor concoctions my childhood nurse had dripped slowly down my throat when it was pained. "How goes the day for my love?" she asked.

"Not well," I grunted, and told of the happenings thus far. She laughed at Katherine's letter, especially at the news that she had ordered costumes with our initials entwined with love-knots. Then her laughter abruptly ceased, and pain crossed her face.

"Poor forsaken woman," she said slowly. " 'Tis hard past bearing to continue to love someone who will have none of you." I looked at her sharply, but she seemed to be talking to herself. "The Irish have a triad. *Three things that are worse than sorrow: to wait to die, and to die not; to try to please, and to please not; to wait for someone who comes not.*"

"You are the cause of my not coming to her. Can you now pity her?" I wondered.

"Yes, and no. No, in that I would not undo it. Yes, in that I may someday be in her place."

The idea was absurd. Anne, fat and fifty and spending her days in prayer and calling after a man who ignored her? Never. Anne would rather be dead.

"Enough of this talk," I said. And I told her about the Papal order.

"So now we play hide-and-seek with him?" she asked gleefully.

"A game at which you excel. Now you shall teach me your tricks, my love."

I looked forward to seeing her put someone else in the position where she had held me for so many years a prisoner—where I could admire and benefit from her prowess rather than being tortured by it.

Dusk was falling. Soon Norris brought in our supper and fresh wood for the fire. It was cosy and close. Anne smiled at Norris as he discreetly performed his duties. His presence did not intrude, yet he managed to make us aware that he was there, lest we say private things in front of him.

The fire crackled; the heat seeped through my veins. I was warmed inside and out, and discreet and functionary as he doubtlessly was, I was glad when Norris cleared away our dishes, added one or two fragrant logs to the fire, and pointedly retired for the night.

I took Anne to my bed, where yet another thoughtful servant had smoothed the fresh linen for us.

"Ah, wife," I said, lying back in her arms. "How I love you!" I pressed my hand to her belly. I felt so complete.

Why, then, was I unable to make love to her? Why did *he* suddenly turn as soft as a maid's breasts? It made no sense. My loins were throbbing, but flaccid.

I wrenched myself away, covering myself in an agony of embarrassment. But Anne knew; of course she did. If she spoke a word, it would hang between us forever.

"Go!" I said. "Go quickly."

Alone in my chamber, I sat staring at the fire. Its jumping, fragrant flames mocked me.

My glance fell on the letter from Katherine, still lying on the chest-top. I picked it up and tossed it on the fire. As I did so, I could not suppress a bitter laugh. We do not always know for what we long.

❧ ❦

The next morning, in bright sunlight, it seemed a singular event, nothing permanent or significant. I whistled as Norris dressed me, and even complimented him on the sweet-smelling fire he had built for us.

"I hope it added to your pleasure," he said modestly.

I managed a great smile that felt real to me. "Indeed!"

He looked pleased.

"I trust the Papal messenger spent an unproductive night?" I was relieved to have this topic to turn to.

"Aye."

"Where is he now?"

"Breaking his fast with the Duke of Suffolk."

Ha! I chortled at that. Charles Brandon hated the Pope almost as much as I, though he had far less cause. Rome had most obligingly granted him annulments of two previous marriages, setting an encouraging example for me at the start of my own negotiations.

"I believe Brandon believes—or so he will tell Clement's envoy—that I am hunting in New Forest, some two or three days hence. He must seek to find me there."

"I shall so remind him," Norris said, his face showing no surprise at these instructions. Even then I wondered how he had taught himself such a trick. He bowed and left to carry my message to Suffolk's house.

I hoped the Papal pet would enjoy his fruitless hunting trip. Perhaps a wild boar would cooperate and yield him some meat, though not the meat he was seeking.

That meat must now attire itself for another day, I thought, heaving myself up; it must apply the sauces and garnishes to make itself palatable to its onlookers.

Before I had finished this overlong task, Cromwell begged leave to see me. Gladly I sent the barber and perfumier away, particularly the latter. He had been offering several new scents for my pleasure, "to stir the sluggish winter blood." But they served only to remind me of what had *not* stirred the night before. Now the offending odours hung in the air, heavy, accusing. Muttering, I turned to greet Cromwell.

"Your Grace!" He had a grin on his face, and it sat so strangely on him that I felt it boded ill.

"What is it?" I tried to keep the alarm out of my voice.

"Your Grace, I have here—our deliverance." He flung out his arms, and two great scrolls rolled down them, like logs down a hill. I saw the Papal seals dangling.

"God in heaven! I will not receive them! Say you were not allowed admittance to my chamber. You *fool!*"

He shook his head, laughing, and came toward me, striding through the repulsive "winter blood" perfume-cloud like Moses through the Red Sea. "Nay, Your Majesty—all your prayers are answered." His voice was soft.

"The bulls," I whispered. "The bulls!"

"Yes." He handed them to me reverently. "They just arrived at Dover on a midnight ship. The messenger rode straight here."

I unrolled them quickly and spread them out. It was true. Pope Clement had approved Thomas Cranmer as Archbishop of Canterbury and accepted his ordination.

"Crum!" The nickname was born in that moment of exhilaration and complicity.

"Congratulations, Your Majesty." Again the eerie grin. "This means you have won."

I stared down at the parchment, at the Latin, at the heavy signature. *I had won.* It had taken six years since the first "enquiry" into my matrimonial case.

The coveted parchment now felt so light, so attainable. Six years. Lesser men would have turned back, been intimidated, counted the costs. Lesser men would not now, in March of 1533, be holding the parchment that Henry VIII of England now held.

It would be the last time I ever required approval or permission from another person to do or not to do anything.

"Yes. I have won."

"And how does it feel?"

"It feels right."

While the other Papal messenger was slogging his way along muddy March roads toward the New Forest near Winchester, I entertained his more successful compatriot at Greenwich. I toasted Clement with the best wines and enquired solicitously after his health and praised his bravery during his imprisonment, and so on. Then I packed his messenger straight back to the Continent on the first available ship. Cranmer I prepared for his consecration as Archbishop.

"And quickly," I explained. "Before Clement can change his mind. I see now why he sent the order to separate from Anne and take Katherine back. It was meant to go hand-in-hand with the patent for you to become Archbishop. I was not to get the one without swallowing the other—like a child taking purge-medicine in a cake. He sent them separately to guard against robbers or accidents en route. His mistake! God clearly favoured us in making sure the messengers did not meet up again in England."

"I thought it was Cromwell who made sure they did not meet," said Cranmer quietly.

"It must have been God's will, or He would never have permitted it to come about so easily." I dismissed it. "You will be consecrated at St. Stephen's, here in Westminster. But first, my dear Thomas, we must discuss my actions, and my intentions. Doubtless you found them puzzling. How did they appear on the Continent?" Cranmer had spent January on a diplomatic mission to the Emperor.

Cranmer's clear blue eyes registered nothing. "They did not appear any way at all. Begging your pardon, Your Grace, your Great Matter was not on everyone's tongues there as it seems to be here."

"Nonsense! Of course it is of great concern and importance to the Emperor! I think that you were more involved in your own 'great matter' while in Germany. Were you not? Well, you can bid farewell to *her*. A married Archbishop! Let *that* be known, and we will be discredited."

Still, Cranmer looked back at me unblinkingly. Really, there were times when he annoyed me.

"Keep her as a mistress. Mistresses are allowed by the True Church; wives are not."

"Does that not strike you as hypocritical, Your Grace?" Again, the quiet question.

Now I lost all patience. "God's blood! Are you a Reformer? Do you intend to turn on me after you are in office? To become a Protestant Becket? Because if you have such intentions, my dear Thomas, I warn you: you will not succeed. I will not tolerate betrayal. So speak now—declare yourself. Do not practise the hypocrisy of which you are so intolerant in others."

A long pause—too long. Then: "I am your man."

"Good." The cloying fragrance was still in the air. I wanted to get away from it. "Come. Let us sit over here, in the morning light." I led him to a sunny window-seat. "It is complicated," I began.

"Do not condescend to me, Your Grace."

He was right; that was what I had been doing. I began again. "Our goal is that you replace the Pope as the highest spiritual authority in England. Thus, a decision made by you cannot be appealed over your head to the Pope. To do that, we must sever certain connections with Rome. Parliament is doing just that."

"How? By what authority?"

"By its own authority. By what authority, after all, did Rome first assert her jurisdiction here in England? By her own. Yes! This whole intricate structure of the Church that you see in England—the cathedrals, the abbeys, the parish priests, the wandering, preaching friars, the monasteries—all rest on such a flimsy base of authority. Rome's say-so! Which Parliament will now examine and repudiate."

"With what specific laws?"

Ah! His mind now quickened to the legal, canonical subtleties of the issue. Good. Let him lose himself there. I smiled. "Two." He looked surprised. "Only two. The first: the Act Forbidding Appeals to Rome. The second: an act providing for the nomination and consecration of bishops without consulting Rome first. I have not thought of a name for this one yet—something innocuous, I hope."

"I see. Rome will not have the power to name the clergy in England, nor to pass judgment on its subsequent actions. Rome will be impotent."

Why must he use that word? "Just so."

"Why should Parliament agree to pass such laws?" he asked blandly.

"Because I have lulled them into believing the laws are as innocuous as their titles. I have gone to great lengths to paint a picture of myself hand-in-glove with Clement. Would such a loyal son do anything to harm his spiritual father? Of course not. These laws are but trifling matters, so they think. Whose name goes on a bishop's roll-call . . . which court hears an appeal . . . it is not a matter of concern to common people."

He rose slowly from the window-seat and rubbed his forehead. "You are making a mistake," he said, with great sadness.

Now I must listen to yet another "warning." I was beginning to accept it as one of the occupational hazards of kingship. I sighed and waited.

"To use Parliament thus is to grant them a power you will regret. If they have the power to confer a right, they also have the power to take it away. Should they decide to do so later, and by your own will the Pope is divested of moral, ecclesiastical, and legal authority in England, to whom will you turn for support? You are making Parliament King in England. I fear that, Your Grace. You are taking away a distant, inconsistent, but morally based ruling partner and replacing it with a nearby secular one."

Was that all? "I can manage Parliament," I scoffed. "It is a child in my hands."

"Children grow up, Your Grace. And when your son is but a child, Parliament will be his elder brother. Who will rule then?"

"I do not intend to let Parliament grow out of bounds. I shall trim it back after the break with Rome is complete."

"Trimmed hedges grow back fast, as any palace gardener will affirm. And in human beings, a taste for power is seldom lost." He looked at me oddly, as if about to add something, then thought better of it.

"It is all I have to use at the moment. Would you have me dispense with it entirely and rule by my own decree, like Nero? By heaven, what a lovely thought!" I smiled. "But I fear the people would never tolerate that. And I work and live with what is, not with what would be, should be, or could be."

I looked out the window at the muddy Thames sliding by, bleak and March-dismal.

"Nevertheless, your warning is well taken." I reached over and patted his shoulder. "I do believe you have some political instincts after all, Thomas. That's a relief!"

He smiled wanly.

"Now to more pleasant things. Your consecration. It is a lovely ceremony. . . ."

So it was. But more lovely, to my ears, was the simple one preceding it in a private chamber in Westminster. There Thomas Cranmer, in the presence of myself and discreet witnesses, solemnly protested that he did not intend to keep any oath of obedience to the Pope if it involved going against the law of the land, the will of the King, or the law of God. The first two were my creatures, and the third was certainly open to royal interpretation.

The transition had begun.

XLVIII

Now it was Holy Week, which the new Archbishop prepared to celebrate in grand fashion, under my orders.

"Must we have it *all*, Your Grace?" Cranmer looked as distressed as he dared. He indeed leaned toward the Reformers, but dared not openly show it.

"Aye."

"Even . . . ?"

"Even creeping to the cross on Good Friday. I myself will lead the procession of penitents."

Cranmer tried to smile.

" 'Creeping to the cross'?" laughed Anne. "That ancient relic! My love, you will rub your knees raw."

"I intend to. It is necessary that I observe all the old forms, even the 'ancient relics,' to reassure the people that the break with Rome does *not* mean we are abandoning the True Faith. And after Good Friday comes Easter."

"When your new Queen is paraded out."

We were standing near a large window in the King's chamber at Westminster, whence we had come to spend Holy Week. Young priests were going in and out of the Abbey below like a line of ants, carrying sheaves of willows for Palm Sunday on the morrow.

"Yes. It is our own time of rejoicing; we have certainly spent more than forty days in preparation for this day."

She laughed, and the early April sunlight struck her face—all youth and hope she was, and I felt my heart sing within me. "We shall not wait until the sun rises on Easter. No, you shall come out with me on the first Mass of Easter—Easter Eve at midnight."

Her eyes danced. "My new gown is cloth-of-silver. It will look best by torchlight!"

"Like a faerie queen," I said.

The entire court was to celebrate Palm Sunday together. I had made it clear that that was my wish, and although they could not know why it was important to me, they naturally acceded. Some hundred of them assembled in the Great Hall of Westminster Palace just prior to the High Mass in the Abbey adjoining. Colours were drab; they were saving their best and newest for Easter Eve. Oh, what a blaze of colour there would be that night!

Anne was with her ladies; officially she was still but a lady of the court, serving a Queen who was no longer Queen but merely Dowager Princess of Wales; and no longer at court, either. Just so are appearances honoured which are absurd and fool no one, yet we are fond of them.

She stood, Anne the secret Queen, surrounded by her own lady-servers, who were casting flirtatious looks toward the gentlemen of my Privy Chamber. These were generally young and well-favoured men from leading families. Norris, as my personal attendant, was the oldest, near my own age. The others ranged in age as low as Francis Weston, who was twenty-two.

I thought back to the handsome young men who had crowded round my Privy Chamber when I first became King. Where were they now? William Compton, Edward Guildford, Edward Poyntz—all dead. Those remaining, like Carew and Neville, were aging boys, grown stout, with sagging jowls, yet with no more matter in their heads than twenty years ago.

Fleetingly I wondered how Weston would look in twenty years. He was so pretty he looked almost like a she-man, and such did not age well; at forty they resembled over-experienced courtesans whose best experiences were past. He had best marry quickly, and well. Even then I noticed how solicitous Anne was of him. It was one of those things one takes in without being aware of it—like whether a certain tree has lost its leaves.

Now Cranmer appeared before us, all stately in his glittering new robes of episcopal estate. He held up his hands and conferred a blessing upon us.

A priest walked up and down, shaking holy water upon us from a silver vessel. Behind him came two servers, their purple penitential robes gleaming, handing out willow branches to each "pilgrim."

Cranmer blessed them. "As men long ago welcomed Our Lord into Jerusalem by honouring Him with palms, let us do the same in our lives. Keep and use these humble branches to the glory of God, and to aid you upon your spiritual journey."

Then he turned, slowly and gravely, and led us in measured steps into the Abbey, where he celebrated the Triumphal Procession into Jerusalem with a

Mass so grand and so complete that no Papalist, no matter how ardent, could accuse us of leaning toward Lutheranism or abandoning the True Faith.

Spy Wednesday. The day, traditionally, when Judas spied on Jesus, asking him questions, prying to find out where he would be the next day—so he could inform Caiaphas and the others and earn his thirty pieces of silver. All that day, most likely, Judas was asking softly worded questions: "My Lord and my Master—with whom shall you share the Passover meal?" Then must he wait awhile before asking offhandedly, "And on what street is the house where we must gather before sundown?"

Spies. I hated spies. I could not imagine what a man must feel who spies. Nor a man who employs spies. It seemed to me that once a man began relying on spies, he put himself in their power. At first the information they feed him is true, but it is a bait to catch him, and then nothing is as it seems. I preferred to base my actions on what was obvious and could be seen with my own eyes.

Night was falling, and it was time to go to the Spy Wednesday Mass— the public chanting of Tenebrae. In the great Abbey, all candles would be extinguished one by one—to reenact Jesus' abandonment by everyone, down to the last disciple.

The day itself had been one of gloom, and so the mood of despair and loss was already in the air. But it was intensified by the dirgelike chanting of the priests and the snuffing of all light in the great Abbey nave.

It felt like a tomb—all cold and dark and enclosed by stone. I tried hard to imagine the mind of Our Lord as He found Himself alone on the earth. There was an awesome period stretching between the fellowship of the Last Supper and the glory of the Resurrection; theologians called this time Satan's Hour. It was a time when Christ experienced all human desolation, felt Himself to be abandoned by God.

I shivered in my cloak. How quickly they ran to abandon Him! How soon the Passover wine and candles and warmth faded away. Our attempts to keep Satan at bay are so weak and pitiful. He always runs us to ground and we must stand and face him—alone.

I looked around me, but saw nothing. I could hear coughs and body movements, but all the men about me were hidden from my sight, and separate one from the other.

This is how Satan rules—by separating us.

But nothing can separate us from the love of God, Saint Paul says.

Nothing save despair.

Despair, then, is Satan's handmaiden.

Holy Thursday. Following the Last Supper, Christ washed the feet of the disciples, saying, "If I wash thee not, thou hast no part with me." Now, as Kings of England had done time out of mind before me, I must wash the feet of beggars—as many beggars as I am years old. Now, in the well-lighted Chapter House of Westminster Abbey, forty-one poor men await me.

I enter. They are seated on the stone bench that runs along one wall, looking around them in wonder. They are barefoot, not because they have removed their shoes, but because they have no shoes to remove. . . .

I kneel before the first man, representing the first year of my life. He is old, scrawny like a diseased fowl, and his feet are callused and hard as claws. I pour the warm, rose-scented water over them, dry them gently with a new linen towel.

The next man has festering sores all over his feet. The greenish pus runs into the water, clouding it in its silver basin. I beckon to Norris to bring a clean basin for the next man. It takes over an hour until the last man's feet are washed.

During all this, I do not feel a thing. Except shame that I feel nothing.

Good Friday. Fasting all day, shut up in our smallest, plainest room. No one at court is allowed to speak to anyone else, to smile, to sing, to eat, to wear anything but black. Even the church bells' metal clappers are replaced by wooden ones, to make dull, muffled sounds. A single piece of meat is left out on the table to grow maggoty and remind us of the corruption that awaits us all.

Three o'clock—the Hour of Death, the Hour of Satan. The Temple veil is rent in half, and we are given over to the power of darkness.

And then I felt it—felt its cold hand gripping me. And what had been pretence, form, play-acting, became real. I felt the power of the Devil, felt him in my very bowels. And God was far away, and the ceremonies did nothing to recall Him. Powerless, powerless . . .

All in the Abbey again, huddled together, a flock of black crows. Now Cranmer unveiled the great crucifix in three stages, chanting sorrowfully, "Behold the wood of the Cross, on which hung the Salvation of the World."

We knelt and answered, "Come, let us adore!"

The cross was placed reverently upon a cushion on the altar steps. Cranmer crept toward it on his knees, then kissed it and prostrated himself on the flagstones before it.

Now I must follow. I was frightened, frightened at my presumption and arrogance. I had meant to use this ceremony for political show, to reassure people of my innocence of any wrongdoing in appointing Cranmer Archbishop. Now I trembled at the implications of approaching the altar of God for such reasons. Would He strike me down, as He had done other rulers who had mocked Him in His very house?

I began the crawl up the cold stones to the altar steps. My hands were shaking.

"Mercy," I heard my voice whispering. "Mercy, O God! Forgive me." Closer and closer I came. My heart was pounding so rapidly I felt myself go dizzy. He would wait until I presumed to touch the sacred cross itself before He struck me.

Now! I reached out and grasped the wood, clinging to it like a rock. I felt strength, power surge through it to me, fill me with peace, dazzling peace.

I breathed out. Peace. I had always thought peace was the absence of fear, the absence of pain or sorrow. Now I knew peace was a thing in itself, a presence that had its own shape, that displaced all other feelings.

I laid my forehead on the holy wood, pressing it hard as if that would bring a gush of the beautiful Presence into my body. I wanted to be totally filled with it, to *be* pure peace.

Then it was gone; the sacred Presence had flown, leaving a human King hunched over an ordinary piece of wood. Cranmer was waiting for me to rise and make room for the next penitent. Stiffly I arose and passed out of the Abbey.

Saturday morning, Easter Eve. The hard, clear light burst into the room, in its own way crueller and more frightening than the dark of the night before. I could see all the radiating lines on my face as I held the hand-glass up. On the backs of my hands were fine diamonds, little divisions in the skin, repeated over and over—like a lizard's skin. These would deepen, grow ever more pronounced with the years.

Jesus had never reached my age. He never had to wrestle with aging and natural mortality. So how could He actually have shared all human experiences?

I splashed cold water on my face, well aware that my thoughts bordered on blasphemy.

The mocking day eventually drew to a close, and I was able to come back to the present and leave future death and dissolution alone. There was a great stirring about court as the dreary Lent and the fast of the past two days passed away into rejoicing. No Jew had ever waited as eagerly for sundown to begin a Sabbath as Anne and I did that sundown. Together we exclaimed like children as the evening stars popped out in the eastern sky.

"It is here! Easter is here! And they all have their orders!" she crowed.

"Yes, my love," I smiled. "Every priest in the land, when celebrating the Easter Mass, will pray for you as Queen. Thus the announcement will be made, and the people must say your name *aloud* in repetition. Three million English-men will all murmur, 'And so rule the heart of Thy chosen servant Anne, our Queen.' Will you hear each one, do you think? Will that content you, at last?"

She laughed lightly. "Only if I hear a sort of buzzing sound, so that I know everyone is saying those precious words in unison!"

I looked at her. I had fulfilled my promises to her, made so long ago. Tonight all England would call her Queen, and I had brought it about. She for whom I had banished my wife, insulted the Holy See, and jeopardized my kingdom, stood in the falling dark, reaching out to me. I took her hand: it was small and warm. I raised it to my lips, feeling the smooth skin. No lizard-diamonds there—not even their forerunners.

"I must dress!" She snatched her hand away, like a child. "Ah! I have waited so long for this night!"

"Mass begins at ten," I reminded her. "The court will gather in the Great Hall and then walk to the Abbey together."

I waited for her, surrounded by all the men and women of court. We were all attired in new-fashioned clothes, and in the torchlight our costumes and jewellery winked like the iridescent butterflies of summer. What a night of splendour, after long darkness! Now I would speak the words I had imagined myself saying for so long, and to this very company.

"My dear friends," I began, holding up one hand for silence, which fell before I even moved my arm back down. "It is with great joy, yea, greater joy than I can say, that I tell you that at last you have a Queen—my beloved Anne. We are wed."

They stood looking back. Had they not heard?

"Yes!" I repeated myself. "Though I have been your King, your chosen and anointed King for twenty-four years, I have never given you what it is your God-given right to have: a loving and true Queen. By His grace, she is here—"

Anne appeared at the far door of the Great Hall, a blaze of silver. Indeed, she appeared so dazzling and extraordinary she seemed no mortal. I stood, silenced, as she made her way toward me where I stood on the dais. The men and women of the court watched her, their faces still expressionless.

"Queen Anne." I extended my hand and she took it, moving easily up on the dais beside me.

"Queen Anne!" I shouted with joy.

"Queen Anne," repeated the people. But the joy was not there. They bowed and curtseyed only as custom required them to.

"Thank you, my good subjects!" said Anne shrilly. "We thank you."

No, no, I wanted to tell her. Not that way. Not in that tone of voice. Well, I would explain it to her later.

"May you all find the joy that God has given me in so humble and virtuous a Queen and so true a wife," I said. The people attempted to smile.

"Now you may have the traditional cramp-rings," Anne said, in that same high-pitched, haughty voice. She opened a glittering silver bag.

What was this? She was enacting the ancient rite of distributing iron rings to cure those suffering from cramp and rheumatism: rings that received their power only through the Good Friday blessing of a true monarch. She must have obtained the rings and performed the hallowing rite secretly, planning to distribute them tonight. Why had she not spoken to me of this beforehand?

"Come, my good people. These will ease you, will help those who suffer. They were blessed yesterday by your loving Queen." She held out a handful of iron rings. No one came up. Anne gestured once again. I motioned, and then they slowly came up and began to take them—with all the willingness of a housewife removing a dead mouse.

"Bless you!" Anne kept repeating in what she must have believed was a queenly manner; clearly she had rehearsed it. Without consulting me.

At last the hideously embarrassing ceremony was over, and the last of the Good Friday cramp-rings had been distributed.

The trumpets sounded from the Abbey across the courtyard. It was time for the royal procession; Anne and I leading the Duke of Richmond, my handsome fourteen-year-old natural son; the Duke of Norfolk (without his Duchess, from whom he was separated, and also without his laundress, with whom he was now living); the Duke of Suffolk (also without his Duchess, my sister Mary, who lay ill at their country manor); Henry Courtenay, the Marquis of Exeter; Margaret Pole, Countess of Salisbury, and her son, Lord Montague; the Earls of Rutland and of Bath; Lady Margaret Douglas, my romantic niece (daughter of Margaret Tudor and the Earl of Angus) . . . and behind all these, the great throng of untitled court people. Somewhere amongst them was plain Master Cromwell.

The Abbey was dark; dark as *the* tomb. Then there was a scraping, a sound of flint against stone, as the new Easter Fire was kindled—kindled and then quickly caught on a taper and transferred to the great Paschal candle, a cylinder of pure beeswax as big around as a man's thigh.

"Alleluia!" proclaimed Cranmer.

"Alleluia!" answered the people, resoundingly.

"He is risen!"

The silver trumpets blared, the candles blazed into light all over the Abbey.

"Bestow the kiss of peace!" commanded Cranmer.

Everyone stirred as faces were turned toward neighbours and the cheek-kiss was given.

Then the traditional Mass of the Resurrection began. Nothing was omitted—from the procession of newly baptized Christians in their white robes to the public renunciation of the Devil and all his works and all his ways. Let anyone dare to challenge my Church, I thought smugly, to say everything was not intact!

Now the solemn part began, the sacred mysteries of the Canon: the Offering, the Consecration, and the Communion, followed by the commemoration of the living . . . "that it may please Thee to keep and strengthen Thy servant Anne, our most gracious Queen; that it may please Thee to be her defender and keeper, giving her the victory over all her enemies, we beseech Thee—"

There was a scraping and movement in the back, which grew louder and made Cranmer halt in his chanting.

People were leaving.

I turned and stared. It could not be. But it was. And not just a few recalcitrants, but row upon row. They turned, looked mournfully up toward the altar where Cranmer stood, then filed out through the great Abbey doors.

They refused to pray for Anne as Queen, or even to remain in a building where others did so!

I stood, stunned, unable to believe what I had just seen—the spontaneous public rejection of Anne. Such a thing I had never even considered. I had seen the Pope and the Emperor and some conservative Northern lords, like the Earl of Derby, Lord Darcy, Lord Hussey, the great Marcher lords, Katherine's partisans, as Anne's enemies. But the common people! She was one of them. How could they reject her?

Katherine must have paid these people! Her sneaking little monkey of an ambassador, Chapuys, was behind this insulting display. Well, I would have him brought before me and punished.

In the meantime, there was this interminable Mass to endure—this Mass, so long awaited, now so ruinous. Beside me, Anne was still. I could feel her anger; it had a shape of its own.

Alone in our royal apartments that night, she screamed with fury. It was past two in the morning, and by this time I had thought to be drifting off into a sleep of paradise—in Anne's arms, feeling her kisses and murmurs of endearments and pretty thanks for all the dangers I had braved to make her Queen, to have brought her to this moment.

But this moment had turned, like so much else in our lives, into an experience of pain and sorrow, of humiliation and frustration.

"I hate them!" she shrieked for the tenth time. "I shall be revenged on them!" Then, to me: "Why did you not stop them? Why did you stand there like a ploughboy?"

"I was as stunned as one," I muttered.

"You should have rounded them up and had them questioned!"

"No, that would have pleased them, given them importance. Better to ignore them. That is the way of Kings."

"No! I must be revenged on them!"

Was it then that the unbidden thought exploded inside my head, past the barriers of desire and obsession? *This is the behaviour of a commoner, not a Queen. Common she was born, common she remains. She is not the stuff of royalty.* Immediately my love for her intercepted the thought, wrestled it to the ground, and deprived it of its liberty.

"They are long since asleep in their beds. We could not find out who they were, even if we wanted. Forget it." I myself intended to question Chapuys, but privately. "There is always a stir at a change. Even spring brings sadness of a sort."

I patted the bed, for which I still had hopes. "Come to bed, sweetheart. Let me make love to my Queen."

But I was as useless with her as I had been that other time, and I slept not at all the rest of that evil night.

Were we cursed? Side by side we lay, each pretending to sleep, while those words ran like rats through our brains.

XLIX

It had happened all over the land. In church after church, when the prayer naming Anne as Queen had been read, people either fell silent or left the Mass. They spoke as loudly as the madman who had run about the streets the previous summer, yelling, "We'll no Nan Bullen!"; as forcibly as the crowd who had pursued Anne and tried to stone her; as angrily as the Ahab-preaching friar.

Now, for the first time, I had doubts about Anne's Coronation. Anne had coveted it, and I had promised it. But what if the people rejected her as wholeheartedly on that day? How much worse that would be than no Coronation at all.

What could I do to prevent it? I could not physically silence every Londoner; there were more than a hundred thousand of them. Nor could I silence them with money. The Royal Treasury was almost empty, and the Coronation would require every spare pound. Behind the golden garments and sumptuous dinners of state, the Crown was in urgent need of money. Toward the latter end, I conferred with Master Cromwell.

He reminded me of the deplorable moral state of the monasteries, where corruption existed side by side with immense wealth. "The sight of it must surely strike sorrow into the bosom of Our Lord," he said piously. He asked permission to send a group of commissioners to visit and report on each religious house, and promised to have a summary of their findings in my hands within a year. "Then you may judge for yourself," he said, "whether they should be allowed to remain open."

Of course, closing them would mean acquiring their assets for the Crown, since it was now forbidden by Act of Parliament to send ecclesiastical income to Rome.

As for Cranmer, he moved swiftly to fulfil his duties. By mid-May he called and presided over a small ecclesiastical court, discreetly held at Dunstable, some distance from London, but near enough to Katherine that she could have appeared, as she was requested to do. Naturally she did not recognize Cranmer's authority and so ignored the little hearing that found our prior marriage to be no marriage at all, and also (conveniently) pronounced my present marriage to Anne valid.

Now we could proceed with the Coronation, which would fall on Whitsunday, a holy day in itself. I prayed that that would help sanctify it in the mind of the people. I tried not to betray my own anxiety to Anne, who had awaited this day as the culmination of all her dreams.

This was to be Anne's day, I had decided. I had had my own Coronation day twenty-four years ago, and there was no need to repeat it. I preferred to let my own memories stand and to allow Anne her own, personal and unshared. Therefore I would not accompany her at the ceremonies; I would stand back and observe like an outsider. I wanted to savour her Coronation, to revel in the knowledge that I myself had brought it about. It was my will, and my will alone, that had achieved this. Without my will, none of this would be happening. There would be no scaffolds being erected; there would be no sore-fingered seamstresses; there would be no bettors in Milk Lane wagering on rain on Coronation Day. I had created this moment, this event, as I never had my own Coronation. Mine was the will of God; Anne's was the will of Henry VIII.

Each night, when I came to Anne's Privy Chamber, I had to be announced. I would wait impatiently in the antechamber while her maid of honour attempted to entertain me and Anne hastily put away her Coronation baubles lest I see them prematurely.

On the Wednesday before the great day, I was especially anxious to see her, and I paced up and down the small area. All the windows were open, and the sounds of London on a May night came pouring in to my ears.

The moon was near full. The sounds of the hammering (workmen were erecting the scaffolding in the streets, and were grateful that the full moon allowed them extra hours), the cries of youth outside the taverns, enjoying the languid night—all sounded as though real life were somewhere beyond the palace, as if it could actually be grasped. Yet I knew that every drunken Dickon leaning against the wattle walls of his tavern imagined us to be where real life resided, where all things were heightened—and so they were, so they were. There was no man so alive as I.

"Will you have some wine, Your Grace?" asked Anne's sweet attendant.

Wine? Who needed wine on a night like this? "Nay, nay—" I waved her away. How rude of me. I stopped and looked at her, so I could remember this night always. She was part of it.

She was small, and had honey-coloured hair. But these were not the main things I noted upon seeing her. Her overriding feature was paleness. A spider-web. A waning moon. A reflection of an old linen gown in a deep, shrouded well.

"Oh, perhaps so." I smiled and tried to be affable. She came forward and poured a portion of Rhenish wine into a chased silver goblet.

"And you?" I lifted it.

She demurred. I insisted. "It is lonely to drink, thus, alone."

She took a small portion, then excused herself, as if timid. I watched her walk to the window and look out.

When *would* Anne be ready? Across the courtyard I could hear my favourite clock—the large astronomical one in the gate-tower—chiming nine. The voices from the tavern were louder but more slurred. I walked over to the lady, who was absorbed in looking out over the rooftops. She had a clean, clear profile.

"Do you not ever—" she began, then faltered.

"Ever what, mistress?" Hearing my own voice, I was surprised at how irritated it sounded. But I was ready to see Anne! Why did she keep me waiting thus?

". . . ever . . . ever look out on those roofs and feel certain—with a great, envious certainty—that all the people sleeping there, or living there . . . are happy?"

Without hesitating, I concurred. "Yes. I am sure of it." Someone had actually felt the same; someone understood. . . .

"And do you ever wish that you could *be* there, come into that entrance hall—that's all muddy—and hear your mother scolding someone for not bringing in enough logs and know that there's warmth and discomfort there?"

"You mean comfort," I corrected her.

"Nay, I mean discomfort. Always warmth and discomfort. They go together, and you hate yourself for swallowing the one because of your hunger for the other. And—"

"My Lord!" The unmistakable voice reached me, the voice I had been waiting to hear. My eyes turned toward its source. Anne stood just beyond the doors to her inner chamber. Her face was hidden, but her voice compelled. I turned from my companion.

Anne laughingly pulled me in and clanged the great doors shut. She looked radiant, and her movements were quick and sure. "I have it at last!" she swung round. "The gown. It is perfect!"

She laughed again. "A gown no one shall ever forget. Do you remember how Wolsey called me 'the night crow,' because my hair was black, my robe black? Now I want all the people to see me as radiant, as much a true Queen in white. Wolsey and the night-robe were darkness. This is to be dazzling high noon."

All the time she was skimming across the polished wooden boards, as if she had no feet at all. The strong moonlight and the torches gave light, and yet her reflection on the oiled wood was shimmering, ephemeral. She never touched it.

"Nay, I cannot show you the design!" she laughed, as she reached her inmost chamber. "I have hidden it well. I wish you to be as dazzled as all the rest!"

I was dazzled even now. She stood in the middle of the room, all beauty and darkness and light. No need to hate oneself because of choosing. To choose her was to have all.

❧ ☙

The Coronation was not a single ceremony, but a nesting set of ceremonies, one within the other, surrounding the precious moment of anointing in Westminster Abbey. First Anne must be transported by water to the Tower, where she would lodge overnight. Then from the Tower she would be carried in a litter through the London streets to show herself to the people. Then, the next day, she would be crowned. And the following week would be a holiday for all.

Carefully I explained the protocol of each of these events to a restless, glittery-eyed Anne.

"The water procession will make a public holiday of it. The Thames is far wider than any street, and allows room for a great pageant, and fireworks, even cannon-fire. There is nothing gayer. Have you ever seen a royal water carnival?"

"Nay. Only the decorated boats we had at Ascensiontide in Norfolk when I was a child."

"Pah!" I dismissed that with a snap of the fingers. "I have been told by the Lord Mayor that there is even to be a dragon upon the water, with a mechanized thrashing tail and a mouth vomiting forth fire. And that is just *one* marvel."

The same Lord Mayor had earlier been instructed by me regarding the Londoners' rude behaviour toward Anne. I had threatened him with heinous punishment if any insults marred the day. Aloud I said, "And the Lord Mayor will call for you at Greenwich in the State Barge."

"What a triumph!" she said, a hard edge to her voice. "My great-grandfather was Lord Mayor of London—and now I am to be its Queen!" The

3 6 3

gloating ill became her. As if catching herself, she quickly said, "My royal barge will make a brave show. It is a merry gold now, and its sails of crimson."

"Katherine has no need of it in the fens," I muttered. "Although she still claims it as her property." The thought of Katherine was like a mound of unmelted snow in an otherwise blooming garden. "I will receive you at the Tower steps," I continued. "And we will spend that night in the royal apartments there."

"I hate the Tower!" she snapped. "It is gloomy and old-fashioned. It oppresses me."

"The royal apartments are newly redecorated—and as comfortable as any other palace. It is tradition to spend the night preceding the Coronation there, and besides, there are the ceremonies creating new Knights of the Bath, and conferring new knighthoods."

"Old things, old ceremonies, old customs, all of it. The old is over and done with and does not concern me," she insisted.

"The old is never over and done with. It is merely dressed in new clothes and presented as new. That you shall do. As you did your sleeves. Are not sleeves an ancient thing? Yet you made them an exciting discovery." (How innocently I said it—I who had been dazzled by the voluminous, jewelled sleeves on her gowns, never suspecting they were fashioned to hide her witch's mark.)

"Yes," she agreed, eager to leave the subject of the sleeves. "I will try to make it all new—to make it a happy memory for everyone."

"That I am sure of, sweetheart. And I shall experience it first-hand. On the Thames, in disguise. Will is arranging it all." I enjoyed the look of surprise on her face. "You are not the only one to attempt something new. I will become one of my own subjects that day, and see your triumph through their eyes."

"What a gift you are giving me," she murmured.

I had no way of knowing it was to be the last great celebration of my youth—the last time I would frolic in a shower of glittering gold and high hopes.

L

It was a glorious day. The bettors were to lose great quantities of money, and I did not pity them in the least. The sun had risen to a flawless sky, and even the water was warm. There was an air of festivity amongst the small craft and the people in them as the water rocked them gently to and fro.

Will and I slipped quietly to take our places in the leaking rowboat that Will had procured for us. We were both properly disguised—I in a moth-eaten cloak and battered hat (discarded by a groom in the royal stables) and he in an old costume left behind by a tinker in the courtyard. How merry to be allowed to be in the background for one blessed day!

The watchword was excitement and the unexpected. Suddenly an odour of garlic reached me. The people in the neighbouring boat were slapping hunks of Kentish cheese on large slabs of bread, then sprinkling them with garlic. They passed them from bow to stern in the boat. They made one too many, then looked about. They saw me.

"Will you have one?" They waved it in the air.

"Aye." I reached out and took it. Will looked at me and frowned. I broke off half and shared it with him. He chomped on it eagerly, as did I. It was good.

A wave reached the boat and rocked it. Our neighbours complained loudly. "The river isn't as quiet as it should be for this late in the year. Only for a Coronation would I sit out here all night and then endure the—"

"Were you here for the previous one?"

"Eh?"

"The King's."

He looked apologetic. "That was so long ago. I was but a lad."

And I, I thought.

"But my father brought me to London. I remember seeing him. My father carried me on his shoulders. The King was very beautiful. He was so young, so . . . so *golden*. Like a jewel he was, and—"

CRACK! The sound of a cannon salvo from the shore cut off the conversation. I turned to see Will raising an eyebrow at me. He hated the way I "drank at vanity's well," as he put it.

"Here she comes," the man exclaimed.

I craned my neck like any provincial. I stood on tiptoe on the seat of the small boat. All I saw was deck after deck, boat after boat: the State Barge, the decorated barges of the craft guilds, the nobles, and the clergy, and countless small craft like ours. They were so thick the Thames itself was all but invisible.

Then I saw a slight parting. The small craft were falling away, leaving a great and broad path for the royal barge. The sun shone off it as if burnishing the way, making it warm.

A snap. The wind had caught Anne's sails. No need for rowers. A hiss. The oars were out of the water, trailing a few drops, then poised like butterflies' wings.

The barge hove into sight. Katherine's barge—but no longer Katherine's. It was transformed.

Everything had been repainted. Where once the Spanish pomegranates and emblems of Spain had been on the prow, now sat Anne's: a white falcon, with her motto beneath. *Me and Mine.* A proud motto, proud as the lady herself.

The wind filled the sails. They were crimson, snapping and billowing with the breeze. Beneath them, seated on a chair of estate, all in white, was Anne.

She did not look at anyone. Thousands surrounded her and gaped, but she looked straight ahead. Her hair blew in the wind as the sails.

I loved her then as at no other time. She was riding on the water like a goddess. I reached out to Will and said, "Is she not lovely?" But I did not hear his answer.

Anne's barge approached, then passed us. "Like Cleopatra, my Lord," said Will, finally. The barge was to be silhouetted by the sun, which it was sailing into, for the rest of the day. Against the sun it resembled a bat—great black wings outspread.

The people around us packed their food and gear to return home. I bade them farewell.

" 'Twas lovely," they said, a trifle sadly. There was a thud as they stowed another item.

"You sound sad," I ventured.

"Aye. She was so lovely." They cast off. "I think—" Their voices were lost in the heave of the water and the noise of sails. I turned to our host and to Will.

" 'Tis time we returned to our home as well."

"Indeed," the boatman said. I settled myself and waited for the short journey back to the common Greenwich quay. Even in small things today, it was a pleasure to give up control to someone else, to sit back and dream.

Dream I did, the setting sun on my eyelids. I dreamt of Anne in a great Egyptian barge, Anne as Pharaoh's wife, Anne as—Potiphar's wife.

At the Tower that night, Anne was feverishly gay. "Did you see it? What did the onlookers say?" she kept asking, never satisfied with my replies. "The dragon—he was magnificent. Did I tell you he spewed fire right up to my feet? One of my shoes was singed—"

"Hush," I said. "Calm yourself."

All around us rose the babble of excited voices. Eighteen young men were preparing for their all-night vigil prior to their ordination on the morrow as Knights of the Bath. The rest of the court was feasting in the hall of the White Tower. And everywhere there were flowers—garlands and petals covered every stone. Bits of broken glass glinted; the boom of the cannons had shattered many windowpanes. Over all this confusion floated string-music.

"Walk with me," she said. "I need the night air."

Gladly I took her hand. "Your cheeks are flaming," I said.

Outside, the White Tower seemed to glow in the luminous May twilight.

"Ah!" She let out a long, shuddering sigh. Then, suddenly, "What of More?"

A jab in my heart. "I sent him twenty pounds to buy himself a new gown for the Coronation. He has not returned it."

This seemed to satisfy her. "And Mary?"

A second jab in the same place. "My sister lies very ill at Westhorpe."

"She has always hated me!"

That was true. Mary had begged me not to persist in this "folly" with Anne. She might as well have requested the rain to halt in its falling halfway to earth. "That is not why she is ill," I stated flatly.

"I insist that she come and pay homage to me as soon as she recovers."

Her pettiness marred the night, and its glory fled for me. But we walked on in silence for another few moments. Then Anne suddenly wished to go to the little Tower chapel to pray.

"No!" I stopped her. "Not in St. John's Chapel. It is—it is where the Knights are preparing to keep vigil all night." It was also where my mother had lain on her funeral bier, surrounded by thousands of tapers, thirty years ago. I would not have Anne pray there before her Coronation.

"But I must pray!" she insisted. Her face looked strained and eager and more vulnerable than I had ever seen it. It also looked different.

"You shall pray," I said. "But in the little chapel elsewhere on the grounds. St. Peter-ad-Vincula."

"Is the Sacrament reserved there?"

"Always."

I guided her to the little stone structure, standing lonely and dark on the far edge of the night's warm noises and light. She hesitated.

"I will come with you and light a torch," I said.

I pushed the warped wooden door open into the echoing interior. A single flame flickered on the altar, signifying the sacred Presence of the consecrated Host.

I lighted a large floor-candle near the door, and reached out to touch Anne's shoulder. "Pray in peace," I said.

"Thank you," she said. "Thank you for not smiling at me." I knew what she meant; to express a genuine urge to piety is to risk ridicule.

"Pray for me," I asked.

June first. In the middle of the night, enchanted May had given way to high summer and the political reality of Anne's procession through the streets of London. Would the city welcome her? Yesterday's show on the water had been pretty, but the string-music and cannonfire and fireworks had masked any jeering, and the malcontents had not bothered to venture out on boats.

The streets were different: freshly widened, gravelled, and lined with scaffolding, with a great "display" at every corner—an open invitation to troublemakers. True, the Lord Mayor had been warned, and he had certainly put on a brave show yesterday, but even he could not control the rabble; he knew that, and so did I, in spite of my threats about "traitors." The idea that two hundred royal constables could keep any sort of discipline over a hundred thousand Londoners was absurd. Today Anne must ride forth, trusting in their goodwill—and God's.

I glanced up at the sun, already a bright hot ball in a clean sky. That, at least, was auspicious. Ascending to the highest ramparts of the square White Tower, I could see westward all across London, whence Anne must cross to Westminster Abbey. Already the streets were choked with people, some of whom must have been there all night.

I myself intended to watch the procession from a window in Baynard's Castle, and it was time I set out, before the crowd thickened.

Cromwell, having no part in the procession, awaited me in the appointed room at Baynard's Castle, actually not a castle at all but a decrepit old royal dwelling that happened to be situated along Anne's route. He had arranged for comfortable viewing-chairs, deep cushions, and music to amuse us as we waited.

"We are quite without a part in today's show," I commiserated with Cromwell. "Which I find consummately amusing, since we are the ones who arranged it all."

He cocked an eyebrow. "The Lady Anne—that is, the Queen—also played a part."

"Not as big a part as you and I." I spoke the words easily, but was well aware of their significance of our partnership. "Today the people will see a passing parade of robes and titles, while the true power stays out of sight."

"It was ever thus," he shrugged, presenting me with a covered silver bowl. I took it; it was icy cold. Curious, I removed the top.

"Sherbet, Your Majesty. They have it in Persia to cool themselves on hot days like today." Cromwell nodded. "I can have it made in other flavours, but mint is my personal favourite."

I tasted it; it was a splendid fillip on the tongue. "Marvellous! Crum, you are marvellous!" How did the man find such ingenious ways of making everything pleasant—and feasible? Not only the coronation of an unthought-of Queen, but the sherbet to pleasure it.

By noon I could hear the trumpets sounding from the Tower, and I knew Anne had set out. It took an entire hour for the front part of the procession to pass by. It was led by twelve Frenchmen, all dressed in blue velvet, both they and their horses, signifying Francis's goodwill; after them came squires, knights, and judges in ceremonial robes; the new-made Knights of the Bath in purple gowns; then the peerage: dukes, earls, marquises, barons, abbots, and bishops in crimson velvet. In their steps followed the officers of rank in England—archbishops, ambassadors, the lord mayors of London and other cities, the Garter Knight of Arms. . . .

Finally, Anne. She was borne through the streets like a precious jewel, sitting in an open litter of white cloth-of-gold, borne by two white-caparisoned horses, a canopy of gold shielding her from the rude stare of the sun.

But not from the rude stares and sullen silence of the crowd—nothing could shield her from that, except she bury herself in walls of stone two feet thick.

Her head was held high, the chin lifted insolently, like a swan's. Around her thin curved neck, like a great collar, was a circlet of unnaturally huge pearls. All in white, dazzling—with that long black hair hanging loose down her back. Pregnant, she was dressed as a virgin, all in white with unbound hair. Scorned, she held her head as proud as Alexander the Great.

My will seemed to me a living thing, as I pitied her and *willed* the onlookers to welcome her, give her some sign of affection. If desire could have moved them, every person would have cheered.

Anne's fool, scampering along behind her, attempted to move them to shame and goodwill. "I fear you all have scurvy, and dare not uncover your heads!" he shouted, snatching off his own cap by way of example—an example they did not follow.

As Anne passed on, followed by all her royal household—her Chamberlain, Master of the Horse, ladies in velvet, chariots of peeresses, the gentlewomen, and finally the King's Guard—the people spontaneously began to cheer. The insult could not have been greater.

Beside me, I saw Cromwell's expressionless eyes upon me. "Pity," he said, and I saw that to him it was but another political fact, to be used as suited our purposes best. "More sherbet?"

Anne was shaking with anger when I came to her at Westminster Palace that evening. "The crowds were silent! The common people all but spat on me, and the German merchants of the Hanseatic League—oh, they think the Emperor will protect them, just as Katherine does, she who paid the people with her nephew's money, but—"

"I have never seen you more Juno-like," I said. "But what of the German merchants?" No one else had dared to tell me of their misdeed.

"Where Cheapside runs into Ludgate Hill, the two greatest cross-streets in London, they erected their 'tribute' to me—a triumphal arch, all archways and pilasters and fountains, with Apollo and the muses, and on each side pillars holding up our coats of arms—"

"And? It sounds pretty."

"Crouched over it all, with a nine-foot wingspan—the Imperial eagle, with Charles's features! His talons were reaching out to grasp our crowns. Oh, the message was clear—quite clear!"

I felt hot anger cascade through me, turning icy cold on its way down. "So," was all I said.

Anne sank down in a chair and changed from Juno into a very human woman who had undergone an exhausting ordeal. Even apart from the emotional overtones, physically the day had been gruelling, especially for a pregnant woman.

I knelt before her. "Stupid, spiteful men made a hurtful gesture. It is as hollow as the papier-mâché of which the eagle is constructed. I pray you, be impervious to it. It reflects on them, not on you." She looked so weary and frail, her fatigue showing in every muscle. "God's blood! Must they vent their hatred on a helpless woman?"

She reached out and traced her hand along my face. "Well," she said. "It is done. They can do no more to me."

That was true. They and Katherine's partisans had done their worst, and the day was over, with no real misfortunes. "Would you like some sherbet?" I asked.

When Cromwell's exotic delicacy was offered her, she exclaimed over it like a child, able to make me feel I had presented her with all the jewels of India. That was ever her magic: to make me feel thus—when she chose to do so.

The great bells of the Abbey were chiming ten as she finished the sherbet and put her bowl down. She fidgeted, smiled, and tried to hide her nervousness. There would be no sleep for her that night, I could see. So I must help her.

"You must rest. For the Coronation tomorrow."

"I cannot," she sighed, drumming her fingers on the chair-arms. They rattled like summer rain on a tent.

"Have some syrup. The monks make a special syrup that soothes and assures sleep. There are times when one cannot afford to be restless and tired."

"A sleeping potion?" She looked at me wonderingly. "You employ sleeping potions?"

"They can be good, if used for good reason."

"Yes . . . there are potions like that . . . potions I have used. . . ."

"To make your skin more fair!" How quickly I came forward to provide a harmless explanation for her confession.

"Aye . . . for my skin, of course . . . and for women's needs, at certain times . . . yes, this is a good reason. My Coronation eve—"

"To make you more beautiful. To help you remember always the feeling of the oil on your forehead, the first weight of the crown as it is placed on your head."

"Do you remember?" Her voice was soft.

"Yes. I remember every word, every moment."

I was wrong. I did not remember "every word, every moment." When Anne was escorted the short walk between Westminster Palace and Westminster Abbey early the next morning under a canopy held by four knights, I had no recollection of having ever done such a thing. I watched her as she disappeared into the Abbey, a tiny figure all swathed in ermine-trimmed purple velvet, and then she was lost to sight. I must retire to the secret viewing-place I had had specially constructed in the adjoining chapel of St. Stephen's (where Cranmer had made his private "disqualifying" vows) if I wanted to view the actual Coronation ceremony.

Now, high in the screened balcony, I looked down on the grey stone, splashed with hundreds of human jewels—Anne alone in purple, the colour of royalty. Once she had been a plain knight's daughter, as common as anyone down on the sacred pavement below. But I had seen her, had raised her up and fashioned her into a Queen; she was my creation.

Now the solemn moment was upon her. Cranmer, robes trailing, came toward her, took her hands, and led her past the rood-screen to the high altar. There she was seated on the ancient, crude wooden crowning-throne.

Yes, I remembered that. I remembered the cold, uncomfortable wood, and I remembered thinking fleetingly of the barbaric chieftains crowned here long ago, clad in fur and leather and sword, who had found this rude seat of kingship hewed to their taste.

Now the sensual memories began to return. Smell: the lulling incense rising in columns around me; the rich scent of new velvet; the damp, clean odour of freshly washed stone. Sounds: the murmur of the holy oil as the Archbishop poured it into the golden Ampulla; the soft padding of holy feet on the cold stones; the detached chanting that echoed far back into the chapel where my father and mother slept their marbled sleep.

A hush had fallen. The moment of anointing was here, and the clink of the Anointing Spoon against the Ampulla was clearly heard. I looked down at Anne in wonder. Walked I so? Appeared I so as I knelt? Was I flanked by candles so? Why could I not remember?

Now, suddenly, Anne was Queen. It was over. What was done could not be undone. But why would I think of undoing even at this moment?

The Coronation banquet followed immediately in the enormous Hall of Westminster Palace, where we had assembled, weeks earlier, for Easter Eve. Tables to serve five hundred awaited the Coronation guests. I myself would watch from yet another window in yet another adjoining room.

From my vantage point, the tables below me, set with linen and golden plates and goblets, could not have been more perfectly appointed. And Anne would preside at last at the royal table on the dais, with no need for me.

She swept in, like a great burst of Nature. Not the hesitant coming of spring, all shy and in bits and pieces, but a trumpet-sound, the cracking of ice in winter. Anne was here!

She took her place, shining over them all, a column of purple. Then she sank down on her seat. Servers swarmed over the Hall, goblets flashed, platters laden with the season's plenty passed to all. The traditional "Champions" in armour clattered on horseback up and down the Hall, challenging any who questioned Anne's right to sovereignty. With their swords and steeds they would vanquish any malcontents.

A quaint, pretty custom. Could they prevail against the sullen, silent crowds lining the London streets yesterday? Like the throning-chair, the Champions belonged to another day of man.

My eyes swept the Hall and saw Thomas More's chair, empty.

It was late that night before Anne and I met again. She seemed the same as always. Thus do changes of great moment disguise themselves as no change at all.

Wordlessly, I took her hand. I led her to my bed, and there, all other thoughts gone, dissipated, flown—I merged with her as I never had with another human being. Even God was forgotten.

LI

The week following Anne's crowning was a respite from all earthly cares. The sun shone constantly; the citizenry were released from work; wine ran from public conduits; every day there was a tournament at the palace tiltyard. And every night there was unparalleled bliss in Anne's bed, where I explored sensual playgrounds whose existence I had never even suspected.

Returning to the workaday world was as difficult as leaving a dream. In the land of the Infidel, I am told, men sometimes sit for days, months, even years in dens hung with silk, and smoke a dream-inducing drug. That was what I felt I had been allowed to do, and I was loth to leave it. Just so quickly is euphoria addicting.

As long as I remained inside my palace, revelling in ceremonies and a woman's arms, all was joy. But outside there was little joy, let alone euphoria. The people still wanted "no Nan Bullen." Thomas More still sat in his study at Chelsea, translating Latin, but never sending even a note of felicitations to me. He had returned the twenty pounds wordlessly. The Pope still tried to inveigle Charles into going to war with me to defend Katherine's—and the Church's—honour. Katherine herself, the "wronged lady," continued to style herself Queen from Buckden, the red brick palace in the fens, where she had grudgingly allowed herself to be transferred.

Also in East Anglia, my sister Mary still lay ill. As soon as his Coronation duties were over, Charles Brandon rode back to be with her. I promised to follow by the end of June, and sent a basketful of strawberries, which she had always loved, from Hampton Court, with affectionate orders that she eat them immediately and be cured.

And now came the short, cruel message: Mary lay dead. The strawberries had reached a woman who had no need of eating.

She was to be interred in Suffolk, where she had spent the years since she married Brandon. She, who had once been Queen of France, had loved jewels and dancing and court gaiety, had lived a quiet country life for eighteen years—all for love of one man. Friend though he was, I envied Charles that. Suddenly, an unbidden thought: Would Anne have done such for me? Mary had gone from Queen to Suffolk lady gladly. Anne's personal journey had been in the exact opposite direction—from simple knight's daughter to Queen.

"She will be buried as Queen," said Charles in a choked voice. He had returned to court while Mary was being prepared for her funeral. "Queen of France. It is the least I can do—I who deprived her of the rightful title in life."

"She chose you, Charles," I reminded him. "She chose to be your wife, to live in Suffolk and have children, rather than remain in the French court and be Dowager Queen."

That was no consolation to him. He seemed determined to believe that he had stolen her youth and privileges of rank from her.

"To have a Queen's burial—will that not be . . . extravagant?" I meant "expensive." The costs of following protocol for a royal interment were staggering, and I knew well that Charles's finances were questionable.

"I will manage," he mumbled, turning begging eyes toward me.

Now was the moment when I should have offered, as a brother and a friend, to pay for the funeral. But I could not. I had no extra money, not even a shilling unaccounted for. Soon I would start reaping the former Church revenues: Parliament had already obligingly passed the Act of Annates, an act that would funnel one-tenth of Church income, which had hitherto gone to Rome, to me. But that future river of cash was a mere trickle as yet.

The moment passed.

"I will have the Lady Willoughby's inheritance," Charles said, the begging look still there.

"What?" I did not understand him.

"Lord Willoughby's daughter—"

"The child who was made your ward," I remembered. "Katherine." Ugh—that name. She had been named after *the* Katherine, for her mother, Maria de Salinas, had come from Spain with Katherine in 1501, when she came as a bride for Arthur.

Soon thereafter the pretty Spanish girl had caught the eye of the amiable Lord Willoughby and they had married. After Willoughby's death, Charles had assumed the daughter's wardship. This meant that for a fee he provided her with a home until she married. It was commonly done; many peers kept several wardships at a time.

"But the income from her wardship can hardly be sufficient to cover the costs of a royal funeral," I persisted. Charles had never had any money sense, although he had had sense enough to betroth young Katherine Willoughby to his son, so that her lands and property would not escape his family.

"We are to be married," he said bluntly. "In three months—after the deep mourning period."

"But—she is betrothed to your own son!" was all that I could think of.

"I broke the betrothal." He shrugged. "She always had a fancy for me. I could see it. The way she'd look at me, coming to enquire about Mary or Henry—" The pride of a natural lecher shone through the eyes that only a moment ago had been so abject and grieving. I felt sick. I turned away; I was afraid I would strike him.

"You must understand," he wheedled. "Money. It is only for money. I did what I had to do to survive. I *did* love Mary, I was not unfaithful to her, but a man must live—why, I cannot even bury her otherwise!"

"Yes," I said quietly, the word a little stone dropped precisely into the charged air between us. "A man must live. It is not honour that gives him life, nor love, nor his heart beating, nor his chest moving. . . . I see now these cannot work at all, save in the presence of money. Money is the fuel that powers us all, that makes love and honour possible."

"Yes. I knew you would understand. You love Anne, do you not? Yet without—"

Say it not! Say it not! "Without the crown she would not have had you."

"—plundering the Church, you could not sustain independence from the Pope and Emperor."

I whirled around and stared at this broad-faced, aging soldier of fortune. "How dare you compare our actions?" I screamed. "You grasping, covetous seducer, prostituting yourself on your wife's bier! I am reforming the Church because it cries out for purging, for purification! Out of my sight!"

"As you wish." He bowed and left the room, his long black mourning cape an insolent swish behind him.

And Mary had loved him! Sorrow and anger fought within me, and as usual, anger won.

Outside, the bright June day seemed crueller than the ugliest day in winter. With Mary gone, I had lost the last link to my real family—and to the boy I had once been.

WILL:

As that past was laid to rest in Framlingham Church in Suffolk, the present Henry, severed from his past, strode across the summer, brave as a lion. To all outward eyes he was at his peak, still healthy, handsome, having attained his heart's desire in a wife and coming heir, as well as a new concubine: the Church. He was fortune's minion that day—his forty-second birthday.

LII

❧ HENRY VIII:

Where was my son and heir to be born? Where else but Greenwich, then Anne's favourite residence—now a place I avoid, as it is thick with ghosts. At the time nothing else would do but that Anne must have her royal confinement there. So, by July, workers were already busy transforming one wing of the airy waterside palace into that strange sanctuary, a lying-in apartment. One month prior to her delivery date, Anne would have to retire there, with only a few trusted women, and remain in seclusion until after the birth. It was a velvet prison, designed to prevent any possible counterfeit babe from being switched with the true Prince. It was for the Queen's protection.

Anne, however, did not see it that way. "To be shut up during August, in high summer!" she lamented. "Kept secluded like a Turk-woman! No man to see me except a physician. 'Tis cruel, sweet Harry!"

" 'Tis custom. We have broken so many large ones, we are bound all the more to observe the small ones."

"And you will be away on progress!"

"No," I assured her. "I will never be more than a half-day's ride from your side. I would not leave you, no, not for all the jewels in Becket's tomb. We will be together up until the day you take your chamber with your women."

"*Women!*" She almost spat the word. "A lot of dull, boring creatures, who talk of nothing but milk possets and childbed fever and 'how it was when I bore my Johnnie,' " she mimicked cruelly—and perfectly.

"You do not care for the company of women?"

"No! I do not! I want wit and music and poetry about me. You give me that. My brother George and his friends, Tom Wyatt, Will Brereton, Francis Weston—*they* are amusing. But a gaggle of gossiping, stupid women!"

It was true. She always surrounded herself with men, and had no women friends. Her closest companion was her brother George, not her sister Mary.

"It is but a short while. You will be glad enough of their presence when your time comes. I cannot fancy your wishing Tom Wyatt to see you in the hours when you give birth. The women will know what to do. After all, they have borne their Johnnies, as you say, which is of more value in a birth-room than knowledge of Italian sonnets."

She made a sour face.

"Now enough of this," I said. "Besides, I have a jewel to tempt you into your lying-in chamber: a great bed that was once part of a Prince's ransom. I am having it taken from my royal treasury-house and reassembled in your chamber."

She brushed aside my bribe, like a cunning child. "Being walled up delights me not. Can I not even have Mark Smeaton to play for me, to amuse me during those endless hours of waiting?"

Mark Smeaton. That beautiful commoner, whose skill on the lute was near to genius. Where had he come by it, I had often wondered.

"It is not possible," I said, tight-lipped. Would she never understand? Things that Katherine, bred royalty from the womb, knew in her bones, were entirely missing in Anne.

"But—" she began, and I cut her off.

"I have decided upon Edward as his name," I announced.

"Oh." She looked puzzled. "I assumed you would choose Henry."

"I have had a son named Henry who did not live." How could she not know that? It seemed impossible that she did not know, would not have taken the trouble to find it out.

She shrugged, as if it were of no consequence, my son Henry, the child of my youth—and Katherine's.

"I have been thinking of the christening ceremony," she said dreamily. "It should be a great state occasion. Yes—the splendour should linger in everyone's mind for a lifetime. I should like thousands of candles, and a font of pure gold, with Edward's name engraved upon it, so that no lesser person can ever be baptized from it. As for my own gown, I think red satin—"

Was not the magnificent, bankrupting Coronation enough for her vanity? I felt annoyance turn to anger within me. Ceremonies, pomp, show; gowns and gold and candles. She had no interest in her son's name, only in the design of his baptismal font. She saw the birth of our son, England's heir, as a showcase for herself, nothing more.

"Mary's christening gown!" she babbled on. "I must have Mary's christening gown! What better way to impress upon the people who is rightful heir to the throne? What better way to humiliate Katherine and Mary? Yes, I shall send for it at once!"

Now her eyes danced, in the way I had once found so enchanting, as they always did when she planned some mischief.

"You are foolish," I said with distaste. "Why do you wish leftovers, remnants of another's life? Why do you not order a new christening robe to be made expressly for *our* child? You can cover it with pearls. It will become a treasure, to be admired for generations. Instead you covet something old that belongs to another woman."

Like myself? As Katherine's husband, I had had value. As her own, was I diminished?

"I want the gown," she insisted. "And I will have it."

❧ ☙

A few days later a furious letter came from Katherine, refusing to give up the gown with all the moral righteousness at her command.

Anne was irate over her rival's stubbornness and hauteur. *"Make her surrender the gown!"* she shrieked at me, snapping the letter up and down and beating the air with it.

"I cannot," I replied. "The gown is not Crown property, as were the royal jewels. Katherine is within her rights to keep it." The fact that Katherine treasured it pleased me.

"Her *rights?* What rights does she have?"

I was shocked. "The same rights as any English subject. Amongst them, the right to own personal property."

"She deserves no rights! She refuses to acknowledge me as Queen! That makes her a traitor!"

"There is no law saying all citizens must formally acknowledge you as Queen. At this time we rely on the old precedent that 'silence gives consent.' "

"You will have to change that law soon enough," she taunted. "There are many different kinds of silences, and soon—very soon!—it will be important to differentiate between them. You will be forced to do so, for your son's sake. Then the executions will begin!" Her eyes narrowed. "Executions. All traitors will be executed, Harry—Katherine and Mary, and that stupid Thomas More. You will have no choice!" Her voice rose to a crescendo.

"Anne!" I grabbed her shoulders and shook her, hard. It was like breaking a demoniac spell. She changed before my eyes, melting from a vituperative fiend to a confused, honest creature.

"You excite yourself," I said lightly. "It is not good for the child. Come, I shall show you the great bed of which I spoke. It has, as I remember, the most delicate carvings. . . ." I spoke soothingly, thus calming her.

Alone in my bed that night (as the physicians had forbidden Anne and me to come together again as husband and wife until after the child's birth),

I was thankful that I had been able to quell her rising hysteria so quickly. Time enough later to reflect on her accusations about Katherine and Mary and her predictions about the measures that might be needed to combat their continuing popularity.

Popular they were. Just the previous week the villagers at Buckden had surrounded the little palace and cried out to Katherine, "God save the Queen! We are ready to die for you. How can we serve you? Confusion to your enemies!" Whenever Mary was glimpsed, people shouted similar things to her. It was quite clear where the populace stood.

The next week I had an edict printed and proclaimed to the sound of trumpets throughout the land: Katherine was no longer to be addressed as Queen. Anyone doing so faced death. But they were free to shout anything else, so long as that one word was omitted—and English is a language rich in synonyms and substitutions.

However, the publishing and proclaiming of the edict served to pacify Anne, as a concrete and external thing always did. Laws and jewels and titles had always been her comfort and security, her refuge.

In only another six weeks, all would be changed, I reminded myself. Once the heir was safely born, and Parliament had sworn fealty to him as Prince of Wales, the country would smile upon Anne and Prince Edward and abandon Mary.

Announcements of the forthcoming solemn event were being readied. Three dozen scribes were copying out "deliverance and bringing forth of a Prince." I selected two of the creamiest vellum parchments, without blemish or wrinkle, to be sent to Francis and Charles, and assigned my two most skilled scribes to write upon them. In my mind the announcements were already at their destination. Just running my fingertips over their blank surfaces gave me a feeling of victory and completion.

Anne's day of confinement drew closer, and whenever she shrilled or pouted or moped, I found myself counting the days until the ceremony of "taking her chamber" would be held. It had been prescribed in my father's reign, and every detail of ritual must be followed, to ensure a good delivery. First a group of noblemen and ladies must conduct Anne to Mass in her private chapel, then serve her with spice and wine under a cloth of estate in her Chamber of Presence. Then her Chamberlain would pray aloud that God would send her a good hour.

Then two men would escort her to the doors of her inner chamber, through which she would pass to her fate, sealed off from any contact with males. Even male lap-dogs and male songbirds were not permitted in the lying-in chamber, and no portraits of men or even illustrations of male beasts.

Before she was immured, however, Cromwell came to me with grave news indeed.

"It has come," he said, simply. "I have word that it has already crossed the Channel and landed at Dover, last night."

There was no need for him to pronounce the hated word: *excommunication*.

"Clement signed it a fortnight ago."

"Curse him! Could he not have waited another two weeks? Anne takes her chamber on Assumption Day. But if she hears of this beforehand . . . ! O, I must intercept it first! Crum, meet the Papal envoy, tell him I shall receive him at—at"—what convenient house lay between London and Dover?— "Crowley. Hurry!"

Crum looked amused. "Are you so eager to receive your own formal damnation?"

Odd, I had not even thought of it in those terms. "The Pope has no power to damn me," I said naturally, without scrutinizing my words. "All he has power to do is write a proclamation designed to alarm my wife and endanger her unborn child. It is the nasty, petty gesture of a weak bully."

Just so, in one unguarded moment, I revealed my mind to myself. Most of life's tests swoop down on us similarly unrehearsed, and so we carry a lurking fear that we will fail them.

Quickly I prepared to ride to Crowley. It meant missing the entertainment Anne had planned for midday, with a poetry contest between some courtiers, an indoor fountain making cool sounds in the oppressive summer heat, and her dessert of sherbet (Crum had presented her with the recipe), with which she was planning to surprise her guests. It was cherry-flavoured, and she had spent hours perfecting the taste. I myself had helped with it; now I must give an offhanded excuse and hurry away. Anne was disturbed, and was not fooled; she sensed that something important had happened.

It took four hours to reach Crowley, a rudely furnished hunting lodge used by my grandfather Edward as a favourite place to relax after a day's excursion with his brothers, Clarence and Richard. I had always liked it, in spite of its unsettling associations from the wars. It was comfortable there; it was the sort of place where a man could take off his boots and snore by the fire. And it was here, too, that Anne and I had passed those heated days during the progress of 1531, when she almost let me into her chamber time and again, but always barred me at the last moment. Was that truly only two years ago?

Now I came to meet a different challenge, in the person of Clement's representative. I strode into the lodge, happy to have arrived first, as that gave me a subtle advantage. I looked round. How different it looked by day, when I had no fire in my blood, no desires I sought to have satisfied. Those who compare victories in war with victories in love are fools, and probably have experienced neither.

I had time enough to become bored before a glint of sun on a helmet far down the road to the east signalled the approach of Clement's proxy.

A foreign power on English soil, trudging along to exert its jurisdiction—this was the last time such an anachronism would be seen, I thought. Never again. I had banished such pretensions from Continental minds and made them unacceptable for any patriotic Englishman.

Even in my own boyhood, things foreign were seen as "better" than things English. Arthur must have a foreign bride; the Tudor dynasty would not be confirmed as "royal" until a European royal family condescended to marry into it. And so Katherine had come, and yokels had cheered the Spaniards and stood in awe of them as they passed along muddy paths. And because of that curious journey more than thirty years ago, another band of foreigners was snaking along another muddy path in another attempt to meddle in English affairs.

I grinned. I could hear the rapid Italian in the distance. This was 1533, not 1501. Their time had passed. I was an English king and my wife was pure English as well, and we ruled a nation proud to be counted "mere English."

The tittering Popish popinjays drew up to the lodge's entrance and sat, brown and slight and sly, waiting to be received.

As they were shown in to stand before me, I appraised them. What had begun with antagonism on my part ended in bafflement. Was it these men of whom I had, for so long, stood in awe? What a fool I had been!

Their leader, travel-soiled and tired beyond the point of nervousness, merely handed me the Papal scroll, as unceremoniously as a farmer passing on a sausage. Doubtless he had been instructed otherwise, but the lulling informality of the lodge and the lack of court witnesses made it too easy to skip the ceremonial.

I took it just as carelessly, and made a show of unrolling it and reading it without emotion.

It should not have disturbed me. I knew—or, rather, decreed that I knew—that Clement (born Giulio de' Medici) was not the Vicar of Christ, but just a misguided bishop. He had no power to pronounce spiritual judgment on me. No power, no power . . . I had staked my kingdom, my soul, on that belief. Why, then, did I stagger, even for a moment, under it?

Wherefore in the name of God the All-powerful, Father, Son, and Holy Ghost, of the Blessed Peter, Prince of the Apostles, and of all the Saints, in virtue of the power which has been given us of binding and

*loosing in Heaven and on earth, we deprive Henricus Rex himself and
all his accomplices and all his abettors of the Communion of the Body
and Blood of Our Lord, we separate him from the society of all
Christians, we exclude him from the bosom of our Holy Mother the
Church in Heaven and on earth, we declare him excommunicated and
we judge him condemned to eternal fire with Satan and his angels and
all the reprobate, so long as he will not burst the fetters of the demon, do
penance and satisfy the Church; we deliver him to Satan to mortify his
body, that his soul may be saved on the day of judgment.*

*He who dares to despise our decision, let him be damned at the
coming of the Lord, may he have his place with Judas Iscariot, he and
his companions.   Amen.*

The words were baleful, ugly, designed to strike terror into the victim.
But I knew them to be powerless. I *knew*. I did not feel cut off from God. Quite
the contrary. Instead, I felt closer than ever to the Divine Presence, the Divine
approbation.

Clement was a fool. A *political* fool. That was all.

The ride back from Crowley seemed drearier than the ride out. Carrying
the Papal scroll felt a bit like clasping a dead thing to myself. It was harmless—why, then, did it feel so eerily evil?

I had forgotten about Anne's "entertainment," and so was puzzled for a
moment when I heard all the voices and merriment coming from her apartments. I had no desire to go in and dissemble before guests; what I really most
wanted was to go alone to my Privy Chamber. I was exhausted, and not from
the ride to and from Crowley. But in only three days Anne would be sealed
away, and I would not see her until I held our son in my arms. I owed it to
her to join her party. Wearily I walked in.

People had reached that stage at the end of a gathering where they were
relaxed and, having fulfilled protocol, could do as they liked. And what they
liked, evidently, was to cluster around Anne.

She reclined back in a padded chair, a courtier on each side of her, one
in back, one at her feet, and Mark Smeaton a respectful ten feet away, paying
homage on his lute. All I could think of was Mount Olympus, surrounded by
cherubs and sighing mortals.

She smiled languidly as she saw me come in, but did not move or wave
any of her admirers away. Perhaps she felt naked without them; in any case,
they seemed a natural part of her.

"I trust your business went well," she said. "Pray join us. You appear
tired."

Tired? Yes, to receive one's excommunication, to read about one's present and future damnation in explicit terms, was draining. I grunted and took a seat nearby. But I had no heart for the merriment, and soon excused myself.

When Anne eventually sent them away and came to see me, I was deeply asleep, in a blank, starless world.

LIII

Only two days before the chamber-taking. As always when great events were scheduled, I attempted to honour them in advance. As always, I failed. The truth was that both Anne and I were on edge with the waiting, and had little to say to one another. So it came as a relief when, on August fifteenth, the prescribed ceremony began, and Anne was conducted to the Chapel Royal for Mass, then served her traditional cup, then, her Chamberlain having prayed fervently for God to send her a good hour, her brother George and her uncle the Duke of Norfolk escorted her to her Privy Chamber door. In she went, followed by her women, and the doors slowly closed behind her, sealing her in.

"We are only lacking a great stone to roll across the door," observed Norfolk.

"So that the saviour—the heir, that is—can roll it away?" asked Nicholas Carew.

In spite of myself, I was shocked at their blasphemy. How dared they speak this flippantly of Christ in front of me, the Defender of the Faith? Remembering the damning Papal parchment, I felt a spot of darkness spreading out over myself, my court, my kingdom. . . . No, that was nonsense. The secret parchment had nothing to do with it.

"You will answer to a heresy charge if you voice such things!" I snapped.

Norfolk looked startled. "I meant no harm, Your Grace. 'Twas but a jest—"

"A jest in my son's name! A poor jest indeed!"

The two of them shot each other a look that said, "The King is vexed. Stir him not." They bowed and took leave. It was a look I was to see more and more often: a look that managed to be both condescending and fearful at the same time.

The end of August was a glorious burst of fulfilment. The harvests were coming in, heavier than any in recent memory. The fruits were so swollen on every tree that their sun-warmed, dusty skins seemed near to oozing. To sink my teeth into a fresh-plucked pear or plum always sent juice spurting all over my mouth. The sun lay warm and golden on my head, and I took it all as an omen, as the hand of God upon me.

September seventh. The wedding day of Charles Brandon and Katherine Willoughby, if all proceeded as planned. That thought cast a pall over the morning as I proceeded to arise, to say my prayers, to begin the day. I prayed for their happiness, but found that it was words only, words without attachment to my heart. Instead of seeing Katherine in her bridal wreath, I saw Mary in her marble tomb. She had been dead just three months to the day.

Hoping to shake off this sadness, which was spreading like a stain across the day, I called for a horse and took a solitary ride toward Eltham Palace. It lay some three miles from Greenwich, farther back from the river, and up on a windy hill, through ancient forests.

How many times had I ridden here as a Prince! Every hundred yards took me back some five or six years, until I was barely ten years old, and still a second son, by the time I stood on Eltham hilltop. How many times had I stood just here, dreaming of the future, watching the Thames shining far away, like a bright ribbon? That boy seemed very close to me now—that lonely, odd little boy— and I longed to reach out and reassure him, say, "It all came right, my lad!"

"Your Grace!" A page galloped toward me, his voice shaking. It was now—and Anne's time was here. I looked no more at Eltham, at the old grounds where I had played and fought Father and envied Arthur. That was gone; the future awaited me at Greenwich. I turned back toward the river and rode crazily to reach the red and white palace where Anne was in labour.

I had but one thought—my son! I did not care what colours Greenwich was, I did not care how sweaty and dirty I was, or how I stank. I tethered my horse and rushed inside, waving aside grooms and others who would have hindered me.

It was a long way to Anne's lying-in chamber. Along the way, beautiful and well-groomed servitors appeared, bent on dissuading or slowing me. Why? At that moment my mind could not absorb it.

"Your Majesty, if you would just bide—have a cup of wine—"

"Your Majesty—the ladies are still with her—"

I brushed them aside, as so many insects, and stood at last at the outer doors to Anne's chambers. Two very ill-at-ease women appeared to bar my way.

"Your Majesty, the Queen is tired—"

Tired! Of course Anne was tired! I pushed the women to one side and opened the great doors myself.

At first the chamber just within seemed deserted. I expected there to be wine and merriment, people dancing about. This was a glorious day, a day of celebration for all the kingdom. The last time I had had a living healthy son was more than twenty long years ago.

Motes danced upon the sun-rays. The world itself must surely be dancing! I stood stock-still, sheer exuberance making me plant my legs, throw back my head, and cry, "A son!" Then I ran, I galloped like a boy, across the polished boards of that long chamber, toward my wife and heir. I leapt over the slanting rays and reached the final, inner set of doors. As I was wrenching them open, someone grasped my arm. A serving woman. I shook her off like an annoying puppy and rushed into the room.

"Anne!"

She was lying against the birth-pillows, great goose-feathered rotundities specially made for the occasion. Her usually beautiful dark hair was damp and matted and her face was drawn. She reached out her hand to me, but it fell limply on the coverlet.

I picked it up and covered it with kisses. "Thank you," I heard myself saying. "Thank you, my beloved."

"Henry—" she began, but I stopped her. She looked so very tired.

"I know it was difficult for you," I babbled, all my earlier apprehensions drowned in a waterfall of excitement and gratitude. "Please rest. Do not talk." I looked around me. "Where is he?"

I rose from my knees. I did not see Anne's hand waving feebly in an effort to distract me.

"Here, Your Grace." One of Anne's ladies-in-service held out a crimson-wrapped bundle and thrust it toward me.

Nestled deep within was the face I had so longed to see. I drew back the covering a little.

"The Tudor red!" I said. "He has the Tudor red hair!"

"She, Your Grace," murmured the lady. "The Queen hath borne Your Grace a fair daughter."

I looked down at the sexless face. "A daughter?"

"Aye. And healthy and with a mind of her own, already." The lady was beaming. I turned wordlessly toward Anne.

"Forgive me," she whispered.

So it was true! The thing in my arms was a wench, after all! I nearly flung it to the floor in disgust. Controlling myself, I merely handed it back to the nurse.

Anne was looking at me imploringly. Never had I seen her so abject.

"I did not know," she began, her eyes swimming with tears. "All this time—with your desires . . . the soothsayers' assurances . . . God's needs for England . . . alienating the Pope—and for yet another useless girl-child!"

She shared my unhappiness. We were alike victims of ill luck. Instead of anger, I found myself wanting to comfort her.

"Take cheer," I said. "She is a beautiful child. We will name her after both our mothers—Elizabeth. And she will have brothers, never fear."

Chapuys, the gloating Imperial ambassador waiting outside the birth-chamber doors, offered his "condolences" on Elizabeth's birth. I walked on in a daze to the chapel, ignoring him.

The Sacrament was in its monstrance. I could see its pale substance through the quartz opening in the intricately worked vessel. That was Christ Himself. I needed to see, to behold, His Presence, so I could ask Him certain questions—questions to which I must have answers.

I knelt on the cold stone, forgoing the richly worked kneeling-cushions on the floor. I needed to *feel* something, to anchor myself to something real. At that instant I did not feel real; I felt like a floating ghost, a mass of disembodied emotions. Perhaps that is all a ghost really is. . . .

I had a daughter. My son had never existed. All this time when I had been imagining him, naming him, already living with him and through him, he had been someone else. A daughter.

England still had no heir. Where there had been one Princess, now there were two. God could do all things. He had given a son to Sarah in her old age. He had given a son to Hannah, after she prayed with Elijah. He had given a son to Saint Elizabeth, who was also too old to bear children. "With God, nothing is impossible." That was what the angel told Abraham when he doubted God's promise of a son. Since God could easily have given me a son, but had not, I must face the truth: He had deliberately withheld a son from me. But why? Why?

I stared at the Sacred Host so long and so ardently that it seemed to melt, shimmer, and dance before my eyes. Answer me! my mind screamed. Answer me!

It only pulsated before me, and my mind strained eagerly to hear . . . nothing. How dare God do this to me? I came before Him, heartbroken and confused, to receive an insolent silence. Was this the way He treated His servants?

Answer me! If God had shoulders, I would have grabbed them and shaken Him. As it was, I felt a strong temptation to go up and grab the Sacred Host and shout at It.

Blasphemy of blasphemies! What was I thinking of? Just so does Satan grab us at our weakest moments, and rush us into sin.

O God—I am so frightened—the Devil has taken hold of me just now, and I have little strength to fight him. My heart is heavy and in pain. Where have I displeased you? Why are you punishing me in this way? Answer me!

Nothing but profound silence. God had utterly deserted me, then. I had so displeased Him that He would not even speak to me. He had abandoned me to the Devil.

Feeling so drained I could hardly stand, I made my way out of the chapel.

There were people waiting outside. The whole court, indeed, had gathered to see me and study me. I must not reveal my altercation with God just now, must not let anyone know that the Supreme Head of the Church in England had had a falling-out with his Commander.

I held up my hands. "God be praised!" I shouted. ("God be thrashed," I meant.) "He has sent us this day as fair a Princess as ever came to England!"

They cheered halfheartedly, and their bewilderment showed on their faces. Still, they were relieved to follow my lead, and I was pleased to have kept my head and played a part. More and more, I was coming to realize the immense advantage in keeping one's true thoughts to oneself. There are no windows into one's mind; this simple truth had failed to serve me before now.

"Aye!" I grinned. "The Princess Elizabeth will be christened ten days from now—and we trust you will attend the ceremony."

Lacking any further reason to stay, and thwarted in their desire to see me weep or rage, they dispersed.

All except Cromwell, who followed me to my chambers, at a discreet distance. I motioned him in, where he slid in like an obedient snake. And stood watching.

" 'Tis bad," I began. "Very bad." Crushing, in fact. My heart ached within me, but to Cromwell I would put a mere political colouring on it.

"It looks bad," he agreed. He often began his treading by repeating back what you had just said. That was safe ground.

"I look like a fool!" I burst out, suddenly seeing myself through the common man's eyes—through Francis's and Charles's eyes, as well. "I shall have to—to have 'ss' added to all the proclamations: 'in the deliverance of a fair Prince-*ss*,' " I barked irrelevantly, thinking of the fair, blemishless parchments selected for those rulers. O, my vanity! How God must have laughed at me, looking down from heaven.

"Yes. You look . . . foolish. At this moment, perhaps. But this time next year you will have a son, and what is a year more, after all the years you have already waited?"

"Already *wasted,* you mean!" I knew what he meant, all right. Anyway, all this was mere noise, against the great question: Why had God allowed this to happen? Why, why?

"Not wasted. Nothing that goes in preparation is ever wasted. You needed the time to prepare England for your Church. Things have proceeded there at great speed. Ten years ago you had scarcely returned from the Field of Cloth of Gold. Think back on what the world was then. Today it is entirely different. Redrawn by your hand, and by your will."

"And God's."

"And God's." He gave due concession to the Deity, then scrambled along to his true target. "However, these gains must be consolidated in law."

"They are," I grunted. "Parliament has seen to that."

"I mean *explicit* laws. Let me be frank. For the moment, you have two Princesses, by two wives, and a son by a mistress. Now, how is a good, honest Englishman to choose between them? They each have claims upon his loyalty or common sense. Mary is seventeen and the child he—the mythical 'common Englishman'—is used to bending knee to. Henry Fitzroy, Bessie's son, is a fair lad, and bastards have risen to thrones before. And then"—his face fell—"there's Elizabeth. One day old. Which one, Your Grace, would *you* support?"

"Not Elizabeth. The other two, at least, have survived infancy. She is the least desirable."

"Exactly. Therefore you must extract an oath of loyalty from all Englishmen of note who might otherwise, in their hearts, support Mary or Henry. Only then—"

"If only I had a son!" I cried. "Why is Elizabeth not a son? Why has God—"

"Because He has not," said Crum coldly. "And we must work with that."

The Oath was simple to frame. It required a man to swear—upon his immortal soul—that he recognized the Princess Elizabeth as my sole legitimate issue. That was all. It was to be administered to every adult English subject. Crum was right: had such an Oath been framed and circulated in earlier generations, dynastic wars would have been prevented.

"But it could not have been done, Your Grace," he reminded me happily. "In those days there were no administrators such as you have now. The great lords of the North and the West were wild beasts growling around the throne. You domesticated and housebroke them, Your Grace, when you executed the Duke of Buckingham. Now they are just districts. *Administrative* districts," he said contemptuously.

"O Marcher lords, where is thy sting?" he crowed. "Bravo, Your Grace. They have laid themselves open to this simple, sweet little Oath. Whatever it costs—the officials, the bookkeeping—it is still a great savings over a war. A few arrests, a few executions—in an orderly fashion—cheap."

"I would have an heir whom the people would love on their own, not grudgingly mutter oaths to."

Crum smiled. "A beautiful thought. But such did not even occur with the Christ Child. Can we hope for more?"

"If Herod had had you for a Secretary, the Holy Family would never have escaped into Egypt."

"I like to think so, Your Grace."

LIV

Anne regained her strength slowly, for such a fiery creature. I had expected her to spring right from childbed into the salon, but she did not. First she developed milk-leg and had to lie for days suspended in a sling—a silken sling, but a sling nonetheless. Nothing but Mark Smeaton's playing would soothe her during those hours. Then she developed melancholia and lay for hours with her eyes blank and expressionless.

Melancholia: the strangest of all afflictions, the one most difficult to banish. Perhaps it was the Janus-face of the strained gaiety I had seen in her at times. She kept muttering that she had failed me, had failed England. She refused to see Elizabeth or even to help plan for her little royal household, which I was having to organize all on my own.

"Hatfield House is a godly, healthy, and comfortable house," I told Anne, feeling as if I were addressing a statue. "It is here in Hertfordshire, only a day's ride away."

She smiled at me, as if doing me a great favour.

"We want her to thrive, do we not? The court is not healthy for her. She might take sick and die. By Christmas, when everyone gathers and exhales foul contagions, she must be safely away."

Anne finally spoke. "Christmas. That is only a few weeks away. I must bestir myself. I must!"

"It is but a holiday. Whatever time you need to be well, please take."

"Christmas is more important. I must be up, and gowned, by Christmas!"

"That you shall, my love. I pray for it daily."

"Elizabeth's household?" she suddenly said. "It will have a full staff of attendants?" She looked more interested than I had seen her in weeks.

"Aye. I am just in the process of appointing them. Perhaps you would like to choose them yourself?" That would be a good sign.

"There is only one I would appoint. The Lady Mary to serve her! To carry her robes and clean up her messes!"

I was taken aback at the suddenness, and the forcefulness, of her request. Could it be granted? Should it be granted? What would such a thing do to Mary's spirit?

"So! You hesitate! On one hand you assure me that I am your true Queen and Elizabeth the only true Princess, yet you balk at this simple request—a natural request, if what you claim is true! What better way to show the people that Mary yields her claim as Princess?"

"Crum and I have devised an Oath to be administered to the people—"

"All very well," she said airily. "But this can serve as Mary's oath." She sounded eminently logical, until she added viciously, "It will break Katherine's heart."

"If Mary comes to serve Elizabeth, it must not be aimed at Katherine," I replied. "Such a thing—"

"Oh, defend her again! I know you long to take Katherine back, that in your heart you either still love her or fear her—" Anne's voice was rising in the familiar tirade, the obsession.

I cut her off. "I will consider appointing Mary. The plan has merits."

She lay back on her daybed, draped in deep soft furs against the coming cold. It was where she spent most of her time now, positioned as it was near the great fireplace, and with a view out toward the Thames. I looked at her nestled down there, the rich sables around her face no richer, darker, or thicker than her own hair, and suddenly I was inflamed with desire for her. It came over me with such dazzling swiftness that I marvelled at it even then. What powers did she possess? Trembling, I took my leave. Behind me in her chamber I heard Mark Smeaton's discreet music start up.

How long had it been since we had lain together as man and wife? How much longer would the physicians keep me away? Seeking to drive the demon of desire from me, I forced myself to consider the idea of sending for Mary to serve Elizabeth.

I had not seen Mary for one and a half years, since she had insolently refused even to listen to my side of the story, but had wholeheartedly been Katherine's partisan in the matter. To be sure, it was natural, as realizing that she was illegitimate must have been painful for her. But perhaps now she would welcome the opportunity to make her peace with me and accept her new position. After all, being an acknowledged and titled royal bastard was no disgrace. Yes, I would write her and tell her that I desired her to come and join the Princess's household at Hatfield. And I would sweeten it with the hint of Christmas at court. . . .

A fortnight later, as I sat having my freshly scissored beard combed with a rosemary branch, Norris handed me a thick letter from Mary. It was weighted down with seals, including that of Princess of Wales, which she no longer had the right to use. A bad beginning.

The letter was blunt. She refused to come and serve at Hatfield House, and as for the "Princess," she knew of no Princess save herself in England; but if it pleased me, she would acknowledge Elizabeth as "sister" in the same way she did Henry Fitzroy, Bessie's bastard, as "brother." My mention of the Queen drew the "puzzled" response that she would welcome the help of Madam Pembroke in reuniting her with her mother, Queen Katherine.

I flung it down. Stubborn fool! What was I to do with her? I needed her. I needed her to cooperate—

No. That was not it. The truth was that *I* needed her; I needed her as a father needs a daughter. I had loved her too long to crush those feelings now, try as I would. I remembered her as a child, as the pretty baby in the jewelled cap, being betrothed to the Dauphin; as the joyful child playing on the virginal for me. How she had laughed, and how we had taken turns on the keyboard . . . and then, the changes in her face and form as one day I looked at her and realized, with a jolt, that she was beginning to make the transition into womanhood.

Proudly she had gone to Ludlow Castle to practise for the court life she would lead, out from under my shadow. And at her leaving, I had felt the same pang of coming loss that any parent does. Not so soon, my little one, not so soon. . . . But I had Anne by then, and my love-madness to blunt what it meant to be losing Mary. And like every parent, I thought, there's Christmas, she'll be back for that. . . . How was I to know that she would never come back? There was an emptiness there that no Anne, no son, and certainly no Elizabeth could ever fill.

I picked up the parchment with the harsh, stilted words of my estranged daughter. Had it hurt her as much to write them as it hurt me to read them?

Anne's recovery took place overnight. It seemed, even then, unnaturally swift. She informed Cranmer that she was prepared to undergo the ancient ceremony of the "churching of women."

"Yes, Thomas," I answered his unspoken question. "We will retain that ceremony. You may proceed with it."

He looked as if there were a stone in his shoe. "I—I have been studying the origins of this ceremony," he finally said, "and it appears to me to be pagan. Even its common name, 'purification of women after childbirth,' sounds heathen. Would not a 'thanksgiving of women after childbirth' be more appropriate to these times and the Church of England?"

I sighed. "Yes. I suppose so. But it smacks of reform. A ceremony here, a phrase there, and where does it end?" I was more distressed than I cared to admit about Cromwell's persistent hunger to "investigate" the monasteries, and any reminders of it made me uncomfortable. "It is better to retain too much than to dismantle over-hastily."

Whatever it was called, the ancient significance of being "churched" was that a woman could now lie with her husband again, with the Church's blessing.

Perhaps it was the excitement, or that it had been so long forbidden us. Or that I desired her more than any man had ever desired any woman. Or that—I know not what, or why, but once again I had ... difficulties. Difficulties of a most delicate nature.

I would go to her chambers, as if to perform a ritualistic act in some ancient temple, and find myself, as it were, a supplicant before an unearthly creature. I was all flame, all fire—then, abruptly, it would depart. All would disappear, and she would lie back, judging, tantalizing.

In the beginning, I made jests. Then I fortified myself with wine. Armed with that assurance, I came to Anne again. Yet again the thing would happen. I conjured other women in my head. I told myself that we were not married, only lovers. But there was no remedy, it seemed.

In fairness, Anne said nothing, betrayed no disappointment. For which I was thankful. Pity and courtesy are also somehow more insulting than outright insults.

I was deeply troubled. What had befallen me? I had always been able to perform. Was it my age? I was forty-two. I felt young, but my father had died when only nine years older than I.

And there was something else. I had, that past autumn (just about the time of Elizabeth's birth), noticed a little sore on my left thigh. I applied ground-pearl ointment to it. But it did not clear. It festered for a while, then closed over. I thought no more about it. Then, a few weeks later, it reopened. This time there was pain, considerable pain.

I had Dr. Butts put a dressing on it, but I had to select doublets that were longer than usual to conceal the telltale bulk of the bandage. I avoided standing as much as possible. I was unable to ride or play tennis; naturally I did not come to Anne's bed during these times. I was inordinately fearful that someone—anyone—should discover my secret. Used to thinking of myself as a whole man, the paradigm of health, I was disgusted and frightened by the thought of any unexplained weakness. My very anger against my body probably delayed its healing.

The Christmas revels came and went, and instead of Mary visiting me at court, I had other, uninvited guests: my impotence and leg ulcer. The festivities were gruelling for both. The dancing and heavy, tight costumes exacerbated the mysterious thing on my thigh; and the sight of Anne, displayed in all her splendid dark beauty for all the court to see, mocked my incapability so cruelly that I wept in the privacy of my chambers.

LV

January, 1534. The year that, supposedly, was to be the best of my life was off to a bitter start—as bitter as the weather outdoors. The Thames had frozen a fortnight earlier, and the sun had not shone for twenty days. The earth was hard and bare; no snow had fallen, and none was foreseen.

What should I do? I knew the answer, of course. It was the one thing I had not done, should not do, but must: go on pilgrimage. Ask Our Lady to remove my infirmities: go to any lengths to enable me to serve God as King.

"Your Grace! You cannot!" For the first time ever, Crum's composure dropped. "To go publicly to one of the monk-run shrines, when we—when you—are in the process of investigating them—what will people say? What will they think?"

"Say that I go there to inspect their vileness for myself."

His expression changed to one of admiration.

Cranmer was equally flustered. "But we pronounced these Virgin-shrines 'excesses.' *Popish* excesses."

"But have we the right to condemn them sight unseen? That seems most unfair."

"The people will misinterpret it. They will think you *worship* there, not inspect there. Then when you order them torn down, will they not be confused?" He blinked at me. I could read his mind so easily. He was thinking, *Is this King sincere in his break with Rome? He is like a man who would break with his sweetheart, yet keeps going out of his way to pass by her house.*

"Never fear, Thomas," I reassured him. "This is a private, passing matter. All will proceed later as God intends." It would never do for him to know my secret.

Anne wanted to go. I said it was a journey for men only, owing to the severity of the weather. She begged me to wait until spring. But my urgency was such that I must needs go immediately, although I could not tell her why, could not let her know of the agony I was suffering in not being able to make love to her—and to endure it a day longer than absolutely necessary was unthinkable.

"Afterwards I will see Mary at Beaulieu House and settle this business. It is not meet that you come and entreat her; but I as her father and King will bring her to heel."

Anne nodded. "Good."

Suddenly an idea came to me. I would not go alone. "Tell your brother George I would have him accompany me. I would become better acquainted with him." I remembered the shy but ambitious youth I had met at Hever so long ago. I had brought him to court with Anne, then forgotten about him. What was he like? "And let him select one or two companions of his own. And young Howard, that poetry-making cousin of yours—"

"Henry, Earl of Surrey?"

"Aye. I would fain know the youngsters about court. A new generation has grown up around me." Another idea came. "I'll bring Carew and Neville, those from my generation. Let me see them play together. And then"—the brilliance of this broke upon me—"Chapuys must come, too! Let him see for himself how stubborn Mary is, but how well guarded. The Emperor can chew on that for a while! And the Pope as well."

"Best have Cromwell join the company, if you truly wish to make Chapuys miserable."

I roared with laughter. "Aye! Yet they get on well together in company, so I am told."

She smiled slyly. "Try them and see."

᯽ WILL:

And so the King brought all these odd bedfellows together for his own amusement, to see what sort of music they would make together. Indeed, there had grown up two generations at court by now, and none reflected this change better than the Howards themselves.

The older Howards—Thomas, the Duke of Norfolk, and his mother Agnes, his wife Elizabeth, and all eleven of his siblings—were conservative, stiff, unimaginative Catholics. The men fought and the women served as chatelaines on their great northern estates. That was all they knew, and all they cared to know.

Their offspring, the network of young cousins—Henry, Earl of Surrey, his sister Mary; the Boleyns, and all eight of Edmund Howard's children—were at best modern and liberal court-creatures, at worst dissolute. The King was left on his own to discover first-hand which were which.

⚓ HENRY VIII:

So it was that on the last day of January an odd assortment of pilgrims left Richmond Palace and set out for the shrine of Our Lady of Wrexford.

We turned east, heading into the rising sun, riding along the same route I had taken to London that first morning I had arisen as King of England so long ago. Then the breezes had been scented and I had felt stronger than any man among the thousands lining the path. It was no longer a slender path now, but a wide, well-trodden road, and I had a special pad on the side of my saddle to ease my troublesome leg. Before leaving, I had smeared the leg with ointment and bound it in luxurious thick layers of gauze, knowing they would be undetectable beneath my bulky winter travelling cloak. How much better it felt to be swathed so protectively. Now if no one jostled me—

"Magnificent, Your Grace." Chapuys came perilously near, his sparkling eyes seeking any idiosyncrasy that might betray a person's weakness. I reined in a little to the right, keeping him well away from my leg, laughing nonchalantly all the while. "I am impressed by your devoutness. To make a pilgrimage in January is highly unusual—and must betoken a need of some sort."

I felt anger burst in me like sparks from a dry log. *He knew!* No, impossible. He merely tried me, probing to see where my weakness lay. "I go to inspect the 'holy' site before deciding its fate. I would be loth to condemn anything without a hearing."

"As you did the Queen? Riding away that July morning and never seeing her in person again?"

I sighed. Our little round-robin concerning "the Queen" was to begin again. It had a number of set lines:

> *I:* I assure you, I left no Queen behind at Windsor.
> *Chapuys:* I assure you, you did. A grieving Queen who loves you sore.
> *I:* I do not understand. Oh—you are referring, perhaps, to the Princess Dowager?
> *Chapuys:* Nay, to the Queen.

And so on. The exchange had once been mildly amusing. Now, like so many other things, it had become tedious and irritating to me. Perhaps we should have the lines copied out on two cards such as actors use, so the next time we met we could merely exchange them and be done with it.

I cut off his amiable baiting. "You will see her daughter, the Lady Mary, in a few days. Then you can decide for yourself how the Princess Dowager's stubbornness is causing hardship for Mary."

"She is Your Grace's daughter as well," smirked Chapuys. "Unless the pious Queen is truly what you claimed she is, the chaste relict of your brother Arthur, and Mary was begotten by the Holy Ghost."

Another voice spoke: "Such levity with the Holy Spirit's name is scarcely fitting for a devout Catholic like yourself. 'All manner of sin and blasphemy shall be forgiven unto men: but the blasphemy against the Holy Ghost shall not be forgiven unto men.' " I had not heard Cromwell's approach, and now his smooth voice, sliding into the conversation as slickly as a wet knife, startled me. And Chapuys as well. The two glared at each other across my horse's neck.

"It is exactly this attitude that has corrupted the Church and the monks until, alas, they stink. You see, you profess to love the Church, but you mock her with men. Fie, Chapuys! No earthly lady would be served by such a knight. Had I daughters, *I* would not let them give you their colours," continued Cromwell.

"Nor would I wear them for low-born damsels, the offspring of a self-seeking peasant." Chapuys sat in Spanish arrogance, his agile frame sitting his horse easily. His silver-studded saddle gleamed in the thin sunlight, reflecting little dancing rays onto Cromwell's plain brown leather one, and his coarse wool mantle. A great block of a man, Cromwell.

He looked down at his plain attire. "I? Self-seeking?" He chuckled. "I am plain Master Cromwell, sir. No titles, no jewels, no lands. I seek naught but to serve my King. I have only one master—he who rides here beside me."

Chapuys snorted, almost exactly in time with his horse's noisy exhaling.

Behind us rode Will, silently. He was to accompany us to the shrine and then take leave to visit his sister and her family, who lived a day's ride farther away. I had worked poor Will hard in the past year or two, with scarcely a thought as to his own needs. I was glad to grant his request. He, in turn, agreed to endure the (to him) unappetizing religious aspects of the journey. But he would enjoy the bickering and tension en route, I could tell—it was what he throve on. Well, he would get a feast of it long before we reached our destination.

The six others rode in a clump behind Will, chattering, their frosty breaths rising above them and creating a common cloud. George Boleyn, Nicholas Carew, William Brereton, Edward Neville, Francis Weston, Henry Howard: what did they have in common? A thirty-year gap separated Henry Howard and Edward Neville. Of what were they talking? But talking they were, and animatedly. A few words carried on the brisk air: *sir . . . France . . . Elizabeth . . . fortnight. . . .*

Elizabeth. Would Mary finally come to serve her? What a stubborn child she was! I would let her know this behaviour would no longer be tolerated. She would serve Elizabeth as Princess, or—or—

Or what? I did not know, I did not want to consider what action I might be forced to take. Back in London, scribes were readying shiny stacks of Oaths to be distributed throughout the realm once the weather broke. Commissioners would sit before the stacks in each town and village, witnessing the signatures of all guildsmen, officers of the law, clergymen, apprentices, swearing—upon their eternal souls—that they recognized my marriage to Anne as true, and Elizabeth as my sole (for now) heir. On their left would lie a deadly scroll, to be inscribed with the names of those who refused to sign the Oath in the presence of witnesses. The scroll would not list their reasons, merely their names.

What would I do with those heaps of scrolls? For I did not delude myself that they would be returned to the palace blank.

The sky was clear, the sun small and shrunken, like a withered apple. Nothing was alive on the land; there was no movement anywhere. How easy to believe that this reflected the state of the kingdom: silent and suspended. It did; but by May all would be altered.

Chapuys moved close to me again. "My knee feels a sudden ache," he said. "There will be a change in the weather, I fear."

How womanish southerners were! Coming from a land of pomegranates and soft breezes, they could not endure the shift of a breeze. Or was this a trick, an excuse to gallop ahead to Beaulieu House, to speak with Mary in private? How transparent he was.

I patted my silver flask, filled with a blood-warming drink from Ireland called *uisgebeatha*. I handed it to Chapuys. "Drink this. It will stifle your knee."

He took a draught and wheezed. " 'Tis poison!"

"Not to the Irish, so I am told."

Chapuys shook his head. "My knee—I beg you, it tells the truth. I suggest we seek shelter—"

The sky was ringing clear. "What, in broad daylight? We have another five hours of good riding ahead of us," I assured him.

On we went, stopping for a brief rest and refreshment, then continuing, to make the most of the short winter day. The sun swung over and behind us, throwing long shadows before us.

And then the shadows faded, although the sun had not set. Exactly when this happened I know not—only that I suddenly became aware that we had been shadowless for some time, heading into a blue twilight. Then I turned and saw it: a great woolly blanket of clouds swathing the sun, and the wind running before it, stinging cold. And hanging from the cloud like a weighty grey curtain was the snow, moving faster than any horse could gallop. It would catch us in less than an hour.

My hands shook, and I felt colder inside than the wind on my face. There was nothing around us—no village, no manor house, not even a peasants' dwelling. I had exulted in the stark open spaces we had passed through since noon, bare fields lying exposed to the sky, but now they were more threatening than any enemy fortress.

"How far to Thaningsford?" I called, signalling for my men to halt. I kept my voice cheerful.

"Two hours' ride," answered Brereton. "I know; my father had tenants—"

"Due north there's a hamlet, called something 'Grange,' " said Carew. "I think it may be closer."

"Are you sure of its location?" I shouted. No time now for his bumblings. He had always been slipshod about details.

"Yes—no—" The wind whipped his cap off, and he snatched it back in midair. "I think—"

Obviously he did not know. I looked round at the others. Chapuys sat regarding me with irritation, and the others merely looked blank, as if expecting me to conjure up a shelter by sleight-of-hand.

I indicated the coming storm. "We can either ride hard to the north or south and hope to go around it, or we can use our time to make a shelter here."

"We cannot go south; the river is there and we cannot be sure it is solidly frozen so we can cross it," said Boleyn.

A clear head. A sensible statement. I warmed inside toward him.

"Ahead of us lie nothing but open fields, at least as far as Edwardswold. But a half hour to the north is a forest," said Will.

My mind leapt at this. A sheltered area, and then a half hour needed to construct some sort of shed. Yes, we could do it.

"North, then!" I had to cry loudly to be heard above the rising wind. I wheeled my horse around and motioned them to follow.

They had to. Whatever I said, they must obey. I prayed that I led them toward safety. But as I changed direction and the wind hit me sideways, it felt wrong, misguided. Every instinct within me cried, *Not this way. Run before the wind, not across it. Seek ready-made shelter. What can you possibly construct in less than an hour that will prove of adequate protection against this gale?* I ignored that voice. Logic told me to go the way I was.

The wind snapped my cloak like a woollen sail, swirling and dragging behind me. I felt naked, so easily did the cold and wind penetrate to my bare skin.

I buried myself in my horse's mane, seeking warmth. His flesh seemed cold underneath the hair, and sweat-foam froze in little clumps on his neck. I felt the surge of muscles working rhythmically as he ran, his headway slowed because of the wind's force against his left side. My own left leg was completely numb, and the cold seemed to be draining my strength, pulling my blood down into a core somewhere. I glanced behind me and saw the others struggling. The bank of clouds was closer now, visibly closer, and the promised forest was nowhere in sight. Where was it? Had Will been mistaken? But he was usually so sure of his facts.

The first stinging bits of snow hit my cheek. God, but I was cold. Suddenly my horse shook his head questioningly and veered off to the right, plunging down a dirt bank into a field.

My hands had lost their grip; the fingers were so numb they seemed severed from the rest of my body. I could no longer control the reins. Cold, cold, cold—I could think of nothing but the cold, it drove everything else from my mind. I must escape this cold, I must—

Ahead . . . way ahead, a good five to seven miles . . . a black line, a *something*. Whatever it was would break the force of the wind. I kicked my horse as hard as I could, then wrapped each rein round and round my senseless hands. Let the arms do the work of the hands.

"Come!" I yelled.

Another slap of snow across my left cheek. I scarcely felt it on my exposed flesh.

Ahead, the fine black line grew prickly. Trees. The forest. Will's forest.

The trees ahead were oaks. It was an old forest, an original forest that had existed since Becket's time, waiting for us. With a last burst of speed, my horse plunged into it, and immediately I felt the wind lessen as it broke upon the oaks instead of on us. A hush like a mother's sigh enveloped us.

I turned to see the others galloping in. Chapuys . . . Will . . . Carew . . . then the rest, indistinguishable figures now, totalling nine. All accounted for.

Only now did I look about. The forest was deep and dark, and the terrain rough with fallen logs and rocks. Dangerous ground for horses. Should we lead them but a little way into the gloom, then stop and make our shelter, or take a chance of riding farther in hopes of finding better protection or even, possibly, an abandoned shelter? As soon as the choices had presented themselves, I knew the answer: the one with the greatest risk, but the greatest possible reward. We would ride deeper in.

When I announced this, the men protested. I silenced them, and they had to obey.

With the snow still a distance away from the line of trees, I turned my back on it and urged my horse forward into the unknown terrain. Within five minutes the overcast sky and high trees made a murkiness so oppressive it seemed almost to be a living thing. The thick branches overhead moved over us, a writhing roof over an evil, still chamber strewn with traps.

And all the while there was this otherworldly cold, a cold that seemed a creature in its own right. I looked about. There was plenty of wood, but it would be so cold it would be difficult to light. Brittle old oak leaves carpeted the ground; these would serve as tinder, but now they effectively concealed treacherous holes where a horse could easily break his leg. There was no sign of a ridge or protection of any sort.

"Your Grace! We must stop!" shouted Will—the only one who would have dared to tell me what to do. "It is about to catch up to us, and we will have no time to construct anything. We must stop now and hold our ground!"

"No, Will! Farther in! Farther in!" My voice, loud and sure, hung in the air between us. The others were all of Will's mind, and we were all reduced to animals seeking our own survival.

Then tradition and habit took command, made them disobey their own animal promptings to obey their crowned and anointed King; and that King, secure in the belief that he obeyed *his* King, led them on.

WILL:

We thought he was quite mad at this point. It was clearly folly to continue into the forest. But he seemed so absolutely certain of himself. Is that the secret of commanding unquestioning obedience?

HENRY VIII:

Now the storm caught up to us, hitting us from behind. The trees caught a great deal of it, but there was still enough blinding, swirling snow filtering through to disorient us. There was no north, no south, no east or west, almost no up or down or sideways. We were lost in an enormous cloud of white butterflies, their millions of wings beating frantically, soundlessly, icily. I could almost have stood still amidst their swirling, frigid whiteness, and let them blanket me until death. The temptation was there, the lure of a beautiful, still death. . . .

Shuddering violently, I dismounted and began to lead my horse. Keep moving, keep the blood warm, do not let the ice-death goddess take hold. . . . I could not see more than ten paces before me, and could only hope my men had not become separated. "Stay close! Each man right behind the next!" I cried.

A ridge ahead: jagged stones all along its face. We were face to face with a barrier that we could not climb over. Had God brought us here just for our death, then?

Then I saw it, just a glimmer—a slit, a dim opening, a crevice in the cliffside. Perhaps we could squeeze in there, huddle together? One hand out in front of me, I stumbled toward it, feeling my way along. The rough rocks tore at my hands, which were so numb I felt nothing and was surprised to see bloodstains on the stones. Suddenly my arm plunged into darkness. I thrust the other one after it, all the way to my shoulders. But the space around them was greater still. A cave.

How far back did it go? Its entrance yawned a little farther to one side, and it was wide—about ten feet. "Cave!" I yelled. "Cave!"

"Halloooo!" came an answer, and figures emerged out of the whiteness, struggling toward me. I bent down and began to crawl awkwardly along the cave floor, feeling for a back wall. When none appeared, I motioned for the men to follow me.

"I can stand!" cried Cromwell, shuffling forward, testing the ground at every step. I raised myself up, expecting to bump my head, but did not. Even raising my hand, I encountered no rock overhead. But I felt a series of soft, silken bumps, which rustled and resettled themselves.

"A chamber with bats as ladies-in-waiting," I said. "Let us make a fire, and quickly."

Within a few minutes the men had brought in a large pile of wood and several armloads of leaves and dead matter. Will struck his flint and steel, showering sparks upon the cold, inert stuff. It took a good quarter-hour before one cooperative leaf began to smoulder, and again as long before its neighbours caught fire. The cold within the cave was even more intense than without. I had the feeling that this cave harboured cold even on Midsummer's Eve, stored it up from successive years like a miser with his gold.

Now the larger branches began to catch fire, sending out a mass of evil-smelling smoke. Choking, the men crowded closer. But the warmth was so feeble I could scarce feel anything. I rubbed my hands hard, hoping to bring them to life. They felt like two blocks of wood—wood that dripped blood.

"Courage!" I said. "It will not be much longer now."

" 'Well, comrades. Now that we have suffered in the beginning, fortune promises us better things, God willing,' " muttered Neville.

Those were my own words on the first miserable night at camp in France in 1513. How had he remembered them all these years? I was touched. But looking at him, I saw only sullen discomfort on his face. Perhaps that was all he remembered of the old French campaign—cold discomfort. It hurt me to think that my companions-in-arms did not treasure the experiences we had shared, especially those noble war experiences of our youth. "Ah, that was a glorious night!" I said.

"In the French mud?" scoffed Carew. " 'Twas almost as miserable as this cold."

"The French campaign was a blessed one," I insisted. "How I wish you others here had shared it with us."

"I was scarcely born," said George Boleyn. "It was my father who accompanied you."

"And mine," said William Brereton, unwrapping his cloak from about his eyes, which peered out of his pudgy, lamblike face.

"My father made me the night before he sailed for France with Thomas Howard and his knights," said Francis Weston, as if reciting a Biblical miracle.

"I was not born until long after," said Henry Howard, son of that selfsame Howard, Duke of Norfolk. He wore his proud youth like an heraldic badge.

Cromwell, squat and bearlike, remained silent.

"And where were you in 1513, Crum?"

"I was in Italy, Your Grace."

"Learning the arts?" asked George Boleyn.

"Yes. Learning the arts," Cromwell said.

The fire made a halfhearted crackle, and we moved toward it. Would it never blaze?

"It needs more air," said Cromwell. "We must stand back, as we would round a dying man."

"Curse the thing!" Brereton cried. "I am cold!"

"Stop whining," Cromwell said. "Whining never won a man anything, even from a deaf and dumb fire."

I, too, longed to kick the fire and curse at it. "Someone will have to gather more wood, so it will be ready when needed," I said, feigning optimism.

Each man looked at the fire, as if by so doing he could make himself invisible and unobligated.

"Lord Rochford." I cited George Boleyn formally. "Bring back as much as you can, and when you weary, let Sir Weston take your place. And then Sir Brereton. We should lay in enough to last us through the night, at least." For it was clear that we must not stir from here until the storm ceased—and who knew when that might be?

The others, spared for the moment from the hateful task of wood-gathering, turned again to the smouldering fire. Carew dropped to his knees and began to puff on it, making it glow hotter. Excited, he blew harder, then suddenly collapsed, falling headlong almost into the fire.

"Pull him away!" Neville leapt even as he spoke, hauling him backwards, where he lay wincing and moaning.

"My chest . . . I cannot breathe . . ." Carew cried, clawing at himself. His face was dead white.

I gasped. I knew little of medicine, save the moods and agonies of my leg-sore.

Cromwell was beside him, bending down, nodding knowledgeably. "Does anyone here have a pain-soother?" he asked.

I did, hidden away in my saddle-pouch, but it was on hand only to treat my leg. Sometimes the pain was so bad . . . but if I revealed that I carried it, would that not cause speculation as to why? And it lay amidst the clean bandages and salve. How to conceal them?

"Uhhhh—" Carew groaned, sounding as if he were dying.

"Has no one a medicine?" demanded Cromwell.

One by one the men shook their heads. The stealthy bandage-changing, the hidden fester, were things unknown to them.

"I have something," I finally said.

The pill, of ground poppy powder, had an almost alarmingly calming effect on Carew. His breathing grew less laboured and shallow, and he stopped clutching at his chest. Colour came back into his cheeks. Then he fell asleep, like a baby.

Cromwell nodded. "Yes, that's what I expected. I think henceforth he should not stir without a supply of these." He held up the vial of pills.

Surely he wouldn't need more! Those ten were all I had with me, and what if I were stricken with the excruciating leg pain? With no way to dampen it, I might betray myself and my weakness. I took them back from Cromwell in what I thought was an offhanded manner. "What is wrong with him?" I asked.

"A bad heart. He will get these 'attacks' from exertion from now on."

"Exertion? Blowing on a fire is exertion?" demanded Neville.

"At his age, yes. After the strain of the journey—"

"Nonsense!" Neville barked. "Age—exertion—" Carew and he were the same age. "Preposterous!"

The neglected fire now burst into full flame, like a contrary child. I turned to it with relief, glad to be done with this conversation. Where had Cromwell learned so much about medicine? During his "studies" in Italy? I knew so little about him, really. I wondered if he had detected my leg weakness. And how would I manage to change my bandage amongst all these men? Perhaps it did not need to be changed; perhaps it could stay on overnight.

Boleyn returned, white as a corpse, dragging several branches inside. He looked relieved to see that there was warmth at last.

"It was all I could find," he said, gesturing toward the outside. "Already the snow is so deep it is hard to see where wood lies. And it is getting dark."

"Warm yourself," I said. I detected an edgy defensiveness in his words.

After allowing them enough time to lose the deepest part of their chill, I asked, "What provisions do we have? Let each man check his saddle-pouch."

As it turned out, there were nine flasks of wine, two of the fiery *uisgebeatha*, twelve loaves of bread, five large cheeses, and several portions of dried, smoked meat. "Enough for a meagre meal for one night," I said.

The bats rustled overhead. "We will postpone the inevitable bat stew as long as possible," I promised. "For now, let us share the bread and cheese."

We fell on it like robbers. It helped but little. I have often found it so, and wonder why. When one is greatly hungry, eating only provokes the appetite further.

Bellies teased and quickened rather than quieted, we began to stretch ourselves out before the fire. As I leaned back on my elbow and extended my legs, I felt the revoltingly familiar trickle of liquid from my sore. So the thing was festering. When the men settled down, I would attend to it. Later, when we would drift away in the darkness to relieve ourselves, I could have access to my saddle-pouch with the necessary things. I held up my flask of *uisgebeatha*. In the meantime, this would kill the pain and miraculously make time pass. I took a deep draught, feeling its extraordinary warmth attack the inside of my mouth and then run its hot course to my stomach. Soon it would spread its mysterious balm through all my veins, bringing peace, delight . . . and the hint of special care hovering over me. I took a second draught to keep the first company.

"Here." I passed it to Will. "You know what it is, and what it can do."

WILL:

Indeed I did. Ever since Anne's wild Irish cousin-kinsman, the Earl of Ormonde, had sent Henry three barrels of the stuff, he had been sampling it. I did not like what it did to him; but I must confess that night in the cave I liked very much how it felt inside me. And I could not see how it made me behave.

HENRY VIII:

"This is a magic potion, to be sure. Sent to me by the Queen's Irish cousinage." I passed it on to the others, and they all took it. Before Brereton, the last of the nine, had finished, the transformation within me had already begun. I felt the delicious, creeping lightness, the divine peace. . . .

Suddenly I loved all the faces around the fire. Save Chapuys. And that was because he had a Spanish face. I hated Spanish faces—ugly yellow things. Thanks to God, Mary did not have such colouring. Lady Mary . . . no longer Princess Mary . . .

"Have another draught, all!" I said, taking a third myself. The men followed suit, and when Brereton handed it back this time I was floating. "Tincture of ecstasy," I said.

No more now. I replaced the cap with exaggerated care, as my fingers were hard to manage. "The fire chases the cold from without, and this from within."

Outside the wind screamed, but it was no longer frightening; instead it seemed purposeful and part of a greater whole. And these men gathered around the fire with me, my preordained companions. Except Chapuys . . .

Chapuys's face glowed so yellow it seemed bathed with sulphurous hell-flames.

"Will you see for yourself how foolish Spanish pride is?" I said. "And how hopeless the Papal cause is in England?" I hectored him.

"He is an intriguer," said Cromwell bluntly. "He has a web of would-be rebels ready to betray you. The plan is simple: Mary is to be spirited away from her country-house at Beaulieu and taken to the Continent, whilst the discontented people here overthrow you. Is that not so, Chapuys?"

"You know no names, Master Cromwell."

He laughed. "Indeed I do. In the West, you believe you have Lord Abergavenny, Sir Thomas Arundel, Sir Henry Parker, Sir George Carewe, certain members of the Pole family, and dear old Sir James Griffith ap Howell. In the North, the discontented Lord Hussey and Lord Darcy, Lord Dacre of the North, and the Earl of Derby. In the South—ah!—there's Lord Edmund Bray, Sir Thomas Burgoyne, Sir Thomas Elyot, and the Earl of Rutland. Did I leave any out? You carry letters from them to the Lady Mary right this moment."

Chapuys looked up in alarm, and stirred.

"Do not bother, good Ambassador. I have already read them—and had copies made before we even departed. A good plan you have. The only weakness is the disorganization and dependence of the conspirators themselves. They are united only through your ceaseless industry on Katherine's behalf. By themselves they are unwilling and unable to carry out any plan, even the simplest."

I listened eagerly. The *uisgebeatha* had loosened their tongues until they babbled like men on the rack.

"The people of England support the Pope and Emperor," retorted Chapuys recklessly. "In their hearts they are ashamed of the sham Queen Anne and of the King's unlawful Acts. In Cardinal Wolsey's day, England sat on the highest councils of Europe. Now she is a laughingstock, a bastard amongst legitimate nations."

I pressed more *uisgebeatha* on him, and he unwittingly took it.

"No. England is now respected for shaking off the shackles of servitude, of minionhood," I corrected him.

"When my father was ambassador to France and to the Pope, they laughed at us," put in Boleyn. "They laugh no more. Their day is over, Master Chapuys. The future is not with the Pope or Spain, but with England and Protestantism."

"Protestantism?" I snapped. "I'll have no Protestants in my realm. They are heretics."

"So seemed Our Lord's disciples to the Pharisees." It was Henry Howard, the youngling. His voice was thin with lack of years.

Everyone looked at him in surprise. "Fie, Sir Henry," said Carew. "You, from an ancient and honoured house—you are not one of those 'new men' who must needs embrace the latest fad, like Lutheranism and this Zwingli-madness in Zurich." His voice was soft, as if he were afraid really to use it for fear of bringing on another "attack." His face still looked drained.

Henry Howard smiled. He was known even at his age as a fashion-setter. He wore wide-brimmed Italian silk hats, with one sweeping feather; he wrote verse in the new "blank" fashion, which meant that it did not rhyme. (As if poetry should not rhyme!) "The past fascinates me not," he said. "It is a charnel-house, shut up, encrusted, airless. I want to open wide the doors—"

As I had at his age, when Father died. . . .

"French doors?" asked Weston. "Like the ones you have been installing in Kenninghall?" Weston cocked his head.

I liked Weston not, I admitted freely to myself. He was too pretty. His habit of wearing only blue, to emphasize his pale blue eyes, set off by black spiky eyelashes, seemed to me most effete and un-English.

"Yes, we have heard about your remodelling," said Cromwell, his eyes steady. "There are many of us who share your interest in remaking our English homes."

"I think we all yearn to create ourselves anew," I said. "With ordinary men, it can express itself in installing French windows. For a King, it must be in refining and reshaping the kingdom itself. England has long been in need of a master gardener—a gardener who will weed her, root out poisonous growth, chase away unhealthsome beasts—wolves, vultures, moles, snakes— and make her bloom."

Now they were staring at me, but I went boldly on. "When a garden is thus planted, there is much initial destruction, and seeming chaos. But out of the upheaval comes order, beauty, peace." I looked at them deliberately. "Do you understand? I must do cruel things in order to bring forth the glory of England, a glory that has long lain choked by weeds."

I took another deep, full draught of Irish-water. "The weeds, the beasts, the Devil himself, will scream and seek to save themselves. But I can tell the true from the false, and I will not be hindered from doing what I must do, for England's sake."

"You are mad!" cried Chapuys. "You speak as Caligula, and as every tyrant since Pharaoh. 'I can tell the true from the false!' Can you not hear yourself, you self-deluded Caesar?"

"I told you they would cry out, did I not?" I asked my men. "Of course you do, you Papal viper. You have everything to lose, you and your Emperor-master, if England grows stronger. Too long have you meddled with us, seeking to use us, taking our money to finance your self-seeking wars, wars that have benefitted Charles, not us! The Bishop of Rome has coughed and waved his excommunication at us. The Emperor seeks my gold and my daughter, whilst Clement spits on my head. Fie, I say! I will root you out, every vestige of you. Get you out of England, foul carrion!"

"Aye," said Cromwell. "I think we all stand united on this. Oh, some of us are more forward-looking than others"—he nodded at Henry Howard and Weston—"but even the most conservative, like Neville and his rusting chivalric manners—can you still get into your 1513 armour, Edward?—are English, pure English, and want our country back to ourselves."

"Your King is mad," said Chapuys. "That is the main thing which you seem determined to overlook in all this blather about 'England.'"

"Madness and greatness oft keep company," said Cromwell. "Make no mistake. Whatever the grumbling about Queen Anne, the people love her Englishness. Your stupid Katherine does the one thing calculated to infuriate them, did they but know it: she appeals to foreign powers to right her cause. My agents are busy throughout the land, however, making them aware of this . . . disloyalty."

"Your *agents,*" whispered Chapuys. "You have indeed 'studied' in Italy."

"The Renaissance has many facets."

Later that night, as they slumbered and snorted by the fire, I crept away to do what I must with my ailing leg. Far back in the dark I flung the pus-soaked bandage and applied a new one by feel, covering it with my hose. The Irish *uisgebeatha* had faded, and nothing masked the fitful throbbing of the leg. Hastily I shook out two pain-pills from the medicine pouch and swallowed them whole. Then I crept back to my place by the fire.

As the medicine took effect and the fire dwindled before me, then passed into a dream, I thought it curious that Cromwell had not refuted Chapuys when he said I was mad.

LVI

There was no real dawn, just a lessening of darkness, as we stirred painfully. I was numbingly cold and stiff, and ravenous with hunger. The fire was almost burnt out, and outside the wind was still howling. I walked stiffly to the mouth of the cave and peered out. Snow lay waist-deep, and in some places the drifts were the height of Goliath. It was twenty miles yet to Beaulieu. Could we reach it by sunset?

In less than an hour we were mounted, miserably, and foundering through the drifts. The bats were no doubt pleased to be left to resume their dark rest undisturbed. I wondered if we had been wise to refuse to feast on them, regardless of how repulsive they seemed.

By noon, our folly in venturing out was clear. We had not gone even five miles, and it was impossible to go faster because of the uneven ground with its treacherous snow cover. We were forced to pick our way along, shaking with exhaustion atop our weakened horses. Beaulieu might as well have been in Scotland, for all the good it would do us. There was no sign of it on the horizon; there was nothing save empty space and a small road, visible only because it was bordered by a stone fence.

The men were silent, each clinging to his saddle and praying to his God. Chapuys's silver-festooned saddle seemed the epitome of false security, betraying us no less than him, useless in this white wilderness to do anything but wink mockingly.

A blast of wind hit me full in the face. My eyes smarted and watered in protest, and the horizon before me shimmered, swam, then cleared. In the blur, though, I had seen something, or thought I had. I blinked and strained to catch it again. Yes, there *was* something . . . and was that a smudge of smoke above it?

"There. Ahead," I grunted. My lips were cracked and bleeding in spite of the grease I had smeared on them.

Cromwell started, stifled a smile. He knows, I thought. He knows what it is, and is pleased that I have discovered it for myself.

"What is that before us?" I asked.

"St. Osweth's," he said, the answer ready.

A small monastery—one that Cromwell's agents had already visited and pronounced especially corrupt. The papers condemning it to dissolution lay on my inlaid work chamber desk amongst others awaiting my royal stamp.

"How providential," I said, wheeling my horse around. "A religious house ahead!" I called to the men. "We will go there."

"The good brothers will doubtless be astonished to welcome a royal party," said Cromwell.

"Doubtless." Thanking God for their location if not for their morals, I turned toward the monastery. The dull spot in the sky that betokened the sun was already halfway to its setting-slot.

The house was rough and tumble-down. Around it were not the neatly trimmed fences and ordered fields of my imagination, but the neglect of a slattern's yard.

Cromwell knocked on the door like a wrathful archangel at the Last Judgment. It creaked open, and a face like a vulture's peered out.

"The King is here," announced Cromwell.

To his credit, the vulture proudly flung open the door and gestured welcome, as if he had expected us. His thick cowl and gleaming pink point of a head above his tonsure made his resemblance to that bird truly striking.

The odour of decay was so strong upon first stepping into the priory antechamber that I wondered what they fed upon.

"I will fetch the prior," the vulture-monk said, bowing low.

Gagging, I willed myself to endure the putrid odour. It was warm in here. That was all that mattered.

The vulture returned, bringing one of the fattest men I had ever seen. He swung each leg in a half-circle, propelling himself forward in a series of curious half-turns, rather than walking as ordinary men do. This exertion caused him to pant and wheeze. He scowled at the effrontery of any presence, even a royal one, that required him to move.

"Prior Richard," said the vulture-monk, presenting the sweating human pig before us. For an instant I had a passing fancy that we had stumbled into a bizarre enclave of talking animals, like those in fairy tales. What would emerge next from the inner door?

"Your Majesty," he wheezed, like an old bellows. Rivulets of sweat ran down his face. "The honour—the magnificence of your presence—it maketh me to rejoice exceeding, yea, I am unworthy that you should come under my roof"— he mixed the Psalms with the Mass, freely—"only say the word, the royal word, and I am your obedient servant."

"We must partake, alas, of your hospitality," I said. "The storm has stranded us and prevented us from reaching our destination. In fact, we spent last night in a cave."

Now he looked alarmed. "How many are you?" He counted us rapidly. "Tell Brother William to lay nine extra," he said to Brother Vulture. "It'll be after High Mass. Meanwhile you can settle yourselves in the dormitory, Your Eminences."

He wheezed and waddled his way down a long stone cloister, all stained and leaking and covered with rook-droppings. At the end a warped, worm-eaten door flapped on its hinges. He kicked it open with one rough motion. Inside was a prisonlike, bare stone chamber with pallets scattered all over the floor. A number of monks were lying abed.

"What, is there plague here?" I asked in alarm.

"No," said Cromwell. "Merely corruption and laziness. Admit it, Prior Richard. Your monks spend half their time lying in bed. Drunk!"

He strode over to a pallet and nudged the man with his toe. Groaning, he sat up.

I was appalled. The man was unshaven, covered with sores, and reeking of wine. Beside him something else stirred. A woman.

"Did I not tell you of such things, Your Grace?" said Cromwell softly.

I spun round and grabbed the prior by his cowl. "You swine! Is this how you honour the Lord?"

"They are ill," he wheedled. "I did not wish to alarm you—"

"Then put them in the infirmary!"

"The infirmary is full, Your Grace." *Prove otherwise,* he dared me.

"What is this woman?" I demanded.

My men guffawed.

"My niece," said the prior, encircling her with his arm in what he supposed was an avuncular manner.

"She has the Devil for an uncle, then." I looked at her. She was scarcely more than a child. And to think of her serving the monks' lust!

All around us the "sick" monks began to stir. Half the pallets held bleary-eyed, bloated men, emitting that characteristic odour of drunkards. One vomited directly on the floor, then turned over and went back to sleep. A ratlike boy scurried over and began to clean it up.

"This is no fit place for human beings," I said. "We will sleep elsewhere."

"There is no place else," he claimed.

"In *your* quarters, Prior."

"I doubt you will find them much to your liking, Your Grace," said Cromwell, "if this fellow is any reflection of their condition."

"Let him sleep in his own dormitory for a night," I said, "amongst his own monks. How long has it been since you have even set foot in here, knave?"

Without waiting for a reply, I turned and went toward what I surmised must be the prior's lodging, in the southeast corner of the priory garth. He wheeled around with surprising speed and attempted to get there first.

"Stop!" I said. "I forbid you to enter first. I will see it undisturbed. Stay with my men!"

At this, the young and old warriors in my party made a circle around the prior, holding him hostage. I strode alone toward the private door and flung it open.

Yawning before me was someone's febrile attempt to recreate an Eastern pleasure-den. The entire floor was covered with pillows, and the walls and ceiling were hung with cheap, brightly dyed cottons. There were no chairs or proper beds, just pallets and cushions and lounging-areas. Several coloured wicker baskets were scattered about. The smell of incense tried unsuccessfully to blot out the odour of rot.

I burst into laughter. The whole thing was so pitiful, so ludicrous. Then I noticed the jewel-chests in the corner.

I opened them, expecting to find imitation jewels as outlandish and preposterous as this Sultan's lair. But they were real. Wonderingly, I took out a great ruby, pigeon's-blood red and swollen with its own preciousness. Next to it lay a pearl, a black pearl—not truly black, of course, but an oily deep grey.

"Where did you get these?" I asked the prior, glowering from the doorway where he was guarded by Neville and Boleyn.

"They were . . . given to the Priory."

"In good faith, were they not? In exchange for which you vowed to pray daily for the souls of the donors?"

"Yes."

"And do you? Do you fulfill your promise?" Before he could wheeze forth another lie, I cut him off. "Do not forswear yourself. We know the answer to that!"

What loot did the large covered baskets contain? I flipped off the lid of the nearest one.

"No!" screamed the prior, trying to twist free. "No!"

There was a quick movement, and a dark shape fairly leapt from the basket. I slammed the top back on, but not before I saw a long dark thing disappear like quicksilver amongst the pillows.

"They are my pets. They—they"— he thought to find some convincing reason—"keep the rats away."

"You fool! Your monks are supposed to keep rats away!" I roared. "Am I mad? Do I dream? Here I find a priory with a dormitory full of lewd, drunken monks, its buildings and grounds in disrepair, no praying being done, and the master of all this living in some schoolboy's idea of a love-nest and keeping snakes as domestic beasts!"

"It is all in the report I gave you, Your Grace," said Cromwell smugly.

Loosed from his captors, the prior began feeling between all the pillows for the snake. "It was Cuthbert who escaped," he said.

At that my men began to laugh hysterically, falling all over the silken cushions.

"You'll hurt Cuthbert! Please, sirs—"

"Cuthbert!" I said. "So you name your snake after a saint? Truly, you condemn yourself by this act alone."

The men enjoyed the pretend Infidel-den. I left them rollicking about, tormenting Cuthbert (if indeed he had remained in the chamber) and awaiting dinner, while I strolled out, drawn to the area that customarily housed the monks' solitary cells. Here, if anywhere, I would find whatever glimmer of religion remained in this fallen house of God.

Along one side of the original priory, judging from the age of the stones and the type of architecture, were the small stone cells. Perhaps St. Osweth's had come into being because of a group of hermits. Some foundations had such a beginning. One holy man and his followers would withdraw from the world, and then their piety and reputation for saintliness would attract pilgrims, and the site would turn into a religious centre—exactly the sort of busy place the holy men had sought to escape in the first place. But no holy hermit could have borne the shame of what St. Osweth's had grown into. Even the houses of prostitution in Southwark were (so I am told) clean and cheerful by comparison.

This side of St. Osweth's was deserted, and in frank decay. Roofs had fallen in, and seedling trees grew in the crevices. Ice hung on the empty windows like grotesque panes of glass. Yet I felt cleaner and clearer here than anyplace else on the grounds. Perhaps thoughts, desires, motives remain in a place long after the men who thought them are gone, leaving an aura to hover about. Whatever it was, I suddenly felt blessed and knew I stood on holy ground. I had made a pilgrimage after all.

Immediately I began to pray. First, hesitantly and silently, for England. Then, softly, for more personal things.

"God, I beg You, fill me with the wisdom to serve You better. Let me know Your will in all my doings, so that I may obey. Show me when I go astray so that I may correct myself straightway." Do not let me become an abomination in Your sight, like the prior.

The wind rose. I felt the cold all about me, and it caused my leg to ache. "O Lord God, take this infirmity away from me!" My words turned to puffs of smoke on the frigid air. "Please, I beg You, I beseech You . . . I can bear it no longer! I know it is a mark of Your disfavour"— the words were tumbling out now, without modesty or seemliness—"but wherein have I failed? Show me clear, bid me do a thing, and I will do it! But tease me no more with bodily infirmities!"

I was angry with God—yes, furious with His way of punishing me for an unknown sin. Was this fair? No earthly ruler would behave in so devious a fashion.

"When *I* punish a subject, I always give him a chance to repent first. Why have You not granted the same courtesy to *me?*" A shot of pain ran through the leg. "Is this how You talk to me? Indirectly? Can You not find a better translator than a diseased leg?"

Now He would strike me—surely! Anything but this insolent silence, this celestial detachment. The leg throbbed, then quieted.

"And to take away my manhood! I beg You, let me be a husband to my wife!"

Anger and fear flung me to my knees, and I shut my eyes and cried out in undisguised pain to God.

I know not how long I remained thus, but it seemed a different sort of time than worldly time. Stumbling to my feet, I felt a fleeting sweetness that promised all would yet be well.

Or did I but deceive myself?

That night in the comical Sultan's den, my men commented several times that I seemed subdued, softened.

"He grows fond and familiar in his old age," said Neville.

" 'Tis we who grow old," said Carew. His heart trouble had frightened him. "The King merely grows more regal."

But Cromwell studied me with narrowed eyes. He was trying to detect something—he who lived by being able to read the secret thoughts of other men.

As early as possible the next morning, we left St. Osweth's behind, as a man will leave a sickbed. It would be closed as soon as I could sign the orders. In the meantime there was no point in punishing the prior. Let him enjoy his snake-lair a little longer before he was turned out to earn an honest living. Prudently, we had deprived him of the jewels and treasury. My saddle-pouches now bulged with gemstones.

The storm had passed out over the Channel and was now harassing France. I hoped it would ruin Francis's hunting. Of late it was reported that he spent inordinate amounts of time hunting, restlessly moving from one lodge to another, feverishly chasing game. Feverish . . . yes, the rumours said he was suffering from the dread French Disease, and this caused his glittering eyes and unpredictable behaviour.

Rumours. I wondered if any had reached Francis or Charles about my infirmity?

LVII

In the morning light, St. Osweth's, now behind us, seemed as dreamlike as the days that had just passed. They were set apart, outside anything in our regular lives. Therefore it was jarring when Cromwell rode alongside me, murmuring about the monasteries, saying that it was necessary to act now about them, that St. Osweth's was but a mild example and mirror of what I might find in over eight hundred other such establishments throughout England. He pressed for permission to seize and close them all.

His thirst for their ruin seemed primary, his concern for their morals secondary. His emphasis distressed me.

"Not *now,* Crum!" I barked, and the cold, clear air seemed to encapsulate my words, to surround each of them with a box. Did the fool not understand that I was about to meet my daughter, whom I had not seen in almost two years? My daughter, whom I loved and with whom I was yet at enmity. Human emotions: these did not reckon in Crum's scales. Except as something to be used to undo a man.

And I was so nervous, so anxious, my heart was pounding louder than my empty stomach was growling. I felt it not, so filled with joy and dread was I to be approaching Beaulieu. I would see Mary; we would talk; all things would be resolved, for love could overcome any barrier.

Beaulieu: a beautiful red brick royal residence, almost a miniature Hampton Court. Mary had been ordered here to separate her from her mother, so that Katherine would know that things were no longer as they had been. It was all aimed at Katherine; I had not meant it to sunder Mary from her past as well. Nor I from mine. Mary kept residence here, as she had at Ludlow, in full state as a Princess Royal. Her household included some hundred servitors, as befitted her supposed rank.

Beaulieu was closer on the horizon, its russet bricks seeming to slap the wild blue sky above it. As we approached, before us groundsmen and manservants were shovelling the snow, tossing the sparkling white stuff over their shoulders.

In the outer guardroom we waited. The household was thrown into confusion at our unannounced visit, and struggled to straighten and order itself. This I did not want.

"Nay, but we'll come in!" I announced, pushing our way inside to the receiving chamber, all tiled and empty.

"Your Grace—Your Majesty—" A young servitor stood awestruck.

"Is . . ." (What title to use?) ". . . my daughter's Chamberlain in attendance?"

Lady Coopey, Mary's chief attendant and administrator, came into the chamber, adjusting her head-covering. "Your Majesty." She knelt.

I raised her up. "No more of this. I would speak with my daughter. The rest"— I motioned toward my group, half frozen and starved—"would appreciate a fire, and to share your dinner. It is near dinner-hour, is it not?" The smell of stew, and breads baking, had told me it was. My own hunger had been suppressed by my desire to see Mary.

"Yes, Your Majesty."

"Then see to it." I waved my hand. "As for ourself, we would wait in a private place."

In the little oratory off the chapel, I looked over the furnishings. Priedieus. Paintings of the saints. And two stones, placed side by side under a painting of the Virgin. This puzzled me.

The door opened. Mary came in.

She was a woman.

This was the sudden, unexpected thought that came to me upon beholding her.

"Mary!" We embraced. Then I held her away and looked at her.

She had been yet a child when I saw her last, and I had hardly seen her at that, so fired was I with Anne-madness. At sixteen, she had preserved some vestiges of the little child, the girl, I had known.

At eighteen, all that was gone. She had transformed herself, and in my absence.

"Your Majesty." She bent herself low.

"No. Father," I insisted, raising her up.

"As you wish." Those words, so precise, so proper, so distant, said many things.

"Mary, I"—I wish to embrace you, to talk with you, to laugh—"it is good to see you."

"And it is good to see you."

And also with you. Must she sound like a Mass?

"Let me look at you." The perpetual parent's request.

She was tiny. She had grey eyes and a chalky complexion. Her hair was golden, in the process of turning muddy, like Katherine's. She had my small-lipped mouth, which was my least attractive feature, and hers as well. When we clamped our mouths, our lips seemed to pucker from tightness. She was beautifully dressed, wearing jewels even before midday, and had great dignity. She kept her eyes on me all the while, never dropping them. What a marvellous, miraculous mixture she was of us both.

"Do I meet your liking?" Her voice was low, gruff, as if to remind me: I am myself, not merely a blend of you and Katherine.

"Entirely." I beamed. Her responding smile was reluctantly given, wary.

That wariness: I was responsible for it. Therefore I must banish it straightway. "Mary, I have . . . missed you."

It was true, and never more so than now. The heart is a peculiar thing; it cannot always choose where it will love. Regardless of my head, my heart always chose Mary.

"And I you, Your Majesty." Her little white hands clutched one another.

"You could come to court," I suddenly said.

"The court is ruled by . . . oh, I cannot bear it!" Without permission, she turned away, and sobs began to shake her. "No, I cannot come there. Pray let me, if I go anywhere, go to my mother!"

That could not be. Not with the network of possible conspirators coalescing around Katherine. Should Mary join her, that would be a lodestone few malcontents could resist.

"I cannot, alas."

"Cannot? No, *will* not! I long for my mother, and she for me! For how long will you separate us? No matter how long," she answered herself, "it can never truly separate us! My heart is with her, as hers with me!"

"And I? Where is my heart? Excluded?"

"With the Great Whore!" She turned, not defiantly—defiance I could have broken—but sadly. "That is where your heart is. Not with me, nor with the Queen. I must reconcile myself to it. Is that what this visit is for? To teach me to reconcile myself to it?"

No, I wanted to say, *it was to see you, persuade you to sign the Oath.* Filthy reasons. The first selfish, the second political.

Our reconciliation was not to be. Nothing was to be. Anne had made us enemies, now and forever.

"What are these rocks for?" I asked irrelevantly, as my eyes rested on them.

"A pilgrim brought them back from Nazareth," she said. "To remind himself that the rocks Our Lord walked on were ordinary rocks. Also to remind himself that all things are equally holy and hard."

"Mary! I need you! I want you! Can you not—will you not—frame a way in your mind that you can come back to me?"

"If it means repudiating my mother, saying she was not your true wife, no. If it means repudiating my greater mother, the Church, then no."

"Can you not even consider my claims, my side?" Was she so completely her mother's partisan?

"Oh, I have studied them. I have read every proclamation that you have worded, have studied the proceedings of Parliament, and followed all your reasonings. I even read the form of excommunication, and knew it applied to you, and trembled for you. I read your *Assertio Septem Sacramentorum* and knew every word. Father, I understand your anguish, and your spiritual intelligence and integrity. But you are *wrong!*"

She reached out her hand and took mine. "I cannot champion wrong even in one I love—against my will!—much as I may wish to. For even if he believes himself right, and I, knowing better, convinced otherwise, follow him—it is *I* who am damned!"

Mary and I: loving each other, even though urged by others not to. I heard her anguish and keened to it. But I could not say other than, "Then you are an ungrateful, disloyal daughter! You must submit to me as your lawful sovereign. And no longer shall you live in the estate of a Princess, for you are no Princess, but a bastard, like Henry Fitzroy.

"It grieves me," I added. I would be gentle. "Sin does not always feel like sin. But we must acknowledge it as sin if it is declared by Our Lord or Holy Scriptures to be so, regardless of our personal feelings in the matter. The truth is that your mother—in spite of her personal piety—was not my true wife."

"And the Great Whore is?" she cried. "God Himself calls mock on it!"

"It is not for you to interpret or speak for God!" I shouted. "Therein lies the deception of Satan!"

"No, I do not interpret for myself. That is Protestant, and I am certainly none of *that!* It is the Church's interpretation I follow, hard as that may be."

"I *am* the Church!" I cried. "God's law has made me so!"

"With all respect, Your Majesty, it is *you* who have made yourself so. Not God, nor His law."

Out upon her! She was irreconcilable with my life.

"I am sorry, Mary, that you speak these words."

Take them back! I begged her, in my mind. I wanted her so desperately. She was silent.

"I know they were spoken without thought."

More silence.

"I will overlook them."

"No, Father. Do not deceive yourself so. For I spoke true."

Will you not even allow me the mercy of self-deception, then? Perhaps it is not a mercy, but a curse. One that I seek too often.

"So here you stand? Even as Martin Luther?" I attempted a joke.

"Eventually we all must." She stood, blanched and stiff and imperious. Not the sweet, soft girl I had loved. I had lost her, back in time and her own growing.

"Very well, then. Know this: that thou art"—I switched to the impersonal form—"a most disobedient, disloyal, and unloving daughter. That thou no longer shalt style thyself 'Princess' but be content with 'Lady Mary,' and no longer abide at Beaulieu, with a mighty staff of servants to do your bidding, but go serve as a handmaid to the true Princess, Elizabeth, at Hatfield . . . there to learn humility and resignation to the station to which God has called you."

I expected some start, some protest. There was none. "I am Your Majesty's most obedient handmaid," she said, sweeping to the floor.

I longed to lean down, embrace her, tell her I loved her. But if she could be hard, she would learn that I could be harder still. Ruby must crack against diamond.

"Indeed," I said. "I acknowledge your fealty. Know, then, that you must go straightway to Hatfield House and begin to serve in the Princess's household."

"Be it unto me according to thy wish," she said.

"Stop echoing Scripture! You shame it, and yourself! You are no Virgin Mary, lass, so do not style yourself thus!" Had she inherited Katherine's tendency to religious excess?

On the way back to London, my men, well fed now, were eager to know the cause for my stormy and hasty departure. I had stamped into the dining hall, bade them tuck the food straight into their bellies, and leave. I did not seat myself, but grabbed several pieces of meat pie and white manchet bread, and ate them ravenously, all the while standing and directing my party to get their cloaks.

Now the dry-eaten food seemed lodged in a series of little lumps from my mouth to my stomach. That, and my choler, choked me. I longed for Will to ride beside me, but he had departed from Beaulieu to his sister's house. None of the others would do, not at this moment when I realized that I had lost my daughter; that my Great Matter was not resolved upon my clever juggling of Papal bulls and decretals and consecrations and Parliamentary acts; that treason lurks in hearts and goes unconverted and undetected in most cases. The line must be, would have to be, drawn across families and old loyalties. Even my own.

But to have lost my daughter—no, it was too hard. I could not bear it, I would soften it somehow. Then I was minded that I had tried to soften it, and it was Mary who would not have it so.

So be it.

I motioned for George Boleyn to come forward and ride with me. That he did, looking gratified and puzzled.

"George, I love you well," I began, for the pleasure of confusing him further, "and therefore I will make a present to you. From henceforth Beaulieu is yours."

Yes, Mary must surrender it to Queen Anne's brother.

He looked dumbfounded, as all are at receiving utterly undeserved gifts.

"As soon as the *Lady* Mary has removed herself, and her household has gone, you may take possession of it."

I waved away his stammering, inadequate thanks.

Another few miles farther on the ride, I beckoned Chapuys to take his place beside me. I was holding audience on the road, as surely as if I had a secretary to direct my appointments.

Chapuys rode forward, his entire being as eager as ever for some sparring. I would not disappoint him.

"Ambassador," I said, "You must be made privy to the conversation betwixt the Lady Mary and myself. I have forbidden her to continue to style herself 'Princess,' and her household has been disbanded. I just gave Beaulieu to Boleyn." I nodded back at the grinning George. "She is being sent to wait upon the Princess Elizabeth. By implication, she has refused the content of the forthcoming Oath of Succession. That makes her a traitor."

"Of what does this Oath consist?"

How many times was this question to be asked—this cursed, hateful question?

"That the subscriber recognizes the Princess Elizabeth as the rightful and sole heir to the throne. That is all."

"And, by implication, that Mary is illegitimate, because your marriage to her mother was no marriage, because it was founded on a dispensation that was false, because the party granting it had not the power to do so, because he had no power at all?"

"The implications—they are not worded! One swears only to the words as stated, not implied!"

"A lawyer's answer. Well, then, your former Chancellor More should be able to take it readily."

"More will take it. He is a sensible man, he will not quibble over 'implications.' But your . . . concerned parties . . . will not be able to, as what is *stated* in the Oath is what is odious to them, not what is implied."

"God will have to sustain them." He smiled smugly. "And God's agents," he added.

"So you threaten me? Of course. I thank you for your honesty." I dismissed him as easily as in a palace audience. He understood the rules.

I rode by myself in silence. All around me the January afternoon was piercingly bright and seemingly benign. The same winter that had sought to kill me two days ago now wooed me with all her skill. She displayed the pure blue sky that was her trademark, and all the play of light peculiar to herself: the shadows that were blue, not black; the yellow-red syrup of sun lying in little pools and cups of snow-formed landscape; the dazzling glow of a mound of snow, seemingly pulsating from within. Then London appeared on the horizon.

It was time for yet another audience. I motioned Henry Howard to come to me. He galloped up to my side, his pretty face seeming even more fresh than the snow.

"You are of an age with my son," I said. Mary was lost to me, but not Henry Fitzroy. I must not neglect one for the heartbreak of the other. "You were born in 1517, am I correct?" I knew I was. I was master of just such minutiae.

"Yes." He was surprised, then flattered, as we all are when someone remembers a personal fact about us.

"Seventeen. My son, Henry Fitzroy, is two years your junior. I would give him a companion to share tutors and pastimes with. Would you find that to your liking? I would treat you as princes together, at Windsor. What say you?"

"I say—I say yes," he said. "Oh, yes!"

Two not-quite-princes, but both having princely blood. "Good. My son needs a noble friend. And you, I think, need to be with others of your age and station. Both of you have been too long confined with women and old men."

His laugh told me I was right.

"In the spring you shall come to Windsor," I said. "Directly after the Order of the Garter ceremony, in which both you and he shall take your places in that noble company." In one offhanded phrase I had elevated him to the highest order of knighthood in the realm. Words, words. Words were so easy.

We arrived back at Richmond long past sunset. Across the frozen Thames the lights of London shone as we passed by, amber and warm, and here and there jagged fingers of ice picked it up, glowing like elongated jewels. I was weary, weary. Since leaving Richmond three days before I had come close to death by white extinction; had encountered the insanity of St. Osweth's; had seen my lost Mary transformed into an exact replica of Katherine, my enemy. The original reasons why I had sought this journey were overwhelmed by its findings.

In the great torchlit palace courtyard, snow-packed and still, I bade my companions good night. Neville and Carew I embraced. A surfeit of affection, unable to reach Mary, now flowed over onto my old friends. "Beware of Cuthbert," I joked.

To Cromwell I said, "I must meet with you before Parliament opens. I have decided to attend the opening in person."

Then we went our own ways, to our separate chambers, I to the royal apartments—and Anne.

I must confess I did not wish to see Anne, or anyone, tonight. I was glad that Will was away. One of the most irksome things about matrimony was that one was never alone. *It is not good that the man should be alone; I will make him an help meet for him.* God intended marriage to counteract that paralysing loneliness which grips you at unexpected moments. But never to be alone with one's thoughts or one's Maker . . . why must it always be too much of one condition or the other?

My own Privy Chamber was full of idle, questioning men. But I passed through them, seeking out the refuge of the inmost chamber within my private suite. There I sat for long moments, unblinking, aware that my body was starved, strained, and crying for the oblivion of sleep.

I must see Anne. It was a duty, a duty of courtesy, like all knightly duties. We would have supper together, and I would tell her of all that had befallen me. Wearily I rang for an attendant, told him my wishes, and lay back awaiting my food and my wife.

Anne came to me sooner than I would have wished, since I wished for no company at all. She appeared at the doors of my chamber, her cheeks dimpling with pleasure. I must appear likewise, I told myself, rousing myself from a sweet lethargy that had just taken hold.

"O Henry," she said, "you are safe! You are safe! I heard of the snow-storm. . . . I feared so, for your life!" Her eyes expressed all sorrow and concern.

"It was an adventure," I said, willing myself to rise up and embrace her. "In faith, I felt like Gawain in his quest for the Green Knight, passing through forests of ice and seas of snow." Suddenly I was too tired to tell it, nor did I wish to. "We spent the night in a providential cave, and the next morning were on our way. All's well . . . sweetheart." There, that satisfied the recounting.

"I fear, however, that my mission to Mary was unhappy. She refused to acknowledge the way of things. She is a replica of Katherine."

Anne smiled smugly. "As I knew. And far more dangerous."

"How so?"

"To be brutal, the old woman's almost fifty, and ill. Mary is young and healthy. Katherine has been a Queen already; Mary is a potential one. A great man once said, 'Never fear your predecessors, only your successors.' "

"You will be pleased to know, then, that I have ended Mary's 'reign' at Beaulieu. I ordered her to depart immediately to serve Elizabeth at Hatfield House. I have also"—I paused at this; I was so infernally *weary!*—"given Beaulieu to your brother George, to do with as he likes."

She squealed with triumph, clasping her hands together in the age-old sign of greed.

"George is a good lad," I said. "May he use it well."

Just then the servitors appeared with our supper, carried on silver trays and covered with great domes of heat-keeping metal. We must suspend all intimate conversation while the small dining table was spread with linen and all the dishes set out with their condiments of pepper and salt and cloves. There was rabbit stew, all savoury and swimming in rich sauce; little pancakes to lie under it; wild berry jelly and lentil soup. As the servitor arranged each item with precise artistry, I watched, my hunger a captive to his art; and Anne and I spoke in whispers and code.

"Your cousin who makes poetry shall teach another to do so," I murmured. "Starting straightway at Windsor."

I expected a smile; instead she glowered. We would discuss this later.

"I have brought back jewels from a lax monastery," I said. I opened the saddle-pouch and handed her the prior's lost treasures. "All these were to pay for Masses unsaid," I told her.

"So many fallen people," she murmured, stroking the stones and gold.

The servitor's ceremony of silver-laying yet went on, slowly, deliberately. Would he never be done?

"Aye. A shame and a disgrace."

The goblets were now set in place, the wine poured into them.

"We thank you," I said. I indicated the fire, and the young servant put two solid oak logs onto it, then withdrew.

I seated myself before the repast, so hungry that by now I was past hunger. I was precise, careful in all my movements. I picked up the goblet, of fine Venetian glass. I had lately ordered a hundred of them. Glass was better than metal for flattering wine's taste.

"Let us drink to all reunions," I said. Our glasses touched. Reunion: the reuniting of that which is severed. If only wine could accomplish that.

The touch of wine in my mouth caused an explosion of hunger. I helped myself to the stew, the pancakes, and savoured each bite. My hunger rose up and sported with the food.

"What meant you about my cousin Howard?" she asked sharply.

"Why, that he and my son Fitzroy shall spend some time together at Windsor. Fitzroy needs to be with other noble lads his own age; he's been too isolated. And as for Howard . . . it would do him good to feel loved, and appreciated. The situation in his family—his parents living apart, no brothers to sustain him—they could help one another."

"So you continue to elevate your bastard son!" she said. "Forget him! He's of your past! Why do you hark back to *him,* when we shall have sons of our own?"

"When we do, I shall honour them as heirs to the throne. I honour Fitzroy only as my son, and as a lad who needs attention and affection. As does Henry Howard. They are both sorely neglected."

"Henry the Good Samaritan," she mocked—or did she? "That is not as others perceive you."

"If you are to be Queen," I reminded her, "you must cease to be concerned with how ignorant people perceive you. Only be concerned with how God, who sees all, perceives you."

We finished our stew—it was delicious, seasoned with herbs I could not identify—in silence. Then I said, "Parliament opens two days from now. They will be enacting the bills concerning our marriage and Elizabeth's primacy of succession."

This is the moment, I wanted to say. *The moment that makes my love for you a matter of law. And treason.* My private passion had become a concern of lawmaking bodies.

"This Oath that will be required . . . it will first be administered in Parliament."

"And then to everyone." Her voice was calm.

"All it will require is that . . . that the person swears that Elizabeth is the heir to the throne, excepting any sons we may have."

"So simple. How many words?"

"Twenty, thirty. But . . . there are meanings behind the words. We know what those meanings are. There will be some, perhaps many"—how many?—"who may find it difficult to take the Oath."

"Because they are not hearing the words of the Oath, but the imaginary words behind it."

"Yes."

The dinner was done. The food, the plates, like all meals finished, were repulsive. I could not leave them soon enough. I stood, and we sought a padded bench on the far side of the chamber. I rang for the leavings to be removed.

"The Oath is my pledge of love to you," I assured her. "It is the greatest offering I can make you."

She laid her gentle hand on my shoulder.

Just then the servitor came to clear away the things, so we remained frozen in our words and actions, but not in our thoughts. Those continued to race, change, rearrange themselves. By the time he left, they were of another order entirely.

"You will not flinch?" she said. "Even though perhaps those you care for, consider dear, may refuse the Oath?"

"Flinch?"

"Refuse to punish them? To let them suffer the penalty of treason?"

"I never flinch."

Who would not sign? Some would; I refused to predict the actions of individuals . . . of those I loved. . . .

Anne was with me, Anne for whom all this had come about. The restorative magic of food was spreading itself all throughout my body, with wine following in its wake. I was floating. . . .

Anne was beautiful, worth all I had had to move to have her. Now I wanted her.

Yes, wanted her! The miracle was here, it had happened after all. My powers were back. . . .

We entwined ourselves in the ancient and magical way, becoming truly one flesh.

And Adam knew his wife. I knew Anne, or felt I did. Knew her to every sinew and bone, so very like mine. . . .

Or so I believed.

LVIII

At midday, three days after my return, I went to Parliament in state. The Thames being frozen, I could not be rowed in the royal barge to Westminster, where both houses were meeting for the opening. Instead I had to walk, with a full complement of retainers and advisors, under a canopy of royal estate, carrying the mace of England, along the Strand. I was gratified to see that windows were still opened and people still hung over the sills to glimpse their King, and that their cries were gladsome ones. What would they change to after Parliament had finished making its bills?

Inside the antechamber at Westminster Palace, I fastened on my heavy gold-and-ermine robes and had the crown placed on my head. *The King in Parliament* was about to take place: my presence, united with Parliament, was the highest law of the land.

Both the Lower House (Commons) and the Upper House (Lords) were gathered together in the Lesser Hall today, a chamber tiled in green and white. In the middle of the room, four ceremonial woolsacks—enormous tasseled bundles saluting England's foundation of financial greatness, wool—served as seats for judges and record-keeping clerks, as well as for Sir Thomas Audley, the Lord Chancellor, More's successor.

The House of Lords consisted not only of fifty-seven peers ("Lords temporal") but of fifty high-ranking clergymen ("Lords spiritual") as well. Commons were about three hundred strong, elected knights and burgesses from all the shires of the realm.

The Lords sat on benches arranged in a great double rectangle around the room, prelates on my right and peers on my left; the Commons had to stand outside, at the bar, behind their Speaker. I sat upon a throne overlooking them all, under a white embroidered canopy of estate, set up on a dais covered in blue and gold—gold Tudor roses and fleurs-de-lis. Flanking me on the dais were my advisors and councillors, particularly Cromwell.

This was the fifth time this Parliament had sat. It was to last for seven years, and become known as the Long Parliament. Thus far it had enacted many things, but they had been aimed primarily at abuses that had long rankled good Englishmen: the separate privileges of the clergy, the taxes and tithes to Rome. This time was different. This time I would ask them to define treason—according to my terms.

Standing before them, my crown heavy on my head, I spoke.

"Before you are bills which will define the meaning of treason. We had always thought we knew the meaning of treason. It was instantly recognizable, as we recognize toads, snakes, vermin. Who could mistake a toad for a tabby cat?"

Laughter.

"But in these perilous days, it is not so simple to distinguish. Our ancestors had only to be alert for snakes and rats. But in our sad days, alas—even Satan can disguise himself as an angel of light.

"That is a quotation from Scripture," I continued. "That is just an example of how things have changed. For translated Scriptures abound, and any man might chance to read them—aye, read them, and misunderstand them!"

I looked out at them. There was no laughter now. They waited to see what I was leading up to.

"With this in mind, and as your loving King, I know you need guidance. We would be derelict in our duty and love of you if we did not provide it. Treason sneaks about on little cat feet, whispering first in one ear, then the other. But he who knows what treason is, who has been alerted, can turn aside . . . and stop the mouth of him who whispered it."

Now there was rustling in the seats. Their apprehension was turning into dread.

"Treason is that which seeks to deprive you of your King, to lessen him in any way. That means attempting to deprive him of any of his rightful titles; speaking scandalously of his marriage to Queen Anne; failing to recognize the Princess Elizabeth as his true and legitimate heir. It means maliciously slandering him, in *words* or deeds. It means protecting those who do."

The true import of these words did not seem to have hit home to them. The gathering of men before me had bland faces as yet.

"Now, as no good and loyal Englishman would wish to be guilty of such a crime, there will be provided an opportunity for all to swear themselves as not being numbered among the hidden traitors." I motioned to Cromwell, who stood and brandished a scroll.

"For your protection," he said, "there will be administered an Oath throughout the land. When you take the Oath, your name will be entered in the register for your district. Then you will be safe in the knowledge that your loyalty is a matter of record, and no enemy can undo you." He looked about. "You in Parliament will be privileged to be the first to take it. Then you may deputise others to administer it." I motioned him to sit.

"The Oath will be simple," I said. "It requires only that a person acknowledge the Act of Succession—which you will enact in this session, stating that the marriage to the Princess Dowager was against God's law, and not subject to any earthly dispensation, and that the Succession passes to the King's issue through Queen Anne. That is all. All adult subjects will take the Oath publicly to observe and maintain 'the whole effects and contents' of the Act. You may swear to it by kissing the Bible, or, if you prefer, a holy relic. It will take only a moment or so. But just as baptism takes only a moment, yet cleanses Original Sin, so this will preserve your earthly body against the taint of treason."

They seemed to understand and stand ready to accede to my wishes.

Parliament enacted the statutes, just as I had asked. Treason was no longer merely a word in the English language, subject to individual interpretation; it was now embodied in the law of the land, and there were certain things one did in regard to it, or failed to do. It was in the latter capacity that I consulted Crum.

I had originally taken to calling him "Crum" because I had no other way of expressing fondness toward him. Although affable, he, like a slippery rock, afforded no grasping places by which to ascend to what was truly Thomas Cromwell. He stood quite alone: no wife (she having died, and he seemingly having no inclination to remarry), no marriage ties at court, no known past. A strange, solitary man. I envied him his self-sufficiency.

Now, this bleak and cheerless day in March, when all the world lay torpid, I spoke with Crum.

"Parliament has taken the Oath, and all the heads of London guilds," I said. "When the weather breaks, then we shall send the commissioners to the rest of the realm."

"It will be June before Northumberland and the Marches are accessible," he said. "You will have to rely on the Percys to protect the commissioners and smooth their task. The Percys . . . a thorn in Your Grace's palm. Henry can be trusted, but he's dying, so they say."

Anne's Henry, her girlhood love. Dying? He was so young, Anne's age.

"He was puny." Crum—as always—answered my unspoken question. "The North did not agree with his delicate constitution—neither the climate nor the manners. He could thrive only in the softness of a court."

But you made that impossible. Tactfully, he did not say it.

"The French court, more like."

"Indeed. Where one could be—what was it 'twas said about Caesar?—'every man's woman and every woman's man.' He evidently could not satisfy his wife. She left him and returned to her father's home. Wretched creature, Percy. A decrepit boy."

"So by August the Oaths should have been given, and received, in every reach of the realm." Enough of Percy, of his dyings and inadequacies.

"Yes. The names of the loyal will be in our hands, also of the dissenters."

"Then we shall have to decide how to deal with them."

"Death is the penalty prescribed by law."

Yes, the law was very clear on that. But executions . . . there had been no executions in England except for heinous, active treason, like the Duke of Buckingham's, for thirteen years. (The Duke had intended to conceal a knife on his person and assassinate me during an audience.) But automatic executions for refusing to sign a paper?

"The sentences must be carried out, else no one will trust the law or believe Parliament can enforce what it passes," Crum insisted.

"I pray that all may take it," he added. "For their sakes, and ours."

Was I duty-bound to try to warn those who might consider refusing? Those who might not realize that the time for temporizing had run out, that the law would show no mercy? It would be on my conscience if I did not.

Conscience? No, that was my excuse, a high-sounding one. The truth was that love—if I had love for these people—commanded me to do it.

Mary I had already gone to. Katherine I could not, as she was near Cambridgeshire, and travelling was impossible just now betwixt there and London. I could write her, advising her of the danger she was in.

More. Thomas More, in Chelsea, keeping to himself since he had resigned as Lord Chancellor. Writing his everlasting books, his letters, his devotions. The Bishops of Durham, Bath, and Winchester had sent him my twenty pounds to buy proper robes to come to London and attend Anne's Coronation with them. He had declined the invitation, with an impertinent "parable" about losing his innocence thereby. It had gone as follows:

Your proposal put me in remembrance of an emperor that had made a law that whosoever committed a certain offence, except it were a virgin, should suffer the pains of death. Such a reverence had he to virginity! Now, so it happened that the first committer of that offence was indeed a virgin, whereof the emperor hearing was in no small perplexity, as he would now have to put that law into execution. Whereupon when his council had sat long, solemnly debating this case, suddenly arose there up one of his council—a good plain man among them—and said: "Why make you so much ado, my lords, about so small a matter? Let her first be deflowered and then after she may be devoured."

And so, though Your Lordships have in the matter of the matrimony hitherto kept yourselves pure virgins, yet take good heed, my Lords, that you keep your virginity still. For some there be that by procuring Your Lordships first at the Coronation to be present, and next to preach in favour of it, and finally to write books to all the world in defence thereof, are desirous to deflower you; and when they have deflowered you, then will they fail not to devour you. Now, my Lords, it lieth not in my power but that they may devour me. But God, being my good Lord, I will provide that they shall never deflower me.

I had looked for him in vain at the Coronation banquet, not as an "emperor" cheated of his quarry, but as a friend sorrowed by another friend's absence. Now I knew that similar bravado and ignorance of the consequences might well lead him blithely to refuse the Oath.

I must go to him. I had no choice.

LIX

As his King and sovereign, I could have ordered him to appear before me in any place I chose, and at any time I chose. I could have routed him out of his cosy quarters, upset his routine, stood his life on its head. But I would not do that. I came as a friend. So I consulted with my astronomers and astrologers and found an eclipse of the moon coming in four weeks. This heavenly disturbance was something we could study together that had no earthly overtones. Afterwards we could talk.

I wrote, inviting myself to come to him in Chelsea and watch the eclipse with him. "For there are none at court nowadays who share my enthusiasm," I wrote ingenuously (so I hoped), "and I have some new sighters, which I trust may surprise you. I bring the old astrolabe from Greenwich as well." Would he remember?

I had humbled myself, yet I did not begrudge it. I only prayed that he would see the danger he was in, and respond to my offer of help.

Indeed, he replied, he would be honoured to sight this eclipse with me. His calculations (so he had known of it all along, but never thought to invite *me!*) showed that the eclipse would begin at slightly after eleven at night and be over by one. He would be pleased if I would honour him by coming early, in time for supper and Compline, and then spend the night in his home.

The air was chill in the late April afternoon as the watermen rowed the royal barge up the Thames to Chelsea. Some trees had begun to unfold their leaves, copper-coloured, feathery things, whilst others were still bare. The grass along the bank was already bright green, almost artificially so. Grass is always the first to awaken after the winter sleep, and it hurts our eyes when it does.

Rounding the bend in the river, I saw the pier that belonged to More's household jutting out a little way into the water. Not only had it not been enlarged to accommodate larger vessels, but it had declined sadly from what it was. The planks were gamely mended, but still warped and sagging; the entire thing swayed under my weight.

Down at the watergate More was waiting, leaning against the wicket. He was as brown and plain as a wren, weathered like the planks of his decaying pier.

"Thomas!" I said, hoping not to betray my surprise at his appearance. "I have so looked forward to this time!" I motioned to my servitors, carrying the fitted box with its precious set of one-of-a-kind lenses, and the astrolabe swathed in velvet. "Now we shall catch her out—Dame Luna."

He reached out his hand and grasped mine. "You are heartily welcome, Your Grace." He opened the gate and bowed low. I strode in and encircled his shoulders with my arm, hugging him close to me. He did not resist. Together we walked toward the house.

In the fragile, cold twilight it was quiet. Unlike that happy, lazy summer afternoon (the only other time I had visited him), there were no servants scurrying, no children romping on the grass. The beehives were dormant, and even the goats were nowhere to be seen.

"My children are married," he said, seeming to read my very thoughts. "Grown up, gone away. Elizabeth married William Dauncey, and Cecily, Giles Heron. My father died recently. Even my little ward, Margaret Gigs, has married my former page, John Clement. Dame Alice and I are left quite alone. It happens much sooner than you think."

"And Margaret?" I remembered his bright, shining daughter.

"She married her Will Roper," he said. "Another lawyer. Our family is beset with them. We need a farmer or a goldsmith to give us diversity."

"You had a Lord Chancellor and a Parliamentarian." I could not help saying it.

"Three generations of lawyers," he said, ignoring my gibe. "But the house will not be entirely empty and sedate tonight. I have asked Margaret and Will to join us. Ah!" He gestured toward a glowering, dumpy figure standing in the doorway. "Here is Alice."

If More looked like a wren, she looked like a buzzard. Thickened and soured since our last meeting, she was a pudding gone bad.

"Your Grace." (Such venom in the words!)

I passed into the winter parlour, and was shocked. Much of the furniture was gone, the tapestries taken down, the fireplace cold.

We have you to thank for this, Lady Alice seemed to be saying, in everything but words. But which "you" did she mean? Me, for my Great Matter? Or her husband, for not bending himself to it, for absenting himself from power and court? They went hand in hand: my Great Matter was his as well.

More never sought to explain or to apologize for his reduced state. He seemed to accept it as natural, as he accepted the coming of spring. "We will kill the fatted logs," he joked, "for we have a great and honoured guest." In that way he ordered a fire to be kindled, lest I take cold.

It was not servants who brought the logs in, however, but Margaret and her husband. They were wearing rough old clothes, and kindled the fire with a surety born of much practise. The blaze was scarcely less cheerful than their chatter and movements.

I settled myself before it, and the sole remaining lady-servitor brought us spiced wine. The goblets were wooden ones. It was only then I noticed that not only was there no silver or pewter in the cupboards, but there were no cupboards, either.

How did he have the courage to entertain the King in such reduced circumstances, and as self-assuredly as Wolsey had ever done at Hampton Court?

I had not actually seen Thomas More in almost two years. Since leaving court he had kept entirely to himself, writing long religious books, like the half-million-word *Confutation of Tyndale's Answer,* living through his correspondence with other humanists and scholars abroad. The little circle of such in England was broken now—some by death, most by politics. Erasmus, deprived of his post at a university, along with all Humanists, by the Emperor, languished in exile like More. Vives and Mountjoy, Katherine's partisans, were in disfavour here. It was a great pity that these men had had to embroil themselves in the matters of the day. They should have stuck with the dead Romans and Greeks.

More had visibly aged. Perhaps so had I. He was less able to mask his changes than I, because he dressed so plainly and wore no jewels to divert the eye. (Loyal servants, jewels. They perform so many tasks so well.) I inquired after his health, as politeness decreed. He answered that his lungs had been troubled by a flux all winter, but that with the coming of warmer weather, he looked to its easement.

Perfectly reasonable words, a civilized exchange. Yet they seemed worse than shouting, worse than curses, because of all they did not say; and the unsaid loomed over us, demanding attention. To sit thus, the silences and the pauses embroidered by designs of "conversation," seemed a monstrous sin. And yet I kept committing it.

"News of your *Confutation* and its fine reasoning has reached me," I said.

"God has given me the opportunity to devote myself to it fully," he replied. "Otherwise I might never have been so thorough."

The fire hissed and a spark jumped out toward us, as though trying, in its own way, to ease and distract our awkwardness.

"Have you much time for astronomy?" I asked. "The skies are clear here."

"I have, but only with homemade instruments. Alas, your New Year's gift of 1510"—he remembered the year; I was gratified, absurdly thrilled—"had to be sold to buy candles for this winter. I have missed it."

So it was difficult for him to part with the astrolabe? And my coming now, with my new playthings . . . it was actually a favour, not an imposition? I would make him a present of them. My heart swelled with goodwill and bounty.

But my tongue was leaden, and the silences persisted. I was relieved when supper was announced and we could begin the soothing ritual of eating, and perhaps make the transition to easiness by the time the plates were cleared.

"Your Majesty, would you bless our table and lead us in prayer?" More opened his palm to me.

He acknowledged my divinely appointed spiritual guidance! What else could this gesture mean? How subtle of More. The rest would be easy, then, the evening pleasant.

"O Divine God," I intoned, "bless this gathering of those who love one another in unity of hearts and souls. May our words and actions and inmost desires be pleasing to You. Fill us with the Holy Spirit, so that we may always speak truth and act according to Thy wishes."

We all crossed ourselves. I looked up. My prayer, far from loosening everyone, seemed to have stiffened them.

"Your Majesty," said Lady Alice, "as it is Friday, and Lent, I have prepared the most festive dishes permissible under the circumstances." She rang her little bell, and the serving girl appeared, bearing a great tureen of soup.

"Slete soup," she said, setting it down carefully in the middle of the smallish table.

"Leeks are Welsh emblems, are they not, and Your Majesty is Welsh?" Margaret More Roper spoke up.

"Do you speak Welsh?" her husband suddenly asked. It was the first thing he had said.

"Yes . . . a little. I learnt it from my father." Strange, I had forgotten that. Forgotten that he had spoken it to me as a child. I hardly remembered him speaking to me at all.

"Leek soup is *cawl cennin,*" I said. "It is usually better on the second eating, when it is called *cawl ail dwym.*"

The Celtic words did what my formal prayer could not: blessed us, gave us unity. A miracle.

"Do you ever wish to visit Wales?" asked Thomas.

"Yes. They are strange people, and yet I am part of them. I sometimes feel I have gotten all the best of myself from them: my music, my love of poetry."

And the worst, I thought to myself. The black moods, the melancholy, that strange feeling of homesickness wherever I find myself.

"Will you make them part of England?" Lady Alice was blunt, as always.

"They *are* part of England," I said. "They cannot help that, nor can I. 'Tis more convenient for all parts to be united under a single government."

The slete soup was nourishing, and filling. I relished it in my belly; but more than that, I relished the free and loving conversation about the table.

"Now for my favourite Lenten dish," said Thomas. "Perhaps it is not a penance, because I love it so." He rang the bell, gaily. I could see he truly looked forward to this dish.

"Deep-dish eel and onion pie."

Presented before us was a magnificent coffer of decorated pastry.

More took the knife and broke open the golden-glazed covering. A great gush of steam issued forth; and then I could see the succulent pieces of eel swimming in their sauce of butter, raisins, and milk. To accompany it was a good dish of boiled garlic.

It was all finer than any royal banquet. And to this day I do not know why. Of course, More would have an explanation: Christ was a guest as well —as the Israelites always leave a place for Elijah at their Passover feasts.

Supper over—there was no dessert, owing to Lent—we went straightway back to the winter parlor for Compline.

Compline was, strictly speaking, a monastic ritual. Even Katherine never said Compline, despite her allegiance to the Third Order of St. Francis. But More had, after all, once been a novice for the Carthusian Order, although he had turned aside, saying, "It is better to be a chaste husband than a licentious priest." Like many men who have served two masters, he had never completely forgotten the first one.

The fire was dying. More ordered tapers to be brought so that he might read the Office. Although he offered me place of honour, I declined. I desired to see him in his customary role.

I desired to know him. Truly to know him.

First came the admonition. "Brothers, be both sober and vigilant," he read.

Then followed silent meditation. Then confession:

"I confess to Almighty God, to blessed Mary ever Virgin, to blessed Michael the Archangel, to blessed John the Baptist, to the holy Apostles Peter and Paul, and to all the saints, that I have sinned exceedingly in thought, word, and deed, through my fault, through my fault, through my most grievous fault. Therefore, I beseech Mary ever Virgin, blessed Michael the Archangel, blessed John the Baptist, the holy Apostles Peter and Paul, and all the saints, to pray to the Lord our God for me."

Then Psalm 133:

"Ecce nunc benedicite Dominum.

"Behold, how good and how pleasant it is for brethren to dwell together in unity!

"It is like the precious ointment upon the head, that ran down upon the beard, even Aaron's beard, that went down to the skirts of his garments.

"As the dew of Hermon, and as the dew that descended upon the mountains of Zion: for there the Lord commanded the blessing, even life forevermore."

The fire died, as More's words did. I felt embraced by God, by this blessed family, by the moment, by the words.

"And now to bed," said Lady Alice, breaking the spell.

"Except for the moon-watchers." Margaret smiled at me.

"Margaret once had a fancy for astronomy," More said. "But when I continually had to point out the difference between the moon and the sun—"

"Nay, I never excelled at astronomy," agreed Margaret. "It baffled me." She looked at us all. "I must to bed. Father is right."

Lady Alice likewise excused herself. Thomas More and I were left entirely alone. As I had wished, had dreamt of.

"Show me your secret," he said. "I am anxious to see what you have brought."

Carefully I opened the velvet-lined fitted wooden box. Inside was a set of lenses, and a board where they could be affixed into a series of holes.

"If these are paired and aligned in a certain way, they bring things closer, I know not how. My eyeglass maker showed me this trick. I can play with them and see objects on the far side of the room as if they were within arm's length. I must confess I have not tried them on the stars. But perhaps tonight?"

"Yes! Yes!" He sounded genuinely interested, and extracted one and studied it intently.

"I had my eyeglass maker grind them," I said. "I have had to resort to wearing reading glasses these days, alas." I was now obligated to wear what were called "forty-year glasses." They also made "fifty-year-glasses," "sixty-year-glasses," and so on.

"We have awhile yet before the eclipse begins. Let us adjust them when it is less chilly, and avoid the condensation on the lens." He rose, gathering his drab grey wool about him.

He ushered me outside, through the rear door of the Great Hall—silent and dark now—and out onto the little meadow behind his manor house. The sharp, sweet smell of promised spring was in every breath.

The land rose slowly to a little knoll. More took a torch and led me toward it. Only as I came closer did my torch show something else to be there. As my eyes took in the structure, so my nose smelled new, oiled wood.

More indicated it. "A moon-watching platform," he said. "The Chinese, I am told, call all balconies such, and so they should."

He had built it for me. For my visit. In his reduced circumstances, still he had seen fit to honour me, and my wishes. . . .

I mounted the steps of the small deck, encircled with a railing.

"I built it on my highest land," he said.

"You built this . . . for my visit? The wood, the workmen's fees—"

"I built it myself," he said. "That is why it tilts so." He laughed. "I hope our calculation table can stand steady."

My men were busy setting it up. They could manage.

"It is steady, Your Majesty," they said. They had made all the necessary adjustments to the legs and the angle of the top.

"You may keep pastime in the winter parlor," More told them. "Request more wood if you like."

Now we were alone. No ceremonies, no mitigating forces, and there was still an hour before the eclipse. It was most inconvenient of the Almighty to schedule it so late.

More walked around the new-smelling platform, rubbing his hands in the cold. There were two chairs on the deck, obviously fetched up from the house, as they were indoor chairs.

"We could look at Venus first," he suggested.

"But there is little to see," I replied. "It is always of a uniform appearance, and so bright. I prefer Mars."

"The God of War," said More. "Spoken like a true prince. Of late it has seemed brighter, at least to my naked eye. May I?" He indicated the larger lens, the one to be held at arm's length.

"If you insert the handle into the hole at the far edge of the board, then tilt it"—I showed him how—"that can serve well for stars near the horizon. It will free one hand."

He was delighted with the innovation.

"I wonder what the red is?" he mused. "Does Mars have red seas, do you think?"

"Yes," I said. "Most likely. Or perhaps it burns with a red flame? Or perhaps it is covered with blood?"

He sighed. "To think there are other worlds, so different from ours. . . . Sometimes I cannot comprehend, truly comprehend, in my soul, the depth of God's great universe. I have recently read of a Polish man's theory that all the planets circle the sun—he has not published, of course—"

"It is not for us to 'comprehend' with our finite minds, but to seek to obey Him in whatever world He has placed us," I said. "It is not, of course, always so plain. . . . God confounds us, tests us."

I hesitated. But the moment was here, the moment when I must speak. "Thomas, I came to see you tonight not only to view the eclipse, but also to warn you. I do not know what you hear from London of worldly matters. Gossip and rumours distort and are no friend to truth. But I am speaking the truth, as your friend, when I tell you that Parliament will require an Oath to support their Act of Succession, which they are even now in the process of making law."

"Of what will the Oath consist?"

That question again.

"That the swearer believes the Princess Elizabeth to be the only legitimate heir to the throne. That the swearer will support her claims against all others"—I paused—"should I suddenly die." How remote that seemed, standing out on the brave little moon-platform.

"That is all?"

"Yes. I believe so. Perhaps a few words to the effect that my marriage to Anne is a true one, the one to Katherine null and void—"

" 'A few words'?" He dashed his hands against the railing of the platform. "Always 'a few words'! Oh, would that they were many—then it would be so much easier. *A few words.* God, why are You so cruel?"

His voice was sharp in the still air, rising like a rapier, rattling itself against God.

"Yet it is all the same." His voice quieted at once, before he turned back to me.

"I hope you will not refuse the Oath," I said. "For it will be law that those who do not subscribe to it are guilty of treason."

His expression—of course, I could not see it well in the starlight—seemed not to alter.

"I thought it best to warn you, so when you are called to swear, you will know," I continued. "You will swear first, and then your household. It will only take a few moments. Commissioners will come to your household, at crown expense. You will not be disrupted." I sounded apologetic, and that would never do. "See that you take it," I said.

"And if, in my conscience, I cannot?"

"Then you must die a traitor's death. For you will have acknowledged yourself a traitor, according to law."

"Then surely the Princesses Katherine and Mary must die as well. For they, above all others, would damn themselves in so swearing."

"You must not consider others when taking the Oath. That is no concern of yours. Consider only yourself, and your immortal soul."

"I shall remember that, Your Grace."

"You can hide no longer!" I said. "The Oath will hunt you out, even here. Know that."

"The best thing is to maintain my silence. Silence gives consent, in common law."

"That is not good enough! There are all sorts of silences. Few of them are good. They range from the hateful, through the mocking, to the indifferent. Silence is never an ally."

"Perhaps it may be mine," he said.

"Do not delude yourself," I answered. "He who keeps silent is my enemy. It must be so, when I make it so easy to declare yourself my friend. The expense, the trouble, are all mine. All you must do is accept. Like the guests summoned to the divine wedding feast."

"Yes, but the invitation was not as open as it appeared. Guests wearing the incorrect apparel were turned away, and sent to hell. Would you do that to me?"

"To refuse to put on the correct apparel is insulting!" My voice was rising. "Especially when the host has provided it!"

Just then the moon rose, a great pale disk. Her rays bathed the observing platform in a silver pallor.

"Our guest," said More. "Or is she our hostess? Sometimes it is hard to be sure."

Just so, he turned my adamant warning into a pleasantry. I longed to shake him, shout louder. But he, who had heard and hearkened to the words of dead scholars and saints—what more could a living man do to capture his attention?

" 'He who is not with me is against me,' " I finally said. "The law will interpret it so."

"I hear you, Your Grace," said More. But had he truly?

We watched the eclipse begin, and could make out the great dark shadow creeping across the splotched face of the moon, higher now, and more lonely. The two lenses used together enabled us to see how very dark and irregular the features of Man in the Moon were.

"Of what do you suppose they are made?" More wondered, aloud. "Ashes? Or some substance we do not have on earth? Could they be liquid? No, then they would shimmer and we would see them sparkle. Could they be tarlike?" He sounded like an excited little boy.

Whatever they were, they were fading from sight as darkness fell upon them.

"Could there be anything living there?" I thought of the tales of moon creatures and the old pagan goddesses and Artemis and Diana. The moon seemed a sentient being, one so involved in our lives.

"God has seen to that."

God. Always such a surety with More.

"Aye. Although we will never know in what way."

"He has populated the earth with odd creatures enough," More said. "Enough for three lifetimes of study."

Should I say anything else? I had come to warn More, to advise him. I had tried to do so, and had been rebuffed. How many warnings was I obligated to give? Was I quit now? Could I enjoy the eclipse in peace?

"Thomas," I said, "my business tonight was serious. Deadly serious. I wish you to know that. If you have any questions—"

"I will ask them, Your Grace. Surely you can believe that."

"Then ask them!"

The compromised lunar disk was left on her own as we faced one another.

"I have none. I know the answers. Once one knows the answers, however much one dislikes them, then there are no more questions to ask."

"But *do* you know the answers?"

"Yes, Your Grace. I knew them before you came here. But I thank you for coming."

"As long as you understand."

"I understand," he insisted. "I understand."

The eclipse having ended, we made our way slowly down the slope to his house, dark now. Off to the right I saw a small building, and I asked, out of a sort of politeness, what it was.

"I call it the New Building," he said.

"But what is it used for?"

"All the things the Old Building had not room for," he answered.

"Private things?" I understood—or thought I did.

"Yes." He actually stopped, and framed his words carefully. "Private things."

I was to sleep in the upper chamber in the rear of the house. The bed had been fitted out with a feather mattress, and laid over with furs. I must confess that by the time I reached the chamber I was groggy and ready for sleep. I would have slept on a stone altar.

"I thank you, Thomas," I murmured. As soon as the door was shut, I staggered toward the bed, and fell upon it, neglecting to remove my clothes. I flung myself full length and passed into a deep sleep. I had meant to think upon Thomas and his obvious disregard of my warnings, but I thought of nothing at all.

Sometime in the middle of the night I awoke, as wide awake as if I had slept a fortnight. The little candle across the room jumped and danced. It had burned halfway down from where I had lighted it. Hours before? Moments? I had no sense of time.

I knew only that I could not sleep. A peculiar sort of energy flowed through me, and I knew I must be up. I swung my feet over the side of the bed, fished for my shoes. They were there, cold and hard, the left transposed with the right, so sleepy had I been upon retiring.

I padded across the room to take hold of the candle, use it to find a praying place. For I knew that was what I needed to do: to pray. I had not prayed in days. My soul was starved for it. I grasped the candle, held it aloft. Of course there was a devotional niche, complete with kneeler and pictures of the saints: the one essential in a Thomas More room.

But in passing over to it I saw a deep yellow light shining from outside the window. It came from somewhere on the grounds. Was it the cooks, lighting the day's fires? Yet it seemed too early. Then I remembered that More had let most of the servants go.

It was in the New Building. Could there be thieves? More had refused to tell me what purpose the New Building served. Had he secreted his jewels there? Perhaps he had kept more than he admitted.

No matter; thieves were there. I would not wake More; I would rather confound them myself.

I attired myself fully, then drew on my cloak. I crept down the darkened stairs and made my way to the great outer door which opened (I remembered) from the Great Hall to the outside.

Poor More. He had so little, had given up so much, and yet men sought to rob him. Anyone associated with court, no matter how remotely, was always assumed to have hidden riches.

The building was close now. I pressed at the door and was relieved to find that it swung open easily. I came inside and shut it.

Now. I was obviously within range of the robbers. The thought that I could confront them, frighten them away, somehow relieved my conscience. I had brought More to lowered circumstances (or had he brought himself?), and yet I could personally prevent their being lowered further. One somehow ransomed and redeemed the other.

Inside the building, it was icy cold—colder, even, than outside. That startled me, and I had to draw my mantle closer about me as I felt my way about. I could not ascertain where the light had come from, for all seemed to be dark within. Perhaps the thieves had extinguished their light.

I pressed my way past one door, taking care not to make it squeak on its hinges. Now I could see light, faint light. It originated around a corner.

I flattened myself against the wall and peered around it.

I expected robbers, filling their bags with More's reduced belongings. They would be laughing, flinging the things in, desecrating them, already spending the money in their heads.

But there was no intruder there. Only More himself, bare to the waist, kneeling on a pallet.

Over his shoulder was a whip. But no ordinary whip. I recognized it as the "discipline": a small metal ring with five chains suspended from it, each chain ending in a hook. As I watched, he beat himself with it, slowly, rhythmically, reciting all the while, "It is for You, Lord, for You. Let my imagination and my memory be effaced. For You, Lord, for You."

He rocked back and forth on his knees, thrashing himself and chanting.

His entire upper body was cut and bleeding. There were slashes all over his back. But they were superimposed on flesh that was already irritated and infected. Yellow pustules were scattered like the blooming of evil little flowerets all over his chest and back, and his whole skin was bright red. There was not an inch of unmarked skin on his upper trunk.

"Forgive me, Lord, that my sufferings do not approach Yours," he intoned. "I will increase them, so as to please You." Then he picked up the "discipline" again, and began to flog himself. He gasped with each fivefold lash, yet continued. Blood oozed from the new-created gashes down to his waist, where it dribbled to the floor.

"I cannot begin to appreciate Your sufferings, O Lord," he murmured. "This as yet feels like pleasure." He whipped himself until his shoulders were completely raw and laid open. "It is not enough!" he cried, flinging himself forward, prostrate upon the ground. "I cannot go the full length. Only give me strength."

There was no crucifix before him, yet he seemed to see it.

His hand—twitching now, but obedient to his will—reached out and grasped the "discipline" once more. He held it out at arm's length, then flicked it full in his face.

"As You wish, Lord, as You wish."

Blood spurted from his face, ran down onto his shoulders, where it traced an obscene pattern.

"I will give You more," he murmured, as though in a trance. The whip hit him full in the face again. I feared for his eyes. "More, O Jesus." Another lash. The blood was swelling now like a spring stream, running down his neck.

Suddenly he flung himself prostrate before his inner vision again. "Enough? But, O Lord, I would do so much more . . . give You so much more!"

He lay motionless for long moments, then eventually pulled himself to his knees.

"As You wish, Lord," he repeated, and crawled toward a dark garment lying nearby. He began pulling it on, and as he did so, he screamed in pain.

"As You will, Lord!"

He continued to draw it down. But it stopped at his waist, and was sleeveless. A hair shirt. I knew then what had caused the hideous, tormented redness of his delicate skin, and brought about the boils and infections. The ends of the horsehairs—tied, to be prickly and blunt—worked their way into the skin of the wearer within a few hours. Hair shirts were woven and constructed thus, to torment the flesh of the wearer.

Worn on top of fresh lashings and scourgings—what agony would it inflict? Too little for More and his torturing God, evidently.

Now he was fastening a linen shirt over his hair shirt. Did he wear the hair shirt always? Every day? For how long had he worn it? I would never know the answers to those questions, as More would never give them, and I could never ask them.

But I knew the answer to my own tormenting question. More would seek the full punishment of the law as yet another "discipline." And I would, perforce, be the one chosen to administer it.

I hated him in that moment—hated him for making me his scourge. That was all I had been all along: his scourge, his temptation, his test. I was not a man to him, but an abstract trial, a representation of one of his confounded Platonic ideas. He had never seen me at all, but only the symbol he had chosen to assign to me.

I despised him. He was a blind fool, taking living beings and recasting them in the image of his abstract honour.

Farewell, More, I bade him silently. May you enjoy the "discipline" you have chosen. Remember always that it is *your* discipline, not mine. For I would keep you with me, veil mine own eyes, imagine that you were as *I* would cast you in *my* own imagination. . . .

Before he could come upon me, I was out the door and into the free cold air, then back to my own chamber. When I awoke again it was mid-morning, and the sun was cheerful.

"Good morrow, Your Grace," said More, at breakfast. "I trust you slept well."

"Indeed," I said. "As well as you."

"Then did you pass the night calmly," he said. "For never have I slept a fairer sleep."

The smile was remote.

"May you sleep many another such," I replied.

LX

It was May Eve, and I lay at Oxford. I had come to inspect Wolsey's "Cardinal College," which of course had been abandoned upon his death. I was considering whether to rescue it and put it under royal sponsorship or to let it continue to languish. The Great Quadrangle, a beautiful cloister-courtyard, only half constructed, had suffered through four winters' ravages. It must be restored and finished soon, or it would be a complete loss.

But royal colleges took a great deal of money. My grandmother Margaret Beaufort had founded two at Oxford's young rival, Cambridge. To honour my reign, and to further the higher learning, I *should* found and support one, I knew. But the money! O, the money!

Now I had spent the day with the learned deans, hearing all the reasons why I should assume the responsibility for Wolsey's lost college. Bishop Fisher, Katherine's fierce partisan and holder of the chair of theology at the University, sought to speak with me and to persuade me. I refused to hear him. I would not speak to the man under the present circumstances. Oxford would soon be needing a new theologian for his chair! Was he aware of *that?*

In the small "withdrawing room" in the suite of rooms I occupied for this visit—courtesy of Wolsey, as these had been his quarters—I sat down with Cromwell. I had brought him with me for my own reasons, reasons he would soon find out.

A number of uncharacteristic settees were stationed about the room, draped with rich fabric and heaped with pillows. In contrast to this, the floors were old, worn stone, grey and cold. The windows were arched and high and filled with tracery. One had the impression of a parish church outfitted with a caliph's couches.

I stretched myself out on one of the settees. But how did one lounge regally? Half lying down seemed a sloppy way of presenting oneself. In any case, it did not lend itself to business. Therefore I sat straight up.

Cromwell looked at the bare table between us. "A shame," he said, shaking his head. "Wolsey would have had it heaped high with dainties. Fisher sends nothing."

"Except, perhaps, a message. This bare table proclaims his asceticism." The ugly scrubbed wood, with its mournful scars, looked at me in scorn. "We would not have accepted his gifts, in any wise. There is only one thing we wish of him. And that he refuses."

The Oath.

They had begun to administer the Oath shortly after my visit to More. The commissioners had gone out to towns and guild halls, to marketplaces and monasteries. Men and women had signed readily, taking their Oath as a pause between planting their fields and going to market. The most popular time was mid-morning, when they could gather and chat while waiting, over a cup of ale.

Only a very few so far had refused.

Thomas More.

Bishop John Fisher.

And a few lone monasteries.

Altogether, only a few score of men. A few score—out of three million!

Katherine and Mary had not been presented with the Oath yet. Undoubtedly they would also refuse. I had received letter after letter from Katherine, alternately admonishing me and crying for my love. They saddened me and mired me in guilt. Would she never leave off?

The Pope had finally heard and hearkened to her pleas. At long last, dragging himself out of some primordial sleep, he had pronounced sentence on the matrimonial case of Henry VIII of England and the Princess Dowager, relict of his late brother, Arthur: the dispensation was good, the marriage valid, and we were to return to one another immediately. Failure to comply would . . . would . . . he would do such dreadful things . . . would we be sorry . . . !

The tantrums of a tardy child.

The stupid fool, Clement. If he had given immediate judgment, on the heels of Wolsey's first request . . . would it have made a difference?

"Clement says he will make Bishop Fisher a Cardinal," said Cromwell, softly.

"What, in the wake of this refusal?" I said. "Then I'll send the head to Rome to receive its hat!"

"The executions will begin?"

"They must." But I would accept changes of heart at the last hour. In fact, I prayed for them.

"When?"

"After the parties have had a decent chance to clear their heads and change their minds. In the Tower, of course." And not the prettied-up part.

"How many months will you allow them?"

Why was he so precise, so pressing?

"A year and a day. Then I can never lament my haste."

"On the contrary, you are most lenient. Slow to anger, like the Almighty. The Princess Dowager, now—there's a one to try a man's patience. She dangles at Buckden as the bait for a rebellion. And Chapuys dangles her."

"She will be offered one last opportunity to co-operate. I have sent Brandon, with a delegation of commissioners, to take her the Oath. If she refuses, she becomes a prisoner, forfeit of all rights." I had thought it a suitably unpleasant assignment for Brandon.

He looked at me questioningly.

"You need not doubt me," I said. "I will not flinch." Everyone, it seemed, counted on my flinching. That was a mistake. Especially for those who staked their lives on it.

More, I knew, counted on my *not* flinching. Otherwise I would not be the ultimate "discipline" that he sought so ravenously.

"So it will be next summer until all is . . . tidied up?"

"Can you bear to wait that long?" Crum was so anxious that I show my power.

"The question is, can *you,* Your Majesty?"

"I would prefer that they repent, yes! So I will provide them with ample opportunity. And the leisure to consider their peril."

"The ninety and nine do not satisfy you. . . . Ah, you do take your title, Supreme Head of the Church, in earnest."

"Do not mock me." Of course I took it in earnest. "Cromwell," I said, turning to other matters, "there will never be another Wolsey. But surely it is time I recognized your position in a title that somewhat describes your function. Therefore I have decided to name you Principal Secretary. You know what that means."

"No, I do not."

"Then make of it what you will." It would be interesting to observe just how he wore the label, and into what sort of garment he fashioned it.

My sleep that night, on the hard, straw-stuffed pallet in Wolsey's old sleeping chamber, was light and restless. Therefore I knew not whether I slept or woke when, in the cold blue dawn, I heard voices. My ears perceived a faint melody, so faint it seemed almost to be a dream-fancy, floating light and clear, celestial. . . . Angels? I gave myself over to them, feeling myself borne upwards, lightly, arms outstretched. So this was death . . . and being brought into God's care. . . .

I awoke in full daylight, knowing that I did not belong yet on earth, reluctant to come back, to put on shoes and comb hair and see others.

As I stepped out into the dining chamber, a great tumult assaulted my ears. Looking out the window, I saw a throng of students in the streets below, wearing costumes and waving May branches.

May Day. It was May Day.

Shaking my head slowly, I turned to see a young student servitor spreading plates upon my table. He wore an outlandish antler-helmet on his head, and was covered in streaming ribbons of all colours.

"Blessed May to you, Your Majesty!" he said.

"Thank you. I had forgot."

"Then you did not hear the singing?"

Aye. I had heard singing. But—

"What singing?"

"The Carol to the May. 'Tis sung by choristers at the top of Magdalen Tower at dawn every May Day."

So the voices had been human, after all.

"I was not informed."

"I am heartily sorry, Your Grace." He truly seemed to mean it.

"These costumes," I said. "Do you wear them all day?"

"Oh, indeed! Even though they always get rained upon, or at the very least, we shiver in them. 'Tis all part of it. The legend has it that the Devil keeps his bargain still. The Devil is a reliable fellow."

Yes, he was. "How so?"

"Well, we generally prefer cider to beer, here in Oxfordshire. But a local beer brewer, he sold his soul to the Devil in exchange for a promise for a spell of nasty weather around May Day, to kill the apple blossoms. And so May Day is cold and damp, always."

"Always?"

"The Devil honours his promises."

"The Devil is a gentleman."

"Indeed, Your Grace! That's just the way to put it!"

LXI

Just after Michaelmas, when all the feasting was done and the last of the goose-carcasses were cleaned away, my son was married.

Henry Fitzroy was now fifteen and had fallen in love with his companion's sister, Mary Howard, Henry's two-years-younger sibling.

It would have been in vain to tell him to wait until the fancy passed. In vain, not because it would not have passed (as it most surely would have done), but because when the time came for him to marry, I could never have selected a more suitable bride than this daughter of the house of Howard. Therefore I gave my blessings to the nuptials and arranged that the wedding should take place at St. George's Chapel in Windsor.

It was not to be a state affair, even though Fitzroy's titles gave him formidable rank as a peer of England: Duke of Richmond and Somerset, Lord Warden of the Marches, Lord Lieutenant of Ireland, and Lord High Admiral of England, Wales, Ireland, Normandy, Gascony, and Aquitaine. It was not to be a state affair simply because to do such a thing, at the very time that the Oath of Succession was being administered, would be to focus undue attention upon yet another claimant to the succession. The issue was heated enough already when loyalties were pulled between two females, Mary and Elizabeth. Reminding everyone of a comely royal lad of marriageable age was not politic.

He *was* comely. I was proud of him, proud of his Tudor looks and his sensitivity and regal bearing.

And still another reason was that Anne did not care to be reminded of my living son, since she had not given me one of her own. That Bessie had was a continual insult to her.

It puzzled me then, why Anne had not. It was not for lack of coupling, or for lack of joy in our bed. Since I had returned from my "pilgrimage," there had been no more of that earlier trouble. Our bodies spoke even sometimes when our words could not bridge the gap between us—by that I mean the gap that separates each individual from any other. Nonetheless we were son-less.

The Princess Elizabeth was a year old now, thriving at Hatfield House, attended by her sister Mary, who insisted on referring to Anne as "Madam Pembroke" even now. She was as stubborn as Katherine. . . .

Katherine. As I selected my rings from an octagonal inlaid Spanish box, I thought of Katherine. She had refused the Oath, as I had expected. But her manner of doing so was to barricade herself in her rooms at Buckden and refuse to admit Brandon or to speak to him and his commissioners. He waited two days in her Great Hall for her to emerge so he could apprehend her and force her answer.

When he ascertained that she had a cook, provisions, and her confessor locked up with her, he knew she would not come out for six months, would perhaps even starve herself to death in there and call herself a martyr for it. Her confessor would give her last rites and send her soul right up to heaven. In disgust, he left, after dismissing the rest of her servants and carrying off her furniture. The townspeople reviled him and threatened his life even for that. An ugly mob, they surrounded the house and harassed my commissioners, waving their stupid pitchforks and hoes.

That was enough. I needed no Anne to urge me to end this childish, stubborn, and aggravating behaviour of Katherine's. Brandon could do nothing, but I was King. I ordered her removed immediately to the gloomy fortified manor of Kimbolton, and put under house arrest. Henceforth she would have two "keepers," Sir Edmund Bedingfield and Sir Edward Chamberlayn, loyal to me. She would live in total isolation, with no visitors and no correspondence permitted her. She was now politically dead.

But even there, she found a way to be contumacious. She refused to speak to anyone who did not address her as Queen. Since there were only fifteen who did—her confessor, her physician, her apothecary, her "master of the rooms," two grooms of the chamber, three maids of honour, and six menial servants—she shut herself up with them and would not set her foot beyond her own doorsill out into the "contaminated" parts of Kimbolton where her keepers and the staff lived. She would not eat food prepared in their kitchen, but set up her own little stove and made her own pitiful meals.

Alone in her extreme isolation, she willed things to be different than they were, as if by sheer force of mind she could control others. Faith can move mountains, so Scripture says. She believed that I was the mountain that could be moved by her faith.

I was running late. I must hurry. Which rings for today? There was the oval ruby I had acquired in France, that first time I had crossed there. The lapis lazuli, set in Arab filigree, a gift from Suleiman in token of my marriage to Anne (and repudiation of Katherine, thereby insulting Suleiman's enemy, Charles: *the enemy of my enemy is my friend*). The square-cut emerald that

Wolsey had given me to "celebrate" his Cardinal's hat. I never wore fewer than four rings. I chose the last, a garnet that had been mine in childhood. It barely passed the knuckle of my little finger now.

The attendant snapped the box shut, flashing the Spanish-Moorish design before my eyes once again: triangular ivory teeth biting into an ebony field, repeated over and over, until that carefully guarded, red and green geometric flowering center. Lush and abstract, guarded and yet sensual . . . the Levant. Katherine in her chamber within a suite within apartments within her royal prison. . . .

I must transfer the rings to the carved ivory box lately presented to me by the new French ambassador, Castillon, as his introductory gift. No more Spanish reminders.

Anne professed to be pleased that there was to be a secondary joining of her mother's house (Howard) to mine. She planned the wedding feast at Windsor and even took it upon herself to select a wedding gift of a pair of falcons, a peregrine and a tiercel, along with an able trainer.

"I love to plan wedding celebrations," she said, "especially since I could never plan my own."

Even after all this time, she still lamented her lack of a proper wedding and its celebration, although at the time she had professed not to care. Why do women set such store by them, as if nothing less makes a marriage real and seals it?

The wedding day in mid-October was as clear and sweet as the children getting married. All the colours were pure and bright and clean in the sky and in the autumnal trees and harvest. Gold and blue in earth and sky; gold and blue in their hair and eyes.

There are many ages at which one can marry, and I am not sure which is best, or brings more happiness. But I do know that youthful love, first love, early love, is the prettiest for others to watch.

The feast afterwards, to be held in the Great Hall of the royal apartments across from the chapel, was already laid and waiting as we lingered outside and talked in the lemony October light. I embraced Fitzroy and his new Duchess, feeling their slight bodies, young and elastic, under their formal velvets.

"May you find joy in one another," I said, "and live out your lives in rich contentment." Two perfect stages of life; what more could they be granted?

"Thank you, Father," said Henry. He had a thin and musical voice, one that was a vague echo of another such.

"I shall honour you, Your Majesty, as father and sovereign," his bride said. She sounded older than he; why is it often so with women? She was a plain thing, yet she evidently incited lust and love in young Henry.

454

"The feast awaits!" Anne was standing in the doorway, beckoning us. Yet it was unseemly for the Queen to call us like a farmer's wife summoning her field labourers.

The guests left the warm courtyard and came obediently into the Great Hall. They stared, entranced. Anne had transformed the Hall into a faerie-place of silver. Diana, the moon-goddess, had spun her web here.

The feast was all of silver—the central presentation was a silver-feathered swan swimming on a beaten silver mirror. The wedding cake was sprinkled with silver leaf, and was to be cut with a silver knife. All dined from silver plates and drank from silver goblets.

Afterward, the entertainments were hers as well. She had arranged an elaborate tableau about men doing obeisance at the temple of the virgin goddess, Diana, after the French style. All this would have been proper had she not elected to play the part of Diana herself.

Excusing herself from the dais and the royal table, she slipped away to change into her costume. Surrounding her in adoration upon the raised stage were men from the court: Francis Weston, William Brereton, Francis Bryan. Her brother George acted as Apollo, and Mark Smeaton, her favourite musician, provided the lute music, specially composed for the occasion. Diana, adored by worshipful attendants, blessed the marriage. A poem by Thomas Wyatt was read.

It made no sense. This was a wedding, not a celebration of virginity. It should have featured Hymen, the goddess of marriage, not a cold, chaste moon-goddess. There was no point to it at all, except to glorify Anne and hint that she reigned over a court of moonstruck, celibate youths. If it had not ended when it did, I would have ordered it stopped.

On the way back to York Place, I upbraided her. "The Queen does not participate in tableaux," I said. "It demeaned the celebrations."

"How so?" She sat up straight in the litter we were sharing. "That I would act, and costume myself? What greater honour could your *bastard*"—she paused before and after the word—"son have?"

"The honour of a discreet and proper stepmother."

Bessie would not comport herself in such a manner, I thought. Bessie had proved a loyal and long-suffering wife of the weak Tailboys. I knew, because Cromwell's spies had reported it, and also because I knew Bessie. I admired her in so many ways. She had not travelled from the North to attend the wedding, but had sent a gift of a pearl-encrusted gold goblet and cover. Gold from Bessie: she was not a silver-chaste woman, nor would she encourage it in others.

"You should be delighted that men find me attractive," Anne countered.

"Not nearly so attractive as you find it yourself," I snapped. "You are

Queen of England, and my wife, not Thomas Boleyn's daughter and a maid of honour at court, acting in tableaux, collecting beaux."

"Just because no men ever paid court to Katherine—"

"Your absurd rivalry with her shall *not* excuse this! Katherine was royal, and she knew how royalty should comport itself!"

"And I do not?" she flared, and held herself up like a cobra about to strike.

"Evidently not," I said.

Yet that night I sought her bed. I wanted her as seldom before. I wanted to tear away her silver-gossamer veil, penetrate to that guarded chamber of hers, violate her strange, solitary, private eroticism. Anne, Anne . . .

LXII

I needed to remember those silver moments when I faced the hard, ugly fact that Thomas More had spent the winter months of 1534–35 in the Tower, along with Bishop Fisher (confined shortly thereafter). They were lodged in the more "comfortable" parts of the Tower, not in the dungeons below, where a dozen or so recalcitrant monks languished in darkness and deep chill, chained and helpless.

Only three orders of monks had defied the Royal Supremacy and refused to take the Oath: the Franciscan Observants, a group of highly devout and visible "preaching" friars; the Carthusians, an order that stressed individual discipline and prayer, and was less a monastery than a collective group of hermits (this was the order that More had almost joined, naturally); and the Bridgettine order at Syon.

The Observants I had a special fondness for. Their main chapel at Greenwich was where I had first been married, to Katherine, and where both Mary and Elizabeth had been christened. I knew them to be good and holy men. But their order stressed preaching. It was here that I had been denounced as "Ahab" by the Friar Peto.

The Observants were vocal, and their preaching and pronouncements carried great weight not only in England, but also abroad. It was my duty to silence them, and silence them I did. In August, 1534, there were seven houses of Observants, with two hundred friars. By December there were none. By refusing to submit to the Royal Supremacy, they ceased to exist as an order in England. They were scattered and their houses closed. That was that.

The Carthusians were another matter. They insisted on obstructing the earthly agents of both God and their divinely appointed King. They fought, argued, and threw up annoying barriers in every way possible—like their heroine, Katherine. How alike they were! What similar spirit infused them!

Both of them met the same fate: imprisonment and isolation.

The Bridgettines, a "double" order of both monks and nuns, had only one house, at Syon, near Richmond. Richard Reynolds, their scholarly prior, was proving as stubborn as Katherine.

The rest of the realm had taken the Oath. Even More's household had taken it. My commissioners had returned from the North with their listings, and there were no names subscribed on the refusal list.

My rebellion had succeeded. My defiance of the Pope, of my false marriage with Katherine, had been accepted, sworn to as a law of the land. The astounding thing was not that it had been possible, but that there had been so few resisters. Doom-sayers and ill-wishers had predicted that Englishmen, the Pope, and Francis and Charles would never tolerate such an affront. Yet the Englishmen had acquiesced, the Pope had yet to order a Holy War against me, and for all that, Francis and Charles had yet to obey. A great company of "yets." In the meantime I reigned supreme, and honoured Anne as Queen, and forced others to do likewise.

I prayed daily that More and Fisher would repent and come to swear the Oath. They were not senseless men, and surely the Holy Spirit would talk with them, convince them.

Anne, however, seemed to hope the opposite. She harboured an especial rancour toward More, one I could never understand, as she had scarcely met him, and certainly he had never failed to be courteous and respectful toward her.

"He refused to attend my Coronation," she said spitefully, "and made up that insulting parable about losing his virginity by so doing." She rolled her eyes heavenward and pointed her hands together in a Gothic spire.

I laughed. "He is a man from another time," I said. "He is fifty-seven years old; when he was born, my grandfather was King. He thinks in those terms."

"I am pleased, then, that you have outgrown him. That world is *passé*."

"*Passé*. Always French with you, my courtesan!" I reached out to enfold her in my arms.

"But it *is passé*," she laughed, sliding away. "He pledges his troth to something that has died. Beautiful as it may be, it died. And *I* did not kill it!" She looked agitated.

We were in her winter sitting-parlor at Richmond. In Katherine's day, this very chamber had been hung with Biblical tapestries and fitted with prayer-niches. Now the windows were naked, giving out onto magnificent views of the frozen Thames below.

People were sporting on its surface. There were young lads with bones strapped to their shoes, sliding about, playing all sorts of games. There were others swatting stones back and forth with sticks. The figures all looked black, their sticks and legs making them appear as insects.

"I did not kill that world!" she repeated. "Any more than these gamesters killed summer."

"Yet you sport upon its surface, and that seems to be a desecration," I said. "To some."

"To More and his like!" She turned to me, her black eyes hard and gleaming. "You will not permit those slanderers to live?" she asked. "For if they live, they insult me daily by their existence."

"Unless they change, they will not live," I said. It was not a promise but a fact. One that I deplored and prayed would soften and give way to something else, something more . . . malleable.

"Good," she said. "I was afraid that a softened version of the Oath might yet be offered to them."

In the privacy of my midnight chamber I had framed a version of the Oath that encompassed only Parliament's enactment and left the Pope and his dispensation untouched. I had thought to offer it to More and Fisher. But I had never worded it to my own satisfaction. How could she know of it?

"There are no variations in the Oath," I insisted. This seemed to satisfy her—or did it?

"I know full well you love More!" she burst out. "And I know in what way, and in what manner! In an unnatural manner!"

"Unnatural?" Her cryptic allusions baffled me.

" 'Thou shalt not lie with mankind, as with womankind; it is abomination.' Leviticus, Chapter eighteen, verse twenty-two."

"Anne!" I cried. "This is unseemly! And where did you read the Old Testament?" I asked, irrelevently. Was her Latin that proficient?

"It is true, is it not?" She ignored my question. "You have 'lain down with him' in the meadows of your mind; sported and frolicked with him there, excluding all others. Craved his approval and love, sought it and cried for it? And now, even now, when he defies you and throws that love back in your face, you seek to mollify and placate him! Your darling must have a special Oath, handmade and tailored and tenderly fashioned by his lover— the King!"

"His lover is not me," I said.

"Pity!"

"His lover is pain, disguised as Christ." And he will wed her, with my executioner officiating as priest, I thought.

"Very allegorical," she sniffed. "But it fails to clarify just how you intend to rescue your beloved from the pit he has diggèd for himself, as the Bible puts it."

"There are only the regular steps by which to ascend. The Oath, and utter loyalty."

"No special hand extended from the King? In an allegorical sense?"

"You should know well of allegories! You stage enough of them—insipid, mincing things, but all the same. You as a goddess, surrounded by worshipping fops! Do you enjoy the fawning, the stylized, false verses and compliments? Fie, lady, I outgrew them by the time I was twenty!"

"By then you had been King three years. When I have been Queen three years, perhaps I shall follow suit."

"No, you shall follow suit now! Lent is soon approaching, and you will cease these 'entertainments' for the duration. Do you understand me, Madam?"

"Indeed." She managed to infuse the word with disdain.

More and more our times together were like this: acrimonious, full of rancour and mistrust, a collapsing of respect. Yet I continued to desire her and crave her presence; I knew not why. She vexed my soul, not comforted it.

During the next few months it became increasingly clear that the refusers of the Oath would have to stand trial. At the end of 1534, Parliament passed another act, the Act of Supremacy, acknowledging my title as Supreme Head on Earth of the Church of England and defining it as treason to "maliciously seek to deprive" me of any of my rightful titles. Now the men in the Tower would have to be judged on that aspect as well.

Bishop Fisher was calm throughout his imprisonment, never seeking any deliverance. The Pope made a belated gesture of support by naming him a Cardinal. But Fisher cared not. He was an old man, an extension, really, of my grandmother Beaufort, never comfortable in the world that had grown up around him since her death. From the beginning of my Great Matter (styled by some "the divorce"), he had taken a stand against me. In the formal hearing of the divorce case at Blackfriars, Warham had presented a list of signatures of all bishops supporting my cause, including Fisher's.

Fisher had risen in gaunt dignity and said, "That is not my hand or my seal." Warham had admitted that Fisher's signature had been "added," but only because it could be done in surety. Fisher grunted, "There is nothing more untrue, My Lord."

In the beginning there had been others against me—Warham himself, for example. But in the end, alone of all the clergy, Bishop John Fisher stood unconvinced and unswayed.

He was finally brought to trial on June 17, 1535, on a charge of high treason for depriving the King of one of his titles by denying that he was Supreme Head of the Church in England. He admitted that he did not accept me as Supreme Head, but sought to exonerate himself by denying that he had "maliciously" done so. But the verdict came in: guilty, and he should die.

The Carthusian priors of the houses of London, Beauvale (in Nottinghamshire), and Axholme (in Lincolnshire) were hauled up out of the Tower and made to stand trial. Along with them were three stubborn monks from the London house. They all refused, for the last time, to take the Oath. They all tried to say they had never intended their own private thoughts and opinions to be "malicious." But this failed to convince the examiners. They were sentenced to be hanged, then cut down alive and their entrails pulled out and burnt, and to be drawn and quartered, on May fourth. Reportedly they went to their deaths singing and with glad countenances, watching each of their fellows being torn limb from limb, absolutely undeterred.

Now there was no one left but More.

More must stand trial, and it must be a grand and public trial in the largest hall in the kingdom: Westminster Hall, where Coronation banquets were held. More was too monumental a public figure to command less.

First he had had several "pre-trials," or examinations. These examinations were led by Cromwell, Cranmer, Audley (who had replaced More as Chancellor), Brandon, and Thomas Boleyn. In all of them he maintained his "silence." I could report all the intricate reasonings he used, but I will not. The truth of the matter is that he based his case (clever lawyer that he was) upon legal hair-splitting—basically upon whether his silence was "malevolent" or not. It was the legal implications of silence that were on trial, not More himself.

His sophistry and legalisms did not impress his judges, and they found him guilty.

Once he saw that silence could do him no good (and that his judges had fathomed him true, in any case), he asked to make a statement. This request was granted.

"This indictment is grounded upon an act of Parliament directly repugnant to the laws of God and His Holy Church," he said. He went on to explain that no one portion of Christendom could make laws governing the Church in that particular land, if they ran counter to the laws in every other land. England could not declare herself above the laws binding other Christian countries. We—Parliament and I—claimed that we could. And there the argument ended.

I have restrained myself from describing More's trials and arguments in all their details, since the end was the end. It is torture to retrace each step and say where one action, one word, could have altered the outcome. His family came to visit him in the Tower and did their utmost to persuade him to sign the Oath, excuse himself, liberate himself.

In the Tower he spent his time writing. There were several books, some in Latin—*Of the Sorrow, Weariness, Fear and Prayer of Christ before his Capture* was the longest—and others in English: *A Dialogue of Comfort Against Tribulation; The Four Last Things.* The latter described the four things that a man on his deathbed must deal with: death, the Day of Judgment, the pains of Purgatory, and the eternal joys of heaven.

More examined the moment of death carefully and concluded that there was no "easy" death: "for if thou die no worse death, yet at the leastwise lying in thy bed, thy head shooting, thy back aching, thy veins beating, thine heart panting, thy throat rattling, thy flesh trembling, thy mouth gaping, thy nose sharping, thy legs cooling, thy fingers fumbling, thy breath shortening, all thy strength fainting, thy life vanishing, and thy death drawing on" was in store for you.

From his window in the Tower, More saw Richard Reynolds of Syon and the Carthusian monks being carted out of the Tower for their felons' execution at Tyburn. Reportedly he looked at them longingly and then said to his daughter Margaret (who continued to visit him and beg him to recant), "Lo, dost thou not see, Meg, that these blessed fathers be now as cheerfully going to their deaths as bridegrooms to their marriage?"

Then he berated himself for his "sinful" life. He was ever obsessed with his own sinfulness and even of the sorrow of the world at large and its purpose. He wrote:

> But if we get so weary of pain and grief that we perversely attempt to change this world, this place of labour and penance, into a joyful haven of rest, if we seek Heaven on earth, we cut ourselves off for ever from true happiness, and will drown ourselves in penance when it is too late to do any good, and in unbearable, unending tribulations as well.

More had at last embraced his dark side. When he closed the gate at Chelsea on his way to his first examination, he was said to have murmured, "I thank God, the field is won at last." He had turned his back on that quietude of Chelsea, on his wife and family, too, and thanked God that they would no longer be there to torment him, keeping him from becoming that monk who had first, in youth, served with the Carthusians as a novice. He never wished to see them again. That was what neither I, nor others, for a great long time, could comprehend.

He had said it clearly, himself, to Margaret, when she came to visit him in the Tower. "I assure thee, on my faith, my own good daughter, if it had not been for my wife and you that be my children, I would not have failed long ere this to have closed myself in as strait a room—and straiter, too."

Now he had passed the test, forsworn—albeit belatedly—the things of this world, and could pledge his vows in blood. Undoubtedly, to one of that mind, it was a great relief. He had not disappointed or betrayed himself to a lesser life.

The execution was fixed for July 6, 1535. He told his daughter, "It were a day very meet and convenient for me—Saint Thomas' Even." His assignation with eternity was neatly fitted in with the Church calendar, which seemed to soothe him.

How could I feel upon receiving this news? Like a father whose daughter has chosen to marry unwisely, yet is deliriously happy in the meanwhile? Should I rejoice with her, grieving in my heart? Or should I use my authority to forbid the match?

I knew no action I could take would prevent this marriage. It had been contracted since More's earliest days.

Yet I wanted him here with me, on earth!

Even had I tried to bring that about, he had already answered that to his satisfaction in a poem he wrote immediately after Cromwell visited him in the Tower and sought to convey my anguish and love.

> Aye, flattering Fortune, look thou never so fair,
> Nor never so pleasantly begin to smile,
> As though thou wouldst my ruin all repair,
> During my life thou shalt not me beguile!
> Trust I shall God to enter in a while
> His haven of Heaven, sure and uniform:
> Even after thy calm, look I for a storm.

So he longed always to be beyond any possible ties or recall to earthly matters.

LXIII

Fisher was executed on June twenty-second. His judges had pronounced the same sentence on him as that meted out to the Carthusian monks.

"I cannot imagine such a death," Anne had said, upon reading the sentence.

"It is the usual felon's death," I replied. "Have you never known of what it consists?" Every English child had witnessed executions. Tyburn, where commoners were executed, was a popular public excursion place. People took their food and blankets and forced their children to watch, "lest you fall likewise into crime." It was instructional. I had always thought it was a pity that hell was not equally observable.

"No. I have never watched an execution. Nor do I wish to." She was agitated.

"Perhaps you should. As Queen, you should know to what we condemn felons."

"It is the fire part I cannot bear!" she said. "To be burnt, to be touched by that evil, hot, licking, consuming thing—oh, they knew well what they did when they made hell a place of flames! I would never go there, never, never—"

"Then do not sin, my sweet." I smiled. The remedy was at hand. Those who did not wish to go to hell knew precisely what they should do to avoid it. It was all laid out.

"Spare Fisher!" she said. "Do not let the flames touch him. No one deserves that!"

"A signature on a paper would have prevented it."

"Even so . . ."

I had intended all along to commute his sentence, to allow him a painless beheading. But Anne's outburst puzzled me. It showed me yet another side of her.

"Have you long been troubled by this fear of fire?" I asked her.

"Always. Since I was a child, when once in my room a lighted piece of wood escaped from the fireplace. It landed on a stool nearby. It glowed and then subsided. I went to sleep watching it—and then awoke, suddenly, to a blaze. The horrible heat, the diabolical grin of the fire—'I fooled you, now I have you. . . .' " She shuddered. "And the crackling, the roasting . . ."

"Be at peace. Fisher shall not face that," I assured her.

Indeed, Fisher was led out onto a tidy scaffold at Tower Hill, just outside the Tower walls. He had always been ascetic and gaunt, but his fourteen months in the Tower had turned him into a "death's-head," as witnesses described him. He went to his death calmly and insisted on wearing his best shirt, as it was the garment with which he would enter Paradise.

That should have been that. But it was the beginning of a set of different challenges to my reign.

Fisher's severed head was parboiled, as was the custom, and set up on London Bridge. The midsummer weather was hot and stagnant; foul odours rose from the Thames, which sloshed back and forth in an enervated fashion. Fisher's head (minus its Cardinal's hat—that would have been too macabre a touch) should have rotted and turned into a horror. But it did not. Instead, it seemed to glow and become more lifelike every day. People began to gather on the bridge to pay homage to it, to tell it their troubles. . . .

To ask it to intercede for them.

Fisher was on the way to becoming a saint.

I ordered this ended. In the night my servants took down the head and threw it into the river.

Fisher, the incipient saint, was checked in his progress. But the weather, and the mood, continued ugly. There were pestilential vapours about, infecting the entire populace. It was best to do More now, and have the whole business finished. Then, that being done, I could go out on progress, ride out amongst the people, talk with them, soothe them. They needed me.

An unhappy languor had fallen over the court, as in one of those tales of enchantment wherein a witch has put everyone under a spell. Anne seemed particularly affected, alternately nervous and apathetic. Others moved about as though their brains had flown, or were held for ransom.

Then Anne told me her news, and that broke my spell.

"I am with child." Magic words. Words that called to action.

"Praised be God!" I exclaimed. All would be right: out of these present troubles and hideous upheavals, the original purpose of which I had all but forgotten, a Prince would come.

I clasped her to me, feeling her slender supple body, all encased in silk. "Praised be God."

More's execution was to be July sixth, a fortnight after Fisher's. I granted his daughter Margaret permission to witness the actual execution. He bequeathed her his hair shirt (yes, he had continued to wear it all through his captivity), and hearsay is that it has been preserved in the family as a relic to this day. He sent no message to his wife.

It was an oppressive summer day, not columbine-fresh as some can be, but lowering and heavy. The humours in the air hung waiting, malevolent.

Anne, in her characteristic, brave fashion, had attempted to mock it by staging a "Pope Julius" party in her apartments. She had had a number of boards painted up for the game that had been invented in the summer of 1529 featuring Pope Julius (he who had granted the original dispensation in 1503), with stops called Intrigue, Matrimony, War, and Divorce. She had set up tables with rounds to determine which players should be matched, culminating in a Master Board with a grand prize. The "tournament" was to begin directly after the summer dinner at ten in the morning and play until a Grand Master emerged.

All the windows of the Queen's apartments were opened, and servants stood by with fans to make artificial breezes. Rose-scented incense supplied the sweetness that was lacking in the reeking outside air. As we were at Greenwich, there was the blessing of some slight breezes, borne inland from the sea. It was undoubtedly worse in the other palaces.

The entire court was assembled for Anne's "tournament," from the Privy Council through the ladies-in-waiting. Crum was there, looking eager for the gambling; the Seymour brothers, Edward and Tom, back from a fruitless diplomatic mission in Paris; Norfolk, Anne's uncle; and . . . as I have said, everyone.

Anne, looking almost as yellow as her gown in the oppressive heat and her condition, flitted about explaining the rules of both the game and her tournament to everyone. At the tinkle of a bell, all began. I was seated at table with Thomas Audley, Richard Riche, the Solicitor-General, and Jane Seymour, Edward and Tom's younger sister, whom I had not seen before.

They were all people of velvet: Audley so yielding and cautious; Riche so smooth and pleasing; Mistress Seymour, so soft and comforting. They played according to character, and as a result I won the game easily, being the only one to play boldly and abrasively.

Pope Julius. It was a clever game, but belonged to simpler times. The truth was that Pope Julius was dead, and there had been three Popes since. My enemy, Pope Clement (or had he been my friend? Certainly I could never have had a more apathetic foe) was now dead, succeeded by a much more hardheaded gentleman, Alessandro Farnese, called Paul III. Rumour had it that Paul intended to implement what Clement had only threatened: a Holy War against me. The Roman Catholic Church was on the offensive at last, having gathered its forces after being stunned by the initial successes of Martin Luther. Pope Julius was simple to understand and manipulate; he made a fitting board game.

I was vaguely disappointed when the game ended, although it ended under my own aggressive bidding. I had enjoyed my partners, enjoyed especially Mistress Seymour and the way she held her cards and pushed her token about the board. I cannot explain why observing the hand and arm motions of a graceful woman should prove so appealing, like a ceremony of sorts, a dance.

The bell was rung; we must change tables. Outside I saw the heat waves reflected in the light coming in the windows, rising from the river.

Noon. More was being led out.

Going up the scaffold, he turned to the Lieutenant of the Tower. "I pray you, Master Lieutenant, see me safe up and, for my coming down, let me shift for myself."

"Now you come to this game with points already," explained Anne. "You may keep them, only demerits will subtract from the total score—"

He put his head down on the block and made a joke with the executioner. In the Tower he had not shaved, but had grown a long beard. He smoothed it neatly down and asked the headsman not to strike it, as "it has done no treason."

We played a second round. At my table were those who had already won—Cromwell, Norfolk, and Edward Seymour. This game was more difficult. My opponents did not hold back and kept strategies in their heads the entire time, not merely one or two plays, but contingency plans as well.

The air grew stifling. Sweat gathered about my neck, wilting my fair linen collar.

I had told More "not to use many words." Brief was best. Looking his last at the crowd gathered on Tower Hill, he asked them to pray for him, and to bear witness that he was suffering death in and for the faith of the Holy Catholic Church.

"You have overlooked this Intrigue point, Your Majesty," said Cromwell. "Now you must lose this round."

"Careless of me," I granted him.

More turned to the executioner, who was growing faint-hearted. "Pluck up thy spirits, man, and be not afraid to do thine office. My neck is very short. Take heed therefore thou strike not awry, for saving of thine honesty." A bungled stroke with the axe meant torture and humiliation.

"I have a turn here in reserve," said Seymour. "I have been saving it all the while."

"He is a deceptive knave," smiled Norfolk. "Thinking all the time, never showing his hand."

"I have two turns," I said. "One to cancel out yours." I shoved his Matrimony token off the board.

"You should be betting, Your Majesty," said Cromwell.

"I have no coins with which to do so," I replied. "And a man must always make good his debts."

"You know where to obtain that which you seek," he said. " 'Knock, and it shall be opened unto you.' "

His snide Scriptural quotes did not sit well on this fetid July day.

"I die the King's good servant, but God's first."

The cannon from the Tower sounded, carrying across the water, coming in through the open windows of our gaming room.

More was dead. His head was cut off.

"Your move, Your Majesty." The three at my table waited politely.

I made my move. I had known several rounds before what it would be. All the time I looked at Anne, walking between tables, overseeing her obscene card party of death.

It was obscene, and she was obscene, and my inordinate desire for her was likewise obscene.

It all stank as the polluted July Thames outside the windows. There was nothing fine about it.

Choking, I pushed back my chair and left the game room.

LXIV

I sat in a great crystal palace—or perhaps it was ice. I could not tell because I could not touch the pillars or the walls. They gleamed and shone like icicles. But there was no dripping, and I was not cold.

I was interviewing someone, only this was his palace, not mine. I wanted him as my servant, or counsellor. Yet it was he who seemed to be setting the rules and conditions. He was unusually articulate and self-possessed. I was frustrated because I knew I would not have him after all. I wished him to demonstrate his powers, but he seemed uninterested in doing so. Was it true, what they claimed for him? I wished to see, before I felt regret at not having him . . . or not serving him myself.

I asked. He laughed (a smug, hateful laugh) and waved a gloved hand. The walls crashed and turned to water, and bubbled up under the chair I was sitting in. I was carried away, spinning, my arms frantically clasping the chair arms, my legs on the rungs, carried down a dark watery chute. . . .

I awoke. The sound of water was a deluge around me. It was beating against the windows, and I could hear trickles. Somewhere it had found an entrance, had nosed open a little crack between stones or through a piece of loose mortar.

My mind cleared. Rain. There could be no rain tonight. It was impossible. The sky had been absolutely clear at sunset. The soaked fields had been granted respite. The crops would recover, and the harvest be normal. That was what the clear sky had promised.

The downpour, which had penetrated even into my sleeping mind, continued to soak the already waterlogged earth outside.

It has not stopped raining since More died, the common people were saying. On the night of July sixth it had begun to rain, and it had continued, intermittently, for the six weeks since. The vegetable crops had already been drowned, rotted. The grains—oats, barley, wheat—by far the most important, as yet were salvageable. But if they were lost!

Damn this rain! I leapt from my bed and went over to the window. It was not a sweet, soft rain. Ugly, hard thrusts of water were striking against the glass.

Henry Norris stirred on his pallet and rolled over. He no longer slept at the foot of my bed, as it was too close to the outer, waterlogged wall and invited mildew. Instead he had moved to an inside wall.

It was raining on More's head, which had turned black impaled on Tower Bridge (so they told me). At least it was not growing into an object of veneration and superstition like Fisher's. I myself had not seen it, nor did I intend to.

This whole business disgusted me, sickened me. Only let this summer be over, let a year's cycle come round, so that every vicissitude of weather (all normal, all normal) was not converted into an "omen" or a "judgment." This time next year there would be an heir to the throne; Anne's boy would be born. Then see how they would remember More—not at all! They were fickle, shallow creatures, the people. Anne's son would give them instant *lethe,* instant forgetfulness, on the subject of More, Fisher, the Oaths.

One thing cancelled out the other—did it not? There could be no gains without payments. And these things were my payment for Anne.

The rain hissed at me.

Do your worst, I dared it. *Do your worst, and I shall yet prevail.*

I badly needed to make a summer progress about the realm, to reassure my people and to take readings on their minds. Yet, because of Anne's pregnancy, I dared not risk her travelling, even in the comparative comfort of a litter, at this time; and I myself would stay with her, watching over her and taking care of her.

She was difficult during this pregnancy, hard to please. She had fancies, one of which was that as long as Katherine and Mary lived, she could not bear a living son. She needed music to soothe her, and therefore Mark Smeaton must be promoted to become her personal musician, for only his lute-playing "chased away the demons." She needed entertainments to amuse her, and therefore I brought the Oxford players to court, and bade them write and perform some "fantastical history of times past," so as to entertain the Queen.

They did so, writing a history of Dr. Faustus and performing it most grandiosely, with red-tinted smoke and demons dragging the damned Faustus down to hell. Anne was delighted with it and showed lively interest in the red smoke and sudden apparitions of the Devil, since she had attempted a similar effect in "Cardinal Wolsey Descending to Hell." Hell always interested people from an artistic standpoint.

She exhibited none of the behaviour I had come to expect from a pregnant woman: the happiness, the contentment, the interest in the coming child. She was restless and self-absorbed, with glittering, feverish eyes. Yet that was of no moment, as long as the child was healthy. Anne was like no other woman in the world; her pregnancy was as singular and disturbing as she herself.

The cursed rain kept up all through the remainder of the summer. There were occasional fair days, as if to tease us, like a beautiful woman who has no intention of yielding her favours but continues to make promises. The first grain crop was now ruined, and the flooding of the fields made it impossible for a second to be sown. This winter there would be hardship at the least and starvation at the worst.

The people had stepped up their visits to shrines, imploring Our Lady, Thomas à Becket, and all the others to hear them. The monasteries reaped a tidy profit from all this, as Crum never failed to remind me. I had allowed him to appoint inspectors to compile records of the assets and holdings of all the clergy in England, to be summarized in a *Valor Ecclesiasticus*. They had fanned out eagerly over the realm to get their information.

Crum liked the fact that offerings were pouring into the shrines' coffers all across the land. I found it ominous. More's head had disappeared from London Bridge. Who had taken it, and why? Were they setting up a shrine to him, too?

I had no one to confide these apprehensions to. Crum was not a man to tolerate apprehensions, either in himself or in others. He would discuss only the realities of a situation, not its intangibles. Cranmer, close as I was to him in many ways, had so many apprehensions himself that I did not wish to encourage them.

As for Anne, she had isolated herself completely in that court world where she whiled away her time. What happened beyond the doors of the Queen's apartments was not of the remotest interest to her. As her spirits alternated between high-pitched nervousness and melancholia, I let her suit herself. Anything to keep her happy and to protect the pregnancy. Except dancing, which was too vigorous. I forbade her to dance.

Thus it was with stunned disbelief that I beheld her dancing with great abandon late one evening after she had ostensibly retired. We had had supper together, a quiet one, as I had given leave in August to all the courtiers who wished to return home for visits. Court was always closed during the summer hunting season, and I was usually on progress. Anne had kept on the men in her retinue, but given the women leave to go. As we dined, I could hear Mark Smeaton playing plaintive love songs in the next room; the incessant rain muffled the actual melodies.

Anne picked at her food until, despite myself, I cautioned her to remember the child, to nourish him. How she hated admonishments! Yet I could not help myself. Was she trying to starve my son?

"I do! I do!" she argued. "I eat well—"

"You do not look it. You are thinner than ever. In how many months is the child to come?"

"Five."

I thought back to how Anne had looked the April before Elizabeth's birth. That was just after the Easter Eve fiasco. There had been panels in her skirts then. . . .

"Yes. I put the panels in before May Day."

She had read my thoughts. Astonished, I reacted to that rather than to what she said.

"But the second is not the same as the first," she continued. "Each child is different—my body is different." She suddenly began to eat. "Nonetheless I shall feed him. Yes, so he'll grow."

"Is he unnaturally small?" Another apprehension to add to the others. "What does your physician say?"

"Dr. Beechey?" She shrugged. "Oh, he is not concerned. . . ."

After the supper, she had bade me good night, as she said she was tired and wished to sleep early. All would have been well for her, but I wished to help her sleep by taking her a sleep-posset which I would prepare myself. So I returned to her apartments an hour hence, and found:

A wild dance going on, with Anne leaping about acrobatically, being handled and passed between men, including her brother. She lacked but a tail to complete the resemblance to a monkey. The men were leaping about, clapping, tapping, bowing; wearing fantastical hats and clicking castanets. The music was wild, thumping, and rhythmic. The tambourines, the heel-stamping, and the castanets drowned out the sound of the door opening. No one saw me—not for a full two minutes. Then George Boleyn, passing opposite, did. And stopped so suddenly that Francis Weston, following, ran into him.

"Your Majesty!" George cried, yanking off his feathered cap. The music died. Nonetheless Anne kept swirling, defiantly, for what seemed forever in the profound silence, with all eyes upon her, until she suddenly cast herself at my feet, executing a perfect touching of the floor.

Then she turned her face upward. "We imitate Spain," she said. "And the Spanish dances from Valencia." She waited for approval. I did not give it.

"Go," I said to the men. "All of you. Now."

Anne started to rise, but I put my hand on her head and kept her from standing. She was forced to remain thus while all her accomplices filed silently from the room. When the last one had left, I removed my hand.

"Why?" I asked.

Rising in that supple motion that had once so entranced me, she tossed her hair after the old manner.

"The Imperial ambassador had just presented me with a gift of Jerez—a drink." She indicated the small cask resting on her table. "The men sampled it, and it went to their heads." She laughed. "It is stronger even than red wine," she said. "Dangerous."

Her pretty lies. Always, the pretty lies. I could not help but admire them, as I admired proficiency in any art.

"Why did you lie about the child?" For she was not with child, I knew that now. She never had been.

"Because you wanted him so." Clever woman—none of the denials a less cunning pretender would have used. Admit it with grace, then turn the *reason* for the lie into something plausible and endearing. "I wanted so much to give you a son. Perhaps in saying I was with child, I believed I could make it be true, could create the event—"

Excellent. Falsehood made a virtue. "I could have gone on progress, but you kept me with you. If ever I needed to show myself about the realm, it was now. Yet you kept me here, for a lie. You deceived me in public, and you deceived me in private. While it was raining outside and the people were murmuring against me, growing the only crops possible under the circumstances, rebellion and treason, you danced with your men."

I stepped back from her. I did not want to touch her. "Lies. You are nothing but lies. There is no truth in you. Nay, do not touch me!" She had reached out for me. My flesh actually shrank from her.

"Please—" she cried, stretching out her hand in supplication.

"You are foul," I said, feeling myself in an evil presence. The sensation was overwhelming, and I felt such revulsion I could think only of fleeing. The presence was not only evil but angry and powerful.

She threw back her head and laughed: a guttural, wolfish laugh.

I turned and quickly left her, before she could spring and—do what? I knew not.

As I passed through the last of her chambers, I noticed her costumed guards standing at attention on both sides of the great double doors that separated her quarters from the rest of the palace. They were impassive, muscular things, clutching their halberds and staring ahead with empty eyes. For an instant I wondered if they were enthralled by their Queen, and whether, if I bade them bind her, they would obey me or their mistress. . . . Those blank, emotionless eyes . . . nay, it was but a fancy, a fancy.

Within my own quarters, I made quickly for my inmost chamber, the one forbidden to everyone. Here I had always found a refuge. Tonight it felt close and pressing, like a coffin. I felt not as though I had barely escaped something, but as though instead I were trapped by it.

In my ears I could still hear Anne's ugly laugh, and the powerful feeling of revulsion swept over me once more, making my flesh tingle. All at once the feeling was familiar; I had felt it many times before. It had clamoured for my attention, striving to warn me for a long time.

It had been there from the moment I had heard her name, that night in France—that apparition of black and white on the dark plain, that feeling of nameless dread and malevolence about me. . . . To name something is to call it into being, evoke a presence.

I had felt it in the garden that first time at Hever when I had sought her out by the willows, and we had come face to face. My arms and neck had prickled in an eerie, disturbing way, and I had thought, fleetingly, of supernatural things, and felt unreasoning fear.

Revulsion in the presence of evil.

That was the earmark of evil: a warning that things are not as they seem, that contact has been made with something malevolent and harmful. It causes healthy people to flee from it, as to stay in its presence is dangerous. It is a protective grace God gives us: just as He causes tainted meat to taste foul, so He makes tainted people "feel" foul, although they may be passing pleasant to the other senses, especially that of sight.

It was not I alone who had perceived it. The people as a whole had been repulsed by Anne. Now the sullen refusal of the crowds to cheer at her Coronation, the mob of women who had attacked her at the boathouse, the country people who spat at her as she rode past, the fact that even her uncle Norfolk referred to her as "the Great Whore" . . . all showed the truth. The truth to which I had been so blind.

But then, it is in the nature of evil to confuse us; that is one of its weapons.

I sank down on a window bench, only to leap up. The oaken bench, with an intricately carved lid, had vines and branches entwining the initials *H.–A.:* Henry and Anne. Mad with love, I had ordered dozens of things carved with those initials. They were now everywhere—from furniture in my inner sanctum of privacy to the gigantic choir screen in the chapel at Cambridge. *H.–A.* flaunted itself all over England.

Revulsion is one proof of evil. But the foremost one, the *sine qua non,* is lies. Lies emanate from evil just as heat radiates from a fire. "Father of Lies" is Satan's oldest and most descriptive name. He delights in lies, he is an artist of lies, he constructs the most subtle and delicate lies and admires his handiwork. He lies even when the truth might serve him better, because he prizes lies for their own sake. His pride in his lies means he often betrays his presence this way.

Lies for their own sake, even when the truth might serve better purpose.

Of what purpose was Anne's lie about the pregnancy? The truth was bound to undo her, as it could not be hidden longer than a few weeks. It had weakened her cause, not strengthened it.

Disguises, covertness, hiding—all are watered-down versions of lies. Anne and her masques, her make-believe . . .

What other signs were there? I felt confusion, a great confusion and despair coming over me. I could barely think, or order my mind; it was as though a stick were stirring mud up from the bottom of my brain, clouding all my thoughts. With a great effort of will I fought against it. Other signs . . . ?

Pride. Satan's pride, his desire for power and conquest. Anne made "conquests" of people. Those captive people in her chamber tonight, dancing as if in a trance . . . nay, not *people,* she made conquests of *men;* she had no use for women, nor they for her. She kept these men-creatures in literal thrall to her . . . as she had done me, had done *me.* . . .

I had performed as one under a spell, had turned against my oldest supporters and strongest beliefs. My erstwhile friends had become my enemies —the Pope, Wolsey, Warham, More, the people themselves. I was divided from my own family, cut off from my daughter, excommunicated from the Church.

I was damned. And all for love of Anne.

I had severed More's head . . . for Anne. I had tortured and executed monks . . . for Anne. I had taken unto myself a servant, Cromwell, who sometimes seemed malevolent himself and who urged total destruction of the monasteries. Something in me had withstood his evil suggestions, until now. Yet not completely; I had given way to his "commissioners" and "inventory-men" who were even now visiting the religious holdings. . . .

Satan seeks to destroy. Through me, Anne had destroyed much.

Satan is a murderer. Jesus said so. *He was a murderer from the beginning.*

From the very beginning: Anne had cursed Wolsey, and he had fallen from power and died mysteriously. I had thought of poison, but self-administered.

How blind I had been!

Warham had suddenly died, just when Anne needed him to.

Percy, who had abandoned her under duress from his father and Wolsey, had been unable to perform with his wife, and was now dying of an unspecified wasting disease.

My sister Mary had openly criticized my passion for Anne and supported Katherine, had refused to attend Anne's coronation. Mary had become mysteriously "ill," wasting away and dying at the age of thirty-five.

Someone had tried to poison Bishop Fisher at a dinner at his home. Two servants had died, but Fisher, though ill, had survived. Survived, to be more surely destroyed through me, for denouncing the lies, the forged signature. . . . *Under your correction, My Lord, there is no thing more untrue.*

My gut contracted. I felt ill myself—poisoned. Could it be?

Yes, she had struck at me, too. The mysterious leg-ulcer, appearing from nowhere, disappearing on the instant that I had done that which Anne wished —humiliated Mary, sent her to serve Princess Elizabeth, turned her home over to Anne's precious brother George . . . her *creature*.

My impotence . . . had it been a curse from her, or just the natural revulsion of my flesh from joining itself to hers, even though I knew not why? But she had overcome it, lifted it away, so as to bind me more closely to herself.

I had begun dying, both in body and certainly in spirit. Like Fisher, I was not an easy victim, but the decline had begun. Anne's slender little hands were guiding me on the sloping path leading to the grave.

Her hands!

I was violently ill; vomit rushed up into my mouth and I spat it into the basin on my sideboard.

Anne's sixth finger.

She had a sixth finger on her left hand, a clawlike nub that branched off from her little finger. She wore long sleeves to cover it and was skilful past reason at concealing it. I had only glimpsed it once or twice, and such was her magic, and my resulting blindness and confusion in her presence, that I saw it, but did not see it.

A witch's mark.

I was sick again, vomiting up green bile, bile that dotted the sides of the basin in mocking imitation of the emeralds thereon.

She could read my thoughts. Even now, she knew what I was thinking. I remembered her knowledge of my substitute Oath for More, one I had never committed to paper.

No. Her powers were not that strong, they could not penetrate even here. I was safe as long as I was not in her actual presence.

Yet the confusion, the roar in my head, persisted. She could stir my thoughts, muddy them from afar, but not control or read them.

She must be contained. I would order her apartments guarded. And then take myself away, far away out into the country, where my thoughts could run free and clean once again, and I could grow strong and plan what I must do.

I would give orders. In the morning. When it grew light.

LXV

I waited for that light with a fervency I thought I had lost forever. It belonged to childhood, to that time when the dark was an enemy, and only the light was friendly. A daytime moon was called a children's moon because we preferred seeing it in the light. . . .

Dawn came and released me. In the clear light my revelations about Anne did not seem absurd, as is usually the case the next morning. Instead they seemed even more obvious and certain.

Anne was a witch. She was tainted with evil and practised evil, nurtured evil and harnessed it for her own worldly advancement.

Last night was her time. This morning was mine. And before night fell again, I must be far away.

I had not hunted in a year. The season for stag and roe, my favourite game, had opened while Anne's "pregnancy" kept me close at hand. I would go hunting, have clean sport in the daylight.

The nearest forest where such game abounded was the Savernake in Wiltshire, three long days' ride west of London. Sir John Seymour, my old companion-at-arms, had retired to his manor there several years ago, and was warden of the royal hunting preserve at Savernake.

I would go there, pass some days at Wolf Hall, and wrestle with the terrifying revelations that had been thrust upon me. I would go alone. There were no companions whose company I wished. Nay, I needed one, for safety's sake. Someone I loved, who was quiet. I would ask . . .

I heard rustling outside my door. I had not slept in my own bed—indeed, had not slept at all—and Henry Norris was searching for me. Henry Norris would be the one. Discreet. Silent. Committed to me.

I opened my door to him. "Make yourself ready," I said briskly. "I leave today to hunt in the West Country, and I wish you to accompany me." To his surprised expression, I said, "It is for a few days only."

I must give no hint of haste, or of fleeing. Yet Anne must be contained, prevented from stirring. I knew not what to do with her, or what was required. I could not think. I was numb with what I now knew. It changed everything, but now it was I who must wear a mask. I needed time, time to think and recover myself and, yes, time to grieve. I was bereaved. I had lost a wife, and my own innocence.

I rode in silence to the West. The setting sun warmed and consoled me, drawing me toward a resting place. I was tired, and longed for some respite.

That first night, we stopped near Wokingham. The brothers of Reading Abbey were gracious (unlike those of St. Osweth's!). We were given quarters that were snug and comfortable and told that we could join them for Compline in their chapel. We did so, and it was with profound relief that I joined in the prayers. They asked me to lead them, but I declined. I was in no spiritual condition to lead others in prayer.

Night had fallen in the small priory. The monks filed away, silently, to bed. The Prior, Richard Frost, motioned us to follow him, and at our quarters he blessed us. Then, after lighting our candles, he bowed and was gone.

A single candle on a bare table. That was my light, and I lay down on the cot where I would spend the night, and pulled the rough wool blanket over me.

Cromwell said monks were evil, and that all small priories were filled with corruption, worse than St. Osweth's. Yet this one was holy and well run. I thanked God for it, even if it were an exception, for my soul ached. I cried that night, cried for Anne and myself. I had loved her, and been wrong.

❧ ❦

We reached Wolf Hall late on the third afternoon, after passing through a small portion of the Savernake forest. It was a woodland forest, not as dense as one would imagine; not solid trees, but broken with open spaces, coppices, and hedgerows. Wolf Hall, situated on a hill like an island in the midst of a sea of green leaves, was a small, half-timbered manor house.

The most striking feature of the holdings was a gigantic barn, with an enormous dovecote attached to it. It dwarfed the manor house and was silhouetted by the rays of the setting sun.

Edward Seymour met us, with pursed lips and proper manner. He reminded me, uncannily, of Bishop Fisher. Both were thin, ascetic, and controlled. Both had searching, myopic eyes. Both said less than they thought.

"We welcome you," he said. "We are overwhelmed with the honour." He ordered our horses taken, then motioned us inside. We stood in a dark receiving room, built long ago to accommodate knights in bulky armour.

"My father is not well," he said. "In the last year, he has become . . . let me be frank. He has become a child."

"This is common," murmured Norris. "It happened to my mother. It was . . . painful."

"It is pitiful," agreed Edward. "My heart cries out whenever I see him. I keep thinking it is something he can control, something he could change if he wished. My father is gone, and in his place sits an infant, an imbecile. My mind knows he cannot help it, but my heart does not. I have consulted with my priest—"

"A local one?"

"Aye. One who has known us always. And he says that sometimes God changes us back to children before He calls us home. But that makes no sense. God is a God of creation, not of destruction. I cannot understand."

"Nor I," I said. God had let me wed a witch, and given me a child by her. It was not as simple as depicted. God was more perverse, and the Devil stronger.

"You will see him at supper," said Edward. "You will see him as he is now, and you will remember him as he was when you knew him."

How much more pain and change could I stand?

The Great Hall was really only a large room, with a double row of windows and no upper gallery. It was evidently quite ancient, from a time when all things were smaller. Once the Savernake Forest had been deep and dark and haunted, and men had taken refuge here in a Seymour's—a St. Maur's, as they had originally been called—hall.

Now it was properly fitted out with long tables, and the rough walls had been plastered over, whited, and hung with shields and ceremonial swords in a decorative pattern.

There were only a few of us to dine, that September twilight; and we were clustered up around the head of one table. I was seated in the place of honour, at the right hand of the host. They led him in, Edward steering his right elbow, Thomas his left. They seated him kindly.

He did not look different. He was the same John Seymour who had fought with me in France, had shared my dining table. His features were yet intact, his eyes the very same. Outwardly, all is as it should be; therefore the rest is preserved as well. So we think.

His blue eyes rested on me. They looked at my hair, my face, my costume.

"Who is this?" he asked querulously.

"It is the King, Father," said Edward. "He has come to hunt with us."

"The King?"

He had known me, joked with me, ridden with me.

"King Henry. Henry the Eighth."

He nodded, but there was no understanding in his eyes. I wanted to say, *Remember the Battle of the Spurs, you rode right behind the French that day. Remember how they ran!*

He smiled, an idiot's smile. It was all gone. But no, it could not be. Behind that face, it was there yet. He lived, he nodded, he ate—how could Sir John be vanished? He was there yet, we just did not know how to call him forth.

"Oh, 'twas merry!" he said. "Merry, merry . . . no one's merry. Not now." He pushed his spoon about his plate.

An infant. He had become an infant; his clock had run backward. But it was against nature. Either we were killed or we expired in weakness. We did not turn back into infants.

"Now, Father." A gentle voice, and two hands caressing him, arranging his plate. The vegetables—carrots and parsnips—separated from the mutton. He smiled and patted her hand.

I looked to see who this was. At first I could discern nothing beyond the dull brown costume of a maidservant with a white headdress. I caught her hand.

"You are kind, mistress," I said. She was so unobtrusive, yet so competent. She pulled back from me, not demurely, but in insult.

"It is hardly a kindness to minister to one's own father," she said, extricating herself from my grasp.

"Jane?" I asked, but she was gone.

"The French are foul," said Sir John. "They lie in wait for us. They have not improved. But the Pope is worse. This new one . . . he is much harder than Clement." He shook his head, seemingly all alert and involved in politics, as he once had been. "They say he sucks his toes." He cackled, fiendishly.

Edward and Thomas continued eating.

"They say he sucks his toes!" insisted Sir John, so loudly that the ancient timbers above us absorbed it. "And furthermore, the north tower needs repair!"

As soon as was decently possible, I left the hall. Servants got Sir John to bed, and I sought mine. The bed was narrow, hard, and musty. Morning Mass in the nearby parish church was at six. I would attend. Meanwhile I fell asleep with my prayers—for Sir John, for Anne, for myself.

We all attended Mass—the entire Seymour household, save Sir John. It was quick and unembellished. The priest mumbling his Latin was as colourless as the grey stones surrounding him. He must have served his entire religious life here, shuffling back and forth between the little altar and his living quarters, with never a surprise or challenge. Just to continue functioning in such a setting made him a hero, a silent soldier of Christ.

Emerging from the little church, I turned to Jane, Edward's younger sister. She was paler than ever in the wan early light.

"You serve your father well," I said to her. "It is a thankless task, and one you perform with love." I could not tell her how distressing I had found it that Sir John was no longer himself.

"It is not thankless," she said. Her voice was familiar. It had a slight accent, or catch. "He thanks me for it. And it is good to be able to repay the things he once did for me, as a child. Few children are given that privilege."

Privilege? To wipe the slobber of a dribbling jaw, to cut meat for a grown man?

"For how long has he been . . . not himself?"

"For at least two years. When I first went to court he was himself. But by my first leave—"

"You were at court before this year? Did you ever—?" The delicate question was asked.

"Yes. I served Princess Katherine, in her last days at court." Her smooth voice showed no sign of hesitation at naming Katherine. She was no turncoat, no disavower. There was no shame in having served Katherine.

"My brother called me back to court later. I have served the Queen since before the Coronation. But . . . it would have been better if I had remained here, with Father."

"Why so?"

"He needs me." A slight breeze blew at her, lifting her skirts and teasing her headdress. It should puff colour into her cheeks. She was far too pale. She laughed and pulled her filmy headdress back.

Her motion . . . the laugh . . . her slightly accented voice . . . I knew her: the girl in the antechamber before Anne's Coronation—that strange, moonlit girl.

"You are a loyal daughter," I said. Sir John was blessed. Would Mary have done the same for me? What of Elizabeth, half witch as she was?

"Not loyal enough," she said. "For every morning, and every night, I pray for him to be restored to his former self. I cannot love him as he is. I have tried, but I cannot. I want my father back; I cannot accept this shell!"

"Yet you minister to him," I said in wonder. "Hold him, and cut his meat."

"And wish he were something other than he is," she said. "What sort of love is that?"

In the days that followed I hunted much, and we dined on buck, roe, hare, or hart every evening. On September seventh, the priest said a special Mass for the Princess Elizabeth's second birthday, and all prayed for her long life and health. Only two years ago things had stood so differently. I had believed in

Anne, and old Sir John had been himself. Now Sir John drooled and clapped his hands when the priest pronounced the benediction.

And what did Anne do? I did not wish to know.

Jane ran the entire household, I came to see. Not only did she soothe Sir John and coddle him, but she oversaw the servants, tended the beehives, supervised the dairy cows, and sorted the linen, folding it neatly and laying it away. She clipped herbs and hung them to dry in the hot, dark rafters of the old barn, and when they were ready, she slipped them in with the bleached and folded clothing. She did all this as silently and silkily as a moonbeam, making it look simple and effortless.

I was drawn to her, for in her presence I felt whole and calm—two things I had not felt since first beholding Anne. In her curious, milky way, she was an antidote to the poison Anne administered.

I sought her out every day, but she was elusive and difficult to detain. Her tasks called . . . Sir John needed her . . . the wind was tugging at the linens stretched out on the grass to dry . . . the cat was up a tree and mewing. . . .

At last I found her one afternoon tending the beehives. Sir John had a small apiary, set at the nether end of the orchard, and Jane was thrusting a smoking torch near one hive. She wore great thick leather gloves, and was swathed in white veiling—a strange echo of a bridal costume. She was humming to the bees, singing them a lullaby. I stood by the side of a pear tree and watched the curious ceremony, for it was passing strange. The humming inside the hive had ceased, as surely as if she had cast a spell over the insects. Gently she lifted up the lid over the tray inside, and took it out. It was laden with wax combs and dripping with honey: the bees had performed well. She replaced it with an empty wooden tray and spoke softly to the bees.

"I thank you for your honey," she said. "I am so sorry to disturb you. I trust you may use this new tray for your winter storage."

She turned to the next hive, her white veiling billowing out beside her, her smoke-torch giving off grey clouds which lulled the bees to sleep.

She was purity, and innocence. Just when I had despaired of such and believed that evil had all things in its grip, Jane was here, whole and uncontaminated, white and immaculate and simple.

꿹 꿹

The days passed swiftly—too swiftly. Sir John had kept a fine kennel of hounds: greyhounds for hunting the roebucks and stags; harriers for weasels, squirrels, and hares; mastiffs for the pests like polecats and stoats. It was soothing to ride out in the yellow mid-morning and pursue the quarry.

So straightforward and simple; so obvious who was the hunter and who the hunted. Even the kills were clean—no confessions, no motivations, no guilt. Then, afterwards, a fine dinner. Impossible to be afraid, to think of anything other than the moment at hand, of the bow and arrow and one's aim.

There were no messages for me during those amberlike autumn days, nor did I send any. I wanted nothing but the slow reassurance of each sunrise and each self-sustaining day, while I gradually accustomed myself to what I now knew about Anne. Strange how quickly one can become accustomed to the unthinkable, once the first horror and shock are past.

By the time my last day of hunting was over, and the beaters were heaping up the piles of game, sorting them into lots for skinning and eviscerating, it seemed that I had always known Anne was a witch, infused with the Devil, had always felt and feared her destructive power over me and those I loved or needed. She had done her worst to Wolsey and More, to my sister Mary, and now she would turn to Katherine, my daughter Mary, Fitzroy . . . and me as well. Perhaps even . . . Mary Boleyn's child Catherine? Anyone she suspected might be a child or a love of mine, she could strike against.

What would I find when I returned? Who would be "ill"? Chapuys had spoken of poison, and I had scoffed at him, thought it another transparent ploy to end Katherine and Mary's political exile. Katherine's insistence on preparing her own food—perhaps it had saved her life until now. What was it Anne had said of Katherine? "I am her death, as she is mine." *I am her death. . . .* Yes, she meant to be.

But to what end were all these deaths? Was the extinction of life, any life, the goal? Or was it more precise than that? Only certain lives?

The halcyon days at Wolf Hall must close, and I must return to London, to Greenwich, where Anne was waiting. I must dispose of her somehow, and make it so that she was utterly and completely stripped of all power, and all opportunities for power.

The ride back showed me, achingly and clearly, what it meant to discover that I had imbued hundreds of inanimate objects with meaning. On my flight to Wolf Hall, I had been in such shock and confusion that I had not seen anything around me. Now, calmer, I saw everything.

The great round tower of Windsor came into view. Windsor, where on an autumn day like today I had made Anne a Marquess. My pride, my joy in her that day, all echoed back, mockingly, from the old stones there.

The greyhounds, bounding ahead of us . . . Anne's greyhound, Urian, had killed a cow on a hunting progress once. (Urian! One of Satan's minions! She had even named her dog that, and I had been too blind to see what it betokened.) I had recompensed the farmer, so besotted with love, I remembered, that I counted it a privilege.

A small wayside shrine, with a Madonna in yellow-painted robes. Yellow, that day at Hampton Court, Anne's gown, and the flowers.

Would an object never be just an object again, a building merely a building, a colour purely a colour, rather than a red-hot nail of memory? If only things would restore themselves to that, half the pain would be gone.

LXVI

We returned quietly, and I made no announcement to the Queen's Chamberlain. The only person I wished to see, and straightway, was Cromwell. Cromwell, and possibly Cranmer. But Cromwell first.

We conferred in his town house in London. It was located next door to the house of the Augustine Friars (soon to be disbanded) and conveniently close to York Place. Unlike anything of Wolsey's, it was small and unostentatious. Cromwell never entertained "in state"; the idea of his hosting banquets for ambassadors and princes was outlandish. He was known to set a good table, and his private guests enjoyed tasty dishes and engaging conversation—much as More's had done—but on an intimate scale.

More. The remembrance of More gripped me so painfully I ached. I let it wash over me, because then it would recede. Otherwise it would never, ever abate. I knew that, but the attacks of guilt and sadness were debilitating.

We were seated in Cromwell's day chamber, a pleasant little room with a view out to his walled orchard. The apples were hanging heavy on some three or four trees, the leaves around them turning yellow. The other trees, the pears and cherries, had already been plucked bare.

"A fine crop of pears this year," said Cromwell, once again picking up my own unspoken thoughts. "The warm, clear May when they flowered, followed by all the rain, was just what a pear tree wants."

A good thing that something wanted More and Fisher's wretched rain and storms. Certainly the grain crops hadn't, nor had the people.

"Try some of its elixir," said Cromwell, handing me a small silver cup of perry—a fermented drink made from pears. Saluting one another, we sipped. The liquid was smooth and delicate.

"Yes, the rain did them well."

He put down his cup and looked at me, waiting, his black eyes deep and understanding.

"Crum, I have been hunting in the West for the past fortnight." I knew he knew that—undoubtedly one of his spies had found his way to Wolf Hall —but it was courteous to volunteer it.

He smiled. "And was the hunting good?"

"Indeed. Hares, stag, roe—we dined to bursting on game every night. I had forgotten how very much I enjoy being a hunter. You hunt, do you not, Crum?"

"With hawks, yes."

"I'm told you have a fine collection of hawks. Where are your mews?" Not here in London, surely.

"In Stepney."

"We must hawk together soon."

"I would be pleased."

Pause. Enough pleasantries. "We must hawk together indoors first. There is one who flies at too high a pitch, one who never should have been empowered to fly at all—one who must be brought down and sent away," I said. "Her feathers must be plucked, and she must be sent away, out of the royal mews."

Was there the smallest hint of a twitch in his lip, a suppressed smile? "The Queen does fly high," he said, slowly but boldly.

"It is in my power to lower her as surely as I raised her up. I would be rid of her, Crum, I would be rid of her. She is no wife to me." More than that I would not say; it was not meet. Crum should be privy only to my conclusion, not the reasons behind it.

"You would send her away, or un-wife her? Which is your wish?"

"To un-wife her. That, above all!"

Crum stood up—with my leave—and began to walk a bit. Up and down, up and down, upon the fine polished wood floor of his chamber. He stood by the window and placed his fingertips squarely on a large globe he had mounted on carved legs, and twirled it. The world spun, a glossy pattern of coloured countries and seas.

"If there is a fault with the marriage that invalidates it, the world will consider the Princess Dowager vindicated and restored to her rightful place."

Katherine. Here in London she seemed nonexistent, vanished into the mists of the fens. Certainly she had ceased to exist for me. But to the Emperor and the Pope, all of England was the same, London no less remote than Kimbolton.

"You will have to take Katherine back," Crum said, spinning the globe again. It creaked on its axis. "It is unfortunate that Your Majesty's surplus wife is still about."

All that to float up to the surface again, like a corpse three days in the water . . . no, I could not endure it. But Anne, the witch . . . I could not endure that, either, as she meant to kill me.

"What if it is not the marriage that is at fault, but the Queen herself?" I whispered. "A flaw, a deep and fatal flaw, that makes her . . ." *not a human being,* I wanted to say, but dared not . . . "not fit to be Queen?"

"A moral failure?" he asked eagerly.

Yes, selling one's soul to the Devil could be described thus. I nodded.

"Stealing, lying, false pretences?" He thought aloud, shaking his head and discarding each one.

"They call her the Great Whore," I said softly.

"That would taint Your Majesty as well." The mocking, the self-assurance, had drained from Cromwell's manner. He leaned on the windowsill, and outside a playful breeze swirled some of the loose leaves off the apple trees. The weighted branches bobbed and dipped. "We do not wish such a solution. Treason—that is heinous, and infects only the traitor, not his object."

"She has broken every one of the Ten Commandments!" I cried.

Now Cromwell abandoned all visible composure. "Your Majesty! I cannot believe . . . surely . . . not *murder.* The Queen has not murdered!"

Yes, she has, I thought. Wolsey, Warham, Fisher, my sister Mary, Percy . . . and even now she is practising the black arts against others.

"In her heart, Crum. In her heart," was all I could reveal for now.

"So have we all," he said. "In the law, in the common law of the realm, it is *deeds* which condemn a man, not thoughts. You do see things as Supreme Head of the Church of England, where, of course, in spiritual terms, the intention itself is a weighty sin." His shrewd use of flattery, he thought, would win the argument and dissuade me.

The First Commandment: I am the Lord thy God; thou shalt not have strange Gods before me.

Anne had taken Satan as her lord and master.

The Second Commandment: Thou shalt not take the name of the Lord thy God in vain.

In participating in Christian rites, by "praying" publicly, Anne was doing so, mocking the Lord.

The Third Commandment: Remember thou keep holy the Lord's Day.

Her Sundays and holy days were spent in idle masques and banquets, glorifying herself.

The Fourth Commandment: Honour thy father and thy mother.

Anne was on bad terms with everyone in her family, except her brother George.

The Fifth Commandment: Thou shalt not kill.

Oh, here she had . . . she had. . . .

The Sixth Commandment: Thou shalt not commit adultery.

She would not do that, no, she was too vain to give herself to anyone besides Satan . . . and pride. Diana the moon-goddess: this commandment she had not broken.

The Seventh Commandment: Thou shalt not steal.

She had stolen the throne, had stolen the rites and anointing appropriate to a true Queen.

The Eighth Commandment: Thou shalt not bear false witness against thy neighbour.

It forbids lies, rash judgment, detraction, calumny, and the telling of secrets we are bound to keep. She did not *tell* lies, she *was* a lie! The Father of Lies had lain with her. . . .

The Ninth Commandment: Thou shalt not covet thy neighbour's wife.

She coveted others' husbands. Me, in the beginning; then Thomas Wyatt, Francis Weston, even her brother George. All were married, yet she demanded that they pay court to her.

The Tenth Commandment: Thou shalt not covet thy neighbour's goods.

Greedily, Anne had always looked to the possessions of others, wanting them to spite their owners. I remembered the insistence on depriving Katherine of the christening gown, of the royal jewels, on taking over Wolsey's York Place. She desired the things only because they were treasured by an enemy.

"Thoughts lead to deeds," I said. "Must we wait for a murderer to murder?"

"We must, as God Himself must. Besides, in the eyes of the *law,* he is not a murderer until then. Your Majesty . . . can you not clarify the problem regarding the Queen? I could help you so much better if I knew your meaning exactly."

No. To let him be privy to my knowledge might endanger his life. The Witch would know.

"No. It is enough for you to know that I must be rid of her, divorced from her. Find means to effect this! Use all your subtleties, use all your powers, but bring it about!" The same instructions I had once given Wolsey about Katherine, and he had failed. "Fail me not; it is a desperate situation!" Crum was not bound by his own glory and reputation; he was much freer to act than Wolsey had ever been. His own ambitions did not hobble him from serving his King. Our self-interests were perfectly in harmony.

"I will need time," he said. "It would perhaps be beneficial if I were to attend the Queen's Michaelmas festivities to observe. If you could secure me an invitation?"

So Anne was planning yet another of her fêtes. "Yes, of course. Is it to be a large one?"

"The entire court, so they say. I did not receive an invitation. The Queen has never . . . cared for me."

"How ungrateful, considering that you masterminded the great revolution which she now uses as her throne."

He shrugged in mock humility. "I have not exhausted my capacity to mastermind, and nothing is secure forever." His eyes were alight, like those of a small boy given a great wooden puzzle. His ingenuity was being challenged and given a chance to fly, hunt, and bring down prey—like one of his beloved hawks.

⁂

I had received an invitation from Anne regarding the fête in honour of Saint Michael the Archangel and All Angels, to be given by Her Majesty the Queen, the time, the particulars, all interwoven with a curious pattern of black and white, in which gradually the design changed from one to the other, turning itself inside out. Of course: the feast of Saint Michael signified the annual autumnal struggle between light and dark, with dark triumphant. Clever of Anne. But then she was always clever, in a feral sense—just not very wise.

I would stay away from her until the cited evening. That was simple enough to arrange, with the press of returning courtiers and the start-up of the law courts and the foreign ambassadors clamouring for interviews. I thanked God that the Queen's and King's apartments were separate. In the meantime I sent Anne friendly, courteous greetings, hoping to placate her and still any suspicions she may have had that I had not "forgiven" her for the false pregnancy.

For the truth was, I was afraid of her. She had certain powers (to what extent I knew not, and that was half the fear of it), among them perhaps the ability to discern one's thoughts, and certainly the ability to wreak bodily harm on enemies. I had no doubt that soon she would turn those powers on me, once she knew I had found her out. My task was to keep her from knowing as long as possible, until I could act first.

In the meantime, Chapuys confirmed my worst fears. The Imperial ambassador, in an all-but-demanded interview, stood before me in anguish. Was my own equally visible, I wondered, as we faced one another: I seated on my throne, wrapped in the royal ermine, holding the sceptre of state; he bareheaded, clutching his hat.

"Your Majesty, the word is that the Princess—the Lady Mary"—he made no quibble about the title—"is gravely ill. Her life is feared for."

He handed me the worn letter, folded and unfolded many times, with a message from Mary, and one from her confessor. I felt a slap of pain that she had chosen to write to Chapuys instead of me, but reason told me, assured me, that it was only natural she would appeal to her partisan. Still, it hurt.

Mary did not describe her illness, but asked Chapuys to plead for her to be allowed to be nursed by Katherine, "my own dear mother and worth a thousand physicians." Her handwriting was feeble and erratic, wandering about the page like a mongrel lost in the desert wastes. The confessor described the onset of the mysterious malady as "sudden, beginning on the Princess Elizabeth's birthday, and causing the Lady great pain in her stomach and bowels, so that she is scarce able to retain any food, and wastes daily. Black bruises appear on her during the night, from what source we know not."

Anne's signature, her mocking signature, was there for those who recognized it: *beginning on Princess Elizabeth's birthday*. This was Anne's way of celebrating.

They say the Devil is so prideful that he often behaves stupidly, just to boast and brag. This was such an instance. Anne had not been able to resist the elegant touch of using September seventh as her starting date to vanquish Elizabeth's rival.

"—I myself will stand surety," Chapuys was saying. I had not heard a word.

"I beg your pardon?" I asked.

"Let her go to Katherine! She needs her mother, she is suffering in spirit as well as in body, and one cannot heal without the other. I offer myself as a hostage. Put me to death if anything untoward comes of their reunion. But—"

"Impossible. What good would your death do, once Katherine has raised a rebellion against me?" Holding Mary's letter in my hand, I hated the cruelty of refusing what I knew would cheer, if not cure, her. I was always being forced to play the villain, only because I knew things others did not, was responsible for the many, not just the one.

"Katherine would act only as a mother—" he began.

"God's blood, she is not as you think!" I motioned for my private letter box to be brought to me, and I unlocked it and drew out a heavy envelope. Cromwell's spies had procured it for me just three days previous. There was no doubt of its authenticity; I knew Katherine's handwriting, its great black boldness, too well. "Read this. Her treason is here." It had grieved me to read it, and to know it.

It was written to the Pope, which in itself broke the Statute Forbidding Appeals to Rome. But even had it not, its contents, calling for foreign intervention in England, were manifest treason.

"Your Holiness knows, and all Christendom knows, what things are done in England, what great offence is given to God, what scandal to the world, what reproach is thrown upon Your Holiness. If a remedy be not applied shortly, there will be no end to ruined souls and martyred saints."

" 'If a remedy is not applied shortly,' " I said softly. "In other words, she implores the P—the Bishop of Rome to urge Charles and Francis to invade England, to implement the Excommunication and Interdict he placed us under. She calls, Chapuys, for me to be deposed. Her 'dear husband,' whom she would 'obey in all things.' Ha!" Anger replaced sorrow at Katherine's duplicity. She pretended to be so holy, so honest—she, too, was full of lies!

Lies, lies! Everyone was lying! I was surrounded by liars.

"Can no one speak truth to me?" I roared.

Chapuys pointed to Mary's letter. "It speaks true."

"Oh, that she is ill, I doubt not. But that Katherine and her partisans—including you, my dear Imperial lackey—would restrict her care to nursing, *that* I doubt. No, Mary shall stay where she is. Katherine shall not stir out to find her. Why, she might have to speak to someone who would forget to call her 'Queen'!" I spat. "I'll send Dr. Butts to Mary," I said. "He can effect a cure, if anyone can." And an exorcist as well, I thought, disguised as an apothecary. She would need his services to recover truly.

Disappointment and disgust flooded Chapuys's face. He indicated the letter.

"We shall retain the letter," I said. That I wanted it to give to the exorcist, I could not betray. Chapuys thought me mean and petty. Well, let him. In his innocence lay his safety.

Anne's net was closing in. Mary was stricken. I had no doubt that Katherine would soon become "ill." But I was taken by horrible surprise when, in three days, came word from Windsor that Henry Fitzroy had begun to cough blood.

If prayer alone could overcome the black arts, then I saved him that night, as I prayed beyond what I had ever thought possible.

Now I must take my terrible knowledge and act, to overcome Anne and her evil. In two days, at the fête . . .

What then? I had no plan, no certainty of what remedy lay at hand.

LXVII

The sun set on Michaelmas evening, and its last glow in the sky was like a reluctant parting, a giving-over into the hands of darkness which must now reign for twelve hours. I stood watching the last light fade, even as I saw the inner lights of the Great Hall glowing brighter. The fête was being readied.

I was the last to enter the Great Hall. It was brilliantly lit, with some sort of white light that had a blue tinge to it, reflected by mirrors. It was an ugly, cruel light that showed lines on faces and made pupils narrow into pinpoints.

Anne came toward me. She was dressed half in white, half in black, her costume divided down the exact middle, and she had turned half her hair white as well. The nails on one hand were painted black, the other gleamed white. It was the first time I had seen her since the dreadful night in her chamber when she had betrayed herself to me.

The court knew we were estranged. Our deep separation had been impossible to conceal, and now they watched, motionless, as Anne and I approached one another.

I alone had no suspense. I knew that her actions would have no effect on me, that I was beyond her machinations. The woman I had loved had never existed, and this vixen was no part of her.

"My Lord," she said, and smiled. Her teeth . . . her blood-red lips . . . they called something to mind . . . something. . . .

"My Queen." I let our hands touch. We lifted them up together, and turned for the people, ceremoniously. I would give them no food for their curiosity.

Anne signalled for the music to begin. From the minstrel's gallery came abrasive, cacophonous sounds, wailing and piercing. Stringed instruments were being tortured, and their cries smothered by brutal drums.

"Do you like it?" she asked. "I had it composed especially for tonight—winter and darkness, overcoming summer and light."

Never had her courage been more brightly displayed: make no mention of our parting, or of our estrangement, or of my accusations; instead, ask my opinion of an experimental composition. I admired her bravery, while despising her person.

"It is hideous," I answered. "As hideous as all darkness and evil."

"Then it is a successful composition," she replied, "for that is what it is meant to represent."

"Who is its creator? Mark Smeaton?" I answered my own question.

She nodded. Then she said, "Will you take your seat of honour? All is in readiness."

She was to be seated at my side. So she was not to perform in this drama, respecting my wishes. Oh, she was so submissive, so pleasing. Too late—all too late.

The Hall was full, packed with the so-called New Men, the young opportunists of the day. There was burly, winsome Edward Clinton from Lincolnshire, his broad shoulders straining his dark satin doublet. Recently become Baron upon his father's death, he was rumoured to have his eye on Bessie Blount, to pluck her upon the sickly Tailboys' demise. But did he wish her for gain? I must ascertain. Certainly he was looking lasciviously at the Chancellor's wife, standing beside him. He would never be faithful.

Sir Richard Riche, one of Cromwell's men, recently made Solicitor-General, was standing between Chancellor Audley and his wife. His utterly featureless, forgettable face smiled blandly, blankly. His lips moved, saying nothing. Yet his testimony had helped to convict More.

More.

His replacements and inheritors milled about: Thomas Wriothesley, another "find" of Cromwell's, strutted about pointing and mincing. He had lately aristocraticized his name from Risley to Wriothesley and talked in what he assumed was a fashionable soft tone. Beside him stood Ralph Sadler, a pleasant little rodent of a man; William Petre, sweet and malleable; Bishop Stephen Gardiner, calculating but inept—an unfortunate combination.

They all left a bad taste in my mouth. I found myself wishing to spit, particularly on the plume of Risley's rakishly affected hat.

It was with relief that my eyes found another group of "New Men." There was William Parr, barely twenty, but with a gravity of manner that suggested an earlier era. He was from a northern family, one that had served me well against the Scots. His sister, Katherine, married to old Lord Latimer, was beside him, her youth not at all compromised by her husband's needs. Although he was also from Lincolnshire, he kept a London town house and brought his wife often to court, where she sought out the few remaining scholars and Humanists, pointedly avoiding Anne's suite. I was surprised—pleased, but surprised—to see her here this evening. Jane Seymour, in pale autumnal gold, stood talking to her, and beside her were Edward and Tom Seymour—the former wooden and mannered, the latter preening like a multihued cockatoo.

The older men stood off in another clump by themselves—the Duke of Norfolk, looking as though he had an indigestible lump of suet in his belly that was turning his face yellow as well; next to him the Duke of Suffolk, untroubled as always. God, I envied him that. It was a special gift never to spend unrecoverable moments in worry or regret. Now that I knew the true reason for Mary's death, I did not begrudge Brandon's remarriage; it seemed a revenge on Anne that he did not grieve overlong. Where was his young wife? Not with him. That was no cause for alarm. Ah, I spied her with Lady Latimer, an equally young but serious woman. So different from Anne, they were. . . .

There was William Fitzwilliam, the Lord Privy Seal, of an age with myself, standing with the two Dukes. He disliked Anne (not that he had ever said so directly, but he conveyed it in every disdainful gesture. I would have enjoyed seeing him take the Oath, as he undoubtedly did it with a mockery that belied the words), and his weathered face was set like an obstinate donkey's as he rocked on his heels and waited for the latest manifestation of her foolishness. By his right elbow was good, solid John Poyntz, of Gloucestershire, with a face like those I had seen lining the roads whenever I went out on progress, and his friend Thomas, Lord Vaux, made a Knight of the Bath at Anne's Coronation. Vaux bore a remarkable resemblance to Thomas Wyatt, but he had no literary ability whatsoever, even though he attempted to write poetry. Beside all these stood Cranmer, primly and eagerly, as though he really enjoyed this and awaited the "entertainment."

In another self-contained circle were Edward Neville, Nicholas Carew, and Henry Courtenay, a sort of old snowbank of privileges and ideas. Left over from an earlier time without ever having achieved or striven for anything then, they were melting in the new times and felt themselves trickling away. Chapuys was with them, his swift movements and nervous energy always a pleasure to observe; did the man never grow old? But then, attached to the little knot like an odd growth were the two Pole brothers remaining in England: Henry and Geoffrey.

At the thought of the Poles I got a feeling inside like that which visited me at the thought of More. Reginald, the youngest Pole, whom I had educated in Italy at my own expense in his youth, had fled abroad and refused to return to England. He was a brilliant scholar, and much esteemed in Padua and the Papal court, and he had just written *Pro Ecclesiasticae Unitatis Defensione* as his answer to my Great Matter. He was Katherine's great champion, so much so that she and her nephew the Emperor thought many problems would be solved if Mary and Reginald would marry, uniting the Red and White Roses in an outlaw union. The Poles, through their mother Margaret, were Plantagenet. And they were cousins of the defunct de la Pole family.

The two English Pole brothers left behind were sad blooms on the White Rose bush. Henry, Lord Montague, was so unimaginative and plain he was like a paving-stone, and Geoffrey, nervous, timid, and sickly, needed to sleep with a night-candle. The pride of the family, its genius and courage, was all with Reginald, who chose the Pope over me.

Standing discreetly some feet away was Cromwell, fashionably attired for the evening. In defence, the little group kept its distance, not realizing that Crum had posted one of his spies (a pretty woman) on the opposite side, and that the farther they withdrew from him, the closer they came into her range.

Anne moved on the Chair of Estate beside me. I knew I should say something to her, but I could not. I hated her with so pure a hatred, feared her with so pure a fear, that I did not trust myself to speak. Not speaking would betray me more, I knew, so I forced myself to make the effort.

"Have you had this long in mind?" I said. I did not want to look at her; she was repulsive to me. So I spoke out of the corners of my mouth.

"Since I saw the first leaf fall, this year." Her voice was beguiling, as of old. It promised important things.

"Is this to be a new form?" Still I would not look at her.

"Yes. There are new elements. Now watch you! The wings I fashioned all myself, while you were away from me. . . ."

A small platform was erected for Anne's players. Little tin shields were placed all along the borders, and behind them nestled candles, to provide the illumination. Within the Great Hall, the eerie blue-filtered lights were extinguished, until only the stage lights were left.

The musicians began to play, the softest harp music ever heard, suggesting eternity and ecstasy. Out upon the platform appeared pale, amorphous beings with great white wings, glistening with feathers. It was as I had always imagined angels, particularly their wings, hovering and close, sweet and comforting. As a child I had been told I had a guardian angel who kept my foot from danger; and when I had played, narrowly missing accidents, I had almost seen that Henry-angel. . . .

Onto the stage erupted black, crisp beings—had they come up from a trap door?—crawling about like insects. There were swarms of them, and they attacked the angels, pulling at their wings, scattering feathers as in a great wind. The music changed to shrill cries of hurt and fear and discord. The angels took rods and hit the devils; one fell in front and his insides poured out, great sticky molten globs. Then their prince appeared—Satan, wrapped in a black satin cloak, masked by smoke.

I was surprised to see that Satan was handsome. His face was even familiar, but, in the flickering footlights, appeared altogether new. It shone with supernatural beauty.

"I am he, the light-bringer, Lucifer, the morning star," he said, and indeed he was all these things.

Evil was not always ugly; it was at its strongest when disguised as an angel of light, and who knew that better than I?

"Fight with me!" he exhorted us all. "Together we shall defeat the angels and reign forever in heaven!"

A battle ensued, and only the Archangel Michael and his hosts of extra angels routed Lucifer and his black legions. All about the Great Hall, braziers were lit, and clouds of smoke poured out, enveloping everyone. The fight on the stage extended to us as well; suddenly both angels and devils were amongst us, shrieking and struggling. A great heavy wing smashed against my chair, scattering feathers; and three demons scurried after its owner and crawled between the rungs of my chair. I recognized one: Francis Bryan, with his eyepatch. Then a familiar gesture, the way he tossed his hair, betrayed another, and my heart froze: Henry Norris was decked out as a demon in Anne's masque. The fight turned real; swords were drawn. The onlookers joined in the pandemonium, and yet I cared not. A drowsy lethargy had sunk over me, paralyzing my limbs and dazzling my mind. The smoke . . .

"Opium." Anne, once again, read my thoughts. "Purchased at great expense and trouble from the East. It is the Great Lethargy, Sloth in a powder. . . . But watch now, it will prevent any harm."

The swords slowed their momentum, dropped by their owners' sides. Motion turned to heaviness. Only the demons retained their quick movements, as if immune. They shrieked and raised their arms, and from beneath the black-draped platform swarmed a horde of evil beings: werewolves, phantoms, mummies, banshees, ghosts, grave-worms, corpses, witches, warlocks, decay, regret, remorse. . . .

Anne rose beside me, crying out with them, her red mouth open and curved, and I knew her for a vampire, eager for blood, as she had sucked mine and turned me, too, into a creature of the night, a creature who had changed into something alien, and lived by others' blood, even the blood of his friends.

She took my hand, and I rose with her. I had become as she was: just as evil, just as bloodthirsty, just as tainted. Her lips had infected me, corrupted my being. Yet I would not be that way, I would be redeemed. . . . In vain I looked for an angel. I saw only a dismembered wing lying on the floor, torn from its shoulder harness and with its wax frame sagging and trampled.

My head spun; my senses were suspended. I felt myself following Anne, letting myself be pulled along a dark, muffled, secret passage leading away from the Hall. Westminster was full of such secret ways and connections, fashioned as it was in ancient times. Anne was taking me away, away from the safety of the others, and this moment was one I could no longer avoid or postpone.

Her fingers were slender and cool as the jewels upon them. Her face was seen only in brief licks of light from the guttering torches in their iron sockets. Behind her, her costume streamed out—great, billowing, smokelike puffs. I was drugged; the opium smoke had stunned me, like the smoke from Jane Seymour's torch putting the bees to sleep.

We were in a chamber. It was a small chamber, hung with filmy draperies. There was a strange odour within. I had never smelled it before, and it bore no likeness to any other; therefore I cannot describe it, save that it was sweet and caressing.

"The end of the fête," I said slowly. It seemed my lips were numb.

She drew back her hood, which shrouded her face. The coverings fell and her face, unique and entrancing, was revealed. To see it was to remember, and to relive, and then to enter once more into the past, when it had commanded supreme obedience and longing in my heart.

I knew better, and yet I loved her once again. Almost all of me did. The conquest was not complete, for there were parts of me new-formed since first I had loved her, and those were not in her power to reclaim; those stood apart in clucking denunciation. But for the rest, they rose up like the dead at the Day of Judgment. And once again there was that rush of feeling, of transport, of excitement.

But not quite. It was not quite the same. I knew more now, it had all been spoilt somewhere along the way, and that lodged itself like a stone in a shoe; we may run, and leap, and bound, yet the landing is sharp, and so we do not bound quite so high or exuberantly ever again.

I loved her with all my might and heart; but soul and mind did not enter in. This time they demurred.

She came to me and kissed me.

How many months, how many years ago had I longed for her to do exactly that? There had been a time when I felt near death because she did not. Yet here it came to me, unbidden and unsought, with her body pressed up against mine, and all the gestures I had once so coveted, and while it was exciting, it was not soul-satisfying. I had grown beyond whatever hunger she once could have satisfied.

Yet my body—my Judas-body, ever the betrayer—responded and for an hour or so helped me believe that I had not changed, that all was as it once was.

"My Lord, my love, my dearest—" Her words poured, molten, in my ears. There was, of course, a bed, all bedecked in the sheerest linen, laid with furs and pillows of swan's down. Anne had arranged all this, had had servitors set it all up, much as I had once done in heated anticipation in my own chambers.

Her words, her hands, her voice, all reached out to me and sought to claim me. Because I was stronger now, and essentially free of her, the appeal was all the more poignant. I could appreciate, as I never had before, the exquisite little things about her: the way she drew aside her clothes, even folding them without actually folding them; her dramatic ability to turn a little storage room into a chamber of carnality; the sensuality behind her desire to watch the light playing on the opalescent surface of the draperies, so that they seemed to pulsate and throb from within. I saw all this, and appreciated it; but the appreciation itself was somehow an enemy to, and acknowledgment of, lust sapped by time.

Was it all gone? Of course that is always the question. If I wade out into a pond, it may seem, on the surface, calm and empty. How safe to shrug and clamber ashore again, never venturing to plunge below the cold, demanding, slimy surface. If I lay with Anne upon the bed, what would happen? Could I predict how I would feel? Did I dare to find out?

She pulled me, and I followed. Yes, I would do it, because if only I could feel those feelings once again, it would redeem all that had passed since. I did not like, or want, what had passed since. I would be what I was.

I would like to claim that only the subtle poison of the opium-smoke caused me to behave as an alien to myself; that my pulling off of my clothes and my following of Anne into the bed was none of mine own doing. But it was. It was entirely I, Henry, who did these things, who loved the Anne he had once known in hopes of bringing back the Henry he had also once known. Passion is sweet and restorative, and in loving Anne again I was younger, stronger, happier. I would be that Henry again. The recent past, the ugly knowledge, would vanish.

We coupled, there upon her black-hung bed. And it was but a coupling, there was no magic to it. I felt each physical sensation, each creak of flesh against flesh. But it was only flesh, and as such had so little power. Her arm was only an arm, her body and face only a body and face. She was Anne, robbed of her extra dimension, her aching splendour—splendour and dimension that I had breathed out around her, emanating from my own passion and desire.

I rolled away from her. Now it was worse. In doing this, I had destroyed even the glory of the memory. For in retrospect it had all been as ordinary as this, only I could not have known it until now. I had broken the seal that held those memories inviolate; instead of resurrecting the past, I had killed it.

I have just read these words over. Words, that is all they are: *in retrospect . . . resurrecting . . . emanating. . . .* The only true thing I have written is "I had broken the seal that held the memories." That I had done, to my own sorrow.

Yet it was a brave action. For had I found more of what I had previously found, I would be willing to pursue it, wherever it might lead.

Anne lay beside me, a slim and sensual being. The candle and torchlight had an affinity for her skin, turning it to creamy vellum. She turned to light a bedside candle. I watched her as she did so, remembering how that very motion had once seemed hers entirely. Now I knew, and had seen how others lit candles.

Yet I hated knowing, and seeing.

No one had ever loved as I had loved. I believed that. No one had ever loved anyone as I had loved Anne.

The sorrow was in the tense.

LXVIII

"**I** am with child."

Anne stood before me, triumphant, and spoke those words. This time I knew she did not lie; she would not have been so bold else.

So her great gamble had paid off handsomely. Her expense for the opium, the fête, the preparation of the private chamber, all to procure my services, had been rewarded. How had I been so compliant? How could the timing have been so right? Of course, it was because *she* had controlled the timing, had planned the celebration around her body's rhythm. Or perhaps she even controlled her body's natural courses? Her powers were, literally, extraordinary.

"I am pleased." I rose to encircle her shoulders with my arm, as courtesy dictated.

We would have a son, and that would save her. If she gave me a son, I could not repudiate her. She knew that and, like an endangered animal, had looked to protect herself.

And with the child firmly anchored within her womb, she could dispense with me. She could be Dowager Queen and rule through her son. Already she had begun to work her spells upon me, to bring back my malady. For within a few days of the Michaelmas fête, I had felt a tingling in my leg, then a throbbing pain, and now the ulcer had reopened and was larger than ever. Ugly black streaks spread out on all sides of it. Dr. Butts was still with Mary, and I did not wish to separate them, so I was forced to treat my affliction myself. None of Dr. Butts's associates was knowledgeable enough—or discreet enough —to involve himself with my illness.

Meanwhile, the reports were that Mary did not improve. Neither did Fitzroy, who was wasting away before Henry Howard's devoted eyes. I could not bring Mary here, for security's sake (unless, of course, she took the Oath), but I could bring Fitzroy.

Then came word that Katherine had fallen ill—"obviously," said the report, "of poison." Thus, in spite of Katherine's precautions and suspicions, Anne had prevailed. Whether by natural methods (bribed cooks, powders) or supernatural, no longer mattered. What mattered was that Anne had prevailed. And she was now pregnant, carrying a child, with the Act of Succession vested in that child, and we had all become dispensable, I most of all. As the pain shot through my leg, I had a constant reminder of that.

Chapuys was frantic with worry about both Katherine and Mary, and betrayed his very real personal affinity for them, apart from political maneuverings. He begged for permission to visit Katherine, but I withheld it for a time. I knew that any attention from Chapuys, with its representation of outside concerns, might stir Anne to injure Katherine further, until she was beyond help from any quarter. To flatter me, Chapuys pestered me for a tennis match, something I had long ago urged upon him.

"In the enclosed court at Hampton, we can play during the nasty weather," he said.

"Perhaps. Perhaps." I could not run about on this infected leg, but I hoped it would diminish by Christmas. "At the holiday time, when we move there."

Would I even be walking by then? What would Anne's hand have done to me by then? I must consult with Cromwell, my totally unscrupulous and utterly discreet Cromwell.

"I must be rid of her!" I cried.

"We have already determined that as long as Katherine lives—" he began.

"Aha!" Therein her own hatred and jealousy was her undoing! For, out of spite, she was causing Katherine to languish and fail. "If Katherine should die, then Anne can be set aside," I finished.

"In a special limbo designed for ex-wives," suggested Cromwell.

"By God, you sound as if you expect it to be a permanent position, created by me!" I barked.

"No, no, Your Majesty," he assured me. "Nothing of the sort. It would be an unnecessary expense to the Exchequer—on a permanent basis."

I settled myself more comfortably on my chair, and rested my leg upon a padded footstool. I wished I could mention my leg to Crum, but I dared not. I realized with a start that I trusted no one now; there was no one I knew to whom I could reveal any intimate thing about myself without fear of betrayal. So that was what Father had meant. It was loathsome, this aloneness. He claimed it was the price of kingship. Was it? At present, the answer was yes. Was it worth it? The answer to that was also yes. One can get used to anything.

"Divorce us, Crum," I ordered him. "Call it what you will, but find a legal way to sunder us. She used illicit means to effect our union; now use licit ones to undo and confound all her cleverness."

A wad of pain worked its way up my leg, and it was all I could do to keep from crying out. "So that the moment the child is born . . . she may be sent away." My belly contracted with the pain, but my will kept the cry of pain from escaping. Crum never heard it.

"There are rumours," he said. "Rumours that the conspirators stand at the ready in Northumberland and along the West Marches to spirit Katherine away."

Would he never be gone? I could not mask this pain much longer. "So the dream has come about, and the Papal forces are ready to move," I said. "It was inevitable. Yet"—another spasm of pain—"if Katherine is ill enough, it all comes to nothing." Yes, the Devil was stupid to wound Katherine.

"Out of England, she might rally."

True. Beyond our shores, treated as her vanity dictated, hearing words of flattery and submission, she would mend quickly enough.

"Out of England she shall never go," I said. "And as for her misguided knights-errant, we shall disempower them, subtly, so that when and if the time ever comes when they might *try* to move . . . they shall find themselves stuck fast."

Poor Katherine. She would never know of her would-be rescuers.

"I would send the Princess Dowager a token of encouragement in her illness," I told Crum. "Not Chapuys. But a box of delicacies, and one of my musicians. . . . See to the land arrangements."

There, that should occupy him. Else I might scream if he did not immediately quit my presence and allow me to massage my leg.

Anne's pregnancy fared well; the most healthy being in all England was that one which lay within her womb. While her magic blighted all of her enemies, her child and her salvation waxed strong.

The year slipped further toward the dark bottom of its wheel. My leg did not mend, but at least it did not worsen. Fitzroy, whom I had brought to court under the pretext of inviting him to keep Christmas with us, remained pale and wracked with a cough (it sounded the very same as Father's), but likewise did not worsen. Mary hung in the limbo of not-truly-ill/not-truly-well, and I was given the painful task of refusing Katherine's natural pleas to help her. She had written Chapuys:

> *I beg you to speak to the King, and desire him from me to be so charitable as to send his daughter and mine where I am, because if I care for her with my own hands and by the advice of my own and other physicians, and God still pleases to take her from this world, my heart will be at peace, otherwise in great pain. Say to His Highness that there*

is no need for anyone to nurse her but myself, that I will put her in my own bed in my own chamber and watch with her when needful.

I have recourse to you, knowing that there is no one else in this kingdom who will dare to say to the King, my lord, that which I am asking you to say. I pray God to reward your diligence.

From Kimbolton. Katherine, the Queen.

The picture of old, sick Katherine hobbling about, "tending" to Mary, thinking herself capable of nursing her back to health, was piteous. She wished her heart to be at peace. But the truth was that Katherine had two other jealous claimants on her person: illness and the network of those who would "liberate" her to give the Emperor and Pope cause to invade us. Mary would doubtless urge such a course as well. Mary was obstinate and wilfully disobedient and subversive, where pious Katherine was not. Katherine still loved me, Mary did not. No, I could not permit them to be reunited and lodged under a common roof, no matter how well guarded.

I had noted the persistent signature, even when in the position of a supplicant: *Katherine, the Queen.*

Christmas was a sham. It was necessary to keep the Twelve Days, necessary for Anne and me to appear together, necessary for her to be lauded as the mother of the hoped-for heir. Princess Elizabeth was brought to court and dressed up and shown about. She was now two and a half years old, and—I was forced to admit—a winsome thing. Her hair was golden red and abundant, her spirits always exuberant, and—most telling of all—her mind sharp and quick. She knew a number of surprising words like "scabbard" and "oak" and "edict." She was exhibited as promise of the even better things to be expected of the heir —for if God was so profligate with gifts for a female, think what He would bestow upon a male.

Through all this, Anne and I exchanged no private or personal words. We were enemies now, locked in a duel: a duel of wits and ruthlessness, the rules understood on both sides.

LXIX

Katherine was dying. Her illness had passed beyond the realm of mere illness, which implies recovery, and into that of "last sickness." On New Year's Day, 1536, I received word from her physician. "Breathing laboured," "colour poor," "unable to take nourishment for a fortnight," "insufficient strength to leave bed," "heartbeat irregular," wrote Dr. De la Sa, and I knew what it signified. I granted Chapuys leave to go to her —accompanied by Crum's "assistant," Stephen Vaughn.

For a week, while the new year was in its first days, Katherine entertained the Angel of Death in her private chamber at Kimbolton. She also entertained Chapuys, who arrived on January second.

She, like the Queen she still was in her own mind, attempted to welcome the Imperial Ambassador ceremoniously. She opened her chambers to Bedingfield and Chamberlayn, her "keepers," who had not seen her since first she shut herself up in royal pride, and included them in the ritual. All her faithful servitors, as well as her gaolers, were required to line up and form an aisle about the sickbed, which Chapuys approached on his knees. Katherine extended her hand and allowed Chapuys to kiss it, saying, "I can die now in your arms, not abandoned, like one of the beasts."

Chapuys then told her a pack of lies (that I promised prompt payment of all the arrears of her pensions, and that when she was better, she could transfer to any manor in the realm), and reminded her of her duty to recover—"as the peace, the welfare, the unity of all Christendom" depended on it, he claimed.

Katherine then ceremoniously dismissed him and let all the witnesses, keepers, and spies depart. When they were safely gone (so she supposed), she sent a secret message for Chapuys to return to her.

So even the pious Katherine was capable of duplicity—a character trait that none of her admirers ever acknowledge.

What they discussed, Stephen Vaughn was unable to ascertain. But they conferred for hours, far into the night.

Chapuys stayed three days, and Katherine rallied during his visit. She was able to eat, and to retain her food. Her spirits soared as yet another gift came to her: Lady Willoughby, the Maria de Salinas of her youth. She had heard of Katherine's dying and, without leave or permission of any sort, had travelled dangerous and foul winter roads to come to Kimbolton. Arriving near midnight of the night before Chapuys's departure, she had stood across the moat and demanded that Bedingfield admit her.

"I cannot," he said. "I have no orders to."

"You must," she said. "I have endangered myself coming here; have fallen; have almost come into the hands of highwaymen. I am a noblewoman, and shall not risk my person further, regardless of your orders. Admit me at once!" Her delicate voice must have rung across the dank, icy moat waters.

The chivalrous, confused Bedingfield lowered the drawbridge and admitted her.

Chapuys left, but committed Katherine to Maria's devoted hands. She seemed much improved. She sat up, combed and arranged her hair, had long talks with her girlhood friend. But in the middle of the night her nausea and pain returned fourfold. Her confessor was sent for, and he immediately saw she was not likely to live until dawn, the earliest permitted time to say Mass. Under canonical law, when death was imminent, a dispensation was allowed. But Katherine—for whom no rules were ever to fashion themselves to human needs —forbade him, murmuring citations from ancient authorities against it. She would wait, she insisted, for the dawn.

God gave her the grace to do so. She received the Sacrament at dawn, then dictated two letters. One was to the Emperor. I know not its contents. One was to me. I received it a few days later.

She lived until two in the afternoon of January eighth. At ten in the morning she received Extreme Unction, and then prayed until noon, in a clear voice, for Mary, for the souls of all the people in England, and especially for "my husband."

Katherine was dead. Katherine, who had been a part of my life, a counterpoint like a second melody to myself, for as long as I could remember. Before I was seven years old, I had known about the Princess of Spain who was coming to England to be its Queen someday.

I tried not to remember her as she was then. I tried to keep only the image of the obstinate, recalcitrant, troublemaking old woman before me. Her pursed, dry lips; her perpetual indignation and gravity that had carved two parallel lines between her brows; her ugly wooden headdresses and her boxlike figure, swathed in coarse dark wool.

Her infuriating lectures on morality; her political duplicity; her treasonous letters to the Emperor; her Popish plots and affectations . . . the list multiplied itself, romped on its own.

Yet, unbidden, came images of the laughing young Princess, her eyes glistening with love and joy of life; the young mother's pride in Mary's musical progress; the young wife's eager attempts to delight and amuse and please me, to put on silver masks and dance in her chamber on Twelfth Night, even though she thought it silly; to pretend not to recognize me when I came dancing, in a costume from Turkey. . . .

The wife of my youth. She had been the wife of my youth, and in dying she took that with her. Those lost days gleamed now more brightly than ever.

I mourned for the Spanish Princess, angry that her life had been, on the whole, so sad. And now there was no hope for anything better, no last-minute changes. She lay beyond all changes.

What sort of faith did I have, then? Presumably she had passed into another world, where all such considerations were cast aside. She was in glory, clothed in a spiritual body, no longer the Spanish Princess or the crippled, sickly old woman she had changed into, but changed yet again into something glittering and immortal. While her physical body was being cut open and embalmed, the immortal Katherine was long since departed, rewarded beyond anything I could ever have bestowed on her.

So I believed . . . so I believed. . . .

But if it were not so? If the poor old body was all there was, then what a cruel reward. I wept, alone in my private box in the Chapel Royal, astonished and bewildered at my tears. Did I not believe? Were all my beliefs hollow, worthless? That was what my tears betrayed.

For if the dead are not raised, neither has Christ been raised. It follows also that those who have died within Christ's fellowship are utterly lost. If it is for this life only that Christ has given us hope, we of all men are most to be pitied.

I should not be weeping for Katherine's bitter life, if I truly believed that each particle of that bitterness was pleasing to God and was now earning her tenfold of glory and reward.

I was a liar, then, a hypocrite. No, I was a doubter. There was a difference. One was honest and human, the other was not. Even Peter had doubted.

God, most almighty and everlasting, please remove these doubts that burn and torment me far worse than my leg. Remove them, or I cannot go on.

Somewhere I heard a stirring. There was someone else in the chapel, down below. I decided to go. I felt more oppressed and troubled than when I had first sought the silence and darkness. Perhaps it would do for another what it had failed to do for me.

I was halfway down the long gallery when I heard the door open and turned to see a figure stealing away from the chapel. It was Jane Seymour, and she was rubbing her eyes. She walked slowly until she came to a window seat, then sat down. She stared, blinking, at the floor.

I approached her carefully. She looked up at my approach, and her eyes and the tip of her nose were red. She attempted to smile, as if that would render them invisible.

"Mistress Seymour," I said, settling down—uninvited—beside her. "Can I be of help? Are you troubled?"

"I am troubled," she admitted. "But you cannot be of help." She fumbled for a handkerchief.

"Only give me the chance," I offered, glad of the opportunity to take my mind off Katherine.

"I would leave court," she blurted out. "As soon as the roads are passable, if Your Majesty would so graciously permit me."

"But why?"

"I am not meant for court," she said. "It is not as I thought it was, not as it will ever be again. I think I was—forgive me, Your Majesty—thinking that the Princess Dowager and the Lady Mary might return again. I had prayed"—her voice faltered—"that they would take the Oath, and return, and . . . but it is never to be, and I can wait no longer. And I mourn for the Qu—the Princess Katherine." Unable to stop her sobs, she lowered her face into her hands.

I felt tears rush to my eyes, as if to be companions to Jane's. "I as well," I admitted, wishing my voice did not tremble slightly. I put my arm around her. "I mourn for her. And, Jane"—I hesitated—"I am touched that you dare to mourn her, to grieve for her openly."

Jane was good, and like all truly good persons, she underestimated the power of the evil around her.

She nodded. Still her tears came, even as she sought to bring them under control.

"Jane, when my mother died, I felt that I had lost everything of love and beauty in my life," I said. "I felt deserted. Already the Princess Katherine was there, already a new person of kindness and grace was in my life, but in my grief I could not see her. I only felt betrayed, lost, and powerless. Do not let your grief blind you that way. Thus evil robs us twice."

My words made no sense to her, I could tell.

"My mother had a locket, which I have kept always. I will send it to you, and wish you to wear it, to accept it as a gift from my mother. Will you do that? And wait six months before leaving court? If you still wish to, then I shall not keep you." I paused. "Oh, Jane—by then you shall truly be as wise as a serpent. You are already as gentle as a dove; therefore the court needs you, whether you need it or not."

I meant not "the court" but "the King."

Katherine's death was formally announced to the court, and then proclaimed throughout England. She would lie in state at Kimbolton, and then her funeral cortège would proceed to Peterborough Abbey, where she would be interred. I appointed the chief mourners and ordered the principal gentry of the neighbourhood to attend her coffin from Kimbolton to Peterborough, two days' slow journey, and sent the necessary black cloth for their mourning apparel. At court, there would be solemn obsequies in honour of Katherine. I commanded all the court to attend, dressed in mourning.

Katherine's letter to me arrived two days after the news of her death. It was with a sort of fear that I opened it, for there is a dread in reading, for the first time, words from a dead person.

> *My most dear Lord, King, and husband. The hour of my death now drawing on, the tender love I owe you forces me, my case being such, to commend myself to you, and to put you in remembrance with a few words of the health and safeguard of your soul which you ought to prefer before all worldly matters, and before the care and pampering of your body, for the which you have cast me into many calamities and yourself into many troubles.*
>
> *For my part, I pardon you everything, and I wish and devoutly pray God that He will pardon you also. For the rest, I commend unto you our daughter Mary, beseeching you to be a good father unto her, as I have heretofore desired. I entreat you also, on behalf of my maids, to give them marriage portions, which is not much, they being but three. For all my other servants I solicit the wages due them, and a year more, lest they be unprovided for.*
>
> *Lastly, I make this vow, that mine eyes desire you above all things.*

I felt stunned. Her last sentence . . . I had expected Scripture quotes, prayers, Latin. But she was done with all that; she had strength only to set down her true thoughts. And, above all, she had desired to see me? The young Princess, then, was there within the old woman, right up to the end? All that we are survives within us, nothing extinguishes the rest. . . . I ached: for the young self in me would, above all things, have granted that wish.

Her will, following, showed her few earthly concerns. She wished to be buried in a convent. She wished Mary to have the gold collar which she had "brought out of Spain." She wished all her servants to be paid their wages in arrears, and extra besides. She wished church vestments to be made of her gowns.

The court obsequies were to be held on January twentieth. Cranmer would lead the prayers on behalf of the soul of the deceased. The day was the coldest yet that winter, raw and blustery, with a stinging wet snow coming from the west. Even in the early afternoon, the gloom was so deep that it appeared twilight.

Anne and her party were not present. The Queen's chair was empty. By her absence she shamed herself, not Katherine.

Returning to the palace from the chapel, I saw, through the thick blue gloom, Anne's apartments all lighted, including her Presence Chamber with its throne. The twinkling lights mocked us below, all the people in black who had honoured Katherine.

I gave no indication that I had seen it, lest I give further scandal. But when the court had gone its own way, each to his or her own quarters, I went to Anne's and demanded entrance. Her chamberlain admitted me. He was costumed in a festive manner.

From within I could hear music, glimpse movement. There was dancing.

"Your Majesty, the Queen did not expect the honour of your presence."

"Obviously." I pushed my way past him and walked slowly out into the middle of the grand chamber where a thousand tapers were burning, and a whole company of men and ladies were dancing. They were all clad in yellow, bright lemon yellow, and in the center were Anne and her brother George, looking as though they had been dipped in gold, touched by Midas himself.

"So," I said quietly, but my one word and the presence of mourning black snapped them to attention. They stopped dancing, and the music faded.

Anne came proudly to me, while all eyes watched.

"You shame yourself," I said, not attempting to lower my voice. "Exulting at Katherine's death reveals only your own spite and shallowness."

"Do you not exult also? 'God be praised, now we are safe from all threat of war,' you said upon hearing the news."

I had said it only for political expediency, to let the Pope know he was done for now. I had not meant it in my heart.

"For the benefit of the Bishop of Rome," I replied, "whose spies are about."

"I am grieved for the attention the Princess Dowager has received for her 'good end,' " said Anne, loudly. "There is talk of little else but her saintly departing. Already people are directing prayers to her, asking for her intercession. Can you afford to have created another saint? First Fisher, then More—now Katherine?"

I signalled for the musicians to take up their playing again, to drown out this conversation.

"You push me too far," I said. I wished to choke her for her taunting words.

"It is true," she answered. "The people *have* canonized Fisher and More, in their hearts—never mind what Rome pronounces—and they are well on their way to doing it with Katherine. You should be dancing with us, to counteract it, not leading them in honouring her! Your own security demands it, regardless of your feelings."

"Fie! You dress your own evil gloating in political wrappings. Dance, my love, all you wish. Soon the time for your dancing will cease."

I turned and left her in yellow, as I had first beheld her.

The embalmer at Kimbolton, who performed an autopsy on Katherine, submitted a secret report to me. He had found all the internal organs as healthy and normal as possible, "with the exception of the heart, which was quite black and hideous to look at." He washed it, but it did not change colour; then he cut it open, and inside it was the same.

"Poison," I said softly. I had known it all along. Anne's poison. It was that triumph she celebrated at her Yellow Ball. I wondered if the particular poison she had chosen was, indeed, yellow. How like her if it were.

Now only Fitzroy, Mary, and I were left to dispatch. Emboldened by her success, she was foolhardly enough to commit her plans for Mary in a letter to Mrs. Shelton, Mary's "keeper": "Go no further. When I shall have a son, as I soon look to have, I know what then will come to her."

Go no further. No more poison for now? Mary was safe, then, for the present.

LXX

A tournament had long been scheduled for the end of the month. I did not wish to cancel it now, as it would indeed seem as though England were mourning a Queen rather than a Princess Dowager if I did so. Holding the tournament would signal that the time for observing the death was past. In addition, it was necessary that I quench the rumours and questions beginning to circulate about my health. If I rode in this tournament, it would be proof that there was nothing wrong with me.

I was forty-four now, well past the age when most men participated in tournaments. Brandon had retired from the lists several years ago. But I still enjoyed the challenge, enjoyed the whole ritual associated with it, and I was loth to give it up.

That January afternoon, one had to be a Northman born to relish the idea of putting on cold metal armour. It was a bright, blue-and-white day, the edges and outlines of all things appearing extra sharp. The air seemed thinner and harder than normal, and even the sounds of the trumpets and pendant bells on the horses were as brittle as icicles. The tournament colours, bold and primary, made a great heraldic shout against the white snow as the challengers rode out. Today the clash of metal against metal would ring and echo coldly, and sparks would be struck, like showers of stars.

My leg was not well. The inflammation had increased until it was beginning to be difficult to walk without betraying my infirmity. Sitting a horse was not any easier; it required different muscles and squeezed the ulcer in a different way but was just as painful.

I rode out, twice around the lists, armed *cap-à-pie,* as they say, with a surcoat of silver bawdakin, accompanied by thirty footmen, dressed all in white and silver. Then the jousting proper could begin. There were some twenty of us competing.

Unlike the knights in King Arthur's time, no Black Challenger or Unknown Green Knight appeared to enliven matters. There had been times, long ago, when I myself had ridden as a disguised challenger, but these days no one did that. Pity. A lot of things were a pity.

My destrier pawed the ground and snorted, sending great clouds of breath-smoke from each nostril. Across the barrier, at the far end of the tiltyard, waited my opponent. He wore the colours of the Marchioness of Exeter. It was my cousin Courtenay I faced (unless his wife had taken a bold lover). He was a fair fighter.

I gave my horse his signal; he leapt forward in the clear, thin air, and even inside my metal helmet I could hear the thunder of his hoofbeats heavy, heavy, heavy on the frozen ground. Through the row of slits in my visor I saw the Marquis coming toward me; the slits framed him so that he was all I saw. I raised my lance and dropped its butt into the great cupped notch on my breastplate where it was designed to rest, braced myself in the stirrups, and aimed.

Something hit me so hard that I was paralysed, utterly unable to move. I saw sky wheeling above me, like a falcon's lure, faster and faster, bits of white and blue chasing one another, and it was not cold at all, but balmy and with the scent of white roses. . . .

I felt fur beneath my cheek, and I heard voices: gentle, murmuring voices, like Jane's bees. I lay still and listened, because I had no strength to do otherwise. It was soothing to be here and let the voices wash over me; to take my own time to awaken, without chamber attendants on a schedule to assist me.

". . . it cannot be kept from her. Nor from *them*." I wondered of whom they spoke. Eavesdropping is a dangerous pastime, to be hazarded more easily by adults than by children.

"I have sent for Cranmer. I took it upon myself to do so."

"*You?*"

"He will require the Last Rites. To let him depart without them is murder."

"Why? Because he stands in mortal sin at the present?"

"All men have something to confess, or to be forgiven. Even the saintly More, and Katherine, required it."

"So much more *him,* eh?"

"You speak treason!"

Silence.

"No, I meant not that. Only that *he* has the souls of the realm on his soul. More and Katherine were free to indulge and pamper their individual souls."

Why could I not discern the speakers? Their voices were anonymous.

"I've told the Queen." A known voice at last. The Duke of Norfolk's.

"What were your words?"

"That the King had been unseated in the lists and his horse had fallen on him, and as he is yet unconscious and barely breathing for these three hours past, he is not like to recover."

"What did she say?"

She rejoiced, I answered them silently. She rejoiced that her spells and witchcraft had been strong enough to bring this about.

"She—laughed. But she is ever wont to laugh when she is taken by surprise," her uncle explained.

In a few minutes I spoke, and took *them* by surprise, my early mourners. They seemed genuinely exultant to have me back. True or false?

WILL:

True. Henry had been King for so long that no one remembered anything else, and he had led his people out into a confusing landscape from which only he promised a map for deliverance. They were terrified at the thought of his leaving them in that place. This was the first time the shadow of the King's death had crossed their minds, for they were accustomed to thinking of him as robust and eternal.

HENRY VIII:

I was recuperating—discreetly, of course, making my resting seem like "musing," my bland food passed off as "fasting Lenten fare" and my curtailed activities as "attention to personal matters." My leg was scabbing over; evidently the fall had shocked it into involution. But my senses were not right. I felt light-headed, and I kept forgetting why I had walked into a room.

It was Dr. Butts who came to me with the news: "The Queen has been brought to bed before her time. She is calling for you."

Before her time . . . yes, it was months before her time. No child could survive, born so untimely. The child was lost, the son that was to be her salvation.

"She calls for me?"

"Indeed. The attendant midwives say she is fighting so hard against the birth because of her fear of you. But what is dead, or not fit for life, must pass out of her body. She hinders it for her own purpose. Please, Your Majesty, come and assure her."

I drew on my furs. It was a long distance to the Queen's apartments here in Greenwich, and ever since my fall I had felt constantly chilled. It was still January. January twenty-ninth. With a start, the significance of the date snapped into place: today Katherine's coffin was being lowered into the vault at Peterborough. Her last earthly act, as it were, before she resolved herself into a memory. Anne's travail had come while Katherine was yet above ground.

There was no merriment about the Queen's apartments today. The servitor who admitted me was quiet, and the furniture was set in order against the walls of the Audience and Presence chambers. As I penetrated further within, the number of attendants increased, but their silence was as heavy as great snowfalls in northern forests. I passed through the Privy Chamber, with its musical instruments mutely arranged on the window seats, and into Anne's inner suite. Dr. Beechy met me.

"All is lost," he said. "The Prince is dead." He indicated a blanket-wrapped mound in a basket, resting on Anne's writing desk. The basket had pushed aside her Italian pens, her inlaid letter-boxes.

"It was a Prince?"

"It had the appearance of a male, of some sixteen weeks. Do you wish to—?"

I nodded. A physician's attendant brought the basket to me. I pulled back the coverings and stared at the jelly-like creature there, almost transparent, and only a few inches long. The male genitalia were recognizable. I pulled the cloth back over it.

"I will see the Queen now," I said. "When was she—when was this delivered?"

"Not above half an hour ago," Dr. Beechy said. "She strove, with all her might, to keep it within her womb. She quite exhausted herself by her efforts, making this issue more painful than a normal birth. She needs . . . comforting."

"The Queen has miscarried of her saviour," a diplomat wrote that week. Indeed, Anne had lost the son upon whom she had based all her schemes and visions of triumph. She was done for.

"So," I said, as I approached her bed, where she was still being sponged and ministered to by her women, "you have lost my boy."

She looked up at me. Stripped of her jewels, her immaculately coiffed hair, her stunning costumes, she was as ugly and wiry as a sewer-rat. Like one of those, she swam for safety.

"O my Lord," she cried, "he was lost for the great love I bear you. For when my uncle, the Duke, brought me word of your accident, and that you were not thought like to live, my pains began—"

Liar. That was two days ago.

"Has Her Majesty been in labour since Thursday?" I asked Dr. Beechy blandly.

The honest, frightened physician shook his head. "Friday it began, Your Majesty."

"It was for despair that your love had left me!" she cried. "On Friday

I saw the locket that Mistress Seymour wore." She used her thin arms to hoist herself up to a sitting position, where she glared at me. "Can you deny that you are giving her tokens? *I will not have it!*"

"You will not have it? You'll have what I dictate that you have, and endure it as your betters have done."

"Katherine?" she screamed. "No, I'm no Katherine! And your maids shall never live to flaunt their tokens in *my* face!" She opened her hand, and lying on her palm was the locket I had given Jane—my mother's locket.

"I tore it off her neck, her thick, bullish neck. She's plain, Henry, and has a fat neck. It's pale and lumpy-looking."

Her whole body was straining forward, and the cords stood out on her neck. I could see a vein throbbing slowly, right under her ear.

"Your neck is prettier," I allowed her. "Slender and with a curve. Yet the head it bears up is filled with evil and curses and malevolence. You'll get no more boys from me." It was not a threat but a statement, and a promise to myself.

She hurled the locket at me. I caught it easily, although she meant it to hurt me or damage itself against something hard.

"When you are on your feet again, I shall speak to you," I told her, closing my fingers over the locket.

I left her chambers.

I was free. She had no further hold over me.

LXXI

March had come in like a lamb, the country folk said, so it was bound to go out like a lion. They were correct, but not for the reasons they thought. This mid-March day, I, the lion, was hawking with Cromwell, my presumed "lamb." At least he was always obedient and docile; in that way he was lamblike.

The day was one of those March oddities—glum and yet alive with potential. Everywhere ice was melting, and one could hear the water flowing in streams and brooks, trickling out of woodland snowbanks, oozing into our horses' hoofprints. One felt the growth ready to spring out of the dry, tightly packaged stems, one could see the glimmer of green beneath the trampled, brown, straggly grass. The wool-puff clouds against the sky seemed rinsed clean and purified. March was a tonic, a scourge, an astringent.

It was a fine day for hawking. Cromwell and I needed to confer, and what better excuse to betake ourselves deep into the countryside and leave the palace spies and eavesdroppers behind? Crum had long been eager to show me his birds, and I had been eager to see the creatures for whom he actually seemed to have warm feelings.

He kept both peregrine falcons and goshawks. By law, one must be at least an earl to fly peregrines. I intended to make Cromwell Earl of Essex—depending on how well he served me in what he judiciously refrained from calling the King's Greater Matter.

He asked me which I preferred to fly today, and I chose the peregrine. He chose its smaller mate, the tiercel. We took them from the hawk-house, hooded, upon our gloved wrists, and rode west beyond Richmond, until we were in the open country near Hampton. All the while the falcons were quiet, but Crum chattered on, uncharacteristically, about them.

"Her name is Athena. I had a difficult time training her to the lure. But she's strong. She even takes big old hares. Isn't afraid of them!" He made sweet clucking noises to her.

"Mars, here"—he lifted his wrist—"enjoys rook-hawking best. He loves to plummet out of the sky and fall on a rook, break its neck, let it drop, in a shower of black feathers. It's a lovely sight!" he sighed. "Mars can even take a jackdaw. I get particular pleasure out of watching that. The 'daw tries to outfly him, but can't." Crum frowned. "Now, now!"

I noticed that Mars was flexing his talons, and one tip had almost penetrated Crum's leather hawking glove. "I love to see them kill," he said simply. "They are spectacular in flight and fight."

"Would that we could emulate them," I agreed. "Our best methods are clumsy by comparison, and there's no sport in our executions."

"A subject that, alas, calls for our attention."

We reined in and prepared to slip the falcons. There was a flock of rooks nearby. We pulled off the hoods and let the falcons take off from our wrists after the unfortunate black birds.

"Have you obtained the evidence?" I asked quickly. I had been forced to reveal the truth about Anne—Black Nan!—so that he would understand the force he was working against.

"Of witchcraft? No, Your Majesty."

The sleek, dark shapes of the falcons, climbing quickly above us, were breathtaking.

"But she is a witch! Why can you not find the evidence? Then— execution will be demanded."

"I thought to discover it. I assumed there would be certain potions, powders, books. But all I found was . . . adultery." He looked apologetic. "Her serving-woman, Lady Wingfield, has told me a strange tale . . . of men hidden inside closets in the Queen's bedchamber, waiting for code-words bidding them to emerge and come to her bed. It is all . . . bizarre." He handed me a piece of parchment, long, stained, with many entries and inks. "Oh, look!"

The falcons had overtaken the rooks, and were now above them, singling out their targets. Then they would drop, perpendicular, wings folded close to the body, like smooth, dark stones of death.

"Yes, yes." I had seen falcons kill before.

I glanced at the paper in my hands. I felt myself go weak, felt my hands tremble. I did not wish to see this, but at the same time I was compelled to read it.

It detailed that the musician Mark Smeaton and "others" had had regular sport in Anne's bed.

A great thud in the sky, which carried to our ears: the falcons had hit the rooks, attacking straight from above. The rooks were dead, and plummeting. The falcons swooped yet again, catching them as they fell. A lazy swirl of black feathers followed them, like a funeral party.

My eyes were forced back to the paper. The details went on and on, relentlessly.

This list would be read out in court, to her shame.

She was even fouler than I had imagined. My hands were contaminated in touching this filthy compilation. "The Great Whore," I murmured.

I raised my eyes. Cromwell had been watching me all the while, his black button eyes riveted on me.

"I thank you," I finally said. "It is time I knew the full truth."

Cromwell nodded. "Truth somehow always seems connected with pain. 'The painful truth,' we always say. Never 'the joyous truth.' I am sorry, Your Majesty," he said quietly.

"God sends pain to correct us," I said, by rote. I had been taught that. Did I truly believe it?

"Nonetheless, it hurts. The only way to avoid it is to cease to care."

Was that what Cromwell had done, after his wife's death?

"It would be restful not to care," I agreed. It would be a peace, an absence I could not imagine. All my life I had cared—about everything.

"Shall we?" He indicated the field, with the fallen rooks. "If we don't remove them, the falcons will feed full, and will hunt no more today."

Feeling outside myself, I watched as I walked toward the kill. I walked, and used a lure to remove the falcons so we could stuff the poor, mangled rooks into our bags. All the while there was another Henry along, one whose wife had just been irrevocably revealed as an adulteress, a whore.

Why could I not feel? Why this strange detachment, this jumpiness, along with a perpetual shadow, an inner tolling of a bell?

The falcons were off again, and Cromwell and I continued the eerie conversation.

"I have had Master Smeaton to dinner," he said. "I entertained him last week, at my London house. He was flattered to be invited. I was able to . . . persuade him to talk. He admitted everything. That he had had carnal relations with the Queen."

"He said . . . 'carnal relations'?"

"I have his words," said Cromwell. "Allow me?" He indicated the horses, and his saddle-pouch. We walked back, and he drew out a sheaf of papers.

"The details of the conversation," he said. "I thought it best."

I read the entire hateful thing, wherein Smeaton confessed his adultery and named William Brereton, Francis Weston, and Henry Norris as her lovers as well.

Henry Norris. My companion of the chamber, my friend.

Did she take an especial relish in bedding him?

He must have protested. I knew Norris, an honourable man. He must have been a difficult quarry, a challenge to her ingenuity and persistence. But she had evidently succeeded.

According to Smeaton's confession:

> *Anne had asked Norris why he had not been more eager to conclude his arranged marriage with Margaret Shelton, and, answering for him, said, "Ah, if any accident befell the King—such as his jousting accident this January—you would look to have me for yourself. You look for dead man's shoes!"*

So I was reduced to this teasing formula. I felt diminished, depersonalized, weakened.

> *Francis Weston was likewise neglecting his wife in favour of Norris's fiancé. When Anne chided him, he had replied, "There is one in your household I love more ardently than either my wife or Mistress Shelton."*
>
> *"Why, who?" asked Anne, innocently.*
>
> *"It is yourself," he confessed.*

> *When she came upon Mark Smeaton alone, skulking and looking forlorn, she asked him, cruelly, "Why are you so sad?"*
>
> *"It is of no importance," he answered, with as much dignity as he could command.*
>
> *"No, please tell me." Her voice was full of luring concern, and he wished to believe it. "Are you unhappy because I have not spoken to you in company?"*

After bedding with him, she had undoubtedly taken a taunting delight in ignoring him when others were present.

> *"You may not look to have me speak to you as I should to a nobleman, because you are an inferior person," she had explained, sweetly.*
>
> *"No, no. A look sufficeth me," he had answered. "And so fare thee well," he wished her.*

There was more of this sort of thing. Anne had given Mark gold pieces "for his services."

I had no desire to read further, any more than a man would wish to plunge headfirst into a cesspool.

"There is one thing more," Cromwell said. He produced another paper. "George Boleyn's wife, Jane, has confided in me that—that—here, you may read her very words." He looked embarrassed for the first time.

I took the paper. It stated, simply, that Queen Anne Boleyn and her brother George were lovers. That they had committed incest together many times.

"This is abomination," I finally said. "It is so filthy, so perverted, so—" I could think of no word to describe it adequately, to describe *her*. "She is the English Messalina," I whispered.

Satan . . . and our pride. He attacks us through our pride. He had heard me assure myself that the Sixth Commandment was the only one she had *not* broken. I had believed her chaste, though evil. Satan had taken that as a challenge. . . .

"A Queen's adultery is treason. Imagining the King's death is treason. When shall we make the arrests, and hold the trials?" asked Cromwell.

"Soon. Let it be soon."

The falcons had made another kill. I cared not what it was. I knew they could kill; what was the surprise in it? It was when a thing acted against its nature that there was surprise in it.

> " 'When the Tower is white and another place green
> There shall be burned two or three bishops and a queen,
> And after this be passed we shall have a merry world,' "

Cromwell recited. "It is a popular rhyme. We have not burned a bishop—how could we, burning is only for heretics and witches. Perhaps this is the start?"

Anne would burn. The Witch would burn. And she had known it all along; her fear of fire had been due to her foreknowledge.

LXXII

A month passed—a careful, watchful month on my part. I gave Cromwell leave to do what was necessary to arrange the arrests. He should move stealthily and avoid causing the parties alarm, lest they take flight or move (in Anne's case) to strike at us first. My leg still ailed me, but had not worsened, and the same held true for Fitzroy and Mary. I had no doubt that she planned more fatal measures for each of us, but was biding her time, as four royal deaths in four months would arouse *anyone's* suspicions.

During those days, I had to continue to allow Henry Norris to serve me daily in my chamber. Whenever he laid out my shoes and hose, I wondered if he thought, *Dead man's shoes, dead man's shoes . . .?* It took every particle of self-control I possessed not to betray my knowledge of him. I felt surrounded by betrayal, dissemblance, and vice.

Without Jane's presence at court, there would have been no clean thing in my sight, and then I truly would have known despair. I glimpsed her often in the company of Anne's maids of honour, but as I did not frequent Anne's chambers, I never saw her close. Other times I would see her passing in the gallery, or walking in the palace gardens below, always in the company of two or three other women. Just watching her move, seeing her gentle gestures, was soothing.

But at length evil thoughts about her came to me. Immersed as I was in corruption and the dark side of human nature, it was inevitable that my mind became tainted by association. I listened to the spiteful remarks made about her, and then to the ones my own head put forth.

Jane is a tool in her ambitious brothers' hands. They are prompting her every move, calculated to appeal to your tastes—and your weaknesses.

Jane is not the virtuous woman she pretends to be; she but plays a part.

Jane sees an opportunity to make her fortune from your misfortune. A pale little opportunist, Mistress Seymour, beneath her prim manner and righteous words.

But if Jane were not true, then everything in the world was false. . . .

I would know the truth. I had never shunned the truth, and I would not begin now.

Those were my high-sounding words. In actuality, I was desperate to silence those mockers, for they were undermining my last source of earthly serenity.

So I succumbed to their tactics, and devised a test for Jane, disliking myself for needing to do so, telling myself all the while that it was necessary.

I wrote her a letter, in which I told her that I knew the circumstances of her loss of my mother's locket, and that, by God's good grace, I had recovered it. I told her that there were troubling doubts in my mind concerning her. Along with the letter I sent a purse bulging with gold sovereigns, more than a hundred of them. I gave the purse and letter to a groom of my chamber, and told him to present this to Mistress Jane Seymour in private, and then to wait for her answer.

That evening he came to me, with the letter and pouch as I had given them to him.

"Have you not obeyed me?" I protested.

"Yes, Your Majesty. I found Mistress Seymour walking alone in the privy orchard, in the rows of pear trees, and I approached her, and handed her these things. She took them, and after glancing at them, she—she fell to her knees, Your Majesty."

"What, in the mud?"

"There was no mud. The ground was quite hard. I remember that the petals from the pears were lying quite dryly all around . . . there was no mud."

"Why did she not read my letter?" I must know every moment of what passed.

"She examined the royal seal, then kissed it, but did not break it. She took the purse and opened it. But then she closed it all up again. She looked at me, as if in distress, and said, 'Pray tell the King to consider that I am a gentlewoman of good and honourable parents without reproach. I have no greater riches in the world than my honour, which for a thousand deaths I would not hurt. If his Grace wishes to make me a present of money, I beg him to do it when God might have sent me a good and honest marriage.' "

"Those were her exact words?"

"Yes, Your Majesty. I took the liberty of writing them down immediately after quitting her presence, lest I forget." He shrugged. "Perhaps it was foolish?"

"No, no. You did well." I appreciated caution and thoroughness. I opened the purse and gave him a sovereign. "We thank you."

I put the purse away, and the letter. Jane had shown herself to be all that

I hoped for. Let this, then, silence the murmurs in my head. Let me not yield to the temptation to test her further. Let there remain some semblance of innocence and trust in me, lest I have nothing to offer Jane Seymour in myself.

April. The very word has a green sound. *April.* It should have a green look and a green smell as well, and this year it did. A strange odour perfused the air, as a green wind swept over the land. It was a sharp odour, a deep odour, of warmth and primitive beginnings.

I rode alone in the meadows when I smelled it. I would have had Jane beside me, but I could not seek her company unchaperoned, and so I did not. The pastures and meadows turned velvety emerald; and the woodlands were a display of pastel colours, as the baby leaves of a thousand trees uncurled: not green at all, in their first hours, but lavender, pink, red, gold.

Cromwell had all in order. The arrests would be made on May Day, following the customary jousts.

"Everyone will be all together then, and that should simplify matters," he explained. "The ceremonial presence of the Yeomen of the Guard will serve to disguise their true purpose."

Disguise, true . . . the tortuous theme of the past half-year.

"The arrests can be made unobtrusively. In the confusion and high spirits, no one will notice. They can be imprisoned by nightfall, all at once. Interrogation the next day, May second. Trial by May tenth. Execution by May fifteenth at the latest," he said.

"Good." The sooner it was over, the better.

"It will be necessary for you to attend with the Queen," Cromwell said apologetically.

"Quite so." If she could play her part, so could I.

We sat in the royal box, Anne and I. This was the first year I had not participated in the May Day tournament. The reason I gave out was my fall in the January jousts. Still, it was difficult to play the part of a spectator, as if I were an old King, one who existed only as a voyeur. It was a world with which I had no wish to acquaint myself, had always disdained and rejected.

Humility, I thought. Being *thought* old and infirm and accepting it with grace is humility. Just as Christ pretended to be powerless before Pilate. (Although he could not resist the cryptic comment about only "allowing" Pilate to have power.) But comparing myself with Christ was pride. I extracted pride even from humility; I could squeeze it from any situation, like juice from an orange.

Anne was in white, the same white she had worn, and so well, at her Coronation. She knew how fairly it set off her dark hair, her creamy skin; and such were her powers that for a few moments, as I sat beside her, I strained to believe her innocent, maligned, so lovely was she, so far from anything morbid. But I knew what I knew.

We did not speak. Each of us waved to the spectators, to the participants. The sun was bright on the field, and shone on the knights' armour. I longed to be with them, instead of penned up in this watching box.

Anne's lovers all rode in the contests. I watched her carefully out of the corner of my eye to see how she behaved toward them. Weston and Brereton caused her no notice—poor men! did they suspect how little she regarded them? —but she quivered with attention to her brother George, who performed well enough. (Not as a champion, but certainly passable.) Then Norris took his place, riding against Francis Bryan. Before beginning, he made the customary bow to the royal box.

Suddenly Anne leaned forward and flagrantly dropped her handkerchief. He picked it up, kissed it, passed it along his brow, then handed it back up to her. Their hands met, caressed.

This effrontery was a spark to my tinder. It was so brazen, so blatant, that I could not endure it. The insult was too great.

I stood up and said softly to Anne, "So, Madam. You shall have your reward." I looked my last at her. I should never see her again upon this earth.

I left the royal box, and informed Cromwell that I was returning immediately to the palace. "Make the arrests as soon as this course is over," I ordered him. "Do not delay."

The handkerchief had been the last liberty Anne would take with my folly of having loved her. There is required a small act to kill love utterly; for reasons known only to God, large, heinous acts do not do it. Perhaps they are too great, have too many chinks and explanations. Only a small act of malicious disregard can achieve the final killing. A lace-edged handkerchief did what even Smeaton's confession had failed to do completely, that is, in every corner of my being.

Norris had not ridden, after all. He had divested himself of his armour and left the grounds straightway, riding after me. He overtook me before I was in sight of Westminster, and rode boldly up to me. I refused to look at him.

"Your Majesty, you are angry at me," he said.

I did not reply.

"Pray tell me my offence, so that I may amend it."

"The handkerchief . . ." I began. "Was it necessary to mock me so? Or was that *her* doing?"

"As God is my witness, I do not understand."

"Stop the pretence!" I hissed. "You are the Queen's lover. I know the truth, and you shall die for it."

"It is not true!" His voice rose in terror. "It is not true! Never have I betrayed you with the Queen, in thought or deed!"

"Come, Norris. She has betrayed us all; you are not alone." He, too, was a victim. "Confess the truth, and you shall go free." Suddenly I meant it. How could I punish him for a fault I shared with him?

"Confess the truth!" I repeated. "Let someone, at last, speak truth to my face!"

The whole truth was a different creature from the half-truth. I wanted him not to deny the accusation, for I knew the physical facts were true, but to somehow redeem it, to acknowledge the bald facts but to give them some interpretation I could live with and assimilate. I wanted it to be kinder and simpler than it sounded, and perhaps it was, but I needed his help in making it so. . . .

"It is completely untrue, Your Majesty."

That was of no use. Norris, you did it, but you must have reasons, please explain them, please put some note of honour and cleanness in this by your very presence . . . your involvement. . . .

"Confess! Confess and you'll go free, be pardoned, I promise it!"

"There is nothing to confess. And I am willing to undergo trial by combat to defend the Queen's honour—"

"She has no honour!" I cried. "Abandon this course, it is hopeless."

"True combat will reveal otherwise," he insisted.

Anne had blinded him, then. He was entirely her creature, ready to defend her to the death.

Another victim, I thought. She has garnered another victim. The honourable ones made the easiest prey; they ensnared themselves in their own nets.

"Arrest him!" I cried to my guards. "Arrest this man!" I reined my horse away from Norris, and pointed at him.

The Yeomen of the Guard closed in, and Norris vanished from my sight. All I saw was a clump of mounted horsemen in the clear spring sunlight, their weapons drawn and sparkling.

LXXIII

WILL:

As night fell, Norris, Brereton, and Weston were all in the Tower. Smeaton had been taken there earlier in the day.

Anne and her brother were still at liberty. It was the last night they would be so. Reportedly, Anne, distressed at the King's behaviour at the jousts, had asked frightened questions and been met with silence. That something was wrong was clear from the deserted royal apartments and the ominous silence of Anne's servitors at dinner. As representatives of the King, they customarily presented her dishes with the salute, "Much good may it do you!" This evening, however, they omitted the phrase.

She was left to spend an apprehensive night by herself. Mark Smeaton had been taken away, she was told. He could not play for her. She attempted to send for her brother George, but was told "it was not meet." Like one of the wild beasts in the Tower menagerie, she was to spend the night in a cage, prowling restlessly, not knowing why she was confined, or what awaited her.

The King spent it weeping and storming. Those of us about him knew not whether to attempt to comfort him or to look away. In the end we chose to look away. Even a King needs to be ignored at times; indeed, he probably craves it.

In the morning the King called first Cromwell, then the rest of the Privy Council, and explained the circumstances. They were to arrest the Queen and take her to the Tower, first setting forth the charges.

Meanwhile, Anne ate her midday dinner and made jokes. "The King keeps this odd behaviour to test me. To test my courage," she insisted.

At about two in the afternoon a deputation of the Privy Council came to her chambers to speak with her and interview her household. It was led by her uncle the Duke of Norfolk, and by Cromwell.

They came into her presence boldly, not deferentially.

"You have committed adultery," the Duke accused her, "with five known men. These men are already imprisoned and have confessed. You, too, must confess. There is no more need to hide and lie. All is known." He also accused her of incest and intent to murder her husband.

Anne angrily denied it. "I am clean from the touch of any man but my true wedded husband, the King!" she screeched.

Her uncle shook his head sadly at her stubborn lie. Already the State Barge, which would convey her to the Tower, was waiting by the water-steps of the palace, manned by Kingston, the Constable of the Tower, and four enemy women spies chosen by Cromwell to report every word Anne uttered henceforth.

"Tut, tut, tut," murmured the Duke, shaking his head like the clapper of a bell.

That afternoon Anne was rowed to the Tower, while the bright spring sunlight glanced off the Thames and common folk waved excitedly at the State Barge.

When she was received at the entrance, she fell to her knees. "God help me!" she cried. "I am not guilty of the accusation!"

Then Kingston and his men took her away—to the selfsame rooms she had lain in the night before her Coronation. There she would stay, alone, with no kind person nearby. Where there had been flatterers and singers that other May night three years ago, now there was silence and mystery.

"Where is my sweet brother?" she cried.

"I left him at York Place," Kingston answered. The truth was that George Boleyn had been taken to the Tower that very morning.

"I hear say that I shall be accused with five men; and I can say no more but nay without I should open my body," she cried, flinging open her skirt hysterically. No one understood her words.

"O Norris, hast thou accused me?" she asked the air. "Thou art in the Tower together, and thou and I will die together; and Mark, thou art here too."

When the King heard how she called upon her brother, Norris, and Smeaton, he wept.

Cromwell knew the Queen well. He knew that she was "as brave as a lion," as someone had once described her, but that even a lion needs an adversary. Without an adversary, without a clear-cut accuser, she would nervously babble and betray herself. He directed every word she spoke to be recorded. Anne Boleyn had never known how to keep silent. Cromwell, who had heard the "I have a longing to eat apples" speech, knew well how to exploit her fatal weakness.

The very first day he reaped a bountiful harvest. She recalled her conversation with Weston in which he had professed his love. She compared him with Norris. "I more fear Weston," she said, and explained why.

The next day she came to her brother. Her spies had told her that he had been arrested.

"I am very glad that we both be so nigh together," she said.

Kingston confirmed that five men had been arrested and now lay in the Tower because of her.

"Mark is the worst treated," volunteered one of the women. "He is chained in irons."

"That is because he is no gentleman," said Anne, callously. She looked about. "They shall make ballads of me now," she said dreamily. "But there is none but my brother to do so. Shall he die?" she asked Kingston.

At his refusal to answer, she descended to threats. "We shall have no rain until I am delivered out of the Tower!" she cried.

Kingston shrugged, unmoved. "I pray it may be shortly because of the fair weather," he replied.

In the meantime the King stormed and screamed. He was wilder than Anne. The night after Anne had been taken to the Tower, his natural son, Henry Fitzroy, had come to call upon him and bid him good night. The distracted, sorrowing King fell on his thin shoulders and cried, "God be praised you are safe from that cursed and venomous whore, who was determined to poison you!"

The bewildered, coughing Fitzroy merely held him fast: son comforting father.

Then an eerie silence descended. The Queen and all her accused paramours and conspirators were held behind the stone walls of the Tower. Juries were being assembled, and formal accusations drawn up. Parliament was prorogued, not to meet again for a month. The King forbade any mail or ships to leave England. The outside world wondered what was happening there. They knew it must be something terrible and momentous.

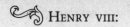

I started receiving letters. First Cranmer wrote me, in amazement and condolence:

> And I am in such a perplexity, that my mind is clean amazed; for I never had better opinion in woman than I had in her; which maketh me to think she should not be culpable. And again, I think that Your Highness would not have gone so far, except she had surely been culpable.
>
> Now I think that Your Grace best knoweth, that next unto Your Grace I was most bound unto her of all creatures living. Wheretofore I most humbly beseech Your Grace to suffer me in that which both God's law, nature, and also her kindness, bindeth me unto; that is that I may with Your Grace's favour wish and pray for her, that she may declare herself inculpable and innocent. And if she be found culpable, I repute him not Your Grace's faithful servant and subject, that would not desire the offence without mercy to be punished.

Then Anne took pen in hand to persuade me. But the letter venomously accused *me* of shortcomings rather than addressing her own:

> Your Grace's displeasure and my imprisonment are things so strange unto me, that what to write, or what to excuse, I am altogether ignorant. Whereas you send to me such a one, whom you know to be mine ancient professed enemy; I no sooner received this message by him, than I rightly conceived your meaning; and if as you say, confessing a truth indeed may procure my safety, I shall, with all willingness and duty, perform your command.
>
> But let not Your Grace ever imagine your poor wife will ever be brought to acknowledge a fault, where not so much as a thought ever proceeded. And to speak a truth, never a prince had wife more loyal in all duty, and in all true affection, than you have ever found in Anne Boleyn—with which name and place I could willingly have contented myself if God and Your Grace's pleasure had so pleased. Neither did I at any time so far forget myself in my exaltation, or received Queenship, but that I always looked for such alteration as I now find; for the ground of my preferment being on no surer foundation than Your Grace's fancy, the least alteration was fit and sufficient (I knew) to draw that fancy to some other subject.
>
> You have chosen me from a low estate to be your Queen and companion, far beyond my desert or desire; if then you found me worthy

of such honour, good Your Grace, let not any light fancy or bad counsel of my enemies withdraw your princely favour from me, neither let that stain—that unworthy stain—of a disloyal heart toward your good Grace, ever cast so foul a blot on me and on the infant Princess your daughter Elizabeth.

Try me, good King, but let me have a lawful trial, and let not my sworn enemies sit as my judges; yea, let me receive an open trial, for my truth shall fear no open shames; then shall you see either mine innocency cleared, your suspicions and conscience satisfied, the ignominy and slander of the world stopped, or my guilt openly declared. So that whatever God and you may determine of, Your Grace may be at liberty, both before God and man, not only to execute worthy punishment on me, as an unfaithful wife, but to follow your affection already settled on that party, Mistress Seymour, for whose sake I am now as I am; whose name I could some good while since have pointed unto:—Your Grace being not ignorant of my suspicions therein.

But if you have already determined of me, and that not only my death, but an infamous slander, must bring you to the joying of your desired happiness, then I desire of God that He will pardon your great sin herein, and, likewise, my enemies, the instruments thereof, and that He will not call you to a strait account for your unprincely and cruel usage of me at His general judgment-seat, where both you and myself must shortly appear; and in whose just judgment, I doubt not (whatsoever the world may think of me) mine innocency shall be openly known and sufficiently cleared.

My last and only request shall be, that myself may only bear the burden of Your Grace's displeasure, and that it may not touch the innocent souls of those poor gentlemen, whom, as I understand, are likewise in strait imprisonment for my sake.

If ever I have found favour in your sight—if ever the name of Anne Boleyn have been pleasing in your ears—then let me obtain this request; and so I will leave to trouble Your Grace no further; with mine earnest prayers to the Trinity to have Your Grace in His good keeping, and to direct you in all your actions.

From my doleful prison in the Tower, the 6th of May.

Anne Boleyn.

If ever the name of Anne Boleyn have been pleasing in your ears. Yes, once it had been. Once I had been so bewitched. But no more, no more!

I walked my corridors. I kept sleepless nights. I prayed for guidance. But it was all a waking nightmare. Day and night blended together in a way that has never occurred since, even in the grip of illness. Outside it was clear and pure, and lily-of-the-valley was in bloom, green and white. Along the south bank of the Thames the grass was thick and wildflowers were open. Inside the palace it was seasonless, detached from all other concerns. The palace made its own seasons.

WILL:

The "crimes"—that is, the bodily crimes—were allegedly committed in the counties of Middlesex and Kent, and indictments must be returned from there. Grand juries sat, deliberated, and returned recommendations during those ugly May days. The evidence was so overwhelming that the five men must stand trial.

The commoners—Smeaton, Brereton, Weston, and Norris—were to be tried on May twelfth, at Westminster Hall, that all-purpose condemnation and celebration chamber. They were dragged out of the Tower and marched through the streets of London to the salivating curiosity of the local citizens. The jury was made up of "the King's commissioners," including Thomas Boleyn himself.

At the Hall, they were faced with an axe with its edge turned temporarily away, and charges were entered against them of having conspired the death of the King, having had carnal knowledge of the Queen, having committed treason against the heirs of the King and Queen and against the King's peace.

Smeaton admitted the second charge, of having "known and violated" the Queen. All the other charges were denied by all of them. But they were all found guilty, and the cutting edge of the axe was turned toward them. They were marched back toward the Tower in silence.

Their date of execution was fixed for May seventeenth—five days after their trial. They were to be shut away and ignored until that day.

The King was troubled that only Smeaton had confessed. He would have preferred that they all had broken under the questioning and admitted their guilt. Not that there was any question in his own mind of their guilt. "I am convinced that these are but a token, that over one hundred men have had intercourse with her," he said.

Three days after the courtiers' trial, the Boleyns were tried—separately—in the King's Hall, within the precincts of the Tower. Twenty-six peers of the realm were to sit in judgment. The Duke of

Norfolk served as the King's representative, High Steward, under a canopy of estate. On one side was the Duke of Suffolk, and on the other Audley, the Lord Chancellor. Amongst the peers was Henry Percy, now Earl of Northumberland.

More than two thousand observers were crowded into the Hall— the Mayor and aldermen of London, members of the principal craft guilds; the courtiers, ambassadors, merchants, and commoners; and myself. I could not help thinking how very public Anne's end was to be, compared to her secret wedding. The King did not care if every commoner heard the nasty details of his cuckolding; indeed, in some strange way, he invited them to come and drink at the well of his shame.

Anne swept into the Hall with arrogance and grace, as if she were presiding over these people, not being called to answer to them. She was, once again, the person who had bewitched the King. Clearly she meant to perform her magic as she had done before.

The Duke read out the indictments found by the juries of Kent and Middlesex:

Whereas Lady Anne has been Queen of England, wife of our Lord Henry VIII . . . for more than three years . . . she not only despising the most excellent and noble marriage solemnised between the said Lord our King and the lady Queen herself, but also bearing malice in her heart toward the said Lord our King, led astray by devilish instigation, not having God before her eyes and following daily her fickle and carnal appetite and wishing that several familiar and daily servants of our Lord the King should become her adulterers and concubines . . . contrary to the duty of their allegiance . . . she most falsely and treacherously procured them by foul talk and kisses, touchings, gifts and various other unspeakable instigations and incitements . . . in accordance as her most damnable propensity to crime drove her on: that, moreover, for the perpetration of that most wicked and treacherous crime of adultery by the Queen certain servants of the said lord King, through the most vile provocation and incitement day after day by the said Queen, were given over and attached to the said Queen in treacherous fashion, and that from here and from other sources this is the account, as here follows of the treacherous deeds and words.

The list of actual acts and adulteries began:

On 6 October 1533 at the palace of Westminster . . . and on various other days, before and after, by sweet words, kissings, touchings and other illicit means, she did procure and incite Henry Norris, a gentleman of the Privy Chamber of Our Lord the King, to violate and carnally know her, by reason whereof the same Henry Norris on October 12 violated, stained, and carnally knew her.

As for her own brother George, Lord Rochford, on November 2:

. . . with the Queen's tongue in the mouth of the said George and George's tongue in the mouth of the Queen, with kisses with open mouth, with gifts and jewels, by reason whereof Lord George Rochford, despising all the Almighty God's precepts, and by every law of human nature, on November 5 violated and carnally knew his own natural sister.

The rest of the list (filled in with lascivious details) was:

—On Nov. 19, 1533, at Westminster, with Henry Norris.
—On Nov. 27, 1533, at Westminster, with William Brereton.
—On Dec. 8, 1533, at Hampton Court, with William Brereton.
—On May 19, 1534, at Greenwich, with Mark Smeaton.
—On May 20, 1534, at Greenwich, with Francis Weston.
—On June 20, 1534, at Greenwich, with Francis Weston.
—On April 26, 1535, at Westminster, with Mark Smeaton.
—On Dec. 29, 1535, at Eltham, with George Boleyn.

In addition to her "foul and insatiable lust," she had conspired with her paramours against Henry's life. She had told them "she had never wished to choose the King in her heart" and had "promised to marry one of them when the King died." To keep them her love-slaves, she had played one off against the other, giving them outrageous gifts.

Cromwell and his Attorney-General, Sir Christopher Hales, introduced two other charges: that she had poisoned the Princess Dowager and attempted to do the same to the Lady Mary; and had injured the King's health maliciously—for when the King became aware of her evil, he "had conceived in his heart such inward displeasure and sadness . . . that certain grave injuries and perils had befallen his royal body." This certainly was true, as I knew, regardless of how others snickered at it.

She had mocked the King behind his back, her accusers said, made fun of his poetry, his music, his clothes, and his person. She had also written her brother George concerning her pregnancy, indicating that the child was in fact his.

Anne rose to defend herself. Standing as proudly as ever I had seen her, she tossed her head and spoke in a loud, ringing voice that carried to the farthest reaches of the stone chamber.

Significantly, she did not answer the latter charges. She addressed only the adultery ones, claiming that she was innocent, although she *had* given Francis Weston money, and had asked Mark Smeaton to her chambers to play the virginal. She spoke with eloquence and wit, and with unearthly charm.

But it did her no good. When the verdict was called, the majority of peers pronounced her guilty. Then her dread uncle Norfolk rose to pronounce sentence:

"Guilty of high treason, adultery, and incest. Thou hast deserved death, and thy judgement is this: That thou shalt be burnt here within the Tower of London on the green, else to have thy head smitten off as the King's pleasure shall be further known."

A great silence, then a movement from the peers. Henry Percy has collapsed. He must be carried, lying limply on his attendant's shoulder, from the Hall. Anne watches him, and something in her face changes, withers.

She speaks now, but without fire.

"O God, Thou knowest if I have merited this death." She pauses. "My Lords, I will not say your sentence is unjust, nor presume that my reasons can prevail against your convictions. I am willing to believe that you have sufficient reasons for what you have done, but then they must be other than those which have been produced in court, for I am clear of all the offences which you then laid to my charge. I have ever been a faithful wife to the King, though I do not say I have always shown him that humility which his goodness to me and the honour to which he raised me merited.

"I confess I have had jealous fancies and suspicions of him which I had not discretion and wisdom enough to conceal at all times. But God knows, and is my witness, that I never sinned against him in any other way.

"Think not I say this in the hope to prolong my life. God hath taught me how to die and He will strengthen my faith.

"Think not that I am so bewildered in my mind as not to lay the honour of my chastity to heart now in my extremity, when I have maintained it all my life long, as much as ever Queen did. I know these my last words will avail me nothing, but for the justification of my chastity and honour.

"As for my brother and those others who are unjustly condemned, I would willingly suffer many deaths to deliver them; but since I see it so pleases the King, I shall willingly accompany them in death, with this assurance, that I shall lead an endless life with them in peace.

"I beg you, good people, pray for me."

She rises wearily, and Kingston leads her out of the Hall and back to her imprisonment.

Her uncle is crying openly. Moments pass until he has himself under control and can confront the last accused prisoner, George Boleyn, Lord Rochford.

The charges are read. They consist of the incest and adultery with his sister, the Queen. He denies it. Of plotting the King's death. He denies it. Of implying that he is the father of the Princess Elizabeth.

At this he smirks and keeps silent, raising one eyebrow mockingly.

A last charge, written on paper, is presented to the peers, then shown to Lord Rochford; it is forbidden to speak the charges aloud before the people. The information has been supplied by Rochford's own wife, Jane.

"Ah, yes," George Boleyn says loudly, and reads the paper word for word. 'My sister Queen Anne has told me that the King is impotent. He no longer has either vigour or virtue in his private parts.'" He laughs, jarringly. Cromwell protests, scolding like an angry jaybird. Boleyn smiles, saying, "But I will not create suspicion in a manner likely to prejudice the issue the King might have from a second marriage."

In one sentence, the King is now the accused. The next marriage has been mentioned, the unspoken thing the people are wondering about. Is it true the King has already chosen a successor? Could it be that all this is arranged merely to facilitate a new marriage?

But Cromwell has a higher trump: yet another statement by Jane Boleyn, Lady Rochford. She swears that there is an incestuous relationship between her husband and his sister the Queen. The "accursed secret," known heretofore only to herself, she must in conscience reveal.

Now the accuser is discredited by his own wife, shown for the foul thing he is.

The twenty-six peers pronounce him guilty, and the Duke reads the sentence:

"You shall now go again to the Tower from whence you came, and be drawn from the said Tower of London through the City of London, there to be hanged and then, being alive, cut down—and then your members cut off and your bowels taken out of your body and burnt before you, and then your head cut off and your body divided into four pieces, and your head and body to be set at such places as the King shall assign."

A cruel hush descended on London after the trials, a breath-holding until the executions. Those who passed by the Tower could hear hammering, and knew the scaffolds were being reassembled, dragged out of storage where they had lain since More's execution last summer.

It was said that the King passed these spring nights on his barge, courting Jane, and that the sound of music and the glow of lanterns carried across the water. They said he was rowed back and forth under the shadow of the Tower. They said a great deal of nonsense, but it made a striking story and painted a picture of the King as a satyr. The truth is that he went out on his barge only once, and not to "the shadow of the Tower," but to visit Jane at Nicholas Carew's house on the Thames.

LXXIV

Henry VIII:

It was over, then. The trial was over and the Witch had not escaped her just sentence. Crum reported it all to me—even, sadly, the personal attacks on me. I was not affected by that; my only fear was that somehow, even yet, Anne would manage to escape.

To be burnt or beheaded at the King's pleasure—I remembered her horror of fire. Would it not be revenge for my "pleasure" to inflict that on her? For her to meet her death, bound and screaming, for her flesh to be roasted, her blood boiled in her veins? I could smell the charred flesh, the stench of her hair aflame. . . .

But I could not. I could not do that, knowing that she was bound for hell as soon as her soul quitted her body—where there would be fire aplenty, the everlasting fire that burns but does not consume. I would not imitate or mock the Devil in providing an earthly substitute. Let Anne quit this earth without bodily pain.

But there was one thing I would have of her, one thing that only she could give: information, a confession that our marriage had been false all along. I would send Cranmer to her, to receive her confession, holding out the promise to spare her the flames if she only admitted it, admitted that she had brought this marriage about by witchcraft, and now abjured it. For I would be freed of her before her death. She would not breathe her last as my wife. I would not be linked to her!

"Go to her," I commissioned Cranmer, "to her suite in the Tower, and extract an oath from her regarding this matter." I noted the questioning look on his face. "Yes, she still keeps state, under my express command. She has her royal quarters, her jewels and gowns." I remembered More in his bookless cell. "They were what she sold her soul for, were they not? Let her enjoy them to the end."

She would keep everything to the end (except her title as my wife), and suddenly I envisioned the fitting way for her to depart this life. I would send for a French swordsman, and he would perform the execution deftly and with style. She had always loved the "French way"; doubtless a good English axe would be too crude for her sensibilities. I wrote out the order for the Lieutenant of Calais. What a surprise I was giving her, right up to the last. . . .

I began to laugh—first a little, then hysterically.

✒ WILL:

We heard the screams of laughter coming from the King's private chamber, but dared not enter. It sounded as if a madman were within, and we feared that somehow an intruder had gained entrance. The laughter was not recognizable as the King's; that was the reason why at length a guard opened the door and checked inside.

There was no one there but King Henry, seated before his writing desk, and red in the face, looking apoplectic.

I approached him—I was the only one who dared—and stood ready to summon the physician. He had suffered a seizure, I was sure.

"Now, good my Lord, help is coming," I said, in what I meant to be my most reassuring tone.

"Help?" he said, in a quiet voice. The red was draining from his face. "Nay, there's no help for it. 'Tis done, 'tis done." He indicated a letter, ready to be sent. "A pretty French death," he said. "One's death should be consistent with one's life, should it not? Only we seldom can arrange it. Well, I shall oblige."

Had the strain, the grief, quite overwhelmed his mind? "Yes, Your Grace," I said, gently. "Lord Privy Seal will see to these dispatches. Come now. You have overworked yourself."

He started to rise, then shook his head. "One thing more. I must give them an easy death as well. Commute the sentence to a simple beheading. There, that'll do." He began scribbling orders on parchment. "But they must content themselves with a local headsman and a regular axe."

On the morning of May seventeenth, with Anne watching from her window, her five lovers and co-conspirators were marched out to the hill beyond the Tower moat, there to mount the scaffold. It was a fine high one, so that all the onlookers (and the crowd was vast) could have a clear view.

Sir William Brereton was the first to stand upon the platform. He whined like a coward and shook bodily.

"I have deserved to die, if it were a thousand deaths," he cried. Then, at the motioning of the headsman to lay his head upon the block, he protested, "But the cause whereof I judge not—but if you judge, judge the best." Seeking further delay, he repeated himself three or four more times.

But at length his voice failed, and he was forced to put his head down. The headsman raised his great axe and chopped clean through Brereton's neck. The head rolled in the straw, and the headsman held it up, as was customary.

It took some few minutes to remove the body and head, lay fresh straw, and wipe clean the block and axe. The dead man was taken down by steps on the opposite side of the scaffold.

Next came Henry Norris. He said little, but what he did say was flattering to the King.

"I do not think that any gentleman of the court owes more to the King than I do, and has been more ungrateful and regardless of it than I have. I pray God to have mercy on my soul." Then he cooperatively laid his head on the block. The headsman struck, and it was over in the time it takes to draw a good breath.

Sir Francis Weston, that pretty boy whose wife and mother had offered a ransom of one hundred thousand crowns to redeem his life, stood fresh-faced on the scaffold, the blue May skies no clearer than his eyes.

"I had thought to have lived in abomination these twenty or thirty years, and then to have made amends. I thought little it had come to this," he said, seeking to be clever and fashionably lighthearted right up to the end. When the headsman held up his severed head, though, the eyes were no longer a sweet blue but glazed-over grey.

Overhead, black shapes were gathering. The buzzards had scented blood and seen moving creatures suddenly cease to move.

Mark Smeaton stood proudly on the scaffold. "Masters, I pray you all pray for me—for I have deserved the death." The lovelorn lute-player fell eagerly upon the block, as if afraid he might be contradicted or denied his death.

Last was Lord Rochford, George Boleyn. He could not help but see the stacked coffins to his right, and the shadows of the buzzards circling overhead, making spots on the scaffold. He looked out at the crowd, then over across the moat to his sister's apartments.

Everyone was silent, awaiting his speech. But, strangely, he began speaking of Lutheranism (he had long been suspected of leaning toward heresy). "I desire you that no man will be discouraged from the Gospel at my fall. For if I had lived according to the Gospel—as I loved it and spake of it—I had never come to this." He went on at length exhorting his hearers to live according to the Gospel.

The hearers were not interested in a sermon, which they could hear from any friar or court preacher. It was not religion that they wanted, but blood and sins.

"I never offended the King," he suddenly said, defiantly. "There is no occasion for me to repeat the cause for which I am condemned. You would have little pleasure in hearing me tell it," he said petulantly, cheating them of their fun. "I forgive you all. And God save the King." He might as well have stuck out his tongue. The nasty salute was his farewell to the world. The axe struck, and his head was disconnected.

The five coffins were borne away in the warm May sunshine, and the disgruntled buzzards flapped away.

Anne was to die the next day. But Henry's "surprise," the French swordsman, had not yet arrived, so the execution was postponed. The original day proved to be windy, and full of thunderstorms, so it was just as well.

Anne was to be executed within the precincts of the Tower, on the little green outside the Queen's lodgings. No more than thirty people were allowed to witness it, and the legs of the scaffold were lowered so that no one standing beyond the Tower walls could glimpse the proceedings inside. Invitations to the event were eagerly coveted. The Chancellor, the three Dukes (Norfolk, Suffolk, and Richmond), Cromwell, and the Privy Councillors were called upon to be witnesses, as well as the Lord Mayor of London, with the sheriffs and aldermen. A cannoneer would be stationed on the battlements, to fire the cannon the instant the Queen was dead.

The King would not attend. Nor would Cranmer. Nor any of the Seymours.

All the night before, Anne kept awake, praying and singing. She composed a long dirge-ballad for her lute, as if in defiance of the fact that her brother could no longer do it. She was determined to be celebrated; and distractedly, on her last night on earth, she wrote these verses, and set them to music:

Oh death, rock me asleep
Bring on my quiet rest
Let pass my very guiltless ghost
Out of my careful breast.
>*Ring out the doleful knell,*
>*Let its sound my death tell;*
>*For I must die,*
>*There is no remedy,*
>*For now I die!*

My pains who can express
Alas! they are so strong!
My dolour will not suffer strength
My life for to prolong
Alone in prison strange!
>*I wail my destiny;*
>*Woe worth this cruel hap, that I*
>*Should taste this misery.*

Farewell my pleasures past,
Welcome my present pain
I feel my torments so increase
That life cannot remain.
Sound now the passing bell,
Rung is my doleful knell,
For its sound my death doth tell,
>*Death doth draw nigh*
>*Sound the knell dolefully,*
>*For now I die!*

Defiled is my name, full sore
Through cruel spite and false report,
That I may say forevermore
Farewell to joy, adieu comfort,
For wrongfully he judge of me;
Unto my fame a mortal wound,
>*Say what ye list, it may not be,*
>*You seek for that shall not be found.*

Besides her praying and composing her ballad, she had one other bit of earthly business to attend to. She asked one of her women attendants to seek Mary's forgiveness for the wrongs she, Anne, had done her and for the severity with which she had treated her, for, until that was accomplished, her conscience could not be quiet. The woman promised to do this in Anne's name.

Dawn came before five, and Master Kingston was already exhausted from the tasks of the day ahead. As host for the execution of a Queen, he naturally had many details of both practicality and protocol to attend to. The witnessing dignitaries must be properly received and grouped about the scaffold according to rank; the twenty pounds in gold alms, provided by the King, to be distributed by Anne before her death, must be got up in little velvet bags; black drapery must be hung about the scaffold; and all chronicles mentioning the execution of a King or Queen must be consulted for the last time, in hopes of finding some overlooked detail that would provide the proper embellishment for the hideous occasion.

In addition, there was the matter of meeting the French headsman and giving him instructions; having the grave already dug and waiting; and procuring a coffin. Kingston was all in a dither, as he had received no instructions from King Henry about either the grave or the coffin, and yet the Queen's body would have to be disposed of somehow.

He was running late. And then came the welcome news: the King had postponed the hour of the execution from nine o'clock until noon. But still no word about the coffin!

Kingston sought out Anne to tell her of the delay. She was disappointed. "I had thought by noon to be past my pain," she said sadly. Rushing toward her gaoler, she whispered, "I am innocent!" She grabbed Kingston's arm, gripping it painfully. "I am innocent!" Then, in one of her characteristic mood shifts, she suddenly cried, "Is it painful?"

"No," said the Constable. "It is over too quickly. There should be no pain, it is so subtle."

She circled her neck with her hands. "I have a little neck," she said. "But the axe is so thick, and rough."

"Have you not heard? The King seeks to spare you that. He has sent to France for a swordsman to perform the duty."

"Ah!" She smiled, a little sliver of a smile. "He was ever a good and gentle sovereign lord to me." She began to laugh, that hideous, raucous laughter which cut itself off as abruptly as it began. "Will you carry a message to His Majesty on my behalf?"

Kingston nodded.

"Tell him he has ever been constant in his career of advancing me: from a private gentlewoman he made me a Marquess, from a Marquess a Queen, and now he hath left no higher degree of honour, he gives my innocency the crown of martyrdom." She gestured sweetly. "Will you tell my Lord that?"

"Never have I seen one to be executed who has such joy and pleasure in death," he said, to himself rather than to her, in wonder at her spirits. He went to take his leave, but she called after him.

"Master Kingston! Master Kingston! The people will have no difficulty finding a nickname for me. I shall be *la Reine Anne sans tête* . . . Queen Anne Lack-Head!"

Frightened, he slammed the thick oak door on her shrieking laughter, but it carried right through the wood.

All this I heard later from the Constable himself. As for the actual execution, I witnessed it in the King's stead. As the hour approached, Henry dressed himself all in white. I dared not ask him why, but there was a dreadful deliberateness in his choice of clothing, as if he were performing a secret ritual. He had kept entirely to himself for the past three days: beginning with the executions of the five men, then on the next day, wild and windy, when he had awaited the arrival of the ship from Calais carrying the swordsman from St. Omer. Now he made ready to go out, ponderously and methodically. His face was expressionless, but I was shocked when I beheld it. The three days had aged him a decade.

"Go there for me," he said. (No need to ask where "there" was.) "Watch it all. Tell me of it later. I shall be at Westminster. Outside. Perhaps I shall ride."

Yes, outside was the place of choice, this sweet May morning, when all the meadows were springing mint and violets. A warm wind had come up out of the south.

To die on such a morning would require extraordinary courage.

It was just noon when the door from the Queen's lodgings opened and Anne emerged, escorted by her only known women friends, Thomas Wyatt's sister and Margaret Lee. She was exquisitely dressed, reminding us all of her extraordinary ability to radiate beauty when she so chose. We were all struck by the high colour in her cheeks, the glitter in her eyes; she was more alive than any other person on the green.

Her neckline was low, to expose her neck and make it easier for her executioner.

She mounted the scaffold carefully, holding up her skirts, then presided over the proceedings as if she addressed Parliament.

Before her was the great wooden execution block, with a cupped indentation for her chin, and a four-inch span for her neck to stretch across. Around its base was enough straw to soak up the blood.

The Frenchman, slender and athletic, stood to her right, his steel sword pointed downward. To her left stood his assistants; their grisly duty was to tend to her headless trunk. A length of black cloth was at the ready, to cover her with. They smiled at her.

Overhead the sky was clear, and no cloud was visible. The damnable birds, lately returned from the winter, insisted on chirping and singing, flaunting their freedom and careless disregard.

"Good Christian people," she spoke, "I am come hither to die, according to law, for by the law I am judged to die, and therefore I will speak nothing against it." Her words rose, and her eyes seemed to fasten on each of us individually. She looked directly into mine, and in an instant I recalled—nay, relived—every meeting we had ever had.

"I come here only to die," she repeated. "And thus to yield myself humbly unto the will of my lord the King." She looked at each of us, dolourously. "I pray God to save the King, and send him long to reign over you, for a gentler or more merciful Prince was there never. To me he was ever a good and gentle sovereign lord."

Her words were respectful, but there was irony and mockery in them. The message was the same as that which Kingston had not dared to carry. Anne would make sure it reached Henry's ears.

She closed her eyes for a moment and fell silent, as if she had finished. "If any person will meddle with my cause, I require them to judge the best. Thus I take my leave of the world and of you, and heartily desire you all to pray for me."

Her words were ended. There had been no protestations of innocence, no mention of her daughter, no pious exhortations, no jests. Anne had arranged her exquisite death as she had arranged her fêtes and masques: out of the bare materials she had fashioned something of memorable, fragile beauty.

She turned to her ladies and gave them their farewell remembrances—a gold and black enamelled book of devotions, a few private words.

Then she calmly removed her headpiece and collar to ready herself for the swordsman. Refusing any blindfold, she closed her eyes and knelt down beside the block.

Then, suddenly, her courage deserted her. She heard rustling on her right, and, terror-stricken, looked up to see the swordsman advancing on her. Her eye froze him, and he retreated. Trembling, she lowered her head again, squeezing her eyes shut.

"O Jesu have mercy on my soul O Jesu have mercy on my soul—" she rattled on. Again her head jerked up, and she caught her executioner as he raised his sword.

She forced her head back onto the block, her whole body straining to hear her executioner move. "To Jesus Christ I commend my soul, to Jesus Christ I commend my soul, O God have pity on my soul; O God have pity—"

We saw the clever Frenchman signal to his accomplices on Anne's left. They moved, and shuffled forward.

"—on my soul. O God—" She started up toward her left, and saw the assistants moving toward her. While she stared at them, her head turned toward the left, the swordsman struck. His thin blade flashed in an arc behind Anne's line of vision. It cut through her slender neck like a cleaver through a rose stem: some initial resistance, a crunching, then a clean sever.

Her head dropped from her shoulders like a piece of sliced sausage, and landed, *plop!* in the straw. I saw the cut neck: a cross-section of tubes, about six or seven of them, like a geometrical drawing. Then two or three of the tubes began to spurt blood, for Anne's heart was still pumping. Bright red gushes of blood squirted like milk from an obscene cow's udder—even the sound was the same. The squirting kept on and on. Why was there still so much blood left in her?

The hands hung down, trailing, beside the block. The suave French swordsman strode forward and felt in the straw for the round object that was Anne's head. It had landed some two or three feet to the left. He held it up by its long, glossy hair.

The cannon boomed, once, upon the battlements.

It still had her appearance, as in life. Her eyes moved, and seemed to look mournfully at the bleeding body still kneeling at the block. The lips moved. She was saying something. . . .

The witnesses broke ranks and sought to remove themselves from this incomprehensible horror. There was no one who would dare tell the King of these last moments; certainly I would not, either.

Everyone scattered, leaving the severed head (the swordsman had departed) and the blood-drained trunk slumped on the scaffold.

The King had not provided a coffin.

In the end, her ladies found an empty arrow-chest in the cellar of the royal apartments. It was too short for a normal person, but it would serve for a decapitated trunk, with the head tucked inside. They wrapped the cooling body with its congealing bloody neck-stump in the black cloth so courteously provided by the Frenchman, and insisted that the sexton of the Tower chapel of St. Peter-ad-Vincula reopen the fresh grave of George Boleyn and lower the makeshift coffin on top of his.

There was no service, no funeral. Anne's remains were left literally to shift for themselves.

HENRY VIII:

Beyond the environs of London, the wildness of the country was the same as that which must have greeted Julius Caesar. It was all pristine, new, untouched. I took my horse up the wooded hills which, even in the shade, were recreating themselves in green. I tried not to think of what was taking place in the Tower and its grounds. The world was recreating itself; could I not do the same?

Behind me the Thames wound in the low areas, a happy ribbon, reflecting the sun. Across from Greenwich lay my ships at anchor, their masts bristling, making splinters against the rippling waters, downstream from the Tower . . . the Tower. . . .

I heard the cannon: a small, faraway sound.

Anne was dead. The Witch was no more, not upon this earth.

I should have felt elated, delivered, safe. But this heaviness of spirit was not to be removed, ever. There was to be no rebirth in green. I was permanently changed, never again to return to my former self. Outwardly I might retain my original appearance, like a rotting melon: all ribbed and rounded on the outside, all fallen and decayed in the secret inward parts.

The cannon spoke of her death. What of mine?

It is not all or none, I told myself. There is a vast tract stretching between the beginning, in health and simplicity, and the end, in disease and convoluted compromises. I tread it now; that unsung territory is my challenge, my making, my own private landscape.

"Jane," I called, from the courtyard. "Jane." It was not a command but a cry.

Jane appeared in the upper window, above the doorway of Nicholas Carew's house. She had sought the cleanness of the open country once Anne had been arrested and there was no more Queen to serve, no need to remain at court.

"I am here," she said. She left the window, came down the stairs, and walked slowly out the front door. I dismounted and stood waiting, weary, yet accepting that weariness as something that would never go away, would only have to be shared.

She came to me silently, extending her hands. Her face shone with an otherworldly love and kindness. She understood, without being contaminated by her knowledge.

"Jane," I said, making no move to touch her. "Will you be my wife?"

"With all my heart," she answered. "And all my soul and body, too."

This is what heaven is, then: to come home from a long exile.

LXXV

W e did not return to London, but, after spending the night in Carew's house, set out early the next morning for Wolf Hall. Jane was a Wiltshire girl, and all who meant most to her were contained in her neighbourhood and its surrounding villages. The Seymours had held the wardenship of Savernake Forest since 1427, and had resided in the area of Bedwyn nearby since the early 1300s; it was from this little piece of England that they drew their strength and pleasure, not from court appointments. Jane was to be wed, and it was with her Wiltshire friends and neighbours that she wished to celebrate, like any village bride.

We came to Wolf Hall in the late twilight, when all the servants had finished work and old, feeble Sir John had been fed, bolstered, and put to bed in his upper chamber. Jane flew up the stairs and I followed, marvelling that I had never done a thing like this before—climbing the stairs to confront a sweetheart's father and ask his blessing. I was King. But I was acutely aware that many fathers would not consider their daughters well served in marrying me.

"Father!" Jane pushed open the door and saw Sir John lying abed, a flannel nightcap on, even in May. She ran to him and knelt before his bedside.

"Janey," he said. "You're home?"

"Yes. I wish to ask your blessing. On my marriage. To the King."

I moved forward, into the little circle of light. "I love your daughter," I said. "I wish to make her my wife, and my Queen."

He stared at me. "My Janey? Queen of England? She knows no Latin."

"She knows more than Latin," I said.

"Will you bless us, Father?" Jane asked.

"Aye." He frowned, as if gathering his wits like a shepherd his flock. "Aye." He extended his hands. "Be to him a blessing, as Sarah was to Abraham." He turned to me. "Cherish her. Do not choke her with jewels." He nodded at his sagacity.

Within a few days, others streamed to Wolf Hall, sickened by the real and moral stench of London. Edward and Thomas Seymour, of course, came straightway, arriving in the morning. They were followed by Francis Bryan, Anne's cousin, who fled from her shame; Sir John Russell; William Fitzwilliam; and John Dudley. Immediately upon congratulating us, Edward set about to arrange the betrothal feast, which every proper bride should have. It would be held in the barn, as Wolf Hall had no suitable Great Hall to accommodate all the well-wishers. It was to be a country reception, and I would leave all of it to the Seymours, revelling in the freedom from having to preside over pageants and royal rituals.

The great barn was cleared of hay and livestock, and a floor was quickly laid down. Next, the rough walls were hung with silk, and neighbouring children spent three days gathering wildflowers and vines and weaving them into long, thick garlands, which were hung over the silk. Torches were planted all along the half-mile path to the barn, and Sir John's kitchens were consumed with preparations for the feast. In the village of Tottenham Park, the bakers left off making bread in order to bake the layers of the great betrothal cake in several ovens at once.

In my palaces I took such things for granted; the cakes appeared, and I never thought who baked them. Here I was holding my breath, waiting to hear if the middle layer of the cake had fallen when the baker's son opened the oven door prematurely. (It had not, although the middle sagged a bit.)

Jane's betrothal feast, served to a hundred neighbours and kinsmen, was simple and lovely. Three long tables had been set up in the transformed barn, and the brothers had procured enough white linen to cover them all, and enough pewter, gold, and silver to serve everyone from metal. (They refused all my offers to send to London for rolls of linen and boxes of gold plate.) French claret sparkled in the goblets, and Sir John managed, in spite of his malady of mind, to give the initial toast and make the formal announcement of Jane's betrothal. Then Edward took over.

"To my sister, who has won the heart of our sovereign lord the King, I wish all joy and happiness," he pronounced, flourishing his cup. All rose and drank.

Jane sparkled even more than the claret, revealing a side of her I had thought she lacked. Although I had been willing to forgo it, finding that I did not have to was an unexpected gift.

Others rose and spoke—of Jane's gentleness, of her great promise, of her humour and humility. In a peculiar way, I was envious of these Wiltshire yeomen and gentry. They had known Jane as a child, had seen her grow up. They were bestowing her on me. (Reluctantly?)

The great cake was wheeled into the room. It had been iced with an ivory-coloured almond frosting, and its base was decorated with wildflowers and candied fruits, which resembled jewels. Jane laughingly cut it, and the inside was dark and filled with currants and spices. Pieces were passed out, and not a crumb remained at the end.

Now the dancing. Fiddlers assembled, local lute-players and musicians with rebecs, citterns, humstrums, and little harps. Twin cousins, two pretty little girls, came up and crowned Jane with a circlet of wild roses. She laughed, and we danced, and the entire company joined us, in the transformed barn. . . .

We were married on the next-to-last day of May in the small private chapel at York Place. Jane was quiet that day, not the sunburnt country girl of Wiltshire that I had discovered and adored. We must be married in London, that she understood. There must be no secret about it, no "unknown" priest. But she and I always thought of our marriage as truly having taken place that night in the great barn.

Jane came to my bed a virgin, both in body and mind, as neither of my other "wives" had done. I came to her a bachelor, for I had never truly been married before. All was as it was meant to be, and so seldom is. . . .

I introduced Jane to the realm as my Queen by presenting her with a new barge, modelled on that of the Venetian Bucentaur, and staging a great water-carnival on the Thames to salute us as we made our way upstream to attend Whitsunday Mass in Westminster Abbey. The day was glorious and clear, and the entire city populace had put aside its winter woollens and cavorted in sheer cottons and silks in every sunlit street. The Abbey was thronged, and the cheering mobs, showering us with flowers, transformed our appearance at the festive Whitsun Mass into a sort of semi-Coronation for Jane.

Afterward, at York Place, I gave a great afternoon banquet, ostensibly to celebrate Whitsun—for the centerpiece was a huge cake of crushed strawberries, seven layers to commemorate the seven gifts the Holy Spirit conferred upon the Apostles at Pentecost—but it was in reality a bride-cake, and a bride-feast.

England had a true Queen at last, and no one begrudged her me.

I ended the celebrations by bringing her with me to the Opening of Parliament on June eighth.

Seated beside me on the Chair of Estate, looking out over both Lords and Commons, she heard Chancellor Audley exclaim, "Ye well remember the great anxieties and perturbations this invincible Sovereign"—he nodded toward me—"suffered on account of his first unlawful marriage. So all ought to bear in mind the perils and dangers he was under when he contracted his second marriage, and that the lady Anne and her accomplices have since been justly found guilty of high treason, and have met their due reward for it." He shook his head as the ugly black shadow passed over the entire Parliament, and over my soul as well.

"What man of middle life would not this deter from marrying a third time? Yet this our most excellent Prince again condescendeth to contract matrimony! And hath, on the humble petition of the nobility, taken to himself a wife, this time, who by her excellent beauty and pureness of flesh and blood, is apt—God willing—to conceive issue." The company rose in acknowledgment of this.

"The lords should pray for heirs to the crown by this marriage," Audley concluded.

Jane was now my wife, and Queen indeed: wedded by a true rite, saluted by the common people, and honoured by Parliament. It was done, and I was happy at last.

Happy at last. Why is it so difficult to describe happiness? There are words aplenty for anguish, despair, suffering, and these are full of vitality. But happiness is left with weak verbs, supine adjectives, drooping adverbs. A description of happiness moves a reader to skip over those passages and causes a writer to flounder in treacle.

Yet how can we recall it if we do not write of it? We put up summer in preserved fruits and conserves, we trap autumn in wine made from late-ripening grapes, we make perfumes of spring flowers. That way we can recall, albeit in a slanted or altered way, some essence of the moment.

But human happiness . . . all our words for it are so bland, as if the thing itself were bland, or merely an absence of pain. When in fact happiness is solid, muscular, and strong; its colour all the spectrum of light; its sounds as sweet as water splashing in a Pharaoh's desert palace; and its smells those of the flesh and its life: fur, heat, cooking.

I was happy with Jane, as happy as one of the great cats stretched out in the sun around Wolf Hall. Only touch them and feel their deep, rumbling purrs, as they rest entirely in the present moment. That was me, that summer Jane and I were one.

LXXVI

Happiness begets courage, inasmuch as we raise our eyes from hud-dled self-absorption and, secure behind the ramparts of our solid, sun-warmed castles, survey all the land surrounding us. There seems to be no truth we are not capable of confronting and withstanding, and so we go seeking it.

Since that June day seventeen years ago, when Katherine's last pregnancy had brought forth its irrefutable summation of accursedness, I had been a pawn of the truth, never its comrade. The truth was that hideous, malformed infant, and if that were the truth, then everything I had espoused was false. My marriage to Princess Katherine had been false; brought about by a dispensation that was obviously false, granted by a personage (the Bishop of Rome) whose claims were equally false. And so the whirlpool of falseness enveloped me, drowning me. I went under the waters, pulled under with foul, dark things, and swam as best I knew how, blindly.

Now I was, miraculously, on dry land again. Like a shipwreck survivor, I sat on the beach, feeling my arms and legs for injuries, looking all round at the wreckage, but marvelling that I lived. A stroll down the beach would undoubtedly disclose further debris, surprise losses, and capricious survivals. Curiosity would draw me to the inspection, but not fear. Whatever remained in the larder of fate, that was good; I would make a meal of it and dine on it.

So, in July, when the so-called Long Parliament dissolved at last and the land set about its lengthy and earnest business of producing grains, fruits, and vegetables, I took my inventory.

Katherine was dead, and with her the threat of war from her nephew the Emperor Charles. She had died signing herself "Katherine the Queen," but the matter of her title did not concern the coffin-worms, or anyone else at this point. That gigantic mistake in my past had now been crossed off.

I wrote "Katherine" on a piece of parchment and drew a thick black line through it.

Next I wrote "the conspirators." For there had been a great network of them, poised and at the ready for a signal of some sort, a signal that never came. Chapuys had teased them into existence and served as their center; Cromwell had spied on them and supplied me with names and information. I wrote a "?" and resolved to talk to Cromwell about them.

Mary. Now that both Katherine and Anne were dead, would Mary see her way clear to a reconciliation with me? She stood alone, deserted by her mother's death. While Anne yet lived, pride would have prohibited Mary's yielding in any way. But the Great Whore, Mary's enemy and mine, had perished and would never triumphantly witness Mary's softening. The hated half-sister, Elizabeth, was now no longer Princess, and Mary did not need to serve her in humiliation.

I wanted Mary back. Our estrangement had been caused by people who were now nonexistent. Jane, Mary's partisan, was eager for Mary's return to favour; and Cromwell had shown interest in persuading her to lower her pride and open herself to change. I wrote another "?" and moved on.

The Emperor Charles. Relieved by his aunt's death from posturing for "honour" any longer, he was overwhelmed by the virulent, infectious Protestantism that was causing disruptions in his own lands. The Netherlands had become a hotbed of heresy; stately Lutheranism had whelped the ugly dogs of Sacramentarianism and Anabaptism—heresy in its purest form. Antwerp and Amsterdam were publishing centers for heretical tracts, and provided sheltering arms for radicals and subversives of every description. I drew a great line across Charles's name.

Francis had proved more successful in controlling the heretical ideas in his domains and had even appointed an Inquisitor-General. But by himself, he was unlikely to heed the Pope's call to arms against me. I drew another line across "Francis."

Pope Paul III. There was no doubt that in this gentleman I had a tireless, clever adversary. He, unlike Clement, had drawn a line, and I was clearly outside it. Thereafter he made no apologies. His goal was to dethrone me or, failing that, to discredit me. It was he who had made Fisher a Cardinal, and it was he who had published the Papal bull which called for a Holy War against me by foreign powers and absolved all Englishmen from allegiance to me on my own soil. He was also grooming young Reginald Pole, a sort of latter-day Thomas More who had fled abroad, to be his weapon against me, deploying him on missions to implement Papal policy. I had been Reginald's patron, paying for all his education, both here and abroad. The Pope had taken him from me and turned him against me. I left his name unmarked.

The monasteries. There were more than eight hundred of them scattered over the realm, and Cromwell's report, *Valor Ecclesiasticus,* divided them into "lesser" houses and "greater." Some three hundred of them were "lesser" and had an income below an arbitrarily selected point. These houses had only a few members and were likely to be lax and poorly run. Certainly it was inefficient of the orders to have a great number of tiny monasteries in operation. Cromwell had recommended dissolving these establishments, letting the truly committed monks transfer to other, more disciplined houses of their orders, and releasing the rest from their vows. The property, of course, would revert to the Crown, as it was treason to send it to Rome. He reckoned that millions of pounds would accrue to me. I left the word "monasteries" un-inked. More to discuss with Cromwell.

Now for a personal inventory. I wrote "poison." I feared that Anne's poison was slow-acting and irreversible. For my leg had not healed, as I had assumed it would do upon her demise. And Fitzroy—his cough had not lessened, and his colour paled day by day. I prayed that I could outlast the life of the poison, and ultimately defeat it, like a city under siege. Sooner or later its power must wane and abate. But it looked to be a long bodily siege. I was determined to withstand it. Would Mary? All the more reason for us to make peace. I was convinced that isolation increased the power of the poison. Under "poison" I included my impotence, which obviously had been due entirely to Anne's malevolence, for it had disappeared with her.

General health. Since my fall in the lists, and the permanent state of ulceration on my thigh, I had had to curtail my athletic activities. The lack of exercise had caused me to gain weight for the first time in my life. My very flesh seemed to expand and change from tautness to looseness. I tried every means of moderate exercise to reverse the process and bring it under control: walks with Jane, long, slow cantering rides, archery, bowling. But the tide of creeping slackness and fat was relentless. It seemed I needed the violent excesses of long hunts with hounds and horses, wherein the horses would tire before ever I did; the sweating tennis matches wherein I would bet upon myself; the foot combat at the barriers in tournaments when I must leap and swing swords while encased in one hundred pounds of tortoiselike armour; even the rigorous dances in court celebrations. Deprived of these tests, my flesh sighed, expanded, and began to sag.

I left "general health" with no black line across it.

Cromwell had shown me his hawks; now I would show him my hounds. I was proud of the royal kennels, and although Edward Neville held the honorary title of Master of the Buckhounds, the actual day-to-day work was done by kennel-masters and dog-breeders, a staff of ten.

This fine day in late July the dogs were being exercised in the open fields not far from Blackheath. Like men, they grew restless and despondent if they were kept indoors and inactive too long; they were meant to run, especially the greyhounds and Scottish deerhounds.

The latter were an interesting breed. I had only lately been successful in obtaining puppies of this noted dog of the open northern country, which hunted by sight and not by smell. Of course, a man had to have a fleet horse and be an expert rider to keep up; in our southern areas, "chases" had been cut through forested areas in order to hunt in this manner.

"They say these dogs have been in Scotland since ancient days," I explained to Cromwell. "But clansmen also claim that they were bred originally from Irish 'swifthounds'—when Ireland and Scotland were exchanging families and settlers back and forth. 'Tis all the same, the wild North. Savages." I admired a pack of deerhounds bounding off together. "But they breed good animals."

Cromwell smiled, and sighed expansively. It never failed to surprise me how well the outdoors became him. I was used to thinking of him as a purely indoor breed. "Perhaps one day they will be tamed and civilized. But not in our lifetime," he said. "Now we must merely contain them."

How quickly he came to the point. The open country gave us the opportunity to discuss it, as I had planned. "The disaffected lords assembled by Chapuys—what of them? In my experience, a group never disbands without having made a gesture of some sort." I threw it out to him.

"Yes, it is like a woman all dressed for a ball. She *must* dance to some tune."

"Whose tune?"

"A northern one, most like. But as yet there's nothing. Wait long enough, and eventually the maiden takes off her finery and goes to bed."

We walked together, smiling and seemingly discussing the dogs. We approached another trainer, with a group of short-legged, dark hounds. He was offering them a piece of cloth to smell.

"How are the slow-hounds progressing?" I asked him.

"Excellently. They have been able to track three different men through a forest, a market-square, and a graveyard—right after a funeral!—and each time identified the proper one in a crowd." He grinned.

"These track by scent," I said. "They are of great use in tracking outlaws, kidnappers, and so on. My breeders are attempting to purify the strain even more—to make their scent keener and their endurance greater. Then they'll be almost on a par with your agents, Crum." Why I needled him in front of others,

I knew not. Crum smiled, a poisonous smile. It said: *Why must I endure this?*

We nodded and moved on.

"You have read the report of the monastic visitations?" he asked, the moment we were out of earshot.

"Yes. The immorality your commissioners found was . . . a disgrace." I had hoped that St. Osweth's was a degraded, atypical example. I had known good monks, and I wanted to believe that the monastic ideal was still alive and calling to the best parts of men. It was true that the original Benedictines had drifted from their austerity and purity; but other orders had arisen to reclaim the spiritual inheritance and reinvigorate it: the Cistercians, the Dominicans, the Crutched Friars, the Premonstratensians. I did not wish to believe that the entire vocation had become moribund. Yet that was what the commissioners reported.

"It is worse in the smaller houses, the ones with scarcely a dozen brothers. Close them, Your Grace. Gardeners prune roses and herbs to make the mother plant grow back more vigorously. This is the same."

A pack of spaniels was coming toward us.

"Taking them to the water, are you?" I called to their keeper.

"If we can find a suitable marsh, yes," he answered. "Be interesting to see how many woodcocks they flush out."

Spaniels—descended from old English "water dogs"—were odd creatures. In their larger state, they were excellent for spotting and flushing game in low, wooded, marshy areas. Shrunk to a toy size, they became "ladies' dogs," lap-dogs. One almost forgot their hunting origins when one saw them only in the Queen's apartments.

I turned back to Cromwell. "I know it must be done. So I shall do it. As Supreme Head of the Church in England, I cannot know of these abominations and yet permit them to continue." But, oh! I would not know. There was so much I would not know, that I knew nonetheless.

Cromwell nodded, keeping his eyes straight ahead, as if the matter were of indifference to him. In fact, he had made it of prime importance to himself. "I shall give orders," he said.

"One last matter," I said, "and then we can truly enjoy the hounds. My daughter Mary. Has she responded to your . . . overtures?" I had instructed Cromwell to approach her again, offering to act as her partisan and advisor. Chapuys had approached her from the other side, urging her to stand fast.

"Surprisingly, yes." He turned and looked at me. The sun caught his eyes and turned their blackness to deep, soothing brown. "I think she may be ready, at last, to . . . come home."

"Ah!" At once, as if a great shade had been lifted from the sun, the landscape grew brighter. The hounds were more richly coloured, the coats of the hound-masters more vivid.

"Her resistance is broken," he said. "She has grown older, wiser—after the recent events."

As have we all, I thought, but did not say.

"When she can see her way clear to us, we will welcome her, the Queen and I," I said instead.

I felt as fleet as one of the deerhounds now, as I walked briskly along the heath, Cromwell in tow.

There were other breeds, clumped together, each with its trainer. One sort of hound was being trained to obey the huntsman's horn. Short-legged and medium-sized, this breed was used to track game into wooded areas. Their short legs assured that they could be adequately followed by huntsmen on foot, armed with bow and arrow.

"You call these . . . ?" asked Cromwell.

"Beagles, Sir. A fine English breed!"

There were also foxhounds and harriers—the latter being those which tracked hares—all being trained to the horn, and the sounds of all the different timbres made rustic music, along with the distinctive baying of each breed.

Another hound-master had a group of small, sparsely haired animals he referred to as "terriers." They had rather ugly, sand-coloured hair and a coarse, grating bark. Their keeper claimed they were invaluable for what they were bred for: chasing vermin like otters, foxes, and rats into their nests and hideaways. "From the Border country," he said.

Naturally. The Borders abounded in vermin, especially of the two-legged sort. It was not surprising they had developed a special breed for it. The dogs seemed as unpleasant as the things they controlled.

"I've a mind to hunt, and soon," I said, to no one in particular. "In the autumn, let us make up a party for it. We'll hunt roe and hare and the beasts of stinking flight—the polecats and stoats." I loved killing these pests.

I was bending down to pat one of the slow-hounds, feeling his thick, silky black fur, when I saw the messenger coming toward me. I felt only annoyance, no premonition. They seek me even here, I thought. Is it asking too much for me to have a scant two hours out-of-doors, inspecting my hounds with my chief minister?

While he approached me, I waited resignedly. He had a sealed message. Some petty thing, I thought, ripping it open.

The Duke of Richmond, Henry Fitzroy, is dead. He died at noon. Your obedient servant and subject, and loyal physician,

Wm. Butts.

Even here, even now, Anne had struck. The sunlight, though yet as bright, was suddenly drained of its warmth.

LXXVII

I could not even openly mourn my son, or permit a public burial. At this point, the people would have been so frightened at reports of yet another death that the presumed hidden current of popular discontent might have broken out. I say "presumed" because it is impossible ever to really know the mind of the people, but there were indications. There was the priest Robert Feron who said, "Since the realm of England was first a realm, was never a greater robber against the commonwealth than is our King. He boasteth himself above all other Christian kings, being puffed up with vain glory. His life is more stinking than a sow; he has violated many matrons of the court." The Prior of Syon Abbey had declared, "Until the King and the rulers of the realm be plucked by the pates, and brought, as we say to pot, shall we never live merrily in England." Then he had added, "I have all the rest of Christendom in my favour. I dare even say all this kingdom . . . for I am sure the larger part is at heart of our opinion."

Throughout the realm, prophecies abounded. "The White Hare shall drive the White Greyhound into the root of an oak, and the King be driven out of England and killed at Paris gate." "There will be no more Kings in England, and such a gap in the West that all the thorns in the realm shall not stop it." "There should come out of the West one that should bring snow upon his helmet that should set all England at peace."

Then there were the treason-leaning statements and grumbles. At Eynsham, Oxford, one John Hill had said that Norris and Weston had been "put to death only for pleasure," and that he "trusted to see the King of Scots King of England." The bailiff of Bampton hoped to see the Scots King "wear the flower of England." The vicar of Hornchurch, Hampshire, had said, "The King and his council had made a way by will and craft to put down all manner of religious; but they would hold hard, for their part, which was their right; and the King could not pull down none, nor all his Council."

A Sussex man, when told about my fall in the lists, had replied, "It were better he had broken his neck." A Cambridge master called me "a mole who should be put down"; his students, "a tyrant more cruel than Nero" and "a beast and worst than a beast."

Other statements reported by Crum's agents were: "Cardinal Wolsey had been an honest man if he had had an honest master"; "The King is a fool and my Lord Privy Seal another"; "Our King wants only an apple and a fair wench to dally with"; and then there was a yeoman's detailed recounting of how I had been riding near Eltham one day, seen his wife, abducted her, and taken her away to my bed.

It was certainly true, what the Kentish man said, "If the King knew his subjects' true feeling, it would make his heart quake." The sample I did hear, did just that. My own unsettled and miserable state, from the beginning of my Great Matter to its end, had transferred itself to them. My new contentment would also transfer itself, but it would take time.

I had lost my son, but I would cheat the Witch of claiming my daughter as well. Under Cromwell's threats to drop her suit, and Chapuys's advice, and the Emperor's final lack of commitment to her cause, Mary gave in. She copied out the "suggested" letter, provided by Cromwell, in which she admitted her mother's marriage to me was incestuous, in which she renounced all allegiance to the Pope and acknowledged me as the Supreme Head of the Church in England, and her spiritual as well as her temporal father. When I received the letter, I thanked God for it. Now all was clear for our reconciliation. I would have Mary back again; I would have my little girl!

Theologians call the parable of the Prodigal Son the sweetest yet strongest story in the Bible. Now I knew how that father had felt. Or was I being presumptuous? I would read the parable over in the new translation that would soon be issued under my patronage.

Already it was nicknamed "the Great Bible" for its size. The recently promulgated "Ten Articles of Faith" required for believers in the—*my!*— Church of England specified that each church should have a Bible in English, and Miles Coverdale's translation was being used for the purpose. Originally it was to be printed in France, for their presses were larger than ours, but the English churchmen had run afoul of the French Inquisitor-General and had had to transfer their entire printing operation to England. The copy I consulted was one of the advance ones, sent for my inspection. One necessary change: Anne's name on the dedication page, as Queen, must be replaced by Jane's, as was being done elsewhere in stone and wood carvings.

I turned to Luke, Chapter fifteen, verse ten.

Likewise I say unto you, there is joy in the presence of the angels of God over one sinner that repenteth.

Or one person who realizes that he is *not* a sinner.

And he said, A certain man had two sons.

Two daughters.

And the younger of them said to his father, Father, give me the portion of goods that falleth to me. And he divided unto them his living.

Just as Mary had asked for her "inheritance"—her Spanish birthright, her title as "Princess"—to the exclusion of all else.

And not many days after the younger son gathered all together, and took his journey into a far country, and there wasted his substance with riotous living.

Mary had "wasted her substance," but in extreme ascetic exercises, in self-made isolation and rebellion.

And when he had spent all, there arose a mighty famine in that land; and he began to be in want.

Yes, Mary was in want. And the "famine" was Anne's attempt to destroy her body and drive away her friends.

And he went and joined himself to a citizen of that country; and he sent him into his fields to feed swine.

She joined herself to Chapuys and his insubstantial dreams of Imperial rescue, and rebellion against my will.

And he would fain have filled his belly with the husks that the swine did eat, and no man gave unto him.

Yes, the Emperor gave pretty words but nothing else. The Pope sent the empty husks of Papal bulls to feed her.

And when he came to himself, he said, How many hired servants of my father's have bread enough and to spare, and I perish with hunger?

Mary realized she had been duped, abandoned, and betrayed—by everyone.

I will arise and go to my father, and will say unto him, Father, I have sinned against heaven and before thee, and am no more worthy to be called thy son: make me as one of thy hired servants.

That was what Mary had done, in her letter of submission.

And he arose, and came to his father. But when he was yet a great way off, his father saw him, and had compassion, and ran, and fell on his neck, and kissed him. And the son said unto him, Father, I have sinned against heaven, and in thy sight, and am no more worthy to be called thy son.

I nodded. Yes, Mary would surely do this in person when we met. She would be moved to.

But the father said to his servants, Bring forth the best robe, and put it on him; and put a ring on his hand, and shoes on his feet; and bring hither the fatted calf, and kill it; and let us eat, and be merry: for this my son was dead, and is alive again; he was lost, and is found.

I closed the Great Bible. Yes, that was it. My daughter was dead, and is alive again. One can be brought back to life, this side of the grave. . . .

I realized how nervous I already was in anticipation of Mary's "surrender" this coming afternoon. She was to come to the palace and there make a formal recitation before me of what she had already put in writing. This would be in private. I needed no witnesses.

By the mid-afternoon, when I had sat, fully dressed in my most august robes (for I must look her King as well as her father) for over an hour in the heat, I knew that she was not coming. At the last moment some new "scruple" had presented itself, some tearing loyalty to Katherine. . . . I felt a disappointment so keen and deep it was in itself a mourning. Hope had died, and the death of hope is the true death; the body merely confirms it after the fact.

To have hoped so fully, so that the thing seemed so assured . . . now this second death. God teases us on the rack of expectations; the earthly ones we construct as implements of torture are poor imitations of His own.

The door opened. I was no longer looking at it, and so Mary was fully in the room before I saw her. And then she seemed a vision.

A tiny young woman—that was my "little girl." She was short, and that made her seem young, belied her true age.

"Father." Her voice was low, gruff. It seemed an odd thing to issue from her throat.

Before I could reply, she flung herself down at my feet and began reciting, in that near-growling voice, "I, most humbly lying at your feet to perceive your gracious clemency, my merciful, passionate, and most blessed father, Supreme Head of the Church of England. . . ." The words were all stuck end-to-end as she admitted her mother's marriage incestuous, abandoned her allegiance to Rome, and acknowledged my claims of overlordship of the Church of England.

I bent down and pulled her gently up, hugged her to me. Her head came only up to my chest.

"Mary, daughter. You need say no more. Thank you for coming back to me."

At once she began to cry, and I knew she wept for her "betrayal" of her dead mother. But to go on living is no betrayal. I said nothing and let her cry. But oh! my heart sang to have her back . . . back from both Katherine and Anne. God be thanked that they were both dead. Their deaths freed me from my past, and my mistakes.

"You are welcome here at court," I finally said. "Come, the Queen wishes to see you again."

"Queen Jane was always kind," she said, in a low monotone.

Jane had come to court when Katherine was already isolated and beginning her stubborn martyrdom. The self-seekers had followed Anne's rising star. But Jane had remained with Katherine and befriended Mary, who was only seven years younger. (Jane had been born the same year I became King.)

Together we walked from my inmost private room and out into the common chamber. I requested that the Queen come straightway. While we waited, Mary and I stood together awkwardly. I no longer felt elated, but almost uncomfortable with a grown woman who was a stranger but also my daughter. Would Jane never come and relieve this tension?

Jane, Jane, help me, as you always do. . . .

Jane appeared, at the far end of the chamber, and came swiftly toward Mary, arms outstretched, a great natural smile on her face.

"Mary, Mary!" she cried, genuine welcome in her voice.

Mary tried to kneel, but Jane embraced her instead. "I have so longed for this day," said Jane. "Now my happiness is complete." She held out her other arm to me and locked us all together, turning the water of awkwardness into the wine of ease, against all odds.

LXXVIII

I held it in my hand: a sacred relic that had been adored from the safe distance of a golden, jewel-encrusted reliquary since the days of Edward the Confessor. Pilgrims had come from far away to see it, and had addressed their most fervent prayers to it. It was a glass vial containing drops of the Virgin's milk—miraculous help for barren women.

Cromwell's inspectors had found it to be a fraud, refilled regularly with ground Dover chalk dissolved in thin olive oil. The slightly yellow tint gave it an authentic look of antiquity.

The monks at that particular shrine had made a tidy living from exhibiting their precious "relic."

"Disgraceful," I said, but more in sadness than in anger.

I turned to the next confiscation. This was a marble Virgin that wept "real tears" and could be petitioned (with money) to share one's own sufferings. I turned it around. There was a small line behind the head, indicating an opening of some sort. I pressed upon the neck, and the stone piece moved outward. I prized it out, and found the head to be hollow. There was a porous container inside to be filled with salt water that oozed through the minute ducts leading to the Virgin's eyes at just the proper rate. It was an ingenious contraption. And it only had to be refilled once a week.

All across the land there were similar versions of these famous hoaxes. They could not be maintained without the conspiracy of corrupt monks. How could one profess himself a follower of Christ and yet practise the same trickery as the priests of Isis or the Canaanites?

Parliament had passed the Act of Suppression of the Lesser Monasteries. The Act began: "Forasmuch as manifest sin, vicious, carnal, and abominable living is daily used among the small abbeys . . ." It was based on the reports that at Garadon there were five homosexuals, "one with ten boys"; that at Selby one of the monks had had sexual relations "with five or six married women" who had come to seek benefit from the Abbey's "Virgin Girdle," which protected one in childbirth; that at Warter, Brother Jackson was "guilty of incest with a nun," and that at Calder, one Matthew Ponsonby "showed peculiar depravity." At Bath Priory—where the prior had tried to buy Cromwell off by sending him a leash of Irish wolfhounds—monks were "more corrupt than any others in vices with both sexes." At Lewes, the prior had "eight whores" and the place was a "very whorehouse and unnatural vices are here, especially the sub-prior, as appears by the confession of a fair young monk."

One by one the houses were being closed. Those monks who had a true calling were being transferred to larger, stricter houses. The rest were to leave and find their livelihood elsewhere. Their monastic property was to be sold and the proceeds to revert to the Crown. The relics were being sent here, for my inspection. It was an unhappy task.

Monasticism had begun as a pure flowering of spiritualism. The great founder of communal Christian living (for until then there had been only desert-living Christian hermits) was Saint Benedict. He thought it better for men to live with other men, and gathered together hermits and wrote instructions, called the Rule, by which they could actually increase their spiritualism by living in a community governed by holy rules. In his view, a man should best divide his time between prayer, study, and manual work.

In time, other interpretations of his Rule prevailed. The Cistercians stressed manual labor and apartness from civilization. The Cluniacs emphasized intricate beauty of worship. The Carthusians sought prayer and solitude. The "preaching friars"—Dominicans, Franciscans—stressed work with the people and impeccable scholarship.

Our own inclinations seem to turn our best strivings first into vanity, then into outright sin. (The Tower of Babel?) The story of the monks was just the story of man, summarized. It now fell to me to drive them from their Garden of Eden. Nonetheless, it was a duty I performed with reluctance, especially as both Jane and Mary disliked it intensely. Ah, but they had not seen the inside of the statue. . . .

The monastic land was sold outright, or leased. (Monks had held between one-quarter and one-third of the land in England.) Usually it was bought by the neighbouring great landholders, who sought to extend their estates.

There were always those reformers who thought it should be distributed to the peasants. But how should the peasants use it? No, the legacy of the monasteries would come to them in other ways; there was much besides land. Land was like hawks: it required great upkeep, love, and expertise. It was not surprising that hawking was "the sport of princes." No one else could afford the time and effort.

The most popular plunder from the monasteries was lead from the roofs. These were stripped immediately, and the lead melted down on the spot with fires made from the ceiling and roof timbers. Next in demand, especially in the London area, were the cut stones used in the monastic buildings. These were hauled away by the cartload and found their way into the new town houses rising along the Strand. I myself appropriated volumes from monastic libraries: old scrolls and manuscripts, some dating almost from Roman times. I also used the bronze from monastery bells for casting cannon.

The buildings themselves were turned to other uses. Often the abbey church was converted into a parish church, while the lodgings of the abbot, along with his cellar and kitchens, became a well-to-do merchant's manor, with the old gatehouse as his porter's lodge.

I will not pretend that I did not rejoice in the profits therefrom. The truth was that the Royal Treasury was almost threadbare, and the monastic income helped reclothe it.

In a greater sense, the Dissolution of the Monasteries was a relief, like emptying out the trunk of a dead man. It is always unpleasant; one has memories of him as he was, and winces at what befell him. But his property must be disposed of, and it would be wasteful and disrespectful just to pitch it all away without inspection, as tender-hearted souls advise—as if one were diminished by having one's goods reused by the living. Surely we are not as the ancient Egyptians, hoarding all for the dead and begrudging it to the living.

Then it all came together—every particle of discontent, nostalgia, and resistance in England—fusing in the North.

The North: two words to describe a territory and a state of mind. England was conquered and civilized from the South upwards, and as one approached the borders of Scotland—first through Yorkshire and then Durham and finally Northumberland—everything dwindled. The great forests gave way first to stunted trees and then to open, windswept moors; the towns shrank to villages and then to hamlets; cultivated fields were replaced by empty, wild spaces. Here the Cistercian monasteries flourished, they who removed themselves from the centers of civilization and relied on manual labour as a route to holiness. The sheep became scrawnier and their wool thicker, and the men became lawless and more secretive, clannish. Winter lasted eight months and even the summers were grey and raw, leading Northumberland men to claim they had "two winters—a white one and a green one."

Since ancient times these peripheral lands had gone their own way, little connected to anything further south. A few great warrior families—the Percys, the Nevilles, the Stanleys—had claimed overlordship of these dreary, cruel wastes, and through them, the Crown had demanded obeisance. But these people knew nothing of me, and I nothing of them. The only touch of love and softness they had ever known was through the great Cistercian monasteries: Fountains, Rievaulx, Jervaulx, Kirkstall. There they could stumble in following a snowstorm and find warmth, food, shelter. There, and only there, could travellers stay the night in safety. There they could be taught to read and write, if they so desired.

Now rumour reached them that their abbeys were to be closed. They had heard, distantly, that ties with Rome were broken. For them, the Church—through Rome—was their one distinction, their one blessing, that set them apart from their wild neighbours even further north. Word had reached them that the newly independent "Church of England" had set forth its beliefs in a statement of Ten Articles that leaned toward Lutheranism and dropped four of the seven Holy Sacraments.

This was the aforementioned Ten Articles of Faith to Establish Christian Quietness, a statement of doctrine drawn up by my bishops in hopes of doing exactly that. The recent changes had so confused the laity that I had thought some clarification of beliefs was in order.

The resulting Ten Articles were a magnificent compromise between the traditionalists and the reformists. Like all compromises, it evidently satisfied no one of either persuasion and unduly alarmed both factions.

The northerners heard, also, in a distorted and distant way, that commoners had replaced noblemen in the King's Council. They had always been served well by "their" noblemen, and feared for themselves without their guardians. But more than anything else they feared change. Like the slow-growing trees in their region—which took three or four years to attain the one year's growth of a similar tree in southern England—they were unable to respond quickly to climactic changes. The plant that grew from their soil was the Pilgrimage of Grace.

༺ ༻

A pilgrimage was what they called it, but a rebellion was what it was. It broke out in spots, like the pox, all over Lincolnshire and Yorkshire. Eventually the mass coalesced into a great pustule—some forty thousand strong —in the area of the middle of Yorkshire. I did not pop the pustule directly —that would have made too great a splatter—but lanced it and let it drain away and dry up.

So much for metaphor. Now let me set down, in summary, exactly what happened in those autumn months of 1536.

I had sent my commissioners north to supervise the suppression of the small monasteries, as stipulated in the Act of Parliament. The first resistance they met was in the hamlet of Hexham, in Northumberland. There an armed mob of monks and townspeople chased them out.

Next, a spontaneous revolt arose in Lincolnshire. The rebels surrounded the castle of Kyme, where Bessie Blount and her new husband, Edward, Lord Clinton, resided, and attempted to force them to join the rebellion. Bessie and Edward refused, and the rebels were unable either to persuade them or to capture their stronghold. As soon as they dispersed, Edward Clinton rode south to warn me.

The irksome rebels went next to Caister, where they killed the Bishop of Lincoln's chancellor, Dr. Heneage, and forced the Abbot of Barking, Matthew Mackerel, to join them. By this point their numbers had swelled to about twenty thousand. They had selected a local shoemaker, Nicholas Melton, as their leader, calling him "Captain Cobbler."

When Clinton reached me and appraised me of the situation, I empowered George Talbot, my loyal Earl of Shrewsbury in the North, to crush the rebels. But he had no need, as their movement collapsed on its own, due to lack of leadership.

In the meantime another group had found itself a leader in Yorkshire: Robert Aske, an energetic, self-made lawyer and visionary. A clever man, it was he who thought to turn their ordinary grumbles into an extraordinary "mission"; to call themselves "pilgrims" and march under a banner with Christ on the cross on one side and a chalice and wafer on the other, and wear white uniforms with red patches for Christ's five wounds.

He devised an Oath of the Honourable Man, which he required his "pilgrims" to take: "Ye shall not enter into this our Pilgrimage of Grace for the Commonwealth, but only for the love that you do bear unto Almighty God his faith, and to Holy Church militant and the maintenance thereof, to the preservation of the King's person and his issue, to the purifying of the nobility, and to expulse all villein blood and evil councillors against the Commonwealth from his Grace and his Privy Council of the same."

This group surrounded the royal castle of Pontrefract, where my heretofore loyal Lord Darcy—"Old Tom," as he called himself—was in command. But Darcy, as Crum's spies had long since informed me, was one of the secret traitors who had allied himself to the Emperor and Chapuys's plot when Katherine was still alive. Therefore it was not surprising that he joined them. (Edward Lee, Archbishop of York, also captured by them, extemporized and escaped.)

The rebels, now with a total force of forty thousand men—twenty-eight thousand on foot and twelve thousand on horse—were in control of the area. They announced their demands: restoration of the monasteries, abolition of heresy laws against Catholics, restoration of the Papal supremacy, legitimation of the "Princess" Mary, and death by burning of the "Protestant" bishops Cranmer, Latimer, and Shaxton. But their express hatred was focused on Cromwell—"Cow Crummock," they called him—whom they detested with a bitterness surpassing reason. He must be removed.

Must be? Sought they to dictate my councillors? Just as Cromwell was their supreme focus, so was my right to choose my own advisors.

I had sent Talbot and Brandon to put down the rebels in Lincolnshire, but the rebellion collapsed before they arrived. Howard, Duke of Norfolk, I was obliged to call out of political exile (whence he had hidden and languished since his niece the Witch's fall) to confront the Yorkshire mob. But my main objective was peacefully to disarm them, both literally and figuratively. I had no wish to fight them, as old ways disperse faster without martyrs.

My herald knelt in front of Robert Aske: a recognized sign of submission. For that he would later be executed. But he was able, at least, to make my offer known: disband, and let your leader come to London and negotiate. You say you are no traitors, but trust your King; now prove it.

The rebels did, and sent Robert Aske to court, where I met with him at Christmas.

Thus ended the so-called Pilgrimage of Grace—neither a pilgrimage nor imbued with grace. But it did alert me to the deep-seated affection for the monasteries and the "Olde Religion" in my far-flung territories. When I met with Aske, one of his requests—and a reasonable one, too—was that I show myself to them, so that they might know me as well as my southern subjects, and that I agree to hold Jane's Coronation at York. It was a pleasant thought, and would make Jane's crowning altogether different from Anne's.

In the end, though, the rebellion in the North failed because it had only the common people's loyalty, not that of the great lords of the North: the Nevilles and Percys; the Earls of Derby, Shrewsbury, and Rutland. These looked at the magnificent Cistercian monasteries and realized the properties could be theirs, if they but supported my policy. And they were right.

The other rebellion, more unexpected and uncharacteristic, came from within the royal apartments. Jane herself took the part of the Pilgrims. Tenderhearted, she hearkened to their complaints and tried to persuade me to capitulate to them.

"Can you not let the monasteries in the North remain?" she begged. "Their needs are different from ours, their land is different. How can you know unless you see for yourself?"

"There can be no exceptions," I tried to explain, gently. "For once exceptions begin, they never end. The Welsh, the Cornish, the fen country—

all will want their special concerns catered to. Besides, this business of the monasteries concerns only myself and Rome."

I had an ugly flash of memory. "These rebels, like Darcy and Hussey and Dacre, Lord Abergavenny, were first seduced into treason by Chapuys's plot to help Katherine's cause. The Pope is part of it—else why would he have dispatched that filthy Plantagenet creature of his, *Cardinal* Pole, to come as Papal legate and lend a hand to the rebels? No one co-operates, of course. The Cardinal languishes in Flanders, unable to find a willing sea captain to sail him across the Channel. May he rot there in the Lowlands!" My voice was rising at the perfidy of it all.

"The Pope! The Pilgrims! They are determined to bring me to my knees! Well, they shall not!" I yelled.

Jane fell at my feet, weeping. "Do not confuse the Pilgrims with the Pope. One is honest, the other not. Can you not consider—"

Now *she* turned against me! "Do you side with them, Madam?" I snapped. "Do not meddle in what you cannot understand!" They had fooled her, but they would not fool me. Did they think me a soft-headed woman?

Jane pulled herself up, staring at me all the while, as if she did not know me. "Yes, Your Majesty," she said.

" 'Bound to Obey and Serve,' " I reminded her. "Is that not the motto you chose for your own?"

"Yes, Your Majesty."

"Then follow it!" I bellowed.

In the North, as the early winter closed in, the rebels laid down their arms and trusted in their representative, Aske, who came to court and spent Christmas with us. I found Aske to be an honourable, thoughtful man—ironically, just the sort of "commoner" I liked to have on my councils and to which his Pilgrims objected.

The Percy family had ruined itself in the Pilgrimage. Earlier, Henry Percy (Anne's erstwhile lover), now the sixth Earl of Northumberland, had bequeathed his familial lands to the Crown upon his death. Whether poor dying Percy did it as a gesture of despair or mockery toward his brothers, I knew not, but it presented an elegant solution to the problem of no Crown holdings in that wild area. Naturally the two younger brothers, Thomas and Ingram Percy, objected, and became traitors and rebels in hopes of reclaiming their ancestral lands. All the while Henry Percy lay on his deathbed, his whole body "as yellow as saffron," they said.

Some of the rich northern abbeys, thinking to protect themselves and win favour, gave shelter and aid to the rebels. Their actions had exactly the opposite effect: they convinced me that all the monasteries must be closed, for they were no friends to me or my government.

After the New Year, two leftover rebels, Sir Francis Bigod and John Hallam, impatient to have their "demands" met, regathered forces and attempted to capture the cities of Scarborough and Hull. Two abbeys, Watton Priory and Jervaulx, joined in, and the next month rebellion broke out in two other shires, Cumberland and Westmorland.

That was enough. There would be no pardon, no promises on my part carried out. The traitors, one and all, would perish, and in the sight of those they had led. Robert Aske was hanged in chains on market day in the square at York; Sir Robert Constable, in the market at Hull; and Lord Hussey was beheaded in Lincoln.

Lord Darcy ("Old Tom," who had shouted at Cromwell, "Yet shall there one head remain that shall strike off thy head!") was beheaded at the Tower, along with Thomas Percy; and Tyburn (where traitors met the prescribed felons' death) took care of the Abbot of Barking, the Vicar of Louth, and the Lancaster royal herald who had knelt in fealty to the rebels. Seventy-four lesser rebels were likewise executed in Carlisle.

The rebel monks, some two hundred of them, were executed as the stinking traitors they were. At Sawley Abbey, they had actually crept back into their officially closed house in arrogant disregard of the law. So I ordered the Earl of Derby to hang the abbot and a score of his monks from the church steeple, on long pieces of timber, so that all his "flock" could see what befell traitors. The white-clad bodies swung from the silent tower (the bells having already been melted down and carried away). I daresay their silent movements spoke louder to the neighbourhood than any ringing bells ever had.

This prompted the first surrender of a monastery. When my royal commissioners took up their work again in April, the Abbot of Furness Abbey, in Cumbria, found it prudent to meet my representatives with a deed of surrender, giving the Crown "all such interest and title as I have had, have, or may have in the Abbey." This unforeseen gift made our task simple—although it rattled Cromwell, who had made out a complex schedule for closing the monasteries, based on their resistance.

"Sometimes it is difficult to appreciate an unexpected victory when one has been bracing for a struggle," I said.

"Yes. This schedule was ingenious," he replied wistfully, running his hands over it, where it lay spread out on our consulting-table. "Now I shall have to expand the numbers sitting on the Court of Augmentations, to handle the gush of new acquisitions."

The Court of Augmentations was the body Cromwell and I had created to process the monastic properties and dispose of them. "I think perhaps a new head is in order, to free you," I said. "I shall appoint Sir Richard Riche."

Cromwell chortled. He looked quite like a jolly uncle when he did so. "A masterful touch, as the Pilgrims demanded his removal from power. After me, of course. They *despised* us."

I looked up from the table to glimpse the cold, promising March sky outside. This time last year I had been hawking with Crum, and had given him the fearsome commission. . . .

"It is all over now," I said in wonder. It *was* all over, and peace had come again.

"I beg your pardon?" Crum looked at me, alert.

"I was only thinking how quiet it is in the land."

"All your enemies are dead, Your Grace."

LXXIX

The day the abbot and monks of Sawley Abbey were hanged, I found Jane crying in her chamber.

I had made arrangements to spend the morning with her looking over the plans for the Queen's New Lodgings, now being constructed at Hampton Court. I had thought my Janey—for so I called her, between the two of us—would relish being able to choose the wood, the artisans to carve it, and all the rest to make the royal quarters a reflection of herself.

Spread out all around her were drawings and samples of colours and materials. But she did not even seem aware of any of them. They surrounded her like dropped petals from an overblown rose, but she did not regard them.

"Well, Janey," I said, stepping into the chamber, "have you decided? You spoke of purple, once—"

My spirits drooped as soon as I beheld her. No, I could not stand another source of sadness today! I could not comfort; I had no comfort to give. I wanted the monks blanked out of my mind.

"Have you not decided, then?" I chided her gently.

"I—they all looked suitable."

"Have you no *preference,* then?" I fought to keep the little saw-edge of irritation out of my voice. "These new lodgings are to be the equal of—"

"Anything in France," she finished for me. "But I am no Madame de Heilly."

"Francis's mistress has no taste," I said. "And these lodgings are for *you,* Janey. For you. Can you not understand how I wish for you to have a place of your own, not inherited from Wolsey or . . . the others?"

"Yes, yes." It was then that I realized the apartments were for me, not for her. I needed to see her in surroundings that had no echoes.

"Choose something, Janey. It will mean a great deal to *me,*" I begged her.

"Very well." She bent forward, picked up a panel of wood. She sounded weary. "This is attractive. I should like the Queen's Privy Chamber done in this."

"Walnut. Very well, my love. And to go with walnut, dark green is always suitable."

"No, I'll not have that. 'Tis too—expected. I'll have scarlet instead." She pointed at a smear of colour.

"The Westminster red." I recognized it. "Most noble."

She smiled. "You will pin down my desires and preferences, in spite of myself."

"I wish to see you captured by them, so that in your absence I can still see you." I hesitated. Should I tell her of what I had seen? "Is the choice really that difficult, that you must cry over it?"

She quickly hid her face.

"There should be no secrets between us," I said, as gently as I could. "Nothing to be ashamed of." She knew me, knew all of me. And I was glad of it.

"It is not I who am ashamed! It is you—or should be!" she cried. "The monks—"

Not this again.

"—that you are having hanged this very moment—"

The arrogant rebels of Sawley, then.

"—in a mocking fashion—"

"The punishment must fit the crime! And should serve as a deterrent for possible converts. These particular monks were arrant traitors."

"It is not the monks," she wept. "It is *you!*"

Now I was completely confused and bewildered. "I do not understand," I finally said.

"What does it do to you to order such things done?" she said. "It changes you, forever."

Poor innocent. Perhaps she did not know me, after all. I was changed that way when I had had to order my first executions after my Coronation, those of Empson and Dudley. After the first they are all the same.

"I hope not," I assured her, reluctant to reveal my true feelings. She would find them ugly. And possibly unacceptable.

"What sort of a world will my children inherit? A world without monks and nuns, a world where abbots hang out of steeples—"

Children.

"Janey, are you—?" I had prayed, I had thrown myself on God's mercy, for there were so many physical hindrances. . . .

"Yes. I have only just now begun to believe it."

So that was what all this was about. The tears, the scruples, the evasiveness. I embraced her, feeling her healthy, compact body against me.

A miracle. For I had thought some punishment lurked, and a child would never be granted me.

That Sunday, a *Te Deum* was sung in all the churches in thanksgiving for the Queen's pregnancy. That meant it was officially announced throughout Christendom, and that everyone would hear of it: the Pope, the Emperor, Francis, the lingering rebels in the North. Truly it was a sign that peace had come again to England, that the horrible upheavals of the past decade were over, like a passing storm.

The year grew flowery and warm, and Jane and I passed that summer in perfect harmony. As I have said, happiness is near impossible to write of, and so I cannot. Although I would, I would—so that I somehow could relive it, in minute detail, not just as a suffused feeling.

She grew fanciful that summer, quite unlike herself. She wished strawberries by the bucket, and cherries, baby peas, and quail. I sent to France for the early cherries and peas, and to Calais for quail. The Lieutenant of Calais returned a full three dozen fat quail (procured across the border in Flanders), with elaborate instructions on how to keep them alive from Dover to London, and how soon after killing they should be prepared. In one sitting she ate a half-dozen quail, laughing all the while as much at her indulgence as at her specific tastes.

I could begrudge her nothing. The people were rejoicing already, so happy were they with the prospect of an uncontested heir to the throne.

Jane's pregnancy was uneventful and healthy. Why, then, why . . . ?

Let me record this briefly, for lingering over it does not assuage it.

Jane's happy pregnancy was countermanded by a labour that seemingly would not end. It lasted three days and two nights, and for the final twenty-four hours she was so weak and disoriented she was given no hope of survival. There was talk—among the physicians—of opening her and removing the child. Even today, there are some who claim I was asked to choose between the mother and the child and that I said, "Choose the child by all means, for another wife can easily be found." This shows the hatred my enemies bore me.

The truth is that I never gave such an order, nor was I presented with a choice.

After what seemed forever, suddenly the child—a healthy, robust boy—

was born. And as soon as he was removed from her body, Jane began to rally. The bonfires flared outside the hills of London; cannon sounded.

A prince was born!

King Henry VIII had a son.

I had a son. I could only repeat those words over and over, as the enormousness of them enveloped and protected me like a shield.

I held him in my arms, and saw how golden and perfect he was. The son denied me with Katherine and Anne—now here, as if it were a simple matter.

He was to be named Edward. He had been born on the eve of St. Edward's Day, and it was my grandfather's name. I told Jane, whispered it in her ear as she lay upon her state bed. My Jane, delivered back to me as well. She smiled, and agreed.

Edward was christened in high state three days later, in the chapel at Hampton Court. The Duke of Norfolk and Cranmer were his godfathers, and Mary was his godmother. Jane, propped up on great bolsters and covered with crimson velvet and ermine, waited in her chambers (and I by her side) to give Edward her blessing following the ceremony. Then she watched the celebrations afterward from her royal couch. She laughed and the torchlight gleamed in her eyes. She was well then, I tell you. She was well.

But from that midnight on she became feverish, then ill. The illness sapped the strength she had regained in the three days since Edward's birth.

The fever and illness turned to debilitation, then hallucinations. For nine days she lingered thus, hovering between our world and some other.

Then, on October twenty-fourth, she died.

WILL:

Everywhere, people sought to fix blame. Some attributed it to "neglect of those about her who suffered her to take cold and eat such things as her fantasy in sickness called for." Monk-lovers and Papalists called Jane a "reformer" who had met her just end (at the Lord's hand). Henry's enemies called it the revenge of Katherine and Anne. (Jointly?)

The common people, who still (despite his enemies' hopes) loved Henry, sought to turn this tragedy into a high romance. Within days after Queen Jane's death, ballads were being sung about her—and one in particular was quite memorable (in contrast to the one Anne wrote to memorialize herself).

Queen Jane was in travail
For six weeks or more,
Till the women grew tired,
And fain would give o'er.
"O women! O women!
Good wives if ye be,
Go, send for King Henry,
And bring him to me."

King Henry was sent for,
He came with all speed,
In a gown of green velvet
From heel to the head.
"King Henry! King Henry!
If kind Henry you be,
Send for a surgeon,
And bring him to me."

The surgeon was sent for,
He came with all speed,
In a gown of black velvet
From heel to the head.
He gave her rich caudle,
But the death-sleep slept she.
Then her right side was opened,
And the babe was set free.

The babe it was christened,
And put out and nursed,
While the royal Queen Jane
She lay cold in the dust. . . .

So black was the mourning
And white were the wands,
Yellow, yellow the torches,
They bore in their hands.
The bells they were muffled
And mournful did play,
While the royal Queen Jane
She lay cold in the clay.

Six knights and six lords
Bore her corpse through the grounds;
Six dukes followed after,
In black mourning gowns.

The flower of Old England
Was laid in cold clay.
Whilst the royal King Henry
Came weeping away.

Henry did indeed "come weeping away," to Windsor, before Jane's embalmed body should begin its lying-in-state at Hampton Court. He said he could not bear to see it, or to take part in any of the funeral ceremonies. He appointed Mary to act as chief mourner, and shut himself up in his chambers at Windsor, where no man saw him for days.

LXXX

There are horrid similarities between a wedding and a funeral. Both cause ordinary life to be suspended until a certain rite has been performed. Both require costumes of a solid colour—one white, the other black. Both must be performed in public and require those who attend to participate emotionally. Both leave things changed forever. Both have objects and superstitions peculiar to themselves: coffin-palls and bridal veils, funeral effigies and wedding rings. Both are costly and must be lavish to show proper respect.

King Henry, in his grief, left his trusted councillors—that is, Cromwell, Cranmer, and Brandon—to arrange and conduct the funeral. There was no need for them to consult him; they knew that there were to be no bounds to the expense for this funeral, that it must be glittering and holy. The monastic gold that Jane had so tried to save would now pay for her funeral.

I attended, for I knew that in later days Henry would want it described to him, although he could not bear to see it now.

Jane's coffin was set up in the middle of the Queen's Chamber of Presence. The freshly decorated room was now hung with black, and all the emblems of death were present: crosses, images, censers. Around her bier were set torches and candles, burning continuously; and a group of mourning ladies, in black habits, kept watch in the chamber all through the day and night.

Mary was chief mourner. It was no ceremonial duty to her, but a heartfelt one. Jane had brought her back to court and made her part of the Royal Family once more, after an exile of five years. But beyond that, from her reddened eyes and grief-slowed movements beneath her long black gown, I could see that it was her mother she was mourning as well. Mary had not been permitted to attend Katherine's funeral.

This chambered mourning, with its incessant dirges, continued for a week. Then Jane's almoner, the Bishop of Carlisle, sprinkled the coffin with holy water and allowed it to be moved to the Chapel Royal, where a catafalque had been erected. Her coffin was taken in long procession, with unlit torches, through the council chamber, into the King's great watching chamber, across the Great Hall, down the stairs into the Clock Court, and along the cloisters, until it reached the door of the chapel.

There she lay in state for a fortnight, until her grave was prepared in St. George's Chapel at Windsor.

The funeral car, drawn by black horses, moved slowly from Hampton Court through the frosty November countryside to Windsor Castle. Death was everywhere—in the fallen leaves, in the dried grass, in the silence of the air. The black procession wound through the brown landscape, and only crows and rooks remained to see.

On top of the great enclosed funeral car, as custom dictated, a wax effigy of Queen Jane rested, wearing her crown and robes of state, her hair streaming out upon the pillow, her neck fastened with jewels. It looked so like her at her best that men gasped at it. For my part, I always felt that these effigies were a taunt and a tease, and made grief sharper; perhaps that was their purpose. After a funeral, they were customarily saved. Henry's mother's and father's were kept, and may be seen to this day, also Edward III's. But Henry ordered Jane's destroyed before he could see it. Perhaps he knew it might come, in time, to serve as an idol for him.

Jane was to be interred near the altar of the chapel. The melancholy rituals of stave-breaking and Requiem Mass, of elegies and incense, were all performed; and at last Jane's coffin was lowered into the vault prepared for it.

There was no one who rejoiced at this death.

That in itself should serve as her epitaph, instead of the trite verse carved on her gravestone:

> *Phoenix Jana jacet nato phoenice: dolendum,*
> *Saecula phoenices nulla tulisse duos.*

> (Here a phoenix lieth, whose death
> To another phoenix gave breath:
> It is to be lamented much
> The world at once ne'er knew two such.)

Certainly Jane deserved a better remembrancer.

I was with her when she died, so there was no need for someone to come and tell me, no blessed time between the hearing and seeing in which I could think, "It cannot be so." No, I was by her bedside, for the physicians had said that if she improved this night, then her battle was won. Of course she would win it; there was no doubt in my mind. My will, my prayers, my love, all would overcome the affliction. And her flushed face, her darting eyes, made her seem no different from a child with a common fever. Sleep was the cure for it; therefore, when she closed her eyes and slept, I thought it all for the best.

I was holding her hand—sweaty it was, and slippery. I meant to hold it until I was sure she was sound asleep, and then disengage my own. (This is the first time I have ever allowed myself to recall, and recount, these things.) Too sudden a movement might wake her. And so I waited. And then, in some imperceptible, subliminal way, I felt a change in the hand. There was less heat there.

I let go of it and took it in my other hand. No, imagination. Her hand was the same; I had just overheld it. But whatever the subtle change in temperature was, it kept on. It was growing cooler with every breath.

Every breath . . . I looked at Jane and saw no movement there. But her breath was always soft.

The stillness of death. It is a stillness peculiar to itself, that the softest breathing, the deepest sleep, cannot mimic.

I shook her, trying to startle her into breathing. The heaviness, the denseness of even her shoulder, proclaimed the irreversible change. Her head lolled forward, as limp as a silk scarf.

I have no memory of what I did after that. Only of my thoughts, which exploded and scattered, like a cage of rats suddenly released.

✵

I awoke in the King's chamber at Windsor Castle. Sunlight shone on the wall. It was either mid-morning or mid-afternoon, I could not tell which. The room was chilly. Therefore it was not summer.

Then it rushed upon me like a maddened dog, fastening its teeth in me: Jane was dead. It gave me no time even to completely awaken before it attacked me. I was savaged by its fangs, bloodied and defeated.

For three days, I am told, I remained thus: unable even to get out of bed, while the hellhound had me to itself. Then an eerie cold light began to shine on me, and I got up, dressed myself, and gave orders for the funeral to proceed. I composed a letter to Francis. (Francis! What clearer evidence of my derangement than that I should choose *him?*) I announced Edward's birth, then added, "Notwithstanding, Divine Providence has mingled my joy with the bitterness of the death of her who brought me this happiness."

I composed an epitaph for Jane. I designed a gravestone for her, and selected Mary as chief mourner. I had my tailor come and measure me for mourning clothes, and ordered cloaks and doublets and hose and shoes, all in black. When he suggested perhaps the quantity was excessive, I insisted that he was mistaken. I ordered Cromwell to select all the black onyx from the Jewel House, and bring it to me. I paced and strutted and consulted books and Scripture.

Then I collapsed, and it was back to bed once more.

All this I remember as in a waking dream. Whenever I stopped moving, I was attacked by paralysing sorrow.

Slowly my head cleared. Then I began to be tormented by recurrent thoughts and obsessions, that in themselves became demoniac. They circled back again and again, as if to drive themselves like nails into my mind. It was in defence against them that I started to write them down, hoping that if I did so they might retreat. Perhaps the act of recording them would placate them, so they would leave me in peace.

I have kept the papers all these years. I do not know what is written on them, nor do I care to reread them. The transcribing did serve as an exorcism. I affix them here, only because I have no other suitable place to put them.

♩ ♩ ♩

If grief is only in my mind, where does my bodily pain come from? In my chest there is a tightness, as if several men with thick arms were squeezing me, pushing my breath out. I feel as if I cannot get my breath, cannot expand my chest. My muscles do not obey. Or when they try, they are weak. I am suffocating. There has come a choking in my throat, something that constricts on its own, and aches on its own. When I cry, it vanishes. But within a few moments it is back again. Like a bear-keeper, it keeps me chained by a short leash.

I have dreaded going into certain rooms, passing by certain things we looked at together, as if it would be too painful. But when it happens —by accident, or necessity—I have been surprised to find it does not hurt, not any more than her absence hurts anywhere else. I feel her absence no more keenly when looking at a beehive than when looking at a book she had never seen. Why is that?

I want Jane back. I would settle for only one minute with her. I would settle for only one question to ask her. I would settle for the chance to say only one sentence to her. Only one!

I see her everywhere. I see bits and pieces of her: in one woman's way of straightening her necklace, in another's timbre of voice, in yet another's profile. As if she were a mirror, broken, and the shards lay everywhere, in the most unexpected places.

I have been blaming God. But how much of it was my fault? The rumours that she took ill on account of bad handling . . . I am beginning to believe them myself. If only I had not forced her to participate in the night ceremony after the christening. If only I had let her rest. . . . The quails. Why did I indulge her fancies and let her eat so many? It was injurious to her health. . . . And then, the infinity of smaller things in which I might have unwittingly contributed to her death. Every day I find more of them. . . .

I remember once someone said to me, describing his wife's death: "First one thinks about it every second of every day, even when one is sleeping; then every minute, then every hour; then only a few times a day. Then comes a day when one does not think of it at all, all day long." That is impossible. The man was a liar. Or else he never cared for his wife.

The season is starting to change, and I hate it. I had somehow "got used" to the absence of Jane in autumn. But now to relearn it all over again . . . to have a whole new set of reminders, and also of things we cannot share, things I can see and she cannot. Is that why there is the traditional "year of mourning"? Because until one has gone through each season in turn, grief will keep pulling out new surprises at every corner?

As the season turns, I realize something I have been fighting so hard against: Jane is now the past. As long as it remained the same month, the same season, it was as if she and the present were still the same. But now they are starting to diverge. There are things occurring now that she cannot see or know about. Enough of these days will make Jane entirely a creature of the past. But I do not want it so! I will keep her here, in the present, with me—if I have to stop every clock in the kingdom to do so.

They say "you must accept God's will." If I accept it, then she is truly gone.

Yesterday I stood in her room, unchanged (I had not let them touch a single article; only to clean away the dust that had fallen since her death, which was an intruder), and knew the sorrow, the yearning, she felt, never to be able to return. Is that what death really is? To leave a room and never be allowed to come back? (And not know it at the time of leaving?) Is it really just that simple?

I saw her yesterday. No, it was not a dream, I am quite certain. I was not even looking for her (as I used to do) and so when I saw her, passing between doorways on London Bridge, it was like . . . I cannot say what. A gift? That one extra instant I spoke of earlier, granted me? I could not speak to her, or ask those questions. I could not even follow her. But she had been there. She looked . . . happy. How could she be? It seemed a horrible betrayal if she could be happy.

My faith was like a potted plant, kept indoors. It could not weather a winter. I had been ignorant of God's true nature until now. God is not "good," He is cruel. And one cannot predict His actions, not through prayer or knowledge or insights.

♂ ♂ ♂

These thoughts held me captive, tortured me, as surely as if I had been chained to a pillar in a dungeon. Indeed, that was how I felt—shackled, paralysed, held prisoner, while the rats of memory, desire, and loss swarmed over me, gnawing wherever they liked, diminishing me.

Then, while I slept one night, a strange change occurred. I awoke on that February morning—almost three months after Jane's death—full of strength and bitter anger. I looked at the crucifix on the opposite wall and despised Christ, hanging there. I wanted to kill Him, if He had not been dead already.

I saw the black-hung walls and despised them as well.

You think I'll weep? No, that I'll not! Never again shall You receive that pleasure as a gift from me!

It was God to whom I spoke. I despised Him, and despised myself for all my weak mewlings and supplications to Him. How He must have enjoyed them! How He must have laughed at my prayers, begging Him to spare Jane; how satisfied He must have been to behold my misery, made visible by these repulsive black hangings. God had robbed me of Jane, now I would rob Him of myself.

I'll serve another master, I threatened Him. In all the legends, this would have been sufficient to have called forth the Dark Presence. At once the Prince of Darkness (or one of his lesser demons) would have appeared in my chamber, contract in hand. It would have specified terms: so many days, so many years, in exchange for one (1) immortal soul of the High and Mighty Prince, Henry VIII of England, Wales, and France, as signed below. . . .

But no one came. There was no puff of smoke, no sulphurous fumes. That angered me, too.

So you are as unreliable as the other one, I sneered to myself. *The least you could do is have a reception for me. I gave grand ones whenever I signed a treaty with a foreign power. You are cheap as well as evil.*

I would serve no master, then, but myself. I would hit out and destroy; I would indulge every whim and appetite that raised itself. I wanted to destroy, to pull down all the ugly rottenness around me. If there was no good left in the world, there was a surfeit of bad, and I would spend myself on it. Not in the name of God—that betrayer, that assassin—but in my own name: King Henry VIII.

LXXXI

I ordered an end to the mourning which I had imposed on the court even through Christmas. (Would that grieve God? Good!)

I began to confer with Cromwell again. Many things were afoot: the bishops had completed their "interpretation" of the Ten Articles of Faith to Establish Christian Quietness, all set forth in a volume called *The Bishops' Book,* designed to answer laymen's questions; it awaited my endorsement. A number of greater monasteries had offered their surrenders: Whalley, Jervaulx, Kirkstead, and Lewes. Rich prizes. I should love to see them demolished. I wanted to hear the groan of the stones being pulled out of their sockets, and the crash of stained-glass windows hitting the ground to explode in multicoloured shards. I wanted to see the "miracle" statues, with their hidden wires and water-filled reservoirs, pitched onto a roaring fire made from monastic choir-stalls and embroidered vestments.

In addition, I was being courted by the Continental powers. It seemed I was an eligible bachelor again, and a rich one at that. Cromwell begged me to "consider the matter and frame it to your most noble heart."

I would never marry again. But for amusement I would look at the portraits. It was sport to order others to perform. "I cannot marry without knowing their appearance. The matter touches me too near my person," I explained.

I dispatched Hans Holbein, More's former painter who had done a passable job on Jane's portrait, to the Continent to take portraits of Christina of Denmark and Anne of Lorraine. That should take months.

I began to order banquets and celebrations. My appetite had returned, and fearsomely. Before, I had cared about my appearance. When I was young, it was important to me that the English King be more awesome than the French monarch. Then, I cared that Katherine, Anne, and Jane should find me desirable, handsome. Now there was no reason not to eat, to steep myself in pleasures of the palate. What else was left to me?

When the fish course came round, I no longer abstained from eels (a notably fatty fish). When the meat was served, I had both beef and lamb. I drank flagons of wine at every meal, so that they passed in a haze of pleasure. I ate all desserts and even called for sweetmeats in my chamber in mid-afternoon. I had no other pleasure but eating. Riding and hunting were taken away from me; there were no women and all the things that go with them: dancing, fêtes, musical evenings. But there was food—marvellous, unbridled food.

WILL:

Now I understand. This was Henry's "Nero" period, when he behaved cruelly and erratically, and from which (unfortunately) much of his reputation is derived. (How unfair, that eighteen months should eclipse almost forty years!) He grew fat. As one eyewitness described him: "The King has grown so marvellously excessive in eating and drinking that three of the largest men in the Kingdom could fit inside his doublet."

His beautiful features expanded and swelled, until his eyes were like little raisins set in a red mass of dough, and his strong neck became enruffed in a series of fat-rings.

He behaved grossly, and uncharacteristically: belching at banquets, eating with his fingers and throwing bones over his shoulder, yawning if he were bored; leaving betimes at entertainments and audiences, insulting ambassadors and councillors, making obscene, scatological jokes; and—most uncharacteristic of all—committing sacrilege. He threw his crucifix in the fireplace and pulled up the Virgin's skirts and spat on her, before likewise consigning her to the flames.

He wrote a mocking, threatening letter to Charles and Francis when they signed a ten-year truce and peace treaty. He called Francis "that quivering husk of a disease-eaten fruit-tree" and Charles a "degenerate, balloon-jawed descendent of a baboon" and said their "feeble union, undertaken under false pretences and for preposterous aims, would bring forth a strange fruit of hideous appearance, pustule-ridden and smeared with excrement, with a hollow but rotten interior."

When Pope Paul III published, publicly, his excommunication of Henry VIII and called for a Holy War against him (as earlier Popes had called for a Crusade against the Turk) Henry laughed uproariously (while wolfing down grouse and woodcock, a dozen altogether) and muttered, "If that Judas-serpent should slither from out his homosexual den of pleasure"—a great wipe of his mouth—"he should find a great shoe, yea, a leather boot, ready to stamp him and make his guts issue from out of his lying, double-tongued mouth." Then a belch, given with a great flourish.

He cared for nothing. He abandoned music (unlike Nero, he did not fiddle while the monasteries burned); all sport was neglected; he never attended Mass, except when required to. He had become a great, slobbering, vicious hulk.

I avoided him as much as possible, and he called for me seldom. I was one of the pleasures for which he had lost delight.

❦ HENRY VIII:

The Bishops' Book was published, and instead of quieting controversy, it sparked it. Because I myself had not authored it, people assumed that it was not authoritative, that further changes in doctrine were possible. The reformers knew exactly where they hoped to see the ark of the Church of England come to rest—near the Lutheran "Mount of Wittenberg." The traditionalists wished only to hold fast, and felt threatened.

Despite all precautions, the heretics took root in England. Reformers did not consider the Church of England to be a domestic affair (*my* affair!). They infiltrated and sought to gain control. Even the filthy Anabaptists established a foothold. I ordered all of them to quit England. But they left their Bibles, tracts, and ideas behind to poison the minds of my people.

At the same time, the Papalist partisans needed to be crushed. I announced that there were to be no more visitations to shrines, no pilgrimages, under pain of death. All "miracle" statues were to be taken from their shrines, sent to London, and examined. If these were truly miraculous, then they should be able to perform, even under adverse circumstances.

They failed the tests. The "Holy Blood of Hailes" remained lumpy (like the dried honey and saffron colouring it was) and did not miraculously liquefy before my commissioners. The "moving" Rood of Halles was exposed with its puppet-wires, and burnt. Bishop Hugh Latimer of Worchester, an ardent reformist, tore away an image of Saint Jerome—using only his left hand—which legend had claimed "eight oxen could not move."

False, false. All as false as God—the Great Charlatan, the Celestial Deceiver.

There were heresy trials, to staunch the Anabaptist pollution. John Lambert was convicted of blatant heresy as a Sacramentarian and burnt.

At the same time, recalcitrant evil abbots defied me and clung to their

Papacy. The abbots of Reading, Colchester, and particularly Glastonbury were all executed. Glastonbury laid lying claim to being King Arthur's Avalon, and boasted a "Holy Thorn" which supposedly sprang from the staff of Joseph of Arimathea, who had come to England with the Holy Grail—oh, the lies, the false *hopes* they would have us hope! The credulous fools who stood by the "Holy Thorn" on midnight of Christmas Eve, expecting it to flower! I hated them as much as I hated all things now. The abbots were hanged on their monastic grounds. My soldiers hacked and uprooted the "Holy Thorn" and set fire to its roots.

I delighted in distributing the monastic property. To Cromwell I gave St. Osyth's Monastery, Launde Abbey, and the Greyfriars at Great Yarmouth. To Sir Anthony Browne I gave vast tracts of land owned by Chertsey Abbey, Merton Priory, St. Mary Overey, and Guildford Priory. I gave Evesham Monastery to Sir Philip Hoby of my Privy Chamber, and Tewkesbury Abbey to his colleague, Edward Harman.

I took a savage pleasure in all these nasty acts. Yet none was nasty enough, none affronted God enough. There was nothing that was purely His which I could mangle.

Holbein returned from his mission with a portrait of Christina of Denmark. But before I could view it, I had already been told by Will of her remark, "If I had two heads, one of them should be at the King of England's disposal."

So that lie was flourishing—that I murdered my wives? Katherine was not murdered by *me,* and neither was Jane. Blame the Witch for the first, and God —that sweet, loving God!—for the second. But that was too difficult for the average dolt behind his wheelbarrow to comprehend. Easier to blame blood-thirsty King Henry.

It is God who is bloodthirsty.

Let us make man in our image, after our likeness.

A killer who kills for sport. You have succeeded, O Mighty One. You even killed Your own Son. How feeble our imitations are—we kill only our enemies, or kill through the law. Will we soon "improve" ourselves, grow more into Your image? Become more God-like?

I am trying, God, I am trying.

I felt an urge for food: not hunger, but an urge for food—they are different. I ordered six tarts, and when they arrived—two apple, one plum, two strawberry, and one raspberry—I ate them all, stuffing them one by one into my mouth before I had even swallowed the first, mingling all their flavours together. I found no pleasure in taste anymore, but in excess . . . there I found *negative* pleasure.

The northern rebellion, which had flared so briefly and visibly in the Pilgrimage of Grace, now died down to a secret, deadly smoulder. I created a Council of the North, headed by Bishop Tunstall of Durham, to govern that area from henceforth. Never again would I leave the northern shires on their own. They should see me, and I them.

But there were those in the realm who had not been pleased, not pleased at all, with the outcome. The Pole family, headed by old Margaret Plantagenet (daughter of the Duke of Clarence, and thus great-great-great-granddaughter of Edward III) and her three "White Rose" sons—Henry, Lord Montague; Geoffrey; and the insufferable Reginald, the traitorous Papal dog-legate—had hoped to restore the fortunes of the nearly defunct White Rose. The North had always been linked to the House of York, and remained sympathetic to Richard III. The various leftover buds from that dynastic stalk—the Poles and Henry Courtenay, the Marquis of Exeter—had haboured ideas of bursting once more into dynastic bloom "if anything befall the King" . . . God willing.

I could recount every article of their treason. But it is tedious. Henry Courtenay and his wife Elizabeth had intrigued with Chapuys in his inept plot to rescue Katherine and Mary. In Cornwall he gathered followers who conspired to proclaim him King.

Henry, Lord Montague, had looked forward to the day that "the King's leg will kill him, and we shall have jolly stirring at last." (What spy had betrayed my secret to him? What traitor had discovered it, and disclosed it?) Reginald Pole had come on a mission from the Pope to help the Pilgrims deprive me of my throne. In fact, the Pope had "entrusted" England to him. These treasons were confessed by Sir Geoffrey, their brother.

Yet another sadness: Nicholas Carew, my old friend, had known of this treason and yet kept it from me; and Edward Neville (my boyhood companion —he who had ridden with me to the White Tower on my accession) had joined the conspiracy.

My father's prediction had come true.

On the day of their executions, I made my way to Father's tomb in Westminster Abbey. I had never visited his tomb before, with its bronze vault resting under the delicate stone lace of his commissioned chapel ceiling. Men praised his glorious chapel, spoke of its beauty, but I had never wanted to come to it, because then I would acknowledge his achievement in some way. Today I was ready to make that acknowledgment, and I had nowhere else to go.

It was colder inside the Abbey than outside. There were places where the roof and windows leaked, and pools of ice lay beneath them, opaque and thick. There seemed to be no one present in that whole vast nave. The chantry offices

—reciting prayers for the dead—had ceased with the abolition of Popish abuses in regard to Purgatory. The praying, muttering monks were no more.

I had to pass through the great choir, and thence past the tombs of Queen Maud, Queen Edith, Henry III, Henry V (the great warrior-king, the perfect Christian) and his Queen, Catherine de Valois. She had always been but a name to me, a royal link between Henry V and my ancestor Owen Tudor. Now as I passed her marble box I saluted her, wondering if my lust and proclivities for commoners had come from her. Certainly she would have understood her great-grandson's yearnings and preferences.

My father's chapel was set off from the rest of the nave by a flight of stairs. One ascended them as if approaching some higher plane of life. Before me opened up the great stone work of art described as "the most beautiful in Christendom." It resembled the woods after an ice storm, and particularly today, in its mantle of cold: the delicate tracery of stems, branches, leaves, all encased in a white, shimmering, brittle hardness.

Father rested within a fence of wrought iron and bronze, fashioned to represent a miniature cathedral. The doors were locked, but I carried the key. Opening the door, I stepped into his secret garden of bronze and gold. Once inside, I found myself in a world apart—sweet, protected, timeless.

He lay within a great black marble sarcophagus, guarded on each corner by a golden angel. A gilded representation of him lay atop, hands joined piously, feet resting on a lion. Beside him lay my mother, in golden effigy, likewise praying.

His bones were in this container. The golden image was not he. But it was hard not to address the representation instead of the box with the bones. No wonder idol-worship and graven images had proved so difficult to eradicate.

I made my way around the tomb, aware, suddenly, of my great bulk. Father was seeing it. He was seeing the enormous, broken thing his athletic, contemptuous son had grown into.

"But I am now a King, Father." I spoke my thoughts aloud. "I behave as you would have me." I had meant to kneel by his tomb, but there was no ledge on the marble sarcophagus, and the stone floor was harder and colder than ice. I remained standing. "I trust no one. This day I see the last of my friends executed for treason. Neville and Carew—the ones waiting for me to come and play after I left you in your sickroom. The ones in my mind's eye when I contradicted you."

Each word left my mouth in a little puff of breath-smoke.

"It is not nearly as lonely as I feared," I said, after a bit. "And loneliness serves as an excuse for all sorts of indulgences. You knew that all along! Why did you not tell me? If I had known, I would have embraced it all the sooner."

I looked at his gilded face, so serene in its representation. He rested in artistic triumph.

"The last of your enemies dies this day," I assured the effigy. "The White Rose is plucked."

Tudor was supreme. There would be no more pretenders. And I had provided the necessary heir.

My body pained me. I was never good at standing, and my legs had begun to ache. I needed to sit down. Father would understand. He and I thought alike, now.

LXXXII

The people were whipping themselves into a frenzy of looting and destruction, all under the guise of religion. At first they had trembled to see their relics taken from their little local shrines and consigned to bonfires. Then, delight in the bonfire itself began to consume them. There is something so deeply satisfying about destroying, trampling, killing. . . . And soon the people themselves outdid the royal commissioners in seizing the relics and desecrating them.

The townsfolk of Maidstone took the ancient Rood of Boxley and reviled it in the marketplace; those at Kirkstall burnt the girdle of Saint Bernard, looked to as helpful in childbirth, and tore up the wimple of Saint Ethelred, used to cure sore throats.

But these were insignificant relics and lacklustre shrines. What the common people did on their level, I would do on mine. I would make a great show of dismantling and utterly destroying the three most ancient, sacred shrines and pilgrimage-centres in England: that of Saint Cuthbert in Durham, that of Our Lady of Walsingham, and, most sacrosanct (and jewel-bedecked) of all, Saint Thomas à Becket's in Canterbury.

Saint? The man was a saint as Thomas More was a saint, as Bishop Fisher was a saint! They were all nothing but filthy and abominable traitors and rebels against their King! Becket had won, in his day, simply because the Pope had managed to intimidate his weak King.

That was in his day. But there was no reason why . . . yes, none whatsoever . . . a man can be brought to trial long after the crime . . . and he must stand for it. . . .

"Dismantle the entire Becket shrine," I ordered my workmen, carefully chosen for both their skill and their honesty. "The gold I want in reinforced wooden carts. The jewels, inventoried and sorted, transported in locked coffers. As for the inner coffin, once you have removed the gold plate covering it, leave it as is. Oh, unfasten the lid, but do not open it." I explained myself no further.

After they had departed for Canterbury, I sat down and began to draft an unusual summons to my Privy Councillors and the ranking members of Convocation.

We stood on the Opus Alexandrinum, the Roman-inspired pavement of intricately inlaid coloured marble that surrounded Becket's tomb behind the high altar of Canterbury Cathedral. There were some forty of us, all told— from the Archbishop of Canterbury himself, Thomas Cranmer, and all his lesser bishops, to my Vice-Regent for Spiritual Affairs, Cromwell, and his Council subordinates.

They surrounded the iron chest, resting on its pink marble arcaded base, that housed the "sacred" remains of Thomas à Becket. The painted wooden lid was loosened and ready to be lifted.

The shrine was bare, otherwise. The canopy of gold netting which had sagged with the weight of pilgrims' offerings—brooches, rings, jewels—had been emptied. The gold plate had been carted away, in twenty-six groaning wagons. Upon my finger glowed the "Regale de France"—a ruby which Louis VII of France had presented when he came to seek the saint's help for a sick child. I had had it made into a fine ring, set round with sapphires, diamonds, and emeralds "recovered" from the golden canopy. I called it my "Becket ring."

"My dear councillors and spiritual advisors," I said, in a soft voice. It carried well in the small area. The acoustics were good. "We are here to try an accursed traitor. Since the defendant could not safely make the journey to London to stand trial, we, in consideration of his limiting condition, have convened the trial here."

I looked about. Cromwell had the proper expression of normalcy on his face. The rest looked frightened, bewildered, or uncomfortable.

I nodded to the serjeant-at-arms. "You may call the defendant."

"Thomas à Becket, Archbishop of Canterbury, come into the court."

I gave another signal, and four royal guards stepped up to the coffin and removed the wooden lid. At that, a silence gripped our party.

I must set an example for them. I approached the dark cavity of the iron box and peered within.

As I did so, I felt suspense, dread of what I might see, what might happen. . . .

Nothing happened, and it was difficult to see inside, in the gloom. I called for a taper and thrust it right into the coffin itself.

There were rotted ecclesiastical vestments swathing a crumbling skeleton. Its mitre had fallen away, revealing a skull with a thin slice taken off its top. Dust and dirt lay an inch thick on the bottom. How did it come to be inside a sealed coffin? I wondered irrelevantly.

"You may view the accused," I said, motioning to my councillors. They filed by, peering into the sarcophagus, lit by the single taper inside. One by one they returned to their places.

When all were silent and waiting, I continued, "The accused, Thomas a Becket, must answer to the following charges." I unrolled a lettered parchment. "One: to the crime of defying and humiliating his King, Henry II of England and Angevin. Two: to the crime of masquerading as a saint."

I turned to Cromwell. "You may present the Crown's evidence against the defendant."

Oh, how I enjoyed it: the delicious recounting of the ungrateful traitor's behaviour, knowing all the while the final outcome. The crushing of one's enemies . . . the Israelites had known that supreme pleasure, had celebrated it even in the Psalms. King David seemed to have had enemies aplenty, and he had been shameless in asking the Lord to do them in.

"A lowly man, Becket, who, gaining the confidence and friendship of the King of England, used that as means to advance his own power," read Cromwell. "Not being content with ingratiating himself with the King and being granted familiarities far above his station, he coveted the Chancellorship and obtained that, then lusted after the Archbishopric and obtained that. He lusted after the power of the Church, and once he was endowed with all he desired, he had no further use for the King. So he turned against him, defied his laws, obstructed his decrees, and trafficked with his sworn enemy, the King of France."

These charges were discussed, as a courtesy to legal niceties. Then I called for the verdict.

"For maliciously misusing the King's affection for his own worldly gain: guilty or no?"

A mumbled response. "Guilty."

"For masquerading as a saint: guilty or no?"

"Guilty."

"For gross ingratitude to his sovereign: guilty or no?"

"Guilty!" Their enthusiasm was increasing.

"Then we find you, Thomas Becket, the accused, guilty on all counts as charged. Guilty as an errant traitor to your divinely appointed sovereign lord. Guilty in that your death was untruly called martyrdom, being canonized by the Bishop of Rome, because you had been a champion to the usurped authority and a bearer of the iniquity of the clergy. There appears nothing in your life and exterior behaviour whereby you should be called a saint, but rather esteemed to have been a rebel and traitor to your prince."

I took a deep breath in the rarefied air of the opened shrine, before continuing.

"The sentence is this: in future you are to be called only *Bishop* Becket, and all mention of you in books of Common Prayer, lists of saints, and so forth, are to be stricken out.

"And we hereby condemn you to be burnt as a traitor, and your ashes scattered."

I nodded to my unquestioning, obedient guards, who came forward, bent over the coffin, and began enfolding the bones within their robes of office. While we watched, they transferred the lumpy bundle—with a corner of the mitre protruding—to a new wooden chest, which they carried away.

A heavy feeling came upon the company, far heavier than when Becket's remains were physically present. We could all hear the neat clicks of the guardsmen's heels as they marched down the long length of the nave with their casket.

"There were, as I said, twenty-six cartloads of gold festooning the abomination that housed Becket's miserable remains. I think an eighth-cartload for each of you who helped examine the justice of the matter would be most appropriate," I said.

Thus I dismissed them. Even enriched as they were, there was no buoyancy in them as they took their leave and melted away into the gloom of the cathedral.

Only Cromwell remained, directly across from the emptied sarcophagus.

"Old bones smell ugly," I finally said. "I would expect a fresh corpse to stink, or a waterlogged body. But this was clean, and dry." I shook my head, wonderingly. The peculiar odour—of centuries of packaged, brooding death—was stronger than ever.

"It is done," I said cheerfully, waving my hand—the one with the Becket ring on it.

Speak, Crum. Say something to banish the odd feeling I have inside ... a feeling I have not felt since ... I know not. ...

"Your Grace, this must end," Cromwell said soberly. The taper lit only part of his face, but his words were chiselled and clear.

They said what I knew already.

"I understand that this was but a political gesture, made to give a little sport to the dull proceedings of dismantling and inventorying the vulgar, Papalist shrines," he continued, putting the most flattering interpretation on it. "I understand it, but I fear it will be misunderstood by the people and exploited by your enemies. You are aware, Your Grace, that many already question your sanity? Your actions of late have played directly into the hands of your sworn enemies. It is you who are a traitor to yourself. For the law defines treason as 'giving aid and comfort to the enemy' and that is what you have been doing —by your lack of self-control, by your actions that are open to unkind, even malicious interpretations. Forgive me, Your Grace—" The boldness of his words now frightened him.

"Have no fear, Crum," I said. "It is finished. It is over."

He had no way of knowing that it had all gone flat, that I was weary of my rebellion and bored with my schoolboyish howl against God, Who seemed—most humiliating of all—not to have taken much notice of it. Certainly He had not responded in any observable way.

LXXXIII

What had the past year of unthinking, pain-filled rampage gained me? I was forced to take a fearless look and confront the results.

I was certainly richer, from the plunder and seizure of the monastic property and shrines. Abbey plate and jewels and manuscripts and vestments now adorned my palaces, and I was buying the loyalty and support of the gentlemen to whom I sold or leased the abbey lands, making sure they had a vested interest in preventing a return to the Papal fold. There was nothing like property and money to sway a man's political leanings.

I was isolated in the larger world. In company with Job, I could lament, *For the thing which I greatly feared is come upon me, and that which I was afraid of is come unto me.* The Pope had called for a war upon me, and lo! a miracle had occurred. Francis and Charles had actually made peace with one another, signed a truce, and loomed as allies against me.

My gleeful rage against the signs and relics of Popery, my allowance of the loosely worded (and interpreted) Ten Articles of Faith to Establish Christian Quietness had caused the Protestants to gain a pernicious foothold in England, and they were now trying to subvert my Church.

My orgy of self-pitying eating and drinking had expanded me beyond all recognition. I was obese, repulsive to look upon.

I had multiplied my troubles and problems. I had solved none and created new ones.

For several months I did nothing. I made few appearances, and those were restrained and circumspect. I passed no new laws and made no pronouncements. I reversed my eating habits, becoming as abstemious as a desert hermit, and found to my horror that the fat on me was firmly entrenched and did not obediently melt away at my command.

To check the dangerous foreign situation that had arisen, I decided to use monastic money to finance the construction of a chain of fortresses and defences all across the southern coastline, stretching from Sandown in the East to Pendennis in the West. I employed a Bohemian engineer, Stephen von Haschenperg, to design these castles, which would be constructed on new principles, allowing for the latest advances in cannon warfare. It would disappoint those who hoped that the monastic wealth might be used to found hospitals, colleges, schools. I was disappointed myself. But there can be no higher learning, no institutions of mercy, unless a country is at peace and not ravaged by her enemies.

I would halt the growing influence of Protestantism by rescinding the Ten Articles. They would be replaced by a conservative Act, setting forth the required orthodoxy of faith.

Parliament duly passed this Act of Six Articles. It affirmed the doctrine of Transubstantiation, noted it was not necessary to receive both bread and wine at Communion, said that priests could not marry, that vows of chastity were perpetual, that private Masses were permitted, and that private confession was necessary. Burning was the penalty for once denying the first article, and a felon's death for twice denying any of the others. I gave the authorities power to enforce it by severe means, for nothing else could prevail. This earned it the sarcastic popular sobriquet, "The Whip with Six Strings."

In spite of my lack of interest, Cromwell had all the while been casting about in Europe for a bride for me. I had let him, for it amused him, and I wished to humour him. In the past year there had been several delicate queries made to Denmark (I have already spoken of the flippant Duchess Christina); to France (there were the three daughters of the Duc de Guise: Marie, Louise, and Renée; two cousins of Francis, Marie de Vendôme and Anne of Lorraine; as well as his own sister), and to Portugal (the Infanta).

None of these was seriously made—at least not on my part; although certainly on Cromwell's—or seriously received. Cromwell's diligence provided Hans Holbein with steady employment and lengthy travels and visits to the courts of Europe, but that was all. I had no desire—indeed, I had a revulsion —against the thought of remarrying. Now, in my personal inventory, I was forced to admit that I was no longer a very compelling object for a woman's desires.

The very fact that I thought of it, grew concerned about it, was a signal that something was beginning to change, to stir. . . .

In the meantime I guarded little Edward's health, obsessively. He was not to be at court, because of the danger of infection, but kept at Havering—a clean manor in the country. His attendants were to be strictly limited in number, and all his linens, hangings, toys, and feeding utensils were to be washed and aired daily. As a result of all this seclusion I myself seldom saw him, but I rested secure in the knowledge that he was safe, and flourished. They said he had inherited Jane's starry eyes. Yes, my Jane's eyes had been like the sapphires from India. My Jane . . .

The line of granite-faced castles was rising steadily on the coasts, like a row of mushrooms after a rain, and just in time. Francis and Charles were growing daily more belligerent toward me, and the Pope was urging them on, like a huntsman to his hounds.

In the early spring of 1539 I rode to Sandgate, near Dover, to inspect my fortifications there. The sea-air was raw and yet restoring, and I felt the first surge of excitement I had felt in a year and a half when I saw the half-completed ramparts of Kentish ragstone surrounding the massive, tripartite fortress in their center. The crenellations on top of the semicircular bastions made them look like three gigantic wheels with interlocking cogs. There were no corners on the castle or its surrounding curtain wall, for corners were vulnerable to cannon-shot.

That for the pretensions of Francis and Charles. They would never prevail against my kingdom, not while I was alive to defend it. I would raise defence after defence, even if I had to beggar myself and the whole of England to do so. As long as there remained a farthing, that farthing would be spent to protect ourselves against our enemies.

Cromwell was walking atop the parapets, with his rolling, bearlike gait. He had become more blocklike of late (unlike Wolsey, whose extra dimensions had transformed him into a sphere). Against the grey sky, Crum was a solid, deeper grey. He waved when he saw me staring up at him.

I was not concerned with Crum, however, but only with the French. Walking round to the farthest protruding rampart, where the cannon would eventually be lined up, I stood on the very edge of the sea-wall, where the cold Channel waters came and made obeisance to England, in little tame waves. Across that water lay France, visible on clear days, but not today.

The water made the soothing slap-and-slide sounds meant to allay my fears. It was hypnotic, and seemed to say, *It is good, it is good, it is good.* . . . False waters. French-tainted waters.

I turned and looked behind me, at the round belligerence of my defence castle, so muted and grey against the equally dull greenish grey grass on the knolls surrounding it. War had the characteristics of an elephant: grey and wrinkled and bulky. Also expensive to feed and house.

Cromwell was no longer visible. He had left the high places and was undoubtedly inspecting the heart of the castle, where men and ammunition must quarter. If there were a weak spot there, he would find it and seek to have it corrected.

I continued to watch the cold, grey-green sea spread out before me. Watching the sea, I did not have to think; and I was weary of thinking. All my thoughts were unpleasant.

"Your Majesty."

Cromwell was beside me. "Ah, Crum."

"The underground provisions are marvellous!" he reported. "Although under the earth, the whitewash and simple designs and open chambers make them aesthetic and even restful. And the decision to have only large chambers is not only practical, but avoids that ugly, cramped feeling of being confined. Von Haschenperg is a genius!"

Even though Crum was no military tactician, he understood the needs of ordinary soldiers—had he himself not served as a mercenary in Italy?—and thus his comments were valuable.

"I am pleased you find it so."

Together we stood and looked toward France. I knew our conversation must tread on this delicate matter. But I was not eager for it.

"My negotiations with the French for your bride have foundered," he finally said, hands clasped behind his back, still staring out to sea.

"How so?" I likewise kept my eyes firmly fastened on invisible France.

"The three daughters of the Duc de Guise have proved . . . difficult," he said. "The first, Marie—"

The widow of the Duc de Longueville, I suddenly remembered. The silly old Duke, held captive in England, who had acted as Louis's proxy in "consummating" his marriage to Mary . . . was his widow yet alive?

"She is young, and although large in person, is thought to be attractive," said Crum, answering my unasked question.

Large. I myself was "large." "Well, as I am large myself—" I began.

"It seems she is betrothed to the King of Scots already," said Cromwell.

James V, son of my sister Margaret. How old could he be, as James IV was killed in the Battle of Flodden in 1513. . . . Twenty-seven, then? Damn the Scots! I had heard little from them in a generation, had mistook their quietness for subservience.

"But her sisters, Louise and Renée, are said to be beautiful. I have sent Holbein to take their likenesses. Unfortunately, Renée, the most beautiful of the three, is said to be religious and determined to enter a convent."

Good. Then I would be spared the de Guise sisters.

"Francis has two cousins, Marie of Vendôme and Anne of Lorraine, which he himself suggested for Your Majesty's consideration. Holbein has agreed to sketch Anne of Lorraine as well, while he is in France doing the de Guise sisters."

This was ludicrous. "What of their looks, these Valois cousins? Perhaps we could have them all transported to Calais, and there let Lieutenant Lisle evaluate the entire French contingent?"

"Alas, no reliable report." He spread his hands wide. "And as for the Infanta of Portugal, Charles would of necessity be involved."

"All this marriage-mongering, and for what?" Suddenly it was no longer a harmless pastime, but something significant and demeaning. Others were becoming involved.

"For perhaps another heir," said Cromwell. "God be praised that you have a son, a fine, healthy Prince," he added hastily. "But as a wise and prudent sovereign, it were better that you provide other sons for the succession—for Edward's sake as well as your own peace of mind. It is difficult to bear the burden of being an only son. And God has proved Himself inscrutable and often cruel."

None knew that better than I: both beneficiary and mourner from the largesse of His "unsearchable ways."

I grunted in response. More princes were all very well to wish, but they must be got upon a woman. Therein lay much happenstance and misery.

"My true opinion," spoke Cromwell near my ear, "is that the Empire and France are no good casting-grounds for you. Charles and Francis are your enemies, and it is in their interest to keep you celibate and unwed, while dangling unattainable brides before you. No, Your Grace. You must outsmart them and seek among your true allies—just as Abraham would not seek among the Canaanites for Isaac's bride."

Where had he come upon all this Old Testament knowledge? Only scholars knew it—and heretics.

"The Duke of Cleves, a non-Papal Catholic like yourself, has two daughters. They are said to be fair. Perhaps we should enquire there."

"Where is Cleves?" It must be an unimportant little duchy.

"Small, Your Grace, but strategic. It is located at the upper end of the Rhine, where that great river spreads out into fingers on the flat plains that finally turn into the Low Countries. It is a troublesome thorn in the Emperor's side," he noted with glee. "The old Duke has just nipped in and taken the Duchy of Guelders right from under Charles's nose. He is quite feisty and independent. And his daughters may be beautiful."

Beautiful. A Rhine maiden, a Lorelei? I confess that my imagination was stirred. It would be so different, with no cruel reminders of the past. Perhaps I was ready for a complete change. If there existed a woman capable of making me forget the Spanish Katherine, the Frenchified Anne, the pure English Jane . . .

"Well," I temporized, "make some inquiries. And if Holbein is free later, perhaps he can take their likenesses."

Cromwell nodded, slowly.

"And ask our ambassadors to the nearby Lowlands to visit their court," I added, "and describe the daughters of Cleves to us."

The daughters of Cleves . . . it had an ancient, poetical ring to it.

The reports were conflicting.

Christopher Mount, who was employed to negotiate a possible treaty of alliance with the Duke of Cleves, wrote to Cromwell, who paraphrased his letter to me:

> *The said Christopher instantly sueth every day, that the picture may be sent. Whereunto the Duke answered, that he should find some occasion to send it, but that his painter, Lucas, was left sick behind him at home. Every man praiseth the beauty of the said lady, as well for her face as for her person, above other ladies excellent. One among others said to them of late, that she as far excelleth the Duchess of Saxony, as the golden sun excelleth the silver moon. Every man praiseth the good virtues and honesty with shamefacedness, which plainly appeareth in the serenity of her countenance.*

Another envoy, Hutton, wrote, "The Duke of Cleves has a daughter, but there is no great praise either of her personage or of her beauty."

Then Holbein's sketch arrived, showing a beautiful and alluring woman, modest like Jane, but bedecked like a Babylonian princess.

My primary commissioner for the marriage, Nicholas Wotton, did not send back any reports from the court of Cleves.

In the meantime, the situation worsened between England and the Catholic powers. Francis and Charles withdrew their ambassadors from court, and there were reports that a French fleet was being assembled at Boulogne, and that Francis was commissioning seven new warships to be built, to attack our shores. The old Duke of Cleves died and was succeeded by his son, who was as anti-Imperialist as his father—a relief for us. He was most interested in allying himself to England, and was in contact with the Schmalkaldic League, an anti-Papal/Imperialist union of northern German states.

Cromwell, who had lived and worked in the Low Countries as a young man (as clerk to an English merchant adventurer), kept assuring me that honour did not reside only in the ancient kingdoms of Hispania, Gallia, and the Papacy, but in the northern duchies and principalities as well.

"You have nothing to fear," he said. "In the future, I believe, England will find her natural allies from amongst these peoples. Indeed, if France and

Spain persist in their outmoded allegiance to the Papacy, new-minded monarchs will have no choice. Is it not better to embrace the future wholeheartedly? Not, like Lot's wife, to keep looking back?"

Again, the Old Testament. And so many Biblical allusions from my "modern" Crum . . .

"To look back avails us nothing," I agreed. The world of Wolsey was gone, and all his assumptions, alliances, and loyalties with it. "Do prod Wotton. I shall not decide until after I have received his report."

LXXXIV

In August, Cromwell reported that he had received word from Nicholas Wotton regarding the Princess Anne, and that it was "favourable."

"What, precisely, did he say?" I pressed him.

That she is intelligent and loyal, and inclined to the match," Cromwell said.

"And she *is* beautiful," I added. Holbein's portrait assured me of that. Intelligent—I needed that. And loyal—no less important.

"Indeed she is!"

"And not too Protestant? I'll not have a Lutheran!"

"No, her house thinks as you do. A rare thing in these troubled times, to have recognized the twin dangers of Papacy and heresy."

"Is her brother content to have her marry away from the Continent?"

"He is content, and ready to sign a marriage treaty."

So here it was. I must marry again. Despite all my restrictions, both political and personal, it seemed a bride had been found to meet them. And beyond that, to provide a bit of exotica . . . a Rhine Princess, whose device was two white swans, emblems of candour and innocence. There was a family legend in Cleves that a faerie swan, drawn in a boat down the Rhine by two white swans, had mysteriously "visited" a Duke of Cleves's daughter long ago, and fathered her child. From him descended my Swan-Princess. . . .

"Then send William Petre to join Wotton and have the treaty drawn up, signed, and witnessed," I finally said.

Cromwell beamed.

Three weeks later he appeared, seeking audience with me. Clutched in his hand was the dispatch from the Duchy of Cleves. Wordlessly he handed it to me, and I broke the seal and read its contents.

Then I handed it back to Cromwell and left him to read it carefully with his lawyer's eye, while I stood at the far end of the chamber and looked out at the dismal little garden below, misted and dying in the autumn rains. My mind wandered, seeking to hide in the dead stalks and fallen leaves.

"So it is to be done?"

"Eh?"

"I said"—Crum thought he disguised the little rise of irritation in his voice—"so it is to be done? All seems to be in order here. Shall I notify the Duke of your decision?"

"Aye. The Duke of Cleves will become my brother." A German brother? The Germans . . . their nature was so alien to me. Their food . . . their great, ponderous legs and haunches . . . even their names: Wolf, Gisella, Ursula. And their leaden ways, so contrary to the English merriment. (But my Anne would not be so; she was different.)

Yes, Anne was like Jane, I could tell by the portrait. I approved of her gown of gold, all studded with gems and elaborately embroidered. Her taste was the same as mine. How well we would look together in public! She appeared dainty and would avoid the domineering blockishness of Katherine and the brazen wildness of Anne. Sweet, like my Jane, with her downcast eyes . . .

At the thought of Jane, the familiar ache, which never entirely left me, came. This mourning seemed to have a life of its own, and had now lived with me longer than Jane herself. I knew I must end it, that it was time. But . . .

The court was delighted that it would once more have a Queen. A court without a feminine half tends to become either dull and entirely businesslike or violent and immoral, depending on the age of its bachelor-King. It was an indication of which stage I was in that the past two years at court had been colourless and boring. Men's concerns were centered on property, religious politics, and foreign trade: middle-aged men's passions.

The realm, too, rejoiced that after so many years it would have a Queen. Having never accepted Anne, and having not been allowed enough time to become accustomed to my beloved Jane, in their minds the people had not had a true Queen since the first rumblings of the Great Matter, in 1527. Over twelve years they had been patiently waiting. Now I would bring them a Princess from across the waters, a dainty, sheltered girl. Anne would become known as "the Silver Swan of Cleves." Even the words had a silken, gliding sound.

So, in November, with the marriage contract signed and witnessed in Cleves, and the Lady Anne promised to depart for England straightway, I announced the good news by proclamation to all England: You are to have a Queen! And they roared back: Hurrah!

Because of the lateness of the year and Anne's delicate complexion, it had been decided that she should travel mainly over land rather than risk a nasty sea voyage. So she and her entourage of ladies were creeping slowly across the face of northern Germany and thence to Calais, where they would cross the Channel in time to spend Christmas in England.

Now that the thing was decided, I was anxious to have the adventure begin. I was suddenly hungry to know every detail about her person, so that I might imagine her and spend time with her in my mind ere I beheld her.

As soon as Nicholas Wotton returned to court, I ordered him to my side and began to ply him with questions. I began with political ones, concerning the new Duke's relationship with the Vatican.

"After all, it affected the one sister's marriage to the Duke of Saxony and raised questions about Anne's possible pre-contract with the Duke of Lorraine," I said.

"Aye, aye." He smiled, his grey wisps of hair making his head look like a dandelion puff-ball. "But she married anyway, although I understand she still must never let her husband see her read a Lutheran text."

"I blame him not! I would never permit a wife of mine to keep heretical tracts! I suppose the Lady Anne spends time with the Scriptures?" I asked idly.

"No. Very little, from what I saw."

"She prefers frivolous works?" Could she have a leaning for love-poems?

He shrugged. "I never heard of it. The Germans do not believe women should study or read overmuch. They think it makes them unfeminine."

True, it could. Look what the New Learning had done to Katherine and Mary—turned them hard and manlike. Elizabeth already showed alarming tendencies that way, and it was making her grave and unappealing—like Arthur! No man would ever want Elizabeth, I thought sadly, even if she weren't ugly and a bastard in the bargain.

"Ah." So the beautiful Lady Anne kept herself as God had originally created women—uneducated, save in the ways of pleasing men. "She must be an enchanting musician."

He looked startled. "Is she?"

"Is she not?"

"I never heard her play."

She was modest about performing before strangers, then. O, excellent! What virtue in a maiden! I could not help but compare her to the other Anne, who could hardly be restrained from showing off her overrated prowess on the lute before whoever happened along.

"I do not think she *does* play," he added. "Her brother, the Duke, thinks that musicians are loose company and have a bad effect on women's morals."

Mark Smeaton. God, would the name—the thought—never lose its power to knife me? Why did it still hurt, after more than three years? Three years, six months, and two days . . . Wotton, remembering too, looked embarrassed. "Perhaps he is correct," I said lightly.

So the Lady Anne would not arrive with an assortment of inlaid lutes, or ivory-keyed virginals, or new compositions to share with me. There would be no musical evenings by the fire on long winter nights. How disappointing. But there would be no Mark Smeatons, either, no delicately fashioned instruments presented as gifts to the Queen from smirking courtiers.

"The King's Musick will provide for our listening pleasure," I said, "and for our dancing, there will be . . ." I stopped. "She *does* dance?"

"No, Your Grace. That is, I have never seen her do so. According to her brother, he regards dancing as a sinful pastime, as corrupting as spending time with musicians."

"God's blood! No dancing?" Even Katherine had danced!

He smiled thinly. "No dancing."

No dancing. Well, my dancing days were past, anyway. I had not danced since Jane's death, and even then I had been hard put to keep up, with my leg-sickness. And since then the leg had grown worse, not better. And there was my weight gain. . . . It would be painful and ungainly for me to dance now. Better that I had a good reason, in the personage of my virtuous young wife, than the true one, in the personage of my decaying old body.

"What *does* she do?" I could not help asking.

"Sewing. I have heard that she does marvellous needlework."

I thought of Katherine and her endless embroidering of my linen shirts —all those *K*'s and *H*'s intertwined. I had had all the stitching taken out as soon as we separated, but still she sent me new ones for as long as she lived. She had been working on another one at Kimbolton when she died. They had sent it to me. It lay in my oldest clothes chest, a silent rebuke.

"Oh." It would be a serene and virtuous life with the Lady Anne. But the truth was that if a woman were beautiful a man could exist on that alone. A Greek statue could not play the lute or dance or debate Scripture, yet one could spend hours in its presence, transfixed and made happy by its beauty.

❦ ❧

While Anne braved the sharp November winds and made her way obediently toward me, it was time for me to choose a suitable wardrobe for my marriage. The truth was that my once-splendid attire had fallen on bad days. I had destroyed my favourite clothes in a fit of grief one day, as I remembered scenes with Jane whilst I had been wearing them. The rest—the ones with no painful remembrances—I had worn carelessly, not bothering to have new ones made. That was also a form of mourning. So now I was reduced to just a few items that still fit me.

Yes, I had remained stout—even, truth to tell, grown stouter, which I had vowed would never happen. I cared, but I did not care. That is, part of me, whatever old part of me was left, cared; the rest, the hollow-shell Henry, did not.

Now, suddenly, I was anxious to acquire new trappings . . . just as I had eagerly refurbished Father's royal apartments so long ago. The tailor had called, and I prepared to be measured and choose fabrics, all in a high good humour.

What brilliant scarlet silks! From Flanders? A new dye process? What depth of satin—like a rich topaz! And now the measurements . . . he laughed nervously . . . the thin tape measure whipped out, a pale snake. Waist: fifty-one inches.

All gaiety gone for an instant. Fifty-one *inches?* Had I gained fourteen inches in my waist? In only four years?

I confronted the mirror set up to one side of me, and looked—truly looked—at myself for the first time since Jane's death. My first impression was of a great white whale. No! And the ripples in the figure—were they entirely of fat or merely the uneven surface of the metal? I was so stunned I was able to put it just this baldly to myself.

A red thing appeared behind the whale, its surface equally wavy. So it was the fault of the mirror after all.

I turned to see Thomas Culpepper standing behind me, a greedy look on his face. "Ah, Thomas," I said. "I should have known you could scent expensive fabric all the way through the door of the King's inner chamber. Yes, you may choose something."

I was fond of the lad, and since he had replaced Henry Norris as the man who attended upon me in my Retiring Chamber, I was not embarrassed to have him see me thus undressed. I knew all *his* secrets—yes, even the sordid business about his meddling with the gamekeeper's wife, and his attack on her rescuers. Shameful!

"Oh?" A grin spread across his handsome face. He never refused favours.

"An early present to one of my groomsmen," I said. "I am being measured for my wedding clothes."

"The wedding will be a public one?" He looked surprised. "I thought—"

"Why ever not?"

"Just that your previous marriage to Queen Jane was so private, quiet."

And the one to Anne Boleyn even more so! I knew what he meant: with your matrimonial history, Sire, is it seemly to make a public show for the *fourth?*

"I shall do as I please!" I roared, reading his mind and answering it. "So you think people will laugh at me? They'll think me an old fool, is that it?"

He looked annoyed, not frightened. But then, his problem lay in lack of prudence, not lack of courage. "No, Your Grace."

"You think I can't afford it?" I couldn't, not very well. Where *had* that monastic money gone, so quickly? On the coastal defences, much of it.

He smiled his dazzling smile. "Only that it will take place in deep winter —hardly a fitting time for great outdoor rejoicings. That is all."

Clever lad. As nimble with his tongue as with his sword . . . and his member. The latter two got him into trouble, and the former rescued him time and again.

"Oh, go choose something." I cuffed him on the back of the head, and put back on my dressing robe. "Make the waist forty-nine inches," I told the tailor. No need to yield to the inevitable yet. A wedding doublet of fifty-one inches? Not for King Henry VIII!

Culpepper held up a garnet-coloured velvet, as rich as a gem of King Solomon's. But it did not suit his colouring. It made him look consumptive and too long indoors. "No," I said.

Still he persisted in studying it. "There is one it would well become," he finally said.

"A lady?"

"Aye. My cousin Catherine. She is orphaned and has little."

Culpepper was not noted for his charitable spirit, so I suspected he meant to seduce her, using the velvet as a bait. "How touching." I did not offer the luscious stuff he craved. "Come, choose something."

The lingering lust on his face was replaced by the original greed. He chose cloth-of-gold, patterned with scarlet threads running crosswise. It would make him appear golden and shining all over, a god of youth.

Envy tore through me. *As you are now, so once was I. . . .*

My bulky figure glistened back at me from the mirror. *As I am now, so shall you be. . . .* I finished the lines with fierce satisfaction. Preen and prance and love your cloth-of-gold looks now, my lad, they can't last, they never do. I kept mine longer than any man has a right to, but they're gone and there's no bringing them back. Damn you! You don't believe I was once magnificent, do you? Wolsey, Katherine, they would tell you, but they're dead. . . .

"Enjoy it, Culpepper," I said, indicating the material.

LXXXV

It was time to talk to Crum. Crum, who had evidently never known a
human passion, and so could never mourn its passing. Jolly, sensible Crum.
Lately I had come to envy him, had come to believe that I had been cursed
in the nature I had—always yearning, always feeling, always hurting. I
wondered what it must be like to go through life as Crum, taking things only
as they are, neither less nor more. Well, his sensible head would help me choose
the Queen's new household.

"It has been a long time since a brand-new household was set up," he
observed. "The seven years between Your Grace's mother's death and Queen
Katherine's Coronation were the last long period England was without a
Queen." He tactfully did not state the obvious: that for a long time I had had
two Queens simultaneously, and my widowerhood after Anne's death had
lasted exactly one day. Probably he thought nothing of it, made no moral
judgment. A rare man, Crum.

"Today I have a new palace to offer her, one no Queen has ever set foot
in—Nonsuch. I would assure that the Queen's royal apartments be readied in
time to receive my bride in January."

"We must make the assignments for her English servitors," Crum said.
"She brings only ten Flemish ladies with her. The rest we must appoint. I have
here a list"—he handed me a roll with at least two hundred names—"of all
the women who have been suggested—or who have suggested themselves."

My eye skimmed the list.

Elizabeth Fitzgerald, the fifteen-year-old daughter of the Earl of Kildare,
and the object of young Henry Howard's poetical fancy, whom he celebrated
in verse as "the Fair Geraldine." She had married old Sir Anthony Browne not
long ago after Surrey's high-minded courting of her. I wondered how marriage
to that withered stalk was satisfying her? Had her practical marriage disillusioned the enraptured Howard? I ticked off her name as approved for court
duty.

Lady Clinton. Wife of the Earl of Lincoln. "Bessie?" I wondered out loud.

"Aye. Evidently she's quite beautiful still, as the young Lord Clinton was mad for her. Could hardly wait till Gilbert Tailboys had expired to wive her. Clinton was a good fifteen years younger, too."

Yes, and he was swaggering, bonny, and bold. The sort Bessie liked. And now they wished to come to court. Yes, of course. I realized with a start that Bessie had become a quasi-relative of mine.

Catherine Howard. Culpepper's cousin. Now living on the dowager Duchess of Norfolk's charity in a loosely run household near London. Culpepper had said she was an orphan.

"Who were Mistress Howard's parents?" I asked Crum. There were so many Howards they were like strawberries in a tangled patch.

"Edmund Howard and the widowed Jocasta Culpepper."

I groaned. Now I remembered. Everyone had thought the widow Culpepper was a fool for marrying that feckless, fortune-hunting Edmund Howard, a younger brother of that vast tribe of which Duke Thomas was the eldest brother. He was a particularly ineffectual fop, who annoyed me so much on his brief visits to court that I had given him a minor post in Calais . . . at which he had failed, of course. He had died in debt, trying desperately to borrow. A weakling. I knew now why Culpepper could see his way clear to Edmund's daughter. But coming from such stock, she could not amount to much. Still, perhaps service to the new Queen would train her in the ways of gentlefolk. Certainly she would not learn such at the Duchess's establishment, known locally as "the Lambeth Zoo." I checked off her name, designating her as a maid of honour.

"Lady Elyot." I snorted. "Too Lutheran. I'll have none such at court." Crum looked pained. "I know about her private 'prayer circle,' " I said. "I know also that she keeps Lutheran tracts and prayed for Lambert. Oh, she keeps attendance at Mass as well, but she deceives me not. No."

Crum shrugged, as if it were no matter. But was it? Lately he had displayed what approached keen interest in heresies and heretics. He kept copies of every seized book and tract, and seemed to know them all by heart.

"The 'Lash with Six Strings' will whip her, then," he laughed.

"There are those who say you have taken the strings from that heresy law," I said slowly. " 'Tis reported that you do not enforce the articles in it, and warn people who are under suspicion. And 'tis true, we have had remarkable few arrests. One would think all England is traditional and devout, with nary a dissenter abroad in the land."

He laughed again. "Perhaps the burnings at Smithfield have discouraged displays of heresy."

"Ah. But *your* job, dear Crum, is to root it out of its secret hiding places. A job that you seem strangely lax in pursuing." I cocked one eyebrow at him. The warning had been well taken. "Now let us continue with the list—"

The lists were complete, and workmen were putting the final pegs in the wooden panelling in the Queen's Audience Chamber at Nonsuch. It was a time of gay anticipation—on the surface, at least. But although I went through the motions of a man eager to greet his bride, doing all the things such a man would do, inside there was no true lightheartedness. I wanted to feel that way, and hoped that feeling would follow actions. Jane would want me to be happy, would she not? I kept her portrait at my bedside. Each night as I saw it I felt sad that soon it would have to be put away, out of sight. But not tonight . . . not yet.

I had had it all planned, down to the very day. Lady Anne would arrive in England on November twenty-fifth, escorted from Calais by the English High Admiral, William Fitzwilliam, and a great company of English lords. She would be met at Dover by members of my Privy Council and conducted from thence to Canterbury. There I would meet her, and the marriage would be solemnized by Cranmer in the Cathedral. Then we would set forth for London, keep Christmas there, and on Candlemas Day in February she would be crowned Queen.

Accordingly, in mid-November I moved to Hampton Court, putting everything aside as I waited to hear of Anne's arrival. Those days were odd, long-shaped. I was awaiting something, I knew not what. It would mark the end of my solitude, and also the end of my youth; for I thought of the Lady of Cleves as the wife of my declining years and pictured us growing old together, companionably. I welcomed the end of my solitude (or did I, truly? for the absence of passion is a much-underrated pleasure) but not the end of my youth (or did I, truly? always having to live up to one's physicality is a wearying thing, as well). One day I realized I had gone all morning without looking at Jane's portrait; had not even thought of it; and then I knew that I had not died with Jane, after all. Only partly—for I thought of her at noon, as usual.

Hesitantly at first, then more eagerly, I began to plan the details of our wedding procession, of the February Coronation. A winter Coronation presented many more obstacles than a summer one, Culpepper was right. But suddenly obstacles were not tiring annoyances, but exhilarating challenges. I amused myself by thinking of ways to put the weather to work for us. If the Thames froze, there could be a glittering Ice Fair set up on it, with blazing fires and skaters and snow sculptures. How magnificent it would be! for dazzling white could far surpass gaudy summer flowers. A winter Coronation for a Queen who would share the winter of my life with me. It would be fitting.

But the twenty-fifth of November found the Lady Anne still in Antwerp, one of her many stopping places on the slow journey between Dusseldorf and Calais.

It was imperative that her first footstep on English soil be properly celebrated, for it was a great moment for myself and for England. In those days of feverish waiting at Hampton Court, each delay in her journey had given me opportunity to add yet another touch, another flourish to her welcome. So when she finally was met at the border of the Pale of Calais by Lord Lisle, what a blinding array of colours must have spread before her, straight to the walled city of Calais itself. No field of wildflowers, no pirate's treasure chest, could have matched it: the garrison cavalry, men-at-arms, and the King's archers clad in green velvet with chains of gold; the lords in four colours of cloth-of-gold and purple velvet; the Lord High Admiral's retinue of gentlemen in blue velvet and crimson satin, his yeomen in damask of the same, and his mariners gleaming in satin of Bruges. In numbers, too, the array was staggering: two hundred archers, fifty gentlemen of the Privy Chamber, thirty gentlemen of the King's household (including Culpepper, Thomas Seymour, and Francis Bryan); hundreds of soldiers in the King's livery of the retinue of Calais; the hundred merchants of the King's Staple, and the ten thousand commoners of Calais.

The Lord High Admiral of England, playing the peacock, with as many men about him in resplendent colours as that noble bird has feathers in its tail, conducted the Lady Anne into Calais by way of the Lantern Gate, where ships lay in the harbour garnished with banners of silk and gold. At her entry, one hundred fifty rounds of ordnance from the royal battleships *Lyon* and *Sweepstakes* greeted her, and thirty-one trumpets as well. The smoke from the cannon was so great, I am told, that for a full fifteen minutes no one could see anyone else, and so a great feeling of carnival and licence prevailed. When at last it cleared away, England had taken the Lady Anne to her heart, and the townspeople and soldiers formed a path through which she passed to her lodgings, cheering her all the way.

Now, across the Channel, I busied myself ordering Christmas festivities for Hampton Court. It had been, of all the royal palaces, the one which measured me at the emotional watermarks of my life. It was here, as a young King, that I had come with Wolsey to inspect his ground plan and fabulous sewers (five feet high!). It was here that I had first been bewitched by Anne Boleyn in her yellow gown that stifling June day. It was here that Edward had been born and that Jane had died. Although it had as many unhappy associations as happy, it was so bound up in what I, Henry, was as a man, that there was no place else where I could rightly have welcomed Lady Anne.

Garlands were hung, five separate Yule logs were brought in; one hundred silver visors were made for guests at the mummings and Twelfth Night masquerades. The King's Musick practised several hours a day for the concerts, and I even composed three new pieces—a motet and two ballads, my first compositions in years.

The peers came from all the realm, at my express invitation, to keep Christmas at court and greet their new Queen. Thomas Howard, Duke of Norfolk, sixty-five years old now, with his sad hatchet face. Charles Brandon, Duke of Suffolk, grown great and bearlike, his hair and beard silver-sleek and glossy. Had I truly forgiven him for remarrying so soon after Mary's death? Inasmuch as I hoped gentle Jane would forgive me, for two years seemed not much longer than two months to me now.

Howard and Brandon: the only two left from the old forest, standing like massive oaks. All around them were the striplings, the "New Men" like Paget, Wriothesley, Southampton, Audley. They were slight, and would remain so, no matter the many titles with which they were bedight: nonentities, civil servants. The true men, like More and Wolsey, were gone, and no one of their caliber had arisen to replace them.

Old men's thoughts! I chided myself. And not fitting ones for a man awaiting his bride. No, although much had changed, to have survived and flourished was a virtue, there was life in us all yet, and we would keep Christmas in ringing fashion.

But as it happened, we kept it as a bachelor court. For high winds kept the Channel clear and made a crossing impossible for Lady Anne and her royal convoy of fifty ships, until the third day of Christmas, that is, December twenty-seventh.

Although I laughed and made merry, it struck a chord of memory in me: the ill-omened, delayed voyage of Katherine of Aragon in coming to England. . . .

Again, old men's thoughts: seeing omens everywhere, cowering like a dog. So the winds blew! So what? A man could face winds, delays, whatever Fate sent, and on his own terms. Whatever the winds blew me, I could grapple with—and win.

The fair Lady Anne made the Channel crossing in only five hours (there —was that not a contradictory omen?), landing at Deal. She was received in high state by Brandon and his Duchess, and the Bishop of Chichester, a retinue of knights, and "the flower of the ladies of Kent," as the romantic Henry Howard described them. They escorted Anne and her ladies and company to Canterbury, there to be received by the Archbishop and high prelates of England.

A white madness of a snowstorm halted her entourage at Canterbury an extra day, but as soon as the skies cleared, the Duke of Norfolk, Lord Dacre of the South and Lord Mountjoy and all their knights and esquires swelled the ranks of the welcoming throng, until it must have resembled a triumphal procession. Then, on New Year's Eve, it was halted once again by a storm. The great party celebrated the beginning of 1540 snug within the walls of Rochester Castle, whilst I did the same at Hampton Court.

But as midnight struck, I could not help but envy all those—some hundreds, already—who had beheld my bride before me. I must, somehow, see her in private myself ere I would meet her before all London in the elaborate ceremony Cromwell had devised. So I informed Crum, who looked pained.

"The ceremony—" he began.

"Yes, I know! I am to be a puppet, a gorgeously dressed doll paraded out to meet another puppet. We have already even prepared a stage by cutting down all the furze and bushes between Blackheath and Greenwich. But, Crum, such a thing cannot foster love!"

He winced at my choice of words. "Indeed it can. Indeed, nothing else is guaranteed to, among the people. They love with their eyes. They want to see gold, silver, rubies, sapphires, emeralds. They want to see armour, all covered with designs, and great horses festooned with silk. *That* is what provokes love in the populace, Sire."

Why, then, did not the splendid Coronation win love for Queen Anne? I answered myself: because they knew her for a witch.

"But in *me,* Crum! In *me!* I would need have love fostered in *me!*"

He stared at me, appalled at his misunderstanding. "Forgive me. I thought you had . . . outgrown your need of that."

"Grown too old, you mean!" The fool! The stupid fool! To hint that I was old! To insult me so!

"No, Your Grace. I meant grown beyond this corrupting need of yours."

Stunned, I felt no anger. Only a consuming curiosity. "Corrupting? Pray, speak. Tell me." Caution and self-protection covered his face. "Nay, have no fear. Speak all your mind on this matter."

"I mean, Your Grace, that your wish to love and be loved is a weak thread that runs through the otherwise extraordinary fabric of your character. I had hoped that it had been pulled from you—as a tailor can remove a discordant or inharmonious thread from a mantle—lest that thread spoil the whole."

"So to love is a weakness in a man?"

"To need that love in order to feel alive is. It renders you dependent on something beyond God, Christ, food, water, and sunshine for your sustenance. A free man needs only those five elements. You need six. Therein are you not free, but a vassal."

I had no answer. "But I will go see Anne alone," I repeated stubbornly.

Alone in my bedchamber that night, I looked at Jane's miniature for a long time before closing the locket firmly. I knew I could not wear it once I had a new wife, and that would be in only a few days' time. Strange that Crum would see the ennobling emotion of love as weakening and corrupting. I had always thought of it as the opposite—strengthening and purifying. Certainly, when I was in the throes of love I was capable of performing the most extraordinary feats. In fact, I could not perform them without it. In between loves, I lay idle, fallow, directionless—awaiting the fresh arrival of love as a becalmed ship awaits a strong wind to fill its sails.

The picture of a becalmed vessel, its sails slack and wrinkled, utterly impotent, was not a pleasing one. But the analogy did not hold, not really. . . . I sought love because it brought out the best in me, made me the man God intended me to be. Everyone was entitled to love, to a helpmate, a wife. It was God's plan. It was Cromwell, with his lonely bachelorhood, who was unnatural.

I kissed Jane's miniature, remembering especially her beautiful white skin. Holbein had captured it so well in the tiny portrait. I would have been content with Jane—I *was* content. But to search no more, to give up: was that not, truly, the mark of the weakling?

No, I would sally forth on the morrow. I would brave this snowstorm and surprise Anne at Rochester Castle. She would scarce expect me, and what a joyous, pretty secret it would be between us.

And now to bed. I mounted the three steps and called Culpepper to bring the bed-furs. In he came, laughing and flushed.

"The sables," I indicated. "I shall need them tonight." The sound of the wind outside rose even above the crackling of the fire. He came over and carefully arranged the glistening dark pelts around me. "And put some myrrh on the fire," I said suddenly. "It is the eighth day of Christmas." He grinned at the extravagance. "Take some for yourself," I said impulsively. "Let all the Privy Chamber attendants share it with me. It is a new decade!"

LXXXVI

arly in the morning, being still of a mind to visit Anne (for often in the night I would change my mind, hence I always preferred to sleep on a thing), I roused eight gentlemen of my Privy Chamber and bade them make ready to accompany me to Rochester. It was not a far ride, and the snow had ceased falling; so we arrived at the castle before dark. Along the way, with each crunch of my horse's hooves in the icy snow, I felt my excitement mounting. I marvelled at it, as a thing I had long thought dead; tried to control it, as along with such wild exhilaration go nervousness and a sick feeling inside, a debilitating shyness and an all but incapacitating fear. But it was useless, and in the end I gave myself up to it, swimming in the heady ecstasy of a lover's anticipation.

Approaching the grey stones, now sleek with ice, I felt my heart pounding so loudly it sounded, in my ears, like the beating of a falcon's wings, just as he leaves the wrist. Be quiet, be quiet, be calm . . . no, do not! Soar all you like, my sweeting.

Into the castle, past the stunned guards. All was quiet, most of the castle empty, drained into the Great Hall, where everyone was gathered on this second day of 1540, drinking, talking. I bade my party join them, and forbade anyone to follow me as I sought out the Lady Anne. They obeyed.

Now I made my way to the great Privy Chamber, wherein Anne was presumed to be, the passage leading up to the door so dark that I had to grope along, feeling as if I were participating in a masque, in an intricately staged New Year's entertainment, as I had done so many times before.

The hard iron of the chamber door was unyielding, stiff. I wrenched it, and it shrieked, like a witch's cry, and the door swung slowly, slowly open. I felt the hairs on my scalp rising, tingling, with the suspense of that groaning, sliding door. . . .

Her dress was of cloth-of-gold. Magnificent! Her back was to me, as she gazed out the tiny, slitted window onto the white landscape below.

"Anne!" I cried.

She jumped, then jerked round. I could see nothing of her, as the light was coming from directly behind her. She made no sound beyond a horrified gasp of terror.

My long brown woollen cloak! I had forgotten to remove it, and now stood before her dressed like a highwayman. No wonder she feared me—feared for her life. I ripped it off me and stood before her, in my golden and green robes of state.

"Anne!" I cried in joy. "It is I, King Henry!"

She screamed, then clapped her hands over her mouth. *"Herr steh mir bei! Wie in aller Welt—!"*

She did not recognize me. "I am Henry, the King!" I repeated.

A woman came scurrying in from the adjoining chamber, along with a guard. The guard, whose face looked young but who had the body of an old hog, bowed. Then he jabbered something in the ugliest language I had ever heard. It sounded like the rumblings of a bowel. Anne replied in the same medium. Then the guard stammered, "For-gif ze Lady, King Henry, a-bot she zhot you vere a grrooom, a horse-master."

Now the Lady Anne had bowed before me, and I saw that her entire head was enveloped in a grotesque hat of some sort, with stiff wings and many folds, a madman's kite. She stood up, and only then did I realize how gigantic she was. A female Goliath. And, in turning to me—

Her face was repulsive! It was as brown as a mummy's, and covered all over with pits and smallpox scars. It was uglier than the faces of freaks exhibited at country fairs, the Monkey Woman, the Crocodile Maid, it was sickening—

A spray of spittle landed on my face. *It* was speaking, and in that language that was no language, but a series of grunts and gas-churnings. Her breath was foul, it was a nightmare, this could not be happening!

I backed out of the chamber, feeling for the door behind me, slamming it shut, leaning against it. I felt nausea fighting its way up in my throat, the acrid stench of it, but I fought it down. As the sickness receded, so did the excitement, the panic, the fantasy. What rose in its place was anger: anger so cold and yet so hot I had never felt its like before.

I had been duped, betrayed. All those people who had seen her—all those envoys who had met her, who had arranged the marriage—they had known. Known, and said nothing. Known, and deliberately led me into this marriage. They were all in it together—Cromwell, Wotton, the Duke of Cleves, Lord Lisle, and the entire company at Calais. And Holbein! Holbein, who could capture the subtlest facial characteristic with his brush; Holbein, for whom no skin was too fair, no hue of cheek too difficult to reproduce, no jewel too faceted to be perfectly captured and rendered—Holbein had made her *pretty!*

I stalked back to the Great Hall, where all the conspirators were gathered. Yes, gathered and drinking their stupid mulled wine and laughing at me. I could hear the laughter. They were all imagining the horrible scene taking place in Lady Anne's chamber, only to them it was not horrible, but comic. They would pay for this!

"Lord Admiral!" I called from the doorway, and the throng fell silent. The Earl of Southampton turned around, grinning—a grin that wilted.

"Come here!" I ordered, and Fitzwilliam came toward me, a puzzled expression on his face. What a fine actor he was! Better that he should not have been quite so fine.

"Sire?" Just the right note of bewilderment.

"How like you the Lady Anne, Admiral?" I asked softly. "Did you think her so personable, fair, and beautiful, as reported, when you first beheld her at Calais?"

"I take her not for 'fair,' but of a 'brown' complexion," he replied—wittily, he assumed.

"How clever you are. I did not know you fenced with conceits and metaphors, along with Wyatt and Surrey." I glared all about the room. "Is there no one I can trust? I am ashamed of you all, ashamed that you dared to praise her, and reported her—by word and picture!—as winsome. She is a great Flanders mare! And I will not have her, no, I will not be saddled with her, nor ride her, nor hitch her to any conveyance in England!"

Never, never, would I touch her! If the propagators of this cruel comedy thought to see me wed her—assumed I would be meek enough to follow through—they did not know Henry of England! What did they take me for? Francis of France, forced to marry "the Emperor's mule"?

"Saddle your own horses, and come with me! You shall answer for this at Greenwich." I would not return to Hampton Court; God, no! Greenwich for business, for unpleasant business. It was at Greenwich that I had married Katherine of Aragon; it was at Greenwich that Anne had borne the useless Princess Elizabeth, and had lost my boy-child. Let Greenwich be the place where the Flemish Mare was turned around and shipped back to the Low Countries to pull her dray!

The bitter cold was heightened by the time we got back to Greenwich, as the sun was setting—a small, shrunken, bloody thing—and the sixteen-hour night was beginning. I rode straight up to the gatehouse and passed through, across the great courtyard and right up to the royal entranceway. "Summon Cromwell," I barked to a page as I strode toward the Privy Council chamber. It was dark and dusty, not having been used these past two months while I kept court at Hampton. Attendants hurriedly brought beeswax tapers and dusted off the Council tables. A fire was laid to drive the dank chill away. In the meantime we kept our travelling cloaks on. I took my place at the head of the table and waited silently.

Cromwell appeared. Upon entering the chamber he looked astonished. "Your Grace—honoured Council members—" he began, playing for time while he figured out what was occurring, the better to be in control.

"I like her not!" I relieved Cromwell of the mystery, and of the need for preliminaries and niceties. There he stood, the man responsible for all this. My enemy.

"I beg your pardon?"

"The Flanders Mare! The Lady of Cleves—I like her not, she repulses me, she is an abomination in a headdress! And *you* would have me wed her, *you* would have me lie with her, *you* would have me make her a Tudor and have her crowned! The woman is hideous, a malformed beast—"

Cromwell knitted his brows in anger. "Oh, Your Grace! To think that we have been so *deceived!*" He turned on the Admiral. "You saw her, you met her at the border of Calais, you welcomed her, with members of the King's household, and lords and gentlemen, and two hundred yeomen, all in blue velvet and crimson satin, and mariners—you saw that she was not what she had been reported. Why did you not keep her . . . penned up . . . in Calais, and notify our sovereign King, our kind King Henry, that she was not as she had been represented?"

Fitzwilliam, the Admiral, looked shocked. "I had no such authority," he whined. "To have done so would have been insubordinate. I was commissioned to receive her and bring her safely to England, and so I did, and anything else would have been treasonous."

Cromwell snorted. "Yet you lied in your letters to His Majesty! After you had beheld the ugly woman, you wrote of her beauty. Was that not a malicious misleading of your King?"

"I did not claim that I myself found her beautiful! I only repeated the opinions of others, who had sworn to her beauty. No one can blame me for not criticizing her, especially as opinions of beauty vary from beholder to beholder—and I believed that she was shortly to be my Queen."

"Enough of this! All of you misled me!" I shouted. "Now you must undo the wrong you have done. You shall find a means of freeing me from this engagement—I care not by what means or on what grounds, but it shall be done. Or *someone* shall pay dearly for making me appear a fool!"

"We will find a technicality, a legality somewhere," said Cromwell smoothly. "Send for Osliger and Hostoden, the Duke of Cleves's ambassadors. They accompanied her to England."

While the unfortunate Germans were being sent for, Cromwell sat down and began to drum his fingers on the table, thinking out loud. "Legality—what's legal? A disease that prevents childbearing . . . but that's after the fact. No, we shall need something ironclad. A consanguinity? Too farfetched. A precontract? She has none, we've investigated that. Not a virgin? Hard to prove. Scandalous conduct? Messy. Besides, we've used that already; it has bad associations. Reflects on the King. No, it will have to be the precontract business. It's dull and dreary, but it's all we've got. And it has nothing to do with character, with personal likes and dislikes."

The Cleves ambassadors, misunderstanding their function (so well did Cromwell play his part), were effusive in their assurances that no precontract existed.

"Ach, that childhood betrothal between our Lady of Cleves and the Duke of Lorraine—it was merely a conditional agreement between the parents of the two parties," said Hostoden, a great, florid burgomaster sort.

They grinned in unison, as if they had practised it. "The formal revocation is attested to in the Chancery of Cleves, in the records for the year 1535."

"Ah!" said Cromwell. "But you have no copy with you?"

"No, alas. But we can send for one."

"That will take weeks," said Cromwell sadly. "And the wedding—which cannot proceed without it, of course—is scheduled for this week. You understand, this changes everything. The nuptials cannot be solemnized—"

"That is no difficulty." They even talked in unison. What *was* this between them?

"I am afraid it is." Cromwell was cold.

"We ourselves will act as surety for the documents. Bind us, toss us in prison, keep us pent up until the documents are safely in your hands. We are yours to do with as you like."

The imbeciles! I turned to Cranmer and the Bishop of Durham. "What think you of this?"

I expected them to agree with me, but they shook their heads sadly. "In our opinion, no impediment to the marriage exists."

"There is the impediment of allying ourselves to the heretical princes of the Schmalkaldic League itself," Cromwell pronounced, turning on his own creature.

"Because the Pope says so?" I said quietly, exposing the weakness of that argument. Truly we were backed into a corner of our own making. "Is there no remedy," I cried out, "but that I must needs put my head into the yoke?" I felt like a trapped animal, a sacrificial bull.

"I am not well handled," I muttered, looking at each face in turn. "No, I have not been well handled in this matter."

WILL:

From these ominous words, the downfall of Cromwell can be dated. Henry was now convinced that his chief minister had engineered the Protestant alliance for secret reasons of his own. From there it was but a short step to believing that Cromwell was a Protestant plotter who meant to make the Church of England Protestant. Cromwell was too clever to have made such a blunder as being misled about Anne; therefore it must have been part of a larger scheme.

HENRY VIII:

Anne had been detained at Dartford on a pretext (also arranged by Cromwell), but now there was no reason for her not to proceed to London. Glumly I gave orders that she was to recommence her journey. The grand celebrations I had planned now rose before me to mock me. I was to be married to a horse in a glittering and staggeringly expensive public ceremony. I was to receive said horse on the heath and common adjoining Greenwich Palace, where golden tents were to be set up, pavilions of silk; even now, a horseman was riding about London, crying out that all who loved their lord the King should proceed to Greenwich on the tenth day of Christmas, to meet and make their *devoir* to the Lady Anne of Cleves, who would shortly be their Queen.

The royal request was obeyed by tens of thousands, who flocked to the environs of Greenwich and the bare fields that had been prepared for the reception of my fourth bride.

I had not slept in two nights, spending every moment searching for a legal barricade to this nightmare. But there was none, although I was ready to try the most obscure reasoning. Once the marriage was performed, it would be even more difficult to set aside, as a thing uncompleted is easier left as is than a standing building dismantled. The possibility of staying married to Anne was unthinkable. I simply would not do it.

But the hour drew closer when I would have to receive her.

It was near dawn when I gave up any hope or pretence of sleeping. I arose and descended the bed-stairs stiffly, taking care not to awaken poor Culpepper, who slept on his pallet at the foot of the bed. I made my way, as quietly as the darkness would allow, over to my prayer-corner. But what began as a cry for God to deliver me from this trial ended with a plea for the revelation of His will and the stalwartness to carry it out.

"O God, Heavenly Father, Maker of all things—spare me from this travesty, deliver me from this cruelty—" Even as I formed the words with my lips in the cold, still air of the room, they died away before the Presence of

God in my mind. I was struck dumb by the glory of God, the shining Presence, the knowledge that He was with me. All my own words and desires faded away —or rather seemed to make up some part of a Whole which I sensed, glimpsed, grasped—a Whole so dazzling and yet peaceful that any earthly thing was blessed merely by being a small part of it. And I was willing—no, eager—to do whatever was assigned to me by God, to co-operate with Him. So my words changed into a lover's murmur of "Yes, yes . . . all that I have or may be, is Yours." It was somehow ordained, meant to be, that the Lady Anne and I must wed. For what reason I knew not, but it would be revealed. Perhaps we were to have a son who would be a great poet or warrior. A son—how was I to get a son upon her? *With men, such things are impossible, but with God, all things are possible.* Such carnal details seemed a trifling matter in that transcendent moment.

I arose from my prie-dieu a committed man, eager to show myself God's man. I rang for my attendants. Time to begin dressing, no moments of dalliance today. Culpepper rolled over and rubbed his eyes. The grooms of the bedchamber appeared, bringing torches, bowls of scented water, and heated towels. It struck me that I was being married as a mighty monarch, a King in his prime, and that this time I would savour all the details and nuances attendant on it. I felt free, detached, observant. (Was this what placing oneself in God's hands meant? If so, it was a curious feeling—to experience oneself as an outsider.)

So I watched myself being made ready, I watched as a large but still muscular man (underneath the fat) was washed in scented water, then patted dry with white linen and massaged with rosemary oil. I watched as his barber combed and clipped his thinning reddish hair, noting casually that there was as yet no balding, but just a general sort of fading and lessening of what, only ten years earlier, had been remarkable hair. The beard, too, was not as thick and showed white in places, but neither was it patchy and scraggly. I saw, in short, a man who was not what he once was, but not yet what he would be. Not young, not old. A transitional man.

And now—the wedding attire. When I ordered it, I had allowed every profligate desire to express itself. Each layer of clothing sought to outdo the one just beneath it. Now they were to be fitted together in one blinding ensemble. Culpepper held out the first undergarment, which was of finest China silk, embroidered with white. It was so light it almost floated as he passed it to me; and the sleek feeling as it slid down next to my skin was like a seductive serpent. But the layers after that became heavier and heavier, encrusted with gold thread and gemstones, Oriental pearls and silver of Damascus, until only a man of my breadth and strength could have worn them all.

I have worn armour and I know how heavy that is; but this was its equal. Yet what are gold and jewels but civilian armour?

My bride awaited me. My fate awaited me. Neither was what I would have chosen, but the ways of God were mysterious, and imperious. In just this frame of mind, I went forth for the public reception of Anne, Princess of the Duchy of Cleves.

The day was fair and clear and cold. Against the hard blue sky the golden tents sparkled, like galleons tossed on a sea. The standards above them snapped smartly like sails. Perhaps someday it would be possible for men to sail on an icy sea . . . if a ship's hull were constructed of very thick wood, several layers. . . . Ah, what could I not do that day, what might I not invent, if only in imagination?

I rode surrounded in glory. Such a company of bravely bedecked knights —six thousand in all, counting the King's Guard, yeomen, pages of honour, spears and pensioners, and all their trappings: the crimson velvet, the antique gold, the knots of gold—shining clearly and sharply in the January morning.

There were thousands more awaiting us on the broad heath—the Germanic merchants of the Steelyard on the east side, glaring across at their rivals, the merchants of Genoa, Florence, Venice, and Spain. In between were our own English merchants—all told, some twelve hundred men.

Down from Shooter's Hill came Anne of Cleves in a carved, gilded chariot, drawn by horses trapped in black velvet. Like Diana drawn by steeds. . . .

So I told myself, and so the noble chroniclers recorded it. On the parchment of the Kingdom, Diana, chaste and beautiful and athletic, was met by Jupiter, mighty and lust-filled and benevolent. You can read how glorious it all was, how the earth shook at our encounter and all the Kingdom rejoiced. Truly that day we all believed it, I as much as any other—and so history is made, so it becomes fixed like fruits preserved in wine long past their season.

Side by side, the Lady Anne and I rode down the hill and across Blackheath, and all my subjects cheered. The Thames (which had not frozen) was filled with boats with satin sails and banners, shooting off fireworks.

That was the public side. But once we reached Greenwich Palace, once the chariot was put away and the black velvet taken off the horses—then I was but myself again, a rebellious small boy inside the magnificent and ordained structure. I squirmed and fought. Once again I did not want to go through with it. The saintly resolve that had begun my day did not outlast the sunset. I gathered Cromwell and my Privy Councillors about me, balked, whined, complained. "If it were not for my Kingdom and that I have proceeded so far in the matter, I would not do what I must tomorrow for any earthly thing."

I fell back into bed, ashamed of my weakness. I was no saint, although I had felt like one in the early dawn. Real saints remained saints all day, through the ups and downs of real weather, real people, real pain—not the wraithlike ones of a dreamy dawn. They did not fall into bed querulous and disappointed in themselves. They were not filled with anger and rebellion.

I did not want to marry the Lady Anne, now or ever. She had a beautiful chariot, but it was not the chariot I must take to my bed. I would *prefer* the chariot—yes, I would prefer to cover its wheels with my bed-furs—rather than its mistress.

Yet it must be. The nuptial ceremony was to take place early on the morrow, at eight o'clock. I had scheduled it for that hour, as if that would get it over with—when in fact it would be just the beginning.

As I lay in bed, berating myself for not being a saint, my thoughts finally became more realistic, more pragmatic. I was about to embark on an arranged marriage. Such things had happened since the beginning. (Were not Adam and Eve an "arranged marriage"?) Ordinary men had the pleasure of choosing their own mates, but to be a King meant to be a pawn in one's own game. I was fortunate in that I had twice chosen from my own subjects, just as an ordinary man might do, for love. Now that was past, just as my youth was past, and I should count myself lucky. I had gotten away with it twice already.

And one of my choices could not have been more disastrous. No arranged marriage could have equalled its horror. So how was I to judge?

My sleep was broken and fitful. I dreamed I was a child again, being held by my mother. It was a wished-for memory, for to my knowledge she had never held me.

LXXXVII

January sixth, dawn. Twelfth Night . . . always my favourite holiday. How ironic that it should be my linkage-day with Anne. . . .

Grunting, I flung aside the covers. Reminiscing—an old man's game. Was it come to this? Truly I would do it no more. Action was always better than contemplation. Any action.

So once again I sank down on my prie-dieu and sought God's blessing and guidance. Once again I felt full with His strength. Was it to be thus every day for the rest of my life? Was that why the manna lasted only one day in the wilderness? Was that why Jesus told His disciples to only ask for *"this day* our daily bread"? I asked; it was given. And I went forth to marry Anne of Cleves.

Cranmer married us. All was in order (save my numb heart). The chamber was filled with well-furred and bejewelled attendants and pure beeswax candles that fluttered only slightly in the draft. I gave Anne a ring inscribed "God send me well to keep," kissed her, and made her my wife. And all the while I felt nothing.

There was a banquet, as was customary. The hours passed, and Anne and I scarcely saw one another. Like Perseus with Medusa, I dared not look at her, lest I be turned to stone and be unable to complete what I knew lay ahead.

The short winter day ended, and the long night began. There would be sixteen hours for us in the bridal chamber—sixteen hours of "transport" for common men, but duty for a King.

We were alone. All the attendants had withdrawn, leaving us in the bridal chamber. It was the very utmost in sumptuousness. Upon the great bed were silken sheets from Persia, and in the corner, urns smoked discreetly with incense. True passion would not have needed such servants, but in its absence we put our faith in them.

How many times had I, in fantasy, made love to a stranger? I imagined it as a circus of voluptuousness, where all impulses might have free reign, because this unknown female would be willing for all, unable to censure or pass judgment. Now I was faced with the reality: a large shadow behind a silken screen, as Anne moved about, undressing. Was it my imagination, or did she deliberately delay? Was she as un-eager, as frightened as I?

The candles burned noticeably lower. I had thought by this time to have it all done with, finished. What was taking her so long? I poured out one cup of wine, then another. I wished to find, and maintain, a state in which I could perform mindlessly. I wanted enough wine in me to dull my trepidations, yet not enough to incapacitate me—a balance not easily achieved.

She emerged, moving slowly out from the screen, walking toward the bed. I approached from the opposite side. The candlelight blurred her features, and I took care only to gaze upon her hair, which was long and golden and shining where she had combed it out over her shoulders.

She climbed clumsily into bed. I followed. Then we sat, side by side upon the slippery sheets, staring ahead, not daring to look at one another.

She is a foreigner, I told myself, far from her homeland, married to a stranger. A virgin in bed with a man, sold into a marriage on the basis of a portrait. How frightened she must be! I at least had had some semblance of choice in the matter; she had had none. My heart went out to her, and in that moment I reached out for her, for the gentle virgin bride. . . .

I kissed her and, shutting my eyes, began to caress her. It was cold in the room, and her natural modesty would cry out to be uncovered only in darkness and under the bed-wraps. I blew out the candles on our nightstand, leaving only the red, jumping flames of the fireplace to light the room. The fire crackled and sighed; Anne sighed, too, relaxing in my arms.

How soft and warm her gown was, how thick and sensuous her hair! Truth to tell, how good it felt to hold a woman, a maiden, in my arms again. I put my hand on her breast, under her gown.

Instead of the firm, high breast of a maiden, I felt the slack dugs of a woman long past her prime. I was so shocked I snatched my hand away with a startled cry. Anne jumped, and I felt her pull away.

It couldn't be true! I couldn't believe my own hand, surely I must have touched a pillow instead. I reached out with my other hand, trying to pull her back toward me, and my hand landed on a soft, quivering, wrinkly mass—her abdomen!

"You lied!" I cried. "You are older than you claim, you are withered, dried up! I have been cheated!"

She leapt out of bed, terrified of my ranting in English. The fraud! I vaulted off the bed and snatched the covers she clutched to herself, revealing her body in all its horror. Her breasts were hanging and shrivelled, her abdomen so paunchy and bloated—

"Pfah!" I cried in revulsion.

She looked at me and her eyes narrowed. "Pfah!" she spat in return, pointing at my member, which was hanging exposed outside my nightshirt. "Pfah!" she repeated, then made a diminutive sign and began laughing. A long stream of that repulsive German followed, as she continued to revile me and insult my manhood.

And why should my member not be small and shrunken up at the sight of *her?* I took it not as a reflection on myself. She looked like a witch as she cackled there in the firelight. I began to imitate *her,* sticking a pillow under my nightshirt to capture her grotesquely ugly belly, but she only laughed all the louder. I began laughing, too. Suddenly I realized that this strange woman had not embarrassed me, but only amused me, and that I felt freer in her presence than in anyone else's I had ever met. Our laughter mounted higher and higher, until we were convulsed by it and gasping for air.

Our laughter then slowly died, and we faced one another. In the dull firelight, which was usually so kind to women, she was still frightfully ugly. No, not frightfully, for I was no longer afraid of her, nor she of me. But the situation—O sweet Jesu, the situation! I was husband to a wife I could be no husband to. And that was no laughing matter.

I sank my head morosely into my hands, and thus I remained for several moments. I became aware, then, of the most debilitating tiredness. I longed for sleep; my head spun. I looked over at Anne and saw her watching me warily, like a bird eyeing a cat.

She *was* afraid of me. Between my fingers (where she could not see me looking) I saw the apprehension and animal fright on her face. Then I remembered what Will had told me the people claimed was Christina of Denmark's answer to my inquiries about her eligibility: "His first Queen he killed with a broken heart; his second was unjustly executed; and his third was killed through lack of care after childbirth." And then, "However, if I had two heads, one of them should be at the King of England's disposal." I had thought it one of Will's jests, and laughed. Now I wondered if he had been truer than he realized.

&⅋ WILL:

"Truer than he realized." Oh, Henry, Henry! It was *you* who were blind and deaf to what you had become in the eyes of Europe. When you sent your envoys out, seeking another bride, you were no longer the great matrimonial catch you had been before your Great Matter. No respectable Princess *wanted* to marry you! She felt it would be taking her life in her hands—that, at the very least, you were jinxed, even if you did not deliberately seek to undo your wives. Luckily, the Duchy of Cleves was so shielded, and the Lady Anne so ignorant of English and gossip, that her brother agreed to your suit. No, Henry, I did not jest. In fact, I censored the worst of the current remarks—the quotes I gave you were the only repeatable ones!

⤷ HENRY VIII:

But those who made refrains were ignorant! They had no idea of what they spoke. And why did they always take the woman's side? Katherine did not die "of a broken heart." She died of Anne's poison and her own foolish pride. If only she had co-operated with me, she would never have ended her days in the fens! No, she would have lived in luxury and shared Mary with me, grown old in honour. And Nan—thank God the common people did *not* know the true blackness of her soul, the degradation of that Witch—lest they tremble and shiver in their beds and never know safety again. Even from the grave she cursed me, headless demon! And sweet Jane. *God* took her from me, and God alone knows how I would have ransomed my kingdom to save her. The people made a ballad for her, and spoke kindly of me then. How had their minds been so poisoned since? It was Anne—Anne operating beyond the grave, in spite of everything I had done to disempower the Witch.

I felt as if she were right there. Oh, wrong was I to have conjured up her shade! I fought to free myself from it; I reached over and touched Anne of Cleves's arm, startling her.

"Let us sleep," I said in as low and gentle a voice as I could. She could understand the intent, if not the actual words. She smiled slowly, then followed me back to bed, so preposterously appointed for love. Together we slid down into the satin and passed the calmest bridal night of any new-wedded pair since Mark and Isold.

We overslept. They awaited us at early Mass in the Chapel Royal, then went ahead and said Mass without us. They awaited us in the Privy Chamber, fresh garments at the ready, a great silver bowl of spiced wine for our comfort. They awaited me at my Council Chamber, where Cromwell, Cranmer, the Admiral, and others expected to detail the plans for the obligatory post-nuptial jousts, tournaments, and banquets. They awaited us impatiently, eagerly, lecherously, like a pack of schoolboys suddenly privy to the private life of their schoolmaster. And I, the schoolmaster, avoided them and played truant like a student: our roles were reversed.

The wan January sun streamed in the windows, warming nothing. I glanced at Anne, sleeping beside me. Yes, she was as ugly as I had thought. The emasculated sun was still strong and merciless enough to shadow all her pockmarks and show her liver-coloured skin. Her yellowish buck teeth protruded from her lips as she snored on. Yet I was no longer repulsed by her. She seemed like an ally, a strange companion in this misadventure of mine—with Cromwell as my adversary.

Yes, Cromwell. I had thought him my ally, yet who was he really? He had appeared conveniently when Wolsey had left court, ostensibly to act as Wolsey's agent in the tangled financial affairs he had so uncharacteristically left behind. In doing so he had established himself as a powerful man, or, if not powerful, a man of consequence, one to be reckoned with. Wolsey's ruin was his gain. And from there he had maneuvered himself into my confidence. How? By his unscrupulous manipulation of the Church. The undoing of the Papacy: Cromwell's insight. The domestication of the English clergy: Cromwell's project. The dissolution of the monasteries: Cromwell's grand design. These moves had made *me* supreme over the Church, and monastic wealth had replenished what I had wasted of my inheritance in French wars. But what had they done for Cromwell? No man does anything that does not ultimately benefit himself most; I knew this now, although I had not always known it. In Wolsey's case that benefit was obvious, and showed itself ostentatiously. But Cromwell had garnered no titles, gloated over no possessions, sported with no women, and exalted in no high rank or office. He was not Chancellor, and wore no gold chain. He did not preside over Court of Star Chamber or over Parliament. What drove him? What did he *want?* Whatever it was, finding himself in my confidence, making himself indispensable to me, and yoking me to the Flemish Mare—all were part of his plan. Although I did not know that plan as yet, I knew Cromwell well enough to know that he would *have* a plan, for nothing in his life was happenstance. So I would watch, and wait. And in the meantime . . . I glanced over at Anne . . . I would have to pretend that we were man and wife. And catch Cromwell out. In that, Anne would serve a purpose.

I let her sleep. I had no desire to be surrounded by people until I had my thoughts on course. Let everyone think we slept late because the marriage was a grand success. It served my plans better.

Thus do we become old. It is not in our aching knees, or in our rheumy eyes. No. It is in the transforming of what in youth is a simple pleasure into something false and face-saving. The wedding night becomes a political ruse. In this we betray ourselves, surprise our own selves in the distance we have already travelled on our life's journey.

Afore noon, Anne and I, attired in our "second day" costumes, greeted Cromwell and the other Privy Councillors before adjourning to a midday feast. In these short winter days, dinner was served when the sun was at its height. I took care not to smile overmuch, lest it be misinterpreted. Let them puzzle over exactly what I felt; let them wonder how pleased I was; let no one be sure of where he stood with me.

A rush of pleasure filled me at the situation. I enjoyed leaving men in limbo, uncertain as to what exactly was happening to them—or was about to happen. It was an ugly feeling, and I was ashamed that I could relish it so. Yet emotions and feelings were not sins, were they? Only actions were sins, and I had done no unkind action. In fact, I was behaving in a most generous and kingly fashion toward them. I spoke vaguely of "our pleasure" in the Lady Anne, and invited them to join us in "our dinner."

Fifty members of the court dined with us in the Great Hall. Anne and her ladies from Cleves, all identically got up in headdresses that reared up around their faces like the wrinkled ears of elephants, chattered away to each other on the dais.

Cromwell, in his customary plain black robes, was seated just down on the table to the right, talking gravely to Brandon. I noticed that he left his wine untouched. Brandon did not, of course.

Across, seated at the other table, were the women. Brandon's new wife, Katherine. (I persisted in thinking of her as his "new wife," even though they had been married as long as Princess Elizabeth had been alive.) Bessie Blount —now Lady Clinton. My eye lingered fondly over her, but she was no longer the Bessie I had known. She was thin and coughed often, pulling her furs as close about her as she dared, for fashion's sake. She was consumptive. I could see it, mark it coldly in one part of me, whilst the other winced. Not Bessie . . . *she* could not grow old. We want the sharers of our youth to remain forever young, to remind us of what we were, not of what we are. Best to die young, then? Certainly, for those to whom your existence is a touchstone, an affirmation.

Princess Mary, dressed all in purple. She loved the colour, and, as she was entitled to wear it, saw no reason not to have her headdresses, her handkerchiefs, her shoes, as well as her gowns, the colour of squashed violets. No reason, save that it was singularly unbecoming to her and made her face look yellow. Next to her was a rare, pretty creature who knew everything about colour and how to use it. She had auburn hair and the fair skin that sometimes goes with it, and wore dusky pink, which made her face and hair seem of sublime tints. She was chattering away to the Princess Elizabeth on her left. Elizabeth's startling red hair was drawn demurely back into a snood, and she was attired in modest brown. Although only six, her manner was so grave and her demeanour so old that from across the room she seemed to be old Margaret Beaufort, come again to taunt and judge me. Her black eyes—keen, sharp buttons—were the very same. But the creature next to her—all froth and frills and foam—was making her laugh. Who was the lady?

A splash of spittle landed before me. Anne was speaking. I turned. Yes, she was saying something, but I could not understand a word. I motioned to one of the envoys from Cleves, Hostoden, and asked him to come and translate.

"She says she is well pleased with such a godly company," he repeated stiffly.

"Tell the Queen"—how strange it sounded!—"that I will engage a tutor for her straightway. She must needs learn the language of her people."

Anne nodded vigorously, her headdress swaying. Again I thought of elephant ears. "They are in England now," I said. "It is time that they lay aside their native costumes and dress according to fashion here. I shall have the court milliner measure the ladies of Cleves tomorrow."

When they heard this, they were indignant.

"They say it would be immodest to lay aside their proper headdresses," Hostoden said. "It is a wickedness to display the hair."

"God's breath! If they cannot conform to English custom and costume, they should return to Cleves!"

They scowled at this pronouncement, then agreed that they would do so. I was flabbergasted, insulted. To quit England so readily? Yet my indignation lasted but a moment, as I saw that in reality it was to my advantage to send away as many of these foreigners as possible and replace them with English-women. In my youth, the court had been a bright place, as bright with youth and beauty as a summer field spread out with wildflowers and butterflies under the sun. There was still youth and beauty somewhere beneath the English sun, and it must be brought to court.

Anne looked startled and frightened at the thought of being left alone. But I reached out and touched her stiff, brocaded shoulder.

"As an English Queen, you should be served by Englishwomen," I said, and Hostoden conveyed my words. "This is your home now. And I shall employ—I shall send—" I motioned for Cromwell, a slight flicker of my eye and finger, and he was instantly beside me.

"Your Grace?"

"You have provided all things for Lady Anne, but no language instruc-tion," I chided him. "I desire straightway that a tutor be found, a person so skilled in his craft that by Candlemas my wife shall speak to me in perfect *English.*"

Having been given an impossible task, Cromwell accepted the commission unemotionally. He bowed, a stiff little smile on his face.

"Yes, my Cromwell," I said smoothly, "I am so anxious to hear my dearly beloved wife speak to me in my own tongue. It will complete my happiness."

A flicker of worry crossed his brow, that brow trained so well in Italy. Then he did his masters well. "As you say, Your Majesty. In your pleasure lies my happiness."

And your welfare, I thought. And your very existence.

I nodded expansively and chucked Anne on the cheek.

That evening, after the light supper of cold venison, pudding, and bread, a slim young man was announced. Anne and I were once again retiring to the "bridal bower," and the rest of the courtiers and attendants had withdrawn—doubtless to jest and pity me. Well, their laughter and their pity would be short-lived.

"Yes?"

"I am sent by the Lord Privy Seal," the lad said. "To teach the King's English to the Princess of Cleves, God save her." He flourished a basket of books, pens, and paper.

Crum—always daring in fulfilling a request. Who would have thought of sending someone to begin lessons this very night? Only Crum.

I motioned the young tutor in, sat him down with my bride before a table.

"I . . . am . . . Anne.

"You . . . are . . . Martin.

"He . . . is . . . King Henry."

I fell asleep to this refrain on the second night of my new marriage.

LXXXVIII

For the next week or ten days, Anne gave herself over completely to her English lessons. I was astounded by her concentration and diligence. Every morning when I left her, I kissed her on the cheek and said, "Good morning, sweetheart." At night before going to sleep, I gave her yet another chaste peck and said, "Sleep well, my dear." By the fourth morning she was able to say, "Good morning"; by that evening, "And you as well, husband"; and before many more days were out she was inquiring solicitously about my state business, my Council meetings, and the forthcoming nuptial tournaments and celebrations. Soon I would have a *talking* horse.

She was also (as befit a domestic beast) docile in allowing her women to be sent back to Cleves, in being assigned a whole new group of attendants, and in being measured and outfitted for a new wardrobe. Her "elephant ear" headdresses were cheerfully surrendered, and she showed a surprising taste for luxurious fabrics and fashionable gowns. She certainly had the frame to carry any extravagance in weight or colour. It was truly like trapping a great horse.

I spent my days closeted in meetings, poring over the latest diplomatic dispatches regarding the "amenity" between Charles and Francis. They must catch no wind of the lack of success in my new marriage, and rather than trust anyone, I must play my part so well that no one, not even Cromwell, would suspect. So I acted the happy bridegroom, watching myself as though I were detached, marvelling at my own ability to dissemble. It is a talent I suspect everyone possesses. Those who lament, "I can never lie, my face gives me away," are the cleverest liars of all.

Forward went the plans for the great national celebrations. Protocol must be served, and on a windy day in late January the jousting barriers were put up in the tiltyard of Whitehall Palace; the brightly coloured flags were raised, and the spectator stands were hung with the Tudor colours.

Crum had employed an innovation: the royal boxes were enclosed, and heated with braziers. We were to gaze out at the contestants through glass plates.

The day of the royal tournaments was blustery and overcast, one of those days that seem grey throughout. But inside the royal glass boxes it was high summer, with all the chattering and uncovered necklines that accompany warmth.

Anne was wearing a square-cut golden velvet and cloth-of-gold gown, and on her hair she had a thin gold wire coronet set with emeralds—quite the latest fashion. She seemed exuberant to be attending this joust.

"In-a Cleves, ve haf no such tang," she enunciated carefully.

No, I supposed not. What an insufferably dull place the Duchy of Cleves must be! Poor thing—coming to England and being hailed as Queen must have been the most extraordinary thing in her very ordinary life. Well, let her enjoy it while she could—for this preposterous charade would last only a few months more, until Charles and Francis had their inevitable falling-out.

The trumpets sounded, ringing out unnaturally clear in the cold. (Why does cold seem to intensify colours and sound?) I stood and gave the signal for them to begin. The flower of England, young men in their prime, rode forth to entertain us, the aging patrons of England.

I glanced over at Brandon, leaning back in his Eastern leather chair. Lately he had been affecting the ways of a sultan, claiming that his old bones felt more comfortable in Persian stuffed chairs, and that smoking their foul-smelling water-pipes improved his mood. Now he was watching the contests with half-lidded eyes. He was not unlike a bullfrog on a giant lily pad; but I remembered his face, fierce behind a visor, as it was in 1524, when he all but killed me in a tournament. . . .

"We could show them something, eh?" I touched his shoulder. He did not respond. Either his hearing was defective or he was lost in thought. No matter. Beside him, Crum made a disgusted motion toward the water-pipe.

I could not help but notice that we seemed to be divided into two groups: old men and young women, the latter watching the young men perform on the field.

On Anne's side of the box were spread out all her newly appointed ladies-in-waiting and maids of honour. I watched them, in a sort of intellectual fascination with youth—or so I fancied.

A flicker of white: lace being waved, a handkerchief . . . *the* handkerchief that day, the black/white May Day when Anne had dropped it to Norris . . . I had not known pain could survive intact like that, as if it had a life of its own, but now it ripped through me, leaving me weak and sick.

The handkerchief moved again, a piece of cloth and lace, a real thing, not a ghost. Holding it was that ethereal creature in pink whom I had seen at the wedding dinner. She waved at Culpepper, who was now fastening her satin colours on his arm. Yet she did not love him, I could tell, by the way her eye wandered and she chattered gaily to her companions. Once he was not looking, she crumpled up the handkerchief and wadded it in her hand. And when Culpepper fell, she scarcely noticed.

She put her plump little hand up to her bosom, and then it all came clear to me: this was the creature for whom Culpepper had requested the velvet, the one he had meant to seduce.

Evidently he had not succeeded. No maiden would ever have regarded her seducer as inattentively as this—what was her name?—this Howard girl regarded Culpepper. They were carrying him off the field now, and there were bright spots of blood in the snow beneath him, but Mistress Auburn-Tresses was whispering to another lady and giggling.

She stuck out her slippered feet to warm them against the brazier, touching them to the singeing metal, then pulling them back just in time. It was a dangerous game, and sure enough, she cried out in pain after the sixth or seventh time.

I made my way down to her, and pulled off her slipper. Her foot was so tiny and warm, like a child's. I had forgotten that there is a time in life when one's feet are plump and rosy. It seemed that mine had been hard, callused, and cold for all my living memory. But this foot was *succulent,* there was no other word for it.

I looked up at her face, and it was as tender and succulent as her foot. She still clutched the handkerchief, but tears glistened on her flushed cheeks, and her cushion-like lips quivered. She was the most sensual creature I had ever touched, the most fleshly and entirely of the senses, of this *earth* . . . and I knew, in that instant, that I must possess her.

I said nothing. I stood up, made my way back to my royal seat.

It was settled. She would be mine. I had but to speak to arrange it. I lived in a world where all desires could be satisfied, but where the lack of desire had been the fearsome thing, the thing that weighed on me and made me feel dead.

Now I lived again. To *want* was to be alive. And I wanted Mistress Howard, wanted her so violently I was ashamed and breathless at the same time.

That night I could not sleep. Truly. For the first time since I had beheld Anne Boleyn at the investiture (June 25, 1525; I would never forget that date) and been bewitched, I had not had such a feeling. Was this, too, witchcraft? No, I knew better now. Anne's witchcraft had come later. That initial feeling I had had was genuine and undesecrated.

To experience it again! I had thought never to do so, and now to be given it, unsought, at my age!

I lay awake all night, enjoying the love yet to come, relishing the fact that I *knew* it would come to pass, for I had power to command, and what I wished, I could take. I was no Culpepper. But in the interval between the framing of a desire and the acting on it—therein lies the torture, and the bliss. A person is never more ours, yet never more unattainable, than in those hours.

Anne snored softly beside me. I felt fondly toward her, knowing that she was the odd means of having brought about my present and future bliss. Without the arranged marriage, I would have been content to languish forever, mourning and feeling myself dead. I had believed myself so. I even felt gratitude toward Francis and Charles. Without their enmity, I never would have had to make this forced marriage, then I never would have had a Queen, and the Queen would never have had a household—

Enough! This was absurd. One might as well be thankful that one's father lay with one's mother on a certain night, and that the midwife was saved from tripping on the stairs because of a fortuitous candle. The truth was, I was gloriously in love—reborn, as it were—and that was all that mattered. Things were as they were, and to care overmuch who brought them to this pass was to busy oneself wastefully. Any action not bringing a lover to the possession of his loved one was wasted, unless it be savouring the moment to come.

❦ ❦

Culpepper's wounds were slight. He had been pricked by a lance-tip that somehow found its way between the overlapping thigh-plates of his armour. The surgeon had cleansed his wound and bound it with pink satin.

"*Her* colours," said Culpepper with a wink, as he reported back to my sleeping chamber for duty. He unwound the satin carefully and placed it reverently on his night-table.

"Whose?" I forced myself to ask, casually.

"My fair cousin's," he replied. "The one I spoke to you about before the Queen's arrival."

"I forget her name."

"Catherine Howard. Daughter of Edmund Howard, the Duke's youngest brother."

I remembered now. I had always held Edmund in the same category of regard I reserved for perpetual drunkards, perverted monks, and deserter soldiers. The wretch had died in debt and unable to perform his duties, of course.

"After her sad father died, she had to be taken in by her step-grandmother, the dowager Duchess of Norfolk."

A part of me sensed danger. Her inheritance was bad, her upbringing pathetic. Blood and training tell. Another part of me was indignant. By those standards, Our Lord would be reckoned of no account.

Her eyes were innocent. They told me all I wished to know. (What had

6 3 7

become of my knowledge that everyone is a consummate liar? Banished, along with all my other painfully acquired knowledge and experience, in the vortex of love.)

"Have you made her your own yet?"

He chuckled. "No. I wait upon a proper time."

The shrug of my shoulders did not betray the rush of relief I felt. She was untouched! I would not have had her otherwise; I could not have stood to know that another had enjoyed her.

Like Katherine, and Anne Boleyn! Other men had held them, other men had parted their legs and inserted their members into their soft flesh, had rubbed back and forth within them, had left a sticky mess . . . foul, foul! That was so sickening, so revolting, to take another man's leavings. No man could do so and remain a man.

People wondered what I had loved in my Jane. Her purity. To know that she was untouched, that no man had soiled her.

I must move quickly with Catherine Howard, lest Culpepper besmirch her. Then I would not want her. No, knowing another had been there before me, had sported himself upon her and within her, would make her diseased in my eyes. I must be first, and only.

"We must find you a wife," I said to Culpepper.

He laughed. "I would rather have mistresses."

"Nay," I insisted. "You need a wife to spend your energy on. Stay away from Mistress Howard. Her only dowry is her virginity. Do not rob her of it."

He shrugged. "Be it as you command. I am thankful I am no woman, to have to trade in virtue."

Virtue. Purity. Modesty. Chastity. All men mock them and denigrate them. Yet all men are struck and awed in their presence.

The next morning, as I made my way to Anne's study, ostensibly to listen in on her English lessons, I glanced all about me, hoping to see Catherine Howard. As a maid of honour, her duties were everyday ones: selecting combs, brushing clothes and inspecting them for lice, cleaning and laying out jewellery. It was the higher ranking ladies-in-waiting who attended the Queen in ceremonies. Therefore it was in Anne's chambers where I must seek to find Mistress Catherine.

Anne was alone with her tutor, however, the stammering youngster who nonetheless seemed to be a genius in the rapid teaching of the tongue.

"In—ze—"

" 'The' "—

"In—the—market iss, apple, pear, cheese, und—"

" 'And' "—

"—turnips."

They crowed with pleased laughter. I enjoyed hearing Anne's delight. Without the shadow of my presence, she seemed a lighthearted person, altogether at odds with her leaden appearance.

"Very good, sweetheart," I said, strolling into the room. The laughter ceased. That hurt me.

"Come, come," I chided. "Do not interrupt yourselves for my sake. What else is in the market? A fat hog, perhaps?"

But they would not resume. Feeling let down, both in my original intention of seeing Mistress Catherine and, unaccountably, in having intruded on Anne and being excluded, I made my way back to my own chamber. This was the time when I would gladly have saddled a horse, gone hunting, left the palace and my feelings behind. But I was not now capable of riding. Lately my leg-ulcer caused me such pain from being rubbed on a saddle that I no longer could endure it. Moping about my chamber on this bleak February day, I called for one of the few pleasures left to me—Will.

Will worked, still, when wine failed and company palled. Almost imperceptibly he had passed from being an entertainer for my private moments, witty and full of scabrous gossip, to being a listener and a wise commentator—especially after Jane had died and I simply could not abide fools about me, I mean *true* fools, not professional jesters. Fools who murmured unctuous platitudes about how "time will heal all" and "you will rejoin her in heaven," and "she would not want you to grieve overmuch." It was Will alone who was honest and brave enough to say, "I know that you would trade the remainder of your life to speak to her for just a quarter of an hour on the most trivial subject." And I could answer, "Yes."

Now I relied on him more and more, telling myself that I must not, as to place so much trust and need on a single person was to court Fate overmuch. I had only to remember Wolsey, More, and Jane herself.

He stood before me in the work chamber, in his ordinary clothes. He seldom wore cap and bells anymore, as the costume offended his sensibilities and was necessary only if he performed in public. Before me, at eleven in the morning, it would have been absurd.

"Will," I muttered, "I am utterly lost, forlorn."

His dark quick eyes searched mine. "No, Hal"—he preferred to call me Hal, as no one else ever did—"you are *bored*. Call it by its proper name."

"What is boredom, then? Define it for me." Already boredom had flown, at Will's magic touch.

"Boredom is that awful state of inaction when the very medicine—that is, activity—which could resolve it, is seen as odious. Archery? It is too cold, and besides, the butts need re-covering; the rats have been at the straw. Music? To hear it is tedious; to compose it, too taxing. And so on. Of all the afflictions, boredom is ultimately the most un-manning. Eventually it transforms you into a great nothing who does nothing—a cousin to sloth and a brother to melancholy."

"You make it sound romantic, and doomed."

He shrugged. "It can be. The odd thing about it is that it is so easily cured. One need only force himself to perform the 'boring' actions, and the condition itself flees. Something about the physical action dispels the boredom. Yet once it has set in, and got its grip on a man, he is usually too enervated to rout it, even by the simple expedient of putting one foot in front of another."

"Will, I *am* enervated. But not from boredom. Will, I am—in love!"

He received this astounding confession calmly. "That, of course, is the most guaranteed cure for boredom. It never fails, in the short run. But it has the disadvantage of always failing in the long run. Well—you stand warned. Who is she?" He did not say "this time." He did not slide his voice sarcastically. He merely inquired, brightly, pleasantly.

"A girl come to court."

"Well, I did not suppose it was someone you had met in the fields. Where else would you meet anyone, save at court? Your choice is quite limited, in truth. I don't suppose you realize it."

"She is young and unspoiled and fresh. A rose without a thorn!"

"Nameless, I see. Equipped with all the standard love-evoking mechanisms to inflame desire in such a jaded old roué as yourself. It's always a 'young girl.' O Hal, how *boring!*"

"How can you say that?"

"To be boring is to be predictable. Have you ever sat down to a Twelfth Night masque, and it is about Cupid and Psyche, and you see, within the first few moments, that you are going to have to watch *all* the tests that Venus sets her: the separation of the rice and wheat, the borrowing of beauty from Persephone, and so on, and so on? And something within you groans and thinks, 'O dear, I have to sit through all this!' There are no surprises, just the known and inevitable. That is how it is with you and your 'rose without a thorn.' Ho-hum. You will idealize her and trust her, and she'll betray you, either with a youngster, or just with Time himself. And you'll be unhappy."

Even Will did not understand! I was stunned.

"Be original, Hal. Fall in love with an old widow. Now there's a story!"

"I am not a story! I am a man! I do not exist to prove theories of tale-spinners. Do I not have a right to happiness?"

"How boyish! A 'right to happiness.' You do not even have a right to life, let alone happiness. That you live, and thrive, is a gift. A gift the gods did not confer on Prince Arthur, or on Queen Jane. There are no 'rights,' only gifts. Although one can increase one's chances of receiving those gifts by acting in certain time-tested ways. Sadly, the doting older husband and child-bride combination is not one of them."

"I cannot help it. I tell you, I am *possessed!*" I cried. Even as I said it, I felt the strength of that possession—impossible to dislodge, save by consummation and attainment.

"You are always 'possessed' by something," he finally said. "Are you never just Hal, without some sort of visiting spirit? Does it not become crowded inside your earthly skin?"

"No! To be alive is to teem with spirits!"

"To be alive is to teem with your *own* spirits, not a host of alien ones."

"Words, words! I will have no more words, but only the Lady Catherine." There, I had stated it.

He laughed. "I would have thought that name would be one you could never stomach again."

"So was Anne! Can I help it if one-third of the women in Christendom are named Katherine, another third Anne, and the last third Elizabeth? Shall I seek amongst the Infidels for a Melisande or a Zaida?"

"Eventually you may have to, if you continue 'falling in love' apace. You are not yet fifty, and have at least another twenty years of lusting—and calling it love—before you. England may prove too small for you."

I could not help laughing. He reduced it all to the manageable, the understandable. Men of logic, who think so differently from men of instinct and passion, always do. They are thus a great comfort for the aftermath, the returning-to-earth part of the love-journey. But not for the beginning; no, not for the beginning. They scoff at magic, and beginnings are magic in their purest form.

He settled himself down on a great cushion before the fire. "Now you must plan your campaign. Shall you win her before Easter, do you think?"

I let him chatter on, but I scarce heard him, as the great obstacle to Mistress Catherine Howard emerged in my mind. That obstacle was in her very name: Howard. The Howards were of the North, and steeped in the Old Religion. "It was merry in England before we had the New Learning come amongst us," the Duke had once grumbled, and as a whole, the family were conservative and against the very changes I had brought about. To entangle myself with a Howard bride meant to turn my back on everything I had done since that mockery of a legatine court in England. Catherine was but a bait in a vast, complicated, political bear-trap. And if I took that bait . . .

But if there were a way to snatch the bait without springing the trap? There must be. I would find it.

Just as her cousin Anne Boleyn had done before her, Catherine managed to elude me, although this time it was accidental. I never found her about Queen Anne when I came to make my formal calls on her, and I dared not increase the frequency or the length of them, lest Anne become attached to me. Above all I did not want that, although she was rapidly becoming alarmingly English. She had progressed to a level of everyday speaking that was on a par with a schoolchild's, had befriended both my daughters, and was busy planning gardens to be laid out in mid-April, after the last frost. If she were disappointed or dissatisfied with our marriage "arrangement," she did not show it. It was going to be difficult to pry her loose when the time came.

It was also difficult to keep Cromwell at bay and soothed. He was by far the cleverest man in my kingdom, shrewd and cunning if not truly visionary; his instinct for personal and political survival was legendary. I took the greatest care that he should be unaware of my reevaluation of him, but to disguise this I had also to conceal my true feelings for Queen Anne.

After the first few days, Cromwell had inquired timidly as to whether the Lady Anne pleased me more than I had originally thought? Since the answer to that was both yes (in her unexpected ability to make any room she was in feel comfortable) and no (in her physical repulsiveness), I merely grunted and said, "Somewhat." This reply made him more nervous than before, so I knew it was a mistake. An apprehensive man notices far more than a contented one, and in the future I must see to it that Cromwell was contented enough to betray himself, or at least to reveal his true feelings about Lutheranism.

The situation in England, though, was this (I could admit it and see it, even though I disliked its implications): we had become, in the eyes of the world, Protestant, and the very things I cherished and relied on depended in large measure on the existence of Protestantism (as it was now being fashionably called, rather than Lutheranism). What were these things? My own conscience, for one. Upon my private conscience I had based my break with Rome and my annulment of the incestuous marriage with Katherine. My conscience I had set up as the highest law of the land. I looked for Divine guidance, and I embraced it. Directly between myself and God there was a relationship, and the intermediaries (Church, holy traditions) were to be leapfrogged en route.

But Lutheranism—I mean Protestantism—was so *social*. It would make man the interpreter of things, and ultimately the focus of all values on earth. In time, no institution or building or objects would be seen as divine at all. It would be all Man, Mankind, and Humanity, and the world would revolve around Man and his little deeds, his little struttings. It would follow, then, that a King is but a man, and every man a potential King. . . .

I despised Protestantism! It led ultimately to anarchy. Therein lay the paradox. England's safekeeping rested uneasily on a justification that ultimately would seduce us to barbarism once more. I was charged with steering a middle course between the destructive extremes of Rome and anarchy. I could do it, although it became more and more difficult. But what of Edward, coming after me?

Protestantism might seem appealing to Cromwell, but he could not foresee where it would lead. Cromwell and his forces must be stopped. Protestantism must be allowed to progress no further in England, lest it wash like a spring tide over Edward when he came to the throne, and sweep him off it.

At court, we prepared to move to Windsor to spend spring and to bring in the May. Carts were readied and drawn up before the courtyard, and workingmen spent two full days carrying out wrapped articles and loading them carefully. Everything was inventoried, and all our favourite objects were to be transported to Windsor. The most delicate ones, of course, were not to be moved. Each palace contained a few of those: a finely tuned clock in one; a ponderous organ in another; a painting whose unstable colours could not withstand exposure to the elements. That was why, each time I returned to a royal residence, I greeted and rediscovered a host of old faithful friends.

Everything had been moved from Greenwich, and I had stayed behind only to review some pesky state papers, which, once signed, would be delivered directly to the Chancellor. I always enjoyed the feeling of a place just deserted, its life gone elsewhere. It gave me a sort of cheap melancholy to roam about the empty rooms, and it was a pleasure I always allowed myself, on one pretext or another.

Today, as I waved away the last of the Imperial messengers (Charles *still* called Francis "brother"; how tiresome!), I decided to walk across the adjoining hallway and into the Queen's apartments. I did so, marvelling not for the first time at how much larger a room appeared without furniture—not just a little larger but double or triple the old size. Without furniture or trappings, it had no personality at all. "Ghosts" were mainly tied up in tangible objects: in the hanging that one was observing when someone said certain words; in the inlaid wood pattern that one had stared at when at a certain hurtful juncture at one's life. Without these, ghosts were flown. Katherine had been here; Anne, too. Jane as maid of honour. Each of them had made the place so different, in her own time, that it seemed surrounded by different bricks; it seemed the windows should give out on different views.

I glanced out the east window from the Queen's Privy Chamber. The same Thames flowed by, rushing now and swollen with the spring waters. I looked about me, rejoicing in the bare boards and open rooms. I always became excited at new beginnings, and that was what empty rooms meant to me.

Within my mind I heard music—vanished music from other rooms, other times. Such was my mood that morning that I did not question it but stood and listened. Slow, long, plaintive . . . things that once had been, but were no more . . . it had a sad beauty all its own.

They were real notes, though. A false one was struck, whereas a false one was never struck in memory. . . .

I moved forward, turning my head. The sound was stronger in my left ear. It was coming from the rooms deeper within the Queen's suite. I passed through the audience chamber, through the outer council chamber. The sound was richer. I stood in the entranceway that branched to both the left and the right, and I could not discern from whence the sound came. I waited some moments, holding my breath. My ears did not decide for me, but my intellect. I knew (being one, myself) that musicians always preferred natural light to artificial. Windows lined the left side of the Queen's apartments, letting in God's light. Therefore I went to the left, and—

Stopped absolutely, my breath frozen, movements arrested, while my mind recorded for all time the sight of a great, ivory-keyed virginal, all naked in a stripped room, with Mistress Catherine Howard leaning against it, picking out notes. I watched her labouring, alone in the room, an expression of pure delight on her face. I knew what it meant to be left alone for a whole day to play a new instrument, to learn and master it with no one listening. It surpassed sensuality, it surpassed almost all other experiences.

Each note sounded out loud and clear, flinging itself jubilantly into the spring air. I stood, hidden, as long as I dared. Then I felt it was deceitful, so to intrude and spy on an artist's solitude, and I stepped out boldly.

"Mistress Howard," I said simply, making my way across the worn floorboards toward her, "I see that you, too, delight in a well-tuned virginal."

She gasped and drew back, like a child caught at something naughty. "Your—Your Majesty—" She stumbled up and grasped at her skirts. The pushed-back virginal bench fell with a crash behind her.

"Nay, nay." I hated it when, in a private situation, I evoked embarrassment and fear. Officially, of course, it was different. "I myself enjoy practising in deserted rooms, where no one can possibly overhear."

She bent over and pulled up the fallen bench.

"Pray you," I said in what I hoped was my most soothing voice, "continue your playing. I always enjoyed hearing the Lady Mary play the virginals, and—"

Not Anne Boleyn. I shut out that horrible memory, of her and her musicians, which kept emerging into my consciousness like a toad after rain.

"—Lady Elizabeth, too. Where did you learn to play so well?"

The lass smiled and smoothed her skirts. "At my grandmother's. I had a tutor."

"When did you begin? You must have studied for many years." I seated myself beside her on the narrow bench.

"No. I"—she thought swiftly—"it was for one year only, when I was thirteen. Yet I studied diligently then. And continued to practise after my tutor had departed."

"You enjoy music, then?"

"I love it." She smiled. I was struck by her composure; but then, when artists come together, it often happens that their calling overcomes shyness, differences in station, everything. We speak a common language, and everything else is hushed. It happened, even, that my love and desire for her were set aside for a moment in the glow of her music, where we became equals.

I reached out and fingered the keyboard, remembering old melodies; she listened. Then she played, and I listened. Midway she laughed, and I glanced at her glowing skin and deep black lashes and was overcome with love, desire, all blended and heightened by the music and even, absurdly, by the virginal before us with its chipped old keys.

She turned to look at me, not averting her eyes, as proper maidens do, but looking me full in the face. Her eyes were ice-blue and rimmed in some darker colour, which only made her appear all the more remote and untouched, waiting for me.

"Catherine," I finally said, astounded at how calm and unwavering my voice was, "I love to hear you play, and I fain would play beside you all my life. There is much of me that has been lost, misplaced—not irretrievably, as I had feared—but for a time. I would share that person with you, and in return I would give you—I would give you—whatever your heart longs for," I finished weakly.

"A new virginal?" she asked. "The keys of this—"

She did not understand! "Certainly, that. But, my dear, what I am asking you—"

What I am asking you is this: Can you love an old man of near fifty? Can you be wife to him?

"—is whether you would be my—"

Whether you would consent to be Queen? One does not beg someone to accept a high state office! It is its own reward!

"—whether you would wed me?"

She stared at me as if I were mad. Then she said, slowly, "I cannot . . . no . . . it cannot be . . . you have a wife already."

Anne Boleyn's words! I felt flung into a vortex of time, where nothing had changed, and we were condemned to repeat the same mistakes and words forever and ever. . . . Your wife I cannot be, for you have a wife already; and your mistress I will not be. . . .

"I have no wife!" Those words, too, were the same. "I have the power to put her aside." Different words, now. Words earned through six long years of testing.

"You mean—I would be Queen?"

"If you consent to become my wife, yes."

She shook her head, dazed. "Little Catherine Howard, to be Queen of England?"

"My dear," I said, choosing my words, "one of the greatest pleasures in being King lies in the power to select others worthy of being elevated to honours and reverence. To discover unseen, unknown personages, who, but for me, would never attain the prominence and recognition they deserve. Think you not there are gifted, talented, and beautiful people aplenty in Ireland? Yet they will be born, live, and die unseen—like human compost. You"—I took her perfect, rounded little chin in my hand—"are born to wear a crown. Catherine, be my wife."

"But the good Lady of Cleves—"

"She will be well provided for. Do not accuse yourself of disloyalty in supplanting your mistress. She and I have never been truly husband and wife. Sister and brother are we, and so shall we remain."

Still she sat silent. Then: "I do not believe it. You trifle with me."

"Never! If you would prove me, so shall it be! I shall never seek to be alone with you until the night Cranmer hath given us the Church's blessings."

"Truly?"

"Aye, truly! A true maid shall you remain until then."

She fell to her knees and began kissing my hand. "Good King Henry, you know not what you do. I am unworthy to become your wife."

Her lips were warm, plump, and moist. I felt my manhood stirring. "Nay. Only the unworthy take an elevation as a matter of course. Your very reticence reveals your worthiness." Her lips continued their work. I disengaged myself and raised her up. "My beloved Catherine," I said. "I thank God for this day. Wait upon me, and trust me. I shall bring all this about so swiftly, you will be amazed!"

The sun streamed into the odd little room; I watched the motes dance in the rich spring light. It was magic, all of it. I kissed Catherine's hands, heard her gasp and pull away, then run from the room, like a child scampering away. A frightened child? Or an excited child? In either case, a child who forgot her manners and did not beg leave to be excused.

A delectable child who would teach me to play again! My palms were sweaty as I closed the cover over the virginal keyboard.

LXXXIX

Every Wednesday evening for the seven weeks between Easter and Whitsun, Cranmer entertained both prelates and courtiers with music recitals in the red brick Archbishop's Palace at Lambeth. It lay close by the Thames, just across from Westminster Palace and Abbey, and offered a delicious indulgence of all five senses on a spring evening: vision, of course, in the sunset lingering on the wide, fresh river; smell, in the delicate spring scents of the damp earth and early flowers all around; taste, in the asparagus and fish served on little white wheat-cakes before the recitals, along with woodruff-flavoured white wine; touch, in the very softness of the May air coming in through the newly opened casements. And sound, from the musicians themselves, and the precision-tuned instruments: viols, dulceuses, lutes, and even a harpsichord from Italy. Sometimes Cranmer would provide an exotic one, like an ivory cornett.

All seemed merry to me those evenings, all a haze of sensual indulgence, for Catherine Howard was there most times, included for her musical interests, along with her uncle the Duke and Bishop Gardiner. Interest in music seemed to be a privilege of the aesthetes and the traditionalists. Protestants frowned on it as a "lightness," which was why the Lady Anne of Cleves had never been trained in it. Truth to tell, most of the delights of the senses seemed relegated to the traditionalists, while the New Men would have everything purged and plain. And chokingly boring!

Those evenings confirmed my commitment to Catherine, to our future, and to my need to check Cromwell. In Catherine I had come home. In the autumn of my life I had a gathering-in place, where I could bring in my stores and sit in the slanting yellow sunlight and know it all well done. And not over yet. In the autumn to come, there would be a new harvest, I knew it. I would have other sons by Catherine, glorious sons, and Mary and Elizabeth would not be needed for England.

They said, later, that I was mad for her. They said the same about Anne Boleyn, and wondered if both women had cast the same spell. They were cousins; had they perhaps learned the same potions, the same incantations? No, it was not the same at all. With Anne I was consumed, caught up in an incandescent swirl that obliterated the world, and myself. With Catherine—ah, that beauty, that perfection. . . .

When I think of my feeling for her, and try to liken it to anything similar, what comes to mind, over and over, is a time I stopped in the woods alone. It was still, and I wanted to let my horse catch his breath. So I tethered him to a tree and walked some little way and found a rock to sit on. It was all brown in that forest—brown leaves above, more brown leaves making a crinkly layer on the ground. My breeches were brown, and my boots too. The toadstools at my feet, growing up all around the rock, were various shadings of brown: fawn, taupe, weasel. I was astonished at how many different ways there were to be brown. And then I saw it—a tiny, iridescent blue butterfly, spreading its wings against an oak leaf. It shimmered against the brown like a jewel in a velvet case.

Catherine was that shining butterfly in the brown autumn of my life. Perfect, jewel-like, with no other purpose than to bring beauty—a purpose she completely fulfilled. I treasured her, guarded her, and doted on her. That was not the same as madness.

Cromwell was not invited to the delicate evenings at Lambeth Palace, and was surprisingly unadept at hiding his curiosity about them. Oh, his spies undoubtedly reported all that went on—whether a composition by Tallis was performed, and which lute was in use, and even to what key it was tuned—but they could not, as yet, read men's minds, although I was told they could lip-read a conversation accurately from fifty feet away. A chilling thought. Cromwell disliked being excluded from cultural events, as though he were still the blacksmith's son from Putney, with manure wet on his shoes. Like most Reformers and purists, he yearned to be invited to the very frivolities he condemned.

He busied himself on those delicious Wednesday evenings as if they were of no account. On those long May twilights, as my royal barge drifted away from the water-steps of York Place (recently re-named Whitehall and expanded) and the red-gold sun reflected gloriously in the hundreds of window-panes on the water-side of the palace, I always saw the dark shape of Cromwell hovering just inside. He never even opened a casement . . . lest the spring air beguile him?

Those evenings at Lambeth, besides being excursions into the realm of the five senses, were also excursions into the past. There, with the Old Men—Howard and Brandon and Fitzwilliam and Lord Lisle—it was always 1520. It was easy there to believe that the world had not changed. There had been no Martin Luther, no suppression of the monasteries. No apprentices had thought to follow trades forbidden them by tradition; no nonsense about a goldsmith's son becoming a lawyer. It had been a safe, domesticated world in 1520, albeit a mummified one.

Real life now lay with Cromwell, back in the palace. Knowing this, the aristocrats delighted in pouring poison in my ear regarding him.

"Your Grace, I know not how to express myself," demurred Henry Howard, Thomas's son, the Earl of Surrey. "But Cromwell is so—so—"

"Not know how to express yourself? Nay, they claim you are the foremost poet in England," I muttered. Yes, "they"—the critics—had lately adopted a phrase, "from Lydgate down to Surrey," implying that nothing in between was worth reading. "Say it, man," I insisted.

"So vulgar."

He was right, of course. But why did I feel as though he had said it about *me?* Cromwell was only my minion. "He is well versed in the paintings and sculptures of Italy," I maintained. Surrey himself had put on airs about his travels in France and his meetings with Florentine poets, as if these made him special.

"A man may look at a painting and not be affected by it. Every peasant in Italy is surrounded by great art, but does it speak to him? Great Rome itself was but a haunt for cowherds until recently. The Forum where Caesar walked, become a place for squatters!"

True, all true. People had forgotten their own history, and lived like savages in the great Temple of Venus.

"Cromwell is a squatter in royal haunts," continued Surrey. "He does not belong. The people of the North instinctively realize that. The demands of the late 'Pilgrims' showed how distressed good, honest folk are at the power of a Cromwell." He smiled at me—a dazzling smile, because he still had all his teeth. That in itself indicated his sheltered life.

"The 'Pilgrims' were traitors," I said softly. "Several hundred were hanged in chains. Are you saying that you agree with them?"

"About the New Men, yes." He made what I privately called his "charming" face. It consisted of an ironic turn of the mouth, along with twinkling eyes. It meant "see how affable and likeable I am, despite my truly impressive credentials." In fact he was neither as affable nor as likeable as he assumed.

"What about the New Men? And who *are* the New Men?"

"Cromwell—"

"Cromwell is but *one* man. You said 'men,' so name another."

"Paget," he said reluctantly. "And Audley. And Denny. And Sadler"—they began pouring out now, like steam escaping from one tiny rent—"and the *Seymours!*" he spat. His hatred stood quivering.

"Which one?" I asked, as if it were of no moment.

"Both of them! Edward, with his pious, grasping ways, and Tom, with his pirate's manner—all swagger and bluster. No man would be taken in by him, of course, so he appeals to the ladies. Oh, he aims high—at the Lady Mary, I do think. And so do many others. The fact that you married their sister has quite gone to their heads."

And the chance to speak has gone to yours, I thought. Call Cromwell what you like, you fool, he never lets himself be flattered, and he never lets down his guard. He would never betray his mind so. I looked at Surrey contemptuously. "They come from good stock. It is upon such honest, decent Englishmen that the future of the realm depends."

"Aye, aye," he quickly agreed, eager to be as beguiling as he imagined himself. "Certainly they are not made of the same material as *Cromwell*, no—for they *are* honest, and have no secret plans of any sort, beyond recognition for themselves. But Cromwell, well, we don't know his desires, do we? He does not seem to want any of the things any normal man would want. There's talk"—he smiled a puzzled smile—"that he's the Devil."

I wanted to laugh, but it never came.

"There are those who, I'm told, can actually strike a bargain with Satan. They sit down and work out a contract with him, just as you do with the money-lenders of Antwerp. 'So-and-so much interest to be paid on the loan of twenty thousand pounds, due on Whitsun of 1542,' you say, and it is done. 'My soul in exchange for such-and-such,' they say, and it is done. Cromwell appears to have—I mean, there are so many signs—"

He meant it. All the playfulness and deceit was gone from his face.

"My dear son, you—"

"Catherine!" said Surrey, as if a spell were being broken. Catherine had seen us deep in talk, and come over. She tugged playfully at her cousin's arm.

"They are taking seats," she chided him, "and you will not be able to see."

Her presence took us out of that dangerous realm where we had entered, just for a moment. She grinned up at Surrey. They were cousins, first cousins. I could see little resemblance between them. Surrey was slender and blonde, Catherine small and auburn-haired. Both had pale skin, that was all.

I reached out my arm to her, and together we found seats and prepared to listen to a series of compositions performed on a reed instrument by a young man from Cornwall.

He was small and dark, like all his people. The melodies were haunting, dreamlike, unlike anything I had heard before. They spoke to a soft, lost side of myself.

Afterwards I talked to him. I had a bit of trouble understanding his accent, as his mother tongue was Cornish. I complimented him on his musicianship and enquired after the sources of his melodies.

"I modelled them on native melodies, Your Grace," he said. "There are similar tunes across the sea in Brittany," he added. "Often my father and I cross there, and while he does his business, I do mine."

"And what is his business?"

"He is a fisherman, Your Grace."

"And yours?"

"A musician."

"And only that?"

"Aye. It's what I'm called to."

"But what of your father's trade?"

He shrugged. "Perhaps somewhere a musician's son longs for the sea."

So simple. He made a revolutionary idea sound so logical. Here was a true New Man, and what Surrey could condemn him? And I had taken pleasure in his offerings!

Often, after the entertainments were over, Catherine and I would stroll about the grounds of the Archbishop's Palace. This area upstream, where Lambeth and, across the river, Westminster Abbey and Palace lay, was quiet and bucolic. Lambeth, with its quiet walks, rounded cobblestones, and faded bricks, invited one to take off one's shoes, put aside one's cloak, and say, "Now, my friend, let us discuss this 'business' of Church taxation—but first, some wine." All things, even weighty state things, were just conversations between two friends. And therefore all things were possible.

Catherine and I stood often by the river's edge at the great water-steps. A dozen lanterns flickered there, lest an unwary foot slip on the wet stones of the landing. Always there were barges of estate tied up there, brave carvings of arms glistening with gold leaf on their prows, waiting to take their masters back to great-houses on the Strand.

We always walked a little distance away, else the boatmen might overhear us. There was a brick footpath along the river's edge, and that was our favourite. We followed it to its end and then stood there, listening to the lapping of the water. In the magic of Lambeth and its ancient accessibility, in the power of May, nothing was beyond reach. Including Catherine as my wife.

I put my arm round her and pulled her close. "I can wait no longer," I muttered. The evening had been intoxicating, a foretaste of what awaited me daily, once my private life was rearranged. "There is no reason to postpone what we both are longing for."

She nodded eagerly, and pressed herself up against me.

"It will not be difficult," I assured myself out loud. "Anne is not my wife in the eyes of God."

"In the eyes of Cromwell, though, she is Your Grace's wife," said little Catherine in a clear, bell-like voice.

"Cromwell . . ." Oh, what was I to do about Crum? "Cromwell must learn to live with disappointment," was my lacklustre reply.

"What he has so adroitly done, set him to work to undo," she said gaily. "As when a child is naughty, her mother makes her toil on the very thing she has ruined. The Duchess often made me take out stitches of the shifts I had embroidered, and done poorly."

My beloved Catherine, granddaughter of a great noble house, forced to do needlework for servants! "Was it tedious?"

"Aye. But it learnt me to notice what I did with my needle. Before that, I was careless, and sloppy."

"You were but a child."

"So is the Lady Elizabeth. Yet she knows well how to follow each movement that her needle makes."

Elizabeth. What matter what Elizabeth did?

"Yes, let us put Cromwell's cleverness to task," I chuckled. "Let him take out his own labouriously contrived stitches."

She laughed. "He caged you. Let him set you free."

"I would not be free, little bird, but bound to you."

She reached out and slid her hand along my cheek. The faint light from the boatmen's torches lit the left side of her face—a half-mask.

"You are a half moon," I murmured, leaning over to kiss her. She returned that kiss heartily, hungrily, sweetly. I quivered, shuddered, erupted with desire.

"Nay, nay—" she was whispering, her voice rising in urgency. "My Lord!"

I was ashamed. I had frightened her, threatened her chastity. "Forgive me," I said. My breath was still coming in short gasps.

She drew her cloak around her. Jesu, how could I have insulted her so? She was crying.

"Catherine, I meant no harm. But this—this is unnatural." At that moment I knew it, felt it. "We must be wed straightway. It is meant to be. No more standing before the Thames, alive with longing." Even the slap-slap-slap of the water against the riverbank sounded sexual to me. "I will speak to Cromwell tomorrow."

Still she kept her face buried in her cloak, her shoulders hunched. I reached out a steadying hand. "Hush now." I soothed her. When she had done crying, I put one arm around her and led her back to her waiting barge. She leaned against me all the way, and yet when the time came to play her part to her waiting uncle Norfolk, she smiled gaily and threw off the hood of the cloak as she joined him in the Howard barge.

Her cousin Surrey, the Lady Norris, Mary, widow of my lost son Fitzroy:

all the Howard youngsters awaited her in the barge, and she outshone them all. As the rowers pulled away from the riverbanks, and the sound of music and the faint lantern light echoed and reflected on the water, I wondered what it was to belong to such a great tribal family, and how it felt.

XC

I awoke well before dawn, savouring the spring sweetness. Every hour seemed precious now, every aspect of the day steeped in a rare perfume. The birdsong outside my window was finer tuned than any human consort of viols. Oh, how beautiful was the world! Catherine would soon be my wife, and I would have someone again to share these exquisite moments of life.

Culpepper stirred on the pallet at the foot of my bed and groaned. He rubbed his eyes and sat up, muttering all the while. His breath was foul. I looked at him, in all his youthful strength and beauty, enmeshed in a hangover; and suddenly it seemed to me a desecration, a perversion of what a man was meant to be. He marred the day, like a boil on a virgin's cheek.

I must see Cromwell, if this thing were truly to come about. And so I sent for him, which I had not done in some time. He appeared so promptly I could almost credit young Henry Howard's tale of diabolical power; only the Devil could travel with such speed.

Clean-shaven and obedient, he stood before me. "Your Grace?" He bowed smartly; only his rising voice betrayed eagerness and compliance.

"Things are breaking up on the Continent, like clouds on a March day," I began.

"Sire?"

"I no longer need the alliance with Cleves!" I barked. "You erected it; you dismantle it."

He looked disdainful. "That is—"

"Leonardo da Vinci—even he!—dismantled the arches and pavilions he created for Princess Katherine's Coronation. He supposedly was a great artist —certainly Francis thought so, buying every small canvas he painted!—and yet he was not above cleaning up his messes. Now you do the same!"

"Sire?" He looked pained and confused. "Pray you, be specific. I am no artist, and have erected no arches filled with cherubim. Nor have I painted Madonnas in strange landscapes."

"No, you have brought a travesty of a Madonna to *my* landscape!"

He looked blankly at me. What an actor!

"I mean the Lady Anne of Cleves! A Madonna—that is, a mother—she will never be, and the political reasons for the marriage are insufficient. Francis and Charles drift apart, like those March clouds, and my good coastal defence system will protect me better than an alliance with the Duchy of Cleves. It was a mistake, a ghastly mistake that robs me of the opportunity to happiness. So undo what you have so dexterously done!"

"I thought . . . that you were fond of the Lady . . . the Queen," he mumbled.

"I am fond of my hunting dogs and of the first lute I had as a boy. But that is not enough for a marriage!"

Instead of responding with abject obedience, he walked about the chamber a bit—though I had not given him permission!—and at length turned back to me, musing. (He acted as if he actually had a choice as to whether to obey or not. Why did he try me so?)

His eyes were narrowed. "It is Norfolk who has put you to this," he said coldly. "He seeks to use you for his purpose."

"No one uses me!" I bellowed. The fool! "Least of all *you!*"

He started; I continued. "Yes, *you!* All over the kingdom they say *you* use *me.* Use me for your own schemes. Protestant schemes. Now prove to me that they lie. Undo this insulting Protestant alliance you concocted for me, that you erected just like one of Leonardo's symbolic arches, all out of papier-mâché and paint. Tear it down. It is as insubstantial as a paper arch."

He looked grim. "Your Grace—"

"Do it! What has been done can be undone!"

In a heartbeat he accepted the challenge. "What provision shall be made for the Lady Anne?"

I waved my hand impatiently. "A manor—a palace—a royal income." Those were Cromwell's concerns. I stopped. Anne was dear to me in a peculiar way. I even loved her, but it was a singular sort of love.

"She shall be my sister," I said. "I will keep her and cherish her as if she were my dear lost Mary. I have no family," I said, almost in wonder. "I would like a sister."

"You must be more specific," he said dryly.

I sat down and the words came. "She shall be titled 'the King's sister.' She shall be given royal residences and . . . shall be my friend."

"A high honour." Did he mock me? I shot a look to his face. "One of which I am uncertain, of late."

"Oh, Crum." I laughed, but did not answer him. A deflection is no answer; it is not even a sop.

I knew deep inside that Crum was becoming dangerous, and had changed since first he came into my service. He had outlived his usefulness both to me and to England. There were signs—signs that even he could not hide: his obvious partiality toward the Protestants on the Continent, his strange leniency toward heretics and Reformers, his uncharacteristic reluctance to enforce "the Whip with Six Strings," and his determined maneuvering for the Cleves marriage.

Yet I hung on that human balance, liking the man, even while knowing he was bad. I lacked the courage to act on my intuition, to just . . . end Cromwell. Eliminate his presence from my government. Each time I would say to myself, "Next time—next time I'll do it—" and yet each time he would walk from my chamber a free man, enveloped in his customary power. Power that I must needs revoke. Next time.

So. Now it would be done. I had no doubt of that. I had frightened him, and a frightened Cromwell was a sure servant. He would untangle me from Anne. But I was pleased at my decision to offer her a place in my family. Of course, such a thing was unprecedented, but then, so was our entire relationship. If Cleves were as dull as it seemed to be, Anne would surely have no wish to return to it.

I felt a contentment fuller than any in years. I paced the chamber a bit, trying to understand why.

Of course. I was being given something few men were ever gifted with: an opportunity to relive my life and have it turn out differently. What was Anne of Cleves but a second Katherine of Aragon—a foreign princess to whom I could not be husband? Only this time, instead of wasting years seeking Papal sanction, I had but to say "Do it" to Cromwell—and it would be done. Instead of appealing to foreign rulers and clinging to her "rights" to me, Anne would co-operate, and we would remain friends.

And Catherine Howard! She was Anne Boleyn before she became hard and heartless and corrupted. By some great miracle (for who can understand God's mind?), I had been given a second chance.

That evening I was to dine with Anne, as I usually did on Thursday evenings; long, comfortable suppers before a hearty fire. I was not disappointed this time.

Anne greeted me affectionately at the door to her withdrawing chamber and pointed to a board set up before the open window, looking out on the summer twilight. My accustomed chair, well bedecked with velvet pillows, was drawn up.

"A new game?" I inquired. How she loved games!

"*Ja!*" She beamed. "It is call-ed 'Var.' " The board had a figure drawn upon it that was funnel-shaped—narrow at one end, wide at the other. To the side were grouped carved horses and men, and wooden coins of different colours.

"Pray explain."

"Ah, *ja*. Vell, it takes ze income from the monasteries, ze New Vorld, ze banks—vool produck-sion, all zose things, and zen buys men with zem, zat is, soldiers, and—zese nations var together."

It was an elaborate and intricate game, based on sources of income for ten countries, and their national goals. Depending on how money was channelled, the outcome could vary tremendously.

As the clock struck midnight I had England mired in a messy war with France, while the Emperor stood on the sidelines with Scotland, and the Pope amassed land wealth.

"Leave it set up!" I cautioned. "I wish to conclude this game, see it through to the end."

She laughed. "I am glad it pleasures you so."

"Where did you find it?"

"I made it up."

I was dumbfounded. "You? You created it?"

She was brilliant! A mathematician, a financier, a strategist. Oh, why was she a woman? Poor Wolsey. If only he had had one-third her grasp of these things.

"You are gifted, Princess. Would I could make you Chancellor of the Exchequer. Or War Minister."

"Und vhy not?" she asked blandly.

"Because you are the Queen," I replied. But will not be for long, I thought. And then, why not . . . ? No, impossible. But I would need *someone* to replace Cromwell. . . . No, absurd!

"Goodnight, sweetheart," I said quickly, nodding and kissing her hand. I walked down the corridor to my own apartments swiftly, lest I suddenly act on my own impulse. Beheading a Queen had not alarmed the populace as much as appointing one Finance Minister would.

❧ ☙

Within a fortnight Cromwell reported that all obstacles were cleared. The "cause" had been found: Anne's precontract with the Duke of Lorraine, but, more importantly, the lack of consummation.

"The *lack* of consummation, or my *inability* to consummate the marriage? Be clear, Crum!"

He shrugged. "Of course it would be more . . . persuasive . . . if you attested to your inability to consummate it. But 'twill serve as well if you present it as a matter of policy that you simply *chose* not to."

"It makes me sound as if my private parts wore the crown instead of my head." He looked over at me, and I could almost read his mind: In you, Sire, they *do.*

"First you made me a public cuckold with Anne, now you'll have me publicly impotent!" I grumbled.

"You said you wanted to be free! Is it my fault that freedom lies through a little play-acting of a personal nature?"

Play-acting? But Nan *was* an adulteress—a witch as well, of course, which is far worse and demands death, but an adulteress in the bargain. . . .

"A King should not be put in the position of public ridicule like that," I maintained.

"You open yourself up to much more ridicule if you try to ride the old 'precontract' horse again. Ride the 'inability' horse and you'll have the support and sympathy of every man in England. There's no one with cock and balls who hasn't suffered a similar attack at some time in his life. That much is certain."

"I am not to be like other men! A King is different—that is what it all rests on." That much was certain, too.

"It is not as if you had no children," he said. "And will have more," he added. "It was merely with a woman the Holy Spirit showed you was not a true wife." He made my selective failings sound moral and brave.

I grunted. Oh, what matter? I would say it and be done. They would laugh for a day, a week, but I should be free nonetheless, and able to wed my Catherine months sooner than going tortoise-like along the dignified precontract route. O my Catherine, see how I love you! I will suffer even this scorn and count it as nothing, just to possess you a week, a day, an hour sooner.

Anne was instructed to leave straightway for Richmond Palace—supposedly because of an outbreak of plague in London. She was told that I would join her shortly. Once she was away, I was at leisure to pull out the long marriage contract with the Duchy of Cleves and spread it on a permanent surface where I could consult it whenever the fancy struck me.

I could invite Catherine to my private apartments without circumspection. I could take her out to Nonsuch and bid her select furnishings for the Queen's apartments.

"They are not yet complete," I said, "and will be decorated entirely to your taste."

She giggled a little. "I know not how to furnish a palace."

"This palace, my love, is a pleasure-seat. It is to reflect entirely our tastes and desires. As such, there is no model—just as there is no one quite like either of us."

"I have no . . . formed tastes." How lovely she appeared as she said this.

"But you have desires!" I reached across and encircled her with my arm, reeling her in and close to me.

Yes, desires. I knew she must pulsate with them. Although her entire bearing was graceful and maidenly, somehow I sensed—perhaps it was her plump fingers, unexpectedly moist; or the way sweat formed a little bird's wing between her shoulder blades when she walked but a little way—that she was a creature of passion. I had but to awaken it. And I would, I would. . . . Before the Michaelmas goose was slaughtered, by God, I'd be churning her into a passion like a choppy sea before a rough wind.

"Aye." She smoothed her hands over her straining bodice. The satin rearranged itself in shining folds all encircling her breasts and accentuating them. O ice-blue satin!—how can you promise such passion? "Desires I hope will find favour and mercy in your sight, Your Majesty."

"Mercy? Nay, I'll give you no mercy!" I chuckled. No mercy until I lay sated on soaked sheets. No mercy until daylight besmirched our chamber. Dirty day! With its ugly peeping eye and neat divisions.

I whispered in her ear. "Come to my bedchamber tonight."

I felt muscles stirring and resistance flowing through her. "Nay. *Nay!*"

So. She was set upon virtue, and would yield her lock only to the key of a marriage rite. So be it. For that she should have, and speedily.

But, oh! How to endure this night? It was as though *I* were but nineteen, and *she* forty-nine. Her chastity made her at one with the oldest woman in farthest Scotland. Unawakened is the same thing as played out.

"I shall groan all through the hours," I said, half-groaning even then.

"I would not be a man, then." She smiled.

Women groan from desire, too, I thought. You shall see.

Instead I smiled. "Good night, sweetheart," I said, unwittingly giving the same farewell that I gave Anne every evening. What else was there to say to an untouched bride?

Cromwell I gave instructions to.

"You have prepared a statement for the Princess of Cleves to sign?" I asked.

"Yes, Your Majesty. It is all set down here, as best I understood your desires." He produced a short document.

"If it said what the true nature of the complaint is, it would be even shorter." The parchment said it, said something—what matter, as long as the game was ended? I laid it down.

"There is another matter, Your Majesty," said Cromwell happily. "A matter pertaining to money." He looked as if he expected me to salivate. Was I perceived as that simple, then? And that greedy?

"In the monastic suppressions, we overlooked one order. The Knights of St. John of Jerusalem."

Ah, yes. The militant order of monks, the sword-arm of Christ. They had formed originally to protect defenceless pilgrims to Jerusalem. They had fought the Infidel and set up hospices all along the pilgrim routes. As always, competence and filling a need where no services existed had made them powerful and then wealthy. Today the order held land and privilege all over Europe. They were true knights, though, in the purest sense of the word. And their name stood for strength, honesty, compassion.

". . . a profit of ten thousand pounds," Cromwell was saying.

"But who will take their place?"

He smiled crookedly. "No one. Because they are not needed today."

"Charity and protection, not needed?"

"Not en route to Jerusalem. Perhaps in other guises, at other stations."

"But with no formal organization?"

"The Knights did not begin as a formal organization. They began with one man's courage and charity. Other men of vision will see the needs today."

I sighed. I was reluctant to sign, as if by signing I would at long last kill something lingering in myself.

"I shall leave it here for you," Cromwell said at length, placing it firmly on top of a stack of lesser documents for my attention, things pertaining to rent-leases in Kent and shipping regulations for Alicante wine.

After he had left me alone, I reread the first parchment carefully. It stated, succinctly and reasonably, why the marriage to Anne was no marriage. It outlined the privileges Anne was to acquire upon becoming "the King's most entirely beloved sister." She would take precedence over all women of the realm, with the exception of my Queen (who was left unspecified) and my daughters. She would be granted a large annual income of about five thousand pounds, and two royal manors, Richmond and Bletchingly.

In exchange, she had merely to sign and acknowledge that we were in agreement on this. Then she had to write her brother and forestall any notions he might have of "avenging her honour." She must assure him that her honour was in no wise threatened and that she and I were in perfect harmony on this matter.

Attached to the document was an envelope containing a terse statement by Cromwell: "It will doubtless be necessary for the King's Majesty to speak personally to selected members of the Court and the foreign ambassadors on this matter, viz, to wit: 'The marriage between the Princess of Cleves and myself has never been consummated, due to our inner conviction that this was no true marriage. The Holy Spirit, the Spirit of Truth and Wisdom, communicated itself to us unmistakably, and we obeyed.' "

How neat and vague and high-minded. But what if questions were asked? Must a King open himself so personally to public knowledge? How much would people demand, and how far was I bound to answer?

I found I could not sign the paper. I would have to search the matter out more fully with Cromwell in the morning.

XCI

That night I could not sleep. And pacing my work room (lest I wake the slumbering Culpepper) I spied Cromwell's lights still burning in his court chambers. He was reputed never to sleep, and now I confirmed the rumour. The great astronomical clock in the gatehouse was striking three as I crossed the inner courtyard to his quarters.

Pushing open his door, I found his immediate receiving room deserted and dark. The lights were farther within. I traversed the distance, drawn on like an insect toward a torch.

A noise inside. Cromwell had heard me.

"Who's there?" he asked in a tremulous voice, not at all his own. "Who's there?"

"The King."

There was a scurrying, and then a wild-eyed Cromwell in a silk night-cover came forth.

"I saw that you were up," I muttered, "and fain would talk to you again about the 'statement' you say I must give, before others are about to overhear us."

"Of course." His eyes darted round nervously. "Of course." He gestured toward his work room beyond, and I entered it.

Two candles were burning on his work desk. It was a large, flat surface made up of a door from one of the suppressed monasteries, laid across two carved capitals. Evidently he took glee in working on the corpse of monasticism, so to speak.

"From whence came these articles?" I asked, as much to gain time as anything else. I wanted an opportunity to look round the room and spy out what he kept about him. I wanted to know, at last, what Cromwell was.

"From St. Mary's, Your Grace. The first monastic house we suppressed." He looked fondly at the spoils.

I nodded. "Sentimental value."

Over in a far corner I saw a stack of books. Of what sort? It was a pity that heresy did not demand the visible props of Popery. No statues, no rosaries, no Reserved Hosts. Just malice in the heart.

"Aye." He had composed himself now, was ready to meet any scrutiny. "There was a matter troubling Your Grace?" he asked.

"The 'statement' regarding the Princess of Cleves. There is something in me which dislikes to sign it."

"In what manner does it offend your sensibilities? I can amend—"

"I know not *how,* precisely. But it disturbs my conscience." What disturbed my conscience, truly, was the putting away of a good woman for no other fault than not exciting me.

"It need not be done at all!" he said merrily. "Perhaps these pricklings of conscience are showing you another way, the most righteous way!"

Any chance that his handiwork would survive elated him. But it could not be.

"Nay, it must be done. It is necessary for the realm that I have a true Queen and perhaps other heirs. It would give Edward comfort, too, not to carry the burden alone."

Cromwell nodded, as he had to; wondering if a new Queen on the throne would represent all manner of connections he had sought to quash.

I turned quickly and swung round to glance at the parchments spread out on his work-surface. They were innocent enough, or seemed to be. One never knew. They might contain codes; I knew he had devised some. To disguise his plans?

I then let my eyes search his chamber. The light was so poor it was difficult to see into the far corners. I thought I saw a shelf laden with odd-shaped vessels. Abruptly I made my way to it, taking one of the candles with me. Behind me I could hear Cromwell following anxiously.

Yes, it was a row of jars and bottles and little boxes. Some were evidently quite ancient; I could tell by the worm-eaten wood.

"What *are* these things?" I asked. I reached out and took one, a rounded container with a hinged lid. Inside was some sort of ointment. I took a smear of it. It smelt vile, like a decaying animal.

"I said, what is in these containers?" I repeated. How dare he not answer forthwith?

"I—it is—medicines seized from the monastic infirmaries," he finally said. "That one you hold—it was used to help failing hearts . . . you remember . . . as Carew had, that time in the cave—"

Carew. Yes. Unfortunately, his heart had finally ceased to beat due to his treason, not to his disease. But for others who had the same affliction . . . ?

"Is it efficacious?"

"Indeed! It saved many lives; the monks of that abbey were noted for that particular cure."

"Why, then, have you not made it available to our own physicians?"

"The monks—it would reflect well on them if it were known that they had devised such cures. No, I prefer—"

"You prefer to hoard these medicines here! You prefer men to die rather than think well of the monks!"

"It is *necessary* to discredit the monks!" he insisted.

"Necessary for whom, Cromwell?" I murmured.

The clock outside struck the half hour. I used listening to the clock as a pretext to approach the window-seat laden with the mysterious books.

"Ah, yes," I mumbled, opening the casement. I stuck my head out and rested my left hand on the sill, quite naturally, and the right on—"Hallo, what's this?" as the pile slipped out from under my pushing hand.

Muffling a curse, Crum came forward, gathering up the books. Suddenly a spitting and hissing from under the window-seat gave way to an angry cat. A black cat. The animal glared at me with fiendish eyes, red by candlelight, but seemingly with a luminosity all their own, an unearthly glow. I felt my skin go hot and cold.

Still, I forced myself to pluck one of the books from the pile. I opened it casually.

Thomas Münzer's letters, edited by Luther. Münzer—the Anabaptist rebel who preached open revolt against princes and led the Peasants' Revolt in Germany in 1524! An heretical book—one of the worst in existence.

I threw it down and took another. Melanchthon's treatise, denouncing me as Nero and wishing that God would put it into the mind of some bold man to assassinate me. This had been printed in Zurich and smuggled into England.

"Crum," I whispered.

"These are all seized from known heretics, Your Grace, and held as evidence pending their trials," he said smoothly and smugly. "By your own reaction, it is clear how very condemning they are. Any man possessing such filth *must* perforce be a heretic. Is it not so?"

"They contaminate your chamber, Cromwell—being kept here so close to your person," I finally said.

These were not "heretical" texts, like the standard ones by Zwingli, Calvin, and Luther. They were calls to revolution by Devil-possessed men. No one would possess such textbooks of insurrection unless he were plotting one himself.

He shrugged. "Unfortunately I must keep them within sight at all times, guarding them. Think you not how quickly they would disappear else?" He laughed, a mirthless laugh. "It's worth a man's life to destroy this evidence. And a man fighting for his life is given strength by the Evil One himself."

Or given clever answers by him, I thought. Satan protects his own.

I knew now what I needed to know. I offered a silent prayer to Christ for showing me these signs, for opening my eyes. But, oh! my heart was heavy as I bade Cromwell a good night. How I wished he had turned out to be something other than what he truly was: the most capable minister a King had ever been granted—seduced and corrupted by heresy and the desire for power.

What few hours remained before dawn I passed in a state of strange consciousness, waiting as the room passed from darkness into a blue fog. At last there was stirring in the outer chamber: the rustling sounds of water being heated, clothes being laid out and brushed, men stretching.

I swung my legs over the side of the bed, acting the part of a sleepy man forcing himself to stir. I groaned and muttered and rubbed my eyes—then recoiled. The odour from the confiscated monastic salve still clung to my hands, like a living thing.

"Water!" I called. "Water!"

The Groom of the Bedchamber appeared, with a silver pitcher of heated, perfumed water and a mound of fatted, herbed soap. So anxious was I to rid myself of the taint of Cromwell's vindictiveness that I skipped the ritual attached to my morning ablutions and plunged my hands straightway into the water, scrubbing them furiously myself rather than submitting to the usual gentle ministrations with cuticle-stick and sponge. Again and again I washed my hands, until the clear scented water grew scummy and my hands were raw. There, now they should be clean! I held them out to receive a coat of perfumed lotion.

∽❧ ❧∽

I called for a Privy Council meeting in mid-morning. I wanted to give them their assignments, make my humiliating "confession," and have done with it. By this time tomorrow, I kept reminding myself, it would all be over.

I sat alone in the chamber, awaiting them. I was all attired in sombre garments, befitting a less than joyous occasion. Brandon and Wyatt would carry the message to Anne, I had decided. As for the horrible acknowledgment—the entire Privy Council would have to hear it, to make it both official and binding.

The first man into the chamber was William Paget. Stolid and utterly colourless and reliable, he was Secretary of the Council. He coughed and bowed deeply to me, then quietly took his place and awaited the others.

Within three minutes William Petre arrived, clad likewise in colourless, drab attire. On his heels came Audley and Sadler. As they took their places, I could not help but think of wrens and poor winter birds sitting in dreary tiers on bare December branches.

Then came the Old Men, all resplendent in luscious colours and sumptuous fabrics. Norfolk, of course, as ranking peer of England, draped in velvet;

Suffolk, in cloth-of-gold; even Gardiner, as Bishop of Winchester and leader of the churchly traditionalists, along with Wriothesley his hanger-on, were brightly attired.

At length the filing-in was complete and they all sat, obedient to the day's business. As the King never personally attended Privy Council meetings, they knew this was no ordinary agenda.

I rose. "My good Council and servants"—I stressed "good" and "servants" —"I am here to share with you a secret matter of mine own heart."

They looked uneasy.

"Yea"—I pulled the prepared statement from its cover—"I, having contracted a marriage in good faith and having participated in a marriage ceremony with all good intentions, find now that my marriage is no true marriage in the eyes of God and the laws of men."

I looked up at their faces. They appeared frozen. Good.

"The Lady Anne of Cleves was not free to make such a marriage, so it seems. There was precontract, from childhood, to the present-day Duke of Lorraine. This evidently is binding in every way."

Now for the difficult part. God, how I hated it!

"Our bodies, in recognition of this, refused to join. We have remained chaste, and have not known one another."

The Earl of Southampton tittered. Then the others followed suit, trying all the while to suppress their mirth. The more they stifled it, the more it grew.

Damn them! ·

"So you wish to know the exact details?" I said sharply. Such a hush fell over them that a man scarce would have credited it. "Very well, then!" *Do not do this,* one part of me said. *Yes, do!* another taunted. *Outdo them in vulgarity and embarrassment.* "When I first came to the bed of the Lady Anne, I felt by her breasts that she was no young maid; their slackness, and the looseness of her belly-flesh, so struck me to the heart that I had neither will nor courage to try the rest."

It was more than they had reckoned for, more than they cared to know.

"And so I have received a Sign, and so has she," I concluded calmly. I dealt out two sets of parchments, one with my left hand, one with my right.

"These papers here"— I tapped gently on the ones resting beneath my left hand—"are to be delivered to the Lady Anne, who is even now at Richmond. They outline the settlement I wish to make her. After all, she is a foreigner here in our realm, and doubtless frightened. The terms are most generous, gentlemen." I outlined them: the rank, the privileges, the income. "I appoint you, Brandon, and you, Wyatt, to deliver these to her this very day."

Before they could look uneasy, I grasped the pile under my right hand. "These are ecclesiastical matters," I explained. "They should be submitted to

Convocation and approved there. Naturally the Church of England will declare the marriage null, and free us both to marry again." I nodded to Cranmer, and he came to fetch the papers. Oh, how very different from the days of Wolsey and the legatine court and Campeggio and the decretal commission. How clean and simple it was now. By sundown it would all be done!

They shuffled out, some of them lingering ever so slightly in case I wanted to consult with them and amplify what I had just said. Amplify? I had said more than I had ever wished to, more than any sane man would wish to.

It was all for Catherine, I thought. For Catherine I had debased myself so, opened myself up to ridicule and speculation. Yet love was a cruel and insane master. I had felt that I had no choice, and even as I burned with shame, I offered it up as a gift to her, perfect proof of my devotion.

XCII

Now there was nothing before me but to wait while Brandon and Wyatt carried the message. Only a few hours until it was concluded—the King's Great Matter this time tamed and turned into only a Small Matter.

I laid down my cloak of state (which I had had to wear in addressing my Council) and felt free in my linen shirt. It was June, and already the sun was high and the air warm. I knew I would be incapable of remaining indoors and attending to state papers and correspondence, although they called to be answered. I would take a turn about the gardens here at Hampton. Wolsey had once been interested in gardening to the extent that he had hired a horticulturist; Anne (the cursed one) had planted beds of bulbs that long spring when she waited at Hampton and I could not bring myself to join her, so revolted was I by her presence. By rights Hampton should have magnificent gardens by now. Today I would inspect them.

I left the royal apartments by the stair-door, and soon found myself in the formal area near the Great Maze. Mazes were expected, required. Every formal garden had to have a maze, so that lads and lasses could spend at least a quarter of an hour getting lost in them, hunting for the end (which gave them a topic of conversation), and then doing their business unobserved. I would have none of mazes today. I nodded to the maze-keeper and his attendant and struck out toward the south side of the Hampton grounds, where great vistas were laid out.

Close to the palace itself was a sunken garden, surrounded by a brick wall. I had seen the wall itself many times from my gallery, but never really inspected what lay inside. That it caught the sun I knew, and that was all.

Now I entered into its secret place, and was dazzled. Along their tidy beds, roses bloomed with such heavy loads of flowers on their stems that it seemed the branches might break for colour, weight, profusion. The south and west exposure of the walls were one mass of climbing roses, so that each brick had some twenty blooms spread out upon it. Taken all together, in a glance, they were "rose"—that is, the sweet blush somewhere between red and white. As my eye took them all in at once, suddenly "rosiness" ceased to be an adjective and became instead a sensual experience.

Loth to spoil the spell, I walked out into the midst of them. Now that I was closer I could see the slight variations: how one was stark white and another more dusky. How even the thorns varied. Some were triangular, with an exuberant crest and hook; others were straight-sided, as if their hearts really were not in the business of tearing flesh. The climbers, I saw as I approached them by the southern wall, had the most tamed thorns of all. I touched one carefully and found it to be soft. I could also feel the heat radiating from the south-facing bricks. Here it was as warm as the lands of the Infidels—where, legend had it, the rose had originated.

An old gardener was crouched down between the bushes, applying dung to their roots from a leather bucket he carried with him. As I approached him, I saw that the beds of roses subtly changed colour, and varied from pure red to a gentler pearly shade. The three bushes where the man laboured bore faint yellowish tinges in the flowers' hearts, though the outer petals were glowing red.

"Master gardener!" I called. Slowly he stood upright. He was ancient. His face was so wizened and wrinkled it was difficult to see the eyes, and a great hat shaded his entire face. But his hearing was evidently in order.

"Eh?"

"Is this garden your special charge?"

"Aye. For twenty years." He gestured toward the wall of climbers. "I started these when they were but small shoots. One came from Jerusalem. The red one. We call it 'Saviour's Blood.'"

"Tell me," I asked, "the colours of roses. Are they but red and white?"

He hitched up his pantaloons and strode out of the plants. "In the wild, yes. But in gardens one can cross them, modify the colours somewhat. But we cannot get two colours on one flower, no, alas." He was thinking I had come to chide him about producing a perfect "Tudor rose" like the ones in carvings, which had red petals on the outside, white inside.

"But these"— I grasped the perfect flower with the hint of yellow in its heart—"could you produce a yellow bloom, eventually, from this?"

He shrugged. "I am trying. That has been my project for nigh on a decade. But always the red outer petals reappear! Once I thought I was nearly there. I will show you. I pressed it. The petals were all yellow, with red streaks only on the very outer petals. But the next season!" He looked disgusted. "It reverted back to red."

He motioned me over to his round, thatched gardener's hut in one corner of the walled garden. He disappeared inside for a moment, then reappeared with a flat, dried flower resting on a piece of parchment.

"My yellow rose," he said with a melancholy look. Indeed it had been nearly gold. What a shame! "Aye." I commiserated with him. "I can see how close you came."

Inside the cottage I saw row upon row of pots and planks laid out with cuttings. "May I?"

He nodded, and I stepped inside. The man had as many cuttings and seedlings as I had state papers waiting my attention. Inside this hut he was monarch and I but a curiosity-seeker, a petitioner.

"Could you develop a rose without thorns?" I suddenly asked. "If you can vary the colour, can you not vary the stalks, the stems, the leaves, and other attributes, including thorns?"

He shook his head. "The thorns seem to be a part of it all, Your Grace. They are always there. Some green, some brown, some sharper than others; but for every stem there must needs be thorns, in my experience."

"Could you breed a bush with negligible thorns, do you think?"

"I never tried."

"But *if* you tried?" Oh, this was the thickness of common folk. Also their protection.

"Try, then!" I said. "I would make it well worth your while to develop such a bush. A rose without a thorn." I came closer to him, fixed his eyes. "It has meaning for me. I need your help!"

"I can try, Your Majesty."

"How long would it take?"

He looked alarmed. "I do not know. I cannot guess. I thought I had a yellow rose"—he nodded again toward the preserved one—"but it disappointed me."

"Aye." I turned away and let up on my stare.

"And then there's winter. All those months when all one can do is wait." Winter. Waiting. Oh, I knew it well.

"Do your best," I said. "Eventually all things yield before a man's best."

I stepped out of the rose-cottage, and once again into the bright sunlight. Brandon must be at Richmond by now; Anne would be reading the terms.

"Until then, take this," he said, handing me a small clay pot with a newly planted cutting in it. Thanks to the old man's expertise and the rich new soil, a bud had opened already. I touched its stem and guided it near to my nostrils. But it was not the sweet rose scent I smelled. The stench from Cromwell's hoarded salve still clung to my fingers, even after all that scrubbing, all these hours.

"Oh!" I jerked my hand away so quickly that the pot fell, shattering. "I—"

Now the old man was offended. He bent down and began gathering up the pieces. But he would still develop my rose without a thorn. He must. I had commanded him.

"Forgive me," I said. "It was an accident." Wiping my hands on my handkerchief, I hurried away.

The stench. The stench of Cromwell's meanness. He befouled even this day. Striding into the hateful indoors, I called for Culpepper. He was nowhere to be seen. Well, then a page would have to do. I must see Cranmer and straightway tell him of what had happened last night. The roses were forgotten.

Cranmer had never left the palace to return to Lambeth after the Privy Council meeting, the page informed me. Instead he had busied himself discussing Biblical translations and theology with the high-ranking clergy on hand for my announcement. Imagine his surprise when I burst in upon him where he sat at a polished oaken table with his fellow churchmen. Spread out before them were all the English translations of Scripture available: the Venerable Bede's, and the heretical Wycliffe's and Tyndale's, as well as Coverdale's and Matthew's. The Holy Word of God was splayed out before them like a man on the rack.

"Gentlemen," I said, striding into the room and making a gesture of respect toward the Holy Scriptures. The prelates all stood upright, spilling some of the contents of their laps. "I am gratified to find you toiling over the Word of God on such a fine June day. Our Lord will surely give you a heavenly reward for that." I smiled. No one smiled back. They feared I tested them.

"It sorrows me to have to borrow the Archbishop of Canterbury for a time," I said, gesturing toward Cranmer. "I shall return him, I promise."

"You may carry on," he said. "Please do sort out the various words for 'angel' used in the Resurrection texts. I would be most grateful." Still they did not smile.

"Come, Thomas," I muttered, putting my arm around his shoulders. I steered him from the room. Around the corner I let him loose. "I apologize," I said. "But these are grievous matters."

Still he shook his head like one awakened untimely from a dream, until I spoke plainly once we had reached the safety of my withdrawing room. Oh, that little oak-panelled room, how well I knew every tree-ring and wrinkle on its walls! How I longed to settle business elsewhere—but nowhere else was safe, and free from Crum's spies.

"Thomas, Cromwell's a traitor. And in league with the heretics."

The tall, calm churchman, with his pale eyes, did not respond.

"I tell you, last night I had the proof!" I told him of all my growing doubts, my fears, apprehensions, intuitions, reports, and finally of the treasonous texts themselves. Still Cranmer stood there like a statue from ancient Rome, with all the drapery of justice and his office cloaking him in a mantle of sense and reason.

"An Anabaptist insurrectionist amongst us!" he finally said.

"Exactly. He has been in league with them since I know not when." (Was it back when he had made me the sherbet? Oh, surely not then! We were friends then.) "And through him they seek power over my realm."

Cranmer was near weeping. "I trusted him, Your Grace. You trusted him. I believed the love of God and of Christ to be truly in him. Oh, dear my Lord, if you cannot trust him, I wot not whom you may trust hereafter."

Those were divinely inspired words, but at the time I heeded them not, so agitated was I, and bound to eliminate Cromwell.

On high treason he'd be arrested, yea . . . as soon as this interminable day came to an end. As soon as the complicated business with Cleves was out of the way—if Anne agreed, and wrote her brother as I'd instructed—then there would be no further administrative need for Cromwell.

The heat of the day broke and even twilight was ebbing before my two matrimonial ambassadors reappeared. They were dust-covered and looked weary. But not afraid. That was good. That meant they had not failed in their assignment. Somewhere in the welter of rolls they carried on their persons (and it seemed they had more than a stag had antlers, so did they protrude all over) were the signature and seal I craved.

"Well?" I rose from my chair.

"She agreed, Your Grace," sighed Brandon, pulling out the one paper that mattered and handing it to me.

I grasped it and let my eyes run like a leaping child to find the requisite signature, down far at the bottom: *Anna, Princess of Cleves.*

"Christ be praised!" I muttered.

Only then did I think to offer them stools to sit upon, and some nourishment. It had been a gruelling day for them as well as for me. Gratefully they seated themselves and held out their dusty hands for bowls of water to wash them. A page performed the duty.

"The Queen—Lady Anne—had a hard time of it," spoke Wyatt in a hushed voice, as his hands were being dried.

It was to be expected. After all, she loved me, and had assumed she would remain Queen of England forever. "Yes, I pity her," I said. And I did. I knew what it was to suffer unrequited love, or to be deprived of a station in life to which one felt called.

"She fainted when she saw us appear round the hedge to her garden," said Brandon.

Fainted? Could it be? No, absurd! She was no Virgin Mary, to bring forth without knowing a man. Where had my fancies taken me? She had done it out of love, out of desperate love.

"Poor lady," I murmured.

"She thought we had come with her death warrant," continued Brandon. "She thought to be arrested, tried, and then executed."

I chuckled contemptuously.

"She was clear frightened, Your Grace. You had shown your disfavour and lack of consent from the start, then sent her away without you. She is no fool. I am sure she is well acquainted with the course of behaviour you took with Anne Boleyn. The withdrawal, the disfavour—all was being repeated."

"Save that she had no lovers!" I shrieked, turning round. "Save that she was no witch! Save that she did not plan my death! Small differences, would you not agree?"

"Aye, aye," murmured Wyatt.

"By all that's in heaven, yea," echoed Brandon. "She revived promptly," he added.

Her strong constitution would see to that, yes.

"She seemed delighted with the agreement, and the terms. In half an hour she changed into the gayest maiden I had beheld in a season."

Gay? Delighted? To lose me as a husband? I remembered Katherine's agony, her insistence on keeping me as her spouse.

"She sent you this token." Brandon took out a velvet pouch and produced her gold wedding band.

"Well, well," was all I could say. Anne had agreed. I had won.

I gestured toward the darkened window. "Tomorrow I'll send flowers from Hampton's gardens," I promised.

"There are lovely gardens at Richmond," said Brandon. "Her own gardens now." He cocked an eyebrow. He knew me well. But must he be so smug?

I shrugged. "The gesture is all."

It was true. Anne had indeed acquiesced, and was content to style herself my dearly beloved sister. The next day she sent *me* flowers, and thus I lost a wife and acquired a sister. Along with the masses of daisies, irises, and lilies she sent, was the letter to her brother, the Duke of Cleves, for which she sought approval before sending.

My Dear and Well-Beloved Brother,

After my most hearty commendation: Whereas, my most dear and most kind brother, lest you take the matter lately moved and determined between the King's Majesty of England and myself somewhat to heart, I had rather ye know the truth by mine advertisement, than for want thereof, ye should be deceived by vain reports. Thus I thought meet to write this present letter to you; by the which it shall please you to understand, how the Nobles and Commons of this realm desired the King's Highness to commit the examination of the matter of the marriage between His Majesty and me to the determination of the Holy Clergy of this realm.

I did then willingly consent thereto; and since their determination made, have also, upon intimation of their proceedings, allowed, approved, and agreed to the same. God willing, I purpose to lead my life in this realm.

Anna, Duchess of Cleves, born of Cleves, Gulick, Geldre, and Berg, and your loving sister.

There. That should persuade him to stay his hand. I changed "willingly" to "gladly," inserted a disclaimer above "intimation."

But it was well done. Oh, Anne pleased me!

And now there was the other ugly matter. The disposal and destruction of Cromwell, lately my servant, but now, it seemed, the heretics'.

He was arrested, upon my orders, as he took his seat at the Privy Council. Earlier that day, as he was walking to the Council chamber, a high breeze had blown his velvet hat off. As he was the ranking man in the group of councillors, by all tradition they should not have kept their heads covered in his presence when he was bareheaded. They should have yanked their caps off in deference. But they did not.

Thus it was that Cromwell knew. "A high wind it must be," he said in a loud, clear voice, "to leave me uncovered and you with all your bonnets on." They bowed and kept silent, enclosing him as he walked, grimly now, toward the Privy Council chamber.

Once he was inside, the Duke of Norfolk approached him, as he had long rehearsed in his mind to do.

"My Lord Cromwell, I arrest you on the King's orders, of high treason."

Then Cromwell fought, and all his composure left him. He flung off the two serjeants-at-arms assigned to escort him to the Tower. He screamed and began flailing. Four Yeomen of the Guard were required to subdue him.

I shuddered at the telling of it.

"He seemed possessed," stammered Cranmer. His shaken manner annoyed me. The highest churchman of England, flinching before a manifestation of the Evil One? How, then, could ordinary men look to him for strength and protection?

"He knew he had failed in his secret mission," I explained to Cranmer. Still, he had almost managed to throw off my men. "And Satan will give him eloquent words in the Tower, we can be sure of that. The only defence is not to read the honeying, lying, beguiling letters. Mark you, he will send them to us both. Destroy them without opening them."

Cranmer continued to pace my chamber, like a sleepwalker. "The people rejoice," he finally said.

"Aye, and well they should." I remembered how one of the issues of the Pilgrimage of Grace was that Cromwell be removed. They had, perhaps, been guided by the Holy Spirit after all. In some things. Not all.

I walked over to Cranmer and put my hand on his shoulder. He resisted for an instant. "In the war of Light and Darkness there is much bloodshed," I said, seeking to comfort him. Still he kept gazing blankly out at the country-side, as though he expected to see a mass of Pilgrims reappear.

"You have studied the Cleves documents?" I inquired.

"Aye, Your Grace. And signed them. The Church finds that, as you and she confessed, there was no marriage at all. By the highest authorities, in union with Your Majesty, the King is a bachelor and his sister a spinster, and both free to marry." (He wisely did not say "again.") "The realm so desires you to be married," he continued, "that at the same time, Parliament will petition you to wed. For the good of the realm and the happiness of your subjects."

O sweet Parliament! To enjoin me to do what I longed for above all else!

Two days later the request was made: the people begged "King Henry to frame his most noble heart to love a noble personage by whom His Majesty might have some more store of fruit and succession to the comfort of his realm."

The Bill of Attainder against Cromwell described him as "a most false and corrupt traitor, deceiver, and circumventor" against the King, and charged him with heresy and treason. He was accused of many things, but the most heinous was that he was a "detestable heretic who had spread heretical literature, licenced heretics to preach, released them from prison, and had been heard to say (so, others had known of his heresy, and merely feared to come forward and expose him!) that the Lutheran Robert Barnes—condemned to be burnt for heresy—taught truth, and that even if the King turned his back on it, "yet I would not turn, and if the King did turn, and all his people, I would fight in this field in mine own person, with my sword in my hand against him and all other."

In addition, when the nobles had recently mentioned his humble birth, he reportedly threatened, "If the Lords will handle me so, I will give them such a breakfast as never was made in England, and that the proudest should know" —proof that he had the secret power to take control of the government, if he could command such forces against Norfolk and the others.

Cromwell was executed for high treason on July twenty-eighth, 1540. As I had foreseen, he sent many letters from his cell in the Tower. I am sure they were persuasive as only the Devil can make them, imparting magic to ordinary words. I dared not read them, but let matters proceed on their own course. It was his own laws, in the end, that killed Cromwell. It was he who had introduced the novelties of holding prisoners without legal counsel; arrest without an opportunity to speak; attainder without legal condemnation; execution without benefit of trial. The harshness that he had visited on others now ensnared him.

As a commoner, he was not given the privilege of execution in the privacy of the Tower green, nor of the aristocratic scaffold and the imported swordsman from France.

WILL:

Although Henry did not read Cromwell's letters, for some odd reason of his own he kept one, unopened, along with his journal. Here is what the condemned, wretched man wrote his master. Ironic that we should be the only ones to read it, long after the fact.

Mine accusers Your Grace knoweth. God forgive them. For as I ever had love to your honour, person, life, prosperity, health, wealth, joy, and comfort, and also your most dear and most entirely beloved son, the Prince His Grace, and your proceedings, God so help me in this mine adversity, and confound me if ever I thought the contrary. What labours, pains, and travails I have taken according to my most bounden duty, God also knoweth. For if it were in my power—as it is in God's—to make Your Majesty to live ever young and prosperous, God knoweth I would. If it had been or were in my power to make you so rich as you might enrich all men, God help me, I would do it. If it had been or were in my power to make Your Majesty so puissant as all the world should be compelled to obey you, Christ knoweth I would. Sire, as to your commonwealth, I have ever after my wit, power, and knowledge travailed therein, having had no respect to persons (Your Majesty only excepted). But that I have done any injustice or wrong wilfully, I trust God shall be my witness, and the world not able justly to accuse me. I cry for mercy, mercy, mercy!

He did not receive it. He was executed, and by a particularly inept headsman. The man kept missing his aim, so that it took several strokes finally to sever Cromwell's head.

The rumours among the people as to Cromwell's downfall were

quite fanciful; for example, that Cromwell had amassed great stores of men and arms, with fifteen hundred men wearing a Cromwellian livery, in order either to marry the Lady Mary or to make himself King; that he had been heavily bribed by the Protestants to arrange the Cleves marriage; that he had boasted that the Emperor was going to award him a crown for his "services." (In making England Protestant?)

✒ HENRY VIII:

A large crowd of his own sort gathered to watch him die. It is a curious fact that they tend to be more bloodthirsty for the punishment of a fellow lowborn who has passed into higher echelons than for that of the nobility upon whose territory he has supposedly encroached. The elevation offends their sensibilities in some basic way. So they cheered loudly (I am told) when Cromwell's head leapt from his shoulders and landed in the hay.

I shuddered when I heard the cannon and knew it done. Had the demon within him perished at that moment? Or did it but seek a new home, and would it wander about till it found a willing host?

Catherine and I were married that day, that very afternoon. It was not intended so, but so it happened. Was it an omen? I tried not to think so, as coincidence had brought about the exact hour on which our nuptials would be performed, but I could not put away the thought of that homeless malevolent spirit, restless without Cromwell's body to inhabit. . . .

XCIII

We became husband and wife at four in the long summer afternoon at Oatlands, a royal manor house in Weybridge, about fifteen miles from London. The ceremony was entirely private, in contrast to that gaudy mistake with Anne of Cleves. There I had been publicly married as a King to a Princess I did not love; now I would be clandestinely married as a man to a woman I adored. Lest anyone say that once before I had had a brief, secret ceremony to a woman I "adored," let me remind him of the differences. I married Anne Boleyn illicitly with a reluctant priest, with none of my family present and in fear and haste. My so-called former wife refused to recognize me as a bachelor, and threatened dire things if I attempted to marry again.

But now the proper dispensation had been granted by the Church of England, acting in Convocation; a bishop performed the ceremony. My former "spouse" sent her good wishes, and all my children attended the ceremony in the Privy Chamber that hot afternoon. True, the Lady Mary was distant, but only because Catherine was some three years younger than she. She could not understand how I could wive someone almost thirty years younger than myself. It is something that maiden women, who wot not what passes between a man and a woman in the dark, do not, cannot, understand. Some day Mary would comprehend—and forgive.

The Lady Elizabeth, however, was pleased to be present, as Catherine was her cousin, and the child needed friends and relatives in a friendless world. She seemed to respond as though she had once again stepped into the warmth of a family, and shyly handed Catherine a carefully arranged bouquet of summer field-flowers.

The chamber windows were wide open and gave out onto the July fields of rye and barley, stretching golden and lazy. All was at its peak, and the harvest would prove worth all that had gone into its making. So I felt, as if the harvest of my life were now pending, and all that had run before (the cold winter of my boyhood; the early spring of my accession—hard, cold, forced before I was ready—the strife and clearing and burning and plowing in England ever since) were fields cleared at last, fertile and calm, ready for this.

"With this ring I thee wed, with my body I thee worship, and with all my worldly goods I thee endow: in the name of the Father, and of the Son, and of the Holy Ghost, amen." I slid the ring onto Catherine's finger, pushing it up slowly, feeling the delicate folds of flesh yielding until the gold reached its limit and stuck there. Waves of heat spread up from my loins as I traced that ring's journey with my finger. "No other will but his" was engraved on its inner circle, and oh! I knew what that will was. It was pure carnality, hallowed now by the Bishop of Winchester and his words. Miraculous words, to turn lust into a Sacrament.

"The Lord mercifully with his favour look upon you: and so fill you with all spiritual benediction and grace, that you may so live together in this life, that in the world to come you may have life everlasting," intoned Gardiner. I turned to Catherine, kissed her heartily, saw her shining eyes turn upwards, then close.

We had a small wedding supper, as any private citizens would do, gathering our friends and family around a table set in the dining hall. No Great Hall existed at Oatlands, just a high-ceilinged chamber on the second storey, hung with hunting trophies. Stags' heads and boars' heads stared at us with their glass eyes.

Catherine and I sat side by side and laughed at everything. We laughed at Brandon when he stood up, cup in hand, and made a solemn toast about matrimony. He himself had been married four times, and had been one of the chamberers on my wedding-night public bedding with Katherine. It all seemed to come together now, all was one. We laughed, and we touched. And touched. O sweet Jesu! That touch!

We smiled at Cranmer's gentle well-wishes. (And touched.) We clapped at the Lady Mary's. (And touched, under the table, lest she see.) We bowed gravely at little Edward's. He spoke three words in Latin, memorized for the occasion. And all the while the sun was lowering, making shadows on the rows in the grain fields outside. At last it set, but the interminable summer twilight lingered on and on, until I longed to order it to disappear.

At long last it grew dark enough in the feasting chamber for candles to be lit, then torches. It was time for our guests to take their leave, and so they did, with kisses and well-wishes. There was to be no ceremonial bedding this time. Like any wool merchant or soldier, I was free to take my bride to my bed unaided.

It was a new bed, purchased from a local magistrate in the nearby village of Weybridge. He had commissioned it from a London artisan, meant it for a grand guest chamber he had had in mind for a manor that never came about. It was of good English oak and agreeably carved, and quite large, in aping the nobility. It stood now in the royal Retiring Chamber, its great four-posts scraping against the sloping ceiling.

I led my sweet Catherine into the chamber, closing the snug, dark door behind me. It was passably dark in there, and the one lighted candle on the wooden chest danced in the billowing summer air. Two dormer windows gave out on the ripening fields. I made to close them. Catherine stopped me, putting her soft hand on my arm.

"On this my wedding night," she said, "I would not be shut up and closed, as in a tomb. I would have a little breath of heaven, of the world beyond."

"Whatever you wish," I said. The windows remained open, and the grain-perfumed air came in, along with the cries of labourers and travellers on the road below.

I wish I could tell exactly what happened in the next few hours. I said thus-and-so. She said thus-and-so. We did thus-and-so. Yet although my senses were fully alert (no wine for either of us that night), I became so transported by her very presence that everything was altered, and I cannot separate one action from another.

It makes me angry that it is so. These were precious hours to me, hours that must now stand after all the nasty tide has swept in against them, and yet I cannot remember! I cannot remember cold details, only my own feelings, which were as strong as Hercules, but formless.

I was with her. I possessed her. She was mine. The very touch of her hand was a gift. A gift which felt simultaneously natural and precious beyond thought. The ordinary me, the true Henry, was not worthy of such a gift, but this special Henry was, the Henry I became in her presence.

All this was entirely natural, was it not? To hold her in my arms, to kiss her lips, to hear those words of endearment gasped out in jerks? The special Henry, the Henry created by this moment and endowed with extraordinary graces (this Henry who was both me and not me, stranger and ever-known) —he felt at ease in this bliss, this homecoming.

I know she responded, created the Henry of whom I speak. In the fleeting moments in which I existed as this extraordinary Henry, I felt I was ever thus: not fading, not temporary. I was bold with her, taking her to bed as this Henry wished. We did not remove all our clothes, so anxious were we to consummate our union and join as one. We left our upper bodies completely clothed, and our lower bodies, naked, sought one another. It happened so quickly, so completely, that the twilight had not faded altogether before our first union was done.

What a contrast was there: our lower selves still fused together in heat and sweat, and enfolded together, whilst our upper bodies touched not at all, save through layers and layers of linen and velvet and jewels.

We rolled away. But no self-consciousness yet: no, none.

I finally spoke, softly. "You are different from my fantasies."

"How so?"

"I never thought you would know, so quickly, what it was you wanted."

"Are you disappointed?" she said sadly. "Because I did not feign reluctance, as a virgin is expected to?"

"No, no," I assured her. But did I speak true?

"I meant to. But the truth is, my desire took hold and I had no will or power to restrain it." Did she speak true?

"Nor I." I leaned over and kissed her gently. The jewel-encrusted doublet I still wore restricted my movement, reminded me of its presence. "It is time to undress," I said softly.

Together we unbuttoned and unclasped the bindings of one another's garments. Then, although naked, we did not look directly at one another, but wrapped ourselves up in the bleached and scented linen sheets and began to talk, like children huddled together.

The talk was awkward, when the bodies had not been. I longed to speak of all my feelings, but sensed that was wrong. Catherine had recovered herself, and began chattering away in a high voice.

". . . and then the most stinking groom in the Duchess's stables, he made gestures toward me. Naturally I was sickened: he was repulsive. How could he ever have thought I would respond? I told my aunt the Duchess. . . ."

Why was she sullying our time together, our first union, with these tales of men who had wanted her and whom she had refused? It made me angry, it hurt me. Yet I let her go on, tried to join in, in a jolly fashion.

From thence she went on about the most inane subjects. Her Howard cousins, Culpepper and Henry the Earl of Surrey; a book she had seen Mary Howard reading; a tale told the Duchess by a returning pilgrim from Jerusalem.

It was all entertaining, witty—and impersonal. Why did she choose to speak of these things on this sacred night? Was it just nervous chatter, the chatter of a maid who feared the unknown? Yet she did not appear afraid or frightened or shaken in the least. Rather she appeared self-possessed, soothing.

I did not understand. I only felt disappointed, somehow. Not in the lovemaking, but in her actions afterward. She was hard and gay, when all I longed for was to take her in my arms.

Then she suddenly broke off her words and turned to me, flinging her arms around me. "Now I would be the bridegroom," she murmured, pressing me on my back, positioning me just so, lowering herself upon me. As she felt me inside her, she leaned back: pulling, pushing, straining. I saw her fair white body, slim and yet big-breasted, in the candlelight, arching away from mine. Her lips were parted, and her chin jutted out. A mass of hair enveloped her, touched even my loins, tickling them. She worked, grunted, cried out. But I felt little. I could not lose myself, although her woman-parts engulfed me, seemed to suck me in. She fell forward, a sheen of sweat upon her back.

"Ah," she murmured, a bubble of saliva forming, and bursting, on her plump lips. Her arms trailed out on either side like those of a drunkard upon a board. Lasciviously she pulled up her left leg, disengaging our private parts. She came away from me with a great sucking noise and a trail of moisture. The drops landed on my belly: small, round, gleaming, and oily. I watched them as they formed, like little pearls.

She gave an animal sigh of contentment.

"It must take a great deal to keep you satisfied," I finally murmured. The drops on my flesh flattened and trickled off, and I felt cold. Outside there was no light. The brief summer dark had taken hold.

XCIV

During the remainder of that unusually hot summer, I fluctuated between two poles of feeling. One part of me rejoiced in Catherine, in my new wife, and basked in her beauty and unrestrained sensuality. She said things I had never thought to hear a woman say. "I dreamed last night of your man-sword, and how it felt inside me, and I could not sleep, for both the memories and the expectations." "The way you move is sinful, and takes me away in thought at embarrassing times. Today when the French ambassador stood before me, all I could think of was the way we had screamed out together at midnight last." Now I myself would never be able to see Castillon, the French ambassador, without remembering Catherine's midnight ecstasies.

On the other hand, it happened again and again—she did not react, did not feel, turned a solemn moment into a trite jest. When I said, "It has never been so good, never in my life," she replied offhandedly, "Oh, it must have been good with the Princess of Aragon, with my cousin Boleyn, with Queen Jane—for there are Princess Mary and Princess Elizabeth and Prince Edward." Smile. Laugh. When I told her of how I loved her, she murmured, "It is carnal only, Henry, pure carnality. I know not else why we find ourselves thus." Giggle. "Have you done this often?" Smirk. And ever: "Tell me, what do you think I—?" Do. Think. Look like. She never tired of hearing how she appeared. Once, when she came upon me writing some music for the virginal, she asked, "Are you writing a tune of our love?" She assumed I was —that she should be my subject and muse and fixation. The fact that it was so was no surprise, no gift. She claimed it as a personal victory, lugged it home with her as the hunters had done the stag and boar heads decorating our wedding-lodge manor.

She was a child, I reminded myself. Children open their presents on the spot. I knew it, and yet I expected more. Or less. I hated her bragging and her strutting. Yet I longed for her kisses and enthusiasms. And her sweet flesh. We remained at royal country manors throughout the summer. After Oatlands we went to Grafton in Northamptonshire. The summer was hot and dry, and caused great unhappiness throughout the land. A drought: the very word had Biblical overtones.

Drought was what God sent when He wished to punish people or, at the very least, compel their attention. But I did not tremble before it. Were not my barns full? There could be other reasons God would give such a rest to the land, and I no longer thought exclusively in terms of sin and punishment, for I had painfully come to realize that God was more grand and intricate than that. Defiantly, I decided to enjoy the drought for what it was: an opportunity to spend a warm golden summer in private with my bride.

In the first week of August I ordered all the clergy to pray for Catherine as Queen during all Masses that Sunday, August eighth. Thus was my marriage announced throughout the land: not by heralds or foreign ambassadors, but simply from the pulpit.

No one walked out, no one denounced me as King Ahab, or as a David with his Abishag. There were no reports of malcontents or ill wishes.

Not that Catherine and I would have heard it, as we kept ourselves secluded in the country with only a skeleton court and the Privy Council in attendance. Even that little was irksome. Early every morning, besotted with love and its demands, I fairly staggered into the bedchamber and collapsed into my private bed. Culpepper would remove my cloak, my slippers, my gold chain, laying them all out neatly on my clothes chest. He would draw the heavy velvet window-hangings, and I would sleep until noon.

Then, with a sigh of exasperation, Culpepper would jerk the curtains open. Hot sunlight would fall on my face or, if not on my face, make a burning patch on my body somewhere. A burning patch that aroused me.

Stirring and turning, I would come back into the world. My days and nights were all topsy-turvy, lasciviously so. I would groan and stretch, mutter and scratch myself.

Culpepper would appear by my side, a steaming basin of orange-scented water in his hands. Indulgently he would bathe me, keeping silence all the while. I was aware that the flesh on my chest quivered overmuch under his demanding strong hands. An inch or so of surplus fat had accumulated. But it was shrinking under my arduous hunting program.

Yes, I was hunting again, which I had thought never to resume. I set aside three afternoon hours daily for hunting in the hushed, dry woodlands about me. I rode like a young man, as I had not done since the summer I had hunted with Anne Boleyn, in 1531. Nine years ago. What do nine years do to a man's body? There are those who hold that they take an irreversible toll. But I believe —no, believed, sad addition of a *d*—that through will and determination a body could be subjugated and reinvigorated. The sore on my leg had gradually faded away, and I tried to forget it had ever existed. I almost succeeded.

The first few days in the saddle, I ached all over. I know this never happened in my youth. Each muscle seemed now to have a voice and a querulous demand of its own. It would be so easy to yield to it, to say, "Ah, well, you've earned your rest, and you *are* forty-nine." Some evenings when I walked I felt a full chorus of them, shrieking, "Be kind. Let us rest in honour." But then I would go to my Queen's chamber and renew my vow to become the hard-muscled man I once had been. Each time we took away our clothes by candlelight I could detect more muscles upon myself and less fat, and the joy I felt in reshaping my physique was second only to the transport I felt in the fleshly love between Catherine and myself.

My bodily and my carnal self: both were being resurrected, reborn, and reshaped.

When the time came for the summer progress to end, I found I had no desire to return to London and immerse myself in affairs of the realm, to read over the rolls of the shires and the tax compilations. There was the horrid task of sorting through Cromwell's records, and this I did not care to do at all. I knew they would be orderly and not difficult to survey. But, oh! to touch them, and see that handwriting. It would be as if he himself stood grinning at my shoulder.

Day by day I was increasing in strength and endurance, both out of doors and between the sheets with Catherine. It was only October. What need to break it all off now? I could return to London, unite my private travelling Privy Council with the London-bound lot, transact essential business in a fortnight, and rejoin Catherine for a long, slow autumn. Then there would be the Christmas revels, and after that, I could return to life as it commonly was.

Or life as it was meant to be. The realm was quiet, at long last, after the murmurings and belligerence at the start of my Great Matter; after the outright rebellion against the closing of the monasteries; after the plots and counter-plots and treachery that went abroad in the realm, masquerading as "conscience" (Thomas More), the restoration of the "old order" (Cardinal Pole), the bringing about of the "new order" (Cromwell); after outside threats and sword-shakings (the Pope and his toady the Emperor, until at last their pawn, Mary, disappointed them by coming over to my side). Oh, it was all over at last, and I was weary, weary. I had fought so many years. Now a golden haze of satiation lay on the land I had harried so, and I would luxuriate in it.

In November, then, I rejoined Catherine at Dunstable. Small manor it was, and it suited me. I enjoyed snugness now, a certain warmth encircling one's being; although I knew I should visit Nonsuch soon, I had at this moment lost my taste for palaces and outsized things. Perhaps I wished to live as a man after living so long as a god.

I decreed that until Christmas, and the obligatory return to London, I would keep only a few about me. Culpepper, of course; Will; Paget, Denny, and Wyatt; and Richard Harpsfield, the hunting-master, along with Edward Bacon, the horse-master. Horses were most important, as I intended to keep riding until well into December. The exercise had already wrought marvels upon my body. In three months I had been hewn anew. Now I would complete the process.

After only two weeks' absence from Catherine, she seemed different—plumper, more pink. She was happy enough in the rooms of Dunstable Manor. "The windows of our chamber give off on the oaks!" she exclaimed. "I love them. They are my favourite trees. The leaves cling all winter, and they turn russet and make a lovely rustling sound when the wind rises."

The November sun was even now slanting through those leaves and shining directly into her eyes. I kissed her and pulled her close.

Was it my imagination? Or was she, truly, thicker?

"Yes," she said, shyly.

I was delirious with joy. "When, sweetheart, when?"

"In October I missed my monthly courses. So it is early yet. Count back three months from October—September, August, July. In June, then."

In June. So quickly! In less than a year of marriage, she would bring forth my child. As Katherine had. Truly, nothing had changed! I was as I ever had been.

"Catherine, my Queen, my love—the joy this brings me—"

"Shhh." She put a finger over my babbling lips. "We are but man and wife yet. The babe is not large enough to alter . . . anything that we might wish to do." Her tongue in my ear. "My body is yours as it always was. Do you remember?" She touched me in a wanton way, triggering a flood of obscene desire in me. I responded as she knew I would.

It was dark when I awoke. I was sprawled out on a narrow bed. Where? My eyes sought for something familiar and found nothing. All was uniformly black. I reached out one hand, numb from trailing on the floor, and felt fur. Fur? A hunting lodge. Yes . . . at Dunstable. Catherine with child. Now, yes . . . then flooded in the memories of our wild and fearless lovemaking. Shameless in the sloping upper chamber and the coveted privacy. Things we did, unthinkable things . . . yet unforgettable. Instinctively I crossed myself, then cursed myself. Popish superstition. What was? The feeling that lust with one's wife was evil. Did not the Scriptures say that Adam, Abraham, Isaac, Jacob "knew their wives"? Yes, but not with such embellishments, or such relish. They knew them, yes, as nature required, but—

My back was exposed, and cold. I groped for a covering, but there was nothing loose. Was Catherine there? It seemed not. I heard no breathing, not even of the softest sort.

I was shivering. I must rouse and clothe myself. I leaned over and fished for garments, and they were there, crumpled at my feet. I drew them on, savouring the warmth they gave me.

By now most of my senses had returned. I knew I perched on the bed where I had lately sported with my dear wife. I was in Dunstable. Night had fallen. Doubtless it was time for supper, and Catherine awaited me in the small room appointed for meals.

I shuffled toward the door and ran my hand along its frame. A sliver of light outlined its edges. Through that crack I saw two profiles. One was Catherine's; the other, a young man's. He had a hawkish nose and a great deal of dark hair that fell forward over his forehead. Their lips were moving rapidly.

I flung the narrow double doors open, and they started.

"My Lord," said Catherine, bowing a little. As if she should bow after what passed between us . . . or was this a wicked sense of humour?

"Wife." If so, I joined in.

"Your Majesty." The young man swept low, then straightened. He was slim and quivering, like an eager rapier. Or something else, something I wished not to think upon.

"This is Francis Dereham," said Catherine, smiling. "A kinsman from Norfolk. I have known him since my childhood, and he is trustworthy. So I have appointed him my secretary."

I looked at him. He looked more like a pirate than a secretary. "It is not seemly to overuse one's prerogative to appoint one's kinsmen to important positions. The Queen's secretary must fulfill certain duties—"

"Let him be my honeymoon secretary, then," she laughed. "Perhaps you are right. In London he would not be adequate. And soon enough we shall return there, and then, dear husband"—she came over to me, took my hand in hers—"we shall become grave and proper, and you will teach me how. In the meantime, cannot our servitors be lighter than usual? We wear cottons in summer, and woollens in winter. Well, then, I would have a cotton secretary for this lighthearted time."

Dereham looked embarrassed, as well he should.

"Secretarial duties will be light until Christmas," I admitted.

"Yes!" she shrieked. "So they shall! So they shall!"

I attributed her edginess to lingering excitement from our time together in the little bedchamber.

November was mild and sweet, with murky fogs rising from the woods, and black, still waters reflecting the stripped trees hovering above. A few last leaves floated on the surface, but they were bleached and limp, companions of the darkness below: souls waiting for a ferry across the River Styx. Great hordes of rooks circled about, selecting certain trees for their gathering places. Glistening and black they settled on the naked boughs, visible from great distances. Birds of winter taking their appointed places. This melancholy transition between gaudy autumn and still winter was a time of its own, a time of which I had never been cognizant. It was abnormally hushed and monochromatic. And holding its breath. I could feel it.

XCV

We spent those hushed weeks in secret pleasure in small royal manors. Every morning I would wake early before the increasingly slug-abed sun, and go to the stables, leaving Catherine still asleep, then gallop for an hour or two after stag and hare and weasel in the soft, shadowless forests. I swear it—the horses tired before I did. I had to change mounts twice or even thrice before I headed back toward the manor for the lavish midday meal, with a roaring hunger and all the blood tingling in my veins.

By the time I arrived back, the manor would be as lively as a Scotsman dancing to his bagpipes. I loved the activity. It made me feel like a tribal chieftain with all his warriors and kinsmen about.

On a day in late November—St. Catherine's Day, to be precise—it was sleeting by the time I handed the reins of my horse over to a groom and strode inside. I was chilled clear through, and went first to my chamber to put on some warm woollens. Catherine was not there. Neither was Culpepper. But Dereham was scowling in the Receiving Chamber, twisting up bits of paper and throwing them into the fire, muttering angrily all the while. He sneered as one large piece snapped and burst. An unpleasant fellow, even if he was Catherine's kinsman. I wondered, idly, why she felt obligated to allow him into her household, if only temporarily. He seemed a bad sort.

It was just a thought, an impression, tearing across my mind like a shooting star. And just as quickly gone.

I shrugged, passed him by, and went into my chamber. A cheery fire awaited me, and a whimsical drawing from Catherine, showing a row of exhausted horses, a grinning King, and a pile of game. I took it and ran my hand over it fondly, then put it where I kept the other tokens she gave me. She was so loving! Her simple, unrehearsed gestures meant more to me than all the sophisticated posturings of court ladies. I hurried down to join her in the dining hall. She was already awaiting me at the high table, although in this small setting it was a rough, stained oak table like any other, and there was no dais.

"My Lord! My Lord!" she called out in her pretty voice, then banged her horn-handled knife and spoon on the table. As if I could not see her! She was all in pink satin, my favourite colour for her, and her auburn hair fell free, unrestrained by any headdress.

"Aye, aye," I said amiably, making my way over to her. As I squeezed between two tables, I was pleasantly aware of how much slimmer I had grown, and of my hard-gained muscular strength. It was a fine feeling, to recapture one's own body.

"Was the hunting good?" Culpepper asked eagerly.

"Aye. Two stags and a dozen hares." I sat down.

He smiled. "Then you'll be wanting to return tomorrow?"

I shook my head. "The weather has turned. Why, did you wish to accompany me?"

"What a disappointment," he murmured.

I laughed. "Your hunting clothes have waited this long to be christened, they can wait another day." Culpepper seemed to choose his activities by the attire required to pursue them. He disliked the heavy breeches and leather shoes sailors must wear; therefore he declined to go sailing.

"Yes. I can wait another day," he admitted.

Catherine touched me. "I am pleased you will be inside tomorrow." I knew what she meant, yet so sweetly and innocently did she say it, she would have fooled the Blessed Virgin. I squeezed her thigh under the table.

"Inside I shall be," I agreed.

Down at the end of the left-hand table, Will looked dour. I knew not what afflicted him of late, but his good humour had flown south with the birds.

ᴄᴅ WILL:

I was sick at heart for you, Hal. All could see what you could not, would not. . . .

I grieved in advance for you.

ᴄᴅ HENRY VIII:

After the rollicking dinner, when we retired to our bedchamber for our afternoon "rest," Catherine's smiles faded. "O Henry," she said, "I know not how to say this, other than just to say it. This morning I learned . . . I am not with child."

I leapt over to her, encircled her with my arms. "You miscarried? O Jesu, why did you not call a physician?"

"I was . . . ashamed. Embarrassed."

Her modesty was too much! "Lie down at once, and I'll send for him!"

Against her protests, I pulled her toward the bed and lifted her into it. I gathered up all the feather bolsters and arranged them behind her back, then arranged a woollen blanket about her. "I will send Dr. Butts in to see you straightway." I leaned over to kiss her, so small and brave in that great bed. "Sweetheart, I grieve for our loss. But you should not have hidden it."

Before she could argue, I left her and searched out Dr. Butts. He was in his room with his assistant, discussing something about anatomy as taught at Padua. It seemed a physician there had actually stolen rotting corpses of executed criminals and dissected them.

I interrupted his impassioned conversation. "The Queen needs you," I whispered directly into his ear. "Bring your birthing instruments."

Clearly puzzled, he left his companion and followed me out of the room. As soon as we were out of earshot, I said, "There has been a miscarriage. She needs you to examine her and tend her. Bring whatever instruments are necessary. Not birthing ones, of course. I know not the proper name for them."

While he was with her, I stood in the outer chamber, pacing and staring at the fire. The dark and querulous Francis Dereham had stalked away, as if it affronted him to share a space with me. Before I could think further on the nasty Dereham, Butts re-emerged. "So quickly?" I was surprised.

"Aye." He stood looking at me, his brown leather bag of implements and herbal potions dangling from both hands. "There was no child. This was just a normal monthly course. No heavier than usual. Apparently the Queen was mistaken."

Mistaken? No heavier than usual? But it was six weeks ago that she had told me. "Would not a delayed course like this result in a greater accumulation of blood?"

"Sometimes. It depends on why it was delayed. Whether by natural or unnatural means."

"Unnatural? But a pregnancy is 'natural,' is it not?"

He shook his head, as if pitying me. "There are ways to alter that monthly function, to meddle with it." He hesitated a moment, then opened his hand. In his palm was a small, smooth pebble.

"This was what the Queen miscarried," he said.

Still I did not understand.

Sadly he explained, "Her womb expelled it. It had been put there to prevent a babe from growing within. 'Tis a custom in the Middle East much practised with beasts of burden, and perhaps with slaves as well. It makes conception impossible."

No! Such a filthy practise, no, Catherine could not have . . .

"Could it have found its way there accidentally?"

"No, Your Grace."

"How long had it been there?"

"Judging from its appearance, for many years."

Jesu! Some evil Arab physician had done this to her as a baby. How? But there were Arab physicians ready enough to be found, even in England. I had found Al-Ashkar. The Duchess must have had one at her service, ready to do her bidding. She did not mean her poor niece ever to conceive—why? Was the old woman that bitter and angry at her charge? At having to bear the cost of raising her worthless stepson's child? There may be children, had she thought, but I'll assure there are no grandchildren? How cruel old women can be.

"Thank you, Dr. Butts," I said. I would reward him well for his discovery.

I re-entered the chamber where she lay. My heart ached for her, so misused all her life. To be orphaned and neglected was one thing, but to be rendered artificially barren. . . .

"All was well?" she asked anxiously.

"Yes," I assured her. I sat down on the bed and soothed her. She was trembling.

"He said there would be more bleeding, perhaps heavy," she said.

It was natural. The womb was rebelling against its misuse.

"It will soon be over." My hopes for a child were even now staining the cloths beneath her buttocks. "Let us plan our Christmas together, now. Shall we keep court? Where?" I sought to distract her, cheer her.

"Hampton," she said without hesitation. She could not know how unsettling a choice that was for me. But no matter—anything to make her joyful.

"As a child, whenever I thought of court, I thought of Hampton. All the great glassy windows, the Italian statues, the astronomical clock; I imagined royal barges all lining the river; oversized kitchen ovens cooking night and day . . . all the world would be there. . . ."

"Stop, stop," I laughed. "You have seen all this in your mind?"

She nodded.

"Then you shall see it all in truth," I promised.

I stood up and looked about the small room. Suddenly I had lost my taste for remote hunting lodges; happiness had proved as elusive here as anywhere else. It was time to return to Hampton.

She bled for a week, following the physician's instructions and drinking a potion of ground dried pennyroyal mixed with red wine three times a day.

"The wine is to replace the lost blood, and the pennyroyal is to staunch the flow," he explained.

When that danger was past, we set out for Hampton Court to keep Christmas, sending notice to all eligible members of court throughout the realm, and even to Scots nobles and Irish peers, to come and join us. All were welcome. Replies came quickly, and the allotments of rooms and servants' quarters were spoken for so greedily that by St. Nicholas' Day there was not a single chamber or even corner of a chamber free.

"You have your wish, sweetheart," I assured her. "By my reckoning, fifteen hundred will lodge here for the entire Twelve Days of Christmas. The kitchen fires will blaze night and day. The Lord Steward requests five thousand geese alone to feed this mighty company. How like you that?"

She smiled. "And there will be balls, and masked dancing?"

"As many of them as you wish," I said.

"Imagine everyone disguised—all fifteen hundred of us," she said dreamily.

"Much mischief would occur." Oh, the maidenheads lost, the husbands cuckolded! All in honour of Our Lord's birth.

I proposed for Will to go about in an Infidel turban and pantaloons, but he refused. As I said, he was most dour and out of sorts these days.

"Costumed or not, you shall not hide yourself away, Will. Too many idle people must be entertained, lest they get into fights. You know the problem of keeping men indoors too long. It transforms them into be-ee-easts." I sucked my stomach in for the tailor who was measuring me for my masquing-coat. All of cloth-of-silver it was to be, with a matching visor and cape.

"Well?" I inquired of the tailor.

"Forty-six inches, Your Grace."

That was five inches less than at this exact time a year ago. But still eleven inches more than the waist of my youth. Another hard season or two of training, of strength-tossing of the caber and wrestling, and riding—that should do it. Even though in June I would be fifty.

I waited for the tailor to leave, then turned back to Will. "I expect your co-operation. God knows, there is enough to poke fun at. There's the Pope and his lecherous Italian family; Charles and his growing piety, more like madness; Francis and his mania for hunting; as well as the pitiful Reformers and their increasing heresies—"

Will stood up, his eyes flat and hard. "By God, I cannot!" he snarled. "It's none of it humourous, or have you grown so blind you see nothing, as inhuman as your enemies depict you? The Pope is no longer Clement, a weak and hounded Italian degenerate, as you would have it, but Paul, a determined and fighting soldier in this war of religion. It *is* a war, and not just one of pamphlets and tracts any longer. The Church is fighting for her very existence, and the battle-lines are drawn—right across the middle of Germany. Pope Paul means to roll that demarcation line back, to recapture Germany and France, possibly to push the Protestants right off the Continent. Paul is no Clement, but the leader of a counter-Reformation. Cromwell was right, you know. It *is* all-out war. It pleases you to see the Pope as a buffoon, defeated by you. But the Old Faith is capable of a vicious fight for its life, and the forces are being readied. Reginald Pole and the Pilgrimage of Grace were but the advance rumblings."

I grunted. True, Paul III was more active than Clement VII. A sea turtle is more active than a land turtle, but both are turtles.

"Charles has grown pious, it is true," Will went on. "But his rehearsing of his own funeral—is that mad? Or is it mad of ordinary men *not* to? We all know we shall die. Yet we fail to draw up wills, fail to have coffins carved. Answer me, Hal—is your will drawn up and witnessed?"

"Not yet. I would not let vain men think they have no longer to please me! Let them wait to know my plans!"

"Ah. And do you know where you will be interred? You are a King. What sort of tomb will you have? Should you not at least have selected the marble for the statues, employed a sculptor? Or are you trusting to fate to entomb you nobly?"

"I shall be buried next to Queen Jane," I said. "And as for all those provisions for grand tombs—Wolsey lies not where he planned. I myself will lie in his sarcophagus. What good is planning?"

Will shrugged. "Francis is eaten up with the Great Pox. Poor man, his only distraction and pleasure lies in hunting. Certainly he can no longer enjoy the delights of women. Do you find that humourous? That his groin and privates are a mass of sores and open putrefaction?"

"If he can no longer enjoy the delights of women, it is because he enjoyed them to excess before. There are those who claim I am smitten with the Great Pox," I snorted. "They lie."

"Then exhibit yourself to the great company assembled here and scotch those rumours," chuckled Will. "Have your hose open for all to see."

I threw back my head and laughed. "Should you fail me, I might have to resort to that. But Will"—I cocked one eyebrow—"my private parts are employed a great number of hours each day, so they may not be available at convenient viewing hours."

He looked disgusted, started to say something, then turned away. A moment passed. Finally he said, "The heretics are no laughing matter, either. Truly, they go further and further afield, until they will never see their way back to the main body of Christianity. They take every aspect of doctrine and expand or alter it in some way. There is that Spaniard, Servetus, who attacks the Trinity, saying Christ has no place there. There is the Dutchman, Menno

Simons, and his followers, who make peaceableness a religion. Then there are those who attack the Sacrament of Baptism, saying only an adult can choose it, therefore all true believers should be re-baptized—"

"The Anabaptists," I sneered. "The worst of the lot!" I hated the Anabaptists, hated everything about them: their smug, fiery self-righteousness, their screaming sermons, their hysterical emotional appeals. I had condemned three to be burnt at Smithfield just a month earlier.

He nodded. "Then there are many who attack the Sacrament of the Eucharist, claiming it is a memorial meal only; others the Sacrament of Holy Orders, insisting priests and laymen are the same . . . some nonsense about 'the priesthood of all believers.' "

"Yes, those ex-priests who lust after women and marry nuns. What, you do not find them humourous?"

"When men commit sins in the name of religion, it is not humourous," he said. "And this is happening more and more. Worst of all, one can no longer count on certain sympathies from one's audience. That terrifies me, Hal—and it should you."

I stared at the crackling fire, as men will do to gain time. He was right. Of the men and their retainers flocking to court to keep Christmas, one could assume nothing about their religious leanings. The ugliness of heresy had seeped into the very fabric of English life, rotting its threads and discolouring its purity.

"It does, Will. It does."

He looked surprised, as if he no longer expected me to listen or understand.

"But what can I do, besides what I am doing? I did not create heresy. I cannot prevent its multiplication on the Continent. Here in England I am fighting a war on both fronts—Romanism and heresy. I formulate a middle way and try to punish extreme dissenters on either side. But I cannot pursue it too vigorously. I wish not to turn England into a terrified state like Spain, with its Inquisition. Nor a battleground like Germany. Even my Privy Council divides into the two camps, and I had to execute Cromwell and More for their extremism. O Jesu—when will men see sense?"

"Not in our lifetime," Will said. "And I fear worse to come in the next generation."

"You have saddened me so that I myself can think naught but gloomy thoughts. What shall we do to make our guests laugh this Christmastide, Will? For we must occupy them with something happy."

"Lechery and lust, the old standbys," he said. "No politics. Just over-hasty youth, impotent old men, cuckolded husbands, swords that will not stand to thrust, young wives with rich old husbands. . . ."

"Aye, aye. That'll be mirthful. And what of young husbands with rich old wives?" I thought of Bessie Blount. Poor woman. Did Clinton truly love her?

"Aye, 'tis a growing custom in our day, as women outlive their men. Mark you, where there's a great discrepancy in age, there's usually an equally great discrepancy in wealth."

I smiled, oblivious of his meaning. O fool!

✺ WILL:

I tried to tell him, but he was deaf and blind. And, oh! the sniggering remarks about his privates and how they were engaged—he sounded like a dirty little boy. I was embarrassed for him, even if he no longer had the good sense to be embarrassed for himself.

As for his assertion that people thought he had the Great Pox, that is simply not true. It was Wolsey who was accused of having the Great Pox and attempting to spread it to others by "blowing in their ears." It is indicative of the state of the Church in England at the time that no one thought it odd or unlikely that a Cardinal might have fallen victim to such a malady.

Although Wolsey was indicted for his malicious attempt, Parliament thanked God that He had seen fit to preserve the King from the Cardinal's alleged illness. "His most noble royal body was saved," the words went.

Incidentally, the Great Pox, alias the French Disease, alias the *Morbus Gallicus,* has acquired yet another name recently: syphilis. Some sensitive soul wrote a poem about a shepherd who had offended Apollo and was sent the disease. Syphilis was the lad's name. Now people want to call the disease that as well. As if a pretty name will change its loathsome nature!

But you, of course, are not concerned with such things.

XCVI

 Henry VIII

I conferred with my master of court ceremonial, William Hobbins, about which festivities should be celebrated.

"By the Grail, we have enough to choose from," he muttered, then quickly checked himself. "By the Grail" was a Popish expletive, like "by Our Lady." Lately the latter expression had been slurred into "bloody," but it fooled no one. Was this man, then, a secret Roman? Will was right—you could assume nothing.

"We should select the ones most suitable for large crowds. Everyone in England is coming, so it seems. Do you know the clan chieftain Donald, Lord of the Isles, is sending a nephew here?"

"I hear they drink blood," he said. "They're still pagans, you know."

"Nonsense." I looked forward to meeting the man. I had never seen an actual Highland Scot, never talked to one. This one was at odds with the Lowland Scots, who were my enemies. The enemy of my enemy is my friend. A fine old saying.

"Here is a list of possible diversions." He proffered a parchment with neat categories all drawn up.

Laboriously we constructed a program that would not leave close on fifteen hundred men and women with nothing to do. If we did not, the Devil would.

By mid-December they began arriving. The first to come were so curious about the palace and one another that that in itself served to occupy them. Daily the numbers swelled, until on December twentieth, I could look out the windows of my Retiring Chamber and see every chimney of Hampton Court smoking. From all around the inner court the plumes of smoke rose, all in a row like soldiers; and other regiments were represented high in the air from flanking courtyards.

"Tomorrow it all begins," I murmured to Catherine, beautiful Catherine, lounging upon my bed. Her silvery satin nightgown reflected the leaping flames in my private fireplace, which burned only the most fragrant logs.

"A royal Christmas," she said drowsily. "What will you give me?"

What a child she was! But I would not disappoint her. I had a gift for her that would make the realm gasp. "Patience, my sweeting." I enjoyed teasing her. I often forced patience upon her in bed, making her wait, suspended, for her ultimate, explosive release. Not until I allowed it did she experience the final shudder. She was greedy for it from the first.

She pouted. "Can you not hint?"

"Gladly. It blooms."

She had no interest in horticulture, so she ceased questioning.

"Tomorrow I take them on a grand hunt. Ladies, too. So prepare to enjoy the Arab horse presented you as a wedding present by the Knights of St. John of Jerusalem." A last, desperate bid for my mercy before they were dissolved in England. I liked not to think upon that.

"What do we hunt for?"

"Boar."

"Upon St. Thomas' Day? Fear you not the Wild Hunt?"

A branch snapped and spat red in the fire-grate.

"'Tis but a legend," I said.

"To hunt . . . on the shortest day of the year . . . in the twilight . . ." She sounded genuinely distressed.

"What happens in the twilight?" Perhaps she knew something I did not.

"If you should go near a churchyard, as it's growing dark . . . Saint Thomas himself will come, driving in a fiery chariot. And then he calls on all dead men named Thomas who are buried there, and they rise from their graves, and go with him to the churchyard cross, which glows deeply and strangely red. . . ."

As she spoke, her face took on an otherworldly look, and it was as if I held a seer, a prophetess. "And sometimes one is compelled to go with the saint, forever, on a ghostly hunt. Or with the other Thomases. . . . Think, O my dear Lord, on the Thomases in your life, the dead Thomases. . . . They take possession—"

I felt fear go through me, as sharp and cold as a rapier that has lain out all through a January night. The dead Thomases in my life: Thomas Wolsey, Thomas More, Thomas Cromwell. What if they *should* rise from their graves and confront me, take possession of my person, hold a trial of me in some distant secluded churchyard? Wolsey's ghost, all shrunken and broken; More, without his head, festering in reproach and self-righteousness; Cromwell, his neck-stump still bleeding, bitter and filled with vicious hatred . . . their rotten shrouds mingling with the mists, tangling me, tripping me, and—

"No!" I snapped. At that exact moment the fire snapped, too, underscoring my thoughts. "It is a country legend, 'tis naught to do with me."

"Culpepper has seen it," she whispered. "He told me once."

"He's a Thomas, too. Most like he made it up to entertain you. And impress you with his bravery. I take it he escaped from their threatening, grasping, bony fingers?"

She turned away sulkily. "You do not believe me. Very well, then, go on the hunt tomorrow. Flout Saint Thomas and all the other Thomases."

O Jesu! Only now as I write the words do I realize: it *was* Thomas, a living one, who made sport of me that day while I was out hunting, leaving my fair wife behind. He came from no grave, but directly from his pallet at the foot of my bed . . . and straightway into my wife's. As I grew breathless and panting with the hunt out of doors, so too did she, coupling with her cousin Thomas in my royal bedchamber. As I thrust the spear home into the bristly boar, so did he spit my wife.

Or was the assignation already arranged, and her desperate tale of the ghostly Thomases her last feeble attempt to avert it and preserve what little remained of her virtue? If I had heeded, would that have made a difference? The hunt was a good one. . . .

As we clattered over the courtyard stones, the three stags and one magnificent boar slung along the carrying poles, a great company leaned out of the inner courtyard windows and cheered. Christmas had begun.

The entire Twelve Days, in retrospect, all blend into one mass of music, colour, and festivity. From the moment we returned with the boar, until the final masked ball, ordinary clothes were cast aside, ordinary manners replaced by elaborate behaviour, and frugality banished. Fires burned for the entire twenty-four hours; candles were not rationed, and the servants had leave to heap their baskets full with them from the buttery, and take as many as they could carry; the ale barrels were to be refilled every two hours, and no one to count the number of pitchers taken away. Individual consorts of viols, recorders, and rebecs roamed the galleries and passageways, playing whatever tunes they fancied or were requested of them. Mary, Elizabeth, and Edward all asked to be allowed to join the groups of musicians, and I happily gave consent. All three of my children loved music and were talented. Mary chose to play the vielle and perform with a standing group in the Great Hall; Elizabeth dressed as a boy and played the flute with a group of "Italians"; little Edward, who could at least play the drum, went round as an accompanist with the children choristers.

On the twenty-third of December I called for the three of them, for a special consultation. It was to be held in the council chamber, a snug oak-panelled room just off the upper gallery.

Elizabeth was the first to arrive, and she came alone, without her nurse, Mrs. Ashley. I complimented her: she looked most businesslike in a plain brown dress, her bright hair pulled back and hidden beneath a cap; a sprightly seven-year-old. She carried a pen and portfolio of papers. Mary came directly after, apologizing for being a trifle late. Edward, plump and rosy in his blue velvet suit, was carried in by his nurse. He was now three.

"Now seat you all," I said happily. Just seeing them all before me—my children!—I felt a great leap of pride. "I need your valuable opinions as to the games to be planned for Christmas Eve."

Both Mary and Elizabeth looked disappointed. Had they expected me to consult them about Parliament, then?

"I do not play games," said Mary, faintly.

"Indeed you do," said Elizabeth. "You love cards, and betting."

Betting? Mary gambled? I had no idea.

"That is why she is always out of pocket," continued Elizabeth. "And in my debt."

Mary scowled. "I shall never borrow from you again," she muttered. "As soon as I have repaid—"

"Which will not be until Christmas, else you shall have to refrain for all the Twelve Days, and with all the interesting players from the kingdom here, too. You will never be able to," predicted Elizabeth brightly.

Mary shrugged.

"So you dice and bet?" I teased. "One would never suspect it, with your sombre clothes. Mary, for my sake—wear something this Christmastide besides purple and black. You look like a spinster."

She stiffened, and Elizabeth shot a glance at me. Mary was acutely aware of her unmarried status and, more than I realized, she feared she would never be wed. She was twenty-four and accounted a bastard internationally. No Protestant prince wanted her, and no Catholic would accept her without recognizing Katherine of Aragon as my wife. Perhaps I should pressure an English peer into marrying her. Yes. I must attend to that.

"I shall order you a scarlet gown," I promised. "The seamstress can measure you by midday, and by working all night—yes, you shall be all in red by Christmas Eve."

She smiled tightly. In truth, she did not know how to smile. She was not unpretty, but her manner would not attract men. I sighed. Her mother had been more appealing, more feminine, at least at the age of twenty-four. What would Mary be like at fifty?

"What games do you propose for the court, Father?" asked Elizabeth briskly.

"Dicing and gaming at boards will keep some busy. But for the rest— those who want lively activity—we must seek other entertainment." I analysed her while appearing to think of games. Not pretty. Clever. But clever enough to hide it. And challenging. Exciting. Just like . . . her mother. Those sharp, appraising eyes. Swift, slender fingers.

"Group games," I said. "Not taxing. Things that enable men and women, boys and girls, to pass time, to meet, to show off their best clothing. What of Blind Man's Buff?"

"Oh, that, of course," she said. "I like Bee-in-the-Middle. One attempts to avoid being stung, or identified."

"Oh! Oh!" said Edward, clapping his hands.

"Can he play it as well?" I asked.

"All ages can play," she assured me. "All the way up to an ancient like Sir Anthony Browne. And Brandon."

Brandon? An ancient? He was in his fifties. Yes, old.

"And my uncle Norfolk. And"—she burst into laughter—"my step-grandmother, the Duchess of Norfolk!"

"That old crone?" scoffed Mary. "I'd like to see her in a corner with her former husband. She'd beat him, as she beat his mistress two years ago!"

"Nay, her husband would sit on her again, as he did the time she spat blood."

How did they know all this about Norfolk and his love-triangle?

"We need another game," I said prissily. "What about Hunt-the-Slipper?" This was one I remembered from my earliest Christmases.

"A nursery game?" laughed Elizabeth.

"We are all children at Christmas."

"Children at their best," she returned. "Children who lose games without a show of temper; who are allowed up past bedtime, as there is no bedtime; who can stuff themselves with cakes and sweets with no reprimand. And who never, never fight—for who fights when he is permitted all?" She sounded like an old man reminiscing.

"I like children," said Mary wistfully, reaching over to ruffle Edward's hair. He pushed her away.

There was a discreet knock upon the council chamber door. Petre, Secretary of the Privy Council, entered apologetically.

"The Laird of the Western Isles has arrived," he said, "and his train is causing a—a disturbance."

I rose wearily. As I stood I felt it—a slight pain, a warmth in my left thigh. No, no! Not the leg-sore again! It had healed, it did not exist any longer. It had been born of the Witch's poison, which had finally spent itself. . . .

There. It had been my imagining. I felt relief flooding through me like warm honey. Truly I could not bear it, could not *endure* it if the thing itself endured.

"I must leave you," I said to the children. "You see how it is. My thanks for your consultation."

Mary nodded, tight-lipped: a gesture I had seen Katherine make when, in later years, some condition displeased her. Elizabeth, impatient herself, looked ready to fly the chamber. As I myself had been in my youth. Why, that was how Wolsey had first ingratiated himself to me—by being my proxy in stuffy council chambers.

XCVIII

The Twelve Days began in solemn splendour with midnight Mass, celebrated privately in the Chapel Royal. It was more glittering and ritualistic than anything in the Vatican, of that I was sure. As incense wafted to the blue and gold ceiling, I felt a sense of triumph against all those who would throw me into the Reformers' camp. One could be anti-Papalist without necessarily being anti-tradition. There were those who sought to use me and label me for their own purposes. What fools they were! *I* used labels and factions, they did not use me.

The Christmas festivities proved a great success. The activities and games we had planned entertained and enthralled the crowds. Catherine seemed delighted, her recent loss forgotten.

I had not danced, exhibition-style, for years. Not since Black Nan. . . . But it was time to reclaim that skill, as I was reclaiming so many others. And so I would dance, on Ninth Night, for the first planned full evening of ensembles and suites. I practised in my chamber, rehearsing old steps and mastering new ones.

O! I had missed dancing, in those dead, hollow years, as I had missed so much, so much that I had not allowed myself to dwell on, or even to recall. I thought I had liked being dead.

There! that was it, the proper turn of the galliard. They called it a "shocking" dance, but the younglings loved it. . . .

My leg seemed submissive, although it had, all during the past fortnight, been sending out ominous tingles. What that betokened, I did not know. Perhaps nothing. I intended to regard it as nothing.

The Great Hall was cleared, and my finest consort-ensemble gathered together, with their woodwinds—recorders, crumhorns, and shawms—and their stringed instruments—viols, lutes, and harps. I had instructed them to begin with popular measures, so that everyone present might join in; only gradually were they to progress to the more demanding dances. I myself would refrain from joining until the saltarello near the end. My entrance would take the company by surprise, as I had long, long ago. . . .

I chatted, and circulated among the celebrants, pretending I had nothing more on my mind, pretending that I planned to stay swathed in my heavy robes, presiding like an old man.

"Yes, yes!" I nodded and clapped. The rondo was ending.

Next was my dance. I unfastened my cloak, laid it by. I readied myself, enjoying the pretence of talking, all the while flexing my calves and rising up and down on the balls of my feet, pointing my toe.

The first beat . . . I moved, thrusting out my leg. And felt excruciating pain in the thigh, suddenly, like a thunderclap. I was frozen with a paroxysm of pain.

The ensemble played on. One would never know that I had missed my entrance cue. Frantically I massaged my leg—the cursed traitor! With each touch I felt fluid ooze up, as if I were pressing on a sponge. Was my leg, then, become a sponge? A sponge of disease? I was wearing black tights, so the stain did not show. Very well. As I formed the words in my mind, a hatred greater than any I had ever felt flamed through me. This was an enemy! An enemy like Anne Boleyn, like Cardinal Pole, like the Duke of Buckingham. It was sent by Satan, like them, to destroy me. But this was more subtle: it would attack from within, rot me out from the inside.

I would dance, despite it. The ensemble reached the entrance point again, and I leapt out on the floor. As I landed, a nail of pain ran up my thigh and into my groin. People backed off to make room for me, to watch the King dance.

And dance he would. And did. I spun and leapt as athletically as a stag, executed all the steps of the galliard perfectly, with a precision usually reserved for clockworks and sword-masters. This particular dance demanded the grace and dexterity of a hummingbird. In this I did not fail.

After the first few beats, I took a mad, savage pleasure in the pain that fought back at me. It was a gladiatorial contest, and I, armed with net and trident, had ensnared and humiliated pain.

The moment the music ended, I was encircled by men and women extolling my skill. They were surprised, oh, yes, they were. The last time anyone had beheld me dance athletically was a decade ago, and many of those faces were gone.

"Dancing is a sport," exclaimed Henry Howard, "and it has seen its champion today."

"Some day this sort of dancing—with leaps and perfect posture and special shoes—will have to be professionally performed, by a permanent troupe," said Wyatt. "But to find some ten or twenty men who dance as your equal . . . there are none such in England, Your Majesty." He said it straight and plain, no flattery in the words. I know flattery and I can hear it in a murmur. He spoke true; he admired me.

But the seepage was bound to be noticed. I felt ooze in my dancing-slipper sticking to the sole of my foot. The discharge had run down inside my hose, then. I must withdraw, and quickly.

"And now to my chamber," I said, with a stage wink. "The reward awaits me there!" I gestured toward Catherine, who was politely talking to Culpepper. For God's sake, come with me, help me in this play-acting, I longed to say. But I could not, because I could never admit to the one person I most wanted to impress that I was, in truth, play-acting. My wife was in many ways the person I was most distanced from, and for whom I wore the most complicated masks. Now she was to help me make this retreat, to save face, but would never be permitted to join me in the inmost chamber.

Together we bowed, smiling. Then we took our dignified, measured steps toward the royal apartments, where the physician would be waiting, help at the ready.

"Come, Catherine." I squeezed her hand in mine. I felt resistance. She did not want to leave. "Do as I say," I muttered, jerking her along in my wake. I hated myself for each separate motion, item piled on item: for having an infected leg to begin with; for being too proud to yield to it; and finally for the pathetic need to use my wife as a camouflage for my own weakness.

Once inside the private suites of the royal apartments, I gestured to her to sit in the withdrawing chamber and keep still. She was clearly angry at this peremptory order, and that forced me to shout at her and demand compliance. I had no time for soft words or persuasion. Another moment and she would see the mess sopping into my shoe.

"I said stay here and wait!"

"You made me leave the young people and the dancing, for nothing! To sit and wait, like a child upon its father—"

Truly, Satan was trying me. The words pierced me like javelins: *young people . . . father . . .* I had taken her from her playmates. . . .

"Silence!" I thundered, glaring at her. Then I stamped away. Did I leave prints with the wet shoe on the polished wood floor?

Safely inside my private close-room, the smallest of all the royal rooms and the one to which no one else was granted access, I slumped on a stool and perched my affected leg up on a cushion. Now that the limb was stretched out horizontal, the fluid dripped straight down off the middle of the calf. It was yellowish-white.

Dr. Butts came in, his long face set like a gargoyle, and stony-coloured as well. Shaking his head, he produced silver scissors from his bag, and began cutting away the hose. Slowly and carefully he lifted off the covering piece of material, as afraid as I to see what lay beneath.

A great reddened area was there, as if the flesh were angry and had grown affronted. And in its midst, a small ulcer.

"So small," I said in surprise.

"Aye." He touched the flesh around it, which was tender and throbbing. "But the sickness has already spread to here and staked its claim. This flesh is not normal. It is in the process of being converted." He moved his fingers slowly outward. "Not until this point does the flesh become like the rest. This area in between"—he indicated the red, hot ring—"is the battleground. The illness seeks to capture it, and your body seeks to save it."

"But what *is* it? What caused it to flare up like this?"

He shook his head. "I know not."

"You *must* know! If you do not, then who does? Have you seen its like before?"

"Skin lesions, yes. But this is more than a mere skin lesion. It erupts by itself and seems to have a life of its own. Evidently it can slumber within your body for years, and then suddenly awake."

"But *why? Why?*" By God, I must know.

"It is characteristic of those with weakness in their veins. The blood is carried, as you know, in little tubes running all over the body. When there is a weakness in the tubes, then they break down, gush, form ulcers. Where they heal up, they have a tendency to break open again, for the true weakness is still there."

"But why is it weak?"

"Something inherent in the walls of the vessels. Look you, Your Majesty, we know that a man inherits his constitution from his ancestors. Now, forgive me, but it seems clear enough to me that the weakness of the Tudors lies, normally, in their lungs. That is the system which carries them off. As they say, a chain is only as strong as its weakest link, and the chain of the Tudors has been snapped over and over by lung-rot, consumption: Prince Arthur, the late King your father, your own son Henry Fitzroy. That weakness which was meant for your lungs was, by God's mercy, transferred to your legs instead. So that, instead of murdering you before your time, it merely forces you to sit upon a cushioned bench whilst others dance. Praise be to God, who has spared you!"

I looked down at my festering leg, and felt a shudder go through me as I tried to imagine this mess inside my lungs. "But is there nothing you can *do?*"

"I have a new salve," he said, "made of several alchemist's metals. But there is nothing that can work while you continue to use the leg. It must be kept quiet and without any weight upon it. Bed rest, Your Majesty."

"Then everyone will know!" I yelped. "If I take to my bed in the midst of the festivities—no! You must devise some means of keeping me on my feet."

"A bandage will be bulky and apparent," he protested. "No, there is no way to hide your secret, and so you would be angering the wound for nothing."

"I shall wear costumes and cloaks. It is only three more days until Twelfth Night. Only a little longer! If you dress the wound every morning and every evening, apply the salve . . . ?"

He looked disapproving. "It is not what I recommend in the best interests of the wound," he said stubbornly.

"Is the wound paramount? What of *my* best interests? What of England's? No, the word must not get out that I, the King, have an affliction. There are those who would rejoice—who would say it is a punishment."

"Very well." He acquiesced. "But the sore must be dressed."

He laid his instruments and dressings out on the flat surface of the window-seat. The first thing he selected was a small sponge, which he applied to the open wound. It stung sharply for an instant, then grew numb. "The pain you feel is the cleansing effect of alcohol. The numbness is from mandragora juice. If you inhaled it, it would put you to sleep."

Mandrake root. An evil thing that shrieked when it was pulled from the ground, that had two legs and a man's pudenda. So it beguiled one's brain, numbed one's flesh . . .

"There is, of course, its association with witches and the Evil One. But sometimes we can turn evil to our own uses, as in sleeping potions and wound-quieters."

The wound was not exactly numb, but warmly and blissfully insensitive to pain.

"Now the salve, which will heal and soothe. Goat's fat, compounded with ground pearls and burnt lead." He mounded it up all over the open sore, like meringue on an open tart. "Now." He looked pleased at his artistry.

"The pain is gone."

"Aye. Now, bandages will enable you to dress and go outside your chambers, but they are bad for the healing. Try to lie abed, unbandaged, as many hours as possible. Tonight you must on no account stir out of your bed."

So I was bedded, with a heap of pillows beneath my hurt leg, and thick coverlets of fur over me. The fire, composed entirely of sweet apple and cherrywood, snapped and sighed with hissing, scented breath.

"To help you sleep," said Dr. Butts, offering me a green syrup in a small silver beaker. The taste was like the feel of the ointment: a sting, followed by bliss. I was happier than I had ever been; it made me so.

"This will help you get through the last few days until Twelfth Night. When it is in your belly and veins, it overpowers the pain. But take no more at any one time than half the beakerful. And no more than three times a day."

"Yes. Yes." I saw him place a full bottle on the mantle, where it glowed as pretty and precious as liquid emeralds. "Catherine . . ." I mumbled. "The Queen . . ." Catherine, still waiting outside . . . poor child . . .

Tell her I am floating in another world, where nothing matters or is felt. . . .

But when he looked for Catherine, my wife was not there. She had quitted the chamber on her own, and gone elsewhere.

🙠 🙡

I slept deeply that night, kept submerged well below the surface of wakefulness by the magical green syrup. When I awoke, it was already past sunrise. The sky outside the windows was clear blue, and little ribbons of sunlight fell in parallel bands to the floor. I had forgotten about the leg-mess until I swung my feet over the side of the bed. Then a wallop of pain like an oaken beam felled me back onto the pillows. My adversary was awake, and alert. Very well, then. I rang for Dr. Butts. He came and dressed my leg in its daytime-going-about bandage, and administered a proper dose of the syrup. Then I called my Clerk of the Wardrobe, and together we selected a jewel-enlivened costume that would draw all eyes to my chest and away from my lower body.

That was to be my strategy for the next three days. Disguise the infirmity. Kill the pain from within. Use dress as an ally in this battle between me and disease.

🙠 🙡

Catherine I let scamper away with her friends. It was she, more than anyone else, from whom I must conceal this weakness. Released from her place by my side, she bounded off with all the court dandies and poets, the Howard clan with all its cousins, and even the peculiar offspring of the Scots and Irish chieftains. These latter were supposedly to stay on and serve a season at court to become "civilized." They certainly needed it. The Scots princeling was huge, covered with freckles, and affected some sort of multicoloured woollen wrapping with a phallic fur-bedecked purse dangling coquettishly over his manhood. The Irish prince had a face as white as ivory and an almost womanish, perverse beauty, and played a native harp, which he suffered never to be separated from. Neither lad knew how to dance, how to present himself to a foreign ambassador, or how to make teasing, insubstantial conversation with ladies.

I had proved myself by the dancing-recital of the night before; no one would suspect that necessity now compelled me to sit quietly amongst the more settled ladies and courtiers. These were the middle-aged—those who had retired from the frivolities of youth, but who were in their intellectual prime. Unfortunately they were much given to discussing theology, philosophy, and politics.

These folk were, in the main, women. Katherine, Brandon's young wife; the widow Latimer; Lady Anne Herbert; Joan Champernown. They were pious, brilliant, articulate. And, I suspected, a bit Protestant—as, I was forced to admit, all young people tended to be. Protestantism was new, radical, engaging. It attracted restive minds. Further along the line it shaded off into heresy, but these pretty ladies were merely dabbling in its water, exercising their minds in the only way permitted them. How dreary it must be to be a woman, I thought, looking round at them. To have so few areas in which you were allowed to stretch yourself. No wonder Protestantism was savoured so. It was an unknown sea in which they could dive deep and taste the exhilaration usually forbidden to their sex.

"Well, Madam Katherine," I addressed the widow Parr, "I am pleased that you could come to court."

"I am gratified that Your Majesty included me," she said, bowing her head. So the "delicate matter" was passed over in a civilized way. Her old husband, Lord Latimer, had been a conservative northern Catholic, a sympathizer with the Pilgrims. My invitation to his widow meant that I did not include her in her late husband's treasonous leanings.

I looked at her. Her gold-red hair, with the deepest widow's-peak (how appropriate!) I had ever seen, was pulled neatly behind a severe little black cap. But her face was pink-cheeked and merry—quite at variance with the asceticism of her mind. She was only twenty-nine. Why was it that a woman seemed to take on her husband's age, and the fact that the widow Latimer had been wed and widowed by two old men stuck to her and coloured one's impression of her? Certainly she herself was not ancient. Then I heard her speaking to Katherine Brandon, and I knew why.

". . . but as Our Lord was constrained, by His Passion, to restrict His forgiveness at the time merely to those nearby—that is, He explicitly forgave the thief beside Him on the cross; He specifically forgave His executioners, who were dicing for His robe—'Father, forgive them, for they know not what they do'—He did not say, 'and thou also, Pilate, and Caiaphas,' although surely in His heart He included them. . . ."

Was this her holiday talk? What, then, was her serious talk?

"Madam Latimer, you are far too joyless," I chided her. "Surely at Our Lord's birth, when He came as a babe, as God's gift to mankind, it is morbid to dwell on His coming betrayal and death."

Her dark eyes danced with excitement. Theology, then, was what inflamed her passion. "Ah, Your Majesty! But it is all one, that is its perfection, its mystery. The Kings brought frankincense and myrrh—shadows of His future death and burial. 'Mary took all these things, and pondered them in her heart.' She 'pondered' them, she did not rejoice, or sing; no, it was a heavy thing. I have often wondered," she said dreamily, like Culpepper stroking a particularly fine piece of velvet, "what Mary did with the gold, frankincense, and myrrh." I noted that she did not say "Our Lady" or "the Blessed Virgin." "Did she store it in a cupboard, somewhere amidst the linen, and look at it once in a long while, or by accident after she had finished her ordinary tasks after an ordinary day, waiting for Joseph to stop work and return? Did she touch it then, and feel the miracle all over again, have an epiphany of her own?" The widow Latimer was the most unabashed romantic I had ever encountered, but only for things unknown, unseen.

"She doubtless sold the gold and spices to pay for the trip to Egypt." It was Elizabeth who spoke, in her practical way. But why was Elizabeth amongst these intellectual matrons? What would attract a child here? Did she long for a mother that much? "After all, the gold would have been heavy to transport, and the exotic spices would have attracted too much attention. However, selling them in Bethlehem might have alerted Herod. Probably they waited until they were in Egypt. The Egyptians would have been more blasé about those items."

The women looked at her, then nodded. "The child speaks true," said Lady Herbert.

Elizabeth laughed. "The Holy Family were people, with all the considerations of any other people." She turned a guileless, smiling face to the widow. "Would you sometime be so kind as to check my translation of Proverbs? I am attempting to translate it into Greek."

The flattered widow nodded.

Charles's wife, the Duchess, produced a small book of devotions. "This I have found so helpful." The others all bent their heads over it, like chickens in a henyard when fresh grain has been heaped on the ground. I cursed my leg, to have confined me in this clucking flock of secular nuns.

"Ach! Zere you are, my child!" A fluster and rustle of material, along with a fine spray of saliva, announced the arrival of Anne, Princess of Cleves. "Und *Henry!*" Her voice rose with genuine gladness. Standing before our group was the great dray-horse herself, all shimmering in yellow satin, spreading her particular brand of good cheer. And I was delighted to see her. Rising slowly (in deference to Sir Leg), I greeted her.

"Sister!"

We embraced warmly. Her sturdy arms almost swayed me off my balance. I was astonished at how glad I was to see her. "Pray join us."

She grabbed a low stool (which a page was sitting on) and sat herself down. I expected her presence to lighten the devotional atmosphere, but to my surprise she joined right in and seemed to know all the translations and prayer books and even the printed copies of sermons which circulated amongst the religious salons. Elizabeth came and sat beside her, clearly fond of her and delighted at her presence. I had done well to make her my "sister."

So the day passed, sedately and in friendly company, and now there were but two more to overcome. That evening, Dr. Butts repeated the medical treatment of the leg. To my disappointment, it looked unimproved. He dosed me well, and sent me to bed at the earliest socially acceptable hour.

XCIX

The next day was easily passed in preparation for the climax and abrupt ending of the Christmas festivities, the Twelfth Night banquet and masked ball. In every chamber the lords and ladies were sleeping late, to store up reserves for the hours of revelry ahead. Then there were costumes to be adjusted, accessories to be located (how to strap on the stag's antlers, carefully transported from Yorkshire?). Arrangements for returning home necessitated visits to the stables and checking harnesses and wagons. The pastry chefs were frantically baking Twelfth Night cakes, with their beans hidden deep inside, to satisfy the appetites of the entire company. The string, keyboard, and reed consorts were rehearsing, for several hours of dancing music would be required, and that allowed each musician to contribute an individual favourite or personal composition. We would hear the regional melodies of Oxfordshire, the Cotswolds, East Anglia, Wales, and even Scotland (if the young Laird could be persuaded to perform, rather than flirt with his contemporaries). O rare excitement, Twelfth Night!

All this busy-ness enabled me to escape scrutiny and also to make the necessary arrangements for my own needs. I had purposely delayed the presentation of my Christmas gift to Catherine. Now I would unveil it at the most dramatic moment possible: midnight on Twelfth Night, at the time of the unmasking.

My own costume? I would be one of the three Kings—Balthazar. He was the most mysterious one, the one about whom least was known. That gave me freedom to construct a most elaborate costume, with a fantastical headgear and beaten silver mask, and long trailing cloth-of-silver cape. Behind me would come my camel. Brown velvet, with two wool-stuffed humps, and proper splayed feet, it took two men to bring him to life. Culpepper would be the front part, Edmund Lacey the rear. They spent Eleventh Day practising in the Great Hall, to ensure that they did not end in a tangled mess on the floor at the important moment.

Will was relieved of his duties for the occasion, and prepared his costume like everyone else.

"You need a holiday," I told him. "Go, join in with my guests. They are so exuberant they will laugh at the most indifferent things. Pity to waste a first-rate comedy master on them. I have engaged the lads in training to provide entertainment. Come, sit at the high table for the feast. I command you!"

He laughed—or was it a laugh? "What? With you and the Princesses, both of them dispossessed or discredited in some way? Do I belong in that company? Truly?"

"We are all misfits up there," I heard myself saying. A King with a malady, I thought, but did not say. "All with some blot on our records, but there, and strong, nonetheless. I would be honoured to have you amongst us."

His face opened up; he was momentarily disarmed, and able to accept affection.

"I would be honoured also," he said quietly.

*

I had not seen Catherine since the onset of my leg malady, and had been grateful for her presence elsewhere. She romped about much more than my daughters, which led me to the conclusion that romping was a trait of personality, not of age. Brandon still romped, and he had passed fifty some time ago. His bride, Katherine, did not, and she was some thirty-five years younger.

All was in order. That evening everyone took his meagre supper in his rooms, freeing the Great Hall for the decorating and festooning. I followed suit, glad to have cinnamon-flavoured porridge and spiced ale, plain black bread and then an early bedtime, all under the guise of resting up for the morrow.

Dr. Butts checked my leg, and although it was no better, he pronounced it no worse. That pleased me. It meant I could dance the following night.

*

It would take a full hour for me to array myself in my costume, so delicate were its lacings and workings. The visor of beaten silver was so thin it was like tissue, and as easily crumpled. Culpepper and Lacey wriggled into the camel costume with much muttering. It was hot in there, they protested, and the pouches of food and flasks of wine they had strapped on themselves would hardly suffice until dawn.

"You must imagine yourselves to *be* camels, able to go days without nourishment," I said. Their grumbling displeased me. It smacked of softness, an abomination in an Englishman. We must be strong, not effete like the whining Frenchman.

They muttered some more. "Silence!" I thundered. The brown velvet humps obeyed.

We delayed changing into our costumes until we were done with the banquet. Visors did not permit for ease of eating.

The Great Hall was bright with the characteristic colour of candle and torchlight. No matter how many pounds of beeswax and tallow one employs, the resulting light is never the clear, bright colour of sunlight or moonlight, but always retains a golden hue. Tonight, ten thousand pounds of wax gave their best, but the upper reaches of the hammerbeam ceiling were lost in haze and shadow, and one was aware that outside this artificial blaze of light and warmth, the winter crouched. The mead hall—wherein all feasted, kept company, and a Norse poet had said life was like the lost sparrow who found his way in while the darkness waited coldly outside. But the passageway was brief, too brief, and all too soon he found himself outside, and dying.

I was inside tonight. No need to dwell on such melancholy, darkling thoughts. My leg was quiescent, whether of its own accord or by the physician's skill, who could say? No questions, ask no questions, accept what is. Questions stink of the rottenness under all the bright things.

I took my place with my Queen and family at the high table. It was the first time in two days I had seen Catherine, and as always, I was stunned by her sheer physical beauty when seen afresh.

"My love," I whispered, reaching over to stroke her cheek, soft and as smooth as ivory.

She smiled.

⚜

The feast was superlative. Even in deepest winter, and after having fed this entire company for a fortnight already, the master cooks presented three separate courses consisting of twenty-five dishes each. There were twenty large Twelfth Night cakes, one for each table. The most elaborate one was presented to the royal table on an ivory board. It had towers and turrets and a checkerboard design: an exact facsimile of Nonsuch Palace!

I cut into its fruited, glazed surface and offered slices to everyone. Last of all, I took my own piece.

Who would find the bean? I must confess I hoped to. The good fortune it foretold I fain would have—some sort of assurance, no matter how flimsy, that the coming year would be blessed.

Mouths moving, chewing, all up and down the table. Who would bite on the lucky bean, the symbolic fortune-bringer?

"Pff—toooo!" Anne of Cleves extracted the coveted bean from her mouth by spitting it onto her plate.

"It is the Princess of Cleves!" announced Will. Everyone nodded, pretending to be relieved that now they could eat without danger of choking or damaging their teeth. Everyone was secretly disappointed.

"It is the year of the Lady Anne," I said to the company at large. "At the royal table, my most noble sister has the lucky bean."

There was clapping, and then one by one the others from the lower tables singled out by Dame Fortune stood up.

"I have it," William Paget spoke, from the nearest table. He sounded apologetic. Next to him, Bishop Gardiner glared.

"And I!" boasted Tom Seymour, arising from the next bank of tables. He waved the silver bean aloft. "Ha-ha!" He sounded like a pagan god of plenty.

"I have it," said Niall Mor, the Irish lad, slowly coming to his feet. He was clad in his familial cloak, with a gold shoulder-brooch as large as a lump of coal and as intricately fashioned as an earring from Damascus. His red hair glowed like the fires of hell.

Catherine kept her eyes on him and did not shift her gaze to the next table when a fat Cambridgeshire baron began crowing, "I have it here!"

✤ WILL:

The Fates were correct. Of all the adults at the King's High Table, Anne of Cleves would certainly be considered the luckiest, at least from our vantage point today. At least she is still alive, on good terms with everyone, and reportedly enjoying life.

✤ HENRY VIII:

The tables were cleared, their great red runners rolled up, the trestles beneath them collapsed. The Great Hall was emptied, ready to be transformed into a staging-place for revels. I could hear the sounds of the musicians assembling, plaintively tuning their instruments in the gallery overhead.

As I made my way back to my chamber to costume myself, I became aware of scuttlings and movements in the darkness of adjoining passageways and alcoves. Hampton Court was blessed with hidey-holes where lovers could steal their privacy. This was curious, as Wolsey had planned the layout and design, and as a churchman he should have had little interest in providing for such needs, as he had allegedly abjured them.

In my inner chamber, I had my leg surreptitiously checked and re-bandaged by Dr. Butts. He wrapped it in fine silk, so although it was tightly bound it would not be bulky.

"For tonight only," he cautioned. "Silk is not an agreeable bandage. It does not absorb. So, should the sore weep, it will leak and be visible. But it looks dry for now. It should keep for a few hours, at least." He nodded. "Take a good dose of the soothing-syrup."

"Nay. It dulls the pain but it also befuddles me, and I must needs remember all the dancing-steps."

I turned to look at myself in the mirror. I was unrecognizable, a vision from the East.

The Great Hall, too, was unrecognizable, utterly transformed from our eating-place of only an hour earlier. A throng of strangers milled about on the floor. A harem-girl. Merlin the magician. Several nuns. There was Pope Adrian, the only English Pope, looking remarkably like myself. (Who had done this?) There was a headsman with a hood and bloody axe, Friar Tuck, painted savages from the New World, werewolves, crusaders. At the far end of the hall, Jezebel. She was wearing a scanty costume that revealed three-quarters of her body, and next to her was a man dressed as Elijah, ranting and raving. As she moved, I knew her—Catherine!

I was appalled. The Queen of England! How dare she appear almost naked in public, dressed as a harlot and an evil queen? Jezebel was wicked, a symbol of wickedness, and an enemy of the Lord. I watched carefully as Elijah harangued her, pointing his fingers sanctimoniously at a mock Torah. Behind them came a pudgy, greasy-haired King Ahab, licking his fingers and giggling. Who were her accomplices? The onlookers laughed and cheered them on, clearly delighting in the sacrilegious display.

No one took notice of *my* elaborate costume, even with the camel trailing behind. No, they were too enthralled with Jezebel.

A Cleopatra entered the hall, with snakes coiling around her belly. They cosied up to her and slithered into the private reaches of her costume. A drunken Mark Antony followed, and then Julius Caesar, falling down regularly in fits. Foam spouted out of his mouth (replenished from a container of whipped egg whites he carried). The crowd cried, "Fall, mighty Caesar!" Every ten feet he obliged.

Troilus and Cressida made the next entrance. They hung upon each other, these lovers of ancient Troy, kissing and caressing. Then a large company of oiled athletes grabbed hold of Cressida and, before Troilus's weeping eyes, pulled up her skirt and made sport of her, fingering her private parts, whilst she swooned in ecstasy and jerked spasmodically in mock fulfilment.

What had become of the gentle, knightly disguises of my past? Was this what Twelfth Night had turned into? I looked round. A few old-timers were decked out in the beautiful, intricate costumes I had expected, whilst all around them rioted obscene youth.

The Abbot of Misrule appeared on the dais, to a great gasp. He was a human-sized private part, complete even to a ring of circumcision. Around his feet sprouted black wires, to mimic pubic hairs, which shook and swayed. The organ itself stood upright, turgid and blushing. The Abbot wiggled back and forth to command attention.

"Dear company," a muffled voice spoke from the organ. "It is not often that I have the opportunity to appear before such a noble group." Scattered laughter. "I stand before you, at your service." Screams of laughter. "Some of you have seen me often. To others I am as yet unknown." He bowed toward the "nuns." "Or perhaps not so?" More laughter. "Now you are all agreed to do exactly as I command you. I desire, therefore, that everyone with a body-part like my own gather at the far end of the Hall. Those who are cloven between the legs, stay here."

Eager to see what he had in mind, the entire company rushed to obey. I was pushed along in the company of men, so that I lost my camel. But what matter? My costume, my entire idea, was *passé*. No one cared about the Wise Men, or their camels.

Game after game followed, under the direction of the Abbot. Obscene, silly games. When the youngsters tired of them (for obscenity runs its course, like any other novelty), they were ready to dance.

The dancing would begin with the basse dance, a stately, slow entrance step designed to show off elaborate costumes and set a tone of solemnity. Set in the midst of this rowdy, bawdy evening, it seemed out of place. But perhaps it would help turn the mood, let me recapture the ambiance wherein I felt most at home. I looked round at the glittering company, all animal-masked and yet half naked. Somehow it made me shiver.

"And so we dance, to bring the days of Christmas to a close. Each man choose a partner, for reasons of his heart," said the Abbot. He sounded weary.

Until now I had refused to speak to Catherine, because I was so offended by her costume. Now I said, "I, the wise astrologer, the magus, would fain dance with . . . Jezebel."

From the midst of the company, Jezebel came slowly and insolently forward and took her place by my side.

As the rest of the men took partners, I allowed myself to gaze at Catherine, in all her wanton disguise. I drowned in the sight of her: her waves of thick auburn hair, her ivory-skinned body, her voluptuous belly, indented like an hourglass.

"We are citizens of the East," I bowed. "It is fitting that we should keep company." Silent, she inclined her head. I took her jewelled fingers. It was the first time in days I had touched her, and it sent pulsations through me.

Behind the Abbot of Misrule the partners lined up, like a great snake. At last everyone was paired off, and the creature began to move, undulating slowly forward to the coaxing notes of flute and shawm. I felt the hairs prickling on my neck at the ancient, commanding music, and at the sexual nearness of this creature by my side. This creature, who was also my wife. But never truly mine, never mine, I always sensed . . . and so it heightened the leaping desire in me.

"Jezebel was evil," I whispered. But it was only words; I did not care that she was evil. She beguiled me. (Or was it merely desire for the moist ecstasy that lay beneath her gauzy skirt? To this day I do not know.)

"She had a fool for a husband," whispered the creature. She made it all sound excusable. "Ahab was so intimidated by the prophets. As More and the Pope tried to intimidate you. Thanks be to God I have not such a womanish husband." She squirmed toward me for a kiss, and as she turned, a gap appeared in her costume's belly-band, and I could see the red hairs guarding her secret places. O God! It triggered my blood, and I felt myself stirring. Had she twisted that way before? Had others seen? Seen what only I was privileged to possess? And have access to?

The tempo livened.

A double bransle. Good. Now I would show myself. About a third of the company left the dancing, knowing they could not compete.

"Play on," whined the Phallus-Abbot. He tilted somewhat. Was he wilting? As if he could read our thoughts, he bent over. "The end draws nigh," he rasped. Then he sought a chair and slumped into it.

The double bransle was a middling sort of dance. It required a knowledge of steps, but did not demand a great deal of rigour. Catherine and I executed it neatly. But she did not speak during all the dances, keeping a mysterious silence. At length there were only the exhibition dances left, at which I intended to perform. Always in the past, this had been the grand culmination of the evening, the performance the entire company yearned for. But now I sensed that it was an indulgence, not a desired offering. It was something the people allowed the monarch to perform, humouring him, not something they truly relished.

I danced perfectly, keeping pace with the music, the increasing intricacy. One by one the others faded back, leaving only me. I commanded the stage as I had done before, as I always had done, or believed I had done. My timing was perfect; there was no fault in my performance. I landed precisely as I should, and stood rigid, my arms outstretched. Applause, as manners dictated, filled my ears. As I stood, slippers clinging to my perfectly positioned feet (and no wetness within), I heard the clock tolling midnight.

"Christmas—Christmas departs," mourned the Phallus. "Our costumes we must lay by, our everyday lives take up." He bowed, shuddered, swayed. "We must unmask." He ripped off his head-covering, that impudent, rounded protuberance. It was Tom Seymour. The company gasped.

The pox-infested Francis I removed his mask. Bishop Gardiner!

When my turn came, I peeled off my own silver visor carefully. "I, Balthazar, King of the East, happily existed for one evening amongst you. Now I am consigned to darkness again, to await another resurrection." People clapped and pretended to be surprised. "There is yet another gift and surprise to be revealed," I announced. "It is this." I held aloft a velvet-lined box, wherein nestled a golden coin, minted but a fortnight past. "A gold sovereign, in honour of my beloved Queen, Catherine. On this side is her likeness. On the other, the seal of England, with her own motto, the motto I have bestowed upon her: *Rutilans Rosa Sine Spina*. The Rose Without a Thorn."

Now true silence fell upon the company. To mint a special issue of coin, in honour of one's bride . . . such a token of love robbed them of speech. As it robbed Catherine.

"O Your Majesty—" she began, then her words died.

I encircled her waist. "Unmask," I commanded.

Stiffly, she obeyed. She peeled the mask from her eyes, said softly, "I disguise myself as what I am not—a Jezebel." She stretched out trembling fingers to grasp the coin of honour. "Thank you," she whispered.

It took over two hours for all to unmask, and after the first few moments it grew tedious. But it was an integral part of the ceremony, and I would not cheat anyone of it. I stood, as if I thirsted to know every identity, and laughed as loudly as anyone.

But by the time it was done, it was past two and my ardour had fled. In my mind I wanted to bed Catherine, but my body betrayed me and cried out for sleep, rest, mending. Duty obliged me to be the last to leave the hall, and I never failed my duty. Besides, there was a sweet satisfaction in seeing a thing through to its end, in surveying the empty Great Hall, strewn with discarded silken scarves and gold-dust and spots of spilled wine, and knowing it all well done. A satisfaction that gave its own benediction.

Then I stumbled to bed, alone, in the odd early hours between Twelfth Night and the dawning of the workaday world.

C

I slept disjointedly for hours, burrowing about in rumpled sheets and mounds of covers. When at last I sat upright, I did not feel rested. Quite the opposite. I should have felt better oriented if I had remained awake all night.

I looked down at the leg, still wound round by its silken bandages. I had neglected to unwrap it last night. Now I did so, expecting to find it saturated with fluid and adhering to the ugly crater beneath. To my surprise it was dry, and as I removed layer after layer of silk, it remained so. The edges of the wound were dry and healing.

I had a desire to spit at it, to aim right in its scabbed-over centre. *Now* it dried itself! Why not a week ago? I hated the sore with a hatred theologians said one should reserve for the Evil One.

❧ ❧

By that afternoon, the courtyard was thick with folk saddling up to embark homeward. The sky was clear. We were blessed in that, for they would have a safe journey. I felt both a loss and a relief at their going.

As soon as the last carts rumbled away, I summoned the Privy Council to meet. There had been no business done for more than a month. Of course, there was less business to transact in winter. All the courts of Europe observed a month-long hiatus to celebrate Christmas. No messengers or ambassadors or spies could travel easily across the frozen, rutted roads, and certainly a sea voyage would be sheer folly. It was impossible to conduct a war, so that all campaigning had to end by October, cancelling battles in mid-fight. Nonetheless, some things needed attention, and the time was at hand.

One by long-faced one, they filed into the Council Chamber, which had been kept pristine and sacrosanct during the revels. Paget, the Principal Secretary, brought his writing materials with him, all arranged in an eelskin case.

"A New Year's present?" I asked him.

He nodded, smiling. It was a most fitting gift for a secretary of the Council.

"Now, most worthy company," I said, leaning forward on my knuckles across the oaken table. "I would be appraised of every situation outside our little world of Hampton Court." I nodded toward Norfolk. "As ranking peer, and lately our ambassador abroad, speak. What word have you received from our envoys?"

He rose, his ermine-trimmed mantle (it was ancient; the fur was yellowing) drawn close about his neck. "France is quiet," he intoned, like a liturgy. "Francis is fevered and restless. Charles is beset all about by the problems of his chop-logic Empire. It was an unlikely concoction from the start, entirely a whim of Charlemagne's. Now Charles V must preside over its dissolution."

"Specifics, Norfolk," I reminded him. Without a Cromwell to keep men to the issue at hand—God, how they wandered. Cromwell . . .

"The Lutheran revolt goes on," he said. "All the Low Countries and half of Germany have been seduced. The other half of the Empire fights back, like a man taken with plague. The heretical outbreaks are the black pustules which weaken and drain the entire system. Spain is the patient's mouth, wherein the medicine—orthodox Catholicism—is poured in full-strength to combat it. Alas, all it does is burn the mouth—as the Inquisition is blistering Spain—without ever touching the buboes themselves."

"My, my. Such poetic analogies. I now understand where your son gets his wild conceits and fantastical metaphors. And to think I thought you merely a tough and literal-minded soldier. But what of the Scots? You have fought them; you know them best of anyone. What news from our spies there?"

"The North mocks you," he said plainly. "They are a nest of traitors you must needs clean out again and again." His eyes danced. He loved killing Scots, riding over the River Tweed and burning their simple homes and terrorizing them. "But they have no truck with the Emperor," he had to admit. "They are not at the moment in league with any of Your Majesty's enemies."

"May I speak?" young Lord Clinton, all bursting with power and prowess, asked politely. I gave him leave. He stood slowly, and as he rose, his physical presence dominated the table—except where it met my own presence. There it stuck.

"I am Lincolnshire born and bred," he said. "A Northman of the realm. You know not, any of you, what it is to be a Northman. We live and take our selfhood from the moors, the wild mountains, far from London and courtish ways. We are conservative, it is said. Those on the frontiers are always conservative. They believe in werewolves and saints. There are no half-measures about them. Percy of the North—Northumberland, to be correct—was called

Hotspur. We are either hot or cold, and our loyalties outlast our lives. We believe—"

"What *is* it, Clinton?" I cut off his inferior poetical ramblings. "Is there something I need to know concerning the North?" I could almost feel Cromwell behind me, sarcastically asking the essential questions.

"The Pilgrimage of Grace began in Lincolnshire. Its leaders were executed, and others as well. But the *spirit,* the spirit lives on! The sight of ruined monasteries infuriates them. They want—"

"By God!" I exploded. "I executed Cromwell. Why, that was one of their very demands! I repudiated the alliance with Cleves and the German Protestants and took a bride as Catholic and old-family as they could have invented. What more could they possibly want?"

"The old ways back."

"What, will they next want the Roman Empire restored, so that they can be protected by a friendly garrison in York, as they were a thousand years ago? Perhaps they'd like the Wall of Hadrian patched up, too—as if *that* ever stopped a Scot!"

"Your Majesty," he protested, "I speak not on their behalf, but to warn the Council of possible trouble."

"Yes, I appreciate that. Your warning is well taken. So my troubles come from the North, rather than from across the Channel?"

"I agree," chimed in Brandon. "Although I prefer fighting on the Continent."

"Ah, your names suit you well. Norfolk for the North, Suffolk for the South." My faithful warriors. But aging. How much longer could they lead my armies forth to battle? Norfolk was sixty-eight, Brandon, fifty-six.

"The Scots are quiet for now," I mused. "I hold Alister MacDonald hostage, as it were. That's what the young Laird is, a surety that his father won't make trouble. But the western Lord of the Isles is not the same as the government—whatever government there is."

Cranmer spoke. "They have never seen you," he said simply. "To them you are but a name. If they but beheld your person—"

True. There was a special bond formed between men whose eyes met, and I had evoked that bond between myself and my subjects on the very first day of my Kingship, when I rode forth to the Tower. They looked upon me, knew my love for them, and were mine. But my own subjects of the North had never seen me. Londoners had; Kentishmen had; even Frenchmen had. But Lincolnshire men, Northumberland men, Yorkshire men, Scotsmen—no.

"Why, I'll go there," I said, almost in wonder.

"A progress," prompted Bishop Gardiner. "A great progress, to show yourself to Scotsmen as you once showed yourself to the French at the Field of Cloth of Gold."

Yes. Of course. I was lost in the vision of it, stunned by its implications. It would solve everything.

As we left the Council Chamber, I touched Lord Clinton's arm. "You shall host us," I said. "You shall show us the hospitality of the North." He looked pleased. "And Lady Clinton? I trust this will be acceptable to her?"

We were two men together, and the fact that we had cared for the same woman served as a bond. "Bessie is ill," he said, after a pause. "Perhaps the North did not agree so well with her."

I could not help but pity women, always consigned to live in localities of their husbands' whim and choosing. "Is it—"

"Her lungs."

Yes, I had noted that consumptive appearance in her, but thrust it away in my mind. "I see." No need to say she'd heal. There was no healing from consumption. I remembered Dr. Butts's words, how it seemed to have staked out the Tudors for its victims. Suddenly the leg-sore, if it were a substitute, looked easy.

"I am grieved," I finally said. I touched his hand. He nodded and, keeping his eyes averted, turned away.

So Bessie would return to her Lincolnshire and spend a last summer there. I prayed it would be a warm one, with field flowers aplenty, and that characteristic wild thyme scenting the air.

Suddenly I felt very naked and stripped by death. All along, he had been plucking people from me, but there had been so many on the branches that I had never begrudged him his due. The way of all flesh, I had murmured sanctimoniously to myself, knowing he had a certain quota and that I, and those dear to me, would not be called up for some time yet. Well, he had run down his list, and now we were at the head of it.

I returned to my own apartments and sat glumly staring at the floor. I wanted to be alone; I did not want to be alone. There was only one person for such a mood—Will.

"You have sent for me?"

I scarce was able to look up. "Yes. I need you." I had never spoken those words before to any man.

"I am here. What troubles you?"

I told him, then. How death had me and those I loved by the throat. How I felt his very fingers on my windpipe, until I scarce could breathe. I named those he had already claimed, and those he was even now in the process of possessing.

"I feel him, too," admitted Will. "Of late I have had to note that there is something chronically wrong with my body. I never have the whole functioning of it any longer. There is always something I must favour, some part I am waiting to have healed. It is disheartening. We are not what once we were. But that is not a signal that death is at hand. Merely that we are being granted a long life. Deaths of those we love en route are also signs we are being spared. Philosophers who discuss the possibility of long life always say that old people long to die, because they are so lonely, having outlived everyone they have had links with. Why is that? Why are they lonely? There are as many people about as in their youth. But the ability to form strong links apparently ceases after a certain age. Affinity arises in youth, and, if we are lucky, endures through to old age."

I nodded. Brandon. More. My sister Mary. Bessie. Will himself. But Catherine, my sweet Catherine . . . her I loved, and that was a new thing. I was still capable of forming bonds. I was not past that stage.

Just as suddenly my unhappy mood was gone, and this melancholy talk annoyed me. I did not think, then, to trace the source of my reactions. I had grieved because Bessie, the love of my youth, was dying, but became indignant when Will suggested that my capacity for loving and being loved was being exhausted. You see, there was the problem of Catherine Howard, and fitting her into all this.

CI

Only a few hours later I lay on the silken sheets of the great royal bed, toying with Catherine. I had drawn the embroidered gold-threaded curtains about us, until we could play at being in a tent on the plains of France. Candlelight leapt up and down in the errant drafts of air seeping under the bed-drapes, but that made it all the more eerie and otherworldly, a playhouse for adults. . . .

Catherine giggled as I touched her throat. I traced its curves and hollows, finding the skin slippery and moist. How was that possible in the dry days of winter?

"For New Year's I was given a cream from Syria," she said, as if reading my thoughts. "It was compounded of substances we have not here in England."

From Syria? "Who has been to Syria?" I could not help enquiring. No one traded openly with the Infidels these days.

"Francis Dereham," she laughed. "He was a pirate in the Irish Sea for a time. Pirates 'trade' with everyone."

I frowned.

"My cousin," she whispered, tickling my ear with her tongue. "You remember."

"He looked like a pirate," I grunted. She was arousing me, and I wished not to be aroused. Not quite yet. "He is not here? He and his like must not be seen with you at true court."

She lay back in the pillows, wriggling like a silverfish. "I sent him away," she yawned. "He will doubtless return to piracy."

"As proper brokenhearted lovers do. Is he brokenhearted?" A casual question.

"He has no heart. Or what he has, 'tis black."

She laughed, lying upon the pillows, a Gypsy herself. Now she was holding out her arms, an expression of utter desire and yearning on her face. I could see how she loved me, wanted me. In her young and unlined face there was lust in its purest form. There—was that not proof of how she craved me?

She was wearing, beneath her gown of velvet, lacy undergarments of silk, and re-embroidered silk. They were warm with her body heat, almost like living creatures as I peeled them away. At last she lay naked before my gaze. Her stomach was so flat and taut I could see it throbbing as her heart beat. It was like the trembling of skin stretched over a drum-head.

I was not ashamed to undress and reveal myself to her. In years past I had been called an Apollo, an Olympic athlete, and I was in the process of reclaiming that body, thanks to my regimen of daily riding, strength-tossing of a great beam, and, in the secret hours in my withdrawing chamber, lifting of weights. As her skilful fingers pushed back the folds of my sheer linen undershirt, I wanted her to see me. I wanted to present myself to her, a sacrifice of my love.

She withdrew the linen shirt, and we were husband and wife, naked as Adam and Eve. She traced her fingertip (polished with red stain; was that, also, a gift of the pirate?) along my chest, midway between my shoulders and my nipples. She raised a wake of gooseflesh.

"Your chest is so broad," she said dreamily. "Half again as wide as a yeoman's."

I looked down at her. Lounging against the pillows, parts of her half-visible in the feather mattress enveloping her, she looked like a sleek, voluptuous snake. She was not Eve, but the serpent.

I wanted to be one with her. I ached to blend myself with her. "Catherine"—I murmured, sucking her mouth into mine—"wife."

She arched herself up toward me, pressing her slippery, perfumed flesh against my own unadorned, natural body. They met, locked.

She flung her legs around my body. They felt like warm serpents, coiling about me, capturing me. Her private parts, her succulent woman-parts, were opened and moistly waiting to receive me. There were so many layers of them, spread open like an intricate flower-heart, with its deep, shadowed core. With a cry of joy, I flung myself into that core, and was swallowed up in ecstasy.

꧁ ꧂

That is the poetical description. Now shall I give it the plain description, that which would be required in a court of law? For I have found myself, as I wrote this, first reluctant, then angry. I write from a vantage point and a knowledge I did not have then. You have had the duped version, as well as I could recreate it, though it sticks in my throat to remember it. Now you shall have the true version, shadowed with later knowledge.

There she was, the harlot, all oiled and anointed, and she bewitched me. In her presence and with her performance I believed myself desired and adored, and when I thrust myself home into her very self, I believed us united, I believed

I had a wife. She moved with me, she returned each motion, shuddering as if she were transported to Paradise, and I plunged into her person, engulfed in the depths, inflamed with my love, and felt her quivering, trembling, then jerking with release. She emitted strange cries, and I felt the squeezing pulsations, coming like waves from her inner parts. My seed had seeped out all around, bathing us both, giving sticky blessing to our love. I lay on her, savouring the pulsations, the emissions. I could feel the last feeble spurts and oozings from my organ and her womb.

Why do I record this? The memory is not sweet, it is disgusting. But it *should* be sweet, it should live on as a cherished memory. Only the truth is this: one-sided love leaves no sweetness, no memories. It is like a puff-pastry, sustained not by actual events but by the intoxicated lover's emotions. When those emotions collapse, nothing remains to remember. There. I have recorded it all. My shame and folly, her treachery, our mutual pleasure. For there was pleasure, that is the pity of it. That is the part I cannot understand—that pleasure. It stands on its own, unassailable, like a god.

A week later I was stricken, felled.

CII

🪶 WILL:

I am intrigued by his remembrances here. He had appeared feverish, almost beside himself all during the Christmas festivities. So naturally when he sent for me on that first day afterward, I assumed it was because he wished to confess. I was his secular confessor, Cranmer his spiritual. And I knew what it concerned: his extravagant gesture in having a coin struck in Catherine's honour. I intended to tell him exactly what public opinion was: that people were scandalized; worse than that (from his point of view), they ridiculed him. They called him a fond old man, a lecher whose private parts were blinding his eyes, an embarrassment. Catherine was not accepted as Queen. The people wanted Anne of Cleves, whom they perceived (thick though they were, they possessed a natural wisdom) as someone of character and noble blood. Catherine Howard? They knew a slut when they saw one, even if the King did not. I meant to tell him this, because I assumed he was troubled. But I never had the opportunity, although I should have been bold and made one. Before I could do so, he fell ill and his life was despaired of.

🪶 🪶

I had been warming myself by a dying fire, wondering how to coax an extra log from the Privy Chamber allotment, when Culpepper tapped me on the shoulder, agitated as could be.

"The King's—dying," he cried.

"How?" I had left him well the evening before, jovially sunk in pillows and making lists for his northern progress. How he loved lists, and busy-work. He was never happier than when swamped in paperwork for one of his beloved projects.

"His leg." I shot a look at him. No one was supposed to know about the King's malady. He kept it a fierce secret. How had Culpepper found out? And was he blabbing it about?

"It closed over, and sent black humours to his head," said Culpepper.

What nonsense. It had closed over after the holidays, leaving as cheery and pretty a pink scar as one would desire.

I stood up. I must go to him.

What I beheld in his chamber was terrifying. Gone was the Henry I had known, served, and (yes) loved since my youth. In his place was a feeble, spasmodic man, his face greenish black. He thrashed about, unable to control his body movements, like a spitted animal. And he was completely speechless.

Outside his chamber they waited, black-robed, like vultures. What would his passing mean to each of them? I shook, a victim of my own fear. Edward was but three years old. Sweet Jesu! We had no King!

I heard wild, metallic laughter echoing. It was my own. *Married for thirty years, to five different women, but he leaves no King behind. . . .*

Someone muffled me and escorted me out. I was crying, laughing, and motioning hysterically. I suppose I was a menace.

✑ HENRY VIII:

The day had started so reasonably, so sweetly. I had drawn on my boots and made ready for the barber. I remember glancing toward the window and thinking how calm and utterly boring a day in late February can be. The sky was an ugly neutral offspring of grey and white, and every naked branch was motionless. The sun was nowhere in evidence, so swaddled was it by the blankets of clouds. Lent was approaching—the dreariest time of the year. The world was enervated.

Then suddenly an intense heat, a squeezing, gripped my brain. I opened my mouth to call out, and I could not. I felt myself pitching forward, the inlaid, polished wooden floor zooming up to meet me, to smash me in the face—but it was I hurtling toward it, and I was unable to spread out my arms to break my fall. I toppled over like a chopped tree in the forest, smashing things around me—the little table with my reading glasses and bedside Psalter, the great chamber candlestick balanced on its three carved legs. I hit, expecting to feel pain, and felt nothing. My nose crumpled, and I could see blood beginning to flow. I tried to crawl away, and heave myself up, but I was paralysed. And then I began to choke and could not clear my throat. I was drowning in my own blood. It ran hot and salty down into my lungs, and breath began to fail.

Someone lifted me, pulled my shoulders back, and a shimmering sheet of blood poured from my mouth. I remember the redness, how it was so much brighter than rubies. Then all brightness fled, and there was nothing.

How long there was nothing I do not know. I awoke—if I can describe it so—to find myself lying upon a daybed. I was heaped round with pillows and furs and evidently had been there for some time. An angry fire spat and gurgled in the fireplace nearby, choked by its overload of logs. From my position beside it, I knew I had been moved there to take advantage of the heat. I stroked the fur of my covers on the fire-side. It was too hot. The pelt would be singed. I made a motion.

Not until I did, did I realize the implications. My body was free again. It obeyed my commands. I stroked the fur once more, feeling its sleek surface, just to test myself. But it was being damaged. They should move me farther away.

Who were "they"? I was alone in the chamber. I could discern no one lurking round in the shadows. Good. That in itself was a favourable sign. It meant no one expected me to die. I remembered the crowds of "observers" in Father's chambers those last few weeks of his life. Sweet Jesu! It was the same time of year! He had taken to his sickbed in January; lingered, hacking, through February and March; died in April.

Suddenly it was very important that I talk to someone. I called.

No sound came.

My throat was swollen, blocked up from disuse. I cleared it, rattling all the membranes. *Now!* I called.

Silence.

I was dumb! God had taken away my speech.

I strained all my muscles. Still, silence.

I was so stunned there was nothing for it but to fall back limply onto the pillows.

It could not be permanent. It must be some laggard part of my healing. When first I had fallen, I could not move my hands. Now I could. This dumbness, too, must fade. It *must*.

The fire exploded with sparks and hissing. Then it subsided into sighing. Like a woman, I thought.

But what had happened? There had been the morning, getting dressed. Then the seizure, the paralysis, the fall. My nose crunching. I put out a hand and touched my nose. It was heavily bandaged, with two wooden supports down each side. I had broken it, then.

Why had I pitched forward? What malady had seized me? I threw all my will and might behind my throat, and called again. Silence.

I had been struck dumb. Like John the Baptist's father, Zacharias. Why? God never acted without reason. Zacharias had been struck dumb because he had argued with the angel Gabriel, when the angel came to announce the Good News.

My Scriptures were in their customary place, and I sought them out, turning to the portion about Zacharias.

> Fear not, Zacharias: for thy prayer is heard; and thy wife Elisabeth shall bear thee a son, and thou shalt call his name John.
>
> And Zacharias said unto the angel, Whereby shall I know this? for I am an old man, and my wife well stricken in years.
>
> And the angel answering said unto him, I am Gabriel, that stand in the presence of God;
>
> And behold, thou shalt be dumb, and not able to speak, until the day that these things shall be performed, because thou believest not my words, which shall be fulfilled in this season.

Had I, too, received a messenger or a sign, and refused to believe?

No. There had been no sign, no message. Of that I was certain. I would welcome a conversation with God, or his angel. All my life I had awaited it. But He had never spoken directly to me.

The door creaked open. Someone was checking on the royal patient. I made gestures for him to come forward. It was a page. I mimicked writing motions.

The lad looked clean frightened out of his skin. Perhaps, after all, they *had* expected me to die.

Dr. Butts followed, looking grave and curious. He carried his leather pouch, crammed with potions and flasks. He sat down on a footstool beside my elaborate sickbed and touched my eyelids, then felt along my neck. He peeled back the coverlets and nightshirt and bent his head to my chest, motioning for everyone to be quiet so he could discern my heartbeats. Satisfied, he restored me to my covered state and then began to tape and probe the leg.

As he removed the herb-soaked bandage, I was astonished. A great round wound festered in the old afflicted spot upon my thigh. It was deeper and uglier than I had ever seen it before. A small clay cup strapped beneath it was filled with foul secretions from the ulcer. Dr. Butts removed it deftly, and put another in its place.

"The ulcer closed," he said slowly, as if he were speaking to a child or a simpleton. "Your life was in danger. It has been three days now since I opened the closure and let it begin to drain. Thirteen cups have been filled with this discharge. It seems to have spent itself. Thanks be to God! It was backed up into Your Grace's body, acting as a poison."

He looked at me, his bright eyes trying to discern any answering spark in me.

"He motioned for writing paper and pen," the page remembered.

"A good sign!" said Dr. Butts. "Pray fetch them." He continued to observe me. It was a strange feeling to be totally passive, unable to participate in one's own life-drama.

The pen in my hand, I wrote out: *How long ago was I stricken? How long till I be well? And why can I not speak?* I put the most frightening question last, as if to reduce its power and importance.

Dr. Butts nodded, pleased with my efforts. "You were stricken on Wednesday last," he said loudly. Did he think me deaf as well? "At the rate you are mending, I would say another fortnight before we have you up and about. As for your speech"—he shook his head—"it puzzles me. I cannot understand why it has not returned. Perhaps the evil humours from your leg have seeped into your throat."

He noted my frown. "But now that the leg is open, and draining, these poisons will flow from your system, freeing your throat." He paused, then added, "God willing."

So he, too, acknowledged this stoppage of voice as a Divine Sign. Behind all his smooth physician's talk he knew the truth. Only God decided when such a mark would be lifted.

O Father, O Son, O Holy Ghost—wherefore had I offended, fallen short? If I had even known my transgressions, I could amend them. But I was ignorant!

There was no way I could hope to find the clue to my failing by use of reason and memory. It might be in some small thing, so small I would have overlooked it at the time. (Although would God be so unfair as to smite me so hugely for a small thing?) I must pray for enlightenment.

I closed my eyes and concentrated on prayer. I addressed God as a King should wish to be addressed: reverently and humbly. I found myself rummaging in the cupboard of my mind for appropriate phrases. After I had exhausted my stock I created new ones, fashioning them lovingly and tenderly. Then I began thanking Him for all His blessings in my life. As I began enumerating them, I slackened my pace, astonished at how richly I was blessed, but at the same time feeling more and more vulnerable. With each good thing we hold, God possesses us more and more, because we tremble lest he whimsically remove it. And even that fear, we are told, is disloyalty, and therefore a sin. . . . Was that my sin? My lack of utter trust in God? What if—

No. I stopped myself. I had promised myself to pray, to pour out my thoughts and wait for an answer, not interrupt the process half through and answer myself. I continued with my blessings, and began to list not the things I possessed, but the things I was lent to enjoy, things no man may own. The seasons. Sleep. Dreams. Memories. Music. Then I thought of specific things *about* those things. I imagined one leaf on one tree, saw it through its entire life, from its swelling as a bud, to its sticky pale green unfoldings, to its flat, dark, dusty prime in high summer.

As I did this, first with the leaf and then with other things, I entered a sort of trance. I began to talk to God directly, yearning to open everything to Him, because only then could I be united with Him, only then could He reach into whatever was diseased in me and heal it. My speech was wordless, if that is possible for you to understand. I gave myself to God as nakedly as little Edward gave himself up to his nurse every evening, and with the same complete abandon.

I felt an odd bliss, a peaceful ecstasy. My eyes were closed—or were they open? I was not in any worldly place.

My answer came, too, but in wordless form. This palpable sense of peace meant that complete surrender was what God required of me: to continue to give myself to Him without reservation, as I had just done. It would take learning, but those moments would have to come more and more frequently. God would keep me dumb until I had learned to pray with my mind and whole being, rather than just with my lips.

CIII

Whilst I waited to be led further into this rich and baffling relationship with God, my earthly body must needs lie on the fur-warmed couch and endure the wait. It must be beguiled, for earthly hours are long to our earthly clay, even though they pass in a trance for the mystic.

Evening was coming on when Timothy Scarisbrick, a chamber-groom, entered with a tray of food for me. Where was Culpepper, I wondered, but it was a fleeting thought, and quickly skipped away. This lad pleased me well. He was straight and pale and Christ-like, at least the way I imagined the young Christ to be during the unknown years when He was simply Mary's son in Nazareth. He set the tray, a delicate ivory-inlaid thing (it looked Syrian—I liked not that association) on my lap, and pulled off the cover. Eggs, chopped chicken, and soup. Invalid's food. Pallid and wan, like the invalid it supposedly nourished.

After this "nourishment," the physician came again, listened to my heart, removed the drainage cup and replaced it with another, and patted my mound of furs solicitously. "Rest well," he pronounced, like a priest giving absolution. I gestured for my pen and pad, and wrote two requests: *1. Applewood for the fire. 2. Niall Mor, for music.* My servers nodded in unison, as if relieved it was so uncomplicated.

The applewood was already hissing and perfuming the air with its incomparable aroma when Niall Mor approached my bedside. He was wearing some sort of dark swirling cape, and his bright hair shone like fire-opals. I half expected spurts of fire to spring up from his footsteps, as he reminded me overwhelmingly of Pluto, god of the Underworld, in a sketch I had once seen as a child—a sketch showing the god with flowing mantle and smoke rising from his sandal-straps and flame on his head-circlet.

"You wish me?" he asked in a soft, pleasing voice. Too pleasing, as it knew it pleased. That spoiled it.

I wrote out: *Play and sing for me. Songs of Ireland. Anything you like. Tell me; explain the verse.*

He unslung his small harp, which he fondled like a woman. "This is a diatonic harp, gut-strung. We use it either alone, in single lines of melody, or else in what we call *Cerdd Dant,* where we sing poetry in counterpoint to the harp." He swirled a bit in preparing himself to play.

"We have, in Ireland, special triads." He began plucking the harp-strings, so sweetly that they seemed to caress the air.

> "Three things that are always ready in a decent man's house: beer, a bath, a good fire.
> "Three smiles that are worse than griefs: the smile of snow melting, the smile of your wife when another man has been with her, the smile of a mastiff about to spring.
> "Three doors by which falsehood enters: anger in stating the case, shaky information, evidence from bad memory.
> "Three times when speech is better than silence: when urging a king to battle, when reciting a well-turned line of poetry, when giving due praise.
> "Three scarcities that are better than abundance: a scarcity of fancy talk, a scarcity of cows in a small pasture, a scarcity of friends around the beer."

I liked it not. It was gloomy; there was something ominous even about the "happy" triads. I shook my head.

He shrugged, clearly not understanding why I did not want more of it. He struck a chord and began a new poem.

> "Lovely whore, though,
> Lovely, lovely whore
> Slept with Conn,
> Slept with Niall,
> Slept with Brian,
> Slept with Rory.
> "Slide then,
> The long slide.
> "Of course it shows."

What peculiar sentiments the Irish had! Why would they celebrate a whore in verse and achingly poignant melody?

I smiled. The music was exquisite, that I acknowledged. I nodded vigourously, so that he might play on.

From his harp came a sparkling sigh, a whispered wave of beauty.

"Ebb tide has come for me:
My life drifts downward
Like a retreating sea
With no tidal return.

"I am the Hag of Beare,
Five petticoats I used to wear,
Today, gaunt with poverty,
I hunt for rags to cover me.

"Girls nowadays
Dream only of money—
When we were young
We cared more for our men.

"But I bless my King who gave—
Balanced briefly on time's wave—
Largesse of speedy chariots
And champion thoroughbreds.

"These arms, now bony, thin
And useless to younger men,
Once caressed with skill
The limbs of princes!

"Why should I care?
Many's the bright scarf
Adorned my hair in the days
When I drank with the gentry.

"So God be praised
That I misspent my days!
Whether the plunge be bold
Or timid, the blood runs cold.

"But my cloak is mottled with age—
No, I'm beginning to dote—
It's only grey hair straggling
Over my skin like a lichened oak.

"And my right eye has been taken away
As down-payment on heaven's estate;
Likewise the ray in the left
That I may grope to heaven's gate.

"And I, who feasted royally
By candlelight, now pray
In this darkened oratory.
Instead of heady mead

"And wine, high on the bench
With kings, I sup whey
In a nest of hags.
God pity me!

"Alas, I cannot
Again sail youth's sea;
The days of my beauty
Are departed, and desire spent.

"I hear the fierce cry of the wave
Whipped by the wintry wind.
No one will visit me today
Neither nobleman nor slave.

"Flood tide
And the ebb dwindling on the sand!
What the flood rides ashore
The ebb snatches from your hand.

"Flood tide
And the sucking ebb to follow!
Both I have come to know
Pouring down my body.

"Man being of all
Creatures the most miserable—
His flooding pride always seen
But never his tidal turn.

"I have hardly a dwelling
Today, upon this earth.
Where once was life's flood
All is ebb."

His voice floated off, flying on the sweet harp-sound. I felt wretched. The cruel selection, celebrating the horrible: the decaying, deceitful aspects of men and women—was it purposeful? What fool would choose such a poem to cheer a stricken King? It must have been unintentional, and therefore an oblique compliment. One sings such a song only to the young and healthy.

Nonetheless, I felt as if my supper lay like a Lenten carp, belly-up, inside me. I gestured for him to leave me. He frowned in disappointment. Oh, the lad had much to learn in court. It was well he had come to do so.

Alone, I lay back and inhaled the applewood. But in my mouth there lay a bitter taste. "Cruel," I murmured, but no sound issued forth. Still waiting. Well, it was God's will that I learn patience and obedience . . . and embrace His mystery. I shivered and drew the fox-fur collar about me. It was a cold and barren vigil I must keep. And where was Catherine?

When all one has to do is lie abed, one quickly loses the normal rhythm of the day, the one that governs everyday life. There is a great wisdom in the orderly arrangement of the hours and the daily passage of light and dark. An invalid can rearrange those units to suit himself, like a child playing with blocks, and he soon makes a jumble of it.

So I lay awake half the night, because I had had no occupation during the day to exercise and tax me. "Christ prayed all night," it says in the Bible. I tried to do so, but fell into that eerie suspended consciousness that bordered on rapture, communing with the Holy Spirit and then waking, or gliding into full awareness, as the dawn stirrings began in the adjoining chamber. By the time Culpepper had appeared with my newly warmed bedjacket, and the beaming young Scarisbrick approached my bedside, grinning, with the laden tray of breakfast food, I was already sleepy, worn out from my night of wrestling with the angel, so to speak. When other men's blood was stirring, mine was settling. O cursed life, an invalid's! No wonder they never mend.

Culpepper was busy and preoccupied. He brought in my clothes, he attended to all my needs, but in a rattled, distracted way. Once he brought a delicately embossed leather envelope to hold all the correspondence from our ambassadors abroad, made with marvellous flaps and pockets, with a special container for wax and the Royal Stamp. He had designed and commissioned it.

I grasped his arm and nodded thanks. I hated this dumbness. Even though I knew it was—must be!—temporary.

Catherine came in directly after Mass, which she attended daily at eight. She had a devout soul, which, like most physically attractive people, she attempted to hide, as if it were a shame, or would cause others to regard her differently. In the young, that is of paramount importance.

But when she came to me, directly after receiving her Maker, she glowed with a beauty beyond the worldly, could she but know it. I smiled at her, reached up and touched her cheek. The evening previous (when the wood was burning and my body settled), I always wrote out a little letter to her, telling her of my thoughts, my love for her, and my observations on her beauty. Each morning she gladly received it, blushing. And each morning (or was it my imagination, my thwarted, lusty imagination?) she seemed more highly coloured, more skittish.

Thus I pretended to be the patient patient. In truth, I longed to throw off my furs and blankets and take my place once again in the councils of men. How long, O Lord, how long?

Whilst I languished, of course I was visited. Will came in regularly to amuse me. Council members called to appraise me of their complaints. It was indeed the New Men versus the traditionalists these days. Churchmen came to read lists of appointments to me for approval. There were many places to be filled. I busied myself filling in those empty lines.

It was all very neat and ordered. When my churning head wished for sleep, my attendants pulled the draperies and converted the chamber into soft night. The sun was barred from my presence like a prattling child. But that ordained a sleepless night to follow. O Lord, how long?

Note that I did not practise upon my throat-instrument every few hours, hoping to find it restored. Each time I blew upon it, I was rewarded with a resounding silence.

It had been ten days, and I was as utterly scrambled as an egg. No voice. An upside-down sleeping schedule. When Cranmer came to my couch-side, after Culpepper and Catherine had taken their leave and Will had bowed out darkly, he carried nothing. No Church-roll or certificates, or even his notes of a national prayer book. *The Book of Common Prayer,* he meant to call it, although he was bogged down within its windings.

"There's an uprising," Cranmer said, in child's English. "In Lincolnshire."

I gestured for him to continue. "It seems some desperate men conspired to meet at Pomfret Fair," he apologized. As though it were his fault! "There are many wretched men in the North, their needs unanswered—"

How many? was all I cared to know. I asked, in my throat, but nothing came. Angrily I grabbed a pen and paper and repeated myself in writing. How cumbersome it is to have to rely on these manual means of communication!

"Three hundred or so. But the reports are garbled. Hourly they change."

And others may join them, I added to myself. There is a nest up there, a nest of malcontents. With the Scots sitting like a crown on their heads.

I flailed about, anger overtaking me. I beat on my pillows, and tore them with my teeth. I was helpless, helpless—a prisoner of my own body! Furiously, I beat even on it. Take this, I thought as I raised both fists up high and brought them down on my thigh. The muscles shifted underneath like stirring dogs. I opened my throat to roar, and demanded that it obey. No sound came forth.

Defeated, I wrote Cranmer instructions: *1. Find out their leaders. 2. Send Suffolk to me. 3. Begin preparations for possible action against them.* He bowed and was gone. I lay back, feeling like Prometheus in chains. In our day, the voice-box has more power than muscles. And mine was bound, enchained.

CIV

I promised myself that I would not test God by repeatedly checking during the long hours of darkness. But when the first light broke through the iridescent frost covering the windows, that would be a Sign.

The first light broke, and I raised my voice. Silence.

Now I was truly frightened. I needed my voice restored; this was an emergency. It was not for myself I needed it, but for England. Still, God did not heed. *And if he did not heed now . . .*

Mid-morning. Brandon appeared. He looked old, I thought. How detached we are in observing the aging of our contemporaries, as if we were somehow exempt from the same process, or as if it were applied unequally, and our poor friend got a double dose, whereas we ourselves got off lightly.

I had already prepared a list of questions, which I handed to him. His baggy eyes skimmed over them quickly.

"Yes, there are more rebels. That is what this morning's dispatch said. Of course, it is four days old . . . the roads this time of year . . ." He shook his head. "All told, they are still fewer than five hundred. They are playing an old tune, Your Grace. Those who wished to dance to it already did their jig during the Pilgrimage. And afterward—in chains and in the gibbet."

Still, they have enough recruits to begin again, I thought. A never-ending supply of malcontents, traitors, like spring weeds.

"Shall I crush them, Your Grace?" A simple request.

I nodded. Kill the thing now. Pluck the plant up, roots and all. And this was supposed to be the place where I must venture forth, taking my Queen. Suddenly I was ferociously hungry to see this mysterious area, the North, which bred mists and rebels in equal quantity.

"Shall I use the utmost force?" *Shall I kill swiftly and brutally?*

I nodded. The softer way was often, in the long run, the crueller.

He bowed and took his leave.

Brandon. I could rely on him. For half a century now, or almost that, he had been my right arm. But when he failed, as my voice had—what then?

The frost on my windowpanes was melting as the sun rose higher. The days had lengthened noticeably since Christmas, although not enough to put winter to rout. And in the North it would be bitter, icy, and locked in darkness and cold until April. Brandon, the old soldier, would have difficulty penetrating the area. Curses upon the ungracious traitors, to call out my dearest friend, whom as King I could not spare from England's service.

I began to scratch off the obscuring frost with my fingernail. I felt impaired all round, but this one thing I could correct. I could at least see out of my window.

It needed a cloth to wipe away the frost-shavings and watery melt. "A cloth," I muttered, and the page stuck one in my hand. I wiped vigorously at the messy pane, until it glistened free and showed me the white world outside as clear as though I were seeing it through my unobstructed eye.

"Ah," I said. Then I started.

I had spoken, and been heard. My voice was freed.

"Thank you," I said quite naturally to the page. He nodded. " 'Tis lovely." I could hear my own voice, as if it were another's. "You may go now." He bowed and obeyed.

Alone, I blinked in stunned excitement. It was back, my voice was back. I crossed myself and whispered, "Thank You. You have answered my prayers." I crossed over to my prie-dieu and looked up at Jesus on the cross. I looked directly into his eyes, and they seemed to smile at me.

Why had God capriciously decided to restore my voice over such an unimportant command? A cloth to wipe off a frosty window: he had loosened my voice for that.

God frightened me. I understood Him so much less than I had always thought I understood Him.

✥ ✥

The page told everyone that I had spoken, and I was soon dislodged from my praying station.

Now that I was able-bodied again, my councillors presented me with all the ugly details of the northern rebellion. The traitorous statements—"the King is the Devil's agent"; "the King is an Anabaptist"; "the King is haunted by the souls of the monks he killed"—bordered on the blasphemous. What sort of people did I rule?

"I have an evil people to rule!" I shouted in answer to myself. "An unhappy people who harbour sedition in their hearts." I looked round at all the smug faces surrounding me. What of them? What secret malice lay in *their* hearts? "I'll soon make them so poor they'll no longer have the time or energy to indulge their disobedience!" And you, too, I thought. Any one of you youngsters, if your youth and health give you fancy ideas, I'll put a stop to *that*. It's Brandon and I who are in control, the old soldiers who know how to rule.

"They'll die for their treason, and we'll go up in the summer to comfort their widows. The grass won't even have grown on their graves yet! But their sons will welcome us with adulation, whatever else lies coiled in their secret hearts. They'll—"

"Your Majesty!" Dr. Butts entered and looked betrayed. His royal patient was up off the sickbed and behaving as normal. "I had heard of your recovery. Why did you not send for me?" He looked hurt. I had insulted him by calling upon him in my need, clutching to him in fear, and then jettisoning him once I recovered. As men do to God.

"I apologize," I said. "Come, let us be alone." The others took their leave, with relief.

"I could hear your voice halfway down the gallery," he admonished me.

"God restored me."

"So it would seem. And in full volume. Is it wise to run a horse at full gallop who has lain ill and languished in his stall a fortnight? Gradual, and by degrees—that is the way to sound health."

He checked my throat, my chest, my leg. The wound had all but disappeared. Drained and healed over, it looked so inculpable and innocuous. The rotten traitor! Traitor no less than my northern subjects!

"Your heart started up suddenly," he said in alarm. "You must avoid exciting thoughts." He put away his listening tube. And smiled. "But I must say, the Lord in His mercy appears to have healed you."

With a few more instructions regarding my food, drink, and rest, he was gone. I was free of my body-bondage once more.

By the time Brandon reached Cambridge, word came that the rebellion had burnt out, having consumed its own fuel. There was no need for him to apply the stern measure of the law, and so he returned by Easter, when spring was breaking on the court.

CV

Spring and Easter were enveloped, for me, in a web of preparations for our northern progress. As the grass brightened and exploded in green, and the bare branches of every tree and bush suddenly turned into feathery brushes, it was hard to believe that there were places in the realm of England where winter still held the land and reigned. Children shrieked and played out of doors—I could hear them from the opened casements—at marbles, skip-rope, and pace-egging, where they cracked their Easter eggs together. Their cries rose lean and eager, like a wild animal kept too long indoors and now celebrating its freedom. Before nightfall there would be skinned knees and lost scarves. That, too, was part of the celebration.

By day I studied dispatches and made up orderly lists of supplies and courtiers for the journey. There was so much protocol to be observed. There must, of course, be a striking difference between how the remnants of the traitorous rebels were received and how the loyal men. It must be a dazzling difference, to strike awe and shame into their hearts, and make forever clear the difference between the two sorts of subjects.

There was also the problem of my cousin, the King of Scots: young James Stuart, the son of my sister Margaret. He had lately married a French Princess (Marie de Longueville, whom I had briefly considered before the Flemish Mare), and she had borne him two sons forthwith. But now, within a week either way of Easter, they had suddenly died, and he was childless and bereft, as he should be, and, I hoped, needful to establish ties with his uncle to the South. It made no sense for Scotland to remain a separate nation. All signs pointed to our union.

My sister Margaret . . . she still lived, and intrigued, and attempted to lead a tumultuous life. Only, as will happen, her looks had fled and left her stranded on the beach of boredom. Pity. Just lately she had complained to Ralph Sadler, my ambassador, that "I take it unkindly that I have had no letter from the King your master, for it is a small matter to spend ink and paper upon me. I should be better regarded here, if it was seen that my brother regarded me."

Well, now she should have her wish. I wrote inviting her, her son James V, and other Scots noblemen to meet me in York in early autumn. There we would all come together at last, and I would see my sister for the first time in twenty-five years, and come to know my nephew the Scots King. The journey for them would be short. I would refurbish St. Mary's Abbey for our meeting. Nothing would be too fine for this momentous greeting. I dispatched master carpenters and masons to the church straightway, so that they could have the five good warm months to work.

Who was to stay behind in London? Who could be trusted? Who would prefer to be spared the sight of the unruly North and its dogged loyalty to the Old Religion? Best to leave Cranmer behind, and to help him, Chancellor Thomas Audley and Edward Seymour. The rest of the court hummed with excitement, like a hive about to swarm. It was an adventure to them. My eyes had not turned abroad since first they were transfixed by the Witch. It was over twenty years since the Field of Cloth of Gold. The younglings had heard of that meeting in the Val d'Or; it had become legendary, but was fading. Now they would go on a greater progress than that, and it would be so glittering and sumptuous that they would have no need to envy their elders.

When Robert Aske had knelt before me during the Pilgrimage of Grace, one of the promises I had given him was that I would come North and have Jane crowned in York Minster. Only a few months later Jane was dead. But the promise of a Queen's Coronation in the North hung over me like a bad debt. Should I have Catherine crowned in York?

I meant to have her crowned, did I not? I was having St. Mary's Abbey grandly refitted for James V. Why not dedicate it with the Coronation? The Scots would surely attend that, and it could be a face-saving reunion for us all, and an incomparable gift of devotion to Catherine.

Why not, then? It was all logical, it fitted like a babe sucking on its mother's breast, forming a perfect union. Why, then, did I balk at it? At length I justified my reluctance to myself by stressing that in the past I had found trying to combine events a disaster. The French visit in 1532, with Anne all bedecked in Katherine's jewels . . . no, one thing at a time.

No one at court was urging me about the Coronation, either. Perhaps, like weddings, they lose their urgency and charm after the first. It is not seemly to repeat important ceremonies too often. So I assured myself. But what was the real reason?

❦ ❧

May and June were passed in preparations for the Great Northern Progress, as it was coming to be called. I felt fully restored to health, as if those horrible days in March had never occurred. The leg was behaving itself. Because

I was so busy and knew there would be much riding and hunting on the progress itself, I refrained from resuming any strenuous exercise for the moment.

✎ WILL:

One of the preparations for the progress involved another "spring cleaning of the Tower." It seemed that the King did not like to travel far afield while leaving traitorous prisoners behind at home. Thus it was that Margaret Pole, the old Countess of Salisbury, followed her son Henry, Lord Montague, to the executioner's block. She did not meekly put her head down upon it, however. She refused on principle, for "only traitors do so, and I am no traitor!" she claimed, and made the poor headsman chase her round the scaffold, chopping madly, like a farmer pursuing a chicken around the barnyard.

✎ HENRY VIII:

I did not see Catherine as much as I would have liked. Duties kept us apart, and she seemed distant and distracted. I could sense it, although she denied it. I knew it was because she was apprehensive about this royal journey, where she would be on display to so many. Seeing this, I was glad I had decided against a Coronation at this time. It would have been too much for her.

In the tangle of activities and demands, I had scarcely noticed the advancing season. My only concern was to be ready for departure in time. Outside, a succession of flowers had come into bloom, then faded. I saw them not.

Then one day Culpepper announced that there was someone in the Audience Chamber, requesting to speak to me. "He's dressed in poor estate," he said. "And carries a burlap sack."

A poor petitioner? I grunted. But the burlap sack—did it hide a knife? Assassins were everywhere, or might be. "Admit him. But stay at my side."

Shortly Culpepper returned with the old master gardener at his side. The man, it is true, was wearing his work-clothes. He must have come straight from his plant-house.

"I have it here, Your Grace!" His voice trembled with delight. "I did not think it would bloom, not so soon!" From out of his bag he delivered a rose. Pure red it was, and blooming on a thornless stem.

"The plant is as yet small. But it looks hardy."

"Astounding!" I murmured. The bud, just opening (like Catherine herself, my sweet Catherine), emerged from a smooth and faultless stem. I would present it to her this evening, after Vespers.

I rewarded the old gardener well for his efforts.

I loved this moment best of all—the moment when, daytime things done, Catherine and I played music together. Tonight she played the virginal while I accompanied on the lute. Sitting behind her, I could dote on the exquisite curve of her neck, as she had put her hair up. My soul was at peace. Not until she grew restless did I break the spell and say, "I have something for you. A gift."

She turned round, eagerly. She never tired of gifts. I must have given her a full coffer, by now, of jewels. And of course she had received Jane Seymour's lands. And Cromwell's.

"Here." I handed her the rose, the unique, commissioned rose.

"Yes?" She took it without looking and smiled, still eagerly.

"You hold it."

Only then did she examine the rose, exclaim over it. When I explained its symbolism, she wept.

CVI

Departure day was to be July first. God thought otherwise and sent deluges from the skies. All told, it was three weeks before the rains stopped and the roads dried sufficiently to permit travel. That gave the Scots extra time to decide how to respond to my invitation to a parley, and gave us longer to ready the great abbey hall of St. Mary's in York to receive them.

I shall not recount the long journey in tedious detail. With so many of us travelling—there were one thousand retainers, officers, and companions—our lodging was of the greatest importance. Even the wealthiest nobles did not have accommodations for so great a company, so we provided two hundred of our own luxurious tents to make up the difference. Yes, the journey itself, the protocol, the lodgings, the obligatory entertainments (which should be renamed "borements") were dull. But the countryside!

Oh, why had I not seen all of England before? I was captivated by the landscape itself, yes. But more by the people. Each population retained the stamp of its origin and past. As we travelled northward, the people became taller and fairer. On the border of Norfolk, their eyes were as blue as a clear October day, almost to a person. "Dane blood," said Dr. Butts, who made a hobby of studying this sort of thing. "This is the side of England where the Danes settled, where Norsemen raided. From the Danes you get the blue eyes, from the raiders the red hair." He pointed to a fiery-haired lad perched on a market cross to glimpse us as we passed. "Sweet child, to bear the marks of such a brutal past."

They talked differently, too. At times I could not make out certain words in the courteous little speeches the locals gave us.

As we passed farther north, settlements fell away and we rode through longer and longer stretches of forest. The days lengthened, too. Twilight seemed almost as long as the afternoon.

"The farther north, the longer the day," said Wyatt, who was fascinated by oddities of geography. "At the highest latitudes, as in very northern Scotland

and the Orkney and Shetland Isles, there is no night at all in June. Just a sort of purple twilight."

Wilder and wilder it became. There was so much game that after the first novelty of it, we did not bother to hunt. Besides, the surrounding forest was so dark and extensive it seemed unwise to chase far into it. We were near Robin Hood territory, and now the sheriff of Nottingham's reluctance to pursue Robin Hood and his merrie men into the fastness of Sherwood made perfect sense. I would have let the outlaw roam, too.

Lincolnshire, which I had once called "one of the most brute and beastly shires of the whole realm," was the beginning of the territory of traitors. It had taken us forty days to reach it from London, travelling at our slow ceremonial pace, it was so remote. Small wonder Lincolnshiremen considered themselves beyond our grasp, a feudal kingdom of their own.

We were welcomed effusively at the Lincoln city gates by the citizens, and the mayor, who presented me with the sword and mace of the city as symbols of submission. So. I beheld at last one of the nests of treachery, all prettied up for the occasion and perfumed with protocol. I could not shake the feeling that here in these northern shires, cities were just floating islands, mock centres of civilization on a great ocean of barbarism and malevolence. It was the land of wolves. I could hear their calls even from the centre of Lincoln itself.

My Rose Without a Thorn—how plump and soft she looked here, and what puzzled and envious stares she elicited! But the very wildness of the land seemed to bring an answer from her. She became more and more Gypsy-like, her cheeks brighter and her hair darker and her eyes more slanting and enticing, the farther north we travelled.

Onward to York, where what passed as roads were just rutted muddy paths. Between Lincoln and York there were a great many former monastic establishments—at Torksey, Willoughton, Selby. Some had been stripped of their lead roofs and had their stones plundered, so that in this green time of year they stood like ruined brides, white and vulnerable. It was the sight of these wronged ladies that had so moved the northerners to righteous anger. And they *were* striking: a plea for the beauty and order of the Old Religion.

Pure sentimentality, though. They had never been as serene and gracious during their lifetimes as they were now in their dissolution. Under those now-vanished roofs had flourished every wickedness.

In all this time on the road, I had not yet encountered a single one of the "indigent monks" of whom so much was made and who were, purportedly, a great problem in the countryside hereabout. These homeless monks and friars were allegedly roaming the kingdom, eating everything before them like locusts, and causing local disruption.

York, at last. The city rose before us, very large, and it was easy to see why it dominated the North as London dominated the South. It was its own kingdom; and I knew now why, for Wolsey, it was tantamount to banishment to another country.

We had turned a former abbey to good use here: it would house the court. Within the walls of the priory, reconstructed and refurbished for royal apartments, we would live. Two hundred golden tents were to be pitched among the ruins, so that all could be accommodated comfortably.

The Lord President of the Council of the North had published my intentions to hear any man with a complaint against the Crown, and he assured me that many had responded to it and were awaiting their chance to talk. And as for the reception of loyalists and the ceremonial penitence service for traitors, that had all been arranged. He prattled on and on, until I was forced to ask directly, "The Scots King? When is he to arrive? I trust St. Mary's is ready."

"The abbey is ready, Your Majesty. The workmen executed the necessary repairs and decorations. It gleams!"

I was pleased. They would see I could build up as well as tear down. "Our nephew will be well received. He arrives when?"

"He—he has not informed us."

"Not yet? But we ourselves were late. The dates I had originally proposed are past. Are there no letters? No messages?"

"None, Your Majesty."

James must be coming. Only that would excuse his silence.

"Very well, then," I said lamely. "I shall await him. In the meantime, the ceremony distinguishing between the traitors and the true subjects must be carried out." I was not looking forward to this, but it was a necessary part of statesmanship that things must be acted out.

The next day, in the Great Hall of the Bishop's Palace, the men of the region who had remained loyal to me throughout the unrest and rebellions were received and rewarded with ample favours. The others, who had wavered or had sympathized with the Pilgrims, were herded into another, rather shabby room, where they were directed to fall on their knees and then stretch themselves out upon the floor. In unison they recited, "We wretches, for lack of grace and of sincere and pure knowledge of the verity of God's words, have most grievously, heinously, and wantonly offended Your Majesty in the unnatural and most odious and detestable offences of outrageous disobedience and traitorous rebellion."

I let them lie there like the abominable creatures they were. How many hours of anxiety had I suffered on their account, when they were but nameless, formless threats, far from my reach? It was *these* vermin who gave nightmares to us in the South. Catherine, standing beside me, looked uncomfortable. She could not understand the deep implications. She saw only a roomful of grovelling men, and soft as was her nature, she squirmed with sympathy for them.

I reached over for her hand, and she jerked it away.

Later, as we sat together at dinner, I tried to explain. But although she seemed to be listening, I could feel that she had hardened her heart against me.

The autumn rains began, and the colourless skies stretched all the way to Scotland. As I waited for my nephew and his entourage, I passed time by hearing complaints against the Crown, as I had promised to do, for "any who found himself grieved for lack of justice." There were quite a number, all involving money in some form or other. I was struck by the singular lack of religious complaints.

One citizen said he spoke for many in his protest about raids from the Scots over the border.

"They swoop down upon us, robbing us and taking our livestock. We have to take refuge in the peel-towers. That's all very well for us, and saves our skins, but when it's safe to come out we find our cottages ransacked and our livestock gone."

"Peel-towers?" I asked.

"You've doubtless seen them on your journey here," explained the Council President. "They are small square towers that are entered on the first floor. Our people built them to withstand raids from the Norsemen. Today they use them more than ever for the Scots." He shook his head.

"Tell me, these Scots—are they the wild men that come from the mountains?" (Like MacDonald's father, only just now being civilized.)

"No," said the farmer. "They're the Border scum. Just bands of bandits and murderers. There's nothing romantic about them, except their music and poetry, which celebrates their blood-feuds."

"Their poetry!" said the President. "It can make your skin tingle. Their way with words is superb.

> 'He is either a devil frae hell
> Or else his mother a witch maun be'—"

he murmured in admiration. "Isn't that beautiful?"

"How can they be steeped in such sensitive language and yet be so bloodthirsty?" I wondered. "How far away do they raid from?"

"They've taken the Roman Wall for their own. The Armstrongs have their hideout in a Roman fort there, at Housesteads. They've come a-raiding as far south as Alnwick and Penrith."

"Twenty miles and more," the farmer nodded. "It isn't only the Armstrongs. It's the Maxwells, the Grahams, the Scotts—redundant name, eh?"

"They're clever, the Scots, as well as cruel. There's only one thing they like as well as the sound of a line of well-turned poetry or the sight of blood covering them up to their forearms: the feel of money in their purses. So they've developed a way to combine both pleasures. They extract what they call 'black-mail' from us to spare us from their terrorizing."

"Mail?" I did not understand.

"A Scots word meaning 'rent.' It's aptly named: black rent. They charge a man for living in peace on his own property. Either way he chooses, they reap pleasure. He pays, and they can fondle money; he refuses, and they can spill blood. And write fine poetry about it afterwards."

I would put a stop to this. Let Norfolk have his fun with these dogs, then. "I shall quell these brutish men," I promised him. I would take this matter to my nephew, the Scots King. Let him curb his subjects or I would do it for him.

But there was no message from James V. By the sixth day it was becoming obvious that he did not intend to accept my solemn invitation or even explain his reasons.

Theories were put forth: "He fears to leave Scotland because in his absence the Earl of Arran might take the throne." (The Scots were divided into rabid parties and factions.) "He thinks this is a trick to take him prisoner." (So he distrusted *me*—his own uncle?) "He does not wish to anger his French allies by consorting with the English." (Absurd. Enemies can talk without compromising themselves, and civilized enemies always do.)

Whatever his own dark reasons, he did not see fit to meet me in York, nor did he even have the courtesy to inform me of his intentions. I had been publicly jilted, as I waited like a deserted bride in the church.

That night I had no stomach for the banquet and mummery, and afterward went directly to my chamber. It was a comforting place, solicitously prepared by my host, even down to stuffing every draughty crack with finest white wool. I was tired, and disheartened. It was time to stop waiting for James, conclude whatever business remained here in the desolate North, and return to London.

I could not sleep, even though I took to my bed early and drank a sweet sleep-posset. At length I decided, late as it was, to come to Catherine.

This involved a lengthy traverse through several chambers, across a gallery, and then again through the Queen's chambers. Only the night-guards stood duty now, and the halls were deserted. A single torch burned in each area, the rest having been put out. The royal residence slept.

As I approached the door to her apartments, a dark shape rose from a chair nearby, and glided toward me.

A spirit . . . or at first I thought so. I was infected by the wild strangeness of this whole region. For it was a face I had thought never to see again: Jane Boleyn, George Boleyn's wife. She who had betrayed her own husband and testified against him at that sordid time of Anne's downfall.

"Why, Jane—" I whispered.

"Your Majesty." She bowed low. It was truly she.

She stood. A hood of the new fashion framed her face, but otherwise it was the same. An ugly face, with a long, bulbous nose and dark, shining, feral eyes too close on either side.

It seemed that she was guarding the doors. But there were yeomen for that. It must be my own imagination, I remember thinking then.

I tapped on the door, and Jane reached out a hand as if to restrain me. There was no response within; everyone must be dead asleep. Perhaps my Catherine was, as well? I produced the proper key (for we always carried our chamber locks with us to protect us from assassins who might have procured a key to the built-in lock), but Jane stayed my hand.

"The Queen sleeps," she said. "She asked me to keep watch in the outer chambers, lest she be disturbed."

"I will not disturb her," I assured her. "I will sleep on a pallet at her bed-foot, if need be. Her presence will aid me to sleep."

"Very well." She nodded stiffly.

The key worked well enough, but the door was barred from the inside as well. I could see the metal rod passing across the door-crack, and a great coffer pressed against the doors. I could not gain entrance without causing a great commotion.

Disappointment flooded me. I had not realized until that moment how much I longed to be with her. I had wanted to tell her how proud I was of her, how my heart was near to bursting as I presented her as my Queen. These recalcitrant northerners had always loved Katherine of Aragon, and remained her partisans. But now there was a new Queen, another Catherine, whose gentle ways and pretty manners had charmed them, a Catherine who bore no taint of Protestantism such as Anne Boleyn, Jane Seymour, and Anne of Cleves had. She had reconciled me with my wayward subjects, as well as with my-self.

"She is afraid of assassins," Jane, Lady Rochford, explained in a whisper. "These tales of bloody Scots have frightened her."

Poor, gentle child. I nodded. They were enough to frighten anyone. I understood her concern. "I would not disturb her," I said. "Let her sleep, sweet Queen."

The next morning she was in my inner chamber, stammering and embarrassed at her makeshift defences. She covered me with kisses and swore that she, too, had been troubled with sleeplessness and would have relished a visit from me. Nothing else could truly calm her or rout her fears. She was chagrined that I had discovered the extent of her childish fear of the Scots. I assured her I was in sympathy, and loved her as much as ever, and no, I did not think less of her for taking those precautions.

It was over. I resolved to wait no longer for the Scots King. Nine days was time enough. But I would exact my revenge at my leisure.

The journey southward, retracing our steps, was orderly. I took the opportunity of travelling to Hull, on the great Humber estuary, to inspect my fortifications. I had spent hours studying the plans for building an experimental castle there, to be linked to two existing blockhouses, then wrestling money to pay for them. Now I would see the finished fort. It excited me to put plans on paper and see them translated into stone and metal. Preparing for war was a very satisfying thing; it both aroused and fulfilled a man.

As we arrived at Windsor almost a month later, we were met by an ugly welcoming party. Edward lay ill, in spite of all my precautions to keep him safe. He suffered from *quartrain ague,* and the physicians thought him so "fat and unhealthy," as they put it, that he was in danger of death.

I sent the bulk of the courtiers and councillors home, and disbanded the Great Progress, as Windsor was our last stopping place. Final banquets and speeches had been planned, but that was unnecessary. We were all well sated with one another's company by now.

Standing by Edward's high carved bed, I asked silently, "Why? Why? Why?" He *was* fat; he looked like a butterball, and his colour was almond-white, with red blotches all over. Did he get no exercise? Did he never play out of doors? In "protecting" him, had the fools of physicians robbed him of any natural mobility? He looked like one of those geese that cottagers keep chained to fatten their livers.

"Open these windows," I barked. The air in the chamber was so foul it made me cough. When only one of the casements was open, the crisp autumn air swept in with startling briskness, banishing the odours. "Give him the proper medicine," I ordered. "Watch him carefully. But when this crisis is past, treat him as a prince, not a dowager. You speak true: he *is* too fat, and unhealthy. But that is your fault, not his!"

I blustered most when I was most afraid.

God was with Edward, and within a day he began to rally. His fever dropped, and his colouring improved. He became restless and intolerant of the bed confinement, a sure sign of returning health. After removing all the contaminating persons from his surroundings, I left him at Windsor and made for Hampton Court. There my journey would end.

CVII

Edward was spared. The northerners were loyal, and the progress had been successful. Catherine was fulfilling the ache in the realm for a true Queen. I felt the hand of God upon me, resting on my head, saying, "Well done, thou good and faithful servant."

On the morrow it was All Saints' Day. I directed my confessor, the Bishop of Lincoln, to give public thanks at Mass in my name for the good life I was leading and trusted to continue to lead with Queen Catherine, after sundry troubles of mind which had happened to me by marriages. This he did; and his silken voice, saying the words, conveyed a peace and fulfillment I had thought never to attain.

I received the Holy Bread, the Word made Flesh—and returning to kneel, I lost all sense of time. When I stirred, I found myself almost alone. Only Cranmer remained, discreetly waiting for me to break my reverie. A King must never be left unattended in a ceremonial stance.

I genuflected and then walked slowly up the aisle, still in a daze of religious ecstasy.

"Your Grace—my dear Lord—forgive me," said Cranmer, thrusting a rolled letter into my hand. He looked ill.

"What? No other greeting? I have missed you, Thomas, in our separation."

"And I you, Your Majesty. Truly."

"I will plough through all the notes you took in my absence, I promise it, tonight. You did well."

"The letter—read it first, I beg you, I—" He looked so agitated I knew immediately that he suffered from rebellious bowels.

"Go, Thomas," I said. Still he stood with a hangdog look. "Yes, yes. I'll read it straightway," I assured him. He slunk away, as if in pain. Poor man.

I seated myself on a wooden bench in the Long Gallery outside the Chapel and unfolded the letter, just to humour him.

It was a joke. It reported the claims of a certain John Lassells that his sister, Mary Lassells Hall, had told him that Catherine Howard was a whore, that she had behaved wantonly from a young age with men of the Duchess's household, giving herself to a "music master" when she was but thirteen and then living in open sin with a cousin until her departure for court.

Who was this Mary Hall? I reread the letter carefully. She was, before her marriage, a servant at the Duchess's Lambeth establishment. When her brother, who was a fervent Protestant, had asked her why she did not seek a position at court, as the other Lambeth servitors had done, she had replied with disdain, "I would not serve that woman! She is immoral, both in living and in conditions." And then she had named "Manox, a music master" and "Dereham, a gentleman," as Catherine's lovers.

Nonsense. It was nonsense. So the Protestants were on the move again. Since the head of the heretical serpent, Cromwell, had been severed, it writhed on its own, in meaningless thrashings. A flush of resentment spread through me. I had spent the summer quashing the pretensions of the Catholics, I thought, and now I must spend the winter curbing the Protestants. I was amused that Cranmer should have been taken in by this bait. But I had left my Protestants in charge in London, I reminded myself. Cranmer, Audley, Edward Seymour . . . they would be approachable by the extremists.

Well, I would have this investigated, and have this Mary Hall silenced. She would regret ever having uttered this slander. Wearily I ordered William Fitzwilliam, the Lord Privy Seal, Anthony Browne, the Lord Admiral, and Thomas Wriothesley, Secretary of State, to round up Mary and John Lassells, and question Manox and Dereham. The slander must be stopped.

In the meantime I enjoyed Catherine heartily, as if in defiance.

Three days later my men returned, and in the privacy of my work chamber they said they had questioned the Protestant brother and sister, the music master, and Dereham, and had been unable to disprove the story. Quite the contrary.

"I fail to believe this!" I muttered. "They must be lying. Oh, why do Protestants abandon their falsehoods only over the lighted fire? Damn their fanatacism! Very well, then—torture them! Force the truth from them!"

Torture was illegal, except in cases of treason, sedition, or suspected treason.

Catherine had planned a supper and "amusement" for me that evening. But suddenly I was not amused; suddenly I did not want to see her or share an amusement. Abruptly I sent word that she must take to her quarters and await the King's pleasure, that it was no more the time to dance.

The King's pleasure had been shattered, and nothing but a full retraction by those blackguards would restore it.

I slept poorly that night, if at all. At my bed-foot pallet, Culpepper was likewise sleepless. I could hear it in his breathing. Ordinarily I could have passed time with him, lighted a taper and set up a chessboard. But a deadly fear had got hold of me, and I did not wish any company. So we passed the long night, each acutely aware of the other's presence, but each alone in an absolute way.

I was relieved when dawn came and it was time to go to Mass. I needed God; I needed some comfort. I dressed hurriedly and made my way down the Long Gallery to the Chapel Royal. There were few people about, as most preferred a later Mass on Sunday morning.

Kneeling there, I poured out every incoherent thought and fear I had, and offered them up to God. The candles flickered on the altar and the Divine Service went smoothly, but I received no answers, no peace of mind.

"—Thee, for that Thou dost vouchsafe to feed us who have duly received this holy mystery, with the spiritual food—" Outside the chapel doors there was a scraping, a scuffling. Then a shriek, piercing and like a banshee's.

"No! No!"

"—of the most precious Body of Thy Son our Saviour Jesus Christ, and dost assure us thereby of Thy favour and goodness towards us; and—"

"Henry! Henry! Henry!" screamed the voice, each naming of my name growing fainter, as from a greater distance.

I shook, even ten feet from the altar and with the Body of Christ inside me.

Another scream, muffled now.

"—that we are very members incorporate in the mystical Body—"

Was I dreaming? Was I the only one who had heard the bloodcurdling calls? The priest mumbled on, the worshippers mouthed the responses.

When I stepped out, the passageway was empty.

There was to be a Privy Council meeting at Bishop Gardiner's residence in Southwark that evening. I called it that afternoon, as Fitzwilliam came to me with still more evidence and depositions. From a field outside Hampton, where I had gone on a pretext of hunting, but in reality to be alone, I issued a command to all the councillors to return to London to attend this emergency meeting. It was to be kept secret, and so I went directly to the royal barge without ever returning to the palace. Rumour had infested Hampton, and now everyone knew something was amiss. Catherine was confined to her apartments, on my orders.

Sitting before me in Gardiner's fine Council Chamber were Audley, the Lord Chancellor; Thomas Howard, ordered back to London for the occasion, looking pleased and important; William Petre, the Principal Secretary; Brandon, Cranmer. . . .

I ticked off their names. Yes, they were all present. I cleared my throat.

"Gentlemen," I began, "you are called here at this inconvenient hour"—I faltered, then plunged ahead—"to consider certain things, evil charged against the Queen." I rattled a paper before my face, the original deposition of the informers. "Whilst we were away, the Lord Archbishop and the Council in absentia"—I nodded toward Cranmer, Audley, and Seymour—"were apprised of alleged misdeeds of my . . . wife. These were sufficiently grave that the Archbishop saw fit to report them to me in writing. Since then, we have investigated further. But these matters are confusing, and so, before proceeding further, we would lay the entire matter before you. The witnesses—defendants—shall speak openly where all can hear."

It was unorthodox. I could scarcely credit my own words. Since this frightful business had begun, it was like a fantasy, and everything seemed like a sleepwalk.

"We shall retrace each step," I said. "John Lassells, speak first."

They led in an elderly man, who seemed the very soul of reason.

"State your name and title."

He bowed. "I am John Lassells, resident of London."

"State your occupation."

"I know what you aim for, so let us be honest and disclose it straightway," he blustered. "I spoke of what my sister Mary, who had served as a nurse in the Duchess of Norfolk's household, told me when I asked her why she did not seek a position at court. It seemed to me that anyone who had known the Queen came requesting a place. There was Joan Bulmer, writing all the way from York; Katherine Tilney, who became her chamberer. Why not my Mary?"

I rapped upon the table before me. "Continue."

"She replied, 'I would not serve the Queen. Rather, I pity her.' I questioned why, and she said, 'Marry, because she is light, both in living and in conditions.'"

I glanced round. The faces were stunned.

"And what did she mean? Did you probe further?" I asked detachedly.

"Aye. And she said"—he hesitated, his voice winding down like a toy doll's—"that there was a music master, Manox, who bragged that he used to feel her body, knew of a private mark on her secret parts—"

The little ladder-mark on her uppermost thigh, a gash stitched together when she was but a child. I used to climb that ladder, it was a game we played, my lips mimicking feet, going rung by rung until they nibbled on the gates of her private parts.

"—and then he was sent away by the Duchess, who found them fondling one another when they were shut up together with the virginals."

Music . . . a music master . . . Mark Smeaton . . . The pain, which I had thought gone forever, now tore my body apart.

Mary Lassells Hall was now brought in. She was as I had envisioned: tall, hard, plain. She quickly told her story.

"After the music master was banished, there came another. A Francis Dereham, some sort of cousin, a gentleman-pensioner of the Duke of Norfolk. He quickly joined the revels in the girls' attic sleeping quarters, became a popular visitor."

Catherine's summer secretary! The pirate-cousin! O Jesu, O Jesu—!

"Pray explain yourself." Norfolk squeezed each painful word out. He was frightened.

"The young maidens were to sleep in a dormitory at night. The Duchess ordered that they be locked in at eight o'clock. But she slept in another wing, and was half deaf, besides. As soon as she'd retired, what a picnic! Every lust-ridden male in the county converged on that 'maidens' chamber.' They climbed in the windows, and brought strawberries and wine, and then spent their lust on the woman of their choice. Their only concession to modesty was to draw the curtains round the bed itself whilst they sported themselves."

"Disgusting," muttered Norfolk.

"Your cousin Sir William Howard had his own key," she said stiffly. "Now this Manox, when he found himself barred from these pagan indulgences, wrote the Duchess a tattling note about them. The Lord William Howard was dismayed, lest he be caught by his wife. He had enjoyed his fifteen-year-old hussy, indeed he had! He scolded Manox and Dereham, saying, 'What, you mad wretches! Could you not be merry but you must fall out amongst yourselves?' His game was spoilt, and he regretted it."

I waved my hand. "Enough." I did not care what Lord William Howard had done. My heart did not break on account of him. "You say others from the Duchess's establishment requested positions from the Queen?"

"Yes. Joan Bulmer, who was her confidante in the old days, now serves as her privy chamberer; Katherine Tilney, as her bed-maid; Margaret Mortimer, as her wardrobe supervisor. They feathered their berths well, to assure their future."

So. She had brought foul reminders of her past life with her. To aid her evil plans. But perhaps it was not her choice, perhaps she had been threatened by them. . . .

"Edward Manox," I called. He came forward and stood before me. I had not expected him to be so handsome.

I repeated the testimony against him. "What say you to these reports?"

760

"They are true, but it is not as it appears! I was the son of a neighbouring nobleman, brought into the Duchess's household to teach her charges music. Catherine Howard was just thirteen at that time, a very . . . forward virgin. She had genuine talent in music"—yes, I knew that, I had rejoiced in that talent, cherished it—"but she was wayward, wanton—and beautiful. She promised her maidenhead to me, but before I could make good that promise, the Duchess caught us kissing on the stairs. She screamed and boxed Catherine's ears. She said she was a fool to waste herself on me, that I was unworthy of her. Then the Duchess dismissed me." He hesitated. "Before I was sent away, Catherine walked with me in the orchard. She said she loved me and would always be true."

I hated the words, hated seeing him, so straight and young and honest.

"I make my living as a musician," he said. "I was living in Chertsey when I was brought here to 'answer certain charges.' Please, my lords. When I knew her she was but Catherine Howard, a girl in the Duchess's household, and I did nothing wrong. She may have promised me her maidenhead, but I never took it. And I have never mentioned to anyone, since she became Queen, that I knew her. It is my own secret."

Oh, get him away! He sickened me. He had shared Catherine, had possessed her in some way that I could not. He had been her first love.

They led him away and dragged Dereham in. Handsome, cocky Dereham. He, too, was read the accusation and called upon to clear himself.

"The Queen is my wife," he said boldly. "She was promised to me two years ago. We lived as husband and wife, and then she went to court and I to Ireland—both to make our fortunes, that was the plan. Well, I had some success in ventures there"—yes, piracy, I remembered—"but imagine my surprise to find, upon my return, that my little wife is now styled Queen of England. Naturally I hurried to reclaim her, and she was most amenable to appointing me her secretary. But, alas, I found I had been replaced in her affections . . . by a Thomas Culpepper."

No. No.

"You say you 'lived as husband and wife,' " said Cranmer dryly. "In what precise sense?"

"In that we coupled often, and had intentions to marry."

Coupled often. I looked at the long-legged pirate, imagining him lying on my Catherine, quivering above her, searching out her secret parts and then depositing his seed within her.

The stone. The stone in her womb . . . that was what it was for. . . . It was Catherine herself who had sought out a practitioner to put it there, to protect herself from her own sexual indulgences.

I felt vomit in my throat.

"Did she promise herself to you?" asked Cranmer reasonably.

"We called one another 'husband' and 'wife.' I entrusted my money to her while I went to Ireland. I remember holding her whilst she said, in tears, 'Thou wilt never live to say to me, "thou hast swerved." ' "

But she had, she had. O God—why did not the pain stop? Why could I not feel anger? Come, clean anger, sweep this agony away!

"Look to Tom Culpepper if you want more!" he cried, as he was taken from the chamber.

Culpepper.

A dozen eyes blinked back at me. I thought my heart would break, I thought myself torn into shreds, as I whispered, "Arrest Culpepper. Question him." A stirring, and my servants went to carry out my bidding.

It was all coming now, the recall, in brutal and torturous detail. Her pretend-chastity, which I had been so loth to violate that I rushed forward the marriage in such haste; her lewd behaviour on our wedding night, appropriate to a jade who was long past sweetness; Dereham's Syrian love-cream; Culpepper and Catherine's absence during my illness, and her skittishness; my attributing her high colouring on those mornings to her religious experiences at Mass; the locked doors on the great Northern Progress, with the trumped-up story about the Scottish assassins, and her kisses and assurances the next morning. O God!

I wept, putting my head down on the Council table. My hat rolled off, revealing my balding scalp. I was naked as I had never been, and I cared not, so great was my grief. I had loved Catherine, had believed her chaste and loving. It was all a lie. She was a whore, a scheming whore, who had gone to court "to make her fortune."

I swayed up and screamed, "A sword! A sword!"

No one stirred.

"Get me a sword!" I commanded. "I shall kill her, kill her—she'll not have had such pleasure in her debauchery as she'll have agony in her death!" I looked round. "I want her to suffer, friends. To suffer! One feels the ecstasy of love in every part of one's body, is that not so? Well, I want pain to pervade her every part, now." It was so simple. Why could they not understand? Pain like that which filled me—that was what I would give her.

"Are you deaf? I said a sword!" Ah, but I could not kill her myself, lacked the dexterity. "A swordsman, then!"

Cranmer flung his arms about me. He, too, was weeping. But there was weeping and weeping, and mine came from my depths. It was unstoppable. The more the pain filled me, the more it welled up.

"Stop it! Stop it!" I could bear no more. I clutched at Cranmer. I screamed, as if to turn my insides out, to rid myself of myself.

Betrayed. I had been betrayed. I could not bear it; the pain was searing.

My life was a lie, my love was a lie, everything was not as it seemed, it was its exact opposite. . . .

I vomited on the table, and watched in revulsion as the stuff dripped down on the Turkish rug. My life was like this vomit; it was myself splattered out and stinking with foul, unrecognizable things.

Someone got me to bed. I was raving, quite mad. Before they led me away, I called for Will and asked them to bring him to me.

I was in bed for two full days, and all that time I lay in a draped room that admitted no daylight. My hands were bound with silken cords, lest I do damage to myself. I wept and raged continuously, with no sleeping. Memory after memory presented itself to me, each one uniquely painful, so that banishing one did not bring surcease. Sleep brought horrible dreams. I was violent, wishing only to be out of my own prison of mind.

It did not subside, only at length I became exhausted, and passed into a state of motionlessness.

CVIII

I came awake to a sorrowing face: Cranmer's. He was standing at the foot of my bed. How long had he been there? What did he want?

"Your Grace—my beloved King—" he began, moving toward me. *Beloved.* Only an old man would say those words to me from henceforth, and I could believe them only from an old man.

Had they feared for me, then? Feared for my sanity, or for my life? Alas, neither had fled, neither had turned tail and deserted me. I was here, fixed, leaden—utterly sane. There was to be no respite from my pain, and my awareness.

"Cranmer." I acknowledged him, bade him come closer.

"We have found this in Culpepper's letter-box—whilst he was out a-hawking merrily—and we searched his rooms. He is arrested—"

He handed me the letter, as embarrassed as if he had written it himself.

Master Culpepper,

I heartily recommend me unto you, praying you to send me word how that you do. It was showed me that you was sick, the which thing troubled me very much till such time that I hear from you, praying you to send me word how that you do. For I never longed so much for a thing as I do to see you and to speak with you, the which I trust shall be shortly now.

The which doth comfort me very much when I think of it, and when I think again that you shall depart from me again it makes my heart to die to think what fortune I have that I cannot be always in your company.

My trust is always in you that you will be as you have promised me, and in that hope I trust still, praying you then that you will come when my Lady Rochford is here, for then I shall be best at leisure to be at your commandment.

I thank you for promising to be so good unto that poor fellow, my man, which is one of the griefs that I do feel to depart from him, for then I do know no one that I dare trust to send to you, and therefore I pray you take him to be with you, that I may sometime hear from you one thing.

I pray you to give me a horse for my man, for I have much ado to get one and therefore I pray send me one by him and in so doing I am as I said afore, and thus I take my leave of you, trusting to see you shortly again and I would you were with me now, that you might see what pain I take in writing you.

yours as long as life endures

Catherine

One thing I had forgotten and that is to instruct my man to tarry here with me still, for he says whatsoever you bid him he will do it.

Catherine. Her frantic, muddle-headed "arrangements." This could be no forgery, for it reflected all too perfectly her personality.

It makes my heart to die to think what fortune I have that I cannot be always in your company. . . .

The "fortune" that kept them apart, that "made her heart to die" was me, my existence, my presence.

Oh, why did it stab me so hotly to realize it, to savour the full meaning? Why did not the full meaning—she was an adulteress, a traitress—cancel out the pain of the little, petty particulars? Yet it was these little things that had the sharpest barbs. . . .

For I never longed so much for a thing as I do to see you and speak with you. . . .

As I had written Anne so long ago, almost the same words—what was it I had said?—"her absence having given me the greatest pain at heart that neither tongue nor pen can express"?

Catherine had had the same madness for Culpepper, then.

No, with her it was not so enduring. It was mere lust, not bewitchment.

Yours as long as life endures, Catherine. . . .

She had never written me a single letter.

"Thank you, Cranmer," I said slowly. "I think it best that you go to her, take her confession now."

It was the next day, while I was awaiting word from Cranmer, that Will received a message from Lady Baynton, Catherine's married sister.

"Dereham did what he did by force," she said, albeit in more elaborate language. The disclaimer had arrived ahead of the original statement it sought to modify.

How like Catherine, I thought. She said one thing and now wishes to retract it, like a child choosing trinkets at a summer's fair. "I like this—no, I'll have this instead." *But it was no more the time to dance.*

At length Cranmer came, so nervous he was trembling. " 'Tis done," he murmured. "She has given a confession. Take it." He thrust it to me, the odious task performed.

"What . . . state was she in?" Oh, tell me something of her, what she wore, how she looked—Sweet Jesu, did I still love her, then? I all but spat.

"In a frenzy of lamentation and heaviness."

Play-acting! As she had play-acted all along. But what if she *were* changed? No, impossible. "What said she of Dereham?"

Cranmer reluctantly opened the page of his personal notes. "Of Dereham she said, 'He had divers times lain with me, sometimes in his doublet and hose, and two or three times naked, but not so naked that he had nothing upon him, for he had always at least his doublet and as I do think, his hose also, but I mean naked when his hose were put down.' "

She remembered every detail, she cherished them! O dear God! And the doublet still on—I remembered our wedding night, when she had had me do the same . . . it excited her. . . .

I thought the top of agony had been reached, but each day brought new heights, and this confession most of all. I would read it, then, read it and die. And be done with death, as I was already done with living.

It was addressed to me. So she wrote me a letter at last.

> *I, Your Grace's most sorrowful subject and most vile wretch in the world, not worthy to make any recommendation unto your most excellent Majesty, do only make my most humble submission and confession of my faults.*
>
> *Whereas no cause of mercy is deserved upon my part, yet of your most accustomed mercy extended unto all other men undeserved, most humbly on my hands and knees I do desire one particle thereof to be extended unto me, although of all other creatures I am most unworthy to be called either your wife or your subject.*

My sorrow I can by no writing express, nevertheless I trust your most benign nature will have some respect unto my youth, my ignorance, my frailness, my humble confession of my faults, and plain declaration of the same referring me wholly unto Your Grace's pity and mercy.

First at the flattering and fair persuasions of Manox, being but a young girl, I suffered him at sundry times to handle and touch the secret parts of my body which neither became me with honesty to permit nor him to require.

Also, Francis Dereham by many persuasions procured me to his vicious purpose and obtained first to lie upon my bed with his doublet and hose and after within the bed and finally he lay with me naked, and used me in such sort as a man doth his wife many and sundry times, but how often I know not.

Our company ended almost a year before the King's Majesty was married to my Lady Anne of Cleves and continued not past one quarter of a year or a little above.

Now the whole truth being declared unto Your Majesty, I most humbly beseech you to consider the subtle persuasions of young men and the ignorance and frailness of young women.

I was so desirous to be taken unto Your Grace's favour, and so blinded with the desire of worldly glory that I could not, nor had grace, to consider how great a fault it was to conceal my former faults from Your Majesty, considering that I intended ever during my life to be faithful and true unto Your Majesty ever after.

Nevertheless the sorrow of my offences was ever before mine eyes, considering the infinite goodness of Your Majesty toward me which was ever increasing and not diminishing.

Now I refer the judgment of all mine offences with my life and death wholly unto your most benign and merciful grace, to be considered by no justice of Your Majesty's laws but only by your infinite goodness, pity, compassion, and mercy—without the which I acknowledge myself worthy of the most extreme punishment.

She lied! She lied even here, even in her "honest" confession, she lied. Where was Culpepper in this, eh? "I intended ever during my life to be faithful and true unto Your Majesty." The effrontery, the brazen deceit, in her very crawling phrases revealed that she did not know yet that Culpepper was taken. Her duplicity was stunning.

All my love for her ceased upon that instant. I saw her entire, for what she was.

I nodded to Cranmer, who was standing by, near to whimpering.

"Thank you. You have done well," I said. "A faithful servant is not one who leaps to attend to joyful tasks, but one who takes it upon himself to shoulder the doleful ones. There are many to serve the bridegroom, but no one to lay out a corpse."

"I am grieved for you, and wish only to help."

"You have proved yourself over and over, but at no time more than now. I had so many to help me marry the Princess of Cleves. Where are they now?"

"The chief one is dead, Your Grace."

So he was brave as well as true, I thought. Not one in a thousand would have voiced that, although all would have thought it.

"Cromwell." I laughed a mirthless laugh. "Oh, how he would have relished these days, to have seen his enemies, the Howards, brought low. To have seen me shamed by that slut! My just reward for having chosen her over Cromwell's Lady Anne." Cromwell must be laughing—if one can laugh in hell. I know that demons cackle and jeer, but the damned?

"No one with any heart or goodness could laugh at these circumstances," Cranmer insisted. Because he was good himself, he could not imagine its absence in others.

"They must be brought to trial," I said, my mind leaving Cromwell in his shroud. "First the men, then Catherine. See how she feels when Culpepper denies her. As he will. He will swear he loved her not. How will she like that, to be denied publicly by the lover for whom she is giving up everything? That will hurt her worse than the sword which is to follow. He *will* deny her, you know. He will deny her and throw himself on my mercy."

I rubbed my forehead. My head was pounding. "The men must have an open trial. Admit everyone at court, and their friends, to attend. Foreigners, too, so that they may spread the word abroad. I want all the world to know how misused and abused I have been! No more will they think I am cruel or bloody, but see for themselves how deceived and betrayed *I* have been!"

He nodded unhappily.

"Do not look so miserable. The worst part is over. Now only formalities and legalisms remain."

He bowed.

Suddenly I thought of something. "Oh, and Cranmer—bring me back the original letter that Catherine sent Culpepper. I would have it in my safekeeping. Such pieces of evidence have a way of disappearing just before a trial or hearing. As the original Papal dispensation for my marriage to Katherine of Aragon did just prior to the opening of the legatine court; as my letters to Anne Boleyn vanished and reappeared at the Vatican. I shall keep the Queen's letter upon my person, so that anyone wishing to steal it must steal it from my very bosom." As my wife was stolen.

But no, she had not been stolen. She had stolen away on her own.

Alone again, I sat down and opened the "confession." I reread it slowly, word by word, as if this time I would see something that had not been there before, something that would redeem and negate the whole of it.

Instead I found more sorrow than ever.

First at the flattering and fair persuasions of Manox, being but a young girl, I suffered him . . . which neither became him with honesty to require. . . .

Francis Dereham by many persuasions procured me to his vicious purpose . . . and used me. . . .

The subtle persuasions of young men and the ignorance and frailness of young women. . . .

The tone stank, the wheedling attempt to excuse herself and shift all the blame onto the men. How much more becoming if she had stood up for herself, shouldered the responsibility! Better a proud Delilah than an excuse-making Eve.

And why had she wanted to marry me?

I was so blinded with desire of worldly glory. . . .

The fool! She was too stupid even to flatter! She just stated flatly that she coveted the jewels and gold.

O, I had loved a stupid harlot. Bad enough a harlot, but a fool as well. A girl too unschooled to write a grammatical letter, and too unclever not to insult the very one from whom she was begging mercy! Evil and subtlety, such as her cousin Anne Boleyn employed, were grand snares which could catch any mortal man. But stupidity! I had been ensnared by the surface charms of a simpleton!

CIX

The ugly secret was out and scampering about the realm like an army of rats. It would undoubtedly reach York and Lincoln far more quickly than the progress had, undoing all the good I had accomplished there for the majesty of the Crown. The trial would clarify and satisfy every morbid curiosity, for I cared not if every foul fact were exposed. Let the full abominations be known. I cared not for my own pride; but let no one afterward accuse the state of injustice, or a trumped-up trial, as they had over the Witch.

Catherine was given orders to surrender her royal apartments at Hampton and move, under guard, to Syon House, a former monastery. Her presence there would certainly deconsecrate it, if the Church had not already done so.

Since her hysterical confession, I had sent Cranmer back to her again, along with Thomas Wriothesley, who was less tender-hearted. It was necessary that she make a statement about Culpepper. We knew her guilt already, and if she hoped to gain absolution for her eternal soul, she must admit to her sin.

Faced with Culpepper's admission, and the evidence of her letter to him, she fainted.

"He could not—he dared not—" she murmured, collapsing. Upon opening her eyes, the first thing she demanded was, "The letter! The letter!"

"It is taken, Madam," she was told. "The King's Majesty hath it."

She keened and wailed. She then confessed to meeting Culpepper in pre-arranged secret places and by the backstairs of palaces; that she had called Culpepper her "little sweet fool" and given him a velvet cap and ring for love tokens.

"But there was no sin between us, I swear!" she wept, with one breath, while with the next blaming Lady Rochford and Culpepper for having pressed her for these meetings.

Lady Rochford had a different tale to tell, one that exonerated her. She had arranged these meetings at Catherine's mysterious urgings. Furthermore, she swore that "Culpepper hath known the Queen carnally considering all things that I hath heard and seen between them."

Enough. Enough of this. Now the entire truth must be driven out. Dereham and Culpepper and Lady Rochford and Catherine Howard and all the other Howards must be brought to trial. The preliminaries, the investigations, were over.

Guildhall, in London. The entire Privy Council, and the foreign ambassadors—the French envoys Marillac and Castillon, and the venerable Chapuys—were in attendance when the men were brought before the company of jurors.

I was told that Dereham was charming. His arrogance was gone and he traded on his background, his good family, and his love for Catherine and honest intentions. He cherished her, he said, and his only thought was to make her his wife. He had been heartbroken when he returned from Ireland (whence he had gone only to make his fortune so that he could offer her the luxuries she so deserved) to find that she spurned and scorned him. She was no longer a simple maiden at the Duchess's, but a girl with a court position, which had quite gone to her head. Her other suitors—particularly a certain Thomas Paston and her cousin Thomas Culpepper (Thomases again!)—did not worry him. It was the King who was his rival, the one before whom he must reluctantly give way. Nevertheless, "If the King were dead I am sure I might marry her," he had claimed.

If the King were dead. He had imagined my death, wished it. Evil intent, malice in the heart. And then—he had requested a position in Catherine's household. Clear proof and evidence that he had wicked intentions.

The Duchess had sponsored him in this request. She, too, had a stake in all this. She was involved.

Culpepper was less abject and co-operative than Dereham when first he was brought in. Clearly he disdained to share the floor with a commoner like Dereham. But in a flash of pride he blurted out that all along the progress they had met secretly, with the connivance of Lady Rochford, and always at Catherine's hot insistence, and that he "intended and meant to do ill with the Queen, and that likewise the Queen so minded to do with him."

With that, and with the reckless nonchalance that was his trademark, he threw away his life, and Catherine's. There could be no mercy now, no mercy for any of them. They were a nest of traitors, traitors who had crouched in the royal apartments planning and wishing my illness and incapacity: Dereham seeking a place in Catherine's household, and Culpepper conveniently near to "serve" me. Yes, serve me poison, as he had done in March, when I was taken so ill. It was not from God that this illness had come, it was from human hands, in Satan's service. I had been stricken, had almost died, so that he could have access to the pleasures of my wife's body.

Die. These instruments of evil must die.

On December tenth, they were taken out of the Tower and transported to Tyburn, the place where commoners were executed.

The Privy Council had advised me that Culpepper's offence was so "very heinous" that it warranted a notable execution, despite his petition to be permitted the kindness of decapitation.

Culpepper. The pretty, lusty boy whom I had loved, as only rogues are lovable. The serpent I had nourished in my bosom, protecting him from the penalties of his own folly and evil. He had raped a gamekeeper's wife and then murdered one of the villagers who tried to save her. This was deserving of the death penalty, but I had been dazzled by his beauty and words, and therefore I had pardoned him. In so doing I had done wrong. He had taken it only as licence to continue his evil, not repent it. In showing misplaced mercy I had created a monster.

The traitor's death: as excruciating a death as human ingenuity could contrive.

Culpepper had earned it. Nonetheless I wrote out on parchment, "Sentence to be commuted to simple beheading," and sent the message straight to Tyburn to meet the executioners.

Let them call me softhearted, womanish. Could I help it if I had a tender conscience and desired to show mercy?

♣ ♣

Christmas. There were no festivities, and Catherine was still a prisoner at Syon House, while I kept to my own apartments and read and reread her letter to Culpepper until I knew every wrinkle on the paper, every ink blot. Why did I do this, like a monk repeating a rosary? Why did I torture myself so? If I thought to make myself insensitive to the wound, it had just the opposite effect: I never allowed it to heal, and by my constant probing, I kept the wound open.

Further investigations, dreary as they were, revealed yet more treason. I was forced to imprison the Duchess because she destroyed evidence relating to Dereham. She had hastily opened his trunks and destroyed his memorabilia and burnt his incriminating letters just before my commissioners arrived to confiscate them.

In truth, the entire Howard clan had conspired to hoodwink me and conceal Catherine's true character, so that they could seize power. They knew the little whore for what she was, but would pass her on to their King, to satisfy their own greed. Now they would pay the price: to the Tower with them all! They were all tried and found guilty of misprision of treason, and thus must forfeit their goods and possessions to the Crown and their bodies to perpetual imprisonment. All of them: Catherine's lascivious uncle, William Howard; her aunt, Lady Bridgewater; and all her brothers and sisters. Several of these cowards disappeared abroad. As for Thomas Howard, the Duke of Norfolk, he wrote an oily letter:

> *Most noble and gracious Sovereign Lord, yesterday came to my knowledge that mine ungracious mother-in-law, mine unhappy brother and his wife, with my lewd sister of Bridgewater, were committed to the Tower, which I am sure is done for some false and traitorous proceedings against your Royal Majesty; which revolving in my mind, with also the most abominable deeds done by two of my nieces against Your Highness, has brought me into the greatest perplexity that ever poor wretch was in, fearing that Your Majesty, having so often and by so many of my kin been thus falsely and traitorously handled, might not only conceive a displeasure in your heart against me and all other of my kin, but also abhor in manner to hear speak of any of the same. Wherefore, most gracious Sovereign Lord, prostrate at your feet, most humbly I beseech Your Majesty to call to your remembrance that a great part of this matter has come to light by my declaration to Your Majesty, according to my bounden duty, of the words spoken to me by my mother-in-law the Duchess, when Your Highness sent me to Lambeth to search Dereham's coffers, without the which I think she had not been further examined, nor consequently, her ungracious children.*
>
> *Which my true proceedings toward Your Majesty being considered, and also the small love of my two false traitorous nieces, and my mother-in-law, have borne unto me, doth put me in some hope, that Your Highness will not conceive any displeasure in your most gentle heart against me, that God knoweth did never think a thought that might be to your discontentation.*

It was true that no one in the family liked the Duke, which was now to his credit. His ungracious and traitorous nieces—oh, he spoke well, and described them perfectly! What was worse than to be uncle of a witch and a whore—unless it was to be husband of them? The Duke was not to go to the Tower with the rest. I would spare him. But would I spare Catherine? That was what the people wondered as the days passed and she remained at Syon House, under guard but not without certain comforts. Her jewels had been taken, but not her attendants. She still had four ladies for companionship. She had not been tried, nor had any trial date been set. Already six weeks had passed since the treasonous disclosure; by this like time Anne Boleyn had been in her grave three weeks already, and I remarried. Some laid the delay to respect for the Christmas season; others said it betokened a still-lingering love for her.

Wagers were that she would live, even though her paramours had perished as felons.

There was a part of me that wished that. And there was a way, there was a way . . . if she would acknowledge her marriage to Dereham, admit that she had been his wife. . . . True, then she would have committed perjury and bigamy by going through a marriage ceremony with me, but that was not treason; the only treason was to the human heart, to have trampled so on an old man's heart. But if she repented, and as a widow retired to a quiet and virtuous life . . . yes, then she could live.

I sent such an offer to her, along with a paper for her to sign. Before it had even reached her, I regretted it. How could I have forgotten, even for an instant, the rest of it? She and Culpepper imagining my death, poisoning me in March, so that only God saved me? Oh, fond old man's fancy, doting so! I had forgot. I had forgot. I had willed myself to forget, as if forgetting made it not so.

She sent proud word back, denying Dereham. There had been no marriage. She was not, and never had been, his wife. She was my wife. She was Queen of England.

So she would cling to that, and die, rather than renounce it, and live? The one thing in her sordid little life that made her special, that would say to later ages, *She lived*. In this, and this only, we have lived, then: to be special for an instant.

I would grant her this. I would allow her to become immortal. If I did not love her, I would force her to sign the paper, un-Queen herself, and live out an obscure life in Sussex. But I did love her, and so I would give her the death she craved.

CX

Some of the Privy Council thought there should be an open trial, so that Catherine could speak and defend herself. I suspected that she would not wish it, but I permitted a deputation to visit her and ascertain this for themselves. A trial meant delay, mess, ugly details. If Catherine had wanted to live, she had had an opportunity to do so, and with a clean record. She had rejected the respectable escape I had offered her through "widowhood." Now she would equally reject any stumbling-block between herself and a blazing death as Queen. Trials and legal proceedings would hinder the drama she was determined to play.

They returned convinced that the Queen wanted no trial. As I had predicted.

Neither did I want a trial, even with her in absentia. I did not want to endure the witnesses and the recounting of details that would haunt me forever. And to what purpose? She was guilty. She had married me only out of greed and ambition, when she was by canon law and usage another man's wife already; had committed adultery with one of my attendants and plotted my death. Did I truly need to have all those wrongs reiterated?

Parliament, which would meet on January sixteenth, would pass sentence on her. I attended the opening session, sitting above the assembly of Lords and Commons as they met in the Chapter House of Westminster Abbey. Lord Chancellor Audley addressed them, congratulating them upon the good fortune that permitted such a fine and wise sovereign to reign over them, Henry the Eighth, by the grace of God King of England and France and Lord of Ireland.

I smelled spring. I smelled apple blossoms and felt the warm air of April on my cheeks, my cheeks which were firm and unbearded. In some far inner ear I was hearing the herald's call at Richmond, that afternoon when I had first become King. I had been bursting inside with fear and eagerness, trembling right on the brink of the veiled future. Now that future was past, the candles burnt to their sockets, and yet the words remained and still brought fear upon me.

One by one, they rose and bowed, until the entire assemblage was standing.

"Let us give thanks to Almighty God who has preserved for so long a time such an exceptional Prince over this Kingdom," Audley said.

Yes, *preserved* . . . like an old thing past its prime. Fish were *preserved* in brine. Exceptional Prince . . . well, the words meant a different thing now.

It was decided that the Bill of Attainder against the Queen would be introduced into Parliament in a week's time, and that I need not be present. I could give my assent by letters-patent under the Great Seal of England, so as to spare myself "the grief and pain of hearing once again the wicked facts of the case." Thus the husband and wife were both ghosts at their own proceedings.

The Bill of Attainder was read in Parliament three times: on January twenty-first, on January twenty-eighth, and finally on February eighth. On February eleventh, the Queen's death warrant became law.

The Bill covered more than just the Queen's high treason. It gave Parliamentary sanction to the trial and condemnation of Culpepper and Dereham and the sentence of misprision passed against the Howards. It also made it a crime, in the future, for any unchaste woman to conceal her state from the King, once he showed an interest in marrying her.

This latter made me a laughingstock. Jokes were circulated to the effect that no woman in the kingdom would be eligible; that only a widow could pass the test; that the competition for my hand would be negligible, and so on. If I had cared any longer about such things, I would have been offended. But I did not intend to marry again. Women disgusted me, and I counted myself fortunate to be at last beyond the need of them.

As I had grown older, my needs grew fewer and fewer. At one time it had been important to me that I have a powerful body and a pretty wife. Both these things were now taken away, and their possibilities were gone. I had wanted riches and beautiful palace furnishings, but now I had them and they delighted me not. Building Nonsuch Palace was a chore, not a pleasure, and I decided on the instant not even to bother to finish it.

All I wanted now was the respect and love of my subjects, and a modicum of health. Dwindling needs, but fiercely coveted nonetheless.

❧ ❧

On February twelfth, Catherine was transported by water from Syon House to the Tower.

I saw them when they made their way upstream, past my windows at Whitehall. A doleful little flotilla, the Queen's boat being guarded between a galley full of Privy Councillors in the fore, and a barge with the Duke of

Suffolk and his soldiers to the rear. Catherine's vessel was curtained and closed and—Jesu be thanked—I was unable to glimpse her, although I tried. Darkness was closing in, as I had forbidden them to start until I was certain that in the short winter afternoon London Bridge would not be reached before total darkness enveloped it. I would not have Catherine see Dereham's and Culpepper's heads impaled above the bridge, and I knew she would look for them, even as I had looked for her as she passed.

The barge stopped at Traitor's Gate, and Catherine, dressed all in black, was taken from the water-stairs to her prison chamber. Her short cold journey was over.

There were curiosity-seekers on the landing, all gaping at her. One of them wrote this ballad:

> Thus as I sat, the tears within my eyen
> Of her the wreck, whilst I did debate,
> Before my face me thought I saw this Queen,
> No whit, as I her left, Got wot, of late,
> But all bewept in black and poor estate.
>
> "To be a Queen fortune did me prefer,
> Flourishing in youth with beauty fresh and pure,
> Whom nature made shine equal with the stars,
> And to reign in felicity with joy and pleasure,
> Wanting no thing that love might me procure,
> So much beloved far, far beyond the rest,
> With my Sovereign Lord, who lodged me in his rest.
>
> "Now I know well," quoth she, "among my friends all
> That here I left the day of my decay
> That I shall get no pompous funeral,
> Nor of my black, no man the charge shall pay;
> Save that some one perchance may hap to say,
> 'Such a one there was, alas! and that was pity
> That she herself disdained with such untruth.'"

She appealed to poets. *All bewept in black and poor estate.* . . . Seeing her mounting those stairs had snared yet another man's heart, got her another partisan.

That was her last outside appearance. Within the Tower there was none to be swayed by her beauty and wistfulness.

That evening she made a startling request: that a block be brought to her cell so she could practise laying her head upon it. She was determined to make a pretty showing before the assembled witnesses on the morrow. I was told she practised daintily upon the thing for upwards of an hour, approaching it from many different angles and laying her head sideways, left and right, and hanging straight down, enquiring of her unhappy attendants which made the better composition.

And how did I pass that night? I lay awake all through it, and in February, the nights are long. It had been night already when Catherine reached the Tower, and it would be still night when she mounted the scaffold to have her head struck off.

It was the same scaffold that Anne had climbed, and More, and Fisher, and Buckingham, and Neville and Carew. Some fancy had arisen among the common people that "indelible stains" marked the spot on the flints below. This was nonsense; I myself had inspected the flints and they were ordinary enough, and nothing remained on them. As for the scaffold, it was still serviceable, and building another one because of squeamishness would serve no purpose.

Nights in February are also cold. This night in particular was damp, with the damp that paralyses you. It was worse than the clean cold of snow and ice. I could scarce move my limbs, even underneath all the furs mounded to warm me. The blazing fire did nothing to aroint the cold. What did Catherine feel, in the ancient Tower? She had always been so sensitive to cold. I remembered how she had sent those furs and blankets to Reginald Pole's traitorous mother, the Countess of Salisbury, in the Tower, lest she take cold. I had chided her for being softhearted. Aye, softhearted she was, toward everyone—the aged, traitorous Countess; the unemployed former secretaries and relations of the Duchess, her accomplices in sin. Toward anyone in need she was melting. She stopped not to question whether they had brought that need upon themselves.

It lightened somewhat in the east—a poor excuse for dawn. Outside my chamber window the vexed Thames slapped more furiously. I could not imagine how chilling those waters must be.

So: it was come. The day of the sentence, the day another Queen of England must die.

I had done my grieving, and arose determined to spend the day with my children. They were the only comfort left to me, the only things I had produced that nothing could mar or sully.

CXI

I had notified them by way of their governesses and chamberlains that February thirteenth was to be reserved for me, their most royal father. They were to spend the entire day in my company, doing what they most loved doing. For I would fain know those things, as to know a man's pleasures is to know his heart.

They were to come to my chamber at eight o'clock, prepared for this day of recreation.

Mary arrived as the very stroke of eight began. She brought a large satchel, and I assumed it contained books. But I was delighted as she pulled out a viol, a viola da gamba, and a recorder. "My greatest pleasure," she said, "is to play music all day long with no one to tell me 'tis time to attend to other things."

Music. I, too, would have music all the day long. I grabbed Mary and kissed her on both cheeks. "You cannot know how that pleases me!" And I spoke true.

Mary pushed herself away and began to ruffle through her music-notes. So much like Katherine . . . I found, to my astonishment, that my fond memories of Katherine had resurrected themselves. Mary was twenty-six now. A woman, four years older than my silly, false wife. She had never liked Catherine, and I had resented that, but brushed it aside as an old maid's envy of a young wife. But Mary had evidently seen things I had not. . . .

Edward now came, brought by his nurse. The sweet-cheeked boy waddled in, so swathed against the cold he was as bloated as a man four days in the water.

"And what would you like to do this day?" I asked him.

"Faith, he has a puppy he loves well," started his nurse.

"I would have the snake," he said quietly.

"A serpent?" I asked.

"He has collected them, Your Majesty," she apologized. "In the fields near Hampton. He seems to have . . . to have a way with them."

He nodded. "Yes, fetch my snakes!"

The nurse brought in a large box. Now I became curious and lifted the lid. Inside were many dark shapes, which did not stir.

"They are sleeping!" cried Edward. "They have no eyelids, so when they sleep it must be dark, and they tuck their heads down, so."

"He found some eggs," said the nurse. "And is trying to hatch them."

"And I shall succeed!" he said.

"Good boy." I chuckled. "I should like to see you succeed." I touched his golden hair. He was so delicate. The fat of the previous autumn had melted away, leaving him luminous and lean-bodied. His skin was so fine it glowed. "And what of your pup?"

"He takes little interest in it," admitted the nurse. "He seems to prefer serpents to true loyal animals."

I shrugged. He was but four years old. The important thing was that he had an interest.

Mary was settling herself with her music and instruments, and Edward was playing with his snakes, when Elizabeth arrived.

"My Lady Elizabeth," I said. "And what have you brought?"

She straggled in, dragging a large box after her. With a sigh, she let it rest. "Materials to make Valentines. Red and white paper, and two volumes of poetry." She ripped off her fur cap. "Tomorrow is St. Valentine's Day."

St. Valentine's Day. O sweet Jesu! I would be fresh a widower upon St. Valentine's Day, my sweetheart having just been beheaded. How fitting.

"And to whom shall you send them? Do you already have a Valentine?" I must keep things at a child's level.

"Perhaps," she said, "but I must make my message cryptic, or sacrifice my pride."

She was wise. Would that it would stay with her as she grew to womanhood, and not be scattered before the look in a man's eye.

"So settle you down, and we shall spend a day together doing as we all like! And at dinnertime, you shall all have your favourite dishes—whether they are healthy or not, or go together or not." I had taken great pains to find out their favourite treats.

"And Father," said Elizabeth, "what shall you do? What is your favourite activity?"

Music. Above all, music. "I shall compose a new ballad. And force myself to be ready by nightfall. Then I shall perform."

We began our tasks, and the sun rose, coming into the chamber.

The cannon sounded from the Tower. It was not easily heard, in midwinter, with all the windows shut tight and stuffed with lambswool against the cold. Mary's playing all but drowned it.

Elizabeth rose, putting aside her red cuttings. "What was that?" she asked quietly, laying her hand on my arm.

I looked into her eyes. "It was the cannon," I said. "Announcing that the Queen is dead."

The Queen was dead. Catherine's head was gone.

"I shall never marry!" cried Elizabeth.

The others looked up: Mary too old to react, Edward too young.

"Elizabeth," I said, reaching for her. I would explain it all to her, explain it to this intelligent child.

She was gone from my reach. "Nay," she said, pretending there were no tears in her eyes. She had cleverly placed herself beyond scrutiny. "Marriage is death," she shrugged. "I would have none of it." She gestured toward the Valentines. "This, and no further. Valentines are pretty."

I went to put my arm around her. When I did, I felt a stiff unyielding thing. She wanted no comforting.

It was I who wanted some comforting, some warmth. But that was beyond reach as well.

The Queen was dead.

Catherine had been led forth onto the scaffold just before dawn. She had worn no mantle against the chilled air. The audience assembled was, for the most part, indifferent. Catherine had had no partisans, no champions.

That in itself was curious. There was none of my Queens who had gone undefended. Katherine of Aragon had had her violent defenders, churchmen who had been willing to die for her, the northern men who had fought on her behalf. Anne Boleyn (due to her witchcraft) had had those who willingly sacrificed their lives and political careers for her. Jane was mourned by the entire realm. Even Anne of Cleves had inspired loyalty and become beloved in certain circles.

But Catherine? It appeared that no one who really knew her loved her, aside from two or three base men who wanted her favours. Once they were dead, no one stepped forward to ally himself with her. Even her "friends" tumbled all over themselves to denounce her and disassociate themselves from her. They had swum toward her like water rats when she first became Queen, demanding places in her household (*black-mailing* her?); now they swam away with equal alacrity.

But why go over this so intellectually? Yes, it was telling and surprising that Catherine was left naked of supporters at the scaffold, but . . .

The scaffold. She had mounted it, helped up by others. This is the part I delayed recounting, this is the grisly part. To omit it would be dishonest, yet . . . oh, would God it had not occurred!

She stood still in the frosty air, all in black. *(All bewept in black and poor estate.)* About the scaffold were all the court, and foreign ambassadors. She had everyone's ear, and every word she uttered would be remembered and whispered and repeated abroad.

Before her was the block upon which she had practised the night before. (Curious that she had not asked for a special swordsman, as had been granted her cousin Anne. But then, she had practised upon the block. Both Queens sought to turn a state execution into a showcase for themselves—to make themselves legends.)

She said, clearly, so that all might hear: "I die a Queen, but I would rather die the wife of Culpepper. God have mercy on my soul. Good people, I beg you, pray for me."

Then she put her head on the block—expertly—and the axe severed it. It rolled but a little way in the hay. Functionaries gathered it up, and spread a black cloth over the body trunk, still kneeling in the black dress beside the block. Blood was gushing from the severed neck, but the cold air quickly congealed it. They lifted her body away, but did not put it in the coffin yet. Let the blood drain out first, else it would foul the coffin.

Two pages scrubbed off the block, to cleanse it of Catherine's mess. The space beside it was rinsed with steaming water from pitchers. I was told that the smell of the water mingling with blood made many bystanders ill.

Then Jane Boleyn, Lady Rochford, was pulled toward the scrubbed-up block. She was allowed to speak, in accordance with custom.

"Good Christians," she said, "God has permitted me to suffer this shameful doom, as a punishment for having contributed to my husband's death. I falsely accused him of loving in incestuous manner his sister, Queen Anne Boleyn. For this I deserve to die. But I am guilty of no other crime." Seeing Catherine's black-covered lump, she began to scream. Then, shaking, she laid her head and submitted to the axe.

After all the blood had run out of her, they put Catherine in the coffin, and buried it in the Chapel of St. Peter-ad-Vincula within the Tower, only a few feet from her cousin Anne Boleyn.

And it was done. Her corpse lay in a box, neatly covered over.

Mercifully I did not hear their scaffold statements until nightfall, when the children had gone. Then I heard them. Then I lay in bed (not warm, merely pretending to be) and heard them.

I die a Queen, but I would rather die the wife of Culpepper.

She had said that. She had actually said that. Was it true? I hurried past that, which was beyond understanding, since her bloodless form now lay buried. I could never ask her, could never wring from her an explanation: Why did you insist on being Queen until the end if all you meant was to reject it?

I die a Queen, but I would rather die the wife of Culpepper.

Perhaps she had only retained the title so that she could, at her own command, do with it as she liked. And what she liked was to glorify her love for Culpepper.

And spit upon my love for her, and the honours I had bestowed upon her.

Tell it true unto yourself, I thought. Shrink not. The truth is that you offered her everything you were. You were sick, yes, and you were old. You did all you could humanly do to minimize those things and make yourself into an offering for her. You devoted yourself to being what you imagined she desired.

And still she did not desire you.

That is what she told you as her farewell. *Do as you like, Henry. You will never be good enough for me. I preferred the charms of a no-one, a nothing. Your achievements, your titles, your gifts, your devotions: I count them as nothing. And you as well.*

Lady Rochford. She claimed that Anne was innocent, that she had perjured her. Was this true? And if it were? Suppose Anne and her brother had not been incestuous lovers? Would that have altered anything? Was that Anne's main crime? No. It was the most unnatural. But remove it, and she yet remained a witch.

Jane Rochford. Jealous of Anne, and now jealous of Catherine. Catherine had made a rejecting scaffold speech, one that would wound me greatly. Jane aped her as best she knew how.

I was exhausted, and brokenhearted. The world before me seemed empty. The teeming stage offered nothing.

I saw no reason to rise from my bed. Nothing was left but little people, little causes, little crusades. The world had shrunk perilously. And I as well.

Such high-flown rhetoric does not truly convey my feelings. After all, it was composed long after the fact. I do not think any man could really explain the desolation I felt that night. I was alone, unloved, as I had been all my life. Only now I finally understood that it was a permanent condition.

CXII

S t. Valentine's Day, and Catherine had now been dead for twenty-four
hours. There had been no embalming, of course, and so her corpse was
in the natural state, exactly like a dog's by the side of the road, struck
by a cart the day previous. I had seen many of these. Usually by this
time they were coated with flies so thick they looked like fur. There were no
flies inside a coffin. But there were maggots, which would hatch and feed on
the flesh. How would the grown flies escape from the sealed coffin, though?
Would they die with the corpse they had consumed?

O God, these nightmarish obsessions! Was I going mad? I was powerless
to stop them, and the fear of them was becoming as terrorizing as the thoughts
themselves. It was my mind that was consumed with maggots, the maggots of
madness.

That night I sat at the banquet I had commanded in honour of St.
Valentine's Day. Cup-bearers and servers were dressed like Cupid, and all the
dishes were to be red and white. Thus the first course consisted of lobsters,
crayfish, custard, apples, red cabbage. "Venus" presided over the other end of
the table, at the place where Catherine should have been. I had chosen Henry
Howard's "Fair Geraldine" to play Venus: another beauty married to an old
man, with an adoring young suitor. I wanted to duplicate Catherine as much
as possible, to watch, as it were, other players playing myself, Culpepper, and
Catherine. I sat staring at her as she tossed her curls (not as thick as Catherine's),
ran her slender fingers lightly up and around her neck-hollow, licked her lips
slowly. If I squinted my eyes, yes, it *could* be Catherine—as she had looked to
others.

Her besotted old husband, Anthony Browne, was down at the end of the
table and to my right. There are two kinds of old men: the fat kind and the
withered-up kind. He was the dried-up, wizened type, who looked like a

preserved lizard. His beady eyes shone with love for her. I noticed that he kept them firmly anchored in her direction, only allowing them to dart occasionally around the room.

I know what you are thinking, went through my mind. You are wondering how you ever came by such a woman. You are remembering what happened between you the last time you bedded her. If it was nothing, you have taken a few potions since then and pray that next time it will be different. If it was satisfactory, you tell yourself over and over that it was for her, too.

Old fool!

I looked now at Henry Howard, the erstwhile lover. Did he gaze at "Geraldine"? I watched as he cut his meat with his elegant personal knife and fork. He took a sip of wine and dabbed daintily at his lips with a lace handkerchief. He was speaking to Petre next him, and did not even look at his love.

Oh, he was clever. Much cleverer than Culpepper, who had betrayed himself in a thousand ways, had I but had eyes to see it. But then Henry was a Howard, and Howards were nothing if not clever. The geniuses of the kingdom, the Howards. They excelled in soldiery, poetry, diplomacy, beauty. But the Tudors were more ruthless. That was why I was King and the Howards only dukes and earls. Not that they would not like to be King, or might not attempt to become so. . . .

I looked once more at the trio, aching as I let them represent myself and my grief. As if by seeing them this way I would somehow gain a new insight, find a new perspective, that would lessen the pain.

Old fool!

In between courses, now, the silly Cupids came bearing large decorated boxes—one with Venus, one with her son. Inside the "Venus" box were pieces of paper with all the women's names, from which each man would draw his Valentine. Likewise the "Cupid" box contained men's names, for the women to choose from.

The company attempted to choose the names with gusto and a light heart, as betokened the occasion. But I knew well how cruel and pitiless they thought me, to stage such a celebration the day after my wife's execution. Their smiles and shrieks did not fool me.

What, did they expect me to wear mourning for the traitress? Did they expect the court to keep itself all in black for a season, as it had for Jane? No, by God! It was divinely arranged that her execution should have fallen just before a happy holiday, so that the court—and I—could be prevented from any facsimile of mourning.

So I wore red, and opened my Valentine. It was from Katherine Parr,

Lady Latimer, the Scripture-quoting widow. I must declare myself to her, present a token, when the mummery was over.

Now the eunuch-like Cupid made his rounds amongst the women, his red loin-covering looking obscenely silly. Each lady took out a sealed note, broke it open, and read therein the name of her appointed Valentine. Who was to be mine? No one betrayed herself. Why did such childish games appeal to grown people?

The second course was presented. It was all in hues of red, made so by steeping and painting with dried rose petals, ground sandalwood, powdered alkanet: pink chicken, scarlet fish, crimson bread. Damask jelly-hearts quivering on plates; garnet puddings, vermilion-tinted parsnips, ruby-red clear soup, glowing like the Black Prince's ruby.

So many shades of red, such subtleties, it was like the great rose garden, where I had been dazzled by all nature's ways of being red. Yes, and where, upon the instant, I had thought of creating the rose without a thorn, for *her*. . . .

Red. Red everywhere. A wife was dead and once again I was swathed in a colour, like Joseph in his coat of many colours, only with me it was one colour, one colour per wife. . . .

When Katherine died, there had been that ball that Anne gave, all dressed in yellow. Blazing, brazen yellow—it had not been seemly, but the Witch said it was mourning, or rather, *her* version of mourning. . . .

When Anne died, I wore white—and all *was* white that day, with the fruit trees all in bloom, and sweet, pure Jane waiting in a country house, as virgin and pure as Anne was tainted. . . .

When Jane died, all was black—my clothes, the court, the chambers all hung with it. . . .

And now, red. Red for blood. The dishes dripped with blood, *that* was what made them red. I could see the oozings, see the clots . . . the cooks fooled me not! Who had done this? Who had dared?

I stood up abruptly. Next to me I saw a cut surface of pudding, with genuine blood leaking out. "Stop!" I smacked Wriothesley's hand and made him drop his fork.

"Tainted! Someone shall pay!"

Everyone stopped and waited upon my command. Obedient, sly creatures. Yet one person had left, had dared to leave the feast before me, and without my permission.

The empty chair mocked me. And then I saw it. Beside the plate, laid across it—a single red rose.

Without a thorn upon its stem.

Fear passed over me, like wind over a grain field.

Catherine. Her ghost was here.

"You frighten me not!" I cried, lying. Could ghosts read thoughts? They came from hell.

The rose shimmered and vanished. The mark of the Evil One. Instinctively I crossed myself, unaware of the frightened stares of my guests.

"Sweet Jesu, preserve us," I whispered. The thing was gone, the Evil Presence was gone. The food no longer dripped blood, and next to me, the pudding reverted into an ordinary pudding.

I sat back down, slowly. No need to give Satan any ground. I must carry on as if this had not occurred. Yield no ground to evil, no, never.

"I did but test you!" I laughed, waving my hand. Everyone bleated back in simulated laughter.

I forked a piece of food and popped it in my mouth. They all followed my example, then chewed with exaggerated motions. Back and forth, back and forth—like a company of goats. The men's beards wagged fiendishly. Their eyes glowed. Fiendishly . . .

The Devil is a goat, some say. He often takes that form, having a particular fondness for it. Now he animated the entire company before me.

The amount of devil in them was revealed by the brightness of the red glow in their eyes. There was Tom Seymour, with eyes like a double Mars at sunrise; Francis Bryan, with his one gleaming, malevolent coal. The Vicar of Hell, they had nicknamed him years back, because he had shifted loyalty from Anne Boleyn and been the first messenger to Jane to announce Anne's condemnation. It was a little thing at the time, but now I wondered if character were truly the handmaiden of such small details, after all.

The others? Edward Seymour, William Fitzwilliam, Anthony Denny, John Dudley, Wriothesley, Gardiner, Sadler, Audley . . . their eyes were faint. Faintly red, faintly "normal," there was nothing one way or the other about them. *So then because thou art lukewarm, and neither cold nor hot, I will spew thee out of my mouth.* The devil had staked a halfhearted claim on them, but their matter was not worth fighting for. The battleground of good and evil should be grander, more sublime than this.

Were there any here in the company with clear eyes, with no tinge of red? Primarily the women: I was startled to see that the Lady Anne of Cleves had such eyes, as did Katherine Parr, as did "Geraldine." Ah, Geraldine . . . then you love your old man, do you? No cuckolding. The revelation was simultaneously a balm and a wound.

That empty place. It was still there. And sitting in it was Catherine, her lower body all encased in pearl-encrusted silk, up to her bloody, clotted neck-stump. Rivulets of blood ran down the sides and flowed gently and warmly around the collar of jewels encircling it, before trickling in streams down into her bodice. Sitting on her platter was her head, the eyes pure red.

Her evil was revealed! I threw my goblet at her, and it struck her head and knocked it off the table. Both the goblet and the head rolled on the floor, like lopsided balls of yarn, coming to rest against the table legs.

Once again the company was staring at me. But protocol forbade their touching me, or making any move of their own.

It was the widow Parr who stood, came over, and laid hands upon my shoulders. They were gentle hands, such as I had not felt since Jane . . . but there was something in them besides, some special grace.

"You are not well," she said, and, in her saying of it, made it natural. "Sleep is what is needed, my Lord." She drew me up. "Come, and rest."

Somehow I was in my chamber, being ministered to by my attendants and put to bed. Somehow all was as it should be.

"I have not forgotten," she said, still there. "You and I are Valentines."

"I have a gift for you, Kate." It was important that she should know that I remembered my duty in these matters.

Then I was alone. My head throbbed, my senses spun. I was overtired, yes. How long since I had slept a natural sleep? Catherine but newly dead. Did *she* sleep? No, she did not. That I knew already.

"Henry."

I heard the voice, sweet and voluptuous, in my ear. She was beside me.

"Henry." A little ways away. A few feet from the bed.

"Henry! Henry! Henry!" Shrieks outside my chamber door.

"No! No!"

The wood registered the vibrations. Only a few inches between us—

I flung open the chamber door, opening on the darkened Privy Chamber. "No! No!"

The voice was behind yet another set of doors. I opened the Privy Chamber doors, leading to the Audience Chamber, but it was empty, vast, alien.

"Henry!"

It came from the gallery, the Long Gallery connecting the royal apartments with the Chapel Royal.

I fumbled at the door latch. It was carved and heavy, to impress petitioners with the gravity of majesty. The doors themselves were great panels, the height of three men. Pulling them open required considerable strength; I felt my belly muscles tighten at the strain.

The passageway outside was deserted. Then I saw it . . . the white figure, being dragged backwards, receding before my eyes. Mournful cries came from it, sorrow beyond telling. . . .

There was nothing there. It had quite vanished, and all its presence with it.

I returned to my bed. Since Culpepper, I had had no intimate of the bedchamber, and I slept quite alone and unattended. In one sense I savoured it. It was tiresome always to consider another's needs in the night, not to dare to light a candle for fear of waking him.

The ghost—for ghost it was, and I might as well name it as such—shrieked and cried in a way no mortal ever had. Would others see it? Or was it meant only for me? I settled the covers about me. I would not sleep, that I knew. But I expected to pass the night in solitary meditation.

It was in the very darkest part of night, when the sun is gone and thinks never to return, that I first saw the monks. They were standing in the shadows of the far reaches of the chamber. I could see straightway that their habits were varied, and that they belonged to different orders. On the left was the light-coloured habit of the Cistercians. I had not dealt kindly with them, that I knew. They were a strict order, living isolated, arduous lives, and a good order, in the beginning. Well, we are all of us good in the beginning. But we must be judged on what we become.

Next to him, a dark habit. Surely a Dominican. This was a hard order to love, just as many in Jesus' time must have found it hard to love a disciple. They were too astute, too caustic, too clever.

Standing a little to the side was a grey-habited figure. Greyfriars, the people called the Observant Franciscans: they had had a priory right outside the palace gates at Greenwich. Once they were my friends; then they became my enemies. Well, I had destroyed that obstructionist order.

Then, in the middle, a dun-coloured habit. Oh, those Carthusians! I had had to take sternest measures against them. They had proved most recalcitrant to my enlightenment. Therefore I was not surprised when the tan-habited one came toward me.

How did I see him? It was dark. His habit did not glow, as country folk would claim. Yet I saw him.

He nodded gravely toward me. I could not see his face, yet I believe it was that of John Houghton, the London abbot whom I had hanged for refusal to take the Oath.

"Henry," he intoned—no, whispered. "You were wrong in what you did. The monks were good, did good."

"They were evil, did evil." Did I speak these words or merely think them?

"No." The sound was soft. So soft I could not quite discover whether it was true or my imagining.

The monks shimmered. Their habits waved and seemed to change colour. Then the sun—only a tiny ray—shone into the chamber. There were no monks.

There were no monks. There was no Catherine. (Yes, there was, only it was a corpse, a corpse without a head. If I bade diggers to dig her up, she would be there, two days rotted now. In winter it is slower. She might yet be beautiful. Her face, that is, printed upon the severed head.) I had fancied it all, in my sick fantasy. "Fantasy" . . . what a powerful word. *The King did cast a fantasy to Catherine Howard. . . .*

CXIII

Soon they would be coming into the chamber—the attendants, the doctors—having heard about my behaviour the night before. (Was it only the night before, when I had confronted the Fiend in all his degrees?) What exactly had happened? Was there any man who would dare to tell me?

The breakfast over, the shaving over, the reading of the daily dispatches over, now the day must begin.

Brandon came to me in my sunny work chamber.

"My behaviour last night," I said straightway. "Describe it as you would if under oath."

"Well . . ." He fidgeted, shifted back and forth on his feet. He had become portly of late.

"Pray seat yourself." I gestured toward a chair, one of two against the wall.

He brought it over, closer to me. "Your Grace." He smiled. "Do you not think it meet that these chairs come to this use?"

I was silent. I did not remember the chairs. Collapsible U-shaped wooden things, inlaid with mother-of-pearl. Some gift from the Patriarch of Jerusalem?

"They were in the Spaniards' tents when the Princess of Aragon first came to England. When your father was not allowed admittance."

In that very tent? When I first saw Katherine, and loved her? I was angry, and I knew not why. Why had they survived? They should have perished, along with all those things of that world.

"That was ten thousand years ago."

"Aye." His grin faded.

"What did I do last night? What did I do and say? And what truly happened? I know you will tell me."

"There was a Valentine's banquet. All was as it should be, all dishes served in order, the colours red and white, the Valentine's box distributed and sweethearts allotted, the red-coloured courses served."

"But?"

"But it was the day after an execution. No ordinary execution. The Queen, my Lord—you executed the Queen. And so the Valentine's feast was a funeral feast. At least, those attending felt it so. There was no merriment, save to please you."

"But what of my . . . my behaviour?"

"You started and stared, and talked to the air."

"I saw Catherine. She was sitting in her seat, with a thornless rose before her golden platter."

"No one else saw her. She was for your eyes alone."

"Did the guests . . . *know* I saw her?"

"They knew you saw *something*."

"So they assume I am mad." I jerked out the words. I had paraded my obsession, my hauntings, in front of the company.

"They assume you were conscience-stricken." His deep brown eyes, the only youthful feature in his lined face, gazed directly into mine. "How you act from today forward will determine whether they judge you as mad."

"I am not conscience-stricken!" I muttered. "She deserved to die."

"That—or mad," said Brandon calmly. "Those are the only two explanations they will allow you. People are simplistic, my Lord."

"You know I am not mad," I began.

"Too strong a strain, for too long, can drive anyone mad." He was cautious.

"I have never been mad, and I never shall be mad! But you are right, it was foolish to plan such a festivity following an execution. Better just to grieve, and admit one's grieving. I should have locked myself up in my chambers and wept all day. Then I would feel clean, not more besmirched than ever."

"Death does not cleanse. Sometimes the loved one—or the hated one—never leaves one's side. I still miss Mary. Katherine is no comfort. I, too, was a fool."

I embraced him. "I misjudged you."

"As others will misjudge *you*," he said. "Unless you are careful."

At once it was important that I tell him all of it. "I was not alone in my chamber. I heard shriekings outside, in the Long Gallery. And then, in the back of the room, there were monks. Whispering together, huddling, pointing, judging."

He started and looked uneasy. "Shrieks? As of a woman? In the Long Gallery, you say?" Suddenly he flung himself up out of the Spanish chair. "Do you remember when you heard Mass at Hampton Court, in the same Chapel Royal, when the first news of Catherine was coming out?"

"Yes."

"No one would tell you, then, as they acted on their own authority and feared your anger. When you were at your prayers, Catherine escaped from her guard and sought to find you at Mass. She eluded her watchers and came down the Long Gallery at Hampton. She reached the very doors of the chapel, where she meant to throw herself on your mercy. But just as she was turning the great door-fastener, she was apprehended. Then—"

"She called for me," I said slowly.

"Trusting that you would hear her. She was so bold she even used your first name, the one forbidden even to me. She dared all. But failed in her attempt. She was dragged away before she could open the doors and intrude on your worship."

"Was she wearing white?" I asked, dully.

"Aye."

"She was dressed, then, as a maiden."

So she would appear, for all eternity. The virgin-whore. I had seen true.

"She attempted to appeal to your sense of sentimentality."

So my "sentimentality" was well known, a weakness for users to play upon. Was there nothing of a king that others did not seek to use? From my "sentimentality" to my time on the evacuation-stool after dinner?

"I will always see her as a maiden." That was true, that was the aching of it. But what of the ghost? Had others seen it?

"I was visited by this sight last night," I confessed. "The same shrieks, the same calling of my name. This time I opened the door, and looked down the gallery myself. *I saw it.*"

Brandon frowned. "Were there any other witnesses?"

"None."

"Set a watch, then. Else you *will* go mad, and she'll have done what she set out to do."

I nodded.

"She hates you," Brandon said. "She wishes you to come to ruin. Remember that. Thwart her."

"But why *Catherine?*" I burst out. "Why not anyone else? I swear, no one else has risen to walk!" I dared not name them, lest that call them forth. Buckingham. Anne. George Boleyn. More. Fisher. Aske. Smeaton. Weston. Norris. Brereton. Dudley. Empson. Neville. Carew. Cromwell. De la Pole. Margaret Pole.

"They were not possessed of the Evil One," he said smoothly. "Only the Evil One gives power beyond the grave."

"Anne—"

He could not answer. "Perhaps her soul reincarnated in her cousin Catherine."

I shook so profoundly I could not stop. Brandon encircled me with his great, heavy arm. "Your list of regrets is no longer than that of any other man," he said slowly. "We live with them. We do not go mad, or sink into melancholy." Still my shaking went on, gathering force. "Regrets. No one sets out to have a list of regrets. It is a mortal condition."

Father, amongst his bloodied handkerchiefs—how I had despised him.

"What now?" I shook my head wildly. "So I now find myself where ordinary men do. But what does a king do?"

"A king spits on the regrets," laughed Brandon.

Then I, too, began to laugh, and the trembling stopped.

I set six unimaginative Kentish soldiers to stand guard in the Long Gallery. I especially noted how dull of wit and irreligious they were, and posted them with the simple instructions that they were to keep watch all night, relieving one another at two-hour intervals. On no account were they to sleep, and they were to report to me any noises or stirrings they even suspected.

"For it has been said that this cold winter has forced an unusual number of rats to seek haven in the spaces beneath the gallery here. If so, I must know, so that appropriate poisons can be set out before they breed in spring. Do you understand?"

They nodded.

"Any unusual stirring," I repeated.

They nodded. Did they truly understand?

I thought my story quite clever. No madman could be so clever. It sounded quite logical and would net me the information I sought.

On the second night I heard the ghost. Its shriekings were quite clear. I cracked open the great doors and looked . . . and saw the apparition, *like* Catherine but *not* Catherine. It merely used her externals. The guardsmen were flailing at it; one stabbed at the air as if to pierce her breast. The other just leapt about like a dazed frog.

I closed the doors. Others had seen it walk. I was not alone. I was not mad.

The next morning the guards claimed they had seen nothing, heard nothing, and had passed a tranquil night.

Liars. Liars. I was surrounded by liars, cowards, enemies who painted every aspect of life false. To what end?

I thanked them and bade them remain on duty for yet another week, just to be sure.

"For if there be rats, we must exterminate them."

They agreed. "One quiet night does not guarantee that they are not present." I looked into their eyes. There was no reluctance there to pass another night on the gallery. Where had this generation got such hardened hearts?

Every night I heard the ghost. Every morning the guards reported an uneventful night. At the end of the eighth day I paid them, thanked them for their honesty and perseverance, and let them go.

"No poisons, then," I said merrily.

"Nothing to poison," they agreed.

No. One cannot poison a ghost. One can only poison others' opinions, and my behaviour at the Valentine's banquet had done that. Well, no matter. I would set about sweetening them. People's minds were like wells. First they run clear, then become polluted—but one can always counteract the pollution. Just throw something else in.

I had had a Valentine's gift for my Valentine, and had promised to give it her. I must follow through, must try to behave as normally as possible. So I sent a note to the widow Parr, asking her to join me for Mass in the morning and for dinner afterward. I knew she still resided at court. Catherine's household remained intact, a body without a head (like Catherine herself, their mistress), awaiting my orders to disband.

The widow Parr appeared promptly, a quarter-hour before the Mass was to begin. I noted she still wore her plain black mourning headdress, in memory of her deceased Lord.

"You are early," I remarked, as my gentlemen ushers brought her into my presence in the Privy Chamber.

"I did not know how long beforehand Your Majesty wished to spend in meditations. I would accompany you, and would not disrupt your pattern of devotion."

"Aye, aye." Suddenly these servers and observers about me were a nuisance. "Come, then. We shall go straightway." I smiled—or rather forced my face to simulate a smile—and held out my hand to her.

Together we entered the Chapel Royal. But instead of going directly to our devotions, I bade her stay and wait until her eyes accustomed themselves to the dimness. Overhead there were great gold stars, all painted in glory on the deep blue firmament.

"This is so dark it is like a Turkish den," she said unexpectedly. "Murky and messed."

Stale incense yet lingered from the previous day's celebration.

"One should come to Jesus in light as clear as Mary did in the early dawn of Easter," she said.

She did not apologize, she did not whittle down her own strength of words. Nor did she steal away to a statue of the Virgin—as I longed to—and fall to her knees in private devotion. Instead, she bent her head down and tried to read from a book she carried in her hand. In the dim light, this was impossible.

Embarrassed, I went over to the private prayer-niche reserved before the Virgin. When Cranmer and his servers appeared, ready to begin Mass, I heaved myself up from the prayer-stool and came once again to Katherine. I took her hand and brought her into the royal box.

She followed all that I did during the Mass. Knelt when I knelt, genu-flected when I genuflected, and even received the host. But I was unable to see her face, deep within the widow's bonnet.

Mass ended. Cranmer embraced us at the chapel doors and conferred blessings on us. I dipped my fingers in the holy water set out; she did not.

Silently we walked side by side down the Long Gallery. Her head was down, and all I could see was the long black tubular bonnet. Her skirts made noises as they dragged along the polished floor.

"God be with you, Katherine," I finally said.

"And with you," she said, but not rotely. She truly meant it.

"Did the Mass speak to you?" I asked. "You could not read your devo-tional book, and you said the chapel was too dark. Yet your late husband was a devout Pope-Catholic."

Pope-Catholic. That was my new term for those who thought no or-thodoxy was possible outside of Rome.

"I am not my husband." Her voice was so low I could scarcely hear her radical words. "The Lord Jesus said"—suddenly her face was upturned, and looking fully at mine—"that households shall be divided. For His sake."

Her face glowed. Her plain little face, which had no real beauty of its own, was infused with spiritual beauty.

I stopped where I was. I had never seen this before. I, who had been privileged to behold beauty in many forms, had never seen that entity called spiritual beauty. In fact I had always thought it a metaphor. Now it made me speechless.

"Aye," I said. "Kate." I reached out and pushed away the ugly widow's bonnet. The sun, coming through the gallery windows, hit her thick red-gold hair, all flattened and combed back. "You must no longer wear mourning," I said. "For you are not in mourning, but are rejoicing with the Risen Lord."

Obediently, she removed the bonnet.

The dinner was awaiting us in the Privy Chamber, laid out on my private dining table. A fair white linen cloth had been spread, and all my gold plate set out.

"This time of year there is little to choose from." Before the meal even appeared, I was issuing disclaimers for it.

"Five loaves and two fishes?" she laughed.

"About that," I admitted.

The bread, made from late-winter rye, was thick and heavy. The drink, made from the same, was nourishing. And yes, there was carp: universal late-winter dish.

"Who minds the carp pools now that the monasteries are abandoned?" she asked, matter-of-factly. It was the monks who had developed elaborate fish hatcheries, and made carp a standard part of the winter diet.

"Villagers. But we are not so dependent on carp any longer, now that there is less fasting."

"A foolish Popish custom," she said briskly. "I am happy that you abolished much of that, my Lord."

"But I have not abolished enough?" I chose my words carefully.

She chose hers with equal prudence. "Things are progressing. True things must build on a foundation."

"What were you reading?" I asked abruptly. "Or, rather, attempting to read?" I indicated her book.

"Private devotions," she said, handing me the book. "Some of the meditations were—I composed some of them myself."

I glanced at it. Key words—"faith," "Scripture," "blood," "justification"—branded it Protestant. "Have a care, Kate," I warned gently, handing it back to her.

She winced at the name. "No one has ever called me Kate," she said stiffly.

"No? But it is a happy name, as you are happy. A young name, as you are young." Was I the only one to have ever seen that side of her? "But if you prefer, I shall return to 'Lady Parr.' "

She did not contradict me. "You invited me, Your Majesty, because you had something for me?"

The Valentine's present: a section of Ovid, and his treatise on love. I had thought she would enjoy translating it. I saw now how utterly inappropriate it would be, how boorish.

"You are my Valentine," I said, thinking as quickly as I could. "We should exchange tokens, and I was remiss in withholding mine."

"You were ill, my Lord," she quickly reminded me.

"Yes, yes. Well, I have here"—sweet Jesu, what *did* I have?—"a jewel. A ruby ring." Red. Valentine's. Yes, it would do.

"I am in mourning," she said.

"We had agreed, as Christians, you were not." I delved into the leather pouch I kept in my private chest, my fingers searching for the ruby. "Here."

Reluctantly she took it. "This is not from a shrine?"

"It is not Becket's ruby, if that is what you fear! A ruby cannot be divided and retain its roundness. Surely you knew that? No, if you must know its origins—this is the girlhood ring of my dear sister Mary. Take it, and wear it in innocence, as she did."

Before she knew men: a brother who married her off for politics; a slavering old first husband, a greedy second husband who remarried before the trees in bloom at her funeral bore fruit. Ruby of childhood and hopes. Odd that a grown woman, twice widowed, should be the one woman I knew who was suited to wear it. Even little Elizabeth was too "old."

"Thank you," she said, putting it on her finger. "It was kind of you to remember the token."

And kind of you to forget that you had to comfort me on that horrible night, I thought. Forgetting is an act of charity—one much neglected.

The widow Parr—nay, Kate—was charity, and love, and light.

But she was a *Protestant!*

Just before she took her leave of me, she fumbled in her gown pocket and brought out a tiny volume of Psalms.

"I wish you to have this," she said earnestly. On her face was that transformed look, the one I wanted never to lose sight of. "Read it," she insisted, pressing it in my hand. "I trust, and hope, my translation is correct."

Then she was gone, and all I had was that little black leather book of Psalms.

Only Protestants made their own translations!

As I sat thumbing through the Psalter, I realized that I had not thought about my "madness" for the past six hours. Her serene sanity had banished it, had made it an absurdity.

CXIV

That afternoon I had scheduled audiences with all the foreign ambassadors. It was time we understood one another. I had been particularly annoyed by a certain Spaniard who, evidently trading on his acquaintance or influence with Chapuys, had witnessed Catherine's execution and then presumed to write a "chronicle" of it, telling of Catherine and Culpepper's romance, of my cruelty, and so on. Already a hundred or so copies had been printed and were circulating, both about London and abroad. They did me a great disservice, painting me as mad, vicious, besotted.

I would have each ambassador visit me upon the stroke of an hour: Chapuys at two o'clock, Marillac at three, the Scots envoy, a Stuart bastard, at four, and the Papal creature at five. Thereafter I would retire to my chamber with a large portion of wine and have baked lampreys for supper. I had already put in my request with the chief cook, as lampreys were tedious to prepare—all those bones to be removed. . . .

I changed into my audience costume. It was necessary, always, to appear as a King, to do as a King. Hence the heavy jewel-encrusted doublet, the cloth-of-gold cape. Over it all, my furred robes of state, much like the ones in fashion when my father reigned. They were now the mark of an older man, a man who, for health reasons, needed extra warmth. So be it. That was true. I had, for so long, refused to put them on. But I needed them, and no longer felt it important that others not know I needed them. I had even allowed Holbein to begin a portrait of me in them, clasping that signature of an old man: a stave. A lovely carved one, presented me by Niall Mor's father. The Irish . . . I must speak to the envoy from Ireland. How could I have forgotten? I had thought of it Thursday last, and made a note—where was the note? Truly this was unacceptable, this misplacing of things, this forgetting. . . .

"Your Majesty, the Imperial ambassador," my page announced.

"We will receive him." I settled myself on the throne of majesty, under the royal canopy. All forms must be observed, else people note there is something amiss . . . like a dog marking a wound, smelling blood. Always wear a bandage. That way they can't smell, can't detect, don't know.

The great high door opened, and Chapuys walked through. How many times had he come through those very doors? Perhaps a hundred? He had come often when Katherine was still a problem, and before Mary and I were reconciled. Lately he had come much less.

"Your Majesty." He dropped to one knee. I marked that it was difficult for him. The fluid motion of old was gone. His knees hurt, I could tell.

"My dear Imperial ambassador." I motioned to a padded chair near my throne. "Pray sit beside us."

He stood as easily as possible and then made his way to the comfortable chair. Once settled, he looked up with wary eyes. "Your Majesty sent for me?"

"Yes, Chapuys." I inhaled deeply. "You and I need no fencing, no probing. We have known one another too long. Therefore let us discuss this like honest, rough men. The truth is, one of your community, a confessed Spaniard, has abused his privilege. That privilege, Sir Ambassador, was being allowed to witness the executions on . . . on February thirteenth past. He has written a description of it, but, more heinous than that, has presumed to "explain" them. Since it was through your influence and permission that he was permitted inside the Tower grounds, it is you whom he has abused and betrayed. For of course, henceforth your privileges to grant such permissions must be revoked."

His little monkey's face glared back at me. "Oh. Are there more executions scheduled? I should be grieved to be excluded."

Oh, that infuriating Spaniard! Ever had he goaded me thus!

"That is not the issue." I kept my voice calm. The days were past when I exploded and revealed all my thoughts, all my passions, all my cherishings. Old man. Old man. Safe and guarded old man. Well, there was advantage in that. "The issue is what you permitted one of your countrymen to do, and on English soil. This thing"—I had it right handy in my working pouch—"is lies."

"Is it against English law to print lies?" he asked blandly. "I mean, against *specific* laws?"

"The printing press is so new we have not had time to formulate laws regarding it! But gentlemen follow certain codes of behaviour, certain standards, and they are as readily applicable to the printing press as to anything else!" But what if they were not? What if all that had been "understood" were no longer so, but some new order must rewrite the rules?

"But when you broke from the Papacy, you set an example." He spread his hands. "It said that none of the old rules, the old deferences, held true any longer. That applies to kings as well as to the Holy Father, you know." He shrugged. "So a common citizen wrote a defamatory 'history'? That will become so common in the new age, which *you* have championed, that no one will take notice of it."

"But it is lies!"

"So?"

"He says here"—I thumbed angrily till I found the place—"that *Cromwell* interrogated Catherine. Cromwell was dead! Did he come to life for the occasion, then?" There. That proved my point.

"Indeed he did." Chapuys chuckled—a superior, amused laugh. "And many more Cromwells will do likewise in this *wonderful*"—he all but spat the word—"new age you have helped birth. Where there is no respect for authority—smite the Pope!—and an exalted respect for the individual—oh, the Englishman is a god!—this sort of thing will abound. You'd best accustom yourself to it. Truth is whatever some ordinary man wishes to hawk, if his credentials are passable and his prose grammatical, and he can afford to have it printed. In this case the man *did* witness the execution; there are his credentials. His prose may be lies, but they are recited in the King's English. His pockets permitted the printing. Oh, but there's a fourth element, without which the others falter: men must hunger for his drivel and be willing to pay to read it."

He spoke true. *The Spanish Chronicle,* as it was called, answered many hungers. The truth was not among them. "So you refuse to refute it or make any gesture to suppress it?" I asked Chapuys.

"I have not the power," he said. Convenient excuse.

"I would you did."

"I also, Your Grace. It is a silly thing, and glorifies Catherine, making her more in death than ever she was in life. She was a"—he hesitated, as if unwilling to yield a point, but compelled by innate honesty to do so—"she was an embarrassing choice for a Catholic figurehead. I fear she has blackened the name of Catholicism in England. Better to have rested it with the Princess of Aragon than to have dragged it through this cesspool."

I appreciated his candour. "Well, the Protestants had Boleyn," I laughed. "It is dangerous for any spiritual body to set up a human being as their representative."

Suddenly he was laughing, a great genuine caw of delight. "Except in the case of the Holy Father," he said.

"No, that is precisely what I *did* say!" Now I, too, was laughing. "He is as bad as Anne and Catherine, in their ways. No, it cannot be a man!"

"But, Your Grace—*you* are now the Supreme Head of the Church of England!"

"Not as a spiritual example." I rose from my throne. My fondness for Chapuys, my old adversary, overcame me. Adversary he might be, but he belonged to my world, my old, known world, and all at once that was becoming very important to me. There were so few of us, and we were dwindling all the while. I threw my arm about his shoulder, his scrawny little shoulders.

He was old. He, too, was marked for passage, passage away from me. I was to be alone. Fear shook me.

"You tremble," he said, almost tenderly. We were enemies come to respect, then tolerate, then love one another. Where were the Princess of Aragon, the Boleyn Witch, Jane, the Princess of Cleves, the Howard whore, in my life now? But Chapuys remained.

"I do, sometimes," I admitted. "In March I can never seem to keep warm enough."

"In July, even, here in England!"

"You retire soon." I knew it.

"Yes. At last."

"The sun will warm you, will heal you. I know it. You have waited a long time."

"I have forgotten the sun. In truth, England feels like home to me. I came here briefly, so I thought. I would serve my time and then go back to the sun, the flowers, the black-and-white of Spanish noon. But I made the mistake of coming to love the Princess of Aragon. I could see her as that young girl, setting out for England—and I wanted to serve her."

"That you did." I released him, old bony man. "You saw her as that Princess when to everyone else she was a dowager. Well . . ." I closed my eyes, bade the images go. "We all need our champions." I had none, but no one need know that. "Your master, the Emperor . . . think you he will implement the Papal bull against me? Heed the call to holy war?"

"You and I both know that if he did not rise on behalf of his aunt, he will scarce stir now. Although he has become more pious and religious of late, that is offset by the turmoil in Germany and the Low Countries. Protestantism there . . . it is *that* which he will battle, not England's. You are quite safe from the Emperor," he conceded. "Only pray do not tell him I said so."

I embraced him again. "Naturally not."

"One thing more, Your Majesty." Chapuys pulled back. "The Princess Mary. Is she to be married soon?"

"I cannot see how that may be. Until the French and the Emperor recognize the importance of an alliance—"

"She is distraught. She *needs* a husband. I speak as a friend, not as an ambassador or as her conspirator. She is twenty-six years old, Your Grace, no longer a child, and soon will pass her childbearing years. Oh, have mercy on her!"

I was astonished at this outburst. "But to whom shall I marry her? A prince of—"

"A duke, a count, anyone! His orthodoxy does not matter! Only see her as a woman, a woman in desperate need of a husband and children. My master, the Emperor, would be irate if he heard me speak thus. But if you loved her as a child . . . Your Grace, her needs are no less now! Only you can free her. She needs to love someone, something. Else her natural goodness will grow all crooked."

Mary. For so many years, an enchanting child. Then a pawn in the war between Katherine and myself. Then—a nothing. I had not thought of her needs, I had been so assiduous in meeting my own. I had thought she would keep, keep until I was at peace.

Nothing keeps. It grows grotesque, or it withers.

"You speak true," I said. "She is terribly alone." Strange I had not realized it. I had ascribed strength and happiness all about me where it did not exist.

Mary. I had loved her so, but when she took Katherine's side I had thrust her aside. What was missing in me, to change allegiances so swiftly? Perhaps the madness reached far back, in an absence of normal feeling.

Madness. No, I was not mad. But these pounding headaches! Where was my head-medicine, the syrup that quieted these ragings? I would have a draught now. The servitor brought it. The pretty emerald syrup. It would course through my veins in time for the next audience.

There. All I had to do now was sit still, wait for it to take effect. But already there was a pounding outside, one that echoed the pounding within my own head.

"Monsieur le Ambassador, Marillac, awaits his audience."

So he was here already? Very well, then. "We are ready," I said.

Monsieur Marillac came into the Audience Chamber. He was virtually a stranger to me, having come to England only a few months previous. Francis did not allow any envoy to remain long enough to form a personal bond with me. Was it because he feared my charm, my influence?

"Your Majesty." He dropped to one knee, then raised his face toward mine, smiling. Such a pretty smile he had.

Wolsey had had a pretty smile. Oh, and such a servile manner, all flattering and obsequious at once.

Wolsey . . . there was no more Wolsey.

"We welcome you, Monsieur Marillac. 'Tis pity we have become so slightly acquainted with you, in all these weeks you have been on our soil. Come closer, Monsieur, and let me see you." I examined his face, his costume. He was stout and placid, that much could I determine. The sort of man with whom I could make no headway. Rather like assaulting one of my new fortifications near the Isle of Wight—I had designed them massive, round, impregnable, and entirely modern, that is, given over to gun-defence and cannon-strategy. No romance or chivalry about them. So, too, this Frenchman.

"How does my brother Francis?" I asked quickly.

"Not well, I fear," he said. "He is stricken with the sorrow that has afflicted Your Majesty."

Yes, I had received Francis's "condolence"—a letter wherein he had intoned, "The lightness of women does not touch the honour of men." I had not known whether to take it as commiseration or taunt. Whatever it betokened, I did not wish to discuss it with this stranger.

"Ummm." I grunted. My head yet throbbed. When would the syrup take effect?

"When you left him, what were his instructions? Were you to woo me as his friend, or raise porcupine-like quills against me?" There, that would startle him, make him cough out the truth.

"I—that is, he—"

I had guessed correctly. The rough-spoken English way had unbalanced him.

"When I left France, he was distant toward you. However, that was prior to—Your Majesty's misfortune—"

"Lies!" I leapt up from my throne and slammed my fist on the arm of it. "It was prior to his own lover's quarrel with the Emperor!" I swung round, then, and glared at him. "Is that not right, *knave?*"

It was all theatrics. Chapuys would have laughed. This greenwood knitted his brows, then did exactly as I had hoped: he blurted out the truth. "There has been a chilling of relations, since the Emperor has failed to recognize—"

"Aha! Yes! The Emperor always 'fails to recognize.' He fails to recognize his nose at the end of his face, eh? Eh?"

Marillac drew back. "Your Majesty?"

"Your master is a fool," I said casually, swinging round once more and sliding into my seat. "He knows he will have to do battle against me. Is he biding his time? Is that his game? Baiting me with foolishness like the money and support he sends the Scots, to incite them against me? Does he think I know not who prevented James from meeting me at York? Does he think I will forget the insult? Well? What does he *think?*"

Marillac stared back.

"Can you not speak for him? What sort of an ambassador are you, then? Have you no powers of representation? What, did you get no letters of instruction?"

He was pitiful. Not even worth sparring with. This was not sport, it was cruelty.

"Tell me this," I finally said. "Is Francis in good health, or not?" I tried to make my tone gentle and disarming.

"Indeed he is," replied Marillac haughtily.

Liar. I knew Francis was eaten up with the Great Pox, and it was beginning its deadly final assault on his mind.

"I am grateful to you for being so truthful." I smiled. "Francis is doubly blessed, then, in both his good health and his true representative. You may tell my brother of France that . . ." I had had a glib remark ready, but what came out was, "I hope we meet again on the plains of Ardes. Yes, if he would be willing, I would come again to the Val d'Or. No fantasy-palaces this time, no tournaments, merely . . . Francis, and myself. You will write him this?"

"This very evening, Your Majesty." The Frenchman bowed low.

That evening what he wrote was, "I have to do with the most dangerous and cruel man in the world." The double-dealing Frenchman! (And how did I know this? I had made use of Cromwell's legacy: his spies and secret police. They served me well. I would not have formed them myself, but as they already existed . . . I had found them useful, and using them myself prevented others from using them against me.)

Spies. There had always been spies. Julius Caesar had his, so 'tis said . . . although they must have been singularly ineffective, since they failed to warn him of the coming assassination. Spies were necessary, I suppose, to run a state. But I disliked the idea, the very fact of their being required.

I preferred to believe I could read a man's visage, could sum him up all by myself. I had realized the French ambassador lied. I did not truly need to have the contents of his letters espied, copied, and presented to me. It demeaned him and added nothing essential to my operating knowledge. But these new times required such machinations as a matter of course.

My head was still pulsating. The emerald syrup had done little to dispel the discomfort. Evidently I had not taken enough. I poured a bit more into the medicinal beaker, and swallowed it.

It was only a tiny bit, and yet within minutes I felt relieved of my symptoms. Why can but a little added to the dosage do that? There is so much physicians have yet to discover.

At four o'clock the Scots envoy was to pay me a call. I sat and pulled out the lengthy chronology I had myself constructed of all our relations, going back to my father's negotiations with James III, when he arranged my sister's marriage. It had been a nasty history of betrayals and distrust on both sides.

Why had the Scots steadfastly set their faces against us? We were their neighbours, we shared a common isle. Yet they preferred to ally themselves with France. When we fought France in 1513, they attacked us from the backside. When I sought a bride on the Continent, James V had entered the same contest and snatched Marie of Guise right from under my nose. And then there was the little matter of the York jilting.

"The Earl of Arbroath," announced the page. I seated myself just in time for the jaunty Earl, who strode in as if he always came to see the King of England.

He was dressed in his formal Scots attire: yards and yards of swirling patterned wool, a dagger in his sock, a great overworked silver brooch holding a sash of some sort.

Daggers were not permitted in my presence, since the Duke of Buckingham's attempt on my life. I nodded to my Yeomen of the Guard, and they ceremoniously removed it.

"Do you truly represent Scotland, Robert Stuart?" I inquired. *"Is* there a Scotland to represent?" That was the true question.

"As much as it is in any man's power to represent that glorious land, I do so." His voice rang in the very mouldings of the ceiling.

"Then you have many questions to answer, questions that have caused me sleepless hours." I motioned him closer. "What is that tartan you wear?" I asked. It was a rather pleasing interweaving of shades and designs. Unsophisticated, but pleasing. "I notice it has white in it. Does that have a special significance?" I was curious.

His great, fishlike mouth broke into a smile. "White is what we wear for dress occasions, woven into the rest of the cloth. It signifies that we will do no hard riding while wearing it. Riding would throw mud."

How primitive! How simple! Dark colours for riding. A stripe of white meaning, "There will be no riding, everything will be indoors and clean, upon my word of honour."

"Aye. I understand. Now, I would you answer me questions which are puzzling me about your master. The Scots King refused to meet with me in York, and I know not his mind. I have received no messages of any sort from him."

"He was afeared of kidnapping."

"Did he think me so little a man of my word?"

"Not from Your Majesty, but that others, antagonistic Scots who oppose him, they would take advantage of his absence."

"Who exactly are these antagonistic Scots? I keep hearing their names invoked, like a charm. There are Lowland Scots and Highland Scots, and chieftains, and Lords of the Western Isles. What sort of country is this?"

"A divided, unhappy country, Your Majesty. The Highland Scots, as you call them, are great families that own certain tracts of land, and have done so since time out of mind. They reside in their little valleys and glens and seek primarily to be left alone. The Border Scots are another matter entirely. They are bandits and extortionists, betraying the English for the Scots, and vice versa, at the same time. Then, the Isles—ah, they are something yet again. They are part Norse, settled by the Norsemen, and don't see themselves as part of any country. They live on those barren, cold rocks out in the Irish Sea, and claim to be Christian, yet . . ." He spread his hands as if to say, *How could they be?*

I held MacDonald, son of the chieftain of the Isle of Rum. I might as well hold the wind hostage, from what this man said. "In such a topsy-turvy country, how came there to be an ambassador selected? What, and whom, does he represent?"

"I am a cousin of King James, albeit from the wrong side of the blanket. I believe I can speak for him. I know his mind."

"But does he *have* a mind?" I barked. "And is it consistent? You knew his mind when you set forth from Edinburgh. Do you know it now?"

"I believe I do. I understand its workings."

"Its turnings, you mean. Very well, then, how turns it in regard to me, his English brother, his *uncle?*"

"He wishes peace."

I stifled a laugh. That outworn old phrase! One might as well say an Ave Maria, for all it meant in real terms. "I know a way to peace," I declared. "Unite the countries. It is unnatural that one island should contain two realms. Let us combine. Through a marriage, at first. Then the two Parliaments would unite—"

"A marriage has been tried, Your Majesty. The Princess Margaret Tudor of England and King James IV of Scotland, in 1503."

"It failed due to the persons involved. My sister Margaret was"—she was lust-ridden, shortsighted, unimaginative—"unequal to the high calling before her. She was but a child when she came to Scotland." And was still a child, at fifty-three. "How does she?" I asked.

He looked dismayed. Margaret was an embarrassment. Betrayed by her lust, her impulses . . . they were all played out now, and no one wanted her. She had many indifferent custodians. Even her son regarded her as a burden—like an old pet that soiled carpets and slept all the time in the sun, its owners just waiting for it to die.

"She is . . . recuperating. At Methven Castle. She suffered a—a—something in her head."

"What of her husband—her so-called husband—Lord Methven?" She had divorced Angus thirteen years ago to marry him, and now sought to divorce him to remarry Angus. The foolish, lustful woman!

"He . . . remains behind, at Stirling."

"The truth is, he has left her," I said brusquely. "He has more important things to attend to than a dying, powerless old woman." I snapped my fingers. The Scot's attention had wandered.

"Your sister," he demurred.

"Aye. My elder sister. Well, I was speaking of a marriage between Scotland and England, one that would do what my father's experiment failed to do."

"Your *sister*," he insisted.

"What, am I supposed to mourn for her? I wrote her in 1528, the year of the Sweating Sickness, when first I heard of her folly in divorcing Angus to marry that fop, Methven. Did she heed me? No! Is it any surprise this has befallen her?" Margaret had been stupid. I hated stupidity. I could forgive any sin, any shortcoming, but that.

He blinked. "It is true, then, the way they paint you."

"Save your rehearsed observations about my cruelty, my lack of human kindness, in which undoubtedly you were tutored by your master, the straight-forward James V! If to call a sister by her true name, and to fail to be swayed by sentimentality for a fool, constitutes cruelty, then I embrace the title."

"You *are* a monster!" He arranged his face in the proper drained, blank manner prescribed for staring at a monster.

"Is that your worst thunderbolt? Come, come!" I taunted him.

"Even the laughter is monstrous," he muttered.

"Now that we understand one another"—oh, that was what audiences were for, the first half hour of them always wasted in this fencing—"let us state it plain. Here is what I wish: that Scotland and England unite, preferably through marriage. That we cease these hostilities, which are nonsensical, if you consult a map; for we *are* one country. All else flows from that."

"Now *you* understand *me*," he said, and his voice was burred and edgy. "I care not what your maps say, or what your 'logic' tells you. We Scots are a different people, entirely different from you. That you understand us not is of no concern to us. We are people of our land, and our land is as different from yours as is Spain."

Spain! Why did he choose *that* country?

"We are people of the sea, of the islands, of the long nights and long days. There is nothing balanced about us. Some of us still speak a different tongue —'tis called Gaelic, and is similar to that on the Isle of Man, the coast of Wales, of Brittany, of all the other rocky, bitter places on the edge of your fat, velvety countries. We cling there, and we thrive there, and we have no need of you!"

"Yes, you do! For without peace, you cannot survive in the world, you'll be crushed, and your Celtic stuff sucked out like an oyster's—"

"You frighten me not!" he snarled. Yes, snarled: like some northern wolf. I had never heard a sound like it from a human throat. Before I could grant him leave, he was gone, his capes all aswirl.

He was right. I knew it deep inside. Scotland was another realm entirely, one so alien to our English way of thought that we could never even comprehend one another.

What was it he had said about his Celtic cousins? Wales, Brittany, Ireland, the Isle of Man? I was Welsh, or partially Welsh. I had spoken their tongue —as a lad, anyway. Was I barred from understanding their minds? Did I share nothing of that?

I knew poetry sometimes made my skin tingle. I knew music transported me to another world, and that my gift for it seemed something external to myself. Was this a corner of what it meant to be a Celt? That corner illuminated, softened, heightened all the rest of me. But what if it were not a corner, but the whole? Suddenly I thought I knew what it was to be Scots, and part of me was drawn to it; the other part recognized it as implacable enemy, one with which I could not coexist.

I had a quarter-hour before the Papal envoy was to appear. I must get myself in hand. My head-pounding had lessened, but not disappeared entirely. I looked at the green syrup. I had had quite enough of that. I did not reach out for the bottle.

I must have a clear head for the Papal nuncio. What was it I wished to hear of him, and wished him to hear of me?

The Papal presence in England reduced to this one little foreigner . . . ah, how impossible it would have seemed a mere decade ago! Then the Papacy was everywhere, dictating, lecturing, controlling. Or attempting to. Now the Pope was gone from my realm, only permitted to retain an inconspicuous presence by my express permission.

"Giuseppe Dominici, the nuncio from the Holy See."

"Let him come forward." I gestured. I was settled now, with all my robes of state about me. It was important to wear them when meeting a Papal envoy.

The doors swung open, and a tiny man appeared. My first thought was, How could the Pope have selected such a small man to represent him? But close on its heels came admiration. Only a man utterly secure in himself could select an unprepossessing envoy to be his voice in a land hostile to him.

The man bowed. "I am Giuseppe Dominici, ambassador of His Holiness,

Paul III." He had the sort of ugly and open face one associated with the most simple-minded.

I waited for him to speak. He waited for me. Silence prevailed.

"Tell me of your journey here," I began.

"It was a year ago," he said. "But it took many months. I had to pass through certain areas of the Lowlands I would fain not traverse again. My habit seemed to incite them, and in Amsterdam I was stoned."

"Is it that serious, then?" I asked.

"There are whole parts of the Netherlands that are not safe for anyone in black."

"Even widows?"

"Even widows," he laughed. "Extreme Protestants do not mourn, you know."

Had they discarded that, as well? Fie! "Turbulent times," I said. A safe remark.

"England is more polite."

"They have a ruler." I never permitted discourtesy to a foreigner. "It is the duty of rulers to tend kindly to their subjects."

"Even to their beliefs?"

There, now we got to it. "Christian rulers are responsible for maintaining truth and Scripture in their realms."

He cocked one eyebrow. "My master, Paul III, His Holiness, would relieve you of that duty."

He was even more direct than I!

"That is the blessed calling of the Holy Father," he continued. "Our Lord foresaw that Christian princes must needs direct their efforts elsewhere, and so, in His glorious mercy, He provided a Blessed Father specifically for—"

"Meddling," I finished for him. "My spiritual duties do not drain my secular resources."

"But it is impossible to maintain both equally," he said smoothly. "No man can serve two masters. You, Your Majesty, are trying to serve both Mammon and God. You are foredoomed to failure."

"I know not the meaning of the word."

"But you will. I tell you, it is impossible. Our Lord said so. I refer to Him, not to any earthly being."

"Then your master, the Pope, is a prime example of misdirection. For he has always tried to do both, and failed in both. His spiritual leadership was at such a low ebb that even common men repudiated it. His worldly leadership has been so misdirected that half the countries of Europe fight against him. Let him heed his alleged Master's words himself!"

"His *alleged* Master's?"

"He claims Christ for his master. Yet do we see Christ in him?"

"No man can see into another's soul, Your Majesty."

I had meant a smart retort. But he spoke true. I could not see into Pope Paul's soul; he could not see into mine. "Only God can see," I finally said. "And we must leave it at that."

"Aye." He bowed, then crossed himself. When he stood erect again, we faced each other in silence, as if the interview had just begun.

"The excommunication still stands?" I finally asked. Someone had to speak.

"He cannot retract it!" The voice of the little man was astonishingly deep, and rich. "There has been too much. The dissolution of the monasteries; the harassment of Princess Mary; the execution of Cardinal Fisher; the burnings of the Carthusians."

I caressed the carved knobs at the end of the throne-arms. Yes, too much to let pass. I would not let it pass. Nor would any man who called himself such. "I understand."

"There is to be a General Council."

"Nine years late. I begged the Pope for one in 1533. My plea was ignored."

"There is to be one now. In Mantua, outside the Emperor's reach. It was an inspired idea to hold one, and surely the Holy Father will recognize your farsightedness. There is so much to be deliberated upon. . . ."

"Yes, how to halt the slide of Europe into Protestantism! But it is too late."

"You will be in a position to name your terms." His voice was crisp and unemotional. "You are not rebellious in doctrine, only in title. A reconciliation between you and the Holy Father would be worth a great deal to him. He needs allies."

"He has Francis, and Charles." I deflected the thrust of this offer, for offer it was.

And, oh! I was tempted by it. To be recognized by Rome, to wear my hard-won titles by consent. . . .

"Inconstant, fluctuating fools," he sneered. "They are not the men you were, to stand firm amidst temptations from all sides. No, they are men of the hour, of the day. . . ."

"Not men of the Light? I fear none of us can claim that title. Nay, nay . . . if Rome and I embrace again, your master and I must agree on several things, none of which has been solved by need or the moment. I will not tolerate meddling, and your master will not tolerate insubordination, and therein we disagree, and disagree mightily. Tell him I'll serve him, if he recognizes my sovereignty over all aspects of England."

That he would never allow. Less I would never agree to. There it lay. The envoy bowed and took his leave.

That night, as I sat morosely slumped before the fire, my lampreys not faring at all well in my stomach, I wondered about what the Scots envoy had said.

Was it true that the two countries would never be united? I had always assumed that someday they would be. It seemed natural. In the back of my mind I had already married one of my children to one of James's. But my father had followed the same scheme, and it had come to naught.

What constituted a country, then? That its inhabitants were of like natures? But the Normans and the Saxons were not of like natures. By that criterion they should have never melded to form England. The Celts—were they as unabsorbable as their spokesman made out? Would Wales never become truly a part of England? And what of the Irish? I meant eventually to absorb that island as well.

If ever I felt decent . . . if this cursed leg would ever heal. . . .

But did one wait to do things until one felt "decent"? Did one order one's life upon a leg? Or did one go ahead anyway, regardless of his personal feelings?

My head-throbbing had returned, and along with it, confusion. . . .

I hated the confusion, hated it worse than any pain I might endure. The confusion was my enemy, the real enemy. It unhorsed me like a challenger in a tournament. . . .

But I would fight it. Or, at the very least, disguise it. None must know.

Now I would take myself to bed. I would call no groom, no servitor. They might sniff out my weakness, hear me call for a candle when I meant for a fur.

CXV

Throughout the spring my remorse decreased and my confusion increased. The ghosts died away. No more did I hear the shrieking outside my chamber; no more food ran red blood and clots. Mercifully, my memory of Catherine, her true physical being, began to recede and fade. I was thankful that I had never commissioned the portrait to be made that I had longed for. Holbein—whom I had forgiven for his Cleves portrait when he explained it was customary to omit pockmarks—had been occupied at the time in executing sketches for a mural for my Privy Chamber, a dynastic one that included my father, myself, and my children. Now there was nothing remaining to recall Catherine's exact features to me.

But I thought of her often. In some way I longed for her—for what she was, had been, to me. And hated myself for it.

All that was human, controllable. But the confusion, the transposing of events and order—I knew now it was not madness. Madness meant not knowing the real from the unreal. Was Wolsey dead, or was he not? No, that was not my affliction. Rather it lay in remembering whether I had put my hand on his shoulder at Grafton, the last time we had met? I hoped I had. But hoping was not the same as knowing.

It continued thus, all the months following the executions. I remember it as a time of continually fighting the adversary, my confusion. Boredom, loneliness, remorse—all these took second place to the urgent need to re-establish some control over my mind, although (pray God!) it was not readily apparent.

WILL:

No, it was not. In fact, I was astonished to read here of his struggles. Outwardly he dressed well, took an interest in diplomatic dispatches, and followed the growing rift between Charles and Francis with his usual alert sarcasm. I was also pleased that he seemed, at last, to be delivered from his dependence on love and women. He showed no interest in romantic matters, either his own or others'. I concluded that the King had come of age at last.

⟨⟩ HENRY VIII:

I let the Howards go, all those I had had arrested and locked up in the Tower. My rage against them had cooled, and it seemed foolish, pitiable, to punish them any further, even though they had been sentenced to forfeit all their possessions and suffer perpetual imprisonment. The old Dowager Duchess; Lord William Howard and his wife, Margaret; Catherine's aunt, Lady Bridgewater; Catherine's brother's wife, Anne Howard: in truth, I did not have the energy to hate with the white-hot hate of which I had been capable in my youth. So they went free, out into the summer air, and pray God they enjoyed it more than I.

No, I did not particularly enjoy it. May Day came, and with it no memories, either good or bad. It was just another day, and a chilly one at that. I saw, from my windows, moving branches that signified the return of the May-revellers, who had gotten up at dawn to gather greens and blooming things. I had no desire to be among them, nor did I denigrate them for doing the thing. I had lost my power to hate, as I said, and that, in its own way, was worse than losing my power to love.

I stayed mostly indoors, taking a sullen sort of pleasure in doing the opposite of what would be "good" for me. My physicians urged me outside, so instead I sat in a close-aired chamber and read dispatches. I saw apple blossoms one morning and closed the curtains.

The dispatches were a devilish mixture of information and lies. From Scotland, it was said my sister had died, of a burst blood vessel in her head. But had she? And if so, had she made a will? She had ceased to matter politically years ago, and personally to me, even further back than that. Yet she was the last of my family, and now I would be survived by no one. I had outlived them all. All those people at Sheen that Christmas of 1498, the Christmas it burnt . . . all gone, as vanished as the rooms they had moved in. Only I moved yet, a shade myself, or near so.

My sister's son, the heavy-lidded, red-haired King, Jamie, looked for another son to replace the two he had lost. His French Queen was pregnant again, and that made Jamie feisty—a foolish way for a King in his position to behave. The Scottish side of the border was far richer than the bleak English moors leading up to it, and Edinburgh was within easy reach of the Duke of Norfolk and his twenty thousand men. That made it simple for us to inflict harm on the Scots, but difficult for them to retaliate in kind. I warned my nephew that I still had in hand "the rod that had chastised his father," but it was his choice to turn deaf on me. So I decided to wait until autumn, when all the grain would have been gathered in, before giving the Duke—now mouldering in disgrace up North—the signal. Poor Jamie. He would wish he had come to York.

The French—and this I found stunning to believe—had made a treaty with the *Turks!* Yes, Francis coyly averted his eyes while Suleiman parted the thighs of Europe and thrust himself deep up inside, right to the gates of Vienna—pissing (to complete the metaphor) right on the bed of the Habsburgs. In fact, it was Francis himself who lifted the bedcovers.

But the Grand Turk: the Caliph of All True Believers! To have embraced him as a brother! True, the man was said to be magnificent, a jewel of his time, a gentleman beyond any in Europe who called themselves such. And a general more brilliant than any we could claim since the Lionheart. He had taken Belgrade in 1521, and the following year he had defeated the hitherto unconquerable Knights of Rhodes, forcing them from their island fortress, although, as befitted a true knight, he had allowed them safe conduct to the island of Malta. Indeed, he had even escorted them there. In 1533, Charles's brother Ferdinand had been forced to recognize Suleiman as overlord of Hungary. And now this treaty with France, which allowed the French to buy and sell throughout Turkish dominions on a par with the Turk; to have resident consuls of their own in Turkish lands; to act as official "protectors" of the Christian Holy Places. And in exchange? What had Francis promised Suleiman in exchange? England?

Oh, Suleiman was ruthless, smooth, and clever. He had expanded the Turkish Empire until it bulged at the seams and oozed into Europe—at Francis's invitation. And he knew how to make an arresting ploy, both to call attention to himself and to amuse others. Such was his sending me a crocodile.

I received word that this creature was awaiting me at the docks of Dover. The florid letter said that in token of the Grand Caliph's great esteem of me, and since we were already neighbours, and soon to be closer ones, he wished me to see for myself one of the grand warriors of his Empire, upon which a general of the Levant should model himself. The animal had been taken, with great fight, in the Nile Delta, and shipped north—first with the Turk's own galley-transport, and then transferred to a French vessel, courtesy of Francis. He had heard I kept a zoo at the Tower, and knew that the Tower had a moat wherein the creature could sport itself. I need only supply it with dogs and cats for food.

"A crocodile? Awaiting me at Dover?" The animal had arrived at the same time as the letter.

"Yes, Your Majesty." Thomas Audley, the Chancellor, smiled.

"Is it alive?"

"Evidently it survived the journey, but it is in poor condition."

"So I must nurse a sick crocodile back to health?" God's blood! What a presumptuous thing for Suleiman to have done! Now I would be forced to cosset the beast, employ means of helping it survive the winter—oh, curses upon him! "Think you we can transport it here to London without its expiring?" I was curious to see it, and see it alive. Not dead, pray God, that might set the ghosts going again in my head. . . . Hush, go back, Catherine is only a skeleton now. It was rotting flesh that disturbed me, not bones.

"Yes, if we bring it slowly. The menagerie-master will know what it needs once it arrives."

The menagerie-master: a strange fellow named Rufus Quigley. He was tall and thin and surprisingly young, and seemed to esteem animals above people. Evidently he understood them better. He lived in a hut on the Tower grounds with a hedgehog and a half-dog, half-wolf creature for companions.

"Well, then give orders to have it transported tenderly to the Tower."

To it, the Tower would be a refuge, a place of succour—how ironic. A crocodile! I was now eager to behold it, the legendary creature of the Nile. . . .

I had always assumed that I would someday experience certain things for myself. The Pyramids. The Nile, where Moses was pulled from the bulrushes. The Holy Sepulchre, where Christ had lain. The blessed city of Jerusalem. Some imaginary day, I would stride upon the sacred pavement of the Crucifixion . . . because I wished it so, and therefore events would arrange themselves to suit my inner needs. I still longed to do so, but without the airy assumption of my youth that it would all come about. In the meantime, the closest reality: a big crocodile that needed to be housed, fed, nursed, transported, wintered.

I received word from Audley that the beast, in its cage, strapped to my best transport wagon, was due to arrive at the Tower on Thursday next. Along with the beast was a special sealed cylinder, from the Turk himself, for which he wished "all dignitaries" to be present for the opening and reading. The crocodile business was to be state business, then.

In the meantime, Master Quigley had been alerted. Consequently I received a request from him to have access to certain monastic manuscripts which the Crown had retained, so that he might peruse them to ascertain the crocodile's feeding habits. I granted it, very impressed with him . . . and pleased that I had retained as many monastic manuscripts as I had done. They would prove of great benefit to future Quigleys.

The beast awaited us. There, in its monstrous crate in the shadow of the Tower's outer walls, it stood. I myself, and the Privy Council, were curious and eager to behold it, although they pretended to be merely performing their duty. I had invited Elizabeth and Edward along to see the spectacle; Mary proclaimed herself above "trips to the zoo."

This was foolish of her. In faith, a trip to the zoo was a coveted experience, and one I rarely granted, upon Master Quigley's advice that human visitors were unhealthful to the beasts.

As I have said, Father had had a zoo, a menagerie. He was attracted to beasts of all sorts, but only in a symbolic sense. A beast was not a creature in its own right, but only insofar as it stood for an abstract trait—honour, kingliness, or some such. He received presents from noblemen and rulers conforming to this fancy. When he died, the poor beasts almost all died with him, having outlived their dynastic symbolism.

Over the years, newcomers had joined the Royal Menagerie, out of happenstance and ill luck: a wounded wolf, a three-legged turtle, a blind snake. Thus the Royal Menagerie had gradually turned into an Animal Hospital, run by Rufus Quigley, where sick creatures recovered and became friends of man. Suleiman's crocodile was the only ferocious, whole beast we had received in years.

Gathered round the ornate crate, we looked respectfully at Master Quigley. He had several muscular men grouped about him, all clad in leather suits (to withstand the crocodile's teeth, so it was thought), holding nets and great prodding spears. From the crate there was only silence.

Standing close by me were those most eager to hear the words of Suleiman—my Privy Councillors, and others concerned with matters abroad. To put it neatly and quickly: there were those who thought action abroad was necessary sport, good for the character and morale; others believed that England should avoid all foreign entanglements and devote herself to home matters, specifically the religious dissension which was growing daily. I held the reins of both factions, keeping them both under control, but they snapped and snarled at each other with increasing fractiousness. As long as I was here to restrain them, all would go merrily. But Edward? What would he do, how could he manage these contentious men?

Before the workmen, with their iron crowbars, were to step forward, I must read the letter from Suleiman. Breaking the seal (which was compounded of Arabian gum, and not like ours at all), I unrolled the creamy vellum (also not like ours in the least; it must have come from a Middle Eastern animal), and read his greeting:

> *Most High and Mighty King, Lord Henry, King of England,*
> *France, and Ireland, we, Suleiman, Sultan of Turkey, Allah's Deputy*
> *on Earth, Lord of the Lords of this World, Possessor of Men's Necks,*
> *King of Believers and Unbelievers, King of Kings, Emperor of the East*
> *and West, we greet you.*

Whereas, we wish to assure ourselves of your continued favour and good will to us, we hereby present unto you a creature from our own dominions. It is a beast of strength, as we ourselves are strong; of endurance, as we ourselves are able to endure vicissitudes of climate and fate; of cunning and power, as our defeated enemies have found us to be. Grant it a home, as I pray you will grant us a home in Europe. Although we, and our people, may seem as strange to you as this beast, yet I assure you that we both can, and will, live in your climes, and thrive there. Your most professed brother, Suleiman.

So! This was meant as a symbol of Levantine adaptability! The fool had no notion of the miserable death to which he condemned the crocodile: an English winter.

I re-rolled the scroll, and motioned to the workmen. "Set the beast free."

"This is insolent, intolerable!" The birds of prey on my Council lost no time pressing close to me. "The Turk announces his intentions to penetrate Europe and remain there," hissed Henry Howard.

"Aye," said Stephen Gardiner, the wily Bishop of Winchester.

"He has *already* penetrated Europe," I muttered. "He took Belgrade in 1521, and almost took Vienna last year. He is in our midst already, however much we would like to believe otherwise. Now the problem is to dislodge him."

"It is God's problem to dislodge him," said William Petre, one of the two Principal Secretaries.

"God needs arms and legs," replied Thomas Seymour. "And I stand ready to offer him mine."

"And I," said his brother, Edward Seymour.

Poor lads. They had never been to war, and ached to go. Perhaps to deny a young man the opportunity to fight, to pit himself against what he believes is evil and the enemy of his soul, is cruelty. Old men, in their day, had tried to prevent me from doing so. They were right, in their way. The issue with France in 1513—today it is entirely forgotten. What was important was the fighting, and my proving to myself, through actions, that I was no coward, no shrinker from violent deeds. Until then I had not known what I was.

Prudence preached caution. Wait and see how well the Turk withstood a European winter—like its creature. Let Charles oust the outsider. It was his task to do so. It was his realms that Suleiman violated; it was he who claimed the title of Holy Roman Emperor. England had no need to become involved; why spend ourselves on distant shores? But there was a gathering force at home, a force which was gaining power, and would explode us: the religious issue. Was it not politic to drain it all off into war, diffuse it for my Edward?

The last of the wooden stays gave way, and fell to the ground. The workmen stood to one side, and Quigley approached the crate, making odd clucking noises. He hesitated before the entrance, as all was silent and dark within. Was the creature merely quiescent, or was it stuporous and near death?

"War is folly," breathed Petre, near my ear. I understood him. It *was* folly. What he did not understand was the other side of folly.

"But when an evil takes root, to avert the eyes is equal folly," I admonished him.

From within the crate came a scraping and, eventually, Quigley's backside. He dragged the crocodile out by its forelegs. The beast lay sprawled, limp, upon the earth.

"I think he is ill," Quigley said. "He barely exhibits any movement. It has been a long, hard journey for him. I must needs resuscitate him with sugar-water."

The company were disappointed. They wished to see the creature thrashing and threatening, not weary and in need of sustenance.

Elizabeth drew near me. "It seems a goodly creature," she said. "I would gladly forfeit my time to attend to it."

A goodly creature? Forfeit her time, from her studies? "Nay, my dear," I said. "It is more seemly for you to attend to your books."

"But if I could help Master Quigley—"

"A girl? Help him? And neglect your studies, your—"

"My studies are for me alone," she said. "They help me naught in ruling, for I shall never rule. They help me naught in being wed, for I shall never wed. Therefore it seems to me that of all persons in Your Majesty's realm, I should have the most freedom to do as I like. I am of danger to no one, being a female, and of use to no one, being judged illegitimate. Therefore I pray you, let me be. If I wish to spend my life and hours tending to a poor dumb beast, who is the poorer for it? Not you, as you have no other use for me."

Her insolent eye, her saucy remark and countenance—these were the very whips of madness to me. Anne Boleyn's daughter, I must never forget it. She was not mine, she was Anne's.

And Mark Smeaton's? There were those who noted a resemblance to him, who made whispered asides. Whispered, because should they come to my ears, such talk was treason. They came to my ears anyway, secondhand, by favour-curriers and gossip-scavengers. Mary was supposed to have remarked once that Elizabeth resembled "her father, Mark Smeaton." I did not reward the person who reported this to me.

"I have a use for you," I answered. "A use close to my heart."

I wanted Elizabeth to like me, to care for me in a filial way. God's blood,

I wanted my children to love me! I had hated my own father; now fate seemed to have arranged it so that my own must hate me in turn.

"I have no place next to anyone's heart," she said. "Nor do I wish to be there."

I could see the tiny beads of sweat gathering on her scalp, the scalp from which sprung hair of the selfsame colour as mine. The sun had climbed high enough now to begin its July oppression, and soon it would be intolerable to stand unprotected under it.

"So young, and yet so hard?" I asked.

She turned away, embarrassed; and in truth, I sounded like a suitor. The only persons I wished to woo now were my children. No more women. I was done with them.

Others were listening. "If you wish to attend to the beast," I finally said, "it could have no wiser or kinder nurse. Only I pray you, be careful—as once its strength returns, it will grow vicious. Never approach it alone, without Master Quigley."

I turned to the gathered company. "Well, we have seen it now. Truly it is a formidable beast, but in need of nursing. Let us leave it." I shielded my eyes against the ever-hotter sun. " 'Tis no time to be out of doors in direct sun. Come—join me in the banqueting house at Hampton. We shall pass the summer afternoon as summer afternoons are meant to be passed."

This impromptu gathering would be the first heartfelt social gesture I had made since Catherine's . . . since the winter. Hitherto I had gone through the motions, in hopes of feeling *something;* today I longed to luxuriate in the intensity of high summer. A long afternoon in the banqueting house—the banqueting house which had not been used for several summers—appealed to me, appealed with no thought of whether it was right, whether it would help me, or whether my physicians would recommend it. It appealed on its own terms.

The banqueting house in question crowned the manmade "mount" at the far end of the Hampton gardens. Anne had laid out all the plans the year Elizabeth was born, but as they were elaborate and called for a great deal of labour, the construction had required another year or so, and the growth of the plants even longer. Only now was it all as we had envisioned it, that summer so long ago, when I had thought Anne Boleyn would always be beside me, and the banqueting house would hear her ringing laughter. . . .

Ghosts, ghosts. I wafted my hand before my face as if to clear the way of cobwebs. They blocked everything, everything, entangling me, dimming my vision of what lay ahead.

The mount, then: it was raised on a brick foundation, and then, atop that, the great sixty-foot mound of earth heaped there by workmen to make an artificial hill. It was now covered with a carpet of thick, fine grass, planted all over with fruit trees—cherry, apple, pear—and with myrtle, box, bay, and laurel cunningly clipped in topiary fashion to resemble beasts and other fancies. Scattered amongst these was a collection of rare sundials I had acquired from the monasteries, as well as gaily painted wooden beasts—dragons, lions, unicorns, greyhounds, griffins—holding shields and vanes for royal arms. The pathway up to the top wound gently round the mount and was planted with daisies, marigold, snapdragon, rosemary, camomile, and lavender. The gravelled path was only wide enough for three or four abreast, and so, as we climbed it, the party stretched out far behind me, like children trooping through the woods.

On top stood the summer banqueting house. It was built on a stone foundation, with wooden trelliswork sides; already, climbing vines and flowers entwined themselves on the inviting ladders, so that inside the house it was all greenish light, and the faint stirring of leaves, which served as a cool filter for the glaring sunlight. Here we would pass the afternoon, supping on strawberries and drinking Verney, a sweet white wine.

I had sent word back to court that some ladies should join us. The only ladies left at court were the wives of my councillors, and some who had official functions, and a few of Catherine's leftover attendants.

They came, almost every one of them. Perhaps they were bored, or perhaps they welcomed an opportunity to spend a summer's afternoon in their husbands' company. Brandon's young wife, Katherine; Joan Denny; Joan Dudley; Anne Seymour, Edward's wife; and Mary Howard, widow of Henry Fitzroy.

I envied them, all those happily married couples. That was all I had wanted: to be a faithful husband, with a loving wife for life. Why had it been denied me? But envy is a corruption, yea, it is expressly forbidden. *Thou shalt not covet thy neighbour's wife. . . .* But it was not my neighbour's wife I coveted, it was his happiness with her. *Nor anything that is thy neighbour's.* Happiness, then, as well.

They gathered about and took their places on the cushioned benches, which were meant to encourage intimacy and lolling about. There were no set places, no protocol. One could move about, too, as one wished.

This was so far from the set masquing, the elaborate formal gatherings I had favoured in my youth. This felt comfortable, a great loosening of the belt—which I had come more and more to appreciate. Now I regretted all the times I had been so blind to the needs of others to do so. For there had been fat old men then, as now—men with stiff joints and expanded bellies, who must have found my "entertainments" a torture.

"Welcome to the banqueting house." I stood up and gestured. "Such a fine day, and such a fine company, complement one another. We have strawberries from William Paulet's garden, as well as from the fields lying above the city wall, in the area called Holborn. We have Verney, and Osney wine, from Alsace—"

"Shall we drink a French wine?" Thomas Seymour rose abruptly, his thick chestnut-coloured hair gleaming. "Would it not shame us to do so? The French have sealed an heretical alliance with the Turk. Shall we, then, drink their wine? I say no!" He turned his goblet and poured the offending wine on the ground. The soil gulped it down greedily.

Shamefacedly, the rest of the company looked to me. Seymour remained standing.

"Seat yourself, Thomas." I nodded toward him. Then I turned to the rest. "He speaks true. I would not have politics becloud this afternoon's pleasure, but it seems we are wrapped in it, like it or not. The Turk has sent us a crocodile, as a welcome-us-to-Europe gesture. The French have helped transport the gift. What say you to this? Shall we drink their wines?"

To a person, they poured their French wines on the ground. In unison it sounded like a company of archers pissing.

"I have my consensus. But now you shall go dry," I laughed.

"English water," said Seymour, "shall quench my thirst readily enough."

"Aye," thundered the rest.

Oh, how heartily they mouthed it! Animosity was pleasant in green arbours, where the deeds were yet to do.

"And would you fight against this unholy alliance?" I asked. "For it may prove necessary."

"Aye! Aye!"

They longed for a war, as I had supposed, longed to spend and sport themselves in some great cause. And it must be great, no petty land boundaries, no religious factions. The Turk was the answer to their Christian prayers.

"Then I shall count you all, when the time comes to cross to France. There, that is done. Now, eat strawberries." I motioned to them.

Their consciences salved, adventure hanging in the future, breathing in their ears, they fell to enjoying the afternoon at hand.

Not all, though. There were many about me who did not wish war with France; they saw it as a foolish waste of time and money, the chasing of an outdated dream. There was a time, they said, when England and France were intertwined, when it was feasible to think in terms of winning large portions of France. But that was when the duchies were independent, when Brittany and Burgundy and Aquitaine did not owe especial allegiance to the French crown.

"—just as in the days when Northumberland and the Palatine of Durham were little kingdoms of their own, before they had to bow to *you*," said

William Paget, who was seated near me. Mr. Secretary, as he was known, was a mild-mannered sort, the exact type of "New Man" so detested by traditionalists. He boasted no glorious ancestors, no knightly accomplishments, and indeed had nothing to recommend him for his high position but decency and common sense. As he had not been brought up on tales of chivalry, he did not see a war with France as anything but a nuisance.

"Practicality is all," chimed in Thomas Wriothesley, Bishop Gardiner's toady. "And a war is impractical for us at this point. What can we possibly hope to gain?"

"To give the French bloody teeth for breakfast!" quivered Henry Howard. He was violent these days; he had changed since the time he and my lost son had lived, jousted, loved, made ballads together at Windsor. Now he was rash and unbalanced, striking men within the palace precincts and challenging them to duels. His hotheadedness had been sent to cool in Fleet Prison already. That it had not cooled much was evident. Perhaps a French gun-ball would ventilate him. "Do you wish to spare France to honour your new-coined name, *Risley?*"

Thus Howard made fun of the Frenchified version of the councillor's plain English name. It was an old story; Risley had become Wriothesley as the Bullens had become the Boleyns. When would we stop thinking that to sound French, feel French, or look French was better? Fie, it was a sickness with us. *That,* then, was the true French Disease!

Risley/Wriothesley was too clever to rise to the blatant bait. Indeed, Henry Howard, for all his knowledge of Greek and blank verse, was a simpleton in dealing with men. "I wish not to spare the French," Wriothesley said smoothly, "but to spare foolish lives like yours. We need a pet poet or two about, someone to dabble in architecture, someone to ape the French in effeteness—if only for a bad example."

Howard's face flushed, and he made as if to grab his sword.

"It is the Scots we should fight," said Bishop Gardiner. "It is the Scots, and they alone, who bar you from your rightful title of Emperor of Great Britain. You have Wales, Cornwall, and Ireland. Only Scotland remains; and I should like to see it crushed—like this." He suddenly picked a tick off Henry Howard's doublet, where it was dazedly wandering after a full meal, and smashed it on the table, sending a squirt of ruby-red blood bubbling out from under his palm. He smiled blandly. "A war against the Scots is a *practical* war."

Gardiner. He was the most intelligent man on my Council, the most ruthless, but curiously lacking in any distinctive personal quirks, so that I find it difficult to describe him. He also was not refined; I could scarcely imagine Wolsey or Cranmer smashing ticks on a table.

"It would be more *practical* to defeat France first and thereby castrate

Scotland forever," I observed, and motioned to a servitor to clean the bloody spot.

" 'He that intendeth France to win, with Scotland let him begin,' " quoted Wriothesley. "I agree with Bishop Gardiner." The ingratiating Wriothesley was always quoting others and agreeing—never initiating anything on his own.

Sir George Blagge, one of the men of my Privy Chamber, had written a hateful poem about Wriothesley:

> From vile estate, of base and low degree,
> By false deceit, by craft, and subtle ways:
> Of mischief mould, and key of cruelty
> Was crept full high, borne up by sundry stayes.

There was more, accusing him of treason, and so on. But the truth was that Blagge's portrait was flattering; Wriothesley simply did not have the imagination to be so brilliantly evil.

The blood . . . it seemed to be spreading out, growing thicker. . . .

"Have we forgotten that the French have betrayed Christendom? That he who makes a pact with the Infidel is himself to be regarded as an Infidel? *That* is the true issue!" snapped Howard. "As if we had a *choice* about fighting him!"

"But one always has a choice about whom one fights," I reminded him. "If you believe otherwise, why, then you deserve your nickname of 'the most foolish proud boy that is in England.' "

The smell of the blood, the fresh blood still warm from Howard's body, just sucked out, now gleaming on the table . . . the smell was rancid, putrefying . . . where was the servitor? I felt sick. Then I saw it: the place on Howard's neck where the thing had lately fastened itself, and it was oozing, a great globe of blood gathering, ready to drip. . . .

How much blood was in him? How many ticks would it take to drain it all out? If he were covered with ticks, would that do it? Blood, blood. There were those who said I "feasted on blood," was "bloodthirsty." They could not know how I hated blood, hated the smell and colour of it.

Outside the leaf-shaded gallery there were cool breezes. But inside, now, it was starting for me again, the blood-haunting. The strawberries before me, gushing red from all their pores, leaving red all over my fingers. . . . I fought down the panic.

"Honour chooses my battlefield," insisted Howard. He moved as he spoke; indeed, he trembled, and the drop fell directly on his sheer linen summer-shirt, making a bright red blossom.

"Then follow your father to Scotland, attend him in the autumn when we thrash King Jamie," I commanded. Such statements from me were to be regarded as commands.

A serving-fellow with a rose-scented cloth wiped up the blood. The gagging feeling in my throat receded; I felt it go, like a tide ebbing, first leaving my throat, then my chest, then my arms. I slumped weakly in my chair. These attacks always left me limp and wrung out. I needed wine.

French wine was not the only wine. There was Germanic wine, from the Rhine valley. I called for that. And yes, they brought it, a pretty goblet of straw-coloured liquid with a flowery taste.

"Let us drink the wine from the vineyards of the Lady of Cleves," I said. "Your offer to drink English water is patriotic, but I fear it may lead you into the flux." Indeed, no one who wished to live drank water.

The flagons of Rhenish wine were passed round the table, and soon everyone had poured a goblet; the women, too.

A pretty picture they all made, faces in shadow against the background of bright green haze; light summer dresses the colour of flowers. Women. But they affected me not. I felt no stirring of longing for them, no desire. Below the waist I was ashes, and in my heart I was numb, and in my mind I was bitter. How foolish I had ever been to spend myself on them, and I disgusted myself even in remembering it. I would not dwell on it, no, it was a foul and nasty place to dwell. . . .

"A riddle. I have a riddle!" cried John Dudley.

The Rhenish was at work when men ceased to talk of honour and began to talk of riddles.

"Tell it, then," urged Anthony Denny.

Denny and Dudley were a pair as close as two yolks in an egg, and even their wives bore the same first name, Joan.

> *"A vessel I have*
> *That is round like a pear,*
> *Moist in the middle,*
> *Surrounded by hair,*
> *And often it happens*
> *That water flows there."*

His voice rose higher as he went along. Shrieks greeted each line.

" 'Tis not from Colchester?" guffawed Tom Seymour.

"Oysters have no hair," retorted Dudley. "Whatever can you be thinking of?"

"*I* know," bragged Richard Riche. "One of Wolsey's great sewers beneath Hampton Court. 'Tis round—'tis a vessel—certainly 'tis moist in the middle—water flows there—and the long weeds growing in it are like hairs—"

"It does not say it has things 'like' hairs, it says it *has* hair," maintained Dudley.

Other guesses were made, as it invited more comments, lewd analogies, and the like. The last thing they wished was for the correct answer to be revealed.

But the correct answer *had* been revealed, for it is true, true above all other things, that women-parts *are* a sewer, are dark and filled with garbage and slime, and are loathsome areas of contagion. Beneath their pretty clean dresses are stinking sewers, where their legs join their bodies. . . .

"The answer is right on your faces," pronounced Dudley. "Your eyes."

The company groaned.

"I have another," offered Wriothesley.

> *"Long legs, crooked thighs,*
> *Little head, and no eyes."*

This turned out to be a pair of tongs.

Tom Seymour proclaimed,

> *"As round as an apple*
> *As deep as a pail,*
> *It never cries out*
> *Till it's caught by the tail.*

"Now guess this—if you be men." He sat back down, a smug look on his face, implying, "men like *me."*

"An eel?" suggested Cranmer timidly.

"Well, you have the correct shape," said the riddler.

"Eels love music," persisted Cranmer. "They swim straight into the nets of singing fishermen."

"I did not say the thing craved music," retorted Seymour.

Old Anthony Browne stood up. "I say 'tis a bell."

"Aye," said Seymour, irritated. He had thought his riddle so clever.

Sir Francis Bryan stood up, swaying. Already drunk on the Rhenish, I noted.

> *"Around the rick,*
> *Around the rick,*
> *And there I found my Uncle Dick.*
> *I screwed his neck,*
> *I sucked his blood,*
> *And left his body lying."*

He bowed all around, thinking himself cute.

"Uncle Dick. Now what could *that* be?" mused Dudley.

Round and round the obscenities went, but for me the phrases rang: *I screwed his neck, I sucked his blood, and left his body lying.* I knew it was aimed at me, meant to tell me what 'they' thought of me.

"Enough!" I interrupted them. "I forbid this!"

" 'Tis but a bottle of wine," demurred Bryan.

"Your humour is offensive," I said. "And I shall have no more of this sort." The traitorous fools. I was surrounded by them.

"Shall I present a different sort, Your Majesty?" asked Gardiner. Before I could give an opinion, he said smoothly,

> *"What God never sees,*
> *What the King seldom sees,*
> *What we see every day;*
> *Read my riddle, I pray."*

"A stinking privy," said Francis Bryan.

"A task one is unequal to," said Edward Seymour, the conscientious courtier. Although there were few tasks he was unequal to, he approached all with wary respect.

"An unearned tribute," said William Paget, my diplomat.

"The answer is, 'an equal,' " said Bishop Gardiner. Oh, it was flattery time indeed!

John Russell—well named, for he was a rustling sort of man, the new Lord Privy Seal, and his hair was russet-coloured—waved his hand.

> *"Highty, tighty, paradighty,*
> *Clothed all in green,*
> *The King could not read it,*
> *No more could the Queen;*
> *They sent for the wise men*
> *From out of the East,*
> *Who said it had horns,*
> *But was not a beast."*

The King . . . the Queen . . . horns . . . horned beast . . . oh, how could he mock me so? Did no one respect or fear their King?

"I marvel at your scurvy wit!" I snapped. "And we shall have no more riddles!"

" 'Twas an oak tree!" he blurted out, trying to absolve himself.

Oaks. *They are my favourite trees.* Oh, foul, foul! That day in the little chamber . . . oaks would forever be ugly for me, soiled by the Howard whore.

"I think we all tire of riddles," said Thomas Wyatt. "Let us turn to poetry instead. Shall we try a rhyming round? I will begin with a verse, then someone else shall add to it, until we have a complete story in verse." He looked round, a great poet himself, but an equally great diplomat. I had sent him on many missions abroad.

I nodded assent. The mood had grown ugly; I hoped this would sweeten it. He began,

> *"Within this tower*
> *There lives a flower*
> *That hath my heart,"*

Francis Bryan continued easily,

> *"Within the hour*
> *She pissed foul sour*
> *And let a fart."*

There were ladies present! Genuine, honest ladies like Joan Dudley, Joan Denny, Katherine Brandon, Anne Seymour—no unwholesomeness amongst them.

This was enough. I stood up slowly, and let the full force of my displeasure rest on him. "Be gone," I said. "Come no more to my table. And look for no more favours at my hand."

He knew enough not to argue, or attempt to excuse himself. He nodded and quit the bower.

Once his small-minded, obscene presence was gone, it was once more a fair summer's day. We sang songs: "Death and Burial of Cock Robin"; "Mouse and Mouser"; "The Milk Maid"; "The Carrion Crow."

> *"Bessy Bell and Mary Gray*
> *They were two bonnie lasses,"*

sang Elizabeth in a thin little voice. I had almost forgotten she was there, at the farthest end of the table.

> *"Bessy kept the garden gate,*
> *And Mary kept the pantry;*
> *Bessy always had to wait*
> *While Mary lived in plenty."*

I was stunned. That Elizabeth would challenge me so publicly about her rights, accuse me before the entire court of withholding her due as a Princess. When all the world knew she was not a Princess at all, but a bastard, the daughter of a witch, who was only given the title "Lady" by my courtesy and kindness! So this was how she repaid me?

"You may keep your garden gate at Hatfield House," I said softly, "by returning there by the morrow. I am grieved that you have not proved fit for the royal bowers at Hampton."

No one else, up and down the long table, murmured a sound. It was only Elizabeth and myself, some fifty feet apart.

"May I take Robert?" she asked. "To take turns with me waiting upon the garden gate?"

I looked at young Robert Dudley, a comely lad, a blue ribbon tying up his pretty brown hair.

"No," I said. "For that would make it play, not work."

His face fell, but hers betrayed no sign of disappointment. So they meant something to one another. Good. Then not seeing each other would hurt.

"Very well," she said. "I am saddened that I must miss tending to the crocodile. For exile from one's source of life and those in sympathy is hard. Nonetheless I shall pray for his survival. May his thick hide and craftiness protect him from all evil-wishers."

By God, she pushed me too far! She was no child; no, she was as political and dangerous as any Pretender of three times her years. As such, she was a danger to my Edward. "You are excused," I said. "No further leave-taking is necessary."

Yet my heart ached to see her go. Who can explain the human heart? Mary was my firstborn, my only child for so long, and nothing could ever alter that. Edward was the gift I had prayed for, so long withheld. Elizabeth? She was a disappointment from the first, she was naught, she was the wrong sex, from the wrong woman, and in the wrong order of birth. Nevertheless she was the most intriguing to me, and I could not fathom why. Perhaps because she was the only one of the three children not afraid of me. As indeed why should she be? She alone, perhaps, of all persons in the realm, was untouchable by my wrath. I could never execute her; I had already illegitimized her, but I would never disclaim her; in short, I had already done to her the worst of what I could do, and she knew that. And I knew that.

All the guests were looking intently at their strawberries. Domestic quarrels are always embarrassing when they spill over into public, but royal ones especially so. No rhyming or Rhenish could rescue this fading afternoon. Best that it end now.

CXVI

The summer dragged to its weary, wilted conclusion. By late August there were droughts in Warwickshire and Northamptonshire, and certain priests wanted to form "Mary processions," as they had done in times past, imploring the Virgin's intercession. Should I forbid them or not? Were they Popish or not? Cranmer and I conferred and reached the decision that a procession in Mary's honour was permissible, while one in any saint's name was not. After all, Christ Himself had honoured Mary from the cross.

"And how is your *Book of Common Prayer* progressing?" I asked him. He had been working on it for so long.

"It progresses. It progresses. And your *Primer*?"

I had set my hand to composing prayers to be said in the vernacular— or, if the person felt more at home in it, in Latin—and I would issue it with my own Imprimatur, my own Nihil Obstat, as Rome had been wont to do. Truth to tell, I was pleased with my little book.

"It is almost done," I said. "I think next year it shall be printed."

Cranmer shook his head. "Your industry and speed are truly gifts. Ones that I envy."

"As I envy yours, Thomas." I spoke true. For his way with words and his purity of heart were rare things.

Others envied Cranmer, not only his gifts but his friendship with me. They sought to bring him down, out of sheer spite and malice. Others saw him as a danger, a gangplank leading to rampant Protestantism. They thought if they tossed that gangplank down into the sea, no radical would ever board the secure ship of England. But Cranmer, who was so naïve about the Original Sin in men's natures (although he described it poetically in his *Book of Common Prayer*), never thought to be on guard against his enemies, or even acknowledged that he *had* enemies.

"I have but one garden to tend, the Church. You have many. How can you oversee the coming war with the French and write prayer books and education books at the selfsame time?"

He referred to my *ABC's as Set Forth by the King's Majesty,* a little reading-instruction book I had prepared.

I could not answer him honestly, for I knew not how I was able to think and attend to many things at once. Only that one gave surcease to the other, and while I laboured on Englishmen's prayers I did not think of how many tents would be needed for a European campaign. "I know not," I admitted. "But it is fortunate I can, else England would need six kings."

Six kings. A council of kings. That is what I was forced to consider, for Edward's minority. My pang of fear with Elizabeth had made me face the worry that had been lurking for some time: Would I live until 1555, when Edward would be eighteen, the same age I had been when I became King? He was only five years old now. And Mary and Elizabeth were tall, rooted plants that threatened my Edward. Mary was a grown woman and could yet be made much of in Catholic circles, in spite of her formal capitulation to me. Elizabeth was clearly clever and winsome, and might harbour secret ambitions for herself. Edward was not safe; no, he was not safe.

I must protect him, must make sure that, even in my absence, he could grow to maturity unmolested. There was no denying that the "New Men," the gentlemen of learning and service whom I had honoured and titled, leaned toward Protestantism. Certainly Edward would have to understand the new ways, the New Learning, in order to deal with those men. And so, with some misgivings but with resignation, I appointed Dr. Richard Cox and John Cheke—Humanistic scholars—to be his tutors.

I also began secretly to draw up a list of those I would appoint as councillors to govern for and with Edward, until he was a man. I knew already that I must leave no Lord Protector, such as Richard Plantagenet had been, for I knew what fate Protectors dealt out to those they "protected." My Council would be composed of equals. My will would insist on that. My will . . .

The idea of my not surviving another thirteen years was chilling to consider. I did not like it, did not care for the queasy, weak sensation it aroused in me. I told myself that making these provisions was the prudent thing to do, that it did not mean I was acquiescing in my own death. Young kings had died in battle, and I myself might yet venture forth in battle—"hazard my person," as they say. . . .

Dare I confess it? I wished to take the field against Francis, to do again what I had done so long ago, but this time do it as I wished, and not be balked and cheated of my spoils by a Ferdinand or a Maximilian. No, I was my own master now, and I would return to that place which had hung, unresolved and insulting to me, for thirty years. I would take the cities in Picardy *I* craved, add them to Calais, and expand the English holdings into a strip extending along the Channel coast.

I confided this to no one. I would wait for things to roll that way, as roll they would. I enjoyed the power it gave me, keeping my thoughts and plans to myself.

In the meantime, preparations for our chastisement of Scotland went ahead. That was no secret. We would wait until their grain was gathered in, until their livestock was wintered, and then we would strike.

In August I had sent troops across the Border, and they had been beaten at Haddon Rig, near Berwick. Nearly six hundred prisoners had been taken, including the commander, Sir Robert Bowes. This was, I must confess, a surprise. The Scots were ever full of surprises. Every time one thought they were quiet, quiescent, beaten—they struck and stung, like an adder.

In retaliation I dispatched Norfolk to persecute them. It was the first communication I had had with him, the first assignment I had given him, since the disgrace of—I cannot write her name again—his niece. He, and his hothead son Henry, managed to burn the lowland towns of Kelso and Roxburgh and about thirty others. But it was an inconclusive, womanish reprisal. I was most displeased. I had given them orders to *defeat* the Scot, not pinch his toe or tweak his nose.

But Jamie, for his own reasons, took the burnings as a call to arms. His honour must be satisfied. He gathered an army, but the nobility would not fight willingly for a King who excluded them from his councils; the Border lords, barons like Argyll and Moray, were smarting from harsh treatment from the unstable, fickle Jamie; and the outcome was that his army refused to march farther south than Lauder, where it disbanded itself.

Another army must be raised, and the industrious Cardinal Beaton managed to gather a force of ten thousand men in only three weeks. Oh, the Cardinal, the Scots Cardinal! He had been commissioned by Pope Paul III to publish the Papal bull excommunicating me, in Scotland. How I despised him! Cardinals, I believe, were created by Rome expressly to torment me in this life.

This Cardinal's army was to be led by Oliver Sinclair, King Jamie's "favourite." He loved him more than he had ever loved any woman, thereby incurring the disdain and derision of his subjects. The hated Sinclair was no soldier. At the edge of the Solway River, in southwest Scotland, Jamie suddenly decided to leave his troops, declaring that he would cross into England from Lachmaben, when the tide ebbed. So that Sinclair could have the battle to himself, and thereby acquit himself? Who knew what he was thinking?

Across the Solway I had three thousand Englishmen, hastily drawn up under the command of the Deputy Warden of the Marches, Sir Wharton.

Although outnumbered, Sir Wharton led boldly and scattered the Scots, driving them into the bog, where his men killed them with spear and sword, or left them to be sucked into the muck or drowned in the river. Twelve hundred were captured, including Oliver Sinclair. The Borderers—who had largely composed the Scots force—took a perverted pleasure in punishing their King by surrendering to us without a fight, and many of the nobles who came into our custody were Protestant. Therein lay a great opportunity.

But God had still a greater one reserved for us. When he heard of the defeat, King Jamie wilted and died. "Fie, fled Oliver?" he said. "Is Oliver taken? All is lost!"

He drooped at Falkland Palace whence he had crawled in abject defeat. His wife was in her last days of pregnancy, but that held out no hope for him. His other sons had died, and any child born at this hour would be foredoomed.

It was a girl, in any case. When he heard of her birth, he said, "Is it even so? The Stuarts began with a lass, and they shall end with a lass." Then he turned his face to the wall, and said, "The de'il take it. The de'il take it," and died. Jamie was thirty-one years old. He left a week-old baby girl, christened Mary, called Queen of Scots, as his heir.

CXVII

What a windfall! What extraordinary fortune! I could scarce credit it, other than that at long last I enjoyed God's favour and basked in His rewards!

Scotland was mine, and for the price of a border skirmish! Sir Wharton and his three thousand men, with no elaborate war machinery, no field provisions, had delivered Scotland squarely into my hands, as if by divine edict.

I was suzerain of Scotland. I was grand-uncle of its infant Queen. I would marry her to my Edward. It was perfect; it was all part of a Divine Plan, I could see it now. Before, it had all been masked in murkiness, and I had floundered like a man in a mist, but still trying to discern the will of God, still trying to follow it when I received no external sighting, relying only on the steerings of my conscience. Now I had my reward, now all the mists were cleared away, and I had steered true. I found myself in a marvellous place.

Scotland and England would be one. Edward would be Emperor of Great Britain: ruler of Scotland, Ireland, Wales, and England. I, who as a child had had to take refuge in the Tower against a rebellion by Cornishmen—I would leave my son a throne that incorporated three other realms. In one generation the Tudors had gone from local kings to emperors. Because of me.

Scotland was mine! Scotland was mine! I would be a kind and gentle husband to her, as I had been to all my wives. I would honour her and treat her with respect. No mistreatment of the prisoners of war, and no (public) gloating over King Jamie's death. Instead, I gave the Protestant-leaning Border noblemen we had taken as prisoners instructions to "woo" the Lowland and Highland Scots upon their release, to convince them their future lay with England. They were to return to Edinburgh and act as our agents there.

As for the infant Queen: I issued an order (as her uncle and guardian) that we would draw up a treaty at Greenwich, arranging for her marriage to Edward.

Things always come round a second time; history never exactly repeats herself, but sets up the pieces of the game the same way. In 1286, the Scottish King Alexander had died, leaving his six-year-old granddaughter, "the Maid of Norway," as his heir. King Edward I of England, who already claimed overlordship of Scotland, immediately moved to have the Maid Margaret betrothed to his son Edward. But the girl had died travelling between Norway and Scotland, and thus the peaceful and natural union of the two countries was averted. But this time there would be no death, this time all "would go merrily as a marriage bell," in More's phrase.

The captured Scots nobles were transported to London, where they kept Christmas with us at Greenwich. I presented them with my terms, which they were to take back to their crushed and demoralized government. They were "to set forth the true and right title that the King's most royal Majesty hath to the sovereignty of Scotland, whereby the late pretenced King of Scots was but a usurper of the crown and realm of Scotland," and uphold that I had "now at this present (by the infinite goodness of God) a time apt and propice for the recovery of the said right and title." Furthermore, the infant Scots Queen was to be betrothed straightway to Edward, then surrendered into English hands, to be brought up in London. These were my demands, and after the Scots peers swore to uphold and enforce them, I released them, speeding them back to their homeland to work for me—but not before I had received hostages in their stead. I housed these "guest" Scotsmen in a former monastic property along the riverfront, where they could act barbarically together and not frighten the horses at court.

I was stunned when, instead of respecting my victory and my clear claim to Scotland, Francis declared that "he would never desert his ancient ally," and began sending ships and money to Scotland. He masterminded a *coup d'état* by the Cardinal and the French Queen Mother, Marie de Guise, in which they defied me. It seems that my rightful claim had "affronted" them, and roused the vexed Scots once again to resist. The curs! Even when they were beaten, they did not acknowledge it; they swore one thing and then betrayed their own oaths. My ambassador in Edinburgh, Ralph Sadler, wrote that "under the sun live not more beastly and unreasonable people than here be of all degrees." They took the infant Mary and crowned her Queen of Scots at Stirling; then they promised Francis that she would wed one of his sons.

In times past, it had always been a French Princess married to a Scots Prince. But the other way round—a Scots Princess married to a French Prince, a Prince who might succeed to the very throne of France—was so dreadful a prospect I trembled to think on it. Scotland would go the way of Brittany, become part of France. . . . No! That I would never permit, even if I had to assassinate the parties involved.

Francis! Francis! I would destroy him, as he was attempting to destroy my island kingdom. Was there no shred of honour in the man? To attack and corrupt sworn men; to ally himself with the Turk, the Great Infidel? Fie! God would give me the strength to crush him, even if it were to prove my last earthly task.

So. I would put my affairs in order, and then I would go and fight Francis. The Emperor was already preparing for war, and it would be convenient were we to join forces. But not necessary. When I was a stripling in 1513 it had been necessary that I have allies. I had needed Ferdinand, and Maximilian, and the Pope. Only the truth is that I had *not* needed them; I had duped myself. They had shackled me and bossed me and taken my money. No, I had not needed them. Now, if Charles wanted to fight alongside me, I would grant him that courtesy. Likewise the Pope. But it was immaterial to me what course they chose.

I sent for Chapuys, to tell his master that I was bent on war with France, for my own selfish reasons, but would welcome fighting company. I knew it would please Chapuys to return to the Continent, and please him as well that his last mission between his master and me was to be a cordial one.

"Tell Charles I will take the field against Francis in person," I told Chapuys. "I mean to fire cannon again with my own hand, to sleep in tents with my men. The terms, my grievances against the King of France, and my tentative battle strategy are all outlined within this document." I handed him a tightly rolled parchment, which I had written myself, past midnight, and which no man had read or witnessed—nay, not even Will. "I have sealed it well, on both ends, and secured the outer case. Tell Charles to ascertain that the seals are unbroken. I know that you will guard it well en route, and no spies will glimpse its contents."

"Cromwell is dead, Your Majesty," Chapuys's dry little voice said. In old age he resembled a scorpion: brittle, desiccated, but still dangerous.

Pity. I could have used Cromwell now; if not the scoundrel himself, at least his methods. Under my direction, Cromwell's leftover spies were quite slipshod and inefficient. I lacked their master's diabolical genius. "Aye. And so letters are safe again." I laughed.

"Is this farewell?" he asked, quite simply.

"Possibly," I said. The Emperor might decide not to send him back to England. It was likely a new ambassador would return with Charles's reply, while Chapuys would be pensioned off to spend his latter days near the Mediterranean, soaking up the sun like a lizard. "I shall miss seeing you, my friend." Farewells hurt, always more than one expected. I hated them.

"Have you considered what we spoke of, regarding the Princess Mary?"

I did not correct him to "Lady." He had earned the right to call her

Princess. "Yes. I had made negotiations with the French, to marry her to Francis's second son. Now—" I twisted my belt, wishing to rend it, as if that would cure my rage. "Now that selfsame son is to marry Mary, Queen of Scots. You see how they betray me. And my Mary is left once again husbandless, unwanted—"

"A Frenchman was unworthy of her," said Chapuys. "But it was loving of you to attempt to arrange it. Perhaps someone from the Spanish royal house . . . even someone younger . . ."

"Or one of His Holiness's illegitimate sons?" I could not resist needling Chapuys. "A good Pope-Catholic, by necessity!"

"Why not? An illegitimate King's daughter for an illegitimate prelate's son?" He returned the parry. But our fencing was mellow, affectionate, as only long-standing adversaries can grow to be. Jesu, I would miss him!

"Yes. That would do. And as part of the marriage settlement, the Bishop of Rome would recognize my title as Supreme Head of the Church of England."

"You dream," said Chapuys.

"A man should dream, and a King *must* do so," I insisted. "And such may yet come to pass. Odder things have done so. Nay, I have not given up hope that someday the Pope and I . . ." I left the sentence vague, unfinished. Unspecified wishes came true sooner than detailed ones.

"May I take a private leave of Mary?"

"Indeed," I said. "She would be grieved if you did not."

Chapuys, gone from England. Another bridge to the past down. Sooner or later, if one stays alive, they all go. The destruction process is inexorable; we behold it so readily in the ruins of buildings but not in ourselves. I wondered what it was like to live to be a hundred. Some men did. There was a region in Wales where a pocket of extremely old people were said to survive, men and women of eighty and ninety, whose parents still lived. Perhaps one got past the point where all the bridges were down. Once that was over, it must be like being reborn. To float in an endless present, with no past whatsoever, but disconnected from the bustling young. . . . This, I think, would be the "limbo" that theologians examine. Was it a reward, or a punishment? Was it the bliss of complete freedom, or just a self-contained nothingness?

Whatever it was, I was unlikely to experience it. Already I had lived as long as my own father, longer than almost any of my immediate and not-so-immediate family. The Tudors were not a race whose days were long upon this earth, no matter how much they honoured their fathers and their mothers.

CXVIII

O ne thing I must attend to, before hazarding my person across the Channel: I would have Holbein finally execute the formal dynastic portrait of the Tudors upon the wall of the great Audience Chamber at Whitehall. There persons attending me could also behold my father, the founder of our greatness, and my gentle mother, who by coming to his marriage bed ended the royal claims of the House of York. On the wall, with Holbein's genius, we would all be united as we had never been in life: Jane and the boy Edward would gaze fondly upon one another; my father would see his grandchildren; Jane and my mother would be both within my arm's grasp, never to leave me. Art is cruel, for it celebrates what never was; art is kind, for it creates whatever we long for, and gives it substance, everlasting substance.

Posing was not as easy as it had once been. I did not relish standing for long sessions, and even sitting had become tiresome. Holbein suggested I might be portrayed seated upon a throne, with the rest of my family grouped around me: the children below, my father and mother behind, standing on a dais. We had brought out, from the Royal Treasury, a bonny throne captured from an Irish chieftain in the 1300s. It was carved with the loveliest, most sinuous forms. But its arms squeezed me so on both sides of my trunk that I grew bilious, and the ancient wood creaked with my weight, straining so that I feared the rungs would pop out.

I had grown huge, and there was nothing to be done about it but to acquire larger thrones. It was impossible for me to reshape my body, and there was a certain voluptuous pleasure in admitting it and passing by the temptation to try to change myself, which brought back too many shameful, burning memories. Now I would be fat, and let chairs and armour and women accommodate themselves to me, rather than the other way round. There was freedom in old age and ugliness; a freedom the young and comely could not possibly imagine.

At length Holbein decided on the composition, the grouping. Of the seven people, three were dead. He would use my father's death-mask as a model, and my mother's wooden funeral effigy. Both were kept in a crypt in Westminster Abbey near their tombs. To paint Jane, he must rely on the picture he carried in his own mind, as well as old charcoal sketches from life in his studio.

Jane . . . As Holbein's skilful touches created an image of Jane beside an image of myself, I ached. There was such an emptiness in my life now, and nothing to fill it. For my disgust of women had not slackened; there was no woman I desired, or could even tolerate. I was done with them.

But something to fill the void, to be companion to me. It was a fearsome thing to be so utterly alone. Why did not needs die with the person who had created them? Appointing someone else to fulfil the needs was grotesque, and never worked.

All through the month of May I sat for Holbein. It was an unusually hot and humid May, wherein to be indoors was stifling, and to pose in my heavy ceremonial robes, trimmed with fur, took the constitution of a Lowlands plough-horse. I was obliged also to keep my velvet hat on at all times, as I combined sitting for the portrait with holding interviews and audiences. I never went without the hat nowadays, except when at long last I drew the bed-curtains about me at night. I was almost completely bald now, and would not shine my pate in public. But the hat was so hot; like having a weasel curled up on top of one's head.

If I was uncomfortable, Holbein was equally so, having to remain standing for hours, concentrating upon every detail of my costume, and imagining an entire person from a ceremonial death-mask. Yes, Father's wax head, mounted on a stand, stood on a little table to my right. It looked so very much like him I felt as though I were once again in his presence.

Toward the end of the month, as I had half expected, a new Imperial ambassador, Francis Van der Delft, came from Charles to present his credentials. As his name implied, he was a Hollander, coming from that peculiar place where the ground oozed constantly. It was also the place where the forces of heresy festered and spawned, where Charles had great difficulty in retaining the people's loyalty.

I received him on a sticky morning, when I wished I could be outdoors in a light linen shirt. The man was pleasant enough, with a wide, flat face and a thick waist; but his news was not. There was trouble over my title. Charles could not grant me my full title of Supreme Head of the Church in England in any treaty document, nor could he promise to defend me should the Pope decide (after Francis was subdued) to turn on me. In short, although Charles would be my ally, he would not be so while calling me by my proper names. And if I accepted that, it meant . . .

Oh, it was an old game, a war of words. We would eventually find an acceptable style, but in the meantime the summer, and good campaigning weather, were fleeing. "And how does your predecessor, Eustace Chapuys?" I asked him.

"Well, Your Majesty. He is with the Emperor Charles now, in Innsbruck, but plans to go south by autumn. He sends you his fond regards."

So he was truly gone. Back home. *Was* it home after all these years? How long does a place continue to feel familiar to one after a long time away?

"And I to him. Tell me, the Emperor—"

Just then I heard a sound of wood hitting wood, followed by a groan. Holbein had dropped his palette, face down, upon the floor.

"It is of no account," I assured Holbein, "except for your own labour lost in blending paints. The floor matters not."

He was kneeling and muttering, trying to pull the palette up, where it had stuck fast. I bent down to help him, bracing for a hard pull. To my surprise, the palette came up easily; a child could have pulled it away. Holbein fumbled with the brushes, his hands shaking.

I looked at him. His face was flushed and sweating. It was entirely too hot to be working inside today. With glee I said, "Enough! We shall not continue. It is cruel to pen ourselves up so." I turned to Van der Delft. "Let us continue our interview out of doors, in the Privy Orchard." To Holbein I said, "You are free to do whatever you like."

While the Imperial ambassador and I strolled beneath the blossoming cherry, apple, and pear trees, caressed by sticky-sweet breezes from the south, Holbein went to his apartments, lay down on his narrow bed, and died of plague.

❧ ☙

Plague! The word itself was a call to fear, but in striking Holbein, it had announced its grinning presence within the heart of the palace itself. And Edward was at Whitehall! I had brought him here to spend the summer, so that he could observe court life and feel at home in a grand palace. Edward had been sketched by Holbein, had seated himself within a few feet of him, just seven days before his death!

I must get Edward safely away, and then flee myself. But where would be the safest place? Already, reports were coming in of the severity of the outbreak in London. Corpse-piles were starting to mount in the cross-streets. No one wanted to touch the bodies, let alone bury them. At Houndsditch, near the gun-foundry, someone doused the pile with hot oil and then set a torch to it. They shovelled dirt over the smoking, greasy ashes, making a gruesome little hill.

The plague was prevalent in the Southeast, all through the villages of Maidstone, Wrotham, West Malling, and Ashford, and at Dover. As yet there were no reports of any sickness to the west. I would send Mary west to Woodstock. I would also go west, with Edward, back to Wiltshire, to Wolf Hall.

The Seymour brothers would come; as Edward's uncles, it was fitting. The rest of the court must scatter, and the Privy Council function as a unit only by means of messengers.

I called together the Council and explained briefly what we must do.

"The plague rages," I said, "and we must flee. No bravery; I want no bravery. Wolsey showed 'bravery' and stayed working in London, until eighteen of his staff died. You are too precious to me for that. I therefore command you to leave London within forty-eight hours. Take as few with you as possible. The plague travels with people, we know not how. If anyone in your household is stricken, move immediately."

They all looked back at me, seemingly healthy. As Holbein had been, when he perched Father's wax death-mask on a stool, just scant days ago. . . .

"Since we must now part, to reunite in autumn, God willing, I must open all my mind to you," I told them. "We prepare for a war with France. The Emperor has already declared war on Francis, and it is our intention to join him, taking the field in person."

At this bold pronouncement, the French-leaning members, such as Edward Seymour and John Dudley, looked unhappy. The non-fighters, like Wriothesley, Paget, and Gardiner, likewise had clouded countenances. But since Seymour and Dudley were essentially soldiers and wanted war, and Paget and Gardiner were Imperialists, there was something for them in the Continental venture regardless.

"At this moment the negotiations are tangled, but only over diplomatic style. England *will* war against France and solve the Scots problem once and for all. Their insubordination has grown intolerable. I will not permit them to flourish unchecked any longer. France is the source of their encouragement and rebellion. We must no longer smite the cub, but slay the mother."

Norfolk and Suffolk looked resigned, but tired. They were old. A Continental army meant that they must lead it. Of course, Norfolk had his flamboyant son to assist him. Suffolk had no one, his son having died betimes.

"I myself am bound for Wiltshire, with my son. I will stay at Wolf Hall."

If Edward Seymour was annoyed by my commandeering of his ancestral seat, he did not show it. He merely sat calmly and nodded, as if he had known it all along.

"I will have at my command a group of trusted messengers, with the best horses from the royal stables. I expect to conduct the business of the realm as well as humanly possible, and I will speed all things to you for your consideration. In the meantime, I pray God will keep us and spare our lives."

One and all, we crossed ourselves.

Let it not be me, each of us prayed. *Spare me.*

CXIX

ould I go alone to Wolf Hall? I would have preferred it; but as King it was necessary that I have a few reliable others to accompany me, preferably including a Seymour, as I was going to their home. Edward Seymour I could not ask after all, I had realized that. He was too important to the realm; better he should go into seclusion at some other place and preserve his life, if our party were stricken. Thomas—now there was company, there was amusement . . . but at bottom he was a man so empty of matter that he had never held a position of importance, and hence would be no loss to England should he succumb to the plague along with myself.

Is there any worse verdict that can be passed on a human life? *He is expendable. His death would make no difference.* I shuddered in even thinking it, as it seemed to be a curse. I liked Tom Seymour, I had not meant it ill. . . . But the truth was, his presence was not essential to any activity or person.

There needed to be a woman, a woman's influence during this exile. A soft woman, a kind woman, a woman concerned with Edward, who could further his studies, as I was not keen on bringing tutors along. The widow Latimer, Kate Parr—was she still at court? I had been remiss in disbanding all the remnants of Catherine's household. As I had no intention of marrying again, I knew that once Catherine's ladies had left, there would be no more women at court. Not that I cared. But my attendants, my Council, my musicians—they cared. A monastic court would not appeal, would not draw the finest minds. So I lingered and delayed, keeping a posthumous court for a dead Queen.

The Lady Latimer was still at court, although she had already submitted a request to be allowed to return to Snape Hall, her late husband's estate in Yorkshire, to take care of her three stepchildren. I sent for her.

She appeared promptly, and when I made what I assumed would be a startling request, she made a startling answer.

"I prefer to go straightway to my own home," she stated. "My lands, my servants, my Lord Latimer's children—they will need me there, with all the confusion—"

God's blood! Did she not understand? There was death about, not "confusion." The plague was not something that needed a competent administrator to direct it. Furthermore, my request was not a "request." A royal request is an order.

"Madam," I said, "I cannot spare the time to debate with you. You will accompany Edward to his mother's home in Wiltshire. You will direct his studies whilst we await the abatement of the plague. We shall depart tomorrow morning. You may spend this evening writing directives to your servants and tenants at Snape Hall."

She glowered; then nodded her head in assent, jerkily.

"I know it is dictatorial," I found myself explaining. "But the times compel it. *I* do not look forward to spending months evading this clever assassin, the plague. I do not ask my subjects to do anything that I myself am not willing to do. England needs you, Madam."

She demurred, but the flattery won her. Only it was not flattery. I had spoken true. I was England, and Edward was England, and at this juncture we urgently needed her.

"Who else accompanies us? Will you bring tutors?"

"No," I answered. "I have ordered Cox and Cheke to depart for their own safety. So you must select the appropriate papers and texts to take."

She looked disheartened. "I am no scholar."

"The plague elects many to fill positions with which they are unfamiliar." Yes, the plague had a terrifying cleansing effect, as inexperienced men and women grasped at openings above their accustomed stations. Priests suddenly were elevated to bishops; apprentices to masters; stableboys to horse-masters.

"Tom Seymour will come," I added. "Edward will need a man's company. He has been too exclusively among women up until now. By Saint Mary, his uncle Tom's as far from effeminacy as anyone I know." I did not add that he had but the external trappings of a man, in my opinion; for to a five-year-old externals would be sufficient.

"He has consented?" she asked.

Oh, she *was* innocent! Consent? There was no "consenting" involved. Obedience was my due, not consent.

"He will," I said dryly. "You may count on his presence."

Early in the morning, before the death-carts had even begun their collection, we left Baynard's Castle, whence we had fled from Whitehall after the first plague attack, riding toward St. Paul's. The great houses near the Thames were dark and still. Occasional crosses marked the doors. But on the whole this area did not appear to be hard hit. Only as we approached the city walls, turning west at St. Paul's Hill, where the dwellings became smaller and more crowded, did the number of crosses increase, until they appeared on almost every door. Then, as St. Paul's Way turned left into Ludgate Hill, right before the Lud Gate itself, there it was: a corpse-pile.

I held my breath as I saw it, for the very air surrounding plague victims was known to be contagious. I motioned to those in my party to do likewise. I would not lose any of them: not Will, not my old familiar Dr. Butts, not Lady Latimer; no, not even boisterous Tom Seymour. As for Edward, he was my life.

The pile of dead were naked. Their limbs protruded like forlorn branches of cut trees. Those at the bottom were already darkened and putrefying; those at the top were so lifelike that you could not believe them dead. This was plague, that breathed on you and left you breathless, but beautifully pre-served . . . for a little while. Flies were thick on the lower portion of the heap, making an obscene humming noise, writhing in iridescent waves over their feed. On top of all, like an offering, lay a naked maiden, pale and lovely, her golden hair serving as a funeral pall. Even as we passed, death-defying scaven-gers climbed on the human pile, searching for jewellery.

Outside the city gate, men were digging trenches. The dead would be thrown in, up to the top, and some little dirt shoveled over them. The men who dared to handle the corpses often followed them within a few hours. As I saw and smelled their sweat, I knew these were braver than any of King Arthur's knights. What Galahad would have fled before, and Lancelot would have avoided altogether, these men faced unflinchingly.

Suddenly I realized that I knew not what had become of Holbein's body. Had it been properly attended to? Surely so!

WILL:

No. Holbein was consigned to just such a trench-interment, where he decayed cheek-by-jowl with a tavernkeeper or a wet-nurse, and their dust is now mingled.

The plague brought about moral dislocations in every aspect of life. Neighbourliness evaporated, as everyone fled from the sick and refused to touch them, leaving only extortionists, whose greed exceeded their fear, to tend the dying.

The plague, and fear of it, reduced people to such terror that they forgot themselves and let their true natures reign. The Seven Deadly

Sins stood revealed, glaring and gigantic, in every man, woman, and child.

Pride? There were groups who withdrew from the plague-ridden people around them and, shutting themselves off completely, thought themselves safe if they embraced "moderation" and "tranquillity." They ate the most delicate viands and drank the finest wines, listened to sweet music, and admitted no one to their quarters, although neighbours were beating on their doors, begging for help. Not only did they refuse entrance to other people, they even refused any news of what was happening beyond their immediate quarters, in London or the realm itself.

Pride wears many hats: another is bravado, as when Charles, Duc D'Orleans, Francis's favourite son (for the plague raged in France as well) rushed into a plague-stricken house and punctured the feather mattresses with his sword, shouting, "Never yet has a son of France died of plague," and died of plague on schedule three days later. Then there was the pride of *not* fleeing, of standing at one's post stalwartly, as Wolsey had done.

Avarice bared its face boldly, with all fear of reprisal and castigation gone. The scavengers, as Hal described, picking over the bloated victims; the extortionistic rates charged for the simplest services; the "pickmen" who appeared, like ghouls, to charge for carrying biers to a burial place, all "respectable" people having fled. Avarice propelled men forward to grasp at positions and possessions abandoned by their rightful owners.

Envy and anger joined hands in letting inferiors wear their masters' clothes and exercise their masters' offices, like evil children let loose to romp in cultivated fields. The anger of the underlings expressed itself in the glee they took in tossing their masters into unmarked graves or in leaving them to decay in public view: the ultimate shame and degradation. Squire Holmes, who had once worn long furred gowns and jewelled hats, must reduce himself, stinkingly, to a skeleton before the eyes of his erstwhile servants.

Gluttony, even in this poisonous time, managed to find a niche for itself. Since one might be dead tomorrow, should not one die with a surfeit in one's belly, one's lips still sticky with spiced wine? There were those who declared that they would as lief die of overindulgence as plague and, in fact, thought they would cheat the plague thereby. So they caroused, eating and drinking continuously, feasting on dead men's stores, going from house to house scavenging, not for gold, but for meat and drink. They passed their last days in an oblivion of wine and pastries.

Others, of course, embraced lust as their answer to plague, preferring to die by an onslaught of Venus. They made their impending release from the moral code their excuse for violating it. They abandoned themselves to licentiousness, setting up orgy-rooms in death-emptied houses, where they indulged in every Roman and French vice known to man. Even respectable women were pawns of lust-inflamed men who came to "minister" to them as they lay incoherent and weak with plague. They were "examined" and exposed and then sported with . . . and left to die.

The law foundered. Lawyers and priests were dying along with those they served, and there were few to administer the law or the Sacraments. Whenever a lone remaining priest appeared to perform a funeral, he would find many other biers falling in behind the original one, as people watched eagerly for any sign of a legitimate funeral, and attached themselves to it. So few remained to enforce civil or sacred law that no one had a mind to observe it, and so there was, in effect, almost no authority at all.

Sloth—that slouching, lurking sin that underlies so many of the others—came into its own, as people declined to tend even to that which they could, such as clearing the streets, removing piles of offal, or gathering in the harvest. They were on a grotesque holiday.

The plague was enough to make a moralist out of me, if not a true Christian. For man's true nature was so ugly, so heinous, that any system, no matter how odious, that modified its evil was to be sought and embraced.

At least until the plague abated.

HENRY VIII:

I had neglected Holbein. I had not cared for his mortal remains, and in so doing, I had behaved as barbarously as any fear-crazed apprentice. The plague had made a heathen of me—I, the Supreme Head of the Church in England. I prayed as I passed the corpse-pile, *Grant them eternal peace.*

Then, *God forgive me for my failings, my lacks, my blindness.*

The more I knew, the more I understood, so it seemed, but thereby my sins multiplied.

Once outside the city walls, the dwellings grew farther apart. But if I thought that the plague was incapable of leaping separated households, I was wrong. Workers had died right in the fields, and their families in their farmsteads had succumbed at the same time. Livestock of all sorts—cows, pigs, sheep, goats—wandered the roads, starving and dazed. Dogs ran loose, reverting to beasts of prey, crouching and growling as we passed. Everywhere the fields were untended, the crops growing as best they could, but with no one to gather them in. Country gluttony manifested itself in people snatching whatever happened to be ripe and, without converting it into flour or beer or preserves, just eating it on the spot, making no provision for the morrow.

Going west, we passed through the villages of Wokingham, Silchester, and Edington. At each one there seemed to be fewer crosses on the doors, fewer corpse-piles, less stench, until as we passed into Wiltshire, we actually came upon an intact village, one in which there were no disturbances, surrounded by fields that were tended and neat. It seemed miraculous, as indeed life and civilization are, however we think of them as normal. They are *not* normal; chaos is.

All the while, as we travelled, I had looked anxiously behind me, like Orpheus, for I feared to lose my followers, feared that I would leave them behind in Hades.

All through Wiltshire the hamlets and villages prospered, untouched by plague, and then we passed through the Savernake Forest, that great wild place that had stood the same since Arthur was King, and came upon the small road I knew so well, the long, wheel-rutted path leading to Wolf Hall.

Wolf Hall: I saw it again, compact, healthy, self-sustaining. Jane's home. My heart leapt with joy, and ached at the same time. *Fool, fool to come here! Did you expect to see Jane, then?*

No. But I am strong enough to endure the not-seeing her. There is a strange pride in embracing God's will, the ecstasy of clasping an armful of thorny branches. . . .

CXX

I settled myself in old Sir John's quarters, with Will and Dr. Butts lodging with me. Edward was to sleep in Jane's girlhood room, and Tom Seymour returned to his original quarters. Lady Kate Parr chose the guest apartments for her own.

Our routine was simple, and I found myself delighting in it. There being no priest, there was no morning Mass. Instead, we all slept until fancy awoke us, usually around seven o'clock. On a summer's morning that meant the sun, and the farmers, had been up three hours already, so one awoke to the smell of cut hay and the play of dancing sunshine on the floor. We gathered for a breakfast of ale, cheese, and dark bread, with sweet butter and plum preserves, out in the courtyard, and sometimes were silent, still groggy, drinking in the odours of a June morning, with the dew still on shaded sweet-williams and chive blossoms. Edward and Kate Parr then settled themselves for the daily lessons; Tom prowled the grounds and the nearby village, restlessly; Will and Dr. Butts took walks and discussed medicine and politics. And I? I attempted to deal with the outside world and keep contact with the Privy Council and with the Continent. Sitting in my little dormered chamber, I could hardly believe that anything I said or did would resound beyond those walls.

Dinner was a lazy, drawn-out affair at midday, consisting of local fare: salads of onions, leeks, dandelion leaves; roasted lark and pigeon pie; cherries with cream and spiced wine. How we would linger, there before the crude table and chairs set up in the stone courtyard, loth to leave, as we talked of many things, freely. The afternoons were given over to long rambles, to music, and to amateurish philosophy. As the evening shadows lengthened, we would gather in the largest upstairs chamber, there to say evening prayers. I led the worship, selecting Psalms and speaking simple prayers, and it was a fitting close to our day.

Such soft days, and hours. I savoured them, without even the awareness of what a balm they were to me. But gradually I began to move about more easily, and my stiff joints and ever-chafed legs grew supple and pain-free. True, they ached at supporting my great bulk (which did *not* diminish) and rebelled sometimes by buckling at surprising moments, but overall I mended, and regained good health.

We spent evenings in each other's chambers, or alone, as we wished. There were no rules, no protocol, no expectations. For the first time in my life I was free of them.

I always visited Edward and asked him to recite the day's lessons to me. It was my own private Compline, to hear my five-year-old son give a summary of his day. Often, Lady Kate prompted him, but not always. They had an easy-going understanding of one another, and in her presence (although, I must admit, not always in mine), Edward softened and acted with self-confidence.

ꞓꙮ ꙮꞓ

Across two fields, with the abandoned beehives in between, stood the great barn where old Sir John had served Jane's betrothal feast. It had stood there, large and glowing in fourteen sunsets, before I dared to go to it. I say "dared" because I had been afraid to do so. The memories it would trigger, the cherished things, lost . . . yet to be here, reside here, and not visit it, seemed a cowardice and a sacrilege I could not permit myself.

So, after our jolly supper of fish caught by Edward in a stream that ran down near the nether pasture, and before bedtime and my unorthodox Compline, I betook myself to stroll toward the barn and make my peace with it. I say "stroll" because my bulk made anything faster out of the question.

The sun was hurrying toward its rest as I tramped along the narrow path. That peculiar long slanting light fell over everything, licking the fields, the crops, the top of the barn.

It had been about this time of year, too, when the feast was served. The twilights were long, and there had been torches all along the path to the barn—which was not a barn, for that day, but a fairy-tale palace. Silks had covered its wattle walls; flowers, in ropes, had hung from its roof; and inside, an oaken floor had been laid down, and long tables covered with linen had been set in gold and silver for the feast.

I looked inside now, and saw it as it was: an earth floor, poor lighting, the smell of animals. The magic was gone, passed on, to some other place and persons.

I sat against the wall, on a little bench there, and rested. The walk had tired me. Sweat was seeping from every seam of my clothing. What had I hoped to achieve by coming here? To assure myself that the transfigured moment had gone? To lay ghosts to rest? To partake of a sacrament of sorts?

Whatever I had wished for, the reality quashed it. This was nothing but an old barn, and a barrier of time separated me from the thing I wished to hold once again. There was no o'erleaping that fixed barrier, even with the pole-vault of imagination and longing.

I was as I was. Now, this moment. A dreary thought, a diminishing thought. And yet, strangely, a *freeing* thought. I was as I was. Now, this moment. All that I was, had been, would be, were here with me now.

I was startled to hear voices. How dare anyone intrude upon my private devotions? For devotions they were, worship of private gods and celebration of private rites.

"This is the great barn of Wolf Hall," Kate's clear voice was saying. "It was built"—a pause while she fumbled with a paper—"in 1452, by your mother's great-grandfather. Your mother had her betrothal feast here."

"In a barn?" Edward's voice. It was whiny and disrespectful.

"Aye. It can accommodate many. What a marvellous barn!"

She appeared in the very midst of it and held up her arms. "How fortunate that it was built so grand!"

"A barn," repeated Edward.

"An enchanted barn," I said, stepping forth. I would eavesdrop no longer.

They both paled, and looked less than pleased to have me join them so unexpectedly.

"I came here to relive my dear wife's betrothal feast. Edward, a barn is nothing to be ashamed of."

I turned toward Kate. I was more touched than I would show that she had brought him here, to teach him of his mother's past. "It is kind of you to instruct him in his personal history as well as in Roman history," I said.

She was silent, only inclining her head.

"Yes, Edward, your mother had her betrothal feast here. And it was a soft May night, and all the neighbours and gentry nearby came to fête her," I said.

He was uninterested. *Now, this moment. All was here.* He cared not at all. An old barn was an old barn, not a magic place where past and present met.

"I wish I could have known her," he finally said.

Only in Holbein's painting, I thought. Only there can you and she know one another.

He went and leapt on the piles of last harvest's hay, mounded at the far end of the barn. I felt suddenly old and ill, and I knew not why. *When we suffer, Christ is speaking to us.* But what does He say? I heard nothing. At this time of my life, I should be able to make a summation, but I could not. In many ways I seemed the same as I had been as a lad. I was young and ignorant, in an old and sick body.

Kate stood beside me as Edward sported in the hay. She smiled.

"He honours his mother in his own way," she said. "I think it is important to him that he has come here and seen the Seymour home and lands. He must know he is a Seymour as well as a Tudor."

"It is on such families that England's greatness rests. The Seymours, the Dennys, the Parrs—those are the true strength of England." I looked at her. "Yes, the Parrs have served England well, and when I speak of 'true Englishmen,' it is the Parrs I mean. Without the 'true Parrs,' there would be no England."

She started to demur, but something would not let her. "Aye," she said. "We are proud to be English."

Mere English. Elizabeth had always used that phrase. She exulted in her English-ness, her pure English pedigree. I must write to Elizabeth. I had presumed Hatfield safe, but perhaps she should join us here. I would not lose her. I would not lose her . . . for I loved her, the saucy rebel. . . .

My thoughts were wandering. I brought them to heel. Kate was waiting.

"That is the source of England's greatness. The pride of her families," I said.

I was tired. I longed for bed. I dreaded the long walk back. I wished I had a litter. At the same time I dreaded the empty chamber. If only I had a companion.

Will was a companion.

Yes, but . . . Will was a man.

I longed for a wife.

The admission was so shocking to me that I shook my head.

A wife.

There would be no more wives, I reminded myself.

A companion, then. A woman companion. Not a wife in the old, ordinary sense.

A monastic marriage?

Yes, why not? You are the King, you can arrange anything.

Someone to read with me, to keep me company, to distract me when the pain is bad.

Who can find a virtuous woman? For her price is far above rubies.

Rubies. I glanced at Kate Parr's hand. Yes, she wore it: the ruby ring I had given her for that shameful Valentine's Day.

"Kate," I said. "Will you be my wife?"

She turned to me, her face masked. Then her mouth twitched and wavered. "Your Grace," she finally said, "it were better to—to be your mistress!"

"Mistress?" I spat. I wanted no mistresses, no fleshly sport, but twining of the *spirit*. The thought of woman-parts disgusted me. The corruption, the secretions, the addiction. No. Not that. "Think you I wish what a *mistress* can offer me? Nay, Madam, then you do not know me!" I flung out my arm, gesturing toward the vast reaches of the shadowy barn. "Think you I came here because I wished to relive the greasy pleasures of a mistress? Do you credit me with no higher love?" Why do we never credit anyone but ourselves with a soul?

"Forgive me," she finally replied. "I meant no disrespect. But I know— I have been told—that normal marriages include this . . . this element. My husbands were old, and I am ignorant of this. I would . . . learn. But at present I know not, truly, what it is to be woman."

"All that is beautiful and healthful in woman, you are already," I said. "The other—oh, remain innocent of it, my Kate! It is naught!"

"How can it be naught, when even the Scriptures themselves celebrate it? 'Thou hast ravished my heart. Thou art beautiful, O my love, as Tirzah, comely as Jerusalem, terrible as an army with banners. How fair and pleasant art thou, O love, for delights! Set me as a seal upon thine heart, as a seal upon thine arm: for love is strong as death, jealousy is cruel as the grave.'"

"I have—never felt this," she said.

O fortunate woman! To have been spared this punishment!

"You are a maiden twice widowed," I said. "And shall remain a maiden with me. O Kate, I need your humanness, not your woman-parts. I need what you, Kate, are."

"And what is that?" Her voice was strangely sad.

"A good Christian lady."

"Aye." Why did she sound disappointed at this high compliment?

"Be my Queen. Should not England's Queen be a good Christian lady?"

"Aye."

"Do you this from patriotic duty, or for . . . personal reasons?"

"Personal reasons," she said. "I am not so patriotic."

Then she cared for me? My heart leapt, strangely.

"I will be good to you, Kate," I promised. "I will be kind, and gentle, and good."

She bowed her head in acquiescence. "Yes, Your Majesty," she said.

Will was alone in our quarters, Dr. Butts having gone to the meadows to gather such difficult-to-find herbs as stonecrop, mugwort, and all-heal, which he had delightedly spotted on one of his rambles. Will was sitting in the window-seat, his head black and featureless against the soft yellow of the midsummer fields. He was slumped a little, as if exhausted. Was he, then, truly growing old, as he had mentioned more than once?

"Will," I said, upon the instant I saw him. "Will, I must tell you . . . it is the most marvellous thing . . . I know not how to explain it. . . ."

Wearily he moved his body and turned round toward me. Now he was a black mountain, blotting out the light.

"Will, I am . . . to be married," I said in wonder.

"Christ, no!"

He leapt from his seat, and light came back into the room.

"Yes," I said.

"No," he repeated. "It matters not who she is, only *you must not wed again.*" He was standing next to me now. "You swore—"

"And I meant it. But this will be different."

"No! That is what you have said each time. And aye, they *were* different, because the ladies themselves were different. O Hal, those who say a much-married man in reality just marries the same woman repeatedly, have never studied you. If you had laboured to do so, you could not have found five women as different as your past wives, and—"

Five? Had there truly been five? "Nay, they were not all true wives!" I protested.

"You went through a marriage ceremony with each of them, Your Grace. Each lady could, for one day at least, call herself a bride, and rejoice."

"It is no matter, God did not rejoice with them."

"He will not rejoice at this!"

"So! Now you claim to know God's will, and God's desires! Well, I have trafficked with God, struggled with Him, consorted with Him, rebelled against Him, and studied Him, more than any man on earth! And I can tell you this—His ways *are* mysterious, and no one can read Him. We can only do, at any given moment, what our limited little consciences tell us to do, and know that that, somehow, fits into the divine mosaic. And I, Henry Tudor, will marry again!"

"So Kate is to be Queen," he said softly. "The prophecy is come true. Her ambition is rewarded."

"What prophecy?"

"One she made herself, according to her brother William. It seems, as a child, she did not take easily to her duties of spinning and weaving. She told her mother that 'these hands are destined for orbs and sceptres, not distaffs and spindles.'"

Perhaps what starts out as a retort, a dream, turns into a drive, takes on a reality of its own. Is that not another cousin to destiny?

"Everyone dreams of becoming royal, even the maids and chimney-sweeps. 'Tis a common fantasy," was my answer.

"When is it to be?" Will indeed sounded tired, whereas I was filled with energy.

"When the plague abates and we return to London," I said. "No, I shall not find a lone country priest and go secretly to him . . . although it would be romantic," I added. A small parish church . . . nuptials in the early summer morning, a walk through the fields, picking wildflowers. . . . "But it is important that this be no hole-and-corner affair. Gardiner or Cranmer must officiate. Pray God they are safe. I have not had word in five days from those in Suffolk. Edward Seymour and Paget, they are well in Gloucestireshire, as of two days ago. . . . Nay, I want them all present."

But the cool secret chapel, the procession through the fields . . . forbidden to me, no need to dwell on it.

"Well, I wish you joy," Will said. "You have had little enough in your weddings."

CXXI

The table was laid in the courtyard, the long wooden one about which we gathered every noon, set up under the spreading hazel tree, as there was no shade from the long wings of the house at this time of day. Jugs of wine were set out on the table, and bunches of flowers, freshly gathered by Dr. Butts, Edward, and Kate.

We all seated ourselves and waited for the cooks to bring out today's fare. I would make the announcement in a moment.

I looked at Kate, seated as always next to Edward. I tried to catch her gaze, but she did not look at me. Rather she looked only at Edward.

The cooks brought out the first course, spring lamb and larks, prepared with scallions and chervil.

After everyone's plate was filled, I took the jug of red wine, thin and sour, but sweetened with honey, and filled my cup. "Fill yours, all," I ordered. When that was done, I took a sip and then raised my cup. "I wish to share with you my great joy this day. England is to have a Queen, and I a wife." I looked at Kate, inclined my head toward her.

Look at me, woman! I ordered her silently, as she continued to study her plate.

"It is our sweet, kind Lady Latimer who will become my wife, and your Queen."

Still she kept her eyes down.

"A modest Queen!" I jested, reaching my cup over to her and touching her vessel with mine. The clunk made her look up.

The company broke into smiles. Kate smiled too, shyly.

"The King has honoured me greatly," she said softly. "I pray that I may ever be a good, kind, loyal, and true wife to His Majesty."

"Nay, you make it sound like a funeral, Lady Latimer," said Tom Seymour. He was sitting at the foot of the table, his accustomed place. He grinned, his elbows on the table, the great sleeves of his white linen shirt billowing out like sails. "Marriage is not decorum, but bliss and abandon and bed-sport." He tasted his wine.

"I wonder that you can speak so," my Kate replied, "as you are a bachelor. You have no knowledge of marriage."

"Nor have you, my Lady; that is, of the side of marriage that belongs to impetuous youth. Alas"—he looked round—"I shall never experience it myself, as I am well past that prime. But the poets do say that it is extraordinary!"

"Mark Antony was forty-eight when he loved Cleopatra," Will said. "And poets make much of their love."

"Shall we debate love this afternoon, then?" asked Dr. Butts.

"No, let us celebrate it," said Will. "For love is a matter of the will as well as of the heart, and can flourish best, perhaps, when the two are combined."

We all drank, and then I reached out and took Kate's hand. She looked at me, and I could not read her face at all.

Edward was the only one at the table who truly rejoiced with me, for he loved Kate, and had no mother. It was all gain to him, as it was to me.

Later that day, Kate came to me. "We must write to Mary and Elizabeth," she said. "For they must not hear of this through gossip or third parties."

"Aye." I had not heard of how Hatfield House had fared, and I was astonishingly worried about Elizabeth. "I will write my own letters, and you yours, and we combine them in a single envelope."

Correspondence was moving a bit more freely now; reports were that the number of plague victims was slackening in Kent and Sussex, the southernmost and hardest-hit counties. But deaths were climbing in Worcestershire, Buckinghamshire, and Northamptonshire, the middle counties. The plague travelled about my realm, making a progress all its own, holding its own audiences and demanding its own obeisance.

That evening I wrote to Elizabeth, inquiring after her health and that of the countryside surrounding Hatfield House. I also told her of my plans to wed, and that I wished her to be present for the ceremony, which would be held as soon as it was healthy for everyone to return to London.

Within the week I had her reply, very prettily worded and yet acknowledging no rift between us, or offering apology for the same. She wrote that Hatfield House, and the immediate neighbourhood, had as yet suffered no attacks of plague, but there had been reports—possibly unreliable—of St. Alban's and Dunstable having been stricken. As for the wedding, and my bride, she would welcome the closer ties with Lady Latimer, whom she greatly esteemed.

Mary, who was at Woodstock, wrote in a stiff manner that she would be pleased to attend the Nuptial Mass, and wished me joy.

⌘ ⌘

In the meantime we whiled away our time at Wolf Hall; and although the June days were pleasant, I was growing increasingly anxious to resume normal life.

For the country was boring, although we delighted in its scents and flowers and sunlight. It is ever a paradox that city-dwellers long for the country, build summer houses there, dream of it in winter—and yet find it stultifying and its native people dull within a very short time.

Tom Seymour was so restless I was tempted to tell him to take his chances and return to London, or even voyage to France to assess the political climate there. From the information that managed to reach me here, Francis, although grieving for his favourite son, was bellicose as ever, and he and Charles were already making sporadic war along their borders. And this while I had to sit and wait for the plague to abate!

Will grew morose; the country did not suit him. He was a city-dweller and had little use for walks in meadows and long afternoons spent napping or reading Homer.

⌘ WILL:

'Tis true I am a city-dweller, but my moroseness arose from my utter inability to do anything to prevent the King from venturing once more into something that boded ill for him. Another marriage! Cared he not that thereby he would be sniggered at not only throughout England, but in Europe as well? What need had he of marriage?

And the war with France! As a youngling, with his vainglorious advisor Wolsey, he had tried that, and found it expensive and wasteful and inconclusive. Had he not learned?

It is hard to see a person whom one loves going down a wrong path, a path that will only bring him grief. What is love's duty? To block the path and prevent the damage? Or to stand aside and respect his right to make errors and be responsible for them? When the loved one is a King, the former choice is not even allowable. Hence my misery.

⌘ HENRY VIII:

Edward and I grew used to one another. We went fishing together; we hunted and built cookfires together; and soon we knew each other's personal quirks. That he grew cross if he were too long in the sun; that he enjoyed dreaming while fishing, and resented the bite of a fish as an interruption; that he tired quickly and had little stamina. This I hoped to correct by including more physical things in his daily life; for it is not good for a King to be so short of vigour.

In turn he learned that I had great difficulty mounting and dismounting, as I had grown so corpulent, and also because my weak leg was of little help to me these days. He saw that I preferred cheese that was hard and tawny to that which was softer and white. He knew that I sunburned easily, and so he took it upon himself to watch my face for redness and then order me out of the sun. From such intimacies grow affection and understanding and subtle ties; and so I was grateful to the plague for giving us this opportunity to come to know one another.

The same applied to Kate. I saw her in the humble circumstances of life, saw how she always was cheerful and calm. I saw, too, how she never emerged from her chamber until an hour past when I saw her first opening the casements. She kept her devotions then, and would not venture forth to speak with men until she had first spoken with God. At night, too, I saw the light burning for some time. Did she keep a private Compline? There were no traditional Holy Offices at that time. She made her own.

One particularly fine day, Dr. Butts announced that he had seen strawberries in the fields near the Savernake Forest, and they were ripe and ready for picking. We made up a party and set out to gather them. Kate and I took one field, discreetly left alone by the others.

"Ah, Kate," I said, "they leave us alone to do as lovers do." It seemed humourous, as we did *not* do what lovers do. I patted my basket. "How we shall disappoint them when we return with our baskets overflowing!"

She turned and gave me a smile, but a sad one. As if to say, *What a pity.* All about us nature was rampantly growing, reproducing, making an abundance of new green stalks, weeds, creepers, and climbers. And here we were in their midst, sterile and restricted.

But it was my time of life. I was autumn now, late autumn. In autumn all these fields and forests would be like me, we would be at one in our cycle. Now November passing through June fields was an outrage, an insult; then we would blend together and I would belong, where today I was but a visitor, a foreigner.

We found the strawberries, mixed in with weeds and self-sown rye. Picking them out was a job, a job I disliked. Bending over was so difficult for me that I was forced to kneel down; but that was also difficult, because the pressure on my weak leg caused it to start throbbing. Disturbing it in any way meant possibly causing it to revert to its festering stage. At length I devised a sort of half-kneeling position to use.

We picked, silently. In truth I had no extra strength to carry on a conversation while bent down in an uncomfortable position. The sun on my hat was rapidly making me overheat, but—last vestige of vanity!—I could never remove it and reveal my baldness.

Sweat began popping out all over my face; then gathered in little streams, running down the troughs and wrinkles of my skin. The red strawberries gleamed and shimmered before my eyes, pulsating like stars. Then everything swirled, and I fell into the patch of meadow, face downward. I felt a strawberry crush against my cheek, and its sweet yielded juice was overwhelming in my nostrils.

I looked up at Kate's face. I was lying on my back in her lap, and she was fanning me with my hat. My hat . . . then she had seen my baldness! Oh, the shame of it!

"The sun made me grow dizzy," I murmured. I was so humiliated, so mortified, that I hated her for seeing this. I would never marry her now. I could not have a wife who looked down upon my weakness, who considered herself superior to me. My legs were forked out. I lay like a helpless frog in her sight.

I sat up, retrieved the hat, clapped it on my head. I must leave this site, her presence, her shaming presence. I struggled to my feet, pushing away her "helping" hands. Her mocking hands, more like!

"Edward does the same," she said, in a natural voice. "He overheats in direct sunlight. It must be the Tudor complexion, for I believe Elizabeth avoids the sun for that reason. Although her white skin is her pride, I know."

I felt a rush of relief. My pride had been spared. But no, this would *not* do. "Kate," I said, "you have seen, now, what I would have kept from you at all costs. I am not what I was. The truth is, the sun has never bothered me before. The truth is, I have many infirmities. My leg periodically goes on a rampage, crippling me. I have had trouble, of late, with my bladder . . . and with raging headaches that leave me spent and weak. And with sick fancies, with shapes that come and talk to me, that stand in corners and run down corridors, shrieking. I am an old, sick man." There, I had said it. Now I would dismiss her, release her from the betrothal, on the understanding that she tell no one what she had witnessed that day.

"Yes. I know." It was a statement, not an apology. "I did not agree to marry you in ignorance of this, Your Grace."

"Then you are doing it from pity?" Of all things, it was pity I could not tolerate, pity that demeaned me more than any other emotion. Pity was the ultimate insult. One who pitied always looked down from superior heights upon the pitiable one. Sympathy came down from its heights to share with you, but Pity sat and looked scornfully below. Pity was useless without action; a vile, contaminated thing. Nay, I would have none of it. I'd gouge the eyes and cut the face of anyone regarding me with pity.

"No, Your Grace."

Liar! "What, then?"

"From—from affection," she said. "Affection and friendship—those are the two loves that care nothing for physical infirmity, to whom the physical being is unimportant. Eros is what is concerned with bodies; although even Eros is a love of sorts, for it wishes to possess the soul as well as the body. Lust is the only attraction that cares exclusively for bodies."

I grunted. "Affection. Can affection move one toward marriage?" I thought affection a weak thing, a watered-down version of Eros or friendship, not something in its own right.

"The Greeks called it *Storge,*" she said. "It is a special family sort of love, in its original meaning. It is a warm comfortableness, a satisfaction in being together. It is the humblest of loves; it gives itself no airs. It is responsible for most of the solid and durable happiness in our lives. Is it *not* a worthy reason to consider marriage?"

Her quick, well-thought-out answer surprised me. This was something she had long since settled in her own mind.

"So you feel affection toward me, Kate?"

"I have felt so for a long time. Else I would not—could not—have consented to be your wife."

"But if I had ordered you, sweet Kate?" A feeling of great fondness and caring and well-being was coming upon me.

"Affection does not order," she said, with a smile.

We finished gathering the strawberries, chattering happily about the philosophical differences among *Storge, Philia, Amicitia, Eros,* and *Caritas,* and returned to Wolf Hall for dinner, feeling married already. Or rather, as married people *should* feel toward one another, although my other marriages had been woefully lacking in such a bond. Excepting my marriage to Jane, of course. Always excepting Jane . . .

CXXII

My messengers were able to come and go more often now, and that alone showed that conditions, at least in the South of England, were improving. The number of plague victims in London decreased abruptly around Midsummer's Eve, and common people attributed it to the magic of the longest day of the year. The scientists and physicians ascribed it to some mysterious effect of the sun's rays upon the disease. Whatever it was, the plague loosened its stranglehold upon London and let the city breathe again.

Within two weeks the number of victims had fallen to nothing. But we must wait another fortnight to be sure. Then it was back to London, back to life as usual.

The dispatches from the scattered Privy Council showed that their minds had returned to business, and they were eager to resume their duties. Bishop Gardiner was bored with tending gardens with Audley in Suffolk; the roses were blooming, but they failed to take much joy in them. Wriothesley and Cranmer, consigned to a parish in Colchester, had attempted to interest themselves in local history and had even compiled a booklet on the baptisms in all the nearby parish churches (spending days copying the parish records). They found themselves becoming quite immersed in it, imagining what these families were like, making up stories to one another to explain the spacing of births and the particular names chosen. But they soon wearied of it, not being particularly imaginative to begin with, and found themselves at a loss to fill their hours.

Petre, in Huntingdonshire, had begun studying the lace woven in the district. There were many different patterns, and the common folk claimed that "Good Queen Katherine" had introduced the skill there. That was nonsense, of course. Katherine did not go out amongst the common women and teach them to make lace. She herself did not make lace, or have any knowledge of how to do so. The fact that much lace was made in Spain meant nothing. *I* did not know how to shear sheep, even though raw wool was England's prime export. At any rate, Petre concluded that Cambridgeshire and Huntingdonshire lace might be exported and serve as a money-making industry for England.

Henry Howard, lounging about his familial estate in Norfolk, amused himself by drawing up plans for a great estate of his own on the site of St. Leonard's Priory in Norwich, to be called Mount Surrey. It was to incorporate all the Italian innovations, and become a Mediterranean villa in the damp mists of East Anglia. Between arranging for builders, glass-masters, sculptors, and painters for his palace, he gave himself over to poetry and heraldry. The unreal world to which he was temporarily consigned was most congenial to him, and he flourished in it.

Anthony Denny and John Dudley, who had gone farther west, one to Devon and the other to Padstow, at the very edge of Cornwall, wrote intriguing descriptions of the region, particularly of Cornwall, where, Dudley said, the inhabitants were tiny and dark, with all the houses and doorways and chairs sized to them, so that a regular man might crack his head in passing from one room to another. On the south coast, he said, they were all pirates, or "wreckers" who lured merchant ships onto the rocks with false lights, and then plundered them. He did not rest well, wondering every night if he would be stabbed in his sleep. "I long for the treachery of civilized men," he wrote.

In mid-July he had his wish, and we all reunited in London, at Westminster Palace, to pursue just that.

How good it felt to be back at work! And to have all my workers ready at hand. Not one had been lost to the plague, and even London, which had been hit most severely, had made a recovery. As we rode back into the city, there was little sign of disruption, and few clues that there had been an injury to the society. With no one to direct them, no one to order them, the surviving Londoners had proceeded to take responsibility for their own little streets and half-streets, and the newly elevated people, wearing offices as yet green to them, seemed to be managing well enough. The heaped plague-pits were already grassing over, and that for some reason both soothed and disturbed me. So quickly . . . yes, why not?

The Imperial ambassador, Van der Delft, had just received a communication from his master. It seemed that Charles had had a successful campaign already, and had scored some notable triumphs in Luxembourg and Navarre. He looked to continue the war on the northern front, but would pass the coming fortnight at Landrecies, directing the siege there. If I wished to enter the campaign after that date . . . ?

"No, no," I said. "It is too late in the season, and we cannot ready an army now, with midsummer already past." Not to mention the plague. "Next season, next season, we shall join him. How long does he plan to campaign?"

"Not past September," Van der Delft replied. "He has family business then—a wedding."

"Ah." I smiled. "I also. I have my own wedding."

The ambassador grinned. "Your own, Your Majesty?"

"Aye. Ah, ah, do not mock me, sir"—I began laughing, as I could see his surprise and unasked questions—"although I know 'tis a temptation."

"I wish you happiness," he said simply.

"I do truly seek it," I answered.

"Then you shall find it." He looked straight into my eyes. I liked him; he seemed honest. We would not spar and parry, as I had done with Chapuys, but that was well enough.

"I pray so. I shall wed the widow Latimer, as soon as all is set in order. Now, though, as to this war business—Charles and I have settled satisfactorily the title confusion, as being addressed as 'Defender of the Faith, *etc.*' will content me. I lack but the proper means—in winds and moneys—to come to France before spring. But I shall do so, and in person. You may tell your master that I will lead my soldiers myself, as I did in the glorious campaign of 1513—the Golden War!"

My God, I grew excited just thinking of it! Oh, my blood stirred! To wear armour again, to camp again, to hold war council meetings in the field-tent . . . how sweetly it beckoned!

❦ ❧

As soon as he returned to London, I spoke to Bishop Gardiner about my intention to wed Kate Parr.

"I wish you to marry us," I said.

"Not Cranmer?" His tone was distant, judging. Yes, Gardiner was jealous of Cranmer, jealous of his closeness to me and his privilege in sharing so much of my life.

"No. It must be someone whose orthodoxy is beyond question, as Lady Latimer is suspected—unjustly, of course—of leaning toward the Reformers. Your performing the ceremony will silence those tongues."

"Will it, Your Grace?" Still he appeared aloof, cool, uncommitted.

"As best they can be," I retorted. "Nothing ever silences tongues altogether."

"Are you so very sure she is not a Reformer?" Each word was measured out and flung at me.

"Because her foolish friend Anne Askew goes about preaching? Each person is responsible for his or her own soul. We are not our brothers' keepers in that regard. Many of my friends have gone astray, misled by false doctrines—does that taint me, so long as I do not follow them?"

With difficulty he smiled. He had such thin lips. I realized, just then, that he seldom smiled; on him it seemed artificial. "No, Your Grace."

"Then you *will* perform the ceremony?"

He could not refuse a royal request.

"I would be honoured, Your Grace."

I myself would have preferred Cranmer, as I loved him and therefore wanted to include him in anything of importance in my life. But I had spoken true to Gardiner; it was politically necessary that a conservative conduct and sanction the marriage ceremony. I would protect my Kate from the enemies who would seek to discredit her, for no other reason than that I loved her and trusted her.

It was to be a family wedding, with all my natural family present—my children, and my niece Lady Margaret Douglas, daughter of Margaret and her second husband, the Earl of Angus—then my family by affection, certain members of the Privy Council and their wives. Altogether that made nearly a score of witnesses.

Gardiner married us on July 12, 1543, in the withdrawing chamber of the royal apartments at Hampton Court. The day smiled upon us, cool and fair, with the distinctive sleepy scent of box trees from the knot-garden below entering the chamber, which had been decorated with lilies and poppies.

My Kate wore a lavender gown, a teasing choice, for purple was royal, yet also betokened penance and mourning. . . . No matter, it was the colour of periwinkles and set off her red-gold hair.

I stood, once again, taking a bride. I had only one prayer: *Almighty God, send your favour upon my marriage, as you never have in the past. Do not let it end in unhappiness, as have all the rest.* Surely I deserved a happy end after all my misfortunes in matrimony.

"I require and charge you both, as ye will answer at the dreadful Day of Judgment when the secrets of all hearts shall be disclosed, that if either of you know any impediment, why ye may not be lawfully joined together in matrimony, ye do now confess it," intoned Gardiner, standing before us in his bishop's robes.

Disillusionment? Bad experiences? Weariness? Were these "impediments"?

"For be ye well assured, that so many as are coupled together otherwise than God's word doth allow, are not joined together by God: neither is their matrimony lawful."

No, there was nothing in God's word forbidding marriage between tired, aching people.

"Henry, King of England, Wales, and Ireland, King of France, wilt thou have this woman to thy wedded wife, to live together after God's ordinance in the holy estate of matrimony? Wilt thou love her, comfort her, honour, and keep her, in sickness and in health: and forsaking all other, keep thee only unto her, so long as ye both shall live?"

All those things I wanted to do, with all my heart. "I will," I answered.

Gardiner turned to Kate. "Katherine Parr, Lady Latimer, wilt thou have this man to thy wedded husband, to live together after God's ordinance in the holy estate of matrimony? Wilt thou obey him and serve him, love, honour, and keep him in sickness and in health"—oh, let it be in health, do not let her have to nurse me—"and, forsaking all other, keep thee only unto him, so long as ye both shall live?"

"I will." Her voice was faint. Had something given her pause? The "sickness"? The "forsaking all other"? For she was young. . . .

"Who giveth this woman to be married to this man?" He looked round at the company, smiled his thin February smile, and said, "I do."

Then, taking our right hands together, he directed me to say:

"I, Henry, take thee, Katherine, to be my wedded wife, to have and to hold from this day forward, for better, for worse, for richer, for poorer, in sickness and in health, to love and to cherish, till death us do part, according to God's holy ordinance: and thereto I plight thee my troth."

Marriage promises. They took in both sides of life: no sooner did they say "better" than they said "worse," no sooner "richer" than a quicker "poorer." In the midst of our greatest happiness they were worded to remind us of woe, and bound us to include wretchedness in with our rejoicings.

Kate then repeated the same vows.

Gardiner took from me the ring I had for her, plain gold, with no engraving at all. I put it on her finger, her cool slender finger. "With this ring I thee wed," I said, "with my body I thee worship, and with all my worldly goods I thee endow. In the name of the Father, and of the Son, and of the Holy Ghost, amen." There. It was done. How differently I would fulfill these vows than I had with my previous wife.

"Kneel," said Gardiner, and we did so, upon the blue velvet cushions laid before us. "O eternal God, Creator and Preserver of all mankind. Giver of all spiritual grace, the Author of everlasting life: send Thy blessing upon these Thy servants, this man and this woman, whom we bless in Thy name: that, as Isaac and Rebecca lived faithfully together, so these persons may surely perform and keep the vow and covenant betwixt them made, and may ever remain in perfect love and peace together, and live according to Thy laws: through Jesus Christ Our Lord, amen."

"Amen," murmured the people.

"Forasmuch as King Henry and Katherine Parr have consented together in holy wedlock," said Gardiner, addressing the whole company, his voice rising, "and have witnessed the same before God and this company, and have declared the same by giving and receiving of a ring, and by joining of hands: I pronounce that they be man and wife together."

He raised his hands over our heads. "God the Father, God the Son, God the Holy Ghost, bless, preserve, and keep you: the Lord mercifully with His favour look upon you: and so fill you with all spiritual benediction and grace, that ye may so live together in this life, that in the world to come ye may have life everlasting. Amen."

We rose, man and wife. The gathered company broke into movement, embracing, swaying together, laughing. We turned to them and accepted their good wishes, joined them in celebrating.

Mary, the bridesmaid, came to us and threw her arms around us both. She kept her eyes averted, but I spied tears spilling down her cheeks. She had known Kate for a long time, ever since Kate first came to London with Lord Latimer and visited court to meet scholars. They had grown fond of one another then; and though she would never consider Kate a "mother," she cared deeply for her as a friend.

Elizabeth came over, as well. Awkwardly she extended her arms to embrace Mary as well as Kate. She said nothing, just hugged us. Words were difficult for her—that is, words from the heart.

Then we were released to the custody of the company. The press of people in the chamber was warm, but it was a close warmth, a happy summer warmth. They were wearing their sheerest linens, and some of the women had left off their headdresses, letting their hair fall free, like maidens—even the strict and humourless Anne, wife of Edward Seymour. Yes, she might actually be attractive, in bed; perhaps Seymour was not the prig he pretended to be.

Bed. I was not supposed to be thinking of bed, even to the extent of other men's beds.

In the adjoining Privy Chamber our wedding feast was laid. There was a bride-cake, and silver bowls of woodruff-flavoured wine, and strawberry tarts. From our loyal lairds in Scotland came a smoked salmon, and the deputy of Calais had sent French cheeses.

Kate and I led the way to the table and ceremoniously took sips from the silver wedding-cup and tasted the bride-cakes. Outside the windows, the sun held itself in the sky for hours, heating the gardens below, so that their scents perfumed the room. I was drowsy, dazzled, entirely a captive of the senses. All I could think was: How delightful this is, to be suspended in time on a summer's afternoon. . . .

And then I saw the shadows growing longer, the hollyhocks casting shadows twice their length; and the air coming in the open casements was subtly different. The afternoon was turning into eventide. The plates upon the white-linened table were empty, and our guests awaited our dismissal.

⤷ ⤶

Alone we were, with the ruins of our wedding feast around us. "Come into my apartments, Kate," I said. They were now her apartments as well. "Come." I held out my hands and drew her in. She came, a little hesitantly, following me into the little private chamber next to the bedchamber.

"Oh!" she cried, seeing a carved oak footstool beside the fireplace. It had been her childhood seating place at her mother's feet.

"I had it brought from Kendal," I said. "So that you would feel at home."

Her stiffness disappeared, and a great smile spread across her tight face. "How did you know?"

"I enquired," I answered. It was simple enough. There were old servants who remembered. Had neither of her doting old spouses bothered to ascertain her preferences?

She flung her arms around me, as if I had given her the pearls of the Orient. "All the way from Westmorland," she murmured, and it might as well have been from the Orient.

"I wanted a bit of your girlhood to follow you here," I said, "so that becoming Queen would not be too abrupt a change."

"Ah. Yes." She fingered her necklace. "Queen. I am Queen."

"Indeed."

Now there was nothing more to say. We stood facing one another, awkwardly, while outside it darkened and a cool wind came up. Soon we heard the gentle drop-drop-drop of rain on the garden below, striking the leaves and rolling off. The sound of summer rain . . . soft, like the murmur of bees.

The tension between us mounted. She feared me, feared that I would demand a husband's rights after all. And the thought was revolting to her; that was obvious.

"Let us retire," I finally said. "I am weary."

Inside the bedchamber there were two beds set up: my accustomed one and a smaller one, of carved walnut with ivory insets, that I had obtained for her. The finest linen lay upon her bed, maiden-linen, never slept on before. A coverlet of white wool was folded at its foot.

"For you, Madam," I said, and I was pained to see her joy at beholding a separate bed.

"I will retire now." This was so formal, more formal than a state banquet. I seated myself upon a padded bench alongside the window and began to remove my garments. First the embroidered silk shirt that I had saved for this, my wedding day. Then the linen undershirt, with its neck-fastenings. Now it was all revealed: my bulging belly, uncorseted. I shot a look at her to see if she were watching, and what her face showed. Indeed she *was* watching, but her expression was . . . expressionless. Next I removed my breeches, then my hose. My legs were exposed, with the purplish veins mapping them all over. She was to see all, see exactly what I was made of, of what infirmities. I stood thus for a full moment or two before ceremoniously pulling my nightshirt on and veiling this ruined work of nature, like draping an obscene statue. With effort I mounted the steps and then climbed into bed.

"You may undress behind the screen," I told her, indicating the silk-hung frame set up in the corner.

"No." She carefully began to remove her own garments, with movements so graceful and deft it was like a dance. There was only a glimpse of nakedness, however, and it was so quickly done that it tantalized rather than soothed. In an instant she was in her bed, her head on the swansdown pillow. She stretched out her hand and took mine.

"Shall we pray, my Lord?" Before I could reply, she began a lengthy conversation with the Almighty.

It was a disappointing act, an insulting one. Yet had I not abjured the pleasures of women, on my own accord? Wherefore, then, should I find fault with her chaste behaviour?

Side by side we both lay for hours, listening to the July rain, pretending to be asleep.

CXXIII

K ate adopted her position as Queen so naturally, easily, and subtly that she made it appear easy to assume the mantle of royalty. She kept her gentlewoman's ways, continuing to correspond with friends and relations in her usual manner, asking them to respond "as friendly as if God had not called me to this honour." She signed herself "Katherine the Queen, K.P." to remind herself—and others—that she was the selfsame Kate Parr she had ever been.

On the other hand, as Queen, she made use of her prerogatives to appoint family and friends to positions at court. Although the number of such positions was greater than the Boleyns or the Seymours had ever filled, I did not find this a threat, for the Parrs were, without exception, such an able and honourable tribe that they became their titles and honours well. There was never a question of loyalty or self-seeking. Kate's brother, William, became Warden of the Marches near the Border; her sister, Anne, became a lady of the royal bedchamber; her stepdaughter, Margaret Neville, was a maid of honour, along with a cousin, Lady Lane.

Kate herself indulged her personal preferences in only two ways, one harmless, one not so harmless. She insisted that fresh flowers must be within her sight at all times, and so her apartments were filled with them; she even hired the old gardener to grow early-spring and late-autumn varieties in his cottage, so that she should have flowers from early February through late November.

The other thing she wanted to bloom was "free discussion" in the "sight of the Lord." What that meant was that she slowly built up a religious *salon*. The slowness of the process appeared to me to contain its own checks and safeguards. Only members of court or their immediate families would be allowed to attend, and that by invitation only. No outlawed texts would be permitted, but only authorized Scriptural translations and my own *King's*

Primer. The intent was to deepen their own understanding of God's Word and their commitment to Christ.

Sometimes I felt that Kate had taken Christ as her true bridegroom. But no matter, no matter . . . she was everything I had wished for as a companion and helpmate, and devoted stepmother to my children. What more could I ask?

My mind was ever now at war. Domestic problems did not concern me, except insofar as they impinged upon our ability to eliminate the French menace once and for all.

Yes, here I must set it down; meet it is that I set it down. I had become convinced that my mission was to eliminate France—and her toadying, backstabbing ally, Scotland—as a threat to England. Then I could die happy.

Then I could die happy . . . always a silly phrase, I had thought, something one said in jest. After eating a large bowl of exquisitely ripe cherries: "Now I can die happy." To expire after a surfeit of pleasure, to extend the ecstasy into eternity . . .

A neutered France (and a harmless Scotland, its teeth drawn) was within my capability. Knowing that, it was my duty as a King and a father to pursue it.

Charles and I bickered over the armies, the routes, and our objectives, just as I had done with his father and grandfather thirty years earlier. This time, however, there was this difference: I knew what I intended to do, and no one could dissuade me from it. I would capture as much of the northern part of France as possible. Normandy and Picardy, those provinces directly across the Channel from England, were my target. Let Charles talk about Paris. If there were time and material remaining after my primary goal, then I would be pleased to push on to Paris. Why not?

My plans were to send an army of forty thousand to France. Simple to say; difficult to do.

Armies need generals to lead them. My two ablest generals, the Duke of Norfolk and Charles Brandon, the Duke of Suffolk, were old. The younger soldiers—Dudley, Howard, the Seymours—were as yet untried and untested in a major campaign. They did well enough with skirmishes and raids on the Scottish Border, but prolonged war with France was another matter. They must earn their experience in France.

Wars cost money. I had little. The monastic properties had not been the great enrichment I had foreseen. I had let them go too cheaply, eager to buy courtiers' goodwill and glue them into loyalty to my regime. It had worked: England would never return to Rome or to the overlordship of great families that my father had had to contend with. It had cost a great deal, but it was worth it. I had bought stability and peace at home. As a result, however, I would have to raise money directly from the people. Or else debase the coinage. Or both.

There was also the problem of my person. My physicians—Dr. Butts in particular—had advised me against going.

"I would not go so far as to *forbid* you," he said. "But your corpulence alone would make it difficult to sit a horse for any length of time."

"For me, or for the horse?" I scoffed. "If it is the horse you are concerned about, I have already had a great courser specially selected, capable of bearing the weight of three bulls. Three *armoured* bulls."

He did not smile. My little joke did not amuse him. "Horses can be replaced. Kings cannot. I truly believe—and you may ponder this as you will—that by going to war, by taking the field in person, you will without question shorten your life."

The words were too close, too immediate. Could he, then, foresee the end of my life from his vantage point? Was it truly so visible?

"Action rejuvenates me," I said stiffly. "I have been too long indoors, concerned with paper matters. Nothing to stir the heart, except in anguish. No honest physical exertion, which is clean and friendly to the body." He had a sceptical look on his face. "Friendly. I insist that it is friendly," I said. "War, that is."

"There is nothing friendly to your body now, Your Majesty," he said.

He knew nothing. Fool of a physician! Action cured me, quiet rotted me.

Charles, too, joined in the harassment. When he heard of my intention to lead my troops in person, he became alarmed and tried to dissuade me. He appealed to my sense of safety, and my age: two things guaranteed to infuriate me. I had never sought safety when honour was at stake, and scorned those who did. As for my age: I was but eight years older than Charles himself.

❧ ❧

Meanwhile, the preparations went forward. As soon as the Channel cleared and it was safe to sail, we would launch our army. All through the winter I was in a fever of preparation. I scarcely noticed Christmas, and so Kate was free to observe it as she preferred: as the birthday of Christ, not as a great public festivity. She and her circle of fellow devotees prayed and kept a vigil. I drew up lists of ordnance and checked the refitting of my warships *Mary Rose, Great Harry, and Matthew Gonnson.* We kept Christmas in our own ways, and praised God according to our own gifts.

Lent came, and Ash Wednesday meant that Easter was only forty days away. And after Easter, as soon as the prevailing winds from the Channel changed direction, it would begin.

At last it was come, the moment I had awaited without even being aware of it, all those years when I had wasted my substance on petty things: *War! War! Glory!* All else led to this. I had begun with war; what more could I ask but to end with it, to complete what I had left behind on the battlefield? The old man would retrieve the muddied standard the young one had dropped, under the restraining hands of Wolsey, Ferdinand, and Maximilian.

Charles had fought Francis in a desultory fashion for a season already. Nothing had been gained. I would not be so haphazard. Nay, I had targeted my initial goal: Boulogne, that city in Picardy, and a neighbour to Calais. Often I had seen it from Dover, or from Hastings, as I stood upon the beach. It glimmered and shone across the Channel, mocking me, saying, *I am as close as Calais.* It looked like a cloudbank, but it was a tough little walled city, daring me. If I captured Boulogne, I could unite it with Calais, make an English strip along the French coast. . . .

Kate was to be Queen-Regent. I had observed her over these months, and she was so trustworthy and competent there was no other logical choice for authority in my absence. The only possible source of trouble for her lay in Scotland. If they made a menace with all my warriors away, Kate would not have at her disposal a general-at-large, as Katherine had had in 1513, with Norfolk and Flodden Field. But Scotland had no King now, only an infant girl as ruler. Nay, there would be no war.

It was May, and I stood on the sands of Dover. Anchored nearby was my flagship, *Great Harry,* which I would board shortly. Already Norfolk and Suffolk had crossed the Channel with the main armies, and they were encamped and awaiting me, the supreme commander.

Kate and I faced one another, and her face was serious; beneath the shadows of her headdress I could see her frown.

"God be with you, Your Majesty," she said. "May He grant you victory." She sounded like an archbishop.

"May He grant you peace," I said, taking her chin in my hand. Her face was very close to mine. I could see the tiny beads of sweat across her forehead. I wanted to kiss her. I did not dare.

"Thank you, Your Majesty," she said, and in moving her mouth, she removed her face from my touch. "I wish you . . . to wear this," she said, putting a ring on my little finger. "And think of me whenever you do see it."

I looked down at it. It was a pretty little jasper ring, from her own hand. It was the first thing of a personal nature she had given me.

CXXIV

We fought well, and Boulogne was taken by siege in a relatively short time. We captured it alone, as Charles was uninterested in it. He had his needs; I had mine. As a youth I would have been unable to accept that, and would have spent fruitless days in trying first to persuade him, then to co-ordinate our armies. This was so much simpler.

I had split the English forces—a total of forty-two thousand men, the largest English invasion ever sent against the Continent—in two, placing half under Norfolk's command to besiege Montreuil, an important city near Calais, while I commanded the other half, directing the siege against Boulogne. I set up camp to the north of the town, by the sea. When I arose in the morning and looked out from my tent, I saw the raw, sparkling sea on one side and the falsely secure walls of Boulogne on the other. I smelt camp-food cooking, a thousand little tails of smoke, each signifying a cook and his skillet.

This time I was living simply. No special bed, no wardrobe-master, no gold plate, as I had required in my youthful campaign. Then I had thought that majesty needed trappings, that a King was not a King unless he appeared always in the proper raiment and slept in a kingly bed. Now I knew I was King even on the meanest cot, and I wished to sleep that way, so that I might experience what ordinary men did.

In my camp-tent I had the following: a cot, a bed-roll, a trunk, a collapsible table, a lantern. I was shorn of all my usual habiliments and felt like a child again, an honest, unencumbered child.

Arising in the morning was so simple. You opened your eyes, got out of bed, and pulled garments from the trunk—or put on yesterday's, draped over the trunk. You relieved yourself (behind the tent, in a trench), then walked over to the cooking area for your group of tents. A mess of dried beef, old bread, and beer were awaiting you. If neighbourhood raids had been successful in the night, then there would be eggs and chicken. The sun warmed your shoulders, and you felt glad. Or the wind whipped off the Channel, and you pulled a woollen shirt over your head and rejoiced in every fibre of that wool.

This stripped-down, simplified life was magically invigorating. It both freed my thoughts and intensified them. I directed the siege, supervising every aspect: where to position the guns, how much powder to give each bombard, which angle would result in the best hit. The walls held fast for a long time, and we were unable to damage them. Then we scored a direct hit on a weak spot and made a large breach. As the stones flew upward and debris rained down on us, I knew Boulogne was ours.

Three days later the city surrendered, and I entered it in triumph.

They shouted at me, waved branches, called me Alexander. Thirty years ago I had believed it—for they had shouted the same things at Tournai. Now I recognized the title for what it was: the tired old phrase used ritually for any conqueror. Charles had been called Alexander, and Francis, too. Everyone had been called Alexander. Yet I smiled and waved, as if I believed them. And perhaps for one instant I did. But only for one instant.

Boulogne was an ugly city. "Ungracious doghole," a member of the Privy Council later called it, and certainly it was much more appealing from without its walls than within. Within, it was the usual French mess of haphazard streets, dirt, and disorder, all suffused with what they mistakenly called "charm." Well, under English command it would straighten itself out. The bombardment had reduced large parts of it to rubble, so that rebuilding would be necessary. I would see to it that it was rebuilt in proper Anglican, not Gallic, fashion.

I remained in Boulogne a dozen days, tasting my triumph. Then, suddenly, the devils came back. I began to be afflicted as I had been at the St. Valentine's Day banquet. I saw red in people's eyes. Not all people's, just some people's. And again the most cursed part of the visitation was that I could not always remember what I had done, said, signed.

I hated it. Why had this come upon me now, *here?* I had thought it a temporary manifestation of sorrow after . . . I will not write her name. But now, in the clear skies of France, when I was content as I had seldom been . . .

Kate wrote sweet letters:

Although the discourse of time and account of days neither is long nor many of your Majesty's absence, yet want of your presence, so much beloved and desired of me, maketh me that I cannot quietly pleasure in any thing until I hear from your Majesty. The time therefore seemeth to me very long with a great desire to know how your Highness hath done since your departing hence; whose prosperity and health I prefer and desire more than mine own. And whereas I know your Majesty's absence as never without great respect of things most convenient and necessary, yet love and affection compelleth me to desire your presence.

And again, on the other hand, the same zeal and love forceth me also to be best content with that which is your will and pleasure. And thus love maketh me in all things to set apart mine own commodity and pleasure, and to embrace most joyfully his will and pleasure whom I love. God, the knower of secrets, can judge these words not to be only written with ink, but most truly impressed in the heart.

Lest I should be too tedious unto Your Majesty, I finish this my scribbled letter, committing you into the governance of the Lord, with long life and prosperous felicity here, and after this life to enjoy the kingdom of His elect.

From Greenwich.

By Your Majesty's humble, obedient, loving wife

and servant,

Katherine the Queen, K.P.

I was blessed in having such a wife. But she must not know I had been revisited by those demons she once had helped lay to rest. No, no . . .

Whilst I kept residence at Boulogne, alternately happier than I had ever been and more miserable, I received a blow that pushed me over into misery's camp. Charles had made a secret peace with Francis, at Crépy, even whilst I was besieging Boulogne. He had disengaged himself from the war and was now, if not my enemy, certainly not my ally. I could expect no help from him. I stood alone against France, Scotland, and even the Turk.

There would be no further aggression in France. Sick at heart, I must return to England and prepare to defend us against possible invasion. I left Brandon in charge and ordered him to hold Boulogne through the winter. I had no intention of surrendering Boulogne, because with it I had doubled the size of the Calais pale.

Kate was overjoyed to see me, and be relieved of the burden of Regentship. She had borne it well, but for shoulders unused to the mantle of sovereignty, it weighed heavily. I did not gallop joyously to lay the keys to the city of Bologne at her feet, as I had those of Tournai at the Princess of Aragon's. Instead I merely showed them to her and said, "This was a good siege campaign, even though the rest was a muddle, and riddled through with betrayal."

"Charles has not behaved honourably," she said. She always said less than she thought. A tactful woman. "Before your arrival, this reached me." She handed me a parchment, heavily studded with French seals.

Francis wished to send his ambassadors to discuss peace, as soon as possible.

"Rather to discuss the return of Boulogne," I snorted. "That I shall never do."

"Naturally not. But discussions will serve to make the time serve *you*."

I smiled. A politic woman. The Lady of Aragon would have talked only of honour. I looked at her hands, grasping other papers she wished me to see. They looked like talons. The fingers were long and bony, ending in curving claws. Some talons wore rings. Mary's little ruby ring was there, but the stone was replaced by a great globule of blood, swelling and about to drop from where it trembled and quivered. . . .

"My Lord, you need to rest. You must be exhausted from your journey. Tell me, the crossing . . . how was it? I have never been upon water. . . ." Deftly she led me by the hand, toward my withdrawing chamber. Her talons rested lightly on my sleeve. I hoped the claws would not damage the material.

I awoke in the late twilight. I had lain down completely dressed, even to my shoes, stretched out on my back. I felt fine, rested, even blissful. I must have been exhausted, I could see that now. That was what Dr. Butts had been concerned about, the sapping of my energy. Yet so enticingly was it sapped, with the excitements of war, I had been unaware of the toll it was taking on me. Now I would rest, and there would be no visitations from my demons.

Boulogne was a prize well worth an hallucination or two. The phantoms would fade, but Boulogne would remain.

The French ambassadors came straightway. I allowed them my gracious permission to cross the Channel in safe conduct, to receive them and hear their proposals. From the start it was hopeless, as my terms—that I keep Boulogne, and that the French cease their provocations in Scotland—were impossible for Francis to accede to. The envoys promptly retreated, and by late October they had made the hazardous Channel crossing and returned to Paris, where Francis intended to spend the winter in cosy ensconcement with his mistress Anne, Duchesse d'Estampes. So much for the French.

As for Charles, he and I sent a volley of accusations against one another. His preposterous claims were that (1) I had evaded the agreed-upon march on Paris; (2) I had used the siege of Boulogne (falsely prolonged) as an excuse to avoid a true mutual commitment; (3) I had agreed that Charles could act as "Arbiter of Europe," and that was what he was attempting now to do, and why he had made separate, private peace with Francis; and (4) I should hand Boulogne over to him in his capacity as arbiter, and he would award it as he saw fit.

I, in turn, had grievances against him, mighty ones. I flung them at him, but he failed to react, or even to refute them. I said that (1) Charles was guilty of treason toward me, that we had agreed that either of us might negotiate separately but neither should conclude a treaty without the other; (2) Charles was bound by treaty to act as my ally, not as a negotiator between France and England; (3) English merchants in Spain were being subjected to the Inquisition; and (4) Spanish troops had entered French employment.

But these were futile, rearguard gestures. The truth was that I had lost my ally and stood naked to whosoever wished to attack me. Even the Pope was proceeding to call his General Council, which would meet at long last in Trent, not in Mantua. I was beleaguered and abandoned, alone on my island kingdom.

Even that would not be so fearsome, if the island itself were only united. But half of it was given over to enemies, French sympathizers. I kept my Border troops busy harassing the Scots, making pitiful little raids into their territory. In one of those, my troops had accidentally desecrated the tombs of the Earl of Angus's ancestors in Melrose. This turned Angus against us—he who had been our stoutest ally—and he and Francis, as well as the infant Queen's council, began plotting for revenge. The form that revenge would take was a Franco-Scottish invasion. The plans were (my spies were able to ascertain this much) for France to send a force to Scotland via the northwest and another just to the Border in the east. Released from bothering with Charles, the rest of the French forces could attack England from the southeast by sea. Francis could raise an immense fleet if he so desired, and since the prevailing winds were from the south across the Channel, he could effect a landing in almost any season.

I was half sick with worry about these things, when Gardiner insisted on a special audience with me to raise alarmist concerns about the growth of the Protestant faction in our midst.

"In your absence this summer they have grown like pestilent weeds," he said. "But unlike weeds, the frost does not kill them. Nay, they hibernate in winter, meeting secretly in one another's homes, spreading their sedition, infecting others with it."

I was weary of this, weary of having to stamp out things, prune the kingdom, control sedition. Ungrateful, malicious dogs! There were always such, prowling and sniffing about the kingdom, lifting their legs and pissing on the rest.

"Let them but show their faces, I'll cut them off," I promised.

The Great Turk continued to correspond with me, for mysterious reasons of his own. He inquired after the crocodile—which was miraculously thriving, having been quartered near the hot springs in Bath, in the southwest part of the country—and offered to send me eunuchs for my court. He himself, he wrote, was luxuriating in winter retreat in Constantinople. How did we ever endure those northern winters, he asked? One January in Vienna had been enough for him. He sent me a Koran. A month later another long, chatty letter arrived. Suleiman was a friendly fellow.

I must confess I enjoyed his communications. They took me far away to a confusing but perfumed land, made me forget the chill-induced misery I grappled with daily in the palace.

CXXV

That I was miserable that winter, I readily record. Only Kate served as a comforter, and I thanked God every day that I had had the grace to make her my wife. For she was a source of grace to me. She was a quiet spot to which I could always return, who was never sharp or cross or unable to give.

The children revered her as well, and she brought out the very best in them. They were gathered together in the palace under her tutelage, and I felt, at last, that we were a family. Kate, mother of none of them, and "wife" (in the carnal sense) of no one, yet made us a family. That was *her* special grace.

Spring, 1545. The French invasion was even now being equipped, and it would certainly come before Midsummer's Day. To ready our coastal defence system, which stretched from Deal to Pendennis, guarding our entire southern flank, I had to extract more money, in the form of loans and taxes, from the people. I expected them to grumble and resist, but they did not.

WILL:

Hal's enemies expected them to rebel, and were sorely disappointed. The theory went like this: the English people were brutalized by a bloodthirsty, rapacious monarch who denied them the religion they desired (Catholic or Protestant, depending on the speaker); made them sign oaths which they detested; repressed them and robbed them. They but awaited the opportunity to rise up and free themselves from his oppressive yoke. But the people of England seemed to agree with "Old Harry" that the French were the enemies, the Pope a meddling foreigner, and the Scots traitors. King Hal was right in fighting them, and they would join him in sacrificing to protect their country. Had not the King gone in person to fight? Had he not spent the winter inspecting and fortifying his southern coastal defences? Did he not intend to captain a warship against the Frenchies? Could his countrymen offer less? Gold, jewels, coin, even touching personal possessions like crosses from Jerusalem, ivory combs, and wedding rings arrived every day at Whitehall. Far from revolting against the "tyrant," the people supported him in his hour of extremity.

HENRY VIII:

I stood prepared for war, to the best of my ability. In the south of England, I had almost a hundred thousand men in arms, divided under three commands: one in Kent under the Duke of Suffolk; one in Essex under the Duke of Norfolk; and one in the west under the Earl of Arundel. My fleet of over one hundred ships lay anchored near the Solent.

In the North, against Scotland, Edward Seymour commanded an army poised right beside the Borders. And standing offshore, the Lord Admiral John Dudley was at sea with twelve thousand men, waiting to grapple with the enemy.

At Boulogne, which the French had vowed to recapture, I had put Henry Howard in charge, to fill the position vacated by Brandon. I prayed that when the time came, his valour would not melt into hotheadedness and bravado.

July 18. It was just after the second anniversary of my marriage, and I had prepared a special celebration for Kate. We would dine aboard *Great Harry*, my flagship, which was waiting in the Solent, that channel between the Isle of Wight and Portsmouth, on our south coast.

Great Harry had gone through many refurbishings and refittings since her launching in 1514. At the time she was built, navies were but "armies at sea" . . . floating platforms carrying soldiers to grapple with enemy soldiers at sea. But now ships were converted into fortresses, stocked with rows of cannon, and the job of sailors was not to engage in hand-to-hand combat with enemy sailors, but to man the killer guns and destroy entire ships. *Great Harry,* although a bit clumsy and old-fashioned in her overall design, had adapted herself well to the renovations, which pleased me. I did not wish to scrap her, as others had urged. Her sister ship, *Mary Rose,* had likewise made the transition and was ready to do battle, as soon as the French were sighted. Our information was that Francis had bade his fleet of two hundred thirty-five ships adieu near Rouen some days ago.

Two hundred thirty-five ships . . . and we but one hundred. Truly, the hour of testing had come.

Nonetheless I was proud of my forces, proud of my fleet, in a way one can be only when one has offered one's best. We had poured every sacrifice into our defence and readiness for war; we had stinted nothing. Now God would have to make up the rest.

Lamps were being lighted in the July twilight when Kate and I arrived at the pier to board *Great Harry.* Kate had dressed in what she laughingly described as her most nautical costume, and I was touched by her efforts to join in the spirit of the occasion.

Stepping on board, I felt a great surge of near-carnal love for my flagship. The smell of the linseed oil which had been used to rub down the seasoned wood; the almost voluptuous creaking of the stout rigging and hemp ropes; the stirrings and rustlings of the bleached linen sails, gathered tidily in their bindings: what a ship was she! She and I had grown and changed together, and in her I felt a summary of myself. . . .

"Your Grace." The captain, Viscount Lisle, Lord Dudley, bowed to us. I acknowledged him. But for this moment I did not wish to speak of common things. The sky was half on fire with the reflection of the setting sun. I went to the rail and looked out to sea, where the waters were flat and untroubled, and there was no wind. At this moment England seemed inviolate, protected by all the elements.

Kate stood beside me. The calm I felt in my person, a sort of afterglow like the departed sun, was crowned in her presence.

"Your Majesties!" A raucous voice sounded behind us. I turned to see Tom Seymour, bending one knee, his plumed hat held at an angle. His uncovered hair glowed, reflecting the red sky.

"Thomas." I held out my hand, indicating that he should rise. "We are pleased that you could join us." I used the royal *we.* The truth was that I never consulted Kate about these things. She was usually amenable to guests; therefore I was acutely aware, by her quick stiffening, that she did not wish Thomas Seymour to be present at this private occasion.

"And I am deeply grateful that you should invite me." He sauntered over to us and took his place at the rail, letting his muscular arms hang over the side. "Are you trying to sight the French?" he said. "They are coming from the south, if they come at all. Such poor sailors!" He shook his head, and all that mane of hair swayed.

"We talk not of the French," said Kate. "We are here to celebrate a private matter, and to inspect the King's flagship."

"Peace be unto you," said an old, familiar voice. Brandon was aboard. I turned to see him, standing bearlike on the oiled deck.

"And unto you." I held out my hands. "We sound like bishops." I laughed.

"Not quite," he said. "We are not discussing property."

We embraced on the deck. "How is your army?" I whispered, for Kate would have no politics to spoil this evening.

"Well," he said. "We are at the ready in Kent to defend England against whatever comes our way. I think they will most likely land there."

"If they do, you know when to light the signal fires?" I had ordered a system of beacon fires to be laid all across the entire southern coast of England, the first torch to be touched as soon as a Frenchman was spotted.

"Aye. There's a great heap near my encampment, and willing torch-bearers to spread the flame."

I was loth to release him. "Think you all of this shall come to pass? Will we truly be invaded, for the first time in four hundred years?"

"I fear so," he said. "The invasion fleet is on its way."

"Invasions fail," I said. I could not hold myself apart from the others much longer.

"If God is willing," he replied.

We were being rude, clinging to each other and whispering secrets. I turned and saw the fair table set up on the deck, and gestured toward Kate and Tom Seymour, who were standing ill-at-ease against the rail where I had left them. I broke from Brandon's embrace and gestured toward the table. "Come."

It was a well-set table, with places for four, laid with gold plate. But the goblets were not proper goblets at all; rather they were wide-bottomed vessels that did not spill when the ship swayed. The decanter of wine was shaped likewise, and was called among glassblowers a "captain's decanter." We must be properly nautical on the King's flagship.

We seated ourselves, Kate and I at either end of the tiny table. "Welcome," I said, raising my glass. "On the eve of our final battle with France, I cherish your friendships."

They all drank. "It is also, by a singular coincidence, the week of my wedding anniversary."

We all drank once again. "I have had two years of great happiness. I know the Seymours rejoice with me, and therefore I wished you, Tom, to share in our celebration. It has been a long, lonely path since your sister's death. Would that Edward could be present as well." I meant my son.

"But he's too busy defending the northern borders with his twelve thousand men," snapped Tom. He meant his brother.

I put down my glass.

"I mean his appointment to command the army of the North," continued Tom. "After his impressive showing in France, it is to be expected he'd be put in some high position."

"He is an able, trustworthy, and brave commander," I said. "England can make use of such. We have had the example of men like Brandon here, a soldier all his life, and of great service to me. Soldiers such as he will likely die in a camp-bed at an advanced age." I clinked my bulbous glass against Brandon's.

"But what of Henry Howard, Earl of Surrey? He's a general's son, playing at being a soldier. He behaved like a moonstruck youth at Boulogne, rushing out and leading raids to no purpose. Near got himself killed. He's a lunatic poet. Why have you left *him* in command of the Boulogne garrison?"

Tom's eyes . . . they were faintly red. No, it was but the sunset's glow. My imagination.

"Because I believe him to be the best man for the task," I said. "Despite his nature. He's wild, he needs a proper channel for his action. War will shape him, calm him."

"Fah." Tom hated Henry Howard, as the new always hates the old that lords itself above all. Several years ago the Duke had attempted to arrange marriage alliances between the families. Tom was to marry Mary Howard, Henry's sister and the widow of my Henry Fitzroy. Henry Howard had put a stop to it on the grounds of the "demeaning" of his family blood. The Seymours had never forgiven or forgotten the slight. If they were good enough to marry with a Tudor king, why not with a Howard lord? But the Howards considered themselves above the Tudors. . . .

"You overspeak yourself," I reprimanded him. "And do insult my hospitality. It is not they whom I have invited to be present on my flagship, but you. Pray attend myself and my guests at table, not absent rivals."

He started, opened his mouth, and then shut it.

"Yes, I said rivals. You envy them, and are filled with malice and rancour. You need not be; you have your own gifts, which they have not."

"And what are they?" He shrugged. "They win me no glory."

The gift of attracting women, I thought. Not men, but women. Even Elizabeth had shown herself susceptible to his charm, which puzzled me. "Your immense energy," I said. "You are like a thousand suns."

Like all shallow men thrown a sop of flattery, he smiled, took the bait to his den, and subsided.

A slight breeze stirred, and we felt it on our cheeks. It was not a soft caress, but a warning. *I fill the French sails,* it whispered. I shivered and looked out at the horizon.

The master-cook brought out the fanciful dessert: a great pastry, in layers, replicating *Great Harry*. Tiny pennants flew from her four masts, and exact miniatures of cannon were mounted on her main deck and gun deck. As the ship was placed before me, two of the cannon "fired," making a snap and a puff of smoke.

"A salute for each of our years of marriage," I said to Kate.

She burst into rare laughter. "O Henry!"

That address between us was forbidden in public. I frowned; Seymour frowned, Brandon frowned. Seymour, indeed, looked angry.

"Nay, gentle wife," I reproved her smilingly. "That is our private talk." Then I changed the subject. "Yet I know we shall look back upon this date as marking a great anniversary for our realm. We stand on the brink of a great battle," I said. "May we prevail, with honour!" I raised my fresh-filled glass.

They solemnly drank. Each of us prayed. For it was a fearful hour for England.

Faces were lit only by the candles set on the table. All around it was now dark, except for the lanterns set up on deck; I permitted no open flames on board ship.

"I must to my post," said Brandon. "I have a far ride to Kent."

"It will be a long night," I said. "My thoughts go with you."

He grasped my hand. "To be alive is to fight the French," he laughed. "Remember, Your Grace, how we planned it all, at Sheen?"

Sheen. Vanished palace. Vanished youths. "Old men fight boys' battles. Well, good night, Charles." I heard his heavy footfalls crossing the gangplank.

"I must take my post as well." Tom commanded *Peter Pomegranate,* a fine, new-built ship. He was much more a seaman than a soldier.

"You are anchored one of the farthest out," I said. "You will see the French first. Set double watches."

"They won't approach in darkness," he said cockily.

"There will be instruments that enable men to come right alongside in darkness, someday," I said. "Perhaps that day is now."

"Not for a thousand years. The stars can tell a captain where he's located on a map, but not what lurks beneath his hull. No, there's no way to read rocks by the stars. And it's rocks—"

"Tom," I said. "Keep watch in the night. That is a royal command."

"Aye." He bowed, took Kate's hand. "I will obey all His Majesty's commands. Bless you in your marriage; I pray daily for you."

His distinctive step, higher and more prancing than Brandon's, sounded on the gangplank.

"I think he has become light-witted," murmured Kate.

"I think he has become dangerous," I said. "Ambitious, cankered, eaten up with envy—dangerous."

"Nay, Your Grace!" Her voice rose. "He does not—does not deserve such weight. He is too insubstantial ever to amount to anything dangerous."

"Perhaps," I said. "But I will watch him. I like him not. I regret that I invited him to join us."

"I do not. It was a kind thing to do, and you are ever kind." She put her arm about my waist, boldly. She had never done this before. "So kind, I think that I have never shown you how my heart warms to your great love." She was pressed up against me, resting her face on my chest. I bent to kiss her, and she did not pull away; indeed, she returned the kiss, deeply.

There was a royal chamber below decks, where I had quartered on my passing to Calais. It was large, well appointed, and completely private. It was held in readiness for me at all times, and afforded a blissful retreat. "Kate—" I murmured, as I made my way toward the steps leading below, with her clinging to me. "Kate, wife—"

In that wooden chamber, well belowdecks, with its stout door and no window at all save a round porthole, Kate became my wife at last. I was gentle with her and she with me, and as it was a prize I had thought never to win, I received it with awe and gratitude and wonderment. I can say no more; to do so is to desecrate it. I will not insult her body by describing it, nor our actions by narrating them.

CXXVI

It was dawn now, and I stood alone at the rail of the ship. I had come out here on deck, in that darkest time of night, to wait for sunrise.

There was a holiness about "watching in the night." The early monks had known this when they set their first worship hour at midnight. And indeed it did possess its own benediction. I prayed as I stood there, prayed for England, and it seemed my prayers might be better heard for the sky being hushed and empty.

I prayed that we would withstand this assault, the largest ever launched against England. It was my fault that this had come to pass; it was my mishandling of our affairs with France. I had done the worst thing one can do in hunting: I had injured the beast without killing him, thereby maddening him, driving him to fight for revenge.

I had done the same with Scotland, I saw that now. "It was not the marriage so much as the wooing," a Scots noble had protested. I had behaved stupidly and rashly in Scotland; so anxious was I to achieve the union almost within my grasp that I had let my impatience gain the upper hand, had insulted and bullied them until they had no choice but to turn to France.

Oh, I had been a fool! But must England pay the price for it?

Let it fall on my shoulders, I prayed. Spare the realm.

But I knew in my heart that I *was* the realm, and the brunt of my shortsightedness and whatever ineptitude still remained in me after all these years must be paid by common Kentish soldiers, by the sailors on these hundred-odd vessels assembled here in the bay.

My hours with Kate were forgotten as I stood there in agony. With her I had been a man, but in this battle and invasion I was a king; and as a king I bore the guilt of having brought my country to this pass. *Deliver us, O Lord, from the hands of our enemies.*

Now the sky was growing light, and I could see the horizon, a faint flat line with nothing on it. The French were not yet in sight. The wind always dropped at sunrise and sunset, and soon would pick up. I knew today was the day we could expect them. I knew it would be today.

The sailors changed watch, traditionally, at four o'clock. Now the morning watchman came out on deck, and I heard him speaking to his fellow, who had stood from midnight until four. They both sounded sleepy.

The sun came up over the eastern rim of the horizon, over land, and struck the tallest gathered sails, touching their puckers and pouches. Men were stirring. I smelt coals being lighted in the galley. My private hour was gone, and I was given back into the hands of the world.

A breakfast was served to Kate and me, and our captain and first mate, on the selfsame table as the night before. This time the table was spread with brownish homespun cloth and pewter plates, and we were surrounded by shouting men. We ate "sailors' fare"—hardtack and salted meat and heated ale—so we could see what provisions our men subsisted on. They were dismal. The hardtack almost broke my front teeth.

" 'Tis said if one rolls off a table, it will kill anyone who might be sitting beneath," the server said, a skinny lad of about sixteen. He laughed in a neighing way.

"The salted meat will make us thirsty in two hours," said Kate. "What do you do upon the high seas to combat that, since you cannot drink sea water? If you must drink on account of your food, does that not add problems in your provisioning? Should you not carry something else?"

"Meat untreated with salt cannot keep," said the first mate. "Carrying live meat in the form of chickens and cattle is even more of a problem than carrying extra barrels of water."

"Why carry meat at all?"

"The sailors cannot work without it. They subsist on bread well enough for a while, but when it comes to doing any strenuous tasks"—he shrugged—"they have no strength on just bread."

"Man does not live by bread alone," bellowed the captain, thinking himself witty.

"Evidently," replied Kate, in her most queenly manner. Those who quoted Scripture to make jokes irritated her.

"So the sailors live on just this?" I asked. It was quite remarkable.

"On long voyages, yes. Pity the Spaniards on those ships to New Spain. It takes weeks to get there, and when they do, half the crews are dead," said the captain. "We are all thankful that Your Majesty, in his wisdom, has shown no interest in this so-called New World."

The New World, with its painted savages and stone cities, had never seemed worth the trouble to me.

"It is astonishing that any vessel survives that voyage," I said. "It seems to me—"

Suddenly an immense boom sounded, followed by a thudding splash in the harbour waters. The ship rocked violently, and the food spilled off the table. The hardtack indeed hit the deck like rocks.

I leapt up, rushed to the rail. The French! French sails filled the line of horizon; sails spaced out like nails hammered at regular intervals into a great board. And coming toward us was a great galleon warship; it was she who had fired the opening shot into the harbour, mockingly. Even while I watched, another round was fired. The war had begun.

I turned to the captain. "I must to shore, to command the land forces," I said. "May God grant you victory." Another boom, and another wave rocked us, this one so fierce that I lost my balance and fell against the captain.

"As soon as we have crossed the gangplank," I said, "cast off to do battle."

I grabbed Kate's hand, and we hurried to shore.

Horrified, I watched as *Great Harry* set sail. It was a long process, and all this time the French were closing in, hoping to sink the English flagship while she slumbered, tied up. What a victory for them that would be! I scarcely breathed—as if not breathing would hold back the time—as my ship cast off, neatly evading the French, who almost ran aground in pursuing her.

Meanwhile, the other galleys were approaching. My navy must meet them, although outnumbered almost two to one.

"We must withdraw to Southsea Castle," I told Kate. I had not meant for her to be present at the actual fighting. But she seemed to have stomach for it—even lively interest. "There I can oversee the battle, and command the forces on land as well. All messengers will be seeking me there." What was happening in Kent, and Sussex? As we scrambled up the hill to the castle, I saw no line of signal fires. But it would take several hours for them to flare all the way across the southern coast.

As I entered the main gate, puffing and panting (for such exertion was almost beyond me now, and added to that, the terror and excitement), I heard the sound of more cannon echoing in the harbour below. I turned to see the host of French galleys approaching, like a great encircling arm, but one that came not with love. My own ships were as yet floundering about, the winds against them. All about them the sea was pockmarked with enemy cannonfire.

I crossed into the inner ward of the castle, and behind me the new portcullis clicked into place. Newly designed levers had been used, and the device slid elegantly into its slots. Even in this hour of extremis, I could appreciate the beauty and power of using the very finest in material, in castles and military hardware as well as in personal adornments. It paid to use the best, to demand it, regardless of the groans of little men, shortsighted, petty "econo-mizers"—

Of what was I thinking? Of portcullis levers, when my country was being attacked! Was this, in itself, not madness? *The old mad King* . . . no, not I. Not I.

From the keep, high and protected, I looked down on the harbour now. The size of the French fleet was staggering. It seemed to expand and fill all the seas, like poppies in a summer field. Against them, cupped in the Solent, was the valiant English fleet.

Take sail, take sail! I commanded them; my mind shrieked it. *Wind, arise!* But their sails fluttered, empty, the inconstant wind against them. Only the most expert seaman could manuever a ship under those conditions.

Mary Rose now moved; her captain had been able to use the antagonistic wind to his own advantage, and the sails caught the waffling breeze and began to pull the ship around.

How gallantly she rode! I felt the same surge of possessive pride as I had about the fortification I had just passed through, only much stronger; I had known this ship a long time, and she was named for my sister.

She was a pretty toy, as war toys always are. As she bobbed on the water, her green-and-white pennons jerked and snapped, and I could see the red of her heraldic flags, including that of the Vice-Admiral, flying from her topgal-lant masts. Her rows of cannon glinted from their crouching places within her belly. She looked almost like the pastry fantasy we had eaten the night before. On her I had hedged my bets, and ordered both soldiers and sailors aboard, to deal with any battle contingency. She was a pastry that had cost my treasury a heap of gold.

I turned and saw my militia leaders approaching, the men under my command here. I would have to lead them out against the French, should the enemy effect a landing. They hailed me, coming up beside me and laying their helmets on the stone wall. Together we watched the engagement below.

The French were bunched at the wide entrance to the Solent. The variable wind hampered them as well. But they were able to send forth oared galleys, small, maneuverable vessels, to harass our great men-of-war. These were small, light ships peculiar to the Mediterranean; and as such, I had deemed them unsuitable for the waters near England. Now we would see if they were of much use to the French, who had elected to retain them in their navy.

Like hunting dogs surrounding their quarry, the galleys darted and feinted with *Great Harry,* which was easing slowly toward the Channel entrance. The French galleys meant, of course, to draw our entire fleet out into open sea, to tease us into rushing out into the ocean, where their superior numbers could destroy us. We, on the other hand, hoped to entice them into the Solent, where our knowledge of local currents and hidden shoals would put them at a disadvantage, and where we could fire upon them from Southsea Castle.

Now *Mary Rose* must tack, must abandon the delicately angled course she pursued, if she hoped to make the open sea. Our strategy was that our premier warships would be drawn out, but only they—*Mary Rose* and *Great Harry*. The lesser warships, *Soverign, Peter Pomegranate, Matthew Gonnson,* and *Regent,* would hold back.

Mary Carew, wife of the Vice-Admiral on board *Mary Rose,* came hurrying over to us, clutching her headdress. It was wishful thinking, as there was little wind, and therein lay her husband's problem.

"O sweet Jesu, bless them!" she cried. She heaved herself up against the stone wall, scraping her arms raw.

"Aye. May He," I said.

"Oh! Oh! Oh!" She pressed herself up against the stones, half-climbing over, like a naughty child. Yet her face was strained, and red drops of blood were appearing, evenly spaced, along her lower lip where she had bitten it. "No, no!" She quivered and groaned.

"Madam," I said, " 'Tis said that it brings ill fortune upon a fighting vessel for its relatives to look upon it whilst under sail. Perhaps you should—"

"Aaaaah!" She gave a choking noise and began clutching at her throat with one hand, whilst pointing hysterically with the other. She *was* tedious; no wonder women were not permitted on board ships. Annoyed, I turned away from her and looked for *Mary Rose* myself.

She was . . . not there. She was gone, sinking. Even as I watched, she turned on her starboard side and slid out of sight beneath the grey waters of the Solent, whilst the most pitiable, hideous cries rose from below decks. Rose—and were drowned. The high-pitched shrieking, which carried across the water like the death-squeaks of rats, turned into a grotesque gurgle, as the entire ship slid as neatly under the water as my portcullis had into its housing. Only two masts remained above water, and frantic men clung to them, gesturing and crying.

Mary Rose was lost; lost in a moment.

"What happened?" I cried. I had had my head turned toward Mary Carew, had been conversing with her. Yet that had been scarcely two minutes.

"The ship—listed," said Kate. "It seemed to be pushed over. The balance was bad; it tipped on the instant—"

"But by *what?*" The wind had been very light.

"It seems—by *itself,*" she said, confused. "I could see nothing that would have pushed it thus. It was almost like a drunken man, losing his balance. A drunken man falls, not for that he is pushed, but because he is drunk. Thus seemed it with the ship."

"A ship does not founder upon nothing!"

"This ship did," she insisted.

"God! God! God!" screamed Mary Carew, seeming to hear her husband's cries from the lost ship.

"He is safe," I assured her. "Only those belowdecks will have—will have—" I could not finish. "Those who could jump clear are swimming. I see them now. Rescue boats will pick them up."

"George cannot swim!" she cried. "He hated water, hated being in it—"

I reached out to hold her, as now I could say nothing to comfort her. Unless the Vice-Admiral were one of the men clinging to the masts, he was lost, if he truly could not swim. Already there were dots surrounding the site of the wreck. Dead men? Or swimmers?

Hysterical, she tried to fling herself over the wall. I pulled her back, and she began to beat on me, pulling at my clothes and clawing at my face.

"Why should you live?" she shrieked. "Why should he"—she pointed at the militia-captain—"and she"—she gestured at Kate—"and even *he*"—she threw a pebble at a lazy circling gull—"and my George not?"

I gestured to the guards. "Take her away. She is a danger to herself. Confine her."

Two huge Hampshiremen encircled her and led her away, making a cage of their arms.

I, too, wished to shriek and cry. *Mary Rose,* with six hundred men, lost. And for no reason, no apparent reason, save—Divine will. God's finger had reached out and touched my pride, my beautiful ship, and sunk her. As punishment? As warning?

The way Kate laid her fingers on my arm, I knew she was thinking the same thing. The masts of the ship pointed at me like the handwriting on Belshazzar's wall. But what did it say? I could not read it clear. O, I was weary of these hateful, muffled messages from Him. . . .

Great Harry swung about, executing her turn perfectly. The fault lay not in the lack of wind, then, or in the captain's skill, but in the very design of *Mary Rose.* But what? She had proved seaworthy for thirty years. What had happened to her now? Truly it *was* the handwriting. . . .

The nettlesome French galleys provoked *Great Harry,* emboldened by the shocking sinking of the man-of-war *Mary Rose.* Now our English row-barges, a counterpart to their galleys, streamed out to engage them. I had thought row-barges, combining both sail and oars, to be transitional vessels that we soon would not need. But here they carried the day, and did what the great warships could not: chased the French away. Now the French fleet lay outside our Solent waters, waiting to pounce.

Night fell, and the action ceased. Our vessels were anchored in the Solent, and the French were around the spit, invisible. The rescue boats had saved thirty-five men from *Mary Rose,* and they had all been on the open top deck, and swept directly into the sea. They were for the most part seamen, un-schooled, superstitious, and hard—unable to describe what had happened to them or their ship. They were of no help at all in reconstructing the tragedy. Sir Gawen Carew, George's uncle, aboard *Matthew Gonnson,* had passed near *Mary Rose* just as she had begun to tack; he claimed that George had cried out, "I have the sort of knaves I cannot rule!" Had they mutinied?

Thirty-five out of six hundred. I sat in my quarters in the granite bowels of Southsea Castle and pondered that fact. Kate was with me, sitting glumly at my side, tracing meaningless patterns with my walking stave on the floor.

"They will attempt a landing during the early hours of dawn," I said. "On the Isle of Wight. Their plans are to establish a camp there, and then take Portsmouth—in reprisal for Boulogne."

"How do you know this?" she asked.

It was obvious. "As an old soldier, I know."

"And you must lead the militia here of twenty-five thousand men, when they land?"

"Yes."

"They have landed no other place?"

"No." The signal fires had not been lighted. The French were, thus far, confined to our area.

"So they concentrate their fury upon you?"

"Yes." Good that it should be so. I worried about Boulogne. Had they left it alone? Or were they harrying it as well? If they did, could Henry Howard and his garrison hold it?

"The ship—" she began, hesitantly.

"Was a great loss," I finished. I did not wish to discuss it, even with her.

Dawn, at five o'clock. I had barely slept. The French were ashore on the isle; I could feel it. I went up to the highest point of the keep to try to spy out the landings. But the island was too big, and if they had effected a landing, it was on the far side, invisible to me.

"Light the signal fires," I ordered a soldier in the warming room. "We have certainly been attacked here, and the coastal defences must be alerted."

If the French took the Isle of Wight, then they would have a secure base from which to mount other attacks. They could be victualed from France as easily as I could victual Boulogne from England. Better, in fact. For the isle was protected by a natural moat of its own, and could serve as a fortified French enclave. The isle was now weakly defended. What was happening there?

The French had indeed made a landing, as we later were told. They had come ashore, shouting and proclaiming the land as Francis's, planting a French flag, and dancing around it with glee. Then they went on a looting and pillaging rampage, in the time-honoured way for soldiers to reward themselves. Unfortunately for them, the isle had few inhabitants to plunder and terrify. Disappointed, they returned to their boats. There was no need for me to lead a militia. The French had departed before I even received official word that they were there.

Where were they now? Still lying in wait outside the harbour? I would leave them there, and leave my fleet, too. That would effectively block their way into Portsmouth.

"Come, Kate, Queen, we must leave this place," I ordered my wife. Mary Carew had spent the night weeping and flailing, at the news that her husband had not been one of the thirty-five saved. I sent word that she was to return to London with me, and be placed under Dr. Butts's care. "We must leave this place of death." Yes, Southsea Castle had become that to me, even though no actual deaths had taken place within its walls.

The air was hot and humid. Sticky salt breezes were stirring, as we made our way out across the causeway and then onto the rutted path called London Road, but only because it led to London. It was certainly not a road. We were strung out along it like pilgrims en route to Canterbury in the olden days, picking their way along dirt paths.

CXXVII

The day was sullen, hot. My mind was entirely occupied by thoughts of the French, and the loss of *Mary Rose*. I did not see the pretty climbing roses on the fences we passed (yet, if I did not see them, how can I here recount them?), nor did I notice the bouncing curls of the village children. I was anxious to know what had happened elsewhere along the coast, and whether the French had been able to effect a landing anywhere.

By late afternoon we were near Basingstoke, and I decided to rest there. I had been up since dawn, and the night before I had scarcely slept at all. Whom could we quarter with? My own Lord Chamberlain, William Sandys, had built a house just north of Basingstoke; I remembered that now. He had built it in the shape of an H, "to honour Your Majesty" he had said, but I knew it was only because that design allowed for the new features he wished to include, such as the long gallery and many windows.

But Sandys had died recently, and the house had come into other hands—I knew not whose. As King, I had the right to quarter in any man's house; yet I preferred to know my host.

I passed the church in the village, a typical parish building dating from the time of Henry II. I certainly would not call upon the priest there to house us. He would insist on doctrinal discussions in exchange for his hospitality, and I had no desire for that.

Outside Basingstoke I found Sandys's house—"The Vynes," a sign announced at its entrance. I looked down its long entranceway, bordered on each side by young lime trees. Someday they would grow giant and sheltering, but for now they were as yet tender and easily felled. They bespoke newness, yet they had already outlived their planter.

Our little party came down the mile-long avenue of struggling trees, and faced the great mansion. It was all of red brick, clean-edged and new. It was beautiful; beautiful as most of my palaces never were, for they were so large, or else built by other men. . . .

Kate pulled up beside me. "Sandys has built a magnificent home." She paused. "Pity he could not live to see this moment." I must have made a depreciating gesture, for she continued, "The moment his sovereign came to visit. Think you not the 'H' was intended for this? Think you not that whatever chamber you lodge in tonight will be designated the King's Chamber, and kept as a shrine forevermore?"

She looked so fierce! "Ah, Kate—"

"Can you not understand?" She sounded angry. "You bring the people joy. They will build an entire house on the hope that someday you might see it, visit it!"

She spoke true. Yet I had seldom allowed myself to consider it enough, to luxuriate in my subjects who revered me so. Instead, I had addressed myself to foreign potentates and powers: Francis, Charles, the Pope. They would never honour or keep a single thing that I had done.

We halted at the end of the brave tree-bordered drive. I sent a groom to the door to announce our presence. It opened; then the groom was left to wait for a quarter-hour whilst confusion erupted within.

At length a man appeared, squinting his eyes as if he beheld an eclipse. "Your Majesty," he stammered. "I am but a merchant, a poor unworthy servant—forgive me, but I cannot—"

"Cannot offer your King a night's shelter?" I kept my voice low and gentle. "That is all I ask. My Queen and I are weary, and would break our desperate journey en route to London. We ask only for a bed, and two small meals. Our party is small"—I indicated our few companions—"and if they cannot comfortably lodge here, they can find a place in the village."

"Nay, nay—" He jumped about and waved his arms. "There is space aplenty here."

"Poor man," whispered Kate. "Your royal presence has quite unstrung him."

"My Lord Chamberlain Sandys built this house," I said. "Oft he begged me to come and lodge with him, but I was never able. Consider this a debt, then, that I pay to my loyal servant; one that I neglected and left too late. 'Tis a personal matter between us; it concerns you not."

He bowed nervously. I knew what he was trying to say. Unexpected events try us most. I put my fingers to my lips. "We do what we can. And if we do that, then that is acceptable to Almighty God." And to anyone else, I added silently. For my part, the greatest favour he could do me was to provide me with silence and a bed.

"Aye. Aye." He kept bowing.

The man was Geoffrey Hornbuckle, and he was a merchant. He dealt in importing steel pins, in exchange for furs; and he had known William Sandys since babyhood. The entire village had been proud when Sandys went to make his fortune at Court; although Hornbuckle had actually made more of a fortune by staying in Basingstoke. No matter, though, to the common mind: fortunes made at court were always magical, and better than those made at home. Sandys's house was the envy of the village. And then, suddenly, the house was for sale, and Sandys entombed in the local church. Hornbuckle had bought the property, feeling both obligation and guilt. His friend was dead; how could he assume his property, walk in his shoes? Yet letting another do so seemed more of a betrayal. At last, reluctantly, he had let himself take possession of the property, although even now he felt himself to be but a caretaker, a keeper of a memory.

"You are not young," I said bluntly. "You may not have the luxury of preferring Sandys's memory, in exclusion of your own living, for years. This is your house now. You must believe that."

He laughed—always a sign someone does not wish to listen. "Would you care to see the chapel? There is dazzling stained glass . . . it honours the Tudors. . . ."

I smiled, and gestured—also a sign of deep disinterest. "The light is fading," I said, "and we are weary. I think I would prefer to rest. Would you ask your steward to send us some refreshments? Light fare. Then we would sleep."

He looked disappointed. Now that he had accustomed himself to our presence, he wished us to act royal and give our blessings to his manor.

We were quartered in a fine chamber on the second floor. I was surprised to see my own arms on the ceiling. Sandys had had them mounted there as a mark of loyalty.

But I was truly too weary, and heartsick, to care about The Vynes. My *Mary Rose* had been sunk (by inhuman hands), and my realm was under attack. God seemed to be showing His angry face toward me once again. And this time I was truly ignorant of where and how I had offended. Exhausted and confounded, I crawled into the great carved bed and fell instantly asleep, even though it was still twilight outside.

The chamber faced north, and so there was no morning sun. Yet I awakened early, agitated and uneasy. Kate yet slept peacefully beside me (for the merchant had no knowledge that we kept separate beds, nor did I feel it politic to so inform him).

I left the bed and stood for some moments before the window. The sun was just now touching the tops of the young lime trees, making the whole avenue glow green. So this was what Sandys had served at court for, and had hoped to return to. . . . Yes, it was peaceful, and a good place for a man.

There were hoofbeats. Someone was riding along that avenue, riding fast. It was no local person intent on informing the squire that he was to attend guildhall; it was someone who searched for the King, and had found him, by his standard planted outside The Vynes.

I pulled on my furred robe; I knew it would be needed. Slipping out of the chamber without disturbing Kate, I made my way down to the entrance porch. The messenger had to make his way past the household guardsman, but his flushed, travel-stained face showed that his business was urgent.

"Your Majesty." He saw past the guard to where I was standing on the stair landing. "I was to deliver this directly into your hands." He clutched a piece of parchment, a field dispatch. The French had landed in Kent. I knew it.

"Our thanks." I took the paper from him. How many enemy, and had they taken a beachhead?

> It grieves me to inform you that yester-even, the Duke of Suffolk, having fallen ill to an ague, died at eleven of the clock. We await your instructions as to the burial of the Duke, for we know he was accounted precious to you.

It was signed by Nicholas St. John, physician of the Kentish army.

I stared at it. The words seemed to shimmer. Brandon, dead?

"He must be royally buried," I said slowly. "Tell them, in Kent, to prepare him for this. If there are no funds, charge them to the Royal Privy Purse. I will—I will"—God, I had not thought of this, had never considered it—"have him interred at Windsor, near my Queen Jane, unless he has family vaults elsewhere that he prefers."

"No, Your Majesty. He expressed nothing of the sort. Death took him unawares."

Does anyone actually meet death with a candle and a book of verses?

"And Kent?" I had to ask. "Have you been attacked?"

"Nay. All is quiet. We sighted your signal fire this morning."

"There has been a naval attack and a landing at the Isle of Wight. They wished to take Portsmouth, but were unable. Where they are now, I know not." All the while I spoke, a great presence was growing in my breast, a black nothingness.

"Be gone!" I said. "Those are my instructions. Carry them well."

I stood in the empty entranceway. I was half-awake, half-asleep. This seemed, still, something of the night and the dawn. A waking dream.

I heard noises in the west wing—the rightmost portion of the H. Cooks were up and about, lighting the fuel for the kitchen. I would fain be alone. But where? Kate slept in the bedchamber, and servants were already stirring.

The chapel. Yesterday the squire had mentioned the chapel. I did not desire it then, but now it would serve as my only refuge.

It was simple to find, as it lay on the opposite side of the H, and I had seen its stained-glass windows from outside. Finding my way into the cool and poorly lit interior, I knew I was safe. No one would disturb the King at prayer. I knelt down and assumed the attitude of prayer.

But I could not pray. All I could think of was Brandon dead, Brandon lifeless, and it was so unthinkable I could not grasp it. We were together, we were almost of an age, he could not die before I. . . .

The rising sun confronted the east windows of the chapel, warming and illuminating them. I looked at them idly, in my confusion. They were fiery and red. I could not make out the pictures in them, or decipher what story they were trying to tell. Brandon was dead. What cared I for the story of Esther?

I knelt there, trying to feel something. But all I felt was emptiness. There should be searing pain. Why was there no pain?

I told Kate, as she wakened in the bed. Immediately she sat upright. "God grant him peace," she said. "And you? I know you grieve."

"Not yet," I admitted. "Not quite yet. Now I feel nothing. As though a block of winter were in my heart, imprisoning it."

"You will," she assured me. "You will feel all of it, but only later. I do not understand it, but that is how it happens." She was out of bed now, fastening on her garments. "Feeling returns only after the person is buried."

"But I *should* feel something besides this ice-locked nothingness!"

"You feel what God allows you to feel. If nothing, now, it is for a purpose. God wishes you to feel other things."

God, God, God. I was weary of Him and His capricious ways.

"Am I supposed, then, to care only for the French war at this time? Because England is in danger?"

"Evidently," she said, and smiled. "One task at a time. God decides which."

Her faith was so simple and sweet. But "simple" so easily slides over into "simplistic."

CXXVIII

At Whitehall, where all messengers had gathered, awaiting me, it seemed that nothing was happening elsewhere in the realm.

Except that Brandon lay dead.

The English fleet yet lay anchored in the Solent and waiting for orders, with the French poised just out of sight. There had been no landings at any place along the southern coast. Nor had there been in Scotland. Francis had failed his promise there, as he failed all his promises. Now perhaps the Scots would understand the nature of their ally.

Across the Channel, Boulogne was quiet. The French interest lay elsewhere, for the moment. Yet Henry Howard was having problems maintaining discipline and morale amongst his men. They broke out in quarrels and rancour continuously. His fault or theirs?

I issued orders: the fleet was to pursue the French, corner them, and do battle with them. In spite of the loss of *Mary Rose,* I believed we could cripple the French fleet and send it limping back to Francis, like a sick child. The Earl of Surrey was to return to England, to attend the state funeral of the Duke of Suffolk. The armies at all points were to continue to maintain their posts.

As I must maintain mine. My health, seemingly so improved by the earlier campaign on the Continent, had deteriorated. (I can safely write it here.) Fluid had accumulated in my leg, so that sometimes I had no sensation in it, and it was swollen and ugly. There was no resurgence of the open ulcer, Jesu be thanked. But I feared that any hour it might be reactivated.

Also (I hesitate to write it even here) . . . there were nights when I thought I heard the monks again. The ones who had been in my chamber when . . . during that time after Catherine's execution. They stood in the corners and mouthed the selfsame words. But now I knew them to be false, so I heeded them not. Why did they continue to haunt me? I had done nothing to encourage them. Was it that they scented a weakened man?

Weakness. It drew forth all the jackals, to snap and snarl and quarrel over their victim. But I was more clever than they, the jackals roaming about my kingdom and Privy Council. They had only their noses, to scent a sick man; I still had brains and power. I would divide the jackals, outsmart them; and in the end, make them serve *me*. Yes, that was the way. . . .

All would be well.

Except that Brandon lay dead.

A state funeral is a formidable thing. I had never attended one, not as an adult. I hated them. All the protocol, all the rank and privileges which must be observed, with the focus of it all an insensate body.

The body, the earthly remains of Charles Brandon, had been disembowelled and soaked in spices for ten days. Then it had been put in a cerecloth, and that wrapped in lead, and that laid in a coffin, and that simple coffin enclosed in another. Around that were arranged garlands and ribbons. I never saw Brandon himself, only the formal outer festoonings of what had once been a man.

Would I have wished to see him, to see his flesh white, his lips set, his great chest sunken?

He had been, after Thomas Howard, Duke of Norfolk, the highest-ranking noble in the realm. I had made him so; taken the mud-spattered orphan and raised him up. I had done well to do so, as he was worthy of his rank.

My sister Mary had loved him.

Now he had another wife who would mourn him. But would she, truly? The truth is, I had loved him more.

Brandon lay dead.

The insistent chorus was coming more often to me now. Feeling had crept back, and was only waiting behind a barricade to burst out.

The Order of the Garter customarily held ceremonies in the Chapel of St. George in Windsor. Brandon was to be buried in the choir of the chapel, only a few yards from Queen Jane. All twenty-five Knights of the Garter were called upon to be present, even though they represented the foremost defence of the realm. For this one day we must be undefended, and pray that God would stand watch whilst we did honour to Brandon.

I had moved to Windsor—even though I disliked the quarters there, as too closely associated with my grief after Jane's death—to oversee this funeral. I wished to make some sort of personal memorial there, to say something. I attempted to write an elegy, but my verse did not come. I tried to compose a prayer, but it sounded pompous. There were words I wished to say. I knew

I had almost heard them before, but they slipped from me. *The fruitful ground, the quiet mind . . .*

Yes. I had read them. They were Henry Howard's, part of a poem. I sent for him.

It was the night before the funeral, and all Windsor was in mourning. My apartments were hung in black, and there was no music. In the Chapel of St. George, Brandon's coffin lay on a catafalque, tapers flickering all around it. I would go down later, would keep vigil as a Knight of the Garter should do. But now there was still the poem to be attended to.

Howard came upon the stroke of nine. He was dressed all in black: I had ordered the court into full mourning.

"Did you bring your poems?" I asked him.

He held out a portfolio of papers. "All I had," he said. "As you requested."

"I wish to read a poem at the funeral," I said. "I have tried to compose one of my own, but grief and exhaustion have, I fear, routed my Muse. Yet I found a phrase echoing through my mind, and I think it to be yours. It is *'The fruitful ground, the quiet mind. . . .'*"

"Aye. 'Tis mine," he said quickly. He must have been pleased, but like all artists he disdained to show it. "Here is the entire poem." He plucked out a sheet and laid it down next to my candle.

Yes! It was exactly what I wished to say. It expressed my own inner feelings.

"It is—my own words," I said, amazed.

Now he blushed. "The highest award one can give a poet. We sit in our little rooms, composing for ourselves, but believing that all men must feel the same. We are alone, but united with every human being—if we are good. If we are bad, we are united with nothing, and no one. The frightening thing is that, sitting in the little room, one does not know to which category one belongs. One must sit there in faith."

"Yes, yes." I did not wish to flatter him overmuch. "I dislike to use borrowed trappings, but I have no choice. My own words will not come, and yours are already there."

"They are to be used by others. I hope that in years to come, when I am no longer here to give permission, they may continue to serve man's inner needs."

I looked at him. I believed his words to be true and heartfelt. As an artist he was noble. But as a man he was petty, unstable, and rancourous. How did the two intertwine?

"I have reports of your difficulties in Boulogne," I said at length, hating to break the spell—the spell that bound us as journeymen in the arts. Now we must revert to ruler and subject. "What seems to be the cause of this trouble?"

"The city is a bastard child of England," he said. "We retain it, but for how long? In Tournai, we were committed to incorporating it into England. Vast sums were assigned for its upkeep. Frenchmen, citizens of Tournai, were to take seats in Parliament. But everyone knows that Boulogne is but a war-pawn, to be returned to France for a ransom. So who shall bother with it? The men are restive, and order hard to keep."

I sighed. His words were true. Keeping Boulogne victualled and defended were enormous expenditures, and I no longer had the cash reserves I had had in 1513. The truth was that I could not afford Boulogne, as I had afforded Tournai.

"Well, do your best," I answered. I knew he was waiting for me to reveal my ultimate plan for Boulogne. And oh, yes, I had one: to unite it with Calais, to double the English holdings. But all that took funds, funds which I did not have. I owed the money-lenders of Antwerp huge sums, plus interest, for the taking of Boulogne.

I was tired. "Thank you, my lad," I told him. "You may go now."

He bowed, stiffly. He was displeased.

"I call you 'my lad' because you were my son's friend," I said.

He smiled somewhat. "There is a poem about our years at Windsor, in that sheaf you have. I still mourn him," he said.

"I also." Now we were, again, two poets together. "Good night, Henry."

"Good night, Your Majesty."

Now I was alone in the room. The candles jumped and flickered, and I remembered yet another reason why I hated Windsor: my son had flowered here in his brief season. He had brought colour to the dead drab stones, a momentary life. But Windsor was death. Nothing survived here.

I began rifling through the poems, looking for the one celebrating his life. Surrey's portfolio was so fragile. Too fragile to entrust a reputation or memory to.

So cruel a prison how could betide, alas?

Surrey had written the poem in prison, then. His imprisonment had served to bring my son back to life for me, if only for an instant.

I knew what I must do. Go to Brandon's coffin, where it stood before the high altar. There I would say farewell to him, privately.

The church was empty. The great catafalque stood, like a building itself, black and square, blocking the altar. All about it flickered tapers, lit hours ago and now burnt half down and guttering. They illuminated the coffin in a ghastly, pagan way, jumping like sacrificial maidens.

I knelt on the stone steps. I closed my eyes and tried to see Charles, tried to conceive of his really being there. In my mind I knew his corpse rested somewhere within the great black-draped box, but in my heart I had no contact with him. Charles . . . what had been my last words with him?

That night he had come on board *Great Harry* . . . what had we said as he took his leave? What was it, what was it?

"It will be a long night," I had said. "My thoughts go with you."

"To be alive is to fight the French. Remember, Your Grace, how we planned it all, at Sheen?"

"Old men fight boys' battles. Well, good night, Charles."

"Good night, Charles," I repeated, and touched the mourning-cloth. "You spoke true. 'Remember how we planned it all, at Sheen?' And we lived it. To live a dream is life's highest reward. Sleep well, my friend. I join you soon."

I started to rise, but now it all came rushing back upon me. His hand-grasp at Sheen, when he had caught me scrambling over the wall. His bedding of me after I had just wed Katherine of Aragon, and I such a frightened virgin. His acting as my champion throughout my madness with Nan, even enduring censure from his wife. His faithful support of me after Jane died. Suddenly I saw his face in all its ages, heard his laughter, felt his love; that love which had always been present, supporting me. The love which I had sought elsewhere, never realizing that I had had it all along.

Now I was alone. The one person who had truly loved me, and known me throughout all my life, was gone. Brandon had loved me when I was yet the second son; had taken my side when Arthur still held favour and sway.

I put my hand up along the great coffin. "I love you," I said, as I had never said to any woman.

As if sealing a pledge, I pressed my hand down upon the black velvet; kept it pressed there as long moments passed and I heard the discreet coughs in the rear of the cavernous chapel. The official watchers waited to take their assigned places by the catafalque and sit up all night. I was robbing them of their paid opportunity; it was already past two, and dawn would be coming up shortly.

Dawn, and the day of Brandon's funeral. I took away my hand and left him to his rest, as I would try to take mine in the short darkness yet remaining.

CXXIX

State funerals, like all other state formalities, were governed by protocol. My grandmother Margaret Beaufort had laid out the precise rules to be followed in childbed, marriage, burial. She felt that a divine mystery attended each of them, and that a certain ritual would tap that mystery and bring one the grace to endure the ensuing condition. Perhaps it did. In any case, I was content to abide by her rules and trust that God had guided them.

The funeral was to begin at eight in the morning, a stately procession, followed by a Requiem Mass. All night, the passing bell had tolled for the Duke. Then began the Nine Tailors, nine strokes to signify that a man had died, followed by sixty strokes, one for each year of his age.

I was chief mourner, and as such I had to array me all in black, a colour I detested.

The coffin was moved outside the chapel, so that it might have a brief cortège and funeral journey for the ceremony. The funeral car—the hearse and six black horses with Brandon's ducal trappings—was to draw him down the long aisle of the chapel, escorted by flaming torches during the reciting of the Dirge.

I had summoned the estate of England, and they were all present. I looked to both sides and saw that the entire Privy Council were assembled, as well as the prelates of the Church of England, with Cranmer at their head, ready to conduct the Requiem Mass. I took my seat, as chief mourner, beside the catafalque.

Cranmer rose. The servers came forward, with their flaring torches, and took their appointed stations around the catafalque with its black hangings. The choir began to chant the Dirge.

" 'I am the resurrection and the life,' " Cranmer proclaimed, from before the coffin. The mourners rose. " 'We brought nothing into this world, and it is certain we can carry nothing out. The Lord gave, and the Lord hath taken away; blessed be the Name of the Lord.'"

"Amen," the company answered.

Cranmer lifted up his hands. "'Lord, let me know mine end, and the number of my days: that I may be certified how long I have to live.

"'Behold, thou hast made my days as it were a span long: and mine age is even as nothing in respect to thee.

"'For man walketh in a vain shadow, and disquieteth himself in vain.

"'Hear my prayer, O Lord. For I am a stranger with thee: and a sojourner, as all my fathers were.

"'O spare me a little, that I may recover my strength: before I go hence, and be no more seen.'"

All of us prayed thus, earnestly, all of us pitting ourselves against the little time left to us. I looked backward at Brandon's children, at his young widow. No matter what, it is only a little that we are spared. Then the matter proceeds.

Now the Requiem Mass began, and followed itself through to the Consecration, the Elevation, the Transubstantiation. The eternal life, Christ's life, beside our puny things . . . the white wafer shining against the black death-pall.

"'Man that is born of a woman hath but a short time to live, and is full of misery. He cometh up, and is cut down, like a flower: he fleeth as it were a shadow, and never continueth in one day.

"'In the midst of life we are in death: of whom may we seek for succour, but of thee, O Lord, who for our sins are justly displeased?'"

Cranmer nodded at me. It was my time to give the eulogy. I left my kneeling-place and walked slowly to the choir steps before the coffin. I was swathed and hooded in the hot August forenoon, as custom demanded. The torches were yet flaring all around the bier, giving off great rolling volumes of smoke.

"Dear friends," I began, "and family." In the front row were Brandon's survivors: his widow Katherine, and his grown daughters Anne and Mary by his youthful marriages; Frances and Eleanor by my sister. Grandchildren were present, as well. All his daughters were married. Suddenly I caught a smile creeping about my mouth. Even in death, Brandon was attended by a flock of adoring ladies.

"I am chief mourner because, as the Duke's boyhood friend and brother-in-law, I am host for this state funeral. When his wife, my sister Mary Tudor, erstwhile Queen of France, died"—I saw Katherine Willoughby stiffen—"he expressly stated that he wished to be buried quietly at the College Church at Tattershall in Lincolnshire, 'without any pomp or outward pride of the world.' He was mindful of his creditors and the debts of his family, and wished to spare any untoward expense. That was the Duke's way. He was ever mindful of others."

Before me I could see the entire Privy Council, like a row of black crows, unnaturally silent, no cawing or pecking amongst them.

"The Duke was my friend. We had known one another since childhood." I paused, to withdraw the poem I would read as an elegy. I was glad to have something written down, as my words were those of a seven-year-old boy; and indeed, that was his chief mourner—an unsure seven-year-old boy from Sheen Manor. I unwrapped Henry Howard's poem, written for some other reason, but now mine.

> " 'Martial, the things that do attain
> The happy life, be these, I find:
> The riches left, not got with pain;
> The fruitful ground, the quiet mind:
>
> " 'The equal friend, no grudge, no strife;
> No charge of rule, nor governance;
> Without disease, the healthful life;
> The household of continuance:
>
> " 'The mean diet, no delicate fare;
> True wisdom joined with simpleness;
> The night discharged of all care,
> Where wine the wit may not oppress:
>
> " 'The faithful wife, without debate;
> Such sleeps as may beguile the night.
> Content thee with thine own estate;
> No wish for Death, nor fear his might.' "

I paused, folded away the paper. More had done so, exactly so, reading for my mother at her funeral as I had stood, listening, a boy of eleven. It was then, hearing his words, that I had first formed that attachment to More which had so fatally bound me, and for which I still yearned in spite of myself. My boyhood self, young self, best self, had momentarily sprung to life at Brandon's bier. Sprung to life—and been soon extinguished.

"The Duke of Suffolk was a true knight," I said, "the truest knight I ever knew. He never betrayed a friend or intentionally took unfair advantage of a foe." I looked out at the Privy Councillors, an antagonistic lot: envious, backbiting, and venomous. Covered by the mourning-cowls (at royal expense) they looked peaceable, like idealized monks. But I knew them. Oh, did I know them!

"Can any of you say the same?"

I then went on to extol the Duke's prowess in war, especially his campaign in France, alone, in 1522, in which he had come close to taking Paris itself. "Only winter and lack of support stopped him," I said. "Like a true knight, he always obeyed his sovereign. Even when that sovereign"—I started to say "was wrong," but that was not a proper sentiment here—"gave orders he did not understand. As a sworn knight, he was bound to uphold them. As a sworn knight, he did."

It was all a chain. Brandon owed loyalty to me, and must obey my confusing, contradictory orders ("Fight the French." "No, abandon Paris, we have no funds.") as I owed loyalty to God, whose orders were even more confusing and contradictory. No matter: we judge the knight on his loyalty and perseverance, not on his understanding.

Cranmer was gesturing to me. My time was almost up.

My time was almost up.

I looked at the assembled mourners and suddenly I felt it: *This was my funeral, and these were my mourners.*

Was I not to be interred in this very ground? Was it not a fact that my coffin would rest on the selfsame bier?

This was a rehearsal for my own funeral. Where I stood now, someone else would stand. Otherwise, all was the same. The same Privy Council, disguised as mourners. The same Cranmer, hurrying along the service.

By the coffin's edge a censer smoked, sending up streams of Eastern odours, thick and mysterious.

The same one would sit by my coffin.

I stared at it. You will be here, I thought, and I not? You will see me dead, and I not see you? You will smoke, when I cannot breathe?

To know it for an absolute fact was terrifying.

Suddenly I could not bear to stand there, witnessing my own end. I was shaking as I placed Brandon's jousting helmet on the cold stones—the helmet that had faced me a hundred times, the one he had worn when I had forgotten to close my visor. . . . Jesu, I could still see it, attached to that mighty body, thundering toward me. . . . The body lay cold and imprisoned now, and I held the helmet.

"This helmet was dear to him. It was his Knight's emblem. It will be mounted up on this stone pillar, to stay there forever. I decree it."

It would be there to see me lowered into a nearby grave-vault.

No, no. I could not believe it. I could not comprehend it. . . .

Cranmer motioned, and grave-attendants came forward to wheel the catafalque over to the great gaping grave opened for it. The paving stones had been removed and stacked neatly, and a deep dark shaft beckoned.

Cranmer then walked twice round the coffin, first sprinkling it with holy water, and then censing it. Brandon's coffin appeared like a summer's morning—gleaming with dew and hidden behind mist.

Neat devices detached the coffin itself from its trappings—all the velvet and flags and flowers—and took it to the hole's edge. These men knew what to do. They were old hands. They knew about slipping the ropes under the coffin, so they would not tear off the gold leaf and ducal escutcheons, and how to lower it smoothly.

" 'O Lord God most holy, O Lord most mighty, O holy and most merciful Saviour, deliver us not into the bitter pains of eternal death.

" 'Thou knowest, Lord, the secrets of our hearts: shut not thy merciful ears to our prayer: but spare us, Lord most holy, Judge eternal, suffer us not, at our last hour, for any pains of death, to fall from Thee.' "

Cranmer stood at the obscene grave-hole.

" 'I am in fear and trembling at the judgment and the wrath that is to come.

" 'That day will be a day of wrath, of misery, and of ruin: a day of grandeur and great horror.

" 'Deliver me, O Lord, from everlasting death on that day of terror: when the heavens and the earth will be shaken.' "

Brandon's day had come. Even now he was being tried—or, having been tried, was serving his punishment. He was screaming in purgatory, begging for surcease, writhing in agony—while we, stupid as only mortal men can be, sat staring at the housing for his corpse.

" 'Lead us not into temptation,' " Cranmer intoned, " 'but deliver us from evil, from the gate of hell.' " He sprinkled the coffin down in its depths, its dark, forsaken depths. " 'Rescue his soul, O Lord. May he rest in peace.' "

The paid gravedigger came forward and threw a spadeful of clods and dirt into the hole. An instant, and then it hit and gave back a distant echo.

" 'O God, Whose nature is always to have mercy and to spare, we humbly beseech You on behalf of the soul of Charles Brandon, Duke of Suffolk, whom You have bidden to depart out of this world: that You would not deliver him into the hands of the enemy, nor forget him forever, but command him to be received by the holy angels, and taken to Paradise, his home, that as he had put his faith and hope in You, he may not undergo the pains of hell, but possess everlasting joys.' "

Pretty words. Reassuring words. But had Brandon ever truly had a relationship with God? We had never spoken of it. And it was my fault, my fault—I had not shared the Light of Christ with him. I had had the Spirit, but hoarded it in my own breast, whilst we talked of campaigns and loves and all earthly things.

I had sent Brandon to hell, unless some other kinder soul had brought him Christ's love. For knightly deeds were not enough, unless they were done for the glory of God. And Brandon had not done them for that.

O God! To have the truth and not share it is as grave a sin as to be lacking it altogether!

Forgive me, Charles! I begged. I did not know—and I did not always know what I *did* know. Even now, I am not sure—what is truth and what is intrusion upon another's private conscience?

Cranmer stood before the open hole.

" 'Forasmuch as it hath pleased Almighty God of His great mercy to take unto Himself the soul of our dear brother here departed, we therefore commit his body to the ground: earth to earth, ashes to ashes, dust to dust: in sure and certain hope of the Resurrection to eternal life, through Our Lord Jesus Christ: who shall change our vile body, that it may be like unto His glorious body, according to the mighty working, whereby He is able to subdue all things to Himself.' "

The Duke's household chamberlains came forward and broke their staves and threw them into the pit, signifying that their master was departed forever.

Now the grave was ready to be filled in.

"Let us now pray as Christ hath taught us," Cranmer said, and led us in the Lord's Prayer.

Out in the dazzling, hot sunshine, we blinked. We were still alive; that was the shock, not the brightness or the incongruity. Inside, all was stopped and cold. But outside, all the while, life was burgeoning. Insects attacked us and bit us. Flowers drooped from the heat of the sun; the attendant had forgotten to water them the evening before. The sheer busyness of life seemed a sacrilege. We were immediately sucked back into its demands.

Outside, people gathered in little knots and began talking—the more frivolous the subject, the better. There is a great need for that after a funeral, and I had no doubt that many would engage in the marital duty as soon as they reasonably could. It almost seemed to be a part of the obligation—or perhaps the rebellion against death.

You see how alive we are? As long as we do this, you cannot touch us. This certifies how alive we are. Nothing of your domain, death.

In the Great Hall of Windsor Castle, the funeral feast awaited. I had ordered the finest cakes and meats to be provided, and the best ale from Kent. The traditional little funeral cakes from Suffolk were provided by the household baker from Brandon's estate of Westhorpe. He had made each one exquisitely, with the ducal arms in miniature on the lid of the pie.

"To honour my master," he had said, when presenting them. They must have taken him days.

"He is honoured," I assured him, "in servants like you."

I eyed them now, neatly arranged upon the royal gold platters. Why are exquisite foodstuffs part of death? The living expect to be fed, even though they have done no labour.

The hall was filling up now, as the mourners came in out of the sharp noon sun. The two factions of the Privy Council grouped about their rallying points—Edward Seymour, Earl of Hertford, and Henry Howard, Earl of Surrey—like eddies of a whirlpool, black cloaks turning slowly about their centres.

About the Seymour centre there were William Petre and William Paget, the principal secretaries; Tom Seymour himself, of course; and important, but missing, was John Dudley, serving now in Boulogne as captain.

Swirling and circling around the hub of their wheel, Henry Howard, were Bishop Gardiner; the Duke of Norfolk; and Thomas Wriothesley—the conservative spokes.

When had these factions arisen? There had not been factions when I had had Wolsey. Perhaps factions were part of the New Order, something that came along with the New Men. Certainly they had existed alongside of Cromwell. He had been the darling of one faction and the curse of the other. Now both parties snapped and snarled at one another like rabid dogs in August. What was the purpose of factions? To steer the sovereign in one direction or another. But this sovereign would not be steered—surely they knew that.

Then it must be another sovereign they sought to control.

Edward.

They foresaw my death, and looked ahead to the control of Edward.

It was *my* funeral they celebrated now; *mine* after which they congregated and ate their meat pies and laid their plans. This was how it would be. This was its true rehearsal. It was one thing for me to realize this; it was another for my enemies to do so.

Damn them! I would stay alive as long as possible, thwart their plans!

In truth, there was no one fit to rule in my stead. There must needs be a balance between old and new, the selfsame balance as existed inside my head. Therefore, therefore—I must appoint both factions to act as Protectorate Council for Edward. They would cancel out the bad aspects of each other. But, oh! so cumbersome . . .

I looked at them. They were such small men. *The meek shall inherit the earth.* But what is the translation, the exact translation, of *meek*? Surely it is not "colourless," "shortsighted," "timid." Such were the men who strove to guide England.

I walked about the guests, smiling and pleasant. My person was now so large that dragging it about was an effort for me and meant that I could address only the person standing directly before me. I spoke to Brandon's widow, Katherine, who, although tear-streaked, seemed reconciled to "the hand of the Almighty." I talked with my nieces, Frances and Eleanor: pretty lasses, and seemingly healthy and intelligent. They had married and had children already —unlike my own childless, bastard daughters. . . .

The sun streamed through the high-placed windows of the Great Hall. I took a seat—a great mourner's bower, all decked in black—and watched. I felt dead myself, and my whole being ached. There was but a little way to go, and it must needs be alone.

Kate was talking with Tom Seymour. I saw them, far down on the floor below. (Is this how hawks see?) I wondered what they were saying. I watched her face, and it was a face I had never seen. She loved Tom Seymour.

I knew it, and even could say the words to myself. *She loves Tom Seymour.*

Now I indeed felt buried in the crypt with Brandon. All he had experienced, as a true knight . . . and yet never, never had a woman he loved, loved another man first and thoroughly. He had died without that wound.

Well, our wounds are our selves.

I swung myself down from my seat, addressed the company, and went to my private apartments.

But not before I began to see strange horns sprouting from the hired mourners' cloaks, shimmering and glowing.

CXXX

ll this took place over a year ago. And what has happened since then? In regard to France, prudence dictated a settlement, although God knows I have no love either of prudence *or* of the French. But for the time being it seemed wise to negotiate something, and so I permitted French envoys to come to London and draw up a peace treaty. That was after New Year's, and there were festivities honouring them, although they were faint and lacklustre compared to similar events in the past. Oh, how we used to celebrate treaties! I remember the Treaty of London in 1518, when Mary was betrothed to the French Dauphine, and Wolsey so happy, and Katherine of Aragon so glum. And then . . . but I ramble. Yes, there once were bright festivities. But brightness has dimmed—or perhaps my eyes can see beyond the lustre to the hollowness now, and so I spare myself the expense and participation altogether. Thus I allowed the French to buy back Boulogne for two million crowns over an eight-year period. It is worth more than that to England, but only if we could truly defend and victual her on a permanent basis. I tried to do that, and failed. Now I had to give her up, like a wife I could not keep.

Wife. Kate . . . ah, Kate. A wife I could not keep. Well, no more of that.

My health continues to improve. I have grown a bit more unwieldy, but the corner has been turned, and as my leg is now completely well—no more attacks!—I hope to begin exercising shortly, and regain my youthful shape. It is still there, hidden, and I will bring it forth, now that my illnesses are past.

Even though I am completely well, daily I work on my will, setting forth the secret governing council for Edward, selecting and culling names, then discarding them. It is a great labour. No one is to know of my plan. I keep them all in the dark. There are surprises in my choices! I outsmart my councillors. They think they know me, but they do not. I have hidden my papers well, inside . . . no, I will not write it here. But I mean for the "changers" to be checked and balanced by the "stayers."

That is why I had to chop off the head of the serpent, the Howard serpent, Henry. He meant to coil round my Edward, imprisoning him. Venomous, ugly thing. I stopped him.

But all is well in the kingdom now. I have kept my naughty factions balanced and soothed, and they have caused no further problems.

Only the voices in my head, the annoying visions, have proved a problem. Occasionally I have done things I could not remember, but always I have rectified them as soon as possible, and no harm has been done.

Oh, yes—there was that fool who just recently (yesterday, or was it longer ago?) asked me what my earliest memory was. I was cross with him. I must send for him and make it up. Those sorts of things, those tidying-up things, occupy me much of late. Yet majesty must always be gracious.

It is time-consuming, making up for the voices in the head. But they are growing less, and then I will have more time to attend to the things dear to my heart. I have waited all my life to do so. At last it is almost at hand. O, to be just a man!

CXXXI

 WILL:

And there it ends, just as the King himself did, some few days later. King Henry VIII died when he was fifty-six years old, in the thirty-eighth year of his reign, expecting to live and reign much longer.

He was never the same after Brandon's death. Despite the brave words in his journal, he was melancholy and ill—either in body or in spirit—for most of the time remaining to him.

The things to which he referred—did he honestly see them as such? If so, his mind was so distorted that he was truly no longer himself. Here are the facts, as every Englishman knows, but perhaps you do not, on the Continent:

The King's health was abominable. His heart began to fail, often beating wildly and erratically, leaving him short of breath and dizzy.

At the same time (I hesitate to write it thus) he stopped making normal piss, so that his body could not rid itself of its water. The physicians collected his urine daily and studied it, could give it a name—"urine of dropsy," very wise!—but were helpless to treat it. This dropsy puffed him up to grotesque proportions and rendered normal movement impossible. Unable to walk much of the time, he had to be hauled about in his palaces on a specially equipped litter, and raised and lowered into his bed by mechanical devices.

His heart thumped like a sick bird while his body ballooned with water. And there was no treatment; it was a common way to die, but it had no name. Except "old age." (Yet not all the old are afflicted thus.)

The fluid, and the swelling throughout his entire body, pressed upon his brain—and that, together with his "visitations," made him erratic and violent and suspicious. When the pressure was especially bad (and one could always tell by a simple glance at his face; puffiness there

9 1 5

meant puffiness in his mind as well), he turned against those dearest to him. He gave orders for both Cranmer and his beloved Kate to be arrested and sent to the Tower—upon the urging of their enemies, who watched for the telltale swelling of their sovereign's face as sailors watch the sky. Coming to himself again, he rescinded those orders and confounded their ill-wishers. But it was an ugly time for innocent and guilty alike.

The prestige and influence of the Protestants increased day by day in England, despite the King's attempts to hold the country to a Catholicism without the Pope: a vision of his own, shared by nobody else. The true Catholics hoped for a restoration of some sort, if not under Edward (who was hopelessly smeared with Protestantism), then perhaps with Mary. The Protestants rubbed their hands with glee that they would soon come into their own. Anne Askew, the "vision-visited-virgin," as Henry described her, was a sacrifice of the Protestants, to prove that the New Religion could produce martyrs as valiant as the much-vaunted early Christians and their bouts with the lions. She was brave, and proved their point. She was the last religious execution in England under King Henry. She was also not a virgin, as veneration would require, but a married woman whose husband repudiated her for her religious fanaticism.

The death of "the most foolish proud boy that is in England"— Henry Howard, the Earl of Surrey—quite broke Henry, in spite of the toss-away words in his journal. I know; I saw the agony he went through in admitting that Howard was indeed a traitor, bent on usurping his ancient familial rights against Edward's new pedigree. What were Tudors and Seymours (diluted scions of Edward III, two hundred years ago) against the Howards, lords of the North from time out of mind? So, Henry Howard must pay the price of his treason, must go to his death, after his arrogant statements about the Howards being "meet to rule the Prince after the King's death"; his adding royal arms to his escutcheon; his obsessive commissioning of paintings of himself with cryptic messages about "H" coming to rule over "T," and "H. Rex" beneath a broken column, and so on. Such a fine mind; such a stupid man.

Both Mary and Elizabeth were reinstated in the line of succession, yet remained illegitimate—a neat bit of legal juggling by their father to increase their rights and desirability as wives without compromising his belief that he had never been legally wed to their mothers. He loved those daughters, and wanted them to have as full and happy lives as possible. (A love sparsely returned on their parts. If the unnatural act reputed to Queen Mary is true, then indeed King Lear was well served by Goneril and Regan in comparison. To curse and desecrate her father's skeleton . . . !)

As to the French, the Scots, the Emperor, the Pope—well, as you know, Francis died directly after Henry, although he rallied long enough to send a teasing, insulting note to his fond old rival before both expired. The Emperor resigned his crowns, the Netherlands one in 1555, the Spanish one in 1556, and retired to a Spanish monastery. The Pope finally led his General Council at Trent, which hardened, rather than softened, the position of the Catholic Church against the Reformers. A battle line was drawn, and the Church seemed ready to fight rather than compromise. Why, it was almost as if she had principles!

The Scots actually show signs of succumbing to the Reformed faith, which would change the entire character of their realm, in relation to both England and the Continent (requiring them to find some Scriptural excuse for their money-grubbing). It is true that Mary Queen of Scots adheres to the Old Faith; but increasingly she is at odds with her Council and countrymen and isolated in this matter of religion, so that she has to import foreigners, Italians and French and such, to buoy her up in her faith. A surprising turn of events, would you not agree— although you hold that the Lord directs the Protestant victory?

As for the King's will: what a troublesome document that turned out to be! He used it to control his councillors, waving it over their heads like a schoolmaster with a whip. Do this, and (perhaps) I shall instate you: do not, and you shall (probably) be omitted from my will. He kept it in a secret place, amending it constantly (oh! he was old: only old men act so!), tut-tutting over it. The price he paid for this old man's—and tyrant's—luxury was that upon his death it was unsigned, almost undiscovered, and questionably legal.

Those constant games that he played with his courtiers led them to play games with him. Hide the document—hide the news. Dangle me— and I dangle you. Divide and rule—unite and outsmart. The last few months were so Byzantine I felt that Suleiman would have been perfectly at home amongst us. Intrigues, flatterers, panderers, betrayers all stalked the corridors and Long Gallery at Whitehall, where the King lay fighting the Angel of Death. Factions in the Privy Council waited to seize power, sure that they could trounce their adversaries. When the old King was dead, when the breath was out of him at last . . . then they would move, sweep into power.

But the Almighty had other ideas, did He not? Little Edward,

Henry's pride: his reign was like a shadow, insubstantial and quickly over. . . .

And all their machinations and arrangements went down like dust, and they had to flee before Mary, Queen Mary, the Catholic angel of vengeance.

Now need I set it down, what Henry's death and interment were.

The King died on January twenty-eighth, 1547, at two o'clock in the morning. He had been quite ill since autumn, and by mid-January he took to his chamber in Whitehall, from which he never emerged. He was confused and comatose, so he was spared the lengthy "death watch" that his father had endured, with smiling courtiers and daily routines. There was no daily routine for him. He knew not when it was day and when it was night, but lived in a world of his own seeing and making. There were moments of lucidity; even an audience with the Imperial and French ambassadors on January sixth. They remembered it well, but it is doubtful that Henry did. It was a great effort to get him dressed that day, as I recall. He was eager to attend to them and make plans for a future conference. He selected his clothes and jewels and, hoisted onto his feet, walked stiffly out to receive the envoys in his Presence Chamber.

It was a brave show. He returned, and divesting himself of his gold-encrusted doublet, his great necklace of rubies, he put on a plain linen nightshirt—eschewing even the embroidered ones—and walked once around his bedchamber before submitting himself, childlike, to be hoisted into bed by his lift-pulley.

He never left that bed again.

As the darkness closed in on him, and his physicians gave up hope, no one dared tell him that his end was near—for to "prophesy" or "imagine" the King's death was treason, as Henry Norris and Henry Howard had found out. I myself did not dare tell him, as I was afraid that he would turn on me and hate me—and I could not bear that, not now. I did not want to lose his love, and so I hung back, cowardly, like the rest.

At length, Sir Anthony Denny—a recent courtier, with no old love to cripple his action—spoke boldly to the King. In the opinion of his physicians, Denny said, the King had not long to live. Was there anyone to whom he wished to confess, or to open his soul?

"Cranmer," whispered Hal. "But not yet." He felt death to be much further away, not standing right at the headboard. Nevertheless they sent for Cranmer straightway, as he was at Croydon, an hour's journey south of London.

And, indeed, when Cranmer arrived, his King was already past speech and barely breathing. "Do you die in the faith of Christ?" asked Cranmer, kneeling, whispering directly in the failing ear.

No response.

Cranmer took his hand. "Give me a sign that you believe that Christ has redeemed you, that you die in firm union with Him." A faint squeeze of the hand, imperceptible but to Cranmer.

"He hears!" he said. "He has affirmed it. He dies in the faith of Christ."

Then I, too, took his hand. (This is unrecorded; I was not a prelate and had no gatekeeping duties over his soul.) I squeezed it hard.

"You have done well, my Prince," I said, directly into his ear. "You have done as well as any man can do, with what God gave you to do with."

Did he hear me? Did he know me? There was life there; then there was not. Just so, he was gone.

Someone pulled me away. "Leave him," they said. "Your time is over. We have no need of fools."

Another cuffed me directly. "Let your King protect you now, all-licenced, hateful, interfering fool!"

My reign, along with Hal's, was over. Already it was ugly in the chamber. I knew they would raven him, tear him.

"The will?" they said. "Where is it? Announce nothing until we have o'er-read the will." They began ransacking the chests, the boxes, the coffers.

I remembered the journal. It was of no use to them but to desecrate. But where had he put it? The last I had seen it, it was at his desk. . . .

Feathers were flying. They were ripping open the mattress underneath him, searching for the will. Cranmer begged them to stop.

"If he'd left the will in a proper place, we'd have no need of this," they replied. "But no! Like the madman he was, he hid it even from his own Council—"

I slid open the hidden desktop, and there the journal lay, right in plain view. I took it out.

"What is that, fool?" Tom Seymour wrenched it from my hands. Upon seeing the tiny handwriting, he lost interest. He could scarcely read.

"My poetry," I said. "Ideas for poems I hope to write, upon

retirement." A journal would interest them, threaten them. Poetry would bore them, and be safe. Henry Howard knew that, as he had attacked King Henry under the guise of writing about the Assyrian king Sardanapalus (". . . with foul desire/And filthy lusts that stained his regal heart . . . Who scarce the name of manhood did retain . . . I saw a royal throne . . . Where wrong was set/That bloody beast, that drank the guiltless blood").

"Fah!" He tossed it back. "Begone. No one wants you now. It's our day, the day of the Seymours, the day I've waited for since my stupid sister married that rotten, evil hulk of a King." He grinned and repeated the last sentence in the dead King's face—the face to which he had always been unctuous and simpering in life. Now I, too, began to see the red in Thomas's eyes, which the King had recognized in his "madness."

I walked out of the death-chamber, the journal tucked beneath my arm. Outside in the adjoining Privy Chamber the remainder of the councillors and courtiers waited to hear the word, to know where the King's soul lingered. No, in truth, they cared not where his soul was, but only where his will and his gold and his heir were.

Nonetheless it was a good reign, and beyond the courtiers, the realm grieved his going. He had done well by everyone but himself.

CXXXII

I fled down the corridors, seeking only to escape the clutching hands and covetous faces of the self-seekers now gathered around the dead King's apartments. I found my own quarters and made my way to a pallet without lighting a candle, lest anyone see the light and come to question me.

When dawn came, I awoke and found that the great palace of Whitehall was still, hushed—pausing for death. The suppliants and mourners had departed, the watchers had gone to bed; the sun was not yet up. Death held sway; Death ruled the realm.

Where had the scramblers for the will gone? Had they found it? What did it say? Had they scampered off to proclaim the news? Or did they hold it fast, like a cardplayer with a losing hand—hoping for deliverance, for some "rearrangement"? Were they themselves working to bring about that rearrangement?

I came up to the royal apartments. I had to knock now; there was no friendly King to let me in. The head of the Yeomen of the Guard grabbed me and searched me.

"What madman would carry weapons against a dead man?" I asked, more in wonder than in anger.

"There are those who seek to desecrate the royal corpse," he said. "In the past hour I found burning-oils and even silver stakes amongst those who have sought to enter; knives and heart-removing devices. Some of these are witches—how else could they have known the King lay dead? For it has not yet been announced, lest the French make war against us in our confusion and disarray. The Council meets tonight."

"To decide what?"

"The details of the funeral. The publication of the will."

"They found it, then?"

He looked confused. "Why, was it lost?"

That is what they would give out. It was lost. Or the King had not made one. To give them time to alter it. O Jesu, chaos reigned!

"I know naught of wills and councils," I said, adopting my most wheedling manner. "I seek only to do honour to my lost King. Tell me, where is he?"

"In the Privy Chamber. The chapel is not prepared to receive him. While it is being readied, he must lie in state in his own Privy Chamber." He waved me in.

They had done something to him in the night: spirited him away, disembowelled him, steeped him in spices and preservatives. Now his corpse lay lapped in Eastern tars and inside a flimsy coffin. It was draped with heavy black velvet palls. The supports underneath it were sagging. No one had been prepared for this eventuality. To "imagine the King's death" was treason, therefore one could not ready even the most elementary props for it. The coffin supports were inadequate, but no one could replace them beforehand without running afoul of Cromwell's leftover secret police.

Sun streamed into the chamber. I felt foolish approaching the death-bier. It was all so makeshift, so un-kingly. I had nothing to say here, nothing to do. I had joined the throng of people who only wished to "check up." I disgusted myself. I left.

☘ ☙

Later I was told that "officials" (what officials?) made it more palatable and seemly. The coffin was surrounded by eighty tapers, and there were Masses, obsequies, and continual watches kept by the chaplains and gentlemen of the Privy Chamber.

Outside this well-ordered respect, the realm trembled and soldiers diced for the seamless garment. No, that is really being too cynical. The truth was that offices must be filled and a nine-year-old King "protected" . . . especially from his older sisters, who represented substantial claims to the throne in their own right.

Here I must digress to comment on the two contradictory deathbed scenes reported by "witnesses," neither of whom was present at the time. The Protestant version is that King Henry had envisioned a great enlightened state in which the Reformed religion would prevail. In this version, Henry deliberately had Edward brought up by Protestant tutors and entrusted the Protestant cause to Mary's conscience by calling her to his deathbed and saying, "Be a mother to Edward, for look, he is little yet." Dying in sanctity, he had commissioned Mary to protect her brother, had cut down the Howards as Catholic weeds that might block Edward's Gospel sunlight, and had created the Governing Council as a safety device to shelter Edward whilst he grew to maturity. He had carefully stricken Gardiner from the list, and from his will, as a troublemaker. "He is a wilful man and not meet to be about my son," he had muttered. "For surely, if he were in my testament, he would cumber you all, and you should never rule him, he is of so troublesome a nature. Marry, I myself could use him, and rule him to all manner of purposes as seemed good unto me; but so shall you never do."

He had sent for Kate and, holding her hands, had consoled her: "It is God's will, sweetheart, that we shall part, and I order all these gentlemen to honour and treat you as if I were living still; and if it should be your pleasure to marry again, I order that you shall have seven thousand pounds for your service as long as you shall live, and all your jewels and ornaments." Kate could not answer for weeping, and so he bade her leave him. Thus the wise, prescient King, having weeded his garden and staked it out to the best of his ability, expired in grace and contentment.

The Catholic version is full opposite. This mysterious eyewitness records that the King, smitten by conscience and devoured by remorse, passed his last hours in his bedchamber, flailing with his arms and calling for "white wine," then sitting upright and seeing shadows. "All is lost," he cried. "Monks, monks!"

In fact both stories are fanciful, albeit fetching.

That Henry tried to plan for the future, and assure Edward's security, is true. That he lamented the mistakes of the past and even longed for the lost world he had helped destroy, is also true. But neither of these things permeated his deathbed. By the time he had come there, his main effort was struggling for breath. Philosophical quandaries are a luxury granted to healthy men.

In five days the Chapel Royal was prepared and readied to receive Henry. His coffin was transferred to the dark, dank, redecorated chapel, where it would rest within a larger coffin for twelve days before being transported to Windsor for interment in St. George's Chapel. The people came to pay their respects. The government published the royal death—along with appropriate bell-tolling and proclamations—and worked at establishing a Protector for the child King. They marvelled at how Henry had omitted it from his will, considering that such a thing was "absolutely necessary" for the peaceful governing of the realm. One would almost have thought, they said, that Henry had feared it: an example of his suspicious nature—or his wandering mind. No matter, they would make it all up, do what the mad King would have done, were he himself. Their unsurprising choice was Edward Seymour, the Prince's uncle. He would be the Protector, the uncrowned King, the ruler of England for nine years, until Edward reached eighteen.

But this is stupid. You already know this, and what happened afterward. I must record the details of the funeral and only that.

CXXXIII

As I have said, the outer coffin stood for twelve long days in the Chapel Royal. To describe this coffin: it was a very large box, made of good English wood, draped with black silk set with precious stones, and garnished with escutcheons and bannerols of the King's descent. Banners of saints, beaten in fine gold upon damask, covered each corner. Stretching over all of it was a great canopy of transparent cloth-of-gold filmed with black silk.

The huge reliquary—for such it was—was surrounded by wax tapers, each two feet long, and weighing, in total, a ton. The entire floor and walls of the chapel were covered in black cloth. It was a chapel of exquisite death.

While Henry was engaged—albeit unwillingly—in this tableau, the realm was seething like an anthill. Chancellor Wriothesley went to Parliament to announce the death formally before both houses of the assembled Lords and Commons. Then Sir William Paget read Henry's will (discovered at last) so it could be proclaimed throughout the land.

The surprise provision in it was that Henry had not ruled out the possibility of children by Katherine Parr; for he placed them directly after Prince Edward in the line of succession, and before Mary and Elizabeth. These were his exact words:

> And for the great love, obedience, chastity of life, and wisdom
> being in our wife and queen Katherine, we bequeath unto her three
> thousand pounds in plate, jewels, and such apparel as it shall please her
> to take of such as we have already. . . .
> And per default of lawful issue of our son Prince Edward, we will
> that the said imperial crown after our two deceases, shall fully remain
> and come to the heirs of our entirely beloved wife, Katherine, that now
> is.

And all this time we had assumed their marriage was of the spirit only! Now the Dowager would have to be carefully watched, and guarded, for the next three months, much as the Princess of Aragon had been after Arthur's death. Truly they were sisters in fate.

The news of King Henry's demise was received with great exultation in Rome. Only Cardinal Pole refused to join in, prompting the Pope to ask, "Why do you not rejoice with the rest at the death of this great enemy of the Church?" Pole stated that the new King, Edward, was steeped in Lutheran and Zwinglian principles, and that his Regency Council was made up of Protestants, so the Church had gained nothing by King Henry's death; indeed it had probably lost something.

But to return to the lying-in-state at Whitehall. At dawn of each day, the Lord Chamberlain stood in the choir-door and chanted in a sad, clear voice, "Of your charity pray for the soul of the high and mighty Prince, our late Sovereign Lord and King, Henry VIII." The mourners —some of whom had been keeping watch throughout the night—then would begin to murmur their prayers before sung Mass would begin, to be later followed by dirges. The Pope would certainly have approved of the Catholicism of the rites.

Then came the day of the removal, so that Henry might be interred in his vault near the altar of St. George's Chapel. Workmen had been busy prying up the great marble paving stones and digging down into the soil beneath. They uncovered Jane's coffin, its royal pall faded and worm-eaten, but still recognizable. Knowing Henry wanted to be as close to her as possible, they excavated a space for his great sarcophagus directly adjoining it.

By mid-February, all was ready. So it was that on the thirteenth day of that cursed month, the coffin was conveyed from the Chapel Royal and loaded upon the funeral carriage to make the slow, two days' journey to Windsor. The great, creaking hearse, nine storeys high and draped in black, swaying from its bulk and awkward shape, was escorted by a four-mile procession of mourners bearing flaring torches. All along the route, curiosity-seekers stood gaping, beholding death reduced to— or was it magnified by?—the ceremonial trappings of a royal funeral.

Along the Thames-side road the hearse bumped along, shaking and rattling and even groaning at times. It was a rutted, ice-pitted path, hastily gravelled for the occasion, and even the stately pace of the wagon horses could not eliminate the beating the hearse must endure. As the short winter day ended, and the pitiful little sun sank directly before us, we reached Syon.

Syon. The suppressed Bridgettine monastery that had resisted the King's dissolution. Syon Abbey—where Catherine Howard had spent her last days, and had been forced out and onto a barge to go down the Thames, in the opposite direction of the King's cortège. Henry would not be happy to rest here. Why had they planned it so?

The horses were to pull the hearse directly into the nave of the little church there, and so they did. The horses then being unhitched, the hearse was left, surrounded by torches in the otherwise dark church. The company retired to the working part of the erstwhile monastery; they were hungry and wanted feeding and wine. The King stood alone. I must confess that I joined them, as my joints ached and I was cold clear through, and there was a fire in the hall.

But the point is that I left Hal alone; left him in that dark and somehow evil chapel. If I had had the wits about me to count sheep, to remember anything, then I would have realized that it was February thirteenth—the anniversary of Catherine Howard's execution. And I would have stayed with him.

Sometime during the night, after the sleepy mourners and choristers had come, sung the midnight dirges, and then departed, the coffin opened, and the King's blood seeped out and dripped upon the stone pavement—thick and ruby-coloured, so it was said. For hours it dripped, as the candle-flames around the coffin guttered and finally went out. And then, the holy presence of light and blessed substance gone, out crept the spirits of hell to do vengeance on the unguarded King. A large black dog, having come from no one knew where, crept forward, upon the final guttering of the flames, before the entire chapel was plunged into darkness. It crept up underneath the hearse, and began lapping up the blood with its long, evil tongue.

It was still there, slurping and grovelling, when the priest came to sing Matins. Dawn had not yet come, and the priest was fumbling with the candles, when he heard the licking and growling.

The beast was eight feet long, and all black. Its tail was snakelike, its eyes red, and its fangs glistened and flashed. Within its eye was no recognition of Man, except as an enemy.

The priest, upon seeing how aggressive it was, refusing to be driven off by natural human activities, fled.

"The Hound of Hell!" he cried, rousing everyone nearby. "The Hound of Hell has come into our chapel, it paces around the King—"

Armed, the men he roused went out to confront the hound. They carried torches and swords. But the beast, snarling and vicious, crouched beneath the coffin and could in no way be driven off. Its muzzle was red with blood.

"We must wait until dawn," the priest finally said. "This chapel has a large eastern window. The light will drive him off. If he is spectral—"

"But why is he here at all? We have no dog that visits us!" asked one of the caretakers of the Abbey grounds. "Never, in the history of Syon—"

"He's here because of the King," said one of his fellows, boldly. "And because of the King's executed Queen. Remember how she wept and grieved?"

"No, it's to fulfil the Scriptural prophecy, the one about King Ahab. A friar said our King would meet the same fate. He preached it to his face. When he wished to marry the Boleyn woman. The Scripture was:

" 'And thou shalt speak unto him, saying, Thus saith the Lord, Hast thou killed, and also taken possession? And thou shalt speak unto him, saying, Thus saith the Lord, In the place where dogs licked the blood of Naboth shall dogs lick thy blood, even thine.

" 'And the battle increased that day; and the King was stayed up in his chariot against the Syrians, and died at even: and the blood ran out of the wound into the midst of the chariot.

" 'And one washed the chariot in the pool of Samaria; and the dogs licked up his blood.' "

Protestants always knew Scripture by heart, and quoted it smugly.

"But this was Queen Catherine Howard," one realist pointed out. "Perhaps she cursed him."

Now you have it, my lad. Now you have it. So evil and hatred can survive the dissolution of the body . . . unlike love and devotion. *Love is stronger than death.* No, hatred is.

"We must wait until light."

In the full light of morning, workmen entered the chapel to re-solder the split coffin. The dog was still there, crouching under the hearse. The plumbers and solderers had trouble driving him off, but by thrusting hot pokers at him, they were able to get him to quit the den he had made under the hangings of the hearse. Once out from under it, he bounded away and seemed to disappear. He did not use any of the church doors to make good his escape.

Peering under the hearse, the workmen saw that it, and the coffin inside it, were cracked. A fluid, thick and repulsive, was oozing down and dripping slowly on the floor. They thought that it was not blood, but corpse-fluids, mixed with embalming fluids and spices. The jouncing and jostling of the funeral hearse over the rough roads had loosened the fastenings and allowed this hideous episode to occur. They worked quickly to patch it up, and then, in the light of day, transport the coffin to its final resting place.

By ten in the forenoon, the funeral cortège was on the road, leaving the fouled stones of Syon Chapel to be cleansed.

The people were thicker now; more lined the road as we approached Windsor. But I could not leave the ugly taste of Syon behind, and the malevolence of Catherine, and the eternity of our past deeds. Nothing is ever gone, it seems, and the past does not wash clean like paving stones. Only the good disappears. I have smelt the potpourris made of last summer's roses, and they are stale and faint. Good evaporates; evil remains and incubates.

The interment at Windsor was a lengthy but simple ceremony. It was almost exactly like Charles Brandon's, eighteen months previous. Bishop Gardiner, that most Catholic of Henry's prelates, led the burial service. There was no eulogy. All of Henry's friends were dead, save myself, and no one invited me to speak. My rank was not sufficient.

The coffin was removed from the hearse, then conveyed to the gaping hole, where it was lowered, by means of a pulley and the help of sixteen burly Yeomen of the Guard. It was a long time making its descent; it seemed to take hours until the final "clunk" was heard and the yeomen could release the ropes.

Then Gardiner began to lead the funeral service, surrounded by the head officers of the King's household: the Lord Chamberlain, the Lord Treasurer, the Lord Comptroller, the serjeant-porter, and four gentlemen ushers, all with staves and rods in their hands. He preached a sermon based on the text, "Blessed are the dead who die in the Lord."

The great funeral effigy of the King, dressed so carefully, fashioned so well, that onlookers had believed him to be yet alive and riding jubilantly on top of his own hearse, was brought forward and stripped and then pitched into the gaping grave.

"Pulvis pulveri, cinis cineri," said Gardiner. Ashes to ashes, dust to dust. Then the entire household of Henry's servers came forward, one by one, and broke their staves with their own hands into splinters, and cast them into the yawning hole. They struck below in only a few seconds;

the gap between the living and the dead was not, as yet, grown very wide. Brandon's jousting helmet, preserved on a stone pillar high up and able to look directly down at the proceedings, was grinning.

"*De profundis,*" intoned Gardiner. "Out of the depths have I cried to thee."

Then functionaries brought forward oiled planks and laid them over the grave-hole; another servant brought out a rich Turkish rug and spread it over the planks, making a sweet and reasonable floor over an open hole with a King's coffin in it.

Gardiner stood upon the makeshift floor, attended by his spiritual officers, and proclaimed young Edward's titles.

"King Edward the Sixth, by the grace of God King of England, Ireland, Wales, and France, Defender of the Faith."

Then his churchmen, and all the mourners, repeated the titles three times.

I want to say there was no spirit in it. That it was all by rote, men dully following other men's protocol. But the truth is, as Henry himself said, "There is magic at the making of a King," and as Edward's name was read, and an involuntary shiver came over us all, I knew that, like it or not, England had a new King.

Then the trumpets sounded, with both melody and courage—and suddenly it was Edward, Edward, all Edward—nothing left of Henry.

The King is dead: long live the King.

Epilogue

There were only a few genuine mourners for the King. By that I mean anyone who felt sad, weak, out of sorts, and disinclined to participate in daily activities. I was one. (Even Kate, the "mourning" Queen Dowager, was taken up with fending off Tom Seymour's wooing.) I found myself praying a great deal and wandering around aimlessly in my chambers. I knew I must soon leave court, and yet my hands were so heavy I could scarcely make them do what I knew they must—clear out my belongings and alert my sister that I was coming to visit her, until I had a more permanent place. The gathering-up process was difficult.

It was hard to remember what I had and what I had not. I had not used some things for many years, and yet they were mine; I knew them. With other things, the ownership was less certain. But as I labouriously gathered them up, I became aware that there was nothing I owned of my King's. I had not sought lands or titles, nor would my life have offered jewels or gold an understanding home. But now I was left with nothing I could touch and say, "This was *his*," or "This was *ours, together*."

I felt so sad over this that I perplexed myself, so bereft that I even shouted at Hal one evening.

"You left me nothing of you! I need something to touch, like an old fond woman! And there is nothing. The vultures have taken everything away, to make an 'inventory.' Even your handkerchiefs have been taken!"

And yet, and yet—was not memory always, and exclusively, within one's head? What good did an object do?

It was a fortnight after the King's funeral, and I had but one day to vacate the royal apartments at Whitehall. I had gathered my things together, and the bundles were bound and strapped and covered by a canvas. They bulged and jutted in strange ways, the implements of an unorganized lifetime. Tomorrow they would be taken away; my sister had said I could join her household in Kent.

My last night in royal apartments. I should have felt something, should have been able to distil some essence of all these years. But I felt uneasy, unwanted, rather than nostalgic. I was anxious to be on my way, out of this house of death and the past.

For the fortieth time I walked around the bundles, checking the knots. All was within. All . . . what had I forgotten? Wearily I bent down to see it, whatever afterthought had been propped up there. Forever, the "afterthoughts" would come trickling in. Now I would have to find room for this, this—

King Henry's little harp. The one he used when composing.

It had not been here earlier. Had someone brought it? But no one had entry to my chamber. And certainly not within the past half hour, which was the last time I had walked around the bundles, checking the knots.

But there it sat, leaning against my belongings, pressing itself to them.

So love can survive, too. Or something close to it. Consideration and kindness.

In my Father's house are many mansions; if it were not so, I would have told you.

It must be a very big mansion, to encompass all it does.